Zimbabwe (ruins) ∴

RHODESIA

Limpopo River

MOÇAMBIQU

MOÇAMBIQUE

Phalaborwa

Transvaal

osega

Pretoria

Johannesburg

Vrymeer ● ● Venloo

Waterval-Boven

Chrissie Meer

SWAZI-
LAND

Lourenço Marques

Vaal River

Veg Kop

DRAKENSBERG

Umfolozi R.

nge
State

Blood River

Kerkenberg

Spion
× Kop

Tugela R.

Dingane's Kraal

Natal

emfontein

Blaauwkrantz

ba Nchu

LESOTHO

Durban (Port Natal)

A

DRAKEN

INDIAN OCEAN

Eish R.

rahamstown

The Nations of South Africa and Surrounding Lands

Jean Paul Tremblay

THE
COVENANT

THE COVENANT

James A. Michener

Random House New York

Copyright © 1980 by James A. Michener

All rights reserved under International and Pan-American
Copyright Conventions. Published in the United States by
Random House, Inc., New York, and simultaneously in Canada
by Random House of Canada Limited, Toronto.

Library of Congress Cataloging in Publication Data

Michener, James Albert, 1907–
The covenant.

I. South Africa—History—Fiction. I. Title.
PZ3.M583Co   [PS3525.I19]   813'.54   80-5315
ISBN 0–394–50505–0
ISBN 0–394–51400–9 (limited ed.)

A limited first edition of this book
has been privately printed.

*Chapter drawings in the style
of Bushmen art by Lois Lowenstein*
Cartography by Jean Paul Tremblay

Manufactured in the United States of America

6 8 9 7 5

*Book design and drawing of baobab
by Carole Lowenstein*

Note

Mr. Errol L. Uys, a distinguished South African editor and journalist now living in the United States, was exceedingly helpful in the preparation of this manuscript. With a rare understanding of his birthplace and its people, he was able to clarify historical and social factors which an outsider might misinterpret, to correct verbal usage, and to verify data difficult to check. Working together for two years, we read the finished manuscript together seven times, twice aloud, a most demanding task. I thank him for his assistance.

JAMES A. MICHENER
St. Michaels, Md.
Christmas 1979

Acknowledgments

On my latest visit to South Africa, I was treated with invariable courtesy, and when it became known that I intended writing about the country, my phone rang daily with offers of assistance, erudite information and untrammeled discussion. When I returned to my hotel at night people waited to discuss points with me, and others offered me trips to places I would not otherwise have seen. This was true of all sectors of the society: black, Coloured, Indian, Afrikaner and English. The number of those to whom I am indebted reaches the hundreds; the following were especially helpful:

General: Philip C. Bateman, a free-lance writer with commendable books to his credit, spent seven weeks guiding me through his country on my hard-research trip. We traveled about five thousand miles, during which he introduced me to most of the experts cited below. I could not have done my work without his informed and congenial guidance.

Diamonds: John Wooldridge, Barry Hawthorne, Alex Hall, George Louw, Dr. Louis Murray of De Beers. Peter van Blommestein took me deep into the mines. I was unusually privileged to spend a morning with Lou Botes, a lonely old-time digger still operating in the Kimberley area, and to share an afternoon with J. S. Mills at his modern operation. Historian Derek Schaeffer was of great assistance, and Jack Young spent a day explaining how diamonds are moved through the market. Dr. John Gurney, head of Kimberlite Research Unit, University of Cape Town, checked details most helpfully. Dr. John A. Van Couvering, American Museum of Natural History, brought recent theories to my attention.

Early Man: Professor Philip Tobias allowed me to spend a day with him at one of his archaeological sites, and Alun Hughes showed me fossils of the great finds. Dr. C. K. Brain, director of the Transvaal Museum, was most helpful. Professor Nikolaas van der Merwe, head of Archaeology at the University of Cape Town, organized an extensive field trip in conjunction with his associate Janette Deacon and others. At the Africana Museum, Johannesburg, Mrs. L. J. De Wet and Hilary Bruce assisted me regarding San (Bushman) materials. Johannes Oberholzer, director of the National Museum, Bloemfontein, spent long hours sharing his conclusions.

Zimbabwe: Curator Peter Wright spent two days instructing me in the intricacies of the monument. Professor Tom Huffman, head of Archaeology of Witwatersrand University, was invaluable in explaining concepts.

Cape Settlement: Dr. Anna Böeseken, the nation's foremost woman scholar, was most helpful both in verbal instruction and in her remarkable printed materials. Numerous Dutch and Indonesian officials instructed me as to operations in Java. Officials of the government of Malaya helped me regarding Malacca. Peter Klein, Rotterdam, offered expert help on the V.O.C. James Klosser and Arthur Doble took me on an extensive field trip of Table Mountain. Dr. I. Norwich showed me his collection of early maps. Christine Van Zyl took me on a tour of Groot Constantia and the Koopmans de Wet Museum. Victor de Kock, former chief archivist, helped. Professor Eric Axelson, distinguished expert on early history, provided numerous insights.

Huguenots: Mrs. Elizabeth le Roux of Fransch Hoek and Dr. Jan P. van Doorn of Den Haag helped with summarizing data. Jan Walta spent three days showing me the Huguenot memorials in Amsterdam. The proprietors of two historical vineyards, Mr. and Mrs. Nico Myburgh of Meerlust, and Mr. and Mrs. Nicolas Krone of Twee Jonge Gezellen, Tulbagh, were unusually hospitable and informative. Professor M. Boucher, Department of History, University of South Africa, provided comment which helped.

Trekboers: Gwen Fagan organized a memorable trek to Church Street, Tulbagh (Land van Waveren). Colin Cochrane spent a day re-creating the old glories of Swellendam. Dr. Jan Knappert, London School of Oriental Studies, gave me valuable perspectives. Dr. D. J. van Zyl, head of History, University of Stellenbosch, offered valued criticism.

Mfecane: Dr. Peter Becker was generous with his time and insights. In 1971 I met with various Zulu leaders during an extensive tour of Zululand.

Great Trek: Professor C. F. J. Muller, leading expert, shared his ideas generously. Dr. Willem Punt, Sheila Henderson, Professor Jack Gledhill, Grahamstown, who is writing a biography of Piet Retief, discussed details.

Salisbury and Old Sarum: Mrs. J. Llewellyn-Lloyd, Surrey.

Oriel College: Donald Grubin, a student of that college.

Afrikaners: P. J. Wassenaar; Professor Geoffrey Opland; Brand Fourie. Martin Spring was especially kind in discussing his book on South African–United States confrontation; Colin Legum; Harry Oppenheimer; The Honorable John Vorster, who spent an hour with me in forthright discussion; Jan Marais, member of Parliament, who entertained me socially and intellectually. Dr. Albert Hertzog spent a long evening sharing his views.

The English: Dr. Eily Gledhill, Grahamstown, took me on an extended field trip to sites of the Xhosa wars. Professor Guy Butler, Rhodes University, was unusually keen. Dr. Mooneen Buys of the De Beers staff discussed her doctoral thesis with me while curators of the Rhodes material provided insights, records and photographs. Professor P. H. Kapp, head of History, Rand Afrikaans University, checked the missionary section.

Black Life: I made continuous effort to meet with and understand black spokesmen. Some, like Bloke Modisane the writer, were in exile in London. Others, like the gifted social analyst Ben Magubane, of the University of Connecticut, were pursuing their careers outside South Africa; I spent three days with Magubane and he commented sharply on the Shaka chapter. Sheena Duncan was most helpful. Credo Mutwa showed me his witch doctor's establishment. Justice A. R. 'Jaap' Jacobs of Northern Cape District advised me. I spent five different days in Soweto, three under government supervision, two at night on my own. During these visits I met with many black leaders, those supporting government policies and those who were determined to end them.

Indian Community: I was able to visit various sites at which Indian merchants were being removed from areas reserved for whites. In Durban, I met with leaders of the Indian community to discuss these measures. Also A. R. Koor, Fordsburg.

Coloured Communities: My contacts were frequent, especially in Cape Town, where Brian Rees and Paul Andrews showed me squatter areas, in which I visited shacks and held discussions.

Boer War: Fiona Barbour, ethnologist at the Alexander McGregor Memorial Museum, Kimberley, analyzed the battlefields; Benjamin and Eileen Christopher conducted a two-day inspection of Spion Kop, Blaauwkrantz and the historical riches of Ladysmith; Major Philip Erskine, Stellenbosch, showed me his extraordinary collection of relics, including much material on General Buller.

Concentration Camps: Mrs. Johanna Christina Mulder, who survived the Standerton Camp, was wonderfully helpful; Johan Loock of the University of the Orange Free State provided much useful information.

Banning: In London, I spent an afternoon with Father Cosmos Desmond, who had just finished a protracted spell of banning. In 1971 I met with four banned persons, two white and two black. In 1978 I spent a morning with Reverend Beyers Naudé.

Sports: Morné du Plessis, major rugby star was most helpful; Louis Wessels, editor of a major sports magazine; Dawie de Villiers, famous Springbok captain (1971); Gary Player, with whom I had an extensive discussion in America.

Mining: I am especially indebted to Norman Kern, who spent a day showing me the deepest levels of the gold mines at Welkom.

Animals: Graeme Innes gave me three days of personal touring in Kruger National Park; Nick Steele showed me Hluhluwe and arranged for me to visit Umfolozi. Ken Tindley, a South African naturalist in charge of Gorongoza in Moçambique, allowed me to work with him for a week. John Owen and Miles Turner gave me unequaled aerial tours of Serengeti.

Vrymeer: I am particularly indebted to A. A. 'Tony' Rajchrt, who allowed me to inspect in great detail his farm at Chrissiesmeer, its operation, its chain of lakes and herd of blesbok.

Various scholars honored me by consenting to read chapters which impinged on their fields of specialization. I sought their harshest criticism and welcomed their suggestions. Where error was identified, I made corrections, but where interpretation was concerned, I sometimes ignored advice. No error which remains can be charged to anyone but me.

For each chapter, I consulted most of the available historical studies and found a wealth of material. Some of it substantiated what I wrote; some contested it. Since many biographers of Cecil Rhodes gloss over or suppress his embarrassment with the Princess Radziwill, I was left with only three accounts: two brief statements by two of his young men, and one excellent full-scale treatment by Brian Roberts: *Cecil Rhodes and the Princess.*

I wrote the brief segment in Chapter XIV concerning Cambridge University two years before the unmasking of Sir Anthony Blunt as the notorious 'fourth man.' My own inquiries had led me to his trail, or to that of someone exactly like him.

Contents

I.	Prologue	*Eland 3*
II.	Zimbabwe	*Rhinoceros 26*
III.	A Hedge of Bitter Almond	*Hippopotamus 63*
IV.	The Huguenots	*Leopard 144*
V.	The Trekboers	*Hyena 217*
VI.	The Missionary	*Wildebeest 294*
VII.	Mfecane	*Lion 371*
VIII.	The Voortrekkers	*Sable Antelope 412*
IX.	The Englishmen	*Zebra 499*
X.	The Venloo Commando	*Basuto Pony 564*
XI.	Education of a Puritan	*Springbok 636*
XII.	Achievement of a Puritan	*Elephant 694*
XIII.	Apartheid	*Cape Buffalo 736*
XIV.	Diamonds	*Giraffe 789*
	Glossary	*876*
	Genealogical Charts	*878*

This is a novel and to construe it as anything else would be an error. The settings, the characters and most of the incidents are fictional. Trianon, De Kraal, Venloo, Vrymeer and Vwarda do not exist. The Nxumalo, Van Doorn, De Groot and Saltwood families do not exist. A few real characters do appear briefly—Van Riebeeck, Shaka, Cecil Rhodes, Oom Paul Kruger and Sir Redvers Buller, for example—and things said of them relate to recorded history. The Battle of Spion Kop is faithfully summarized, as are the principal events of the Great Trek. Great Zimbabwe is accurately presented in light of recent judgments. All incidents in the chapter on apartheid are offered from the research of the author alone and are vouched for by him.

The Covenant comes to its end as of December 1979 and therefore can take no account of subsequent events, such as the independence of Zimbabwe and the extended rioting that is taking place in South Africa as these pages are being proofread. It is believed that the narrative prepares the reader for these happenings and others that will follow.

It has been impossible to avoid certain labels once popularly accepted but now deemed pejorative: Bushman (instead of San or Khoisan); Hottentot (instead of Khoi-khoi); native, Kaffir and Bantu (instead of black). Coloured is capitalized because in South Africa it designates a legal classification.

THE
COVENANT

I. Prologue

I T was the silent time before dawn, along the shores of what had been one of the most beautiful lakes in southern Africa. For almost a decade now little rain had fallen; the earth had baked; the water had lowered and become increasingly brackish.

The hippopotamus, lying with only her nostrils exposed, knew intuitively that she must soon quit this place and move her baby to some other body of water, but where and in what direction, she could not decipher.

The herd of zebra that came regularly to the lake edged their way down the bare, shelving sides and drank with reluctance the fetid water. One male, stubbornly moving away from the others, pawed at the hard earth, seeking to find a sweeter spring, but there was none.

Two female lions, who had been hunting fruitlessly all night, spotted the individualistic zebra and by arcane signals indicated that this was the one they would tackle when the herd left the lake. For the present they did nothing but wait in the dry and yellow grass.

Finally there was a noise. The sun was still some moments from the horizon when a rhinoceros, looking in its grotesque armor much the same as it had for the past three million years, rumbled down to the water and began rooting in the soft mud, searching for roots and drinking noisily through its little mouth.

When the sun was about to creep over the two conical hills that marked the eastern end of the lake, a herd of eland came to drink—big, majestic antelopes that moved with rare grace, and when they appeared, a little brown man who had been watching through the night, hidden in deep grass, whispered a prayer of thanks: 'If the eland come, there is still hope. If that rhinoceros stays, we can still eat.'

Gumsto was typical of his clan, four feet ten inches high, yellowish brown in color, thin and extremely wrinkled. Indeed, there were few areas of his body that did not contain deep indentations, and sometimes within a square inch twelve lines would run up and down, with eight or nine crisscrossing them. His face looked like the map of a very old watershed, marked by the trails of a thousand animals, and when he smiled, showing small white teeth, these wrinkles cut deeper into his countenance, making him look as if he were well past ninety. He was forty-three and his wrinkles had been with him since the age of twenty-two; they were the mark of his people.

The clan for which he was responsible numbered twenty-five; more would prove too difficult to feed; fewer, too vulnerable to attacks from animals. His consisted of himself as leader, his tough old wife Kharu, their sixteen-year-old son Gao, plus assorted males and females of all ages and all possible relationships. The safety of this clan was his obsession, but at times he could be diverted. When he looked up to greet the sun, as he did each morning, for it was the life-giver, he saw the two rounded hills, exactly like a woman's breasts, and he thought not of the safety of his clan but of Naoka.

She was seventeen, widowed when the rhinoceros now drinking at the lake killed her hunter husband. Soon she would be eligible to take a new mate, and Gumsto looked on her with longing. He realized that his wife was aware of his passion, but he had a variety of plans for circumventing her opposition. Naoka had to be his. It was only reasonable, for he was the leader.

His attention was deflected by a thunder of hooves. Zebra lookouts had spotted the two lions and had sounded retreat. Like a swarm of beautifully colored birds, the black-and-white animals scrambled up the dusty bank of the lake and headed for safety.

But the male who had seen fit to wander off, dissociating himself from the herd, now lost its protection, and the lionesses, obedient to plan, cut him off from the others. There was a wild chase, a leap onto the rear quarters of the zebra, a piteous scream, a raking claw across the windpipe. The handsome animal rolled in the dust, the lions holding fast.

Gumsto, watching every movement in the attack, muttered, 'That's what happens when you leave the clan.'

He remained immobile as seven other lions moved in to share the kill, attended by a score of hyenas who would wait for the bones, which they would crush with their enormous jaws to salvage the marrow. Aloft, a flight of vultures gathered for their share when the others were gone, and as these predators and scavengers went about their business, Gumsto proceeded with his.

His immediate responsibility was to feed his clan, and this day he would mount an attack on that rhinoceros, kill it or be killed by it, then gorge his people with one gigantic meal and move them off to some better site. As he reached these basic decisions, his small brown face was wreathed in a contented smile, for he was an optimist: There will be a better location.

Leaving the dying lake, he went to the living area of his clan, which consisted of absolutely nothing except a halting place beneath low trees. The terrain of each family was outlined by sticks and a few piled rocks, but there were no huts, no walls, no lean-tos, no paths, no shelter except grass rudely thrown across a framework of interlocked saplings. And each family's area contained only enough space for members to lie in hollows scooped out for their hips. The few possessions had been meticulously selected during centuries of wandering and were essential and tenderly prized: loincloths and skin cloaks for all, bows and arrows for the men, body powders and small adornments for the women.

Gumsto's family kept its shelter at the base of a tree, and when he had taken his position with his back against the trunk, he announced firmly, 'Antelope are leaving. Water too foul to drink. We must leave.'

Instantly old Kharu leaped to her feet and started striding about the small area, and since each of the other stick-lined habitations was close, everyone could hear her grumbling protests: 'We need more ostrich eggs. We dare not leave before Gao has killed his antelope.' On and on she ranted, a harridan of thirty-two with a horribly wrinkled face and a complaining voice. She was only four feet seven, but she exerted great influence, and when her tirade ended she threw herself upon the ground not eight inches from her husband and cried, 'It would be madness to leave.'

Gumsto, gratified that her complaint had been so moderate, turned his attention to the men in the other areas, and they, too, were so close that he could address them from his tree: 'Let us kill that rhinoceros, feed ourselves, and start for the new waters.'

'Where will we find them?'

Gumsto shrugged and pointed to the horizon.

'How many nights?'

'Who knows?'

'We know the desert continues for many nights,' a fearful man said. 'We've seen that.'

'Others have crossed it,' Gumsto said quickly. 'We know that, too.'

'But beyond? What then?'

'Who knows?'

The imprecision of his answers alarmed him as well as the others, and he might have drawn back from this great venture had he not chanced to see Naoka lolling in the dust behind the thin line of sticks that marked her quarters. She was a marvelous girl, smooth of skin and decked with beads cut from the thick shell of the ostrich egg. Her face radiated the joy of a fine young animal, and obviously she wanted a husband to replace the one the rhinoceros had killed. Aware that Gumsto was staring at her in his hungry way, she smiled and nodded slightly as if to say, 'Let's go.' And he nodded back as if to reply, 'What delight to share the dangers with you.'

It was remarkable that a girl as nubile as Naoka was available for a new marriage; a clan might operate together for thirty years without such an accident, because it was the custom of this tribe for a girl to marry when she was seven and her husband nineteen or twenty, for then trouble was avoided. It was a fine system, for the husband could rear his wife in ways he preferred; when she entered puberty to become a real wife, she would be properly disciplined, knowing what things angered or pleased her man. And he, having been forced to practice restraint while his wife was still a child—ostracism if he molested her sexually prior to her second period—acquired that self-control without which no man could ever become a good huntsman.

There were weaknesses in the system. Since the husband had to be much older than the wife, there was in any group a surplus of old widows whose men had died at the hunt or been killed by falls when searching tall trees for honey. These elderly women were welcome to stay with the band as long as they could function; when they could no longer chew or keep up with the march, they would be placed in the shade of some bush, given a bone with meat clinging to it, and one ostrich egg, and there they died in dignity as the clan moved on.

Useless old widows were therefore common, but beautiful young ones like Naoka were a precious rarity, and Gumsto calculated that if he could somehow placate old Kharu, he stood a reasonable chance of gaining Naoka as his second wife. But he realized that he must move with some caution, because Kharu had spotted his intentions, and he was aware that his son was also eying the beautiful girl, as were the other men.

So as he leaned against the tree, his right foot cradled in the cavity above his left knee, he took stock of himself. He was a normal, good-looking man, rather taller than others in his group. He was compact, angular of shoulder and slim of hip, as the desert required. His teeth were good, and although he was deeply wrinkled, his eyes were powerful, unstained by rheum or brown. Best of all, he was the master-tracker. From a distance of miles he could discern the herd of antelope blending with the sand and find the one that was going to lag, so that it could be detached and struck with an arrow.

He possessed an inner sense which enabled him to think like an animal, to anticipate where the antelope would run or where the great rhinoceros was hiding. By looking at a track days old and noticing the manner in which the sand had drifted, he could almost detect the life history of the animal. When fifteen tracks jumbled together, he could identify the one made by the creature he sought and trace it through the medley.

Night fell, and a woman responsible for tending the fire placed her branches with delicate attention, enough wood to produce a flare to warn away predators, not too much to waste fuel. The swift, sure blackness of the savanna lowered upon the camp, and the twenty-five little brown people curled up under their antelope cloaks, their hips nestled in the little hollows. Two hyenas, always on the prowl, uttered their maniacal laughs at the edge of darkness, then moved on to some less-guarded spot. A lion roared in the distance and then another, and Gumsto, planning his exodus, thought not of these great beasts but of Naoka, sleeping alone not a dozen lengths away.

His plan had two parts: ignore old Kharu's bleating but involve her always more deeply in the exodus so that she would have no alternative but to support it; and lead his hunters on the trail of that rhinoceros for one last meal. In some ways it was easier to handle the rhinoceros than Kharu, for at dawn she had six new objections, delivered in a whining voice, but despite her irritating manner her cautions were, as Gumsto had to concede, substantial.

'Where will we find ostriches, tell me that,' she railed. 'And where can we find enough beetles?'

Glaring at her ugly face, Gumsto showed the love and respect he felt for this old companion. Chucking her on the cheek, he said, 'It's your task to find the ostriches and the beetles. You always do.' And he was off to muster his men.

Each hunter reported naked, except for a quiver of slender arrows, a bow, and a meager loincloth to which could be attached a precious receptacle in which he kept his lethal arrow tips—but only when the rhinoceros was sighted. Few hunters have ever sallied forth with such equipment to do battle with so monstrous a beast.

'From the next rise we may see him,' Gumsto reassured his men, but when he followed the spoor up the hill, they saw nothing. For two days, eating mere scraps and drinking almost no water, they pressed eastward, and then on the third day, as Gumsto felt certain they must, they saw far in the distance the dark and menacing form of the rhino.

The men sucked in their breath with pleasure and fear as Gumsto sat on his heels to study the characteristics of their enemy: 'He favors his left foreleg. See, he moves it carefully to avoid pressure. He stops to rest it. Now he runs to test it. He slows again. We shall attack from that corner.'

On the next day the little hunters overtook the rhino, and Gumsto was right: the huge animal did favor his left front leg.

Deftly he positioned his men so that no matter where the beast turned, someone would have a reasonable target, and when all were ready he signaled for them to prepare their arrows, and now a cultural miracle took place, for over the centuries the clan had developed a weapon of extraordinary complexity and effectiveness. Their arrow was like no other; it consisted of three separate but interlocking parts. The first was a slight shaft, slotted at one end to fit the bowstring. The secret of the arrow was the second part, an extremely delicate shaft, fitted at each end with a collar of sinew which could be tightened. Into one collar slipped the larger shaft; into the other went a small ostrich bone, very sharp and highly polished, onto which old Kharu's deadly poison had been smeared.

When assembled, the arrow was so frail that of itself it could scarcely have killed a small bird, yet so cleverly engineered that if properly used, it could cause the death of an elephant. It represented a triumph of human ingenuity; any being who had the intellect to devise this arrow could in time contrive ways to build a skyscraper or an airplane.

When the final tip was in place—handled with extreme care, for if it accidentally scratched a man, he would die—Gumsto used hand signs to direct his hunters to close in, but as they did so he detected one last avenue down which the rhino might escape if it saw the hunters. Ordinarily he would have placed one of his practiced men at that spot, but they were required elsewhere, so perforce he turned to his son, and with deep apprehension said, 'Keep him from running this way.'

He prayed that Gao would perform well, but he had doubts. The boy was going to become a fine hunter; of that there was no doubt. But he was slow in mastering the tricks, and occasionally Gumsto had the horrifying thought: What if he never learns? Who, then, will lead this clan? Who will keep the children alive on the long marches?

Gumsto had been right to be apprehensive, for when the rhinoceros became aware of the hunters, it galloped with great fury right at Gao, who proved quite powerless to turn the beast aside. With a contemptuous snort it broke through the circle of hunters and galloped free.

The men were not hesitant to condemn Gao for his lack of bravery, since they were hungry and the escaped rhino could have fed the entire clan, and Gumsto was appalled, not at his son's poor performance in this particular hunt, but at the grave danger his clan faced. Twice recently he had sensed his age—a shortness of breath and a weakness at unexpected moments—and the safety of his people weighed heavily upon him. The inadequacy of his son reflected on him, and he was ashamed.

In sore irritation he abandoned the rhinoceros and concentrated on a herd of little springbok. Assuming full control of his men, he brought them to a spot from which they could take good aim at two animals, but neither was hit. Then Gumsto himself stalked another and lodged his arrow in the lower part of the beast's neck.

Nothing visible happened, for the arrow's weight was quite inadequate to kill the beast; all it accomplished was to deposit the tip beneath the tough outer skin, where the poison would be free to disseminate. And now the excellence of this arrow manifested itself, for the springbok, feeling the slight sting, found a tree against which to rub, and had the arrow been of one piece, it would have been dislodged. Instead, it came apart at one of the collars, allowing the shaft to fall free while the poisoned tip worked its way ever deeper into the wound.

The springbok did not die immediately, for the effect of the poisoned arrow was debilitating rather than cataclysmic, and this meant that the men would have to track their doomed prey for most of that day. During the first hours the springbok scarcely knew it was in trouble; it merely felt an itching, but as the poison slowly took effect, strength ebbed and dizziness set in.

At dusk Gumsto predicted, 'Soon he goes down,' and he was right, for now the springbok could scarcely function. Even when it saw the hunters approach, it was powerless to leap aside. It gasped, staggered, and took refuge beside a tree, against which it leaned. Pitifully it called to its vanished companions, then its knees began to crumble and all was confusion as the little men ran up with stones.

The butchering was a meticulous affair, for Gumsto had to calculate exactly how much of the poisoned meat to toss aside; not even the hyenas would eat that. The first concern of the hunters was to save the blood; to them any liquid was precious. The liver and gizzard were ripped out and eaten on the spot, but the chunks of meat were taboo until taken back to camp and ritually apportioned so that every member of the clan could have a share.

Gumsto could not be proud of his accomplishment. Instead of bringing home a huge rhinoceros, he had produced only a small springbok; his people were going to go hungry, but what was worse was that at the tracking only he had foreseen which way the animals were going to move, and this was ominous. Since the clan knew nothing of agriculture or husbandry, it lived only on such meat as their poisoned arrows killed, and if those arrows were not used properly, their diet would be confined to marginal foods: tubers, bulbs, melons, rodents, snakes and such grubs as the women might find. This band had better develop a master-hunter quickly.

Normally, the son of a leader acquired his father's skills, but with Gao this had not happened, and Gumsto suspected that the deficiency was his: I should not have allowed him to drift into peculiar ways.

He remembered his son's behavior at their first big hunt together; when other lads were hacking up the carcass, Gao was preoccupied with cutting off the tips of the horns, and Gumsto realized then that there might be trouble ahead.

'You're collecting them to hold colors?' he asked.

'Yes. I need seven.'

'Gao, our clan has always had some man like you, showing us the spirits of the animals we seek. Every band has, and we treasure the work they do. But this should come after you've learned to track and kill, not before.'

Wherever the San people had traveled during the preceding two thousand years, they had left behind on rocks and in caves a record of their passage: great leaping animals crossing the sky with brave men pursuing them, and much of the good luck the San hunters had enjoyed stemmed from their careful attention to the spirits of the animals.

But before prayers, before obeisance to the animal spirits, before anything else on earth, the band must eat, and for a lad of sixteen to be delinquent in the skills of obtaining food was worrisome.

And then a shameful thought crept up on Gumsto: If Gao turns out to be a proficient hunter, he will be entitled to Naoka. As long as he remains the way he is, I face no trouble from that quarter. That exquisite woman was reserved for a real man, a master-hunter, and he himself was the only one available.

So when the meager portions of meat were distributed, he asked his wife airily, 'Have you talked with the widow Kusha about her daughter?'

'Why should I?' Kharu growled.

'Because Gao needs a wife.'

'Let him find one.' Kharu was the daughter of a famous hunter and took nonsense from no one.

'What's he to do?'

Kharu had had enough. Rushing at her husband, she shouted for all to hear, 'It's your job, worthless! You haven't taught him to hunt. And no man can claim a wife till he's killed his antelope.'

Gumsto weighed carefully what to say next. He was not truly frightened of his tough old wife, but he was attentive, and he was not sure how he ought to broach this delicate matter of moving Naoka into his ménage.

How beautiful she was! A tall girl, almost four feet nine, she was exquisite as she lay in the dust, her white teeth showing against her lovely brown complexion. To see her flawless skin close to Kharu's innumerable wrinkles was to witness a miracle, and it was impossible to believe that this golden girl could ever become like that old crone. Naoka was precious, a resonant human being at the apex of her attractiveness, with the voice of a whispering antelope and the litheness of a gazelle. Desperately Gumsto wanted her.

'I was thinking of Naoka,' he said carefully.

'Fine girl,' Kharu said. 'Gao could marry her if he knew how to hunt.'

'I wasn't thinking of Gao.'

He was not allowed to finish his line of reasoning, for Kharu shouted across the narrow space, 'Naoka! Come here!'

Idly, and with the provocative lassitude of a young girl who knows herself to be desirable, Naoka rolled from the hip on which she had been resting, adjusted her bracelets, looked to where Kharu waited, rose slowly, and delicately brushed the dust from her body, taking special care with her breasts, which glowed in the sun. Picking her way carefully, she stepped the few feet into Kharu's quarters.

'Good wishes,' she said as if completing a journey of miles.

'Are you still grieving?' Kharu asked.

'No.' The girl spoke with lovely intonation, each word suggesting others that might have been said. 'No, Kharu, dearest friend, I'm just living.' And she squatted on her haunches, knees and thighs tightly flexed, her bottom just off the ground.

'That's a poor life, Naoka dear. That's why I called.'

'Why?' Her face was a placid mask of innocence.

'Because I want to help you find a husband.'

Disdainfully the girl waved her right arm, indicating the bleak settlement: 'And where do you expect to find me a husband?'

'My son Gao needs a wife.'

'Has he spoken to Kusha? She has a baby daughter.'

'I wasn't really thinking of Kusha . . . or her daughter.'

'No?' the girl asked softly, smiling at Gumsto in a way to make him dizzy.

'I've been thinking of you,' Kharu said, adding quickly, 'Now if you married Gao . . .'

'Me?' the girl said in what seemed astonishment. Appealing to Gumsto, she added, 'I'd never be the proper wife for Gao, would I?'

'And why not?' Kharu demanded, rising.

'Because I'm like you, Kharu,' the girl said quietly. 'The daughter of a great hunter. And I was the wife of a hunter, not quite as good as Gumsto.' She flashed a look of power at the little man, then added, 'I could never marry Gao. A man who has not yet killed his eland.'

For this terrible dismissal she had chosen a freighted word: *eland.* The clan coexisted with the antelope, finding in them their physical and spiritual needs. They divided the breed into some twenty categories, each its own distinguished unit with its own terrain and individual habits. Any hunter ignorant of the variations of the antelope was ignorant of life.

There were the elegant little klipspringers, not much larger than a big bird; the small impala with black stripes marking their rumps; and the graceful springbok that could leap as if they had wings. There were the duiker, red and short-horned, and a universe of middle-sized animals: steenbok, gemsbok, blesbok and bushbuck, each with a different type of horn, each with its distinctive coloring.

These prolific animals of the middle range the hunters stalked incessantly; they provided much food. But there were four larger antelope that fascinated the little men, for one of these animals would feed a clan: the bearded wildebeest that trampled the savanna in their millions; the lyre-horned nyala; the huge kudu with its wildly twisting horns and white stripes; and rarest of all, the glorious sable with its enormous back-curved horns, so enchanting that hunters sometimes stood transfixed when they chanced to see one. Beast of beauty, animal of wonder, the sable appeared only rarely, as an apparition, and men at their campfires would often recall where and when they had seen their first. Not often was a sable killed, for the gods had given them perceptiveness beyond normal; they kept to the darker groves and rarely appeared at exposed watering holes.

That left the animal which the hunters treasured above all others: the giant eland, taller than a man, a remarkable beast with horns that twisted three or four times from forehead to tip, a tuft of black hair between the horns, a massive dewlap, and a distinctive white stripe separating forequarters from the bulk of the body. To the hunters this stately animal provided food to the body, courage to the heart and meaning to the soul. An eland was walking proof that gods existed, for who else could have contrived such a perfect animal? It gave structure to San life, for to catch it men had to be clever and well organized. It served also as spiritual summary to a people lacking cathedrals and choirs; its movements epitomized the universe and formed a measuring rod for human behavior. The eland was not seen as a god, but rather as proof that gods existed, and when, after the hunt, the meat of its body was apportioned, all who ate shared its quintessence, a belief in no way unusual; thousands of years after the death of Gumsto, other religions would arise in which the ritual of eating of a god's body would confer benediction.

So Naoka, faithful to the traditions of her people, could laugh at old Kharu and reject the idea of a marriage with Gao: 'Let him prove himself. Let him kill his eland.'

It was now obvious to Kharu that unless she made it possible for her son Gao to qualify as a hunter, and thus marry Naoka, that young woman was going to steal Gumsto, who showed himself pathetically eager for the theft. It became advisable for the old woman to encourage hunts, but to do this she must ensure an abundant supply of poison for the arrows. That had always been her responsibility, and she was prepared to find a new supply now.

Like her husband, she was deeply worried about the safe continuance of her clan, and she saw that to protect it she must instruct other women in the collecting of poisons, but none had demonstrated any special skill. Clearly, Naoka was the one on whom the clan must depend in the future, and it was Kharu's job to induct her, regardless of the fear in which she held her.

'Come,' she muttered one morning, 'we must replenish the poison.' And the two women, so ill-matched and so suspicious of each other, set forth upon their search.

They walked nearly half a day toward the north, two women alone on the savanna with always the chance of encountering a lion or a rhinoceros, but driven by the necessity of finding that substance which alone would enable the band to survive. So far they had found nothing.

'What we're looking for is beetles,' old Kharu said as they searched the arid land, 'but only the ones with two white dots.' In fact, they were not looking for adult beetles, only for their larvae, and always of that special breed with the white specks and, Kharu claimed, an extra pair of legs.

It was impossible to explain how, over a period of more than ten thousand years, the women and their ancestors had isolated this little creature which alone among beetles was capable of producing a poison of remorseless virulence. How had such a discovery been made? No one remembered, it had occurred so very long ago. But when men can neither read nor write, when they have nothing external to distract their minds, they can spend their lives in minute observation, and if they have thousands of years in which to accumulate folk wisdom, it can become in time wisdom of a very high order. Such people discover plants which supply subtle drugs, and ores which yield metals, and signs in the sky directing the planting of crops, and laws governing the tides. Gumsto's San people had had time to study the larvae of a thousand different insects, finding at last the only one that produced a deadly poison. Old Kharu was the repository of this ancient lore, and now she was initiating young Naoka.

'There he is!' she cried, delighted at having tracked down her prey, and with Naoka at her side, watching attentively, she lay prone, her face a few inches from earth: 'Always look for the tiny marks he leaves. They point to his hiding place below.' And with her grubbing stick she dug out the harmless larva. Later, when it had been dried in the sun, pulverized and mixed with gummy substances obtained from shrubs, it would convert into one of the most venomous toxins mankind would discover, slow-acting but inevitably fatal.

'Now my son can kill his eland,' Kharu said, but Naoka smiled.

Only two tasks remained before the imperiled clan was free to embark upon its heroic journey: Gumsto must lead his men to kill a ritual eland to ensure survival; and his wife must seek out the ostriches. Gumsto attacked his problem first.

On the night before the hunt began, he sat by the fire and told his men, 'I have sometimes followed an eland for three days, hit him with my arrow, then tracked him for two more. And when I stood over his fallen body, beautiful and slain, tears sprang from my eyes, even though I had tasted no water for three days.'

The effect of this statement was ruined when Kharu growled, 'We're not interested in what you did. What are you going to do this time? To help your son kill his eland?' Gumsto, staring lasciviously at Naoka, ignored the question, and was profoundly excited when the girl winked at him, but on the hunt his desire to find an inheritor of his skills drove him to work with Gao as never before.

'In tracking, you notice everything, Gao. This touch here means that the animal leans slightly to the right.'

'Is it an eland?'

'No, but it is a large antelope. If we came upon it, we'd be satisfied.'

'But in your heart,' Gao said, 'you would want it to be an eland?'

Gumsto did not reply, and on the fifth day he spotted an eland spoor, and the great chase was on. Avidly he and his men trailed a herd of some two dozen animals, and at last they spotted them. Gumsto explained to his son which of the animals was the most likely target, and with caution they moved in.

The delicate arrows flew. Gumsto's struck. The eland rubbed itself against a tree, and the poison collected by Kharu and Naoka began to exert its subtle effect. One day, two days, then a moonless night settled over the savanna and in darkness the great beast made a last effort to escape, pushing its anguished legs up a small hill, slowly, slowly, with the little men always following, never rushing their attack, for they were confident.

At dawn the eland swayed from side to side, no longer in control of its movements. The fine horns were powerless; the head lowered; and a violent sickness attacked its innards. He coughed to clear himself of this undefined pain, then tried to gallop off.

The animal stumbled, recovered, and got to the top of a sandy rise, turning there to face his pursuers. When he saw Gumsto charging at him with a club, he leaped forward to repel this challenge, but all parts of his body failed at once, and he fell in a heap. But still he endeavored to protect himself, lashing out with his hooves.

And so he lay, fighting with phantoms and with the shadows of little men, defending himself until the last moment when rocks began smashing down upon his face and he rolled in the dust.

With intense passion Gumsto wished to utter some cry that would express his religious joy in slaying this noble beast, but his throat was parched and he could do nothing but reach down and touch the fallen eland. As he did so he saw that Gao had tears for the death of this creature, and with a wild leap he caught his son's hands and danced with him beside the eland.

'You were the good hunter today!' Gumsto shouted, inviting the other men to join, and they did, in celebration of the eland and Gao's honest participation. As they danced, one man who stood aside began a song of praise for this eland who had defended himself so gallantly:

> 'Head down, dewlap astray, dark eyes bleeding,
> Sun on the rise, night forgotten and the glades . . .
>   He stands, he stands.
> Hot sand at the hooves, dark pain in the side,
> Sun at the peak, morning forgotten and the lakes . . .
>   He stands, he stands.
>
> Dark head, white line along the flanks, sharp horns,
> Soul of a dying world, eyes that pierce my soul . . .
>   He falls, he falls.
> And I am left with the falling of the sun.'

While the other women dried strips of eland to take on the perilous journey, Kharu attended to the ostriches, and with Naoka at her side to learn this element of survival, she walked far south to where the huge birds sometimes nested. She was not concerned with the birds themselves, for they were barely edible; what she sought were their eggs, especially old ones that had not hatched and were dried in the sun.

When they had collected a score, their contents long since evaporated, they wrapped them carefully in the cassocks they wore, slung them over their shoulders, and returned to camp, where the men were much relieved to see their success.

'We're almost ready to leave,' Kharu said, as if she had satisfied herself with omens, but before the clan dare move, she and Naoka must attend to the eggs. They carried them to the edge of the brackish water, and there, with a sharp stone awl, she made a neat hole in the end of each egg. Then Naoka submerged it in the lake, allowing it to fill. When all the eggs contained water, however poor, Kharu studied them for leakage and instructed Naoka in plugging the holes with wads of twisted grass: 'These will keep the clan alive through two risings of the new moon.'

When the time came to assemble the travelers, Gao was missing, and a young hunter said, 'He's up there.'

High on the rear face of the hill, in a kind of cave, they found Gao standing by a fire. About his hips hung a rhinoceros-skin belt, from which dangled seven antelope tips containing his colors. On a sloping rock he had engraved with a series of puncturing dots his evocation of the dark rhinoceros which had escaped because of his carelessness. With purity of line he boldly indicated the head with one sweep from mouth to horn, using another unbroken line to show the huge bulk of the animal, horn to tail. It was in the representation of the hindquarters, however, that he was most effective, for with one swift stroke he indicated both the form of the ham and its motion in running. The front legs, thundering across the veld, he again indicated in one sweep of line, and the colors he used to show the animal in its swift movement through the grass vibrated against the heavy color of the rock.

Run through the grass, dark beast! Gallop over the unconquered savanna, horns high! For a thousand years and then ten thousand run free, head level with the earth, feet pumping power, line and color in perfect harmony. Even Gumsto, looking at the completed animal, had to admit that his son had transmuted the moment of defeat when the rhinoceros broke free into a glowing record of what had otherwise been a disappointing day, and he was personally proud when a singer chanted:

> 'Earth trembling, sky thundering, heart catapulting,
> He breaks free, earth thundering,
> And my joy gallops with him . . .'

But he controlled his enthusiasm by warning his son, 'You caught him with your paints. Now you must catch him with your arrows.'

Why did the San, these Bushmen—as they would be called later—take so much trouble to depict the animals they killed for food? Was it to release the soul of the beast so that it might breed again? Or was it expiation of the guilt of killing? Or an evocation of animal-as-god? It is impossible to say; all we know is that in thousands of spots throughout southern Africa these hunters did paint their animals with a love that would never be exceeded. Anyone who saw Gao's rhinoceros would feel his heart skip with pleasure, for this was an animal that throbbed with life. It represented one of the purest expressions of art that man would achieve, and it came in the waking hours of human civilization. It was a product of man at his most unsullied, when artistic expression of the highest order was as natural and as necessary as hunting.

But Gumsto's theory on the matter must also be taken seriously. He asked each of his hunters to stand by the fire and look at the rhino over the left shoulder: 'It's bound to bring us good luck.' He knew that art contained a much-needed talismanic power.

In the 1980s experts from other continents would hear of this rhinoceros and come to stand in awe at the competence of the artist who had created it. One critic, familiar with Lascaux and Altamira, would say in his report:

> This splendid rhinoceros, painted by some unknown Bushman, is as fine a work of art as anything being done in the world today. Fortunately, someone built a fire in the cave, so we can carbon-date it to 13,000 B.P.E. (Before the Present Era), which makes us wonder at the excellent technical quality of the pigments, which seem much better than the ones we use today. But the excellence of this work lies in the power with which the animal is depicted. He is real. He flees real hunters whom we do not see. His head is held high in the joy of victory. But there is more. This is an evocation of all animals as seen by a man who loved them, and with this wild and joyous rhinoceros we gallop into worlds we might otherwise not have known.

Since the San could never know when they might kill another animal, when they did get one they gorged outrageously—eat, sleep, eat, fall in a stupor, eat some more—after which an amazing transformation occurred: the deep wrinkles that marred their bodies began to disappear; their skins became soft and rounded once more; and even old women of thirty-two like Kharu filled out and became beautiful, as they had been years before. Gumsto, seeing her thus, thought: She's beautiful the way I remember her. But then he saw Naoka lying insolently in the sun and he had thoughts that were more pertinent: But Naoka's going to look beautiful tomorrow, too.

After the eland was consumed, Gumsto said, 'In the morning we start,' and all that night he stood beside the lake that had comforted his people. He watched the animals come and go and was pleased when the zebra and the antelope stayed close together, each to its own clan, all members obedient to one general discipline which enabled them to survive attacks by the prowling lions.

At dawn, as if to send the travelers on their way, a host of pink flamingos rose from the far end of the lake and flew in drifting arcs across the sky, turning at the other end and doubling back in lovely involuted curves. Back and forth they flew some twenty times, like the shuttle in a loom weaving a cloth of pink and gold. Often they dipped low as if about to land, only to sweep suddenly upward to form gracious designs in their tapestry, the bright pink circles on their wings spilling through the air in vivid color, their long red legs trailing aft, their white necks extended fore.

As Gumsto watched them, they circled for the last time, then headed north. They, too, were abandoning this lake.

When the file formed up, twenty-five persons one behind the other, Gumsto was not in the lead. That spot was taken by old Kharu, who carried a digging stick and about her shoulders a skin garment in whose flowing cape she had wrapped four ostrich eggs filled with water. Each of the other women carried the same supply, with little girls caring for only two.

She was in command because the clan was heading due west for five days to a spot where, two years before, Kharu had buried an emergency nest of nine eggs against the day when stragglers reached there exhausted. Since they were leaving this area, she wanted to recover those eggs and take them with her.

As they moved into land where few lakes or springs existed, she became the spiritual leader, for she knew the curious places where dew-water might be hiding. Or striding along earth so parched that water might never have existed there, she would spy a tendril so brown and withered that it must be dead, but when with her digging stick she traced it far underground, she would find attached to the vine a globular-root which, when dragged to the surface and compressed, yielded good water.

She enforced one inviolable rule: 'Do not use the ostrich eggs.' She was in charge of the water, and would allow no one to touch it. 'Dig for the roots. Drink them.' The ostrich eggs must be reserved for those frightening days when there were no roots.

Gumsto's clan did not inhabit this vast area alone. There were other San tribes hidden away in the savanna, and often they would meet as their journeys crisscrossed, and sometimes a woman from one clan would leave to marry a hunter from another, or children whose parents had died would be adopted from group to group. And in these chance meetings Gumsto's people would hear of other bands less fortunate: 'They went into the desert without enough water and were seen no more.'

It was Kharu's responsibility to see that this did not happen to her people, and often as they walked she would pass many trees without stopping, then notice one with a slightly different look, and when she went to that tree she would find trapped in the fork where branch met trunk a cache of sweet water.

Best of all, she would sometimes walk ahead for two or three days, her ostrich eggs bouncing behind, convinced that water lay hidden somewhere —her eyes sweeping from one horizon to the other. Then, stopping for the others to catch up with her, and in obedience to some signal they could not detect, she would indicate with her digging stick that all must head in this direction, and when they attained a slight rise they would see a far bank covered with vines bearing tsama melons, speckled, smaller than a man's head and filled with loose pulp from which extraordinary amounts of water could be extracted.

A tsama melon, Gumsto decided, was among the most beautiful objects in the world, almost as lovely as Naoka. He had been watching the girl, and was impressed by the manner in which she listened to Kharu's instructions in the rules for survival; at the end of this journey the girl was going to be competent to lead her own band across deserts, and Gumsto intended sharing that leadership with her.

'I am still thinking about Naoka,' he told Kharu one night.

'I think about her, too,' the old woman said.

'You do?'

'She will soon be ready to lead this clan. But she must have a husband, a young one, and if we can't find her one, we should give her to some other clan, for she is going to be a strong woman.'

Gumsto was about to say that he had seen enough of strong women, but Kharu interrupted: 'There are the thorn bushes!' and when she ran to them and uncovered the nine hidden ostrich eggs, she found the water still sweet. Sighing with gratitude, she said, 'Now we can enter the desert.'

Gumsto spent that night beset by two nagging problems: he could not understand how old Kharu could frustrate every plan he devised for taking Naoka to be his extra wife; and he could not cease staring hungrily at that beautiful girl. It was tantalizing to see her, smooth-skinned and lovely in the moonlight, with dust upon her long legs, lying so near to him and yet untouchable.

But as the long night passed, he had to admit that on one basic fact, Kharu was right. If she could instruct Naoka, a girl she disliked, in the principles of survival, he was obligated to speed his son's induction into manhood, and if in so doing, he qualified Gao to marry Naoka, that was a small price to pay for the safety of the clan. So he began investigating the terrain, looking for locations where eland might be grazing.

It was he who now walked at the head of the file, for the clan was penetrating land they had not touched before, and quick decisions were often necessary. They were a curious lot as they walked bravely into the arid lands, with four peculiarities that would astonish all who came in contact with them later.

Their hair did not grow like that of other people; it appeared in little twisted tufts, separated one from the other by considerable space of empty scalp.

The women had buttocks of enormous size, some projecting so far backward that they could be used by babies to ride upon. *Steatopygia* this phenomenon would be called (suet buttocks), and it was so pronounced that alien observers frequently doubted the evidence of their own eyes.

Their language was unique, for in addition to the hundred or so distinctive sounds from which the world's languages were constructed—the *ich* of German for example, or the *ñ* of Spanish, the San added five unique click sounds formed with lip, tongue and palate. One click sounded like a noisy kiss, one like a signal to a horse, one a clearing of the throat. Thus Gumsto used the normal complement of consonants and vowels, plus the five clicks, making his speech an explosive chatter unrivaled in the world.

The male penis was perpetually in a state of erection. When the first observers reported this to an incredulous world, explorers rushed to confirm the miraculous condition, and one French scientist said, 'They are always at the ready, like a well-trained unit of infantry.'

When they were far into the desert, their search for food became so imperative that they could not make much forward progress, but even so, their drift toward the west and south was irreversible, and as the moons changed they passed deeper and deeper into the desert. It was not an endless sweep of white sand, such as the desert of northern Africa would become in historic periods; it was a rolling, brutal mix of isolated rock sentinels, thorn bush clinging to the red sun-bleached surface, little animals scurrying about at night, larger antelope and their predators moving by day in ceaseless search for water, but never seen. To venture forth upon this cruel expanse of blazing noontimes and bitterly cold nights even if one had adequate food and water would be daring; to try to cross it as these Bushmen were doing was heroic.

One afternoon Kharu, always casting about with hungry eyes, leaped in the air like a gazelle, shouted 'Ooooooooo!' and sped across the desert like an antelope with torn and dirty coat. She had spied a tortoise, and when she captured it, with the band cheering, she looked up in wrinkled triumph, her tiny hands holding the delicacy above her head. A fire was quickly started from the rapid friction of two sticks, and when the coals were hottest the tortoise was pitched upon them, upside down, and there it sizzled, sending its precious aroma through the clan.

The steam popped its shell apart, and when it cooled Kharu apportioned its meat and juices, not much more than a smear to each of the twenty-five, and an extra dab to Kusha, who was pregnant, and although the amount each received was scarcely enough to chew, it had a wondrous effect, for it reminded the small people of what food was like. It could not possibly have satiated anyone, but it sustained everyone.

The problem of water was equally acute, for in the desert none was found in the tree forks, and often there were no trees. Tsama melons, which could survive almost anywhere, were sparse and shriveled in this terrain. The wanderers had been forced to draw upon the ostrich eggs until there were only nine left, but Kharu knew from past adventures that this water must be kept for the last extremity, and they were far from that. With her stick she dug for roots that might contain a tiny bit of liquid and allowed her people to chew on these until their mouths were wet. She sought any shrub that might have trapped an accumulation of dew, and always she looked for indications that some deep-hidden trickle was moving beneath the rocky sand.

When she located such a spot she dug as deeply as she could with her hands, then pushed a long reed beneath the surface. If she guessed right, she could painfully suck out small amounts of water, drop by drop, and take them into her mouth but not drink them. Along another reed, which she held in the corner of her lips, she let the water trickle down into an ostrich egg, from which her threatened companions would later drink.

When two days passed with no water at all, it was obvious that she must begin to draw upon the nine eggs, and in accordance with ancient tradition she drew first upon the seven carried by others, reserving hers for what were called 'the dying days.' Each noon, when the sun was hottest, she moved among her people, encouraging them: 'We will find water soon,' and she would refuse them a ration, but in the late afternoon, when they had survived the worst, she would order an egg to be passed, not to drink, but for a wetting of the lips, and as the water diminished a mysterious phenomenon overtook the women who carried the eggs. As long as the eggs were full and heavy they constituted a burden pulling down on the women's shoulders; but even with this weight, they moved with light steps, knowing that they carried the safety of all; but when the water was drunk, making the eggs no longer a burden, the women walked painfully, their shoulders hungry for the lost weight, their minds always brooding upon their inability to be of further service because of their empty shells.

Kharu, feeling the consoling heaviness of her eggs, knew that as long as she could retain them, the clan could live, but the afternoon came when she, too, had to broach one of them, the next to last, and when the journey resumed she could detect the difference in weight, and the terror began.

As the senior woman she had another obligation not to be avoided: it came when Kusha went into labor, forcing the band to halt in a barren stretch of sand. It was the custom for pregnant women about to deliver to move apart from the others, seeking some gully or tree-protected glade, and here, unaided, to bring forth the newborn, and Kusha did this, but after a while she summoned Kharu, and the withered old woman went behind the hillock to find that Kusha had delivered twins, a boy and a girl.

She knew instantly what she must do. Placing the tiny female at Kusha's breast, she took the male aside and with her digging stick prepared a shallow grave. With gentleness she placed the boy in it, and hardened her heart when he began to cry. Quickly she smothered the babe by throwing down earth to refill the hole, for although children were needed to keep the clan vital, twins were omens of bad luck, and when a choice as painful as this became obligatory, it was always the male that was sacrificed. Even one extra infant, during a desert crossing, would consume water that might prove critical.

Kharu, having discharged her obligations, now demanded that Gumsto fulfill his: 'We must take even the boldest steps to secure water and meat. And you must allow Gao to do the killing, for he cannot lead this clan without a wife.'

Gumsto nodded. He had used every stratagem to delay this moment, but now he was satisfied that his son must ready himself for command: 'It's difficult to think of him leading the hunters. Or Naoka gathering beetles.'

Kharu smiled at him. 'You're an old man now. It's time you gave up your foolish dreams.' She moved close to him and took his hand. 'We never suffered in this clan when you were leader. Now teach Gao to be like you.'

He took his son aside and said grimly, 'We are close to perishing unless we have the courage to take daring steps. Those hills to the west, I'm sure they hold eland and water. But they also hold lions. Are you ready?' When Gao nodded, Gumsto led the file west, with everyone surviving precariously on sips of water from Kharu's final egg.

As they headed for the ridge of hills they were kept under observation:

far in the blazing sky, wheeling endlessly to mark anything that moved across the desert, a flight of vultures watched the tiny band impassively. That these forlorn stragglers would accomplish their salvation seemed most improbable, and the vultures waited, patterning the sky with impatience. Hyenas stirred in various parts of the desert, for if the vultures remained aloft, some living thing must be about to perish, and the scavengers moved close, certain that some older person would soon fall behind.

This time they were cheated by old Kharu, her wrinkles so deep that not even dust could penetrate. It was she who apportioned the last water from her final egg and who then strode ahead, determined to keep her people moving forward, and it was she, not her husband, who first saw the eland exactly where he had predicted.

It was a frustrating hunt. Near death from thirst and hunger, the little band watched impotently as the eland moved majestically out of one trap after another; the combined skills of Gumsto and his son were neutralized by the cleverness of the animals. On the second night the fatigued men heard an ominous roaring, and for a long time no one spoke, but finally Gao, who understood animals, uttered the fateful words: 'We must use the lions.'

This strategy was usually avoided, for it entailed so much danger that none of the hunters wished to employ it, but old Kharu, who was watching her clan disintegrate, desperately wanted to encourage the men. She knew that in matters of hunting, decisions must always be left to them; nevertheless, when no one supported her son, she broke ancient tradition by thrusting herself into the midst of the hunters and saying firmly, 'Gao is right. We shall die if we don't use the lions.'

Gumsto looked at his weather-beaten old woman with pride, knowing the courage required for her to intrude upon this meeting. 'Tomorrow we will use the lions,' he said.

This tactic, used only in extremity, would require the united effort of all, even the children, and the probability was great that one or several would lose their lives, but when the continuance of the band was at stake, there was no alternative.

'We go,' Gumsto said quietly, and his little people spread themselves into a half-moon, creeping toward the eland. Gao left the group to ascertain exactly where the lions dozed, and when he signaled their position, Gumsto and another hunter started to move noisily, so that the eland would hear them and edge away. As planned, the big animals did see them, did become nervous, and did run off, directly into the claws of the tawny beasts. A female lion grasped the throat of the biggest eland, bit into its neck, and brought it down.

Now came the time for audacity and precise execution. Gumsto and Gao kept their people in hiding, each person quietly grasping clubs and rocks for the heroic moment. They watched the lions feeding, and the lips of even the bravest grew dry; the hearts of the women beat faster in contemplation of what they must now do; and children who had never previously participated in a hunt knew that they must succeed or perish.

'Now!' Gumsto cried, and with a sudden rush, everyone surged forward, shouting madly, brandishing clubs and hurling rocks to drive the lions from their kill.

It was a most perilous maneuver, for the lions could easily have slain any one or two or three of the San, but to have so many rushing at them and with so much confusion bewildered the beasts, and they started to mill about. It was at this point that Gumsto sprang directly at the principal lions, beating them about the face with his club.

He had volunteered for this suicidal mission because the continuance of his band was more important than the continuance of his life, but at the moment when all hung in the balance—one man against the lions—he was saved by the sudden appearance of Gao at his side, roaring and thrashing, and forcing the snarling lions to withdraw.

But when the eland was taken by the San, with a dozen hyenas chuckling in anticipation, it was neither Gumsto nor Gao who assumed charge, but Kharu, rummaging with bloody hands through the exposed entrails until she found the most precious portion of the carcass, the rumen, that preliminary stomach of all animals called ruminants. When she felt how heavy it was, her old face broke into smiles, for it was here that the dead eland had collected grass for later digestion, and with it a large amount of water to make the grass soft.

Ripping open the rumen, Kharu squeezed the grassy accumulation, expelling enough liquid to fill her eggs, and in a peculiar way this liquid was better than water, for it was astringent, and bitter, and cleansing, and when she doled out a few drops to all, their thirst was assuaged. On this miraculous fluid the band would survive.

At the end of their joyous feasting, the exhausted gluttons lay about the carcass in stupor, their bellies extended; when they revived, Kharu made her speech: 'Since Gao found the eland, and since he drove away the lions, let us proclaim him a hunter and award him a wife. Naoka, step forward.'

One man, a considerable hunter himself, protested justifiably that since Gao had not actually slain the eland, he did not qualify, and there was consternation. But Kharu nudged her husband forcefully, and Gumsto stepped forward. Taking his son by the hand, he stood before the clan and said proudly, 'A lion is just as important as an eland. And this boy drove away four lions that were about to kill me. He is a hunter.' And with emotions that almost tore him apart, he passed his son's hand into that of Naoka.

'Ah-wee!' Kharu cried, leaping into the air. 'We shall dance.' And when the calabash sounded, and hands beat out the rhythm, the little people swirled in joy, celebrating their victory over the lions and the satisfying news that soon Naoka and Gao would have children to perpetuate the clan. Round and round they went, shouting old words and stomping to raise a sanctifying dust. All night they danced, dropping at times from exhaustion, but even from their fallen positions they continued to shout oracular words. Other antelope would be caught; other wells would be found for replenishing the eggs; children would grow to manhood; and their wandering would never cease. They were hunter-gatherers, the people with no home, no fixed responsibilities except the conservation of food and water against the day of peril, and when the allotted moons had come and gone, the dancers would go, too, and others would cross these barren wastes and dance their dances through the long nights.

Gumsto, watching the celebrants, thought: Kharu was right, as usual. The young to the young. The old to the old. Everything has its rules. And when he saw his wife dancing vigorously with the women, he leaped up and joined the men. Kharu, watching him, noticed that he limped slightly, but she said nothing.

The festivities had to be brief, for the clan must move on to safer areas, but in the moving, Kharu saw something else that disturbed her: Gumsto was beginning to lag, surrendering his accustomed position in the van to Gao, and when this had occurred several times, she spoke to him.

'Are you grieving over Naoka? You know she merited a younger husband.'

'It's my leg.'

'What?' The simplicity of her question hid the terror she felt, for a damaged leg was about the worst thing that could happen on a journey.

'When we charged the lions . . .'

'They clawed you?'

'Yes.'

'Oh, Gumsto!' she wailed. 'And I sent you on that mission.'

'You came, too. The lions could have got you.' He sat on a rock while Kharu explored the sore, and from the manner in which he winced when she touched certain nerves she knew that it was in sad condition. 'In two days we'll look again,' she said, but when he walked with a sideways limp, dragging his left leg, she knew that neither two days nor twenty would heal his hurt. And she noticed that aloft three vultures followed him with the same relentless attention he had exercised when tracking a wounded antelope.

Whenever the clan moved onward, she stayed close to him, and once when the pain surged with great force and he bit his lip to prevent tears from showing, she led him to a resting spot, and there they remembered the days when he had taken his eland to her father, that great hunter, and asked for Kharu in marriage.

'You were seven,' Gumsto said, 'and already you knew all things.'

'My mother mastered the desert.'

'You were a good child.'

'I was proud of you. Taller, stronger than the husbands of the other girls.'

'Kharu, they were good days, in those lands around the lake.'

'But the water grew stale. The water always grows stale.'

'The rhinoceros, the herds of wildebeest, the zebras.' He recounted his triumphs from the days when his band ate well.

'You were as knowing as my father,' she conceded. Then she helped him rejoin the band as it moved south, and when it became apparent that he could never again lead the hunt, she told Gao, 'Now you must find the meat.'

Gumsto's accident produced an unforeseen result that both pleased and perplexed him. When the band halted eight days, both to replenish their

ostrich eggs and give him time to recover, Gao quickly left the camp to find
a large slab of smooth stone, on which he worked with furious energy during
all daylight hours. From his resting place Gumsto could see his son, and
guessed that he was creating a memorial to some important animal, but
later, when Kharu helped him to the rock, he was unprepared for the
wonder that was revealed.

Across a broad expanse Gao had formed not one eland but thirty-three,
each as well composed as any he had previously drawn, but done with such
fury that they exploded across their stony savanna. They leaped and quivered and exulted and rushed at unseen targets, a medley of horn and hoof
that would astonish the world when it was discovered.

But there was a deficiency, and Gumsto noticed it immediately: 'You
haven't colored them carefully.'

He was right. Gao had worked so feverishly to record this epic before
his band moved on, that in the end he had simply splashed colors here and
there, attempting to finish some of the creatures, satisfied with merely
indicating the hue of others. The result was a confusion of movement and
color, though it did give the massive composition a curious balance and a
sense of real eland chasing across the timeless rock.

But why had the boy been so careless? Time was pressing, but he could
have pleaded for two extra days. Pigments were also precious, and perhaps he realized he might not have enough to show each of the thirty-
three properly, but he could have enlisted some hunter to help him
find more.

There were a dozen other reasonable explanations for the wild coloring,
but none approached the truth: Gao had created the eland in this arbitrary
manner because at the height of his powers, when his senses were ablaze,
he had experienced a revelation which showed that it was not the faithful
laying down of color within the confines of his composition that would
best indicate the reality of an eland, but a wild splashing that would
catch the spirit of the sacred animals. It was an accident, the kind of
accident that inspired artists contrive, and Gao could not explain it to
his father.

Gumsto did not like the carelessness, not at all, for he deemed it an
insolence to the eland, whose colors should be thus and so, as all men knew,
but as he was about to complain he saw in the lower right-hand corner
of the mural his son's depiction of a San hunter, a man awed by the eland
but facing them with his frail arrow, and he saw that this little fellow
was himself. This was a summary of his life, the recollection of all the
eland he had slain to assure his people survival and meaning, and he
was silent.

Three times he asked his son to carry him back so that he might study
it, and live again with the animals that had meant so much, and whenever
he saw himself so small at the lower corner he felt that Gao was right. This
was the manner of life, that a man live forever with the major concerns, not
with the grubs hiding under the bark of the thorn tree. To be on the savanna
with a tiny arrow tip, and it the difference between death and life, and to
throw oneself among the mightiest of the antelope, not the klipspringer and

the duiker, and to fight them as they came, that was the nature of man—
and it was his son who had shown him this truth.

When the others realized that Gumsto's days were almost finished, for he
was now forty-five, a very old age for these people, they knew that the day
was approaching when they could wait for him no longer, and one afternoon
they watched indulgently as he crawled from his area into the one occupied
by Gao and Naoka, where the young bride lolled in the sand. 'I wanted you
for my wife,' he told her. She smiled. 'We could have . . .'

'It's better this way,' she said without moving. 'Gao is young and you're
an old man now.'

'No more hunting,' he said.

'How good that your son learned.'

'Indeed,' the old man agreed. He had an infinity of things he wished to
say to this splendid girl with the unwrinkled face, but she seemed uninter-
ested, yet when he started to crawl back to his own area she smiled at him
in her ravishing way and said, 'I would have liked you for my husband,
Gumsto. You were a man.' She sighed. 'But my father was a man, too, and
one day Gao will be as great a hunter as either of you.' She sighed again.
'It's always for the best.'

Everyone in the tribe knew that the decision had to be made. Gumsto
lagged so constantly that he was becoming an impediment, and this could
not be tolerated. For two more days old Kharu served as his crutch,
allowing him to lean upon her while she leaned on her digging stick, two
old people striving to keep up, and on the third day, when it seemed that
he must be left behind, Kharu was surprised to find Naoka coming back
to urge Gumsto along.

'Let him lean on me,' the girl said as she assumed the greater burden,
and in the heat of the day, when Kharu herself began to falter, Naoka alone
carried him along. At dusk, when the others were well ahead, Gumsto told
his two women, 'This is the last night.' Naoka nodded and left the old
couple by a thorn tree.

In the morning Kharu overtook the others, asking for a filled ostrich
egg and a bone with some meat on it. These were provided by Gao, but it
was Naoka who carried them back to where Gumsto sat propped against
the thorn. 'We bring you farewell,' the girl said, and it was from her smooth
hands that he took his final supplies.

'We must leave now,' Kharu said, and if she was crying, Gumsto could
not detect it, for her tears fell into such deep wrinkles that they quickly
became invisible. Gumsto leaned back exhausted, able to show no interest
in the meat or the water, and after a while Naoka knelt down, touched him
on the forehead, and departed.

'You must catch up,' Gumsto warned the woman he had tended since
the age of seven.

Kharu rested upon her digging stick, reflected for a moment on the days
they had spent together, then pushed the bone nearer to him and strode off.

For just a moment Gumsto looked up at the gathering vultures, but then
his eyes lowered to follow the disappearing file, and as he watched it move

toward better land he felt content. Gao was a hunter. Naoka was learning where the beetles hid, and the luscious tubers. With Kharu to guide them for a while, they would do well. The clan was twenty-five again, the right number: he was gone, but Kusha's baby restored the balance. The clan had survived bad days, and now as it disappeared he wished it well. His last thoughts, before the predators moved in, were of that zebra: He had insisted on moving away from his clan, and the lions had got him.

Kharu, walking with determination, soon passed Naoka, then overtook the main portion of the file, and assumed at last her place in the lead. There, with her stick to aid her, she led her band not due west, as it had been heading recently, but more to the southwest, as if she knew by some immortal instinct that there lay the Cape—with its endless supply of good water and wandering animals and wild vines that produced succulent things that could be gathered.

II. Zimbabwe

I N the year 1453 after Christ, the effective history of South Africa began
by actions occurring at a most unlikely spot. At Cape St. Vincent, on the
extreme southwestern tip of Europe, a monkish prince of Portugal in his
fifty-ninth year sat in his monastery on the bleak promontory of Sagres and
contemplated the tragedy that had overtaken his world. He would be known
to history as Prince Henry the Navigator, which was preposterous in that
he had never mastered navigation nor sailed in one of his ships with an
explorer who had.

His genius was vision. At a time when his narrow world was circumscribed by fear and ignorance, those handmaidens of despair, he looked far
beyond the confines of Europe, imagining worlds that awaited his discovery,
and although he had studied carefully the reports of Marco Polo and knew
that civilizations existed in the far Orient, he was convinced that until white
men from Europe, baptized into Christianity, had stepped upon a piece of
land, it remained for all reasonable purposes undiscovered, heathen and
condemned.

His target was Africa. Twice he had visited this dark and brooding
continent which lay so close to Portugal, once in grand victory at Ceuta
when he was twenty-one, once in shameful defeat at Tangier when he was
forty-three, and it fascinated him. From much study he had deduced that
his ships, each flying a flag blazoned with the red cross of Jesus Christ, could
sail southward along the western coast of Africa, turn a corner at the
southern tip and sail up the eastern coast to the riches of India, China and
mysterious Japan. Obstinately he had pursued this goal for forty years and
would continue until his death seven years hence, but he would fail.

His defeat was Africa. No matter how forcefully he goaded his captains,
they never accomplished much. They did rediscover the Madeira Islands
in 1418, but it took sixteen more years before they passed a cape jutting out
from the Sahara. They did round Cape Blanco in 1443, and one of Henry's

ships had ventured a little farther south, but there the matter rested. The great hump of Africa was not yet rounded, and by the time Henry would die in 1460 very little would be completed; the notable voyages of Bartholomeu Dias and Vasco da Gama would not be made till long after the Navigator was gone.

His triumph was Africa. For although he was permitted by God to witness none of the success of which he dreamed, it was his dreams that sent the caravels south, and if he never saw a shred of merchandise from India or China coming home in his ships, he did fix Africa in the Renaissance mind, and he did spur its exploration and its conversion to Christianity. It was this latter goal that was of major importance, for he lived a monastic life, eschewing the grandeurs of the court and the intrigues which might have made him king, satisfied in his servitude to God. Of course, as a youth he had fathered an illegitimate daughter and later he did rampage as a soldier, but the main burden of his life was the Christianizing of Africa, and that was why the year 1453 brought him such grief.

The Muslims, those dreadful and perpetual enemies of Christ, had swarmed into Constantinople, lugging their ships across land to break the defenses, and this outpost, which had long protected Christianity from the infidel, had fallen. Since all Europe could now be invaded by the followers of Muhammad, it was more urgent than ever that a way be found around Africa to circumvent the menace, and it was this problem which preoccupied Henry as he studied his maps and laid his plans for new explorations.

What did he know of Africa? He had assembled most of the material available at that time, plus the rumors and the excited speculations of sea captains and travelers. He knew that millennia ago the Egyptians had ventured down the east coast for great distances, and he had talked with sailors who had touched Arab ports in that region. He had often read that amazing statement in Herodotus about a supposed ship which had set south from the Red Sea with the sun rising on its left and had sailed so far that one day the sun rose on its right; this ship had presumably circumnavigated the entire continent, but Herodotus added that he did not believe the story. Most enchanting were the repeated passages in the Old Testament referring to the immense stores of gold that Ophir, somewhere in Africa, provided:

> . . . and they went with the servants of Solomon to Ophir, and took thence four hundred and fifty talents of gold, and brought them to King Solomon.

> Kings' daughters were among thy honourable women: upon thy right hand did stand the queen in gold of Ophir.

> I will make a man more precious than fine gold; even a man than the golden wedge of Ophir.

The happy phrase, 'the golden wedge of Ophir,' sang in Henry's mind, urging him to visualize the vast mines from which the Queen of Sheba had brought her gifts to Solomon. But there were other verses that haunted him: King Solomon built a navy at Ezion-geber; his ships conducted voyages lasting three years, returning home with cargoes of gold and silver, ivory and apes and peacocks; and once King Jehoshaphat assembled a vast fleet to bring back the gold of Ophir 'but they went not; for the ships were broken at Ezion-geber.'

It was all so factual—the fleets, the voyages, the gold. 'And where was this Ezion-geber?' Prince Henry asked his sages. 'It was the city we know as Elath,' they replied, 'lying at a northern tip of the Red Sea.' When Henry consulted his maps it was clear that the Biblical ships must have gone south to Africa; there was no way by which they could have entered the Mediterranean. So somewhere along the east coast of Africa lay this golden wedge of Ophir, immeasurably rich and doubtless steeped in heathenism. To salvage it became a Christian duty.

And now, in 1453, the obligation was trebled, for with Constantinople in Muslim hands and the profitable trade routes to the East permanently cut, it was imperative that Africa be saved for Christianity so that ships could sail around it directly to India and China. Then the soldiers of Jesus Christ could capture Ophir from the Muslims and turn its gold to civilized purposes. But where was Ophir?

While Prince Henry brooded and plotted at Sagres, constantly goading his reluctant captains to seek the cape which he knew must mark the southern tip of Africa, events at a small lake in that region were taking an interesting turn. To the undistinguished village of mud-and-thatch rondavels that huddled along the southern edge of this lake, a gang of noisy children came shouting, 'He comes! Old Seeker comes again!' And all the black inhabitants came out to greet the old man who dreamed.

When the file of newcomers reached the edge of the village it stopped to allow the Old Seeker time to arrange his clothing and take from a bag carried by one of his servants an iron staff topped by a handsome spread of ostrich feathers. Bearing this nobly in his left hand, he moved two steps forward, then prostrated himself, and from this position called, 'Great Chief, I bid you good morning!'

From the mass of villagers a man in his fifties stepped forward and nodded: 'Old Seeker, I bid you good morning.'

'Great Chief, did you sleep well?'

'If you slept well, I slept well.'

'I slept well, Great Chief.' Both the chief and his villagers must have sensed the irony in those words, for he was by no accounting a great chief, but protocol demanded that he be called such, especially when the man coming into the village sought advantages.

'You may rise,' the chief said, whereupon the Old Seeker stood erect, grasped his iron staff with one hand, placed his other upon the wrist, and rested his powder-gray head on both.

'What do you come seeking this time?' the chief asked, and evasively the old fellow replied, 'The goodness of the soil, the secrets of the earth.'

The chief nodded ceremoniously, and the formal greetings ended. 'How was the journey south?' he asked.

The old man handed his staff to a servant and said in a whisper, 'Each year, more difficult. I am tired. This is my last trip to your territories.'

Chief Ngalo burst into laughter, for the old man had made this threat three years ago and four years before that. He was a genial, conniving old rascal who had once served as overseer of mines in a great kingdom to the north and who now traveled far beyond his ruler's lands searching for additional mines, observing remote settlements, and probing always for new trade links. He was an ambassador-at-large, an explorer, a seeker.

'Why do you come to my poor village?' Chief Ngalo asked. 'You know we have no mines.'

'I come on a much different mission, dear friend. Salt.'

'If we had salt,' Ngalo said, 'we could trade with the world.'

The old man sighed. He had expected to be disappointed, but his people did need salt. However, they had other needs, some of them mysterious. 'What I could use,' he said confidentially, 'is rhinoceros horns. Not less than sixteen.' They were required, he explained, by older men who wished to marry young wives: 'They need assurance that they will not disappoint in bed.'

'But your king is a young man,' the chief said. 'Why does he need the horn?'

'Not he! For the rich old men with slanted eyes who live in a far country.'

From the tree under which they took their rest, the two men looked down at the lake, and Ngalo said, 'Tonight you will see many animals come to that water. Buffalo, lions, hippos, giraffes and antelope like the stars.' The Old Seeker nodded, and Ngalo added, 'But you will never see a rhino. Where can we possibly find sixteen horns?'

The old fellow reflected on this question and replied, 'In this life man is assigned difficult tasks. How to find a good wife. How to find sixteen horns. It is his task to find them.'

Chief Ngalo smiled. It was pleasurable to be with this old man. Always when he wanted something badly, he devised sententious and moral justifications. 'Mankind does not want sixteen rhinoceros horns,' he chided. 'You want them.'

'I am mankind.'

The chief could not resist such blandishments, but neither could he comply. 'Look, dear friend. We have no rhinos, but we have something much better.' Clapping for an aide, he cried, 'Tell Nxumalo to fetch the heavy earth!' And in a moment a boy of sixteen appeared, smiling, bearing three roughly rectangular ingots made from some kind of metal. Placing them on the ground before his father, he started to depart, but the Old Seeker asked, 'Do you understand what you have brought me, son?'

'Iron from Phalaborwa,' the boy said promptly. 'When my father's people went there to barter for these, I went with them. I saw the place where men worked the earth like ants. They had done so, they told me, for as long as anyone alive could remember, and many generations before that.'

'What did you trade?' the old man asked.

'Cloth. The cloth we weave.'

The Old Seeker smiled to indicate his pleasure that this lad should know the provenance of things, but once he had done so, he frowned. 'If I had wanted iron from the mines at Phalaborwa, I would have gone directly there. Thaba!' he shouted. 'Bring me the staff!' And when his servant ran up, bearing the carefully wrapped iron staff, the old man uncovered it and thrust it at the boy.

'That's real iron. From our mines south of Zimbabwe. We have all we need,' and contemptuously he pushed aside Nxumalo's rude ingots. Then he drew out from inside his robe a small oval object such as Nxumalo had never seen before. It was a shimmering yellow that glistened when light fell upon it, and it was suspended from a chain, each careful link of which was made of the same substance. When the old man thrust it suddenly upon him, Nxumalo found that it was surprisingly heavy.

'What is it?' he asked.

'Amulet.' There came a long pause. 'From Persia.' Another pregnant halting, then: 'Gold.'

'What is gold?' the boy asked.

'Now, there's a question!' the old man said, sitting back on his haunches and staring at the lake. 'For forty travels of the moon through the stars it was my job to find gold, and like you, I never knew what it was. It's death at the bottom of a deep pit. It's fire engulfing the iron containers when the smithy melts the ore. It's men sitting day after day, hammering out these links. But do you know what it is most of all?'

Nxumalo shook his head, liking the feel of the heavy metal. 'In the end it's a mystery, son. It's magic, because it lures men from lands you never heard of to come to our shores, to ford our rivers, to climb our mountains, to come a journey of many moons to Zimbabwe to get our gold.' Gently, almost lovingly, he retrieved the amulet and placed the chain about his neck, hiding the golden pendant beneath his cotton robe.

That was the beginning of his attempt to persuade Nxumalo: 'What you must do, son, is find eight rhinos and take their horns, then follow my trail to Zimbabwe . . .'

'What is Zimbabwe?' the boy asked one evening.

'How sad,' the old man said with unfeigned regret. 'Not one person in this village has ever seen Zimbabwe!'

'What is it?'

'Towers and soaring walls.' He paused and pointed to the low stone wall that surrounded the cattle kraal and said in an awed voice, 'Walls ten, twenty times higher than that. Buildings that reach to the sky.' A group of elders shook their heads in disbelief and clucked among themselves, but the Old Seeker ignored them. 'Our king, lord of a thousand villages bigger than yours, the great one the spirits talk to, he lives in a kraal surrounded by walls higher than trees.' He placed his hand on Nxumalo's arm and said, 'Until you've seen Zimbabwe, you live in darkness.'

Whenever he spoke like this, telling the boy of the grandness of the city from which he came, he reverted to the problem of the rhinoceros horns and the necessity of bringing them to the city, but one morning as he spoke with Nxumalo and his father he said abruptly, 'Ngalo, dear friend of many searchings, today I leave you to look for the Ridge-of-White-Waters, and I want Nxumalo to lead me.'

'He knows the way,' Ngalo said, pointing directly west to where the prominent ridge lay. It was a four-day journey which entailed some dangers, but the path was a pleasant one. 'Why do you wish to go?'

'In my day, Ngalo, I have sought many things. Women, high office, the path to Sofala, the king's good wishes. But the best thing I ever sought was gold. And I am convinced that in your terrain, there must be gold somewhere.' Contemptuously he dismissed the iron ingots that remained under the tree. Addressing only Nxumalo, he said, 'Iron gives temporary power. It can be made into spearheads and clubs. But gold gives permanent power. It can be fashioned into dreams, and men will come a long way to satisfy their dreams.'

On the third day of their journey west, after they had passed many small villages which the old man seemed to know, it became apparent to Nxumalo that the Seeker knew very well where the Ridge-of-White-Waters lay and that he had insisted on having companionship only because he wanted to convince Nxumalo of something. That night, as they were resting at the edge of a miserable kraal, the old man spied the boy standing alone, in his eyes a mixture of sadness and anticipation as he stared toward the empty lands to the south.

'What is it, young friend?'

'It is my brother, mfundisi,' he said, using a term of respect. 'Last year he left for the south, and I must go too, when it is time.' It was a custom that he must honor: the oldest brother always succeeded to the chieftainship, while the younger brothers moved to the frontier and started their own villages. And this had been done since these blacks came down from the north, centuries ago.

'No, no!' the Old Seeker protested. 'Find me the rhinoceros horn. Bring it to me in Zimbabwe.'

'Why should I do so?'

The old man took the boy's hands and said, 'If one like you, a boy of deep promise, does not test himself in the city, he spends his life where? In some wretched village like this.'

On the fourth day such discussions halted temporarily, for the Old Seeker's troop was attacked by a band of little brown men who swarmed like pestilential flies determined to repel an invader. When their slim arrows began buzzing, Nxumalo shouted, 'Beware! Poison!' and he led the Old Seeker to safety inside a ring of porters whose shields repelled the arrows.

The fight continued for about an hour, with the little men shouting battle orders in a preposterous series of clicking sounds, but gradually the taller, more powerful blacks herded them away, and they retreated into the savanna, still uttering their clicks.

'Aiee!' Nxumalo shouted with exasperation as the little fellows disappeared. 'Why do they attack us like jackals?'

Old Seeker, who had worked with the small people in the north, said calmly, 'Because we're crossing hunting grounds they claim as their own.'

'Jackals!' the boy snorted, but he knew the old man was right.

On the morning of the fifth day, as planned, the file of men reached the Ridge-of-White-Waters, which later settlers would call Witwatersrand, where the Old Seeker hoped to find evidence that gold existed, but the more carefully he explored the region—a handsome one, with prominent hillocks

from which Nxumalo could see for miles—the more disappointed he became. Here the telltale signs, which in the lands about Zimbabwe indicated
gold, were missing; there was no gold, and it became obvious that the
exploration had been fruitless, but on the evening of their last day of
tramping the hills the Old Seeker discovered what he was looking for. It
was an ant hill, eleven feet high, and he rushed to it, breaking it apart with
a long stick and fumbling through the fine-grained soil.

'What are you looking for?' Nxumalo asked, and the old man said,
'Gold. These ants dig down two hundred feet to build their tunnels. If
there's gold here, they bring flecks to the surface.'

At this site there were none, and reluctantly the Old Seeker had to admit
that he had taken this long journey to no avail: 'I didn't come to see your
father. I didn't come for rhino horn. Son, when you have a multitude of
targets, always aim for the one of merit. I came seeking gold, and I'm
convinced there's gold here.'

'But you didn't find it.'

'I had the joy of hunting. Son, have you listened to what I've been telling
you these days?' He led Nxumalo some distance from the spot where his
bearers waited, and as he looked out over the vast bleakness visible from
the fruitless ridge he said, 'It isn't even gold I seek. It's what gold can
achieve. To Zimbabwe come men from all across the world. They bring us
gifts you cannot imagine. Four times I went down the trails to Sofala. Twice
I sailed upon the dhows to mighty Kilwa. I saw things no man could ever
forget. When you seek, you find things you did not anticipate.'

'What are you seeking?' Nxumalo asked.

The old man had no answer.

The task of collecting sixteen rhinoceros horns was proving much more
complex than Nxumalo anticipated when he accepted the challenge, and
after the Old Seeker had departed to visit other tribes who might or might
not know of gold mines, the boy approached his father: 'I want to track
down the rhinos.'

'So the old talker poisoned you?'

Nxumalo looked down at his feet, unwilling to admit that he had been
entrapped by blandishments and singing words. 'Like the iron,' his father
said. 'You went, and you dug for iron, and you found it. And when you
came home with ingots . . . they didn't mean very much, not really.'

'I want to see the city,' Nxumalo said.

'And you shall. And when you come home you'll tell me, "It didn't
matter very much." '

Those of Nxumalo's brothers who remained at the kraal wished him
well in his quest for the rhinoceros horns but showed no interest in joining
him. The tribe was essentially sedentary, with fixed villages, sturdy wattled
huts and a settled agriculture. The women knew how to cultivate fields, the
men how to manage cattle and tend the fat-tailed sheep. One brother
directed the metalworkers who provided tools for the region and another
was gaining a reputation in the district as a herbalist and diviner.

But it was Nxumalo who championed the ancient arts of hunting and tracking in the wild, and because of this he seemed the more regal figure, the young man who best preserved the historical merits of the tribe. He was the only one with much chance of tracking down eight rhinoceroses and delivering the sixteen aphrodisiac horns to Zimbabwe, so on a warm summer morning he and six helpers moved eastward toward the heavily wooded area leading to the sea.

He was an imposing lad, not yet full height but taller than most men, and the principal characteristic that struck those who saw him for the first time was power: his arms and legs were well-muscled and his torso much broader than his hips. His face was large and placid, as if he knew no anger, and when he smiled all his features participated and his shoulders moved forward, creating the impression that his entire body was enjoying whatever sensation had evoked the smile; and when his lips parted, his white teeth punctuated the grin. It was obvious that when he reached the age of eighteen he would be able to marry whom he pleased, for he was not only the chief's son but also a young prince among men.

He was so totally different from the small brown hunters who had once inhabited this area that he seemed unrelated to them, and in a way he was. Earliest man, Australopithecus, had once flourished over a large part of Africa, and as he developed into modern man, one branch settled close to the equator, where the sun placed a premium on black skin, which adjusted to its punishing rays; no primitive tribe of pale-white complexion could have prospered long in those blazing regions which produced Nxumalo's people, just as his heavily pigmented skin would have been at a severe disadvantage in the cold north, where the sun's parsimonious rays had to be carefully hoarded.

Slowly, over many centuries, Nxumalo's black ancestors, herding cattle before them and carrying seeds in their skin bags and baskets, had migrated southward, reaching the lake about four centuries after the birth of Christ. They arrived not as conquering heroes but as women and men seeking pasturage and safe enclaves; some had continued southward, but Nxumalo's tribe had fancied the encompassing hills about the lake.

As they lingered they came into contact with the small brown people, and gradually these had been pushed south or into the mountain ranges to the east. From these places the insatiable little hunters raided the kraals of Nxumalo's people, and there had to be confrontations. Some did live in peace with the invaders, trading the spoils of their hunt for tools and sanctuary, but thousands of others were turned into serfs or put to work at the mines. Association continued over centuries, and occasionally at Nxumalo's kraal some woman of his tribe would have enormous buttocks, signaling her inheritance from the small people. There were fierce clashes between the two groups but never a pitched battle; had there been, the end result might have been more humane, because as things turned out, the little brown people were being quietly smothered.

It was an able group that had moved south in this black migration: skilled artisans knew the secrets of smelting copper and making fine tools and weapons tipped with iron. In certain villages women wove cloth, sometimes intermixing threads of copper. And every family owned earthenware pots designed and crafted by clever women and fired in kilns in the ground.

Their language bore no resemblance to that of the small people. A few tribes, moving south along the shores of the eastern ocean, would pick up the click sounds, but Nxumalo's people had acquired none. Their speech was pure, with an extensive vocabulary capable of expressing abstract thought and a lively aptitude for tribal remembrance.

Two special attributes set these tribes ahead of any predecessors: they had developed sophisticated systems of government, in which a chief provided civil rule and a spirit-medium religious guidance; and they had mastered their environment, so that cattle herding, agriculture and the establishment of permanent villages became practical. And there was one more significant addition: over the vast area trade flourished, so that communities could socialize; Chief Ngalo's people could easily import iron ingots from the great mines at Phalaborwa, one hundred and seventy miles away, and then send fabricated spearheads to villages that lay two hundred miles southwest, beyond the Ridge-of-White-Waters.

In other words, when Nxumalo set forth to find the rhinoceros horns that would carry him to Zimbabwe, he was the inheritor of a substantial culture, which he intended, even at his early age, to augment and protect. He knew that when his father died, his older brother would inherit the chieftainship, at which time he himself would take a wife and move farther west to establish a frontier village of his own, and this prospect pleased him. His impending excursion to Zimbabwe was an exploration, not a removal.

On the sixth day of their march, after passing great herds of buffalo and wildebeest, Nxumalo told his companions, 'There must be rhinos among those trees,' but when they reached the area where the savanna gave way to real forest, they found nothing, and an older man suggested, 'I've never seen rhinos where the trees were so many,' and he pointed back toward the sparser savanna.

Nxumalo was about to rebuke the man, for he had once been with hunters who had found their rhino in heavy woods, but he restrained himself and asked, 'You found rhinos back there?'

'We did.'

'Then let's look there.' And when they did, they saw unmistakable signs of the mighty beast. But these blacks were not Bushmen, and the mastery the brown people had shown in tracking animals was little known; it was obvious that rhinos had been here, but where they had gone, the hunters could not determine. They hunted, therefore, in a hit-or-miss way, moving about in large circles and with such noise that a Bushman would have been shocked. But they were fortunate, and in time they came upon a black, pointed-snout rhino with two massive horns, one behind the other.

Killing so formidable a beast required both skill and courage. The former would be contributed by the six huntsmen with iron-tipped spears, the latter by Nxumalo as leader of the expedition. Placing his men along the route he intended the animal to follow, he moved quietly into position somewhat ahead of the beast, leaped suddenly from the grass and exposed himself to the startled animal, which, with instant impulse to destroy, lunged madly at the boy like some enormous juggernaut launched upon an undeviating course.

Horns low to impale, little legs pumping, snout ablaze and throat utter-

ing deep growls, the rhinoceros charged with enormous power, while the
boy ran backward with beautiful deftness. It was a moment no hunter could
forget, that grand relationship of beast and man, when a single mistake on
the part of the latter meant immediate death. And since the animal could
run much faster than the boy, it was obvious that the latter must be killed
unless some other force intervened, and this occurred just when it seemed
that the powerful horns must catch the lad, for then the six hunters rose
up and thrust their spears to turn the animal aside.

Four of the iron-tipped spears found their mark, and the great beast
began to thrash at the low bushes in his path, forgetting the boy and
wheeling to face his new adversaries, one of whom was stooping to recover
his weapon. With a wild charge the beast bore down upon the man, who
leaped aside, abandoning his spear, which the rhinoceros broke into many
pieces. Then Nxumalo closed in with an axe, taking a mighty swipe at the
beast's back legs. As he did so, another man thrust his spear with great force
into the animal's neck.

The battle was not over, but its outcome was certain, and instead of
trailing the damaged beast for days, as the Bushmen would have done, these
determined men, with their superior weapons, closed in and brought him
down with stabs and thrusts and tormentings. The great black beast tried
to defend himself, kicking and goring, but in the end the seven men were
too persistent, and he died.

'Two of our horns,' Nxumalo said as his men hacked the precious item
from the carcass. They were curious, these horns, not horn at all but heavily
compacted masses of hair, and their presence doomed this magnificent
animal to near-extinction, for silly old men in distant China believed that
rhinoceros horn, properly administered in powder form, restored virility,
and China in these days was rich enough to search the world for horn.
Nxumalo's men, so prudent in so many ways, cut from this dead rhinoceros
only the two horns, cached them beneath a tree blazed with many cuts, and
abandoned the ton or more of choice meat as they set out to find their next
quarry.

They killed three additional rhinos on this hunt, driving them into pits
lined with jagged stakes. The eight horns they carried back to the village,
leaving the carcasses to the vultures, hyenas and ants, and in each of the
killings young Nxumalo had run in the shadow of those piercing horns and
those thundering feet. 'He is a skilled huntsman,' the men told the chief.
'He can do anything.' And when the boy heard this report he smiled, and
his handsome black body glistened as he leaned forward to show his appreciation.

In almost no respect did Nxumalo's village resemble the dwelling place of
the little brown men which had preceded it: now there were substantial
rondavels instead of open space on the ground, and carefully nurtured
grains and vegetables instead of chance gatherings; now there was a fixed
community. But in one regard life was much the same: women and men
wore almost no clothes.

So it was remarkable that one of the principal industries of the village was the weaving of cotton cloth, and when young Nxumalo returned with his eight rhinoceros horns, to be hailed a hero, it was natural that he take notice of one of the girls who sat in a low grass-roofed building by the lake, throwing their shuttles and shifting their looms.

Often as they spun their cotton they would pause to watch the animals grazing on the far side of the lake, and if a zebra kicked its heels or a gazelle danced in the air, the girls would applaud. And if a troop of elephants chanced to move in, or a flight of cranes, there would be cries of pleasure and not much would be accomplished.

Among the weavers was Zeolani, fifteen years old and daughter of the man who knew how to make copper wire from ingots brought south from the Limpopo River. From bits and pieces left over from the consignment, her father had made her the seven slim bracelets she wore upon her left wrist, so that when she threw the shuttle in her weaving she created soft music, which pleased her and set her apart from the others.

The work was not onerous; nothing that the tribe did demanded sustained effort, and there were long periods when the girls spent most of their days in idleness. Zeolani used these times to slip back to the looms and weave for herself cloth made of second-grade cotton adorned with bits of copper taken from her father's hoard. This cloth was not pure white, like that woven for trading; it was a honeyed tan, well-attuned to her blackness, and when its copper flecks caught the sun, the cloth seemed to dance.

Of it she made herself a skirt, the first seen in this village, and when she wrapped it about her slim waist and pirouetted by the lake, her dark breasts gleaming in the sunlight, she made herself a girl apart.

'They say you were brave at the hunt,' she said to Nxumalo as she danced by when he lingered at the silent weaving shelter.

'Rhinos are hard to find.'

'And hard to kill?' As she posed this question, she swung away from him, aware that as her skirt flared outward it showed to fine advantage.

'The others did the killing,' he said, entranced by her gentle movements.

'I kept watching to the east,' she said. 'I was afraid.'

He reached for her hand, and they sat looking across the lake at the desultory animals who wandered down for a midday drink: a few antelope, two or three zebra, and that was all. 'At dusk,' he said, 'that shore will swarm.'

'Look!' she cried as a lazy hippopotamus half rose from the waters, jawed mightily, then submerged.

'I wish the strangers in far lands wanted hippo teeth instead of rhino horns,' Nxumalo said. 'Much easier to do.' Zeolani said nothing, and after a while he touched her skirt, and then, almost as if he were driven to speak, he blurted out: 'When I am gone I'll remember this cloth.'

'It's true, then? You've decided to go?'

'Yes.'

'The old man talked and talked . . . and you believed him?'

'I'll go. I'll see the city. And I'll come back.'

Taking her by the hands, he said fervently, 'When I traveled with the Old Seeker we came upon a fine land and I thought, "We'll leave the lake

to my brothers . . . to tend their cattle and their fields. Zeolani and I will
find a few good hunters and we . . .'

She did not coyly repeat the *we,* for she knew well what Nxumalo had
been thinking, because she, too, had contemplated moving away from this
village and starting a new one with her hunter-husband. Instead of speaking, she took his hand, drew it close to her naked breast, and whispered,
'I shall wait for you, Nxumalo.'

After the next hunt, in which Nxumalo brought down four more rhinos,
the young lovers found many opportunities to discuss their uncertain future. 'Can't I go to Zimbabwe with you?' Zeolani asked.

'So far! The way uncertain. No, no.'

They decided upon a course fraught with danger, but their love had
matured at such a dizzy speed that they were eager to risk the penalties.
At Zeolani's signaling they wandered by different routes into the savanna
east of the village to a spot hidden by the two small hills shaped like a
woman's breasts, and there they made love repeatedly, even though it could
mean the end of his trip to Zimbabwe if she became pregnant. If word of
such condition circulated, the tribe would condemn her for having known
a man without sanction and everyone would know who the man must have
been, and they would be severely punished.

There, between the hills, they kept their trysts, and fortune was with
them, for there was no pregnancy. Instead, there developed a deepening
love, and as the day approached when Nxumalo must march north with the
tribute, their last meetings assumed a mournful cast that could not be
dispelled.

'I will walk behind you,' the girl said, 'and come into Zimbabwe as if
by accident.'

'No, it's man's work,' said this boy of sixteen.

'I will wait for you. You are the only one I will ever live with.'

They went boldly to one of the hills south of the village and looked west
toward the spot that Nxumalo had chosen many months ago. 'It lies far
beyond. There's a small stream and many antelope. When I was sleeping
there I heard a rustle, so I opened one eye. It could have been an enemy.
What do you suppose it was?'

'Baboons?'

'Four sable antelope. Their horns were wider than this,' and when he
extended his arms to their maximum, Zeolani slipped into them and they
embraced for the last time. Tears came to her eyes as her slim fingers traced
the muscles in his arm.

'We were intended,' she said. 'By every sign we were intended.' And she
counted the omens that should have brought them together, and each knew
that never in this life could another mate be found so inevitably right.

'I shall wait for you,' the girl said, and with this childish and futile
promise ringing in his ears, Nxumalo set forth.

It was a journey any young man would want to make, five hundred miles
due north across the heart of Africa, crossing wide rivers, sharing the
pathway with animals innumerable, and heading for a city known only in

legend or the garbled reports of the Old Seeker. Sixteen men would accompany their young leader, and since only the guide Sibisi had made the first part of this trip before, the others were at least as excited as Nxumalo.

He was surprised at how lightly the men were burdened; on one of his hunting trips his helpers would carry three times the weight, but Sibisi explained, 'Much safer if travel light. Use the first days to tighten muscles. Enjoy the freedom and make yourselves strong, because on the twenty-seventh day . . .' He dropped his voice ominously. 'Then we reach the Field of Granite.'

The loading would have been simpler if the rhinoceros horns could have been reduced to powder and adjusted to the men's other cargo, but this was forbidden. The horns had to be intact upon delivery at Sofala to the waiting dhows that would carry them thus to China, so that apothecaries could be assured they were getting true horn and not some admixture of dust to make the packages larger.

The file set forth at dawn on a clear autumn day, when the swollen rivers of spring and summer had receded and when animals born earlier in the year were large enough to be eaten. Sibisi set a pace that would not tire the men at the beginning, but would enable them to cover about twenty miles each day. For two weeks they would travel through savanna much as they had known at home, with no conspicuous or unusual features.

Two men who carried nothing proved invaluable, for it was they who ranged ahead, providing meat for the travelers. 'I want you to eat a lot and grow strong,' Sibisi said, 'because when we reach the Field of Granite we must be at our best.'

On the morning of the sixth day the march speeded considerably, and the file covered at least twenty-five miles a day until they approached the first notable site on their journey. 'Ahead lies the gorge,' Sibisi said, and he regaled the novices with accounts of this spectacular place: 'The river hesitates, looks at the wall of rock, then leaps forward shouting, "It can be done!" And mysteriously it picks its way through the red cliffs.'

Sibisi added, 'Mind your steps. You're not clever like the river.'

The gorge was so extremely narrow, only a few yards across, that the river rushed through with tremendous force, its turbulence well suited to the towering red flanks. The transit required the better part of a day, the porters following a precipitous footpath that clung to the eastern edge of the river and carried them at times down into the river itself. At the midpoint of the gorge the tops of the walls seemed to close in, so that the sky was obliterated, and here birds of great variety and color flashed through, playing a game of missing the cliffs as they darted about.

'Insects,' Sibisi said, showing the others how the turbulence of the water created air currents that tossed insects aloft, where birds awaited, and for a while as Nxumalo paused to absorb the wonder of this place—a river piercing a wall of rock—he felt that his journey could have no finer moment, but he was wrong. The true grandeur of this trip lay ahead, for as the travelers came out of the gorge they entered upon a place of wonder.

The land opened out like the vast ears of an elephant, and across it trees of the most outlandish nature scattered. 'They're upside down!' Nxumalo cried, rushing to a massive thing much thicker than any he had previously known. It was fifteen feet through the center, with bark soft and shaggy like the skin of an old dog; when he pressed against it, his thumb sank deep within. But what was truly remarkable were the branches, for this mighty tree reaching sixty feet into the air carried only tiny twigs resembling the roots of some frail plant, ripped out of its soil and stuck back in, upside down.

'It is upside down,' Sibisi agreed. 'The gods did it.'

'Why?'

'They made this excellent tree. Perfect in every respect. Big branches like an ordinary tree. But it was lazy, and when they came back to gather fruit, they found nothing. So in anger they ripped it out of the ground and jammed it back in, upside down, as you can see.'

When Nxumalo laughed at the sight of this monstrosity, Sibisi gripped his arm. 'No ridicule. Many men owe their lives to this tree, for when you are perishing from thirst you come here, puncture the bark, and out will drip a little water.' Nor was it only water the baobab gave, for its leaves could be boiled and eaten, its seeds sucked or ground to make a tingling drink, and its spongy wood stripped and woven into rope.

It was a tree that festooned the landscape, its great pillars of thick glossy bark and tangled branches spreading far into the sky. Wherever he looked north of the gorge, there stood these trees, as if to cry, 'We are sentinels of a new land. You are coming onto the earth we guard.'

And it was a new land. The savanna sprouted different grasses, and there were different birds and different small animals running between the rocks. But in the distance there were always the same large animals: elephant and eland and galloping zebra. They were the permanent gods that accompanied men when they journeyed north, and at night when they lit their campfire, Nxumalo could hear the lions prowling near, lured by the smell of human beings but repelled by their flames, and in the distance the soft grumbling of the hyenas. It was as if a man traveling across the savanna carried with him a garland of beasts, beautiful and wild and useful. Nxumalo, peering into the darkness, could sometimes see their eyes reflecting the flames, and he was always surprised at how close they came; on nights when it was his turn to keep the fire alive, he would allow it to die perilously low, and in the near-darkness he would see the lions moving closer, closer, their eyes not far from his, their soft and lovely forms clearly discernible. Then, with a low cry, he would poke the embers and throw on more wood, and they would quietly withdraw, perplexed by this untoward behavior but still fascinated by the wavering flames.

On the morning of the seventeenth day Nxumalo saw two phenomena that he would always remember; they were as strange to him as the upside-down baobab trees, and they were premonitory, for much of his life from this time on would be spent grappling with these mysteries.

From a hill three days north of the gorge he looked down to see his first mighty river, the Limpopo, roaring through the countryside with a heavy burden of floodwaters collected far upstream and a heavier burden of mud. The waters swirled and twisted, and to cross them was quite impossible, but

Sibisi said, 'They'll subside. Two days we can walk across.' He could not have said this in spring, but he knew that this untimely flooding must have originated in some single storm and would soon abate.

In the waiting period Nxumalo inspected the second phenomenon, the vast copper deposits just south of the Limpopo, where he was surprised to see women, some as young as Zeolani, whose lives were spent grabbing at rock and hauling it lump by lump up rickety ladders to furnaces whose acrid fumes contaminated the air and shortened the lives of those who were forced to breathe them.

The tribe in charge of the mines had accumulated large bundles of copper wire, which Nxumalo agreed to have his men transport to Zimbabwe, and now the two who had been carrying nothing were pressed into service. Even Nxumalo, whose burden had been light, took four measures of the wire, since the miners paid well for this service.

'We've always traded our copper with Zimbabwe,' the mine overseer said, 'and when you reach the city you'll see why.' His words excited Nxumalo, and he was tempted to ask for more details, but he kept silent, preferring to find out for himself what lay at journey's end.

When the Limpopo subsided and its red-rock bottom was fordable, the seventeen men resumed the exciting part of their march, for now they were in the heart of a savanna so vast that it dwarfed any they had known before. Distances were tremendous, a rolling sea of euphorbia trees, baobabs and flat-topped thorn bushes, crowded with great animals and alluring birds. For endless miles the plains extended, rolling and swelling when small hills intervened, and cut by rivers with no name.

At the end of the first day's march from the Limpopo they came upon the farthest southern outpost of the kingdom of Zimbabwe, and Nxumalo could barely mask his disappointment. There was a kraal, to be sure, and it was surrounded by a stone wall, but it was not the soaring construction that Old Seeker had promised. 'It's larger than my father's wall,' Nxumalo said quietly, 'but I expected something that high.' And he pointed to a tree of modest size.

One of the herders attached to the outpost said, 'Patience, young boy. This is not the city.' When he saw Nxumalo's skepticism he led him along a path to a spot from which a valley could be seen. 'Now will you believe the greatness of Zimbabwe?' And for as far as his eye could travel, Nxumalo saw a vast herd of cattle moving between the hills. 'The king's smallest herd,' the man said. Nxumalo, who had been reared in a society where a man's status was determined by his cattle, realized that the King of Zimbabwe must be a man of extraordinary power.

When Sibisi and the outpost headman settled down with their gourds of beer, Nxumalo, uninformed on the topics they discussed, wandered off, to find something that quite bewitched him: one of the herdsmen, with little to do day after day, had caught a baby eland to rear as a pet. It was now full grown, heavier than one of Nxumalo's father's cows and with twisted horns twice as long and dangerous, but it was like a baby, pampered and running after its mother, in this case the herdsman, who ordered it about as if it were his fractious son.

The eland loved to play, and Nxumalo spent most of one day knocking about with it, pushing against its forehead, wrestling with its horns and avoiding its quick feet when the animal sought to neutralize the boy's cleverness. When the file moved north the eland walked with Nxumalo for a long time, its handsome flanks shining white in the morning sun. Then its master whistled, called its name, and the big animal stopped in the path, looked forward to his new friend and backward to its home, then stamped its forefeet in disgust and trotted back. Nxumalo stood transfixed in the bush, staring at the disappearing animal and wishing that he could take such a congenial beast with him, when the eland stopped, turned, and for a long spell stared back at the boy. They stayed thus for several minutes, consuming the space that separated them, then the animal tossed its head, flashed its fine horns, and disappeared.

Nxumalo now carried only two bundles of wire, for Sibisi had said quietly, 'I'll take the others. You must prepare yourself for the Field of Granite.' In the middle of the plains, blue on the far horizon, rose a line of mountains, and marking the pathway to them stood a chain of ant hills, some as high as trees, others lower but as big across as a baobab. They were reddish in color and hard as rock where the rains had moistened them prior to their baking by the sun.

On the twenty-ninth day as they neared Zimbabwe they saw ahead of them two mighty granite domes surrounded by many-spired euphorbias, and as they walked, bringing the domes ever closer, Sibisi pointed to the west, where a gigantic granite outcropping looked exactly like some monstrous elephant resting with its forelegs tucked under him. 'He guards the rock we seek,' Sibisi said, and the men moved more quickly to reach this vital stage in their progress.

Between the twin domes and the sleeping elephant lay a large field of granite boulders, big and round, like eggs half buried in the earth. Nxumalo had often seen boulders that resembled these, but never of such magnificent size and certainly none that had their peculiar quality. For all of them were exfoliating, as if they wished to create building blocks from which splendid structures could be made; they formed a quarry in which nine-tenths of the work was done by nature, where man had to do only the final sizing and the portage.

The rounded domes, fifty and sixty feet high, had been laid down a billion years ago in layers, and now the action of rain and sun and changing temperature had begun to peel away the layers. They were like gigantic onions made of rock, whose segments were being exposed and lifted away. The result was unbelievable: extensive slabs of choice granite, a uniform six inches thick, were thrown down year after year. Men collecting them could cut them into strips the width of a building block and many yards long. When other men cut these strips into ten-inch lengths, some of the best and strongest bricks ever devised would result.

There was only one drawback to this operation: the Field of Granite lay in the south; the site where the bricks were needed was five miles to the north. To solve this problem the king had long ago decreed a simple rule: no man or woman traveling north to Zimbabwe was permitted to pass this field without picking up at least three building blocks and lugging them to the capital. Strong men, like Sibisi's, were expected to carry eight, and even couriers like Nxumalo, son of a chief, had to bring three. If their other burdens were too great, they must be laid aside, for no man could move north without his stone bricks.

Masons working at the site tied the stones in packages of four, binding them with lianas found in the forest, and these were waiting for the southerners as they arrived. When the masons found that a chief's son was in the train, they prepared a bundle of only three bricks for him, and with this new burden he set off.

At first the stones were not oppressive, but as the hours passed, the men groaned, particularly those who had already been burdened with the copper. That night four men had to share the watch, tending the fire and fighting exhaustion, and when Nxumalo stood guard, he was so tired he forgot the animals and watched only the stars that marked the slow passage of his watch.

At dawn the punished men climbed the last hill, and at its crest they received a reward which made the drudgery acceptable, for there in a gracious valley, beside a marsh, stood the city of Zimbabwe, grand in a manner no one from Nxumalo's tribe could have imagined. There stood the mighty edifices built of rock, pile after glorious pile of gray-green granite rising from the valley floor.

'Look!' Sibisi cried in awe. 'That must be where the king worships!' And Nxumalo looked to the north where a hill of real size was crowned by a citadel whose rough stone walls shone in the morning sunlight. The men from the little village stood in silence, gaping at the wonder of the place. From a thousand huts in the shade of the mighty walls and parapets the workers of the city were greeting the dawn of a new day.

'This is Zimbabwe,' Nxumalo said, wiping his eyes, and no one spoke.

No group of visitors from beyond the Limpopo could expect to enter any of the handsome stone enclosures, so after dutifully depositing the rhino horns with the authorities, Nxumalo and his men were led to the section of the city occupied by the common people, and there they rested for fifteen days before starting their return journey. On the day of departure Nxumalo left his lodgings with a sense of sadness, for he had enjoyed this city and its manifold offerings, but as he reached the area where his men assembled, he felt his arm taken by a firm hand.

'Nxumalo, son of Ngalo,' a voice said, 'this is to be your home.' It was the Old Seeker, come to rescue the boy in whose future he had taken such a deep interest. 'You are to work on the walls.'

'But I am the son of a chief!'

'Since when does the smallest calf run with the bulls?'

Nxumalo did not reply, for he was learning that this old man was far more than a dreamy wanderer exploring the Ridge-of-White-Waters. In Zimbabwe he was a full-fledged councillor at the king's court, and now he told his young protégé, 'In Zimbabwe you do not force your way, Nxumalo. Our walls are built by the finest men in the city. They will not tolerate fools at their side. Satisfy them, and you will gain entrance.' And he pointed to the stone towers in the valley and the walls of the mountaintop citadel.

Zimbabwe in the year 1454 was certainly no duplicate of a European city like Ghent or Bordeaux. Its architecture was much ruder; it contained no Gothic cathedral; and its palace was infinitely simpler. Although its principal ritual and royal centers were made of stone, its houses were of clay-and-thatch construction. No one in the city could read; the history of the place was not written; there was no nationwide system of coinage; and society was less complex by many degrees than that in Europe.

It was, however, a thoughtfully organized, thriving community with a brilliant business capacity, evidenced by the teeming marketplace to which a network of producers and traders gravitated. A mild, healthful place with a fine water supply, it enjoyed the most advanced amenities of that day, right down to an ingenious system of drains. It had a particularized work force and a government which had been more stable than most of those in Europe. But even as it stood supreme over this heartland of southern Africa, dangerous undercurrents threatened the continuance of the place, for it was stretching its control and resources to the limit at a time when other regional forces were in movement, and no one could predict how much longer this great capital would continue to prosper.

It was into this center of grandeur and uncertainty that Nxumalo was projected, and as he labored on the wall, tapping into place rocks like those he had transported, he watched all things.

He saw how a constant stream of porters arrived from the compass points, each man bearing whatever valuable goods his district contributed to the capital, and he began to detect the variations that marked the different regions. There were, for example, noticeable shades of blackness among the men: those from the north, where the great rivers flowed, being darker; those from the west, where there had been more of the little brown people to mate with, being shaded toward brown. And one tribe from the east sent men who were conspicuously taller than the others, but all seemed capable.

They spoke in various tongues, too, when they were among themselves, but the variations in language were not great, and all could manage the speech of Zimbabwe, with amusing dialect differences betraying the fact that some were of the swamps and others from the empty plains. It was the residents of the city who attracted Nxumalo's principal notice, for they moved with an assurance that he had previously seen only in his father. They were in general a handsome people, but among them moved a cadre of officials who were outstanding. Usually taller than their fellows, they wore uniforms made of the most expensive imported cloth into which had been woven strands of gold and silver; they were never seen carrying anything except staffs indicating their office, and even these they did not use as walking sticks but rather as formal badges. Ordinary people moved aside when they approached, and one of these officials came each day to inspect the work being done by the stonemasons.

He was a considerate man who wanted to like the work for which he was responsible; only rarely did he order any section torn down and rebuilt, and one day when he was standing over Nxumalo, pecking at the young man's work with his staff, he suddenly burst into laughter, and no one knew why. 'We should get him to do the heavy work,' he said with a wave of his staff, indicating a baboon shuffling along on its hind legs and front knuckles, stopping to root in the ground near the post of the chief stonemason, who had found the creature abandoned at birth.

The inspector watched the tame baboon for some moments, then tapped Nxumalo with his staff: 'Your job will be to train him.' Chuckling at his joke, he moved along to inspect another part of the wall.

Having identified Nxumalo among the temporary sojourners who came great distances to labor at the walls before returning to their homes, this inspector formed the habit of asking him each day, 'Well, how are we progressing with the baboon?' then laughing generously. One day he asked, 'Aren't you the chieftain's son?' When Nxumalo nodded, he said, 'Old Seeker wants to see you. He says it's time,' and he ordered Nxumalo to lay down the board on which he had been carrying adobe.

The boy was about to descend when he saw a sight below which staggered him, for moving toward the marketplace came two men of astonishing appearance. They were not black! Like the cloth that Zeolani bleached in the sun, the skin of these men was not black at all, but a pale honey-tan, almost white, and they were dressed in flowing robes even whiter than their skins, with filament protection for their heads.

He was still staring when Old Seeker came up, bustling with importance. 'What's the matter, son?' he asked, and when he saw the strangers whose appearance had so shocked Nxumalo he laughed. 'Arabs. Come up from the sea.' And taking Nxumalo by the arm, he teased: 'If we follow them, you can waste the fortune you've been earning on the walls.'

Nxumalo and his mentor fell in behind the two white men as the latter proceeded regally toward the marketplace, followed by thirty black slaves who had carried their trade goods up from the seacoast. Wherever the procession appeared it was hailed with shouts, and hundreds of city residents trailed along behind to watch the strangers halt at a compound, where they were greeted effusively by a short, rotund black who dominated the market.

'What wonderful treasures I've put aside for you,' the round man cried as the Arabs moved forward to greet him. He was about to disclose more, intimating that as in the past, he had secreted a private hoard of goods to be exchanged for his personal gain, but at sight of Old Seeker his voice lost its animation, for the old man was a court official who sat in judgment on such illegal trading. Punishment was lifetime banishment, so the little merchant, much deflated, ended lamely, 'I'm sure you've brought many good things.'

'I'm sure the king will be pleased with our gifts,' the taller Arab said.

Mention of this august and mysterious figure caused Nxumalo to tremble, for in the months he'd been here, only twice had he glimpsed the king and even then not properly, for it was law that when the great lord of Zimbabwe passed, all must fall upon the ground and avert their eyes.

'It's wise of you to double your gifts,' Old Seeker told the Arabs as he watched them put aside the goods they intended to present the king. 'Last season your gifts were scarcely fit for this fat one here.' And he noticed the signs of worry that crossed the short man's face.

When the Arabs had their gifts prepared, Old Seeker surprised Nxumalo by handing him the iron staff of office: 'This day, son, you shall enter the great place with me.'

The young man who had so valiantly defied the rhinos looked as if he would faint, but the old man placed a reassuring hand on his shoulder: 'It's time for the grandeur I promised you, Nxumalo, son of Ngalo.'

There were no guards at the narrow northern entrance to the Grand Enclosure, for no mortal would dare cross that threshold unless eligible to do so. Since it was the custom for councillors to sponsor young men of promise, Old Seeker had been granted permission to introduce the able young fellow from the south.

They all halted just outside the entrance, for here the slaves must deliver their burdens to the court attendants. The Arabs themselves were not permitted more than three paces inside the austere walls, but as the visitors stood at attention Old Seeker moved forward to lead them into a smaller walled-in section of the enclosure.

'We shall wait here,' the old man said. 'We must follow every order with care.' To Nxumalo he whispered, 'Do what I do.'

The boy said nothing, for he was awed by what was being revealed. He had labored on walls such as these which surrounded him but had never guessed the grandeur they hid. The area subtended by the sturdy granite encirclement seemed to stretch to the heavens, and indeed it did, for no attempt had been made to cover the walls or the rooms with a roof.

A group of elder councillors filed into the meeting place and stood to one side. Then came three spirit-mediums attached to the king's person; they squatted against a wall and seemed to disapprove of everything. When an imposing figure in a blue robe appeared from within, Nxumalo assumed this must be the king and started to fall upon his knees, but Old Seeker restrained him.

'Lo, he comes!' the figure cried, and from all present the exciting message was repeated: 'Lo, he comes!'

This was a signal for everyone, and especially the Arabs, to sink to the smooth mud-packed floor. Nxumalo went down quickly, forehead pressed against the hard surface, eyes squeezed shut, and knees tightly pressed to still his trembling.

He was still in that position when he heard laughter, but he dared not move.

The first gust was followed by a chorus of laughter. Everyone in the reception area seemed to be roaring, and then he heard a quiet voice saying, 'Come, little bird, onto your legs.'

It was a kindly voice, and seemed to be directed at him. A sharp nudge from Old Seeker caused him to look up, and he found himself staring directly into the thin handsome face of the king, who looked down at him and laughed again.

Instantly everyone else in the area did likewise, and from outside the walls came the sound of hundreds laughing, for it was a law in Zimbabwe that whatever the king did had to be imitated by everyone in the city. A laugh, a cough, a clearing of the throat—all had to be repeated.

Pleased with the laughter, the king indicated that the Arabs might rise, and as they did, Nxumalo noticed that whereas all those in attendance on the king wore expensive cloth woven with metals, he wore stark-white cotton, completely unadorned. Also, he moved with kingly grace and never timidly like the others.

When he reached the Arabs he nodded and spoke easily with them, inquiring about their journey up from the sea and asking them to share any intelligence they might have acquired concerning troubles to the north. He was interested to learn that traders from Sofala no longer deemed it profitable to risk travel into that agitated area, and he listened attentively as the Arabs reported the staggering victory their people had enjoyed at a place called Constantinople, but he could make little of the information except to observe that the Arabs seemed to think that this strengthened their hand in dealings with him.

'And now the gifts!' the tall Arab said, whereupon he and his companion unwrapped their bundles, one after another, gracefully turning back the cloth bindings until the treasures were revealed: 'This celadon, Mighty One, was brought to us by a ship from China. Observe its delicate green coloring, its exquisite shape.' The dazzling ceramics were from Java, to which gold would be sent. The fabrics, finer than anyone in Zimbabwe could weave or imagine, came from Persia; the filigreed silver from Arabia; the heavy glazed pottery from Egypt; the low tables of ebony from Zanzibar; and the exciting metalware from India.

At the end of the presentation the Old Seeker leaned toward the king, heard his wishes, and told the Arabs, 'The Mighty One is pleased. You may now trade in the marketplace.' They bowed respectfully and backed off, and Nxumalo started to follow them, assuming that his visit to Zimbabwe had ended; soon he would be on his way back to his village.

But the king had other plans for this promising lad, and as Nxumalo moved off, a regal command halted him: 'Stay. They tell me you work well. We need you here.' Old Seeker could not mask his joy at this recognition of his protégé, but Nxumalo showed that he was bewildered. Did the king's command mean that he would never again see his brothers or Zeolani at her spinning?

It was the king who answered that unspoken question: 'Show the young man these buildings. Then find him a suitable place to stay.' With that he strode away while Old Seeker and a score of others fell in the dust to honor his passing.

'Well!' the old man cried as he brushed himself off. 'Honors like this come to only a few, believe me.'

'What does it mean?'

'That you're to live here now . . . to become one of us.'

'But Zeolani . . .'

The old man ignored this question that had no honorable answer. 'You'll see things which ordinary mortals . . .' His eyes glowed as if the triumph were his, and with fast, busy steps he started Nxumalo on their tour of the Grand Enclosure.

They entered a narrow passageway parallel to the high outer wall, and Nxumalo feared it might never end, so long and sweeping was it, but finally it opened into a courtyard so grand that he and the old man intuitively fell to their knees. They were in the presence of a mighty royal scepter, unlike any symbol of majesty seen in Africa before or after. It was a soaring conical tower, eighteen feet in diameter at its base, thirty feet high and tapering sharply as it rose. At the top it was adorned by a chevron pattern built into the stone, and as a whole it represented the majesty of the king. On a raised platform next to the tower stood a collection of handsome unadorned monoliths, each symbolizing some achievement of the king and his forebears.

'Beyond lie the king's chambers,' Old Seeker said. 'His wives and children live there, and no man may enter.' Then briskly he moved toward the exit, beckoning Nxumalo to follow him. 'We must see what the Arabs are accomplishing in the marketplace.'

When they rejoined the traders, Nxumalo studied the two strangers in disbelief, keeping as close to them as possible, watching all they did. Their hands were white and their ankles, and he supposed that if he could see their skin below the exposed neckline, it would be white too. Their voices were deep, displaying an accent unlike any used by workmen from distant regions. But what impressed Nxumalo most was that they exhibited a self-assurance as proud as that of the king's councillors; these were men of importance, men accustomed to command, and when they lounged in the courtyard of the depot, as they did now, waiting for the exchange of goods, it was they who determined what should happen next.

'Spread the gold here, where the light falls,' the taller man directed, and when attendants brought in the precious packages and began to turn back the corners of the cloth, everyone showed excitement except the two Arabs. They expected the gold to be of high quality; they expected a copious amount.

'Look at this!' the round man cried, his voice rising. And from the packages emerged a score of ingots of pure gold, wrenched from mines a hundred miles away, and rings carefully fashioned, and pendants for officials, and a great plaque with a rhinoceros rampant.

'By the way,' the chief Arab interrupted, pushing the gold aside. 'Did you get the rhinoceros horn?'

'We did,' the round man said, clapping his hands, whereupon servants brought in three large bundles. When opened, they produced an accumulation of three dozen horns, which excited the cupidity of the Arabs, who hefted them approvingly.

'Very good. Really, very good.' Rupturing the exchange of pleasantries, the principal Arab barked at one of his waiting slaves, 'See that these are handled properly,' and from the way all treated the horns, it was obvious that they were of great value.

'And what else?' the Arabs asked.

There followed a small parade of Zimbabwe men bringing to the Arabs a treasure of ivory tusks, copper wire and artifacts carved from soapstone. With each new disclosure the Arabs nodded and ordered the goods moved outside for packing by their own men. Then the leader coughed and said evenly, 'And now you will want to see what we bring you?'

'Indeed,' the round man said, his voice betraying his eagerness. He then did a strange thing. Taking Nxumalo by the hand, he introduced him to the Arabs, saying, 'This is the young fellow who brought you the best horns.'

Nxumalo felt the white man's hand touch his, and he was face-to-face with the stranger. He felt the man's hand press into his shoulder and heard the words spoken with heavy accent: 'You bring excellent horns. They will be well received in China.'

Proudly, as if they owned the goods, the slaves undid the bales, producing fine silks from India and thousands of small glass beads—red, translucent blue, green, golden-yellow and purple. These would be sewn into intricate patterns to enhance garments, necklaces and other finery. The Arabs were pleased to obtain gold, which they would use to adorn their women; the blacks were just as gratified to get these beads for the adornment of theirs. So far as utility was concerned, it was a just exchange.

The Arabs also brought a collection of special items for bartering with vassal chiefs, and among these was a small metal disk on which an elephant and a tiger had been carved. This came from Nepal and was not worth much, so the Arab leader tossed it in his hand, judged it, and threw it to Nxumalo: 'For the fine horns you brought us.' This disk, with its filigree chain, would be sent south to where Zeolani waited, and fifty years later when she died it would be buried with her, and five hundred years later it would be found by archaeologists, who would report:

> Indubitably this disk was made in Nepal, for several like it have been found in India. It can be dated accurately to 1390. Furthermore, the tiger which shows so plainly never existed in Africa. But how it reached a remote hill east of Pretoria passes explanation. Probably some English explorer whose family had connections with India carried it with him during an examination of the region and lost it. As for the fanciful suggestion that the disk might have reached some central site like Zimbabwe as an article of trade in the 1390–1450 period and then drifted mysteriously to where we found it, that is clearly preposterous.

The mines of Zimbabwe were scattered across an immense territory, Zambezi to Limpopo north to south, seashore to desert east to west, and it became Nxumalo's job to visit each mine to assure maximum production. Gold, iron and copper had to flow in to Zimbabwe and lesser marketplaces throughout the kingdom so that the Arabs would continue to find it profitable to pursue their trade. His work was not arduous, for when he reached a mine, all he did was check the accumulated metal; rarely did he descend into an actual mine, for they were small and dangerous affairs with but one responsibility: to send up enough ore to keep the furnaces operating, and how this was achieved was not his concern.

But one morning at the end of a journey two hundred miles west of the city he came upon a gold mine where production seemed to have ceased, and he demanded to know what slothful thing had happened. 'The workers died, and I can find no others,' the overseer said plaintively.

'I saw many women . . .'

'But not little ones.'

'If the mine's so small, get girls. We must have gold.'

'But girls can't do the work. Only the little brown people . . .'

In some irritation Nxumalo said, 'I'll look for myself,' but when he saw the entrance to the mine he realized that he could not climb into that crevice. Since he insisted upon knowing how the production of a mine could be so abruptly terminated, he ordered the overseer to summon men who would widen the entrance, breaking away enough rock to permit his descent.

When he lowered himself to the working level, holding a torch above his head, he saw what the overseer meant: there at the face of the gold-bearing rock lay seven small brown figures, dead so long that their bodies were desiccated, tiny shreds of their former being. Four men, two women and a child had died, one after the other over a period of months or even years, and when the last was gone, no further ore had been sent aloft.

He remained in the mine for a long time, endeavoring to visualize the lives of these seven little people. Because the mine was so cramped, only they could work it, forced one time into the narrow opening, condemned thereafter to live underground for as long as they survived, eating whatever was thrown down to them, burying their dead in a pile beside the rock, living and dying in perpetual darkness.

Nxumalo remembered what Old Seeker had said about the wandering bands of small brown people with their poisoned darts. 'Jackals,' he himself had termed them. Prior to visiting this mine he had never before seen them rounded up and enslaved, and certainly the councillors at Zimbabwe would not have sanctioned it, but on this far frontier, out of all touch with the capital, any mine overseer could act as a law unto himself.

'How long do they survive?' Nxumalo asked when he climbed out.

'Four, five years.'

'The children?'

'If the old folk live long enough, the children learn to mine. One family, maybe fifteen, eighteen years.'

'And if the old ones die too soon?'

'The children die with them.'

'What do you propose doing about the mine?'

'Our men are out hunting for some new brown workers. If they find any, we'll be able to mine again.'

'Will you find them?'

'Hunting them is dangerous. They use poisoned arrows, you know.'

'Put your own women to work down there. That's how we do it at other mines.'

'Our women prefer the sun and the fields,' the overseer replied, and in conspiratorial whispers he added, 'You're a man, Nxumalo. You know what fat beauties are for.'

'You opened the entrance for me to go down. A little more, and they can squeeze in.'

'What use could we men have of them if they came home exhausted from laboring underground? Tell me that.'

'When you have the hunger for them, let them rest a day or two.'

'I tell you, sir, our women would refuse to work as miners. You must bring me people from outside.'

Sternly Nxumalo said, 'I shall return next season, and I will expect to see this mine operating at capacity. We must have gold.'

This ultimatum would be met, for as Nxumalo marched back toward Zimbabwe, the mine overseer, who loved his five fat wives, was relieved to see a band of his warriors returning from the desert with nine small brown people. They would fit nicely into the mine; they would eat what was tossed down to them; and never again would they see daylight.

As Nxumalo visited the distant mines he often recalled that moment when he first saw the Limpopo and when he first climbed down into a mine: It was a premonition. I spend my life crossing rivers and descending shafts. Wherever he traveled through the vast domains of Zimbabwe he came upon the old treasured mines, and in time learned how to predict where new ones might be found, and although nine out of his ten guesses proved barren, that tenth repaid all efforts. Each new find, each old mine that increased its output enhanced his reputation.

Although he had made himself familiar with thousands of square miles of the kingdom, there remained one place he had not visited: the citadel atop the Hill of Spirits at Zimbabwe itself, but now as he returned from his latest trip he was summoned to the king's residence to deliver his report in person to the ruler and his councillors. He was guarded about what he said concerning the enslavement of the small brown people at that frontier mine, but he spoke boldly of the problems in the north, and when he finished, the senior councillor indicated that the king wished to speak with him alone.

After the assembly left, this councillor led Nxumalo through a maze of passages to the inner court, where, in a small roofless enclosure, he waited for his private audience. Soon the king appeared in his austere white robes, hastened directly to Nxumalo and said, 'Son of Ngalo from the lands my people do not know, I have never seen you at the citadel.'

'To go so high is not permitted, sir.'

'It is permitted,' the king said. 'Let us go there now and ask the spirits.' And under palm umbrellas the king and his inspector of mines walked down the main passageway through the city, past the area where the joiners and the masons dwelt, past the site where workmen brought stones for the walls. It seemed a lifetime since Nxumalo had helped repair those walls, and it was like a dream to be walking beneath them with the king himself.

They moved swiftly along the royal path that led to the rock-encircled citadel, and now the way became little more than a track, four feet across, but twice each day forty women swept it so that not a blade of grass or a pebble marred its surface. To attain the steep trail that led up to the summit, they had to pass the pits from which women dug wet clay used for plastering walls; and as the king went by, they all bowed their heads against the moist ground, but he ignored them.

The winding path climbed through a grove of trees, then traversed bare, rocky slopes, and reached at last an extremely narrow passageway between boulders. The king betrayed that he was out of breath, and although Nxumalo was well trained because of his distant journeys, he deemed it prudent to make believe that his chest heaved too, lest he appear disrespectful. At last they broke into a free and level space, and Nxumalo saw a grandeur he had not even vaguely anticipated when staring at the citadel from below.

He was in the midst of a great assembly of walls and courtyards twined among the immense granite boulders which gave the place its magnificence; those massive rocks determined where the walls must run, where the gracefully molded huts could stand. Rulers came from far distances to negotiate with the king, and so long as the meetings were held down below in the city, these foreign rulers, often as rich as the king, were apt to be slightly contemptuous of his soft-spoken arguments, but once they had been forced to climb that difficult path to see the citadel, they had to acknowledge that they were dealing with a true monarch.

Nxumalo was startled by the vivid colors that decorated the walls, the sculptures that marked the parapets and the symbolism that abounded. But what interested him most were the little furnaces at which metallurgists worked the gold ingots he sent from his mines, and he watched with admiration as they fashioned delicate jewelry by processes so secret they were never spoken of outside the citadel.

Despite his interest in the gold, Nxumalo was led away to the eastern flank of the citadel, and again he walked with that inner fear that had marked his first meeting with the king, for he knew that he was heading for the quarters of the great Mhondoro, the one through whom the spirits spoke and the ancestors ruled. By accident he caught a glimpse of the king's face and saw that he, too, had assumed a solemn mien.

The Mhondoro's enclosure seemed deserted when Nxumalo entered, but soon a shadowy figure could be seen moving in the dark recesses of a hut that filled one corner of the area. The main feature was a platform, waist-high, from which rose four soapstone pedestals, each topped by a sculptured bird which appeared to hover above the sacred place. Another wall contained a lower platform on which stood a collection of monoliths and other sacred objects of great beauty. Each related to some climactic experience of the race, so that in this enclosure stood the full history and mythology of Zimbabwe, a meaningful record of the past that could be read by the Mhondoro and his king as easily as European monks unraveled the writings of their historians.

The king was permitted by custom to walk to the meeting platform, but Nxumalo had to crawl on his knees, and as he did so he saw that when the discussions began he would be sitting among skull-like carvings, clay animals decorated with ostrich feathers, elaborate collections of medicated beads and pebbles, and tangled clumps of precious herbs. But no single item arrested his attention like the crocodile six feet long, carved from hard wood in such reality that it seemed capable of devouring the holy man; when Nxumalo took his seat beside this monster, he found that its scales were made from hundreds of wafer-thin gold plates that moved and glistened when he disturbed the air.

Now from the interior of his hut the Mhondoro appeared, wearing a yellow cloak and a headdress of animal furs. It was the king who paid homage: 'I see you, Mhondoro of my fathers.'

'I see you, Powerful King.'

'This is the one who was sent,' the king said.

The Mhondoro indicated that Nxumalo must keep his gaze forward, lest his eyes fall upon the symbols of kings long dead and anger their spirits, who would be watching. The young man scarcely dared breathe, but at last the Mhondoro addressed him: 'What news from the mines?'

'The gold from the west declines.'

'It used to be copious.'

'It still is, to the north, but our men are afraid to go there.'

'Trouble, trouble,' the spirit-medium said, and he turned to the king, speaking softly of the problems overtaking their city.

Nxumalo appreciated their concern, for at times on his recent journeys he had felt as if the entire Zimbabwe hegemony were held together by frail threads of dissolving interests. He sensed the restlessness and suspected that certain provincial chiefs were entertaining ideas of independence, but he was afraid to mention these fears in the presence of the city's two most powerful men. There were other irritations too: wood, grazing rights, the lack of salt. And there was even talk that the Arabs might open their own trade links in areas beyond Zimbabwe's control.

The painful afternoon passed, and when fires appeared in the city below, the Mhondoro began chanting in a dreamy voice: 'Generations ago our brave forebears erected this citadel. Mhlanga, son of Notape, son of Chuda . . .' He recited genealogies back to the year 1250 when Zimbabwe's walls were first erected. 'It was the king's great-grandfather who caused that big tower down there to be built, not long ago, and it grieves my heart to think that one day we may have to give this noble place back to the vines and the trees.'

In the silence that followed, Nxumalo became aware that he was supposed to respond: 'Why would you say that, Revered One?'

'Because the land is worn out. Because our spirits flag. Because others are rising in the north. Because I see strange ships coming to Sofala.'

It was in that solemn moment that Nxumalo first glimpsed the fact that his destiny might be to remain always in Zimbabwe, helping it to survive, but even as he framed this thought he looked at these two men sitting beneath the beautiful carved birds and he could not conceive that these leaders and this city could be in actual danger.

When he accompanied the king down from the citadel, servants with flares led the way and stayed with them on their progress through the city. Out of deference to the king, Nxumalo volunteered to attend him to the gateway of the royal enclosure, but the king halted midway in the city and said, 'It's time you visited the Old Seeker.'

'I see him often, sir.'

'But tonight, I believe, he has special messages.' So Nxumalo broke away and went to his mentor's house beyond the marketplace, and there he found that the old man did indeed have special information: 'Son of Ngalo, it's time you took the next cargo of gold and rhino horns to Sofala.'

This was a journey of importance which only the most trusted citizens were permitted to undertake. It required courage to descend the steep paths lined with leopards and lions; it required sound health to survive the pestilential swamps; and it required sound judgment to protect one's property against the Arabs who bartered there.

'The Arabs who climb the mountain trails to visit Zimbabwe have to be good men,' the wise old fellow warned. 'But those who slip into a seaport and remain there, they can be ugly.'

'How do I protect myself?'

'Integrity is a good shield.' He paused. 'Did I ever come armed to your father's kraal? Couldn't he have killed me in a moment if he wished? Why didn't he? Because he knew that if he killed a man of honor, he'd soon have on his hands men with none. And then the whole thing falls apart.'

'You know, I'm sure, that my father used to laugh at your stories. The miracles you spoke of, the lies.'

'A man cannot travel great distances without developing ideas. And now I have one of the very best to bring before you.'

He clapped his hands, and when the servant appeared, he gave a signal. Soon the curtains that closed off the living quarters parted and a young girl of fourteen, black as rubbed ebony and radiant, came dutifully into the room. Lowering her eyes, she stood inanimate, like one of the carved statues the Arabs had presented to the king; she was being presented to Nxumalo, the king's inspector of mines, and after a long time she raised her eyes and looked into his.

'My granddaughter,' the old man said.

The two young people continued gazing at each other as the Old Seeker confessed: 'From the first day I saw you at the lake, Nxumalo, I knew you were intended for this girl. Everything I did thereafter was calculated to bring you here for her to see. The rhino horns? I had all I needed waiting in the warehouse. You were the treasure I sought.'

Because of the pain that comes with all living, Nxumalo could not speak. He was acutely aware of this girl's beauty, but he could also remember Zeolani and his promise to her. Finally he blurted out: 'Treasured Father, I am betrothed to Zeolani.'

The old man took a deep breath and said, 'Young men make promises, and they go off to build their fortunes, and the antelope at the lake see them no more. My granddaughter's name is Hlenga. Show him the garden, Hlenga.'

It was in 1458 that Nxumalo assembled a file of sixty-seven porters for the perilous journey to the coast. The route to Sofala was horrendous, with swamps, fever-ridden flats, precipitous descents and swollen rivers barring the way. As he listened to accounts of the journey from men who had made earlier trips, he comprehended what Old Seeker had meant when he said, 'A wise man goes to Sofala only once.' And yet Arab traders appeared at Zimbabwe regularly, and they had to traverse that formidable route.

This contradiction was resolved by the Old Seeker: 'The Arabs have no problems. They start from Sofala with fifty carriers and arrive here with thirty.'

'How is it they're always the ones that arrive?'

'White men protect themselves,' the old councillor said. 'I went down with the father of the man who gave you that disk. At every river he said, "You go first and see how deep it is." So at one crossing I said, "This time you go first," and he said, "It's your task to go. It's my task to protect the gold." '

Nxumalo laughed. 'That's what one of our mine overseers says when tossing a catch of little brown men down the shaft: "It's your task to go down there. It's my task to guard the gold when you send it up." '

'One more thing, Nxumalo. Arabs in a caravan will be your staunchest friends. Share their food with you, their sleeping places. But when you reach Sofala, be aware. Never go aboard ship with an Arab.'

Nxumalo coughed in some embarrassment. 'Tell me, Old Seeker, what is a ship? The king spoke of it and I was ashamed to ask.'

'A rondavel that moves across the water.' While the young man contemplated this improbability, the old man added, 'Because if you step aboard his ship, the Arab will sell you as a slave and you will sit chained to a bench and never see your friends again.'

This almost casual mention of friends saddened Nxumalo, for the friend he cherished most was Zeolani, and the possibility of never seeing her again distressed him. At the same time he recognized that all things happening in Zimbabwe were conspiring to prevent him from ever returning to his village, and he supposed that if he succeeded with the forthcoming expedition to Sofala, his position at Zimbabwe would be enhanced. Yet memories of Zeolani and their impassioned love-making behind the twin hills haunted him, and he longed to see her. 'I want to return home,' he said resolutely, but Old Seeker laughed.

'You're like all young men in the world. Remembering a lovely girl who is far away while being tormented by another just as lovely, who is close at hand . . . like Hlenga.'

'On your next trip to my village . . .'

'I doubt I shall ever wander so far again.'

'You will. You're like me. You love baobabs and lions prowling your camp at night.'

The old man laughed again. 'Perhaps I am like you. But you're like me. You love rivers that must be forded and paths through dark forests. I never went back, and neither will you.'

On the morrow, with a kiss from Hlenga on his lips, this young man, twenty-one years old, set forth with his porters to deliver a collection of gold, ivory tusks and other trading goods to the waiting ships, and so heavy was the burden that progress under any circumstances would have been

tedious; through the forests and swamps which separated them from the sea
it was punishing. Nxumalo, as personal representative of the king, headed
the file, but he was guided by a man who had made the difficult traverse
once before. They covered only ten miles a day, because they were so often
forced by turbulent rivers or steep declivities to abandon established trails.
They were tormented by insects and had to keep watch against snakes, but
they were never short of water or food, for rain was plentiful and animals
abounded.

At the end of the sixth day everyone had subsided into a kind of
grudging resignation; hour after hour would pass with no speech, no relief
from the heat, the sweat and the muddy footing. It was travel at its worst,
infinitely more demanding than a trip of many miles through the western
savanna or southward into baobab country. This was liana land, where
vines hung down from every tree, tormenting and ensnaring, where one
could rarely move unimpeded for ten feet in any direction.

But always there lay ahead the fascinating lure of Sofala, with its ships,
and Chinese strangers, and the glories of India and Persia. Like a tantalizing
magnet it drew the men on, and at night, when the insects were at their
worst, the men would talk in whispers of women who frequented the port
and of Arabs who stole any black who tried to visit with these women. The
travelers had an imperfect understanding of the slave trade; they knew that
men of foreign cast traveled the Zambezi capturing any who strayed, but
these invaders had never dared invade Zimbabwe and risk a disruption of
the gold supply, so their habits were not known. Nor did the murmuring
blacks have any concept of where they might be taken if they were captured;
Arabia they knew only for its carvings, India for its silks.

When the great escarpments were descended and the level lowlands
reached, the travelers still had more than a hundred miles of swampy flat
country with swollen rivers to negotiate, and again progress was minimal.
It was now that young Nxumalo asserted his leadership, dismissing his
guide to the rear and forcing his men into areas they preferred to avoid. He
had come upon a well-marked trail which must lead to the sea, and as his
men straggled behind, unable to keep the pace he was setting with his lighter
burden, they began to meet other porters coming home from Sofala or were
overtaken by swifter-moving files heading for the port, and a lively excitement spread through the group.

'We must not step inside a ship,' the guide repeated on the last night,
'and all bargaining is to be done by Nxumalo, for he knows what the king
requires.'

'We will wait,' Nxumalo said, 'until the Arabs make us good offers, and
they must be better than what they offer us at home, for this time we have
done the hauling, not they.' He was prepared to linger at Sofala for months,
selling his goods carefully and obtaining only those things his community
most needed.

'What we really seek,' he reminded them, 'is salt.' Even his gold bars
would be bartered if he could find the proper amount of salt.

When his porters took up their burdens next morning, passers-by
confirmed that Sofala would be reached by noon, and they quickened their
pace; and when salt could be smelled in the air, they began to run until the

man in the lead shouted, 'Sofala! Sofala!' and all clustered about him to stare at the port and the great sea beyond. In awe one man whispered, 'That is a river no man can cross.'

The bustling seaport did not disappoint, for it contained features which astonished; the sheds in which the Arabs conducted their business were of a size the Zimbabwe men had never imagined, and the dhows that rolled in the tides of the Indian Ocean were an amazement. The men were delighted with the orderliness of the shore, where casuarina trees intermingled with palms and where the waves ran up to touch the feet and then ran back. How immense the sea was! When the men saw children swimming they were enchanted and sought to run into the water themselves, except that Nxumalo, himself perplexed by this multitude of new experiences, forbade it. He felt that he must face one problem at a time, and the first that he encountered proved how correct he was in moving prudently, for when he inquired about a market for his goods, and traders heard that he had twoscore elephant tusks, everyone doing business with China, where ivory was appreciated, wanted to acquire them, and he was made some dazzling offers, but since he had not intended selling immediately, he resisted. He did allow himself to be taken to an Arab ship, which, however, he refused to board; from the wharf he could see inside, and there, chained to benches, sat a dozen men of varied ages, doing nothing, making hardly a movement.

'Who are they?' he asked, and the trader explained that these men helped move the ship.

'How long do they wait like that?'

'Until they die,' the trader said, and when Nxumalo winced, he added, 'They were captured in war. This is their fate.' They were, Nxumalo reflected, much like the small brown men who were thrown down mines to work until they died. They, too, were captured in war; that, too, was their fate.

Wherever he moved in Sofala he saw things that bewildered, but constantly he was enticed by the dhows, those floating rondavels whose passage across the sea he could not comprehend but whose magic was apparent. One afternoon as he stared at a three-masted vessel with tall sails he saw to his delight that the white man who seemed to be in charge was the same tall Arab who had traded at Zimbabwe.

'Ho!' he shouted, and when the Arab turned slowly to identify the disturbance, Nxumalo shouted in Zimbabwe language, 'It's me. The one you gave the disk.' The Arab moved to the railing, peered at the young black, and said finally, 'Of course! The man with the gold mines.'

For some hours they stood on the wharf, talking, and the Arab said, 'You should carry your goods to my brother at Kilwa. He'll appreciate them.'

'Where is the trail to this Kilwa?'

The Arab laughed, the first time Nxumalo had seen him do so. 'There is no trail. It couldn't cross the rivers and swamps. To walk would require more than a year.'

'Then why tell me to go?'

'You don't march your men along a trail. You sail . . . in a dhow.'

Nxumalo instantly recognized this as a trick to enslave him, but he also knew that he yearned achingly to know what a dhow was like, and where China lay, and who wove silk. So after a night's tormented judging he sought the Arab and said simply, 'I shall deposit all my goods here, with my servants. I'll sail with you to Kilwa, and if your brother really wants my gold . . .'

'He'll be hungry for your ivory.'

'He can have it, if he brings me back here to get it.'

It was arranged, but when his men heard of his daring they protested. They, too, had seen the slaves chained to the benches and they predicted that this would be his fate, but he wanted to believe the Arab trader; even more, he wanted to see Kilwa and discover the nature of shipping.

Toward the end of 1458 he boarded the dhow at Sofala for the eleven-hundred-mile passage to Kilwa, and when the lateen sails were raised and the vessel felt the wind he experienced the joy that young men know when they set forth upon the oceans. The rolling of the dhow, the leaping of the dolphins that followed the wake, and the glorious settings of the sun behind the coast of Africa enchanted him, and when after many days the sailors cried, 'Kilwa, the golden mosque!' he ran forward to catch his first sight of that notable harbor to which ships came from all cities of the eastern world.

He was overwhelmed by the varied craft that came to Kilwa, by the towering reach of the masts and the variety of men who climbed them. He found the Arab equally moved, and as the dhow crept through the harbor to find a mooring place, the trader pointed to the shore where buildings of stone glittered and he said with deep feeling, 'My grandfather's grandfather's father. We lived in Arabia then, and he sailed his trading dhow to Kilwa. On that beach he would spread his wares. What wonderful beads and cloths he brought. Then he and all his men would retire to his boat, and when the beach was empty of our people, the black-skinned traders would come down to inspect the goods, and after a long while they would leave little piles of gold and ivory. Then they would retire, and my father would go ashore and judge the offer, and if it was miserly he would touch nothing, but return to his dhow. So the men would come again and add to their offer, and after many exchanges, without a word being spoken, the trade would be consummated. Look at Kilwa now!'

Nxumalo succumbed to its spell, and for nine days did not even bother to barter his treasures. When he visited the mosque, lately rebuilt and one of the noblest in Africa, he thought: That tower they call the minaret. It resembles the tower I worked on at Zimbabwe. But ours was built much differently. Perhaps someone like me came here to Kilwa, and saw this fine city and went home to do his building.

He visited all the ships then in harbor and the trading points on the mainland, and after a while he began to comprehend the intricate world in which black men and yellow and honey-tan like the Arabs met and traded to mutual advantage, each having something precious to the others. Because he had gold and ivory, he could deal on a basis of equality with Egyptians and Arabians and Persians and Indians and the soft, quick people from Java.

He would have sailed with any of them to the far side of the sea; he would have been a willing passenger on any ship going anywhere; but in the end he arranged for the Arab's brother to sail him back to Sofala for his entire cache of goods. He might have bargained for a slightly more advantageous trade with other merchants, but to do so would have been undignified for an officer of the court of Zimbabwe.

It was a long, drifting trip back to Sofala, and during such a protracted voyage anything might have happened, but the passage was calm and uneventful, with Nxumalo talking at great length with the Arab traders and learning from them of the vast changes occurring in the world. The significance of Constantinople was explained; although he knew nothing of the name, he deduced that the Arabs must now enjoy an enormous advantage. What was of greater interest were tales the Arabs told of changes along the Zambezi: 'Many villages have new masters. Salt has been discovered and tribes are on the move.'

When their ship neared the mouth of that great river the captain pointed out the little trading post of Chinde, and Nxumalo began to recite the melodious names of this enchanted coast: Sofala, Chinde, Quelimane, Moçambique, Zanzibar, Mombasa. And the sailors told him of the distant ports with which they dealt: Jidda, Calicut, Mogadiscio, Malacca.

While these narcotic names infected him with their sweet poison he stayed on deck and watched the moon tiptoe across the waves of an ocean he still could not comprehend, and grudgingly he admitted that he was so enamored of this new world—the towers of Zimbabwe, his register of mines across the country, the fleet of ships at Kilwa and Sofala, the grand mystery of the ocean—he could never again be satisfied with his father's village and its naked men plotting to snare a rhinoceros. His commitment lay with the city, not to any grandiose concept of its destiny but to the honorable task of doing better whatever limited assignment he was given. He would supervise his mines with extra attention and trade their gold to maximum advantage. He would work to strengthen Zimbabwe and help it maintain itself against the new hegemonies forming along the Zambezi. To undertake such tasks would mean that he could never go south to claim Zeolani, and as night faded, the moon sinking into the western sea seemed like the slow vanishing of that beautiful girl. At the moment when the golden disk plunged into the waves it looked much like the Nepalese disk he had sent her, and he could think only of their love-making and of the sorrow that would never completely leave him.

At dawn he sought his Arab mentor and said, 'I must buy one special thing . . . to send south . . . to a girl in my village.'

'You will not take it to her yourself?'

'Never.'

'Then make it something precious, for long remembrance,' and the Arab put before him a selection of items, and from them Nxumalo started to choose his gift, but as he looked past the trinkets he saw the slaves, chained forever to their benches, and he was in confusion.

When Nxumalo led his porters back to Zimbabwe at the close of 1459, he brought with him goods from distant lands and much intelligence regarding developments on the Zambezi, where Sena and Tete were becoming important trading towns. He brought rumors of areas farther up the river where salt was available and the land not exhausted. And he secreted in his bundle a jade necklace from China, which he sent south with the Old Seeker on the trip which that fellow again averred was his last.

For many days he met in the citadel with the king and the Mhondoro, discussing the Zambezi developments. He reported on all that the Arabs had told him, and he started an impassioned description of what steps must be taken to protect and augment Zimbabwe, but he did not get far, because the king cut him short with an astonishing statement: 'We have decided to abandon this city.'

Nxumalo gasped. 'But it's a noble city,' he pleaded. 'Even better than Kilwa.'

'It was. It is. But it can no longer be.' The king was adamant in his decision that Great Zimbabwe, as it was called then and forever, must be surrendered to the jungle, since further occupancy was impractical.

As he reiterated this doleful verdict the three men looked down upon the fairest city south of Egypt, a subtle combination of granite-walled enclosures and adobe rondavels, a city in which eleven thousand workers enjoyed a good and differentiated life. It was a place of constant peace, of great enrichment for the few and modest well-being for all; its faults were that it had spent its energy searching for gold, its resultant income on ostentation. It had ignored clear signs that the press of people in the capital city had impaired the environment; the delicate balance between man and nature which had endured for so long was upset. Its economic stability and assured gold had pleased distant Arabs and Indian princes, but as its natural resources dwindled, its existence was doomed. Those long lines of slaves carrying in precious goods had done nothing to nourish the real city, so at the very apex of its glory it had to be abandoned.

On no one did the decision fall with harsher force than on Nxumalo, for on the dhow that night he had committed himself to the perpetuation of this city, yet on the day he returned to put his promise into action he was informed that the city would no longer exist. For two weeks he was disconsolate, and then it occurred to him that a worthy man dedicates himself not to one particular thing which attracts him, but to all tasks; and he vowed that when the time came to move this city to its new site, he would devote all his powers to that endeavor and, with Hlenga's help, make the new city superior to the old.

It is difficult, five hundred years after the event, to describe in words the precise quality of thought available to the men who made this decision to abandon Zimbabwe, but because the act was so crucial in the history of southern Africa, an attempt must be made without inflating or denigrating reality. The king was no Charlemagne; he was unaware of libraries and monetary systems, yet he had an uncanny sense of how to keep a sprawling empire functional, and if he knew nothing about armies or military policy, it was only because he kept his nation at peace during a long reign. He spoke only one language, which had never been written, and he had no court painter to depict his likeness for foreign princes, yet he knew how to keep Zimbabwe beautiful; the additions he made to both the lower city and the citadel were commendable. He was a ruler.

The Mhondoro was certainly no Thomas Aquinas speculating upon the nature of God and man; indeed, he was sometimes little more than a shaman propitiating dubious spirits that might otherwise destroy the city. But if he lacked a comprehensive theology like Christianity or Islam with which to console his people, he did have remarkable skill in banishing their grosser fears, controlling their wilder passions, and lending them the assurances they needed to keep working. He was a priest.

The condition of Nxumalo was more puzzling. Offspring of a minimal society, child of a family with extremely limited horizons, he had been allowed adventures which lured him always toward larger concepts. He was one of those wonderful realists who can add a tentative two to a problematic three and come up with a solid five. He saw Zimbabwe exactly as it was, a city fighting for its life in a rapidly changing world, but he also saw in his imagination the cities of India and China, and he guessed that they were struggling too. He realized that if there existed something as magnificent as an ocean, there could be no reasonable limit to the wonders its shores might contain. He could not read or write; he could not express himself in scholastic phrases; he knew nothing of Giotto, who was dead, or Botticelli, who was living, but from the first moment he saw those carved birds adorning the citadel he knew they were art and never some accidental thing from the marketplace. He was a pragmatist.

Any one of these three, or all as a group, could have learned to function in any society then existing, given time and proper instruction. The king certainly was as able as the Aztec rulers of Mexico or the Incas of Peru and markedly superior to the confused brothers of Prince Henry, who ruled Portugal abominably; had the Mhondoro been a cardinal at Rome, he would have known how to protect himself at the Vatican as it then operated; and if Nxumalo with his insatiable curiosity had ever had a chance to captain a ship, he would have outdistanced Prince Henry's reluctant navigators. These three might be called savages, but they should never be called uncivilized.

Yet this is precisely what Henry the Navigator did call them as he lay dying in his lonely monastery on the forlorn headland of Europe. He sat propped in bed, surrounded by a lifetime of books and documents, striving to devise some stratagem that would speed his captains in their attempt to turn the southern tip of Africa and 'discover and civilize' places like Sofala and Kilwa. It required an arrogant mind to consider these great entrepôts 'undiscovered' merely because no white Christian had yet traveled up the eastern coast of Africa, whereas thousands upon thousands of dark Arabs had traveled down it, and had been doing so for a thousand years.

These were the closing weeks of 1460, while Zimbabwe still functioned as the capital of a vast but loosely ruled hegemony, with its royal compounds decorated by celadons from China, but Prince Henry could say to his assembled captains, 'Our mighty task is to bring civilization to the dark shores of Africa.' He added, 'That the gold mines of Ophir should be

occupied by savage blacks is repugnant, but that their gold should fall into
the hands of those who worship Muhammad is intolerable.'

So in the final days of his life, while Nxumalo and his king wrestled with
sophisticated problems of management, Prince Henry challenged his captains to round Africa. Two generations of these men would die before
anyone breasted the cape, but Henry approached death convinced that the
discovery of Ophir was close at hand. 'My books assure me,' he told his
sailors, 'that Ophir was built by those Phoenicians who later built Carthage.
It is very ancient, long before the days of Solomon.' He took real consolation
in this belief, and when a captain said, 'I have been told it was built by
Egyptians,' he snorted, 'Never! Perhaps Old Testament Jews drifting down
from Elath, or maybe powerful builders from Sidon or Arabia.' Not in his
worst fever could he imagine that blacks had built an Ophir, and worked
its mines and shipped its gold to all parts of Asia.

And even had he survived long enough to see one of his captains reach
Sofala, and if that man had sent an expedition inland to Zimbabwe, and if
he had reported upon the city, its towers gleaming in the sun, its carved
birds silent upon their parapets—and all managed by blacks—he might
have refused to accept the facts, for in his thinking, blacks capable of
running a nation did not exist.

There were dark-skinned Muslims who threatened the Christian world,
and yellow Chinese of whom Marco Polo had written so engagingly, and
soft-brown Javanese who traded with all, but there were no blacks other
than the unspeakable savages his captains had met on the western coast of
Africa.

'The only people with whom we contend,' he told his captains, 'are the
Muslims who endanger our world. So you must speed south, and turn the
headland which I know is there, and then sail north toward the lands our
Saviour knew. We shall confront the infidel and win a world for Christ, and
your soldiers shall enjoy the gold of Ophir.'

Prince Henry was sixty-six years old that November, a worn-out man
and one of the supreme contradictions in history. He had sailed practically
nowhere, but had provided a fortune to his captains, threatening to bank-
rupt his brother's kingdom, in his rugged belief that the entire world could
be navigated, that Ophir lay where the Bible intimated, and that if only he
could get his ships to India and China, his priests could Christianize the
world.

Henry of Portugal was an explorer *sans égal,* for he was goaded onward
solely by what he read in books, and from them he deduced all his great
perceptions. How sad that his captains, in his lifetime, did not indeed reach
Sofala, so that he could have read their reports of a thriving Zimbabwe. Had
he seen proof of this black civilization, it might have shaken his preconceptions, for he was, above all, a man of probity. And if the few remaining
stragglers in the area had accepted Christianity, he would have found a
respectable place for them in his cosmogony. But his people had neither
reached Zimbabwe nor envisioned its existence.

Even sadder was the fact that after Vasco da Gama did finally reach
Sofala in 1498, the Portuguese considered such ports merely as targets for
looting, gateways to vaster riches inland. By 1512, fifty-two years after

Prince Henry's death, Portuguese traders were beginning a brisk business with the chiefdoms that had grown up in the shadow of Great Zimbabwe, and one priest composed a long report of his dealings with a representative from one settlement who had come down to Sofala leading sixty blacks bearing cargoes of gold and ivory and copper, just as the Bible had predicted:

> His name, Nxumalo, third chief of a city I was not privileged to see but on which I interrogated him closely. He was very old, very black, with hair of purest white. He talked like a young man and wore no adornment or badge of office except an iron staff topped by feathers. He seemed able to speak many languages and talked eagerly with all, but when I asked him if his city was the ancient Ophir, he smiled evasively. I knew he was trying to mislead me, so I persisted, and he said through our Arab interpreter, 'Others have asked me that.' Nothing more, so I pressed him, and he said, 'Our city had towers, but they were of stone.' I told him he was lying, that our Bible avers that Ophir was made of gold, and he took me by the arm and said quietly, in perfect Portuguese, which startled me, 'We had gold too, but it came from mines far from the city, and it was difficult to obtain, and now the mines have run dry.' I noticed that he had all his teeth.

III. A Hedge
of Bitter Almond

THERE was no close parallel to the miraculous thing that happened at the cape called Good Hope.

In 1488 Captain Bartholomeu Dias in a Portuguese caravel rounded this cape, which he considered to be the southernmost point of Africa, and he proposed going all the way to India, but like other captains before and after, he found his crew afraid and was forced by their near-mutiny to turn back.

In 1497 Captain Vasco da Gama landed near the cape, remaining eight days and establishing contact with large numbers of small brown people who spoke with clicks.

In the ensuing century the Portuguese penetrated to the far reaches of the Indian Ocean: Sofala of the gold dust, Kilwa the splendid entrepôt, Aden and its shrouded figures, Hormuz with the metaled jewelry of Persia, Calicut offering the silks of India, and Trincomalee with the rare cinnamon of Ceylon. It was a world of wonder and riches which the Portuguese dominated in all respects, shipping its spices back to Europe to be sold at enormous profit and leaving at the outposts priests to Christianize and functionaries to rule.

As early as 1511 one of the greatest Portuguese adventurers, Afonso de Albuquerque, ventured out of the Indian Ocean, establishing at Malacca a great fort that would serve as the keystone to Portuguese holdings. Whoever controlled Malacca had access to those magical islands that lay east of Java like a chain of jewels; these were the fabled Spice Islands, and their riches lay in fee to Portugal.

During the entire sixteenth century this small seafaring nation transported untold wealth from the area, making irrelevant the fact that Muslims controlled Constantinople. Profit was now made not from tedious overland camel routes but from seaborne traffic. However, it was not this explosive wealth which led to the miracle.

In the opening years of the seventeenth century two other very small European nations decided to seize by force their share of the Portuguese monopoly. In 1600 England chartered its East India Company, known in history as John Company, which quickly gained a solid foothold in India. Two years later the Dutch launched their counterpart, Vereenigde Oostindische Compagnie (United East India Company), to be known as Jan Compagnie, which operated with stubborn troops and very stubborn traders.

The eastern seas became a vast battleground, with every Catholic priest a forward agent of Portugal, every Protestant predikant a defender of Dutch interests. Nor was it merely a commercial-religious rivalry; real warfare was involved. Three hideous times—1604, 1607, 1608—mammoth Dutch fleets strove to capture the dominating Portuguese fortress on Moçambique Island, and the sieges should have ended in easy victory, because the island was small, 3,200 yards long, 320 yards wide, and defended by as few as sixty Portuguese soldiers against whom the Dutch could land nearly two thousand.

But the defenders were Portuguese, some of the toughest human beings on earth. Once when there was little hope that the few could resist the many, the Portuguese mounted a sortie, swept out of their fortress walls and slew the attackers. The Portuguese commander taunted: 'The company defending this fort is a cat that cannot be handled without gloves.' During one of the sieges, when all seemed lost, the Portuguese proposed that the affair be settled by fifty Dutch soldiers fighting a pitched battle against twenty-five Portuguese, 'a balance honoring the character of the contesting armies.'

The Dutch tried fire, trenching, towers, secret assaults and overpowering numbers, but never did they penetrate those fortress walls. How different the history of South Africa might have been had the Portuguese defenders been one shade less valiant. If in 1605 the sixty had surrendered to the two thousand, by 1985 the strategic ports of Moçambique would probably rest in the hands of the descendants of the Dutch; all lands south of the Zambezi River could have been under their rule, and in the ensuing history South Africa would have been the focus, not Java. But never could the Dutch mount that final push which would have carried them to great victory in Africa.

In these years, when a Portuguese soldier disembarked from one of his nation's ships to take up duty within a fort at Moçambique or at Malacca, on the straits near Java, he could expect during his tour of duty three sieges in which he would eat grass and drink urine. Some of the most courageous resistances in world history were contributed by these Portuguese defenders.

One salient fact differentiated the colonizing efforts of the three European nations: the manner in which the effort related to the central government. The Portuguese operation was a confused amalgam of patriotism, Catholicism and profit; the government at Lisbon decided what should be done, the church ruled the minds of those who did it. When the English chartered their East India Company they intended it to be free of governmental interference, but quickly saw that this was impossible, because unless John Company behaved in a generally moral way, the good name of the nation was impugned; thus there was constant vacillation between commercial freedom and moral control. The Dutch had no such scruples. Their charter was handed to businessmen whose stated purpose was the making of profit on their investment, preferably forty percent a year, and neither the government nor the church had the right to intrude on their conduct. Any predikant who sailed in a ship belonging to Jan Compagnie was promptly informed that the Compagnie would determine what his religious duties were and how they would be discharged.

It was soon apparent that three such radically different approaches would have to collide, and soon the English were battling the Dutch for control of Java, while the Dutch stabbed at Portugal for control of Malacca, and all three fought Spain for control of the Spice Islands. Yet ships of these battling nations constantly passed the Cape of Good Hope, often resting there for weeks at a time, with little effective effort to occupy this crucial spot or arm it as a base from which to raid enemy commerce. It is inconceivable that these maritime nations should have rounded the Cape on their way to war and passed it again on their return without ever halting to establish a base. It is even more difficult to believe that hundreds of merchant ships bearing millions of guilders' and cruzados' worth of spices should have been allowed to navigate these difficult waters without confrontation of some kind. But that was the case. In two hundred years of the most concentrated commercial rivalry in Asia and war in Europe, there was only one instance in which a ship was sunk at the Cape by enemy action.

The explanation, as in the case of many an apparent inconsistency, rested in geography. A Portuguese ship setting out from Lisbon made a long run southwest to the Cape Verde Islands, replenished there and sailed almost to the coast of Brazil before steering southeast to round the Cape for the welcoming anchorage at Moçambique Island, from which it headed east to Goa and Malacca. Dutch and English ships also passed the Cape Verdes, but realizing that the Portuguese would not welcome them, continued south to the crucial island of St. Helena, which they jointly commanded, and once they cleared that haven, it was a brisk run to India. From there the English could head for entrepôts in the Spice Islands while the Dutch could anchor at their tenuous foothold in Java. There was really no reason why anyone need interrupt his journey at the Cape.

So from 1488, when Dias 'discovered' it, to 1652—a period of one hundred and sixty-four years climactic in world history—this marvelous headland, dominating the trade routes and capable of supplying all the fresh food and water required by shipping, lay neglected. Any seafaring nation in the world could have claimed it; none did, because it was not seen as vital to their purposes.

Although it was unclaimed, it was not untouched. In this empty period one hundred and fifty-three known expeditions actually landed at the Cape, and since many consisted of multiple ships, sometimes ten or twelve, it can be said with certainty that on the average at least one major ship a year stopped, often staying for extended periods. In 1580 Sir Francis Drake, heading home at the end of his circumnavigation with a fortune in cloves, caused to be written in his log:

From Java we sailed for the Cape of Good Hope. We ranne hard aboard the Cape, finding the report of the Portugals to be most false, who affirme that it is the most dangerous Cape of the world, never without intolerable storms and present dangers to travallers, which come neare the same. This Cape is a most stately thing, and the fairest we saw in the whole circumference of the earth.

In 1601 when Sir James Lancaster arrived with a small fleet—an appalling two hundred and nine days out of London—one hundred and five men were dead of scurvy, with the rest too weak to man the sails. There was one exception; in General Lancaster's own ship the men were in good shape:

And the reason why the Generals men stood better in health than the men of other ships was this; he brought to sea with him certaine bottles of the Juice of Limons, which hee gave to each one, as long as it would last, three spoonfuls every day . . .

Lancaster kept his men ashore forty-six days, plus five more at anchor in the roads, and during this time he was astonished at the level of society he encountered among the little brown men who occupied the land:

We bought of them a thousand Sheepe and two and fortie Oxen; and might have bought more if we would. These Oxen are full as bigge as ours and the sheepe many of them much bigger, fat and sweet and (to our thinking) much better than our sheepe in England . . . Their speech they clocke with their tongues in such sort, that in seven weeks which wee remained heere in this place, the sharpest wit among us could not learne one word of their language; and yet the people would soone understand any signe wee made to them . . . While that wee stayed heere in this baye we had so royall refreshing that all our men recovered their health and strength, onely foure or five excepted.

Year after year the ships stopped by, the sailors lived ashore, and the clerks wrote accounts of what transpired, so that there exists a rather better record of the unoccupied Cape than of other areas that were settled by unlettered troops. The character of the little brown people with their clicking tongue is especially well laid out—'they speak from the throat and seem to sob and sigh'—so that scholars throughout Europe had ample knowledge of the Cape long before substantial interest was shown by their governments. Indeed, one enterprising London editor compiled a four-volume book dealing largely with travels past the Cape, *Purchas his Pilgrimes,* and entered unknowingly into literary history as the principal source for *The Rime of the Ancient Mariner.*

Two engaging traditions endeared the Cape to sailors. It became the custom that whenever the navigator sensed that he was nearing the Cape, he would alert the crew, whereupon all ordinary seamen would strain to see who could first cry out: 'Table Mountain!' After his sighting was verified, the captain ceremoniously handed him a silver coin, and all hands, officers and men alike, stood at the railing to see once more this extraordinary mountain.

It was not a peak; as if some giant carpenter had planed it down, its top seemed as flat as a palace floor, and not a small floor, either, but a vast one. Its sides were steep and it possessed a peculiarity that never ceased to amaze: at frequent intervals, on a cloudless day when the tabletop showed clear, a sudden wind sweeping north from the Antarctic would throw a cloud of dense fog, and even as one watched, this fog would spread out, obliterating Table Mountain. 'The devil throwing his tablecloth,' men would say later, and the mountain would be hidden, with the hem of the cloth tumbling down the sides.

The second tradition was that of the post-office stone. As early as 1501 the captain of a Portuguese vessel passing the Cape came ashore with a letter of instructions to aid future travelers, and after wrapping it in pitched canvas, he placed it under a prominent rock on whose surface he scratched a notice that something of importance lay beneath. Thus the tradition started, and in all succeeding years captains would stop at the Cape, search for post-office stones, pick up letters which might have been left a decade earlier, and deliver them either to Europe or to Java. In 1615 Captain Walter Peyton, in the *Expedition* at the head of a small fleet, found post-office stones with letters deposited by different ships: *James, Globe, Advice, Attendant.* Each told of dangers passed, of hopes ahead.

There are few reports of letters ever having been destroyed by enemies. A ship would plow through the Indian Ocean for a year, fighting at port after port, but when it passed the Cape and posted its letters beneath some rock, they became inviolate, and the very soldiers who had fought this ship would, if they landed for refreshing, lift those letters reverently and carry them toward their destination, often dispatching them on a route that would take them through two or three intervening countries.

What was the miracle of the Cape? That no seafaring nation wanted it.

On New Year's Day 1637 a grizzled mariner of Plymouth, England, reached a major decision. Captain Nicholas Saltwood, aged forty-four and a veteran of the northern seas, told his wife, 'Henrietta, I've decided to risk our savings and buy the *Acorn.*' Forthwith he led her to The Hoe, the town's waterfront, and resting there in the exact spot occupied by Sir Francis Drake's ship in July of 1588, when he waited for the Spanish Armada to come up the Channel, stood a small two-masted ship of one hundred and eighty-three tons.

'It will be dangerous,' he confided. 'Four years absent in the Spice Islands and God knows where. But if we don't venture now . . .'

'If you buy the ship, how will you acquire your trade goods?'

'On our character,' Saltwood said, and once the *Acorn* was his, he and his wife circulated among the merchants of Plymouth, offering them shares in his bold adventure. From them he wanted no money, only the goods on which he proposed to make his fortune and theirs. On February 3, the day he had hoped to sail, he had a ship well laden.

'And if the sheriff abides his word,' he told his wife, 'we'll take even more,' and they went together to the ironmonger's, and as before, their surety was their appearance and their reputation. They were sturdy people and honest: 'Matthew, I want your lad to keep watch on my foremast. If I raise a blue flag, rush me these nineteen boxes. I'll pay silver for seven. You contribute the dozen, and if the voyage fails, you've lost all. But it will not fail.'

At the door of the mongery he kissed his wife farewell: 'It would not be proper for you to deal with the sheriff. I believe he'll come. You watch for the blue flag, too.' And he was gone.

Three bells had sounded when a cart from Plymouth prison hove into sight, bearing ten manacled men guarded by four marching soldiers and a very stout sheriff, who, when he reached the wharf, called out, 'Captain Saltwood, be you prepared?'

When Saltwood came to the railing the sheriff produced a legal paper, which he passed along for one of his soldiers to read, since he could not: 'Ship *Acorn*, Captain Saltwood. Do you agree to carry these men condemned to death to some proper spot in the southern seas where they are to be thrown ashore to establish a colony to the honor of King Charles of England?'

'I do,' Saltwood replied. 'And now may I ask you, has the passage money been voted?'

'It has,' the fat sheriff said, and as he stepped aboard the *Acorn* he counted out the five pieces of silver for each of the condemned men. 'Now the delivery. Captain Saltwood, I want you to appreciate the rogues you're getting.' And as the manacled prisoners came awkwardly aboard, chains dangling, the soldier read out their crimes: 'He stole a horse. A cutpurse. He committed murder, twice. He robbed a church. He ate another man's apples. He stole a cloak . . .' Each man had been sentenced to death, but at the solicitation of Captain Saltwood, who needed their passage money, execution had been stayed.

'Have you granted them equipment to found their colony?' Saltwood asked.

'Throw them ashore,' the sheriff said. 'If they survive, it's to the honor of the king. If they perish, what's lost?' With that the four soldiers climbed into the cart and pulled the wheezing sheriff in behind them.

'Run up the blue pennant,' Saltwood told his mate, and when it fluttered in the breeze the ironmonger hurried down to the ship with his nineteen crates of tools badly needed in the distant islands.

As soon as the *Acorn* stood out from harbor, Saltwood ordered his carpenter to strike off the manacles, and when the convicts were freed he assembled them before the mast: 'During this trip I hold the power of life and death. If you work, you eat and are assured of justice. If you plot against this ship, you feed the sharks.' But as he was about to dismiss the unfortunates, he realized that they must be bewildered by what might happen to them, and he said reassuringly, 'If you conduct yourselves well, I shall seek the most clement coast in all the seas. And when the moment comes to disembark, I shall provide you with such equipment for survival as we can spare.'

'Where?' one of the men asked.

'Only God knows,' Saltwood said, and for the next ninety days the *Acorn* sailed slowly southward through seas it had never traversed before, and the heavens showed stars which none had ever seen. The prisoners worked and partook of such food as the regular crew received, but always Saltwood kept his pistols ready, his defenses against mutiny prepared.

On the ninety-first day out, the *Acorn* sighted St. Helena, where the condemned men prayed to be set ashore, but a congenial port like this was not the intended destination, so the convicts were kept under close guard while the ship was provisioned, and after four restful days the *Acorn* headed south.

On May 23, in rough weather, the little ship, barely visible against the massiveness of Africa, stood off the sandy beach north of Table Mountain, for it was here that Captain Saltwood proposed to cast his convicts ashore. But before he did so, he gave them a selection of implements from one of the crates of tools, and his men contributed food and spare clothes for the apprehensive settlers.

'Be of good cheer,' Saltwood advised the convicts. 'Select one of your group to serve as leader, that you may subdue the land quickly.'

'Won't you sail closer to the shore?' one of the men asked.

'This coast looks dangerous,' Saltwood said, 'but you shall have this little boat.'

As the convicts climbed down into the frail craft he called, 'Establish a good colony so that your children may prosper under the English flag.'

'Where will we find women?' the impertinent murderer called.

'Men always find women,' Captain Saltwood cried, and he watched as the criminals manned the oars and rowed ineffectively toward the shore. When a tall wave came, they could not negotiate it; the boat capsized and all were drowned. Captain Saltwood shook his head: 'They had their chance.' And he watched with real regret as his boat shattered on the inhospitable beach.

But this voyage of the *Acorn* was not remembered for its loss of the ten convicts, because such accidents were commonplace and barely reported in London. When the stormy seas subsided, men from the ship went ashore at the Cape proper, and one of the first things they did was check the area for post-office stones; they found five, each with its parcel of letters, some intended for Amsterdam, some for Java. The former were rewrapped in canvas and put back under one stone; the latter were taken aboard for delivery in the far Far East. Under a special stone engraved with the *Acorn*'s name, the mate deposited a letter to London detailing the successful passage via St. Helena but ignoring the loss of the ten prisoners.

The shore party was about to embark for the long trip to Java when a group of seven little brown men appeared from the east, led by a vivacious young man in his twenties. He offered to trade sheep, which he indicated by cleverly imitating those animals, if the sailors would provide him with lengths of iron and brass, which again he indicated so that even the dullest sailor could catch his meaning.

They asked him his name, and he tried to say Horda, but since this required three click sounds they could make nothing of it, and the mate said, 'Jack! That's a good name!' And it was under this name that he was taken aboard the *Acorn* and introduced to Captain Saltwood, who said, 'We need men to replace the convicts. Show him to a bunk for'ard.'

He was naked except for a loincloth made of jackal skin, and a small pouch tied about his waist; in it he carried a few precious items, including an ivory bracelet and a crude stone knife. What amazed the sailors were the click sounds he made when talking. 'God's word,' one sailor reported to another, 'he farts through his teeth.'

Within a week of watching the sailmaker ply his awls and needles, Jack had fashioned himself a pair of trousers, which he wore during the remainder of the long voyage. He also made a pair of sandals, a hat and a loose-fitting shirt, and it was in this garb that he stood by the railing of the *Acorn* when Captain Saltwood led his little ship gingerly into the Portuguese harbor at Sofala.

'You were daring to enter here,' a Portuguese merchant said. 'Had you been Dutch, we would have sunk you.'

'I come to trade for the gold of Ophir,' Saltwood said, whereupon the Portuguese burst into disrespectful laughter.

'Everyone comes for that. There is none. I don't believe there ever was.'

'What do you trade?'

'Where do you head?'

'Malacca. The Spice Islands.'

'Oh, now!' the trader said. 'We accept you here, but anyone who tries to enter the Spice Island trade . . . they'll burn your ship at Malacca.' Then he snapped his fingers. 'But if you're brave, and really want to trade, I have something most precious that the Chinese long for.'

'Bring it forth,' Saltwood said, and with obvious pride the Portuguese produced fourteen curious, dark, pyramidal objects about nine inches square on the base. 'What can they be?'

'Rhinoceros horn.'

'Yes! Yes!' In the pages of his ship's log, on which he had prepared his notes for this great adventure, he had noted that rhinoceros horn might profitably be carried to any ports where Chinese came. 'Where would I trade them?' he asked.

'Java. The Chinese frequent Java.'

So a bargain was struck, after which the Portuguese said, 'A warning. The horns must be delivered as they are. Not powdered, for the old men who yearn to marry young girls must see that the horn is real, or it won't work.'

'Does it really work?' Saltwood asked.

'I don't need it yet,' the Portuguese said.

Wherever the *Acorn* anchored, Jack studied the habits of the people, marveling at their variety and how markedly they differed from the English sailors with whom he was now familiar and whose language he spoke effectively. At stately Kilwa he noticed the blackness of the natives' skins; at Calicut he saw men halfway in darkness between himself and his shipmates; at resplendent Goa, where all ships stopped, he marveled at the temples.

He gained great respect for Captain Saltwood, who not only owned the

Acorn but ran it with sagacity and daring. For one dreamy day after another the little vessel would drift through softly heaving seas, then head purposefully for some harbor none of the crew had heard of before, and there Saltwood would move quietly ashore, and talk and listen, and after a day of cautious judgment would signal to his men, and they would bring to the marketplace their bales of goods, unwrapping them delicately to impress the buyers. And always at the end of the trading, Saltwood would have some new product to fill his holds.

Like all the little brown people, Jack loved to sing, and in the evening when the sailors idled their time in chantey, his soft clear voice, echoing like some pure bell, joined in. They liked this; they taught him their favorite songs; and often they called for him to sing alone, and he would stand as they lolled, a little fellow four feet ten, his slanted eyes squeezed shut, his face a vast smile as he chanted songs composed in Plymouth or Bristol. Then he felt himself to be a member of the crew.

But there was another tradition, and this one he disliked. From time to time the English sailors would cry, 'Take down your pants!' and when he refused, they would untie the cord that held up the trousers he had sewn and pull them down, and they would gather round in astonishment, for he had only one testicle. When they questioned him about this, he explained, 'Too many people. Too few food.'

'What's that got to do with your missing stone?' a Plymouth man asked.

'Every boy baby, they cut one off.'

'What's that got to do with food?' The Plymouth man gagged. 'My God, you don't . . . '

'So when we grow up, find a wife, we must never have twins.'

Again and again when the voyage grew dull the sailors cried, 'Jack, take down your pants!' and one sultry afternoon in the Indian Ocean they brought down Captain Saltwood. 'You'll be astonished!' they said admiringly as they sought the little fellow, but when they found him and stood him on a barrel and cried, 'Jack, down with your pants!' he refused, grabbing himself about the middle to protect the cord that tied his trousers.

'Jack!' the men cried with some irritation. 'Captain Saltwood wants to see.'

But Jack had had enough. Stubbornly, his little face showing clenched teeth, he refused to lower his pants, and when two burly sailors came at him he fought them off, shouting, 'You not drop your pants!' And there he stood on the barrel, resisting, until Saltwood said quietly, 'He's right, men. Let him be.'

And from that day he never again dropped his drawers, and his self-stubbornness had an unforeseen aftermath: he had been the sailors' toy, now he became their friend.

The part of the journey he liked best came when the *Acorn* slipped past the great Portuguese fort at Malacca and wandered far to the east among the islands of the spice trade; there he saw for the first time cloth woven with gold and the metalwork of the islands. It was a world whose riches he could not evaluate but whose worth he had to acknowledge because of the respectful manner in which his friends handled these treasures.

'Pepper! That's what brings money,' the sailors told him, and when they crushed the small black corns to release the aromatic smell, he sneezed and was enchanted.

'Nutmeg, mace, cinnamon!' the sailors repeated as the heavy bags were heaved aboard. 'Turmeric, cardamom, cassia!' they continued, but it was the cloves that captivated him, and even though guards were posted over this precious stuff, he succeeded in stealing a few to crack between his teeth and keep against the bottom of his tongue, where they burned, emitting a pleasant aroma. For some days he moved about the ship blowing his cloved breath on the sailors until they started calling him Smelly Jack.

How magnificent the East was! When the *Acorn* completed its barter, Captain Saltwood issued the welcome command: 'We head for Java and the Chinese who await our horns.' And for many days the little ship sailed along the coast of Java with sailors at the rail to marvel at this dream-swept island where mountains rose to touch the clouds and jungle crept down to dip its fingers in the sea.

Captain Saltwood found no time to enjoy these sights, for he was preoccupied with two serious problems: he had traded so masterfully that his ship now contained a fortune of real magnitude and must be protected from pirates; but the fortune could not be realized unless he got his ship safely past the fort at Malacca, across the seas, around the Cape of Good Hope, through the storms of the equator, and home to Plymouth. It was with these apprehensions that he anchored in the roadstead off Java and was rowed ashore to bargain with the Chinese merchants who might want his rhinoceros horns.

While the *Acorn* lay at anchor, waiting until the next fleet formed for the journey to Europe, Jack had an opportunity to explore the trading center that the Dutch had established on Java. He lounged by the waterside, learning to identify the varied craft that worked these Asian waters: carracks with their bristling guns, swift flutes from Holland, the amazing proas from the islands—by shifting the location of their mast, they could sail in either direction with equal speed—and best of all, the towering East Indiamen.

It was while watching one of these monsters unload that he became aware of a tall, thin Dutchman who seemed always to preempt the best cargo for his warehouse, which stood close to the harbor. Traders called him Mijnheer van Doorn, and he seemed a most austere person, overly conscious of his position, even though he could not have been more than twenty-three. Jack was awed by his stiff dignity and spoke to him in broken English, which Van Doorn as a trader had to know.

'Where you from?' the Dutchman asked, looking down as if from a great and sovereign height.

'Many days.'

'You're not black. You're not yellow. Where?'

'Setting sun.'

The interrogation was so unsatisfactory that Van Doorn summoned a sailor from the *Acorn* and asked, 'Where's this fellow from?' and the man replied, 'Picked him up at the Cape of Good Hope.'

'Hmmmm!' Van Doorn stepped back, looked down his long nose at the

little fellow, and said, 'The Cape, is it a fine place?' Jack, understanding
nothing of this, laughed and was about to retreat when he spotted a white
person about his own size, a boy of thirteen whom Van Doorn treated
affectionately.

'Your boy?' Jack asked.

'My brother,' Van Doorn replied, and for the last two months that
Captain Saltwood idled off Java, Jack and this white lad played together.
They were of equal size and equal mental development, each striving to
understand the complex world of Batavia. They formed an attractive pair,
a thin little brown man with bandy legs, a stout Dutch lad with blond hair
and wide shoulders, and they could be seen together in each of the quarters
allocated to the different nationalities: Malay, Indian, Arab, Balinese, and
the small area in which the industrious Chinese purchased almost anything
offered for sale, but only at the prices they set.

One day young Van Doorn explained that Dutch children had two
names; his other one was Willem. 'What's yours?' he asked.

'Horda,' his playmate said with a blizzard of click sounds. 'And his
name?' he asked, pointing to the older Van Doorn.

'Karel.' And while Jack was repeating the two names, Willem produced
his surprise. Having noticed that Jack owned only the clothes he wore, he
had procured from the Compagnie warehouse an additional pair of trousers
and a shirt, but when Jack put them on he looked ridiculous, for they had
been cut to fit stout Dutchmen, not dwarfish brown persons.

'I can sew,' Jack said reassuringly, but after the clothes were altered he
reflected that aboard the *Acorn* whenever one man gave another something,
the recipient was supposed to give something in return, and he very much
wanted to give Willem van Doorn a gift, but he could not imagine what.
Then he remembered the ivory bracelet hidden in his pouch, but when he
handed it to Willem it was too small to fit his stout wrist. It was dour Karel
who solved the problem. Taking a silver chain from the Compagnie stock,
he fastened the ivory circle to it, then hung the chain about Willem's neck,
where the combination of silver, ivory and the lad's fair complexion made
a fine show.

That night Captain Saltwood, richer than he had ever dreamed because
of the trade he made on the rhino horns, informed his crew that since no
other ships were preparing to depart for home, the *Acorn* had no alternative
but to make a run up the Straits of Malacca to join with some English fleet
forming in India. 'It will be a grave adventure,' he warned his men, and they
spent that night preparing their muskets and pikes.

At dawn Jack wanted to slip ashore to say farewell to his Dutch friend,
but Captain Saltwood would not permit this, for he wished no interference
from Dutch authorities and intended sailing without their knowledge or
approval. So Jack stood at the railing of the *Acorn*, looking vainly for his
companion. Willem knew nothing of the departure, but toward eleven a
Dutch sailor ran into the Compagnie warehouse, shouting, 'The English
ship is sailing!' and Willem, fingering his ivory gift, stood by the water's edge
watching the ship and its little brown fellow disappear.

It required two weeks for the *Acorn* to transit Java waters, sail along
the coast of Sumatra and past the myriad islands that made this sea a

wonderland of beauty as well as fortune, but in time the sailors could see that land was beginning to encroach on each side of the ship, and they knew they were headed directly into the critical part of their voyage. To port lay Sumatra, a nest of pirates. To starboard stood the massive fortress of Malacca, impervious to sieges, with nearly seventy major guns on its battlements. And fore and aft would be the pestilential little boats filled with daring men trying to board and steal the prize.

The fight, if it came, would be even, for the *Acorn* was manned by men of Plymouth, grandsons of those doughty fellows who with Drake had routed the ships of King Philip's Armada. They did not intend to be boarded or sunk.

It was Captain Saltwood's strategy to remain hidden behind one of the many islands to satisfy himself that there was adequate wind, and then to run the gauntlet at night when the Portuguese might be inattentive, and this plan would have succeeded except that some Malay sailor, lounging on the northern shore, saw the attempted passage and sounded an alarm.

It was midnight when the battle began, great guns flashing from the fort, small boats darting out in an attempt to set fire to the English ship, larger boats trying to ram and board. Jack understood what was happening and knew from conversation with the sailors what tortures he and the others might expect if their ship was taken, but he was not prepared for the violent heroism of his English mates. They fought like demons, firing their pistols, thrusting and stabbing with their pikes.

Dawn found them safely past the looming fortress, with only a few small craft still trying to impede them; like a bristling beetle ignoring ants, the *Acorn* swayed ahead, its sailors shooting and jabbing at their attackers, and before long, pulled away. The dangerous passage was completed.

In India, Captain Saltwood faced a major disappointment: no English fleet would sail this year. So once more he went on alone, a daring man carrying with him enough wealth to found a family and perhaps even acquire a residence in some cathedral town. Getting home became an obsession, and he sailed the *Acorn* accordingly.

At Ceylon, pirates tried to board; off Goa, Portuguese adventurers had to be repulsed. South of Hormuz the Plymouth men ran into real danger, and at Moçambique two crazed carracks lumbered out to give chase on the remote chance that they might take a prize, but when the *Acorn* sailed serenely on, they abandoned the pursuit. Finally Sofala was passed to starboard, with Captain Saltwood saluting the unseen merchant who had sold him the rhinoceros horn. The southern coast of Africa guided them westward, and the morning came when a sailor shouted, 'I see Table Mountain!' and Captain Saltwood himself handed him the silver coin, saying, 'We're one step nearer home.'

When the bay was reached and the longboat prepared, Jack said farewell to his accidental friends, standing on tiptoe to embrace them. Once ashore, he walked slowly inland, pausing now and again to look back at the ship whose victories and tribulations he had shared for nearly four years. But the moment came when the next hill must close him off forever from the *Acorn,* and when he passed this and began to see familiar rocks and the spoor of animals he had always known, a strange thing occurred. He began divesting himself of the sailor's uniform he had worn these many months. Off came the shirt, the carefully sewn trousers, the leather shoes. He did not throw them away, nor the extra raiment given him by the young Dutch boy at Java, but tied them carefully into a little bundle, which knocked reassuringly against his leg as he walked homeward.

When he reached his village he was sucking a clove stolen at Java, and when his old friends poured out to greet him, he breathed a strange odor upon them, and undid his bundle to display what he carried, and to each he gave a clove in remembrance of the many times during the past four years that he had thought of them.

By 1640 the grim-faced Dutchmen who proposed to rule the East from Java had endured enough: 'Those damned Portuguese at Malacca must be destroyed.' In stinging reports to the Lords XVII, the businessmen who controlled the East Indies Company from their dark offices in Amsterdam, they had complained: 'The Catholic fiends in Malacca have sunk our ships for the last time. We are prepared to besiege their fortress for seven years if necessary.'

The Lords XVII might have rejected this daring proposal had not a gentleman whose grandfather was burned at the stake while trying to protect Dutch Protestantism from the fury of Spain's Duke of Alva argued passionately: 'Our fortunes teeter in the balance. Malacca must be destroyed.' His oratory carried, and plans to crush the Portuguese had been approved, not by the Dutch government but by Jan Compagnie. The hard-headed citizens of Holland knew in what kind of hands responsibility should be placed. Merchants with something to protect would know how to protect it.

When authorization reached Java the local Dutchmen responded enthusiastically. Funds were made available. New ships were built. Javanese natives in sarongs were taught to handle tasks afloat. And of equal importance, ambassadors were dispatched to large and petty kingdoms to assure them that when the Dutch moved against Malacca their interest was not territorial: 'We intend to take no land belonging to others. But we must stop the Portuguese piracy.'

Among the ambassadors chosen for this ticklish task was Karel van Doorn, now twenty-five and with a solid reputation as a loyal Compagnie servant. He was severe, honest, humorless, and gifted with an understanding of finance and the profitable management of Compagnie slaves.

Such promotions as Karel had achieved were due principally to his mother, the stalwart widow of an official who had been killed while endeavoring to extend Compagnie holdings in the Spice Islands. He had been a man of enormous energy; by arrogance, bluff, courage and expropriation he had protected the Compagnie; by chicanery, theft, falsification and diversion he had at the same time built up his own clandestine trading interests —a thing severely forbidden—and in so doing, had accumulated a considerable wealth which he had been trying vainly to smuggle back to Holland when he died. His widow, Hendrickje, now found herself with a growing fortune which she could spend only in Java.

Fortunately, she flourished in the tropics, and as soon as the Dutch destroyed the Javanese city of Jacatra and began building opposite its ruins their own capital, Batavia, she appropriated one of the choicest locations on the Tijgergracht (Tiger Canal) and there built herself a mansion. Curiously, it could have stood unnoticed on any street in Amsterdam, for it was done in massive Dutch style, with heavy stone walls and red-tiled roof protecting it from snows which never came. Thick partitions separated the rooms, which were illuminated by very small windows, and wherever a breeze might have entered, some heavy piece of furniture shut it out.

The only concession indicating that this massive house stood in the tropics was a garden of surpassing beauty, filled with the glorious flowers of Java and punctuated with handsome statuary imported from China. In this garden, to the sound of the tinkling gamelan comprised of eleven musicians, many decisions regarding Dutch fortunes in the East were reached.

Mevrouw van Doorn, a voluptuous blonde who might have been painted by Frans Hals, who did paint her mother, had arrived in 1618 when that notable administrator Jan Pieterszoon Coen was running affairs in his harsh, capable style, and she had quickly endeared herself to him, supporting him eagerly no matter what he did. She heard him warn the populace that acts of immorality among servants must cease, and when one of her maids became pregnant she herself dragged the frightened girl to Coen's headquarters and was present in the square when the girl was beheaded. The young man involved was also sharply reprimanded.

Two obsessions controlled her life: business and religion. It had been she who goaded her husband into setting up his illegal private businesses, one after another. It had been she who supervised those operations, earning a profit of sixty percent a year when the Lords XVII could make only forty. And it had been she who sequestered the stolen funds when they reached Batavia. Indeed, her husband's estate was now so complicated that she dared not risk returning to Holland lest it fall in chaos. As she reported to her younger sister in Haarlem:

> I often think of coming home to live with you in our house on the canal, but I dread those cold winters. Besides, I am kept prisoner here supervising the sixty-nine slaves who work for me. By Haarlem standards I know this sounds a lot, but it really isn't. When I go about Batavia, attending my affairs, eight slaves accompany me to assure that coaches, umbrellas and footwear are available. Seven girls tend my clothes, six watch over my retiring room. I need six cooks, nine serving men, eleven members for my orchestra, twelve to tend the grounds and ten for general services. So you see, I am kept quite busy.

Her devotion to religion contained no shred of insincerity, nor should it, considering her family history. Her grandfather, Joost van Valkenborch, had been executed by the Spaniards in 1568 when the great Count Egmont went to his death; both patriots had given their lives in defense of Holland

and Calvinism. Her father, too, had died fighting the Spanish Catholics; Willem van Valkenborch had established the first Calvinist assembly in Haarlem, a clandestine affair whose members knew they would perish if caught. One of her first memories was of secret night worship when her father spoke eloquently of God and the nature of man. Religion was more real to her than the stars over Java, more encompassing than the canals that served Batavia.

Before her husband died they had shared the pleasure of receiving from the Lords XVII a Protestant Bible printed in Dutch, a massive affair published in 1630 by Henrick Laurentsz of Amsterdam, and together they had read in their own language the glowing stories that had sustained her father and grandfather in their martyrdoms. Despite all the wealth her husband had left her, she held her chief treasure to be this Bible; it was the light that ruled her life.

Her next treasures were her two sons, who lived with her and whose fortunes she supervised so carefully, nudging the local directors whenever she thought Karel merited an advancement. It was she who had proposed him for the embassy to governments neighboring on Malacca, and when the trip was in preparation it was she who suggested that young Willem go along so as to witness the vast extent of the Compagnie's trading interests.

'He's only fifteen,' Karel protested.

'Proper time to learn what ships and battles are,' his mother snapped, and on a very hot afternoon when flies buzzed in stifled air, members of the diplomatic mission were briefed by high officials of the Compagnie, who sat like gargoyles in the white-walled council chamber, nodding gravely as an old man who had been fighting the Portuguese for three decades spoke portentously: 'A solemn moment approaches. We're about to crush Malacca.'

Karel leaned forward. 'Assault the fortress?'

The old man, clenching his fists and dreaming of long-gone defeats, ignored him. 'In 1606 we tried to capture that damned place and failed. In 1608 we tried again, and 1623. In 1626 and '27 I myself led the landing parties. We got to the walls but were driven back. During the last four years we've tried to blockade the Straits, starve them out, and always they've laughed at us. Now,' he shouted, banging his frail hand on the table, 'we destroy them.'

'How soon do we sail?'

'Immediately.'

When Karel showed disappointment at missing the siege, where promotions might come quickly, the old man said, 'You'll be back for fighting. We may not attack for at least a year. And remember what your job is. To assure all our neighbors that when we capture Malacca we shall seek no territory for ourselves.'

Another officer said sententiously, 'All we insist upon is trading rights. We'll take the fort but leave the land.'

And then a very large man with a voice that rumbled from much preaching added, 'Explain to them all that if they do business with us, it's only business. An honest deal for all. We will not try to Christianize them, the way the Portuguese have done with their oppressive Catholicism. Mark my words, Van Doorn, your strongest weapon could be religion. Tell them to watch our deportment when we capture Malacca.'

'If we capture it,' someone corrected.

'No!' a dozen voices cried. 'Dr. Steyn is right. When we capture it.'

The minister coughed and continued: 'When we occupy Malacca, nothing is changed. The sultan continues in power, freed of Portuguese influence. Muhammad continues as their God, freed of pressure from the Catholics. The Chinese, Arabians, Persians, Ceylonese, English—and even the Portuguese traders themselves—anyone with a business in Malacca will continue to own it and operate it as he wishes. All we seek is the right to trade, for all men. Tell the rulers that.'

In four days of concentrated argument this point was hammered until Van Doorn understood better than most of the Lords XVII back in Amsterdam what the practical politics of Jan Compagnie were. The Lords, representing all regions and aspects of Dutch life, had to be cautious, aware that whatever they promulgated enjoyed the force of law; indeed, their decisions were stronger than ordinary law because from them there was no appeal. But the governors in the field, who needed two years to send a query and receive an answer, had to be daring. On their own they could declare war, appropriate an island, or conduct negotiations with a foreign power. The governor-general in Java could order the execution of anyone, slave or free, English or Chinese: 'For stealing property belonging to the Compagnie, he shall be dragged to the port of Batavia and keel-hauled three times beneath the largest vessel. If still living, he shall be burned and his ashes scattered.'

The governor-general, accustomed to exercising these powers, glared at Karel and said, 'We expect you to convince the nations that they have no reason to oppose us when we make our attack.'

'I shall,' Van Doorn assured him.

There was at this time riding at the port of Batavia a trading ship heavily laden with goods for China, Cambodia and the Dutch entrepôt on Formosa, and free space for the stowing of such spices and metals as might be picked up in the course of a long journey. To this ship Karel, his brother Willem and their sixteen servants reported. Because of the importance of this mission, the captain had vacated his cabin and assigned it to the brothers, and there, surrounded by books and charts, they started the long voyage to the ancient ports of the East, sailing through waters that Marco Polo had known, past islands that would not be touched by white men for another century.

Wherever they stopped, they assured local leaders that the Dutch had no designs upon their territory, and that Java expected neutrality when the attack came on Malacca. 'Won't these people warn the Portuguese?' Willem asked.

'The Portuguese know. We've been attacking Malacca every ten years. Surely they expect us.'

'Won't they build their defenses?'

'Of course. They're doing it right now.'

'Then why didn't we attack right now?' the boy asked.

'Next year will be just as good. Our job now is to pacify allies.' But later, when the Dutch were dining alone, Karel was inspired to raise his glass to the sailors and soldiers who would participate in the siege: 'To that brave man amongst us who could well be the governor of Malacca before this year is out!' And all the Dutchmen drank in silence, imagining the possibilities: in their army a man did not have to be a nobleman to become an admiral or a governor.

By late April 1640, when the Van Doorns returned to Batavia with assurances that no neighbors would interfere with operations in the Straits of Malacca, and when a fleet of war vessels had been assembled, Governor-General van Diemen decided that the time was proper for the major thrust.

'Karel,' he told the returning ambassador, 'you're to accompany the fleet. Take charge as soon as the fortress is secured.'

'Looting?'

'It will be a long, dangerous fight, Karel. Allow the men three days to capture what they will. Then establish order. After that, no one is to be touched, Muslim or Christian.'

'The sultan?'

'Protect him, by all means. The soldiers will probably loot his palaces and take some of his women. But let him know that he survives with our blessing . . . and only because of our blessing. He'll prove our strongest ally.'

When the sails of the fleet were raised, they covered the sea like a sheath of white lace, and spies rushed overland to launch small boats in which they would scurry to Malacca to inform the Portuguese that the next siege was under way. It required thirteen days for the straggling fleet to reach the Straits south of the fortress, and when young Willem van Doorn looked up at the mighty battlements, thirty feet high, twenty-six feet thick, he gasped, 'No one could break them down.'

He was right to be apprehensive, for the fortress was much greater now than when the Dutch had first assaulted it. Five large churches stood within the walls, two hospitals, granaries, many deep wells, accommodation for four thousand fighting men. The town outside contained twenty thousand people, the harbor and the river more than a thousand small boats. From five towers sixty-nine major cannon controlled all approaches, and most important, the battlements were commanded by a man who had withstood other sieges and who was determined to outlast this one.

For five long and terrible months he succeeded. Two thousand of his people starved to death, then two thousand more, and finally another three. But he exacted a fearful toll on the Dutch assailants; more than a thousand highly trained men died in their attempt to approach these mighty walls.

They did achieve a limited success: by heroic measures they wrestled their cannon ashore, protected them with abutments, and proceeded methodically to knock large holes in the fortifications. Now all that was required was for foot soldiers to charge through the holes and the fort would be theirs, because deserters assured them: 'The Portuguese are eating rats and chewing upon the hides of horses.'

But to reach the holes, the Dutch would have to wade up to their armpits through malarial swamps, then swim turbulent streams while Portuguese on the walls shot at them, and this they were hesitant to do. So a kind of waiting war developed, during which yachts were dispatched regularly to Java seeking reinforcements and advice; in December, Willem van Doorn sailed on one of them, bearing messages:

> Our predikant Johannes Schotanus was an excellent man while the first fighting was under way, but in this waiting period he is again proving most difficult and has had to be suspended. We are sorry, for he possesses wonderful gifts. His teachings are exemplary, if only he would practice them. He could accomplish so much if he stayed sober, but we must not let him act as predikant after we capture Malacca because he would disgrace the Compagnie by his wild insobriety.

In the sixth month of the siege young Willem returned to the fleet in a large ship, bringing fresh supplies, much gunpowder and instructions that the fortress must now be taken. So on a Sunday night in January 1641 every able-bodied Dutchman moved ashore, forded the swamps, and made a predawn attack, driving the Portuguese from the openings in the walls by means of a furious barrage of hand grenades. By ten that morning the keystone of Portugal's empire in the East had fallen.

One of the most enthusiastic victors was Willem, who found that he did not fear gunfire or towering walls. Indeed, he was more resolute than his older brother and much more willing to press forward whether others accompanied him or not. He was among the first into the city, cheering wildly as cannon were drawn inside, lined up, and pointed down the narrow thoroughfares. Ball after ball, huge spheres of solid iron, leaped from the muzzles of the cannon, wreaking fearful destruction. Willem applauded the fires that raged and was in the forefront of those greedy soldiers who rampaged through the treasure-laden buildings that escaped the blaze.

It was a bloody triumph, but as soon as the looting was brought under control, the Dutch behaved with their customary magnanimity: the Portuguese commander was saluted for his bravery and given a ship in which he could transport his family, his slaves and his possessions to whatever haven he chose; the gallant captains who had defended the towers were permitted to accompany him with all they owned; and when an unsuspecting Portuguese merchant ship sailed into the channel laden with cloth from India, it was encouraged to dock, on the principle that since the islands under Dutch control produced little surplus cloth, trade with Portuguese India must not only be permitted but encouraged.

And so the vast eastern empire started by Magellan and Albuquerque dissolved. Only the village of Macao would be retained on the threshold of China, a part of tiny Timor in the waters north of Australia, the minute enclave of Goa in India, and the savage hinterland behind Moçambique Island—these were the remnants. All the rest was gone: Ceylon, Malacca, Java, the important Spice Islands. A man's heart could break at the loss of such glorious lands.

While the fires still smoldered, the victors reported to the Compagnie managers in Batavia: 'Noble, Valiant, Wise, and Honorable Gentlemen, Malacca has fallen and will henceforth be considered private territory and a dominion of the Dutch East India Compagnie.' Now the eastern world was secured and time was ripe for the Dutch to think seriously about establishing a safe resting point between Amsterdam and Batavia where sailors could recover from scurvy. Logic dictated that it be located at the Cape of Good Hope, but its founding had nothing to do with logic. It was sheer accident.

Batavia! This tiny enclave on the northwest coast of Java, this glorious capital of a vast and loosely held empire, had been named after the Batavi, those fierce, sullen men encountered by the early Roman emperors in the marshes that would subsequently become Holland.

It would always be a contradictory place, a walled fortress town perched on the edge of a jungle, totally Netherlandish in disposition, appearance and custom; but at the same time a garden-filled tropical escape from Holland, festooned with lovely flowers and strange fruits in great abundance. It was a heavenly place, a deadly place, and many Dutchmen who came here were dead within ten years, struck down by indolence, gluttony and drunkenness. It was in this period that Compagnie men, returning to Batavia from forced stints in the outlying Spice Islands, conceived the feast that would always be associated with Java.

It could be observed at its best in the spacious dining room of Hendrickje van Doorn, where fifteen or twenty guests would assemble to the playing of her musicians. Javanese slaves in sarongs would pass huge platters of delicately steamed white rice, nothing more, and each guest would form a small mountain on his plate. Then the first group of waiters would retire, and after an expectant pause Mevrouw would sound a tinkling Chinese bell, and from the kitchen out in the garden would appear a chain of sixteen serving men, some of the gardeners having been called to assist. Each carried in his open palms held waist-high two dishes, making a total of thirty-two: chicken bits, lamb cuttings, dried fish, steamed fish, eight rare condiments, ten fruits, nuts, raisins, vegetables and half a dozen tasty items that no one could identify.

As the sixteen servants passed along the table, each guest heaped edibles around his rice until the plate resembled a volcano rising high above the sea. But this was not all, for when these servants retired, others appeared with flagons of translucent gin, from which copious draughts were poured. Thus reinforced, the diners started on their meal, calling back the thirty-two little dishes from time to time lest the plate appear empty. This was 'the sixteen-boy rice table of Java,' and it accounted in some measure for the fact that many men and women who had lived rather circumscribed lives in Calvinistic Holland were reluctant to go home, once they knew Batavia.

Nevertheless, twice each year Dutch merchant ships trading throughout the East convened at Batavia in preparation for the long journey back to Amsterdam; each fleet would be at sea for half a year, rolling and dipping with the long swells of the Indian Ocean, sailing close-hauled into the storms of the Atlantic. On occasion a third of the fleet would be lost, but whenever a ship seemed doomed, it would hoist a panic flag, whereupon others would cluster around, wait for clearing weather, and transfer its cargo into their holds, and in this way the precious spices continued their homeward journey.

The first fleet sailed around Christmas; the second, waiting just long enough to obtain the monsoon cargoes from Japan and China. The holiday sailing was especially popular with the Java Dutch, for just about this time of year they began to be homesick for the wintry canals, and to see the great fleet waiting at anchor was a sore temptation. In 1646 there was no exception; an immense fleet gathered off Batavia under the command of an admiral, and on the morning of December 22 it hoisted sail.

At the last minute three ships whose smaller size and trimmer rigging would enable them to move more swiftly than the others were detached and ordered to wait for three weeks to serve as the after-fleet to carry important last-minute messages and any Compagnie officials who wished to depart after the Christmas celebrations. *Haerlem, Schiedam* and *Olifant* were the ships, and they tied up so that their sailors could roister ashore, and large fights broke out because sailors from the first two ships, which bore honorable names, began to tease those from the *Olifant,* Dutch for *elephant.*

Christmas that year was a noisy time, but at the spacious home of Mevrouw van Doorn it exhibited a lovely Dutch grace. Her musicians were dressed in batiks from Jokjakarta, her serving men in sarongs from Bali. There was dancing, and long harangues from minor officials serving in the Spice Islands, but as the day wore on, with enormous quantities of food being consumed and gallons of beer and arrack, the governor-general found occasion to take Mevrouw van Doorn aside to give her advice concerning her sons.

'They both should sail with the after-fleet,' he said quietly as his assistants snored away their beer and vittles.

'Deprive me of my staunchest support?' she asked, directing the slaves with the fans how best to move the air.

'Your sons are no more staunch in their support of you than I,' the governor said, bowing in his chair. When she acknowledged the compliment, he continued: 'Karel was born in Holland, and this is a permanent advantage. But he has never served there and the Lords XVII are not acquainted with his talents.'

'Karel will prosper wherever he's put,' his mother said sharply. 'He needs no special attention from Amsterdam.'

'True, an admirable son, sure to reach positions of significance.' Dropping his voice, he reached for her hand. 'Positions of eminence, as I did under similar circumstances.'

'Jan Pieterszoon Coen often told us that you were one of the greatest. And you know that Karel is of your stamp.'

'But remember the counsel of prudent men where authority is concerned: "One must stand close enough to the fire to be warmed, but not so close that he is burned." Karel really must be seen in Compagnie headquarters. There is no alternative, Hendrickje.'

For some moments she reflected on this advice and knew it to be sound. Jan Compagnie was a curious beast, seventeen all-powerful men who did not know the East at firsthand, making decisions that influenced half the world. She would never want her sons to be members of that tight, mean-spirited gang of plotters, but she did want them to achieve positions in Java and Ceylon which only the Lords XVII could disburse. It really was time for Karel to put in an appearance. 'But Willem?' she asked softly, betraying her love for this tousle-headed lad. 'He's too young. Truly, he should stay with me.'

The governor laughed heavily. 'Hendrickje, you astonish me. This lad has been to Formosa, Cambodia. He fought valiantly at Malacca. He's a man, not a boy.' Then he grew serious, asking the servants to withdraw.

'Let us keep the fan-boys. They speak no Dutch.'

'Hendrickje, for Karel to be seen in Amsterdam is policy. For Willem to report there is survival. His entire future life may depend on this.'

'What can you mean?'

'What you know better than I. Few boys born outside Holland can ever hope to attain a position of power within the Compagnie. And especially no boy born in Java.'

Mevrouw van Doorn rose impetuously, ordered the fan-boys to leave the room, and paced back and forth. 'Outrageous!' she cried. 'My husband and I came here in the worst days. We helped burn Jacatra and build this new Batavia. And now you tell me that because our son was born while we were here . . .'

'I do not tell you, Hendrickje. The Compagnie tells you. Any boy born in Java suffers a dreadful stigma.'

He did not continue, for there was no need. No matter how angry Mevrouw van Doorn became over this tactless reminder that her son Willem suffered a disadvantage which might prove fatal in Compagnie politics, she knew he was right, for Dutch settlement in the East produced contradictions which simply could not be resolved. The Dutch were honest Calvinists who took their religion seriously, and the drowsy rooms in Batavia contained many persons whose forefathers had died protecting their religion. They were the spawn of heroes, prepared to die again if Calvinism were threatened.

But they were a paradoxical lot. They believed that God in His mercy separated the saved from the damned, and were convinced that the Dutch were saved, not all of them, but most. They firmly believed in sobriety, yet drank themselves into a stupor five days out of seven. They believed in strict sexual deportment, much stricter than the Portuguese or English; they spoke of it; they read those passages in the Bible which condemned lewd living; and their predikants roared at them from the pulpit. They did believe in chastity.

And there was the difficulty. For they were also a lusty lot; few men in Europe had a quicker eye for a flashing skirt than the Dutch of Amsterdam. They rousted and stormed through brothels, chasing girls brought from Brazil and Bali and from God knows where; but always they did this after protestations of virtue and before prayers of contrition. Few men have ever behaved so lustily between episodes of protective devotion.

In Java the problem was trebly difficult, for to it came the most virile young men of Holland to serve five to ten years, but with them came no Dutch women, or few, and these of the worst sort. Hendrickje van Doorn had written to at least a hundred young women in Haarlem and Amsterdam, begging them to come out as wives to these splendid young men who were making their fortunes, but she attracted not one: 'The voyage is too long. I shall never see my mother again. The climate is too hot. It is a land of savages.' A hundred marriageable girls could recite a hundred good reasons for not going to Java, which meant that the young men would have to work there without wives until such time as they could go home with their wealth.

Without wives, but not without women. The girls of Java were some of the most attractive in the world—slim, shy, whispering beauties who created the impression of knowing far more about love than they admitted. The girls of Bali were even more seductive, while the wonderful women of China were strong and able as well as beautiful. It was a Dutchman of stalwart character who could listen to his predikant in church on Sunday and keep away from the glorious women of the compounds during the next six nights.

The Lords XVII and their subordinates were tough-minded business-men out to make a fast profit, but there arose occasions when they had to turn to other issues, and none was more vexing than this problem of the mixing of races. As the directors agonized over miscegenation, two oppos-ing schools of thought emerged: the enlightened ones who saw considerable merit in encouraging their employees to marry women of the East, thus forming a permanent settlement; and the narrow ones who foresaw the degeneration of their own race. The puritan view prevailed, though in practice it meant little whenever a lonely man needed the warmth of a concubine or slave.

The debate would rage for centuries, not only in Java but in other Dutch settlements. At one stage intermarriage was advocated to the extent of offering Compagnie employees a cash bonus if they married local girls and settled permanently; but, bedeviled by conflicting philosophies, the direc-tors were never able to find a satisfactory solution. While they searched their souls for just answers, an endless number of illegitimate children appeared.

Of course, the most delectable local women would have nothing to do with the invaders; many were Muslim and would rather die than convert or carry the child of a kaffir, an unbeliever, as they termed the Dutch. Thousands of others, less committed or concerned, slept with their masters, and the more liberal Dutchmen welcomed the new brown offspring as an enchanting addition, since the parental combination of handsome Dutch blond of clear white skin and slim Javanese woman with orchid complexion produced clever half-caste boys and irresistible girls.

But such sentiments were rare. Most Dutchmen who ruled the tropics were convinced that the races must be kept apart, lest the superior intelli-gence of those from Europe be contaminated. That sentiment was used by one of the Lords XVII, who fulminated against half-castes:

'These piebald gentry are the children of the devil, the spews of sinful lust, and they have no place in our society. The men are not to be employed as scribes and the women must not be allowed to marry our employees. They are a disgraceful accident of whom we cannot be proud and against whom we must protect ourselves.'

The Lords XVII, many of them sons of clergymen, found much delight in exploring the ramifications of this subject, always pointing out that half-castes were a condemnation of orderly rule. They were not unaware that the bulk of those who went to the East were thrown into a society in which they need scarcely lift a finger, and certainly not to labor as they had done in Holland. Such men corrupt easily. Still, the directors consoled themselves with the belief that it was not the laziness of their employees but the lasciviousness of the women with whom they came in contact that threatened Holland's sons.

For this reason, the Lords were always cooperative if a young man in their employ wished to go home to find himself an honest Dutch wife. The men did go home; they proposed to the young women of Amsterdam; and they were, of course, refused. So the young men came back to Java alone, the supply of half-castes multiplied, and Java acquired a malodorous reputation which increased the difficulty of finding wives for the men. The most condemnatory reports were submitted by investigators dispatched from Holland to check upon conduct:

> Java is a moral sink, the white women often being worse than the men. They spend whole days in lechery or idleness, eating themselves into insensibility, drinking to excess, consorting with the lowest of the islands, and accomplishing nothing. I know of three wives who in Holland would be exemplary church members who do nothing from one week to the next but eat, fornicate with strangers, and complain about their slaves, of whom they have an abundance.

Small wonder that the Lords XVII established the iron-clad principle that no position of leadership could be held by a man born in the islands. Such men would lack the moral fiber automatically obtained during an education in Holland; their judgment would be sullied by their contact with the Javanese, their force corroded by the deleterious effects of the East.

'There is one escape for a boy like Willem,' the governor said, calling for the fan-boys again, since the air was becoming oppressive. 'If he goes home now, before contact with Asian women, and if he enters the university at Leiden, he may cleanse himself of his Javanese birth. If he remains here, he condemns himself to third- or even fourth-level positions.'

Disheartened, Mevrouw van Doorn sank into a chair. She was only fifty-one and wanted to keep her sons with her in the big house with the multitude of servants, but she appreciated the dangers of which the governor was speaking. Karel's progress might be impeded if he did not get back to Holland, but Willem would be disqualified for any advancement. She must send her sons home.

'The after-fleet will sail in January,' the governor said. 'I can find them two passages on the *Haerlem.*' When she hesitated, he added, 'God knows, Hendrickje, there's a dark future for them in Java. At best, marrying some local girl of dubious reputation. At worst, sinking into the gutter.'

She sighed, rose and went to the doorway to contemplate the flowers in her garden, and said, 'Arrange for them to go,' and with that she abruptly turned all her attention to her New Year's festival. It would be free and open, like the ones her husband had offered Compagnie people when he was alive, with everyone invited.

She began by borrowing musicians from homes of her friends, and smiled approvingly as the brown-skinned slaves carried their bronze game-lans and bamboo drums into the various rooms where dancing would occur. Then she enrolled cooks from these same houses, until she had more than forty servants in and about the kitchens. The walls she decorated with her own fabrics, hanging them in great festoons until the colors danced. Twenty-four turbaned footmen attended the carriages, and an equal number of women watched after the guests when they entered the halls.

The celebrations lasted three days, and were especially vivacious in that many of the leaders of Batavian society had departed on the Christmas fleet, so that those who remained felt obligated to show extra enthusiasm to replace that which had been lost. People ate and drank till they were near senseless, then slept sprawled on beds and floors until the soft music awak-ened them so that they could sing and dance and eat themselves into another stupor. At times some amorous woman, having dreamed of this party for weeks, or one whose husband had left on the fleet, would catch a stout burgher as he was about to go to bed, and she would join him in one of the smaller rooms, often retaining the fan-boy to keep the humidity lowered.

Mevrouw van Doorn's two sons watched the New Year's celebrations with detached interest; stern Karel had observed the carryings-on in previ-ous years and judged them to be the inevitable release of spirits by people who were far from home and sentenced to live among natives they did not respect. He had no wife as yet, nor any intention of finding one for the present, and whenever some lady far in drink wanted to drag him into a corner, he smiled wanly and moved away. In previous years young Willem had usually been kept away from the rowdier celebrations, but now that he was both a practiced ambassador and a front-line soldier, to do so any longer would be incongruous, so he wandered among the guests, listened to the music and watched with unusual attention the prettier slave girls.

'It's time he should go,' his mother conceded as she saw him follow one serving girl into the kitchens, and when the party was over, and the bor-rowed musicians had returned to their accustomed places, she ordered her carriage with its six attendants and rode down the streets of Batavia to the Compagnie headquarters.

'I should like the two passages on the *Haerlem,*' she said crisply, and the documents were handed over.

Since the three swift vessels would not depart until the seventeenth of January, overtaking the main fleet somewhere in the vicinity of St. Helena, where fresh stores would be taken aboard, the brothers had two full weeks of farewells. Young Willem spent his in visiting numerous friends, but Karel reported each day to the Compagnie offices, mastering details of that year's intended sales and purchases. He took note of the various fleets that would sail east and north, and of the captains who would command them; at times, as he studied the complex operations, he felt that he was sitting like a spider at the heart of a web, controlling the destinies of half a world. There were now no Portuguese in Malacca; those Straits were Dutch. There were no other Europeans at Nagasaki, either; Japan was now exclusively a Dutch concession. English vessels still stopped at their little entrepôt but were no longer allowed in the Spice Islands; and even the occasional French merchantman, its sails ragged from the long voyage out, had to obey regulations set down by the Dutch.

'We rule the seas,' he exclaimed one morning when the full power of Jan Compagnie was revealed.

'No,' an older man cautioned. 'The English are beginning to rule India. And the Portuguese still control Macao and the China trade.'

'Let them have the tea and ginger,' Karel conceded, 'so long as we keep the spices.'

When the brothers approached the three ships, they could smell the spices from a considerable distance, for the holds were crammed with last-minute sacks and bundles from the eastern islands; the ships moved in a splendid ambience, reeking of fortunes and the promise of gold. They were taking the heart of Asia to the center of Europe, and each ship represented a greater wealth than many small nations would handle in an entire year. Jan Compagnie controlled Java, and Java controlled the seas.

On the fourth day, after the little ships had passed through Sunda Strait, a vigorous storm arose, with visibility almost nonexistent. Great winds raged for three days, and when the low clouds lifted, the *Haerlem* was alone. The captain fired cannons, listened for replies, and when none came, followed the basic rule of navigation: 'If separated, proceed to the point of rendezvous.' Without further apprehension as to the fate of the *Schiedam* and *Olifant,* he headed for St. Helena and the body of the fleet.

It would take more than two months to negotiate this distance, and as the *Haerlem* sailed westward, sunrise at her back, sunset glowing ahead, spars creaking and sails filled by reassuring winds, the brothers speculated as to what might have happened to their sister ships. 'They're good captains,' Karel said. 'I know them, and they know the oceans. They're out there somewhere, because if we survived, so did they.'

'Will we see them?' Willem asked, peering always toward the horizon, as if on this vast sea three tiny ships might accidentally converge.

'Not likely. They may have rushed ahead. They may have lagged. We'll see them at St. Helena.'

'You think they're afloat?'

'I'm sure of it.'

On the long reach, it became apparent that the Van Doorn brothers were heading for Holland with conflicting motivations. For Karel, who had been born there and who vaguely remembered both his mother's home in Haarlem and his father's in Amsterdam, it was merely a return to the seats of power where he must establish himself with the Lords XVII against the day when he would become governor-general of Java. For Willem it was quite another matter. He was afraid of Holland, not because he knew anything adverse about it but because he loved the East so much. Those days with the little brown man, wandering through the various quarters and meeting traders from all nations, had enchanted him, while the languorous trip to Formosa had awakened him to the magnitude of his birthland. He was not old enough to comprehend the limitations he suffered as a Java-born Dutchman, and he simply refused to believe that a man born in Amsterdam was inherently superior to one born in Batavia.

When he questioned Karel about this, his austere brother frowned. 'The Java Dutch are mainly scum. Would you even dream of marrying a girl from one of those families?' This perplexed young Willem, for not only had he dreamed of marrying the Van der Kamp girl; he had also dreamed quite actively of marrying the little Balinese who served as his mother's maid.

Next morning, for reasons he could not have explained, he rummaged in his gear, found Jack's ivory bracelet still attached to its silver chain, and defiantly placed it about his neck. When Karel saw this he said sharply, 'Take that silly thing off. You look like a Javanese.'

'That's how I want to look,' and from then on, the bracelet was rarely absent.

In the middle of March unfavorable winds were encountered, and although the crew remained remarkably healthy, the captain grew apprehensive about his water supply and announced that he was planning to stop at the Cape of Good Hope, where fresh water would surely be available and bartering cattle with the little brown people a possibility.

During the reddish sunset Willem remained aloft, savoring his first glimpse of the famous rock, and even after the sun had sunk beneath the cold Atlantic, the curve of earth allowed its rays to illuminate the great flat area, and he noticed that the sailors relaxed, for they considered the Cape the halfway point, not in days, for the run to Amsterdam would be long and tedious, but in spirit, for the alien quality of the spice lands was behind them. The Indian Ocean had been traversed; the homeward passage through the Atlantic lay ahead.

At dawn on March 25 Willem did not see Table Mountain, for as so often happened in these cold waters a wind had risen, bringing clouds but no rain; the flat summit was obliterated. But then the wind abated, and toward noon the lookout shouted, 'Ship ahoy!' and there, nestled at the far end of the bay, rode a little merchant vessel. The chief mate and a few oarsmen were dispatched in the skiff to ascertain who she was, but as they drew away, the weather closed in, a stout wind from the southeast forcing the *Haerlem*'s captain to make sail close-hauled. The other ship became lost to sight as the wind freshened to storm level, pushing the *Haerlem* toward shore.

At this point it was still in no real danger, but now the wind veered crazily, so that sails which had been trimmed to hold the ship offshore became instruments for driving it on. 'Cut the spritsail!' shouted the captain, but it was too late; fresh blasts caught the sails and drove the little ship hard aground. When the captain tried to swing it around, hoping that other gusts would blow it loose, rolling seas came thundering in. Timbers shivered. Masts creaked. Sails that had been cut loose whipped through the air. And when night fell, the *Haerlem* was hopelessly wrecked and would probably break apart before morning.

'Anchor chain has parted!' a watchman's alarm pierced the night, and the Van Doorn brothers expected the ship to go down. The captain ordered four cannon shots to be fired, trusting that this would alert the other ship to the peril, but the message was not understood. 'By the grace of God, our only Helper,' as the captain wrote in his log, 'the power of the waves abated.

We were not ripped apart. And when dawn broke we saw that while our position was hopeless, we were close enough to shore to save those aboard.' In the misty morning the skiff returned to report that the ship in the roads was the *Olifant,* so a longboat was lowered and made for the beach, but the *Haerlem*'s men watched with dismay as the boat foundered in the pounding surf, drowning one sailor who could not swim.

'We must get ashore!' Karel shouted to the captain.

'There is no way,' the captain replied, but Karel judged that if he could lash two barrels together, they would float him ashore, and it was on this rig that Karel and Willem van Doorn landed at the Cape of Good Hope.

The following days were a nightmare. Led by the Van Doorns, the crew of the *Olifant* tried three different times to reach the sinking *Haerlem,* but always the surf pounded their longboat so that they had to retreat. Fortunately, two English merchantmen sailed into the bay, homeward bound from Java, and with daring seamanship a boat from the *Haerlem* succeeded in reaching them with a request for help. To the surprise of the Dutch, the English crew agreed to aid in transferring the smaller items of cargo to the *Olifant,* and for some days they labored at this as if they were in the pay of Amsterdam: '. . . a hundred sockels of mace, eighty-two barrels of raw camphor, eighty bales of choice cinnamon, not wet, and five large boxes of Japanese coats decorated in gold and silver.' And when this arduous work was completed the English captains offered to carry forty of the *Haerlem*'s crew to St. Helena, where they could join the main Dutch fleet on its way to Amsterdam.

But before these good Samaritans sailed, Willem was given a task which he would often recall. 'Fetch all letters from the post-office stones,' he was told, and when he started to ask what a post-office stone was, an officer shouted, 'Get on with it.'

Ashore, he asked some older hands what he must do, and they explained the system and designated two young sailors to protect him as he roamed the beach, even to the foot of Table Mountain, looking for any large stones which might have been engraved by passing crews. Some covered nothing, but most had under them small packets of letters, wrapped in various ways for protection, and when he held these frail documents in his hands he tried to visualize the cities to which the letters were directed: Delft, Lisbon, Bristol, Nagasaki. The names were like echoes of all he had heard on the voyage so far, the sacred names of sailors' memories. One letter, addressed to a woman in Madrid, had lain beneath its rock for seven years, and as he stared at it he wondered if she would still be living when it now arrived, or if she would remember the man who had posted it.

He brought nineteen letters back to the English ships, but six were addressed to Java and other islands to the east. Gravely, as part of the ritual of the sea, the English mate accepted responsibility for seeing that the thirteen European letters were forwarded, after which Willem took the others ashore for reposting under a conspicuous rock.

When the English ships departed, the Dutch had time to survey their situation, and it was forbidding. It was impossible in this remote spot to make the gear that would have been required to refloat the *Haerlem.* It had to be abandoned. But its lower holds still contained such enormous wealth that neither the *Olifant*, nor the *Schiedam* if it put into Table Bay, could possibly convey it all back to Holland. A temporary fortress of some kind must be built ashore; the remaining cargo must then be taken to it; and a cadre of men must remain behind to protect the treasure while the bulk of the crew sailed home in the *Olifant*.

Almost immediately the work began, and the foundations for the fort had scarcely been outlined when the work party heard cannon fire, and into the roadstead came the *Schiedam*. Though marred by the disastrous grounding of the *Haerlem*, it was a joyous reunion of the three crews, and soon so many sailors were working to construct the fort that the captain had to say, 'Clear most of them out. They're getting in each other's way.'

Now came the exhausting task of rafting the bulk of the *Haerlem*'s cargo ashore, and with speed lest the battered ship break apart. The Van Doorns worked on deck, supervising the winches that hauled precious bales aloft, and when three sailors were sent to the lower hold to shovel loose peppercorns into bags, Karel directed: 'You're not to leave a single bag down there. It's precious.'

But soon the men hurried aloft, gasping, and when Karel demanded why they had left their posts, they pointed below and said, 'Impossible.'

But since rich stores lay beneath the deck, Karel leaped down into the hold; the sailors had been right. Salt water, leaking into the pepper, had begun a fermentation so powerful that a deadly gas was being released. Choking and clutching at his throat, Karel tried to get back on deck, but his feet slipped on the oily peppercorns, and he fell, knocking his head against a bulkhead.

He would have been asphyxiated had not young Willem seen him fall. Without hesitating, the boy leaped down, shouting for help as he went. Ropes were lowered and the limp body of Karel was hoisted aloft. Willem, with a handkerchief pressed over his face, climbed out, his eyes smarting and his lungs aflame.

For some time he stood by the railing, trying to vomit, but poor Karel lay stretched on the deck, quite inert. Finally the brothers recovered, and Willem would never forget how Karel reacted. It was as if he had been personally assaulted by the pepper, his honor impugned, for with a burst of vitality, his eyes still watering, he went back to the rim of the hold, still not satisfied that the exudations were too powerful to be sustained by any sailor.

'Tear off the other hatches!' he bellowed, and when this accomplished little, for the hold was large and the cargo tightly packed, he ordered holes to be chopped in the upper deck. This, too, proved useless, so in a towering rage he shouted for a ship's cannon to be moved into position so that it could shoot down into the hold and out the sides of the ship.

'Fire!' he shouted, and a cannonball ripped away five feet of the hull, allowing fresh air into the hold.

'Swing the cannon!' he cried, and from a different angle another shot blasted a tremendous hole in the other side. Three more shots were fired, enabling the gas to escape, and when the hold was cleared, Karel was first down to salvage the precious pepper.

By April 1 the situation was under control. Work was progressing on the mud-walled fort, and a well sixty feet deep dug by the enterprising men was producing fresh water. Transfer of the cargo from the wreck was proceeding so smoothly that the leaders of the three ships could gather on the *Schiedam* to formulate final plans.

The captain gave it as his opinion that the *Olifant* and *Schiedam* should sail for the fatherland, taking with them as many of the *Haerlem*'s crew as possible. He asked what this number would be, but Karel interrupted by saying that the major consideration must be the salvage of the cargo, and that before any sailors were sent home, a determination must be made as to how many would be needed to man the fort until the next homebound fleet arrived. The captain acceded to this sensible recommendation, and the council decided that sixty or seventy men, if well led by a capable officer, could protect the pepper and cinnamon during that time.

The council members looked at Karel, hoping that he would volunteer to stay behind and guard the cargo, but he realized that his opportunity waited in Holland, and he did not propose endangering it by a protracted absence at the Cape. So it was agreed that two tough marine officers would remain at the fort with a cadre of sixty while the Van Doorn brothers would hurry to St. Helena, where they would catch a fast trading vessel direct to Amsterdam. But on April 12, when the *Olifant* and *Schiedam* departed, young Willem van Doorn stayed onshore: 'I feel I'm needed at the fort.' It was the kind of self-confident statement old fighting men could respect, so they concurred. 'Hold the fort!' they called as the two little ships sailed off, leaving history's first group of Dutchmen alone at the Cape.

Only twelve days later, at the end of April when the finest days of autumn came, Willem surprised the fort commanders by announcing, 'I'd like to be the first to climb Table Mountain,' and when permission was granted he enlisted two friends. They marched briskly toward the glowing mountain, some dozen miles to the south, and when they stood at its foot Willem cried, 'We don't stop till we reach up there.'

It was a punishing climb, and often the young men came to precipices which they had to circumvent, but at last they reached that broad, gracious plateau which forms the crest of this mountain, and from it they could survey their empire.

To the south lay nothing but the icebound pole. To the west were the empty Atlantic and the New World territories owned by Spain. To the north they saw nothing but wind-swept dunes stretching beyond the power of the eye. But to the east they saw inviting meadows, and the rise of hills, and then the reach of mountains, and then more and more and more, on to a horizon they could only imagine. In silence the three sailors studied the land as it basked in the autumn sun, and often they wheeled about to see the lonely seas across which winds could howl for a thousand miles. But always their eyes returned to those tempting green valleys in the east, those beckoning mountains.

But looking eastward, they ignored the clouds which had formed almost instantaneously over the ocean to the west, and when they turned to descend the mountain, the devil threw his tablecloth and any movement became perilous.

'What can we do?' his companions asked Willem, and he replied with common sense, 'Shiver till dawn.' They knew that this would result in anxiety at the fort, but they had no alternative, and when the sun finally rose, dispelling the fog, they marveled anew at the paradise which awaited in the east.

From the first days of isolation the sailors had been aware of little brown men who occupied the Cape. They were a pitiful lot, 'barely human,' one scribe wrote, 'dirty, thieving and existing miserably on such shell fish as they could trap.' They were given the name Strandloopers (beach rangers), and to the sailors' dismay, they had nothing of value to trade but wanted everything they saw. It was a poor relationship, marked by many scuffles and some deaths.

But on June 1, when the marooned men concluded that they had seen everything worth seeing in their temporary home—rhinos feeding in the swales, hippos in the streams, lions prowling at night, and antelope untold—an incident occurred, so bizarre that everyone who later wrote his report of the wreck commented upon it:

> On this day at about two in the afternoon we were approached from the east by a group of some twenty little brown men much different from the pathetic ones we called Strandloopers. They were taller. Their loincloths were cleaner. They moved without fear, and what joyed us most, they led before them a herd of sheep with the most enormous tails we have ever seen. We called them Huttentuts from their manner of stuttering with strange click sounds and got quickly to work trying to trade with them. They were quite willing to give us their sheep for bits of brass, which they cherish.
>
> And then the most amazing thing happened. From their ranks stepped a man about thirty years old, quick and intelligent of manner, and God's word, he was dressed in the full uniform of an English sailor, shoes included. What was most remarkable, he spoke good English without any click sounds. Since none of us knew this language, I went running for Willem van Doorn, who had learned it at Java, and when he left the fort, knowing that a Huttentut had come who spoke English, he asked me, 'Could it be?' and when he saw the little man in the sailor's uniform he broke into a run, shouting, 'Jack! Jack!' and they embraced many times and fingered the ivory bracelet that we had seen on Van Doorn's chain. Then they danced a jig of happiness and stood apart talking in a language we did not know of things we had not seen.

Actually, among the Hottentots with whom the Dutch did business during their year as castaways, there were three who had sailed in English ships: Jack, who had been to Java; a man named Herry, who had sailed to the Spice Islands; and Coree, who had actually lived in London for a while. But it was with Jack that these Dutchmen conducted their trade.

This meant that Willem was often with the Hottentots when there was bartering, and as before, he and Jack made a striking pair: Jack seemed even smaller when standing among big Dutchmen, and Willem, now full-grown at twenty-two, towered over his little friend, but they moved everywhere along the bay, hunting and fishing together. Toward mid-July, Jack proposed that Van Doorn accompany him to the village where the sheep-raising Hottentots lived. The fortress commander suspected a trick, but Willem, remembering the responsible manner in which the little fellow had conducted himself at Java, begged for permission.

'You could be killed,' the commander warned.

'I think not,' and with that simple affirmation, young Van Doorn became the first Dutchman to venture eastward toward those beckoning mountains.

It was a journey of about thirty miles through land that gave signs of promising fertility. He passed areas where villages had once stood and learned from Jack that here the land had been grazed flat by cattle. 'You have cattle?' the Dutchman asked, indicating with his hands that he meant something bigger than sheep.

'Yes.' Jack laughed, using his forefingers to form horns at his temples, then bellowing like a bull.

'You must bring them to the fort!' Willem cried in excitement.

'No, no!' Jack said firmly. 'We don't trade . . .' He explained that this was winter, when the cows were carrying their young, and that it was forbidden to trade or eat cattle before summer. But when they reached his village, and Willem saw the sleek animals, his mouth watered; he intended reporting this miracle to the fort as soon as he returned.

His stay at the village was a revelation. The Hottentots were infinitely lower in the scale of civilization than the Javanese, or the wealthy merchants of the Spice Islands, and to compare them with the organized Chinese was ridiculous. But they were equally far removed from the primitive Strandloopers who foraged at the beach, for they had orderly systems for raising sheep and cows and they lived in substantial kraals. True, they were mostly naked, but their food was of high quality.

Living among the little people for five days encouraged Willem to think that perhaps a permanent settlement might be practical, with Dutch farmers growing the vegetables required by the passing fleets of the Compagnie and subsisting on the sheep and cattle raised by the Hottentots; this possibility he discussed with Jack.

'You grow more cattle, maybe?'

'No. We have plenty.'

'But if we wanted to trade? You give us many cattle?'

'No. We have just enough.'

'But if we needed them? You saw the English ship. Poor food. No meat.'

'Then English grow sheep. English grow cattle.'

He got nowhere with the Hottentots, but when he returned to the fort and told the officers of the wealth lying inland, they grew hungry for beef and organized an expedition to capture some of the cattle. Van Doorn argued that to do this might embitter relations with the brown people, but the other sailors agreed with the officers: if cattle existed out there toward the hills, they should be eaten.

The argument was resolved in early August when Jack led some fifty Hottentots to the fort, bringing not only sheep but also three fine bullocks which they found they could spare. 'See,' Van Doorn said when the deal was completed, 'we've won our point without warfare,' but when the officers commanded Jack to deliver cattle on a regular basis, he demurred.

'Not enough.'

The officers thought he meant that the goods they had offered were not enough and tried to explain that with the wreck of the *Haerlem* they had lost their normal trade goods and had only spices and precious fabrics at the fort. Jack looked at them askance, as if he could not decipher what they were saying, so one of the officers procured a boat, and with six Hottentots and Van Doorn, went out to the disintegrating hulk to let the little men see for themselves, and to pick up any stray bits of material they might want in trade for their cattle.

It was a futile trip. All that remained aboard the creaking wreck were the heavy guns and anchors and the broken woodwork, and these had no appeal to the Hottentots, who had been taught by Coree after his return from London, 'Wood nothing, brass everything.' The brass had long since vanished.

But as the others climbed back into the boat, Willem chanced to find a hidden drawer containing an item of inestimable value. Hearing the officer coming down the gangway to hail him, he slammed the drawer shut and followed the Hottentots ashore.

That night when others were asleep he told the watch, 'I want to inspect the *Haerlem* again,' and silently he rowed out to the ship, which had now settled nine feet into the sand. Fastening his line to a stud, he climbed aboard, going quickly to the captain's quarters, where he opened the drawer. And there it was, with thick brass corner fittings and center clasps.

Carefully opening the brass locks, he turned back the cover and saw the extraordinary words: 'Biblia: The Holy Scripture translated into Dutch. Henrick Laurentsz, Bookseller, Amsterdam, 1630.' This was a printing of the very Bible his mother had cherished and he knew it would be most improper to allow a book so sacred to sink at sea, so covering it with his shirt, he carried it back to the fort, where he hid it among his few possessions. Occasionally in the days ahead, when no one was watching, he gingerly opened his Bible, reading here and there from the sacred Word. It was his book, and at the New Year he borrowed a pen and wrote on the first line of the page reserved for family records: 'Willem van Doorn, his book, 1 January, 1648.'

The Dutch sailors at Table Bay were not forgotten. During the twelve months they stayed, nearly a hundred Dutch ships engaged in the Java trade passed back and forth between Amsterdam and Batavia, standing far out to sea as they rounded the Cape. Some English ships actually sailed into the bay, offering help as needed, and in August three Compagnie ships anchored near the fort, providing mail, information and tools.

The captain of the *Tiger,* leader of the flotilla, caused Willem serious trouble, because on the evening prior to his departure for Java, he announced at the fort that any sailors who wished to return to that island for an additional tour of duty were welcome, and three volunteered. 'We sail at noon tomorrow,' the captain said, and all that night Willem wrestled with the problem. Intuitively, with a force he would always remember in later years, he shied away from going on to Holland, a land he did not know and to which he felt no attachment. But if he failed to join the *Tiger,* right now, the next fleet would be Europe bound, and he might never see Java again.

Toward midnight he woke the fort commander and said, 'Sir, my whole heart pulls me toward Java.'

'And mine,' the officer responded, and with swift phrases he explained how any man of character who had once seen the Spice Islands would never want to work elsewhere: 'It's a man's world. It's a world of blazing sunsets. Java, Formosa! My God, I'll die if I don't get back.'

'My mother argued—'

'Son, if I weren't commander of this fort, I'd ship aboard the *Tiger* like that!' And he snapped his fingers.

'My mother says that no Dutchman has a chance with Jan Compagnie if he's born in Java—unless he gets back home for education and proper church training.'

'Well, now!' the commander said in the dim candlelight. 'Well, now, Mevrouw van Doorn is the smartest woman in the islands, and if she says . . .' In some irritation he banged his fist on the table, causing the candle to flicker. 'She's right, goddamnit, she's right. Jan Compagnie has no respect but for Amsterdam trading gentlemen. I'm from Groningen and might just as well be cattle.' Mention of this word diverted him, and he gave Willem no more guidance, for in the darkness he intended to send a troop of gunners out to fetch those Hottentot cattle.

When dawn illuminated Table Mountain, young Willem van Doorn made his decision: the *Tiger* would sail without him; he would obey his mother's orders and sail on to Holland with the March fleet—but as the *Tiger* was about to hoist anchor he set up a great shouting, 'Captain! Captain!' until the commander thought he had changed his mind and now wished passage to Java.

Not at all. He was running to the post-office stone under which he had buried the six letters addressed to Java. Puffing, he ran to the *Tiger*'s longboat, and the documents were on their way.

When the ship pulled away he felt little regret, for as it went he had the curious sensation that he was intended for neither Amsterdam nor Batavia: What I'd like is to stay here. To see what's behind those mountains. That night he read long in his Bible, the sweet Dutch phrases burning themselves into his memory:

> And Moses sent them to spy out the land of Canaan, and said unto them . . . go up into the mountain and see the land . . . and the people that dwelleth therein, whether they be strong or weak, few or many; and what the land is that they dwell in, whether it be good or bad . . .

And as he studied other texts dealing with the reactions of the Israelites to the new land into which they had been ordered to move, he felt himself to be of that exploring group; he had gone up into the mountain to spy out the land; he had journeyed inland to see how the people lived and whether the land was good or barren. It was ordained that he should be part of that majestic land beyond the mountains; and when three days later the swift little flute *Noordmunster* left to overtake the two slower vessels bound for Java, he saw it go with no regret. But how he might manage to stay at the Cape he did not know, for the Dutch were determined to abandon it as soon as a homeward fleet arrived.

In the empty days that followed, Van Doorn occupied himself with routine life at the fort. On a field nearby he shot a rhinoceros. In a stream inland he shot a hippo. He went aboard the English ship *Sun* to deliver mail, which the captain would forward from London, then helped two sick Dutch sailors aboard for the long trip home. Of great interest, he headed a hunting party to nearby Robben Island, where the men shot some two hundred penguins; he himself found the flesh of these birds much too fishy, but the others averred that it tasted better than the bacon of Holland. And twice he led parties that climbed Table Mountain.

Only one unusual event occurred during these quiet days. One afternoon, at about dusk, a small group of Hottentots approached the fort from the east, leading cattle, and when the sailors saw the fresh meat coming their way—animals much larger than those at home—they cheered, but the trading was not going to be easy, because Jack was in charge, and in broken English, said, 'Not sell. We live in fort. With you.'

The officers could not believe that these savages were actually proposing that they move into the fort, and when Willem insisted that this was precisely what Jack was suggesting, they broke into laughter. 'We can't have wild men living with us. You tell them to leave the cattle and go.'

But Jack had a broader vision, which he tried to explain to the Dutchmen: 'You need us. We work. We grow cattle for you. We make vegetables. You give us cloth . . . brass . . . all we need. We work together.'

It was the first proposal, seriously made, that natives and whites work together to develop this marvelous tip of the continent; Jack knew how this might be accomplished, but was brusquely repelled: 'Tell him to leave those damned cattle and begone!'

Van Doorn alone, among the white men, understood what was being suggested, and he had the courage to argue with his officers: 'He says we could work together.'

'Together?' the officers exploded, as if with one voice they spoke for all of Holland. 'What could they do to help us?' And one of them pointed grandiloquently to the Dutch guns, the ladders, the wooden boxes and other accouterments of a superior culture.

Van Doorn suggested, 'Sir, they could help us raise cattle.'

'Tell them we wish only to deal with them for the beasts.'

But when the officers proposed to start the bartering, they found that Jack and his little people refused to trade: 'We come. Live with you. Help you. We give you these cattle. Many more. But no more trade.'

This was incomprehensible, that a band of primitives should be laying down terms, and the officers would tolerate no such nonsense. At Banda Island east of Java when the sultan opposed them over the matter of cloves, the entire population of fifteen thousand had been slaughtered. When the Lords XVII heard of this they demurred, but old Jan Pieterszoon Coen had explained firmly, in letters which reached Amsterdam four years after the event: 'In Holland you suggest what we should do. In Java we do what's necessary.' When the sultan on another island refused to cooperate, he and ten thousand of his people were forcibly resettled on Amboyna. If the Compagnie did not tolerate opposition from Spice Islanders, who, after all, were semi-civilized even if they did follow Muhammad, it was certainly not going to allow these primitives to dictate trading terms.

'Take the cattle,' the officers said, but at this, young Van Doorn had to protest: 'In the villages beyond the hills are many Hottentots. If we start trouble . . .'

'He's starting the trouble. Tell him to take his damned cattle, and if he ever comes back here, he'll be shot. Get out!'

The officers would permit no further negotiation, and the Hottentots were dismissed. Slowly, sadly, they herded their fat cattle and started back across the flats, unable to comprehend why their sensible proposal had been rejected.

Willem saw Jack again under pitiful conditions. A group of six sailors applied for permission to hunt the area well north of the fort for eight or nine days, and since barter with the Hottentots was no longer possible and meat was needed, they were encouraged to see if they could find a hippopotamus or a rhinoceros, both of which provided excellent eating. Because the land they were exploring was more arid than that to the south and east, they had to go far, so that they were absent much longer than intended, and when they returned, there were only five.

'We were attacked by Hottentots, and Van Loon was killed by a poisoned arrow.' They had the arrow, a remarkable thing made in three sections bound together by tight collars of sinew, and so made that when the poisoned tip entered the body, the rest broke away, making it impossible to pull out the projectile.

'We cut it out,' the men explained. 'And he lived for three days, always getting weaker till he died.'

The officers were outraged and swore revenge on the Hottentots, but Van Doorn recalled something Jack had told him during his stay at the village: 'We don't ever hunt north. The San . . . that's their land.' That's all he could remember; it had been a warning which he had overlooked, and now his companion was dead.

He suggested that he go east to discuss this tragedy with Jack, and although the officers ridiculed the idea at first, upon reflection they saw that it would be unwise to engage in open warfare with the little brown men if the latter enjoyed superior numbers and a weapon so frightening. So they gave consent, and with two armed companions Van Doorn set out to talk with Jack, taking the arrow with him.

As soon as the Hottentots saw it they showed their fear: 'San. The little ones who live in bush. You must never go their land.' They showed how the arrow worked and explained that they themselves were terrified of these little men who had no cattle, no sheep, no kraals: 'They are terrible enemies if we go their land. If we stay our land, they let us alone.'

It was amusing to Willem to hear the Hottentots speak of this vague enemy as 'the little ones,' but Jack convinced him that the San were truly much smaller: 'We keep our cattle toward the ocean. More difficult for little ones to creep in.'

And so open warfare between the Hottentots and the Dutch was a-voided. One of the men drafted a report to Amsterdam, explaining that the Cape was uninhabitable, worth positively nothing and incapable of providing the supplies the Compagnie fleets required:

> Much better we continue to provision at St. Helena. There is no reason why any future Compagnie ship should enter this dangerous Bay, especially since three separate enemies threaten any establishment, the Strandloopers, the Hottentots and these little savages who live in the bush with their poisoned arrows.

At the moment this man was composing such a report, an officer was walking through the fortress gardens and noticing that with the seeds rescued from the wreck of the *Haerlem* his special group of gardening men had been able to grow pumpkins, watermelons, cabbages, carrots, radishes, turnips, onions, garlic, while his butchers were passing along to the cooks good supplies of eland, steenbok, hippopotamus, penguins from Robben Island and sheep they had stolen from the Hottentot meadows.

In January the sailors at the fort observed one of the great mysteries of the sea. On 16 September 1647, two splendid Compagnie ships had set sail from Holland, intending to make the long journey to Java and back. This could require as much as two years, counting the time that might be spent on side trips to the Spice Islands or Japan. The *White Dove* was a small, swift flute, economically handled by a crew of only forty-eight and captained by a man who believed that cleanliness and the avoidance of scurvy were just as important as good navigation. When he arrived at the Cape for provisioning, all his men were healthy, thanks to lemon juice and pickled cabbage, and he was eager to continue his passage to Java.

He told the personnel at the fort that the Lords XVII had them in mind and thanked them especially for their rescue of the peppercorns, which would be of immense value when they finally reached Amsterdam.

'Thanks are appreciated,' the fortress officer growled, 'but when do we get away from here?'

'The Christmas fleet out of Batavia,' the captain said. 'It's sure to pick you up.' He asked if any sailors wished to return with him to Java; none did, but his invitation rankled in Willem's mind.

It was not like before. He did not oscillate between Holland and Java. His whole attention was directed to a more specific question: What could he do now to best ensure his return to this Cape? He was finding that it contained all the attraction of Java, all the responsibility of Holland, plus the solid reality of a new continent to be mastered. It was a challenge of such magnitude that his heart beat like a drum when he visualized what it would be like to establish a post here, to organize a working agreement with the Hottentots, to explore the world of the murderous little San, and most of all, to move eastward beyond the dark blue hills he had seen from the top of Table Mountain. Nowhere could he serve Amsterdam and Batavia more effectively than here.

He found no solution to his problem and was in deep confusion when the *White Dove* prepared to sail, for he could not judge whether he ought to go with her or not. His attention was diverted when that ship's sister, the towering East Indiaman *Princesse Royale,* limped into the bay. She was a new ship, grand and imposing, with a poop deck like a castle, and instead of the *White Dove*'s complement of forty-nine, she carried three hundred and sixty-eight. Her captain was a no-nonsense veteran who scorned lemon juice and kegs of sauerkraut: 'I captain a great ship and see her through the storms.' As a consequence, twenty-six of his people were already dead, another seventy were deathly ill, and the tropical half of the voyage still loomed.

When the two captains met with the fortress officers, Willem could see clearly how dissimilar they were: A man who runs a big, pompous ship has to be big and pompous. A man who captains a swift little flute can afford to be alert and eager. He was not surprised next morning when the *White Dove* hauled anchor early, as if it wished to avoid further contact with the poorly run *Princesse Royale,* nor was he surprised when he found that the *White Dove* had taken with it a healthy portion of the available fresh vegetables and fresh meat. After sixty-eight steaming-hot days the flute would land in Java without having lost a man.

When Willem loaded provisions aboard the *Princesse Royale* he was appalled to find that more than ninety passengers lay in their filthy beds, too weak to walk ashore. Many were obviously close to death, and he saw for himself the difference between the management of the two ships. They had sailed from the same port, on the same day, staffed by officers of comparable background, and they had traversed the same seas in the same temperature. Yet one was healthful, the other a charnel house whose major deaths lay ahead. But when he asked the men at the fort about this, they said, 'It's God's will.'

He thought much about God in these days of perplexity, and secretly went to the brassbound Bible, trying like his forefathers to ascertain what God wished him to do. And one night by a flickering candle he read a passage which electrified him, for in it God ordered his chosen people to undertake a specific mission:

> And I will establish my covenant between me and thee . . . And I will give unto thee, and unto thy seed after thee, the land wherein thou art a stranger, all the land of Canaan, for an everlasting possession . . .

God was offering this new land in covenant to his chosen people, and the manner in which a few ardent Dutchmen had been able to withstand for generations the whole power of Spain proved that they were chosen. Willem was convinced that soon the Lords XVII in Amsterdam must recognize the obligation that God was placing upon them. Then they would manfully occupy the Cape, as He intended—and where would they find the cadres to do the job? In Java, of course, where men who understood these waters worked. He would hurry back to Java on the *Princesse Royale* to be ready when the call came.

When he informed his officers of this decision, the man from Groningen applauded: 'Just what I'd do,' but he would have been incredulous had he known why Willem was doing it.

On the night before sailing, Van Doorn sat in his quarters, wondering how to safeguard his large Bible. If he took it aboard ship, it would be recognized as Compagnie property and confiscated; this he would not tolerate, for he felt in some mystical way that he had saved the Bible for some grand purpose and that it was dictating his present behavior. So toward morning, when the fort was quiet, he carried it away, and as he walked through the fading darkness he remembered the post-office stones, where messages of grave importance were deposited, but a moment's reflection warned him that whereas tightly wrapped and sealed letters might survive in such dampness, a book like this Bible would not. Then he recalled that on one of his climbs of Table Mountain he had come upon a series of caves, not deep, and although the mountain was distant, he set out briskly for it, carrying his treasure, and before midnight, with the moon as guide, he found the cave and hid the canvas-wrapped Bible well in the rear, under a cairn of stones. He was convinced that it would be his lodestone, drawing him back. At noon, when the *Princesse Royale* sailed, he was a passenger.

It was a voyage into the bowels of hell. Before the Cape was cleared, sailors were tossing dead bodies overboard, and not a day passed without the quaking death of someone suddenly attacked by fever. When Willem first saw the mouth of a woman struck down by scurvy—her gums swollen so grossly that no teeth could be seen—he was aghast; he had crossed this sea in the *Haerlem* without such affliction and he did not yet fully understand why this ship should be so stricken.

As it limped down the Straits of Malacca, two and three bodies each day were thrown overboard, and when Van Doorn wanted, in his exuberance, to explain how the Dutch had captured the Portuguese fort that had once blocked these waters, he found no one well enough to listen; the great Indiaman creaked and wallowed in the sea, with more than a hundred and thirty dead and many of the survivors so afflicted that the sweats of Java would kill them within a few months.

When the charnel ship reached the roadstead at Batavia, there waited the little *White Dove,* washed and ready for a further trip to Formosa. The two captains met briefly: 'How was it?' 'As always.' 'When do you return to Holland?' 'Whenever they say.' On the return trip the *Princesse Royale* would lose one hundred and fifteen.

Mevrouw van Doorn was not pleased to learn that her younger son had returned to Java. She suspected that some deficiency in character had driven him to scurry back to an easy land he knew rather than risk his chances in the wintry intellectual climate of Holland, and she feared that this might be the first fatal step in his ultimate degeneration.

Willem had anticipated his mother's apprehensions but feared he might sound fatuous if he spread before her his real motivations: a vision from a mountaintop; a friendship with a little savage; a dictate from a buried Bible. Keeping his counsel to himself, he plunged into the solitary job of drafting a long report to his superiors in Batavia, in hopes that they would forward it to the Lords XVII.

In it he made his sober estimation of what the Dutch might achieve if they were to establish a base at the Cape of Good Hope. *A Cautious Calculation* he titled it, and in it he reconstructed all he had witnessed during his months as a castaway, informing the merchants in charge of the Compagnie of the potential riches in this new land:

> Three separate vessels gave us seeds, two from Holland, one from England, and every seed we planted produced good vegetables, some bigger than those we see from home. Sailors who know many countries said, 'This is the sweetest food I have ever eaten.' On my trip to the native village I saw melons, grapelike climbers and other fruits.

He compiled meticulous lists of what had flourished in the Compagnie gardens, how many cattle the Hottentots had, and what kinds of birds could be shot on Robben Island. It was a catalogue of value and should have been an encouragement to anyone contemplating the establishment of a provisioning base, but suspicious readers were apt to linger most carefully over those passages in which he detailed the life of the Hottentots:

> They go quite naked with a little piece of skin about their privities. To gain protection for their bodies they smear themselves with a mixture of cow dung and sand, increasing it month after month until they can be smelled for great distances. Men dress their hair with sheep dung, allowing it to harden stiff as a board. The women commonly put the guts of wild beasts when dry around their legs and these serve as an adornment.

He provided the Compagnie with a careful distinction between the Strandloopers, a degenerate group of scavenging outcasts, the Hottentots, who were herders, and the Bushmen, who lived without cattle in the interior.

He calculated how many ships could take on fresh vegetables if the Compagnie established a place to grow them at the Cape, and then showed that if they could stabilize relations with the Hottentots, they might also obtain almost unlimited supplies of fresh meat. He advised abandoning the stop at St. Helena, with the sensible caution that if the Dutch did not peaceably withdraw, the English would in time throw them out.

It was a masterful calculation, prudent in all important matters, and it accomplished nothing. Officials at Batavia felt that a spot so distant was no concern of theirs, while the Lords XVII deemed it impudent for a man little more than a sailor to involve himself in such matters. So far as he could see, nothing happened.

But a word once written will often accidentally find a life that no one anticipates; it lies folded in a drawer and is forgotten, except that sometimes at moments unexpected someone will ask, during a discussion, 'Isn't that what Van Doorn said some years ago?' The passage from *A Cautious Calculation* which kept reviving in two cities half a world apart concerned ships:

> How is it that two ships of comparable quality throughout, manned by men of equal health and training, can sail from Amsterdam to Batavia and one arrives with all men ready for work in Java while the other comes into port with one-third of its crew so stricken that they must die within a year from our fevers and another third already buried at sea? There are no such things as good-luck ships and bad-luck ships. There are only fresh food, rest, clean quarters and whatever it is that fights scurvy. A halt of three weeks at the Cape of Good Hope, with fresh vegetables, lemon trees, and meat from the Hottentots would save the Compagnie a thousand lives a year.

Many of the Lords XVII felt that it was not their duty to worry about the health of sailors, and one said, 'When the baker bakes a pie, some crust falls to the floor.' He was applauded by those other Lords who had rebuked a subordinate in Java for sending two ships of Compagnie food to starving field hands in Ceylon: 'It is not our responsibility to feed the weaklings of the world.'

But to other members of the ruling body, Van Doorn's comments on the Cape reverberated, and from time to time these men brought the matter of excessive death to the attention of their fellows. One estimated that it cost the Compagnie a goodly three hundred guilders to land a man at Batavia, and that if he did not work at least five years, that cost could never be recovered, and there the debate ended, with no action taken.

Mevrouw van Doorn watched with dismay as her younger son slipped into the dull routine of a lesser clerk at the disposal of less able young men who had been trained in Holland. Willem's brightness dimmed and his shoulders began to droop. He often wore a girlish chain about his neck with an ivory circle dangling from it, and what was most painful of all, he was beginning to drift into the orbit of the few Dutch widows who stayed on at Batavia, but without the family fortunes that Mevrouw had when she decided to remain. They were a fat, sorry lot, 'sea elephants ridden by any bull that wished,' and it would not be long before Willem would be coming to inform her that he proposed taking one or the other to wife. After that, nothing could be salvaged.

And then one day in 1652 as Mevrouw van Doorn, white-haired and plump, arranged for her New Year's celebration, the startling news reached Batavia that a refreshment station had been started at the Cape of Good Hope under the command of Jan van Riebeeck. It was a matter of debate as to which part of this news was more sensational, the station itself or its proposed manager, but as Hendrickje said loudly, to the delight of her audience, 'If a man isn't clever enough to steal from the Compagnie, he won't be clever enough to steal for it.'

Willem van Doorn was in the garden when his mother said this, but he caught the name Van Riebeeck and asked as he came through the doors, 'Van Riebeeck? I met him. What about him?'

'He's been chosen to head a new settlement at Good Hope.'

Willem, twenty-seven and already flaccid, just stood in the doorway, framed in spring flowers, and his hands began to tremble, for the long dry period of his life was over. After he gained control he began to ask many questions regarding how he might win an assignment to the Cape, when an aide to the governor-general called him aside: 'Van Doorn, we've been asked to send the new settlement a few of our experienced men. To help them get started.' And Willem was about to volunteer when the aide said, 'Younger men, of course, and the council wondered if you could recommend some men for the lower echelons. For the higher, we'll do the choosing.'

And so Willem van Doorn, no longer considered young enough for an adventurous post, busied himself with selecting the first contingent of Batavia men to serve at the Cape, and it was a sorry task because none of the men wanted to leave the luxury of Java for that windblown wilderness.

The fleet sailed and Willem was left behind; his essay was kept in chests, both in Amsterdam and Batavia; and the man who as much as any had spurred the establishment of this new station was barred from joining it. The months passed, and Willem ran down to each incoming fleet to inquire as to affairs at the Cape, and then one day a message reached the council that Commander van Riebeeck was wondering if he might have permission to obtain a few slaves from Java for his personal use in growing vegetables, and the same aide who had dashed Willem's hopes previously now offered a dazzling proposal: 'Van Riebeeck's buying a few slaves for the Cape. And since you drafted that report . . . I mean, since you know the land there, we thought you might be the man to handle this courtesy.'

Willem bowed, then bowed again. 'I would be honored to have such confidence placed in me.' And when the aide was gone, he dashed to see his mother, shouting, 'I'm going to the Cape.'

'When?' she asked quietly.

'With the Christmas fleet.'

'So soon!' She had longed for the day when her son would announce that he was returning to Holland, 'to save himself,' as she put it, and was distraught that he was sentencing himself to a place even more demeaning than Java. Now he would never attain a Compagnie position, and only God knew what might happen to him. But even the Cape was better than lingering here in Java and marrying some local slut. So be it.

On the eve of departure she sat with him in her spacious reception room and said, 'When you think of me, I'll be here in this house. I'll never sell it. If I went back to Holland, I'd be tormented by memories of my musicians playing in the garden.'

She seemed so completely the epitome of those Dutch stalwarts who controlled the world—Java, Brazil, Manhattan Island, Formosa—that Willem knew she needed no cosseting from him, but when she took down her

Dutch Bible and said, 'I memorized passages at night when it was death at Spanish hands to own a Bible,' he was overcome with love and confided: 'When our ship was breaking apart I crept back and found this great Bible abandoned to the sea. And when I saw that it was the same as yours, I knew I had been sent to save it, and that if I showed it to anyone, it would be taken from me. So I buried it in a cave, and it calls me to return.'

'I've never heard a better reason to sail anywhere,' his mother said, and when the Christmas fleet departed, on December 20, she was at the wharf to bid him farewell. That night, back in her big house, she began her preparations for what she termed 'the feast of the dying year.' She borrowed the musicians, supervised the roasting of the pigs, and nodded approvingly when servants dragged in the liquor. As the year ebbed she and her Dutch equals roared old songs and wassailed and fell in stupors and slept them off. Java would always be Queen of the East and Batavia her golden capital.

The council had agreed that Van Riebeeck's slaves must come not from Java, whose natives were intractable, but from Malacca, where the gentler Malayans adjusted more easily to servitude, so when the fleet transited the Straits, Willem's ship put in to that fine harbor and he went ashore to inform the commandant of the fort that four slaves were to be delivered, whereupon a sergeant and three men went off to the forests back of town, returning shortly with two brown-skinned men and two women. Before nightfall Willem's ship had overtaken the fleet, and the long journey to the Cape was under way.

One of the slaves was a girl named Ateh, seventeen years old and beautiful in the tawny manner of most Malayan women. She pouted when the sailors confined her and the others in a caged-off section belowdecks, and she protested when food was thrown at them. She demanded water for washing, and the sailors heard her commanding the others to behave. And at some point in each day, no matter how dismal it had been, she broke into song, whispering words she had learned as a child in her sunlit village. They were songs of little consequence, the ramblings of children and young women in love, but she made the dark hold more acceptable when she sang.

By the time the journey was half over, this girl Ateh was so well known that even the captain had to take notice of her, and it was he who gave her the name by which she would later be known: 'Ateh is pagan. If you're going to sing in a Christian church, you've got to have a Christian name.' Thumbing through his Bible, and keeping to the Old Testament, as the Dutch usually did, he came upon that lyrical passage in Judges which seemed predestined for this singing girl: 'Awake, awake, Deborah: awake, awake, utter a song . . .'

'Prophetic!' he said, closing the book reverently. 'That shall be her name —Deborah,' and henceforth she was so called.

Since it was Willem's responsibility to deliver the slaves, and since he wished to keep them alive if possible, it being usual in these waters that thirty percent died on any passage, he was often belowdecks to satisfy himself that they were properly cared for, and this threw him always into consultation with Deborah. Before he came down the ladder, she would be huddled in a corner reviling the ill fortune that had brought her there, but when she saw him coming she would move forward to the bars of the cage and begin to sing. She would feign surprise at his arrival and halt her song in mid-note, looking at him shyly, with her face hidden.

Since the fleet had now entered that part of the Indian Ocean where temperatures were highest, the penned slaves were beginning to suffer. Food, water and air were all lacking, and one midday, when the heat was greatest, Willem saw that Deborah was lying on the deck, near to prostration, and on his own recognizance he unlocked the gate that enclosed the slaves and carried the girl out to where the air was freer, kneeling over her as she slowly revived.

He was amazed at how slight her body was; and as she lay in shadows her wonderfully placid face with its high cheekbones and softly molded eyelids captivated him, and he stayed with her for a long time. When she revived he found that she could speak the native language of Java, with its curious tradition of forming plurals by speaking the singular twice. If *sate* was the word for the bamboo-skewered bits of lamb roasted and served with peanut sauce, then two of the delicacies were not *sates,* as in many languages, but *sate-sate;* to hear natives speaking rapidly gave the impression of lovely soft voices stuttering, and Willem began to cherish the sound of Deborah's voice, whether she sang or spoke.

On most days he arranged some excuse for releasing her from the cage, a partiality which angered both the Dutch seamen and the other slaves. One evening, when the time came for her freedom to end, he suggested that she not go back into the cage but remain with him, and through the long, humid night, when stars danced at the tip of the mast, they stayed together, and after that adventure everyone knew they had become lovers.

This posed no great problem, for scores of Dutchmen working in Java had mistresses; there was even a ritual for handling their bastard offspring, and no great harm was done. But the captain had been commissioned by Mevrouw van Doorn to look after her son, and when he saw the young Dutchman becoming serious about the little slave girl he felt obligated to warn him as a father might, and one morning when sailors reported: 'Mijnheer van Doorn kept the little Malaccan in his quarters again,' the older man summoned Willem to his cabin, where he sat in a large wicker chair behind a table on which rested another of those large Dutch Bibles bound in brass.

'Mister Willem, I've been informed that your head has been twisted by the little Malaccan!'

'Not twisted, sir, I hope.'

'And you've been acting toward her as if she were your wife.'

'I trust not, sir.'

'Your mother put your safekeeping in my hands, Mister Willem, and as your father, I deem it proper to ask if you've been reading the Book of Genesis?'

'I know the Book, sir.'

'But have you read it recently?' the captain asked, and with this he threw open the heavy book to a page marked with a spray of palm leaf, and from the twenty-fourth chapter he read the thundering oath which Abraham imposed when his son Isaac hungered for a wife:

'And I will make thee swear by the Lord, the God of heaven, and the God of the earth, that thou shalt not take a wife . . . of the daughters of the Canaanites . . . but thou shalt go unto my country, and to my kindred, and take a wife . . .'

Slowly the captain turned the pages till he came to the next passage marked by a frond. Placing his two hands over the pages, he said ominously, 'And when Isaac was an old man, having obeyed his father Abraham, what did he say when his son Jacob wanted a wife?' Dramatically he lifted his hands and with a stubby finger pointed to the revealing verse:

And Isaac called Jacob, and blessed him, and charged him, and said unto him, Neemt geene vrowe van de dochteren Canaans.

Willem, seeing the words spelled out so strictly, felt constrained to assure the captain that he meant nothing serious with the Malaccan girl, but the older man was not to be diverted: 'It's always been the problem in Java and it will soon become the problem at the Cape. Where can a Dutch gentleman find himself a wife?'

'Where?' Willem echoed.

'God has foreseen this problem, as He foresees everything.' With a flourish he swung the parchment pages back to the first text, indicating it with his left forefinger. 'Go back to your own country and be patient. Don't throw yourself away on local women, the way those idiots in Java do.' Pointing to the deck below, he added, 'Nor on slaves.'

'Am I to wait perpetually?'

'No, because when you debark with your slaves at the Cape, this fleet continues to Holland. And when we reach Amsterdam, I'll speak to your brother Karel and commission him to find you a wife from among the women of Holland, the way Isaac and Jacob found their wives in their native country. I'll bring her back to you.'

When Willem drew back in obvious distaste over having his life arranged by others, the captain closed the great book and rested his open hands upon it. 'It tells you what to do right here. Obey the word of the Lord.'

The visit to the captain changed nothing. Willem continued to keep his slave girl in his quarters, and it was she who obeyed the Bible, for like the original Deborah, she continued to sing, twisting herself ever more tightly about his heart.

Then abruptly everything changed. One afternoon as the east coast of Africa neared, Deborah sat on the lower deck whispering an old song to herself, but as Willem approached she stopped midway and told him, 'I shall have a baby.'

With great tenderness he drew her to her feet, embraced her, and asked in Javanese, 'Are you sure?'

'Not sure,' she said softly, 'but I think.'

She was correct. Early one morning, as she rose from Willem's bed, she felt faint and dropped to the deck, sitting there with her arms clasped about her ankles. She was about to inform Willem that she was certain of her pregnancy, when the mast-top lookout started shouting, 'Table Mountain!' and all hands turned out to see the marvelous sight.

Willem was overcome when he saw the great flat mountain standing clear in the sunlight, for it symbolized his longing. Years had elapsed since he left it, and he could imagine the vast changes that must have occurred at its base, and he was thinking of them when Deborah came to stand beside him.

Aware of the hold this mountain had on him, she said nothing, just hummed softly, whispering the words now and then, and when he took notice of her she placed her left hand, very small and brown, on his right arm and said, 'We will have a baby.' The mountain, the waiting cave and the indiscernible future blended into a kind of golden haze, and he could not even begin to guess what he must do.

When he was rowed ashore, leaving Deborah behind, for she must wait till an owner was assigned, he found a settlement much smaller than expected; only a hundred and twenty-two people inhabited the place. There was a small fort with sod walls threatening to dissolve on rainy days, and a huddle of rude buildings within. But the site! Back in 1647 when the shipwrecked sailors lived ashore, their beach headquarters had been nine miles to the north, and Willem had seen only from a distance the delectable valley at the foot of Table Mountain; now he stood at the edge of that good land, protected by mountains on three sides, and he believed that when sufficient settlers arrived this would be one of the finest towns in the world.

He was greeted by the commander, a small, energetic man in his late thirties of such swarthy complexion that blond Dutchmen suspected him of Italian parentage. He wore a rather full mustache and dressed as fastidiously as frontier conditions would allow. He spoke in a voice higher than usual in a mature man, but with such speed and force that he gained attention and respect.

He was Jan van Riebeeck, ship's chirurgeon, who had served in most of the spice ports, winding up in Japan after abandoning medicine to become a merchant-trader, a skill he mastered so thoroughly that he was making profits for both the Compagnie and himself. For each hour he spent in the former's interests, he spent an equal time on his own, until his profits grew to such dimension that the Compagnie had to take notice. Accused of private trading, he was recalled to Batavia, where he was dealt with leniently and shipped back to Holland for discipline. Forced into premature retirement, he might well have finished his life in obscurity had not a peculiar circumstance thrust him back into the mainstream and an honored place in history.

When the Lords XVII decided to establish a recuperation spot at the Cape, they selected as their manager one of the men who had guarded the trade goods following the wreck of the *Haerlem*. He had been chosen because of his familiarity with the area, but when he declined, a wise old director said, 'Wait! What we really need is a merchant of proved ability.'

'Who?'

'Van Riebeeck.'

'Can we trust him?' several of the Lords asked.

'I believe he's a case of what we might call "belated rectitude," ' the old man said, and it was Jan van Riebeeck who got the assignment.

In effect, his instructions were simple: 'Establish a refreshment station which will feed our ships, but do so at no cost to this Compagnie!' That charter, in force for the next hundred and fifty years, would determine how this land would develop: it would always be a mercantile operation, never a free colony. The charter already accounted for what Willem was seeing on his brief walk to the fort with Van Riebeeck, but he had the good sense not to share his observations: This is much finer than Batavia, but where are the people? The land beyond those hills! It could house a million settlers, and I'll wager it's not even been explored.

'I often saw your brother Karel in Amsterdam,' Van Riebeeck said.

'How is he?'

'Married to a wonderful girl. Very wealthy.'

Willem, observing that the commander evaluated even marriage in terms of commerce, changed the subject. 'Will there soon be more people?' he asked.

Van Riebeeck stopped abruptly, then turned as if to settle once and for all this matter of population, and from the sharp manner in which he spoke, Willem suspected that he had made his speech before: 'You must understand one thing, Van Doorn.' Although only six years older than Willem he spoke patronizingly: 'This is a commercial holding, not a free state. We're here to aid the Compagnie, and we'll enlarge the colony only when it tells us to. As long as we allow you to stay ashore, you work for the Compagnie. You do what the Compagnie says.'

Within the next few hours Willem learned his lesson. He was ordered where to put his bag, where to make his bed, where to eat, and where to work. He found that a farmer could till a plot of land but never own it, and that whatever he grew must produce profit for the Compagnie. Of course, as an old Java hand he was not alarmed by these rules, but he did recall that in Batavia there had been a lusty freedom, epitomized by his mother, whereas here at the Cape there was somber restriction. Worst of all, the tiny settlement suffered under two sets of masters: from Amsterdam the Lords XVII laid down the big principles, but from Java came the effective rules. The governor-general in Batavia was an emperor; the commander at the Cape, a distant functionary. In Java, grand designs effloresced; at the Cape, they worried about 'radishes, lettuce and cress.'

Three days later, when Willem stood before the commander in the fort, Van Riebeeck thought him a poor replica of his brother: Karel was tall and slim, Willem shortish and plump; Karel had a quick, ingratiating manner, Willem a stubborn suspiciousness; and Karel was obviously ambitious for promotion within the Compagnie, whereas Willem was content to work at anything, so long as he was free to explore the Cape. In no comparison was the difference more startling than in their choice of women: Willem, if the ship captain could be trusted, had formed an alliance with a Muslim slave girl, while Karel had married the daughter of one of the richest merchants in Amsterdam.

'Wonderful match,' Van Riebeeck said. 'Daughter of Claes Danckaerts.' And again he added, 'Very rich.'

'I'm happy for him,' Willem said. Actually, he could scarcely remember his brother and could not possibly have guessed how Karel had changed in the eight years since he had quit the wreck of the *Haerlem* to sail homeward. From what the commander said, he must be prospering.

'What we have in mind for you,' Van Riebeeck continued, 'is the vineyard. Have you ever grown grapes?'

'No.'

'You're like the others.' When Van Doorn looked bewildered, the energetic little commander took him by the arm, led him to a parapet from which the valleys lying at the foot of Table Mountain were visible, and said with great enthusiasm, 'This soil can grow anything. But sometimes we approach it the wrong way.' He winced, recalling one early disaster. 'From the start I wanted grapes. I brought with me the seeds, but our gardener planted them the way to plant wheat. Scattered them broadside, plowed them under, and six months later harvested weeds.'

'How do you grow them?'

'Rooted vines, each one separately. Then you make cuttings . . .'

'What are cuttings?'

Patiently Van Riebeeck explained the intricate proceedings whereby tiny plants imported from Europe turned eventually into casks of wine headed for Java. 'Why do we bother?' Willem asked, for he saw that fruit trees and vegetables would flourish.

'Java's demanding wine,' the commander said sharply. Hustling Willem back to his rude office, he pointed to a large map that showed the shipping route from Amsterdam to Batavia: 'Every vessel that plies these waters wants wine. But they can't fetch it from Holland, because that wine's so poor it sickens before the equator and reaches us as vinegar. Your task is to make wine here.'

So Willem van Doorn, now thirty years of age, was settled upon a plot of ground belonging to the Compagnie and given nine basketfuls of small rooted vines imported from the Rhineland. 'Make wine,' Van Riebeeck said peremptorily, 'because if you succeed, after twenty years you'll be free to head for Holland.'

'You also?' Willem asked.

'No, no! I'm here for only a brief time. Then I go back to Java.' His eyes brightened. 'That's where the real jobs are.'

Willem started to say that he preferred the Cape to either place, but since he had never seen Holland, he concluded that this might be presumptuous; still, the fact that Van Riebeeck thought well of Java made him more attractive.

For a man who had never done so, to make wine presented difficulties, but Van Riebeeck showed Willem how to plant the precious roots, then provide them with poles and strings to grow upon, and finally, prune them along the lines required. He learned how to use animal fertilizer and irrigation, but most of all, he learned to know the howling southeast winds that blew incessantly in some seasons, making the high ground near the mountain a grave for growing things.

'It didn't blow like this when we were here before,' he complained, but the Compagnie gardeners laughed at him, for they were weary of hearing his constant recollections.

'We were up there,' he said, pointing some nine miles to the north, where the winds had been gentler. The men ignored him, for in their opinion there could be no spot in this forlorn land where the winds did not howl. But they showed him how to plant trees to give protection, if they survived, and offered other encouragements, for they, too, needed wine.

Willem realized that he had been handed an unrewarding assignment in which failure was probable, but it gave him one advantage which he prized: everyone else at the Cape lived within the fortress walls in cramped, unpleasant quarters, while he enjoyed the freedom of living in his own hut beside his vines. True, he had to walk some distance for food and companionship, but that was a trivial price to pay for the joy he found in living relatively free.

But his freedom accentuated the slavery in which Deborah lived, and often at night, when he would have wanted to be with her, he was in his hut and she in the fort, locked in the guardhouse. The Malayan slaves had been thoughtfully placed by Van Riebeeck: 'One man and woman will work for my wife. The strongest man will work the ships. The other woman can do general work for the Compagnie.'

Deborah was the latter, and as she moved about the fort, Van Riebeeck saw that she was pregnant. This did not trouble him, for like any prudent owner, he hoped for natural increase, and since Deborah was proving the cleverest of his slaves, he assumed that she would produce valuable children. But he was distressed that the father of the unborn child was Van Doorn.

'How did this happen?' he asked Willem.

'On the ship . . . from Malacca.'

'We need women. Badly we need them. But proper Dutch women, not slaves.'

'Deborah's a fine person . . .'

'I've already seen that. But she's Malay. She's Muslim. And the Bible says—'

'I know. The captain read me the passages. "Thou shalt not take a wife from the Canaanites. Thou shalt go to thine own country and find a wife." '

'Excellent advice.' Van Riebeeck rose from his desk and paced for several moments. Then threw his hands upward and asked, 'But what shall we do here at the Cape? At last count we had one hundred and fourteen men, nine women. White men and women, that is. What's a man to do?'

He wanted to bar Van Doorn from visiting with his slave girl, but he refrained because he knew that to exact such a promise in these close quarters would not be sensible. Instead he warned: 'Keep marriage out of your mind, Van Doorn. What happens in Batavia will not be encouraged here. The child will be a bastard and a Compagnie slave.' Van Doorn, suspecting that what was law now would be altered later, bowed and said nothing.

But when he saw how far with child Deborah had come, he felt a pressing desire to stay with her and make her his wife, even though his experience in Java should have taught him that these marriages often turned out poorly. Such memories were obliterated by his recollection of those exceptional marriages in which Javanese women had created homes of quiet joy, half-Christian, half-Muslim, in which the husbands relinquished all dreams of ever returning to a colder Holland and a more severe society.

Deborah, to his surprise, seemed unconcerned about her future, as if the problems of pregnancy were enough. Her beautiful, placid face showed no anxiety, and when he raised questions about her status, she smiled: 'I'm to be a slave. I'll never see my village again.' And he supposed that this was her honest reaction, that she did not prize freedom the way he did.

'I want to care for you,' he said.

'Someone will,' she said, and when his emotion flared, tempting him to steal her from the fort, she laughed again and said that when the time came, Commander van Riebeeck would find her a man.

'Will he?'

'Of course. In Malacca the Portuguese owners always found men for their slave women. They wanted children.'

'I'll be that man.'

'Maybe you, maybe someone else.'

As the time neared for the birth of their child, Willem endeavored to visit with Deborah as much as possible, and it became known to everyone that he was the father. She walked with him sometimes to the vineyard, thinking with amusement of how a Portuguese grandee at Malacca would have scorned any fellow countryman who dipped his hands into the earth. But she was acquainted with growing things and said, 'Willem, those vines are dying.'

'Why? Why do they die?'

'The rows run the wrong way. The wind hits them too strong.' And she showed him how, if he planted his vines along the direction from which the winds blew, and not broadside to it, only the lead plants would be affected, while the sun would be free to strike all the vines evenly.

She was at the vineyard one day, singing with that extraordinary voice, when Van Riebeeck came to inspect the German vines, and he, too, saw that they were dying: 'It's the wind.' And he added grimly, 'No wine from these plants,' but he assured Willem that replacement plants were on their way from France. He was determined to produce wine for the Compagnie, even if he had to import new plants constantly.

When the women of the fort led Deborah to her confinement, Willem was overwhelmed by the realization that he was about to become a father, and this had an unexpected effect: he wanted to recover his Bible so that he could record in it the fact of birth, as if by this action he could confirm the Van Doorn presence in Africa. Since he had a hut apart from the others, it would be safe to produce the book without being required to offer explanations as to how he had acquired it. So in the evening after his son was born he slipped along the beach till he came to that ancient cave, and when he was satisfied that no one was spying, he entered it to claim his Bible.

A few days later Commander van Riebeeck appeared at the vineyard, said nothing about the birth of the boy, but did ask for Willem's assistance on a knotty problem: 'It's this Hottentot Jack. They tell me you know him.'

'Jack!' Willem cried with obvious affection. 'Where is he?'

'Where indeed?' And the commander unraveled his version of duplicity, stolen cows, promises made but never kept, and suspected connivance with the dreadful Bushmen who had edged south, enticed by Compagnie sheep and cattle.

'That doesn't sound like my Jack,' Willem protested.

'The same. Nefarious.'

'I'm sure I could talk with him . . .'

The complaints continued: 'When we arrived in the bay, there he was, uniform of an English sailor, shoes and all.'

'That's Jack,' Willem said.

The commander ignored him. 'So we made arrangements with him. He to serve as our interpreter. We to give him metal tools and objects.'

'He spoke English rather well, didn't he?'

'But he was like a ghost at twilight. Now here. Now gone. And absolutely no sense of property. Whatever he saw, he took.'

'Surely he gave you cattle in return.'

'That's what I'm here about. He owes us many cattle and we cannot find him.'

'I could find him.'

At this confident offer the commander placed the tips of his fingers together and brought them carefully to his lips. 'Caution. We've had killings, you know.'

'Our men shot the Hottentots?' Willem asked in amazement.

'There were provocations. It was this sort of thing Jack was supposed to—'

'I'll go to him,' Willem said abruptly. So Van Riebeeck arranged for three trusted gunners to accompany him in an exploration of those villages which Jack and his people had occupied when the *Haerlem* wrecked, but Willem refused the gunners: 'I said I'd go. Not with an army.'

That was the beginning of his difficulties with the Compagnie. Those in authority refused to believe that an unprotected Dutchman would dare to move inland, or survive if he did, but Willem was so confident that he could reach Jack and settle differences with him that he persisted. In the end he was ordered to accept the three gunners, and after strong protest which irritated everyone, he complied.

He had been right. When the Hottentots spied the armed men coming after them, they retreated into the farther hills, driving their sheep and cattle before them. In nine days of wandering, Van Doorn spoke with not a single Hottentot, so perforce he started homeward, but as the four men marched, one of the gunners said, 'I think we're being followed,' and after extra precautions had been taken, it was agreed that some brown man—or men—was keeping to the mounds and trees, marking their progress.

'It's got to be Jack,' Willem said, and when they came to those slight rises from which the Cape settlement could be seen—the point at which a prudent enemy would turn back—he told the three gunners, 'I know it's my friend. I'll go to meet him.'

This occasioned loud protest, but he was adamant: 'I'll go without a gun, so that he can see it's me, his friend.' And off he went, holding his hands wide from his body and walking directly toward the small mound behind which he knew the watcher waited. 'Jack!' he called in English. 'It's me. Van Doorn.'

Nothing moved. If the person or persons behind the rise were enemies, he would soon see the flight of deadly assegais, but he was certain that if anyone had the courage to track four well-armed men, it must be Jack, so he called again, loudly enough for his voice to be heard at a far distance.

From behind the hill there came the soft sound of movement. Slowly, slowly, a human form emerged, that of a Hottentot, unarmed and wearing the uniform of an English sailor. For several moments the two men faced each other, saying nothing. Then Van Doorn dropped his empty hands and moved forward, and as he did so, little Jack began to run toward him, so that the old friends met in a forceful embrace.

They sat on a rock, and Willem asked, 'How did these wrongs come to happen?'

It was too difficult to explain. On each side there had been promises unkept, threats that should never have been uttered, and petty misunderstandings that escalated into skirmishes. There had been killings; there would be more, and any possibility of reconciliation seemed lost.

'I don't believe this,' Willem said. His affection for the slave girl Deborah had intensified his attitudes, making it easier for him to look at this Hottentot as an ally.

'We talk too much,' Jack said.

'But we're going to stay here, Jack. Forever. A few now, many later. Must we live always as enemies?'

'Yes. You steal our cattle.'

'They tell me you steal our tools. Our European sheep.'

The Hottentot knew that this countercharge was true, but he did not know how to justify it. Enmity had been allowed to fester and could not be exorcised. But one charge was so grave that Willem had to explore it: 'Did you murder the white soldier?'

'Bushmen,' Jack said, and with his nimble fingers he indicated the three-part arrow.

'Won't you please come with me?' Willem begged.

'No.'

There was a painful farewell, the little brown man and the big white, and then the parting, but when the two men were well separated, with Van Doorn heading back to his gunners, one lifted his weapon and shot at Jack.

He had anticipated such a probability, so as soon as he saw the gun raised, he jumped behind a mound and was not hit.

On a fine February morning in 1657 nine gunners and sailors assembled outside Van Riebeeck's office, and all in the fort stopped work and moved closer to hear an announcement that would alter the history of Africa:

> 'Their Honors in Amsterdam, the Lords XVII, wishing always to do what furthers the interests of the Compagnie, have graciously decided that you nine may take fields beyond Table Mountain and farm them under your own guidance, but you must not move farther than five miles from the fort.'

When the men cheered at this release from drudgery, Willem van Doorn heard the commotion and came in to listen with envy as Van Riebeeck spelled out the meticulous terms laid down by the Lords. The freedmen would work not individually but in two groups, one five, one four, and would receive in freehold as much land as they could plow, spade or otherwise prepare within three years. Their crops would be bought by the Compagnie at prices fixed by the Compagnie. They could fish the rivers, but only for their own tables. They were forbidden to buy cattle or sheep from the Hottentots; they must buy from the Compagnie, and one-tenth of their calves and lambs must be given back to the Compagnie. On and on the petty regulations went—and also the penalties: 'If you break one rule, everything you own will be confiscated.'

The men nodded, and Van Riebeeck concluded: 'Their Honors will allow you to sell any surplus vegetables to passing ships, but you may go aboard to do so only after said ships have been in harbor three days, because the Compagnie must have a chance to sell its produce first. You are forbidden to buy liquor from ships. And you must always remember that the Lords XVII are giving you this land not for your indulgence but in the hope that you will turn a profit for the Compagnie.' Van Doorn, listening to the restrictions, muttered to himself, 'He says they're free, but the rules say they're not free.'

Van Riebeeck, wishing to solemnize this significant moment, and totally unaware that he had imposed any unreasonable restrictions, asked the men to bow their heads: 'Under the watchful eye of God, you are now free burghers,' and to sanctify this status he read from the Bible that glowing statement of God's covenant which had excited Willem:

> 'And I will give unto thee, and unto thy seed after thee, the land wherein thou art a stranger, all the land of Canaan, for an everlasting possession . . .'

With this benediction these nine became the first free white men in South Africa, the progenitors of whatever nation might subsequently develop. Suddenly the quiet was broken with cheers for the commander, after which the two groups set forth to line out their future farms.

One of the Hottentots had listened intently to this ceremony, and late that afternoon he crept off, taking a route past the fields the free burghers were surveying. At a small stream he stopped to watch as two antelope dipped toward the sparkling water; then he moved to break the news to his people: 'They are taking our land.'

The joy with which the nine free burghers had greeted their release was short-lived, for during the first year of backbreaking effort they came to know the Compagnie's interpretation of freedom. Two of the more adventurous, alarmed by their growing indebtedness to the Compagnie stores, began clandestine trading with the Hottentots for elephant tusks, rhino horns and ostrich feathers. For this they were severely disciplined, but Van Riebeeck did reluctantly agree that they might trade for cows, if they never paid more than the Compagnie did.

An argument arose over whether they might kill one of their own sheep for their personal use; the commander recognized this as a threat to the Compagnie's butchery, but he did compromise: 'You can slaughter one animal occasionally, but before you do so, you must pay a fee to the butchery.'

In the evenings, in their rude huts, the burghers grumbled, and sometimes Van Doorn would be present, for the things these men said he understood. No complaint was voiced more constantly than the one regarding labor.

'Is this what freedom means?' one farmer asked. 'We're peasants, working eight days a week.'

'The Hottentots are better off than us,' another said. 'They have their herds and all that free land out there. We're free . . . to be slaves.'

Relations with the Hottentots had deteriorated: few brought animals to be traded, almost none wanted to work for the burghers. Most kept their herds at the edge of the settlement, watching sullenly as the Dutchmen's cattle encroached.

'In Java no man would work like this,' one stout burgher complained. 'I think I'll hide in the next ship and sail back to Holland.'

And that's precisely what several of the free men did, so guards were posted about any vessel that put into Table Bay, and then one morning in 1658 the lookout atop the fort awakened everyone by hammering on a length of metal suspended from a post and shouting, 'Warship coming!'

Apprehension gripped the tiny group of settlers; as far as they knew, Holland was still at war with England, and since this intruder might be carrying a landing party, a quick muster was called, and Van Riebeeck said, 'We fight. We will never surrender Compagnie property.' But as the men prepared their muskets the lookout cried, 'Good news! It's a Dutch ship!' and all ran from the fort to greet the taut little craft.

Van Riebeeck was waiting when the ship's boat drew alongside the jetty his men were constructing, and as soon as the captain jumped smartly ashore the good news was announced: 'Off Angola we ran upon a Portuguese merchant ship headed for Brazil. Short fight. We captured her. A little gold, a little silver, but scores of fine slaves.'

Van Riebeeck could not believe the words; for years he had been imploring his superiors in Java for slaves to work at the Cape, and now the captain was saying, 'We found two hundred and fifty on the Portuguese ship, but seventy-six died in our holds.' Many of the others were seriously ill, and some were boys and girls, of whom Van Riebeeck complained, 'They'll be of little use for the next four or five years.'

'Fetch the big one,' the captain cried. 'You'll want him for yourself, Commander.' Then, lowering his voice: 'In exchange for extra beef?'

When the boat returned, there standing in the bow, shackled heavily, stood the first black from Africa that Willem and the other Dutchmen had ever seen; all previous slaves had been private acquisitions from Madagascar, India or Malaya.

This man must have come from a family of some importance in Angola, for he had what could only be called a noble bearing: tall, broad-shouldered, wide of face. He was the kind of young man a military leader promotes to lieutenant after three days in the field, and as soon as Van Riebeeck saw him he decided to give him an important assignment. He seemed destined to be the leader of the thousands of future slaves who would soon be joining the community.

'What's his name?' he asked, and a sailor replied, 'Jango.' It was an improbable name, corrupted no doubt from some Angolan word of specific meaning, and Van Riebeeck said, in the Portuguese dialect used by all who worked in the eastern oceans, 'Jango, come with me.' And as the tall black, hefting his chains, followed the commander to the fort, Willem thought: How majestic he is! More powerful than two Malays or three Indians.

For the next few days Commander van Riebeeck was occupied with assigning tasks to his new slaves, reserving eleven of the best for the personal use of his wife, and with the arrival of blacks in force he judged that he had better tidy up the status of the slaves already at the Cape. So he summoned Willem to his quarters and asked, 'Van Doorn, what are we going to do about this girl Deborah?'

'Van Valck wants to marry his Malaccan girl. I want to marry Deborah.'

'That would be most unwise.'

'Why?'

'Because you're the brother of an important official in the Compagnie.'

'She's to have another child.'

'Damn!' The preoccupied little man strode back and forth. 'Why can't you worthless men control yourselves?' He had brought his wife with him, and two nieces, so that he felt no lack of feminine companionship; he believed that men like Van Doorn and Van Valck should wait until suitable Dutch women arrived from Holland, and if this took nine or ten years, the men must be patient.

'I'm thirty-three,' Willem said. 'And I feel I must marry now.'

'And so you shall,' Van Riebeeck said, whipping around to face his vintner. Reaching out his hands, he grasped Willem's and said, 'You'll be married before the year's out.'

'Why not now?' Van Doorn asked, and he saw Van Riebeeck stiffen.

'You're most difficult. You spoil everything.' And from his desk he produced the copy of a letter he had sent some ten months before to the Lords XVII in Amsterdam, requesting them to find seven sturdy Dutch girls, no Catholics, and send them south on the next ship. Names of the intended husbands were given, and at the head of the list stood: 'Willem van Doorn, aged thirty-two, born in Java, brother of Karel van Doorn of this Compagnie, reliable, good health, vintner of the Cape.'

'So your wife is on her way,' the commander said, adding lamely, 'I would suppose.'

'I'd rather marry Deborah,' Willem said with that stolid frankness that characterized all he did. A more subtle man would have known that rejecting a woman the commander had taken pains to import, and for a slave, was bound to provoke him; it never occurred to Willem, and when Van Riebeeck pointed out that it would be highly offensive to any Dutch Christian woman to be sent so far and then discarded in favor of a Muslim slave, Willem said, 'But I'm practically married to Deborah.'

Van Riebeeck rose stiffly, went to his window, and pointed down into the fortress yard. Willem, following his finger, saw nothing. 'The horse,' Van Riebeeck said.

'I see no horse,' Willem said in a tone calculated to irritate.

'The wooden horse!' Van Riebeeck shouted.

There it was, a wooden horse of a kind that carpenters use for sawing, except that its legs were so long that it stood much too high to be useful for woodworking. Willem had often heard of this cruel instrument, but it had not seemed a reality until this moment.

Clapping his hands, the commander instructed a servant: 'Tell the captain to proceed.' And from below a prisoner who had transgressed some trivial edict of the Compagnie was led toward the horse, where a bag of lead shot was attached to each ankle. He was then hoisted into the air, poised spread-legged above the horse, and dropped upon it. The fall of the man's body, plus the weight of the lead shot dangling from his ankles, was so powerful that the body was almost broken in half, and he screamed terribly.

'Let him stay there two days,' Van Riebeeck told his orderly, and when the man was gone, he said to Willem, 'That's how we discipline workmen who disobey Compagnie orders. Willem, I'm ordering you to marry the girl I've sent for.'

Van Doorn was transfixed by the hideousness of the event, and that night when guards were asleep and he was supposed to be in his hut at the vineyard, he crept into the punishment area, gave the prisoner a drink of water, and lifted him slightly from the cruel wood, holding him in his arms through the hours. When the sun struck the man he fainted, and remained unconscious till nightfall. This night Van Doorn was kept from administering aid by a guard posted to watch the victim; as Willem stood in the shadows staring at the ugly horse, he understood why its legs were so high: they prevented the two bags of lead from resting on the ground.

Van Riebeeck spent some days pondering the problem of Willem and Deborah, and finally arrived at a solution that left Van Doorn aghast. The commander assigned Jango to the bed next to Deborah: 'Day after day they'll see each other, and I'll have no further problems with Van Doorn.'

But he did. When guards were not looking, Willem slipped into the slave quarters below the grain store to sit with Deborah and Jango, and in broken Portuguese the three discussed their situation. Jango listened briefly, then said, 'I understand. Your baby, when it comes. I care.'

Willem clasped his hand, then added, 'Jango, do nothing to enrage the officers.' He intended that such warning apply only to Jango, for he could not suppose that Deborah would in any way incur Compagnie displeasure. While Willem warned Jango of the horse and other punishments visited upon fractious men, she whispered a song, singing a lullaby as if her baby was already born.

Finally Willem said with a faith that impressed Jango, 'When the predikant arrives with the fleet, I'm sure Van Valck will be allowed to marry his Malaccan girl, and I know I'll get permission, too. Jango, protect her till I do.' The huge black man shifted his chains and nodded.

It was not only slaves that caused Van Riebeeck trouble. The Hottentots gave him no rest, this day smiling and gregarious, the next sullen and contentious, and when one enterprising brown fellow, hungry at the end of a long workday, slipped into the Compagnie kraal and stole a sheep, actual war broke out.

It was not a real war, of course, but when the white population was so small and the native so large, the loss of even one white man posed grave problems. The stolen sheep was soon forgotten, but tempers rose on both sides as cattle were taken, assegais thrown and muskets fired. And the situation was aggravated when many of the new slaves ran away, representing a huge cash loss to the Compagnie.

In the final clash, four men were slain, and then reason prevailed. To the fort came Hottentot messengers, calling, 'Van Doorn! Van Doorn!' He was finally found playing with his son, and Van Riebeeck was irate when Willem, out of breath, finally reported.

'Isn't that thieving Jack's crowd?' the commander asked, pointing to where seven Hottentots stood under a large white flag.

'I don't see Jack,' Willem said.

'Let's talk,' Van Riebeeck said. 'Go bring them in.'

So Willem, unarmed, left the fort and walked slowly toward the Hottentots, and Jack was not among them. 'Where is he?'

'He stay,' replied a man who had helped at the fort.

'Tell him to come see me.'

'He want to know if it is safe?'

'Of course.'

'He want to know from him,' the man said, pointing to the fort.

So a further conflict between Van Doorn and the commander arose when Willem left the Hottentots, returned to the fort, and informed Van Riebeeck that Jack was demanding a guarantee given personally by the commander. Since this seemed an accusation of bad faith, Van Riebeeck refused. 'May I do so on your behalf?' Willem asked. There was a grudging nod.

The Hottentots were invited to approach the outer perimeter of the fort, where Van Doorn assured them that it would be safe for Jack to join them, but the little brown men still wanted recognition from the commander himself. So Willem again confronted Van Riebeeck, and after much angry discussion, he agreed to the meeting.

When Jack received the safe conduct, he remembered Java, and the way men of importance behaved. Donning his faded uniform and mounting his finest ox, he jammed his cockaded hat on his head and rode forth to meet the man whom some of his people were already calling the Exalted One.

The peace negotiations, as Van Riebeeck would grandiloquently call them in his report to the Lords XVII, were protracted.

'You've been taking too much of our land,' Jack said.

'There's room for everyone.'

'As long as we can remember, this was our place. Now you take all the best.'

'We take only what we need.'

'If I went to your house in Holland, would I be allowed to do the same?'

Van Riebeeck ignored this rhetorical question. 'Why don't you bring back our slaves when they run away?'

'We tend cattle, not people.'

'Then why do you steal our cattle?'

Jack said, 'We used to come to this valley for bitter almonds. We must have food.'

'You'll find other almonds.'

'They're far away.'

And so it went, until Van Riebeeck said wearily, 'We will draw a paper that says we shall always live in peace.' And that night, when Jack had ridden off on his ox, Van Riebeeck sat alone with his diary. As he had done every day since arriving at the Cape he penned a careful entry, which would be read with reassurance in both Amsterdam and Java:

> They had to be told that they had now lost the land, as the result of the war, and had no alternative but to admit that it was no longer theirs, the more so because they could not be induced to restore stolen cattle which they had unlawfully taken from us in our defensive war, won by the sword, as it were, and we intended to keep it.

And then the Cape forgot both slaves and Hottentots, for one clear December morning the settlement awakened to a breathtaking sight. In the night hours the ships of a great merchant fleet had moved into the bay and six medium-sized vessels rode tidily near the *Groote Hoorn,* a magnificent East Indiaman bound for Java. Tall and proud, she displayed her fine woodwork and railings of polished brass as if she were boasting of the distinguished passenger who occupied her stateroom, the Honorable Commissioner, personal emissary of the Lords XVII. He came with powers to investigate conditions at the Cape before sailing on to Java, where he would become governor-general: the merchant Karel van Doorn.

When he stepped carefully ashore, he looked disdainfully at the slaves who held his pinnace. He was dressed in black, with broad white collar, ribbed hose and brightly buffed shoes. He wore a broad-rimmed hat, carried a lace handkerchief, and guided himself gingerly with a silver-topped cane. He wore his hair in ringlets, which cascaded over his collar, and his beard in a trim point. He was tall and stiff and handsome, and when he was safely ashore, he turned to assist a lady even more carefully dressed than he. She reminded Willem of his mother, for she looked as if she had the same inborn sense of regal command, and he could visualize her occupying the big house in Batavia.

Karel, of course, did not see his brother; his attention was directed solely to Van Riebeeck as the senior Compagnie official, and even when these two had exchanged greetings, no attempt was made to summon Willem, so he stood lost in the small crowd as cheers were given while the entourage marched to the fort. Even there Karel did not ask to see his brother, for as commissioner, he deemed it necessary to impose his authority upon the settlement as promptly as possible.

'What are your major problems?' he asked Van Riebeeck as soon as the door was closed on the watching subordinates.

'Four, Mijnheer.'

Karel was forty-three years old that year, a man burdened with importance, and since Van Riebeeck was only thirty-seven, smaller and less imposing, Karel would normally have been able to lord it over the resident agent, but he had in addition full and sole jurisdiction to look into every aspect of the Cape occupancy and to draft whatever new instructions he deemed prudent.

Placing a sheet of valuable paper before Van Riebeeck, he asked, 'What are the four?'

'There has been no predikant here since the founding. We need marriages and baptisms.'

'Dr. Grotius is on his way to Batavia. He'll come ashore tomorrow.'

'The slaves run away constantly.'

'You must guard them more carefully. Remember, they're Compagnie property.'

'We guard them. We punish them if we recover them. We chain them. And still they seek their freedom.'

'This must be stopped, and harshly. The Compagnie does not purchase slaves to have them vanish.'

'But how do we stop them?'

'Every man, every woman must assume responsibility for keeping the slaves under control. Especially you. The third problem?'

'Desperately we need women. Mijnheer, the workmen cannot live here alone . . . forever.'

'They knew the terms when they signed with us. A place to sleep. Good food. And when they get back to Holland, enough money saved to take a wife.'

'I've begun to think that many of our men may never go back to Holland.'

'They must. There's no future for a Compagnie man here.'

'And this is the fourth problem. I detect an innate restlessness among the free burghers.'

'Rebellion? Against the Compagnie?' Karel rose and stomped about the room. 'That will not be tolerated. That you must knock down immediately.'

'Not rebellion!' Van Riebeeck said quickly, indicating that the commissioner should resume his seat and waiting until he had done so. 'What I speak of, Mijnheer. The men complain of the prices we pay for their corn . . . their expenses . . .' He stopped at the look Van Doorn gave him. 'They sometimes seem driven to probe eastward—on their own, not on Compagnie business at all. As if the dark heart of Africa were summoning them.'

Karel van Doorn leaned back. On three separate occasions the Lords XVII in Amsterdam had detected in Van Riebeeck's voluminous reports hints that the free burghers at the Cape were beginning to look beyond the perimeters set for them at the time of their original grants. This burgher baker had wanted an additional plot for himself. That farmer had suggested moving out to where the lands were more spacious. Even Van Riebeeck himself had petitioned for a hundred acres more so that he might extend his personal garden. On this heresy Commissioner van Doorn knew the Compagnie attitude and his own inclinations; leaning forward so that his words would have more weight, he said, 'Commander, you and your men must understand that you have been sent here not to settle a continent but to run a business establishment.'

'I understand!' Van Riebeeck assured him. 'You've seen how I protect the smallest stuiver. We waste not a guilder at this post.'

'And you make not a guilder.' Van Doorn did not relax his stern gaze. 'When the *Groote Hoorn* sails we would like to take aboard a large supply of vegetables, mutton, beef and casks of wine. And as of right now, I expect that we shall be disappointed in all four.'

'Wait till you see our cauliflower.'

'The wine?'

'The vines do poorly, Mijnheer. The winds, you know. But we've planted a protective hedge, and if the Lords could send us some stronger vines . . .'

'I bring them with me.'

Van Riebeeck, an ardent gardener, showed his joy at this unexpected bounty, but he was brought back to reality by Van Doorn's insolent questioning: 'The mutton and the beef I'm sure you won't have?'

'The Hottentots trade very few beasts with us. Indeed, I sometimes wonder at the ways of the Lord, that he should allow such unworthy people to own so many fine animals.'

Karel rocked back and forth in silence, then stabbed at the items in his dossier. 'You have cauliflower, but nothing else.'

Van Riebeeck laughed nervously. 'When I say cauliflower, I mean, of course, many other vegetables. Mijnheer will be astonished at what we've done.' Without allowing time for the commissioner to rebut this enthusiasm, the lively little man said, 'And of course, Mijnheer, there's a fifth problem, but this is personal.'

'In what way?' Karel asked.

'My letters. My three letters.'

'Concerning what?'

'My assignment to Java. When I accepted this task, and it's not been an easy one I assure you, it was with the understanding that if I did good work here for one year, I would be promoted to Java. At the end of that year I applied for transfer, but the Lords said I was needed at the Cape. So I stayed a second and petitioned again. Same answer. I stayed a third, and now it's in the seventh year.' He paused, stared directly at the commissioner, and said, 'You know, Mijnheer, this is no place to leave a man for six years.' When Van Doorn said nothing, the commander added, 'Not when a man has seen Java. Please, Mijnheer. Most desperately I long for Java.'

'On this the Lords gave me specific instructions.' From a leather box made in Italy he produced a sheaf of papers, riffled through them, and found what he wanted. Disdainfully he pushed it toward Van Riebeeck, then sat with his lips against his thumbs as the commander read it a-loud: ' "Your strong efforts at the Cape have been noted, as has your repeated request for transfer to Java. For the time being, your skill is needed where you are." ' In a hollow voice Van Riebeeck asked, 'How many years?'

'Until you produce enough meat and wine for our ships.' Van Doorn was quite harsh: 'You must remember, Commander. You and your men are here not to build a village for your own pleasures, but to construct a farm that will feed our ships. Every sign I see about me testifies to the fact that you are wasting your energies on the former and scamping the latter.' With that he reached for a new paper and began reading off the vetoes and decisions of the Lords XVII, none of whom had ever seen South Africa, but all of whom had studied meticulously the detailed reports sent them by Van Riebeeck:

'Item: Hendrick Wouters is not allowed to keep a pig.

'Item: Leopold van Valck is not to plant his corn in the field beyond the river.

'Item: Henricus Faber is to pay nineteen florins for use of the plow.

'Item: Rice imported from Java must not be fed to any slaves acquired from Angola, but only to those who became accustomed to it while living in Malacca.'

On and on went the instructions: the blacksmith could shoe the gardener's horse only if the latter was to be used on Compagnie business; the sick-comforter is encouraged to conduct worship on Sundays, but he must never again preach from his own notes; he must restrict himself to reading sermons already delivered by properly ordained predikants in Holland; the wife, Sibilla van der Lex, must not wear sumptuary finery; there must be no loud singing after eight in the evening and none at all on Sunday; and the names of the four visiting sailors who were caught dancing with slaves last New Year's, everyone naked, must be sent with Commissioner van Doorn to the authorities in Java, where they are to be punished for immorality, if they can be found.

'You must stamp out the frivolous,' Van Doorn said, and only then did he ask, 'Is my brother working well?'

'We have him at the vineyard.'

'You said the vines were poor.'

'They are, Mijnheer, but through no fault of his. They reached us in poor condition. They were packed in Germany. Improperly.'

'The ones I bring are from France,' Van Doorn said sternly. 'I can assure you they've been properly packed.' Then, actually smiling at Van Riebeeck, he said, 'I should like to see my brother. Don't say anything about it, but I bring a surprise.'

Willem had been waiting patiently outside the door, a man of thirty-three sitting with his hands folded like a refractory schoolboy. 'Commander wants you,' a servant said, and Willem jumped from his bench, nodded as if the servant possessed great authority, and entered the office. His brother looked resplendent.

'How are you, Willem?'

'I'm very glad to be here. Very glad to see you, Karel.'

'I'm commissioner now. In Java, I'm to be the assistant.'

'Mother?'

'She's fine, we understand. I want you to meet my wife,' he said, and as he spoke a look of either compassion or amusement crept across his countenance and he reached out to take his brother's arm.

They went to a part of the fort which had been specially cleaned and provisioned for meetings during the visit. It was made of fine brick, recently kilned in the colony, with a floor pounded flat and polished with liquid cow manure that had hardened to a high and pleasing gloss. It contained five pieces of handsome dark mahogany furniture carved in Mauritius by a Malayan slave: a table, three chairs and an imposing clothes cupboard that covered much of one wall. Seated on one of the chairs was the noble lady Willem had seen coming ashore some hours before.

'This is your sister, Kornelia,' Karel said, and the woman nodded, refraining from extending her hand.

She did, however, smile in the cryptic way that Karel had smiled only a few moments earlier. 'And this,' Karel continued, 'is Dr. Grotius, who is to conduct the marriages and baptisms.' He was a fearsome man, fifty years old, angular and with a heavy touch of righteousness. He wore black except for a white collar of enormous dimension and greeted everyone who approached him with a bleak nod softened by no change of expression.

'Dr. Grotius has been sent to vitalize religious observances in Batavia,' Karel explained, whereupon the predikant looked directly at Willem and bowed again, as if including him among the persons to be vitalized.

The marriage which Dr. Grotius performed occasioned no difficulty, once he was satisfied that the slave girl who was marrying Leopold van Valck understood the Christian catechism and was willing to abjure the heathenism of Islam, but when it came to baptizing the children, a real confrontation arose, and Commissioner van Doorn was vouchsafed a new perspective on Van Riebeeck, who up to now had been so obsequious.

Baptism of the children who were clearly white presented no problem; their parents acknowledged Jesus Christ and the veracity of the Dutch Netherlands church, but when the slave girl Deborah, with no husband, offered her dark-skinned son Adam, Dr. Grotius sternly rebuked her, saying, 'Children born out of wedlock can in no way be baptized. It insults the holiness of the Sacrament.'

At this point Kornelia, a self-centered woman, lost interest in theological disputation and demanded to be taken back to the ship. As soon as she was gone Van Riebeeck resumed defending his position: 'Dominee, we live at the edge of a wilderness. A lonely few. After six years we have but one hundred and sixty-six. Nine women only. We need these slave children. Please, do baptize them.'

'The traditions of the Bible,' thundered Grotius, 'are not to be ignored simply because the place is a wilderness. Here more than in a civilized city must the rules be followed, lest we fall into contamination.' He refused to budge, and the ceremony broke up in confusion.

Five participants reacted in five sharply different ways. Dr. Grotius stormed back to the ship, unwilling to stay in the fort where such profanations took place. Deborah showed no concern whatever, her grave, placid face untroubled by the storm she had caused; it had not been her idea to baptize her son; Willem had insisted upon that, coming to her secretly when news of the ceremony became known. Willem was distraught and briefly considered disclosing the fact that the child was his, and that it was he who was insisting upon the baptism. Jan van Riebeeck was just as adamant as Dr. Grotius, except that he was determined that the slave children be baptized for the good of his little settlement. And Commissioner van Doorn, who sensed that sooner or later he would be called upon to break this deadlock, was morally agitated. Quite simply, he was eager to do the right thing. He wanted to be a good Christian patriarch, and when the others were gone, he prayed.

At supper that night Van Riebeeck and Willem discussed with him what ought to be done about the baptism, and Van Riebeeck made a strong plea that his request be honored: 'We are a Compagnie, Mijnheer van Doorn, not a church. You and I are to determine what happens at the Cape, not some predikant. In Java, as you know . . .' Whenever a Dutchman said this magical word he lingered over it: Yaaaa-wa, as if it possessed arcane powers. Whatever had been done in Yaaaa-wa was apt to be right. 'In Java, as you know, we baptized the children of slaves and raised them as good Christians. They helped us run the Compagnie.'

'I would not want to contradict a doctor of theology—'

'You must!' Van Riebeeck thundered. He suddenly seemed taller.

'If he wrote back to Amsterdam that we had profaned the Bible—'

Van Riebeeck pounded the table. 'The Bible says . . .'

And it was these words that sent the three men to Willem's hut to consult the Bible he had rescued from the *Haerlem*. Unclasping the brass fittings, he laid back the heavy cover and offered the book to his brother, who turned the pages reverently, probing those noble passages in which Abraham had laid down the laws for his people living in a new land, just as the Van Doorns and Van Riebeecks had to establish principles for their followers in this vast new territory. What was the right thing to do?

By candlelight they searched the passages, but found no guidance. Karel, accountable for healing this breach, was reluctant to surrender the Bible. Again and again he turned the pages, reading occasionally some passage that seemed to relate to their presence in the wilderness, then rejecting it. In the end he found nothing. They were adrift.

'Could we pray?' he asked, and the three knelt on the earthen floor, their somber faces illuminated by the candlelight as Karel pleaded for divine guidance. God had led the Israelites through such dark periods and He would lead the Dutchmen. But guidance did not come.

Then Willem, vaguely remembering passages in which Abraham faced difficult decisions, looked with real intensity through the chapters of Genesis, and after a while came upon those passages in which God Himself, not Abraham, instructed sojourners in the steps they must take to preserve their identity while in a strange land:

> This is my covenant, which ye shall keep, between me and you and thy seed after thee; Every man child among you shall be circumcised . . . He that is born in thy house, and he that is bought with thy money, must needs be circumcised . . .

> And Abraham took . . . all that were born in his house, and all that were bought with his money, every male among the men of Abraham's house; and circumcised the flesh of their foreskin in the selfsame day, as God had said unto him.

'It's what we sought!' Willem cried, and in the flickering light the two men responsible for this tiny settlement peered over his shoulder to find justification for whatever they might have to propose. Van Riebeeck was delighted: 'It's quite plain. Their covenant was circumcision, and God ordered the slaves to be circumcised. Our covenant is baptism, and He orders our slaves to be baptized.' He was so relieved that he cried, 'Commissioner, we must go to the ship at once, and have Dr. Grotius baptize the children,' and when Van Doorn protested at the lateness of the hour, Van Riebeeck jabbed his finger at the Bible and cried, 'Did not God command that it be done that selfsame day?'

Carefully Karel studied the Bible, and when he read the words *in the selfsame day* he knew he was obligated to have these children baptized before midnight. 'I think we should give thanks for God's guidance,' he said, and the three men knelt once more.

Bearing lanterns against the night, they carried their Bible to the waterfront, aroused the boatmen, and made their way to the *Groote Hoorn,* where they summoned Dr. Grotius. 'Dominee,' Karel cried when the predikant appeared in his nightgown, 'God has spoken!' And they spread the text before him.

For a long time Dr. Grotius studied the passages, reflecting upon them. Finally he turned to his visitors and said, 'Mijnheeren, I was wrong. Can we pray?' So for the third time they knelt, while Dr. Grotius, his hands firmly on the Bible, thanked God for His intervention and begged for continued guidance. But Willem noticed that the doctor was lingering over every item of his conversion, so that when Commander van Riebeeck suggested that he return to shore for the infants, so that they could be baptized within the day, Dr. Grotius said, almost triumphantly, 'That day is now passed. We shall perform the office before this day ends.'

With that he closed the Bible, but as he did so, a corner of the cloth upon which it had been resting caught in the leaves, and he fingered the pages to set the cloth loose, and this led him to reopen the book to the page on which Willem had inscribed the birth-facts of his first-born: 'Son Adam van Doorn born 1 November 1655.'

'Have you a son?' Dr. Grotius asked.

'Yes,' Willem said frankly.

'But . . .' There was a painful silence, after which the predikant asked, 'Wasn't the dark child to be baptized named Adam?'

'He is my son.'

The awfulness of this admission, that the brother of a distinguished merchant who was serving as commissioner for the Lords XVII should have been consorting with a pagan slave girl, struck Dr. Grotius and Karel dumb. Twice the former tried to form words of condemnation: 'You . . . you . . .' But he could think of no damnation proper for the crime. He had never served in the East and had little comprehension of the anxieties and hunger Dutchmen could feel. Karel, however, did know Java and the miseries that could ensue when men of promise married with native women . . .

'Oh, my God!' he cried suddenly. Looking at Dr. Grotius with shock, he indicated with his shoulder another cabin and cried, 'She's in there.'

'Oh, goodness!'

Whipping about, Karel jutted his face into his brother's and asked, 'Are you married?'

'I wanted to—'

'I wouldn't permit it,' Van Riebeeck said.

With fervor Karel clasped the commander's hands and cried, 'You were so prudent.'

'But Deborah—' Willem began. Karel brushed him aside and said petulantly, 'I wanted this to be a surprise.' With grandiloquent gestures he pointed to his right: 'Your future wife is in there, asleep . . . waiting to meet you in the morning.'

'My wife?'

'Yes. My wife's cousin. A girl of fine family, come all the way from Amsterdam.' And on the spur of that moment Karel rushed from the little cabin, ran down the hallway, and banged on a door: 'Katje! Come out!'

Katje, whoever she was, did not appear, but Kornelia did, tall and formidable in her night clothes. 'What's this noise?'

'Go back to bed!' Karel pushed her roughly away from the door. 'I want Katje.' And in a few moments came the girl—short, ill-favored when sleep was upon her, with frizzled hair and red face.

'What is it?' she asked peevishly.

'You're to meet Willem.'

'Not like this,' Kornelia said from the rear.

'Come!' Karel cried, agitated beyond control. And he jerked the protesting girl down the passageway and into the predikant's cabin, where with red eyes and sniffling nose she met her intended husband: 'Willem van Doorn, this is your bride, Katje Danckaerts.'

She was a country girl, a daughter of the poor Danckaerts, but a full cousin of Kornelia's and thus someone to be cared for. A year ago when Kornelia had asked, 'Whatever will we do with Katje?' her husband had said impulsively, 'We'll take her with us to the Cape. Willem needs a wife.'

So it had been arranged, and now the ungainly girl, twenty-five years old, stood in the cramped room where so many others were crowded and mistook Van Riebeeck as her betrothed, but when she moved toward him, Karel said sharply, 'Not him. This one!' and even the predikant had to laugh.

At this moment Kornelia appeared, wrapped in a coat and demanding to know what was happening. 'Go back to your room!' Karel thundered, hoping to prevent his wife from learning about the scandal, but she had been ordered about enough and elbowed her way to Katje's side.

'What are they doing to you, Katje?' she asked softly.

'I'm meeting Willem,' the girl whined.

Kornelia surveyed the men and realized immediately that they were making a botch of whatever it was they were trying to accomplish. Willem looked especially inept, so she said gently, 'Well, if you're meeting your husband, let's meet him properly,' and she pushed her cousin forward. Willem stepped up awkwardly to greet Katje, but she held back, and it was prophetic that the second utterance he heard her speak was also a complaint: 'I don't want to get married.'

She had barely finished this sentence when she felt Kornelia's firm hand in the middle of her back, giving her such a sharp push forward that she fairly leaped into Willem's arms. In that brief moment he looked at her and thought: How different from Deborah. But as he caught her he felt her womanliness and knew that he would be responsible for the years of her life. 'I'll be a good husband,' he said.

'I should think so,' Karel muttered, and then sensible Kornelia, who had acquired confidence from associating with the best families of Amsterdam, said forcefully, 'Now I demand to know what you men have been doing,' and Dr. Grotius, realizing that further dissembling was fruitless, directed her attention to the revealing entry in the Bible. She read it carefully, looked up at Willem, smiled, then read it again. Summoning Katje to her side, she showed her cousin the damaging news, then said quietly, 'It seems your husband has had another wife. But that hardly signifies.'

'She's pregnant again,' Willem blurted out.

'Oh, Jesus!' Karel moaned, whereupon Dr. Grotius reprimanded him.

'Neither does that signify,' Kornelia said.

'He's not really married to the slave girl,' Van Riebeeck said reassuringly, and Karel added, 'But they shall be married now.' When everyone turned to stare at him, he added lamely, 'I mean Willem and Katje.'

'They certainly shall,' Kornelia said, and it was she who proposed that the marriage ceremony take place right now, at one in the morning. But the predikant objected that it would be illegal to solemnize any marriage until banns had been read three times, at which Kornelia said, 'Read them.' So Karel rattled off the rubric, repeating it twice: 'Katje Danckaerts spinster Amsterdam and Willem van Doorn bachelor Batavia.'

'Cape,' Willem corrected.

'Marry them,' Karel snarled at the predikant, so the Bible was opened, with three witnesses to verify the sanctity of the rite about to be performed. In flickering light, while Katje and Willem kept their hands upon the open pages, the glowing phrases of the sacrament were intoned.

When the ceremony ended, Willem startled everyone by demanding a pen, and when it was provided, he turned to the page which had given such offense, and in the little spaces decorated with cupids and tulips where weddings were to be inscribed he wrote: 'Katje Danckaerts, Amsterdam. Willem van Doorn, Kaapstad, 21 December 1658.'

Through the mysterious system of communication that always existed in a frontier area like the Cape, the Hottentots learned that an Honorable Commissioner had arrived to adjudicate matters, and that he was older brother to the man who tended the vineyard. The news was of little significance to most of the brown men, but to Jack it was momentous, for it meant that he could pursue his major objective with someone capable of accepting it. Accordingly, he took his sailor's clothes from the bark-box in which he kept them, dusted off the heavy shoes he had made from cowhide, put on his wide-brimmed hat, and with a heavy stave cut from a stinkwood tree came westward to the fort.

On the parapet a lookout turned at intervals, scanning the land for signs of any trouble from the Hottentots, and the sea for the English or Portuguese ships that might some day attempt to capture the little Dutch settlement. Since the fort itself now contained only ninety-five men of fighting age, plus nine women and eleven children and the slaves, it was unlikely that any enemy from Europe could be repelled by them and the fifty-one free burghers, but a lookout was maintained nevertheless, and now he spotted Jack coming through the dust.

'Hottentot!'

Commander van Riebeeck ran to the wall and quickly saw that it was his old nemesis Jack, shuffling in with some new chicanery. 'Call the commissioner,' he instructed his orderly, and when Karel was rowed ashore and saw the newcomer, he cried, to Van Riebeeck's irritation, 'That's Jack!'

'How do you know him?'

'We were together in Java.' And he hurried out to meet the little fellow.

They did not embrace, Karel was too studious of his position for that, but they did greet each other with unmistakable warmth. 'I'm to be in charge at Java,' Karel said.

'Cinnamon, nutmeg, tin, cloves,' Jack recited, evoking the days when he had known the Van Doorn brothers at the Compagnie warehouses.

'All that and more,' Karel said proudly.

Blowing out his breath, Jack asked, 'You got any cloves?'

'No,' Karel said with a thin laugh. Together they walked to the fort, where Jack asked, 'Willem, he here too?' When the younger Van Doorn was sent for, with Van Riebeeck in attendance, Jack repeated the proposal he had made many years before.

'Time that you men, Hottentots work together.'

'Fine,' Karel said, sitting stiffly in his big chair. 'If you trade us cattle, we'll—'

'Not that,' Jack said. 'We need our cattle.' He was speaking English with a heavy Portuguese overlay and occasional Dutch words acquired lately—that grand mélange which was on its way to becoming a unique language—but everyone in the room understood him and was able to respond in the same vernacular.

'What, then?' Karel asked.

'I mean, we come here. Live with you. Have pasture here, huts, run your cattle, our cattle.'

Willem broke in: 'Nobody tends cattle better than a Hottentot.'

With considerable disdain Karel stared at his brother. 'Live here? You mean . . . Hottentots living in this fort?'

'They learn trades very rapidly, Karel. Those who become carpenters might live in the fort, or bakers, or shoemakers. Look, he made his own shoes.'

With disdain Karel looked at the shoes, big, misshapen affairs, and they epitomized his view of the Hottentot: capable of mimicking a few outward traces of civilization, but worthy of no serious consideration. He was dismayed at the way the meeting had turned, and without ever addressing himself seriously to Jack's proposal, he returned to the problem of the runaway slaves.

'What you can do for us is organize your people for tracking down our runaways. We'll give you weights of metal for every slave you bring back.'

Jack thought, but did not say: When we hunt, we hunt animals, not men. We're shepherds and cattlemen, and we could help you so much.

'As to the possibility of your moving into the vicinity of the fort,' Karel said with a deprecatory laugh, 'I fear that will never happen.'

'Commander . . .'

'He's the commander,' Karel said, indicating Van Riebeeck. 'I'm the commissioner.'

'Commissioner, sir. You white men need us. Not today maybe. Not tomorrow. But the time comes, you need us.'

'We need you now,' Karel said with a certain generosity. 'We need your help with the slaves. We need your cattle.'

'You need us, Commissioner. To live with you. To do many things.'

'Enough of this.' Van Doorn rose grandly, nodded gravely to his one-time friend, and left the room. He left the fort and returned to the ship, where he penned two recommendations for the Lords XVII that became law at the Cape:

> There must be no social contact with the Hottentots. The easy entrance that some have had to the fortress area must be stopped. In everything that is done, effort must be made to preserve the three distinctions: the Dutchman in command, the imported slave at his service, and the Hottentot in contact with neither. They are not to be used as slaves and are under no circumstances to be taken into any family. I would suggest that a fence be built around the entire Compagnie property. It might not be strong enough to repel invad-

ers, but it would serve the salutary purpose of reminding our people that they are different from the Hottentots, and it would forcefully remind the Hottentots that they can never be our equals. It would also impress upon our people that their job is the replenishing of Compagnie ships and not the exploration of unknown territories. If material for a fence is not available, a hedge of thorns might be considered, for this would keep our men in and the Hottentots out.

Already serious at this moment, and of the gravest potential danger in the future, is the fact that our Dutch are beginning to use the bastard Portuguese tongue adopted by slaves and idlers and petty traders throughout the Eastern Seas. During my stay I noticed the introduction of many words not used in Holland. Some were Madagascan, some Ceylonese, many were Malaccan but most were Portuguese, and if this were to continue, our Dutch language would be lost, submerged in an alien tide, to our detriment and the cheapening of expression. Compagnie servants at the Cape must address their slaves in Dutch. All business must be conducted in Dutch. And especially in family life, conversation must be in Dutch, with children forbidden to speak the language of their amahs.

When these new rules were explained at the fort, Commissioner van Doorn judged his responsibilities discharged, and he instructed his captain to prepare the ship for the long trip to Java.

On the evening before departure, a gala New Year's festival was prepared by Van Riebeeck and his gifted wife, Maria. It was attended by their two nieces, attired in the new dresses Kornelia had brought them, and music was provided by Malaccan slaves. Each item of food had come from the Cape: the stock fish, a leg of mutton, cauliflower, cabbage, corn, beets and pumpkin. The wine, of course, was provided by the ship, taken from casks being transported from France to Java, but as Karel said so gracefully when he proposed the toast: 'Before long, even the wine will come from here.' And he nodded toward his brother.

'Now for the dessert!' Van Riebeeck cried, flushed with the good wine. Clapping his hands, he ordered the slaves to bring in the special dish prepared for this night, and from the kitchen came Deborah, heavy with child, bearing in her two hands a large brown-gold earthen crock, straightsided and with no handles. Looking instinctively at Willem, her grave face expressionless, she awaited a signal from him; with a slight nod of his head he indicated that she must place the pot before Kornelia, and when this was done, and a big spoon provided with nine little dishes, everyone saw with pleasure that it was a most handsome bread pudding, crusty on top and brown, with raisins and lemon peel and orange rind peeking through.

'Our Willem makes it,' Van Riebeeck said proudly as the diners applauded.

'Did you really make this?' Kornelia asked as she poised the spoon above the rounded crust.

'I had to learn,' Willem said.

'But what's in it?'

'We save bits of bread and cake and biscuit. Eggs and cream. Butter and all the kinds of fruit we can find. At the end, of course . . .' He hesitated. 'You wouldn't appreciate this, Kornelia, never having lived in Java . . .' He felt that he was not expressing himself well, and turning to his brother and Van Riebeeck, he concluded rather lamely: 'You Java men will understand. When the sugar's been added and the lemon juice, I dust in a little cinnamon and a lot of nutmeg. To remind us of Java.'

'You're a fine cook, Willem.'

'Someone had to learn,' he said. 'You can't eat fish and mutton four hundred days a year.'

At this curious statement the diners looked at one another, but no one thought to correct the speaker. At some spots in the world the year did have four hundred days, and even a small thing like bread pudding helped alleviate the tedium of those long, lonely days.

When the last wine decanter was emptied, two final conversations occurred. They were monologues, really, for the speakers lectured their listeners without interruption. Karel van Doorn told Commander van Riebeeck, 'You must strive very hard, Jan, to comply with all Compagnie rules. Waste not a single stuiver. Make your people speak Dutch. Fence in the Compagnie property. Discipline your slaves. Get more cattle and start the wine flowing. Because if you take care of our ships, I can assure you that the Lords will reward you with an assignment in Java.' Before Van Riebeeck could respond, Karel added reflectively, 'Didn't the spices in Willem's pudding . . . Well, didn't they remind you of the great days in Ternate and Amboyna? There's no place in the world like Java.'

At this moment Kornelia van Doorn was telling her red-complexioned cousin, 'Katje, help Willem grow his grapes. Because if he succeeds, he'll be in line for promotion. Then you can come to Java.' With a flood of gentleness and affection, she embraced her unlovely cousin and confessed: 'We haven't brought you to a paradise, Katje. But he is a husband and his hut is temporary. If you keep him at his work, you'll both soon be in Java, of that I'm sure.'

When Willem saw how meticulously the vines from France had been packed and learned how carefully they had been tended on the voyage, he felt that these new stocks would invigorate the Cape vineyard; the hedge of young trees was high enough to break the force of those relentless summer winds and he now knew something about setting his rows in the right direction. Before Karel sailed on to Java the vines were well planted, and one of the last entries the commissioner made in his report to the Lords XVII commended Willem for taking viticulture seriously and predicted: Soon they will be sending casks of wine to Java.

His last entry was a remarkable one, often to be quoted in both Amsterdam and Batavia but never to be comprehended there or in South Africa; it dealt with slaves and their propensity for running away. In his stay at the Cape he had listened to three days of detailed testimony on the frequency with which slaves of all kinds—Angolans, Malaccans, Madagascans—ran away. It was a madness, he concluded, which no measures open to the Dutch could eliminate, and he reported to the Lords XVII:

> Neither hunger nor thirst, neither the murderous arrow of the Bushman nor the spear of the Hottentot, neither the waterless desert nor the impassable mountain deters the slave from seeking his freedom. I have therefore directed the officers at the Cape to initiate a series of punishments which will impress the slaves with the fact that they are Compagnie property and must obey its laws. At the first attempt to run away, the loss of an ear. At the next attempt, branding on the forehead and the other ear to be cropped. At the third attempt, the nose to be cut off. And at the fourth, the gallows.

When the *Groote Hoorn* resumed its way to Java, it was decided that since the prompt production of wine loomed so important, Willem ought to have more assistance at the vineyard, so the slave Jango was excused from his duties at the fort. This was a happy decision, because he quickly displayed an aptitude for handling vines, and when the new plants took root, Van Riebeeck felt that the pressing of wine would soon be a reality.

But Jango had the weakness of every man of merit: he wanted to be free. And when Willem recommended that the chains be struck off his slave, 'so that he can move more freely about the vineyard,' Van Riebeeck reluctantly agreed.

'You may be courting trouble,' he warned Willem, but the latter said he felt sure Jango would appreciate this opportunity of working outside the fort and could be trusted.

He was partly right. Without chains, Jango worked diligently, but as soon as the new vines were pruned, he escaped into the wilderness. Two days passed before Willem reported his absence to the fort, where the news caused great agitation. Van Riebeeck was furious with Willem for having delayed the alarm, and in anger dispatched a field force to track down the escapee, but when a muster was taken he found that three other slaves had joined Jango, and their tracks indicated that they were heading directly into Bushmen country, where they would probably be slain. 'And that's the end of Compagnie property,' Van Riebeeck groaned.

But after a three-day search, Jango and the others were discovered huddled at the foot of a small cliff, cold and hungry. When they were roped together and on the march back to the fort, the soldiers began to speculate on how Commissioner van Doorn's draconian laws governing runaways would be enforced. 'You're going to lose your ears,' they told the slaves. 'You know that.' One Dutchman grabbed Jango's left ear and sliced at it with his hand: 'Off it comes!'

But when the lookout at the fort spotted the returning prisoners, and everyone gathered to see the mutilations, they were disappointed, for Van Riebeeck refused to lop off ears: 'I do not disfigure my slaves.' Two assistants argued with him, citing both the new law and the necessity for drastic punishment, but the stubborn little man rejected their counsel. The slaves were moderately whipped, thrown into a corner of the fortress that served as a jail, and kept without food for three days.

Five days after they were released, Jango ran away again, and Willem was summoned to the fort: 'We have reason to believe that the slaves have again made union with the Hottentots. Go find Jack and warn him that this must not continue.'

'And Jango?'

'We'll take care of Jango.'

So Willem went eastward to confer with Jack, while the usual troop of hunters went after Jango, who this time had taken only two others with him. Willem found Jack at a distant site, unwilling to admit that he was in league with the slaves, unwilling to cooperate in any way.

'What do you want?' Willem, exasperated, asked his old friend.

'What I said at the fort. Work together.'

'You heard my brother. That can never happen.'

'More ships will come,' Jack persisted. 'More cattle will be needed.'

Willem's frown ended the conversation. There was no hope that the kind of union Jack was proposing could ever be effected; white men and brown were destined to live their different lives, one the master, one the outcast, and any attempt to bridge the gap would forever be doomed by the characters of the persons involved. The white men would be stolid and stubborn like Willem, or vain and arrogant like Karel; the brown men would be proud and recalcitrant like Jack . . .

A visible shudder raced over Willem's face, for he had been accorded a glimpse of the future. Staring down the long corridor of Cape history—beyond the fortress and the branding of slaves—he saw with tragic clarity the total disappearance of Jack and his Hottentots. They were destined to be engulfed, overswarmed by ships and horses. Tears of compassion came to his eyes and he wanted to embrace this little man with whom he had shared so many strange adventures, but Jack had turned away, rebuffed for the last time. In his ragged English uniform and his big homemade shoes, he was walking alone toward the mountains, never again to approach the Van Doorns with his proposals.

When Willem returned to the fort he found that Jango had been retaken and that the heavy iron chains had been returned to his legs. Henceforth he would work at the vines slowly, dragging monstrous weights behind him. But in spite of this dreadful impediment, he ran away a third time, far to the north, where he survived three weeks prior to his recapture. This time, argued the junior officials, his ears really must be cropped, but once more Van Riebeeck refused to carry out the harsh measures which Commissioner van Doorn had authorized, and one of the commander's subordinates dispatched a secret message to Batavia, informing Karel of this nonfeasance.

The garden-hut in which Katje van Doorn started her married life echoed with an incessant chain of complaints; three were recurrent.

'Why do we have to live in this hut? Why can't we move to the fort?

'Why can't I have four slaves, like the commander's wife?

'How soon can we join Kornelia and your brother in Java?'

Patiently Willem tried to answer each complaint: 'You wouldn't like it at the fort. All those people. What would you do with so many personal slaves? And we'll have to prove that wine can be made here before they let us go to Java.' He deceived her on the last point: he had no desire whatever to return to Java; he had found his home in Africa and was determined to stay.

Katje was not convinced by his arguments, but she did appreciate it when he built a small addition to the hut so that she could have space of her own. Of course, when time came to finish the floor, and he brought in bucketfuls of cow dung mixed with water for her to smooth over the pounded earth not once but many times, she wailed in protest. So he knelt down and did the work for her, producing in time a hard, polished surface not unlike that of weathered pine. It had a cleansing odor too, the clean smell of barnyard and meadow.

He was startled upon learning that Katje had gone to Van Riebeeck, petitioning him for a servant. The commander pointed out that the only woman available was Deborah, adding delicately that it would hardly be proper for this girl to move into their hut, seeing that she was far pregnant, and with Willem's child. To his astonishment, Katje saw nothing wrong in this: 'He's my husband now, and I need help.'

'Quite impossible,' Van Riebeeck said, and Katje's complaints increased.

On the other hand, she was steadfast in tending the new vines, and so it was she who patiently watered the young plantings and wove the straw protections which shielded them from the winds. She watched their growth with more excitement than a mother follows that of a child, and when the older vines at last yielded a substantial crop of pale white grapes, she picked them with joy, placed them almost reverently in the hand press, and watched with satisfaction as the colorless must ran from the nozzle.

She and Willem had only the vaguest concept of how wine was made, but they started the fermentation, and in the end something like wine resulted. When it was carried proudly to the fort, Van Riebeeck took the first taste and wrote in his report to the Lords XVII:

> Today, God be praised, wine has been made from grapes grown at the Cape. From our virgin must, pressed from the young French muscadels you sent us, thirty quarts of rich wine have been made. The good years have begun.

But the next year, when a heavy harvest of grapes made the production of export wine a possibility, it received a harsh reception in Java: 'More vinegar than wine, more slops than vinegar, our Dutch refused it, our slaves could not drink it, and even the hogs turned away.' And because sailors aboard the big East Indiamen rejected it too, the Cape wine did not even help to diminish scurvy.

As a consequence, Willem fell into further disfavor at the fort; his deficiency was harming Van Riebeeck's chances—as well as his—of getting to Java; Katje, sensing this, constantly railed at him to master the tricks of wine-making, but there was no one from whom he could learn, and the pressings of 1661 were just as unpalatable as those at the start.

Willem had toiled faithfully at the vineyard and deemed himself eligible to become a free man, but he had to acknowledge that the Compagnie retained total control over all he did, so three times he prayerfully petitioned the commander for permission to proclaim himself a burgher, and three times Van Riebeeck refused, for his own release from this semi-prison depended largely upon Willem's success.

'You're needed where you are,' Van Riebeeck said.

'Then give me another slave to help propagate the vines.'

'You have Jango.'

'Then strike off his chains . . . so he can really work.'

'Won't he run away again?'

'He has a woman now.'

Willem said these words with pain, for on those days when Katje upbraided him most sorely, he could not refrain from contemplating what his life might have been like had the Compagnie allowed him to marry Deborah. On trips to the fort he would see her with her two half-white sons, moving through her tasks with placid gentleness as she softly sang to herself, and he would return to his hut and by candlelight finger through the great Bible until he came to that passage in Judges which the ship captain had read to him during the long passage from Malacca: 'Awake, awake, Deborah, awake, awake, utter a song.' And he would lower his head into his hands and dream of those golden days.

And then one day he learned at the fort that Deborah was pregnant again, not with his child this time but with Jango's, and as an act of compassion for her he insisted that Jango's chains be struck off, and the next day Jango, Deborah and their boys headed for freedom.

It was incomprehensible to the soldiers that these slaves would dare such a venture—pregnant woman and two children—but they were gone, headed north for the most dangerous roaming ground of the Bushmen and their poisons. Van Riebeeck, furious at having been talked into unshackling Jango, ordered a troop of soldiers to bring him back at any cost, and for seven days the fort spoke of little else.

No one was more apprehensive than Willem. He wanted Deborah to survive. He wanted his sons to live into manhood so that they could know this land. And curiously, he hoped that Jango would escape into the freedom he had so courageously sought through all the years of his captivity. Indeed, he felt a companionship with this slave who had tended the grapes so faithfully, dragging his chains behind him. Willem, too, sought freedom, escape from the bitter confines of the fort and its narrow perceptions. No longer did he merely want to be a free burgher; he now wanted absolute freedom, out beyond the flats toward those green hills he had first seen from the crest of Table Mountain fourteen long years ago. He was hungry for openness, and bigness, and at night he prayed that Jango and Deborah would not be taken.

'They caught them!' Katje exulted one morning as she returned from the fort, and against his will he allowed her to take him to the gate when the fugitives were dragged in. Jango was quietly defiant. Deborah, not yet visibly with child, held her head up, her face displaying neither anger nor defeat. It was Van Riebeeck who responded in unexpected ways; he absolutely forbade his soldiers to mutilate the slaves. In his regime there would be no cropping of ears, no branding, no nose lopped off. Back went the chains, on Deborah too, but that was all. Physically, Van Riebeeck was a smaller man than any to whom he gave these orders; morally, he was the finest servant the Compagnie would ever send to the Cape.

The more Willem had observed Van Riebeeck, the higher became his opinion of the man's ability. The Lords XVII had assigned him impossible tasks; like the ancient Israelites, he was supposed to build great edifices with faulty bricks. He was given a dozen things to do, but no funds with which to do them, and he was even begrudged his manpower. When he enticed sailors from passing ships to stay at the Cape, he built his garrison to one hundred and seventy men, but the Lords commanded him to reduce it to one hundred and twenty on the reasonable grounds that they were operating a commercial store and not a burgeoning civil community.

But one unexpected reaction startled Willem: 'I want you, and thirty slaves, and all the free burghers to plant a hedge around our entire establishment. I've been ordered to cut the colony off from that empty land out there.' With a broad gesture of his left hand he indicated all of Africa. 'We'll keep the slaves in and the Hottentots out. We'll protect our cattle and make this little land our Dutch paradise.'

He led Willem and the burghers in seeking the kind of shrub or tree that would make a proper hedge, and at last they found the ideal solution: 'This bitter almond throws a strong prickle. Nothing could penetrate these spikes when the tree grows.'

So a hedge of bitter almond was planted to separate the Cape from Africa.

In 1662 the glorious day arrived when a ship from Amsterdam brought the news that Commander van Riebeeck was at last being transferred to Java. Katje van Doorn immediately wanted to know why she and Willem could not go, too, and was distraught when she learned that Willem had never applied. Upon upbraiding him, she discovered that he had no intention of leaving the Cape: 'I like it here. There's no place for me in Java, with Karel in command.'

'But we must go, and force Karel and Kornelia to find us promotions!'

'I like it here,' Willem said stubbornly, and he refused to plead with Van Riebeeck for a transfer.

The new commander was an extraordinary man, not a Dutchman at all, but one of the many Germans who long ago had sought employment in the Compagnie. He had served in Curaçao, in Formosa, in Canton, in most of the Spice Islands and particularly in Japan, where he had been ambassador-extraordinary that year when more than one hundred thousand persons died during the vast fire that swept the capital city of Edo. When he reported to the Cape he was a weak, sickly, irritable man, much plagued with gout and a moody disposition. During the days of interregnum, when Van Riebeeck was making his farewells but before his replacement assumed command, the German behaved circumspectly. He had a German wife who had mastered the complexities of Compagnie rule, and together they studied conditions at the Cape. They were therefore well prepared to take charge as soon as their predecessor left. Especially they intended to halt—and punish—the evil and costly flight of slaves.

So on the day that Van Riebeeck sailed, his eyes aglow with visions of Java, the new commander faced the problem of a slave who had fled to join a Hottentot camp but had been recaptured by horsemen galloping across the flats. As soon as the escapee was brought within the fortress walls, the commander ordered that his left ear be chopped off and both cheeks branded.

A few days later another slave was caught eating a cabbage grown in the Compagnie gardens; he was promptly flogged and branded, after which both ears were chopped off and heavy chains attached to his legs, 'not to be removed for the duration of his life.' When similar punishments were meted out to other recalcitrant blacks, Willem slipped into the fort to talk surreptitiously with Jango and Deborah: 'I know you still seek freedom. For the love of God, don't risk it.'

Jango, sitting with Willem's two sons on his knees, laughed easily. 'When the time comes, we'll go.'

'The chains! Jango, they'll catch you before sunset.'

'Of course we'll go,' Deborah said quietly, and Willem looked at her in astonishment. He had lived with her, had sired two children with her, and had known almost nothing about her. He had assumed that because she had a quiet, placid face and spoke softly that her heart was placid too. It had never occurred to him that she hated slavery as much as Jango, and it appalled him to think that she would risk losing her ears and having her face branded, just to be free.

'Deborah! Think of what they might do to you,' he pleaded, but she merely looked at him, her eyes resolute, her face immobile. Finally she placed her hand on his and said, 'I will not remain a slave.'

On his way back to his hut he prayed: Oh, Jesus, help them come to their senses. But one night when the guards were inattentive, the four slaves set forth once more.

When they were dragged back, the new commander ordered everyone in the little settlement to assemble for the punishment: 'Jango, for the fifth time you have tried to escape your dutiful labors, depriving the Compagnie of its property.' Willem felt sick, wondering what awful thing was about to be done, but when he turned his ashen face to Katje, he saw that she was stretching forward to watch the proceedings.

'Jango, you are to have your ears lopped. You are to have your nose lopped. You are to be branded forehead and cheeks, and you are to carry chains for the rest of your life. Deborah, twice you have run away. You are to be branded forehead and cheeks, and shall wear chains for the rest of your life. Adam and Crisme, you are slaves—'

'No!' Willem shouted. The commander turned to take note of who had interrupted him. An aide whispered that this was the father of the two boys, which angered the commander even more: 'You are slaves, and you are to be branded on the forehead.'

'No!' Willem shouted again, determined that such dreadful punishment not be visited upon his children, but two soldiers pinioned him, and the sentences were executed.

A week later the slave Bastiaan stole a sheep belonging to the Compagnie and was hanged, and now the new commander had time to study the case of Willem van Doorn. He learned that he was the younger brother of the powerful Karel van Doorn, but he also learned that Karel had little regard for his brother and knew him to be troublesome. He knew that on four occasions Willem had petitioned to become a free burgher, stating that he had no desire to work endlessly for the Compagnie, and at the punishment he had, of course, behaved disgracefully. Here was a man begging for discipline, and the commander was determined that he receive it.

'Willem van Doorn,' he said at the public sentencing, 'you've been a disruptive influence. You've consorted with slaves. You were seen only last week slipping in to the slave quarters, and you require discipline. The horse, two days.'

'Oh, no!' Katje pleaded, but the words had been spoken, so Willem was grabbed and bound, while two heavy bags of lead pellets were attached to his ankles. The high wooden horse was dragged in and stationed where everyone could witness, and four men held him aloft while two others kept his legs pulled apart.

In the moment that he was held thus suspended, the mutilated slaves Jango and Deborah were brought forth to watch, and for the first time Willem saw the hideous face of the man, the deeply scarred face of the woman he had loved. 'No!' he screamed, and all who heard, except Jango and Deborah, supposed that he was protesting the cruel punishment he was about to receive.

'Now!' the commander called, and he was dropped. The pain was so terrible that he fainted.

When he recovered, it was night and he was alone, chained to the horse whose rough edges tore sullenly at his crotch, spreading it, cutting it, wounding it horribly. If he moved to alleviate the pain, new areas were affected. Against his will deep groans escaped, and when he tried to move to a new position, the awful weights on his legs pulled him back.

Twice that night he fainted, partly from the pain, partly from the vicious cold that swept in from the bay. When he awakened, he began to shiver, and by the time the dull sun rose, he was feverish.

Residents of the fort came to mock him, satisfied that he deserved what he was getting. They had envied him his home at the garden, the fact that he had a wife and they didn't, and his relationship to a powerful brother in Java. They noticed that he was shivering, and one woman said, 'He has the ague. They all do after the first day.'

That afternoon, when the wind rose, his fever intensified so that when dusk came, with rain whipping in from the bay, he was in grave danger. His wife, unwilling to visit him while others were mocking him, crept up to the horse and whispered, 'How goes it, Willem?' and he replied through chattering teeth, 'I'll live.'

The fact that he had said this made Katje suspect that he would not, so she forced her way into the commander's office and said, 'You're killing him, and Karel van Doorn will learn of this.'

'Are you threatening me?'

'I am indeed. I am the niece of Claes Danckaerts, and he's a man of some importance in Amsterdam. Take my husband down.'

The commander knew enough of Compagnie politics to appreciate the influences that might be brought against him if a determined Dutch family declared war upon a German hireling, and from the manner in which Katje spoke, he suspected that she would pursue her threat, so against his own best judgment he put on a cloak and went out into the storm.

He found Willem unconscious, his body trembling with fever, and when he twice failed to rouse him, he gave the brusque order: 'Cut him down.'

The stiff body was carried to the garden-hut and placed on the dung-polished floor, where Katje brought him slowly back to consciousness: 'You're home. It's over, Willem.' And their love, awkward and strained as it would always be, dated from that moment.

The ordeal of the wooden horse had a powerful impact on Willem van Doorn. For one thing, it crippled him; he would always walk with his body slightly twisted, his left leg not functioning like his right. And he would be susceptible to colds, a deep bronchial malaise affecting him each winter. An even more powerful result, however, was that he began to frequent the smithy in the fort, stealing pieces of equipment, which he kept sequestered behind the shed in which the vines were grafted.

One evening, when he had assembled a heavy hammer, a chisel and a bar for prying, he grasped Jango's arm as he dragged his chains homeward. Without speaking, he kicked aside a covering of grass, displaying the cache. Jango said nothing, but his eyes showed Willem his gratitude.

It was not easy to look at Jango. Instead of ears he had lumpy wounds. His face, lacking a nose, lost all definition. And the three bold scars on forehead and cheeks imprisoned the glance of anyone who saw that ugly, repulsive face. Willem looked only at the eyes, which glowed.

The two men never confided in each other. Jango refused to tell Willem what his precise plans were, or how he would carry out his final attempt. The instruments for his freedom lay there under the grape cuttings and would be called upon when time was proper, but how and where he would cut away his chains and Deborah's, neither man knew.

Then one afternoon, half an hour before sunset, Jango quietly quit his work and dragged his chains to the grafting shed, removed the covering grass and wrapped the chisel in a canvas bag. With strong blows, well muffled, he cut the chains that bound his legs, then tied them inconspicuously back together. Secreting the tools under his sweaty shirt, he walked unconcernedly past Willem, as he always did at close of day, and for a brief moment the two men looked at each other, one with face terribly scarred, the other with heart in turmoil. It was the last time they would ever be in contact, black and white, and tears came to Willem's eyes, but Jango refused to allow emotion to touch him. Clutching his tools, he moved toward the fort.

'You're very nervous,' Katje said when her husband limped in to supper, and when he stayed for a long time reading his Bible, she said, 'Willem, come to bed.' Desperately he wanted to go to the fort, to stand upon the wall, to witness how Jango and Deborah and the boys made their escape, and where her chains would be struck off, but he knew that he must betray nothing. He was not afraid of the punishment that would be meted out to him if the commander deduced his role in this escape; he was afraid only for Jango and Deborah and his sons. At nine, when Katje went to bed, she saw her husband still at his Bible, his head lowered as if in prayer.

They fled into the desert lands northeast of the fort, Jango the black from Angola, Deborah the brown from Malaya, Adam and Crisme, half-brown, half-white, and the baby girl Ateh, half-black, half-brown. When they were well away from the hedge of bitter almond, Jango struck off his wife's chains, then discarded his own, but she picked them up, thinking that they would be useful in trading with the Hottentots or Bushmen.

This time they escaped. As they entered into a wilderness unknown, uncharted, they exemplified that reverberating report of Karel van Doorn:

> Neither hunger nor thirst, neither the murderous arrow of the Bushman nor the spear of the Hottentot, neither the waterless desert nor the impassable mountain deters the slave from seeking his freedom.

They survived, and in time the descendants of Adam and Crisme and thousands like them would not have to flee to freedom bound in chains. They would be able to live in places like Cape Town, where they would come to know a greater bondage, for they would be stigmatized as Coloured. They would be preached against by predikants, because they would be living testimony to the fact that in the beginning days whites had cohabited with brown and black and yellow: 'They are God's curse upon us for the evils we have done.' The land of their birth would be the home of their sorrow, and they would be entitled to no place in society, to no future that all agreed upon, but they would forever be a testimony.

The German commander was not really sorry about the disappearance of Jango and the Malayan girl. Had they been apprehended, he would have had to hang them, and there would be the ugly question of the three children, two with those heavy scars upon their foreheads.

Nor was he especially concerned when spies informed him that Willem van Doorn was showing signs that he might be preparing to quit the colony to head eastward for a farm of his own: 'He's building a wagon. He's putting aside any objects that fall his way. And he's collected more grape rootings than he needs for his fields.'

'When the time comes, we'll let him go. He's a troublemaker and he belongs out there with the Hottentots.'

In 1664, when one of the homeward fleets brought to the Cape an unexpected visitor, the German commander was pleased that he had not overreacted in Willem's case, because the visitor was Karel van Doorn, bringing the exciting news that he had been summoned home to become one of the Lords XVII. 'My father-in-law had something to do with it,' he said modestly. 'He's Claes Danckaerts, you know, the wealthy merchant.' He moved into the fort with considerable pomp, followed by Kornelia and her two children dressed in lace and satin. Celebrations were held for five nights, during which the commander confided that he was exhausted by this damned Cape, and that he hoped Karel would do everything possible to get him transferred to Java.

'I know how you feel,' Karel said. 'Van Riebeeck told me the same when I was last here. This is certainly no place for a man with ambitions.'

'What's Van Riebeeck doing?'

'Like everyone else, he wanted the supreme job.' Here Karel smiled weakly at the commander. 'But no one from the Cape would ever be given that.'

'What's he doing?'

'Governor of Malacca. And there he'll stay.'

'But at least he's near Java.'

'And you shall be, too. Not near it. In it.'

The commander sighed and started dreaming of that fortunate day when he would again be back in civilization. But he was interrupted when Karel asked, 'What's this I hear about my brother?'

The commander supposed that Karel was referring to the incident of the horse, and said, 'As you know, out of compassion I had him taken down—'

'I mean, his making himself a free burgher.'

'We'd never permit anyone to make such a decision on his own,' the commander said quickly.

'But might it not be a good idea to get him out of here?'

The commander, having served in foreign capitals, recognized a devious suggestion when he heard it: Good God, he's trying to get rid of his brother. Why?

He never discovered Karel's reason for proposing that Willem be allowed, even encouraged, to leave the fort. For some undisclosed family complication, it was to Karel's advantage to get rid of Willem, and sending him into the assegais of the Hottentots might be the most practical way. Maps were produced, sketchy affairs which represented almost nothing correctly, and the two men selected an area where a frontier post might profitably be established, supposing that Willem survived the bleak initial travel and the threats of Bushmen and Hottentots.

It lay to the east, where a lively river debouched from the first range of mountains; exploring parties had commented upon it favorably, and here Karel outlined an area of some sixty morgen: 'Let him try to raise his grapes there. God knows we could use the wine.'

'How was the last batch he sent to Java?'

'Barely acceptable for the hospital. But each year it gets a little better.'

When arrangements were completed, the two officials summoned Willem, who limped sideways into the fort. 'Willem! We've great news!'

'How's Mother?'

'Oh, she died two years ago.'

'Her house? The garden?'

'The Compagnie took it back. It was theirs, you know.'

'Did she . . . was she in pain?'

'She died easily. Now, what we wanted to see you about . . . You tell him, Commander.'

The German said, 'We are going to allow you to become a free burgher. Far across the flats. Here.'

'That's about where I've decided to go,' Willem said softly.

The two officials ignored this rebuke to their authority. 'Look!' Karel said. 'We're giving you sixty morgen.'

'You don't need sixty morgen to grow grapes. I could do it on twenty.'

'Willem!' Karel said with some harshness. 'Anytime the Compagnie offers you something free, take it.'

'But I can't farm it.'

'Take it!' Karel shouted. A Lord XVII was offering a laborer sixty morgen of the choicest land, and the laborer was raising objections. This Willem was beyond salvation; the only good thing about this visit was learning that his brother's two bastard children had vanished somewhere in the desert. It reminded him of Hagar—but did her bastards die?

The meeting between Katje and her cousin Kornelia was equally cold, and shrewd Katje warned her husband, 'There's something wrong about them, Willem. They've done something wrong and are ashamed to see us.' She brooded about this for some time, then one evening at supper snapped her fingers: 'Willem, they've sold your mother's house and are keeping the money to themselves.'

'Let them have it,' Willem said, but Katje was the niece of a merchant, and it galled her to think that she might have been defrauded of property that was duly hers, or at least her husband's, so she went to the ship and confronted the older Van Doorns: 'Did you sell your mother's property?'

'No,' Karel said carefully.

'What happened to it?'

'It was Compagnie property. You know that. Like the house you're living in—'

'It's a hut.'

'But it's Compagnie property.'

'I think you sold—'

'Katje!' Kornelia said sharply. 'You forget yourself. You forget that you were a poor farm girl—'

'Kornelia, you're a thief. You're stealing Willem's share.'

'We will hear no more!' The commissioner did not intend to sit by and listen to a member of his own family, an impoverished member at that, charging him with defalcations. 'Take her back to shore,' he directed the sailors, and during the remainder of the visit he refused to meet with his brother.

His farewell was a gala. There were fulsome speeches from the German commander and his staff, gracious responses from Karel and his wife. The new Lord XVII, the first to have had extended experience in the East, assured his listeners that the Compagnie would always have close to its heart the welfare of the Cape:

> 'We're going to find you additional settlers, not too many, never more than two hundred living here. It was I who proposed the hedge, and it seems a salient idea. Makes this a comfortable little establishment with enough room for your cattle and vegetables. I'm told that my brother Willem, whom you know favorably, is heading eastward to see if he can make some real wine instead of vinegar. [Laughter] But his going must not suggest a precedent. Your task is here, at this fort, which the Lords XVII have decided to rebuild in stone. As Abraham brought his people to their new home and made it prosper, so you have established your home here at the Cape. Make it prosper. Make it yield a profit for the Compagnie. So that when you return to Holland you will be able to say, "Job well done." '

Three days after Karel departed for Amsterdam and his duties as a Lord XVII, Willem started loading his wagon. After providing space for Katje and their son, Marthinus, he tucked in grape cuttings, the tools he had taken from the smithy, all household goods required by Katje, and two items which were of supreme importance to him: the brassbound Bible and the brown-gold crock in which he baked his bread puddings. Without them a home in the wilderness would be impossible.

As he did his packing, he heard from Katje a constant whine of complaints: 'You're taking too many grape vines. You'll never use that chisel.' And he would have shown his irritation at this cascade of words except for one thing: he had grown to love this petulant, difficult woman, for he had seen that when family interests were involved, she could be a lioness, and he sensed that on the frontier she would prove invaluable. Like a chunk of hard oak that grows to appreciate the rasp that grinds it down and makes it usable and polished, so he appreciated his wife.

Before the loaded wagon could reach the trail, it had to penetrate the hedge of bitter almond, and normally it would have gone down the farm road past the fort to the exit, but Willem had no intention of subjecting Katje and Marthinus to the crowd's derision. Instead, he chopped down four bushes, breaking his own path, and when spies reported this vandalism to the commander, they expected him to order Willem's arrest, but the commander knew something the spies did not: that the Honorable Commissioner, Karel van Doorn, wanted his abrasive brother lost in the wilderness.

'Let them go,' he said with disgust as they headed for more spacious lands.

IV. The Huguenots

I N the year 1560 in the little village of Caix in the northern wine region,
when Mary, the future Queen of Scots, was Queen of France, society was
well and traditionally organized. There was the Marquis de Caix, who
owned the vineyards, as petty a nobleman as France provided, but petty
only in land and money; in spirit he was a most gallant man, survivor of
three wars and always prepared for a fourth or a seventh. He was tall, slim,
handsomely mustached, and with a goatee of the kind that would in later
days represent the France of this period. He could not afford dashing
clothes, nor caparisons for his two horses, but he did take pride in his
swords and pistols, the true accouterments of a gentleman. His great weakness, for a man in his position, was that he read books and pondered affairs
that occurred in places like Paris, Madrid and Rome, for this distracted him
from his local responsibilities, and his vineyards did not flourish.

Abbé Desmoulins, the priest of Caix, had infirmities almost as disabling.
An older man who had seen the sweep of battle, he had been deeply affected
by religious events in Germany and Geneva; the preachings of those two
difficult Catholics Martin Luther and John Calvin disturbed him, for he saw
in the fulminations of the former a justified challenge to the sloppiness of
the church as he knew it, and in the transcendant logic of the latter, an
answer to the confusions he was finding in religion as it operated in France.
Had he stumbled into a curacy controlled by some unlettered nobleman
secure in his faith, the Abbé Desmoulins would probably have remained in
line, preached a standard religion, and died without ever having come to
grips with either Luther or Calvin. He had the bad luck to find himself in
a village dominated by a marquis whose faith was as mercurial as his
military exploits, and in a subtle way these two leaders agitated each other,
so that the village of Caix was in a rather tenuous position.

Head of the vineyards was a stalwart, conservative, taciturn semi-peas-
ant named Giles de Pré, thirty years old and the father of three children

who already worked with him in the fields, even though the youngest was
only five. De Pré was a wonderfully solid man with an uncanny comprehension of agriculture. 'You're an oak tree yourself,' his wife often said. 'If the
pigs rooted at your feet, they'd find truffles.' Like many farmers around
Caix, the De Prés could read, and it was their pleasure to work their way
through the French Bible the marquis had given them, noting with satisfaction that many of the noblest figures in that history had been associated with
vineyards. But as they read, especially in the Old Testament, they acquired
a suspicion that human lives had once been arranged somewhat better than
they were now. In the days of Abraham or David or Jeremiah, society had
known a sanctity which was now vanished; in those days men lived intimately with God, and rulers were acquainted with their subjects. Priests
were devoted to great principles, and there was reverence in the air. Today
things were much different, and even if the marquis did rule the area, it was
with a most unsteady hand.

That was the village of Caix, in the year 1560: a marquis who could not
be depended upon except in battle; a priest who had lost the assurances of
his youth; and a farmer whose reading of the Bible confused him. It was
to such men throughout France that John Calvin dispatched his emissaries
from Geneva.

'Dr. Calvin is a Frenchman, you understand,' one of these austere
visitors explained to the Marquis de Caix. 'He's a loyal Frenchman, and
would be living here except that he made an unfortunate speech.'

'Why has he fled to Geneva?'

'Because that city has placed itself in his hands. It thirsts to be ruled
by the institutes of God.' At this mention the emissary said, 'Of course,
you've read Dr. Calvin's remarkable summary of his beliefs?' The marquis
hadn't, and it was in this way that one of the greatest books in the history
of man's search for religious truth, John Calvin's *Institutes of the Christian
Religion,* reached Caix.

It was a profound book, written with strokes of lightning when Calvin
was only twenty-six and published widely the next year. It was beautifully
French, so clear in its logic that even the tamest mind could find excitement
in its handsomely constructed thought. Martin Luther in Germany had
made wild, explosive charges which repelled thoughtful men, while John
Knox in Scotland had raged and roared in a way that often seemed ridiculous, but Calvin in Geneva, patiently and with sweet reason, spread out the
principles of his thought and with irrefutable clarity invited his readers to
follow him to new light springing from old revelation.

But it was also revolutionary, 'like nine claps of thunder on a clear
night,' the Geneva man said when handing over the book, and he
enumerated Calvin's shocking rejections: 'First, he rejects the Mass as
an accretion in no way connected with our Lord. Second, he rejects
compulsory confession as an ungodly intrusion. Third, he dismisses all
saints. Fourth, their relics. Fifth, their images. Sixth, he denies out of
hand that the Virgin Mary enjoys any special relationship to either God
or man. Seventh, he has abolished all monasteries and nunneries as
abominations. Eighth, he rejects priests as power-grasping functionaries.
And ninth, it must be obvious by now that he rejects the Pope in Rome

as unnecessary to the operation of God's church in France.'

The marquis was hesitant about accepting so radical a doctrine, but when he passed the *Institutes* along to the abbé, he confided, 'What I like about Calvin's system is the way it works with civil government to create a stable, just social order. I've become really irritated by the confusions in our land.' He was correct in assuming that Calvin sponsored civil order, for in Geneva he taught that the governance of his church must rest with four groups of serious men: first, a body of brilliant doctors to explicate theology and prescribe how men and women ought to behave; second, clergymen to interpret this theology to the general public; third, a body of all-powerful elders to assume responsibility for the church's survival and act as watchdogs of the community's behavior, and when they uncover a miscreant, turn him or her over to the city magistrates for civil punishment; fourth, a collection of deacons to perform God's great work of collecting alms, running orphanages, teaching children and consoling the sick.

'I like his sense of order,' the marquis said.

'Where would you fit in?' his priest asked.

'Certainly not a doctor. I'm a stupid man, really. I could never learn Greek, let alone Hebrew. And I'd not be pastor, that's certain.' When he shrugged his shoulders, the priest laughed, recalling the scrapes this handsome man had engineered.

'I don't think I'd like to be an elder,' the marquis continued. 'The women, you know. I'm not intended to be a watchdog of other people's morals. But I could be a deacon. I could work for the welfare of a system like Calvin's.' He paused to reflect upon the fact that for most of his life he had been just this, a man trying to help where needed. 'Yes,' he said loudly, 'I could be a deacon.' Then he burst into laughter. 'But I'd want to be very careful who the elders were. I don't want to enforce the rules of some damned snoop-snoot.'

When the Abbé Desmoulins returned the *Institutes* to the marquis he was deeply worried: 'The four orders we spoke about I understand. They're needed to ensure civil tranquillity and order in the church. But the doctrine that even prior to birth all men are divided between the few who are saved and the many who are perpetually damned . . . That's very unCatholic.'

'I knew you'd have trouble with that,' the marquis said eagerly. 'I did myself.'

He led the priest to a corner of the garden, where under branching trees beside a low stone wall erected some three hundred years earlier the two men analyzed this fundamental doctrine of the burgeoning religion, and the marquis offered the bald, simplified interpretation of Calvin's thought that was gaining currency among non-theological groups: 'It conforms to human experience, Abbé. In this village you and I can name men who were saved from birth and others who were doomed from the moment the womb opened. Such men are damned. God has put his thumb upon them and they are damned, and you know it and so do I.'

'Yes,' the priest said slowly, 'they are damned, and proof of their damnation is visible. But by faith they can be saved.'

'No!' the marquis said sharply. 'There is to be no more of this salvation by faith.'

'You speak as if you'd accepted the teachings of Calvin.'

'I think I have. It's a man's religion. It's a religion for all of us who want to move forward. There are the saved who do the work of the world. There are the damned who stumble through life headed only for a waiting grave.'

'And you're one of the saved?'

'I am.'

'How do you know?'

'Because God has given signs. This vineyard. My castle. My high position in this village. Would He have given me these if He did not intend to assign me to some great task?'

But when the abbé studied the *Institutes* with his background of religious speculation, he found that Calvin had preached no such fatalistic doctrine. Only God in the secrecy of His wisdom and compassion knew who was saved and who not, and high estate on earth was unrelated to one's ultimate estate in heaven. All children were to be baptized, because all had an equal hope for salvation: 'But I judge that most will not be saved, according to Dr. Calvin.'

An assignment which would encourage the marquis to believe that he was among the saved was at hand, for when the king in Paris heard of the growth of Calvinism in the towns along the Flemish border, he dispatched a Catholic general at the head of twelve hundred stout Catholic yeomen, and they lashed about the countryside, maiming and killing, and leading errant Protestants back into the customary fold. In late 1562, with the boy king dead and Mary on her way back to Scotland a widow, the Marquis de Caix rallied two hundred of his men who had never heard of John Calvin or Geneva, either, and marched forth to do battle. It should have been a rout, twelve hundred against two, but the marquis was so able in the saddle and so grand a leader to his men that they repelled the invaders, chasing them fifteen miles south and inflicting heavy damages.

Among the foot soldiers who routed the Catholics was the wine-maker, Giles de Pré, who, when he returned home weary and triumphant, announced to his wife that he was now a Huguenot. When she asked what this word meant, he could not explain, nor could he tell her what his new religion stood for, nor had he heard of the *Institutes,* or Geneva. But he knew with striking clarity what his decision entailed: 'It's an end of priests. No more bishops shouting at us what to do. That big monastery, we'll close it down. People will behave themselves, and there will be order.'

Slowly the village of Caix became a Huguenot center, but with almost none of the changes predicted by De Pré in effect. The good Abbé Desmoulins continued as before, arguing forcefully with the marquis against the theory of predestination. When the bishop arrived from Amiens he thundered in the same old way, except that now he fulminated against Calvin and the Huguenots. In 1564 John Calvin, the most significant Frenchman of his era, died in Geneva, but his influence continued to spread.

In 1572 the Marquis de Caix, veteran of nine battles in which Huguenots confronted royal armies, decided to visit Geneva to see for himself what changes Calvinism sponsored when it actually commanded a society, and with his chief farmer Giles de Pré, set out on horseback for the distant city. Any Huguenot had to be careful these days in traveling about France, for that old tigress Catherine de Medici waged ceaseless war against them, even though she had long since ceased being the legal queen; and if a Protestant like the Marquis de Caix, with his powerful military reputation, dared to move about, he was apt to be pursued by a real army and slain on the spot. So the two travelers moved cautiously, like two rambling farmers, eastward toward Strasbourg, then south to Besançon and across the low mountains into Geneva.

The visit was a disaster. The free-and-easy marquis found that Calvin's successors were terrified lest their Protestant Rome, as some called it, be overturned by Catholic princes storming up from the south. Extreme caution ruled the city, with synods condemning men to be burned for theological transgressions. When the marquis, wearied by his long journey, sought some inn where he could employ the services of a maid to ease his bones and comfort him, the innkeeper turned deathly pale: 'Please, monsieur, do not even whisper . . .'

'You must have some girls?'

The innkeeper placed his two hands upon the wrist of his guest and said, 'Sir, if you speak like that again, the magistrates . . .' He indicated that at some spot not far from there—where, he never knew—there would be spies: 'Catholics trying to destroy our city. Protestants ready to trap men like you.'

'I seek some merriment,' the marquis said.

'In Geneva there is no merriment. Now eat, and say your prayers, and go to bed. The way we do.'

Wherever they moved, the two Frenchmen encountered this sense of heavy censorship, and it was understandable. The city, inspired by fear of a Catholic attack on the one hand and Calvin's severe Protestantism on the other, had evolved what later historians would describe as 'that moral reign of terror.'

'This is not what I had in mind,' the marquis confided to his farmer. 'I think we had better quit this place while we have four legs between us. These maniacs would chop a man in half . . . and all because he smiled at a pretty girl.'

They slipped away from Geneva without ever having announced themselves to the authorities, and during the long ride back home they often halted at the edge of some upland farm, sitting beneath chestnut trees as they discussed what they had seen. 'The trouble must rest with Geneva,' the marquis said. 'We're not like that in France, spies and burnings.'

'The good far outweighs the bad,' De Pré argued. 'Perhaps they have to do this until the others are disposed of.'

'I caught the feeling they were doing it because they liked to do it.'

The travelers reached no conclusion, but the marquis's suspicions deepened, and he might have changed his mind about Protestantism as the solution to the world's evils had he not become aware that along the roads of France there was a considerable movement of messengers scurrying here and there, and he began to wonder if perchance they were looking for him. 'What are they after?' he asked De Pré, but the farmer could not even make a sensible guess.

Since it was mid-August, there was no necessity to frequent towns or cities in search of accommodation, so the men slept in fields, keeping away from traveled routes, and in this way moved across northern France toward the outskirts of Rheims. On the morning of August 25 they deemed it safe to enter a small village north of that city, and as they did so, they found the populace in a state of turmoil. Houses were aflame and no one was endeavoring to save them. Two corpses dangled from posts, their bowels cut loose. A mob chased a woman, caught up with her, and trampled her to death. Other fires were breaking out and general chaos dominated the village.

'What happens here?' the marquis called as one of the rioters rushed past with a flaming brand.

'We're killing all Protestants!' the man cried as he ran to a house whose inhabitants he did not like.

'Careful, careful!' the marquis whispered as he led his horse gingerly into the center of the rioting. 'Why are you hanging him?' he shouted to members of a mob about to throw a rope over the lower branches of a tree.

'Huguenot.'

'On whose orders?'

'Messengers from Paris. We're killing them everywhere. Cleansing the country.'

'Sir,' De Pré whispered. 'I think we should ride on.'

'I think not,' the marquis said, and with a sudden spur to his horse he swept down upon the rioters, knocked them aside, and grabbed the doomed man by his shoulders, striving vainly to swing him to safety. The man's feet were lashed so that he could not help himself, and he would have been stamped to death by the mob had not De Pré dashed in, grabbed him by the thighs, and galloped off beside the marquis.

When they were well out into the country they halted, and the nobleman asked the bound man what had taken place. 'Midnight, without warning, they leaped upon us. I hid in my barn.'

'Huguenot?'

'The same. My wife hanged. They had a list of every Protestant and tried to kill us all.'

'What will you do?'

'What can I do?'

'You can come with us. We're Huguenots too.'

The frightened man rode with De Pré until they reached an isolated farm, where the marquis asked, 'Is this a good Catholic farm?'

'It is indeed,' the owner said.

'Good. We'll take that horse. We're Huguenots.'

It would be remembered in history as St. Bartholomew's Day, that awful August massacre which the Italian queen mother, Catherine de Medici, instigated to destroy Protestantism once and for all. In cities and towns across France, the followers of Calvin were knifed and stabbed and hanged and burned. Tens of thousands were slain, and when the joyous news reached Rome, Pope Gregory XIII exulted, and a cardinal gave the exhausted messenger who had brought the news across the Alps a reward of one thousand thalers. A medal was struck, showing the Pope on one side, an avenging angel on the other castigating heretics with her sword. In Spain, King Philip II, who would soon be losing his Armada to Protestant sailors from England and Holland, dispatched felicitations to Catherine on her meritorious action: 'This is one of the greatest joys of my entire life.' Lesser people celebrated in lesser ways.

Even in a village as remote as Caix the slaughter raged, and if the marquis and his farmer had been at home that fateful night, they would have been slain. As it was, the marquis' barns were burned, his vineyards ravaged; and Giles de Pré's wife was hacked into four pieces. It was a fearful devastation, one of the worst in French history, and its hideous memory would remain engraved on the soul of every Huguenot who survived.

Some did. The Marquis de Caix resumed his residence in the village, always ready to sally forth on whatever new battle engaged his fellow Protestants. Giles de Pré married again, and took as his assistant in the refurbished vineyards the man he had helped rescue at Rheims. And in due course the Abbé Desmoulins found that he was more attuned to the sober precepts of John Calvin than to the rantings of his bishop at Amiens; like hundreds of priests in Huguenot areas, he changed his religion, becoming a stout defender of his new faith.

In this quiet way the village of Caix became again solidly Huguenot, and in 1598 held joyful celebrations when that fine and sensible king, Henry IV, issued the Edict of Nantes, assuring the Huguenots that they would henceforth enjoy liberty of conscience and even the right to hold public worship in certain specified locations outside towns. And as far as Paris was concerned, no closer than twenty miles.

The De Pré family continued as wine-makers, servants to the successive Marquis de Caix, until that fatal year of 1627 when the last marquis rode off to help defend the Huguenot city of La Rochelle against the Catholic armies that were besieging it. He fought gallantly, and died amidst a circle of enemy swords, but with him died his title; no longer did Caix have a marquis.

In later years members of the De Pré family stayed with their vineyards and the church started by Calvin, but never did these rural people descend to the harshness practiced at Geneva or to the burnings conducted there. French Calvinism was a quiet, stable, often beautiful religion in which a human being, from the moment he was conceived, was registered in God's great account book as either saved or damned. He would never know which, but if life smiled on him and his fields prospered, there had to be a supposition that he was among the saved. Therefore, it behooved a man to work diligently, for this indicated that he was eligible to be chosen.

This curious theology had a salutary effect in Caix: any person who presumed that he was among the elect had to behave himself for two reasons. If he was saved, it would be shameful for him to behave poorly, for this would reflect upon God's judgment; and if God saw him misbehaving, He might reverse His decision and place the offender among the damned. Prayer on Wednesday, church at ten on Sunday, prayer at seven Sunday evening was the weekly routine, broken only when some fanatical Catholic priest from a nearby city would storm into Caix and rant about the freedoms the heretical Huguenots were enjoying. Then there might be insurgency, with soldiers rioting and offering to slay all Protestants, but this would be quickly suppressed by the government, with the inflammatory priest being scuttled off to some less volatile area.

In 1660, when even these sporadic eruptions had become a distant memory and when all France glowed from the glories attendant upon King Louis XIV, the De Pré family celebrated the birth of a son named Paul. With the extinction of Marquis de Caix's title, distant female relatives had sold off the vineyards and the De Prés had acquired some of the choicest fields. At ten, young Paul knew how to graft plants in the field and supervise their grapes when they were brought in for pressing. The De Pré fields produced a crisp white wine, not of top quality but good enough to command local respect, and Paul learned each step that would ensure its reputation.

He was a sober lad who at fifteen seemed already a man. He wore a scarf about his neck the way old men did and was fastidiously careful of his clothes, brushing them several times a day and oftener on Wednesdays and Sundays. At sixteen, he astonished his parents by becoming in effect a deacon; he wasn't one, technically, but he helped regulate life in the community and served as visitor to families needing financial help.

'I should like to be an elder one day,' he told his parents that year, and he was so serious that they dared not laugh.

They were not surprised when, at the age of eighteen, he announced that he had decided to marry Marie Plon, daughter of a neighboring farmer, and he rejected their suggestion that they accompany him when he went to seek permission of the elders for the marriage. Gravely he stood before the leading men of the community and said, 'Marie and I have decided that we must get on with our lives. We're going to work the old Montelle farm.'

When the elders interrogated him, they found that he had everything planned: when the wedding was to be, how the Montelle farm was to be paid for, and even how many children they proposed to have: 'Three—two boys and a girl.'

'And if God should give you less?'

'I would accept the will of God,' Paul said, and some of the elders laughed. But they approved the marriage, and one man made Paul extremely happy when he said at the conclusion of the interrogation, 'One day you'll be sitting with us, Paul.' It was with difficulty that he refrained from retorting, 'I intend to.'

The marriage took place in 1678, launching the kind of strong, rural family that made France one of the most stable nations in Europe, and promptly, in accordance with the master plan, Marie de Pré gave birth to her first son, then her second. All that was now required was the daughter, and Paul was certain that since God obviously approved of him, a daughter would appear in due time.

But now, once again, there were ominous signs in French society. Devout Catholics were shuddering at the blasphemous liberties allowed Protestants under the Edict of Nantes and pressed for its repudiation. Always assisted by the mistresses who exercised the real power over the kings of France—Henry IV would have fifty-six named and recorded—the clerical faction succeeded in annulling one after another the liberties enjoyed by the Calvinists.

The minister at Caix explained to his congregation the restrictions under which they all now lived: 'You cannot be a teacher, or a doctor, or a town official, even though Caix is mostly of our faith. You have got to show the police that you attend one meeting a month to listen to government attacks on our church. When your parents die, Protestant burial services can be held only at sunset, lest they infuriate the Catholics. If you are heard speaking even one word in public against Rome, you go to jail for a year. And if either you as a citizen or I as a minister try to convert any person to our faith, we can be hanged.'

None of these new laws touched Paul de Pré, and he lived a contented life regardless of the pressures being applied to his community. But in 1683 two events occurred which terrified him. One morning two of the king's soldiers banged on the door and told Marie that they had been billeted to her home, whereupon, pushing her aside, they stamped into the farmhouse, selected a room they liked, and informed her that this would be their quarters.

Marie ran to the vineyard, calling for her husband, and when he reached the house he asked quietly, 'What happens here?'

'Dragooned,' the soldiers said.

'What does that mean?'

'We live here from now on. To keep an eye on your seditions.'

'But—'

'Room. We'll use this one. Bed. You can move the blue one in. Food. Three good meals a day with meat. Drink? We want those bottles kept filled.'

It was a dreadful imposition, which worsened when the lonely soldiers tried to drag local girls into their quarters. Forbidden by the Catholic priest from a neighboring village to behave so coarsely, they retaliated by inviting dragoons from other homes into the De Pré rooms, shouting through the night for more food and drink, and handling Marie roughly when she brought it.

But even so, the senior De Prés did not appreciate where the real danger lay until one Sunday morning when they found the soldiers behind the barn talking earnestly with the two boys. When Paul came upon them, the soldiers seemed embarrassed, and that afternoon he sought out the Calvinist minister for guidance.

'I might have killed them, for it seemed ominous,' he confessed.

'Indeed it was,' the clergyman said. 'You're in great peril, De Pré. The soldiers are interrogating your boys to trick them into saying something against our religion or in favor of theirs. One word, and the soldiers will take your boys away forever, claiming that they said they wanted to be Catholics but that you prevented their conversion.'

It happened in several homes. Children were tricked into saying things of which they could have had no understanding, and away they went, to another town, in another district—and they would never be heard of again. 'You warn your sons to be careful,' the minister said, and then came the anguished nights when mother and father secretly instructed their sons what to say.

'Do your parents lecture you at night?' one of the soldiers would ask the boys.

'No,' he must say.

'Did they ever take away pictures of the saints that you loved?'

'No.'

'Wouldn't you like to attend Mass with other boys and girls?'

'We go to our own church.'

Now nights became sacred, for when the family was alone in their part of the house, and the soldiers rioting in theirs, Paul took out his Geneva Bible and patiently read from the Book of Psalms those five or six special songs of joy and dedication which the Huguenots had taken to their hearts:

> 'As the hart panteth after the water brooks, so panteth my soul after thee, O God. My soul thirsteth for God, for the living God: when shall I come and appear before God?'

And the elder De Prés drilled their sons in how to avoid the peril which menaced them: 'Our lives would end if you were taken from us. Be careful, be careful what you say.'

In 1685 the axe which had been hanging over the Huguenots fell. King Louis XIV, judging himself to be impregnable, decided to rid himself of Protestants forever. With grandiloquent flourishes he revoked all concessions made to them by the Edict of Nantes and announced that henceforth France was a Catholic country with no place for Huguenots. Dragoons were dispatched to Languedoc, that ancient hiding place for heresy, and whole towns were depopulated. The massacre of St. Bartholomew's Day might have been reenacted across France, except that Louis did not want to inherit the moral stain of his forefathers.

Instead, a series of harsh decrees altered French life: 'All Protestant books, especially Bibles in the vernacular, to be burned. No artisan to work anywhere in France without a certificate proving him to be a good Catholic. Every Huguenot clergyman to quit France within fifteen days and forever, on pain of death if he return. All marriages conducted in the Protestant faith declared null and all children therefrom designated bastards. Protestant washerwomen not to work at the banks of the river, lest they sully the waters.'

And there was another regulation which the De Prés simply could not accept: 'All children of Protestant families must convert immediately to the true faith, and any father who attempts to spirit his children out of France shall spend the rest of his life on the oar-benches of our galleys.'

What did these extraordinary laws mean in a village like Caix, where the population was mainly Huguenot? Since it had long been an orderly place, it did not panic. The pastor summoned the elders, and when the deacons assembled, a large percentage of the adult males were present. 'First,' said the minister, 'we must ascertain if the rumor be true. Probably a lie, because four kings have assured us our freedom.'

But in due course official papers arrived, proving that the new laws were in effect, and a few families converted on the spot, parents and children noisily embracing the traditional faith. Other families met in conclave, and fathers swore that they would die with their infants rather than surrender them to Catholicism. 'We'll walk to the ends of the earth till we find refuge,' Paul de Pré cried flamboyantly, and when the pastor reminded him that the new edicts forbade taking either one's self or one's children out of France, De Pré astounded the assembly by shouting, 'Then the new laws can burn in hell.'

From that moment, others drew away from him. The pastor announced that he would go into exile at Geneva, and the Plons proclaimed loudly that they had never really approved of John Calvin. Paul observed such behavior without comment; they could abandon their religion and their duties at Caix, but not he. And then came the assaults that shattered his confidence.

One morning the soldiers billeted at his farm brought in a mob to ransack the place, searching for Huguenot books. With loud, triumphant voices the soldiers shouted, 'Calvin's *Institutes!* The Geneva Bible!' And he watched in sick dismay as these testaments were pitched into a bonfire, and as the flames consumed the books, with men roaring approval, one of the soldiers grabbed him by the arm and growled, 'Tomorrow, when the officials come from Amiens, we take your children too.'

That night Paul gathered the family in a room with no candles and told his sons, 'We must leave before morning. You can take nothing with you. Our vineyards will go to others. The house we abandon.'

'Even the horses?' Henri asked.

'We'll take two of them, but the others . . .'

Marie explained to the children in her own words: 'Tomorrow the soldiers will take you away. Unless we go. We could never give you up to others. You are the blood of our hearts.'

'Where are we going?' Henri asked.

'We don't know,' she said honestly, looking at her husband.

'We're heading north,' he said, 'and we've got to cross dangerous lands owned by Spain.'

'Won't they arrest us?' Marie asked.

'Yes, if we're careless.'

He had no clearer concept of where he was going than his infants; all he knew was he must flee oppression. Having once experienced the calm rationalism of John Calvin, he could not surrender that vision of an orderly world. He told his sons, 'I'm satisfied that God will lead us to the haven for which we are predestined,' and from that conviction he never deviated.

After midnight, when fowls were asleep and roosters had not yet crowed, he led his family north, abandoning all he had accumulated. How did he have the courage to take a wife and two small children into uncharted forests toward lands he did not know?

Calvinism placed strong emphasis on the fact that God often entered into covenants with his chosen people; the Old and New Testaments were replete with examples, and Paul could have cited numerous verses which fortified his belief that God had personally selected him for such a covenant. Lacking a Bible, he had to rely on memory, and his mind fixed upon a passage from Jeremiah which Huguenots often cited as proof of their pre-destination:

> They shall ask the way to Zion . . . saying, Come and let us join ourselves to the Lord in a perpetual covenant that shall not be forgotten.

Each sunset, when the travelers rose from their daytime sleep to risk the next stage northward, Paul assured his sons, 'The Lord is leading us to Zion, according to his covenant with us.'

When De Pré arrived in Amsterdam in the fall of 1685 he had with him only his wife, his two sons and a ragtag collection of bundles; the two horses had been sold at Antwerp, where Paul received for them a great deal more than the guilders involved. A crypto-Protestant had given him the address of a fellow religionist who had emigrated some years before to Holland, and it was to this man that the De Pré family reported.

His name was Vermaas and he held two jobs, each of which proved crucial to De Pré: during the week he worked in a dark, drafty weigh-house where shipments of timber, grain and herring from the Baltic were weighed and forwarded to specialized warehouses; on Sunday he served as custodian of the little church near the canals where only French was spoken. Here Protestants from the Spanish Netherlands and Huguenots from France gathered to worship God in the Calvinist manner, and few churches in Christendom could have had a more devout membership than this. Each person who came to pray on Sunday was an authentic religious hero who had sacrificed position, security and wealth—and often the lives of family members—to persevere in Calvinism. Some, like the De Prés, had crept at night across two enemy countries or three in order to sing on Sundays the Psalm that Huguenots had taken specially to their hearts:

> 'I called upon the Lord in distress: the Lord answered me, and set me in a large place.'

Amsterdam with its burgeoning riches and crowding fleets was indeed a large place, spacious in wealth and freedom, and Vermaas epitomized the spirit of the town, for he was a big man, burly in the shoulders and with a wide space between his eyes.

Intuitively he liked Paul de Pré, and when he learned how this resolute family had fled French tyranny, he embraced them. 'There's a good chance I can find you work at the weigh-house,' he assured Paul, and to Marie he said, 'I know a little house near the waterfront. Not much, but it's a foothold.'

Vermaas was master weigh-porter, and Paul sensed immediately the importance of this position. Never before had he seen such scales: huge timbered affairs with pans that weighed as much as a man, but so delicately balanced that they could weigh a handful of grain. To these scales, each taller than two men, came the riches of the Baltic. Stout little ships, manned by Dutch sailors, penetrated to all parts of that inland sea, selling and buying at a rate that would have dazzled a French businessman. At times the weigh-house would be occupied with timber from Norway; at other times copper, iron and steel from Sweden would predominate; but always there were tubs of North Sea herring waiting to be cured by a process known only by the Dutch, after which it would be transshipped to all the ports of Europe.

'Gold with fins,' the men at the weigh-house called their herring, and De Pré learned to tell when a ship with herring was about to unload; this was important, for when the workmen hauled in the tubs of gold, they were permitted to sequester a few choice fish for their families.

De Pré had deposited his wife and children in the miserable shack near the banks of the IJ River, trusting that he would in time be able to find them better quarters. It was a vain hope, for Amsterdam was crowded with refugees from all parts of Europe: Baruch Spinoza, the brilliant Portuguese Jew, had lived here while unraveling the mysteries of God; he had died only a few years ago. René Descartes had elected to come here to conduct his work in mathematics and philosophy, and a score of great theologians from all countries had considered Amsterdam the only safe place to conduct their speculations. The English Pilgrims had rested nearby before sailing on to Massachusetts, and it was still the major center for the rescue of Jews from a score of different lands.

Houses were not easy to find, but with the aid of timber Paul acquired at the waterfront and cloths with which to stuff the windy cracks, he and Marie converted their shack into a livable home, and although the dampness caused much coughing, the family survived. The boys—Henri, six, and Louis, five—reveled in the canals that cut across the city and the endlessly changing river up which the Baltic ships came.

'The Golden Swamp' Amsterdam had been called in the old days, for it was then four-fifths water, but engineers were ingenious in filling in the shallow lakes to build more land. Son Henri's first comment on his new home was apt, and the De Prés often quoted it: 'I could get in a boat, if I had a boat, and row and row and never come back.' And every year men dug new canals, so that the city became a network in which every house was connected by water with every other, or so it seemed.

The French church, seated on one of the most interesting small canals, had started in 1409 as a Catholic cloister, but during the Reformation it was converted into a refuge for generations of fleeing dissidents. Rebuilt many times, it became a monument not only to Protestantism but also to the essential generosity of the Dutch, for its ministers, a courageous lot of French-speaking Walloons, who had dared much in coming here, had always been given pensions by the Dutch government on the grounds that 'we are seekers after truth and are richer in having you among us.' No other nation in recorded history gave immediate pensions to its immigrants, or profited more from their arrival.

With pride Paul led his family to this church on Sundays, pointing out to the boys the various other Frenchmen who worked along the waterfront. It was an impoverished congregation, with many families subsisting only through the generosity of Dutch patrons, but invariably someone in the group provided flowers for the altar, and it was because De Pré commented on this that his good fortune commenced.

One Monday morning, as Paul and Vermaas were hefting bales of cloth onto their weigh-scales, the big man said, 'You like flowers, don't you, Paul?'

'Where does the church always find flowers?'

'The Widows Bosbeecq send them over. They're looking for someone to tend their garden.'

'Who are the widows?'

'Aloo! This one doesn't know the Widows Bosbeecq!' And the workmen came to joke with him.

'What ship have you been unloading?' When De Pré pointed, the men cried, 'That's their ship. And that one and that one.'

It seemed that seven of the best ships sailing the Baltic belonged to the widows, and Vermaas explained, 'Two country girls married the Bosbeecq brothers. The men were fine captains who worked the Baltic for many years. In time they had seven ships, like that one.'

'How did they die?'

'Fighting the English, how else?'

In 1667 the older Bosbeecq brother had accompanied the Dutch fighting fleet right into the river Thames, threatening to capture London itself; he had gone down with his ship the next year. The younger brother helped in three notable victories over the English, but he, too, had died at the hands of the English, and the family's profitable trade with Russia might have evaporated had not the two widows stepped forward to operate the fleet. Choosing with rural skill those captains who would best preserve their profits, they continued to send their doughty potbellied vessels to all parts of the Baltic.

Sometimes the widows would appear at the docks, always together and with parasols imported from Paris, and would primly inspect whichever of their ships happened to be in the harbor, nodding sagely to their captains and approving of the manner in which their cargoes were being handled. They were in their sixties, somewhat frail, dressed in black. They walked carefully, attended by a maid who shoved idlers aside for them. One was tall and very thin; the other was roundish, always with a broad smile. Never once did they complain about anything, but Vermaas assured De Pré that when they had their captains alone in the family office, they could be quite tart.

A few days after their conversation Vermaas ran up to De Pré with exciting news: 'It happened by accident. When the Bosbeecq factor was here the other day I told him you liked flowers. He became quite interested, because the Widows Bosbeecq are still looking for a gardener.' So it was arranged that Paul quit work early one afternoon and accompany the Bosbeecq factor to the tall, thin house on the Oudezijdsvoorburgwal (Old-sides-forward-city-dyke) where the widows waited.

'We have a large garden,' they explained, and from a narrow window Paul could see a garden so neatly trimmed that he could scarcely believe it was real. 'We like it neat.' There was also much work to be done inside the house, and the widows wondered if Paul had a wife. 'Is she able?' they asked. 'Is she encumbered with children?'

'We have only two boys.' Quickly he added, 'They're quite grown, of course.'

'How old?'

'Six and five.'

'Oh, dear. Oh, dear.' The sisters-in-law looked at each other in real dismay.

Paul sensed that his entire future depended upon what he did next, and he started to say, 'Those boys have walked all the way from . . .' Dramatically he stopped, for he knew that this was irrelevant. Instead he said quietly, 'Please! We live in a cold, damp shack, and my wife keeps it like a palace. She could do wonders here.'

The Widows Bosbeecq liked their servants to be at work at five in the morning; it discouraged sloth. But once on the job, the workers enjoyed surprising freedoms, the principal one being that they were exceptionally well fed. The widows liked to prepare the food themselves, leaving to Marie de Pré the cleaning of rooms, the sweeping of the stoep and the ironing of clothes sent upstairs by the slaveys. They were good cooks, and being country women, felt that one of man's major requirements was an adequate supply of food, and where growing boys were concerned, downright gorging was advisable.

'It must have been God who brought us here,' Paul said frequently, and on Sundays he led his brood across the canal to the French church for prayers. One Sunday the widows intercepted him as he was about to leave: 'You should attend our church now. It's just as close.'

The idea stunned De Pré. It seemed almost blasphemous that he should abandon the church of his fathers, the place in which French was spoken, and attend a different one which used Dutch. He had never considered this before, since he was convinced that God spoke to mankind in French and he knew that John Calvin did. It would have surprised him to know that Calvin's principal works had been written in Latin, for the solemn thunder of Calvin's thought had reached him in French translation, and he could not imagine it in Dutch.

He discussed this with his family, even though the boys were scarcely old enough to comprehend the difference between French, the correct language of theology, and Dutch, an accidental: 'Within the family we must always speak French. It's proper for us to speak with the widows in Dutch, and you boys must always thank them in that language when they give you clothes or toys. But in our prayers, and in the services at the church, we must speak French.'

He told the widows, 'I went to see your church and it must be the finest in Christendom, because ours is certainly a small affair. But we have always worshipped God in our own language . . .'

'Of course!' the widows said. 'We were thoughtless.'

The fact that De Pré now lived in the Bosbeecq house, with no further obligations at the weigh-station, did not mean that he lost touch with

Vermaas. On Sundays, after church, they would often meet to discuss affairs pertaining to the Bosbeecq ships, and one fine April day they stood together at the bridge leading from the French church as the two widows came down the cobblestones, attended by their servant.

'Pity you're married,' Vermaas said.

'Why? Marie's wonderful . . .'

'I mean, if you weren't married, you could take one of the widows, and then the house . . .'

'The widows?'

'Never be deceived about widows, Paul. The older they are, the more they want to get married again. And the richer they are, the more fun it is to marry them.'

'They're older than my mother.'

'And richer—'

'Who are those men?' Paul interrupted, referring to the horde of strange-looking men who seemed always to be clustered about a building which abutted onto the French church.

'Them?' Vermaas said with some distaste. 'They're Germans.'

'What are they doing here?'

'They line up every day. You must have seen them before this.'

'I have. And I wondered who they were.'

'Their land has been torn by war. A hundred years of it. Catholics against Protestants, Protestants killing Catholic babies. Disgraceful.'

'I knew war like that,' Paul said.

'Oh, no! Not like the German wars. You French were civilized.' He made an ugly sound in his throat and drew his finger across it as if it were a knife. 'Slash across the throat, the Frenchman's dead. But in Germany you would . . .'

'Why do they stand there?'

'Don't you know what that building is? You've been working here for more than a year and you don't know?' In amazement he led De Pré across the bridge and into the Hoogstraat (High Street), where a sturdy building surrounding a courtyard bore on its escutcheon the proud letters V.O.C.

'What's that mean?' Paul asked.

'Vereenigde Oostindische Compagnie,' he recited proudly. 'Jan Compagnie. Behind those doors sit the Lords XVII.' And he explained how this powerful assembly of businessmen had started more than eighty years ago to rule the East.

'But the Germans?' Paul asked, pointing to the rabble that waited silently outside the courtyard.

'There's nothing in Germany,' Vermaas explained. 'These are men who fought for some count . . . some baron. They lost. For them there's nothing.'

'But why here?'

'Jan Compagnie always needs good men. The clerk will come out tomorrow morning, look them over, try to spot those likely to survive. And poof! They're off to Java.'

'Where's Java?'

'Haven't you seen the big Outer Warehouse of the East Indies Company?'

'No.'

'Well, after we weigh the goods here and assess the taxes, they're stored in the proper warehouses,' and on Sunday he took Paul on a leisurely stroll along various canals, past the house in which Rembrandt had lived and the place once occupied by Baruch Spinoza before he had to grind lenses to keep himself alive. They crossed a footbridge to an artificial island that contained a vast open space surrounded by row upon row of warehouses, a very long rope-walk and a majestic, five-storied building for holding valuable importations.

'The treasure chest of the Lords XVII,' Vermaas said, and he summoned a watchman, who granted admission. In the darkness the two men moved from one stack of goods to another, touching with their hands casks and bales worth a fortune.

'Cloves, pepper, nutmeg, cinnamon.' Vermaas repeated reverently the magic names, and as he spoke De Pré grew sick at heart for contact again with the soil, the real soil of trees and vines and shrubs.

'Now, these bales,' Vermaas was saying, 'they're not spices. Golded cloth from Japan. Silvered cloth from India. Beautiful robes from Persia. This is from China, and I don't know what's in it.'

'Where's it come from, all this richness?'

'From the gardens of the moon,' Vermaas said. All his life he had wanted to emigrate to Java, where a purposeful man could make his fortune. He had an insecure idea of where Java was, but he proposed one day to get there. Grasping De Pré by the arm, he said in a whisper, 'Paul, if you can't marry a rich widow, for God's sake, get to Java. You're still young.' And the sweet promise of this dark warehouse was overpowering.

In the morning De Pré asked permission from the widows to visit the offices of Jan Compagnie. 'Whatever for?' the women asked.

'I want to see what the Germans are up to. About Java.'

'Java!' The women laughed, and the older said, 'Go ahead. But don't you start dreaming of Java.'

So he walked only a few blocks to the Hoogstraat, where the crowd of Germans was vastly augmented, men extremely thin and pinched of face, but willing to undertake the severest adventure if only it would provide sustenance. He stood fascinated as clerks came out of the Compagnie offices to inspect the supplicants, selecting one in twenty, and he saw with what joy the chosen men leaped forward.

But when he returned to his work the widows said that they wished to talk with him: 'Don't get Java on your mind. For every guilder that reaches us from Java, six come from the Baltic. Yes, you'll see the big East Indiamen anchored off Texel, transshipping their spices and cloth-of-gold, and you'll hear that one cargo earned a million of this or that. But, Paul, believe us, the wealth of Holland lies in our herring trade. In any year our seven little ships serving the Baltic bring in more money than a dozen of their Indiamen. Keep your eye on the main target.'

They spoke alternately, with one making a point and her sister-in-law another, but when the roundish one repeated, 'Keep your eye on the main target,' the taller wished to enforce the idea: 'We've been watching you, Paul. You and Marie have been chosen by God for some great task.'

No one had ever spoken like this to him before; he had for some time suspected that he was among those elected by God for salvation, the basic goodness of his heart emitting signals that he was predestined. As of now, he lacked the financial wealth which would have proved his election, but he felt certain that in time it, too, would arrive, and in his self-congratulation he missed what the widows said next. It was apparently something very important, for one of them asked sharply, 'Don't you think so, Paul?'

'I'm sorry.'

'My sister said,' the taller woman repeated, 'that if you learn shipping, you could become one of our managers.'

With the bluntness that characterized most French farmers, and especially the Calvinists, De Pré blurted out, 'But I want to work the earth. You've seen what I can do with your garden.'

The widows liked his honesty, and the roundish one said, 'You're an excellent gardener, Paul, and we have a former neighbor who might use your services, too.'

'I'd not want to leave you,' he said frankly.

'We don't intend that you shall. But he's a friend, and one of the Lords XVII, and we could spare him three hours of your time a day. You can keep the wages.'

His hands dropped to his side, and he had to bite his lip to control his emotion. He had wandered into a strange land with no recommendation but his devotion to a form of religion, and in this land he had found a solid friend in Vermaas, who had gone out of his way to help him, a church whose members were encouraged to worship in French, and these two widows who were so kind to his wife, so loving with his sons and so generous with him. When the Huguenots fled France they found refuge in twenty foreign lands, where they encountered a score of different receptions, but none equaled the warmth extended to them in Holland.

On Tuesday morning at nine o'clock, after De Pré had put in his usual four hours of hard work, the Bosbeecq women suggested that he accompany them to the stately Herengracht (Gentlemen's Canal), along which his new employer lived, and there they knocked at the door of a house much grander than theirs. A maid dressed in blue admitted them to a parlor filled with furniture from China and bade them sit upon the heavy brocades. After a wait long enough to allow Paul time to admire the richness of the room, a gentleman appeared, clad in a most expensive Chinese robe decorated with gold and blue dragons.

He was tall and thin, with a white mustache and goatee. He had piercing eyes that showed no film of age, and although he was past seventy, he moved alertly, going directly to De Pré and bowing slightly. 'I am Karel van Doorn, and I understand from these good women that you wish to work for me.'

'They said you could have me three hours a day.'

'If you really work, that would be enough. Can you really work?'

De Pré sensed that he was in the hands of someone much harsher than the widows, but he was so captivated by the idea of Java that he did not want to antagonize anyone who might be associated with that wonderland. 'I can tend your garden,' he said.

With no apologies to the Bosbeecqs, Van Doorn took Paul by the arm, hurried him through a chain of corridors to a big room, and threw open a window overlooking a garden in sad repair. 'Can you marshal that into some kind of order?'

'I could fix that within a week.'

'Get to it!' And he shoved Paul out the back door and toward a shed where some tools waited.

'I must explain to the—'

'I'll tell them you're already at work.' Van Doorn started to leave, then stopped abruptly and cried, 'Remember! You said you could do it in a week.'

'And what do I do after that?' Paul asked.

'Do? You could work three hours a day for ten years and not finish all the things I have in mind.'

When De Pré returned to the Bosbeecq house, where the widows were preparing a gigantic meal because they knew he would be hungry, the two women suggested that he sit with them in the front room, and there, in forthright terms, they warned him about his new employer, speaking alternately, as usual, like two angels reporting to St. Peter regarding their earthly investigations.

'Karel van Doorn will pay you every stuiver you earn. He's fiercely honest.'

'Within limits.'

'And he can afford to pay you. He's very wealthy.'

'He is that. The Compagnie in Java had an iron-clad rule. No official to buy and sell for himself. Only for the Compagnie.'

'But his family bought and sold like madmen. And grew very rich.'

'And the Compagnie had another iron-clad rule. No one in Java to bring money earned there back to Holland.'

'She knows, because her uncle was one of the Lords XVII.'

'But when Karel's mother died in the big house along the canal in Batavia, he hurried out to Java, and by some trick which only he could explain, managed to smuggle all the Van Doorn money back to Amsterdam.'

'And he should have shared half with his brother at the Cape—'

'Where's that?' Paul interrupted. It was the first time in his life he had heard mention of this place.

'It's nothing. A few miserable wretches stuck away at the end of Africa, trying to grow vegetables.'

'Is Mijnheer van Doorn's brother there?' Paul asked quickly.

'Yes. Not too bright a lad. Born in Java, you know.'

'And Van Doorn should have shared the family money with his brother.'

'But he didn't.'

'He smuggled it into Amsterdam, and with it bought himself membership in the Lords XVII.'

'He took my uncle's place.'

'He's one of the leading citizens of Amsterdam. You're lucky to be working for him.'

'But watch him.'

'At the Compagnie, you'll see his portrait painted by Frans Hals.'

'And at the Great Hall of the Arquebusiers, you'll see him in Rembrandt's painting of the civic guard. He's there with my husband, standing beside him.'

'And you'll notice that her husband has his right hand closely guarding his pocket, which is a good thing to do when Karel van Doorn's about.'

'But for a young man like you, he's an influential person to know.'

'If you guard your pocket.'

The relationship was a profitable one, even though Karel van Doorn expected his gardener to work at such a speed that at the end of three hours he was on the verge of collapse. Anything less than signs of total exhaustion indicated laziness, and Van Doorn was apt toward the end of the third hour to slip away from his desk at the Compagnie and watch through the back wall, hoping to catch his workman resting. When he did, he would rush in and berate Paul as an idle, good-for-nothing Frenchman who was, if the facts were known, probably a Papist at heart.

But a hard-nosed French farmer was an adequate match for any avaricious Dutch merchant, and De Pré devised a score of ways to defeat his employer and end the daily three-hour stint in moderately rested condition. In fact, he rather liked the game, for he found Van Doorn meticulously honest in his payments, and when occasionally De Pré returned to the gardens on his own time to finish a job, his employer noticed this and paid extra.

'The one thing that perplexes me,' Paul told the widows one afternoon, 'is that during all the time I've worked for him, he's never once offered me anything to eat or drink.'

'He's a miserly man,' one of the women said. 'Anyone who steals from the Compagnie in Java and from the government in Amsterdam and from his own brother . . .'

'He never steals from me.'

'Ah! But don't you see? The Bible says that you must treat your servants justly. If word got out that he maltreated you, his entire position might crumble. He would no longer be among the elect, and all would know it.'

'I don't understand,' Paul said.

'It's very simple. A man can steal millions from the government, because the Bible says nothing about that. But he dare not steal a stuiver from a servant, because on that both the Bible and John Calvin are very strict.'

'But doesn't the Bible say anything about a little food and drink?'

'Not that I can recall.'

And then, on the very next day, Karel van Doorn offered his gardener Paul de Pré a drink, not at his house but in the Compagnie offices. He had come home at the beginning of the third hour and said abruptly, 'De Pré, let's go to my offices. I need your advice.'

So they walked across town to where a new batch of German mercenaries waited, imploring Karel as he passed, for they knew him to be one of the Lords XVII, but Van Doorn ignored them. When he was seated behind his desk he said without amenities, 'They tell me that in France you made wine.'

'I did.'

'What do you think of this?' From a drawer in his desk Karel produced a bottle of white wine and encouraged the Frenchman to taste it.

'How is it?' Van Doorn asked.

Pursing his lip and spitting onto the floor, De Pré said, 'The man who made that ought to be executed.'

Van Doorn smiled thinly, then broke into a laugh. 'My brother made it.'

'I'm sorry. But it's a very bad wine. It shouldn't be called wine.'

'My own opinion.'

'They told me your brother's in Africa?'

'This comes from his vineyard. He's been working it for thirty years.'

'He must have a very poor vineyard.'

'I wonder if he mixes in something beside grapes?'

'He wouldn't dare.'

'Then how can it be so bad?'

'In making wine, there are many tricks.'

'Could this wine be saved?'

Gingerly De Pré took another sip, not enough to strangle him with its badness but sufficient for him to judge the miserable stuff. 'It has a solid base, Mijnheer. Grapes are grapes, and I suppose that if a vintner started fresh . . .'

'I have a report here. It says the vines are still healthy.'

'But are they the right kind of vine?'

'What do you think should be done?'

De Pré sat with his hands in his lap, staring at the floor. Desperately he wanted to get back to the soil, in Java preferably, where gold proliferated, but his heart beat fast at the possibility of once more raising grapes and making good wine. Since he did not know what to say that might further his plans, he sat dumb.

'If the Compagnie were to send out some men who knew wine,' Van Doorn was saying as if from another room. 'And if those men took with them new strains of grape. Couldn't something be done?'

Ideas of wonderful challenge were coming at him so fast that De Pré could not absorb them, and after a while Van Doorn said, 'Let's look at the map,' and he led the way to a council chamber decorated with a Rembrandt group portrait and a large map done by Willem Blaeu of Leiden. On it four spots showed conspicuously: Amsterdam, Batavia, the Cape of Good Hope, Surinam in South America.

'We're concerned with these three,' Karel said, jabbing at the Cape, which stood midway between Amsterdam and Java. 'If our ships sailing south could stop at the Cape and load casks of good red wine and strong vinegar, they could maintain the health of their men all the way to Java. And we'd save the freightage we now spend on bottles from France and Italy.' Suddenly the spot representing the Cape assumed considerable importance.

'But the soil—will good vines grow there?' De Pré asked.

'That's what we intend to find out,' Van Doorn said. 'That's why I've been watching you so closely.'

De Pré stepped back. So the watching had been spying—and since his experiences with the Catholics of France, this fact troubled him deeply.

'You didn't think that I hired you to clean up my garden?' Van Doorn laughed. 'I could have hired a hundred Germans to do that, good gardeners some of them.' He actually placed his arm about De Pré's shoulders, leading him back to the first office. 'What I sought, De Pré, was an estimate of you Huguenots. What kind of people you were. How you worked. How dependable you were religiously.'

'Did you find out?' De Pré was angered with this man, but his own canny approach to life made him respect the Dutchman's caution.

'I did. And your honest reaction to my brother's wine has made up my mind.' He rose and strode nervously about the room, galvanized by the prospects of new engagements, new opportunities to snaffle a florin here or there.

Resuming his seat, he said softly, 'De Pré, I must swear you to secrecy.'

'Sworn.'

'The Lords XVII are going to send three shiploads of Huguenots to the Cape. We like you people—your stubborn honesty, your devotion to Calvinism. Your family is going to be aboard one of those ships, and you'—he reached over and slapped De Pré on the knee—'you will take with you a bundle of first-class grape vines.'

'Where will I get them?'

'In France. From some area whose vines you can trust.'

'They won't send vines to Amsterdam. Forbidden.'

'No one sends the vines, De Pré. You go get them.'

'I'd be shot.'

'Not if you're careful.'

'The risk . . .'

'Will be well paid for.' Again he rose, storming about the room, tossing his white head this way and that. 'Well paid, De Pré. I hand you this first bag of coins now. I hand you this second bag when you return to Amsterdam with the grapevines. And if you get them to the Cape, you and I will sell them to the Compagnie and share the profits.'

De Pré studied the offer, and he was glad that the Bosbeecq women had alerted him to this canny gentleman: he was buying the vines with Compagnie money, then selling them back to the Compagnie for more of its money. He remembered something one of the women had told him: 'Van Doorn has a mind that never stops working. As a Compagnie official, he imports cloves from Java. And whom does he sell them to? To himself as a private trader. So he earns double, except that he trebles the price of cloves, since he's the only one who has any, and makes a princely profit.' Here was a man to be wary of, but he also remembered something else the women had said: 'But he dare not steal a stuiver from a servant.'

'Will you pay me the two other times?' he asked directly.

'Would I dare do otherwise? A member of the council?'

And then De Pré's stolid French honesty manifested itself: 'You didn't share with your brother.'

Van Doorn ignored the insult. 'In life,' he said, 'accidents occur. My brother was a dolt. He gave me no help in spiriting the family fortune out of Java. He was a man to be forgotten. You're a man to be remembered.'

When Paul informed his wife that he intended smuggling their eight-year-old son Henri into France with him, she was appalled, but after he explained that this might prove to be the one disguise that would disarm the border guards—'A father traveling back to the farm with his son'—she consented, for she had long suspected that French families ought not to stay too long in congenial Holland. The boys were beginning to speak only Dutch, and the strict Calvinism of the French was being softened by the easier attitudes of the Dutch. She knew also that her husband longed to get back to the making of wine, and this seemed an opportunity engineered by God Himself. So she packed her son's clothing, kissed him fondly, and sent him off on the great adventure.

There was no problem as long as the pair remained in Holland: Amsterdam to Leiden to Schiedam and by boat to Zeeland, where another boat skirted Antwerp and set them down in Ghent. But on the approaches to Amiens, spies could be expected, so the pair shifted eastward and slipped by back roads into the country north of Caix, and when Paul saw the fine fields his eyes filled with tears. This was the good land of France, and it was only an error of magnitude that had driven him from it.

When he passed several small villages where Protestants had once worshipped freely and saw the ruined churches, he was desolated, and late one night he tapped lightly at the window of a farm he knew to be occupied by his wife's family, the Plons.

'Are you still of the true religion?' he whispered when an old woman came to the door.

'It's Marie's man!' the woman cried.

'Sssssssssh! Are you still of the true religion?'

When no one dared answer, he knew that they had reverted to Catholicism, but it was too late to retreat. He must rely upon these farmers, for they controlled his destiny. 'This is Marie's boy,' he said, thrusting Henri forward to be admired by his kinfolk.

'If you're caught,' an old man said, 'they'll burn you.'

'I must not be caught,' Paul said. 'Can we sleep here tonight?'

In the morning he told the cautious Plons that he must have four hundred rootings from grapes which made the finest white wine. 'You'd not be allowed to take them across the border, even if you were Catholic,' they warned.

'I'm taking them to a far country,' he assured them. 'Not Holland or Germany, where they would compete.'

He spent four days with the nervous Plons, carefully compacting the vines they brought him, and when he had three hundred and twenty he realized that they formed about as big a bundle as he could reasonably handle on the long journey back to Amsterdam, and the work ended. On the last night he talked openly with the Plons, who by now were satisfied that officials were not going to break down their doors for harboring a

Huguenot, and the old people told him, 'It's better now that the village is all one faith.'

'There are no Protestants?'

'None. Some ran away, like you and Marie. Most converted back to the true religion. And a few were hanged.'

'Did the priest escape to Geneva?'

'He was hanged.' Plon's wife interrupted: 'He offered to convert, but we couldn't trust him.'

Then Plon summed up the matter: 'Frenchmen were supposed to be Catholics. It's the only right way for us. A village shouldn't be cut down the middle. Neither should a country.'

'You'd like it much better here,' his wife agreed. 'Now that we're all one.'

But when Paul went to bed on that last night he realized that he could never turn his back on Calvinism; the cost of his emigration was modest in comparison with what he had gained by remaining steadfast. The quiet rationalism of Amsterdam was something the Plons would not be able to comprehend; he wished he were able to explain how content their daughter Marie was in her new home, but he judged he had better not try. He had come back to Caix for its good grape rootings, and he had them.

When he delivered the vines to Mijnheer van Doorn at the Compagnie offices, Karel paid him promptly, but Paul noticed that the sum was slightly less than promised, and when he started to complain, Van Doorn said crisply, 'We contracted for four hundred, you remember,' and Paul said, 'But it would have been impossible to carry so many,' and Van Doorn said, 'Contract's a contract. The solidity of Holland depends upon that.' And Paul dropped the subject, pointing to the large black bow resting on Van Doorn's left arm.

'A death?'

'My wife.' The chairman of the Lords XVII lowered his voice as if to say, 'That subject's closed,' but then he realized that Paul would be interested in what was about to happen as a consequence of his wife's death. 'She was a wonderful woman. Sailed to Java with me. Helped arrange matters there.' Paul wondered why the great man was telling him this, and then came the thunderbolt: 'I'm marrying Vrouw Bosbeecq next Saturday.' Lamely he added, 'At the Old Church. You'll be invited.'

'Which widow?' Paul asked.

'Abigael, the tall one,' and when he saw the incredulity on Paul's face, he explained, 'This way we can combine our two houses and save a good deal of money.'

'What of the other widow?'

'She moves to the Herengracht . . . with us. The other good part is that the seven ships will come . . . ' He hesitated, then said, 'Well, under my management.'

Paul wanted more than anything else at that moment to run out and find Vermaas, who might be able to explain this absurdity, a wealthy man over seventy conniving to get hold of a few ships, but Van Doorn wished to discuss news that was even more exciting: 'We're assembling a Compagnie fleet right now. They sail for Java within the week, and two hundred and ninety Huguenots will be aboard. It works out well, Paul, because when we close down the Bosbeecq house you and your wife won't be needed any further . . .'

Paul was disgusted. He had risked his life to find three hundred and twenty vines for an experiment, and while he was gone this tall Dutchman had sat in this office scheming, burying his wife and proposing to another before the earth on the grave had settled.

'Mijnheer van Doorn, my trip to Caix was possible only because my little boy Henri accompanied me. He's eight, and I wonder if you would like to make him a special present? For his bravery?'

Van Doorn reflected on this, then said judiciously, 'I don't think so. The contract was with you.' He showed Paul to the door, where he said warmly, 'I hope the boys will enjoy life aboard ship. It's an exciting trip.'

As soon as Paul was free of the Compagnie quarters he ran to the weigh-house to consult with Vermaas: 'I heard the Widow Bosbeecq with my own ears warn me that Van Doorn was a thief, that he could not be trusted . . .'

'And you come home to find she's about to marry him?'

'Yes! It passes understanding.'

'Except for what I told you, Paul. Every widow who ever lived wants to get married again. I said even you could marry one of them, if you were single.'

'But I know she despises Van Doorn.'

'If a widow can't find a real man, she'll take Van Doorn.' Then, with a cry of animal delight, he shouted, 'Good God, Paul! Don't you see how it happened?'

When De Pré looked blank, the big warehouseman cried, 'They took you over to Van Doorn's to work his garden because they wanted to be close to him in case his wife did die. They were using you as bait.'

Paul reflected on this for some time, then asked, 'Do you not think, Vermaas, that Dutchmen make use of everybody?'

'They're in business, Paul.'

The wedding was a solemn affair, with most of the business leaders of Amsterdam in attendance at the Old Church beside the canal. Some came in barges, poled along by their servants, but many walked, forming long processions in black, as if this were a funeral. The church was filled, and when the choir chanted the metrical Psalms so beloved of Calvinists, the place reverberated. The Widows Bosbeecq did not weep; they marched steadfastly to the front of the church, where they waited for the arrival of Karel van Doorn, tall, stately, handsome and whiskered. The marriage couple made a fine impression, two old people joining their lives and their fortunes for the remaining years of life.

'Oh, no,' the roundish widow said that night in the old house as she talked with De Pré about his adventures in France. 'They're not uniting their fortunes. You think a woman as clever as my sister would allow a scoundrel like Van Doorn to lay his hands on our ships?'

'But Mijnheer van Doorn told me himself—'

'When did he tell you?'

'Last week.'

'Aha!' the woman chortled. 'That was last week. Well, this week we presented him with a contract, specifying everything. This house? We sell it and keep the money. The farmland? We join it to his. The seven ships? They're all put in my name, not his.'

'I should think he'd back out.'

'He wanted to. Said we were robbing him. So we revised the contract to keep him happy.'

'Did you give him the ships?'

'Heavens, no! But we did agree that when my ships took their salted herring to Sweden, he should be the agent for selling them, and he keeps the commission.'

Paul was amazed at the cold-blooded quality of this transaction, and started to comment upon it, when the old woman placed her hand on his arm and said softly, 'You know, Paul, it was partly your fault that Abigael decided—that we decided, really—to get married.'

'How me?'

'Because Mijnheer van Doorn came to us the night of his wife's burial and said, "Good women, your man De Pré is sailing shortly for the Cape. You'll be alone again, so why don't we arrange something?" And he was right. We would be alone again, and you reminded us how pleasant it was to have a man in the house.' She laughed. 'Any man.'

When the Bosbeecq house was emptied and the shutters closed, the widows suggested that the De Pré family move with them to the Van Doorn house for the few days before the ships loaded for the Cape, but Mijnheer would have none of this. 'Let them sleep in the old place,' he said, and a few blankets were taken there. But the widows did carry hot food to them, which they ate sitting on the floor.

'You must be sure that Van Doorn pays you all he owes,' they warned Paul, and on the last day in Amsterdam, Paul went to the Compagnie offices and reminded Van Doorn that the third part of the payment was still due him.

'I have it in mind,' Mijnheer assured the émigré. 'I'm handing this packet to the captain of our ship, and the moment you land the vines at the Cape, you get your final payment. See, it says so here. Ninety florins.' But Paul noticed that he did not hand over the promissory note; he kept it, saying, 'This goes to the captain of your ship.'

At dusk that night the Huguenots gathered in the old French church, two hundred and ninety children and women and men who had dared the terrors of this age to retain their faith. They had braved dogs that hunted them, and men who rode after them on swift horses, and frontier guards who shot at them. They had crossed strange lands and come to towns where their language was unknown, but they had persevered, these woodworkers, and vintners and schoolteachers. They had sought freedom as few in their generation had sought it, volunteering their fortunes and their lives that they might live according to the rules they believed in. And now they were embarking upon the final adventure, this long passage in rolling ships to a land about which they knew nothing—except that when they reached it they would be free.

'Cling to your God,' the minister cried in French. 'Cling to the inspired teachings of John Calvin. And above all, cling to your language, which is the badge of your courage. Bring up your children to respect that language, as we in exile here in Holland have respected it against all adversity. It is the soul of France, the song of freedom. Let us pray.'

In the morning Paul led his family from the Bosbeecq home and lined them up on the bridge over the canal. 'Oudezijdsvoorburgwal,' he said for the last time. 'Always remember that when we were naked, the good people on this canal clothed us, as it says in the Bible. Keep that name in your heart.'

He then led them to the house of Mijnheer van Doorn, where he knocked on the door, asking that the Widows Bosbeecq appear, and when they did, he told his sons, 'Remember these good women. They saved our lives with their generosity.'

Next he took them to the French church, where the doors were opened for families to say their last prayers, and inside its warm hospitality he and his family prayed in French, committing themselves again to the promises made the night before.

When they left the church and started toward the waterfront where the ships waited, Paul saw as if for the first time the quiet grandeur of this city, the solid walls behind which sat the solid merchants, the stout churches with their stout Dutch ministers, and above all, the charity of the place— the simple goodness of these burghers who had accepted refugees from all the world because they knew that if a nation could feed and manage itself, it could accommodate strangers.

He was sorry to leave. Had he reached Holland sooner in his life, he might have become a Dutchman, but he was French, indelibly marked with the mercurial greatness of that land, and Holland was not for him.

Seven different Compagnie ships would carry the Huguenots to their new home. They left at various times and encountered various conditions. Some made the long run in ninety days; the poor *China,* buffeted all the way by adverse winds, required a hundred and thirty-seven, by which time many of its Frenchmen were dead. The De Prés and sixty others were loaded upon the *Java,* but not by plan. There were two ships at the wharf that day, *Java* and *Texel,* and Paul was inclined to choose the latter, but his friend Vermaas would not allow it: 'Look at the planking, Paul.' He looked and saw nothing amiss, but Vermaas said, 'It's uneven, not laid on carefully. Bad in one, bad in all.' And he led the family to the gangway of the *Java.*

This occasioned some difficulty because friends of the De Prés were already aboard the *Texel,* and the boys wanted to stay with them. But Vermaas had convinced Paul that the *Java* was safer, so there were tearful farewells, and kisses blown and promises to farm together in the new land —and it was appropriate that the parting should have been sorrowful, for after the *Texel* passed Cape St. Vincent at the tip of Portugal, where Prince Henry the Navigator had dreamed of voyages like this, it ran into heavy seas and perished.

The *Java* was a medium ship, not small and swift like a flute, nor large and wallowing like an East Indiaman. It was a slow ship, requiring a hundred and thirty days for the tedious passage, and it carried no lemons or pickled cabbage. For four long months the passengers ate only salted meat, and scurvy rampaged through the lower decks.

They were dreadful, these low-ceilinged hovels below the waterline. Fresh air was unknown, cleanliness impossible. Men emptied their bowels in corners and children lay white and gasping on filthy bunks. During the transit of the equator the temperatures were intolerable and dying people pleaded for a breath of air, but when the lower latitudes were reached, the next to die cried for blankets.

At the hundredth day Paul became aware that his wife, Marie, was not handling the long passage at all well. Her life in the cold, damp shack close to the river IJ in Amsterdam had started a lung congestion which had never really mended, and now, with worsening conditions belowdecks, she began to cough blood. Frantically Paul sought assistance among the passengers, but to no avail. There were scholars aboard the *Java,* and a failed clergyman, and some excellent farmers, but no doctors or nurses, and Paul had to watch in despair as his wife declined.

'Marie,' he pleaded, 'we must walk on deck. To catch the breezes.'

'I cannot move,' she whispered, and when he forced her to her feet, he saw that her knees crumpled, so he returned her to the filthy bed.

He sought counsel among the women passengers, and all they could do was look gloomily at the stricken Frenchwoman and shake their heads lugubriously. It was no use appealing to the crew, for they were a miserable lot. Dutch sailors of merit preferred to work the Baltic ships, from which they could return to their homes periodically; also, the pay was better. For the long passages to Batavia, the Lords XVII had to rely principally on those untrained Germans whom De Pré had seen outside the Compagnie offices. They were not sailors, nor were they disciplined. For twenty years they had been conducting religious warfare back and forth across Germany, and it was unreasonable to think that they would now settle down and obey orders. Uncertain of what their Dutch officers were saying, totally unable to comprehend the French emigrants, they barely kept the ship afloat, and it was probably they who had been responsible for the sinking of the *Texel*: the Dutch captain had surely shouted the right order at the moment of peril, but his sailors had not responded.

So the *Java* rolled and pitched through the South Atlantic, with all hands praying that the wind would steady so they might make land before everyone was dead. Under these circumstances it was not strange that Marie de Pré should sink closer and closer to unconsciousness; her husband watched in horror as her vital signs diminished.

'Marie!' he pleaded. 'We must go aloft. You must walk and regain your strength.' As he argued with her three sailors moved through the filthy quarters collecting bodies, and Paul ran to them begging for fresh water for his wife. The Germans looked at him and grunted. The Cape would soon be reached and then these troublesome passengers would be gone, such of them as had survived.

Long before any sailor could win his silver schilling for crying, 'Table Mountain!' Marie de Pré fell into a coma, and since there was no proper clergyman aboard the rolling ship, the Dutch sick-comforter was summoned. He was a small, round fellow with rheumy eyes and the self-effacing manner of one who had tried to pass the courses at Leiden University and failed. Forbidden to preach like a real minister, he discharged his deep convictions by serving as general handyman to the Dutch church; especially he comforted those who were about to die.

As soon as he saw Marie he said, 'We'd better fetch her children,' and when Henri and Louis appeared he took their hands, drew them to him, and said softly in Dutch, 'Now's the time for courage, eh?'

'Could we pray in French?' Paul asked, hoping that his wife would be heartened by the language she had used as a child in Caix.

'Of course,' the sick-comforter said, but since he spoke not a word of French, he nodded to Paul, indicating that he must do the praying. 'It will ease her,' he said, even though he knew that she would never again hear human speech.

'Great God in heaven,' Paul prayed, 'we have come so far in obedience to Thy commands. Save Thy daughter Marie that she may see the new home to which Thou hast brought us.' When he finished, the sick-comforter clasped the two boys and prayed with them in his language, after which he said in a low voice, 'We can call the sailors now. She's dead.'

'No!' Paul shouted, and the fury with which he embraced his wife, who had accompanied him so far and with so gentle a compliance, made those about him weep.

'Call the sailors,' the sick-comforter said forcefully. 'Boys, you must kiss your mother goodbye,' and he edged them toward the pitiful bier.

In due time two German sailors shoved their way through the passengers, took the corpse away, and holding it aloft, pitched it into the sea, after which the sick-comforter indicated that he would lead public prayers for those who were still ambulatory. A stout Dutch merchant who had once served as deacon at Old Church pushed him contemptuously aside as unworthy; he would do the praying, and all on deck bowed their heads.

When the *Java* finally anchored in the lee of Table Mountain, Paul de Pré, thirty pounds lighter than when he sailed, reported to the captain, asking for his final payment for acquiring the grapevines, but instead of handing over any money, the captain informed Paul that Mijnheer van Doorn had arranged for the delivery of some one hundred and twenty acres of land toward the eastern mountains, and he produced a document affirming this: 'The Compagnie Commander at De Kaap is directed to give the French emigrant Paul de Pré sixty morgen of the best land, contiguous to the farm of Willem van Doorn in the settlement of Stellenbosch, there to raise grapes and make wine.'

By paying De Pré in Compagnie land rather than his own money, Van Doorn had saved himself ninety florins.

Paul—brooding over the loss of his wife—was halfway across the desolate flats before the immensity of Africa struck him, and he was suddenly overcome with dread lest this enormous continent reject him, tossing him back into the sea. The land was so bleak, the vast emptiness so foreboding that he began to shiver, feeling himself rebuked for his insolence. Clasping his sons to protect them from the loneliness he felt, he muttered in French, 'Our grapes will never grow in this godforsaken soil.'

That night the Dutchman in whose wagon he was riding pitched camp on the loneliest stretch of the flatlands, and Paul stayed awake, listening to the howling wind and testing the harsh, sterile earth with his fingers. Driven with fear, he rose to inspect his grape cuttings, to see if they were still moist, and as he replaced their wrappings he thought: They are doomed.

But toward the end of the second day, when the laden wagon completed its traverse of the badlands, he was allowed a gentler view of Africa, for they now traveled along the bank of a lovely river edged by broad meadows and protected by encompassing hills. He thought: This is finer than anything I knew in France or Holland! A man could make his home here!

Begging the driver to halt, he lifted his sons down so that they could feel the good earth that was to be their home, and when he had filtered it through his fingers he looked up at the Dutchman and shouted in French, 'We shall build a vineyard so great . . .' When the driver looked at him in stolid unconcern, for he understood not a word De Pré was saying, Paul cried in Dutch, 'Good, eh?' and the driver pointed ahead with his whip: 'Ahead, even better.'

They camped that night beside the river, and by noon next morning they saw something that sealed Paul's love of his new home. It was a farmhouse, low and wide, built of mud bricks and wattles, and so set down against the hills rising behind it that it seemed always to have been there. He noticed that it stood north to south, so that the west face looked toward Table Mountain, still visible on the far horizon. From this secure house a lawn of grass reached out, with four small huts along each side for tools and chickens and the storage of hay; they were so placed, and at such an angle, that they seemed like arms stretching to invite strangers, and when Paul had seen the entire he whispered to himself, '*Mon Dieu!* I should like to own this farm!'

'Has the master a daughter?' he asked the driver.

'He does.'

'How old?' he asked casually.

'Nine, I think.'

'Oh.' He said this in such a flat, disappointed voice that he added quickly, lest he betray himself, 'That's good. Someone for my boys to play with.'

'He has sons, too. Nine and eight.'

'Interesting.'

'But you understand, the farm really belongs to the old man.'

'Who?'

'Willem van Doorn. And his old wife Katje.'

'Three generations?'

'Working the fields, you live a long time.'

When they reached the farmhouse, walking down the lane between the eight huts, a tall Dutchman, broad of face and open in manner, came out to greet them: 'I'm Marthinus van Doorn. Are you the Frenchman?'

'Paul de Pré, and these are my sons Henri and Louis.'

'Annatjie!' the farmer cried. 'Come meet our neighbors!' And from the house came a tall, gaunt woman with broad shoulders and big hands. She was obviously quite a few years older than her husband, in her late thirties perhaps, and she bore the look of one who had worked extremely hard. She did not smile easily, as her husband had done when greeting the strangers, but she did extend a practical welcome: 'We've been waiting for your knowledge of grapes.'

'Is it true, you've made wine?' her husband asked.

'A great deal,' Paul said, and for the first time the woman smiled.

'The old man is out with the slaves,' Van Doorn said. 'Shall we go see him?'

But before they could depart, a high, complaining whine came from the back of the house: 'Who's out there, Annatjie?'

'The Frenchman.'

'What Frenchman?' It was a woman's voice, conveying irritation that things had not been explained.

'The one from Amsterdam. With new vines.'

'Nobody tells me anything,' and after a bit of shuffling, the door creaked open and a white-haired woman, partially stooped, came protestingly into the sunlight. 'Is this the Frenchman?' she asked.

'Yes,' her daughter-in-law said patiently. 'We're taking him into the fields to meet the old man.'

'You won't find him,' the old woman muttered, retreating to the shadows of the house.

They did find him, a crippled old man in his mid-sixties, walking sideways as he supervised the slaves in pruning vines. 'Father, this is the Frenchman who knows how to make good wine.'

'After thirty years they send someone,' he joked. Since that first joyous pressing decades ago, hundreds of thousands of vines had been planted at the Cape, assuring a local supply of wine, but even the best vintage remained far inferior to those of Europe.

The old man jammed his pruning knife into his belt, walked awkwardly to greet the newcomer, and said, 'Now let's figure out where your land's to be.'

'I have a map . . .'

'Well, let's fetch it, because it's important that you get started right.'

When the map was spread, the old man was delighted: 'Son, they've given you the very best land available. Sixty morgen! With water right from the river! Where will you build your house?'

'I haven't seen the land yet,' Paul said hesitantly.

'Let's see it!' the old man cried, almost as if the land were his and he was planning his first house. 'Annatjie, Katje! Get the boys and we'll go see the land.'

So the entire Van Doorn establishment—Willem and Katje; Marthinus and Annatjie; and the children Petronella, Hendrik and little Sarel—set off to see the Frenchman's land, and after they had surveyed it and assessed its strengths, all agreed that he must build his house at the foot of a small mound that would protect it from eastern winds. De Pré, however, said with a certain stubbornness, 'I'll build it down here,' but his reasons for doing so he would not divulge. They were simple: when the Van Doorns indicated the spot they were recommending, he immediately noticed that it did not balance the house they had built, and he wanted his home to be in harmony with theirs, for he was convinced that one day these two farms must be merged, and when that time came he wanted the various buildings to be in balance.

'We'll put it here,' he said, and when several of the Van Doorns started to protest the obvious unwisdom of such a location, old Willem quieted them: 'Look! If the house is put here, it balances ours over there. The valley looks better.'

'Why, so it does,' Paul said, and soon the building commenced. The Van Doorns sent their slaves to work on the walls, as if the house were to be their own, while the three De Prés toiled alongside the swarthy Madagascans.

'De Pré's a Frenchman,' Willem said approvingly. 'He knows how to work for what he wants.' And as the house grew, its mud bricks neatly aligned, the Van Doorns had to concede that it was not only spacious, but also solid and attractive.

'It's a house that needs a woman,' old Katje said, and on the next evening when the Frenchman ate at her house, she asked him bluntly, 'What are your plans for finding a wife?'

'I have none.'

'You better get some. Now, you take Marthinus'—she pointed to her sturdy son—'he was born at the Cape when there were no women, none at all available for young men. So we moved out here to Stellenbosch, except it wasn't named that in those years, and here I was—the only woman for miles around. So what to do?'

Paul looked at Marthinus and then at Annatjie, and asked, 'How did he find her?'

'Simple,' Katje continued. 'She was a King's Niece.'

This news was so startling that Paul stared in a most ungentlemanly manner at the tall, ungainly woman. 'Yes,' Katje said, 'this one was a King's Niece, and you'd better be sending for one of them, too.'

'What do you mean?'

'Orphans. Amsterdam's full of girl orphans. No one to give them in marriage, no dowry, so we call them the King's Nieces, and he gives them a small dowry and ships them out to Java and the Cape.'

'How did . . .'

'How did Marthinus know that Annatjie was his? When news of the ship reached out here, we supposed all the girls would be gone. But I told

Marthinus, "Son, there's always a chance." So he rode at a gallop, and when he got to the wharf all the girls were gone.'

She placed her work-worn hands on the table, then smiled at her husband. 'I was what you might call a King's Niece also. My rich uncle shipped me out here to marry this one. Never saw him before I landed. Thirty years ago.'

'But if the girls were all gone, how did your son . . .'

Old Katje looked at Marthinus and laughed. 'Spirit, that's what he had. Like his father. You've heard that Willem chopped down four bitter almond so we could escape from the Cape. I predicted he would be hanged. I said, "Willem, you'll be hanged." '

'What did Marthinus do?'

'Got to the ship, all the girls gone. But before he rode back empty-handed he heard that one of the men at the fort didn't like the girl he got, so he shouted, "I'll take her!" And one of the other men said, "You haven't seen her!" But Marthinus shouted again, "I'll take her," and the girl was sent for, and there she is.'

Paul could not determine in what spirit the woman pointed to her daughter-in-law, whether in derision for being so much older than her son, or in disgust at her being so ungainly, or in pride for having had the strength to surmount such a poor beginning. 'Look at her fine children,' the old woman said, and Paul noticed that the three youngsters were looking at their mother with love. He would never have told his children such a story, but when he got his sons back into their house, he was startled to hear Henri say, 'Father, I hope that when you go to the ship, you get someone like Annatjie.'

The Huguenot boys were finding their new home even more exciting than the canals of Amsterdam. The spaciousness enchanted them; they loved the flashing sight of animals moving through the swards of long grass; and playing with the Van Doorn children was a joy. But the Dutchman they loved was old Willem. He moved slowly among his vines, his left leg out of harmony with his right, and he coughed a lot, but he was a reservoir of stories about Java and the Spice Islands and the siege of Malacca.

He took delight in arranging surprises for them: cloves to chew on so their breath would be sweet, and games with string. He let them watch the Van Doorn slaves, great blacks from Angola and Madagascar, and then one afternoon he told them, 'Boys, tomorrow night I have the real surprise. You can try to guess what it's to be, but I shan't tell you.'

At home they discussed with their father what it might be: perhaps a horse of their own, or a slave boy whom they could keep, or a hunting trip. They could not imagine what the old man had for them, and it was with trembling excitement that they crossed the fields at dusk to join the seven Van Doorns.

The old lady was complaining that too much fuss was being made, but even so, no one told the French boys what the surprise was to be, and with some anxiety they sat down for the evening meal, where the old ones talked endlessly as a slave woman and two Hottentots served them.

'Tell me in simple words,' Marthinus said, 'what a Huguenot is.'

'I'm a Huguenot,' Paul said. 'These two boys are Huguenots.'

'But what are you?'

'Frenchmen to begin with. Protestants next. Followers of John Calvin.'

'You believe as we do?'

'Of course. You in Dutch, we in French.'

'I hear you Huguenots were badly treated in France.'

'Tormented and thrown in jail and sometimes killed.'

'How did you escape?'

'Through the forests, at night.' No one spoke. 'And when we were safely in Holland, your brother, Karel . . . He's an important man, you know, in the Lords XVII. He sent me back to fetch the vines I've brought you. I took my son Henri with me to confuse the Catholic authorities. This boy crept through the forest with me to steal the grapevines, and if we'd been caught by the soldiers . . .'

'What would have happened?' young Hendrik asked.

'I'd have been chained to a ship for life. He'd have been put where they turn Huguenot boys into Catholic boys in a jail, and his brother here would never have seen him again.'

'Was it really so cruel?' Marthinus asked.

'It was death to be a Calvinist.'

'It was in our family, too,' Willem suddenly said. 'My great-grandfather was hanged.'

'He was?' Louis asked in awe, all thoughts of the surprise buried in this revelation of family courage.

'And my grandfather died in war, fighting for our religion. And as a little girl my mother used to gather with her family like this and do something that would have caused her execution . . .'

'What do you mean?' Louis de Pré asked.

'She would have been hanged if they had caught her.'

'What did she do?'

'Blow out the candles,' Willem said, and when only one flickered he produced from the next room the old Bible, which he opened at random, and when the children were quiet he read a few verses in Dutch. Then, with his hand spread out upon the pages, he told them, 'In those days your grandfathers died if they were caught reading like this.' Closing the heavy cover, he told the children, 'But because we persisted, God came to comfort us. He gave us this land. These good houses. These vines.'

Young Hendrik van Doorn had heard these tales before, but they had made no impression on him. Now, with the Frenchman telling comparable stories, he understood that tremendous things had happened in France and Holland, and that he was the recipient of a powerful tradition. From that night on, whenever the Dutch Reformed Church was mentioned, he would visualize a young boy creeping through the forest, a man chained to a galley bench, one of his ancestors hanged, and especially a group of people huddled over a Bible at night.

'Light the candles!' old Willem cried. 'And we'll have the surprise!'

'Hooray!' the Huguenot boys shouted as Annatjie left the room, to reappear bearing a brown-gold crock with no handles. As she came to the table she looked momentarily at her father-in-law, who nodded slightly toward Louis. Going to him, she placed the crock before him, and he looked in to see the golden brown crust with the raisins and lemon peel and cherries peeking through.

'Oh!' he cried. 'Can I have some?'

'You can have it all,' Willem said. 'I made it for you.'

The three Huguenots stared at him, unable to conceive that this wrinkled old farmer could also cook, but when the crock was passed to Paul, so that he could serve, he jabbed his spoon into the crust and they applauded.

While the others ate, Paul studied the old Dutchman and was confused. Willem had proved the most generous of neighbors, lending slaves whenever needed; he laughed with the children and now proved himself an able cook. He was in no way the dour and heavy Dutchman Paul had expected, but he did have one mortal failing: he could not make good wine. In a way, this was not surprising, for none of his countrymen could, either. For a thousand years Frenchmen to the south of Holland and Germans to the east had made fine wine, but the Dutch had never mastered it.

'Van Doorn,' Paul said one day in exasperation, 'to make good wine requires fifteen proper steps. And you've done all of them wrong except one.'

Willem chuckled. 'What one?'

'The direction of your vines. They don't fight the wind and the sun.' De Pré studied the lines and asked, 'How did you get that right?'

And then an inexplicable thing happened. The old man stood among his vines, and dropped his hands, and tears came to his eyes. His shoulders shook, and after a long time he said, 'A girl instructed me a long time ago. And they branded her on the face, here and here. And she fled into the wilderness with my sons. And by the grace of God she may still be alive ... somewhere out there.' He placed his hands over his face and bowed his head. 'I pray to God she's still alive.'

So many things were implied in what the old man said that Paul concluded it was wisest to ask nothing, so he returned to the making of wine: 'Really, Mijnheer, you've done everything wrong, but because your vines know you love them, they have stayed alive, and when my good grapes join them, I do believe we can blend the musts into something good.'

'You mean, we can make wine they won't laugh at in Java?'

'That's why I came,' De Pré said, and his jaw jutted out. 'In two years they'll be begging for our wine in Java.'

Inadvertently he brought dilemmas into the Van Doorn household. One day, while listening to his sons at play, he realized to his dismay that they had shouted at one another for upwards of half an hour without once having used a French word. They had begun to conduct their lives wholly in Dutch, and no matter how carefully he spoke to them in French at mealtime or at prayers, they preferred to respond in Dutch. He recalled the farewell sermon of the clergyman at the Huguenot church in Amsterdam: 'Above all, cling to your language ... It is the soul of France, the song of freedom.'

When it became apparent that no discipline from him was going to make his sons retain their language, he appealed to the Van Doorns for help, but they were aghast at his effrontery. 'You're in a Dutch colony,' Katje said bluntly. 'Speak Dutch.'

'When you want to register your land,' Willem said, 'you'll have to do it in Dutch. This isn't some French settlement.'

'It's quite proper that church services should be in Dutch,' Marthinus continued. 'Ours is a Dutch church,' and when De Pré pointed out that in Amsterdam the Dutch had not only permitted a French church to operate but had also paid the salary of the foreign minister, Marthinus growled, 'They must have been idiots.'

Despite their arguments, Paul still felt that the Compagnie should duplicate the Dutch government's generosity and provide the Huguenots with a church of their own, and he started looking about for fellow Frenchmen, but found none, and for good reason. The Lords XVII, afraid that the immigrants might coalesce, just as De Pré was now proposing, and form an indigestible mass within the settlement, speaking an alien language and demanding extraterritorial rights, had issued an edict to prevent this error:

> The Huguenots shall be scattered across the countryside rather than settled in one spot, and every effort shall be made to stamp out their language. Legal proceedings, daily intercourse, and above all, education of the young must be conducted in Dutch, and no concession whatever shall be made to their preferred tongue.

The threat of a divided colony was not trivial, for although the number of Huguenots was small—only one hundred and seventy-six in the main wave of immigration—so was the number of Dutch, for in 1688 when De Pré and his first group landed, the entire Compagnie roster listed only six hundred and ten white people, counting infants, and a frightening portion of these were of German descent. At times it seemed that the Germans must ultimately submerge the Dutch, except for two interesting factors: on the rare occasion that a German found a marriageable woman, she was invariably Dutch; and the Germans tended to be ill-educated peasants who readily accepted the Dutch language.

Not so the Huguenots. They were both well educated and devoted to their language, and if left to cluster in xenophobic groups, might form an intractable minority. Since the Dutch did not propose to let this happen, the French were scattered, some to Stellenbosch, some higher up in a place called Fransch Hoek, and others in a choice valley well to the north. But no matter where they found refuge, they encountered this driving effort to eradicate their language, which De Pré was determined to resist. In the letters he dispatched to the other settlements he wrote:

> The most sacred possession a man can have, after his Bible, is his native tongue. To steal this is to steal his soul. A Huguenot thinks differently from a Dutchman and expresses this thinking best in his

native language. If we do not protect our glorious French in church, in law and in school, we surrender our soul. I say we must fight for our language as we would for our lives.

This was such open subversion that Cape officials felt obligated to send investigators to Stellenbosch, and after brief questioning, these men proposed throwing De Pré into jail, but the Van Doorns protested that he was a good neighbor, needed for the making of wine. The latter point impressed the officials, who lectured De Pré at a public hearing: 'Only because your friends have defended you do you escape imprisonment. You must remember that your sole duty is to be loyal to the Compagnie. Forget your French. Speak Dutch. And if you circulate another inflammatory petition, you will be ejected from the colony.'

Despite this censure, De Pré did gain one of his objectives: the refugees were given permission to build a small church for the minister who had sailed in one of the ships from Amsterdam, and behind its whitewashed walls only French was heard. But the children, and especially Henri and Louis de Pré, continued to speak mainly in Dutch, and it became apparent that the Compagnie's efforts to stamp out French would in the end succeed.

It was agreed between the Van Doorns and the De Prés that the question of language would be discussed no further; each side had made its position clear and only animosity could ensue if the arguing continued. Of course, no one supposed that any peace treaty would be honored by old Katje, and whenever she gave the De Pré boys a goodie she would tell them, 'Say thank you, like a good Dutch boy,' and the boys would say, 'Hartelijck bedanckt, Ouma!'

One night she asked Paul, 'Why did you come to a Dutch land if you don't like it?'

'I do like it,' Paul said. 'Look at my fields.'

'But how did you get here?'

'Your husband's brother sent me to steal the grapevines, as I told you.'

'How is the old thief?'

'Katje!' Willem protested.

'Well, he is an old thief, isn't he?' she demanded of De Pré.

'If he is, he's a smart one,' Paul said. 'He married one of the richest widows in Amsterdam.'

'I'm sure of that,' Katje snapped, and when De Pré revealed the clever manner in which the Widows Bosbeecq had outmaneuvered Karel in the matter of their seven ships, she chortled.

'Nine cheers for the widows!' she cried, then grabbing her granddaughter Petronella, she said solemnly, 'If you ever become a widow, outsmart them, Petra. Keep your wits about you and outsmart them.'

'Grandmother!' Annatjie said sharply. 'Don't talk like that to a child.'

'And you too!' the old lady said. 'If you become a widow, which God forbid, watch yourself. Women are smarter than men, much smarter, but in times of emotion—'

'But you see,' Paul broke in, 'the Widows Bosbeecq were forewarned about Karel. They knew he was a tricky man.'

Suddenly Katje leaned forward, and reaching out to grasp the Huguenot by his arm, she asked, 'How did they know that?'

'They warned me about him when I went to work at his big house. They were ready to marry him, you understand, either of them, but they knew he was a thief . . . because of what he had done to you.' At this point he addressed Willem.

Katje tugged at his arm: 'What do you mean?'

'The way he stole from your husband.'

Sharp tug: 'Stole what?'

'When he sold your mother's house in Batavia. Everyone knew that half the money was for Willem, but he kept it for himself . . . all of it.'

'I knew it! I knew it!' the old woman shouted, jumping from her chair and rampaging back and forth from table to door. 'I told you he was a thief.' Halfway back to the table she stopped, remembered old days, and cried, 'I told him to his face. "You're stealing from us." ' On and on she recalled scenes of that last confrontation when she had divined what the couple was up to. At the end she fell into her chair, dropped her head on the table and wept.

'There, there,' Willem whispered.

'But we could have had that money. We could have gone back to Holland in style. We didn't have to work like slaves . . .'

'I would never have gone,' Willem said, and his wife looked up at him in astonishment, then with slow understanding as he asked, 'Would you have missed this valley for a smelly house on a smelly canal?'

But as the De Prés started to walk home they could still hear the old woman haranguing her family: 'Always remember, your uncle was a thief. He stole what was rightfully yours.' On and on, until they could hear no more, she lectured on how she had been right, back in 1664.

It annoyed Paul that his sons used Dutch to refer to Katje. It was 'Ouma gave us a cookie.' 'Ouma said we could sleep over there.' It meant *old mother,* hence *grandmother,* and was a term of endearment, for if Ouma gave her husband a bad time over the various mistakes he made in his life, she compensated by her love for children. She knew they needed discipline and she was the one to dispense it, but she also knew they needed love, and she was as indulgent with the De Pré children as with the Van Doorn.

One morning, when Henri and Louis had gone to the big house to beg sweets from the old lady, they ran home in tears. 'Ouma's dead! Ouma died last night!' Three days later she was buried at the foot of a hill, and on the way back from the grave Marthinus said, 'She's had time to get to heaven, and right now she's advising St. Peter, sternly.'

Her death had a curious aftermath. Old Willem, recalling how often she had badgered him to enlarge the farmhouse—seeking by this means to finally compensate for the cramped hut at the Cape—decided that he would at last accede to her wishes. When he announced that he was riding to the Cape to buy a Malay carpenter, his son asked why, and he replied to Annatjie, as if she were old Katje's surrogate, 'It's about time I made this house the way she wanted it.'

By starting early and riding hard through the heat of day, the old man reached the Cape before dusk, and what he saw always delighted him. The bay now had a quay at which ships could tie, a handsome new fort of gray stone, streets with solid houses and spacious orchards growing pears and lemons and oranges and plums and apples. More than half the white people in the colony lived in the town, which had every aspect of a thriving community—except one: the entire place contained not a single formal store; the Compagnie felt that the duty of the Cape was to refresh its fleets and collect goods for use in Java. What local buying and selling might be necessary would be done by the Compagnie, from its offices, and no merchant class would be allowed in the Cape.

But Amsterdam was a world away from the raw settlement in Table Valley, and its restrictions had the opposite effect from those intended: practically everyone at the Cape became a secret huckster, dealing directly with passing ships, hoarding clandestine stores in their homes, selling, bartering, smuggling until they became so skilled that they earned their entire living at the business. Corruption was also rife among Compagnie officials, as poorly paid as they were resentful of service at this insignificant and forsaken outpost; venality reached to the top, as proved by the vast private estates operated by some Compagnie men.

The Lords XVII had never sought a proper settlement here and constantly proclaimed that free burghers were to keep within the bounds established by the authorities in Amsterdam. Physical and spiritual lives alike were minutely prescribed, for the truth was that the Lords were both perplexed and frightened by the vastness of Africa. Holland was a small, hemmed-in country and provided the scale by which their Cape entrepôt would always be judged. The Lords believed that if, through their Council of Policy at the Cape, they were able to dictate what could be read, or spoken in church, or discussed publicly, they would retain control; so they instructed the farmers how to conduct their leisure hours, their wives how to dress, and all citizens when to go to bed at night.

But Willem had the Lords XVII to thank for providing him with an opportunity to purchase a carpenter; the Lords had ordered: 'No homeward-bound official may bring his slaves with him to Holland.' So Willem picked up a bargain and hurried to the Castle, as the new five-bastioned fort was now called, to register his property, but he found the officials more interested in Paul de Pré than in the deed of sale.

'Tell us, does De Pré still converse in French?'

'Not with us. We don't speak it.'

'But with his children?'

'When his boys are with us, they speak Dutch.'

'Is he circulating any more petitions?'

'He's too busy with the grapes.' Had De Pré been manufacturing grenades, Willem would not have betrayed him.

With visible reluctance the Compagnie granted permission to buy the young Malay carpenter, Bezel Muhammad, whose name betrayed his mixed origin—the first deriving from his black Madagascan mother, the second from his brown Malaccan father. He spoke five pidgin languages, none well, and was a master of saw and hammer. He was reluctant to leave a town which contained other Coloureds, with whom he liked to associate, but he saw advantages in moving closer to where trees grew. He preferred the timber of Africa to the mahogany of Mauritius or the heavier imported woods from Java. He also liked the forthright manner of Van Doorn, and promised, 'I build good.'

As they were leaving the Castle an official called out after them, 'Remember, you're responsible for that slave! See that he doesn't run away!' Willem agreed, thinking: How men change. When Jango wanted to run, I helped him. But for this slave I paid my own money, so I must guard him.

Willem could not have foreseen the effect that Bezel Muhammad would have upon the valley. The children loved helping him with his tasks, accompanying him into the forest in search of stinkwood, that heavy dark wood which smelled so foul if a tree rotted, but looked so grand when planed down and polished. Annatjie, now in sole charge of the house, appreciated his helpfulness, but it was Paul de Pré who was affected most deeply.

He quickly discovered that Bezel was an artist, not only in wood but in all building, and it was he who argued Willem into allowing the slave to refinish the west façade of the house, the side facing Table Mountain: 'What we should do, Willem, is make the long house not only a little bigger, but a little more pleasant.'

'That's what Katje always wanted.'

'We'll do it for her,' Paul said, but often as Willem watched the energy with which the Huguenot worked he gained the impression that Paul was building not for Katje, but for himself. On important points the Huguenot was adamant.

'The front must be kept long and low, but over the door we want a beautiful gable, like the ones I knew in Holland.' He sketched the graceful curves that would define the gable and determine its height, and although he consulted the two Van Doorn men on what materials Bezel Muhammad should use, it was he who directed each stage of the construction.

It was De Pré's idea also to build a wing projecting backward from the front door, so that the house took the form of a T, with the kitchen and serving areas in the stem at the rear. When the house was completed, he found a way to finish off its long clean walls with cow manure, which hardened like stone, and then to whitewash them so that they gleamed pure-white. But because the mud-and-manure produced an uneven surface, when the whitewash was applied, it assumed magnificent planes and dips and protuberances which reflected light in a thousand different ways. Like a crystal jewel set among trees, the gabled whiteness symbolized the scintillating Dutch-Huguenot alliance which, with its strong German component, was forming a new society.

'And now the surprise!' De Pré announced as all looked with pleasure at their new dwelling. 'What I have in mind is something else Katje would have liked.' And he sketched in the dust his plan for a stoep, a front porch on which to rest when the sun went down behind Table Mountain. It was agreed by all that Katje would indeed have liked this, would have sat there at the end of day; so the gallant old woman, who had rarely been given a moment to rest while alive, was memorialized by a stoep on which her descendants would sit doing nothing.

'It mustn't be a high stoep,' De Pré cautioned, 'for that would mar the face. Just two courses of stone and only wide enough for two rocking chairs.' When it was finished, the Van Doorns applauded, and on the first evening when Annatjie tested the rockers, looking out to Table Mountain, she told her son Hendrik, 'It will be your job to care for these fields when your grandfather and your father are no longer here.' Later she would remember that when she said this, her son had turned away from the Cape and said, 'Grandfather always wanted to go that way. Didn't you?' And old Willem had agreed with his grandson: 'Go beyond the mountains. If I were younger, I'd build my farm out there, and to hell with the Compagnie.'

Bezel Muhammad had his own surprise for his new family. Having found several large stinkwood and yellow-wood trees, he had built a standing clothes cabinet, nine feet high, with finely polished swinging doors in front, a set of four drawers below, and feet carved in the form of an eagle's talon grasping an orb. In simple design the closet would have been handsome, but when the two woods, near-black and glowing gold, were alternated, the result was quite dazzling. It was a gift for Annatjie, but everyone agreed that Katje would have loved that armoire.

When De Pré used this word the Dutchmen looked at him askance, and even when he explained its meaning they resented it. 'That thing's a wall cupboard,' Marthinus said, and he was aghast at what De Pré suggested next. Leading the entire family to a spot well west of the remodeled house, he asked them to look at its quiet perfection as it nestled among its hills: 'See how all things fit together. The gable not too high, the stoep not too big, the walls reflecting the light. It's our palace in Africa.'

The Dutchmen did not like the analogy. Palaces were occupied by Spaniards and Frenchmen, and they had meant death to Calvinists. 'I want no palace on my land,' Marthinus said.

De Pré ignored him: 'There's a new palace building near Paris. Trianon it's called. Our African palace should be called that, too.'

'Ridiculous!' Marthinus cried, but De Pré said quietly, 'Because when we start to sell our wine, we'll need a good name for it. And if we call it Trianon, we'll catch everybody. A few will know it to be a good Cape wine. The main will think it's French.'

This made sense, and when De Pré saw that the Van Doorns were wavering, he dispatched Henri to fetch a bundle by the door, and when the lad rolled in the wrapped parcel, Paul carefully folded back the covering to display a beautifully made oaken cask, capable of holding a leaguer of wine, which Bezel Muhammad had decorated with a most handsome replica of the gabled house and the single word TRIANON.

Old Willem accepted the cask, and after he had studied it in various lights, said: 'We'll call it Trianon. Because my wine wasn't worth a stuiver till this fellow came along.'

In the years that followed, when the wine of Stellenbosch was gaining favorable attention both in Java and Europe, Bezel Muhammad continued to build, but only occasionally, his wall cupboards of the two contrasting woods, and whereas he took great pains to design each one in lovely balance

—making his art the only one of high degree that flourished in the colony in these decades—he never exceeded that first handsome design. It stood in the bedroom to the left as one entered Trianon and was admired by all.

His cupboards were sold as soon as he could finish them, and at various farms in the Stellenbosch area they were prized. The slave who made them was in great demand when it came time to build a gable or enlarge a house, and this caused Annatjie some uneasiness, for although she was quite willing that her family profit from the work of their slave—Marthinus sold the cupboards and kept all but a few rix-dollars on each—she was not content that this skilled man should be without a wife, and it perplexed her as to how she might find him one.

When she raised the question at supper one night, Marthinus said, 'Most men who come out here live without women for years. Look at De Pré.'

'Yes,' she said, 'and I wonder about him, too.'

'Let him get one of the King's Nieces. The way I did.'

When next De Pré ate with them she raised the question: 'Paul, it's time you should ask the Compagnie to bring you a wife. You could write to Karel. He'd find you someone.'

'He'll not deal with that one,' Willem said sternly.

'But he can't always live alone,' Annatjie said, and she was so persuasive that De Pré drafted a careful letter to his old employer, asking for a wife. A year later Trianon received word that Karel van Doorn had died, his estate going to the Widows Bosbeecq.

So Annatjie turned her attention to Bezel, dispatching letters to the Cape to ascertain if there were any Muslim slave girls, or black ones, for that matter, seeing that he was half-black, who might be purchased, but there were none, and Bezel continued to live alone, building the houses and the furniture that became a feature in the elegant town of Stellenbosch.

It had a fine church now, broad streets lined with young oak trees, and a score of tidy small houses whose floors were smoothed brown with cow manure. It looked nothing like Holland, not too much like Java; it was a unique little gem of a town born of the South African experience, and no house excelled that one called Trianon.

And then a farm family moved nearby with a marriageable daughter, Andries Boeksma and his pretty child Sibilla. 'She's God's answer to our prayers,' Annatjie told Paul as soon as she heard the good news. Using the excuse of taking spiced apples to the newcomers, she studied Sibilla and drove back to Trianon, exultant—'Paul, Marthinus! She's just what we've prayed for'—and she insisted that the two men dress properly, kill a lamb and take it to the Boeksmas. She very much wanted to go along, but felt that to do so might betray her interest in having Sibilla meet the Huguenot widower.

'What happened?' she asked breathlessly when she and her husband were alone.

'I don't really understand,' Marthinus said. 'They took an instant dislike. They were barely civil.'

'What could have happened?'

'Well, Boeksma walked to the cart with me, and while Paul was saying goodbye to Mevrouw he confided that Sibilla would never marry a Frenchman, and on the way home Paul confided that he had no interest in her. He was most emphatic. Told me, "None whatever." '

With the most obvious stratagems Annatjie endeavored to ignite a romance between the two, inviting the Boeksmas twice to her table and lending Bezel for the building of their house, but Paul wanted nothing to do with Sibilla, and she in turn showed herself to be most uneasy in his presence. Before long she was betrothed to a widower from a farm at the north edge of town, and Paul was still without a wife.

When he left his sons with Annatjie for two weeks so that he could journey to Fransch Hoek, she was convinced that he had gone in search of a wife among the other Huguenots, but when he returned alone she found that he had only been agitating—as he had so often before—for the establishment of a French school. When Marthinus upbraided him for this, he repeated stubbornly, 'If a man loses his language, he loses his soul.'

Two interests kept the families united: their desire to produce a good wine, and their deepening faith in Calvinism. Like all Huguenots, Paul was fanatically devoted to his religion, and because his experience of repression was recent, he was apt to be more fiercely protective than his Dutch neighbors, none of whom had known the Spanish persecution personally. Had the Dutch of Stellenbosch wanted to relax the austerity of their Calvinism, the Huguenot immigrants would have protested. Back in Holland the Dutch were making gestures of conciliation with Catholics, especially their German neighbors, and occasionally a strain of this liberalism would surface at the Cape; when French ships put into the bay, officers and men were treated with respect, even though they were Catholic; but for the Huguenots that religion remained unspeakable, and whatever steps their church took had to be diametrically opposed to Rome.

This preoccupation with religion was illustrated when a band of raiders struck at the cattle of the Stellenbosch farmers. The attackers were a wild bunch of outcasts, slaves and renegade Hottentots who crept into Dutch kraals and in repeated sorties carried off many of the best animals.

Neighboring farmers assembled to retaliate, but their efforts made little impression along a hundred-mile frontier, so the burgher militia had to be summoned to launch a serious offensive. Every adult male in the district reported to Stellenbosch, and it was to this meeting that Farmer Boeksma rode up with three of his Hottentot servants equipped and armed for war.

'Madness!' several of the old-timers argued. 'You heard what the governor told us. "To allow them to bear arms is nothing less than putting a knife in their hands to slash our throats." '

'He was talking about slaves,' Boeksma reminded the men.

Over the years the Dutch had had so much trouble with their slaves, who persisted in trying to escape to freedom, that the most bizarre punishments were instituted: when one black woman enraged the community, the commander ordered that she be stripped, broken on the wheel, and tied to the ground while her breasts were ripped off by red-hot pincers, after which she was to be hanged, beheaded and quartered. When certain settlers protested this barbarity, the commander granted clemency: the woman was sewn into a canvas bag and thrown into the bay, where she struggled for half an hour before drowning.

'We must never arm slaves,' a cautious man warned.

'But these aren't slaves,' Boeksma pleaded. 'They're loyal. They believe in me like my own children.'

As he spoke, the armed servants stood silent. One could still be classified as a Hottentot, but the other two were Coloureds, and when Boeksma called them part of his family he spoke the truth, for there was no tribe or captaincy surviving in this area to which they could give their allegiance, no homeland, no human being except 'Groot Baas Boeksma.' They had accepted his God, his church, his way of life, and this was demonstrated daily in the language they spoke, an exciting mixture of Dutch-Malay-Portuguese-Hottentot. It was a good patois and it served them well in field and kitchen. A farmer might not be able to afford many slaves, but every settler was able to attract his complement of Hottentot-Coloured families; they tended the vineyards; they served his meals; they nursed his infants and minded his children, scolding when needed and whispering instructions in the language they were building from their disparate backgrounds.

Still, the idea of arming even such placid dark men was repugnant, and an impasse was reached between Boeksma, who wanted to do so, and the sager heads, who warned against it. It was the Huguenot De Pré who resolved the argument: 'I seem to remember a passage in our Bible. In the years when Abraham was still called Abram, his nephew Lot fell into trouble, and there was discussion as to how the commando might rescue him. And did not Abraham arm his servants and sally forth to save his nephew?'

None of the Dutchmen remembered this incident, but all agreed that if Abram really had armed his servants, that would constitute permission for them to do the same, so they consulted Willem, who offered his Bible to the worried men, and in the fourteenth chapter of Genesis, De Pré found specific instructions telling them what to do, but when he encountered trouble reading the Dutch he almost spoiled things by saying, 'In French it's clearer.' It had never occurred to his neighbors that God's word had ever appeared in any language but Dutch:

> 'And when Abram heard that his brother was taken captive, he armed his trained servants, born in his own house, three hundred and eighteen, and pursued them . . . And he brought back all the goods, and also brought again his brother Lot, and his goods, and the women also, and the people.'

What astounded these devout men was that when they added up those servants in the Stellenbosch region capable of fighting, they totaled three hundred and eighteen, and Andries Boeksma shouted, 'It's a revelation— a revelation from God Himself! A thousand years ago, nay, ten thousand, He foresaw our plight and instructed us to arm our servants.' And he asked the men to pray, expressing their thanks for this guidance, and when they rose they organized a punitive expedition, and for every animal the Hottentots had taken away, the Dutchmen brought back three.

From then on, no commando sallied forth without its complement of Hottentot-Coloured fighters, and few farmers would venture into the wilderness without their dark families trailing along with them. For generations this alliance would maintain, fortified sometimes by bloodlines when lonely men needed companionship, but more often based on a kind of acknowledged and gentle servitude, for they were, as Boeksma had said, 'Loyal.' As the Dutchmen traveled, the little dark men and women might not be visible, and they never ate at table, but they were there, one step behind the Groot Baas.

Willem did not accompany the raiders, and he refused for a good reason: he still hoped that some kind of peace might be brought about between white settlers and brown. 'You're no longer a good Dutchman,' Andries Boeksma chided when the victorious commando returned. 'You don't think like a man from Holland, and you don't act like a man from Java.'

'I've thought of that myself,' Willem said. 'I suppose I'm an Afrikaner.'

'A what?' Boeksma cried.

'An Afrikaner. A man of Africa.' It was the first time in history this designation had been used, and never would it apply more accurately. And when the day came that Willem's persistent lung disease, incurred by his hours on the horse, attacked and he lay dying, he counseled his grandchildren never to war with the Hottentots: 'Share Africa with them in peace.'

His sickbed stood in the left-hand room facing Bezel Muhammad's first cupboard, and he passed the pain-choked hours by studying afresh the lovely relationship between the two woods, dark and light. They seemed an augury of what the country he had discovered and settled might become.

No amount of Biblical glossing helped when the Van Doorns faced their real catastrophe, nor were the teachings of the Dutch Reformed Church of much assistance, either. One spring morning when Marthinus was working at the vines and the three De Prés were far away, he was summoned by the frantic ringing of a bell, and suspecting that this meant fire, he ran toward the big house, shouting, 'De Pré! De Pré! Where in hell are you?' But when he reached the house, and found only Annatjie, tall and red-faced, standing in the kitchen with Petronella, he was glad he had come alone.

'Send the boys away,' his wife said brusquely, and the two lads were dismissed, even though Hendrik, now thirteen, could guess that the emergency had something to do with babies.

When the boys were gone, Annatjie gasped, 'This one wants to marry Bezel Muhammad!' And when Marthinus looked at his fifteen-year-old daughter, she nodded so vigorously that her pigtails bobbed, giving her the look of a child.

Marthinus sat down. 'You want to marry a slave?' When his daughter nodded again, he asked, 'Does he know about this?' And before she could reply, he demanded, 'Do you have to get married?'

She shook her head and held out her hands to her father. 'I love him, and he's a good man.'

Marthinus ignored this for the moment and said, 'I could find you a dozen husbands at the Cape.'

'I know,' Petronella said, 'but I would not be happy with them, Father.'

The way she said *Father* melted Van Doorn. Extending his arms, he said, 'Before he died, old Willem told me he had wanted to marry a slave. Said he regretted not doing so every day of his life. Oh, he loved old Katje, you could see that . . .'

'Then, I can marry him?'

Marthinus looked at his wife, a woman who had contracted a marriage almost as bizarre: in her case she accepted a white husband she had never seen; Petronella was taking a black-brown man she had known for three years. When Annatjie shrugged, the girl took it as a sign that her marriage was approved, but her father said quietly, 'Leave us now, Petronella,' and when she was gone he raised questions too delicate for her ears: 'You know how the Compagnie feels about white and black . . .'

'The Compagnie's worried only about their sailors and soldiers who creep to the slave quarters.' Annatjie sniffed.

'And about men like Boeksma.'

'We all know about Boeksma and his servant girls.'

'With Petronella it is different. She's in love with her slave.' In his confusion Marthinus turned to his Bible, but found no guidance. Abraham had married his slave girl Hagar, and her offspring had populated half the earth, but they could find no account of an Israelite woman's taking a slave husband. There was, of course, constant fulmination against Israelite men marrying Canaanite women, but nothing about the reverse, and it began to look as if God was much more concerned about young men than about their sisters. They even found the obscure text in Ezra in which God, speaking through His prophet, commanded all men to put away their strange wives. They read aloud that extraordinary list of nearly a hundred men who had taken wives from among the Canaanites:

> 'And of the singers also; Eliashib: and of the porters; Shalum, and Telem, and Uri . . . And they gave their hands that they would put away their wives; and being guilty, they offered a ram of the flock for their trespass.'

In the end Marthinus realized that the decision must be made by the Van Doorns alone, and when reached, must be defended by them against whatever opposition the community might organize, so one afternoon he asked his wife to sit with him at the kitchen table, to which they summoned the young lovers.

'Are you determined to marry?' Marthinus asked.

'We are.'

The Van Doorns sat with folded hands, looking at the couple, and the more they studied Bezel the more acceptable he became. 'You are clean and hard-working,' Marthinus said. 'You're a good carpenter. You never praise your own work, but I can see you prize it.' Annatjie said, 'It's as if you combined the best of your two races, durable like the blacks, poetic like the Malays.' But then Marthinus observed ominously, 'And you also represent two very difficult problems.'

When Petronella asked what these were, he said, 'First, he can't marry a white woman while he remains a slave.'

'That's simple,' she said. 'Set him free.'

'Not so simple,' Marthinus said. 'Bezel, you must buy your freedom.'

The slave, having anticipated this impediment, nodded to Petronella, who from the folds of her dress produced a canvas bag containing coins, which she emptied onto the table.

'How did you collect them?' Marthinus asked.

'From the wall closets he makes,' Petronella explained. 'I save the money for him.'

Head bowed, Marthinus fumbled with the coins but did not count them. After a while he cleared his throat and pushed the money back toward his daughter. 'He is free. Keep the coins.' Then, sternly, he added, 'But the marriage will still be impossible unless he's a Christian.'

'He's willing to become one,' Petronella said.

'I was speaking to Bezel.'

'I think I'm already a Christian,' Bezel said, and when this was explored, the people at the table were satisfied that he told the truth, but when they approached the predikant to have him verify the fact, Paul de Pré heard of the negotiation and fell into a rage.

He was so eager to gain possession of Trianon, a house he had practically built, with vineyards he alone had saved from decay, that he had been quietly devising his own plans for Petronella. True, she was only fifteen and he thirty-four, but on a frontier where wives often died in childbirth, it was not uncommon for a patriarch to take himself four wives in sequence. The bride was always about seventeen, the man growing older and older. He had been giving serious thought to Petronella and now he heard with dismay that she was about to be married to a slave.

Frantic, he ran across to Trianon, bursting through the doors he had rebuilt. 'I've come to seek your daughter's hand in marriage.'

'She's already taken,' Annatjie said.

'Muhammad? The slave?'

'Yes.'

'But there hasn't been a wedding!'

'Perhaps there was, perhaps there wasn't,' Annatjie said calmly.

'You would never allow a slave . . .'

'Perhaps we will, perhaps we won't,' she said, and when he started to rave, she said without any show of anger, 'Neighbor De Pré, you're making a fool of yourself.'

Paul appealed to Marthinus, but he remembered too vividly his father's dying comment on what marriage meant at the edge of a wilderness: 'Tell Hendrik and Sarel to find the best women they can and cling to them. I could not have lived my life without Deborah's singing in my ears. I could never have built this refuge without Katje's help.'

'I think we'll let things work themselves out,' Marthinus said, and for

five months he did not see De Pré at the vineyard, but when the time came
to blend the wine, with Trianon's harsher grapes giving character to De
Pré's gentler ones, Paul could not stay away, and it was he who made the
final selections: 'This wine in barrels, for the slaves in Java. But this good
one we put in casks for Europe.' And it was with this vintage that Trianon
became an established name, even in Paris and London.

It was Annatjie who first detected Paul de Pré's grand design. She was a
hard-minded woman who even as a child had learned to calculate what
others might be wanting to do to her. Other unmarried girls at the orphanage had been afraid of emigrating to Brazil or South Africa, but she had
perceived this as her only avenue of escape and had never moaned over the
consequences of her act. When the man who chose her first at the Cape
rejected her, she did not fly to tears, satisfied that someone else would want
her in this lonely outpost, and when Marthinus stepped forward to claim
her, she was not surprised.

She remembered that first long ride across the flats; how bleak they
seemed, how destructive of hopes! But at the worst part of the transit she
had known that something much better must lie ahead, and she had gritted
her teeth, held fast to the reins, and thought: He wouldn't have settled here
if the land were all like this—so that when the river appeared, with ibis and
cranes gracing its banks, and ducks of wild variety diving to its bottom, she
did not feel triumphant relief, but only that this was what she had expected.

Her life with Katje had been difficult at times, for that quarrelsome
woman loved to complain, accusing her daughter-in-law of being too lazy
or too careless, but after two or three harsh battles in which Annatjie stood
her ground, Katje realized that she had a strong woman in her house, and
the two mistresses worked out compromises. Occasionally it had been
necessary for Annatjie to shove Katje aside, when something had to be done
quickly and in what she thought was the proper way. When this first
happened, her mother-in-law exploded, but Annatjie said, over her shoulder
as she did the work, 'Yell your heart out, old lady, but don't get in my way.'
In later years, when the younger Van Doorns had three children, Annatjie
appreciated Katje's presence, for she proved a loving grandmother, instilling decent behavior into the children while stuffing them with goodies.

Annatjie's relationship with Willem had been more placid. She felt sorry
for the crippled old farmer and admired the stalwart way he tended his
vineyard, never complaining of the pain that kept him walking sideways,
always ready to help any newcomer get started in the Stellenbosch area. She
had worked with him in building the huts that had accumulated about the
farmhouse: one shed for pigeons, one for farming tools, one for the storage
of grain. She enjoyed that heavy work, for with every building that went
up, she felt that the Van Doorns were securing their hold upon the land;
she, more than his son Marthinus, was a projection of Willem's dream for
South Africa.

With her three children she was a firm-minded mother, insisting that
they work on the land with the slaves and Hottentots during the day and
learn their letters at night after the table was cleared. She was desperately

afraid they would be illiterate, and made them read with her from the only book the family owned, the big Bible whose Dutch words were printed in heavy Gothic script—and for a child of seven to try to decipher them was much like unraveling a secret code, but the ability to do so was the mark of a good human being, and patiently she drilled her offspring. In this she succeeded, but in her determination to make them hard-working farmers, like the ones she had known as a girl in Holland, she failed, for as the years passed, the white men of Africa grew accustomed to seeing black bodies bent down over the fields. It seemed God's ordination that labor be divided so that men like the Van Doorns could supervise while slaves and servants toiled. The expression 'Oh, that's slave's work' became current.

Annatjie was distressed when Hendrik showed no real interest in reading, and learned only under duress. For some reason that she did not understand, he inclined toward the wilderness, the tracking of animals and the exploration of valleys yet unsettled. She often wondered what would happen to him, for he was not tractable like the De Pré boys; he had a quick temper, a stubbornness much like his grandfather's; indeed, the only hopeful aspect of his character had been his affection for Willem. It was he who had listened most intently to what the old man had said about the siege of Malacca and his voyages to Japan. The De Pré boys were hungry for news of the France their father had known, but her children were content with Africa.

Petronella she always loved with special affection; the girl was much as she had been, stubborn, helpful, considerate of others and with a vast capacity for love, and it was with this in mind that Annatjie had approached her daughter's marriage to Bezel Muhammad, a free man and a Christian. She had learned to look not at a man's skin but at his soul, and she was quietly amused when Farmer Boeksma revealed his. A hypocritical man, he ranted in church, but at home had three little servant girls who bore a remarkable resemblance to him; their black grandfathers had ridden at his side on commando; their black mothers had served at his table. But now he denounced the proposed Van Doorn marriage: 'It's all right, when the pressure's on a man, to sleep with a slave, but, by God, you never marry them.'

Quickly another farmer corrected him: 'What you mean, Andries, it's all right for white men to sleep with black women. Never white women with black men.' When this was enthusiastically approved, Boeksma endeavored to prohibit the marriage, and might have succeeded except for two reasons: local people needed the wine Marthinus made and the wall closets Bezel built. So the slave became free, the dark man married the white woman, and in a score of unexpected ways the community profited.

Not long after the wedding, Boeksma approached Annatjie with an interesting proposition: 'Mevrouw, would you allow your slave to build me a stinkwood closet?'

'He's a free man. Ask him direct.'

Bezel accepted the commission, and Annatjie was pleased to see the beauty of the gigantic piece. It was, she believed, the best work her son-in-law had ever done, and she watched with wry amusement as he loaded it on his cart for delivery to the man who had been his adversary.

With her daughter married, Annatjie's concern turned to little Sarel, whose reticence had worried her from cradle days. As long as he had to be compared only to Hendrik, who was himself quiet, she could rationalize: 'Sarel's a good boy. He just doesn't attract much attention.' But when he had to be judged against the De Pré lads, his deficiencies became apparent. He spoke more slowly, reacted tardily to externals, and never showed anger the way boys should. She was not yet prepared to admit that Sarel was slow-witted and would have fought anyone who said so, but she did worry: 'He's a slow developer. Not to be compared with the others.'

Annatjie herself was without vanity, or envy, or senseless anger. She was a woman born without prospects who had stumbled into a life infinitely better than she could have anticipated, with a young husband who appreciated her, an older son who gave promise of becoming outstanding, and parents-in-law who had been exceptional. Furthermore, she lived in a valley that had no equal in South Africa and in a house that would one day be hailed around the world as a masterpiece of Cape Dutch invention.

She was therefore quite capable of handling Paul de Pré's obvious determination to gather all the land in this valley into one vast holding, of which the principal part would be the vineyards of Trianon. The Van Doorns now owned their original sixty morgen, plus an additional hundred and twenty acquired since coming to the valley. Paul de Pré owned only the sixty granted him by Karel van Doorn in lieu of cash, but already he had plans to pick up another farm, and had sharp eyes for several bits of unclaimed land beyond that.

He had tried to marry Petronella in order to establish some kind of claim on Trianon, and had been rebuffed. Indeed, he had been ridiculed by Annatjie, who had told him he was making a fool of himself, but this had not deterred him from proceeding with his ambition, and one evening some months after the funeral of old Willem he came to the Van Doorns with an astonishing proposal: 'Why don't we merge the two farms? I'll contribute mine so that we can operate the vineyards as a single unit.'

'But what would you do?' Marthinus asked.

'Work with you. We can make this the best wine farm outside of France.'

'You'd give up your morgen?'

'We'd be partners. What difference does it make who owns this piece of land or that?'

Marthinus said, 'But we own one eighty morgen. You have only sixty. What kind of partnership is that?'

'If I stop tending the grapes, how much are yours worth, eh?'

'We'd farm it, some other way. But we'd never give up our land.'

'Think about it,' De Pré said, and after three weeks, when the subject was not returned to, he announced one night, 'I now have a hundred and six morgen and will soon have two hundred.'

When he was gone, Annatjie sent the boys to bed and talked seriously with her husband. 'I'm sure Paul has plans to take over Trianon. He rebuilt our house to his taste. He named it. He designed the motif for our casks. And his slaves work the fields better than ours do. I often wondered why he never planted a hedge between our properties. Now I know.'

'I think he just wants a good relationship. As he said—working the fields as a single unit.'

'Marthinus, he's a peasant. A French peasant. And French peasants do not surrender their land easily. Never.' When her husband started to uphold the Huguenot, she interrupted: 'Remember how you defended your land when he proposed a partnership? "We'd never give up our land." What made you say that? Old Willem's sacrifices to get the land? Old Katje's long years of hardship here? Well, if you love your land, Paul de Pré worships his. And if he's willing to give us his, it's only because he thinks he sees a way to gain control over the whole estate later on.'

Marthinus pondered this. He and Annatjie were older than De Pré and would probably die sooner. But there were the three Van Doorn children to inherit Trianon.

'Don't count on that,' Annatjie warned. 'If Petronella has a dark husband, they won't try to hold the land. And I've had grave suspicions that Hendrik won't want to stay here. He's like his grandfather. Eyes to the east. One day he'll wander off and we'll see him no more.'

'There's still Sarel. He loves the soil.'

'De Pré is sure he can outwit Sarel. De Pré knows that Petronella and Hendrik don't count. It's him against Sarel, and he intends to win.'

'But he could well be an old man before this happens. You and I aren't going to die tomorrow.'

'De Pré himself—yes, he will be old, but his boys will be young. And able. And older than Sarel. Three determined Huguenots against one young Dutchman who's not . . .'

'Not what?' Marthinus asked aggressively, and the words she had sworn never to utter came forth: 'He's not too quick.'

'What do you mean?' He spoke in anger, for his wife had opened a subject he had for some time been trying to avoid, and he reacted defensively: 'There's nothing wrong with Sarel!'

The forbidden subject having been broached, she plowed ahead: 'He's a wonderful child and we both love him, but he's not too quick. No match for the De Prés.' And when she began slowly to recite the deficiencies which could no longer be masked, Marthinus had to admit that his young son was limited: 'Not a dull boy. I'd never confess that to anyone. But I do sometimes see that he's not . . . well, as you say . . . quick.' Then he voiced the hope that kept him working so hard at the vineyard: 'One of these days Hendrik will see the light. When the time comes for him to take command.'

'Hendrik has seen other horizons,' Annatjie said. 'He talked too long with old Willem. One of these days he'll be gone.'

'So how do we protect ourselves against De Pré?'

'I think we look first at the land,' she said. 'What's good for the land?'

Marthinus sat for a long time, staring at the flickering candle, and finally said, 'The sensible thing would be to join the two farms, operate them as one, and make some really fine wine.'

'I think we should do so,' Annatjie said.

'But you said you were afraid of De Pré?'

'I am, but I think that together you and I will prove a match for him.'

So to De Pré's astonishment, the Van Doorns came to him and said that papers should be drawn combining the two holdings and that De Pré should go to the Cape to formalize the documents, for such joining of land would never be permitted without Compagnie sanction. And it was this trip which altered everything at Trianon, for when Henri and Louis had a sustained opportunity to see the bustling town, now with about a thousand inhabitants of myriad coloring, they were enchanted by it.

Malays in turbans, Javanese in conical hats, swarthy Madagascans in loincloths, handsome dark women from St. Helena, and high Compagnie officials in fine suitings with lace at the collar—these were the people that formed the Cape parade. While the elder De Pré arranged for the uniting of the farms, a French East Indiaman put into the bay, and stately parties were held at the fort, and one night the Huguenots, as fellow Frenchmen, were invited to attend, and the boys heard their native language spoken with elegance, and saw for themselves what a superior group the French were.

The captain of the French vessel, impressed by the manliness of the boys, invited them to visit his ship, where they ate with the officers and spoke of France. When the ship departed, the boys stood on the quay, saluting, and after that they had no interest whatever in working the fields at Trianon or inheriting the grand design their father was putting together.

In 1698 Henri announced that he was sailing back to Europe. This was not unusual; every return fleet which stopped at the Cape enticed a few free burghers to abandon the settlement, disgusted with the difficulties of farming or terrified by the prospect of being forever lost in the African wilderness. Soldiers, too, who served at the Cape without acquiring land usually wanted to return home at the earliest possibility, and over ninety percent of Compagnie officials quit the Cape when their tour of duty ended. It was the unusual man who followed the steps of Willem van Doorn, choosing the Cape once and for all as his future home and committing himself totally to its development. Young Henri de Pré was not such a pioneer; he was haunted by the gracious canals of Amsterdam, the good fields of France, and he longed to see them once more.

As for young Louis, eighteen years old, the sights and adventures of the Cape had corrupted him. He wanted no more of the wilderness farm or the placid offerings of Stellenbosch: 'I want to work at the Cape.'

'But what can you do, with no land?'

'The Compagnie's wine contractor needs an assistant. I'll join him. I'll work with the men at Groot Constantia, and learn the wine trade. The Huguenots at Paarl will need help.' With that quickness of mind that Annatjie had detected, the boy had visualized a complete way of life: 'I'll marry some Dutch girl.' He could have said, had he wished to confide his entire dream, 'And we'll have many sons and our name will live here forever.'

It was in this way that the Huguenots, that small group of refugees, would make their mark on South Africa. Their names, modified in passing generations, would reverberate in local history and would at times seem to monopolize elite positions: the athletic DuPlessis; the legalist DeVilliers; Viljoen, adapted from the name of the poet's family Villon; Malherbe; the

poet Du Toit, who would help build the Afrikaans language; the military
Joubert; the Naudés of religious fervor; the extensive, rugged Du Preez
family. All of them were devout Calvinists, dedicated to learning and to
conservatism. It was no accident that the man who would lead the Afrikaners to their final nationalist victory and become prime minister came from
this stock—Malan, whose ancestors had fled persecution from a small town
in southern France.

In 1700 Louis de Pré left the aggrandized vineyards of Trianon and
settled in at the Cape, where, according to plan, he married a Dutch girl
and prospered in all he attempted. He would have seven sons, who would
in time be called Du Preez.

His father's plans fared less well. He was forty years old, the best
wine-maker in the district, full partner in the profitable Trianon winery, but
a man now without children or a wife. He lived alone in his small house,
took some of his meals at Trianon, and fended off the Van Doorns when
they persisted in trying to find him a wife. 'Why is he so obstinate?' Marthinus asked one night after Paul had left to walk the short distance to his
lonely house.

'You know what I think?' Annatjie said to her husband. 'I think he is
interested in only one thing—he still hopes that Hendrik will leave us and
that he can bring Louis and his sons back here to take over. He intends that
this shall be a De Pré farm before he dies.'

'He is dreaming.'

'I saw him the other day drawing designs in the dust—uniting all the
little huts into fine buildings stretching out like arms from this one. It could
be quite fine, as he plans it.'

'Let him do it. Bezel likes nothing better than to start carpentering a
new building.' The wings that De Pré had sketched could easily be erected
between seasons, but Annatjie guessed correctly that he would not start
until the farm was more securely in his grasp.

Trianon now comprised about three hundred and eighty acres, all with
access to water. It owned more than thirty slaves from various parts of
Africa, the eastern ocean and Brazil. Fifty Hottentots and Coloureds
worked also from five-thirty at dawn till seven at night, receiving no wages;
they were given food, tobacco, an occasional blanket, and the right to graze
the few animals that remained from their once-vast herds. Once each day
they would queue up with the slaves for a splendid reward: a pint of raw
wine.

One evening Farmer Boeksma arrived to buy a cask of Trianon at the
very time the slaves and servants were lined up for their tot, and he observed, 'Maybe they have bartered away their freedom, but what a marvelous way to forget the past.' Marthinus, thinking of what old Willem had
told about Jango's lust for freedom, and the prices he had been willing to
pay, said nothing.

And then the Bushmen struck. The little brown people had watched with
dismay as white farmers kept extending their holdings farther into traditional hunting grounds. At first they had merely observed the invasion,

retreating ten miles ahead of the plow, but now they were beginning to fight back, and on many mornings a farmer on the outskirts of Stellenbosch would awaken to find his kraal broken, a prize ox slaughtered in a gully, and the spoor of Bushmen leading north toward the open country.

Every tactic had been used to combat the voracious raiders: armed Hottentots had been sent against them, commandos had been mounted, guards had been posted on twenty-four-hour duty, but the little men loved animal meat so much, and the placid cows of the Dutchmen were so inviting, that they circumvented every device the farmers tried. Losses were beginning to be intolerable, and in August of 1702 most of the farmers of Stellenbosch decided they must eliminate the pests.

They were led by Andries Boeksma, who argued that since the Bushmen were not human, they could be wiped out ruthlessly. Others, guided by Marthinus van Doorn, contended that Bushmen did have souls and must not be shot down like wild dogs; he was willing to have the worst offenders disciplined and even hanged if they persisted, but their basic humanity he defended. At first the community divided evenly, the tougher old men insisting that the Bushmen were not much different from dogs or gemsbok, the younger granting that they just might be human.

After a week of debate it was agreed that the argument be settled by recourse to the Bible, but no guidance could be found there, because little people with enormous bottoms and poisoned arrows had never molested the Israelites. When a vote was taken, it stood eleven-to-six in favor of exterminating the Bushmen, since it was decided that they were animals and not human. But before the commando could be started north, young Hendrik van Doorn, twenty-one years old, startled the assembly by volunteering a special piece of evidence:

> 'When I was tracking with the Hottentots we followed a rhinoceros for some days, and when we had it well located in a valley, we went to bed expecting to shoot it in the morning, but when we reached its resting spot, we found that the Bushmen had slain it in a pit. This angered us, and we started tracking the Bushmen, and at last we came upon where the clan was camped, and we saw that they had tame dogs with them, and we concluded that if they could tame dogs, they must be human beings like us and not animals as many had proposed.'

His evidence stunned the eleven men who had voted to kill off all the little people in the way hyenas were destroyed if they came too near a farm, and Andries Boeksma said gravely, 'If they can tame dogs, they're human, and we cannot shoot them all.' To hear the leader of the commando reason thus impressed the others, and the final vote was sixteen-to-one that the Bushmen were human, the lone dissident arguing, 'Human or not, if they steal my cattle, they have to be dealt with.' He would say no more in public meeting, but he planned to kill every Bushman he saw.

The seventeen horsemen found a substantial spoor to follow, the trail of five or six Bushmen dragging cattle parts back to camp, and for several days they narrowed the gap between the two parties. On the fourth day

Andries Boeksma saw signs which satisfied him that the Bushmen must be close at hand, hiding perhaps behind low rocks: 'They know we're after them, so they won't lead us to their camp. That proves this bunch are scavengers, and we can kill them all.' This was agreed upon, even by those who had defended them: the little things might in principle be human, but this particular group were cattle thieves who must be slain.

So the commando, practicing extreme caution, since everyone feared that terrible flight of thin arrows which brought agonizing death, moved toward the rocks that could be hiding the thieves, and when Boeksma saw twigs move, he shouted, 'There they are!' and his followers cheered as they swept down on their target.

There was so much gunfire that none of the Bushmen had any chance of escape, but as they fell, one man maintained control and calmly aimed his arrow at a specific rider, launching it just before he collapsed with four bullets through him. The arrow struck Marthinus van Doorn in the neck, lodged deep within, and broke apart.

By nightfall he felt painfully dizzy and asked Andries Boeksma to cut the arrowhead out, but the big Dutchman said, 'I can't do it, Marthinus. I'd cut your throat.' So the agony increased, and at dawn Marthinus was again pleading that the arrow be cut out, but the men agreed with Boeksma that this was impossible. They built a litter and slung it between two horses, hoping to get Van Doorn back to the apotheek at Stellenbosch, but by midday the poison had spread furiously, and in the late afternoon he died.

'Shall we bury him here?' Boeksma asked Hendrik. 'Or would your mother want him at Trianon?'

'Bury him here,' Hendrik said. The Van Doorns had never feared the veld. So the men of the commando broke into two groups, one to dig a grave, one to gather stones that would mark it, and when the hole was deep enough to keep away hyenas, Marthinus van Doorn, forty-three years old, was buried. Andries Boeksma, as leader of the commando, said a brief prayer, then tied the bridle of Van Doorn's horse to his and started homeward.

Hendrik would never forget what happened at Trianon when the mournful procession rode in to inform Annatjie of her loss. It was not what his mother did that shocked him; she was resolute, as he had expected—a tall, gaunt woman of fifty-one, with rough hands and deep-lined face. She nodded, started to cry, then pushed her knuckles into her eyes and asked, 'Where did you leave the body, Andries?'

'Decently buried . . . out there.'

'Thank you,' she said, and that was all.

Nor was it her impersonal reaction that appalled young Hendrik—he knew that she was not the wailing kind—it was what happened after the commando had ridden off. No sooner had the horsemen left Trianon than Paul de Pré hastened over from his house, crying in a loud voice, 'Mon Dieu, is Marthinus dead?'

'Why do you ask?' Hendrik said.

'I saw the empty horse. The way the bridle was tied to Boeksma's.'

'And what did you think?'

'I thought, "Marthinus must be dead. I must go comfort Annatjie." '

'He's dead,' Hendrik said. 'Mother's inside.' And he saw the avidity with which the Huguenot hurried through the door. Hendrik should not have listened, but he did, hearing De Pré say with great excitement, 'Annatjie, I've heard the dreadful news. My heart is pained for you.'

'Thank you, Paul.'

'How did it happen?'

'Bushmen. Poisoned arrow.'

'*O mon Dieu!* You sorrowful woman.'

'Thank you, Paul.'

There was a silence which Hendrik could not interpret, and then De Pré's voice, urgent and nervous: 'Annatjie, you'll be alone, trying to work the vineyard. I'll be alone, trying to do the same. Should we not join forces? I mean . . . well, I mean . . . What I mean is, should we not marry, and hold the place together?'

Hendrik quivered at the brazenness of such a question, at the awful impropriety of its coming on this day, but he was restrained from bursting into the room and thrashing the Frenchman by what his mother replied: 'I knew you would come quickly to ask that question, Paul. I know you've been plotting and scheming and wondering how you could gain control of the Trianon. I know you're nine years younger than I am and that not long ago you wanted to marry my daughter, not me. And I know how shameful it is of you to ask that question this night. But you're a poor, hungry man, Paul, with only one desire, and I have pity on you. Come back in seven days.'

De Pré spent those days in drawing plans, in adding up acreages and in supervising the slaves and the Hottentots as they prepared the grapes for harvest. He neither went to the big house nor attended the memorial service in Stellenbosch at which the predikant and the members of the commando told the community of Marthinus van Doorn's heroism. He stayed completely apart, working as he had never worked to get Trianon in top condition, and at eight o'clock in the morning of the eighth day he walked over to Trianon in his pressed and dusted clothes.

He did not find Hendrik there. The young man had loaded his wagon —first putting in it, carefully wrapped, his grandfather's Bible and brown-gold crock—with the equipment necessary for a life on the veld, and with a slave and two Hottentot families, had departed for the lands beyond the mountains, taking with him a small herd of cattle and sheep. Before leaving he had said farewell to Petronella and Bezel Muhammad; he judged they were as happy as human beings were allowed to be on this earth, but he could not know that their two dark children would soon be lost in that human wilderness called Coloured; for a brief while they and their descendants would be remembered as Van Doorns, but after that, their history, but not their bloodline, would vanish as surely as would the antecedents of the three little girls fathered by Andries Boeksma. Later, it would become fashionable to claim that all such half-castes were the spawn of those lusty . sailors who could not control their urges at the halfway house between Europe and Asia. That a Van Doorn or a Boeksma had contributed to the Coloureds would be unthinkable.

Hendrik had no feeling about his brother Sarel; the boy showed no courage, no deep interest in anything, and he guessed that with the De Pré boys gone, Sarel would inherit the vineyards; but in this development he had no interest whatever. He did have enormous feeling for Annatjie and supposed that in her place he would do as she was doing; she had been a most excellent mother, loving and understanding; he had seen how tenderly she cared for old Katje when the grandmother was troublesome, and she had been just as attentive to Paul de Pré's two motherless boys. Tears came to his eyes as he admitted to himself that after this day he might never see his mother again, that this break was final; Trianon and the lovely river and the white walls and the gables were lost forever.

With his wagon he headed eastward, as old Willem had done years before; the difference was that he traveled without a wife.

The wedding took place in the church at Stellenbosch at eleven in the morning, and by three that afternoon Paul de Pré, now master of Trianon, had his slaves tearing down the huts that stood in front of the house, and when the space was cleared, he and Bezel Muhammad paced off the dimensions of the proposed wings.

'It's important,' Paul explained, 'that they come away from the main building at an angle, and that the two angles are the same.' When the stakes were driven and the two men had gone far down the entrance road to satisfy themselves that they had found the proper relationships, Paul said, 'I think that's it,' and he could visualize the finished buildings, stark-white but with shadows playing across the surfaces like breezes in a glade, the arms extended in welcome, with the two flanks helping to form with the house a spacious enclosure such as farms in France sometimes had.

'It will be glorious!' he cried with deep pleasure as the sun began to sink, throwing bold colors on the hills behind the house, and he could visualize travelers from the Cape approaching this haven of white buildings and generous spaces.

Construction started immediately. Ten slaves dug foundations, piled rocks, and mixed mud for the walls. Cadres were sent into the fields to cut the heavy thatch that would form the roofs, and Bezel Muhammad led still others into the forests to find yellow-wood for the rafters. Under the constant urging of De Pré, the two rows of buildings seemed to spring from the soil, and when they were nearing completion, and Muhammad's supervision was no longer needed, Paul took him aside to explain what would later prove to be the most engaging aspect of the buildings.

'What I want,' he told Bezel, 'is for each of the eight compartments to have over the door, in the darkest stinkwood you can find, an oval plaque, carved in high relief, indicating what goes on in that segment of the building.' And he stepped along the two flanks, suggesting by big movements of his hands what he had in mind.

'As we ride in, first door on the left, a pigeon, dark against the white wall. Next a pig, because we'll use this as part of the sty. Next a stack of hay, and over this door near the house, a dog. Now let's go back and look at the right-hand side. First a rooster, then a measure for grain, then a pot of flowers, and on the one nearest the house, a rake and a hoe.' Bezel nodded, already planning in his mind how he would carve certain of the signs, but as he started for the two-room home he had built for Petronella some distance from the main house, Paul called him back: 'On the right-hand side, have the tools over the next-to-last door. Save the flowers for the door nearest the house, so that Mevrouw de Pré can get to them easily.'

In all he did, he consulted the wishes of Mevrouw. He might have been tempted to be unpleasant with Annatjie, for she was both older and plainer than he; fifty-one years of ceaseless work had roughened her face, while he remained a handsome youngish man of only forty-two. Girls from surrounding farms, and sometimes their mothers, too, had looked at him with affection, but he had so desperately yearned for control of Trianon that he was willing to pay the price, and that was faithful attention to Annatjie, through whose hands he had acquired it. He would never belittle her, or mention her advanced age, or in any way fail to pay the debt he owed her.

He gave evidence of this attitude on the day the two outreaching buildings were completed, each door with its splendid identifying oval, for after Annatjie had inspected everything and approved this handsome addition, Paul said, 'And now we attend to your needs.'

'I have none,' she said.

'Oh, yes. Your house is too small for you.' She noticed with approval that whereas he often said 'my farm, my vineyard,' and even 'my fields at Trianon,' he invariably referred to the house as hers. There she was mistress, and he proposed making it worthy of her.

Leading her inside, he showed how the T could be improved by the simple device of adding two large rooms to the stem. 'What we'll do,' he explained, 'is change it from a T to an H.' And he pointed out that if this were done, she would also gain two small gardens in the empty parts of the H. 'In hot summers, the cool wind will come at us from all sides.'

When the H was completed, it worked exactly as he had foreseen, and the De Prés now had the finest house in Stellenbosch, a low gracious set of buildings beautifully associated with meadow and mountain. But still his insatiable urge to build drove him on: 'Bezel, I want you to carve me a monstrous oval, six times bigger than the little ones.'

'Showing what?'

'Wine casks decorated with vines.' And while the Malay carpenter carved the symbols, Paul directed his slaves in building a huge wine cellar at the rear of the house but closely attached to it, so that a Spanish-style patio resulted. Trianon now had four lovely gardens: the big one in front, the two little ones tucked into the angles of the house, and this quiet, restricted one at the rear, closed in by white walls and dotted with small trees. When Bezel Muhammad bolted his carving into position, Paul said, 'Here's a building in which wine of distinction might be housed.'

His building mania was almost ended. When the great wine casks from France were placed in position, and the pigeons and chickens and pigs were in their cubicles, he informed Annatjie that he would build one final thing for her, and when she tried to guess what it might be, he told her to visit with the Boeksmas in Stellenbosch for five days. When he came to the Boeksma farm to fetch her, she asked what he had done, and he told her, 'You must see for yourself,' and as they drove up the lane, and into the areaway between the two embracing arms, she could detect nothing new, but as they approached the house she gasped, for at each end of the low stoep on which they sat in the evening Paul had directed his workmen to build two ceramic benches perpendicular to the front wall and faced with the softest white-and-blue tiles from Delft. They showed men skating on frozen canals, women working at the river, views of old buildings and sometimes simply the implements of Dutch farm life. They converted ordinary benches into little jewels, glistening in sunlight, and the great house of Trianon was complete.

It was great in neither size nor height, nor was it Dutch. Its chief characteristics had been borrowed from Java, its secondary ones from rural France, but the spirit that animated it and the manner in which it hugged the earth came only from South Africa. Dutch workmen had helped build it, and a French megalomaniac, and a Malay carpenter, and slaves from Angola, Madagascar and Ceylon, with Hottentots doing much of the light work. It was an amalgam, glorious yet simple, and its chief wonder was that when one sat on the Delft benches at close of day, one could see the sun setting behind Table Mountain.

Paul's attitude toward his five children would always be ambivalent. Concerning Annatjie's boy Hendrik, who had vanished into the wilderness, he was glad to see him go, for he recognized him as a threat. He did not worry about his own son Henri, now in Amsterdam, for he judged this one would never have wanted to farm; indeed, he felt some relief at the boy's disappearance, for he sensed that sooner or later he would have had trouble with him. Annatjie's boy Sarel he considered a dolt and was pleased to see that girls thought so, too, for the boy was not married, would produce no heirs to claim the vineyards, and could be dismissed. His son Louis was a different matter; Paul was still convinced that after a few years at the Cape, the boy would want to come back to the farm, and it would be to him that Trianon would ultimately revert; often he consoled himself by thinking: The experience with the Compagnie will make him a better manager. He'll know about ships and agents and markets. That the boy would ultimately return he never doubted, and that Louis could wrest the vineyard from silly Sarel was evident. 'Trianon of the De Prés' he saw as the ultimate title, and if the French name should be submerged in the Dutch Du Preez, that would be all right with him.

It was his attitude toward Petronella that surprised Annatjie, for he had bitterly opposed her liaison with Bezel Muhammad, but now his opinion changed radically. One day he said, 'Annatjie, I'm not using my house, and the boys seem to have fled. Why not give it to Petronella and Bezel?'

'I think they'd like that,' Annatjie said, and she was astonished when he not only gave the young couple the house, but also helped Bezel erect a workshop in which his tools would have an orderly place. He even assigned three slaves to the task of cutting stinkwood trees for Bezel and shaping them into timbers.

Later, of course, Annatjie discovered that Paul had talked Bezel into building only wall cupboards, which were carted to Louis de Pré, who sold them at top prices at the Cape. Bezel was given less than a third of the profits, but he and Petronella did occupy their new home rent-free, and he appreciated the fact that Paul's patronage was of great value to a carpenter who had been a slave.

Then came the years of conflict. Paul was determined that Louis come back to inherit the vineyard; Annatjie was equally insistent that her son Sarel pull himself together, take a wife, and produce the Van Doorn children who would supervise Trianon far into the future. In this struggle De Pré used vicious weapons, denigrating Sarel at each opportunity, spreading in the community rumors that he was an imbecile. He spoke casually of the day when Louis would return to take command: 'He's studying the wine business, you know. The Compagnie has sent him to Europe to ascertain who the trustworthy merchants are.'

The struggle took an ugly turn whenever Annatjie maneuvered her self-conscious son into contact with any marriageable girl, for then Paul would arrange to meet, by happenstance, her parents, to whom he would drop bits of intelligence: 'I don't really suppose he's an idiot. He can buckle his shoes.' And since Sarel, who blushed beet-red at the sight of a girl, did nothing to advance any courtship, the meetings arranged by his mother came to naught.

She wondered what to do. She was fifty-seven now and did not expect to live far into her sixties; Sarel was not deficient, of that she was certain, but he was shy and awkward and he needed a wife most urgently. But where could she find one for him?

She arranged an excuse for taking him to the Cape, but accomplished nothing, so in desperation she looked toward Holland and the orphanage from which she had come. She very much wanted to commission Henri de Pré to make contact with the women who supervised the girls, but her peasant instincts warned her that Henri could be trusted no more than his father, so in desperation she sat in her corner of the big house and penned a secret letter to a woman she had never seen, the mistress of the orphanage where the King's Nieces resided:

Dearest Mevrouw,

I am a child of your house, living far away where there are no women. Please find me a healthy, strong, reliable, Christian girl of seventeen or eighteen, well-bred and loyal, who can be trusted to come here to marry my son. She will have to work hard but will be mistress of nearly four hundred morgen and a beautiful house. My son is a good man.

Annatjie van Doorn de Pré
Trianon, Stellenbosch, The Cape

She forwarded the letter without letting her husband know, and nearly a year of anxiety passed before a courier arrived with news that a Compagnie ship from Amsterdam would soon be putting in with a wife for Sarel van Doorn.

'What's this?' De Pré demanded.

'Someone's sending out an orphan, I suppose. The way I came.'

'But who asked for an orphan?'

'Many people know that Sarel needs a wife.'

'What would he do with a wife?' This was a difficult moment for De Pré. Never had he transgressed his resolve to treat Annatjie with respect and even love, and he did not propose to treat her poorly now; but he was determined that Trianon stay in his family, and if Sarel married and had children, such inheritance might be in question. If he forbade himself to abuse Annatjie, he felt no such restraint where Sarel was concerned, and now he made gross fun of the hesitant young man.

'What would that one do with a wife?' he repeated, and Annatjie, wanting most earnestly to slap his insinuating face, left the house.

She ordered slaves to inspan her horses, then asked Bezel Muhammad to accompany her to the Cape, where she would greet the arriving bride. 'Why not take Sarel?' he asked, and without thinking, she replied, 'He might not know what to do.'

She would. When they reached the Cape, the promised ship had not yet arrived, but others of its convoy assured the officials that it was on the way, so she waited. And then one morning guns fired, and a pitifully small ship limped into harbor with almost half its passengers dead. For a dreadful moment she feared that she might have lost her orphan, but when the survivors came ashore Geertruyd Steen was among them, twenty-two years old, blond, squared-off in every aspect, and smiling. She had a large square face, a stout torso, big hips, sturdy legs. Even her hair was braided and tied so that it accentuated the squareness of her head, and Annatjie thought: Dearest God, if there was ever a woman destined to breed, she is it.

The girl, not knowing what to expect, looked tentatively about her for some young man who might be awaiting a wife, but saw only sailors and Hottentots, so she took hesitant steps forward, saw Annatjie, and knew instinctively that this woman must be her protector. There was a slight pause, after which the two women ran at each other and embraced almost passionately.

'You've come to a paradise,' Annatjie told the girl. 'But it's a paradise you must build for yourself.'

'Are you to be my mother-in-law?'

'I am.'

'Is your son here?'

'It's an important story,' Annatjie said, and on the spur of the moment she directed Bezel Muhammad to take one of the horses and ride on ahead. It was important that she talk with this girl, and a long ride across the flats would give her just enough time.

She whisked Geertruyd out of the Cape that morning, afraid lest she be infected the way Louis de Pré had been, and as they entered the flats, she began talking: 'I shall have to tell you so much, Geertruyd, but every sentence is important, and the order in which it's told is important, too. My husband, your father-in-law, is a remarkable man.'

She explained how he had fled persecution in France, the courage with which he had made his way to Holland, and his great bravery in risking a return trip to fetch the vines which now accounted for the prosperity of Trianon. She told how tough old Willem van Doorn and his nagging wife had ventured out into the wilderness to build their farm, and how Paul de Pré had transformed it into a rural palace.

The first hours were spent in these details, but when they stopped to have their midday meal, Annatjie changed the tone of conversation completely: 'You'll see a dozen kinds of antelope, and hear leopards at night, and maybe one day you'll find a hippo in the river. We have a flower called protea, eight times as grand as any tulip, and birds of all description. You'll live in a land of constant surprises, and when you're an old woman like me you still won't have seen everything.'

She asked Geertruyd to look about her at the endless flatness. 'What do you see?' she asked.

'Nothing.'

'Always remember this moment,' Annatjie said, 'for soon you'll see such a place of beauty that your eyes will not believe it.' Geertruyd leaned forward as her mother-in-law-to-be added, 'If you do your work well, you'll build a little empire here, but only you can do it.'

All elderly people claim that the future lies in the hands of the young people, but few believe it; Annatjie de Pré knew that alternatives of the most staggering dimension depended upon how this particular young girl behaved herself and with what courage she attacked her problems.

'What problems do you mean?' Geertruyd asked.

'Inheritance,' Annatjie said. 'Yesterday you were an orphan girl owning a few dresses. Tomorrow you'll be a significant factor in the ownership of the finest vineyard in the land.'

Geertruyd listened and did not like what she heard. 'I am not penniless,' she said. 'I have guilders in my package.'

Annatjie liked her response, but goaded her still further: 'You come bringing nothing. Except your character. You're being offered everything, if you demonstrate that character.'

'I am not a pauper!' Geertruyd repeated, her square face flushing red.

'I was when I came across these flats,' Annatjie said, and without emotion she told the girl of how she, too, had left that orphanage, and of how her first man had rejected her, and of how she had slaved to improve the farm. 'You say you have a few hidden guilders. I had nothing.'

Abruptly she turned to the problem of her son, the proposed husband: 'Sarel is a fine, honest young man. He's always been overshadowed by the four children he grew up with. My husband, who despises him because he's afraid of what he might become, will tell you within the first ten minutes that Sarel's an imbecile. Sarel will be especially afraid of you, and if you believe my husband, you may shy away.' She paused and took Geertruyd's hands. 'But we never know, do we, what a man can become until we treat him with love?' They talked no more.

When they came off the flats, and the river hove into view, and the horses entered the long lane leading to Trianon, Geertruyd Steen saw for the first time the stunning sight of those enveloping arms, the clean white façade of the house and the two Delft benches defining the ends of the stoep. 'It's beautiful,' she whispered.

'And remember,' Annatjie whispered back, 'it was Paul de Pré who made it this way.'

'Halloo there!' Paul cried as he bounded out of the door to greet his wife and the stranger from Amsterdam. As soon as Geertruyd stepped forward, shining like a red Edam cheese, he thought: *Mon Dieu!* That one was bred for having children. 'Sarel!' he called. 'Come out and meet your bride!'

These were words well calculated to embarrass the young man, and Annatjie sought to soften them by calling, 'Sarel, here's the most pleasant girl I've ever met.'

From the doorway came the young man, twenty-six years old, weighing not much more than his intended and many times as shy, but when he saw Geertruyd and the frank joy that wreathed her face, he was drawn to her immediately and came forward, stumbling in his eagerness.

'Mind your step,' Paul said, extending a hand to help.

Sarel brushed aside his stepfather's hand as he moved to greet Geertruyd. 'I'm Sarel,' he said.

'My name's Geertruyd.'

'Mother says you come . . . from the same place she did.'

'I do,' the girl said, and the meeting was so agreeable that Sarel was put at ease. He wondered if he should volunteer to kiss the girl, but the question was resolved for him; she stepped forward and kissed him on the cheek. 'We're to be married soon, I think,' she said.

'Let's not rush things,' Paul said cautiously, but Annatjie said, 'It will be arranged. The banns will be read.'

Paul objected seriously to having Petronella and her husband attend the wedding, but when Annatjie insisted, a compromise was worked out. Petronella and Bezel would sit in the rear of the church but not participate; Annatjie said that this was a strange way for Paul to act, seeing that he had given the young couple his house, but Paul said, 'What we do at home's one thing. What we do in public is quite another,' and he simply would not listen to Annatjie's further plea that the couple be allowed to sit in the family pew.

When the wedding party returned to Trianon, Paul said graciously, 'Isn't it lucky we built the extra two rooms? The young people can have one of them.' So they were installed, and he began to watch Geertruyd meticulously, to see if she showed any signs of pregnancy, for with the birth of her first child, the Van Doorns would have a potential inheritor of the vineyard, and his own design would fall into confusion.

He knew it was inevitable, yet the possibility made him irritable, and one night at supper he threw down his spoon and cried, 'Damnit all, it's been four months since I've spoken a word of French. Everybody in this house speaks Dutch, even though I own the place.'

'You don't own the place,' Annatjie reminded him, 'You own part of it.'

'Then we should speak part French.'

'I know not a word,' Geertruyd said, and this simple statement angered him further.

'They're even threatening to halt the sermons in French,' he wailed.

'Every time I attend a funeral, it means one less French voice in the colony. And none to come to replace it.'

'Paul,' his wife said with a certain harshness. 'Stop this. It's long past the time to acknowledge what you already are, a good Dutchman.' The tone of her voice, her easy assumption infuriated him, and he stomped from the room and slept that night among the wine casks.

There in the darkness the ugly thought leaped forward in his mind: Annatjie can't live forever. She's almost sixty. One of these days she's got to die. He had respected her for all she and her family had done for him, and had honored his obligation to treat her with civil affection, but now the world that he had built was being threatened, and he wished that she were dead—and he began to watch her health as closely as he did Geertruyd's.

Annatjie did show signs of rapid aging. Her hands were withered and heavy lines marked her face. She moved more slowly than when he had married her, and her voice cracked now and then. Her deficiencies were the more notable in that he continued as young as ever—a vital, hard-working man with a smooth face that displayed his enthusiasm: After all, I am nine years younger. If I had this place by myself . . . He was thrilled by the prospect of what he could accomplish; and this was not fatuous, for one had only to look at the buildings of Trianon, those handsome, well-proportioned masterpieces, to realize what this man could achieve.

And now the battle for Trianon began. Sometimes at meals De Pré would seem to strive for breath; he felt surrounded by enemies who were trying to wrest his vineyard from him, and all he could see in the kitchen were hostile faces. Annatjie he could dismiss; she was almost sixty and must soon die. Sarel showed no signs of improving because of marriage, and could be ignored. With peasant cunning Paul saw that his real foe was Geertruyd, this deceptively quiet orphan from Amsterdam. Watching her closely, he found to his dismay that she was watching him. No matter what he did to make his good wine, he could feel Geertruyd spying on him, noting how he acted and why.

She never confronted him, for in the orphanage it had been drilled into her that the sovereign quality in any woman was meekness. So when De Pré railed at her, she kept her eyes lowered and made no response. She also refrained from trying to defend Annatjie when Paul shouted at her, for she was determined to avoid diversionary squabbles. But when De Pré, in his strategic assault, humiliated Sarel, trying to convince the young man that he was incompetent, she felt her anger rise. But still she fought to maintain self-control.

Four times, five times at supper Paul scorned his stepson, without rebuttal from Geertruyd or Annatjie, and this convinced him that he could beat down these women. One evening he launched a series of destructive attacks: 'Sarel, wouldn't it be better if you kept away from the slaves? They ignore your orders.'

Sarel said nothing, only fumbled with his spoon, so De Pré stormed on: 'And don't meddle with the wine casks. Certain things around here have to be done right.'

The young man reddened and, still silent, looked down at his plate, but when De Pré dredged up a third humiliating point—'Stay clear of the new vines'—Geertruyd had had enough. Very quietly, but with frightening determination, she interrupted: 'Monsieur de Pré . . .'

'Haven't I told you to call me Father?'

'Monsieur de Pré,' she repeated menacingly, 'since Sarel will take over the vineyards when you are dead . . .' She delivered the word with such brutal finality that De Pré gasped. He had often contemplated his wife's death, never his own.

'So Sarel and I have decided,' she continued, her face flushed with anger, 'that he must become familiar with all stages of making wine.'

'Sarel decided?' De Pré burst into derisive laughter. 'He couldn't decide anything.'

Everyone turned to look at Sarel, and he realized he ought to respond, both to combat his stepfather and to support his wife, but the pressure was so ugly that he could not form words.

So in her first attempt at defiance, Geertruyd lost, and she noticed that this made De Pré even more arrogant. For the first time he put aside his pledge to treat Annatjie with the respect due a wife and became publicly contemptuous. This grieved Geertruyd, for quite properly she placed the blame on herself; she went to Annatjie and assured her: 'I shall do whatever I must. Let his wrath fall on me, but you and I together are going to make Sarel strong. You'll see the day, Annatjie, when he runs this vineyard.'

'Have we the time?' Annatjie whispered.

'I hoped last month I was pregnant,' Geertruyd confided. 'I was wrong, but one of these days you'll have a Van Doorn grandson. This vineyard must be protected for him.'

So in the second year of Sarel's marriage the two women intensified their efforts in educating him to be a responsible man and themselves to be masters of viticulture. They studied everything about the process and compared notes at night, but what gave them greatest hope was that Sarel appeared to be learning, too. 'He's not dull,' Geertruyd whispered one night when De Pré had left the table, 'it's just his inability to express his thoughts.' They found that he was developing sound ideas on how to tend vines, make casks, protect the must, and manage slaves effectively, and one afternoon, out in the bright sun, Geertruyd cried joyously, 'Sarel, you'll run this vineyard better than De Pré ever did.' He looked at her as if she had voiced some great truth, and he tried to convey his appreciation, but words did not come easily. Instead he embraced her, and when he felt her peasant body, warm in the sun, he was overcome with love and said haltingly, 'I can . . . make wine.'

That night Paul was unusually obnoxious, for he sensed that Geertruyd, this orphan from nowhere, was on the threshold of transforming Sarel, and it embittered him to think that all the good things he had done at Trianon —and he had done many—would ultimately be for the benefit of strangers. 'Sarel!' he lashed out. 'I told you to stay clear of those casks—'

'Monsieur de Pré,' Geertruyd interrupted instantly. 'I told Sarel to mind the casks. How else can he run these vineyards when you are dead?'

There was that horrid word again, thrown at him by this twenty-three-year-old peasant girl. He beat on the table till the spoons rattled, and cried, 'I want no imbecile meddling with my casks.'

'Monsieur de Pré,' Geertruyd said with an infuriating smile, 'I think Sarel is ready to take complete charge of the casks. You won't have to bother any longer.'

'Sarel couldn't . . .'

Annatjie had heard enough. Sternly she said, 'Paul, must you be reminded that I still have authority in this place? It was I who decided that Sarel must learn how to run it.'

Geertruyd, strengthened by her mother-in-law's support, said firmly, 'Sarel will start tomorrow.'

'That one couldn't line up three staves,' De Pré snarled, and he was about to hurl additional insults, but under the table Geertruyd quietly pressed her hand against her husband's knee, and with courage thus imparted, Sarel spoke slowly: 'I am sure that I . . . can build good casks.'

The battle for the control of Trianon was interrupted by an event so arbitrary that men and women argued about it for decades: it seemed that God had struck the Cape with a fearful and reasonless scourge. One day in 1713 the old trading ship *Groote Hoorn* docked with an accidental cargo that altered history: a hamper of dirty linen. It belonged to a Compagnie official who had been working in Bombay; upon receiving abrupt orders to sail home, he had been required to depart before he could get his shirts and ruffs washed, so he tossed them into the hamper, proposing to have them laundered while he stopped over at the Cape. Unfortunately, the hamper was stowed in a corner where men urinated and where a constant heat maintained a humidity ideal for breeding germs. This condition was pointed out to the owner, who shrugged and said, 'A good washing ashore and more careful stowage on the rest of the trip will correct things.'

At the Cape the hamper was carried to the Heerengracht, the canal where slaves did the laundry. Six days later these slaves began to show signs of fever and itching skin; three days after that, their faces erupted in tiny papules, which soon enlarged to vesicles and then to pustules. The lucky slaves watched these festering sores change to scabs and then lifetime scars; the unlucky ones died of shattering fevers. Smallpox, that incurable disease, was on the rampage, and whether an afflicted person lived or died was not related to the care he was given.

Forty out of every hundred slaves died that year. Sixty out of every hundred Hottentots at the Cape perished, making their survivors totally dependent on the Dutch. The turbulent disease traveled inland at the rate of eight miles a day, ravaging everyone who fell within its path. One strain leapfrogged the flats to strike at Stellenbosch, and on some farms half the slaves died. The Hottentots of this region were especially susceptible, and many white farmers perished also.

It struck with peculiar fury at Trianon, killing Petronella in the first days and annihilating more than half the slaves. No one in the area tried more diligently to stem the awful advance than Paul de Pré; he went to every afflicted house, ordering the people to burn all clothes related to the dead, and in certain instances, when an entire family had died, he burned the house itself. He quarantined the sick and dug a clean well, and in time the tide abated.

But on the sixteenth day he fell ill, and began to tremble so furiously that Annatjie and Geertruyd put him to bed in the little white outbuilding marked with rake and hoe. There these good women cared for him, assuring him that they would send for Louis at the Cape—if that young man had survived the plague. Wrapping their faces in protective linen, they moved like ghosts about the improvised hospital, comforting him and promising to protect his vineyards.

They were heartsick when the pustules on his face proliferated until they covered all parts of his skin; and when his fever rose so that he shook the bed, and his eyes grew glassy, they knew he could not survive. Still wrapped in cloth to protect themselves from infection, they stayed with him through the night, their candle throwing shadows on the white interior, their forms moving like phantasms come to haunt him for the ill will he had borne them.

He did not become delirious. Like the fighter he was, he followed each step of his decline, and asked, when morning broke, 'Am I dying?'

'You still have a chance,' Annatjie assured him.

When he began to laugh wildly, she tried to ease him, but he would not cease cackling. Then, looking at the ghosts, he pointed at Annatjie and said in a hollow voice, 'You should be dying, not me. It was intended that you should die, you're so much older.'

'Paul, lie still.'

'And you!' he shouted at Geertruyd. 'I hope your womb is dry.'

'Paul, stop—please stop!'

But the agony of death was upon him. The vast dreams were vanishing. His sons were alienated; the slaves were dead; the vineyards would be withering. 'It's you who were supposed to die!' he screamed, and the sores on his face showed fiery red as he dragged his fingernails across them. 'It wasn't planned for me to die. You infected me, you witches.'

He tried to leap from the bed to chastise his tormentors, but fell back exhausted. He began to weep, and soon pitiful sobs racked his body as mortal grief attacked him. 'I was not meant to die,' he mumbled. 'I am of the elect.' He stared accusingly at the shrouded figures waiting to collect his fever-wasted body—and then he died.

Geertruyd, shattered by his hideousness, tried to throw a sheet over him, then broke into convulsive sobs, whereupon Annatjie took hold of her, shook her vigorously, and whispered, 'These are things that are not to be remembered.' And they prepared his body for quick burial.

As soon as Paul was buried, and trenches were dug for the accumulated corpses of the slaves, Annatjie and Geertruyd made a sober calculation of their position, and it was the younger woman who perceived most clearly the danger threatening Trianon and the strategy by which it might be averted.

'At the Cape, in Java, and in the offices of the Lords XVII men will argue, "No women should be allowed to operate a treasure like Trianon," and steps will be taken to deprive us of it.'

'They will not remove me from these fields,' Annatjie said.

'They will try. But we have two very strong points in our favor. The wines that De Pré blended three years ago are still in our casks. They'll protect us at the beginning.'

'But when they've been shipped?' Annatjie asked.

'By that time we'll have our second protection.'

'What?'

'Sarel. Yes, Annatjie, by the time Amsterdam orders you and me off the place, because a man must run a vineyard, we will put Sarel forth, and convince the authorities that he can run this place better than any other man they might propose.'

'Could he do that?'

'We shall help him do it,' Geertruyd said. And then, looking away, she added, almost in a whisper, 'Each night of my life I shall seek God's help to become pregnant. When Sarel realizes that he is to be a father . . .' Suddenly she whipped about and caught Annatjie's hands. 'He is a good man, Annatjie. We shall prove to him that he can run this vineyard.'

Geertruyd was right in expecting that the men of the system would resent leaving two women in charge of a property upon which the Compagnie depended for revenue, but she was quite wrong as to where that animosity would originate. Their good neighbor, Andries Boeksma, who could not resist sticking his nose into everything, including his maids' sleeping quarters, began raising doubts both at Stellenbosch and at the Cape.

'The young wife knows nothing, an Amsterdam castaway, and as you know, the boy's an imbecile. The old lady was capable, but she's dying, and I ask you, what's to happen with this valuable property?'

Carrying his concern to the officials at the Castle, he encouraged them to ask the very questions that Geertruyd had anticipated, and one night after drinks when the governor asked Boeksma, 'Who could we get to run the vineyards,' Andries said boldly, 'Me. I know the wine business better than De Pré ever did. We don't need Huguenots to teach us how to make wine.'

'That's a sensible idea,' the governor said, and next morning he dispatched letters of inquiry to both Java and Amsterdam.

No one warned Geertruyd that her good neighbor Andries Boeksma was plotting to steal Trianon, but one day as she came from the fields where she had been inspecting grapes, she saw him with his wagon stopped beside their fields, inspecting them, and when she walked over to speak with him, she saw that he was smiling and nodding his head as if engaged in pleasing calculations.

Hurrying home, she sought Annatjie, and found her in bed, too weak from illness to rise, and for a moment the perilous position in which Geertruyd found herself overwhelmed her, and she fell into a chair beside the bed and wept. When Annatjie asked what had happened, she whimpered, 'Now I lose your help, my dear, lovely mother, when I need it most. I just saw Andries Boeksma spying out our land. Annatjie, he intends stealing it from us, just as I warned.' She wept for some moments, then broke into sardonic laughter: 'Stupid me! I thought the enemy would be in Java or Amsterdam. And he was waiting in the next village.'

'My fever will subside,' Annatjie assured her. 'If we can hold off the Lords XVII, we can hold off Andries Boeksma.' And from her bed, which held her prisoner far longer than she had expected, she took charge of everything, dispatching slaves to perform specific tasks and explaining to Sarel her reasons for each act.

She was especially eager to have the Compagnie import large numbers of new slaves to replenish the work force, but in this she was disappointed; a young official from Amsterdam had landed at the Cape during the last stages of the epidemic and had seen it not as a vast destruction but as a heaven-sent opportunity for reform. In his report to the Lords XVII he wrote:

> The pox, which did have grievous consequences, offers an opportunity to set Africa on the right path. Our Dutch farmers living there have accustomed themselves to a life of ease. Their daily routine carries them away from their lands to partake of wine, smoke sundry pipes of tobacco, gossip like women, complain about the weather, and pray constantly that their afflictions might pass. It is ironical that they call themselves Boers, for farmers they are not. They regard all such work as our farmers perform at home as labor fit only for slaves.
>
> I recommend that you use this plague as a God-sent opportunity to halt further importation of slaves, and to curtail the use of Hottentot and half-caste labor. Let us comb from Holland honest men and women who know how to work, Boers who will create in Africa a peasant class of true Dutch character, unspoiled by sloth and privilege.

For a brief moment in history there was a chance that this advice might be followed, converting South Africa into a settlement much like the northern American colonies and Canada, where in good climates free men built strong democracies, but before the proposed Dutch farmers could be imported, the problem was resolved in an unusual way.

Hottentots from independent captaincies east of Stellenbosch had been cruelly ravaged by the pox. Their cattle dead, their traditional hunting lands depleted, they wandered in pathetic groups to farmhouse doors, begging for any kind of work so long as it provided food. This was their only chance of survival, and before long, Geertruyd had accepted so many that Trianon was back to its full complement of workers, proof that if the white man succeeded in his economic enterprises, the brown and the black man would find a way to participate in his prosperity. The only requirement was that the black do his sharing not for free wages but in some form of servitude.

When the fortunes of the plantation were at their lowest ebb, and rumors circulated that it might be taken from the women, Annatjie in her sickbed conceived a strategy which had to be acted upon quickly. Summoning Sarel and his wife, she told them, 'Now's the time to buy back any claims the De Pré boys might have on their father's share of Trianon. They'll think it's worthless. We know it's going to be invaluable.' To her delight, it was not Geertruyd who responded, but Sarel, who said very slowly, 'They will know our troubles . . . and they will sell . . . at a lower price.'

'Oh, Sarel!' his mother cried. 'You do understand, don't you?'

'And this year . . . the three of us . . . we will make even better wine.'

That night Annatjie composed a letter to Henri de Pré in Amsterdam, offering him a shockingly few rix-dollars for his share, and she wanted to carry the letter herself to the Cape, where she would bargain with Louis, but her health would not permit, so she coached her daughter-in-law: 'Sarel's not quite able yet to conduct such a negotiation. And when you've paid Louis his money, you must go to the Castle and meet with the governor and sound him out.'

'I would feel ill-at-ease,' Geertruyd said, looking at her work-stained hands.

'We do what we must,' Annatjie said, and when the cart was ready, she left her bed to bid the girl farewell.

The meeting with Louis went much better than she had anticipated, but it contained one very painful moment. After the deal was concluded, and the papers signed, Geertruyd was led into another part of the house, where coffee and rusks had been prepared, and there she saw De Pré's four sons, and gasped, 'You have four and I have none,' and her barrenness lay heavy upon her.

At the Castle the governor said it was most fortunate that she had come to the Cape, for an Honorable Commissioner had arrived from Java and was awaiting a ship from Amsterdam which would bring him instructions from the Lords XVII. 'We're particularly interested in Trianon,' the governor said as he led her in to dinner.

When she entered the Compagnie mess she was startled by two things: the richness of the huge teakwood table set with gold-and-blue plates kilned in Japan, each bearing the august monogram V.O.C. and accompanied by five pieces of massy silver from China; and the presence of her neighbor Andries Boeksma, who had obviously been instructing the Honorable Commissioner from Java about what he considered the troubles at Trianon.

It was a chilly dinner. The three men, each so much older, wiser and more capable than she, stared down their noses at this girl who presumed to manage a great vineyard. 'What are your plans for restoring Trianon?' the man from Java asked.

Taking a deep breath, she said, 'My husband Sarel already has the fields in good order.'

'Sarel?' Boeksma echoed.

'Yes,' she replied, looking straight at him. She hesitated, wondering if she dared say what was in her mind, but then she found her courage. Turning to the governor, she said with the tenderness of a young wife, 'I'm sure you've been told that Sarel's not capable. I assure you that he is. It's just that he expresses himself slowly.'

'Why isn't he on this mission?'

'Because he is very shy. And I am doing all I can to cure him of that affliction.'

'Many call him slow-witted—' Boeksma said.

'Sir!' the man from Java interrupted. 'This lady . . .'

'It was a most rude remark,' the governor said, 'but I would like to know . . .'

'Three years from now, your Excellency, you will bring important visitors to Trianon . . . to show them with pride what my husband has accomplished.'

During the journey back to Trianon, Geertruyd van Doorn sat very erect, staring straight ahead as if she were a wooden doll, and when she reached the welcoming arms of her little buildings she did not even glance at them. At the big house she ignored the waiting servants and ran directly to Annatjie's room, where she threw herself on the bed beside the sick woman and broke into convulsive sobs.

After her mother-in-law had comforted her, she controlled herself enough to report on her disastrous visit to the Castle: 'They humiliated me. Three great men staring at me, making fun of you and me. Forcing me to say whether or not Sarel was an imbecile. Oh, Annatjie, it was so shameful. And they mean to take Trianon from us.'

Leaping away from the bed, she stormed about the room, uttering curses she had learned in whispered sessions as a child. 'I will not let them do it. Sarel van Doorn will stand before them and face them down. He will run this vineyard to perfection, and within one month I will be pregnant with the son who will inherit Trianon.'

'That's up to God,' Annatjie said.

'I am telling God. "Make me pregnant. Give me the son I need." '

'You are blaspheming, Geertruyd.'

'I am taking God into my partnership. Annatjie, we have two months at most. They're waiting for instructions from the Lords.'

Annatjie, against her children's advice, rose to supervise fields while Geertruyd worked with Sarel: 'It all depends upon you, my dearest friend. When the men come here to inspect us, you must meet with them, and assure them that all is well.'

'Men?'

'Yes, three tall men, old, powerful.' She acted out their roles: 'The Honorable Commissioner is a gentleman, but he can be very stern. He'll ask the difficult questions. The governor . . . well, he knows everything. Andries Boeksma . . .' She studied how to characterize this evil, unpleasant man: 'He's a worm. But if you try to step on him, Sarel, the others will rise to protect him. Let him insult you.'

Since the ship bringing instructions from Amsterdam was tardy in arriving, the committee of inspection had to postpone its visit for more than half a year, which gave the Van Doorns added time to organize their efforts; but Andries Boeksma also had time to establish his attack, and when the long-awaited letters arrived, with instructions that their commissioner from

Java must settle everything, Boeksma convened a planning session at the Castle.

'I've been keeping an eye on the vineyard,' he reported. 'Dreadful shape.'

'The wine seems to be standing up,' the governor said.

'But don't you see, your Excellency? These women are clever. That's wine that De Pré blended.'

'What will the three people do if I dispossess them?' the commissioner asked, turning to the governor.

'They own the land. We'd compensate, one way or another. Maybe a little farm that they could handle. Perhaps a gin shop here at the Cape . . . for sailors.'

'When we get there,' Boeksma coached his superiors, 'you must insist that we meet with Van Doorn alone. The women will protest, but you must order them away. So that you can see for yourselves how defective he is.'

And when the three men finally reached Trianon, Geertruyd awaited them on the stoep, gloriously pregnant, and smiling broadly as she brought Annatjie forward to greet them.

'I was right,' Boeksma whispered. 'They aren't going to let us see Sarel. I told you they kept him locked up.'

At that moment, from the lovely half-door that marked the entrance to the house, Sarel appeared, a tallish, good-looking, thin young man whose smile showed two rows of very white teeth. 'Distinguished gentlemen,' he said, emphasizing each syllable, 'we welcome you . . . to Trianon.' With that he offered the two women his arms and held them back as the visitors entered the hallway.

There they received another surprise when Geertruyd detached herself, smiled at the men, and led them into the room designated for their meeting. It had been decorated with flowers and a small cage of goldfinches, and after arranging the four chairs she graciously excused herself: 'My husband feels it would be better if he met with you alone.' She bowed and left.

Once removed from the room, she ran into the one adjoining it, pressed her ear against a small hole in the wall, which had been covered at the other end by the flowers, and listened nervously as Sarel started the discussion. 'Please, God,' she whispered, 'forgive me for when I was insolent. Help Sarel to do what we planned.'

In the opening minutes Sarel's interrogators were quite insulting, treating him as if he were indeed defective, but when Boeksma completed his charges of mismanagement at Trianon, Sarel surprised them by answering slowly and intelligently, 'Gentlemen, aren't you referring to the days when we all suffered . . . from the loss of servants to the plague? We have none of those problems now.'

Boeksma started to refute this claim, and Geertruyd listened anxiously to hear how her husband would handle him, and she was relieved when Sarel said firmly, 'So I have asked our servants to bring before you a selection of our wines.'

He waited until Boeksma started to protest that these had to be wines that Paul de Pré had been responsible for, then added quietly, 'I know that you must suspect . . . that I am offering you wine laid down by De Pré.' He laughed. 'That would be a naughty trick. These are my wines, as you shall see . . . when we visit the cellars.'

Geertruyd, hearing this complicated statement, left her listening post and ran to where Annatjie waited. Taking her mother-in-law by both hands, she exulted: 'He's even better than we had hoped!'

The visitor from Java tasted the new wines and was impressed: 'This is very good, really.'

'And next year it will be great,' Sarel said. 'We intend to make great wines . . . at Trianon.'

Geertruyd, back at her post, clasped her hands and held her breath. What Sarel was to say next represented an enormous gamble, but also a vindication, and as a fighting woman, she had deemed it a proper risk. 'Honorable Commissioner, we at Trianon have no desire to force our product on Java. That's unfair . . . to Java. So what we did two years ago was make quiet inquiries of European . . .' He hesitated, trembling at the bold thing he must say next. Then he smiled and continued: 'What we did was seek buyers in Europe. And I am pleased to inform you that both France and England will buy our wine . . . at an excellent price.'

'Wait!' the commissioner protested. 'If you can make wine this good, we would . . .'

'But where did you get the authority,' the governor asked, 'to make inquiries in Europe?'

'Not in Europe, your Excellency. My wife carried samples to captains when their ships docked at the Cape. I wanted to save you trouble, your Excellency.'

And there the discussion ended as Geertruyd appeared in the doorway. 'Oh,' the man from Java cried. 'Here's your wife now, coming with tea and rusks. You must be very proud, Mevrouw van Doorn, of the excellent wine your husband is making.'

'I am,' she said, and when the interrogators were gone, and Sarel had laughed at how Andries Boeksma had tried to insert irrelevant probes, Geertruyd took her husband's hand and led him to where Annatjie, exhausted, slumped in a chair.

'Your son was magnificent,' Geertruyd said. 'He saved our vineyard.'

'Did I?' Sarel asked, and from the way he straightened up when he spoke, his women were satisfied that he was at last ready to be the master of Trianon.

V. The Trekboers

I N 1702 Hendrik van Doorn became a trekboer, one of those wandering graziers who moved eastward across virgin land at the slow pace of an ox.

Turning his back on any further claim to Trianon, because his mother had married the Huguenot only eight days after his father had been slain by Bushmen, he had penetrated the mountains, taking his wagon apart and carrying it piece by piece up precipices, then reassembling it for tortuous descents into the valleys.

He kept on till he reached a stream where kingfishers flashed blue as they dived toward crystal water, and when he saw the good pastures nearby, he knew he had reached his temporary home. For the first years he grazed his cattle and sheep, lived himself in the meanest reed-and-mud hovel, and shared his austere food with the one slave and the two Hottentot families who had come into exile with him.

Each spring he swore, 'This summer I shall build me a real house,' but as the season lengthened, his resolve weakened, and he watched idly as his Hottentots ranged deep into surrounding valleys, seeking their own people who still dwelt in the region, raising their own cattle, which they would readily barter. His herd increased, and every other year he was able to drive some of his stock back to a Compagnie buying-station; there he would acquire the supplies needed for the approaching two years, then vanish, for he was growing to treasure the freedom he had attained and feared contact with the merchants of the Cape.

Each year, two or three wandering white men might pass his way, or some other young trekboer 'finished with the Cape,' or one of the hunters who ventured far into the interior for months at a time, seeking his fortune in ivory or hides. Once Hendrik joined with a hunter who probed far to the south, where a mighty forest of stinkwood and yellow-wood concealed a herd of elephant.

In the fourth year, drought struck, spreading its ashen terror, choking the river where the kingfishers danced and destroying the pasture. The Hottentots, always aware of water, led them sixty miles to the edge of a great pan containing a little water, and here Hendrik remained with two other trekboers. When the rains finally came, he returned to his stream, but it was never quite the same again, for in the evenings when he sat near the fire with the Hottentots and his slave he felt a sense of restlessness, of loneliness. It never occurred to him that this feeling might terminate if he married, for there were no Dutch girls in that vast region.

In 1707, on a journey home from the cattle station, the Hottentot who guided the oxen realized that Hendrik was not pleased. There had been talk among the Compagnie buyers of a proposed rent for farms such as Van Doorn occupied—nothing definite . . . no legal placaats . . . just rumors of rix-dollars to be paid. 'Verdomde Compagnie!' the Hottentot heard the baas mutter over and over, and it was in this mood that Hendrik stomped alongside his wagon as it approached his hut. It helped his temper none to see another trekboer outspanned there.

The man shuffled toward him and held out his hand. He, too, had braved the mountains and carried his wagon piece by piece down the precipices. The difference was that he had women with him, a haggard wife and a pigtailed daughter named Johanna. Hendrik was twenty-six that year, the girl sixteen, and during the three months the itinerant family stayed at the hut he became enraptured of her. She was willow-thin, a most energetic worker, and the one who held her small family together, for her father was irresolute, her mother a complainer. It was Johanna who mended the clothes and did the cooking. Hendrik, who had lived off the simplest fare, learned to enjoy the curries this girl made; she had acquired the trick of making even the poorest meat taste acceptable by adding the fragrant spices concocted by the Malays at the Cape. She carried with her a plentiful supply, and when Hendrik asked, after a particularly fine supper based on steenbok flanks, 'On eastward, how will you find curry?'

'We have enough for three or four years. You don't use very much, you know. By that time traders will be coming through, won't they, Pappie?'

Pappie was an optimist: 'Smous . . . two, three years, there'll be a flow of such peddlers.'

One evening at supper, when they were rested and well prepared for the journey ahead, the father said, 'Tomorrow we move on,' and it was then that Johanna became aware that she did not wish to leave Hendrik. At the edge of the mysterious wilderness she had found a man, sturdy, gentle, and reasonably capable, and although he had said or done nothing to reveal his interest in her, for he would always be hesitant about his own capacities, she felt assured that if she could stay with him a little longer, she would find some way to encourage him.

She was not yet distraught about the passing years—sixteen years old and no husband—but she did foresee that if her family moved far east, it might be some time before a marriageable man came along, so after everyone had gone to bed she crept close to her parents and whispered, 'I would like to remain here with Hendrik.'

The old people fell into a frenzy: 'Would you leave us alone? Who will help us?' They had a dozen reasons why their daughter must not desert them, and each was compelling, for they were an inadequate pair and knew it. Without Johanna they saw little chance of survival in the bleak years ahead, so they pleaded with her to come with them. Tearfully she said she would, for she knew that without her they could perish.

But when she was alone, staring at the empty years ahead, she could not bear the thought of the solitude that was being forced upon her, so she moved silently to Hendrik's litter and wakened him: 'Our last night. Let's walk in the moonlight.'

Trembling with excitement, he slipped into his trousers, and barefooted they left the hut. When they had gone where none could hear them but the ruminating cattle, she said, 'I don't want to leave.'

'You'd stay here? With me?'

'I would.' She could feel him shivering, and added, 'But they need me. They'll not be able to survive without me.'

'I need you!' he blurted out, and with that she dropped any maidenly reticence and embraced him. They fell on the ground, grappled hungrily with each other, and assuaged the loneliness and uncertainty that assailed them. Twice they made fumbling and inconclusive love, aware that they were not handling this matter well, but also aware that gentleness and love and passion were involved.

Finally she whispered, 'I want you to remember me.'

'I'll not let you go. I need you with me.'

She wanted to hear these reassuring words, to know on the eve of her departure for strange fields that she had been able to inspire such thoughts in a man. But now when Hendrik said in a loud voice, 'I'm going to speak with your father,' she grew afraid, lest a confrontation occur that could have no resolution.

'Don't, Hendrik! Perhaps later, when the farm . . .'

Too late. The stocky trekboer marched to the hut, roused the sleeping pair and told them bluntly, 'I'm going to keep your daughter.'

Perhaps they had anticipated such a denouement to their extended stay; at any rate, they knew how to deal with it. With tears, accusations of filial infidelity and pleadings they besought her to stay with them, and when morning came she had to comply.

After they left, Hendrik experienced the most difficult days of his life, because now, for the first time, he could imagine what it would be like to live with a woman; he would lie in his hut and stare at the rolling land she had traversed, picturing himself on horseback galloping after her. He went so far as to worry about how they could marry, with no predikant in the region.

Four times he resolved to leave his hut and herds in care of his servants and ride east to overtake her, but always he fell back on the dirty paillasse he used for a bed, convincing himself that even if he did find her, she might not want to come back with him. But then the awful reality of how impoverished his life would be if he had no wife overcame him, and he would lie for days immobile.

After a year he conquered this sickness, and had almost forgotten Johanna, when his slave came running with news that people were ap-

proaching. Leaping from his bed, he instinctively looked to the west to see
who had come across the mountains, and when he saw nothing, the slave
tugged at his arm and cried, 'This way, Baas.' And from the east, shattered
and nearly destroyed by their experiences on a bleak and distant tract, came
Johanna and her family.

For two weeks Hendrik and his servants treated the sick, defeated
travelers: 'Our Hottentots ran away with most of our cattle. We planted a
few mealies, but in the wrong soil. The winds. The drought and then the
flooding rains. We had to eat our last sheep.'

The father assailed himself. His wife complained bitterly of their wrong
choices. And Johanna, pitifully thin, lay exhausted on Hendrik's paillasse,
blaming no one, but obviously near death from having had to do all the
work. For ten days Hendrik tended her gently, washing her wasted body
and feeding her with broth made by the Hottentots at their open fires; on
the eleventh day she got out of bed and insisted upon doing the cooking.

This time the family stayed for six months, and when it came time for
them to resume their westward journey to the Cape, Hendrik gave them
four oxen, a small cart and a servant, but as they were preparing to depart,
Johanna moved to his side, took him by the hand, and without speaking to
her parents, indicated that this time she would stay with him. Her thin face
showed such anguish at the thought that they might force her to go with
them that they could make no more protest; they knew that she loved this
man and had lost him once through filial obedience, but she would not
surrender him a second time. It was a solemn moment, with no minister
to confer society's approbation, no ritual of any kind to mark one of the
great rites of human experience. There was no talk, no prayer, no chanting
of old hymns. The girl's father and mother faced a perilous mountain
traverse on their retreat to the Cape, and there seemed little chance that
they would ever return to see their daughter.

The Hottentot flicked his hippopotamus-hide whip. The oxen moved
forward, and the broken couple retreated from their sad adventure.

In the fifteen years since that informal marriage, Johanna had borne nine
children, each delivered in the corner of the harsh hut with the assistance
of little Hottentot women, whose wails of apprehension and joy equaled the
howls of the newborn. Two children had died, one struck down by a yellow
Cape cobra in the dust outside the dwelling, another taken by pneumonia;
but the seven survivors swarmed about the huts and hillsides. Johanna kept
track of her brood, fed and swept and sewed clothes for them all, and kept
her ramshackle home in reasonable order.

But she herself deteriorated, and one traveler described her as a slattern,
a word she merited, since she had no time for her appearance. At thirty-
three she was used up and practically dead, except that she refused to die.
She had entered that seemingly endless period in which a scrawny woman,
inured to work, moved almost mechanically from one bitter task to the next,
perfecting herself in a ritual of survival.

'The only attention she allows herself,' the traveler wrote, 'comes at
dusk when, with her brood about her, she holds court as her two Hottentot

women servants bathe her feet. Whence this custom came, I know not, nor would Mevrouw van Doorn explain.'

No matter how bleak her life, no matter how unattractive she became, she retained one assurance: Hendrik loved her. She was the only woman he had known, and that first night in the fields she had shown him that she needed him; without books to read or the ability to read them, without other Dutch people to consort with, she had been content to hold Hendrik as the core and source of her life, while he, able to read the great brassbound Bible, could envision no life other than the one he led with her. Sometimes, after reading a chapter of Genesis or Exodus to his family and relating the wanderings of the Israelites to the tribulations of a trekboer, he would speculate on the future of the children: 'Where will the girls find husbands?'

And then in 1724 came the worst drought Hendrik had known, and even when the Hottentots galloped to the edge of the northern pan, thinking to herd the cattle there, they found that it, too, had retreated to a mere pond. Hendrik now had four hundred cattle, three times as many sheep, and he realized that his depleted lands could no longer support them. Even the modest garden that Johanna tended had withered, and one evening Hendrik directed all his clan to go down on their knees and pray. With thirty-five supplicants around him—his own eight, the twenty-two Hottentots, plus the slaves—he begged for rain. Night after night they repeated their prayers, and no rain came. He watched his cattle, his only wealth, grow scrawny, and one dark night as he crept into bed Johanna said, 'I'm ready,' and he replied, 'I do believe God wants us to move east.'

'Should've moved five years ago,' she said without rancor.

'I figure to move east. Maybe sixty, seventy miles.'

'I been east, you know.'

'Was it as bad as you said?'

'It was worse. We was seventy miles east of here, just where you're heading, and it was even worse than Pappie said.'

'But you're willing to try again?'

'This place is used up. We better go somewheres before the drought ruins us.'

'You'd be willing to try again?'

'You're a lot smarter than Pappie. And I know a lot more now than I did then. I'm ready.'

The older children were not. Conservative, like all young people, they complained that they wanted to stay where they were, especially since families were beginning to move into the area, but there were two boys at the farm who looked forward to the proposed move with considerable excitement. Adriaan was a mercurial stripling, lean and quick like his mother. He was twelve that year, illiterate where books were concerned but well versed in what happened on the veld. He understood cattle, the grow-ing of mealies, the tracking of lost sheep and the languages of his family's slaves and Hottentots. He was not a strong boy, nor was he tall; his principal characteristic was an impish delight in the world about him. To Adriaan a mountain had a personality as distinct as that of a master bull or his sisters. He certainly did not talk to trees, but he understood them, and sometimes when he ran across the veld and came upon a cluster of protea, their flowers as big as his head, he would jump with joy to see them whispering among themselves. But his chief delight lay in walking alone, east or north, to the vast empty lands that beckoned.

The other boy who was cheered by news of an eastward trek was the half-Hottentot Dikkop, fathered nineteen years earlier by a Coloured hunter who had lain with one of Hendrik's servants. It was unfair to call him a boy, for he was seven years older than Adriaan, but he was so unusually small, even for a Hottentot, that he looked more like a lad than Adriaan did. He had a large bottom, a handsome light-brown skin and a shy nature that expressed itself principally in his love for the Van Doorn children, especially Adriaan, with whom he had long planned to set forth on a grand exploration. If the family now moved a far distance eastward, after the new hut was built and the cattle acclimated, he and Adriaan would be free to go, and they would be heading into land that few had seen before. Nothing could have pleased Dikkop more than this possibility, and when the wagons were loaded he went to Hendrik: 'Baas, come new farm, Adriaan, me, we head out?'

'It's time,' the baas agreed, and that was all the promise Dikkop required. On the journey he would work as never before, proving to his master that the proposed exploration was justified.

Two wagons heavily loaded, a tent to be pitched at dusk, a white family of nine, two slaves, two large families of Hottentots, two thousand sheep, four hundred cattle and two span of oxen—sixteen in each—formed the complement of the Van Doorns as they headed into totally unfamiliar land. Johanna had a meager collection of kitchen utensils, five spoons, two knives but no forks. Hendrik had a Bible published in Amsterdam in 1630, a few tools and a brown-gold crock in which on festive occasions he made bread pudding for his family. He also had a small assortment of seeds, which he was confident he could expand into a garden, and sixteen rooted cuttings of various fruit trees, which, with luck, would form the basis of an orchard. In the entourage he was the only one who could read, and he took delight in assembling all people connected with him for evening prayer, when he would spread the Bible on his knees and read from it in rich Dutch accents.

The trekboers traveled only modest distances on any day. The oxen were not eager to move and the herds had to be allowed time to graze. Hottentots had to scout ahead to locate watercourses, so that five miles became a satisfactory journey. Also, when a congenial spot was found, the caravan lingered three or four days, enjoying the fresh water and the good pasturage.

At the end of three weeks, when some sixty-five miles had been covered, Hendrik and Johanna stood together on a small rise to survey a broad expanse of pasture, where the grass was not excessive or the water plentiful, but where the configuration of land and protective hills and veld looked promising.

'Was your father's farm like this?'

'Almost the same,' Johanna said.

'And he failed?'

'We almost died.'

'This time it's different,' Hendrik said, but he was reluctant to make the crucial determination without his wife's approval. At a score of intervals in their life together she had been so prescient in warning him of pitfalls that he relied on her to spot weaknesses that he missed.

'Would you worry, Johanna, if we chose this spot?'

'Of course not! You have sons to help you. Trusted servants. I see no trouble.'

'God be praised!' he shouted with an exuberance which startled her. 'This is it!' And he started running toward the center of the plain he had selected, but Johanna cried, 'You won't have time before sunset! Wait till tomorrow!'

'No!' he shouted with an excitement that activated his children and the servants. 'This is ours! We mark it out tonight.' And he kept running to a central position, where he directed his Hottentots to collect rocks for a conspicuous pile. As soon as it was started, he cried to everyone, 'Where's north?' He knew, of course, but wished their confirmation for the sacred rite he was about to perform.

'That's north,' Dikkop said.

'Right.' And he handed Johanna a pistol. 'At half an hour, fire it. I want everyone here to witness that I walked only half an hour.' And with that he strode off to the north, not taking exaggerated steps, and not running, but walking with grave intent. When he had covered about a mile and three-quarters, Johanna fired the pistol, whereupon he stopped, gathered many rocks and built a pile somewhat smaller than the one at the center. Then, shouting with joy, he sped back to the center, leaping and kicking like a boy.

'Where's south?' he yelled.

'Down there!' several voices cried, whereupon he said again to his wife, 'Give me half an hour,' and off he went, never running or cheating, for the testimony must be unanimous that he had defined his land honestly. When the pistol fired, he built a cairn and hastened back to the central pile.

'Where's west?' he shouted with wild animal spirits, and off he went again, taking normal strides but with abnormal vigor. Another shot, another cairn, another dash.

'Where's east?' he cried, and the men bellowed, 'There's east!' But this time, as he headed for the vast unknown that had so lured his crippled grandfather, and had seduced him away from the pleasing security of Trianon, it seemed to him that he was participating in a kind of holy mission, and his eyes misted. His steps slowed and diminished much in scope, so that his farm was going to be lopsided, but he could not help himself. He had walked and run nearly eleven miles at the close of a demanding day, and he was tired, but more than that, he was captivated by the mountains that ran parallel to his course, there to the north, hemming in the beautiful plains on which the great farms of the future would stand. And to the south he could feel the unseen ocean, reaching away to the icebound pole, and he had a sense of identification with this untrammeled land that none before him had ever felt.

'He's not walking,' Adriaan said at the center.

'He's slowing down,' Johanna said.

'Give him more time,' the boy pleaded.

'No. We must do it right.' But Adriaan grabbed his mother's hand, preventing her from firing, and of a sudden his father leaped in the air, throwing his arms wide and dashing ahead to recover the lost time.

'Now!' Adriaan said, dropping his hand. The pistol fired, the eastern cairn was established, and Hendrik van Doorn tramped slowly back to his family. The new loan-farm, six thousand acres of promising pasture, had been defined.

The next three months, April through June, were a time of extraordinary effort, since the farm had to be in stable operating condition before the onset of winter. A spacious kraal was built of mud-bricks and stone to contain the precious animals, trees were planted, a small garden was dug and a larger field for mealies was plowed and allowed to lie fallow till spring planting. Only when this was done were the servants put to the task of building the family hut.

Hendrik paced out a rectangle, forty feet by twenty, then leveled it with a mixture of clay and manure. At the four corners long supple poles were driven into the ground, those at the ends bent toward each other and lashed together. A sturdy forty-foot beam joined them, forming the ridge pole of the roof. The sides of the hut, curving from base-line upward, were fashioned of wattles and heavy reeds interwoven with thatch. A crude door entered from the middle of one side, but the two ends were closed off and the whole affair was windowless.

The house contained no furniture except a long table, built by the slaves, with low benchlike seats formed of latticework and leather thongs. Wagon chests held clothing and the few other possessions, and atop them were stacked the plates, pots and the brown-gold crock. The fireplace was a mud-bricked enclosure to one side, with no chimney. Children slept on piles of softened hides, their parents on a bed in the far corner: four two-foot posts jutting above ground, laced with a lattice of reed and thong.

The name for the rude domicile in which the nine Van Doorns would live for the next decade, and the other trekboers for the next century, would occasion endless controversy. It was a hartbees-huisie, and the contradictory origins proposed for the word demonstrated the earthy processes at work shaping a new language for the colony. The hartebeest, of course, was the narrow-faced, ringed-horn antelope so common to the veld, but there was no logical reason why this lovely animal who roamed the open spaces should lend his name to this cramped residence. A better explanation is that the word was a corruption of the Hottentot /harub, a mat of rushes, plus the Dutch huisje, little house. Others claimed that it must be harde plus bies plus huisie, hard-reed house. Whatever, the hartbees-huisie stood as the symbol of the great distance these Dutchmen were traveling physically and spiritually from both the settlement at the Cape and their progenitors in Holland.

The first winter was a difficult time, with little food in store and none growing, but the men scoured the hills and brought in great quantities of springbok and gemsbok and handsome blesbok. Occasionally the Van Doorns, in their smoky hartebeest hut would dine on hartebeest itself; then

Johanna would cut the meat into small strips, using a few onions, a little flour and a pinch of curry. Hendrik would roam the lower hills, looking for wild fruits which he could mangle into a chutney mixed with nuts, and the family would eat well.

The children begged their father to make one of his bread puddings, but without lemon rind or cherries or apples to grace it, he felt it would be a disappointment, and he refrained, but toward September, when the long winter was ending, an old smous driving a rickety wagon came through from the Cape with a miraculous supply of flour, coffee, condiments, dried fruits, and things like sewing needles and pins.

'You'll be the farthest east,' he said in a high, wheezing voice.

'How'd you get over the mountains alone?' Hendrik asked.

'Partner and I, we broke the wagon down, carried the parts over.'

'Where's your partner?'

'Took himself a farm. Down by the ocean.'

'How you getting back to the Cape?'

'I'll sell the things. I'll sell the wagon. Then I'll walk back and buy another.'

'You plan to come back this way?' Johanna asked.

'Maybe next year.'

'This'll be a nice place then,' Hendrik said. 'Maybe I'll build us a real house.'

No one believed this. Four years on this farm, a drought or two, a more fertile valley espied on a cattle drive, and the Van Doorns would all be impatient for a move to better land. But now there was food at hand, and a few rix-dollars to pay for it, so the entire family joined in fingering through the old man's stock.

'I'm not eager to sell,' he said. 'Lots of people on the way back want my things.'

'How many people?' Hendrik asked.

'Between here and the mountains . . . ten . . . twenty farms. It's becoming a new Stellenbosch.'

Johanna saw to it that they bought prudently, but at the end of the bargaining she said, 'Bet you haven't had a good meal in weeks.'

'I eat.'

'If you let us have some of that dried fruit, some of those spices, my husband will make you the best bread pudding you ever tasted.'

'That one?' The old man looked almost contemptuously at Hendrik, but when Johanna pressed him on the exchange, he began to waver.

'You got any mutton? Just good mutton?'

'We do.'

'Mutton and pudding. I'd like that.' So the barter was arranged, and while Johanna and Hendrik worked inside the hut, the old man sat on a rickety stool by the entrance, savoring the good smell of meat. Trekboers liked their meat swimming in grease.

It was a gala meal, there at the farthest edge of settlement, and when the meat had been apportioned and there was much surplus, Adriaan said, 'I'd like to give Dikkop some.' No one spoke, so he added, 'Dikkop and me, we're going on the walk, you remember.' So it was approved that the

Hottentot could come to the doorway of the hut while Adriaan passed him a tin plate of mutton. 'Stay here,' he whispered.

Now Hendrik brought forth the crock with no handles, placing it before the old man: 'You first.'

This was a mistake. The old fellow took nearly half the pot; he hadn't had a sweet in ages, and certainly not one with bits of lemon rind and dried apples. The Van Doorns divided the remainder evenly, but Adriaan split his portion in two. 'Whatever are you doing?' Johanna asked, and her son said, 'I promised Dikkop a share,' and he passed it quickly out.

Their journey was planned for November, when protea blossoms were opening like great golden moons. Dikkop, brown and barefooted, nineteen years old and well versed in frontier living, would be in charge. Adriaan, well clothed in rugged leather vest and moleskin trousers, and exceptionally informed regarding animals and trees, would be the spiritual leader. They would head for a wild terrain with lions and hippos and elephants and antelope unnumbered. And in the end, if they survived, they would wander back with nothing whatever to show for their journey except rare tales of cliffs negotiated and rivers swum.

In the late spring of 1724 they started east, carrying two guns, two knives, a parcel of dried meat and not a fear in the world.

It was a journey that could rarely be repeated, two young fellows heading into unexplored land without the least concept of what they might be finding, except that it would be an adventure which they felt confident of handling. Dikkop was an unusual Hottentot, skilled as a carpenter, like a Malay, but also beautifully adapted to the wild, like many Hottentots. He had a sense of where danger might lie and how to avoid it. He dreaded physical confrontations and would travel considerable distances to escape them; he was, indeed, something of a coward, but this had helped him stay alive in difficult surroundings and he did not propose altering his philosophy now.

Adriaan, in the wilderness, was a remarkable boy, afraid of nothing, confident that he could confront any animal no matter how big or powerful, and alive to all the sensations about him. If his grandfather Willem had been the first Afrikaner, he was the second, for he loved this continent more devoutly than any other child alive at that time. He was part of it; he throbbed to its excitement; he lived with its trees and bushes and birds; and if he could not read books, he could certainly read the documents of nature about him.

They had no tent, no blankets. At night Dikkop, drawing upon knowledge ten thousand years old, showed Adriaan how to form a declivity in the earth for his hip and then to place bushes against his back to break the breeze. They drank whatever water they came upon, for none could be polluted. They ate well, of ripening berries, nuts, roots, an occasional river fish, grubs and abundant meat whenever they wanted it.

They climbed trees to survey distant areas, guided themselves by the stars, keeping a middle path between the mountains to the north, the ocean to the south. Occasionally they spied Hottentot clans, but they preferred to avoid them, for this was an adventure they did not want to share with others. In this way they covered more than a hundred and fifty miles due eastward. On the banks of one river, where all things seemed to be in harmony—grass for cattle had they had any, flat fields for seed, good water to swim in, fine trees for timber—they remained two weeks, exploring the river north and south, testing the herds of game. In later years Adriaan would often remember that river, and would ask Dikkop, 'What do you suppose the name of that river was? Where we stayed those weeks doing nothing?' But they could never deduce what river it must have been: Groot Gourits, Olifants, Kammanassie, Kouga, Gamtoos. It was a river of memory, and sometimes Adriaan said, 'I wonder if it was real. I wonder if we dreamed that river.' It was statements like this, heard by practical men, that gave him his name Mal Adriaan: Mad Adriaan. Daft Adriaan. Crazy Adriaan who sleeps in trees.

Thus the great journeys of boyhood mark a man, showing him possibilities others never see, uncovering potentials that stagger the youthful mind and monopolize an entire life in their attaining. A boy of twelve, sleeping in a tree, looks down upon an alien landscape and sees a lioness, lying in wait to trap an antelope at dawn, and as he watches in silence, a zebra moves unconcernedly into the arena, and the antelope skips free when the lioness leaps upon the zebra's back, breaking its neck with one terrible swipe of claw and snap of teeth. Mal Adriaan, the boy who knows how a lion thinks.

At the midpoint of their journey, when it was about time to turn back with enough stories to fill a lifetime of evening recollections, an accident occurred—nothing of great importance and no harm done—which in its quiet way symbolized the history of the next two hundred and sixty years in this region. Adriaan and Dikkop, white and brown, were traveling idly along a swale that showed no sign of animals, when suddenly Dikkop halted, lifted his head, pointed eastward and said, with some concern and perhaps a little fright, 'People!'

Instinctively the two boys took cover, fairly certain that their movements had been so silent that whoever was approaching could not have detected them. They were right. From the far end of the swale came two young men, shimmering black, hunting in an aimless, noisy way. They were taller than either Adriaan or Dikkop, older than the former, younger than the latter. They were handsome fellows, armed with clubs and assegais; they wore breechclouts and nothing more, except that around the right ankle they displayed a band of delicate blue feathers. They had apparently failed in this day's hunting, for they carried no dead game, and what they intended eating this night, Adriaan could not guess. However, on they came at a moderate pace which would soon put them abreast of the hiding watchers.

It was a tense situation. The newcomers might pass on without discovering the two boys hiding, but then the problem would be how to skirt either north or south to avoid them. More likely, the newcomers would soon spot the strangers, and then what might happen no one could foretell. Dikkop was trembling with apprehension, but Adriaan merely breathed deeply. Then, without preparation, he spoke loudly but in a gentle voice, and when the two blacks turned in consternation, he stepped forward, holding his empty hands forth and saying in Dutch, 'Good day.'

The two blacks automatically reached for their clubs, but now Dikkop moved out, his hands before his face, palms out with fingers extended: 'No! No!' The two blacks continued their movements, held up their clubs, brandished them, and faced the strangers, whose hands were still extended. After a very long time, while Dikkop almost dissolved in fear, they slowly dropped their clubs, stood looking at the unbelievable strangers, then moved carefully forward.

In this way Adriaan van Doorn became the first of his family to meet blacks inhabiting the land to the east. Willem van Doorn had landed at the Cape in 1647, but it was not until 1725 that his great-grandson stood face-to-face with a South African black. Of course, from the early days at the Cape, men like Commander van Riebeeck had owned black slaves, but these were from Madagascar and Angola and Moçambique, never from the great lands to the east. Thus the Van Doorns had occupied the Cape for seventy-eight years before this first contact, and in those fatal generations the Dutch had become committed to the policy of Europeans in whatever new lands they encountered: that whatever they desired of this continent was theirs. During all those years they had paid scant attention to reports from shipwrecked mariners and Hottentot nomads that a major society existed to the east. Because of arrogance and ignorance, the impending confrontation would have to be violent.

'Sotopo,' the younger said when the matter of names was discussed. He came, he said, from far to the east, many days travel, many days. The older boy indicated that they, like Adriaan and Dikkop, had gone wandering at the end of winter and that they, too, had been living off the land, killing an antelope now and then for food. But this day they had been unlucky and would go to bed hungry.

How did they say this? Not a word of the black language was intelligible to the farm boys, and nothing that Adriaan or Dikkop said was intelligible to the other pair, but they conversed as human beings do in frontier societies, with gestures, pantomime, grunts, laughs, and incessant movement of hand and face. The problem of talking with these strangers was not much different from the problem of talking to strange slaves that the Van Doorns would buy from time to time. The master talked, and that was it. The slave understood partially, and that was enough. What really counted was when Dikkop tried to tell them that with the stick he carried he could catch them an antelope for supper. They were too smart to believe this. A witch doctor could do many things with his magic, but not to an antelope. So the four boys crept quietly to the edge of the swale, waited a long time for animals, and finally spotted a herd of springbok drifting along the veld. Very patiently Dikkop moved into position, took aim at a healthy buck, and fired. When the noise of the gun exploded, the two black youths exclaimed in fear, but when the springbok fell and was collected by Dikkop, they marveled.

The canny Hottentot, aware that this night would probably be spent in the company of these two, used many gestures to warn them that if his stick could kill a springbok far away, it could certainly kill them close at hand. And he further showed them that even if they stole the stick, they would not be able to kill the white man, because they would not have the mystery, which he was not going to explain. They understood.

Onto the embers of the blazing fire went the springbok meat, and as it roasted, the four young men made careful calculations of their situation, each pair speaking freely in its own language, assured that the other could not understand whatever strategies were proposed. Dikkop, who was terrified of the situation, suggested that as soon as they finished the evening meal, he and Adriaan should start back toward the distant farm, relying on their guns to keep the blacks at bay should they attempt to follow. Adriaan laughed at such an idea: 'They can run. You can see that from their legs. We'd never escape.'

'So what we do, Baas?' Dikkop asked, almost impertinently.

'We stay here, keep watch and find out as much as we can.'

To Dikkop such a strategy seemed irresponsible, and he said so, sternly; the compromise that evolved was ingenious. As Dikkop explained it, 'We sleep in that tree, Baas. With our guns. You sleep first and I keep guard. Then I waken you, you keep your gun trained on them. Shoot them down if they try to kill us.'

But after they had eaten, the strangers licking the antelope fat from their fingers, Adriaan and Dikkop were astonished to see that the blacks headed immediately for a tree, disposing themselves so that they were protected should the two young men try to kill them in the night. Adriaan, as he hollowed out a place on the ground from which he could aim his gun at the tree, noticed that they had taken their warclubs aloft with them.

And so they spent the night, two above, two below; two awake, two asleep. Only when daylight came did the blacks climb down out of their tree.

They were together four days, with Dikkop in a state of near-exhaustion because of the fear that gripped him. The blacks were so much bigger than he, so powerfully muscled, that he could not avoid imagining them swinging their clubs at his head, so that even at the moment when he fired his gun to bring down another antelope, he expected to be brained. He was not unhappy when the accidental partnership showed signs of breaking up, the blacks explaining that they must return eastward eighteen days walking, Dikkop saying with relief that he and Adriaan must go westward their thirty days. He told Adriaan, 'About same distance, Baas. They move much faster.'

The parting involved no great emotion, but all felt it to be a pregnant moment. There was no shaking of hands, no *abrazos* in the Portuguese style, only a moment of intense quiet as the two pairs looked at each other for the last time. Then, as if to epitomize the unfolding history of these racial groups, Sotopo thrust out his hand to grasp Adriaan by the arm, but the Dutch boy was frightened by the unexpected movement and drew away. By the time he recovered his senses and wanted to accept the farewell touching, Sotopo had stepped back, mortified that his gesture had been rejected. Dikkop, the Coloured man, merely stood aside and watched, participant in nothing.

The two blacks moved off first, but after they reached the eastern end of the glade they stopped and turned back to watch the strangers walking to the west, and there they stood as the two figures grew smaller and smaller, their miraculous fire-sticks over their shoulders.

'Who were they?' Sotopo asked his older brother.

'Like the ones who came across the sea, before Old Grandmother's time.' The lads had been told about these mysterious creatures; they had arrived by sea in a floating house that had broken to pieces on the rocks, and they had come ashore. There had been a few killings, on each side, after which the strangers had split into two parties, one walking overland and perishing in the empty spaces, the other waiting by the shore for many moons—many, many moons—until another floating house came to take them away.

They had left no visible impact on the tribes, only memories to be talked about at night by warriors in the kraals. But clearly, the little fellow with the white hair had been of that breed. As for the other? 'Who was he, Mandiso?'

'He looked like one of the brown people from the valleys,' the older boy replied, 'but there's something different.'

And when the strange pair vanished in the western distance, the two black travelers turned toward their own homes.

They were Xhosa, members of the great and powerful tribe that lived beyond the big river, and when they returned to their family they were going to have much explaining to do. They could hear Old Grandmother screaming at them: 'Where have you been? Where did you take your little brother? What do you mean, a white boy with a stick that threw flame?' Each night as they moved closer to home, they devised a different strategy.

'You explain it, Mandiso. You're older.' And that night it was arranged that Mandiso would tell how they had wanted to know what lay west of the big river, beyond the hills where the red-paint earth lay.

But on the next evening it would seem desirable that Sotopo do the speaking, since he was younger and would be accorded a more sympathetic hearing: 'We followed the spoor of a large beast, but could not find him, and before we knew it we were beyond the hills.'

On some nights they would mutually acknowledge the fact that neither of these explanations sounded convincing, but how to explain their hegira they did not know. The truth would surely be rejected. 'The reason we were away so long,' Mandiso said as they gnawed on roots from a succulent shrub, 'was that day after day we felt that when we reached the top of the next hill we would see something of magnitude.' He hesitated, and Sotopo continued the narrative: 'But whenever we reached the crest of the hill, all we saw was nothing. More forests, little rivers and a great many more hills.'

'Shall we tell them of the two boys?' Mandiso asked.

'That's difficult,' Sotopo said, 'because the little one with the yellow skin —I don't think he was a boy. I do believe he was a Khoi-khoi, maybe twenty summers.'

'I liked the big one,' Mandiso said. 'He wasn't afraid, you know. The little one, you could smell him sweating in fear. But the white-haired boy, he seemed to like us.'

'But at the end he, too, jumped back in fear.'

'He did,' Mandiso agreed. 'You moved toward him and he leaped back, afraid like the little one.'

When they reached the banks of the big river and knew that they must soon encounter other Xhosa, they stopped speculating and faced up to the fact that before nightfall they would have to explain their absence. 'What we'll do,' Mandiso said with a touch of resignation, 'is simply tell them that we wanted to see what lay far to the west.'

'But shall we tell them of the two strangers?'

'I think we better had,' the older boy said. 'If we could smell fear in the little one, Old Grandmother will see excitement in our eyes, whether we speak of it or not.' So it was agreed that they would tell the entire story, embellishing nothing, hiding nothing, and this resolve pacified their fears, and they went forward boldly to meet the scouts that guarded the perimeters, and with them they were quite brave and forthright, but when Old Grandmother started shouting at them, they crumpled and told a very disjointed story.

The Xhosa people took their name from a historic chieftain who ruled around the year 1500. Among his many accomplishments was securing for them the lovely chain of valleys they now occupied between the mountains and the shores of the Indian Ocean. For half a thousand years they had been drifting easily south and west, enticed from in front by a succession of empty pasture lands, edged from behind by the movement of other tribes. They had been traveling at the rate of only a hundred and twenty miles a century, and although this had accelerated recently, as their population and especially their herds increased, they could have been expected to reach the Cape, and the end of their expansion, about the year 2025 had not the Dutch occupied the Cape and started their own expansion eastward. After the meeting of the four young men, it became obvious that trekboer and Xhosa would have to come face-to-face, and that this would take place rather soon, probably along the Great Fish River.

Well to the east, in a valley unusually well protected, lived the Great Chief, who had never even visited the western frontier where the family of Sotopo and Mandiso lived. All tribes owed allegiance to the Great Chief, though his effective powers over them were limited to precedence at festivals and rituals, and determination of the rights of the royal family, to which all chiefs of the tribal group belonged. The constituent tribes were organized geographically, Sotopo's being the westernmost. Tribal chiefs appointed headmen of various clans or 'neighborhoods,' which were large enough to permit their members to intermarry. The 'neighborhoods' were broken down into kraals, where intermarriage was forbidden, and Sotopo's father, Makubele, was kraal headman; he carried orders from above, served at ceremonies and postured a good deal, but everyone knew, especially Makubele himself, that the kraal was really ruled by the tongue of Tutula, Old Grandmother. The family consisted of forty-one members.

To say 'They owned a wooded hillside well inland from the sea' would confuse the entire point of this story, because nobody *owned* any part of the land. Sotopo's father owned many cattle, and if the cows continued to produce calves, he might well become the next chief. Old Grandmother owned the beautifully tanned animal skins she used as coverlets in winter. And Sotopo owned his polished hard-wood assegais. But the land belonged to the spirits who governed life; it existed forever, for everyone, and was apportioned temporarily according to the dictates of the tribal chief and senior headman. Sotopo's father occupied the hillside for the time being, and when he died the older son could inherit the loan-place, but no man or family ever acquired ownership.

The beauty of the system was that since all the land in the world was free, when a dispute over succession occurred or a kraal became crowded, the aggrieved could simply move on; if an entire kraal decided to move west, as happened continually, they left behind unencumbered land open for others to occupy. In some other distant valley as acceptable as the one they had left, they would settle down, and life would continue much as it had done for the last eight hundred years. All that was needed to ensure happiness was unlimited land.

'What we should get on with now,' Makubele said, puffing his pipe after the excitement over the boys' trip quieted, 'is Mandiso's circumcision.' Everyone agreed, especially Mandiso, who was seventeen years old now and eager to become a man. The running away to the west had been a last childish adventure; now girls in the valley were beginning to look at him with extra interest, and unless he went through the painful ordeal of officially becoming a man, there was no chance that he could ever attain one of them, no matter how much lobola he assembled for a purchase. Their valley already contained one man, now in his forties, who had evaded circumcision, and no one would have much to do with him, women or men, because he had not certified his manhood.

Young Sotopo, only fourteen that year, had become aware during their expedition that his brother was changing, growing more serious; sometimes Mandiso had remained silent for most of a day, as if he were anticipating the rites that lay ahead, and now no one was more attentive to the impending rituals than Sotopo. He kept wondering how he would perform, were he Mandiso.

He watched as the family elders visited other families to ascertain which of their boys wished to participate, and he stayed with his father when the men visited the witch doctor to determine when the moon would be in proper position to build the secluded straw lodge in which the manhood-boys would live for three months after the ritual. He saw the designated boys set out to collect red-earth clay for ceremonial adornment, watched as they wove the curious rush-hats they would wear for a hundred days: three feet long, tied at one end, open at the other, but worn parallel to the ground, with the tied end trailing behind. He could imagine Mandiso in such a hat; he would look much like the crowned crane, sacred bird of the Xhosa.

The day came when the man who had been appointed their guardian assembled the nine manhood-boys and led them to the river, where in the presence of men only, with a few lads like Sotopo watching from hiding places among the trees, they stripped, went into the waters, and painted themselves totally with white clay; when they emerged, they were like ghosts. In this uniform they marched to the secluded lodge, where the guardian entered with them, initiating them into the verbal secrets of the tribe. After a long time he led the boys outside, where all checked to be sure there were at least nine ant hills; Mandiso identified his with two sticks, and the guardian left.

All that night the boys chanted old songs inherited from the days when the Xhosa people lived far to the north, long before the time when Great Xhosa gave them their name, and Sotopo, still watching, envied them their fellowship, and the singing, and the fact that they would soon be men.

Next morning, when the sun was well up, the guardian returned with his knife-sharp assegai, strode purposefully into the lodge and cried in a loud voice, 'Who wishes to become a man?' and with pride Sotopo heard his brother answer, 'I wish to be a man.' There was a silence during which Sotopo could imagine the flash of the assegai, the burning pain, and then the triumphant shout: 'Now I am a man!' Against his will, Sotopo burst into tears of pride; his brother had not cried out in pain.

When the nine were initiated, they left the lodge one by one, each carrying in his right hand the foreskin that had been cut away. This was hidden in the ant hill, each to his own, so that evil spirits could not find them and create spells. For three days a guard was posted at the ant hills to keep sorcerers away; by then the ants would have devoured all traces of the ritual.

It was important, in this valley, to watch out for spirits, and when the nine boys had been in their shack for six days, the dreaded fire-bird struck to remind everyone of his power. Only a few people had ever seen this bird, which was fortunate, because it was so terrifying. It lived behind the mountains and ate prodigious quantities of stolen mealies, growing so fat that it became larger than a hippopotamus. Then, because it was a hellish bird, it set itself on fire, its body fat throwing long flames as it flew through the sky, screaming with a mixture of joy at destroying kraals and pain at the consuming of its own body: thus came thunder and lightning.

When the fat was nearly burned away, the fire-bird dove to earth in a tremendous clap of thunder, buried itself deep and laid one egg, large and very white, which burrowed underground till it reached the bottom of some river. There it ripened until another full-grown fire-bird leaped out of the river to gorge mealies, set itself afire, and bring more thunder and lightning.

On this day, when Mandiso and his eight companions huddled in their lodge, the fire-bird was especially vengeful, sweeping back and forth across the valley until the earth seemed to tremble, so loud were the claps of thunder. As at any kraal, it was imperative that the headman go out into the storm with his assegais, stand by the kraal where the beasts lowed in confusion, and with such magic as he had, defend his cattle and his family from the lightning. If the fire-bird did succeed in blasting a kraal, it was proof that the occupants had done something wrong, and then they would have to pay excessive fees to the witch doctor to get themselves made clean again.

Indeed, one had to pay the witch doctor for almost every act of life, but when the fire-bird wept, that was powerful proof that someone had transgressed. In certain storms, when the bird's fat burned too swiftly, the pain became unendurable, and the wild-flying bird began to cry, just like a baby, and as its tears fell they turned to hail, each grain bigger than a bird's egg, and this peppered the valley unmercifully.

In this storm the fire-bird wept so pitifully that vast sheets of hail came thundering down, breaking thatch and hurting cows until their cries penetrated the hut where Sotopo and his family huddled. One flurry of especially heavy stones struck Makubele as he stood outside endeavoring to protect his family, and he fell to the ground. Sotopo, seeing this, realized that if the witch doctor heard of it, he would take it as proof that it was Mandiso who had sinned in some way, causing the fire-bird to torment the valley. So although it was forbidden, Sotopo jumped from the safety of the hut, ran to his father, raised him to his feet, and then assisted him in fighting off the bird.

When the fire-bird left the valley to dive into the earth behind the hills, and the lightning ceased, Sotopo quietly gathered the three assegais he had laboriously made and his one calf, harbinger of the herds he would one day own, and walked purposefully to the witch doctor's hut.

'I come seeking aid,' he said twice at the low entrance. From the dark interior a heavy voice said, 'Enter.'

Since the boy had never before visited a diviner, he had little concept of the mysterious world he was entering: the owl on the dead branch; the stuffed hornbill in the corner, red-wattled and forlorn; the sacs of dead animals; lizards and herbs; and above all, the brooding presence of the old man who wrestled with evil spirits, preventing them from overwhelming the community.

'I hear your father was knocked down by the fire-bird,' the witch doctor said.

'No,' Sotopo lied. 'He slipped when rain made the slope muddy.'

'I hear you left your hut.'

'I went to help fight off the fire-bird.'

'Why do you come to me? What other great wrong have you done?'

'I come to plead for my brother.'

'Mandiso? In the circumcision lodge? What great wrong has he done?'

'Nothing. Oh, nothing. But I want you to intercede for him, that he conduct himself bravely during these weeks.'

The diviner coughed. This was a bright boy, this Sotopo son of Makubele, grandson of Old Grandmother. He knew that it was all-important how a young manhood-boy behaved himself during the initiation; two years ago one applicant fainted with pain, and although it was discovered that his wound had festered, that was no excuse for fainting, and he was consequently given second status, which would mar him for the rest of his life. That Sotopo should be enough concerned about his brother to offer three assegais and a cow . . .

'You bring me the assegais?' the witch doctor asked.

'Yes, and my cow.'

'You're a strong boy. You'll be a wise man one day. Leave them with me.'

'And you will protect my brother?'

'He will do well.'

'And you'll forget that my father slipped in the mud?'

'I will forget.'

'Diviner, we thank you. All of us thank you.' Sotopo told no one of his clandestine visit to the witch doctor, and he was much relieved when he heard rumors from the ritual lodge that Mandiso was conducting himself especially well.

In the days that followed, Sotopo became aware that another resident of the valley was taking an unusual interest in his brother's progress; it was Xuma, the attractive girl who lived in the kraal at the far end of the valley. She was fifteen, a year older than Sotopo, with a smiling face, supple lips, and an accumulation of ear bangles, beads and ankle charms that made her approach a musical interlude. Sotopo had known Xuma all his life and liked her better than any other girl, even though she was older than he and in some ways stronger, and it pleased him that this lively girl, above all others, had focused her attention on Mandiso.

'How do they say, about the lodge?' she asked as she came easily down the path to Sotopo's kraal.

'They say well. He's strong, Xuma.'

'I know.'

It was permissible, in Xhosa custom, for boys who were not yet men to play at night with girls past puberty, always mindful that there must not be any babies, and Sotopo was aware that Xuma had begun to go into the veld with his brother, even spending nights with him, so he was not surprised that she should now be inquiring after him, and he was pleased. Because he loved his brother, and cherished the long exploring trip they had taken together, he looked forward to the day when Mandiso would be chief of the clan and he the assistant.

His family lived in a collection of huts, seven of them, scattered about the kraal in which the cattle were kept. They were dome-shaped, formed by rows of saplings implanted in a circular pattern, bent inward and bound together, then thickly thatched. The huts were handsome of themselves, and when seen against the rolling hills, formed pleasing patterns.

Xuma, honored to become part of this family, volunteered to help collect thatch for replenishing the huts, and often she went down to the river with her shell knife to cut rushes. Sotopo went with her, to help carry the large, but light, bundles homeward, and on one trip Xuma confided that her father had fallen into trouble with the witch doctor and had been forced to pay him excessive gifts.

'That's troublesome,' Sotopo said, not revealing that he, too, had had a minor confrontation with the powerful diviner.

'I don't know what Father did that was wrong,' Xuma said. 'He isn't a man who angers anyone easily, but the witch doctor was most angry.'

It was like that among the Xhosa. As a nation, the tribes were a gentle people, eschewing vast armies for war against their neighbors, but there were clashes with the Hottentots. Some of the conquered little people allied themselves with the Xhosa, intermarrying and occasionally even attaining power within the hierarchy. This interaction with the Hottentots continued through many centuries, and one of the lasting legacies was a unique language: from the Hottentots, the Xhosa borrowed the click sounds, and these distinguished their speech from that of the other southern black tribes.

Although they did not war on the grand scale, no Xhosa warrior ever hesitated to snatch up his assegais if his cattle had to be defended, or if he saw a good chance to capture his neighbor's. Cattle raiding was the national pastime; success conferred distinction, for cattle were in many ways more important than babies. Everything depended upon them: a man's reputation derived from the number of cattle he held; the kind of bride a young man could aspire to was determined by how many cattle he could bring as lobola to the girl's parents; and the good name of a kraal like Sotopo's sprang almost entirely from the number of cows and oxen and bulls it possessed. The cattle did not have to be good beasts, nor produce copious milk, nor excellent eating meat; there was no merit in having a prepotent bull which threw fine animals. Only numbers counted, which meant that year by year the quality of the great herds deteriorated, with five thousand beasts needed to perform the functions that nine hundred really good animals could have fulfilled.

So although the Xhosa lived without fear of warfare, they lived in dreadful fear of what might happen to their scrawny cattle, and it was the diviner who established and policed the intricate rules for the preservation of the herd. For example, during her entire lifetime no Xhosa woman could ever approach or lay her hand upon the rocks which enclosed the kraal, and if any dared to enter the sacred area, she would be punished. A boy set to tending his family's cattle as they roamed the hills had better come home with every calf, or his punishment would be savage. There was a time to perform every function connected with cattle, a proper way to handle them. No boy dared milk a cow, and for a girl to do so was a grave offense; of course, in special circumstances, when no adult males were available, a daughter was permitted to milk a cow, but she was forbidden to touch the milk sac itself. Every act of life, it seemed, was circumscribed by rules, and Xuma's father had broken one of them. He was, as Xuma intimated to Sotopo, in deep trouble.

But this was forgotten as the time approached when the nine manhood-boys in the lodge reached the end of their confinement, and now a sad thing happened: Sotopo, who had been so close to his brother, became aware that henceforth a gulf would exist between them. Sotopo was still a boy; Mandiso was a man, and his allegiance to the eight others who had undergone the ordeal with him would always be much stronger than his friendship for his own brother, who had not, and it was with sorrow that the boy watched the emergence of the man.

The lectures on manhood delivered by the headman and the guardian were now ended. The intricate rituals, the secrets of the tribe had been shared, and the time for burning down the lodge and all its pains was at hand. But first the nine new men must go to the river in sight of the entire community and cleanse themselves of the white clay that had marked them for the past hundred days. In stately procession, naked, with the mark of their circumcision plain for all to see, the new-men marched to the river, immersed themselves, and spent several hours trying to clean away the adhesive mud. When they emerged, their bodies, long protected from the sun, were lean and pale. Anointed with butter and red-earth, they glimmered in the unaccustomed light; never again in their lives would they appear so manly, so promising of noble conduct.

Then came the celebration! Dried gourds, their seeds intact, were rattled in fine rhythms. Musical instruments, consisting of a single cord of cured gut tied tight between the ends of a bowed piece of wood, were plucked, the musician keeping one end of the wood between his teeth, and altering the sound by altering the movements of his mouth. Old women held two sticks, beating them together, and young men who had completed their ritual three or four years before dressed themselves in wild costumes of feather, rush and reed, ready to dance till they collapsed in exhaustion.

Before the manhood-boys were free to join the celebration, their guardian lighted a brand, carried it solemnly to the ceremonial lodge and set it ablaze. Now the nine inductees rushed from their place of seclusion for the last time, dressed in gaudy costumes topped by their elongated hats, which they still wore horizontally. Turning their backs to the blazing lodge, they kept their eyes rigidly forward as they walked away, for if they dared look back, evil spirits would doom them.

Free of the lodge, they became like wild men as they joined their exultant families and friends, cavorting without rule and leaping into the air as if to challenge the fire-bird himself. Then slowly order began to take over, the clapping of hands assumed a stately rhythm, and all associated with the ceremony leaned forward to see which new-man among the nine would step forward as spokesman for the group.

It was Mandiso, and at this moment of honor Sotopo gave a cry of joy and nodded to the diviner, who did not nod back.

'Today we are men,' Mandiso said, and with these words he began the great dance of the Xhosa, keeping his feet planted on the ground but gyrating all parts of his body as if each were a separate entity. He was especially adroit at sending his belly in one direction, his buttocks in another, and at the moment when he did this to perfection, the other eight new-men leaped in the air, tore about the dancing ground and settled into their version of this dance, so that the entire area was filled with wildly twisting bodies, cries, and the rumble of approval.

The feasting lasted two days. At times both the young men and the spectators collapsed in exhaustion, slept in a kind of daze, awakened, drank large draughts of mealie-beer, and with fresh shouting and renewed vigor, resumed the dance. Dust rose from the kraals; soot from the burned shack was scattered joyously; Sotopo, numb with pride because of his brother's outstanding performance, watched the proceedings from the edge of the crowd and observed how carefully Xuma followed the dancers, never participating herself but applauding quietly whenever Mandiso performed his solos.

When Mandiso returned to the family kraal, the first thing he did was to ask Sotopo's help in laying out the floor for a new hut; it was not as big as his father's, nor would it be as tall; it was a hut for two people, not ten.

'You can attend the ant hills,' the new-man told his brother, and Sotopo was delighted to be given this honor. Taking a large basket, he circulated among some fifteen large ant hills, scooping up excess earth in which the ants had deposited their larvae, dead bodies and bits of their saliva. This fine, granular earth, when spread in a thick layer and watered down and allowed to bake in the sun, formed a substance harder than most stone, and when polished with cow manure, made the best possible base for a hut. Sotopo, guessing that he was building for Xuma, made a floor that would last a generation.

The young women of the family had to gather the saplings for the walls, but when it came to the thatching, that all-important part, Old Grand-mother herself wanted to go down to the fields and cut the grass, and although she was too weak to gather all that would be required, she did deliver the first bundles and then stood noisily directing the design of the lovely, rounded finish.

It was a jewel of a hut, and now Mandiso was eligible to visit Xuma's parents, but on the eve of doing so, the most disturbing word reached Sotopo via one of his playmates: 'A sorcerer has placed a curse on Xuma's father.' This could be such a fatal impediment to any union of the two families that Sotopo borrowed two of his brother's best assegais and a goat and went directly to the witch doctor, hailing him from a distance: 'All-powerful One! May I approach?'

'Come' echoed the mournful voice.

'I seek counsel.'

'I see that this time you bring only two assegais.'

'But they are better, All-powerful.'

'And a cow?'

'The boy is holding a goat outside.'

'What is the question?'

'Will my brother marry Xuma?'

There was a long silence, perhaps five minutes, during which the old man carefully weighed the complex problems raised by this inquiry. Sotopo's family was one of the most powerful in the valley and could be expected, in the years to come, to provide both leadership and wealth; it would not be wise to affront them. But on the other hand, Xuma's family had long been troublesome and there was good cause to believe that the last flight of the fire-bird had been evoked by malperformances on the father's part. Twice the witch doctor had warned the man, and twice the injunctions had been ignored. Now he was under a curse, and it seemed highly improbable that he would ever be allowed to escape from it, for it was the duty of a diviner to police the health of his clan, to remove all forces that might work against central authority, and Xuma's father was an irritation.

But what to say about this proposed marriage? And the more the old man pondered this difficult question, the angrier he became at this boy Sotopo who had raised it. Why had he dared to come with such an imperti-nent question? Why had he stepped forth as champion of the girl Xuma, which was clearly his intention in this affair? Damn him. Sotopo, son of Makubele, a boy to be marked for remembrance.

The old man temporized: 'I suppose that Xuma herself has had no part in her father's misbehavior. I suppose a marriage could go forward.'

'Oh, thank you!' Sotopo cried, but after he had surrendered the two assegais and the goat and had gone running down the footpath, the diviner stared after him, mumbling, 'Two assegais, not three. A goat, and not one of the best. Damn that boy!'

The wedding ceremonies covered eleven days, and in certain respects they were a triumph for Mandiso, since he got himself a strong, beautiful and darling wife; but in another way they were a disaster, for through her he acquired the enmity of the diviner. As to the wedding itself, there was a good deal of marching back and forth between Mandiso's kraal and Xuma's: he had to take a heifer there as proof of his good intentions; she had to bring rushes here as an indication of her willingness to work; he had to go there in his finest ornaments to dance before her family and break two saplings across his knee, thus pledging that he would never beat his wife; she had to come and dance before his cattle kraal to show that she revered the cows and would show them the respect they merited. And through it all, the old witch doctor watched sardonically, aware that no matter what rituals they observed, nothing good could come of this marriage. It was doomed.

But he did not interfere, and even officiated in certain of the hallowed rites, going so far as to protect the new hut against evil. He did this for good reason: he suspected that within a year Mandiso and Xuma would flee the place, after which he could see that one of his nephews gained possession.

To that end, as soon as the young couple moved into the handsome hut, he began asking questions through the community, never directing them at Mandiso, but always at Xuma's father: 'Who do you think it was that caused the fire-bird to fly?' and 'Have you noticed how the mealies at his kraal have grown bigger than any others? Could he be casting spells?'

Week after week these poisonous suspicions were broadcast, never a substantiated charge, only the nagging questions: 'Have you seen how Xuma's cattle become pregnant so quickly? Could her father be weaving a spell there, too?' The assumption in this question was most effective; that her father was casting a spell over the new hut was problematic, but that he had done so at his own was accepted: 'He's bringing this valley into sore trouble.'

During this time Sotopo was preoccupied with the last days of boyhood. Having seen his older brother through the twin ordeals of circumcision and marriage, he returned to those things that gave his own life significance. Beyond the family kraal, at the edge of the river, there was a level place where in the morning the wagtails danced, those delicate little gray-brown birds that bobbed their tail feathers up and down as they paraded. They loved insects, and darted their long bills this way and that, plucking them off dead leaves.

They were the good-omen birds, the ones that made a kraal a place of joy, and Sotopo had always found delight in being with them, he on a log, they on some rock at the edge of the river; he sprawled out on the ground, they dancing back and forth oblivious of him, for they seemed to know that they were protected: 'No one but a man near death from frenzy would disturb a wagtail, for they bring us love.'

He also felt increasingly attached to Old Grandmother, as if, like Mandiso, he must soon move away from her influence. He stayed with her about the house, watching as she prepared the dish he liked the most: mealies well pounded in the stump of a tree, then mixed with pumpkin, baked with shreds of antelope meat, and flavored with the herbs which only she knew how to gather.

'Tell me again,' she said as she worked. 'When you ran away from us, you say you met two boys, one brown, one white?' When her grandson nodded, she asked, 'You say one spoke like us? The other didn't? How could that be?'

She had a dozen questions about this meeting; the men in the family had listened to the story, nodded sagely and forgotten the matter, but not Old Grandmother: 'Tell me again, the brown one was small and old, the white one was young and big. That goes against the rule of nature.'

But when he explained, with increasing detail, for he enjoyed talking with the old woman, she told him what he had heard many times before: 'I didn't see it myself, because it happened before I was born. But men like that boy came to our shore once in a house that floated on the waves, but they died like ordinary men.' It was her opinion that what the white-skinned boy had said was probably true: 'I think there are other people hiding across the river. I don't think I'll ever see them, but you will, Sotopo. When you marry and have your own hut and move to the west . . .'

At this point she would always stop what she was doing and ask her grandson, 'Sotopo, who are you going to marry?' And he would blush beneath his dark skin because he had not yet addressed this problem.

But one day he did ask the question whose answer could reveal the dangers that lay ahead: 'Old Grandmother, why do you always say that when I take a wife, we'll move across the river?'

'Ah-hah!' she cackled. 'Now we're ready to talk.' And she sat with him and said, 'Can't you see that the witch doctor is determined to drive Xuma's father out of the valley? And that when he goes, Mandiso will surely go with him? And that when Mandiso and Xuma flee, you'll join them?'

She had uncovered thoughts which had been germinating deep in the boy's mind; he had chosen to stay by himself, away from the others, to communicate with the wagtails and his other friends of river and forest, because he was afraid to face up to the tragedy that he saw developing in the valley, with families quietly turning against Xuma's father, and by extension, against Xuma and Mandiso. He knew instinctively what he had been afraid to voice: that before this year was out he would have to choose whether to stay with his parents, whom he loved, and with Old Grandmother, whom he loved most dearly, or go into exile with Mandiso and Xuma.

His solution for the moment was to draw even closer to his grandmother, for she was the only person who would talk with him; even Mandiso was so occupied with starting a new family that he had little time for his brother.

'Why does the diviner torment us?' he asked the old woman one day.

'He doesn't. No, he doesn't. It's the spirits. It's his job to keep the spirits happy or they'd devastate this valley.'

'But Xuma's father . . .'

'How do we know what he's done? Tell me that, Sotopo! How do we
know what evil things a man can do without the rest of us being aware?'

'You think he's guilty?'

'Of what? How should I know. All I know is that if the witch doctor
says he's guilty, he's guilty.'

'And Mandiso must go into exile with him, if he leaves?'

'Oh, now!' She thought about this for some time, sucking at her corncob
pipe, then said to her grandson, 'I think the time comes for all of us when
we should move on. The field is no longer fertile. The neighbors are no
longer kindly. For an old woman like me, death comes to solve the problem.
For a young person like you, move on.'

Neither of them said another word that day; they had stepped too close
to the ultimate realities of life, and it would require weeks of reflection
before complete meaning could be known, but in those days of silence
Sotopo became aware that all things had deteriorated sadly in the community. Xuma's father had been found one morning in a ditch with a gash on
his head. Xuma's cooking pot was shattered when she left it drying in the
sun.

So young Sotopo, now approaching sixteen, gathered the two assegais
he had made of dark wood and went for the last time to see the diviner.
'Come in,' the old man said.

'Why is Mandiso being punished?'

'You bring me only two assegais? And a calf, perhaps?'

'I have no more cattle, All-powerful One.'

'But you still ask my help.'

'Not for me. For my brother.'

'He is in trouble, Sotopo, deep trouble.'

'But why? He's done nothing.'

'He's associated with Xuma, and her father has done much evil.'

'What evil, All-powerful?'

'Evil that the spirits see.' Beyond this fragile explanation the old man
would not go, but he allowed his visitor to sense the implacable opposition
all good men ought to show against a member of the tribe guilty of evil
practices, even though those practices were never identified.

'Can you do nothing to help him?' Sotopo pleaded.

'It isn't him you're worried about, is it?'

'No, it's Mandiso.'

'He shares the guilt.'

'Can he do nothing?' the boy asked.

'No. The evil is upon him.' And no amount of pleading, no amount of
future gifts would alleviate this dreadful curse. The community, through the
agency of their diviner, had named Xuma's father as a source of contamination, and he must go.

Shortly after this visit he was found beaten to death at the gateway to
his kraal, an especially ominous way to die, implying that even the sleek and
growing cattle had been powerless to protect him.

That night Mandiso and Xuma came to the big hut, the wife sitting
circumspectly to the left among the women as the fateful discussion began.

'You must leave us,' Old Grandmother said without any show of sorrow.

'But why must I surrender . . .'

'The time has come to go,' she said forcefully. 'Tell him, Makubele.' And the boys' father referred only to his own selfish interests: 'The old one's right. You must go. Otherwise the curse will apply to us all, won't it, Old Grandmother?'

But she refused to allow her own predicament or that of her family to intrude in this matter: 'What is important, Mandiso, is not what will happen to your father, but what will happen to you and Xuma. What do you think your future is now, with her father killed in that manner, at the gateway to his kraal?'

'If there is one sacred place—' Mandiso began, but Xuma broke in: 'We must go. And we must go before nightfall tomorrow.'

'Can it really be so!' her husband said, appalled at the implications of what Xuma had said.

'Isn't that true, Old Grandmother?' the girl asked.

'I'd go tonight,' the old woman said. And it was agreed that before the next sun set Mandiso and Xuma would start for the west, to a new settlement, to a new home. They would take cattle, and skin bags of mealies for seed, and other oddments—but they must go, for the consensus of their community, arrived at in complex ways, had decreed that they were no longer wanted.

But where did this leave Sotopo, not yet a man but deeply devoted to his brother and his brother's wife? When the family conclave broke up, he remained with his grandmother a long time, discussing his difficult alternatives: remain, with the diviner probably opposed to him; or flee, when he had not yet been ordained a man? He had absolutely no hard evidence that the witch doctor had declared war upon him, but he knew it had happened and that sooner or later the rumors would begin to circulate against him. But he also knew that to face the future without the sanctions of circumcision entailed dangers too fearful to contemplate. Having watched his brother's joyous entrance into married life, with a girl as admirable as Xuma, he had begun to sense how awful it would be to have the girls of his community categorize him as less-than-man and to be deprived of their companionship.

This was something he could not discuss with his grandmother, so in the dead of night he crept to his brother's kraal and whispered, 'Mandiso! Are you awake?'

'What is it, brother?'

'I shall go with you.'

'Good. We'll need you.'

'But how will I ever become a man?'

Mandiso sat in the dark with his left hand over his mouth, considering this perplexing question, and then, because he felt he must be truthful, he listed the impediments: 'There'd be no guardian to bless the hut. There'd be no other boys to share the experience. We probably couldn't find clay to cover your body. And at the end there'd be no grand celebration.'

'I've thought of that, Mandiso. I've thought of it all, but still I want to stay with you.' And he added, 'With you and Xuma,' for he was not ashamed of his love for his sister-in-law.

'It seems to me,' Mandiso said, 'looking back on everything that happened, that a boy becomes a man with the pain, with the courage. He becomes a man not with the dancing and the food and the cheers of others. He becomes a man within himself, through his own bravery.'

They pondered this for a long time, during which Mandiso hoped that his brother would speak up, would volunteer proof of his courage, but Sotopo was too confused by this necessity to make at age sixteen a decision more difficult than most men make in their entire lives. So finally Mandiso tipped the scales: 'In the woods that time, when we met the two strange men'—in his thinking, they were men, now—'it was you, Sotopo, who devised the plan for sleeping in the tree. I believe I might have slipped away.'

'Really?' the boy asked, and the possibility that he had been brave, there in the woods, so captivated his mind that he said no more that night. Nor did he sleep. At dawn he was at the river saying farewell to the wagtails. At full-sun he was watching a pair of monstrous hornbills waddling across the fields, and at midmorning he had collected his remaining goats, falling in line behind five of the young men who had shared the ritual circumcision with Mandiso and who now elected to go with him because of the profound brotherhood they felt. Three girls who hoped to marry with the young exiles trailed along for a short distance, then turned back tearfully, knowing that they must wait till their suitors brought lobola to their fathers.

In this way units of dissidents had always broken off from the main body of the Xhosa. Perhaps the diviners performed a vital function in identifying those potentially fractious individuals who might ultimately cause trouble in the community; at any rate, the diviners served as the agencies of expulsion. For eight hundred years groups like Mandiso's had broken away to form new clans on the cutting edge of expansion. They never moved far; they retained contact with the rest of the tribe; and they still acknowledged a hazy kind of allegiance to the Great Chief, who existed far to the rear but whom they never saw.

This time the wandering unit proceeded to the east bank of the Great Fish River, which they settled upon because of the vast empty grazing fields on the west bank. 'We'll use those fields,' Mandiso told his followers, 'for the cattle that like to roam.'

In this time-honored tradition the Xhosa innocently launched a westward move which would bring them into direct conflict with the Dutch trekboers, who with equal innocence were drifting eastward. These two great tribes were so similar: each loved its cattle; each measured a man's importance by his herds; each sought untrammeled grazing; each knew that any pasturage it saw belonged to it by divine right; and each honored its predikant or diviner. A titanic confrontation, worse than any storm the fire-bird had ever generated, had become inevitable.

When, in February 1725, Adriaan and Dikkop approached their farm at the conclusion of their wanderings, they faced none of the uncertainties that had perplexed the two Xhosa lads. True, they had been gone almost four months when only three had been intended; but their people knew what they were doing, and the extended absence was no cause for alarm. As Hendrik assured his wife several times: 'If the lions don't eat them, they'll be back.'

So when they straggled in, with the dust of distant horizons on their eyebrows, no one made much fuss, for Hendrik, too, had been wandering, six weeks to the north to trade for cattle with the Hottentots. He had returned with two hundred fine animals, the largest-ever addition to his herd. He asked Adriaan to ride with him to the easternmost part of the grazing lands, and from a low hill the two Van Doorns looked down approvingly. 'God has been good to us,' Hendrik said. ' "All the land that is Canaan He has given to us and the generations which will follow you." ' For a long time they sat astride their horses, watching the cattle, and there was joy in their hearts.

The hartebeest hut had been lived in so thoroughly that it could scarcely be distinguished from the one on the previous farm, and on the perimeter of the holding, Hendrik had placed four more cairns, midway between the compass points. In less than a year the Van Doorns had themselves a stable farm, six thousand acres well marked and so far removed from any neighbor that intrusion of any kind was unlikely for years to come.

The family was deeply interested in Adriaan's report of the two black youths and this proof that a tribe of some magnitude occupied the lands farther east. Again and again the older Van Doorns asked their son to repeat exactly what he had learned during his four-day meeting with the blacks.

'They speak with clicks,' Adriaan said, 'so they must be of the same family as the Hottentots, but Dikkop understood none of their words. They were a strong, really handsome people, but their only weapons were clubs and assegais.'

Hendrik was so interested that he summoned Dikkop, who conveyed the important information that so far as he could discern, they called themselves the Xhosa: *Hkausa,* he pronounced the word, giving it a pronounced click in the back of his throat. 'They said they were the Xhosa, who lived beyond a big river.'

'What river?' Hendrik asked.

'There were so many,' Adriaan and Dikkop said together, and for the first time they spelled out the geography of the vast lands to the east, and it was this report, laboriously written down in archaic language by Hendrik van Doorn, that ultimately reached the Cape, adding to the Compagnie's comprehension of the lands they were about to govern, whether they wanted to or not:

> The land east of our farm is not to be traversed easily, because heavy mountains enclose it on the north, a chain unbroken for many miles that cannot be penetrated, for there seem to be no passes across it. Travel to the south along the seacoast is no easier, because deep ravines cut in from the shore, running many miles at times, not passable with wagons. But in between these impediments are lands

of great productivity and greater beauty. Our farm lies at the western edge of what must be the finest lands on earth, a garden of flowers and birds and animals. Copious rivers produce water for every purpose, and if fruit trees can be made to grow there as easily as they do here, you will have a garden paradise. But we have reason to believe that black tribes are pressing down upon it from the east.

When Hendrik finished this writing he was proud to have remembered so much of his education, and ashamed that he had neglected it. At Trianon his parents had taught him his letters and to speak correct Dutch, but long years in the company of Hottentot and slave, and then with an illiterate wife, had caused him to speak in rough, unlettered sentences. Worse, he had taught none of his children to read.

But he engaged in no recriminations, for life was bountiful. With June came harvest time, and the family was busy gathering not only enough vegetables for the long winter, but also more than enough to dry for seeds: big yellow pumpkins, gnarled green squash, mealies, radishes, onions, cauliflower and cabbage for pickling. The fruit trees, of course, were too young to bear, but in his explorations of the surrounding terrain Hendrik had found wild lemons whose thick and oily skin proved so useful, and bitter almonds like the ones from the hedge his grandfather had cut down during his escape from Compagnie domination.

One heard little of the Compagnie out here. The farm was so distant from headquarters—one hundred and sixty-two miles in a straight line, half again more according to the wandering path over the mountains—that no official could easily reach it. No predikant ever arrived for marriages and baptisms, and certainly no assessor or tax collector. Still, a kind of supervision prevailed, distant and unenforced, but ready for implementation when roads should penetrate the area. A petulant Compagnie official who crossed the mountains in vast discomfort had come as far east as four farms short of Van Doorn's, and he had written upon his return to the Cape:

> Wherever I went I heard of divers Dutchmen who occupied stupendous farms, Rooi van Valck to the north, Hendrik van Doorn to the east. They graze their cattle on our land without the Compagnie deriving any benefit. They plant their seeds on Compagnie land without any profit to us, and I think the Compagnie deserves better treatment from these rascals. I recommend that every man who occupies a farm pay to the Compagnie a tax of twelve rix-dollars a year plus one-tenth of whatever harvest of grain or fruit or vegetables or animals he produces. But how this tax is to be collected from farms as distant as Rooi van Valck's and Hendrik van Doorn's, I have not decided.

The loan-farm law was passed, but as the perceptive emissary had predicted, it could rarely be enforced. Distant farmers were instructed to carry their taxes to either the Cape or Stellenbosch, and they simply ignored the law. On farms close in, the officials did make a brave show of riding out in midwinter to demand overdue tithes, but with obstinate and dangerous renegades like Rooi van Valck, no collector dared approach his outlaw domain lest he be shot through the neck.

In these years Adriaan had little concern with tax collectors; he was so occupied with extending his knowledge of the wilderness that weeks would pass without his being seen at the farm. It was then that the soubriquet Mal Adriaan was fastened most securely to him; he would come home from an exploration and say, 'While I was sleeping in the tree . . .' or 'As I climbed out of the hippo's wallow . . .' or 'In the days when I lived with the gemsbok . . .' He caused outrage among his family and the slaves by insisting that lions could climb trees, for it was commonly accepted that they could not and that a man was secure if only he could find refuge in a tree.

'No,' said Adriaan, 'I've seen a tree with seven lions sleeping on the higher branches.' This was so crazy that even the slaves called him Mal Adriaan, and once when he was twenty he experienced for the first time the loneliness that comes upon a young man when he is ridiculed by his peers. The family was eating in the hut, scraping away at bones of mutton and cabbage, when his father asked, 'Have the animals moved closer to our valley?' and he replied automatically, 'When I was staying with the rhinoceros . . .' and his brothers and sisters said simultaneously, 'Oh, Adriaan!' and he had blushed furiously and started to leave the table where they huddled, except that his mother placed her hand upon his arm to restrain him.

That night, as they sat outside the hut, she told him, 'It's not good for a man to wait too long. You must find yourself a wife.'

'Where?'

'That's always the question. Look at our Florrie. Where's she to catch a husband? I'll tell you where. One of these days a young man will come by here on his horse, looking for a bride. And he'll see Florrie, and off she'll go.'

And sure enough, within four weeks of that conversation Dikkop, always frightened of new movement, came rushing to the hut, shouting, 'Man coming on horse!' And in came a dusty, lusty young farmer who had ridden a hundred and twenty miles on hearing the rumor that Hendrik van Doorn out beyond the river had several daughters. He made no secret of his mission, stayed five weeks, during which he ate enormous quantities of food, and on the night Hendrik offered him a bread pudding crammed with lemon rind and cherries and dried apples, he belched, pushed back the soup plate from which he had gorged himself, and said, 'Florrie and me, we're heading home tomorrow.'

The Van Doorns were delighted. It might be years or never before they saw this daughter again, but at her age it was proper that she ride away. Illiterate, barely able to sew a straight line, a horrible cook, a worse housekeeper, off she went with her illiterate husband to found a new farm, to raise a new brood of tough-minded trekboers to occupy the land.

Two nights after they departed, Johanna sat with Adriaan again and said, 'Take the brown horse and be going.'

'Where?'

'Three people now have told us that Rooi van Valck has a mess of daughters. Ride up and get one.'

'They also say Rooi's a bad one. Defames the Bible.'

'Well.' She hardly knew how to say what was required, but she had thought about this matter for some time, keeping her mouth shut lest she irritate her husband. But now she said in a low voice, 'Adriaan, it's possible to take the Bible too seriously. I can't read it myself—never had my letters—but sometimes I think your father makes a fool of himself, scouring that book for instructions. If Rooi van Valck has a daughter, and she looks as if she'd be good in bed, grab her.' When Adriaan said nothing, for these ideas were shocking to him, raised as he was with absolute faith in the Bible, even though he could not read it for himself, his mother added, 'Living in a hut is no pleasure. It's not much better than what the Hottentots have. But to love your father and go to bed with him when you children are asleep. That can be enough to keep a life going.' With a sudden jerk of her hand she pulled him around to face her in the darkness. With her eyes close to his she whispered, 'And never forget it. You leave for Van Valck's at sunup.'

Adriaan took the brown horse and rode far to the north, across the empty plains, across the muddy Touws River, and well to the west of the Witteberge Mountains, until he saw ahead the columns of dust that signified a settlement. It was the farm, the little empire, of Rooi van Valck, and to get to the hartebeest huts in which Rooi and his wild collection of attendants lived, he had to pass through valleys containing twenty thousand sheep, seven thousand head of cattle.

'I'm looking for Rooi,' Adriaan said, overwhelmed by the magnitude of his wealth.

'Not here,' a Madagascan slave growled.

'Where is he?'

'Who knows?'

'Can I speak to his wife?'

'Which one?'

'His wife. I want to speak with his wife.'

'He's got four. The white one, the yellow one, the brown one, the black one.'

'Which one has the daughters?'

'They all got daughters, sons too.'

'I'll see the white one.'

'Over there.' And the slave pointed to a hut not one bit better than the one the Van Doorns occupied.

All these cattle, Adriaan said to himself as he crossed the clearing to the hut. And he lives in a hut like us. He was pleased rather than disturbed, and when the white Mevrouw van Valck invited him to sit with her, he was relieved to see that she was much like his mother: old beyond her years, well adapted to the dirt, independent in nature.

'What do you want?' she asked, squatting on a log that served as a bench.

'To see your husband.'

'He's around somewheres.'

'When will he be back?'

Like the slave, she answered, 'Who knows?'

'Today? Three days?'

'Who knows?' Looking at him carefully, she asked, 'What farm?'

'Hendrik van Doorn's.'

'Never heard of him.'

'Trianon. Those Van Doorns.'

The name had a startling effect on her. 'Trianon!' she roared, following the name with a string of Dutch and Hottentot curses. Then, going to the open end of the hut, she bellowed, 'Guess who's here? A Van Doorn of Trianon!'

'I'm not from Trianon,' Adriaan tried to explain, but before he could establish this fact, numerous people had erupted from the many huts, women of varied colors bringing with them children of the most mixed appearance.

'This one is from Trianon!' Mevrouw van Valck shouted, hitting him in the shoulder playfully and ringing out a new string of obscenities. 'And I'll wager he's come to find him a wife. Isn't that right, Van Doorn? Isn't that right?'

And before he could control his blushing and explain in an orderly manner the purpose of his mission, the tough woman had yelled for different people, and a procession of bewildering types came to her hut. 'You can have this one,' she shrilled, pointing to a nubile girl of seventeen with dark skin and black hair. 'But you can't have that one because he's a boy.' This occasioned great laughter among the women, and the parade continued.

'This one you can have,' she said more seriously, 'and I'd advise you to take her.' With these words she brought forth one of her own daughters, a girl with bright red hair that fell almost to her waist. She seemed to be about fifteen or sixteen, not shy, not embarrassed by her rowdy mother. Going directly to Adriaan, she extended her hands and said, 'Hello, I'm Seena.' When her mother started to say something obscene, the girl turned in a flash and shouted, 'You, damn fool, shut up.'

'She's the good one,' Mevrouw van Valck shouted, cackling with the other wives, who formed a circle of approbation.

'She has lovely hair,' a Malay woman said, reaching out to fluff the girl's red tresses.

Adriaan, overcome with embarrassment, asked Seena, 'Is there somewhere . . .'

'Get away, you . . .' The girl uttered an oath equal to her mother's and chased the women back. 'We can sit here,' and she indicated an old wagon chest at the entrance to the hut in which she lived with a ramshackle collection of other children.

'Where's your father?' Adriaan asked.

'Out killing Bushmen,' she said.

'When will he be back?'

'Who knows? Last time it took him four weeks to clean out the valleys.'

'Can I stay here?'

'Was my mother right? Are you looking for a wife?'

'I'm . . . I'm . . . looking for your father.'

'You don't have to wait for him. He doesn't care what happens. Have you a farm?'

'I live a long way off.'

'Good.' That was all she said, but the single word conveyed her longing to get away from this tempestuous place.

It was worse when Rooi himself roared in from the manhunt. He was a huge man with a flaming head of red hair that gave him his name. He was really Rupertus van Valck, from a family which had settled early at the Cape. Rooi van Valck, Rooi the Falcon, the red-haired terror who submitted to no control, whether from the Cape governor, the Lords XVII, or God Himself.

The Van Valcks first had trouble with authority in the time of Van Riebeeck, when Leopold, the stubborn soldier who had founded the family, sought permission to marry a Malaccan girl. The Compagnie dillydallied so long that when permission was finally granted, Rooi's grandfather was a sire twice over. The next serious clash came when Mevrouw van Valck, a lively, independent-minded woman, wanted to dress in a way becoming her prettiness. From Amsterdam the Lords XVII specifically ordered that 'Mevrouw van Valck must not wear bombazine, and certainly not a bright yellow bombazine, and especially since she is not the wife of a senior Compagnie official.' When she persisted, with her husband's encouragement, soldiers were sent to rip the dress apart, whereupon Van Valck thumped the soldiers—and spent a long day on the wooden horse.

Since he had not been dropped onto the killing horse from any height, he escaped the permanent injury that had marred Willem van Doorn's later life, but he never escaped the corroding resentment, and when some months later one of the soldiers who dropped him was found with his throat cut, it was assumed that Van Valck had done it. Nothing was proved, but subsequently, when Willem and Katje made their escape through the bitter almond, this Van Valck followed the same route. But he went north.

There, in a wild and spacious valley, he built his huts, assembled slaves and runaways, and launched the infamous Van Valcks. He had four sons, and they proliferated, but all kept to the initial valley, where they farmed vast herds of animals and planted whole orchards of a single fruit. They sheared their own sheep, wove their own cloth, and tanned their hides to make leather shoes. They timbered, built rude roads, and had a community which needed to move out for nothing except periodic journeys to graze, and into which officials were afraid to enter.

It was the other side of the African coin. At the Cape, citizens came to attention when the Lords XVII handed down a directive; they lived for the Compagnie's profit, from the Compagnie's largesse, and in obedience to the Compagnie's strict laws. But at Van Valck's frontier, the red-haired adventurers said, 'To hell with the Compagnie!' and enforced it.

No predikant had ever preached at Rooi van Valck's, or ever dared to castigate the master for having four wives. For two generations no Van Valck had been legally married, and in this generation none wished to be. The mélange of children could not be distinguished, and their bounding health and good spirits belied the Compagnie's belief that children must be reared in strict accordance with the Bible. At Rooi's, there were no Bibles.

'So you come looking for a bride?' the huge man said as he studied Adriaan. 'You the one they call Mal Adriaan?'

'How did you hear of me?'

'The smous. In what way are you crazy?'

'I like to wander. I study the animals.'

'Eh, Seena! Kom hier, verdomde vrouw.' When she came to him, he rumpled her hair and said, 'No question she's my daughter. Look at that hair! I don't have to worry the smous got to her mother.'

When Adriaan blushed a deeper red than Rooi's shock of hair, the renegade tossed his daughter in the air, catching her under the arms. 'If you get her, you're getting a good one,' he cried. And again he snatched her up, throwing her far into the air, but this time she fell not back to his arms, but across the open space into Adriaan's. The first time he touched Seena, really, was as she came flying at him.

'She's yours, son, and don't go wandering too much, Crazy Adriaan, or the smous will catch her when you're not looking.'

'Shut up, damn you!' the girl cried, making a face at her father. 'If Adriaan was bigger, he'd thrash you.'

With a huge hand, Rooi reached out, grabbed Adriaan, and almost broke his collarbone. Shaking him like a dog, he said, 'He better not try. And, son, you treat this girl right, or I'll kill you.' It was obvious that he meant it, but to Rooi's surprise, Adriaan broke loose, swung his fist in uncontrollable fury, and smashed the huge man on the side of his face. It was like a monkey swatting an elephant, and Rooi roared with delight.

'He's a spunky one, Seena. But if he tries to hit you, kick him in the stomach.' And with a sudden swipe of his right boot, he aimed a shot at Adriaan's crotch. Perhaps the fear of the awful pain that impended activated the young man, for deftly he sidestepped, caught the up-swinging foot, and toppled the big redhead.

While still flat on the ground, Rooi lashed out with a swinging leg, caught Adriaan at the ankles and brought him down. With a leap, the big man fell upon him, wrestling him into a position where he could gouge his eyes with big knuckles. As Adriaan felt the man's superhuman strength and saw the dreadful knuckles coming at him, he thought: I am wrestling with the devil. For the devil's daughter. And he jerked his knees up to smite the evil one in the gut, but Rooi fended off this last attack.

'I'll teach you,' he grunted, and he would have done so had not Seena grabbed a log and struck him on the head, knocking him quite silly. When he recovered, blinking his eyes and spitting, he roared, 'Who hit me?' and Seena said, 'He did.' And there stood Adriaan, fists clenched, waiting for what might come next.

'By God!' the huge redhead shouted as he raised himself to his knees. 'I do believe Seena's got herself a good one.' And when he hoisted himself back onto his feet, still groggy, he embraced Adriaan in one huge arm, Seena in the other, and dragged them into his hut, where he broke out a jug of brandy.

They drank through the night, and toward four in the morning, when Adriaan was almost insensible, Rooi insisted that the bridal couple be given a hut to themselves, so children were swept out of the hovel occupied by the Malayan wife, and onto her filthy pile of straw the young pair were thrown. At first Adriaan wanted only to sleep, a fact which was circulated through the camp by youngsters who watched from a peephole, but Seena certainly did not propose to spend her wedding night in that manner. So, as the children shouted to the elders, she roused him from his stupor and indoctrinated him into the duties of a husband.

'That's good, that's good!' Rooi van Valck said when the children reported to him. 'I think Seena's got herself a man to be proud of. He's a little crazy, that's obvious, but he's quick with his fists, and I like that. What's his name again?'

'Adriaan,' the children said. They knew everything.

Sotopo's achievement of manhood did not come easily. As his brother Mandiso had predicted when the matter of the boy's joining the exodus to the Fish River was discussed, the new settlement had no guardian to supervise the circumcision rites, no other boys to share it, and certainly no large community to arrange a celebration. But Sotopo knew that the ceremony had to be performed, and it was, in a lonely and gruesome way.

A small hut was built, big enough for one boy. Since white clay could not be located, red had to suffice. There being no older man familiar with a sharp cutting edge, a young amateur volunteered, and with a dull assegai performed a hideous operation. Without the proper herbs to medicate it, the wound festered so badly that Sotopo almost lost his life. For a hundred days he remained in isolation, only his brother slipping in occasionally to share the experience he had had when he was inducted into manhood.

When the seclusion ended, the small hut was set aflame, as custom required, and time was at hand for him to dance. He did so alone, with no gourd, no stringed instrument; tail feathers projected from the rear as he waved his buttocks, and the shells about his ankle reverberated when he stomped. At the conclusion he delivered a speech of profound import. Looking at the adventurous little band, he said in a loud, clear voice, 'I am a man.' It was toward men like him that the trekboers were advancing.

Seena and Adriaan met Nels Linnart of Sweden in a most improbable way. In 1748 a horseman came rushing up from the south with the exciting news that a great ship had foundered off Cape Seal, with so much cargo to be salvaged that all farms in the area could replenish their stocks for a dozen years. At Van Doorn's, every able man saddled his horse to participate in the looting, and when Adriaan galloped south, Seena rode with him, her long red hair flashing in the wind.

They arrived at the wreck about two hours before sunset the next day, to find an even richer store than the messenger had indicated. Some thirty trekboers had formed a rescue line with ropes and were bringing the ship's passengers ashore, but as soon as the lives were saved, these same men rushed back through the waves to plunder the ship, and the eager Van Doorns arrived in time to reach the foodstuffs before the water damaged them. Whole barrels of flour and herring were rafted ashore. One family concentrated on every item of furniture in the captain's cabin, and when he protested, a huge trekboer glowered at him and said, 'If you'd kept your ship off the rocks, we wouldn't be plundering it.'

All that night, with the aid of a shadowy moon and rush lanterns, the avaricious trekboers ransacked the ship of its movable treasures, but at dawn a young man not over thirty came to Adriaan and said, in highly accented Dutch, 'Please, sir, you and your wife look decent. Will you help me get my books?'

'Who are you?' Adriaan asked suspiciously.

'Dr. Nels Linnart, Stockholm and Uppsala.' When Adriaan's blank face showed that he understood nothing, the young man said, 'Sweden.' Adriaan had never heard of this, either, so the man said, 'Please, I have fine books there. I must save them.'

Still Adriaan registered nothing, but Seena said impatiently, 'He needs help,' and in the doctor's wake the two Van Doorns swam out to the ship, clambered up the side and boarded the vessel that could not stay afloat much longer. To them it was a weird universe of dark passageways, pounding waves and the dank smell of steerage. The treasured books were in a cabin, forty or fifty large volumes published in diverse countries, and these Dr. Linnart proposed to move ashore, but to get them through the waves without destroying them posed a problem.

Seena devised a way. She would jump down into the waves, grasp the rope, then accept an armful of books, which she would hold aloft as Adriaan struggled beneath her, holding her above the waves as they moved slowly ashore. 'Bravo!' cried the doctor from the deck as he saw the couple deposit his books well inland and come back for another cargo.

In this manner the little library was rescued; it would form the foundation of a notable collection of books in southern Africa: Latin, Greek, German, Dutch, English, Swedish, and fourteen in French. They covered various branches of science, especially mathematics and botany, and among them was *Systema Naturae* by Karl von Linné, also of Stockholm and Uppsala. 'He's my uncle,' the young doctor said, stamping the water out of his boots.

'What kind of book is this?' Adriaan asked, for it was the first one other than his father's Bible that he had ever held in his hands.

'It deals with plants and flowers.'

And there on the beach by the wrecked ship Adriaan said the words that would determine the remainder of his life: 'I like plants and flowers.'

'Have you seen many here?' the young scientist asked, concerned always with his basic subject even though his ship had sunk.

'I have walked many miles,' Adriaan said with immediate recognition of the young man's intense interest, 'and wherever I went, there was something new.'

'That's what my uncle said. My job is to collect the new plants. The ones we haven't heard of yet in Europe.'

'What do you mean, collect?' Adriaan asked, but before the young doctor could explain, Hendrik shouted, 'Come on! There's lots more to take before she sinks.' And the two young Van Doorns continued with the plunder, but when there was nothing left and the ship started to break apart,

Adriaan was drawn back to the scientist, and while the other trekboers helped the shipwrecked passengers build temporary huts to protect themselves till rescue ships arrived, he and Seena stowed the precious books upon their two horses and started walking back to the farm, accompanied by the young Swede.

> I had intended [he wrote in his report published by the London Association] doing my collecting in India, but Providence sent my ship upon the rocks at the southern tip of Africa, where I was rescued by a remarkable couple with whom I spent the four happiest months of my life, living in a wattled hut. The husband, who could not read a word of any language, had made himself a well-trained scientist, while his wife with flaming red hair could do positively anything. She could ride a horse, handle a gun, drink copious quantities of gin, swear like a Norwegian, prune fruit trees, sew, cook, laugh and tell fabulous lies about her father, who, she claimed, had four wives. I remember the morning that I cried in my bad Dutch, 'God did not intend me to go to India. He brought me here to work with you.' They opened a new world for me, showing me wonders I had not anticipated. The husband knew every tree, the wife every device required for a good life, and when the four months ended in their hut, I was better prepared to start my collecting than if I had matriculated in a university. To my great joy and profit, this wonderful pair wanted to join me, even though I warned them that I might be gone for seven months. 'What's that to us?' Mevrouw van Doorn asked, and they rode off with me as unconcerned as if headed for a *fête champêtre* in some French park.

They traveled farther east than Adriaan had gone on his first exploration, then due north into a type of land which not even he had ever seen. It lay well north of the mountain range and was desert, yet not desert, for whenever rain fell, a multitude of flowers burst across the entire landscape, submerging it in a carpet of such beauty that Dr. Linnart was amazed: 'I could spend a lifetime here and identify a new flower every day, I do believe.' When Adriaan inquired further as to why the Swede was collecting so avidly, Linnart spent several nights endeavoring to explain what the expedition signified, and in his report he referred to this experience:

> Van Doorn wishing to know what I was about, I decided to unravel for him the full extent of my interest, holding back nothing. I laid forth Karl von Linné's organizing principle of *genus* and *species,* and within the first hour this natural-born scientist understood what I was saying better than most of my students at the university. He then asked me why Linné bothered with such a system, and I informed him that my uncle intended to catalogue every plant growing in the world, which was why I had come to South Africa, and he asked me, 'Even these flowers on the veld?' and I said, 'Especially these flowers, which we do not see in Europe.' So with that bare instruction, he proceeded to collect some four hundred flowers, not

less, arranging them in grand divisions according to Von Linné's principles. It was a remarkable feat which few scholars in Europe could have duplicated.

The caravan consisted of Dr. Linnart, the two Van Doorns, Dikkop in charge of everything, and ten Hottentots paid by the Swede. Two wagons accompanied the expedition, loaded with small wooden boxes into which the specimens collected by Adriaan went. On four separate occasions Linnart said that he could not credit the wealth of flowers on the veld, and each time Adriaan assured him that if he went farther, he would find more.

But interested as Dr. Linnart was in botany, he was even more captivated by Seena's remarkable capacity for keeping the camp lively, and he was enchanted one morning when she said briskly, 'Biltong's gone. You, Linnart, shoot us an eland.' So he and Dikkop had gone hunting, and although they failed to get one of the huge antelopes, they did knock down two gemsboks, which they butchered on the spot, bringing back to camp large stores of thinly cut strips of the best lean meat.

'Looks good,' Seena said approvingly as she tended a pot in whose liquor the meat would be marinated.

Linnart, hungry to know the procedures of every operation, asked, 'What's in the pot?' and she showed him: 'A pound of salt. Two ounces of sugar. A heavy pinch of saltpeter. A cup of strong vinegar, a little pepper and those crushed herbs.'

'What herbs?'

'Any I can find,' she said. And into this cold mixture she dropped the strips of meat, stirring them occasionally so that each would be well penetrated. When she was satisfied that the gemsbok was properly marinated, she directed Linnart to remove the strips, take them to the sunny side of the camp where the wind could strike them, and leave them there to dry.

When they were hard as rock, with flavor permeating every cell, they were packed in cloth, to be gnawed upon when other food was lacking. 'The best meal for the veld,' Linnart exclaimed as he nearly broke his teeth chewing. 'Better than the pemmican our Reindeer People make. More flavor.'

The best part of each day came in the late afternoon when Seena and the Hottentots were preparing supper, for then Dr. Linnart sat with Adriaan, discussing Africa and comparing it with other lands he had seen. He liked to take down his atlas and press flat the maps of areas he spoke of, and then little Dikkop would crowd in, look at the incomprehensible pages and nod sagely in agreement with whatever the Swede said. Adriaan, who could not read the words, grasped the geographical forms and he, too, approved.

'Look at this map of Africa,' Linnart told the men one evening. 'Your little colony is truncated. It ought to run all the way north to the Zambezi, its natural boundary. And east to the Indian Ocean.'

'Here in the east,' said Adriaan, tapping the map, 'are many Xhosa.'

'Who are they?'

'Tell him, Dikkop.' And the Hottentot expressed his apprehension over the large tribes of blacks that Sotopo had described during their meeting in the glade.

'Mmmm!' Linnart said. 'If that's the case, sooner or later . . .' And with his forefinger he indicated the blacks moving westward and the trekboers eastward. 'There's got to be a clash.'

'I think so too,' Dikkop said.

'But up here? Toward the Zambezi? Have any of you gone up there?'

'The Compagnie wouldn't allow us,' Adriaan said.

'But the Compagnie lets you live where you are, hundreds of miles from the Cape. What stops you from exploring the north?' When neither of the men responded, he said, 'Men should always move out till they reach the final barriers. East to the ocean. North to the Zambezi.'

If he implied that the trekboers were delinquent in comparison with other peoples who had explored other lands, he had some justification, but if he thought that they held back through lack of adventurousness, he was wrong, as he discovered when at the end of seven months they came back south through the mountains, looking for signs of the Van Doorn farm:

> Then I learned what *trekboer* means, for when we approached the farm where I had spent those four happy months, I saw to my horror that the place had been wiped out. The roof of the hut was flapping in the wind. The kraal was deserted. The gardens had gone to weeds and there was no sign of sheep or cattle or human beings. It was total desolation, and I looked with anguish at the young Van Doorns, trying to anticipate how they would accept this tragedy. They were unconcerned. 'Father moved, I suppose' was all my extraordinary guide said, and with no more concern than if the journey involved perhaps a mile, we set off eastward toward a destination we could not guess. At the forty-mile mark I asked, 'Will they be here?' and Van Doorn merely shrugged his shoulders, saying, 'If not here, somewhere else.' I was especially impressed by the indifference of red-haired Seena. When I asked her one night after an especially difficult day fording rivers, 'Where do you think they are?' she spoke like a sailor: 'Who cares a goddamn? They've got to be out here somewhere.' And at the end of the seventy-fifth mile, by my calculation, we came upon a handsome valley in which the old man had staked out a circular farm comprising, I calculated, not less than six thousand acres of the best. For this he paid only a handful of rix-dollars annually, was not obligated to fence it, and when he judged the pastures to be exhausted, he was free to abandon it and move some seventy miles to some other spot of equal beauty, to treat it as roughly. 'Tiptoeing through paradise,' they call it.

It became a tearful moment when this brilliant young man left the Van Doorn farm and headed toward the Cape with his two wagons filled with specimens. Adriaan and Seena did not cry, of course, for they had known for some time that he must leave them. The tears came from Dr. Linnart, who tried three times to make a flowery farewell speech to the effect that he had lived for nearly a year with nature and with two people who understood it better than he did, but every time he looked at Seena he was so overcome with love and fellowship that tears choked him and he had to start over. It was an expedition, he affirmed, that he would never forget; he ended his comments rather awkwardly: 'My cousin, who publishes his books under his Latin name, Carolus Linnaeus, would send you a copy of the volume in which this material will appear, except, of course, neither of you can read.'

Several of his comments regarding his trip to the Cape were widely circulated in Europe and America; after recounting his horrendous experience in crossing the final mountains, when his specimens ran the risk of being lost in a sudden fog, he told of coming to Trianon:

> It was impossible to believe that the same family which occupied the huts in the wilderness also owned this delectable country mansion, laid out as meticulously as any French palace. It boasted four separate gardens, each with its special quality, and a façade which, while not ornate in any way, displayed an elegance that could not be improved upon. These Van Doorns make two kinds of wine, a rich sweet Trianon for sale in Europe, where it is highly regarded, and a pale, very dry white wine of almost no body or fragrance until the last bottle has been drunk. Then it remembers beautifully . . .

> At last we reached the Cape, which had been described by several Dutchmen as something comparable to Paris or Rome. It was a miserable town of less than three thousand souls, unkempt streets and flat-roofed houses, with some recollection of Amsterdam in the canals that brought water down from mountain streams. The Castle and the Groote Kerk, a fine gabled octagonal building, dominate life here, the former telling the people what their hands must do, the latter instructing their souls.

> The avaricious Compagnie utilizes the Cape not as a serious settlement but as a provisioning station on the way to Java. Compagnie law dominates all: the church, the farmer, the clerk and the future. There are no schools of any distinction, the scholarchs barely able to keep ahead of their students. Yet the Compagnie officials and the few persons of wealth live indulgently, as I witnessed during a splendid dinner at the Castle, where no fewer than thirty-six fine dishes were offered, and even the ladies, who ate separately, partook most liberally of the governor's largesse.

> My visit to the Cape occurred two years prior to my collecting tour in the English colonies of America. These colonies were launched more or less at the same time as the Dutch venture in Africa, and I was constantly oppressed by comparison of the two. The colonies had scores of printing presses, the most lively newspapers and journals, and books in every town. I was able to consult with scholars at several fine colleges, Harvard, Yale and Pennsylvania among them. But my most doleful concern grew out of my extended meeting with Dr. Franklin in Philadelphia, that self-educated genius. He

reminded me precisely of Adriaan van Doorn, for the two had identical casts of mind. But because of the cultural opportunities in the English colonies, Dr. Franklin is acknowledged to be a great scholar, while Van Doorn, who can neither read nor write, is called at home Mal Adriaan, Crazy Adriaan . . .

It was my own ignorance that caused a major disappointment. Although I knew some Dutch, I had expected to speak mostly French, because of the large number of immigrants who reached the Cape from that country. I had taken mainly French books with me, but when I tried to use the language, which I speak moderately well, I found no one to talk with. Custom and the stern measures of Compagnie rule have eradicated the language, and throughout the colony no sound of French is heard.

Adriaan and Seena had four children, who were reared in the same slapdash manner that prevailed at Rooi van Valck's, and to a degree, at the hartebeest huts of the Van Doorns. They were raised with love and boundless physical affection, much as if they were young puppies, and they showed signs of becoming close copies of their wandering father or their rowdy and profane mother. The first and third had red hair inherited from the Van Valcks; the second and fourth, light blond hair like the Van Doorns; and in 1750 it seemed probable that they would be frontier nomads like their parents, illiterate, contemptuous of Compagnie authority, and delightfully tied to the soil of which they were a part. In a few years strange young men would wander in to court the girls and then start eastward to launch loan-farms of their own, stepping off the six thousand acres to which they felt they would always be entitled. 'The land out there is limitless,' the trekboers proclaimed. 'We can keep moving till we meet the Indian Ocean.' And if a man kept his farm for about ten years before leapfrogging to virgin soil, the process could continue for another hundred years.

'Of course,' Adriaan said when such predictions were being made, 'sooner or later you're going to run into the Xhosa.'

'The what?' the newer trekboers would ask.

'The Xhosa.'

'And what in hell are they?'

'The blacks. They're out there, beyond the big river.'

But since he was one of the very few who had seen them, and since the farms were prospering in the new lands, the Xhosa barrier was ignored.

In many ways the Van Doorn farm now resembled that of Rooi van Valck: grandfather, grandmother, Adriaan's family and his brothers', the numerous grandchildren, and many servants, and the large herds of cattle. Life was good, and when one of the women cried at midmorning, 'I want someone to chop this meat,' any man in hearing distance was eager to help, because this meant that the cooks were going to make bobotie, and there was no dish better than this on the veld.

Seena, who had often made it for her father, usually took command. In a large, deep-sided clay baking dish she placed the chopped beef and mutton, mixing in curry and onions, all of which she allowed to brown while she pounded a large handful of almonds mixed with additional spices. When all was blended and seemingly done, she whipped a dozen eggs in such milk as was available, and threw this on top, baking the entire for about an hour. While the smell permeated the area, she boiled up some rice and took the lid off her crock of chutney. No matter how big the baking dish, no matter how few the diners, there were never any scraps when Seena made bobotie. 'All credit to the curry,' she always said.

To sit at a table after a hard day's work and to have a mug of brandy and a huge plateful of bobotie was the kind of treat that kept a farm contented.

Occasionally Grandfather Hendrik brought out his big Bible, hoping to instruct the children in their alphabet, but they felt that if their parents and their uncles and aunts survived without reading, so could they. But once or twice the youngest boy, Lodevicus, who was now eleven, showed signs that he might be the one who would return to the earlier scholarship of the Van Doorns who had lived in Holland. He would ask his grandfather, 'How many letters must I learn if I want to read?' and Hendrik, referring to the Dutch alphabet, would reply, 'Twenty-two.' And he would show the boy that each letter had two forms, small and capital, taking unusual care in explaining that in Dutch, unlike other languages, capital IJ was not two letters but one. It was all too confusing for Lodevicus, and soon the boy was out rampaging with the others.

However, old Hendrik noticed that it was this same Lodevicus who was beginning to show impatience whenever Adriaan disappeared on one of his explorations: 'Why isn't Father here to help with the work?' And he became quite agitated if Seena accompanied her husband, as she liked to do: 'Mother ought to be home, making us bobotie.' The three other children accepted their father's strange behavior and showed no concern when he was absent for months at a time. Moreover, they enjoyed it when their parents began to say, 'People are crowding in. Too many Compagnie rules. That valley where the cattle grazed last year looks better.' But Lodevicus said, 'Why can't we stay in one place? Build us a house of stone?'

Hendrik and Johanna, always willing to move when they were younger, now sided with their grandson: 'Lodevicus is right. Let's build a house of stone.' And they argued that this piece of land was good for another twenty years, if properly managed. But Adriaan became increasingly restless, and red-headed Seena backed him up: 'Let's all get out of here!' So the wagons were loaded, the huts were abandoned, and with little Dikkop in the lead, everyone moved eastward, but along the way, Hendrik whispered to his grandson, 'Lodevicus, when you're older, you must stop wandering and build your house of stone.'

It was during one such journey that old Hendrik, now sixty-nine, collapsed and died. This was no great tragedy; his years had been full and he had lived them at the heart of a lively family whose future seemed secure. But there was the matter of burial, and this posed a difficult problem, for whereas Hendrik had been a religious man who would have wanted God's words to be read over his grave, the family no longer contained anyone who could read. Johanna brought out the old Bible and there was serious talk of burying it with the old man who had loved it, but at this moment Lodevicus happened to look away and saw a rider coming down the hills to the west.

'A man comes!' he called to the mourners, and Dikkop hurried off to ascertain who it might be. Within a short time a stranger rode up, tall and thin, wearing dark clothes and broad-brimmed hat, but no gun of any kind. When he reined his horse he looked with piercing eye at each of the Van Doorns, and said in a voice that seemed to come from deep within the earth, 'I have been searching for you, Van Doorns, and I see that my arrival is timely.' Alighting, he strode to the grave, looked down and asked, 'What sinner has been called to face the judgment of his Lord?'

'Hendrik van Doorn.'

'The same,' the tall man said. 'He alone among you was saved, is that not true?'

'He knew the book,' Johanna said, pointing to the Bible.

'Let us bury him with prayer,' the stranger said, and while the commingled family bowed, he launched into a long supplication, beseeching God to forgive the grievous sins of his wayward child Hendrik, whereupon red-headed Seena began to snicker, for if there had been any Van Doorn who was not wayward, it was Hendrik.

The stranger paid no attention to this irreverence, but continued his endless prayer. The Hottentots who had worked for Baas Hendrik, some from the earliest days, stood respectfully to one side. They had loved the old trekboer as a father, and the old patriarch had often seen them as children, using the whip when he felt it was needed, rewarding the industrious when he returned with cloth and implements from the cattle trading. He never understood why they so readily drank themselves into a stupor, or why their children ran away to become vagrants rather than work for him. He had acknowledged them to be master herdsmen, far better than the pesky Bushmen still out there sniping at colonists with their poisoned arrows. When the prayer finally ended, the stranger said peremptorily, 'Now you can bury him. He's on his way to meet his Maker.'

'He's dead,' Seena said brusquely. 'He had a damned good life and he's dead.'

'I take that you're the daughter of Rooi van Valck. By your red hair, I mean.'

'I am.'

'I have been sent by the Compagnie to bring the word of God to the wilderness. I am Dominee Specx, of Huguenot lineage, and I have been living at the new town of Swellendam. I am commissioned to marry and baptize, and to bring families like yours back to the ways of the Lord.'

'You're welcomed,' Johanna said, as matriarch of the sprawling family.

'You're on your way to a new farm?'

'We are.'

'They're going to collect the rents on farms now.'

'They'll get none from us,' Adriaan said sharply. 'We've farmed where we willed and paid taxes to no one.'

'That's ending,' the stranger said. 'Beginning this year, all will be collected.'

'All but us,' Adriaan said. 'We explored this land. We occupied it alone. And it belongs to us, not the Compagnie.'

Predikant Specx asked if he could ride with them to the new site, and Johanna said, 'Yes, if you will read to us from the Bible.'

And it was in this way that Lodevicus van Doorn memorized the great, stirring passages of the Old Testament, the experiences of Abraham and Joshua in their wildernesses, the love stories of David and Ruth. Night after night, as the tall dominee sat by the candle, intoning timeless stories of men who wandered into strange lands, Lodevicus reflected on how much he had missed in the years when he could not read the Bible, and he asked Specx how long it would take him to learn, and the dominee said, 'One week, if God commissioned you.'

To the surprise of the Van Doorns, he proved to be a congenial traveling companion, eager to share the work, willing to share the hardships. At the riverbanks he was often up front with the Hottentots to guide the oxen across, and he was a strong man with an axe when they settled on their new land and it came time to cut wood. Nor was he reticent, as some predikants were apt to be. He entered any argument, made his statement, and listened to those who tried to rebut him. He was fun at meals, for he had a most voracious appetite and startled the children with the amounts of food he consumed: 'I do believe I could eat that entire bobotie.'

'I'm sure you could,' Seena said. She alone displayed animosity toward the predikant, an inheritance from her father, who had fought the church incessantly, and one afternoon he took her aside and said, 'Seena, I know your father. I've fought with him. Last year he threw me off his farm when I went there to talk with him about God. He roared, "I need no God meddling in my affairs." And now you're roaring at me.'

'We don't need you here, Dominee. We're doing very well.'

'I'm sure you are, Seena. You and Adriaan are falling into the footsteps of your father—'

'Not a bad way to fall,' she said sharply.

'I'm sure it isn't. I've shared great love and happiness living with you.'

'And great pans full of bobotie, too.'

'I would gladly pay, Seena, had I the money. But I travel alone, I travel with nothing, like the original men who did the work of Jesus.' When Seena started to comment scathingly on his acceptance of charity, he took her by the hands and said, 'For myself, I am ashamed to come to you with nothing. But I bring you a gift greater than any you will ever know. I bring you the love of God.'

'We have His love,' Seena said harshly. 'He prospers our farm. He increases our flocks. We worship Him in our way.'

'But you cannot always accept everything and give nothing.'

'You seem to.'

'I give you the greatest gift, salvation.'

'You just said the greatest gift was love, or something. Now it's salvation. Dominee, in some ways you're a fool.'

He was not insulted by her rejection. Without ever trying to divert her criticism, he plodded on with his message: 'Seena, I've come to marry and baptize. I want the first marriage to be yours.'

'I need no prayers said over me. I have four children . . .'

'Legally, if you are not properly married, and Adriaan died . . .'

'Adriaan dies, I keep this farm,' she said defiantly.

Specx ignored this bravado and said, 'But your children should be baptized, Seena.' And when she started to protest that they were getting along all right as it was, he interrupted sharply: 'Seena, the world's changing. Swellendam has legal offices now. Soon there'll be an effective arm of government out here. Taxes will be collected. Laws will be enforced.'

'You mean this noble land will be hammered down till it looks like the Cape?'

'Exactly. God and law and decency follow each the other. Seena, allow your children to be baptized.'

But Seena was adamant, and for the time being, Specx dropped the subject. Working alongside them, he helped the Van Doorns establish themselves on what might be called a double farm: six thousand acres to Adriaan van Doorn, six thousand to his brothers, side by side. But when the hartebeest huts were started, the dominee returned to the matter of baptisms: 'I most urgently plead with you to have your children brought into the holy family of the church. You owe it to them. They're not going to live out their lives in this wilderness. There will be churches here before they marry, and they must belong or their lives will be cut off.'

'I've lived without churches for thirty-four years,' Seena said. 'Now get back to work and leave me to my cooking—so that you can gorge yourself before you leave.' He replied that he did not intend to depart before the children were baptized.

The argument changed dramatically when Seena's two daughters rode up from the south, accompanied by their husbands and two baby girls: 'We want to be married. We want our children to be baptized.'

'God be praised,' the dominee said, and Johanna said, 'We'll make one of Willem's bread puddings to celebrate,' and Adriaan was surprised at how vigorously his mother participated in the preparations, for Johanna was visibly delighted that her granddaughters were to be properly married, that her great-grandchildren were to be baptized.

None of the huts was finished when the various ceremonies were performed, but this did not stop the women from preparing a grand feast of mutton, dried fruits, baked cauliflower, carrots, pickled cabbage and pudding, with a whole ox roasted for the servants. And the conclusion of the day was marked by a strange occurrence: the boy Lodevicus came before the dominee and said, 'I, too, wish to be baptized.' And when this was done, he added, 'I want it written in the Bible.'

So the old book was brought out, and Predikant Specx shuddered when he saw how it had been neglected, lacking a whole generation on the page of marriages and births; he called for some implement for writing, but of course there was none.

So he sat with the Bible on his lap and pointed at the various squares where Johanna should have been entered as the wife of Hendrik, and Seena as the wife of Adriaan. He showed them where the daughters and their husbands should be printed, and then where Adriaan's two sons should be placed: 'Lodevicus, this is your square, right here, and when you learn to write, you're to put your name here, and your wife's here, and your children down here. Do you understand?'

Lodevicus said he did.

Adriaan made a fearful mistake when he confided to his four children the thoughts he'd had while wrestling with Rooi van Valck for the hand of his daughter: 'You have no idea how big your grandfather was. Tell them, Seena.' And with profane descriptions she told the awe-struck children of her life at the Van Valcks', and of the numerous wives and the score of children. Three of the young Van Doorns relished these tales, for they explained the red hair in their family and the lustiness of their mother.

But when Lodevicus, the youngest child, robust, white-haired, very Dutch in appearance, heard his father actually say, 'I knew I was wrestling with the devil, and he would have gouged out my eyes, except your mother bashed him in the head with a log,' he was overcome by a feeling of loathing, for he was convinced that Rooi van Valck was the devil. Judging his mother and her harsh ways, he was convinced that she was the devil's daughter, and that if he did not exorcise himself, he would forever be contaminated with hellish sin.

In 1759, when he was twenty years old, he experienced a theophany so palpable it would dominate the remainder of his life. Whenever a crisis approached he would be able to evoke this sacred moment when God spoke to him beside the stream, commanding him to go to the Cape to find for himself a Christian wife who would counteract the satanic influence of his mother: 'You cannot read. Go to the Cape and learn. You live in sin. Go to the Cape and purify yourself. Your father and mother are of the devil. Cross over the mountains, go to the Cape and find a Christian wife to save them.' The Voice stopped. The night fell silent. But a light glowed to the north toward the mountains, and he fell on his knees, begging God for strength to obey His commands, whereupon the light intensified and the Voice returned: 'You are the hammer who shall slay the infidel.' There was no more.

For the next few weeks Lodevicus walked by himself, pondering how he might get to the Cape to fulfill God's commandments, and he spent much of this time watching his parents for signs of their satanism. He found none in Adriaan, whom he dismissed as an ineffectual, but he did see in Seena's robust paganism much evidence of her damnation. She swore. She drank gin whenever any was available. And she was most offensive in teasing him about when he was going to find himself a wife.

'Get on a horse, ride in any direction, and grab the first young thing you see,' she said. 'One's about as good as another, when it comes to running a farm.'

He shuddered at such blasphemy, remembering that the Voice had told him that he was destined for a special bride who would bring light and

Christianity to the trekboers. And one night, when he could bear his mother's abuse no more, he went to the kraal, saddled a horse, and rode westward in the darkness.

He moved from farm to farm, always aware that when he and his bride returned they would bring decency into this wilderness. On two occasions he stayed with families that had marriageable daughters, and there was a flurry of excitement when he rode up, for he was a big and handsome man, with broad shoulders and blond, almost white, hair, but he had no eye for these girls, dedicated as he was to his commission. At this stage in his life he knew the Bible imperfectly, but he imagined himself to be a son of Abraham heading back to the homeland to find a bride of decent heritage.

In this frame of mind, his entire being focused on the Cape, he approached the small settlement of Swellendam, nestled among hills and distinguished by some of the loveliest white houses in the colony. As he entered the village he wondered where he might stay, for already people in towns had become less hospitable than those in the country, where a traveler could expect an enthusiastic welcome wherever he stopped, and he was walking aimlessly when he heard the resonant voice of Dominee Specx: 'Isn't this Lodevicus of the Van Doorns?' When Vicus said, 'Yes, Dominee,' the predikant asked, 'And what brings you to this fair village?' and the young man made the startling explanation: 'Because God has ordered me to the Cape to take a wife.'

By no gesture did Predikant Specx betray any reaction to this extraordinary statement; instead he invited Lodevicus to the parsonage, informing him that a widow nearby would provide him housing for a small fee; then, sitting him upon a chair, he asked, 'Now what was it that happened to you?' When the epiphany was described, Specx said, 'I believe God has visited you.' And he suggested that they pray, but before they could do so, a young woman of twenty-two, her hair drawn tightly back against her head, revealing a face of calm austerity, came into the study with a forthright question: 'Who came here with you, Father?'

'Lodevicus, of those Van Doorns I told you about.'

'Oh, yes. How are your parents?'

'Poorly,' Lodevicus said, and before she could say she was sorry, he added, 'They know not God.'

'Yes, Father told me.'

'He has been called of God,' the dominee said, 'and we were about to give thanks.'

'May I join?' the girl asked.

'Of course. This is my daughter, Rebecca,' and the first thing young Van Doorn did in the presence of this quiet, stately girl was kneel beside her and pray.

When they rose, Specx explained to his daughter: 'The Lord commanded him to learn how to read and write. I think we could teach him.'

So for the next four weeks father and daughter instructed Lodevicus in his letters, and by the end of the period he was reading in the Bible. He also attended every service conducted by Specx, and later asked for extensions of the sermon's main theses. It was a time of great awakening, with ideas ricocheting about the white walls as the young man formulated the large concepts that would animate him the rest of his life. So powerful was the influence of his epiphany that not once in these days did he contemplate terminating his journey at Swellendam and asking for Rebecca's hand in marriage; the Lord had said that his bride awaited him at the Cape, and he intended setting forth for that town as soon as he was satisfied that he could read.

But when he reached the Cape he felt like one of the angels who looked down upon Sodom and Gomorrah. Sailors roaring off the ships to riot with the slaves and Coloureds. Indecencies at night. A world so alien that the idea of taking a wife from these quarters was repellent, and he prayed for guidance. He had been instructed to come here and take a wife, but to do so was repugnant. And now he did not know where to turn.

For three weeks he remained in this state of indecision, obedient to God's major dictate but unable to accept the detail. Again and again he walked along the shore, expecting another revelation, but none came. He saw only the vast and frightening sea and he wanted to run from it to recover the sweet assurance of the valleys across the mountains, and he was reminded of that lovely phrase in the Bible, 'the other side Jordan,' where he felt sure goodness would be found.

In profound conflict of spirit, he decided to quit the Cape, recross the mountains, and seek counsel from Predikant Specx; it never occurred to him that he was seeking not the dominee, but his daughter. All he remembered in later years was that when he came down off the hills and approached the beautiful town, he broke into a run, galloped like a runaway animal down the main street, and burst into the parsonage with the cry: 'Dominee Specx, I've come back.' But all members of the predikant's family knew why he had come back.

Three prayerful sessions were held, with Lodevicus laying bare his inability to obey the final detail of his conversion and Dominee Specx explaining that God often moves in mysterious ways, His wonders to perform: 'When you departed, I prayed that you would return because I knew that you and Rebecca were destined for majestic things.'

'Rebecca?' Lodevicus asked.

'Yes, she planned to marry you from the day you arrived.'

'But the Lord told me to find my wife at the Cape.'

'Exactly what did the Voice say?' Dominee Specx asked, and when Lodevicus replied that he could not remember exactly, the clergyman said, 'You told me that it said, "Go to the Cape . . ." and then "Find a Christian wife." That doesn't mean that you must take your wife from the Cape. It merely means that God wanted you to have the experience of the Cape. And you were quite right to come back here for your bride. God directed you, don't you see?'

The explanation was so logical that Lodevicus had to accept it, and neither then nor afterward would he admit to himself that he had returned to Swellendam to marry Rebecca, for she had seemed too mature and superior to be attainable.

They were married by her father in the newly built church, and after a honeymoon that revealed the quality of the two young people—he fanatically determined to exhibit God's handiwork, she unflinching in her resolve to take Christianity to the frontier—they saddled two horses, and with a minimum of possessions, set forth to tame the wilderness.

Their reception at the Van Doorn farm was not a pleasant one. On the trip east Lodevicus had warned his bride that Seena might prove troublesome: 'Adriaan's an infidel, but he's quiet. My mother's the daughter of Rooi van Valck, and she'll be difficult, even hostile.'

When they rode into the farmyard the first voice they heard was Seena's, loud and raucous, shouting to her husband, 'Adriaan! He's back. With a bride.'

When the family assembled, Lodevicus, with new-found assurance, attempted to share with his parents the miracle of his epiphany: 'God called to me to go to the Cape to take a wife.'

'Adriaan heard a call like that once,' Seena said, 'but I doubt God had much to do with it.'

'So I stopped at Swellendam to pray with Dominee Specx, and Rebecca taught me the letters and how to put them together . . .'

'I'll warrant that wasn't all she taught.'

The young couple ignored these interruptions, and Lodevicus continued: 'And when I learned to write, I got down on my knees and thanked God and told Him that as soon as I returned home I would write our names in the Bible. Fetch it.'

He issued this request as a command, and Seena was somewhat irritated when her husband complied. Going to a wagon chest in which he kept the odd valuables that accumulate even in a hartebeest hut, he brought forth the old Bible, opening it to the page of records between the two testaments. 'This time,' Lodevicus said gravely, 'we have a pen,' and with everyone watching, he carefully inscribed the missing names: 'Adriaan van Doorn, born 1712. Seena van Valck born . . .'

'Maybe 1717,' she said.

'Father, Rooi van Valck. Mother . . .'

'I never knew for sure.' Lodevicus and Rebecca stared at her, and he said, 'We've got to put something.'

'Put Fedda the Malayan. I liked her best.'

'Put Magdalena van Delft,' Adriaan said. 'You know she was your real mother.'

Seena spat: 'That for Magdalena.'

Hurriedly Lodevicus wrote in the names of his brother and his two sisters, then, with a flourish and a smile for his wife, he wrote: 'Rebecca Specx, Swellendam, daughter of the Predikant.'

When he put the pen aside, satisfied with his work, Seena asked, 'When you reached Swellendam, were you married?'

'Oh, no!' her son said. 'When I had learned to write I marched on to the Cape, as God had directed.'

'Over the mountains?' Adriaan asked, showing respect for such a trip.

'Over the tall mountains, but when I reached the Cape, I found Sodom and Gomorrah. Indecencies everywhere.'

'What indecencies?' Seena asked.

Again he ignored her, telling of his revulsion, his rejection of the town and his return over the mountains. 'We were married and spent the next weeks in a revelation. The four of us, Dominee Specx and his wife, I and my wife, we sat together and read the entire Bible.'

For the first time Rebecca intruded. In a low voice, but with great firmness, she said, 'The Old Testament, that is.'

'And we discovered,' Lodevicus continued, 'how we trekboers are the new Israelites. That we have reached the point where Abram was when he changed his name to Abraham and settled in Canaan while Lot chose the cities of the plain, to be destroyed. And I learned that the time of our traveling is ended. That we must settle and build our houses of stone.'

'Did you and the dominee,' Adriaan asked, 'ever discuss the fact that you new Abrahams would be building your houses of stone on land that can be worn out? That we have to move on from time to time to find ourselves better land?'

'They're not moving at Swellendam,' Lodevicus replied, whereupon his mother said, 'We are. This verdomde farm is worn out.'

And while the old couple planned their next leap eastward, the young couple journeyed to the southern farms, there to advise the people how they ought to live.

It was on their return journey that Lodevicus first shared with another human being the mysterious fact that at the stream God had told him that he was to be the hammer, the trekboer who brought order into shapeless lives, and as soon as he said the words, Rebecca understood. With great excitement she said, 'It was why Father and I prayed that you would return from the Cape. And take me with you. That we could perform the tasks that lie ahead.'

'God spoke to you, also?'

'I think He did. I think I always knew.'

It was with this common understanding of their salvation and their mutual reinforcement that the younger Van Doorns came back to the farm, secure in their knowledge of what was required, and the first person their wrath fell upon was Dikkop, now fifty-seven years old and as inoffensive as always. Because of the many years they had shared, and the adventures, Adriaan gave the little fellow unusual prerogatives, and Lodevicus decided that this must stop: 'He is of the tribe of Ham, and he must no longer live with us or feed with us, or in any way associate with us, except as our Hottentot servant.'

When Adriaan protested such a harsh decree, Lodevicus and Rebecca explained things carefully, step by step, so that even Seena would understand: 'When the world started the second time, after the flood, Noah had three sons, and two of them were clean and white like us. But the third son, Ham, was dark and evil.'

'Now, Ham,' Rebecca continued, 'was the father of Canaan and all black people. And God, acting through Noah, placed a terrible curse on Canaan: "Cursed be Canaan! A servant of servants shall he be to his brethren." And it was ordained that the sons of Ham shall be hewers of wood and drawers of water, for as long as the world exists. Dikkop is a Canaanite. He is a son of Ham, and is condemned to be a slave and nothing more.'

It really didn't matter to Adriaan and Seena what the Hottentot was called; he was necessary to their lives, and as such, he was well treated. Seena especially liked to have him in the hut when food was being prepared or eaten, and it was this that caused the first open rupture with her daughter-in-law, for one day Rebecca said in some exasperation, 'Seena, you must not allow Dikkop in the hut ever again.' Then she added, in a voice of honest conciliation, 'Except, of course, when he cleans up.'

'But he's always been with me when I cook.'

'That must stop.'

'Who says so?' Seena asked belligerently.

'God.'

With the snap of a cloth and a sharpness of tongue that invited trouble, Seena said, 'I doubt that God troubles Himself over a woman's kitchen.'

'Lodevicus!' Rebecca called. 'Your mother refuses to believe.' And when Vicus came into the hut to hear the complaints, he, of course, sided totally with his wife, taking down the Bible and turning to those short, inconsequential books that end the Old Testament, and there in Zechariah he found the concluding passage which had loomed so large in the teaching of Predikant Specx at Swellendam: ' "And in that day there shall be no more the Canaanite in the house of the Lord of Hosts." ' He added that from this time on, the hut was the house of the Lord, and since Dikkop was clearly a Canaanite, he must be banished.

Curiously, Adriaan did not support his wife in this argument, for he was coming to believe that Rebecca spoke for the future; it was time that order be brought to the frontier, although he himself wanted none of it. The truth was, he rather liked his daughter-in-law, for she was capable, intelligent and forthright, and he suspected that Lodevicus had been lucky to catch her. Seena, however, saw her as a moralizing menace to be consistently opposed: 'You think your Bible has an answer for everything?'

'It has.'

'Well, when you and Vicus make the Xhosa mad, and they come clicking over that hill armed with assegais, what does your Bible say about that?'

With absolute assurance Rebecca said, 'Vicus, fetch me the Bible, please,' and in later years he would often remember this moment, when his wife and his mother argued over what might happen if the Xhosa struck.

Turning the pages expertly, Rebecca came to that passage in Leviticus which formed a keystone of her father's belief, and read triumphantly: ' "And ye shall chase your enemies, and they shall fall before you by the sword. And five of you shall chase an hundred . . ." ' And then, as if this solved all problems of the frontier, she glared at her mother-in-law and said, 'We will have five to defend this farm.'

Of course, the little brown men knew nothing of this prophecy and had no difficulty whatever in breaking through. One night a clan of Bushmen living beyond the mountains crept down, found large numbers of cattle roaming freely, and made off with some sixty fine beasts.

'That's enough,' Lodevicus said, his voice betraying iron but no fire. 'That's just enough. And now we settle the problem of the Bushmen.'

He organized a commando, all the men from thirty miles around, and he set forth, inviting Adriaan to come along but ignoring him when decisions were required. They went north about seventy miles, so far that Adriaan was certain they had left the Bushmen far behind, but when he started to alert his son to this fact, Vicus, grim-lipped, sat astride his horse, saying nothing.

The old man was right. The commando had far outrun the little brown raiders, but Vicus had devised a super strategy, and when the riders reached a spot where whole families of Bushmen might be expected to congregate, he ordered his men to dismount and hide themselves near a spring that broke out from between the rocks. Adriaan, unable to discern his son's plan, expected the hunting party to arrive with the stolen cattle and walk into an ambush, but instead, just at sunset, a huge rhinoceros lumbered in to catch his evening swill of water, and as he drank noisily, switching his wiry tail, Lodevicus dropped him with one powerful shot behind the ear.

There the great beast lay, beside the spring, and before nightfall vultures gathered, perching in trees and waiting for the dawn. They were seen, of course, both by the Bushmen families awaiting the return of their men and by the cattle stealers coming north, so that by midafternoon some sixty Bushmen, counting the women and children, had gathered at the spring to gorge upon the unexpected feast of the dead rhino.

During the first excitement as the little people butchered the huge beast, Lodevicus kept his men silent, and this was prudent, for the wait allowed another thirty brown people to assemble, and when they were all there, about ninety of them, cutting the rhino steaks and laughing as the blood ran down their wizened faces, Vicus leaped up and cried, 'Fire!'

Caught in the crossfire of a score of guns, the banqueters fell one by one. Cattle stealers, grandmothers, the makers of arrows, the young women who collected the beetles from which the poisons were made, and the little children, even the babies—all were exterminated.

Lodevicus the Hammer he was called after that exhibition, God's strong right arm, and whenever trouble threatened he was summoned. He organized the first church in this remote region and served as its sick-comforter during the years when it had no predikant. He read sermons from a book printed in Holland and sent him by Rebecca's father in Swellendam; he was punctilious about never posing as a real clergyman, for that was a holy vocation requiring years of formal study and the laying on of hands, but he did enforce religious law on both his own family and the scattered farms. Whenever a young man and woman started living together, he and Rebecca would visit them, take their names down in a book, and make them promise that as soon as a predikant came their way, they would marry. He also kept a register of births, threatening parents with damnation if they failed to have their infants baptized when the dominee came.

One night as he rode back after lecturing two young couples living carelessly down by the sea, he took Rebecca by the hand and led her a safe distance from the hut: 'I'm sorely worried. I've been reflecting on Adriaan and Seena. It's an affront to God for me to travel far distances to enforce His ordinances when in my own home . . .'

'What are we going to do about them?'

'It would be a dreadful act, Rebecca, to evict one's own parents. But if they persist in evil ways . . .'

When he paused to weigh the gravity of the problem, Rebecca enumerated the nagging difficulties she faced with Seena, the worst being her mother-in-law's paganism: 'She sneers at our teaching, Vicus. When you were gone she brought Dikkop back into the hut, even though she knows the Bible forbids it. When I pointed this out, she snapped, "Either he stays or you starve." '

'Rebecca, we should pray,' and they did, two earnest and contrite hearts seeking the right thing to do. They considered themselves neither arrogant nor unforgiving; all they sought was justice and sanctification, and in the end they resolved that Adriaan and Seena would have to leave: 'They're still young enough to build their own hut, they and that Canaanite Dikkop.'

They rose early so as to be strengthened for the unpleasant scene that must ensue, but when they looked out to the meadow they found Adriaan and Dikkop already up, two horses laden with enough gear to last them for an extensive journey.

'What are you doing?' Lodevicus demanded.

'Seena!' Adriaan shouted. 'Come out here!' And when the redhead appeared, her husband said, 'Tell them.'

She did: 'He's tired of your preaching. He's ashamed to keep a hut in which his friend is not welcome. And he doesn't like the new type of life you're trying to force on us.'

'What is he going to do?' Rebecca asked.

'He and Dikkop are going up to the Zambezi River.' The blank look on her son's face betrayed the fact that he had no idea of where such a river might be. 'The Swede told us about it. It's up there.' And with a careless wave of her arm she indicated a wild river of the imagination some fifteen hundred miles to the north.

'And you?' Rebecca asked.

'I'll stay here. This is my farm, you know.'

And in those few words Seena underlined the impossible situation that faced the young Van Doorns. They could not force his mother off this farm, nor could they in decency abandon her here. They would have to share the hut with her until her husband returned. 'How long will you be gone?' Lodevicus asked in chastened voice.

'Three years,' Adriaan said, and with a flick of his whip he started his oxen north.

It was in October 1766, when Adriaan was at the advanced age of fifty-four, that he and Dikkop left. They took with them sixteen reserve oxen, four horses, a tent, extra guns, more ammunition than they would probably need, sacks of flour and four bags of biltong. They wore the rough home-made cloths of the veld and carried a precious tin box containing Boer farm

remedies, medicinal herbs and leaves, their value learned through generations of experience.

They moved slowly at first, seven or eight miles a day, then ten, then
fifteen. They let themselves be diverted by almost anything: an unusual tree,
a likelihood of animals. Often they camped for weeks at a time at some
congenial spot, replenished their biltong and moved on.

As the two went slowly north, they saw wonders that no settler had ever
seen before: rivers of magnitude, and vast deserts waiting to explode into
flowers, and most interesting of all, a continual series of small hills, each
off to itself, perfectly rounded at the base as if some architect had placed
them in precisely the right position. Often the top had been planed away,
forming mesas as flat as a table. Occasionally Adriaan and Dikkop would
climb such a hill for no purpose at all except to scout the landscape ahead,
and they would see only an expanse so vast that the eye could not encom-
pass it, marked with these repetitious little hills, some rounded, some with
their tops scraped flat.

In the second month of their wandering, after they had rafted their
luggage wagon across a stream the Hottentots called Great River, later to
be named the Orange, they entered upon those endless plains leading into
the heartland, and late one afternoon at a fountain they came upon the first
band of human beings, a group of little Bushmen who fled as they approached. Throughout that long night Adriaan and Dikkop stayed close to
the wagons, guns loaded, peering into the darkness apprehensively. Just
after dawn one of the little men showed himself, and Adriaan made a major
decision. With Dikkop covering him, he left his own gun against the wheel
of the wagon, stepped forward unarmed, and indicated with friendly gestures that he came in peace.

At the invitation of the Bushmen, Adriaan and Dikkop stayed at that
fountain for a week, during which Adriaan learned many good things about
the ones his fellow Dutchmen called 'daardie diere' (those animals), and
nothing so impressed him as when he was allowed to accompany them on
a hunt, for he witnessed remarkable skill and sensitivity in tracking. The
Bushmen had collected a large bundle of hides, which Dikkop learned
would be taken 'three moons to the north' for trade with people who lived
there.

Since the travelers were also headed in that general direction, they
joined the Bushmen, and twice during the journey saw clusters of huts in
the distance, but the Bushmen shook their heads and kept the caravan
moving deeper into the plains till they reached the outlying kraals of an
important chief's domain.

The Bushmen ran ahead to break the news of the white stranger, so that
at the first village Adriaan was greeted with intense curiosity and some
tittering, rather than the fear which might have been expected. The blacks
were pleased that he showed special interest in their huts, impressed by the
sturdy, rounded workmanship in stone and clay and the walls four to five
feet high that surrounded their cattle kraals. As he told Dikkop, 'These are
better than the huts you and I live in.'

News of their arrival spread to the chief's kraal and he sent an escort
of headmen and warriors to bring these strangers before him. The meeting

was grave, for Adriaan was the first white man these blacks had seen; they came to know him well, for he stayed with them two months. They were excited when he demonstrated gunpowder by tossing a small handful on an open fire, where it flamed violently. The chief was terrified at first, but after he mastered the trick, he delighted in using it to frighten his people.

'How many are you?' Adriaan asked one night.

The chief pointed to the compass directions, then to the stars. There were so many people in this land.

When Adriaan studied the communities he was permitted to see, it became obvious to him that these people were not recent arrivals in the area. Their present settlements, the ruins of past locations, their ironwork traded from the north, their copious use of tobacco—all signaled long occupancy. He was especially charmed by the glorious cloaks the men made from animal skins softened like chamois. He liked their fields of sorghum, pumpkins, gourds and beans. Their pottery was well formed, and their beads, copied from those brought to Zimbabwe three hundred years earlier, were beautiful. He accepted their presence on the highveld as naturally as he accepted the herds of antelope that browsed near the fountains.

In succeeding months he would never be far from such settlements, scattered over the lands they crossed, but he rarely contacted the people, since he was preoccupied with reaching the Zambezi. Besides, he worried that other chiefs might not be as friendly as the man who danced with joy at the flash of gunpowder.

As they moved north they shot only such food as they required, except one morning when Dikkop became irritated with a hyena that insisted upon trying to grab her share of an antelope he had shot. Three times he tried in vain to drive the beast away, and when she persisted he shot her. This might have occasioned no comment from Adriaan but for the fact that when she died she left behind a baby male hyena with fiery black eyes; she had wanted the meat to feed him, and now he was abandoned, snapping his huge teeth at Dikkop whenever he approached.

'What's out there?' Adriaan called.

'Baby hyena, Baas,' Dikkop replied.

'Bring him here!'

So Dikkop made a feint, leaped back, and planted his foot on the little beast's neck, subduing him so that he could be grabbed. Struggling and kicking but making no audible protest, the baby hyena was brought before Adriaan, who said immediately, 'We've got to feed him.' So Dikkop chewed up bits of tender meat, placing it on his finger for the animal to lick off, and by the end of the third day the two men were competing with each other to see who would have the right to feed the little beast.

'Swartejie, we'll call him,' Adriaan said, something like Blackie or the Little Black One, but the hyena assumed such a menacing stance that Adriaan had to laugh. 'So you think you're a big Swarts already?' And that's what he was called.

He showed the endearing characteristics of a domesticated dog without losing the impressive qualities of an animal in the wild. Because his forequarters were strong and high, his rear small and low, he lurched rather than walked, and since his mouth was enormous, with powerful head muscles to operate the great, crunching jaws, he could present a frightening appearance, except that his innate good nature and his love of Adriaan, who fed and roughhoused with him, made his face appear always to be smiling. Short tail, big ears, wide-set eyes, he made himself into a cherished pet whose unpredictable behavior supplied a surprise a day.

He was a scavenger, but he certainly lacked a scavenger's heart, for he did not slink and was willing to challenge the largest lion if a good carcass was available. But once when the two men came upon a covey of guinea fowl and wounded one, Swarts was thrown into a frenzy of fear by the bird's flapping wings and flying feathers. As winter approached and the highveld proved cold, whenever Adriaan went to his sleeping quarters—eland skin formed like a bag, with soft ostrich feathers sewn into a blanket—he would find Swarts sleeping on his springbok pillow, eyes closed in blissful repose, his muscles twitching now and then as he dreamed of the hunt.

'Move over, damnit!'

The sleeping hyena would groan, lying perfectly limp as Adriaan shoved him to one side, but as soon as the master was in the bed, Swarts would snuggle close and often he would snore. 'You! Damnit! Stop snoring!' and Adriaan would shove him aside as if he were an old wife.

They saw animals in such abundance that no man could have counted them, or even estimated their numbers. Once when they were crossing an upland where the grass was sweet, they saw to the east a vast movement, ten miles, twenty miles, fifty miles across, coming slowly toward them, raising a dust that obliterated the sun.

'What to do?' Dikkop asked.

'I think we stand where we are,' Adriaan replied, not at all pleased with his answer but unable to think of any other.

Even Swarts was afraid, whimpering and drawing close to Adriaan's leg.

And then the tremendous herd approached, not running, not moving in fear. It was migration time, and in obedience to some deep impulse the animals were leaving one feeding ground and heading to another.

The herd was composed of only three species: vast numbers of wildebeest, their beards swaying in the quiet breeze; uncounted zebras, decorating the veld with their flashy colors; and a multitude of springbok leaping joyously among the statelier animals. How many beasts could there have been? Certainly five hundred thousand, more probably eight or nine, an exuberance of nature that was difficult to comprehend.

And now they were descending upon the three travelers. When they were close at hand, Swarts begged Adriaan to take him up, so the two men stood fast as the herd came down upon them. A strange thing happened. As the wildebeest and zebras came within twenty feet of the men, they quietly opened their ranks, forming the shape of an almond, a teardrop of open space in which the men stood unmolested. And as soon as that group of animals passed, they closed the almond, going forward as before, while newcomers looked at the men, slowly moved aside to form their own teardrop and then pass on.

For seven hours Adriaan and Dikkop stood in that one spot as the animals moved past. Never were they close enough to have touched one of the zebras or the bounding springbok; always the animals stayed clear, and after a while Swarts asked to be put down so that he could watch more closely.

At sunset the western sky was red with dust.

In the next months the landscape changed dramatically. Mountains began to appear on the horizon ahead, and rivers flowed north instead of east, where the ocean presumably lay. It was good land, and soon they found themselves in that remarkable gorge where the walls seemed to come together high in the heavens. Dikkop was frightened and wanted to turn back, but Adriaan insisted upon forging ahead, breaking out at last into that wonderland of baobab trees, whose existence defied his imagination.

'Look at them!' he cried. 'Upside down! How wonderful!'

For several weeks he and Dikkop and Swarts lived in one huge tree, not up in the branches, which would have been possible, but actually inside the tree in a huge vacancy caused by the wearing away of soft wood. Swarts, responding to some ancient heritage in a time when hyenas had lived in caves, reveled in the dark interior spaces, running from one to the other and making strange sounds.

He had become an exceptional pet, perhaps the finest animal Adriaan had ever known, placid like the best ox, brave like the strongest lion, playful like a kitten, and of tremendous strength like a rhinoceros. He enjoyed playing a fearsome game with Adriaan, taking the trekboer's forearm in his powerful jaws and pretending to bite it in half, which he could have done. He would bring his teeth slowly together and impishly watch Adriaan's face to see when pain would show. Tighter and tighter the great teeth would close until it seemed that the skin must break, and then, with Adriaan looking directly into the animal's eyes, Swarts would stop, and laugh admiringly at the man who was not afraid, and he would release the arm and leap upon Adriaan's lap and cover him with kisses.

At times Adriaan would think: These years can never end. There will be enough land for everyone, and the animals will multiply forever. When he and Dikkop left a carcass it was good to hear the lions approaching, to see the sky filled with great birds waiting to descend and clean the feast.

They came at last to the river, not the Zambezi, as Adriaan had promised, but the Limpopo, that sluggish stream that marked the natural northern borders of the subcontinent. Dr. Linnart had said the natural border was the Zambezi; Portuguese explorers had said the same; and anyone who had a map, rude and rough, saw that the Zambezi was the natural boundary, but reality dictated that this boundary be the Limpopo. South of here, the land was of a piece; north of here, it altered radically and could never be digested as an inherent part of a manageable unit.

Perhaps Adriaan realized this in December 1767 when he stood at the Limpopo beside his irreparably broken wagon and his oxen and horses dying from disease. 'Dikkop,' he said, 'we can't go any farther.' The Hottentot agreed, for he was tired, and even Swarts seemed relieved when the trio started south on foot. It was as if the hyena had a built-in compass which reminded him of where home had stood; he seemed to have known that he was heading away from where he ought to have been, and now that he was homeward bound he manifested his joy like a sailor whose ship has turned into a proper heading.

They formed a curious trio as they came happily down the spine of Africa. Swarts, with his big head and small bottom, took the lead. Then came Dikkop, with small head and enormous bottom. Finally there was Adriaan, a lean, white-haired trekboer, fifty-six years old and striding along as if he were thirty. Once Swarts insisted upon leaving the trail made by antelope and heading to the west, and when the men followed they found a small cave which they were about to ignore, until Dikkop looked at the roof and discovered a marvelous canopy showing three giraffes being stalked by little brown men; it had been painted there millennia ago by the ancestors of the Bushmen they had met. This way and that, men and animals moved, colors unfaded, forms still deftly outlined. For a long time Adriaan studied the paintings, then asked, 'Where have they gone?'

'Who knows, Baas?' Dikkop replied, and Adriaan said, 'Good boy, Swarts. We liked your cave.'

Summer that year was very hot, and even though the trio was moving south, away from concentrated heat, Adriaan noticed that Dikkop was exhausted, so he looked for routes that would keep them away from the hot and dusty center and lead them out toward the eastern edge of the plateau, where they were likely to encounter cooling rains; and on one such excursion they came upon that quiet and pleasant lake where the flamingos had flown and Nxumalo had hunted his rhinoceros.

It was at its apex now, a broad and lovely body of water to which a thousand animals came each evening, in such steady profusion that Swarts was benumbed by the possibilities he saw before him. Lurching here and there, chasing birds and elephants alike, he watched for any weakling, placing himself well back of the lions that were also stalking it, and ran in for bits of meat whenever an opportunity arose. When the bigger predators were gone, he would waddle into the lake to drink and wash himself, and he obviously enjoyed this part of the trip above any other.

Dikkop was faring less well. It was 1768 now and he was sixty-three years old, a tired man who had worked incessantly at a hundred different tasks, always assigned him by someone else. He had lived his life in the shadow of white men, and in their shadow he was content to end his final days. He was not indifferent about his fate; eagerly he wanted to get back to the farm to see how Seena was doing, for he loved her rowdy ways and usually thought of himself as 'her boy.' He would be very unhappy if anything happened to him before he saw her again.

He was to be disappointed. As the summer waned, so did he, and it became apparent that he would not be able to endure the long return journey: 'My chest, he hurts, he hurts.' Adriaan berated himself for having brought so old a man on so perilous an expedition, but when Dikkop saw this he said reassuringly, 'Impossible to come without me. But you get back safe, I think.'

He died before the chill of winter and was buried beside the lake he had grown to love; it was when Adriaan collected the stones for Dikkop's cairn from the ruins of an ancient village dating back to the 1450s that he began talking seriously to his hyena: 'Swarts, we're piling these stones so your filthy brothers don't dig him up and eat him, you damned cannibal.' Swarts showed his enormous teeth in what could only be a grin, and after that whenever Adriaan consulted with him about which eland path to follow or where to spend the night, Swarts bared his teeth and nuzzled his master's leg.

Adriaan now had every reason to pursue vigorously his way homeward, but for reasons he could not have explained he lingered at the quiet lake, not exploring its hinterland but simply resting, as if he realized that this was a place to which men fled for refuge. From his sleeping place he studied the low mountains to the east, the twin peaks that looked like breasts, and the flatlands hungry for the plow. But most of all he kept his eyes upon the rim of the lake, where animals came to drink and across whose placid surface the flamingos flew.

'Vrijmeer!' he cried one day. 'Swarts, this is the lake where everything that moves has freedom.' That night he could not sleep. Restlessly he stepped across the inert body of his hyena to stand in moonlight as undisciplined thoughts assailed him: I wish I were young again . . . to bring a family here . . . to live beside this lake . . .

It was not easy for Adriaan to admit that he was growing lonely. He had never talked much with Dikkop, nor looked to him for intellectual companionship. He was not afraid of traveling alone, because by now he knew every trick for avoiding dangers; he sensed where the kraals of the black people lay, and he swung away from them; he slept where no lion could reach him, relying upon Swarts to alert him if unusual developments occurred. The hyena was not really a good watchdog, he slept too soundly on a full belly, and with his master's constant hunting he had a good supply of guts and bones to gorge upon; but he had a marked capacity for self-defense, and many animals that might have attacked Adriaan sleeping alone would think twice before risking a hyena's great jaws and flashing teeth.

The loneliness came from the fact that he had seen Africa, had touched it intimately along the mountains and the veld, and had reached the point where there were no more secrets. Even the fact that a majestic waterfall lay only a short distance to his northwest would not have surprised him, for he had found the continent to be greater than he had imagined or Dr. Linnart had suggested.

Again the vagrant thought struck, this time with pain, and he said in a loud voice, 'God, Swarts, I wish I were young again. I'd cross the Limpopo. Go on and on, past the Zambezi all the way to Holland.' He had not the slightest doubt that given a good pair of shoes, he could walk to Europe. 'And I'd take you with me, little hunter, to protect me from the dik-diks.' He laughed at this, and Swarts laughed back at the idea of anyone's needing protection from the tiniest of antelopes who leaped in fear at the fall of a leaf.

Perhaps this recurrent loneliness was a premonition, for as they came down off the spacious central plateau to cross the Great River, he saw that Swarts was becoming restless. The hyena was two and a half years old now, a full-grown male, and as they came into territory where other hyenas hunted in packs, Swarts became aware of them in new ways, and sometimes at dusk gave indications that he wanted to run with them. At the same time he knew deep love for his human companion and felt a kind of obligation to protect him, to share with him the glories of the hunt.

So he vacillated, sometimes running toward the open veld, at other times scampering back in his lurching way to be with his master; but one night, when the moon was full and animals were afoot, he suddenly broke away from Adriaan, ran a short distance into the veld, stopped, looked back as if weighing alternatives, and disappeared. Through his sleepless night Adriaan could hear the sounds of hunting, and when day broke, there was no Swarts.

For three days Adriaan stayed in that area, hoping that the hyena would return, but he did not. And so, with regret almost to the point of tears, Adriaan set out for the mountains that protected his farm, and now he was truly alone, and for the first time in his life, even afraid. From the latitude of the stars he calculated that he might be as far as three hundred miles north of his destination, afoot, with a diminishing store of ammunition and the necessity of covering that expanse of open country when he was not quite sure where he was.

'Swarts,' he shouted one night, 'I need you!' And later, as he lay fitfully sleeping, he heard the sound of animals, many of them, trampling near to where he was hiding, and he began to shiver, for he had not heard this noise so close before. Then slowly he came awake, and was aware of something pressing upon him, and it was Swarts, snoring in the old manner.

Now he talked with the animal more than ever, as if the hyena's return laid bare his need for companionship; Swarts, for his part, kept closer to his master, as if after tasting the freedom of the wild, he realized that partnership with a human being could have its rewards, too.

Down the long plains they came. 'It must be over this way, Swarts,' Adriaan said, looking at the last line of hills that rose from the veld. 'The farm is probably down there, and when you meet Seena you two are going to have fun. She's red-headed and she'll throw things at you if you don't look out, but you'll like her and I know she'll like you.' He was not at all sure how Seena would take to sharing her hut with a hyena, but he kept assuring Swarts that it would be all right.

But the hyena's recent experience in the wild had revived animal habits, and one evening after Adriaan shot a gemsbok, a beautiful creature with white-masked face and imperial horns, a lioness thought it safe to move in and command the kill, whereupon Swarts leaped at her, receiving a horrible slash of claw across his neck and face.

When Adriaan, screaming at the lioness, reached his companion, Swarts was dying. Nothing that the man might do could save the beast; his prayers were meaningless, his attempts to stanch the blood fruitless. The great jaws moved in spasms and the eyes looked for the last time at the person who had been such a trusted friend.

'Swarts!' Adriaan shouted, but to no avail. The hyena shuddered, gasped for air, got only blood, and died.

'Oh, Swarts!' Adriaan moaned repeatedly through the night, keeping the misshapen body near him. In the morning he placed it out in the open where the vultures could attend it, and after an anguished farewell to a constant friend he resumed his journey south.

Now he was truly alone. Almost everything he had had with him at the start of his exploration was gone: ammunition, horses and oxen lost to the tsetse fly, the wagon, the trusted Hottentot, his shoes, most of his clothing. He was coming home bereft of everything, even his hyena, and his memories of the grandeurs he had seen were scarred by the losses he had sustained. Most of all he mourned for Swarts; Dikkop, after all, had lived his life, but the hyena was only beginning his, a creature torn between the open veld and the settled farm that was to have been his home.

As he slogged his way south Adriaan began to feel his age, the weight of time, and idly he calculated the farms he had used up, the endless chain of animals he had bred and passed along, the huts he had lived in and never a house: 'Swarts, I'm fifty-seven years old and never lived in a house with real walls.' Then he braced his shoulders, crying even louder, 'And by God, Swarts, I don't want to live in one.'

He came down off the great central highland of Africa—not defeated, but certainly not victorious. He could still walk many miles a day, but he did so more slowly, the dust of far places in his nostrils. From time to time he shouted into space, addressing only Swarts, for now he was truly Mal Adriaan, the crazy man of the veld who conversed with dead hyenas, but on he went, a few miles a day, always looking for the trail he had lost.

When he broke through the mountains into unfamiliar terrain he calculated correctly that he must be a fair distance east of his farm, and he was about to turn westward to find it when he said, 'Swarts! If they had any sense, they'd have moved to better land over there.' And like earlier members of his family, he headed east.

But when he reached the territory that ought to have contained the new farm, he found nothing, so he was faced with the problem of plunging blindly ahead into unknown territory or turning back, and after long consultation with Swarts he decided on the former: 'Stands to reason, Swarts, they'd be wanting better pastures.'

At the farthest edge of where he could imagine his family might have reached, he came upon the shabbiest hut he had yet seen, and in it lived a man and wife who had taken up their six thousand acres with only the meagerest chance of succeeding. They were the first white people Adriaan had seen since setting out, and he talked with them avidly: 'You hear of any Van Doorns passing this way?'

'They went.'

'Which direction?'

'East.'

'How long ago?'

'Before I got here.'

'But you're sure they went?'

'We stayed in their old huts. Four months. Trekboer came through, told us they had gone.'

Since Adriaan needed rest, he stayed with the couple for a short time, and one morning the woman asked, 'Who's this Swarts you keep talking to?' and he replied, 'Friend of mine.'

After two weeks, during which the trekboer gave him a supply of ammunition, which he used to bring meat to the hut, Adriaan announced casually that he was about to try to locate his family. 'How long you been gone?' the woman asked.

'Three years.'

'Where'd you say you were?'

'M'popo,' he said, using a name the blacks had taught him.

'Never heard of it.' For a moment Adriaan felt that he owed it to his hosts to explain, but upon reflection, realized that to do so adequately would require another two weeks, so he departed with no further comment.

On and on he went, well past the place where he had met Sotopo, the Xhosa, and one morning as he reached the crest of a substantial line of hills he looked down to see something which disturbed him greatly; it was a valley comprising some nine thousand acres and completely boxed in by hills. 'It's a prison!' he cried, alarmed that people would willingly submit themselves to such confinement.

What dismayed him especially was that at the center, beside a lively stream that ran from the southwest to the northeast, escaping through a cleft in the hills, stood not the usual Van Doorn huts but solid buildings constructed of clay and stone. Whoever had planned this tight enclave intended to occupy it not for the ordinary ten years, but for a lifetime. It represented a change of pattern so drastic that in one swift glance Adriaan realized that his old trekboer days were ended, and he groaned at the error these people were making: Stone houses! Prisons within a prison! To reach this at the end of three years on the most glorious land in Africa was regrettable.

But he still was not certain that this was his new farm until an older woman with fading red hair came out of the stone house and walked toward the barn. It was Seena. This stronghold was her home, and now it would be his.

He did not call out to his wife, but he did say to Swarts, 'We've come to the end, old fellow. Things we don't understand . . .' Slowly and without the jubilation he should have felt at reaching the end of so long a journey, he came down the hill, went to the door of the barn, and called, 'Seena!' She knew immediately who it was and left the gathering of eggs, running to him and hugging him as if he were a child. 'Verdomde ou man,' she cried. 'You're home!'

After the children had screamed their greetings and Lodevicus, now a solid thirty, had come forth with Rebecca, Adriaan asked the adults, 'How did our farm get to this place?'

'We wanted security,' Lodevicus explained. 'The hills, you know.'

'But why the stone houses?'

'Because this is the last jump that can be made. Because on the other side of the Great Fish River the Xhosa wait.'

'This is our permanent home,' Rebecca said. 'Like Swellendam, a foothold on the frontier.'

'I saw a place up north. It had hills like this, but they were open. There was a lake, and it was open too. Animals from everywhere came to drink.'

The younger Van Doorns were not interested in what their father had seen at the north, but that night when Adriaan and Seena went to their bed after the long absence she whispered, 'What was it like?' and all he could say was 'It's a beautiful country.'

That had to stand for the thundering sunsets, the upside-down trees, the veld bursting in flowers, the great mountains to the east, the mysterious rivers to the north, but as he was about to close his eyes in sleep, he suddenly sat upright and cried, 'God, Seena! I wish we were twenty . . . we could go to a place I saw . . . that lake . . . the antelope darkening the fields.'

'Let's go!' she said without hesitation or fear.

He laughed and kissed her. 'Go to sleep. They'll find it in time.'

'Who?'

'The ones who come after.'

Lodevicus and Rebecca never once asked about the northern lands; their preoccupation was in building a paradise at hand; but in the afternoons their children gathered with Adriaan to hear of Swarts, the cave with leaping giraffes on the ceiling, the boisterous blacks who danced at the flash of gunpowder, and of the place he called Vrijmeer.

When the excitement of his return died down, the battle between Seena and Rebecca resumed, with each woman confiding to her husband at night that the other was intolerable, and Adriaan would lie awake listening to his wife's litany of complaint: 'She's a nasty tyrant. She has a withered lemon for a heart. It's her intention to run this entire area, and Lodevicus supports her.'

He shared with her his impression upon first seeing their new home: 'This room with its tight walls is a prison cell—within the stone house, which is the small prison, within these hateful hills, which form the biggest prison of all.'

'No,' she corrected. 'The big prison is the ideas he wants to enforce. Every person on every farm must behave the way he says. You know, he's started fighting with the Xhosa when they come over the river to feed their cattle.'

When Adriaan asked his son about this, Lodevicus said, 'Three times I've heard you speak poorly about having our farm within these hills. Well, war with the Xhosa is inevitable. They're pressing westward more strongly each month, and soon we'll have real warfare.'

'Let them graze their cattle,' Adriaan said.

'They'll never be content with that. Mark my words, Father, they'll want everything. They'll overrun this farm. That is, if it wasn't protected by hills.'

In 1776 Lodevicus was proved right, for a large group of Xhosa, led by Guzaka, son of that Sotopo with whom Adriaan had spent four days of friendship, became increasingly angered by the constant pressure from the white farmers.

As in the beginning days of Dutch-Hottentot contact, when an attempt was made to confine the settlement so as to avoid irritations, once again the Compagnie, trying vainly to rule an area already ten times greater than Holland, forbade any further barter with blacks. But on the frontier their proclamations were like sand thrown in the wind. Daring white men crossed into the lands occupied by those they called Kaffirs, Arabic for infidels, reasoning that it was simpler to fire their guns and take what land they needed rather than sit out a protracted bargaining session with the Xhosa. No bitter-almond hedge could possibly demark hundreds of miles of border-land; also, Sotopo's people provoked rage, for, when the white men's herds moved placidly within range, they reverted to old ways, sang old songs, sharpened their assegais, and shouted with glee as they stole the trekboers' cattle.

And so the battles began, the blacks claiming land which was theirs by hereditary right, the trekboers grabbing for the same land because it had been promised to the children of God.

Guzaka's men struck south, smiting an isolated farm not far from the sea, killing everyone and driving some five hundred cattle back across the Great Fish. They then rushed northward to the Van Doorn farm set among hills, recognizing it as the major impediment to their westward expansion.

'It will not be easy,' Guzaka warned his men.

'You said that about the other farm,' one said.

'It was not defended. At this place there are the hills.'

'Which means they're trapped inside.'

'It could mean something else,' Guzaka cautioned.

'What?'

'That we will not be able to break in.'

'We have so many. They have so few.'

'But they have the guns.'

'The others had guns.'

'But only two to use them. Here there will be many.'

'Are you afraid, Guzaka?'

'I am,' and before the others could ask if they should turn back, he added, 'But we must wipe out this farm, or it will oppose us always.'

It was he who led the charge down the eastern hill, coming first to the cattle byres and the other small buildings, and it was here that the Xhosa met their punishing taste of what real trekboers could do in defense of a farm. From crannies that the blacks could not have anticipated, gunfire snapped at them, cutting and killing until they had to retreat. No invader even came near the house.

On the hillside, surveying what amounted to the first trekboer fort, Guzaka and his men consulted on what to do, and their leader reminded them: 'I told you this would be different.' He did not yet know that his father's friend, Adriaan of the Van Doorns, occupied the stone house, nor would he have recognized the name had it been spoken, but he carried in the back of his mind stories his father had told of that compelling meeting with the white man and of the man's capacities. Guzaka understood that there were degrees in manhood and that the futile defenders of that first farm stood rather low on the rod of measurement. The men in this house resembled more the one that Sotopo had encountered.

'Shall we turn back?' his men asked.

'No. Then they would think it was too easy to defeat us. We will attack from two quarters.' And he devised a plan whereby one group would come down the eastern hill, while a larger body would swing in from the south.

In the stone house Adriaan said, 'They're not stupid. This time they'll come at us from two directions.' Looking at the hills and the position of the stream, which though small would prove difficult to ford under gunfire, he concluded that they would have to come in from the south, so along that wall he stationed three of his guns.

'But they'll try the east again,' he warned. 'Just to test us.' So he alone went to the byre, satisfied that the number of eastern invaders would be smaller than before.

When Guzaka saw that his own groups were in position, he gave the signal and dashed for the outlying buildings; to his delight, there was no gunfire, so with a wild yell he urged his men on to the house, but when they were abreast of the cattle byre, a deadly fusillade struck from the flank, and two of his men fell.

Then from the south wall of the house, gunfire erupted, and that invading contingent was also thrown back.

When the Xhosa regrouped on the eastern hill it was obvious that this farm could not be taken. Turning away from that stronghold, the blacks forded the stream well east of the house, rounded up such cattle as grazed in the far fields, and retreated through the northeast opening.

'They'll be back,' Lodevicus warned. 'Not today, but they'll know that ours is the kraal that must be reduced.'

'Kraal?' Adriaan asked.

'This refuge enclosed by hills,' and from that time on the farm was called De Kraal, the protected place.

The trekboers, having lost none and slain seven, should have celebrated, but they didn't, for old animosities between Seena and Rebecca continued to smolder, always ready to burst into flame. Usually the brawls involved religion, with Seena ridiculing her daughter-in-law's stern devotion and Rebecca complaining of her mother-in-law's agnosticism. No compromise seemed possible, and when the old folk were alone, Seena resumed her pestering: 'Let's leave and build a little hut where we can live the way we used to. I'm tired of having the Bible thrown at me.'

'It's being thrown at your father, too,' he said, referring to the rumor that a military expedition had been sent to eliminate Rooi van Valck's outlaw empire. Some even claimed that Rooi had been hanged.

Seena doubted this: 'They'd have to catch him first. And then they'd have to get a rope around his neck. Not many at the Cape would like to try.'

'If you'd be more patient with Rebecca,' Adriaan began, whereupon his wife gave him a lesson on the future of South Africa: 'She'll never let up. With her quiet manners she'll press on and on. The way her father did.'

'What do you mean?'

'He came here singing Psalms. Accomplished nothing with you and me.

But he worked on Lodevicus, sowing seeds. And later on he trapped him.'

'What do you truly think of our son?'

'He's going to grow stronger every day. As a boy he was like a piece of soft limestone lying in water. You can cut it with your fingernail. But when it stands clear of the water, and dries in the sun, it becomes harder than granite, and no one can cut it. Rebecca and Vicus, they'll form a terrible partnership.'

As she uttered this prediction, Rebecca was arguing with her husband: 'Vicus, I know I've said it many times before, but I can no longer tolerate that woman. I can't have her godlessness continue to contaminate my house.'

'In point of fact,' Lodevicus said, 'the house is hers and my father's, not yours.'

'Very well, we'll leave it to them and go build our own.'

'But I worked three years building these walls. Be patient. They can't live forever.' Lodevicus was hardening, but he had not yet reached the point at which he could throw his parents out of their own house.

Rebecca was sterner: 'God has directed you and me to bring a new order into a pagan land. We're to form a new life here among the trekboers. We're to raise children according to the Holy Book and not the way that godless old woman raised you and the others.' When Vicus started to protest, she silenced him: 'Don't you realize that God performed a miracle so that you could be saved? Suppose Father had not stopped at your farm to plant the holy seed? Suppose you had not visited Swellendam to have it nurtured? You've been set aside for a noble mission, and we cannot allow it to be diverted.'

Of the four adults engaged in this continuing battle, Mal Adriaan was the only one who saw its dimensions clearly, for he possessed a childlike simplicity which he was willing to turn even upon himself: 'I'm a man of the past, Seena. There's no place in this family for wanderers. Frightened people want to retreat into stone forts.' When his wife asked what he thought of her, he laughed. 'You're a pagan. Daughter of a pagan. There'll be no place for pagans in the world Vicus and Rebecca are building.'

As for Lodevicus, Adriaan supposed that Seena had been correct when she described him as limestone-about-to-become-granite: 'I don't think I'll like the finished result. Too stiff, too unforgiving. And I pity those who cross him.'

Rebecca he saw with unflinching clarity: he sensed that she had declared war upon Seena and him and was probably agitating for their expulsion; but he also saw that she was an exceptional woman whom he might have wanted to marry had he been younger. She was passionate and clean and shining, like a white stone at the bottom of a moving river. Her courage merited enormous respect, for in her zeal to discipline the trekboer world, which he had to admit was lawless, she was like some great mother elephant crashing through the underbush, headed for a destination which she alone perceived, and nothing would stop her. That she felt herself to be driven by God only made her more formidable. She was not cruel, nor did she try to overwhelm her opposition; like a cascade running to the sea, she simply kept moving in her predestined direction.

She would be the inner strength of the new religion developing in South Africa, the silent woman who sat serene in church while the men roared and ranted and announced the Psalms to be sung; but in the privacy of the home it would be she who determined what the day-to-day applications of that public religion were to be, and if ever the men carelessly fumbled their way toward some wrongdoing, she would summon them back to the stern path of duty. She would be against change, against relaxation, against new ideas from abroad, against any bizarre interpretation at home. She would form the granite core of the church, and her quiet teaching would prevail.

In short, Adriaan had grown to respect his daughter-in-law not only as the inexorable force of the future but also as the hard-grained, just human being who was needed at this moment in history. She was a stalwart wife, a compassionate mother; he liked her caustic wit and her capacity to hew to a single line. She was, all told, a good woman, and if she opposed him, the fault must be his.

It was always this way when generations clashed: the best of the old found it easy to appreciate the merits of those among the new who displayed integrity. It was the second echelons, deficient in understanding and empathy, who caused the trouble, and now Lodevicus was prepared to do just that.

It was the second expedition against the Bushmen which demonstrated how stonelike he had become and how justly he merited the title Hammer. This time there had been no massive theft of cattle, only the constant spiriting away of a cow here, an ox there, but all farmers in the region were enraged with the little brown men, and when Lodevicus said, 'They're like vermin. Periodically they have to be exterminated,' they agreed, and once more a commando was sent north to cleanse the area.

On this expedition no rhinoceros was used as bait, and for good reason: there were now no herds of large animals in the region; most had been killed off or driven away. Rhinoceros, hippopotamus, lion, zebra, those glorious beasts who had roamed these hills had vanished before the horse and gun, and now these dreadful weapons were to be turned against the Bushmen.

What Lodevicus did was separate his commando into three groups operating like a vast pinwheel, riding in circles that tightened toward the center, and as the men rode they watched for little brown men who might be trapped within their circle. As the bewildered Bushmen ran this way and that in sad confusion, the horsemen picked them off, one by one. There was no mass slaughter of ninety, as before, but only the deadly attrition of knocking down running targets—until two hundred were slain.

Adriaan, remembering his friendship with the Bushmen, had spoken against the hunt, but he had been ignored. He was appalled at its inhumanity, and when one old man, hampered by a kind of belt he wore, stumbled about in confusion, Adriaan rode to rescue him, but Lodevicus swept in, lowered his rifle, and killed the man.

'What have you done?' Adriaan cried.

'We're clearing the land,' Vicus shouted from his horse.

'Damn you! Look at him!' And Adriaan dismounted to inspect the dead man's belt, and found it to be of rhinoceros hide imbedded with eight tips of eland horn. Holding the belt aloft, he cried, 'What is it, Vicus? Tell me, what is it?'

His son reined in his horse, rode back, and looked contemptuously at the leather. 'Seems like a belt.'

'Dip your finger into one of the horns,' and when he did, the finger came out a deep-stained blue.

'What is it, Vicus?' And when his son said he didn't know, Adriaan cried in pain, 'They're the pots of an artist. Who paints the living veld on the roof of the cave. And you murdered him.' Looking up at his mounted son, he said with bitter scorn, 'Lodevicus the Hammer. I won't share my house with you one day longer.'

'It's my house,' Lodevicus said. 'I built it.'

Whereupon the old man cried in terrible rage, 'Read the Bible you prate about! It was Abraham's house as long as he lived. But you've tainted it . . . with red blood . . . and blue paint. And I'll have no more of it.'

Turning his back on his son, he mounted his horse, hurried over the hills, and shouted as he rode into De Kraal, 'Seena! Come on, old Redhead. Get yourself ready to leave this pitiful place.'

'Good!' she shouted back. 'Where do we go?'

'I'll find a place,' he assured her, and at sixty-five the old wanderers began scouting far lands to determine where they would build their own hut.

In 1778 the Hollanders who came to Cape Town to govern the colony, spending temporary terms in a land that confused them, gave honest proof of their desire to administer the area justly, for they devised a solution to frontier problems that was more humane and considerate than any being offered at this time by either the British or the French in their colonies. The governor himself trekked all the way from Cape Town, on horseback and by slow oxcart, to talk with trekboers like the Van Doorns and native chieftains like Guzaka, and after painful consideration of what was best for all, sent an emissary back to De Kraal with a written order that was concise and unmistakable:

> We have decided that the only practical solution to the problem of having settled white farmers mingling with roaming black herdsmen is to separate the two groups severely and permanently. This will provide justice and security for each segment, leaving each free to develop as it deems best. Since the Compagnie plans to import no new settlers, and since the blacks certainly have sufficient land for their purposes, we order that each shall stay in their present places and move no farther. There shall be no contact of any kind between white and black.
>
> The Great Fish River shall be the permanent dividing line between the races, and a strict policy of apartness shall be maintained, now and forever. No white man shall move east of the Great Fish. No

black man shall move west. In this manner, peace can be maintained perpetually.

When the emissary rejoined the governor's party he was able to state with assurance: 'The frontier problem is settled. There can never again be conflict, because each side will keep to its own bank of the river.'

The day after he said this, Adriaan van Doorn loaded his wagon, handed his wife a walking stick, and bade farewell to his son's family. To Rebecca he said with sorrow, 'You and Lodevicus have set a course so harsh I cannot follow. May your God give you strength to finish it.'

'He's your God, too.'

'Mine is a gentler God,' he said, but when this rebuke caused blood to leave her face, he kissed her and said, 'The world throws up mountains, and sometimes we must live in separated valleys.'

And he forded the river and built his hut right in the center of the area which the governor had promised would never again be touched by white men.

When Xhosa spies informed Guzaka that a trekboer had violated the order before it was seven days old, he concluded that the only reasonable response was warfare, so he assembled a party and led his men in a swift charge that engulfed the trespass hut.

Before Adriaan could reach for his gun, assegais flashed and Seena was dead. Swinging the butt of his rifle, he tried to beat off the attackers, but they overwhelmed him, and when his arms were pinioned, Guzaka lunged at him with a spear.

Now Lodevicus became indeed the Hammer, exacting a terrible revenge. Inflamed by the knowledge that it had been he who forced his parents' exodus, he confessed his guilt to no one, but led his commandos far across the Great Fish, rampaging deep into Xhosa lands, destroying forever the hopeful truce the governor had arranged. He burned and slaughtered, and for every cow the Xhosa had stolen, he took back a hundred. With flashing guns he rode against unmounted men armed only with spears, shouting, 'Kill! Kill!'

When he returned to De Kraal he claimed, in his apologetic report to the governor, that he had been lured across the Great Fish by Xhosa infamy, but that the border was now secured for all time. Although he convinced the governor, he was not persuasive with Guzaka, who heard of this report, and now it was he who planned revenge.

'Every kraal must be destroyed,' he thundered at night meetings, and if Vicus van Doorn had sought retribution after the death of his parents, Guzaka wanted nothing less than extermination.

It was, in most respects, as uneven a war as would ever be pursued in Africa, with each side having outrageous advantages. Blacks outnumbered whites by a ratio of one hundred to one and could extirpate any single white farm; but the whites possessed guns and horses, and when the latter galloped through a kraal, they spread such terror that one white gunman could methodically reload and shoot a dozen fleeing natives.

It was a confusion, a clash of interests that could not even be defined. Guzaka was committed to moving his cattle slowly onward, as his people had been doing for eight hundred years, while Lodevicus felt that God Himself had ordered him to establish on the far bank of the Fish River a Christian community obedient to the rules of John Calvin. Land ownership was a constant problem, Guzaka's tribe having always held their land in generality and believing that they were entitled to every lush pasturage reaching to the Cape, while the trekboers cherished a tradition which their Dutch forebears had defended with their lives: that a man's farm merited the same respect as a man's soul.

It was impossible to detect at any moment in this vast struggle who was winning. At the beginning of 1778 Guzaka gained a signal victory by razing the hut of Adriaan van Doorn, but in the spring of that year Vicus retaliated with his famous 'tobacco commando.' Recalling his tactics with the Bushmen, when he used a rhinoceros to wipe them out, he scattered tobacco on the ground a Xhosa war party would traverse; when they bent to grab at this prize, they perished in a hail of lead. In 1779 recognized warfare erupted, black regiments pitted against white field forces, and this was repeated in 1789 and 1799, bloody preludes to the more terrible wars that would continue through the next century.

During the battles Lodevicus never equated the Xhosa with the Bushmen, those troublesome little animals that had to be exterminated. Since the Xhosa were large men like himself, they commanded respect. As he told Rebecca, after one arduous expedition, 'When we pacify them, they'll be good Kaffirs.'

Guzaka had no intention of becoming a good Kaffir. Six separate times he threw his warriors against De Kraal, still convinced that if he could humble it, he could break the spirit of the trekboers, and six times the protecting hills enabled the embattled farmers to repel the invaders, and in the chase that always followed, to massacre them. But on the seventh try, in 1788, Guzaka and his warriors broke into the valley unexpectedly and came upon Rebecca van Doorn as she was going from the cattle byre to her house. With flashing assegais they cut her down, and she died before Lodevicus could reach her.

In contrast to the rage he felt at the similar death of his mother and father, this time he fell silent, brooding upon the harsh fact that God was not giving him the easy victories Dominee Specx had spoken of in those exciting days of revelation at Swellendam. He was also plagued by memories of that morning when his wife and his mother resorted to the Bible to answer the question of what would happen when the Xhosa struck, and the mocking words reverberated: 'An hundred of you shall put ten thousand to flight.' One of that ten thousand, the damned Guzaka, had killed his father, his mother and his wife. The New Jerusalem had not been established on the far side of the Great Fish; the Canaanites had not been expelled from the house of the Lord; indeed, they seemed to be chopping that house to bits.

And then, in the depth of his despair, when it seemed that his mission and that of the trekboers had been completely frustrated, God visited him again, in the person of a girl of nineteen who came riding alone into De

Kraal on the back of a white horse. She was Wilhelmina Heimstra, from one of the irreverent families down by the sea, and her mission was forthright: 'I cannot live in idolatry. I cannot exist without the presence of God.'

'You can't stay here,' Lodevicus said. 'I have no wife.'

'That's why I came,' the girl said. 'When the messenger told us that the Xhosa had killed Rebecca, whom I knew . . .'

Lodevicus, then forty-nine, the Hammer of the frontier, stood silent. In all the territory he commanded there was no predikant to give direction, not even a sick-comforter other than himself, and he did not know what to do. But then he recalled the patristic figures of the Old Testament and how often they had been faced by such problems on their lonely frontiers: older men without wives, heads of families with no one to assist them, and his mind fell especially on Abraham, that first great trekboer:

> And Sarah was an hundred and seven and twenty years old . . . and Sarah died . . . and Abraham came to mourn for Sarah, and to weep for her . . . Then again Abraham took a wife, and her name was Keturah.

It became apparent that God had sent this girl to comfort him in his old age, but the problem of how a Christian marriage could be performed without a cleric was perplexing. 'You cannot stay here, when I have been so demanding of others that they follow in righteous paths.'

'You demanded, Lodevicus, that's true, but no one obeyed. Everyone to the south lives as they always lived. I'm the one who listened and obeyed.'

This was so similar to his own experience, when Predikant Specx, now dead three years, had preached to scores who did not listen, and to one who did, that Lodevicus had to be impressed, and when he looked at the flaxen-haired girl, so smiling and so different from rigorous Rebecca, he was tempted.

It was really quite simple. Wilhelmina pointed out that since she could not very well return to the south, having run away, there was no alternative but for her to stay at De Kraal, and this she did, moving into the room that Adriaan and Seena had once occupied; and on the third night, as she slept, her door opened and Lodevicus said, 'Are you willing to be married of God? Without a dominee to enter it in the books?' and she replied, 'Yes,' and nine months and eight days later the boy Tjaart was born.

In 1795 news reached De Kraal which stunned the Van Doorns, news so revolutionary that they had no base for comprehending it. A courier from Cape Town had dashed across the flats to Trianon, then over the mountains to Swellendam, then along the chain of farms to De Kraal, and wherever he stopped to give his report, men gasped: 'But how could this have happened?'

'All I know, it's happened. Every Compagnie holding in South Africa has been surrendered to the English. We're no longer attached to Holland. We're citizens of England and must be obedient to her.'

It was incomprehensible. These frontier farmers had only the vaguest notions of a revolution in France or of the new radical republic that now controlled Holland. They knew that France and England were at war, but they did not know that the new government sided with France while the old Royalists supported England. They were bewildered when they heard that their Prince of Orange, William V, had fled to London, and from that refuge had ceded the Cape to his English hosts.

And what they heard next was even more confusing: 'The English warships stood in the bay. But Colonel Gordon behaved valiantly.'

'Was he English?'

'No, Scot.'

'What was he doing in the fort, fighting the English?'

'He was a Dutchman, fighting for us.'

'But you just said he was a Scot.'

'His grandfather was, but he came to live in Holland. Our Gordon is a born Dutchman . . . joined something called the Scots Brigade.'

'So the Scots made him a colonel, in Scotland?'

'No, the Scots Brigade is Dutch. We made him a colonel, and he was in command at the Castle.'

'Did he drive away the English?'

'No, he surrendered like a craven. Never fired one of our guns and invited the English to take everything.'

'But you said he was brave.'

'He was. Brave as a tiger defending her young. Because after the disgrace of surrender, he blew his brains out, as a brave man should.'

Lodevicus and Wilhelmina asked the courier to go over the details again, and at the conclusion the courier returned to the astonishing truth: 'This colony is now English. You are all to be confirmed in the ownership of your farms. And English soldiers will be here soon to establish peace on the border.'

When the young messenger rode on, to spread his confusion among the other trekboers, Lodevicus assembled his family, and with little Tjaart upon his knee, tried to pick out the truths that would govern their new life: 'What do we know about the English? Nothing.'

'We know a great deal,' his wife contradicted, bowing quickly to ask forgiveness for her impertinence. 'We know they don't follow the teachings of John Calvin. They're little better than Catholics.'

That was bad enough, but soon a man rode in from Swellendam announcing himself as a patriot, and he lectured the Van Doorns about America, where England had once had colonies and where the citizens had risen in revolt against English rule. 'What I learned when I was in New York,' he said, 'is that when English magistrates come ashore, English troops are always ready to follow. Mark my words, you'll see Redcoats on your frontier before the year is out. They'll not have Lodevicus van Doorn telling them how to handle Kaffirs.'

From a corner of the room, where he had been sitting with Tjaart, Lodevicus spoke of the real problems facing the Dutch in Africa: 'New rulers who have not our traditions will attempt to alter our church, recast it in their mold, destroy our ancient convictions. To preserve our integrity, we shall have to fight ten times as hard as we fight against the Xhosa. Because the English will be after our souls.

'Since they do not speak our language, they'll force us to speak theirs. They'll issue their laws in English, import books printed in English, demand that we pray from their English Bible.' Pointing like an Old Testament prophet at the various children in the room, he said with an ominous voice, 'You will be told that you must not speak Dutch. That you must conduct your affairs in English.'

In later years Tjaart would say, 'First thing I remember in life, sitting in a dark room while my father thundered, "If my conqueror makes me speak his language, he makes me his slave. Resist him! Resist him!"'

And when the Redcoats came, followed by the magistrates, the Van Doorns did resist, and looked very foolish for having done so, because within a few years everything was thrown again into wild confusion, for the same messenger came galloping eastward over the same route with news more startling than the first: 'We're all Dutch again! England and Holland are allies, fighting a man called Napoleon Bonaparte. You can ignore English laws.'

So the Redcoats were withdrawn; Van Doorn's fears proved groundless; and life resumed its orderly way, which on the frontier meant without any order at all. Guzaka continued his raids across the Great Fish, and Vicus hammered him for his insolence. Killing became so commonplace that often it was not even reported to Swellendam.

Restoration of Dutch rule had one curious side effect: a minor but condescending official came out from Holland to inspect the frontier, and upon finishing his tour he commented on the sad deterioration of speech in the colony: 'At times I would scarcely know I was listening to Dutch, the way your people mishandle the language.' From his pocket he produced a slip of paper on which he had noted certain unfamiliar words. 'You borrow words with a most careless abandon, adopting the worst of the native languages and forgetting your good Dutch words.' And he read off neologisms like *kraal, bobotie, assegai* and *lobola*. 'You should purify yourself of such abominations,' he said, proceeding to criticize also the local word orders and mispronunciations. When he was finished, Lodevicus said with some asperity, 'You make us sound like barbarians,' and the visitor said, 'That's what you'll become if you lose your Dutch,' and that was the beginning of the Van Doorn family's distrust of the homeland Dutch. They were a snobbish, metropolitan, unpleasant lot, with no appreciation of what frontier life involved.

When the stranger left, Lodevicus called his group together and said, 'We'll speak Dutch the way we want it to sound.' And the result was that they drove an even deeper wedge between their inherited Dutch language and the new tongue they were building.

Despite these years of uncertainty and war, Lodevicus prospered as a stock farmer, extending his acres far beyond mountain-girt De Kraal. When he required more help and found it impossible to lure Xhosa warriors to work his farm, he grumbled about their arrogance, then drove his wagon to Swellendam, where he purchased slaves: two Madagascans, three Angolans. Because of his visible wealth, he was appointed veldkornet for his district, and he presented a dominating appearance; tall, heavy, white-haired, with whiskers down the sides of his face, he wore substantial clothes, holding up his heavy trousers with both belt and suspenders. When he walked among strangers he strode ahead, with Wilhelmina a respectful four paces behind. In public she always referred to him as the Mijnheer, and he was gratified to see how easily she assumed Rebecca's role as a driving religious force, but of a different quality. She was amiable, forgiving of minor defections and most eager to be of help to everyone who came past the farm. She sang as she worked and was overjoyed to learn that a real church had been built at Graaff-Reinet, ninety-odd miles to the northwest: 'We must report to the predikant for our marriage.'

'I can't leave the farm.'

Wilhelmina laughed. 'You call yourself a trekboer?'

'No more. The Van Doorns are through wandering. This is our home.'

'But Tjaart's got to be baptized,' she said with such simplicity that he could not refuse her. So the older Van Doorn children were left in charge while their stepmother led Lodevicus and young Tjaart to their religious duties.

It was a glorious ride, with Tjaart old enough to recall in later years the vast empty spaces, the lovely hills with their tops flattened. He would never forget the moment when his parents halted their horses some miles south of the new village to observe that extraordinary peak which guarded the site: from flat land it rose very high in gentle sweeps until it neared an apex, when suddenly it became a round turret, many feet high, with sheer walls of solid gray granite. And at the top, forming a beautiful green pyramid, rose wooded slopes coming to a delicate point.

'God must have placed it there to guide us to things important,' Lodevicus said, impressing upon his son the stunning significance of the place, and Tjaart remembered this peak long after he had forgotten his parents' marriage and his own baptism.

The boy now had three memories upon which to build his life: that the Dutch way of life must be defended against the English enemy; that Graaff-Reinet was a center of excitement; and that far to the north, as Grandfather Adriaan had told the other children before he died, lay an open valley of compelling beauty which he called Vrijmeer.

And then, in 1806, when the Van Doorns were congratulating themselves upon having resisted the English threat and preserving the countryside for Calvinism, the final shocking news arrived. Because the ordinary citizens of Holland had joined forces with Napoleon, England felt it must reoccupy the Cape to keep it from falling into French hands, which would cut the life line to India. It was now an English possession, and neither the local Dutch government nor the mother country Holland would exercise further control. All of Lodevicus' apprehensions about suppression at English hands revived.

The Cape, having been a stopping place between Holland and Java during the years 1647 to 1806, now became one between England and India, and the indifference with which Holland had always treated this potentially grand possession would now be matched by English imperiousness.

In these days of change it was inevitable that assessments be made of Holland's long rule, and it was remarked by certain observers—Dutchmen who had known their country's holdings in other parts of the world, Englishmen who had fought in the American war, and Frenchmen who knew many parts of the world—that her rule had been almost without parallel in world history. The home country had allowed neither its royalty, its parliament nor its citizens any voice in the rule of this distant possession; control had rested in the hands of a clique of businessmen who made all decisions with an eye to profit. True, these profits had sometimes been widely distributed, with the government grabbing a healthy share, but in essence the colony had been a narrow business venture.

This had imposed limitations. The surging colonization that marked the French, Spanish and English settlement of North America, with excited citizens pushing exuberantly into the interior, was discouraged in South Africa. Always the Lords XVII preached caution, a holding back lest rambunctious elements like the Van Doorns stray so far afield that they could not easily be disciplined. If one major charge could be leveled against the Compagnie, it was that it restricted normal growth. The borders which should have extended to logical boundaries, perhaps the Zambezi, as Dr. Linnart suggested, never did, which meant that the generic entity never came into being. Absentee businessmen, seeking only profit, do not generate a sense of manifest destiny; indeed, they fear it lest it create movements that get out of hand, and without this spiritual urge, no nation can achieve the limits to which geography, history, philosophy and hope entitle it. Because of Compagnie policy, rigorously enforced through sixteen decades, South Africa remained a truncated state, with only a few single-minded pioneers like the Van Doorns eager to dare the unknown.

Comparison with North American development was inescapable. In 1806, when the English assumed final control, South Africa had 26,000 white settlers. Canada, which had been started at about the same time as Cape Town and on less favorable soil, had 250,000, and the young United States more than 6,000,000. Mexico, a century older than South Africa, had 885,000. The main reason was simple: the Lords XVII were so reluctant to allow any immigration from which they could not immediately profit that during the entire eighteenth century they permitted only 1,600 new settlers to land! Sixteen newcomers a year cannot keep any new society healthy, or an old one, either.

But the Lords XVII were not entirely to blame, for on the rare occasions when they did advocate immigration, the response from those already living at the Cape was uniformly negative. 'It is absolutely impossible,' those holding land reported, 'to introduce any more whites into the country because they could find no livelihood.' What this really meant was that positions of advantage already filled by those in place would not be shared. There were no vacancies for the tough, impoverished migrant seeking a new country and a new chance, because the work that such people would normally start with was already being done by slaves.

In the time it took the cautious Lords XVII to approve inward movement of a hundred miles, settlers in North America had penetrated a thousand. While the Compagnie grudgingly allowed the establishment of a few small towns like Stellenbosch and Swellendam relatively close to the Cape, the free French and English settlers were already building communities like Montreal and Detroit far inland, thus laying the foundation for further movement westward.

It was not that the Dutch were commercially minded and the English not; had the English merchants been allowed to dominate North America they might have duplicated the folly of the Dutch, but English commercialism was never free to dictate to their colonies the way the Compagnie did.

Wherein lay the difference? The Dutch system of government not only permitted but encouraged its businessmen to rule without supervision, whereas the English government, which started in the same direction, quickly turned matters over to Parliament, a free press, and the innate longing for freedom of its citizens overseas. English businessmen might have wanted to ape the Dutch precedent, but the institutions of freedom forestalled them.

In no respect did the Dutch deficiency show itself more clearly than in the field of education and the dissemination of culture. Because the population was meager and dispersed over thousands of square miles, the development of large schools was impractical, and those that were attempted in the towns were atrocious. On the veld, where countless children like the Van Doorns grew up, education was left to a group of vagabond itinerants with only a meager knowledge of reading and writing. Usually discharged servants of the Compagnie, these inept clerks roamed from farm to farm dispensing their rudimentary wisdom while they supplemented their income with anything from composing love letters to making coffins. The trekboer Van Doorns were not alone in producing children who were illiterate; one traveler estimated that seventy-five percent of the colony's children were unable to read.

This was not surprising, because the Compagnie ran the colony for nearly a century and a half before it allowed the colonists to import a printing press, or publish any kind of book, or print a newspaper. In Canada these things happened almost automatically, and America could not have been the same without its itinerant printers, inflammatory broadsides and contentious newspapers; but it was precisely such potential troublemakers that the Compagnie sought to inhibit, and did.

In such a climate there could, of course, be no institutions of higher learning, and here the comparison with other colonial settlements was shocking. The Spaniards, who conquered Mexico in 1521, had by 1553 opened a major university. They took Peru in 1533 and sponsored a university in 1551. The English, who landed at Plymouth Rock in 1619, had a functioning college at Harvard in 1636, and before the revolution started in 1776 they had sixteen great colleges in operation. During the entire Dutch rule the Compagnie never even came close to starting a college.

Of course, bright boys at the Cape sometimes found their way back to Leiden or Amsterdam, where splendid universities were available, but an emerging nation needs speculative intelligence bred in local institutions; they provide the fine yeastiness that produces strong new ideas applicable to local situations. The entire history of South Africa might have been modified if there had been a strong school system topped by a university staffed with local luminaries dedicated to the creation of a new society. Instead, fresh ideas either did not germinate or were stamped out.

Much of the blame must be shared by the church; its leaders were convinced that they could trust only predikants trained in the conservative centers of Holland, and they were terrified of the possibility that a Cape seminary might arise to sponsor alien ideas. Missing in South Africa were those gaunt Pilgrim ministers of New England who cut themselves off from European dictation and initiated a local approach to religious problems.

'The Night of Darkness in which the South African nation had its birth,' some historians would describe this period of the trekboers, when the merchant mind stifled the scientific, creative and political urges of the citizens.

But there was another side to this coin, and it shone brightly. A few Dutch children, through assiduous teaching within the family, did gain an education almost comparable to that available in the average European country, and although the Boers lacked an Oxford or a Harvard, they did have their own unique university, and its curriculum was one of the most effective in the history of education. They had a massive Bible, which accompanied them wherever they went; their curriculum was the Old Testament, whose narratives predicted each event that might arise. There were, of course, many trekboer families like the Rooi van Valcks and the Adriaan van Doorns who ignored the Bible, through either illiteracy or indifference, but the majority studied and obeyed.

Few nations were ever as solidly indoctrinated in one group of principles as the Dutch in South Africa, and this begat a Volk—a people—with tremendous driving force, self-assurance and will to persist. With constant support from this theological university, which each man could carry with him as he moved, the Dutch colony became a conservative, God-fearing state, and so it would remain despite English occupation, English persecution, English wars and the constant threat of imposed English values. In South Africa the Old Testament triumphed over the university because it was the university.

On one major point Lodevicus was wrong. When he thundered 'South Africa is Dutch and will always remain so' he misrepresented the composition of his white community: Dutch ancestry, forty percent; German ancestry, thirty-five percent; Huguenot component, twenty percent; and although this would later be denied by Van Doorn's descendants, a Malay-Hottentot-black component of at least five percent. This creative mix had produced a handsome, tough, resilient Volk infused with the trekboer spirit, and no English governor would have an easy time trying to discipline them into the ways he wanted them to go.

VI. The Missionary

T HE Englishmen who came so late to South Africa, and with such
pervasive power, were men of courage, as the Saltwoods of Salisbury,
that cathedral town southwest of London, proved. On Midsummer
Day 1640, after three years of daring enterprise among the Spice Islands,
Captain Nicholas Saltwood of the little ship *Acorn* came sailing into Plymouth harbor with a bulging cargo of nutmeg, clove and cinnamon. It was
so valuable that it made all his partners—who had counted him dead, and
their investments lost—men of substantial wealth.

His own fortune was increased when he sold the *Acorn* within two hours
of anchoring. When his partners, eager to send him forth again, asked why
he had acted so precipitately and against his own best interests, he snapped,
'You invested money. I invested my life against pirates, storms and Portuguese forts. No more.'

When he was alone with his wife, Henrietta, who had spent these three
years in near-poverty, he kissed her vigorously and led her in a small dance
about their meager rooms: 'Years ago, sweets, I saw the cathedral at Salisbury, and I swore that if I ever reached the Spice Islands and made my
fortune, you'd have a home in the meadow, beside the River Avon. And
you shall!'

With his bags of silver and his drafts upon the spice merchants of
London, he packed Henrietta in a diligence and his household goods in two
drays. Taking his position at the head of his armed guards, he led the way
through the lovely lanes of southern England until he reached that broad
and noble plain in the middle of which stood Salisbury Cathedral. There,
on the right bank of the Avon, he purchased nine good acres and the seven
swans that guarded those gentle waters.

Like many a prudent Englishman, Captain Saltwood planted a garden
before starting on a house, but since he was a man of vigor he preferred
trees, and he located his so that they framed the handsome cathedral on the

far side of the river. To the left he placed nine cedars, well rooted, whose dark limbs swept the ground. In the center, but not exactly so, he planted eleven strong chestnuts; in spring they would be white with flowers; in autumn, heavy with fruit for children to play with. Well to the right and safely back from the river, he started a group of slender oaks; in time they would be massive of trunk and stout of limb, and under them swans would nestle when they came ashore.

Sentinels he called his trees, and that name was given the house that later rose among them. It was notable as reflecting an older style of construction known as hang-tile. It was two-storied, with the lower walls built of conventional brick; nothing unusual about that. But the top story was faced in a most peculiar manner: instead of using brick, ordinary roof tiles had been hung vertically! The effect was resoundingly fourteenth century, as if the roof had slipped, abandoning its accustomed place to come down and cover the walls. The true roof was of thatch, sixteen inches thick and carefully trimmed like the hair of a boy about to leave for choir.

Generations of Saltwoods had gathered under the sentinel trees to discuss family problems while contemplating the spire of the cathedral; under strictures laid down by Captain Nicholas, they continued to be cautious in protecting their investments but daring in investing their profits. About 1710 a Timothy Saltwood had had the good fortune of making the acquaintance of the Proprietor, that gentleman of august lineage who owned much of the region, and before long Timothy was serving as the Proprietor's agent, an occupation of dignity which passed from one Saltwood to the next.

One afternoon during the first years of the 1800s, Josiah Saltwood, the present master of Sentinels, sat with his wife on a bench beneath the oaks and said, 'I deem it time we meet with the boys.' He paused, as if matters of gravity impended, then added promptly, 'Nothing serious, of course. Merely their entire future.'

His wife laughed. 'They're all about somewhere. I could summon them.'

'Not just yet. I must ride to Old Sarum with the Proprietor. The election, you know.' And with his wife at his side, and the swans following, he walked across the lawn to where his horse was being saddled.

The beautiful cathedral had not always stood in its present location. In the early days of Christianity in England a much different cathedral-castle-fort, keystone to security in this part of the country, had rested on a low hill some two miles to the north, and here devout bishops exercised as much leadership as the masters of the castle would permit. It was called by a bewildering variety of Roman and Saxon names, but in time it came to be known as Sarum, and from it came that set of orders and regulations for worship known as the Use of Sarum, which would be adopted by much of the English church.

The first cathedral, begun in 1075, was a large, rugged building in the French manner, set down within the walls of the castle-fort; between the two groups of occupants, clergy and soldiers, so much friction arose that rupture was inescapable. Rarely has a formal complaint been more comprehensive than that issued by Pope Honorius III in 1219 when he summarized the difficulties of his priests at Sarum:

> The clergy cannot stay there without danger to their persons. The wind howls so furiously that priests can hardly hear each other speak. The building is ruinous. The congregation is so small it cannot provide repairs. Water is scarce. People wishing to visit the cathedral are prevented by the garrison. Housing is insufficient for the clergy, who must buy their own houses. The whiteness of the chalk causes blindness.

The bishop solved these difficulties by offering to move his cathedral from Sarum to a vacant field well to the south, where the town of Salisbury would belatedly arise. The exchange worked and the cathedral at Sarum was abandoned, to the pleasure of the bishop; he owned the vacant field and sold it to the church for a nice profit.

With the loss of its cathedral, Sarum declined. Once it boasted more than two thousand residents, then one thousand, then five hundred, then only a handful, and the day came in the early 1700s when it had almost none. Cathedral and castle alike were in ruins.

But tradition dies hard in England, and in rural England, hardest of all. When Parliament convened in the late 1200s, Sarum as a major settlement and support of the king, was awarded two seats; in its heyday it sent some mighty men to London. With the disappearance of its cathedral and its population, those seats, in any other country, would have been lost. But not in England, where precedent was prized. If Sarum had once been entitled to two seats, Old Sarum, as it was now called, was still entitled to them, and these empty fields with barely a single human being residing on or near them retained the right to send two members to Parliament and arrogantly exercised that right.

It became famous as 'the rottenest of the English rotten boroughs,' referring to those former towns, now abandoned or much reduced in population, which clung to ancient privileges on the principle that 'Parliament represents land, not people.' So that even in these early years of the nineteenth century one-fourth of the members of Parliament came from boroughs which in common sense should have returned nobody, and a shocking percentage of these were from boroughs like Old Sarum, which contained almost no one.

When a sitting Parliament was dissolved and a new one authorized, who selected the men to represent a rotten borough, especially when it had no voters? Custom said that whoever owned the land reserved the right to nominate whom he wished to represent it. What made this system repugnant to people of sensible intelligence was that an empty spot like Old Sarum could have two members of Parliament while great towns like Birmingham and Manchester had none.

At Old Sarum, in the first decade of the 1800s, an election was held for members of the new Parliament that would soon be convening, and the Proprietor rode out to the site in his carriage from Salisbury Town, while his factor, Josiah Saltwood, forty-nine years old, accompanied him on horseback. They started from the south side of River Avon, crossed the stone bridge five centuries old, passed the marvelous cathedral with its tall, clean tower, and made their way through the cluster of inns from which the stagecoaches departed for London. As they left the North Gate they entered the lovely rolling hills that led to Old Sarum, and after a pleasant rural passage, came to the south side of the rise on which the ancient ruins stood.

They did not climb that hill, but stopped at an elm tree whose spreading branches created a kind of shady amphitheater. Stepping carefully from his carriage, the Proprietor, an old man with white hair and kindly blue eyes, looked about him and said, 'Rarely have we known a finer voting day, eh, Josiah?'

'It was thoughtful of the old Parliament to end when it did,' the factor agreed.

'I can remember storms,' the old man said, recalling voting days when rain dripped from the elm. 'But our work never takes long, be praised.'

The coachman led his horses some distance from the tree, and after another servant placed a collapsible table on cleared ground, steadying the legs with twigs, the Proprietor unfolded a set of legal papers.

'I trust you find everything in readiness,' Saltwood said.

'Seems to be,' the old man said. He wore white side whiskers and showed a military bearing, for he had served his nation in many capacities abroad. It was curious that he had never elected to take one of his Parliament seats for himself; always he had picked other men who showed promise of good judgment, as had his father before him, so that whereas Old Sarum was indeed a rotten borough and an offense to reason, it had sent to London a succession of notable politicians, most of whom had never set foot in Old Sarum or even Salisbury. Indeed, none had ever lived within fifty miles of the dead town, but they had accepted the nomination as their right and had performed well. William Pitt the Elder, one of the outstanding English statesmen of the previous century, had been able to function as independently as he did only because he was sent to Parliament from Old Sarum, whose invisible electors he did not have to appease.

'Who's it to be this time?' Saltwood asked.

'A surprise, and not a surprise,' the Proprietor said, taking from his pocket a private memorandum. 'Dear old Sir Charles is to keep his seat, of course. He never speaks in the House, proposes no bills and might as well stay at home, but he's never done any harm, either, and many of us deem him the best member in recent history.'

The name was properly entered in the report of the election that Saltwood would forward to London. 'It's with the second name we get our surprise,' the Proprietor said, thrusting the paper at his factor. 'See for yourself.'

And there it was, in second position in the memorandum: 'Josiah Saltwood.'

'Me, sir?'

'You've a better head than most, Josiah, and I wish to reward it.'

The factor gasped. A seat like this, from one of the rotten boroughs, could cost an aspiring politician as much as a thousand pounds, and it might have to be paid anew periodically, but considering the money a clever man could come by if he held a seat, the cost was minimal. To have such a boon handed to one was only to be dreamed of, and here came a gift he had not even solicited.

'You're the man for the job,' the Proprietor said. 'But I want you to take it seriously. During the first four years it'll be better if you say nothing. Just listen and vote as I instruct, and after four or five years, you might begin to do things. Nothing flashy. You're not to be noticed. Men from the provinces are apt to make asses of themselves and don't last. Show me one from Old Sarum who ever spoke much and I'll show you one who lasted only a session.'

Saltwood very much wanted to ask, 'How about William Pitt?' but had the good sense to keep his mouth shut. Indeed, as he stood silent in the manner the Proprietor liked, the old man said, 'Even Pitt, he talked too much. Much better if he'd sat silent more often.'

With the necessary papers signed, and endorsed by Saltwood, the old gentleman signaled for the horses, and when he was safely inside his carriage for the ride back to the cathedral for evensong, he flicked his hat to his factor, riding behind, and said, 'We've done a good day's work.'

Behind them stood the great elm, its branches covering an immense spread. For three hundred years this venerable tree had witnessed elections like this, but never one conducted so speedily. A significant percentage of Parliament had been elected by one man in the course of seven minutes.

When Josiah Saltwood assembled his family under the oak trees to inform them of the surprising event at Election Elm, his wife Emily did not try to anticipate what her husband was about to announce; her task had been the rearing of four sons, and it had occupied her exclusively. Her principal recreation had been walking the mile or so to the cathedral to listen to the choristers; she did not care much for the sermons.

The four boys came to the meeting with eagerness; for some time they had been speculating on what they must do to find a settled place in life, and any sudden change in their father's position excited them for the possibilities it might uncover for them. Peter, the eldest, had come down from Oxford some years back and was serving as a kind of junior clerk for the family estate while vaguely learning the tasks involved in his father's role as factor to the Proprietor. He was not accomplishing much.

Hilary Saltwood, twenty-four years old that day, presented a serious problem. As a younger son he could not look forward to inheriting either the Saltwood house or his father's occupation. He must look to the army or to the church for his life's sustenance, and up to now he had decided on neither. He had done well at Oxford and could possibly have aspired to work in India, but he had dallied, and now all positions for which he might have been eligible were filled by young men with greater concentration. In some respects he was brilliant; in others, quite confused, so that the family often speculated on what might become of him.

Richard Saltwood, however, though he had done poorly at Oxford and left with the most meager degree awarded, had bought his way into what was always called 'the Gallant Fifty-ninth,' a regiment stationed in India. His father had told the Proprietor, 'That boy was destined for the army

from birth, and I'm damned relieved he's found a place!' Then, with proper
deference, he added, 'Thanks principally to you.' It had been the Proprietor
who had put up the money to purchase the commission and who had
recommended young Saltwood to the commanding colonel. Richard would
soon be on his way to India and was delighted with the prospect.

It was young David who was most worrisome. He had managed to stay
at Oriel in Oxford—the college to which Saltwoods had gone time out of
mind—only one term, after which he was sent down 'with prejudice,'
meaning that he need not reapply when and if he ever learned Latin. To
be dismissed from Oriel was rather shameful, for even the most backward
scholar should have been able to get a degree from that feckless college. If
a lad had real promise, he went to Balliol; if he sought preferment, he went
to Christ Church; and if he wanted to cut a figure, he went to Trinity. If
he came from some rural cathedral town like Salisbury, with little Greek
and less social footing, he went to Oriel. Indeed, the archetypal Oriel
student was a Saltwood from Sentinels, and had been for over a hundred
and fifty years. What with four Saltwood boys of child-producing age, it
looked as if the college was assured of an endless future supply of its
preferred students.

What to do about David, no one knew. As his father once said, 'If a boy
can't handle it at Oriel, what on earth can be expected of him?'

Saltwood coughed as his family sat in the picnic chairs, awaiting his
revelations. 'It's rather surprising news,' he said modestly. 'I'm to be the
new member of Parliament from Old Sarum.'

'Father!' It was difficult to separate what the various boys were saying,
but that they were honestly pleased with this turn of fortune was apparent,
and they were gratified not only because of what it might mean to them,
but especially because their father had been such a hard-working, responsible citizen.

'No better choice!' Richard said. Striking the pose of a politician arguing
a point, he cried, 'Sirs, sirs! I beg of you! Attention, please.'

'When do you leave for London?' Peter asked, but before his father
could reply, young David leaped to his feet, ran to his father, and embraced
him.

'Good on you!'

Quietly Mrs. Saltwood said, 'Let's hear your father's plans.'

'They're simple,' Josiah said. 'You and I leave for London immediately,
find a flat, and stay there for the season.'

'I shouldn't like to leave the trees,' Emily said, pointing to the cedars
and chestnuts.

'We've new fields to consider,' he said abruptly, and his wife spoke no
more.

'Who's to mind our interest?' Peter asked hesitantly, afraid lest his
question seem like begging.

'You, Peter. And you're to become the Proprietor's manager. He asked
for you.'

'And I'm off to India,' Richard said brightly. 'How about you, Hilary?'

The second son blushed, for he was being importuned to disclose his
plans before he was entirely ready, but in such a conclave, when issues of

gravity were being decided, he could not refrain. Very softly he said, 'I've been wrestling . . . for many days . . . I've been away, you know, in the fields mostly . . .'

'And what did you decide?' his father asked.

Hilary rose and slowly moved among the oaks, coming back to stand before his mother. 'I'm to be a missionary,' he said. 'God has called me out of my confusion.'

'A missionary!' Emily repeated. 'But where?'

'Wherever God sends me,' he replied, and again he reddened as his brothers gathered to congratulate him.

'I'm going overseas, too,' David broke in.

'You're what?' his father cried.

'I'm emigrating. Four chaps I know in London . . . we're off to America.'

'Good God, those rebels!'

'It's a settlement scheme. Ohio, some place like that. I'm sailing next month.'

'Good God!' his father repeated, aghast at the prospect of a son of his in such a wilderness. 'David,' he said seriously. 'We'll be at war with those rebels within a year. As soon as I get to Parliament, I'm to vote for war. The Proprietor said so.'

'I'll be fighting your troops somewhere in Ohio, wherever that is.'

'When will you be back home?' Emily asked.

'It'll take some years to get the plantation going,' the young man said. 'Slaves hoeing the cotton, and all that. But I'll be back.'

'You must never take arms against England,' Josiah said gravely. 'You'd be shot for a traitor. And there will be war.'

'Father, America's a sovereign nation. Don't send a lot of silly troops like Richard—'

'Brother against brother!' Richard cried. 'Wouldn't that be jolly?'

So under the oak trees at Sentinels in the County of Wiltshire the Saltwoods reached decisions on the destinies of their sons. Peter, who had brains, would take charge of the family business. Hilary, who had character, would go into the ministry. Richard, who had courage, would enter the army. And young David, who had neither brains, nor character, nor courage, would emigrate to America.

The shock caused by Hilary's announcement that he intended becoming a missionary instead of a proper clergyman grew into a firestorm when his family learned that he proposed joining the Missionary Society operated not by the Church of England but by the dissidents, and more especially, the radical Congregationalists. 'You'll ruin your prospects,' his mother warned, but he was adamant, assuring his family that when he reported to the training headquarters at Gosport, not far from Salisbury, he would not be required to convert to the rebellious faith. 'I'll serve my time with Jesus overseas and come back to Salisbury,' but even as he promised this he announced that he was not going to be a part-time missionary but one wholly dedicated to the cause: 'I've elected to go for a complete theological education, terminating with ordination as a full-fledged minister.' His father, now in Parliament and a resident of London, encouraged him in this decision: 'In for a penny, in for a pound. Choose the highest possible, because one day, when this missionary foolishness is over, your mother and I expect to see you dean of Salisbury Cathedral.' At tea one afternoon, during the later stages of his training, his mother said, 'Hilary, you must discharge your duties quickly, because the Proprietor has promised most faithfully that when you're through and safely back in the Church of England, he plans to exert every influence for your assignment as dean of the cathedral.'

Hilary's brothers approved heartily: 'We could sit here under the oaks and look across the meadows and tell each other, "That cathedral's in good hands." Do hurry and finish with the savages, wherever you go.'

He would have made a flawless dean, tall, slightly stoop-shouldered, his head bent a little forward as he walked along the cloisters, as if he were looking for something a few yards ahead, diffident, rather brilliant in his studies and of deep conviction religiously. He should have stayed at home, progressing from one small living to another until his reputation as a sound young man was established, then moving into the larger positions from which he would write two incomprehensible books. Such books were a prudent step in English advancement; no one bothered to read them, but one's superiors were gratified that the effort had been made. And in due course, fortified with credentials from the noble houses of the county, including the Proprietor's, he would move on to professor at Oriel and then the deanship.

What had interrupted this pleasant, routine progression? Hilary Saltwood had religious insights far deeper than those of the ordinary Oxford graduate, and he had paid attention to those ringing commandments of Paul in the New Testament in which young men were charged with the duty of spreading the gospel. Indeed, his favorite book in the Bible was Acts, in which the birth of a new religion, and especially of a new church, was portrayed so vividly. With Paul he had traveled the Holy Lands and penetrated to those surrounding nations which knew not Jesus and where Christianity began as an organized religion.

He felt a deep affinity with Paul, and a thorough knowledge of Acts prepared him for the Pauline letters that outlined the next steps in the spread of Christianity. His own discovery of Christ was less dramatic than Saul's conversion into Paul on the road to Damascus, but it had been real. He was not, like others he knew, turning to religion because as a second son he had nowhere else to turn; the church was by no means his secondary choice. Long before his father had been nominated for Parliament he had been on the verge of announcing his commitment to Jesus, and would have done so regardless of his family's fortunes.

His conversion was deep if not spectacular, and he enjoyed the opening months of his ministerial education; the London Missionary Society, as it was being called in some quarters, was becoming famous in various parts of the world, even though it had been in existence for barely a decade. Its stern, intense young devotees, coupled with the older, practical artisans, had penetrated to remote areas, often serving as the cutting edge of civilization as it reached unsettled lands. The LMS was a revolutionary force of the most persistent power, but in his early months at Gosport, Hilary did not discover this.

Instruction was principally in the propagational theories of the New Testament, an extension, as it were, of Acts and the missionary letters of St. Paul. He enjoyed the abstract philosophizing and profited especially from the droning lectures of an older scholar who expounded the basic theories of the New Testament, instructing him in facts that sometimes surprised him:

> 'The Book of Acts is significant for two reasons. It was written by the same hand that gave us the Gospel According to St. Luke, and that unknown author is extremely important because he is probably the only non-Jew to have composed any part of our Bible. All the other authors were rabbis like Jesus and St. Paul, or ordinary laymen like St. Matthew, the tax collector. In Acts we receive the first message about our church from a person like ourselves.'

But apart from knowledge, there was also deep conviction. These mature ministers truly believed that it was the duty of young men to 'go forth unto all the world' to spread the word of God; they were convinced that unless this word was taken to the remotest river, souls worthy of salvation might be lost.

For these simple English clergymen there was no predestination whereby all men were sorted out as either saved or damned; such belief would make missionary work a futility. The Society taught that every human soul was eligible for salvation, but this could be attained only if some missionary could instruct it. The task was to deliver Christ's precious message to savages who were in darkness, and few young Englishmen of this period who absorbed that teaching ever doubted that they personally could bring this salvation.

There was much prayer, and many learned discussions as to how salvation might be conveyed, and crude geography lessons outlining the problems to be encountered in Africa or the South Seas, where the young men were to go. It was studious and pious and soporific. But when Reverend Simon Keer, after having served four years on the frontier, burst into headquarters, every aspect of Hilary Saltwood's life was altered.

Keer was a Lancashire activist, son of a baker and lacking a university education. He was a short, round man, not over five feet two, with an unruly mop of red hair and a pair of wire spectacles that he kept shoving back onto the bridge of his nose. His station had been South Africa, a land that Hilary had scarcely heard of; vaguely he knew that through some accident or other a vast area had fallen under English rule. The students were spellbound when Keer, bounding up and down like the bobbin on an active line, launched his impassioned speeches:

> 'There is a land down there in our care which cries for the word of God, a land of black souls thirsting for redemption. Lions and hyenas ravage these people by night, slavery and corruption by day.

We need schools, and hospitals, and printing presses, and trusted
men to teach farming. We need roads and proper houses for these
children of God, and dedicated men to protect them from cruel
abuse.'

After he had listed another dozen things the natives required, one young
man whose father was a butcher asked, 'Don't we need churches, too?' and
Reverend Keer replied, without halting the flow of his impassioned oratory,
'Of course we need churches.' But in the days that followed he never again
mentioned any need for them. Instead, he captivated his eager listeners by
his explicit accounts of what it was like to be a missionary:

'I landed at Cape Town with my Bible and my dreams, but before
I preached my first sermon I traveled three hundred miles over
almost impassable mountains, across arid lands and up and down
ravines where there was no road. I lived for weeks with white men
who spoke not a word of English and black men who knew nothing
of Jesus Christ. I slept on the barren veld with only my coat to cover
me and ate food that I had never seen before. The first task I was
called to perform was aiding the birth of a baby girl, whom I baptized. The first service I conducted was under a thorn tree. When
I finally reached my post I was alone, with no house, no food, no
books and no congregation. All I had was another thorn tree under
whose spreading branches I conducted my second service. Young
men, in South Africa a thousand thorn trees wait to serve as your
cathedrals.'

He had an overpowering effect upon the young dreamers of the LMS, for
with his exhortations to face the practical problems of the world he combined a devout conviction that what he had done, and what they must do,
was missionary work over which God exercised a personal supervision.
Again and again he cited those stirring commands issued by St. Paul when
he struggled with his frontiers, and as he lectured, the reality of the New
Testament materialized before the eyes of his listeners.

It was not till the third week of his fiery declamation that he began to
confide the real problem that had brought him back to London. In his
preliminary lectures he had disposed of the physical world of the missionary
and in subsequent ones he had treated knowingly the theological basis of
conversion. Now he sought to instruct his future replacements in the realities:

'I care not whether you have planned to work under the palm of the
South Seas or the frozen wastelands of Canada. I care not what
commitments you have made to your parents or your ministers here.
We need you in Africa, and I implore you to dedicate yourselves to
the salvation of this continent. Especially do we need you in our new
colony, for nowhere else on earth are the challenges to Christ's
teaching more clearly dictated. A dozen men like you, dedicating
your lives to the task, can set patterns for a new nation.'

Whenever he spoke on this theme, and he returned to it constantly, he became like a man possessed of special insights: his voice soared; he seemed to become taller; his eyes flashed. He was engaged in a kind of spiritual Armageddon and conveyed his thundering sincerity to any listener. In the fourth week, after a series of such flights, he told the young missionaries what the great problem was:

> 'Slavery! The Dutch who have occupied the Cape for a hundred and fifty years are among the finest people on earth. They're all good Protestants, much like the Presbyterians of Scotland. They tithe; they listen to their predikants; they support their churches; but they have fallen into the great evil of slavery. For generations they have been owners of imported slaves, and now the wonderful brown and black people with whom they share the land they also hold in cruel bondage, and it is our solemn, God-given mission to rescue all these souls from that bondage. If you join me in this task, and I pray that you will, you must expect that men will revile you, and misrepresent your motives, and even threaten you with bodily harm. But you will persist. And God will strengthen you, and in the end we shall build an English nation of which God will be proud.'

In the fifth week, realizing that he had been painting too somber a picture of the missionary's life in South Africa, he stopped ranting, and began to amuse his listeners with affectionate stories of his life there, using an exaggerated North Country dialect:

> 'Half an hour before dawn comes a rrrroar! It's a lie-yon, but he's retreating from the sunrise. You learn to know that by the manner in which his voice rrrrecedes. Comes a knock on your tent, and it's the little girl informing you that her baby sister is about to be born and Mother says can you hurry. There are days on the veld with hunters and nights under the starrrrs with more lie-yons and protea flowers, bigger than your mother's washbasin.'

What the young men never forgot, however, were the two brief sermons Keer delivered in the Kaffir language—in them they heard for the first time the click sounds which the Xhosa had borrowed centuries before from the Hottentots. He explained to them that he had mastered the language in order to compile a dictionary, from which a translation of the Gospels for the Xhosa would soon be made.

His first sermon dealt with the Good Samaritan, and since he played all the roles, dancing about the stage, his red hair flying, and since he altered his voice and manner for each of the participants in the parable, the missioners could easily follow the story without understanding the words. But his second sermon dealt with Christ's love for all people, and now there were no clues to its meaning except the overwhelming conviction that filled the room when he stood on his toes, eyes closed, deep voice throbbing with the repeated words *Jesus Christ.*

As he reached the climax of his preachment a hush fell over the room, and when the last click sounds had echoed, Hilary Saltwood knew that his destiny lay in South Africa. Waiting till the other students had left the room, he stepped forward to the podium, but before he could speak, Reverend Keer jumped down and held out his hands: 'Laddie, you've decided to join the Lord's work in Africa?'

'I have.'

'God be praised.'

That night, after he had written explanatory letters to his parents, he felt an enormous sense of having been set free. He had been impelled toward this decision both spiritually and intellectually, and would never question it. It had been God's miracle that sent Simon Keer at this particular time, and Hilary thanked Him for that with a full heart.

But before he fell asleep a most curious reflection flashed across his mind: In all the time I've been here, I've rarely heard the Old Testament mentioned. We're men of the New Testament, the personal followers of Jesus and St. Paul . . .

When Hilary completed his studies, Parliament was not in session, so before sailing for South Africa he returned to Sentinels on Salisbury Plain, and there he sat under the oak trees with his parents and his two brothers. Peter was now in full charge of family affairs and spent half his time on them, the other half devoted to the interests of the Proprietor. Richard had his commission in the Wiltshire regiment and was on leave prior to embarking for India; he joked that when he was a general he would stop off at Cape Town to meet with his brother, the bishop. Their father did not appreciate such remarks, for he still insisted that what Hilary ought to do was serve routine time as a missionary, then hurry back to enter competition for the deanship of the cathedral: 'When a young fellow has backing as strong as the Proprietor's, and as vigorous . . .'

One day the entire family went for a picnic at Old Sarum, where Josiah showed them the ancient elm under whose noble branches he had been elected to Parliament, and the older Saltwoods remained there while the three brothers climbed the low hill to view the ruins. It was both remarkable and moving that they could pick out the lines of those very old buildings which represented a heroic age of England, but after the first moments they paid scant attention to the ruins, for this was a cloudy day, and while they were standing among the fallen rocks a portion of the sky cleared, allowing great shafts of light to fall upon Salisbury to the south, and there the cathedral stood, bathed in radiance, a most noble monument, perhaps the finest in all England, situated on its almost empty meadow with no smaller buildings encroaching, and beyond it, outlined in the same accidental light, the three clumps of trees at Sentinels.

'Oh, look!' Peter cried. 'It's a signal!'

'For what?' Richard asked.

'For us. For us Saltwoods.' Grasping the hands of his brothers, he cried in excited syllables, 'Wherever you go, you're to come back here. This is always to be your home.'

Richard said, somewhat gruffly, 'It looks a far distance from India.'

Peter ignored his brother's dampening comment and asked, in a flush of emotion, 'Hilary, will you say a prayer for us?'

It seemed a most natural thing to do when three brothers, who had shared an old house beside a river of heavenly beauty and in the shadow of a great cathedral, were parting: 'Dearest God, Thy home is everywhere. Ours is here. Let us cherish both.'

'Damned fine prayer, Hilary,' Richard said, and the outing ended, but four days later their father proposed a more serious expedition, one that would require horses and considerable preparation.

'You'll be gone for some time,' he said to Hilary and Richard. 'I've spoken to the Proprietor and he wants to come along. Says it may be his final visit.'

'To where?' Peter asked.

Their father had a welcome surprise. Through the centuries when Salt-woods sent their sons to Oxford, the boys invariably went by carriage north through Wiltshire and then easterly through Berks, a route that carried them past one of the noble monuments of the world, and generations of the family had come to look upon this place as symbolic of their fortunes, so that occasionally, when no lad had gone north to university for some decades, the Saltwoods would convene and go that way without excuse, simply to renew their acquaintance with Stonehenge.

The monument lay only eight miles north of Salisbury, and a visit could be completed within a day, but the Saltwoods liked to pitch a tent there overnight so as to catch the dawn rising over the ancient stones. This expedition consisted of the Proprietor, still traveling by carriage, with the four Saltwood men on horseback and five servants following with tents, the food and the flagons of wine. The road was a rough one, not much traveled, since most people leaving Salisbury headed either east to London or west to Plymouth. Only the occasional scholar on his way to Oxford went north to Stonehenge, or someone headed to the port at Bristol or the towns in Wales.

Toward the close of day Josiah said, 'I rather think that at the rise of the next hill we shall see it,' and he told the boys to rein in their horses and allow the Proprietor to be in the lead when Stonehenge was first sighted.

'There they are!' the old man cried, and to the east on a small mound which caught the first rays of the rising sun and the last light of day stood the hallowed stones, some fallen, some leaning, some erect in the location they had occupied for more than four thousand years. It was an awesome place, and no Englishman conversant with his nation's history could fail to be humbled upon approaching it.

'D'you think it was the Druids?' the Proprietor asked as the group surveyed the somber monument.

'It was here centuries before anyone heard of Druids,' Josiah suggested.

'My own thoughts,' the Proprietor said. 'Sturdy bastards, whoever they were.'

Hilary had always been enchanted by Stonehenge. He had seen it first as a boy of ten on a family excursion much like this. He had seen it again when he accompanied Peter to Oriel, and of course on his own travels to Oxford. It was timeless, old beyond counting when Jesus was born, and it reminded men of the long sweep of history and the periods of darkness. The stones turned red as the sun dipped to its horizon, shimmering in the fading light.

'We'll pitch the tents over there,' the Proprietor suggested, and that night they slept within the shadowed circle.

Long before dawn the Proprietor was up, cursing the night and abusing his servants for not having lighted candles. 'I want to see the sun striking it,' he grumbled, and as the Saltwoods joined him he said, 'I'm sure they used to conduct human sacrifice here. At the solstices, anyway. Probably killed off two old men like me and three young virgins. Let's go to the sacrifice.'

And they stood among the ancient stones, hauled here from sources far removed, as the sun broke upon them.

'D'you think you could offer us a prayer, Hilary?' the old man asked.

'Let us bow our heads,' the new minister said, and as day came in earnest he prayed: 'God, Who marks our passage back to Salisbury and to India and to South Africa, and also to America where our brother hides, watch over us. Watch over us.'

The Proprietor said that while these were fine words, he would have appreciated some mention of the fact that this might be his last journey to the stones, whereupon Hilary uttered another short prayer, instructing God on this additional matter, and the old man was appeased.

They spent that day inspecting the fallen rocks and making cautious guesses as to how old they might be, but as dusk approached, Hilary experienced a surge of religious emotion and moved apart from the others. Standing among the untoppled pillars, a gaunt, angular, stoop-shouldered figure who might well have been an ancient priest of this temple, he whispered, 'O God, I swear to Thee that I shall be as faithful to Thy religion as the men who erected these stones were to theirs.'

He landed at Table Bay one morning in the spring of 1810, expecting to be greeted by representatives of the LMS who would probably spend some weeks indoctrinating him in his duties and perhaps even accompanying him to his place of assignment. Instead, as soon as he stepped ashore he was grabbed by a sturdy Dutch farmer with very broad shoulders and full beard who asked in heavily accented English, 'Is it true, you're a disciple of Simon Keer?'

Modestly Saltwood conceded that he was, whereupon the farmer pushed him away, muttering, 'You ought to be ashamed, spreading lies.'

He was not allowed even one night's rest in Cape Town, for at noon he found himself in a caravan of sorts heading eastward to a river on the far side of the mountains, where he had been directed to launch a mission. During the arduous journey he learned much about South Africa but even more about Reverend Keer, for wherever he stopped, people asked about the red-headed Lancashire man. The few Englishmen spoke of him with obvious regard, the many Dutchmen with unmasked contempt, and one night he asked an English missionary's wife to explain this contradiction.

'Simple,' she said. 'Simon Keer always stood up for the Hottentots and the Xhosa.'

'Isn't that our duty? To bring them to Jesus Christ?'

'Reverend Keer treated the Hottentots more like workmen in England.

Always fighting for their rights. Decent pay. Decent homes for them to live in. Things like that.'

'Did the Dutch object?'

She put down her cooking pans and turned to face Hilary. 'You must keep one thing in mind, if you're to be an effective missionary. We English have been here four years. The Dutch have been here a hundred and fifty-eight. They know what they're doing and they do it well.'

'Keer says that what they do so well is slavery.'

She placed her two hands on Hilary's and pleaded, 'Don't use that word. Reverend Keer was given to exaggeration. He lacked education, you know.'

'He's translating the Gospels.'

'Oh, he was excellent at identifying himself with the Xhosa. He could stay up all night transcribing their words.'

'I thought it was my duty to do the same.'

'To bring them Christ, yes. To become their advocate against the Dutch, no.'

'You speak harshly.'

'The Xhosa killed my son. They'd have killed me, too, except that a Dutch commando arrived in time.'

'And you stay?'

'It was an incident. We were at war and our troops had killed their people. Simple retaliation.'

'Aren't you afraid?'

'I am, and you will be, too. And pray God that you don't get caught up in it.'

As he penetrated farther into the country he became increasingly aware of how different the long-established Dutch were from the lately arrived English, and in his first letter home he shared his observations with his mother:

> The Dutch speak of themselves in three distinct ways. Those in the environs of the Cape call themselves Dutch, although many of them have never seen Holland or ever will. In truth, they speak harshly of the old country, holding in contempt those real Dutchmen who came out from Holland to lord it over the locals with sneers and assumptions of superior education. Some of these long-time Dutch have taken themselves a new name, for they are more of Africa than of Europe. 'We are *Afrikaners,*' they say, but where I am traveling now these Afrikaners are named *Boers* (farmers). But farther east toward the lonely perimeter of the country, where the roughest of the Dutch dwell, they call themselves *trekboers* (migrating graziers), which is appropriate, for they are constantly moving on with their herds, until I am reminded of Abraham and Isaac. My mission is to be established in the lands of those trekboers who have stopped their wanderings.

At his next halt, where only Boers lived, Hilary received his harshest view of Reverend Keer: 'Arrogant, stupid man. Kept saying he loved the Xhosa and the Hottentots, but every action he took damaged them.'

'In what way?'

'Made them dissatisfied with their lot.'

'What is their lot?'

'At school in England, did they teach you the Book of Joshua?'

'I've read it.'

'But have you taken it to heart? God's story of how the Israelites came into a strange land? And how they were to conduct themselves there?' It was obvious to the Boer listeners that the new missionary knew little of Joshua, so the oldest farmer took down his huge Bible and slowly leafed the pages until he came to the familiar instructions, which he translated roughly for the newcomer:

> 'You shall not marry with the daughters of Canaan . . . You shall keep yourself apart . . . You shall destroy their cities . . . You shall hang their kings from trees . . . You shall block up their graves with stones, even to this day . . . You shall take the land, and occupy it and make it fruitful . . . One man of you shall chase one thousand of them . . . You shall keep yourselves apart . . . And they shall be your hewers of wood and your drawers of water . . . And all this you shall do in the name of the Lord, for He has commanded it.'

Closing the big book reverently and placing his hands upon it, he stared directly into Hilary's eyes and said, 'That is the word of the Lord. It is His Bible which instructs us.'

'There is another part of the Bible,' Hilary said quietly, leaning his thin shoulders forward to engage the debate.

'Yes, your Reverend Keer preached quite a different message, but he was an idiot. Young friend, believe me, it is the ancient word of God Himself that we follow, and you will break your teeth in this country if you contradict it.'

Across the southern plains of Africa, wherever he stopped, Hilary found himself engaged in argument over the merits of Simon Keer, and the Boers were so forceful in their rejection of the little redhead that in his quiet moments Hilary began to read Numbers and Joshua, finding in them not only the passages which his first Boer mentors had cited, but scores of others which applied directly to the position of the Dutch who had come into this land like the Israelites of old, who had entered their land of Canaan. The parallels were so overwhelming that he began to see local history through Dutch eyes, and this was a salvation when he opened his own mission.

The spot selected for him lay on the left bank of the Sundays River, four hundred miles from Cape Town. When he reached it, not a building stood, not a roadway existed. The river, suffering from drought, carried little water, and there were no trees. But the spot itself was congenial, perched on a broad bend of the river and graced with level fields acceptable to plowing. In the distance was a forest with an abundance of usable wood; and at hand, enough stones to build a city. Hilary, visualizing what this bleak spot might become, named it from a passage in the twentieth chapter of Joshua, where God instructs His people to erect cities of refuge to which any accused could flee and be assured of temporary safety:

> And on the other side Jordan . . . eastward they assigned . . . Golan
> . . . that whosoever killeth any person at unawares might flee thither,
> and not die . . . until he stood before the congregation.

This will be Golan, my city of refuge, Hilary thought, and when the last members of his caravan disappeared, leaving him majestically alone in the heart of a strange land, he prayed that he might be allowed to build well.

The first night, as he lay on the ground close to his belongings, he listened to strange sounds, and the darkness of Africa assailed him with a wild discordance, a sense of awe and anticipation rather than fear. When he awakened at dawn, he found a group of brown people watching him, squatting on their haunches a hundred feet away. For months there had been rumors that a missionary was coming.

Hilary beamed at the sight. Surely the Lord Himself had brought this little gathering into the arms of His servant Saltwood. Dusting himself off, he rose to greet them, overjoyed when one man spoke to him in broken English.

'We stay with you. We your people now.' His name was Pieter, son of that Dikkop who had traveled with Mal Adriaan. It was ten years since he had lived with the Van Doorns; he had run away after a beating for eating a melon from the family garden. He had drifted from farm to farm, working just enough to avoid being classified as 'Vagrant Hottentot,' which would allow his being assigned arbitrarily to any farmer who wanted him.

In truth, Pieter was a man who saw virtue in idleness; he could happily pass an entire day with his back against a tree, eyes firmly shut.

But before sunset that first day the Hottentots had shown Hilary how to dig a foundation to keep out rain, and by the second nightfall they had cut enough saplings to frame out a dwelling. Hilary saw in his imagination how Golan should look: rows of huts facing each other, a meeting hall and a church to close off one end of the rectangle.

He was pleased with the rapid growth of his little community—six Hottentots to forty within three weeks—and within a short time Hilary and his followers had the mud-and-clay walls of a mission church in place. Before the thatching of the roof was complete he preached a message of dedication inside the little structure. Having mastered several words of the Dutch-like language these people spoke, and some Hottentot with its click sounds, he delighted his congregation by offering the benediction in their language. In the days that followed he heard members of the mission saying gravely to one another as they worked, 'Peace be unto you.'

Peace was a commodity almost unknown. Young Xhosa warriors persisted in raiding cattle from white men's farms, and not long after Hilary's first sermon English troops, fortified by a Boer commando, had launched a massive attack against the black men, driving twenty thousand of them back across the Great Fish River and liberating, as they phrased it, vast herds of cattle. The gallant leader of this rout would be honored by having a newborn town named after him: Grahamstown.

Hilary was untouched by these events; but it grieved him that after six months he had not met one Xhosa, and he began to fear that he had made a mistake in locating Golan here. During his studies at Gosport he had imagined himself bringing Christianity to black savages, wrestling with their pagan beliefs and finally welcoming them to Jesus. Instead he was surrounded by brown Hottentots, more than ninety in the huts that faced the rectangle, while all the Xhosa lurked far across the river, a gang of cattle thieves.

In his reports to the LMS he called his flock 'my Hottentots,' knowing that few were of the pure strain; they ranged from light, yellow-skinned half-Malays to very dark half-Angolans. They were not inclined to hard work, and a distressing number loitered about the mission doing nothing. But Hilary always remembered the name he had given this place, Golan the refuge, and he believed that these 'mild and peaceable folk,' as he wrote of them, merited all the sanctuary they could find. Many had come to him with terrible tales of beatings, chains, and years of labor without pay from Boers who made their lives a misery. Simon Keer's impassioned indictment of the colonists echoed in his ears, and he saw it his duty to succor the weak.

Even his hopes for the Xhosa soared when a black man finally came to Golan, an elderly fellow from a kraal to the east. He proclaimed himself to be a Christian, stating in halting English that he had been baptized by a missionary with red hair called 'Master Keer,' and he indicated that his village contained several other blacks who had been converted by 'our dear little man who could speak Xhosa.'

His Christian name was Saul, and Hilary promptly sent him back to Xhosa lands to spread joyful news about Golan, and because of Saul, at the end of six months the mission was home to one hundred and forty Hottentots and twenty Xhosa. The latter taught Hilary the traditions of their people, and he developed respect for the ease with which they adjusted to life at Golan. As he worked with them he found himself constantly referring to the practical instructions he had acquired from young Simon Keer, rarely to the theological indoctrination of the older LMS clergymen. 'Missionary work,' Keer had predicted, 'is one-tenth disputation, nine-tenths sanitation.'

The first white man Hilary met was a Boer living at a remote spot twenty-eight miles to the northeast, across hills that separated the Sundays River from the Fish. He rode into Golan one afternoon, a tall, rough-clad, white-haired old man who looked like someone from the early books of the Bible, his beard trembling in the wind. 'Name is Lodevicus,' he said in halting English. 'Lodevicus van Doorn.' He had come to warn Hilary not to allow any Hottentots from the north to take refuge at Golan.

'Why not?' Hilary asked.

'They . . . my laborers . . . they signed papers,' he growled, obviously disliking the necessity of speaking in a foreign tongue. 'They to work . . . not pray.'

'But if they come seeking Jesus Christ . . .'

Lodevicus showed his irritation that Saltwood made no effort to address him in Dutch: 'If you here . . . missionary . . . damnit . . . learn Dutch.'

'I should! I should!' Hilary agreed enthusiastically, but to continue the conversation it was necessary to find someone who had both languages, which put Lodevicus in the awkward position of lodging a complaint against Hottentots through the agency of a Hottentot. It was fortunate that Lodevicus did not recognize the melon thief, and insensitive to the impropriety, went on talking, with Pieter listening respectfully and saying 'Ja, Baas' at least once a minute.

'Baas say, "His Hottentots not come seek Jesus. They run away from work his place." '

'Tell him that even so, if any of his workmen were to come seeking refuge with me . . .'

No sooner had the interpreter started this sentence than Lodevicus interrupted.

'Baas, he say, "My goddamn workers come here, no trouble for you. I come gettim." '

'Tell him that if any Hottentot or Xhosa seeks Jesus Christ . . .'

Once more Lodevicus issued a string of threats, only some of which the Hottentot bothered to repeat. So this first meeting between the Boer and the Englishman ended in disarray, with Lodevicus shouting as he remounted his horse that Saltwood was no better than that damned idiot Simon Keer. He sputtered what sounded like curses, and Hilary was told: 'Baas say damn-fool Master Keer come back, he meet him with sjambok.'

'Assure him that Reverend Keer is safely in London and will not be seen again in these parts.' When this was delivered, Lodevicus directed the Hottentot to say, 'Damn good thing.'

As a Christian, Hilary could not allow his first acquaintance with a neighbor to end so poorly, and with a complete change of attitude he said to the Hottentot, 'Ask Mijnheer van Doorn if he will join us in evening prayer?'

This sudden switch to the Dutch *mijnheer* softened the old man somewhat, but only for a moment, for he soon realized that the prayers would be conducted in English, whereupon he spat: 'I pray Dutch church.' And with that he galloped off, even though night was almost upon him.

And that was the way things stood between the mission station of Golan and the nearest white man to the north until the end of the first year—when the Reverend Simon Keer burst upon the South African scene with a reverberation that would last for two centuries, making his name accursed. He did not appear in person, which was prudent, since he would have been whipped, but a booklet that he published in England did arrive by ship. It bore the pejorative title *The Truth About South Africa,* and was a compilation of accusations against the Dutch so horrendous that the civilized world, meaning London and Paris, simply had to take notice.

It charged the Boers with having already killed off the Bushmen, annihilating the Hottentots, and beginning to abuse the Xhosa—expropriating their land, stealing their cattle, and killing their women and children. It was especially harsh in allegations that the Hottentots and Coloured brethren were being tricked into slavery and denied ordinary decencies. It was a blanket indictment, its charges so melodramatic that they might have been ignored had he not added one accusation which more than any other inflamed the Christians of England and Scotland:

The Boers refuse to allow their Hottentots to attend mission schools or to convert to that one true religion which could save their immortal souls. Indeed, one gains the impression that the Boers refuse to believe that their laborers have souls, and each day that dawns sees Jesus crucified anew in order for the Boer to gain a few more shillings through the toil of these mild and peaceable people forced into a servitude worse than that of the true slave.

Such charges ignited action throughout England, especially since that nation now had responsibility for the governance of South Africa, and protests of the most vigorous force were launched. What made government intervention inevitable was Reverend Keer's closing statement that he personally could indict a hundred Boers for forced enslavement, criminal abuse and even murder.

When the four dozen copies of *The Truth About South Africa* reached the Cape and were distributed, with Dutch translations being rushed to the frontier, a sullen resistance developed. Even prospering townsmen in Cape Town and Stellenbosch who had clearly benefited from the English takeover protested that Keer had unjustly maligned the entire colony. And the frontier Boers! Each man felt that he was being specifically accused, and wrongfully. Pamphlets were prepared, rebutting the absent missionary, and practically the entire population combined to defend South Africa's reputation.

But the power of an inspired missionary to inflame English public opinion would always be great, and while at the Cape a few people were defending South Africa, in London a multitude called for action, and before long, commissions were on their way to the Cape to look into Keer's charges, and the mournful day came when formal accusations had to be lodged against some fifty Boers, who were commanded to stand trial before judges who would circulate throughout the colony. The Black Circuit, this exhibition would be called, and in due course it would reach Graaff-Reinet, several days' ride to the northwest, and there Lodevicus van Doorn would be tried for physically abusing his Hottentots, starving them and denying them the right to attend religious services. He was also accused of murder.

Before the Black Circuit reached Graaff-Reinet, Lodevicus, convinced that no judge appointed by the English would accord a Boer justice, swallowed his pride and rode back to Golan, where he found that Hilary could now speak moderately good Dutch. The two men conducted an impassioned conversation.

'All I ask, Saltwood, is that you come with me, now. Look at my farm. Talk with my Hottentots and slaves.'

'I'll not be party to this lawsuit.'

'It's not a lawsuit. It's a charge of murder.'

'And other things, if I hear correctly.'

'And other things. Trivial things. And it's those you must inspect.'

'I'm not a witness, Mijnheer van Doorn.'

'All men are witnesses, Dominee.'

The sudden use of this Dutch appellation caught Hilary's imagination, and he had to admit that in a situation so grave, all men were witnesses, so that even though Van Doorn had been an unpleasant man, if he now appealed for help, it had to be given. On the spur of the moment he said, 'I'll ride with you, but I'll not testify in court.'

'No one asks you to,' Lodevicus said gruffly.

Leaving Golan in care of Saul, Hilary left for the north, finding a ride with Van Doorn a moving experience: 'These vast lands with no markings —how do you find your way?'

'The look of things,' Lodevicus said, and Hilary thought: That's what I'm being asked to judge—the look of things.

As in the days when Mal Adriaan wandered these lands with Dikkop, this Van Doorn and his English clergyman formed a bizarre pair, the first an old man with heavy frame and white whiskers, the second a tall and gawky young man with the open face of a child. They were unlikely associates, Boer and Englishman, with different heritages, different attitudes toward life and vastly different religions, one Old Testament, the other New. Yet they were joined in a forced association that would prove, for better or worse, inescapable.

When they entered the low hills that separated the mission station from the farm, a wholly new vista opened, the vision of a land immense in its dimensions, softly varied in the rise and fall of its low ridges, but ominously grand in the substantial mountains that rose to the north. They seemed to warn Saltwood: This is a greater land than you have envisaged. The challenges are vaster than Simon Keer defined.

At the crest of the last rise Lodevicus reined in his horse and pointed down to a small valley hemmed on all sides by hills of varying height. It was as tight a little world as Saltwood had ever seen, a secure haven cut by a river which brought fruitfulness to the rolling fields. The river entered the area at an opening to the southwest, ran diagonally across the meadows and exited at a pass in the northeast. If ever a frontier settler had a farm that was secure, this was it.

'De Kraal,' Van Doorn said gruffly but with evident pride. 'Safe place for keeping cattle.'

'Have you cattle?'

'The Hottentots have taken our herds north to graze. But this kraal is for human beings. A nest within the hills.'

Hilary turned in his saddle to inspect the land, and from his experience with meadows on the Salisbury Plain estimated that De Kraal ran five miles west to east and something less than three north to south. Making such calculations as he could, he said in astonishment, 'You have nine thousand acres down there.'

'Yes,' said Lodevicus. 'This is the land of the Van Doorns.' And he rode down into his little empire as if he were Abraham riding a camel to Canaan.

The three days Hilary spent at De Kraal were a revelation, for he was in an enclave removed from any outside influence and ruled by one man. It was into this fortress that English justice presumed to force its way. Lodevicus had a wife, of course, and Hilary was surprised when he met her, for she seemed not at all awed by her austere husband, even though he was at least thirty years older. Wilhelmina van Doorn was a big, amiable woman who obviously set the laws to be observed in her house. She had one son, Tjaart, a square-bodied young farmer with a lad of his own.

De Kraal had nine Madagascan and Angolan slaves, few by comparison with the intensively farmed vineyards near Cape Town, but it also had thirty-two Hottentot and Coloured workers and their families, some whose ancestors had become affiliated with the Van Doorn family generations ago. By law they were contract laborers duly registered at Graaff-Reinet; whether they were de facto slaves was moot. No outside observer like Saltwood would be allowed to ascertain the facts.

'Thirty-two Hottentots?' Saltwood asked. 'Isn't that a lot?'

'They have to herd our cattle sixty miles north of here.'

'Sixty miles! Doesn't that put them on other people's land?'

'There are no other people.'

Lodevicus invited Saltwood to inspect every aspect of De Kraal, where the slaves and Hottentots ate and where they slept and worked. Since Hilary now understood much of the Dutch-Portuguese-Malayan-Madagascan dialect spoken between master and servant, he was able to conduct his investigations without the interference of Van Doorn. He was especially eager to interrogate the Hottentots, for Golan's people had said that the Boers were constantly abusing them, but when the herders were brought in he found them a jovial lot who loved their horses and the open range.

'How much do you get paid?' he asked the lead man.

'Paid? What is paid?'

'Wages. Money.'

'We got no money.'

'Not now, but how much does Mr. Van Doorn pay you?'

'He not pay nothing.'

Saltwood started again: 'You work? Seven days a week? How much do you get paid?'

'Baas, I no understand.'

So with great patience the missionary explained that everywhere in the world, when a man performed a certain task, like herding cattle . . .

'We like cattle . . . sheep . . . big land.'

'But what do you get paid?'

After many false starts Hilary discovered that they got paid nothing in cash. They did receive their clothes, and their horses, and their food, and when they fell ill, Mrs. Van Doorn medicated them.

'Are you free to leave De Kraal?' Hilary asked.

'Where would we go?'

Three times Saltwood questioned the Hottentots, trying to ascertain whether they were in fact slaves, but he never reached a satisfactory answer, so he broached the subject with Van Doorn himself: 'Would you call your Hottentots slaves, like the Madagascans?'

'No! No! They can leave any time they wish.'

'Have any ever left?'

'Why should they?'

Hilary dropped this line of investigation, turning his attention to the slaves, whom he found to be in good condition but surly in manner, unlike the Hottentots who worked the free range. One of the Madagascan men showed scars, and when Saltwood inquired about them, he found that the man had run away, been recaptured and punished.

'Why did you leave?' he asked.

'To be free.'

'Will you run away again?'

'Yes, to be free.'

'Will you be punished again?'

'If he catch me.'

When Hilary asked Van Doorn about this, the Boer could not mask his disgust: 'He's my slave. I paid good money for him. We can't let our slaves get the idea they can run away at will. Of course they have to be punished.'

'You seem to have whipped him rather harshly.'

'I disciplined him.' When he saw how Saltwood flinched, he said sharply, 'Dominee, in the old days he'd have had his nose cut off, his ears, one hand if he persisted. These are slaves, and they must be disciplined, as the Bible says.'

Apart from the Madagascan, the Van Doorn slaves and Hottentots showed evidences of good treatment, and Saltwood said so, whereupon Van Doorn confessed: 'We live at the edge of the world, Dominee. We spend years without seeing a predikant. We must have slaves to operate the farm. We must have Hottentots to run the cattle and sheep. We rely upon instructions from God and the direction we receive from this.' He indicated a huge old Bible, and when Saltwood took it in his hands, and pried open the brass clasps, and saw the heavy pages within, and the one on which Van Doorns had for a hundred and fifty years kept their family records, he was awed by the simple righteousness of this frontier Boer, and knew that if Van Doorn asked him to be a witness at his trial in Graaff-Reinet, he would out of simple decency have to at least testify as to his character.

He was little prepared for what Lodevicus asked him to do now: 'Dominee, we live alone, terribly alone. Would you baptize our grandson?'

Saltwood stiffened. 'At the mission you refused to pray with me.'

'I was a fool,' the old man said. 'Wilhelmina, come in here!'

The smiling Wilhelmina came into the room, bowed to the missionary, and stood with arms akimbo. 'Tell the dominee,' her husband said. 'Tell him what I told you when I reached home.'

'From where?'

'From the mission,' he snapped. 'When I got home from that visit to the mission.' When she stood bewildered, he said more gently, 'When I told you I had refused to pray with him.'

'You said you were a damned fool, and you were.' Smiling at the visitor, she started to retire, but her husband said, 'I've asked him to baptize the boy, and he's agreed.'

'I do indeed,' Hilary said, and the little boy, struggling with a puppy, was brought into the room, and water was provided by one of the slaves, and the solemn rite was performed. But as it ended, Reverend Saltwood noticed that the little girl who had fetched the water lingered, twisting her fingers in her gray dress, and it was in this sanctified moment that he met the child Emma, daughter of the Madagascan.

She was ten that year, a bright child often perplexed by what she witnessed. Her face had that sooty-blackness which seemed almost blue, and was so attractive, as if God had said, 'Emma, since you're to be black, why not be really black?' Her face was composed of handsome interlocking planes, so that when she smiled, showing her white teeth, it broke into

lovely patches of light and shadow. When she was six and living on the farm
from which Lodevicus had purchased her parents, she had been instructed
sketchily in Christianity by Simon Keer and had from him acquired a vision
of a world somewhat different from the one the slaves knew. Now, as the
Van Doorns took their baptized grandson out in the yard to resume play
with his puppy, she lingered to ask Reverend Saltwood, 'Can I come to your
mission?'

'You are a slave, my child,' he said softly. 'You belong to Baas.'

'Baas, he follow me, cut off my nose?'

'You know he wouldn't do that. But you also know what happened to
your father when he ran away. If you run away, you'll be punished.' As he
spoke he recalled the words of Jesus: 'Suffer the little children to come unto
me'—and he knew that he was being less than heroic in failing to support
this child. But his reflections were broken by a shout from one of Van
Doorn's Hottentots: 'Riders! Riders! From north!'

A bailiff from the Black Circuit sitting at Graaff-Reinet had come to
inform Lodevicus that he must appear before that court. 'For what?' the old
man blustered, whereupon the nervous little Dutchman who had joined the
English service puffed out his chest and in faltering voice recited the
charges: 'Enforced slavery of Hottentots. Abuse of slaves. Murder of a
slave.'

'By God, I will destroy that judge,' the old Boer cried, but the bailiff
whispered in rapid Dutch, 'Lodevicus Hammer, you have friends at Graaff-
Reinet. Many Boers owe their farms to you. You'll never hang.'

'But I'm to be dragged into a Kaffir court . . .'

'Please, Lodevicus, I'm just starting in my job. Don't make trouble.'

It was humiliating, but the old fighter realized he must comply, so after
giving orders to his son and bidding Wilhelmina farewell, he came to
Saltwood and said humbly, 'Dominee, you must ride with me.'

Despite his earlier resolution, Saltwood now faltered, and asked weakly,
'Why?'

'To testify. You've seen me. You've seen my slaves.'

'But the charge of murder—'

'Ask the slaves.' And Lodevicus was so obviously shaken by his arrest
that Hilary wanted to help in some way. Certainly he could testify that by
Boer standards, the De Kraal slaves and Hottentots were reasonably
treated, and he was willing to say so to the court, but he was not willing
to be called on to aid any man charged with murder. Van Doorn, seeing his hesitation and guessing as to its cause, said again, 'Ask them.'

So Hilary took the girl Emma aside. 'Do you know who God is?'

'I do,' she said in a childish voice.

'And do you know what hell is?'

'Master Keer, he tell me.'

'And do you know that if you don't tell the truth, you will go to hell?'

'Master Keer tell me.'

'The old baas, has he ever killed a slave?'

The little girl's dark face froze into a scowl, her soot-black features
betraying her agitation. Finally she said, moving nervously from foot to
foot, 'He beat my father. Sometimes he thrash my mother. But he never kill
nobody.'

'Do the slaves ever talk at night, Emma?'

'All the time.'

'Do they ever speak of a killing? Long time ago? When the old baas angry?'

'No killing.'

Saltwood was impressed by the girl's willingness to speak but also by her obvious fear, so he asked abruptly if she would fetch her parents, and when they appeared, as nervous as their daughter, he asked them in their dialect, 'Has Baas ever killed a slave?'

They looked at each other, then at their daughter, after which the husband said, 'He beat me too much. He beat my wife sometimes.' He showed Saltwood the scars that he had shown before. They were gruesome and deep.

'But has he ever killed a slave?'

'No.' When he said this, his wife tugged at his shirt sleeve and they whispered for a while.

'What's she saying?' Hilary asked Emma.

'About the other time.'

'What other time?'

And the father told in broken, agitated words that on another farm, where they had lived prior to being purchased by Van Doorn, the master had killed a slave, and had been arrested at the insistence of Simon Keer, and had been fined two pounds. Also, his right to own other slaves was taken away, which was why these Madagascans had been sold to De Kraal. There had been murder, but never by Van Doorn.

'Does your father know who God is?' Hilary asked the little girl.

'No.'

'Then he does not know what hell is, either?'

'No,' the girl said. 'But he knows what true is. There was no murder.'

Saltwood went to the door and called to Van Doorn: 'I'll ride with you.'

The Black Circuit at Graaff-Reinet was an explosive affair. Inspired by Simon Keer's incendiary reports, a score of indictments had been issued based on the accusations of missionaries, Hottentots and Coloureds, all charging the Boers with gross abuses. Granted, there had been serious evils: Hottentots had been forced to work on after their legal contracts had expired; their women and children had been threatened with violence if they left; slaves had been excessively flogged; there had been murder.

But many of the charges were wild, without foundation, so that what should have been a serious judicial inquiry became a shambles. The countryside rallied so strongly in support of the Boers, and perjured itself so willingly, that no demonstrable lawbreakers could be found guilty, while dozens of reasonably honest frontiersmen like Lodevicus van Doorn were publicly humiliated by being forced to stand in the dock and answer to preposterous accusations.

Three Hottentots were brave enough to testify against Van Doorn, but what they said was so chaotic that the court had to be suspicious, and when Reverend Saltwood stepped forward to defend him, the court had to be attentive. The verdict was 'Not guilty,' but this absolved nothing, for the

Boers who had been so abused by the English courts would never forget their humiliation. Thus the Black Circuit joined that growing list of grievances, some real, some fancied, which would be recited in every Boer family for the next century and a half.

The English were mortified that one of their own ministers had given testimony enabling a Dutchman to escape punishment: 'He was guilty as sin, you know. Indictment said so.' A rumor was floated that Saltwood had defended the Boer in anticipation of favors to come: 'Perjured himself, of course. They're taking up a collection for him right now, among the Boers.' It was agreed that Hilary Saltwood must be ostracized insofar as the English community at the Cape was concerned: 'From now on he's the darling of the Boers.'

How wrong they were! The Van Doorn–Saltwood armistice lasted only two days, for when they rode back to De Kraal, Wilhelmina van Doorn met them at the gate, crying, 'Lodevicus! Emma's run off.'

'Get her back.'

'We don't know where she's gone.'

'Set the Hottentots tracking. They'll find anything.'

Saltwood found it difficult to visualize that little child in her gray dress running anywhere, but if she was indeed gone, he was fairly sure why: 'Probably went to the mission.'

As soon as he uttered these words he knew they were ill-advised, for Van Doorn's look of petty irritation turned to one of hatred: 'She cannot do that.'

'But if she wants to know about Jesus.'

'I teach my slaves and Hottentots all they need to know about Jesus.'

'But, Mijnheer van Doorn—'

'Don't Mijnheer me!'

'Obviously, this child hungers for Jesus. It's been four years since she heard about him and still she—'

'Where did she hear about Jesus?'

'At the other farm. From Simon Keer.'

What a sad mistake to have spoken that name! Van Doorn began shouting Dutch phrases so fast that Hilary could not follow, then jutting his white-whiskered face forward and growling, 'Any slave of mine has dealings with Simon Keer, I'll beat her till she's—'

He stopped, aware of the dreadful thing he had been about to say, and aware also that his new friend, Saltwood, knew how the sentence would have been completed. It was then, at the moment of their triumphant return from the Black Circuit, that the veil dropped between these two men.

Saltwood was first to speak: 'If Emma has run to Golan, she will have my protection.'

'If my slave is at your mission, you can be sure I'll come and take her.'

'Van Doorn, don't fight the law.'

'No law gives you my slave. I paid good money for her. She belongs here.'

'She belongs in the care of Jesus Christ.'

'Get out!' Throwing open the door, he ordered Saltwood to be gone, but when the latter headed for the hill, he summoned two Hottentots and directed them to speed west, keep out of sight, and fetch the slave girl Emma from the mission.

Saltwood, anticipating such a maneuver, traveled at forced speed, but when he reached Golan he found the place in an uproar, for the Hottentots had preceded him and were in the process of carrying off the little girl, who was weeping and struggling in their arms.

Without hesitating, Saltwood dashed to his quarters, grabbed his gun, and confronted the kidnappers: 'Drop your hands. Back on your horses and ride home.'

'Baas say bring Emma.'

'I say take your hands off her.'

'No! She belong us.'

At this moment Emma broke loose and ran to Saltwood, throwing herself at him, and when he felt this child seeking his protection, he determined to rescue her at any cost; and as the Hottentots reached out to seize her, he fired his gun over their heads, frightening them and terrifying himself. Fortunately, the two brown men scuttled to their horses and galloped away, for had they lunged at Saltwood again, he would have been quite incapable of firing at them, even had his gun contained a second chamber.

Hilary now placed the child with Saul's family, where she began learning the alphabet, the catechism and the refulgent promises of the New Testament. She proved an able student, as gifted in singing as in sewing, and before long it was her glowing black face and gleaming teeth that showed in the front rank of the mission choir.

She was practicing under the trees one evening when Lodevicus van Doorn rode in like a white-haired avenging angel, two guns resting carelessly on his saddle. 'I've come to fetch you, Emma,' he said quietly.

'She will not go,' Saul said, trembling at the sight of the menacing guns.

'If you try to stop me, Kaffir, I'll blow your head off.' Lodevicus did not touch either of the guns, but he did move his horse closer to Emma.

With a dignity many of the blacks acquired at the mission, old Saul moved to protect the child, whereupon Lodevicus raised one of his guns.

'For God's sake!' a voice cried from one side. 'Are you mad?'

It was Saltwood, coming to lead the choir. Unarmed, he walked directly to the muzzle of the gun, looked up at Lodevicus, and ordered: 'Ride back to De Kraal.'

'Not without my Madagascan.'

'Emma lives here now.'

'I have an order from the court at Graaff-Reinet which says—'

'Such orders apply to runaway slaves, not to little girls seeking Jesus.'

Van Doorn's neck muscles stood out like the vines of a squash. 'You goddamned meddler . . .'

'Old friend,' Saltwood said quietly, 'get off that horse and let's talk.'

'I'm going to take my slave.'

'Come here, Emma,' and the little girl in her blue mission dress ran to clasp her protector.

Van Doorn was infuriated. Emma was his property, worth a great deal of money, and he had a proper order directing her return. If he shot this Englishman now, the frontier Boers would support him and to hell with the

English, but as he raised his gun, Saul stepped quietly in front of the missionary and the child, extending his arms to protect them, and there was something in this gesture which caused the Boer to hesitate. If he fired now, he would have to kill three people, and one of them a little girl. He could not do such a thing.

But as always, Saltwood said the wrong words: 'If you kill me, Lodevicus, the entire force of the British Empire will hunt you down to the ends of the earth.'

From his saddle the Boer burst into a contemptuous laugh. 'You English. You goddamned English!' Without further comment, he wheeled his horse and headed back to the veld. He would ride through the night rather than spend it with fools like this English missionary.

When word circulated through the farms of the Boer community that the English missionary Saltwood had stolen the slave girl Emma and provided her refuge at Golan, consternation spread among them, and meetings were convened to which participants might have to ride for fifty miles. At each the principal orator was the patriarch Lodevicus the Hammer, who saw more clearly than most the dangers men like him faced.

'I can see the inevitable,' he ranted. 'The English want our Hottentots to live like Boers. Our lands are to be whittled down till we crowd together like Kaffirs. And mark my word, one day our slaves will be taken from us. And then our language will be outlawed and we'll hear predikants delivering their sermons in English.'

A farmer from near Graaff-Reinet, who had seen the fairly amicable relations that existed there between Boers and English officials, said, 'False fears. We can abide the English till they leave again.'

Quiet happenings proved that he was wrong. This time the English invaders showed no sign of quitting the country, and indignation ran through the isolated community when three new clergymen were assigned to remote districts; all were Scotsmen.

'You'd think we had no predikants of our own,' the farmers cried, truly distressed at this radical change.

'It's England pressing us under the heel,' Lodevicus announced, and he refused to send any further tithing to the church.

The fault was not England's. The government knew that frontier congregations longed for predikants who could speak Dutch, and those in charge wanted to send out such men, but there simply were none. Considering all the colonization under way throughout the world at this period, South Africa was the only major settlement in which organized religion failed to provide enough ministers to accompany the outward thrusters. When this deficiency became apparent, the government did the next best thing: it imported large numbers of young Scots Presbyterians who made the easy jump from John Knox to John Calvin; they were fine public servants, men of great devotion and a tribute to their religion.

Lodevicus, of course, was unaware of England's good intentions in this matter, and even if they had been explained to him, he would have damned them; all he was concerned with was that the new predikants were from an alien country, and would be bringing alien ideas. It was clear to him that they had been inserted to destroy Boer influence; one element of his gloomy prediction was being proved true.

Since there were no schools anywhere near De Kraal, Lodevicus was not personally involved in the next scandal, but he was outraged when he heard from farmers in settled areas like Swellendam that English was invading the schools.

'Shocking!' one man told a group of Boers. 'My son Nicodemus goes to school on Monday—what does he find? A new teacher. An Englishman who tells him, "From now on we speak English," or something like that. Nicodemus, he don't speak English, so how does he know?'

Bitter resentment developed among the Boers, and many a family, after the Bible reading at night, reflected on the warnings Lodevicus had uttered: 'It's coming around the way he said. First our church, then our school. Next we'll be forbidden to speak Dutch in court.'

This prediction had scarcely been voiced when a farmer near Graaff-Reinet who wanted to lodge a complaint about a boundary was informed that he must submit his brief in English. This provoked further argument, with Lodevicus resuming his role as prophet: 'Most sacred possession a man can have, even surpassing the Bible, I sometimes think, is his native tongue. A Boer thinks different from an Englishman and expresses that thinking in his own language. If we don't protect our language everywhere, church and court, we surrender our soul. I say we must fight for our language as we would for our lives, because otherwise we can never be free.'

Lodevicus, like all the Van Doorns, was obsessed with freedom, but only for himself. When one Englishman argued: 'Historical parallelism, old man. When the Huguenots came here, you Dutch were in command and forbade them to speak French. Now we're in charge, and we want you to speak English. Only fair.'

At such reasoning the old man exploded: 'Goddamn! This place was never French! Only Dutch! It will never be English either. You learn the Dutch of the Afrikaner, damn you.' He would have chastised the visitor had not others intervened. The Englishman sought to apologize, but Lodevicus was caught in a mighty rage and, his neck muscles bulging, he shouted, 'Never, never will our soil be English.' Storming about the room like a Biblical patriarch, he thundered, 'You will have to kill me first . . . and then my sons . . . and then their grandsons . . . forever.'

It was against this background of rebellious thought that Lodevicus the Hammer rose against the English in 1815. Tjaart was absent with the herds when a horseman came riding up to De Kraal late one evening. 'Van Doorn! Lodevicus van Doorn!' he shouted, leaping from the saddle.

The white-bearded old man stepped outside. 'Ja, broeder, wat is dit?'

Breathlessly: 'Hottentots are killing Boers!' And when Lodevicus grabbed him by the neck, he stuttered: 'Frederick Bezuidenhout . . . lives thirty miles north of here . . . the court at Graaff-Reinet . . .'

'I know that court,' Lodevicus snapped. 'What's it done now?'

'Summoned Bezuidenhout . . . charges of abusing a servant.' It seemed that when the accused, a rough, unlettered renegade, refused to appear, a lieutenant and twenty soldiers were sent to fetch him. Unwisely, all the soldiers were Hottentots, and when Bezuidenhout retreated to a cave, gunfire was exchanged, and the highly trained Hottentots shot him dead. The Bezuidenhout family vowed vengeance.

Lodevicus reacted spontaneously: 'Good riddance. Those thieves.' He knew the Bezuidenhouts as border ruffians who respected neither English rule nor Dutch, and as veldkornet he had often been required to discipline them. 'Afrika voor de Afrikaner!' was their battle cry, and they hated the English with a passion equaled only by their abhorrence of those Dutch who served what they called 'The Lords of London.'

They were an unregenerate lot and Lodevicus could not feel sorry over the death of Frederick. 'Van Doorn!' the messenger shouted. 'Are you listening? Hottentots sent by the English Kaffir-lovers murder a Boer.' He shook the master of De Kraal and cried almost plaintively, 'We need you, Lodevicus Hammer.'

'For what?'

'To lead the Boers.'

'Against who?'

'The English. Who plan to kill off all us Boers.'

Van Doorn, much as he hated the English, could not accept this ridiculous statement. He started to tell the messenger that he was forgetting the early days when trekboers armed their Hottentots to fight the Xhosa, but the man was persistent.

'Lodevicus Hammer, if we let the English do this thing to one of us, they will do it to all,' and his arguments were finally so persuasive that the old man asked, 'What do you want of me?' and the messenger said, 'Lead us against the English.'

'And where would we get the troops?'

Softly the messenger said, 'The Bezuidenhouts say we must go to Kaffirs.'

Neither man spoke, for this was the moment of treason, the moment when loyalties and moral judgments hung in the balance. Lodevicus van Doorn knew well that the ultimate battle his people would have to fight would be against the blacks, and he had seen how fearful that struggle could be. His father Adriaan, his mother Seena, his wife Rebecca had all been slain by the Xhosa, and he in turn had decimated their ranks. To ally with them now was unthinkable.

'The only Kaffir this Boer wants to speak with is a dead one,' he growled.

'No, no! Van Doorn, listen to me. With the Kaffirs we can drive out the English. When that's done we can settle with the Kaffirs.'

'They butchered my family,' Lodevicus said grimly.

'And now we use them for our purposes.' He explained how this could be done, and concluded: 'I've heard you say yourself, Vicus, that the English will destroy us. They will stamp on the backs of the Boers. They will make us say "Mister" to the Hottentots eating at our own table.' On and on he went, driving home the message that the Englishman was the real enemy: 'Look what he did to you in the Black Circuit.'

This was the telling blow. Lodevicus, who had hammered the Kaffirs, took a great step down the road to treason: 'The enemy that matters is the enemy of today. He is white and English.'

'I know where we can meet with the Xhosa generals,' the messenger whispered, and without conceding that he would actually unleash these fearsome warriors against the English, Lodevicus did agree to talk with them.

Through the dark night the two conspirators rode east to the Great Fish, forded it upstream from a rude fort, and sought the dwelling of Guzaka, son of Sotopo. When at last Lodevicus faced the warrior, the two adversaries glared at each other in silence. Guzaka had slain three members of the Van Doorn family; the Hammer had captained the destruction of more than three thousand Xhosa. Finally Guzaka rose, extended his two hands, and said, 'It is time.'

They sat outside Guzaka's hut, two grizzled warriors licking their wounds like old tomcats, their claws blunted by the years. 'Ja, Kaffir,' Van Doorn said slowly, 'here stands a Van Doorn asking your help. God knows it's not right, but what else is there?'

'The Redcoats will destroy both of us,' the white-haired Xhosa said.

'We must kick them out.'

'Killings, too many killings,' Guzaka said.

'Settle with them, then we'll settle peace between us.'

'But you Boers steal our lands, too.'

'Did we ever drive twenty thousand across the Big Fish? It was the English who did that.'

'It's still our land,' Guzaka said, confused by the drift of the conversation.

'Old man, you and I don't have too many years. Let us solve the land question now. We drive out the English, then you and I make peace. We each herd cattle. We share the land.'

'Can we defeat the Redcoats?' the old warrior asked.

'Together we can do anything,' Lodevicus said with fervor, and impulsively he clasped his enemy's hand, for at that moment he truly believed those words.

Inspired by this show of friendship, Guzaka said, 'Tonight I shall discuss this with my headmen. Tomorrow we make the treaty.' It was a word he knew well, for along this contested border there had been more than fifteen treaties, none with prospects more hopeful than this: Boer and Xhosa against the enemy.

But during this parley, which might have meant so much to the frontier, a young Xhosa warrior with wild and shifting eyes who claimed to see visions and exercise prophecy—a thin man with a ridged scar across his forehead—had sat off to one side, carefully watching, his heart smoldering with hatred for Van Doorn. He remembered that years ago this huge Boer had scattered tobacco on the ground as a trap; his father had stooped to retrieve it—and fifty warriors had perished.

So after Lodevicus and the messenger withdrew, the trembling prophet harangued his tribesmen: 'Jackals! Cowards! Men without skins! Who is this Van Doorn who comes begging? Is he not the sorcerer who uses tobacco to slay his enemies? The blood of my people is on his hands.'

'The blood of his people is on our hands,' Guzaka replied. 'This is the time to halt the bloodshed.'

'What can this monster do for us?' the prophet demanded.

'He will help us fight the English,' Guzaka argued. 'With the Boers we can live in peace. With the English, never.'

'If we help these Boers today,' the scarred prophet warned, 'they will steal our land when the battle is over. I say kill them tonight.'

But Guzaka saw a chance to gain that lasting peace without which his people would suffer unbroken travail, and he tried vainly to support the concept of a combined attack on the English; he achieved nothing, for the prophet, inflamed by an apocalyptic vision of long-dead Xhosa generals rising mysteriously to launch an attack on both the English and the Boers, expelling them from the land, cried, 'He is old and frightened!' And three young warriors struck Guzaka, leader of many battles, to the ground and killed him.

They then raged out into the night, seeking the trail by which Lodevicus had left the camp. In the mists, sixty warriors, spurred on by the prophet, fell upon the tent where Lodevicus slept. The old man reached for his gun, but before he could fire even one shot, assegais pierced his chest and he fell back.

As he lay dying in treachery he moaned, 'Merciful God, forgive me. Forgive me.' As he fell back, blood gushing from his lips, he mumbled, 'Adriaan, Seena. Rebecca, me. The circle . . .'

News of the death of Lodevicus had not yet reached De Kraal when Hilary Saltwood entered the valley with Saul. Tjaart, returning from the cattle drive, eyed the missionary suspiciously, seeing him only as the Englishman who had stolen the slave girl Emma. Clasping the sjambok at his side, he flicked the long hide over the grass and growled, 'Off these lands, Saltwood.'

Hilary, perched on the riding seat of a small cart, felt Saul trembling next to him. 'Put that down, Tjaart. This is no time for argument.'

'Back to your Hottentots, Englishman, and take that damned Kaffir with you.'

Saltwood's eyes followed the line of the menacing whip, then crept up to Tjaart's face. The Boer recognized a look of anguished appeal, and his next words were less intemperate: 'What is it you want?'

'It's your father, Tjaart.'

Wilhelmina and Tjaart's wife, who had been listening inside the house, stepped outside and stood glaring at the intruder; at the sight of the women Saltwood held back his words.

'What about my father?'

'He rode with the rebels.'

'Damnit, man, I know that. And I join them tomorrow.'

Lord, why me? Hilary asked himself as if in prayer. Why does it always have to be me who faces this family.

'Tjaart, your father is dead.'

The younger Van Doorn ground out his words: 'What you say, Englishman?' Till now they had been conversing in the language of the Boers, but in his agitation Tjaart used the missionary's language.

The color drained from Wilhelmina's face. Putting her arm about her daughter-in-law's shoulders, she drew her close to her bosom, and in that instant she thought of the long years since the day she rode north from a godless past to offer herself to Lodevicus the Hammer. They had been good years and violent. Twice her lips formed his name, and when she looked up at the stricken, bean-thin missionary she knew that he was telling the truth. Her wild old man was dead.

'The Kaffirs killed him,' Saltwood repeated. Quietly he explained that his Xhosa, Saul, had been visiting across the Great Fish and had learned of the mission to Guzaka and of the dual tragedy that ensued. When he assured them that Saul would be able to lead them to the body, Wilhelmina said softly, 'Dominee, you must be tired. Come in.'

That afternoon they started the grim journey; Wilhelmina was insistent that the Hammer should be buried where he fell. 'He was a man of God but not of churches,' she said, and she refused Saltwood's offer of burial at the mission. At noon next day, while the Xhosa were lamenting the death of the general, Guzaka, the white men and women piled rocks above the grave of Lodevicus, whereupon the missionary offered a prayer in Dutch, after which he recited the somber passages of the Ninetieth Psalm:

> 'The days of our years are threescore years and ten; and if by reason of strength they be fourscore years, yet is their strength labour and sorrow; for it is soon cut off, and we fly away . . . So teach us to number our days, that we may apply our hearts unto wisdom.'

On their return, the mourners reached the point at which Saltwood and Saul must head east for Golan, and it seemed to the missionary that his life and Tjaart's were as divergent as the directions they would now follow; he had been as close to a Van Doorn during these past days as he would ever be, and this moved him to say fervently, 'Tjaart, don't ride with the rebels. Don't seek tragedy.'

'You?' Tjaart asked. 'You worry about my soul?'

'Concerning the slave girl, Emma, who has caused so much bitterness. I want to buy her.'

'A dominee? Buying a De Kraal slave?'

'Her and her parents.'

'Where would you get the money?'

'I'd write home . . . to my mother.'

The fatuousness of this statement amused all the Van Doorns, and for the first time since the death of the Hammer they broke into laughter. 'He'll write home to his mother!' Tjaart mimicked. But he did agree to sell the slaves.

Even as the laughter echoed, the final scenes of the futile uprising were being enacted to the north, where well-trained English soldiers pinned down a ragtag commando of seventy dissident Boers, most of whom surrendered without a shot. A few of the ringleaders escaped to fight a bitter-end clash, but when it ended, Johannes Bezuidenhout, brother of Frederick, who had started the troubles, lay dead. The first abortive rebellion was ended.

It was a sound that never before had been heard in this part of the world: two slow-footed drummers marching alongside a cart in which stood six manacled men and beating out the pace of death. The two horses, groomed for the occasion, hauled the last of the Bezuidenhout rebels into a beautiful valley surrounded by comforting hills. The six men had been sentenced to death, but one had been reprieved: before his life in jail began he must stand tied by the neck to the gallows while his five companions were hanged.

The place chosen for the hanging was so appallingly named, and the events it would witness so hideous, that it would reverberate in South African history: Slagter's Nek—The Neck of the Slaughterer.

The crowd of witnesses was great. All revolutionaries not condemned were required to stand in the shadow of the gallows, as were members of the men's families, and the two widows of the Bezuidenhouts already dead. Near three hundred militia were present to control passions: English troops in red, Hottentot militia in marching gear, and loyal Boers in the rough dress of the commando. And in command of all rode a most extraordinary man: the son of the mayor of Albany, New York, in the new United States of America.

Colonel Jacob Glen Cuyler, forty years old and a fine figure of a man, had been born on the eve of the American Revolution into a loyalist family. When his parents refused to support the revolution, they fled to Canada, where young Jacob joined the British army. Because of his Dutch heritage, it seemed sensible to send him to South Africa, where he landed with the second English invading force of 1806. A man of courage and intelligence, he prospered in the new colony, rising to rank of colonel and magistrate of a large district south of Graaff-Reinet.

He was a foe of revolutionaries. They had driven him from his home in America and left him with indelible memories: when he came to South Africa he brought with him two handsome portraits of his parents, completed shortly before his death by Major John André, who lived with the Cuylers before his execution as an English spy.

Colonel Cuyler, acting under strict orders from Cape Town, was determined that these hangings be conducted with propriety. It was he who had suggested the two drummers; it was he who had stopped at Golan Mission on the way north to tell Missionary Saltwood: 'It's always proper to have a clergyman present at a hanging. Gives religious sanction and helps control the doomed men.'

No one who attended the hangings at Slagter's Nek would ever forget them; women and men would sometimes cry in the night, not because of the hangings, which occurred often in those days, but because of the soul-wrenching thing that happened.

When the five condemned men were led to the gallows, they were forced to climb upon movable platforms and stand at attention, hands and feet tied, as the ropes were attached to their necks and knotted. Some of the men accepted blindfolds, others ignored them, and when all was in readiness Cuyler ordered the drums to roll, and the platforms were kicked away. For a long, terrible moment the doomed men struggled in the air—and then the miracle happened! Four of the five ropes broke, allowing those men to fall free.

When this occurred a great shout of joy rose from everyone, even the rows of Hottentot corpsmen. Reverend Saltwood actually jumped up and down, throwing his arms in the air and crying, 'God be praised!' In a frenzy of relief he clasped the men who had been so miraculously saved and knelt in the dust to untie their ankle fetters. Then he led them in prayers, which seemed to gush forth as if God Himself were rejoicing. In his exultation at this happy escape from tragedy, even though the unlucky fifth rebel dangled dead, he found himself next to Tjaart van Doorn, and in mutual joy the two enemies embraced. 'Thank God, thank God!' Hilary mumbled repeatedly as he and Tjaart danced in the shadow of the gallows.

'Tjaart!' Saltwood cried ecstatically. 'You must come and worship with me. We can be friends, truly we can.'

'Maybe we can,' Tjaart said, and it was in that moment of reconciliation that the awful thing happened.

'Re-form!' Cuyler shouted. 'Bring new ropes.'

'What?' Saltwood cried, unable to comprehend what he was hearing. 'New ropes!'

'But, Colonel! In English law . . . if the rope breaks, the man goes free!'

As soon as Hilary voiced this ancient edict, and a good one it was, for it acknowledged that God Himself sometimes intervened to save the condemned, the crowd took up the cry, and those relatives who had been rejoicing with their reprieved men ran to the officer, reminding him of this honored tradition.

'They are saved!' the people cried. 'You cannot hang them a second time.'

'True,' Saltwood pleaded, tugging at Cuyler's sleeve. 'It's a custom all men honor. The hanging was completed when God intervened.'

Suddenly Cuyler's eyes hardened. He had a job to do, a revolution to quell. Having been driven away from Albany, he understood the terror that could engulf a land when revolutionary ideas were allowed to gallop across a countryside, and he intended having none of that in Africa. These men must die. So it was frustrating when this damn-fool English priest started making trouble. With a vigorous shove he knocked Saltwood back and cried to his orderly, 'Bind that silly ass and take him away.'

'No, sir, no!' Hilary protested. 'You will defile this land if you—'

'Take him away,' Cuyler said coldly, and soldiers seized the missionary, clapping a hand over his mouth so that he could protest no further, and dragged him off.

Then the four survivors whom God had touched were placed once more upon the platforms, their faces ashen as fresh ropes were tied about their necks.

It was not a roar that came from the crowd. It was not a military challenge to the new government. It was only a vast sigh of anguish that so foul a thing should be done on so fair a day. Then, from the area in which he was being held, came Saltwood's high begging scream: 'No! No!'

Once more the platforms were kicked aside. This time the ropes held.

When Tjaart van Doorn returned to De Kraal he was silent for a long while, then grimly he summoned his mother, his wife, his children, and in solemn conclave lined out the mystical litany that would be recited in die-hard Boer families from that day forward: 'Never forget the Black Circuit when Hottentots and liars bore testimony in English courts against honest Boers. Never forget how the English have tried to banish our language. Never forget Slagter's Nek, where an English officer hanged the same men twice, in disobedience to God's law.'

Tjaart was twenty-six now, a quiet, stubborn man emerging slowly from the shadows of his father's flaming exuberance to assume responsibility for De Kraal. His character was not yet fully formed; he supported all his fiery father had done, even his near-treason, convincing himself that 'Father was driven to it in desperation over the illegal acts of the English.' But he knew he could never take the Hammer's place as champion of the Boers; his was a calmer approach, that of the self-confident bull who rules the pasture without bellowing. It became obvious to him that English rule would have to be challenged, but when and how, he could not guess. He supposed that the invaders would make one small mistake after another, digging their own graves, until that day when the Boers would be able to resume control of their native land.

When Colonel Cuyler returned from the hangings at Slagter's Nek, he was so disgusted with Reverend Saltwood's pusillanimous behavior—for so he considered it—that he submitted an angry report to Cape Town, confirming what many government officials had begun to suspect: that Hilary was an irresponsible character whose loyalties were questionable. From then on, the English segment of South Africa had little to do with the gawky missionary at the eastern edge of settlement.

During these years Captain Richard Saltwood was conducting himself rather well in India; at Hindu hangings, of which he saw not a few, he gave way to no hysterics: 'Blighter was caught, he gets hanged, that's that.'

In 1819, as a newly commissioned major with six campaigns to his credit, two with Ochterlony against the Gurkhas, losing 1814, winning 1816, he shipped home to England from his regiment, and when his transport lay to at Cape Town he fully expected to unite with his brother, who was serving somewhere as a missionary, but when he found that Hilary was four or five hundred miles distant, he was amazed: 'This place is as big as India.' And he surrendered any idea of trying to find him.

He was not pleased with what he heard in Cape Town regarding Hilary's curious behavior; one army wife said, 'It's the frontier, Richard. The Kaffirs, the Hottentots, the Boer farmers who can't read or write. Our army men are stationed there only seven months. That's about all they can take. How long's your brother been there? Nine long years? No wonder he's acting up.'

An army captain who had been stationed at Graaff-Reinet was more specific: 'It's the moral loneliness . . . the intellectual loneliness. The church in London sends them books and all that, but there they are, stuck away and gone. I wouldn't dare leave one of my men out there for even two years. They'd go to rot.'

'In what way?'

'They begin to see everything from the point of view of the natives. They learn the language, you know. Eat Kaffir food. Some of them, God forbid, take Kaffir wives.'

'Not missionaries, certainly.'

'Yes, even marry them. And there have been cases . . .' He dropped his voice significantly to allow Major Saltwood to guess what those cases had consisted of.

'Is there anything I can do?' Richard asked.

'There certainly is. Find him a wife.'

'Can't he find—'

The captain interrupted, wishing to elaborate on a point which he had often considered: 'Fact is, men everywhere are sounder stuff if they have wives. Keeps them responsible. Go to bed earlier. Eat better-prepared food. Missionaries are no different. Your brother needs a wife.'

'Why doesn't he take one?'

'None to be had.'

'I saw lots of women at the dance last night.'

'None single.' He ran off a list of the pretty women Richard had met, and every one was married.

'They didn't seem so last night,' Richard said.

'What you must do,' the captain said, 'is when you get home, find your brother a good wife. One who accepts missionaries.'

'And ship her out?'

'That's the way we all do. Every ship comes into Table Bay has its quota, but never enough.' He looked reflectively into his cup. 'When you're in England, and women are everywhere, they seem rather ordinary. But when you're overseas and there are none—no white ones, that is—damn, they seem important.' It was under this urging that Richard Saltwood drafted a letter to his brother:

> I was most fearfully disappointed not to have met you during my visit. The regiment's home to Wiltshire with me a major, thanks to some lucky work against the Gurkhas. I find myself quite homesick for Sentinels, and wish to God you were going to be at home when I get there.
>
> Several people in Cape Town, religious and military alike, urged me to find you a wife when I get back to Salisbury, a task I face for myself. Send Mother a letter, quickly, telling us whether we should proceed and how. Your woman could be aboard one of the next ships to Cape Town, and I could be, too, because I've taken a great liking to your land. I think an English soldier could do well here, and I'm afraid I've gone about as far as I can in the Glorious Fifty-ninth.

When Hilary received the letter he was at low ebb, for Golan Mission was not doing well. The rows of huts were filled with Hottentots and Xhosa seeking to avoid work under the Boers, but few were sincere Christians. Not even Emma's parents had converted, and there was a problem with Emma herself. She was nineteen now, and a true Christian, but plans of some kind had to be made for her future; the most she could hope for was marriage to some half-Christian Xhosa; more probably she would slip back into servitude at some Boer kraal.

Funds to support the mission were slow in coming from England, and one young man who had been seconded to relieve Hilary had taken one look at South Africa and scrambled back aboard his ship, preferring to trust his luck in India. Hilary kept himself insulated from such disappointments by cherishing his trivial accomplishments and sharing them with Emma: 'Phambo appeared at prayers again, and I do believe he is on the way to salvation.' Three days later, when Phambo ran off to the Xhosa camp on the other side of the Great Fish, taking with him three Golan cows, Hilary did not condemn him: 'Poor Phambo heard temptation and could not resist, but when he returns, Emma, as I am convinced he will, we must greet him as our brother, with or without the cows.'

Hilary refused to acknowledge the ostracism directed against him by both the Boers and the English: the former because he was an agent of the English repression; the latter because he had 'behaved poorly' at Slagter's Nek. And both sides viewed him with scorn for supporting the Kaffirs against white men. One good reason why he was able to ignore the ostracism was that he rarely participated in any public gathering. His world was his church.

But his brother's letter suggesting that he take a wife made great sense; he was thirty-four now, worn and wasted by his exertions on a difficult frontier, and he felt the need for someone to share his spiritual burdens; if his mother, in consultation with her other sons, could comb the Salisbury scene and locate a suitable wife, the years ahead might prove more profitable both to Jesus and to His servant Saltwood. So he wrote a careful letter, advising his mother as to the requirements for a missioner's wife in South Africa.

He was distracted from such personal matters when Tjaart, accompanied by four Boers, galloped into the mission one morning, shouting in anxiety, 'We need every man! The Kaffirs are marching on Grahamstown.'

The commando waited some fifteen minutes for Saltwood to arm himself, and Hilary spent ten of these in agonizing inner debate as to whether it was Christian for him to participate in armed combat against the Xhosa, a people he loved; but he realized that until the frontier was pacified, not even missionary work could proceed, so reluctantly he took his rifle.

'Bring your Hottentots, too!' Tjaart cried, and six of them eagerly mounted up. For the English to have used armed Hottentots against the Boers had been criminal; for the Boers to use them against the Kaffirs was prudent.

It was seventy miles from Golan Mission to the little military post at Grahamstown, and as the Boers urged their horses onward, Saltwood reflected that only Englishmen lived in the village, yet here were the Boers galloping full speed to aid them. He was aware that Tjaart despised the English, inveighing against them at every chance, but when an English outpost was threatened by Kaffirs, the Boer commandos were always ready to saddle up. It was confusing.

The twelve newcomers were given a cheering welcome at Grahamstown, where fewer than three hundred English and Hottentot soldiers, plus two cannon, awaited the Xhosa attack. Tjaart's contingent meant that thirty civilians would aid the soldiers; he was distressed when the English commander divided his troops: 'Half to the barracks southeast of town, half here with me to defend the empty town.' He sent the women and children to the safety of the barracks, except for five, who said, 'We'll fight with our husbands in the town.'

Throughout the night Hottentot scouts crept in to report the steady advance of the Xhosa horde, but Tjaart and Saltwood could not credit the numbers they recited. 'Hottentots always exaggerate,' Tjaart explained. 'Whites and blacks are so much bigger, they think there's more of us.' But at dawn the defenders gaped in sickening awe as the slopes northeast of Grahamstown showed more than ten thousand warriors descending in three massed divisions. The noise of this multitude as they began dashing toward the settlement caused fear in every heart.

The brow-scarred Xhosa prophet had predicted certain victory: 'When Grahamstown falls, we have a clear run through every frontier farm from the ocean to the mountains at the north!' Behind the exulting regiments came hundreds of women with their cooking pots and gourds, for the prophet had promised them: 'At sunset we shall feast as never before. Redcoats and Boers alike, destroyed.'

Tjaart, imbued with the spirit of the Hammer, perceived the impending attack as one more clash in a never-ending battle. There stood the enemy, here stood the men of God—and the only obligation of the latter was to chastise the former. Turning to the men near him, he said, 'Anyone afraid to fight, ride off now.' And he looked directly at Saltwood, half expecting him to flee, but throughout history no Saltwood had ever deserted, and Hilary would not break that tradition. Turning to his six Hottentots, he asked, 'Are you ready?' and the brown men nodded.

'Then let us pray,' and when he had done so in English, Tjaart asked if he might add words of his own, and in Dutch he prayed: 'Like Abraham we face the Canaanites. Like him we place our lives in Thy hands. Great God, guide us good Christians as once again we smite these Kaffirs.'

The attack came in early afternoon, wave after wave of shrieking Xhosa roaring down the hill to hurl themselves against the soldiers in the town. Those in the barracks had to watch, helpless, as the regiments rushed at the little houses.

'We must go to help them,' Saltwood said.

'Stay!' a lieutenant ordered. 'Our time will come.'

The most daring of the Xhosa got to within one hundred feet of the soldiers, but then massed gunfire raked their ranks and the two cannon wreaked devastation. Hundreds of blacks fell in the front ranks, until their commanders, seeing that the English line could not be broken, gave the order to swing onto the barracks. Here they were more successful, penetrating the small collection of buildings. This landed them in the center of the barracks square, where they were safe, since the cannon could not be brought directly against them for fear of killing fellow Englishmen and Boers. The fighting would have to be hand-to-hand.

Tjaart and Saltwood were in the midst of it, shoulders pressed. They saw two Hottentots go down, a Redcoat fall. A huge Xhosa leaped at Saltwood, swinging his war club, but Tjaart twisted about to drop him with a pistol shot. For almost an hour the battle raged in the square, then finally the gallant Xhosa, facing gunfire they had not anticipated, had to retreat. A jubilant cry arose from the white and Hottentot fighters as the warriors fled in uncontrolled panic. Grahamstown had been saved!

In the aftermath of battle Saltwood was missing, and for a while Tjaart wondered if this missionary, who had fought so bravely, had been dragged away by the fleeing Xhosa, but as Tjaart searched a field he saw Hilary, bloody and disheveled, kneeling beside a dying Xhosa. Tears streamed down his face, and when he saw his neighbor Van Doorn approaching he looked up in bewilderment.

'Seven hundred of them dead,' he mumbled softly. 'I've counted more than seven hundred lying here. Three of our men dead. May God forgive us for this slaughter.'

'Dominee,' Tjaart reasoned. 'God wanted us to win this battle.' When the missionary muttered something incoherent, Van Doorn added, 'In warfare like this, so few of us against so many of them, it's no time to love thy enemy. Destroy him. Because where would you be now if they'd broken through? Can you see Golan burning?'

Saltwood looked up at the man who had saved his life. He tried to justify his feelings of repugnance, but he could form no words. 'It's all right, Dominee,' Tjaart said. 'We taught the Kaffir bastards a lesson they'll remember. Till next time.'

'Next time?'

Tjaart tugged at his beard. 'It will never stop, Dominee. Not till one side is victor in this land.'

Saltwood had to admit, though reluctantly, that what Van Doorn was saying was true, but he did not voice this thought, for next to him the young Xhosa warrior, no more than a boy, shuddered and lay still.

When Hilary Saltwood's letter reached Sentinels in the shadow of Salisbury Cathedral, his mother was fifty-four years old, a widow and eager to help her distant son find the proper wife. The commission was not an unusual one in rural England. Sons of distinguished families would venture to all parts of the world, serving for years as outriders of civilization in places like India, South America and Ceylon, without ever thinking of marrying local women the way Portuguese and French colonizers did. An Englishman remembered the girl left behind, and when he was in his mid-thirties he would come home, and some gaunt woman in her early thirties, who in another society would never find a husband, would be waiting, and they would repair to the village church, two people who had been terrified of missing life, and they would be married, and flowers would be scattered, and the local curate would dry his eyes at this little miracle, and soon the pair would be off to some other remote spot.

Or, as in this case, the son would write home to his parents and ask them to pursue his courtship for him, and they would visit only the daughters of families they had known for a generation, and again some older woman who might never have married would find that she was needed in some far country by a man she could only vaguely remember. This was the English pattern, and men who deviated from it by marrying local women were apt to find their lives truncated, if not ruined.

Emily Saltwood, upon reading her son's appeal, retired to her room for two days and reflected upon the marriageable daughters of her friends, and after trying her best to judge the girls from a man's point of view, and a missionary's, she decided that the family she must visit was the Lambtons, who lived across the bridge within the purlieus of the cathedral.

Wishing not to share her secret mission with any servant, she elected not to use her carriage but to walk to the village, where she sought out the bricked path leading to the Lambton residence, at whose door she knocked quietly. After an interval that troubled her, because it seemed that no one was at home, she heard shuffling feet approach, and an elderly maid creaked open the door. 'Mrs. Lambton is not at home,' she said. Nor was Miss Lambton there, but there was a possibility that they could be found near the cathedral grounds, for they had planned on having tea in that vicinity.

Emily said, 'You know, it's frightfully important that I see Mrs. Lambton immediately, and I think you'd better go fetch them.'

'I couldn't leave the house, ma'am.' The maid was insistent.

'On this day you'd better.' Emily Saltwood could be just as insistent. 'Couldn't you go and meet them at the cathedral?'

'No, I couldn't. Because what I have to discuss is not for an open park. Now you scurry off and find your mistress, or I'll take this umbrella to you.'

This the maid understood, and after a while she returned, leading both Mrs. Lambton and her daughter Vera. This was rather more than Emily had expected, so she said quite brusquely, 'It was your mother I wished to see,' and the tall girl, twenty-nine years old and somewhat timid, dutifully vanished.

'I've had a curious letter from my son Hilary, in South Africa,' Emily began, and without another word being spoken, Mrs. Lambton grasped the significance of this abrupt meeting. Keeping her hands under discipline, lest they tremble, she said, 'Vera and I remember Hilary well. The soldier, wasn't he?'

'The missionary,' Emily said.

'Yes, yes.' Her hands were now trembling furiously, but she kept them hidden. She knew she'd made an unforgivable mistake, confusing the Saltwood boys, but she recovered admirably by throwing Emily on the defensive: 'Didn't you have a son who went to America?'

'Alas, we did. Never hear of him.'

'They tell me that your boy Richard's thinking of returning to India . . . without the regiment.'

'He's headstrong. He'll be off to some remote spot.'

'Tell me, Emily, how does a mother feel when her chicks are so scattered?'

'You may soon know, because Hilary has asked me to ascertain whether Vera . . .' It was most difficult to say such a thing bluntly, without preparation of any kind, but it was inescapable. 'He wonders if Vera would like to join him in South Africa—in the mission field, that is.'

'She's a devout girl,' Mrs. Lambton parried. 'All us Lambtons are devoted to the church.'

'I know, I know. That's why it's been so easy for me to approach you on so delicate a matter.'

'I don't know how Vera . . .' Mrs. Lambton spoke defensively, as if her daughter were accustomed to weighing such proposals, but Emily Saltwood was not going to have any of that. Abruptly she said, 'Vera's at the age when she must make up her mind . . . and quickly. Hilary's a fine lad and he needs a wife.'

'How old is he?' Mrs. Lambton asked sweetly.

'Thirty-four. The proper age for such a marriage.'

'And has he prospects?'

'His older brother—Peter, that is—he'll inherit the house, of course. But we expect Hilary to be dean of the cathedral one of these days. When his tour ends, of course.'

'Most interesting.' Mrs. Lambton knew of three young clergymen who were being considered for that promotion. Besides, Hilary suffered an impediment which completely disqualified him, and it was important to knock down Mrs. Saltwood's bargaining position early in the game: 'Didn't I hear that your son took orders with the Methodists, or something quite awful like that?' She beamed her benign Sunday-in-church smile.

'Merely for his ordination to do Christ's work. He'll scamper back into the proper fold, once he returns.' She, too, smiled. 'You've heard, I'm sure, that before he died, the old Proprietor, who was extremely fond of Hilary, made special overtures for him at the cathedral.'

'Pity he died,' Mrs. Lambton said. She had other solid objections to sending her daughter to a land so remote as South Africa, but she was realist enough to know that Vera was aging and had better catch a suitor promptly. Even a ghost like the absent Hilary had to be considered, so she extended Mrs. Saltwood a courtesy she did not fully feel: 'I think we should discuss this, Emily.'

'Shall we involve Vera?' Mrs. Saltwood asked.

'Not at this point, I think. And certainly not the two of us. It would make everything seem too important.'

'It's just that,' Emily said with that charming frankness that characterized so many elderly English women who no longer felt restraints. 'It's very important for my son, and frankly, it ought to be for Vera too. She's not getting any younger.'

She walked home across the old bridge, turned right, and went down the quiet lane leading to Sentinels, where she felt vaguely uneasy, although unaware that national events were about to do her work for her.

In London her eldest son, Peter, now a member of Parliament for Old Sarum, had become a leader in the movement to alleviate English unemployment by the device of granting large funds for shipping unwanted families out to South Africa:

> This interesting action will serve two noble purposes. In England it will remove large numbers of unfortunate people from our charity rolls, and in South Africa it will correct the imbalance that now exists between the many Dutch and the few English. If our new colony below the equator is to become properly English, as it must, we shall have to throw many Englishmen into the balance pans, and this act will do just that.

A gigantic effort was mounted to convince impoverished Englishmen that they must quit their hopelessness at home and venture into the new paradise. Articles were published extolling the agricultural possibilities, the beauty of the landscape, and the salubriousness of the climate on the right bank of the Great Fish River, in the vicinity of that splendid rural capital Grahamstown. No mention was made of the recent attack by ten thousand assegaied Xhosa on said capital or the deaths among those who had defended it.

Most helpful were the speeches and writings of Reverend Simon Keer, who assured Englishmen that those lucky enough to be included in the roster of immigrants—whose boat fare would be paid by the government and whose land would be given free, a hundred rolling acres to each family—would be entering a paradise to which America and Australia were niggardly in comparison. To residents of crowded England, where a family could live well on twenty acres, the vision of a hundred, rent-free, tax-free, was compelling.

Ninety thousand citizens, well mixed as to occupation, education and ability, volunteered to emigrate, a superior lot, really, to those who had emigrated earlier to Canada and America, and had they all been moved to Cape Town, the history of Africa would have been sharply modified, for at this time there were only some twenty-five thousand Boers in the entire colony, and the infusion of so many Englishmen would have made South Africa much like any other British colony. But enthusiastic members of Parliament, such as Peter Saltwood, promised much more than they could deliver, and when the time came to fill the ships, only enough money to transport four thousand settlers was provided, so that the eighty-six thousand who might have restructured a nation had to be left behind.

Among those lucky enough to be included was a young man of twenty-five named Thomas Carleton, a carriage builder by trade, whose enthusiasm matched the rhetoric of speakers like Peter Saltwood and Simon Keer. From the first moment he heard of the emigration plan, he wanted to go, and with letters of approval from his minister and sheriff, he was among the first interviewed: 'My business is solid, but it's not really thriving. I want to go where distances are great and men must have wagons.'

'Have you any money saved?'

'Not a penny, but I have strong arms, a willing back and a complete set of tools fully paid.'

The examiners doubted if they would find many men so qualified and unanimously recommended that he be accepted, so he was given a slip of paper guaranteeing his passage and the allocation of one hundred acres. He was to report three months hence to Southampton, where the ship *Alice Grace* would be loading. 'That'll give you time to find yourself a wife,' the examiners explained.

'Not me!' Thomas said. 'I haven't a penny to feed a wife.'

When the news of this grand scheme reached Salisbury, the Lambtons listened with more than casual attention, and the more they heard, the more convinced they became that this was the kind of adventure to which an unmarried girl of good breeding might subscribe. Of course, Vera would not be sailing as an ordinary charity case, her way paid by the government; as the intended bride of a clergyman who might one day be dean of the finest cathedral in England, and the sister-in-law-to-be of an important member of Parliament, she would have preferment.

But the grand decision hung in the balance until Salisbury was visited by the one man in England who spoke as if he knew most about the new colony, Dr. Simon Keer, as he now called himself, a power in the LMS. He announced a public meeting in the cathedral cloisters, where chairs lined the hallowed square and where against a background of gray stone he explained everything. He was now middle-aged, a short, plump little man with red hair, a Lancashire accent and a powerful voice that boomed as it echoed from the noble walls; his oratory rolled like thunder as he spoke of challenges and flashed like lightning when he outlined the potentialities:

> 'If we grapple courageously with the problem of slavery in this colony, we shall show the way for Canada and Jamaica and Barbados and, yes, the United States itself. Any English man or woman who accepts this invitation to perform God's duty will be serving all of mankind. I wish I could sail in those ships, for all who do will be rebuilding the world.'

When the Lambtons lingered to ask him if he knew anything of Grahamstown, where the new settlers would be given their land, he showed his frank astonishment that a family as distinguished as theirs might be interested in emigrating: 'It's for the poorer type, you know. The solid workers of the world.'

'Of course,' Mrs. Lambton said. 'But we're told that the Golan Mission, run by your Society . . .' She had to say no more. With a wild clap of his hands and a leap in the air he cried, 'I know! I know!' And he took Vera's hands and danced a jig with her, even though she was a head taller than he. 'You're going out to marry Hilary Saltwood.'

He spent an hour assuring the Lambtons of how fine a man this missionary was. He reviewed the steps by which Hilary had reached conversion, and said that whereas he himself had not yet visited Golan Mission, for it had not been in existence when he served in that area, he had excellent reports of it. But then Vera took him aside for a confidential assessment.

When he finished she was convinced that she could profitably sail to South Africa, but her mother raised one serious objection: 'With whom can Vera travel? I don't fancy her alone on a ship for four months, surrounded by God knows whom.'

'That's a real problem,' Dr. Keer conceded, 'but I've been working closely with the shipping companies. Real gentlemen, you know.' To hear the former missionary speak, he consorted only with the best families, stayed only at the great houses, and one gained the impression that he enjoyed missionary work far more when lecturing in England than he had when serving on the Xhosa frontier. 'I'm sure we'll find persons of quality among the ship's officers. I'll make inquiries.'

This wasn't necessary, for within a week of Dr. Keer's lecture in the cloisters, Richard Saltwood came down from London, where he had been consulting with his brother in Parliament, and his news was exciting:

'Mother! I've resigned my commission. Wasn't going anywhere down that lane. And Peter's arranged with the colonial secretary for me . . . Point is, I'm to have a government job at Grahamstown! David lost in America. Me lost in South Africa.'

'Are you contemplating staying there?' his mother asked.

'There's nothing for me here. I've neither the money nor the talent to be a colonel of the regiment. So I'm off to the new land. I saw it and liked it. Much better than India.'

'This could be providential,' his mother said. 'We've found a bride for Hilary. The Lambton girl. You knew her years ago. She's a tall, thin thing now and is desperately hungry for a husband, although she won't admit it.'

'She's sailing to Cape Town? Splendid for Hilary.'

'She's ready to sail,' Emily said hesitantly, 'but she's afraid of going out with the emigrant mob—unattended, as it were.'

'I'll take her!' Richard said with the spontaneity that had gained him the affection of any troops with whom he served in close quarters.

'That's what I had in mind, the moment you spoke. But there are grave dangers . . .'

'Our laddies have the savages whipped into shape. A skirmish now and then, nothing to fear.'

'It wasn't that I was thinking of. Richard, will you go fetch Vera? Right now?'

They sat under the oak trees in the picnic chairs John Constable had used for his paints two years earlier when doing the large canvas showing Salisbury Cathedral in sunlight; as an appreciation for his constant use of this lawn, he had dashed off a wonderful watercolor sketch of the towers, which he had given Emily on his departure; it hung in the main room in a fine oak frame which she had cut and nailed herself.

The Saltwoods of Salisbury had not survived for nearly two centuries, during which people of influence had tried to wrest Captain Nicholas Saltwood's fortune from them, without acquiring certain shrewd skills, one of which was to marry young women of the vicinity who showed ability. Emily Saltwood had been one of the most resilient, mother of four good boys and counselor to all. She had never been afraid to pinpoint inherent dangers, nor was she now.

'How old are you, Richard? Thirty-one?' He nodded. 'And you, Vera? Twenty-nine?' She nodded.

'Then you're old enough to realize that a four-month sail to Cape Town, aboard a small ship, in close confinement . . .'

The couple found it embarrassing to look at her, so she spoke with extra vigor, demanding their attention: 'Inherently dangerous, wouldn't it be?'

'I suppose so,' Richard said.

'Old romances are full of this sort of thing. Tristan and Iseult over in Cornwall. One of the Spanish kings, if I recall, and his brother escorting the bride. Are you listening to what I'm saying?'

Richard placed his hand on his mother's and said, 'I'm taking a little girl I knew at playtime . . . out to marry my brother. When I seek a wife, I'll find one for myself.'

'Those are insulting words,' Vera snapped, and for the first time the two Saltwoods looked at her as an individual and not as a prospective answer to a Saltwood family problem. She was, as Emily said, twenty-nine, tallish, thinnish, not especially beautiful of face, but lovely of voice and smile. Like many young women her age she knew how to play the piano and had taken watercolor instruction from Mr. Constable when he stayed in the village. For the moment she was reticent, but as she grew older she would become much like the woman now counseling her: a strong English wife with a mind of her own.

She had never yet been kissed by any man other than her father, and by him only rarely, but she had no fear of men and had always supposed that when the time came, her parents would find her a husband. She was a girl of spirit and rather looked forward to an interval on the frontier, always supposing that her husband would return to a position of some importance at the cathedral, in whose shadow she had been raised and intended to die.

'I'm fully aware of the dangers,' she told her putative mother-in-law, using a low, calm voice even though she realized that Mrs. Saltwood's questioning reflected on her as much as on her son.

'That's good,' Emily said with an inflection that signified: 'This meeting's over. We understand one another.' But Richard had one thing more to say: 'You must tell Vera where the idea came from that sent you to her house . . . seeking a wife . . . for Hilary, that is.'

Emily laughed vigorously and took the young people's hands in hers. 'Vera, when Richard passed through Cape Town various army friends advised him that Hilary needed a wife. It was Richard who set this all in motion. And now he proposes to complete the transaction.'

'I don't think of myself as a transaction,' Vera said.

'We're all transactions. My husband married me years ago because the Saltwood holdings needed close attention, much more than he needed a wife.'

They rose from their chairs under the oak trees and looked across at the stunning beauty of the cathedral—which some of them might never see again.

The *Alice Grace* was a small commercial barque accustomed to freighting cargo to India but now commissioned to carry some three hundred emigrants to Cape Town, in conditions which would have terrified owners of cattle being shipped across the Channel to France. Her burthen was two hundred and eighty tons, which was significant in that by law she was entitled to carry three passengers for every four tons; this meant that she should have sold passage to no more than two hundred and ten emigrants. Thus, when she left port she was ninety over complement, but since most of the passengers were charity cases, government inspectors smiled and wished her 'Good voyage!'

She departed Southampton on 9 February 1820 on a gray, wintry day when the Channel looked more immense than the ocean, its waves far more menacing. For seven painful days the little craft tossed and pitched in waves that seemed determined to pull her to shreds, and all aboard who had not sailed before were convinced that they must perish. Major Richard Saltwood, retired, who had sailed to and from India, reassured the cabin passen-

gers that once the Bay of Biscay was reached, the passage would settle into
a pleasant monotony in which the limited movement of the ship 'would be
like a gentle lullaby, no worse.'

Especially pleased to hear this was the woman whose welfare lay in his
hands. She did not accept the violent motion of the ship easily, and this
irritated her, for she was grimly determined to 'make a brave show of it,'
as she had promised her mother she would, and when her stomach was
wrenched into convulsions by her sickness, she was ashamed of herself. She
was the sole occupant of the cabin next to her brother's, as she called him,
but he shared his with a captain going out to join the Gallant Fifty-ninth
on the Afghan frontier, so that during the bad days she had two gentlemen
to assist her.

Sure enough, when the *Alice Grace* entered the great Bay of Biscay the
storms subsided and the gentle, reassuring motion which Saltwood had
predicted replaced the tossing. Vera came to like the motion of the ship, as
he was certain she would, and for the third and fourth week the three
travelers had a congenial time together, with Richard discovering what a
sterling person this Vera Lambton was. Her determination was obvious, her
sense of humor reassuring. When children were ill, she acted as general
nurse, and whenever any of the women passengers in steerage needed
attention, she was eager to help. My brother's getting a strong woman,
Richard told himself, but because of a reticence which he could not have
explained, he did not inform his cabin mate of Vera's destination. 'She's a
family friend' was all he'd say. 'Heading out to South Africa.'

'She'd make some chap quite a decent wife,' the captain observed several
times, but since he was much younger than Vera, and since his regiment
would not allow him to marry till he was thirty, his interest in her could
only be that of an observer.

Once Cape Finisterre was passed, that bleak and ominous last outpost
of European civilization, the long reach to the bulge of Africa began, and
now the three travelers began to be aware of a remarkable young man, a
wagon builder by trade, who had more or less assumed command belowdecks. He was an attractive fellow, careful of his appearance even though
the ship provided him no water for washing. His curly head and broad grin
appeared wherever there was trouble. It was he who organized the teams
that handled the slops; he supervised the distribution of food; and he sat
as judge's clerk when the rump court belowdecks handed out penalties for
such infractions as theft or pummeling another passenger.

'Name's Thomas Carleton,' he told Saltwood and the captain when they
asked if he could fix their door, which had come off its hinges during a blow.
'I can fix it, sirs. With wood I can fix anything, it seems.' And as he worked,
devising ingenious tools for getting around corners, he told them of his
apprenticeship in a small Essex village and his removal to the more important town of Saffron Walden, not far from Cambridge University, which he
had once visited.

He was a chatterbox, intensely excited about his prospects for starting
a new life in the colonies: 'I can work eighteen hours a day and sleep four.
Saffron Walden had prospects for everyone except me, so I kicked up me
heels and was off to sea. The town's a fascinating place, you understand.
Named by the father of Henry VIII, him with the wives. One of the two

places in England entitled to trade in saffron, precious stuff. It makes meat taste better, but in all me days I never took a pinch of it into me mouth. Reserved for rich people.'

Vera, returning to her cabin after a stroll on the minute deck—fifteen steps forward, fifteen back—heard this last observation and interrupted: 'Saffron's a yellow powder, I think, and it's not used for meat. It's used for rice.' She blushed and added, 'Here I am explaining India, and both you men have been associated with it.'

'Not I, not yet,' the captain said gallantly.

'But she's right,' Richard said. 'Saffron is yellow—orange, really—and they do use it a great deal in India. You'll grow to like it.'

'While you're here,' Vera said to the wagon builder, 'could you fix the lock on my box? The workmen threw it aboard, I'm afraid.'

Thomas Carleton left the men's cabin and moved a few paces to Vera's, where, after one quick glance at the portmanteau in which she kept her dresses, he told her that a small piece of wood must be replaced so that the screws holding the hasp could catch. 'It's no problem,' he assured her, 'always providing we can find the wood.' Together they made a quick tour of the deck, finding nothing, but when they went to the 'tween deck, where the ship's carpenter kept his cupboard, they found the piece they needed, and it was so small that the carpenter refused any payment from Vera: 'Take it and be blessed.' He was giving it not to this amiable girl but to the wagon builder, whose good work among the passengers he had noted.

When the box was fixed, Vera thanked the young man, four years her junior, and then talked with him about conditions belowdecks. She was by no means a philanthropist, as those seeking always to do good for others were called in England—those busybodies who were agitating against slavery in Jamaica and child labor in Birmingham—because families like hers in Salisbury were too sensible for that. But she was interested in whatever was occurring on this tedious voyage, and on subsequent days she visited various parts of the ship with Carleton, and one night about half after ten the captain who occupied the bunk closest to the dividing wall in Richard's cabin whispered, 'I say, Saltwood! I think something interesting's going on next door.'

'Mind your business,' Richard said, but any chance of sleep was destroyed, so toward three in the morning, after assuring himself that the captain was asleep, he peered into the night and saw young Thomas Carleton, he of the glib tongue, slipping out of the next-door cabin and down the ladder to his proper place below.

The next weeks, half of March and half of April, were a dismal time for Richard Saltwood; it was apparent that Vera Lambton was entertaining the young man from belowdecks three and four times a week. During the day their behavior was circumspect. They spoke casually if they chanced to meet each other as he pursued his duties, but they betrayed no sign of intimacy. On one very hot day after the Cape Verdes had been passed and the ship was heading sharply southeastward, the ship's captain summoned both Saltwood and the young officer to assist him in a court-martial; the accusing official was young Carleton, who, as an officer in charge of maintaining discipline belowdecks, had brought charges against a pitiful specimen who on four different occasions had been caught stealing.

When the court learned that he had been shipped aboard after a chain of similar offenses in London, there could be only one logical verdict: 'Twelve lashes.' And Thomas Carleton was charged with bringing on deck all the passengers so that they could see for themselves how crime was punished. When all were in place, ship's officers led the convicted on deck, where he was stripped to the waist, tied with his arms about the mast, and lashed with a club from whose end dangled nine cattails of knotted leather. He made no sound till the fifth stroke, then cried pitifully and fainted. The last seven lashes were delivered to an inert body, after which he was sloshed with salt water. There was no more stealing.

The flogging had a sobering effect upon theft belowdecks; some of the passengers were a sorry lot, but most were from the sturdy and moral lower classes, women and men who would engage in no misconduct, and they rebuked those who did. One man, nearing fifty and with two sons, grabbed Carleton's arm as the young man hurried past one afternoon and pulled him into a corner.

'Laddie,' he said bluntly, 'you're treadin' on very dangerous ground.'

'What do you mean, old man?'

'Meddlin' with a lady of quality, that's what I mean.'

'I'm a man of quality,' Thomas said quickly. 'I am as strong—'

'Those men in the cabin next hers, they're officers. They'll shoot you in a minute, laddie.'

'Those men are not involved with the lady, and take your hand down.'

This the older man refused to do. Instead he tightened it, saying, 'Laddie, this is a small ship. If I know, don't you suppose they know?'

For six days the warning deterred young Carleton from visiting Vera, and Richard sighed with relief at having avoided the necessity of intervening where his brother's honor was involved. At night he listened for sounds that would betray an assignation, and was pleased when none came echoing through the thin wall. But on the seventh day he spotted Vera talking intently with the young wagon builder, and that night, about eleven, her door creaked open and someone slipped in.

It was, in many ways, the worst night of Richard Saltwood's life, for the lovers, having been separated for a week, clutched at each other with such passion and noisy delight that the young captain was awakened.

'I say, Saltwood, listen to this! I say, like a pair of goats!'

The noise of love-making could not be masked. There were rumblings of the bulkhead, the squeals of a woman who had waited till her twenty-ninth year for love, and harsh pantings. Without even moving to the captain's bed, Richard could hear the lascivious echoes, and after a long, wild ecstasy in the other room, when the captain said, 'I say, that's prolonged!' confused Richard blurted out, 'And she's going out to marry my brother!'

In Saltwood's room there was silence, broken by the sounds bouncing off the bulkhead, and after a long time the captain asked in barrack-room accents, 'Well, whad'ja goin' to do?'

'What do you mean?' Saltwood asked in the darkness.

'Damnit all, man. Aren't you goin' to shoot him?' And Richard heard the hard clang of a revolver being slammed onto their table.

It was there when daylight came into the cabin, accusing him. He did not shave that morning, nor take any food. The young captain left him severely alone, but at midafternoon he returned, picked up the revolver, and banged it down again: 'Good God, man! It's your duty. Shoot the filthy blighter.' When Richard was unable to respond, the young man said, 'I'll testify. I've heard everything, God knows. If you want to shoot 'em both, I'll testify for that, too.'

But the Saltwoods of Salisbury were not a family that solved problems by shooting. In Parliament, Peter had been challenged to a duel by a foolish city member and had ridiculed the man into retreating. In the wilds of Illinois, young David had refused to gun down an Indian caught trespassing, although his neighbors shot them for much less. And in the South Atlantic, with storms rising as the coast of Africa hove into sight, Richard could not bring himself to shoot a young wagon builder and perhaps the man's mistress as well. Instead he waited till dusk, then told his cabin mate to put away the revolver while he went next door to talk with his sister-in-law, as she had sometimes phrased herself.

'Vera, your behavior's been shameless.'

'What do you mean?' she said, bristling.

'The bulkhead. It's very thin.' She looked at the wall in amazement, tapped upon it and heard nothing. 'We don't make noises, the captain and I,' Richard said. 'We're gentlemen.'

She tapped again, whereupon the captain, lounging in bed, tapped back. It sounded like the explosion of a gun. 'My God!' she said, covering her face.

'Yes. The captain offered me his gun, wanted me to shoot you both.'

This had quite the opposite effect from what he had intended. Vera stiffened, lost any sense of contrition, and faced him boldly. 'I'm in love, Richard. For the first time in my life I know something that you've never known, will probably never know. What it's like to be in love.'

'You're a foolish woman on a lonely ship . . .'

Instead of attempting to defend herself, she laughed. 'Don't you think I know that your poor little Hilary is sadly damaged? That you're desperate to find him a wife . . . to get him back on course? I know that. Everyone knows it.'

'Who told you?'

'Simon Keer. The Reverend Simon Keer. Oh, at the public meetings he extolled your brother. So did your mother. But when I spoke with Keer alone, what do you think he said? That Hilary's a bit of an ass. Those were his words. He said I might be able to do something with him, the LMS certainly wasn't able to.'

'He told you that?'

'What else could he tell me, if I asked him in all honesty?'

'But Keer's the reason . . . He sent Hilary to Africa.'

'What he said was "Some young men, especially from Oxford . . ." '

'Natural envy from a man without an education.'

' ". . . some young men from Oxford take religion too seriously. It addles them." '

'But Keer marches up and down England, lecturing about the missions.'

'He does so for a purpose, Richard. He wants to end slavery. Doesn't give a damn about religion . . . in the old sense.'

'What do you mean?'

'And neither do I.'

The blasphemy staggered Saltwood, and he sat down abruptly, whereupon Vera confided in a rush of words that it had been she, not her mother, who was desperate to find a husband. She loathed being a spinster, the afternoon teas, the sober dresses. Hilary, off in Africa, had been a last chance and she had grabbed at him. 'Your mother was so afraid I'd be put off by the long sea voyage.' She laughed nervously. 'I'd have fought my way aboard this ship. It was my last chance.'

Richard had never heard a woman talk this way, had never imagined that a Lambton of Salisbury could. And now the girl was saying, 'The journey's changed everything. You're no longer responsible for me. I'm going to marry Thomas.'

'No minister would—'

'Then we'll marry ourselves. When we reach South Africa he'll go to his land, and I'll go with him.'

'But Hilary will be there. Waiting.'

She did not even reply to that. She laughed in a way that caused. her shoulders to shake, after which she took Richard by the arm, pulled him to his feet, and helped him out the door. She would discuss the matter no further, and that night both Richard and the captain could again hear rumbles from the adjoining cabin.

'You goin' to shoot 'em?' the captain asked.

'No! No! Stop such questions.'

'Then I will.' And there had to be a scuffle before Richard could wrest the captain's revolver from him. But this did not deter the violent young man, who felt that somehow his honor, and that of his regiment, had been impugned, for he burst out of his cabin, knocked loudly on the adjoining door, and demanded that Carleton go below 'to your proper quarters, damn you.' When the young wagon builder tried to slip past, the captain swung a mighty blow at his head, knocking him down the ladder.

'I hope he broke his neck,' the officer growled as he returned to bed, and after some painful moments of silence he felt compelled to say, 'Saltwood, I can understand why you had to leave the regiment. You were a disgrace to the uniform.' For two days he refused to speak to his cabin mate, but on the third day, with tears in his eyes, he clasped Saltwood's hand as if they were brothers and said, 'Richard, dear boy, is there anything I can do to help?'

'There is,' Saltwood replied in deep gratitude. 'When we stop at Cape Town, have that miserable blighter thrown ashore. I promised Mother I'd deliver this girl to Hilary, and by God, I shall, damaged or not.'

So when the *Alice Grace* put in for replenishing, none of the passengers belowdecks were allowed ashore, for they were docketed to Algoa Bay, three weeks more sailing along the coast. But the young wagon builder who had dared to make love to a lady of quality was thrown onto the wharf, with his axes and angles, while the lady of quality wept for him from the railing.

She was rudely dragged away by Richard, who said with fierce determination, 'You must go on to Hilary. As you promised Mother.' And all the time the *Alice Grace* stayed in Cape Town, she was kept prisoner in her cabin, guarded by the brother-in-law who stood guard outside, relinquishing his position to the captain when sleep was necessary. Even when the governor invited all the captain's guests to a gala, she was not allowed to attend lest she meet with Thomas Carleton and run away.

She remained in her cabin even when the ship resumed its journey, as did everyone else who had one, for a wintry gale blew up, driving the vessel far south, reminding the sailors of Adamastor, the tempestuous giant who guarded the Cape in the time of Vasco da Gama, and of whom Luis de Camoens had written with such brilliance.

Day after day the winds raged, forcing waves so high across the bow of the ship that they flooded cabins. At times the vessel plunged downward in such steep and sickening falls that everyone belowdecks was sent flying in one direction and then another as shrieks and wails competed with the howling winds. Sleep was impossible and food unthinkable; at numerous times, when her wet and lonely cabin shivered as if its bulkhead might splinter, Vera huddled in a corner, fearful of the moment when the voyage would end, terrified of its continuance, but never did she give way to superstition and castigate herself or her actions with Thomas as being in any way the cause of this violent storm. She was glad she had known him, even for just their brief passage through the tropics, and she prayed that in some mysterious way she might meet him again.

Alone, at the heart of a shattering tempest, she changed from being a meek English spinster and became a mature woman with a surprisingly independent mind. She had enjoyed being loved by a strong man and realized that she could never return to the dreamy afternoons of a cathedral town. As for marrying a missionary, that was quite impossible, but what she would do she did not know. Once, as the ship fell sideways in a plunge that could have torn it apart, she clung to her bed to prevent being swept away and cried, 'If we make land, I'm an African.' And she shook her fist in some wild direction, supposing the storm-girt continent to lie in that quarter.

On the seventh day of the storm, when the little barque was well down toward polar waters, passengers began reciting old tales of ships, rudderless and sails gone, being driven relentlessly southward till ice entrapped them, holding them forever in its embrace: 'A graveyard of ships down there, masts erect. Everyone aboard frozen stiff and standing erect till judgment day.' They told also of the Flying Dutchman: 'Captain van der Decken, out of Rotterdam. One of his great-grandsons settled at the Cape years ago. Swore he could round the Cape in a storm like this, swore an oath to do so. He's out there somewhere, still trying to breast the Cape, and will be till the people frozen down there are called to judgment.'

The poor ship was so knocked about that when the storm finally abated and the sun allowed the captain to calculate his position, all were shocked to learn how far south they had been driven; they were indeed on their way to the ice, and now, as they turned north toward Algoa Bay, they were humbled and chastened in spirit, so that even the young captain felt remorse at the way he had wanted to treat the awakened young woman in the cabin next to him, and he knocked on her door to apologize.

'I'm sorry,' he said.

'I'm not,' she replied.

'In the storm,' the captain confided, 'I thought once or twice we must surely sink. And do you know what I thought next?' He smiled at her engagingly, a man much younger than herself, endeavoring to reach understanding. 'I thought how utterly insane I'd been to interfere in your affairs. I wanted to shoot you, you know.'

'I was told.'

'Madam, would you allow me to make amends? I was such an ass. Whom you love makes no difference to others.' And to her astonishment, he fell to one knee, took her hand—and kissed it.

The scene at Algoa Bay in the winter of 1820 was one of historic confusion, confusion because five ships like the *Alice Grace* were trying to unload passengers in the open roadstead without a wharf to aid them, historic because a whole new type of person was coming ashore to add a new dimension to South African life.

The confusion was monumental, both in the bay and ashore. Captains endeavored to anchor their ships as securely as possible, but wind and tide tossed them vigorously, so that anyone trying to debark was in peril. Long ropes were led ashore through the water; they would be used to haul the boats to the beach. Women and children, of which there were aplenty, were crowded into the rude boats and taken ashore through the surf. Occasionally a boat broke loose to wander off, passengers screaming, until some stout-hearted swimmer came to rescue it.

Some women, having come seven thousand miles to their destination, flatly refused to debark, trusting neither the frail boats nor the men guiding them, but bellowed orders from the ship's officers usually forced them loose from the railings to which they clung; a few had to be dropped bodily into the tossing boats, and these ran the risk of broken limbs. Some daring children, unable to wait any longer to reach the paradise about which they had been constantly told, leaped gaily into the water as the lighters neared the beach, gasped and spat and spluttered toward shore, screaming their delight. Their mothers watched anxiously till they were lifted out of the water and onto the shoulders of men who would carry them through the surf. Among those who helped the immigrants to safety were some Xhosa who only a year before had flung themselves against Grahamstown.

Ashore the confusion worsened: 'The party from Manchester, over here! Liverpool, over there! Glaswegians, stay by that dune. Please, please! The Cardiff people must come over here to the big man with the top hat!' Dashing from one end of the beach to the other, instructing everyone what to do, was Colonel Cuyler of Albany, New York, now in charge of a much more pleasant task. But even here the energetic man encountered troubles, for the government had appointed him to instruct the immigrants in harsh facts overlooked in England when the glories of South Africa were being extolled: 'This is not yet a land of milk and honey. It's a land of guns. Never, never go into your fields without your muskets.'

In addition to the scrambling immigrants, the shore was cluttered with Boer farmers who had driven in, from sixty and seventy miles away, in heavy wagons pulled by fourteen or sixteen or twenty oxen, and these men forced hard bargains with the newcomers, offering to cart them and their possessions to their new homes for outrageous prices. But what alternative did the immigrants have? So day after day wagons were loaded, whips were cracked, and teams of stolid oxen began the long journey to the new paradise.

In the waiting crowd ashore was Reverend Hilary Saltwood, come to greet his bride. He was still extraordinarily thin and visibly entering middle age, for he was thirty-five and showed the effects of his hard life. He was certainly not an attractive bridegroom, and few women would have sailed so far to claim him, but when his present duties ended and he could be got back to England for some fattening up, and settled in some quaint rural parish, he might prove acceptable. The outstanding thing in his favor was the gleam that suffused his face: it was the countenance of a man who believed in what he was doing and found constant reassurance in the honesty of his calling. He loved people; his expedition to Grahamstown with the commando had taught him even to love the Boers who opposed him so vigorously, and the fact that he had fought well against the Xhosa warriors had earned him respect, so that the ox wagon that waited to take his bride to Golan Mission had been volunteered by Tjaart van Doorn himself.

There the two men waited amidst the wild confusion: the tall dark-suited missionary so ill-at-ease; the short, squared-off Boer with the heavy beard; the sixteen lumbering oxen indifferent to the whole affair. 'Dear God!' Hilary cried. 'It's Richard!' And he ran to the beach to embrace his brother coming wet and dripping out of the waves.

'Where's the lady?' Hilary asked in some apprehension, forgetting to introduce Van Doorn, who stood nearby, testing his hippopotamus-hide whip.

'She'll be coming,' Richard said. 'Who's this?'

'Oh, this is my neighbor, Tjaart van Doorn.'

'You live at the mission?'

'Thirty miles north.'

Richard blinked. Neighbors at thirty miles? But then he heard a shout from the *Alice Grace*'s lighter. It was the captain, with Vera Lambton beside him: 'Richard! Ho, Saltwood! Here comes the bride!'

His cry was so hearty, and the message so warm in this scene of new lives beginning, that everyone in the vicinity stopped work to watch the arrival of Miss Lambton, who looked quite pretty in her rough traveling clothes. Three cheers went up as the lighter was slowly pulled ashore, strong hands grasping the rope and guiding it to the beach.

Ashore, men quickly learned that she was the intended of Reverend Saltwood, and cheers were raised in his behalf. Even Tjaart van Doorn, moved by the spectacle of a wife arriving in such manner, relaxed and clapped the minister on the back: 'Exciting, eh?' And he moved forward to help bring his neighbor's betrothed ashore.

In the boat Vera sat rigid, her eyes down; she did not want to scan the shore lest she see the missionary she had been sent to marry. She did not want him, her heart lay elsewhere, and she doubted she could ever mask that fact; but the fierce rejection she had voiced during the storm had subsided, and now, faced with the prospect of making her way alone in a strange continent, she supposed that she must accept him: God forgive me for what I am about to do.

At the last moment she looked up, and what she saw banished all her fears—and although she endangered herself, she stood up in the boat, waved both hands, and screamed, 'Thomas!'

Thomas Carleton, wagon builder of Saffron Walden, had galloped at breakneck speed across the flats, across the mountains and the long reaches, to intercept the boat, and there he stood, arms outstretched, to greet his love. Disdaining the hands that waited to lead her onto dry land, Vera leaped into the shallow water, lifted her skirts, and ran through the waves, throwing her arms wide to embrace the one man she could ever love. She was twenty-nine, he twenty-five; she was educated in Bible, painting and music, he in wood-handling; but they were joyously committed to living in South Africa the rest of their lives. They were the English settlers of 1820.

Vera's arrival in this dramatic manner dominated the attention of everyone, even Richard Saltwood, who stood aghast as he watched her. Reverend Hilary was left standing alone, off with the oxen and the waiting wagon that would never carry his bride to the mission. Gradually people on the shore became aware of him, and turned to look at the forlorn figure, and as they did so, they broke into laughter. Harsh words were thrown, and ribald ones, and he stood apart, allowing them to fall over him like a cascade of icy water. He sought condolence from no one, nor did he try in any way to dissuade Miss Lambton from her extraordinary behavior. He could not guess what had precipitated it, but he was sure it must have been an emotion of powerful force, and certainly it was God's will that she should go with the other and not with him.

He did not demur when Tjaart came back and said apologetically, 'Since I'm here, I'll cart the couple to their new home . . . if it's all right with you.'

'That's what you should do,' and when Richard, having assembled his own gear, said that he, too, must find a carter and be on his way, Hilary nodded. In the end, all the immigrants found transportation of some kind or other and were off to try raising wheat and mealies on land that could scarcely grow weeds; the government had not been entirely honest with these settlers, neither in Cape Town nor in London. They were not supposed to be farmers and merchants in the old sense; they were to form forward hedgehogs of self-defense along the border, keeping the Xhosa away from the established farms farther inland. Vera and Thomas, in their frontier home, were supposed to take the brunt of any Xhosa attack, so that established settlements like Grahamstown could exist in safety.

Hilary, who understood this conniving strategy, was saddened to see his intended bride and his brother heading eastward into such a situation, and as he stood alone he prayed for them, that God would give them strength for the trials that lay ahead. That done, he watched their wagons disappear, then mounted his horse and rode slowly back to Golan Mission.

He would never forget 1820. For him it was a year of tragedy, with both the Boer and the English communities sneering at him, not even conceding that he was a well-intentioned dominee. His mission was characterized as a farce where blacks could escape honest work; his attempts at agriculture were pitiful; and his constant insistence that Hottentot and Xhosa be given fair treatment was seen as weakness of character. The Boers despised him for his antagonism to coerced labor, the backbone of their existence, while the English dismissed him as socially unacceptable.

His position worsened whenever Dr. Keer, in London, issued a new publication or caused an inquiry to be made in Parliament. The little agitator was finding that his diatribes against the Boers were popular with the English press and his passkey to the highest ranks of English society. He wrote and preached and lectured, uttering the most inflammatory accusations against the Boers, but whenever he thundered from the safety of London, the lightning struck Hilary Saltwood in his exposed mission, and there was serious talk among the farmers of burning the place.

He seemed sublimely indifferent to the ostracism and to the threats. He maintained a kind of Christian charity at his mission, accepting all who stumbled in, finding them clothes and food in unlikely quarters. He kept the converts working, more or less, and spent much time with the choir, believing that a soul that sang was closer to God than one that brooded in silence, and many travelers of that period wrote amusingly of coming to Golan and hearing at evening prayers a glorious choir singing old English hymns, all faces dark except that of the missionary, which stood a good foot higher than the others. The writers always implied that Saltwood was out of place, but that was not accurate. He belonged with these people.

It may have been that God devised this loneliness, when all white men scorned him, so that his attention could be focused on the future of South Africa; at any rate, one night as he lay sleepless he was vouchsafed a vision of such crystal purity that in the morning he had to share it with his parishioners. He spoke in a mélange of English, Dutch, Portuguese and Xhosa:

> 'With the coming of our English cousins, and in such numbers, we can see that this land can henceforth never be of one unit. It must always be broken into fragments, many different people, many different languages. We stand this morning, in 1821, like a river moving along the crest of a ridge. Sooner or later it must come down one side or other, and how it comes will make all the difference in this land. Let us pray that it will come tumbling joyously down as a cascade of love and brotherhood, in which Hottentot and Xhosa and Englishman and Boer share the work and the rewards. Golan Mission must no longer be for blacks alone. We must open our hearts to all people, our school to all children. [Here he frowned.] I cannot

believe that our great river of humanity will go rushing down the wrong side of the mountain, creating a hateful society in which men of different colors, languages and religions will go their separate ways in bitter little streams, each off to itself. For we are all brothers in God and He intended that we work and live together.'

Among his listeners that morning, when he shared his vision of a new South Africa, were many who could not comprehend what he was talking about; common sense told them that white men who had wagons and guns and many horses were intended to rule and to have lesser people work for them. But there were a few who understood that what the missionary was saying was true, not at this moment perhaps, but in the long reach of a man's whole life, or perhaps within the lives of his grandchildren.

Among this latter group was the gifted soprano Emma, whose family had escaped slavery through Hilary's charity, or rather his mother's, for she had sent the funds which purchased their release. Emma was now twenty-one, smallish in size, and her face was as jet-black as ever, her teeth even and white. She had a wonderfully placid disposition, worked well with children, and guided the mission whenever Saltwood had to be absent.

For some time she had been thinking of Golan's future, and because she was a Madagascan and not a Xhosa, she was able to see more clearly than some. She found the Xhosa in general a superior people, and could name a dozen ways in which they excelled: 'Baas, they could be as good farmers or hunters as any Boer.'

'Never, never call me Baas again,' Hilary admonished. 'I am your friend, not your baas.'

She was aware, of course, that Hilary had gone to Algoa Bay to fetch a wife, and speedy rumors had reached even Golan, describing the hilarious scene in which he had stood on the shore, arms open to receive his woman, while she ran right past him to embrace another. Emma, better than most, appreciated the agony this sensitive man must have known then, and upon his return she had discharged most of the managerial duties until he had time to absorb his disgrace, and bury it.

Emma, with no last name, understood the subtle process by which Saltwood had sublimated his personal grief and found, in doing so, his vision of South Africa as a whole, and she supposed that no one would ever understand this country, in which she, like Hilary, was a stranger, until he had experienced some sense of tragedy. She supposed also that once he expressed his vision, he would see its impossibility and would shortly thereafter leave the area and return to England, which must lie very far away.

So she was surprised one day, and perhaps pleased, when he said, 'I shall stay here the rest of my life. I'm needed for the building.'

She believed him, and knowing this, moved closer to him, for it was apparent that no man as fragile as he could survive without strong assistance, and she further observed that he was held in such scorn by the two white communities that there was little possibility that he could ever find a wife in those quarters.

She was, in some respects, even more solidly informed than Saltwood himself and exercised a sounder judgment, and this had been true when she was ten and realized that her life depended upon escaping from slavery at De Kraal. Her parents had been afraid; the other slaves, all of them, had been terrified of consequences; but she had fled into the night without horse or guide and had made her way to freedom. Now it was she who saw that Hilary must have a partner, and she perceived this on the simplest base: that he could not survive without one.

Reverend Saltwood, after his vision and his willingness to commit his life to it, was thinking along much different lines. He felt that God had brought him to Golan for some specific and perhaps noble purpose, and he was sure that it was God who had vouchsafed him the vision; in this respect he was much like Lodevicus the Hammer, except that Lodevicus had known that God had visited him personally.

Therefore, if he had been chosen for some exalted design, it was obligatory that he conform to the inherent patterns of that design—and what were they? That all men in South Africa were brothers, that all were equal in the sight of God and that all had just rights, none standing higher than another. He recognized that there were managerial degrees, and he was certainly no revolutionary; in the Missionary Society, for example, he stood on the very lowest rung of the hierarchy, and in his humility he suspected that he deserved little more. In Cape Town lived officials who gave him orders, and in London lived other officials who sent orders to South Africa, and above all, stood the little group of powerful thinkers like Simon Keer who directed everything. He was quite satisfied with the abstract structure, but he was somewhat troubled by the fact that everyone in the chain of command was white, as if this were a prerequisite for power. At Golan he had delegated command and it had worked rather well.

He had turned the mission choir over to Emma, and it was she who had trained the voices into a beautiful instrument, not he. He had found that in his absences Emma had run the establishment at least as well as he, and perhaps better. She certainly was as good a Christian, having braved true hardships in forging her allegiance to Jesus, and she was kind and humble in dealing with Boers when they came to complain about their runaways. 'Humble, but firm,' he wrote in one report, 'she displays the true sense of Christ's teaching. If she is required to face down some arrogant Boer screaming for the return of his Hottentots, she stands there, a little figure in a gingham dress, hands on hips, defying them to desecrate the house of the Lord. One man thrashed her with his whip, but she would not move, and in some confusion he rode away.'

Another line of thought was pushing its way into Saltwood's reflections, and he would have been astonished if its historic parallel had been pointed out to him, but like many men from superior cultures who are placed in association with large numbers of persons of inferior mechanical culture, he was beginning to think that salvation lay in rejecting the inherited superior culture and marrying some simple woman from the less advantaged, and in so doing, establishing connection with the soil, with the elementary. Thus, at this very time in Russia young men of the ruling class were coming to believe that they must marry serfs to attain contact with the real Russia, and in France writers and philosophers contemplated marriage to fallen women, so that together they might start from a solid base, as it were, and climb to new understandings. In Brazil gruff Portuguese planters defiantly married blacks: 'To hell with Lisbon. This is my life henceforth.' And in India certain mystic-driven young Englishmen were thinking that to understand the land to which they were now committed, they must take Indian wives.

There was a sense of self-flagellation in all this, and many observers were amused by it, but there was also a sense of primordial experience, of identification with a new land, and of deep-rooted psychological suspicions that in a flowering culture marked by too many books and far too many parties, something fundamental was being lost. When religion, with its example of Jesus Christ's abnegation, was thrown into the scales, there built up a solid impulse toward actions that would never otherwise have been contemplated, and one bright morning when life at Golan Mission was as placid as it would ever be, Reverend Hilary Saltwood entered upon three days of prayer and fasting.

He was thirty-six now, and as far in promotions as he would ever go. He was aware that his mother still fondly imagined him coming home to the deanship at Salisbury, but he knew that lustrous prize was lost forever; indeed, he sometimes doubted that he could even secure some inconspicuous English living. He suspected also that his term at Golan had better be ended; he had built so well that any new man from London could take charge. But his productive life was by no means finished; he felt an urgent call to the north, where many lived in ignorance of Jesus, and he envisioned his life as spent in one lonely outpost after another. But to live like that he needed a companion.

He remembered how excited he had been when his mother wrote that she was sending him a wife. How often he had read that letter, how carefully he had studied his mother's description of Miss Lambton, visualizing her working with him in outpost stations. In his loneliness he would sometimes recall every item of her dress as she came through the surf that day in Algoa Bay. 'I need a wife to share the veld,' he cried aloud.

But what wife? Dare he ever again enlist his mother in a search? He thought not. Could he ride over to Grahamstown to see if it contained any eligible women, new widows, perhaps, among the immigrants? Not likely. There they would laugh at him and jeer, and no woman would want to share that humiliation. Should he return to Cape Town? Never. Never. His life was on the frontier with the black people he loved.

Loved! Did he love Emma, his marvelous little assistant with the laughing eyes? He believed he did, but he wondered whether God would approve of such a union.

His thinking thus far had required one full day; he spent the next two in trying to ascertain whether a man totally devoted to Jesus Christ dared risk such a marriage, and just as the Boers searched the Old Testament for guidance in their time of tribulation, so he took down the New Testament and tried to decipher the teachings of Jesus and St. Paul, and the old familiar phrases leaped and tumbled in contradiction through his mind: 'It is better to marry than to burn . . . He that is unmarried careth for the things of the Lord . . . Husbands, love your wives . . . It is good for a man not to touch a woman . . . So ought men to love their wives as their own bodies,' and St. Paul's specific command to celibacy: 'I say therefore to the unmarried, "It is good for them if they abide even as I." '

It was a confusing doctrine, generated in a time when people were living in agitated communities much like the South Africa of 1821, and a searcher could find Biblical justification for either marrying or not marrying, but in the end one incident in the New Testament superseded all others: when a poor couple in Cana were being married without enough money to provide wine for their guests, Jesus stepped forward and converted water into wine so that the celebration could proceed. Laughter possessed Hilary when he thought of it: I've always liked that miracle best of all. A celebration. A blessing. And at the end the governor himself saying, 'At most parties they serve good wine at the beginning, rubbish as soon as the guests are drunk. But you've brought us the best wine at the end. Stout fellow!' I believe that Jesus and his disciples must have danced at this wedding.

He spent the third night praying, and in the morning he went to Emma and said, 'Jesus Himself would dance at our wedding. Will you have me?'

They were married quietly by Saul, who now served as deacon at the mission—this tall white man, this short black woman. They shared a wattled hut beside the church, and since no announcements were broadcast, news of the extraordinary marriage did not circulate.

It certainly did not reach Grahamstown, seventy-five miles to the east, where Richard Saltwood had found himself a saucy bride, Julie, the Dorset girl who had ridden her own horse to Plymouth to take passage on one of the last emigrant ships. Alone and unprotected, she lacked the funds to hire a sixteen-oxen wagon to freight her to Grahamstown, so she had walked, bringing with her barely more than the clothes on her back. Within a week six men had wanted to marry her, and in her flirtatious way she had chosen Richard. She could not read, but when he explained that one day he would take her back to the cathedral town of Salisbury, she said brightly, 'Then, by God, I better learn,' and she had sought out Mrs. Carleton to teach her, and the two women, so unlike in breeding, so similar in courage, had a fine time wrestling with the alphabet.

When Richard proposed that he send for his brother to conduct the wedding, Julie cried, 'Capital! It'll give us a chance to introduce him to the town.'

So a servant was sent west on horseback to invite Hilary to perform the ceremony, and the invitation seemed so sincere and the opportunity to establish connections with the new settlement so favorable that the missionary accepted. He would take Emma with him so that the Grahamstown people could witness the depth of his conviction that a new era was beginning in the colony.

Hilary, Emma, Saul and the servant made the eastward journey, with Bible reading each evening, prayers each dawn, and much conversation about Richard and his experiences in India. Hilary, having found great happiness in his own marriage, speculated on what kind of bride his brother was taking, and in his prayers repeatedly asked God to bless Richard.

As the quartet rode into Grahamstown, Hilary pointed out the little houses that had seemed like secure fortresses that day when he faced the screaming Xhosa, and he showed Emma the site on which Tjaart van Doorn had saved his life.

As they rode down the principal street they came to the spacious parade ground where a small church stood on land which would be occupied later by a fine cathedral, and another of Richard's Hottentot servants hailed the procession to say that Baas was at the shop of Carleton, the wagon builder, so the horses were turned in that direction while the slave hurried on ahead, shouting, 'De Reverend kom! Look, he kom!' And to the door of the rude shed in which Carleton worked came his wife, his friend Richard Saltwood and lively Julie, the intended bride. All four looked up at the horsemen and saw Hilary sitting high among them.

'Hullo, Hilary,' Richard said with the casualness that had always marked his behavior toward his brother. 'Glad you could come.'

'Hello, Richard. I hear God has blessed you with a bride. He has blessed me, too. This is my wife, Emma.'

From her horse the petite Madagascan smiled warmly at the two women, then nodded to their men. She remembered them later as four gaping mouths: 'They were astounded, Hilary. Didn't you see them, four mouths wide open?'

No one spoke. Emma, with a deep sense of propriety, felt that it was not her duty to do so first, since she was being presented to them, but they were too dumbstruck even to speak to Hilary, let alone his extraordinary wife. Finally the missionary said, 'We'd better dismount,' and he extended his hand to his wife.

The story sped through Grahamstown: 'That damned fool Saltwood's married a Xhosa bitch.'

It was an agonizing three days. No one knew where to put Emma, or how to feed her, or what to say to her. They were surprised to learn that she could speak good English and write much better than Julie. She was modest, of good deportment, but very black. There was no way to alleviate the awfulness of her reality, no explanation that could soften the dreadful fact that a decent Englishman, although a missionary, had married one of his Xhosa Kaffirs. When it was pointed out that she was really a Madagascan, one man said, 'Know the place well. The bastards ate my uncle.' And now a rumor circulated that Emma had been a cannibal.

Richard quietly insisted that the marriage proceed as planned, with his brother officiating, and the temporary church was crowded, most of the spectators having come to see the cannibal. It was a moving ceremony, filled with the soaring phrases of the Church of England wedding ritual, perhaps the most loving in the civilized world.

> 'Dearly beloved, we are gathered together here in the sight of God, and in the face of this company, to join together this Man and this Woman in holy Matrimony; which is an honourable state, instituted of God in the time of man's innocency . . . which holy estate Christ adorned and beautified with his presence, and first miracle that he wrought in Cana of Galilee . . . Wilt thou love her, comfort her, honour, and keep her in sickness and in health . . . so long as ye both shall live . . . forsaking all others . . . for better for worse, for richer for poorer, in sickness and in health, to love and to cherish, till death us do part . . .'

When Hilary intoned these mighty words, standing tall and gaunt, like someone St. Paul might have ordained in Ephesus, he gave them special meaning, for it seemed to him that he was solemnizing not only his brother's marriage but his own, and when he came to the cry, ' "O Lord save thy servant and thy handmaid!" ' he felt that he was asking blessing upon himself, and some of the congregation suspected this and looked with horrid fascination at Emma, wondering if she could qualify as a handmaiden whose fate concerned God.

The highlight of the ceremony came with the singing of Psalm Sixty-seven, required by The Book of Common Prayer, for then little Emma, who stood facing the crowded church, let her voice soar as she did at the mission, and other singers stopped to listen:

'O let the nations rejoice and be glad: for thou shalt judge the folk righteously, and govern the nations upon earth.'

The congregants heard the song but not the words.

On the return trip Hilary said, 'It was a dreadful mistake to have come. They saw nothing. They understood nothing.'

'What did you think when you met Vera?'

'It was strange. I'd never seen her, you know. Not really. I moved forward. She moved back. And I thought, "How lucky I was not to have married her." '

'You never had the chance,' Emma said.

'I'm convinced God took care of that. He had you in mind.'

'I liked Thomas very much,' she said. 'He'll do well in this country. We need wagons.'

'You and I need one, particularly.'

'Why?'

'Because we've got to move north. We're not wanted here any longer.'

So when they reached Golan and satisfied themselves that Saul could maintain the mission with Hottentot and Xhosa deacons until some young clergyman arrived from England, they started packing in earnest. They acquired a small wagon and sixteen oxen, a tent of sorts and some wooden boxes for their goods. With this meager equipment they set forth.

They headed northwest for a destination unknown, one man, one woman traversing barren lands that held no water, moving into canyons where desperadoes might be lurking, and crossing lands often ravaged by wandering bands of Hottentot and Bushmen outlaws. They had no fear, because they carried almost nothing of value that could be taken from them, and if they were to be slain, it would be in God's service. They were traveling to take His word into a new land, and they would maintain their steady progress for fifty days. Alone, walking slowly beside their oxen, they went into lands that no white man had ever penetrated before.

In later decades much would be made of treks conducted by large groups of Boers armed with guns, and these would indeed be remarkable adventures, but equally so were the unspectacular movements of solitary English missionaries as they probed the wilderness, these lonely harbingers of civilization.

By accident, and surely not by design, the Saltwoods came at last into that bleak northern country which had provided refuge to the slaves Jango and Deborah, who had fled here with their children. The land was now occupied by a few Bushmen, a few Hottentots who led a vagrant life after their last herds had been bartered away, quite a few runaway slaves from various parts of the world, and a scattering of ill-defined ne'er-do-wells and outcasts. In the veins of these fugitives there was Dutch blood aplenty, German, too, from settlers and sailors off ships, and not a little contributed by English officers on their way home from India and freed during their Cape Town leaves from the confines of British respectability. There was every color, from the purest black to the fairest white, the last being provided by the new missionary, Hilary Saltwood of Oxford.

He had settled on land in the northern part of the Great Karroo, that rolling semi-desert which occupied so much of the country. It was a thirstland whose treeless expanse frightened most people but enchanted those who found refuge here. The Saltwoods built their meager hartebeest hut close to a meandering stream, which went dry much of the year. When it was finished, they surrounded it with a thicket of protective thorn, exactly as Australopithecus had done five million years earlier.

The site would have seemed quite miserable, except for the cluster of five hills, each separated from all the others, perfectly round at the base, handsomely leveled off at the top. Their beauty lay in their symmetry, their classic purity of form; from a distance they resembled five judges huddling for an opinion, but from within their circles—say at the entrance to the missionaries' hut—they became protective sentinels guarding the Karroo from the vast herds of animals that wandered by and from the titanic storms that swept across it. When a man elected to serve God at this forsaken spot, he had the presence of God with him at all times.

One traveler, standing at the door to Saltwood's hut, avowed that he could 'see north to portals of heaven and west to the gates of hell without spotting a human being.' He was, of course, wrong. In various nooks and secret places families had their huts. Behind the flat-topped hills there were whole villages whose residents hunted small animals for their hides, great ones for their ivory tusks. Others traded to the north, crossing the Karroo to where substantial numbers of people congregated. And others, with remarkable diligence, actually farmed the area—one hundred and fifty acres to feed one sheep—and found it profitable. One man mended wagons for customers as far distant as a hundred miles.

But everyone in the Karroo shared in one miracle, and joyously. When spring rains came to this arid land, usually in early November, the rolling plains exploded with flowers, millions of them in a sweeping carpet of many hues. It seemed as if nature had hidden here her leftover colors, waiting for the proper moment to splash them upon the world. In one of his sermons Hilary Saltwood said, 'The stars in heaven, the flowers on the Karroo, they're God's reminder that He stays with us.'

His duties were many. It was he who marked with ritual the passages of life: to christen, to marry, to bury. He served as arbitrator in family brawling. He taught school. His wife was general nurse to the scattered community. Messages were left at his rectory, the hut by the water pan, and he counseled with all who sought advice on anything. He helped at brandings, attended slaughterings in the hope that he might come home with a leg of something. And he participated in extended hunts when food was needed. He was a vicar of the veld.

But most of all he conducted services, in the open, beside the stream, with the five hills looking down. He read from the New Testament, lingering on its revolutionary messages of social justice, equality and brotherhood. In simple terms, devoid of cant, he talked with his people about new fashions of living in which all men would share responsibility, and he bore constant testimony to the fact that black and white could live together in harmony:

> 'That the white man is temporarily in a position of command be- cause of his gun, his horse and his wagon is as nothing in the eyes of the Lord, or in the passage of history. How brief is the life of man. A hundred years from now it may be the black man who will be in a position of authority, and how little that too will matter in the eyes of the Lord. White man up, black man up, the perpetual problems remain. Where do I get my food to eat? How do I pay my taxes? Am I safe at night when I go to sleep? Can my children learn the lessons they need? It is answers to those questions that we seek, and it matters not who is powerful and who weak, because in the great rolling away of history, all things change but the fundamentals.'

Whenever he spoke like this on Sunday morning, he spent Sunday afternoon wondering about the education of his own children. He and Emma now had three dark-skinned rascals, with their father's height and their mother's flashing white teeth. They were bright children, masters of the alphabet at five and their numbers at six. With others in the area, they studied with Emma and took their catechism from Hilary; some of these children were instrumental in bringing their parents to the mission, encouraging them to go through the motions of worship, and all participated when Reverend Saltwood organized a picnic with games and songs and food.

Then the young ones, twenty or thirty of them, of every shade, would venture outside the five hills and play on land that reached forever. A dozen kinds of antelope would watch from a distance, and sometimes lions would move close to listen and then to roar with chilling thunder.

Adults always sought permission to join these safaris, and sometimes it seemed as if they enjoyed the outings more than their children, especially when great flocks of ostrich loped past or when boys found a settlement of meerkats. Then there was joy indeed as everyone gathered to watch the furry little animals scamper to their burrows, stand upright to see who was watching, and duck swiftly below ground. 'Meerkats are like people,' Emma told the children, 'they must run around, but they're happiest when they go back into their homes.'

Hilary could find in the Bible no precedent for a picnic, and he some- times wondered if he was sponsoring a pagan ritual. There was no instance in which Jesus had participated in such a gathering, but the missionary felt sure that the Master would have approved this glowing combination of fellowship in watching the meerkats and reverence in singing the hymns that followed. And one night he asked Emma, 'Isn't it possible that the miracle of the loaves and fishes should be considered a picnic? Or when He asked that the children be allowed to come to Him. Maybe the Cana wedding guests assembled on the side of some hill in Galilee.'

Such days imparted a happiness that Hilary had never known before. His wife was a woman of infinite richness; her children were a joy; the tattered people who comprised his congregation loved his curious manners and forgave his intrusions into their spiritual lives; and the great, barren land, once one became accustomed to it, provided a congenial home. Best of all, there were no Boers and Englishmen contesting for power, no social stigma because this man was white, that woman black.

And then the relative peace was broken by Dr. Simon Keer, thundering back to South Africa to collect incidents to be used in another book. He was in his fifties now, at the apex of his political power and a furious fighter for causes worthy of his support. He had recently assumed leadership of the philanthropic movement, as it was now called, and had learned how to excite huge crowds in London and Paris with his fiery oratory and dramatic examples of Boer misconduct. His first book, *The Truth About South Africa,* had run its course, and he felt he could best inflame opinion by producing a sequel showing that the horrors of Dutch occupancy at the Cape still persisted, even though Englishmen of higher moral standards held the reins of government. A supporter had given him a generous loan to fund this trip, counting upon Dr. Keer's sensationalism to cover the investment.

In short, the volcanic little man had found in the philanthropic movement his golden Ophir, and he was coming back to South Africa to increase his treasure.

Wherever he went he caused turmoil, lecturing the locals about morality, threatening them with the laws his friends in Parliament were about to pass, and accusing the Boer farmers of crimes that would have been rejected even by the Black Circuit of 1812. Always he made the confrontation one between the honest Englishmen of the empire and the dishonest Boers of the backveld, and when one man who had seen the real horrors of slavery in the English islands of the Caribbean said in public meeting, 'Don't come preaching to us. Clean up your own islands,' he silenced the man with the thundering response: 'Your observation is irrelevant.'

When rumors circulated that two Boers had tried to assassinate him at Swellendam, his audiences increased in size, as did his fury; he was certainly not without courage, for he took his message to all parts of the colony, and in due course he convoked at Grahamstown a meeting of all LMS personnel, and when messengers had ridden to the outposts, a strange, ungainly group of men and women began to straggle in. They were the forward agents of God, an impassioned, dedicated, unlikely lot made old before their time by the bleak conditions under which they lived, but intensified in their beliefs by the problems they had succeeded in solving.

Strangest of all the couples were the Saltwoods of Great Karroo, he walking in long strides, staff in hand, his black wife riding a small horse. They had come three hundred miles, their eyes ablaze at the prospect of meeting the leaders of their calling. When they entered the thriving mercantile center the first sign they saw was THOMAS CARLETON, WAGON BUILDER. It was a real building now, with stone walls, tiled roof; in fact, it was two buildings, one the foundry and carpenter's shop, the other a sturdy house.

'We must halt here,' Hilary said, anxious to try to heal any wounds that might still exist between him and the man who had stolen his bride. 'Hello, Thomas!' he called, and when the builder appeared at the door of his forge, Hilary was astonished to see how the years that had handled him so roughly had scarcely touched this bright-faced young man.

'I'm Saltwood,' Hilary said hesitantly.

'Why, so it is! Vera, come here!' And from the house beside the shop came the former Miss Lambton of Salisbury, now a matron with two blond children. No longer the timid spinster studying watercolors, she was now in her mid-thirties, mistress of a house and keeper of accounts for her husband's thriving business.

'Good morning, Hilary,' she said graciously. Then, with a mischievousness she could never have disclosed back in Wiltshire, she teased: 'You're the reason I sailed so far.'

'Are these your children?'

'They are.'

'I have three now,' he said quietly.

'We haven't stopped, you know,' Carleton said, putting his arm about his wife.

'Has my brother any little ones?'

'Like all of us. He has one.'

During this colloquy Emma had remained on her horse, quietly to the rear, and now Vera cried warmly, 'Here is your wife!'

'It is. Emma, as you know.'

The wagon builder helped her alight, took her by both hands, and asked, 'Didn't you tell us you're a Madagascan?'

'I did.'

'How in the world did you get down here?'

'I was born here,' she said in the slow, beautiful English she had acquired from her Oxford-educated husband. 'But my parents were . . . How do you say it, Hilary?'

'Kidnapped.'

'They were kidnapped by Portuguese slavers. It was quite common. Still is, I think.'

'Little woman like you, three children!' Carleton shook his head and returned to his work.

In the days prior to Dr. Keer's arrival, the Karroo couple participated in many friendly meetings like this, for the indignation caused by their marriage had abated. Grahamstown was now a typical rural English settlement with a thriving marketplace to which many Boer wagons came. They were heartily welcomed, not only for their trade but also because of the commandos they provided whenever untamed Kaffirs from across the Fish River attacked.

Hilary overheard one tough English farmer joking with a Boer: 'After we were here eighteen months, and the Kaffirs had attacked us once and you Boers five times, our minister said on Sunday, "See how the heathen restrain themselves in the face of God! They always prefer to raid the

Boers." And a man in the back of the church cried, "It isn't God, Dominee. It's cattle. We don't have any and the Boers do!" '

Hilary was particularly pleased to renew acquaintance with his brother Richard, whose exuberant wife Julie had undergone a transformation somewhat similar to Vera Lambton's, except that whereas the latter had descended from the role of Salisbury elite, Julie had climbed the ladder from Dorset illiterate to solid gentlewoman, wife of a former major in the Fifty-ninth. She found no difficulty in accepting Emma Saltwood as her sister-in-law, partly because everyone knew that Emma would be returning to the Karroo as soon as the convening ended, and could thus pose no problem with her miscegenation, but partly also because of Christian charity. Julie saw that Emma was a remarkable woman and no doubt a fine mother, and as such she merited acceptance.

The trouble came with Dr. Keer, for when he dismounted, tired and hungry after the long ride from Golan, he gasped when he saw Hilary, and thought: Dear God, this man's ten years younger than me, and look at him! To reach Keer's hand, Hilary had to stoop, which made him appear even older and more haggard than he was; in missionary work a man on the frontier aged much more rapidly than an official back in London. And when Keer realized that the little black woman trailing behind must be the Kaffir his informants had spoken of, he almost gagged: It's another case of a man's taking his missionary work too personally.

In private discussions with the people of Grahamstown he spoke with some force against the awful error of a missionary's marrying a woman of any tribe with which he worked: 'It's a fatal mistake, really. Look at poor Saltwood. How can he ever return to England? I need an assistant. Work does pile up. Parliament and all that, you know. But could I ask him to help me? With a wife like that, how could he solicit funds from important families?'

One night, at a small gathering, he asked Richard Saltwood directly, 'My dear boy, how did you ever allow this to happen to your brother?' and Richard replied with amusement, 'I think you'd better ask Mrs. Carleton over there. You and she were responsible, you know.'

'Me? Carleton? Never met the man. What's he do?'

'He builds wagons. It's his wife you know.'

'Can't believe it,' Keer said, but when he was led across the room to where Vera stood, she reminded him that they had met in Salisbury when she was still Miss Lambton. 'Of course, of course! When I was giving my lecture on slavery.' He coughed modestly. 'I visit the entire country, you know. Becomes very tiring.' He was rambling on so that he might have time to collect his thoughts, and suddenly he remembered: 'But you were to marry Hilary Saltwood!' He stopped, then added in a pejorative way, 'But I hear you've married the carpenter.'

It fell to Vera Carleton to puncture this little man's balloon, and with the quiet assurance she had gained from doing hard manual work to aid her husband, she said, 'Yes, I did marry the carpenter. Because after your lecture that night I took you aside and asked for your personal opinion, and you confided that Hilary Saltwood was rather a silly ass. Which I confirmed later, so I thank you for your good advice.'

Dr. Keer was nonplused at the direction this conversation was going,

but Vera forged ahead, her voice rising: 'So on the ship coming out I decided
not to marry Hilary. I sought out Thomas Carleton, the wagon builder, I
asked him to sleep with me, and then to marry me. So I am doubly indebted
to you, Doctor.'

When Keer retreated several steps, she followed him. 'And I am indebted in a third way. For when I see what a great fool you are, and what
a man of nobility Hilary Saltwood is by comparison, I realize that you aren't
fit to tie his boots, or my husband's, or, for that matter, mine. Now you
scamper back to London before the Boers hang you.'

She was still fuming when she reached home: 'It was awful, Thomas,
that little prig. I suppose you'll have to apologize tomorrow, but Hilary
really is Christ-like, and Keer's so stupid he wouldn't recognize Jesus if that
carpenter walked in here tonight.' Then she laughed. 'Didn't you see the
way Keer patronized you? And me? He seems to forget that a carpenter was
once important in this world, and may be so again.'

Angered by Keer's open abuse of one of his missionaries, Vera was
inspired to move closer to Emma Saltwood, and when the two had tea
together, or when they walked with Julie Saltwood, there developed a kind
of frontier solidarity which was possible among these pioneer women who
had come long distances to a strange land and who had conquered it in
limited ways. No one of the three had escaped battles—ten-year-old Emma
running away from De Kraal, Vera battling the physical and emotional
storms south of the Cape, wild Julie riding a horse to Plymouth to escape
stupid parents and more stupid brothers—and each had won through to the
reassuring plateau of strong husband and lively children.

Common experience allowed them to be friends, but this could happen
only in their generation. Already forces were at work which would drive
them forever apart, and in the second generation companionship like this
would be unthinkable. Then a woman of good heritage from a cathedral
town would not care to associate with a runaway illiterate from Dorset, and
neither would dare invite into her home a Kaffir, whether married to a white
missionary or not.

The cruel wedge that would separate people was driven deeper by
everything that Dr. Keer did or said during his convention. In public
meetings he excoriated the Boers, making any future relationship between
Boer and missionary impossible. In private he continued to ridicule Saltwood for having taken a Kaffir wife; on this subject he did make one
important observation: 'What Hilary's done, the silly fool, is place a weapon
in the hands of our adversaries. Critics accuse us of being nigger-lovers—
kaffir-boeties, the Boers call us—and when one of our own people makes
such a disastrous marriage, it proves that everything they said against us
is true. It sets missionary work back fifty years.' In general, he spoke and
acted as if the welfare of the world depended upon his conciliating the better
families of England so that they would bring pressure on Parliament to pass
the laws he wanted.

His damage to the Hilary Saltwoods was mortal. As head of the LMS,
he dictated that Hilary was to be kept in seclusion on the farthest veld, and
at the final reception, when it seemed that he had done as much damage
as an intruder could, he delivered his ultimate insult.

He was standing in a reception line, bestowing grace upon the locals, when the wagon builder Carleton and his sharp-tongued wife approached. Since apologies had been made, he was able to nod austerely, as he would to anyone in trade, but then he saw Hilary Saltwood, who had lacked the common sense to leave his Kaffir wife at home. She trailed along behind him, and when she reached Dr. Keer she held out her hand, intending to bid him safe journey home, but he found an excuse to turn away so that he would not have to acknowledge her. She kept her hand extended for just a moment, then—without showing any disappointment—dropped it, smiled, and passed on.

The wagons that arrived to carry Dr. Keer back to the Cape brought a parcel of mail from London, including a letter from Sir Peter Saltwood, M.P., Old Sarum, advising Richard that their mother was failing. Sir Peter was providing passage which would enable Richard to sail immediately, and it was hoped that he would bring his wife, whom the Salisbury Saltwoods were eager to meet.

This was quite impossible, for after a shaky start, the Richard Saltwoods had now developed a good business in trading ivory, and it was imperative that he journey to the eastern frontiers to buy such tusks as he could from the Kaffirs, but it occurred to him and Julie that since the Hilary Saltwoods were in town, they should go. Much argument was advanced, with Emma pleading that she must return to her children, but as Hilary said, 'Those children love to stay in the veld.' So a messenger was posted north with news that the Saltwoods were extending their absence for a year or two.

In their innocence, they supposed it to be what essentially it was, the visit of a son to his aging mother, the presentation of a wife at the ancestral home. Just as Emma had been untouched by Reverend Keer's refusal to take her hand, so she and Hilary would be unmoved by either acceptance or non-acceptance. And it never occurred to them that in places like Cape Town, London and Salisbury they would encounter open hostility. Raised eyebrows, yes. Amused chatter, yes. Even the repugnance which the Boer farmer felt toward an Englishman who had taken a Kaffir wife, they expected some of that, too. But they had lived so amiably together that they felt certain there could be no cruel surprises.

They were wrong. Even while their wagon traveled slowly westward toward the Cape, curious people clustered to see the long-legged missionary who had taken the short Kaffir wife, and there were many giggles. At some houses where transients customarily slept, they were not welcomed, and occasionally they encountered real difficulty in finding quarters. At Swellendam they were a surprise; at Stellenbosch, a scandal.

When they were safely across the flats and entering Cape Town, they assumed that there they would escape the unkind curiosity, but again they were mistaken. Dr. Keer had spoken rather harshly of his stupid outcasts in the Karroo, and many people went out of their way to see them, not as missionaries, but as freaks. They spent a trying time before their ship arrived, but once aboard it, their real troubles began. Four families of some distinction, returning home from India, refused to be seated in the same salon as the blackamoor, so Hilary and his wife had to take their meals apart. They were not welcomed on deck, nor were they included in any of the ship's activities. On Sundays church services were held without the participation of a clergyman, since none but Hilary was aboard, and he was not invited to preach, for his presence would be offensive to the better families.

The ostracism worried him not at all. As he told his wife, 'We're in an age of change, and it's going to take time.' That it would require two hundred years or more would have stunned him, for he moved about the ship unconcerned with the present, assured that the future would see a better balance between the races. With anyone who would speak with him, he talked quietly of mission life, explained the various regions of South Africa, and shared his vision of the future:

> 'In India you'll have every problem we have. How can a few white Englishmen continue to govern huge numbers of people who aren't? In a hundred years situations will be quite different from what they are now. I see the same happening in Java with the Dutch, or in Brazil with the Portuguese. In New Zealand and Australia, I'm told, the problem is somewhat different, because there the white man forms the majority, but he's still got to rule decently or he'll lose out. Like it or not, we must devise systems of government to meet unforeseen conditions, and I for one am convinced it must be done on a basis of Christ's brotherhood.'

He was so persuasive in his quiet way that toward the end of the voyage certain passengers approached the captain and said that they would like to recommend Reverend Saltwood as minister for one of the last Sundays, but this was dismissed abruptly: 'Passengers wouldn't hear of it.' To which the men replied, 'We're passengers, and we think the others would accept.' The appeal was denied.

However, little Emma had been active among the children, telling them outrageous accounts of lions and leopards, of hippos in the river and rhinos crashing through the forest. Strangely, what interested the children most was her depiction of the Karroo:

> 'Think of a land as flat as this deck. Here, here and here, what do we have? Little hills, round at the bottom, flat on top, never touching. Scores of them. And from these hills one morning comes a blesbok. You want to see what a blesbok looks like? [Here she took some blacking and transformed a boy's face into the white-and-black glory of the blesbok.] So here comes our blesbok. And then another. And another. You're all blesboks, so get in line. And then another and another, until the world is full of blesboks. Marching in line. As far as you can see, faces like this. That's where I live.'

When Blesbok number one returned to his parents, they wanted to know what in the world had happened to him, and he said, 'I'm a blesbok, on the Great Karroo.' This started inquiries, and several parents discovered that Mrs. Saltwood had been entertaining their children for some time, and when they discussed this with their boys and girls, they found further that she had become something of an idol: 'She can sing, and make games with string, and she tells us about ostriches and meerkats.'

So now certain women joined their husbands in an appeal to the captain, but he was adamant against allowing Saltwood to conduct services, on the very good grounds that whereas a few families may have come to accept the missionary, those that really counted were still set against it; he knew from past experience that to irritate the rabble signified nothing, but to infringe in the slightest upon the prejudices of the ruling families meant that letters would be written to management and black marks cast. He'd have none of that on his ship.

On the second to last Sunday those families who still wanted to hear Reverend Saltwood preach arranged an alfresco worship on the afterdeck, and to it came most of the children, hoping to hear the missionary's wife tell one of her stories about ostriches, or perhaps even to sing. She did the latter. When her husband called for one of the Church of England hymns, and there was no organ to set the tune, her voice rose in unwavering volume, a beautiful voice that seemed to fill that part of the ship. Then her husband spoke briefly of Christ's mission in Africa. He raised no difficult points, ruffled no sensibilities, and when the service ended with another hymn, many of the families congratulated him on an excellent performance. 'We're so glad you sailed with us,' one man said at the exact moment when the captain, in something of a rage, demanded to know who had authorized the service on the afterdeck.

'It just happened,' a junior officer said.

'Don't let it happen again,' the captain said. Several passengers had already protested that such a service was a mockery, since the real service was being held in the salon.

At Salisbury there was confusion. Emily had expected her son Richard to appear; she was not prepared for Hilary, and certainly not for his black wife. Had she wanted them to come, she would have sent for them, but when they arrived she simply could not behave poorly. She was glad to see Hilary again, even though he did look older than she, and she was respectful of his choice of a wife.

In the second week she confided to her friend Mrs. Lambton: 'Thank God, I behaved myself. That Emma's a treasure.'

'Can you stomach the blackness?'

'I'm happy if my son's happy. You must feel the same way about Vera, married to the wagon builder. Emma tells me your daughter is quite content, with two—or was it three?—lovely children.'

'To tell you frankly, Emily, long ago, before you talked with me, I dreamed that about this time Vera would be coming back to Salisbury with Hilary—that he'd be taking up his duties at the cathedral . . .' Suddenly she burst into uncontrollable tears, and after they were stanched she said bitterly, 'Damn! Damn! How dreadfully wrong things happen. How can you stand having that blackamoor in your house?'

Emily wanted to weep, too, not for the black woman in her house, but for her son David, lost God knows where in Indiana, for Richard with his illiterate stable girl, and most of all for Hilary, that sad, mixed-up man about whose head such ugly rumors flew.

'You know what they're saying in London?' Mrs. Lambton said after her sniffles were brought under control. 'Dr. Keer himself said to a small gathering . . . Our Cousin Alice was there and heard him. He says that poor Hilary is an outcast, that he's made a perfect ass of himself, with English and Dutch alike.'

'I suppose it's true,' Emily said. 'But I wonder if it matters. In God's eyes, I mean. The other day I received a letter from London. Someone who'd been on the ship with Hilary. They said his sermon on the voyage was like Christ Himself walking among men and restating His principles. He said he thought I'd like to know.'

At this Mrs. Lambton dissolved completely, and after a series of racking sobs, mumbled, 'I had so wanted them to marry. Vera could have saved your son, Emily. She'd have made him strong and proper. He'd have been dean over there, mark my words. He'd have been dean.'

'The rest of the letter,' Emily continued, 'said that Hilary had been denied use of the proper chapel aboard ship. The salon, I think they call it. He had to preach in the open. I think Jesus often preached in the open. I don't think even Vera could have gained permission for my son to preach inside. I think he was ordained to—' Against her will she broke into fearful sobs: He was so gaunt. He looked so sickly. The house they lived in on the desert, it sounded like a peat-gatherer's hut. He looked so very tired. And his poor wife had to make all the decisions.

With an unexpected thrust of her hand, she took hold of Mrs. Lambton's arm and cried, 'Laura, why do these things happen? I'll never see Richard or David again in this life. You'll never see Vera or the children. We sit here like two old spiders in a web, with the flies far, far away. Karroo! Karroo! Who gives a damn about Karroo? Or Indiana, either? Life is here, and we've let it slip away. We have a cathedral, the loveliest in England, but the choristers have fled. I feel such grief for that poor black woman in my garden. Laura, I could die of grief.'

Things improved not at all when Sir Peter came down from Parliament, well aware of what an embarrassment Hilary's visit was causing. Several London newspapers had run cartoons showing an elongated missionary accompanied by his fat dwarfish wife with bare breast and grass tutu, entitled 'The Bishop and His Hottentot Venus' or other amusing jests, and the ridicule was beginning to have wide effect. Lady Janice was both mortified and apprehensive, fearing that it would be hurtful to the good work her husband was trying to accomplish, and she came to Salisbury intending to take stern measures and insist that her brother-in-law and his wife leave immediately.

But when Sir Peter saw his younger brother and was reminded of that emotional moment at Old Sarum when he had invited his brothers always to come back to Sentinels, he relaxed, and pleaded with his wife to do the same, so although he could not express any warmth over this reunion, he did extend courtesies. Even Lady Janice was reasonably decent to her black sister-in-law.

In long discussions on the benches under the oak trees, Sir Peter sought guidance from his brother as to how England ought to conduct itself in this new colony: 'You know, Hilary, that I'm rather the leader in the House on these matters. Yes, government's given me free reign to work something out. Close touch with the Colonial Office, and all that. And you create such a different impression from what Simon Keer's been telling me that I wonder if we shouldn't call him down here for some serious consultation.'

'That would be capital,' Hilary said, not the least vengeful over Keer's treatment of him at Grahamstown. So the fiery leader of the Africa philanthropists was sent for, and in the meantime Emma Saltwood was exploring Salisbury. Each morning she helped serve breakfast, then donned a little white cap, took an umbrella, more as a stick for walking than for rain, and crossed over the Roman bridge into the village, where she spoke softly with anyone who wished to ask her about Africa and nodded deferentially to those who did not. She frequented all the shops, marveling at their intricacies, purchasing one small gift after another for her children.

Her reception was uneven. Women of good family who enthusiastically supported Dr. Keer's philanthropic movement loved the blacks in Africa, which they proved by their generous contributions, but were uneasy when a specific black took residence in their village and looked askance when Emma passed their way. It was the clerks in the shops and the housewives marketing who came to regard the missionary's wife as one of themselves, greeting her warmly when they met. They began to talk with her about lions and mealies and meerkats and the tanning of hides. But mostly they marveled at her clear voice when she sang at services, and one man who knew music said, 'I cannot believe so much voice can emit from such a small frame.' He asked if she would sing for him in his study, and there, with the assistance of two pupils, he tested the range and power of her voice. She liked the experiment, took deep breaths, and sang a chain of wonderful notes.

Now cartoons appeared entitled 'The Hottentot Nightingale,' and she was asked to sing at various affairs and even to travel to Winchester to sing in the cathedral there. Always she maintained her smile, her willingness to work and talk with others. England at this period had an insatiable interest in her colonies and the strange peoples they contained, and many persons like Emma had been imported to serve as nine-day wonders, but only a few reached the provinces. In Wiltshire, Emma Saltwood was a sensation.

Therefore, when Dr. Keer arrived in town he could no longer ignore the little Hottentot, as everyone called her. Remembering that she was Sir Peter's sister-in-law, he had to treat her decently, and insofar as he could unbend to an inferior, he did.

Hilary, who could bear no animosity toward anyone, was actually pleased to see the dynamic little agitator, although, as he told Emma, 'He doesn't seem so little now. Success and moving with important people have made him taller.'

'It's a game with him,' Emma said shrewdly. 'The pieces on the board are no longer plain checkers. Now they're knights and parliaments.'

'But don't forget. It was this man who taught me to love Jesus,' Hilary said.

'Don't you forget!' Emma laughed. 'He taught me, too. He was like thunder and lightning.'

They speculated on what could have caused the profound change, and reached no conclusion, but when the three men sat beside the River Avon, admiring the swans that moved through the rippled reflections of the cathedral, Hilary was willing to concede that Keer was motivated by one ambition: to end slavery. Everything else was secondary; he had moved from the veld onto a world stage: 'The pressing task no longer concerns the Cape Colony. It focuses solely on Parliament. We must pass the anti-slavery measure. We must force the colonial secretary to issue the ordinances I've drafted. We must press forward, always forward.' It was obvious that he had little concern with Boers, Kaffirs or Englishmen as human beings, but only with a rationalized system, and confessed this: 'In the government of nations the time often comes when the establishment of a principle ensures freedom for centuries to come. We're at such a marking point.'

'You don't agree?' Sir Peter asked his brother.

'Oh, but I do. Dr. Keer's right. We are at a turning point. But I believe it involves specific human beings and not abstract principles. Peter, in whatever you do, you must ask how this will affect the Boer farmer, for he is white South Africa. And how it will affect the Xhosa—'

'You mean the Kaffirs?'

'I never use that word. They're individual tribesmen. The Xhosa, the Pondo, the Tembu, the Fingo, the Zizi. And one day they'll be Africa. So be careful what you do to them. And finally you ought to ask yourself, "How will this affect the Englishman?" Because I assume we'll govern the place for generations to come, and we must do so with justice.'

'Can't we protect both Dr. Keer's general interest and your specific ones?'

'I'm afraid not. I think that when governments regulate in general, they stifle the individual, and then he festers and grows revolutionary and upsets everything. Start with individual justice and you'll guide the general.'

'Quite wrong,' Keer said with some force. 'Unless the principles are laid down, nothing good can follow.'

Sir Peter addressed his brother: 'How about the abolition of slavery? Surely Dr. Keer is right on that.'

'Indeed, indeed,' Hilary said, twisting his long, thin legs in knots as he tried unsuccessfully to make his point. 'What I mean is, the abolition must be done without infuriating the white. Otherwise we've accomplished nothing.'

'With a stroke of the pen we accomplish everything,' Keer said, his voice assuming the messianic glory he adopted when addressing church groups.

Hilary, twisting his legs into even tighter knots, began to laugh. 'Peter, you've never known a Boer, and, Simon, you've forgotten. Let me tell you about my neighbor Tjaart van Doorn. Built square like a corncrib. No neck. Big whiskers down the side of his face. Wears a belt and suspenders, and shoes he makes himself. Controls maybe sixteen thousand acres and lives in a fort. How many slaves? Half a dozen?'

'What's your point?'

'South Africa is filled with Tjaart van Doorns, and one day his white ox runs away. He goes after it, brings it back, and puts it to work. No punishment. No swearing. Two days later the ox runs off again. Again Tjaart goes after him. Same thing. I was there, baptizing a baby, and I saw him. Not a harsh word. So next day the white ox runs away a third time, and this time I go with Tjaart to help surround the beast, and when I get a rope around its neck, Tjaart comes up, blue in the face, and with a mighty roar he hits the ox between the eyes with a huge club. The ox drops dead, and Tjaart says to the fallen body, "By damn! That'll teach you." '

The two listeners said nothing, and before either could respond, Emma appeared with glasses of a drink she and Emily Saltwood had made: cold cider with honey and a dusting of cinnamon.

'Point I'm making, Peter, is that if the laws you pass goad the Boers, they'll listen once and accept what they don't like, and they'll listen twice. But I assure you, if you come at them a third time, they'll grab that club and bash you between the eyes.'

Very carefully Simon Keer delivered his next observation: 'What it comes down to—it appears to me—are we ruling South Africa, or are the Boers, from whom we took the colony some years ago and whom we have cosseted outrageously?'

With equal calm Hilary said, 'We did not take it from them. We took it from their supine government in Europe. They're still there, every one of them, and increasing by the year.' Then he became urgent: 'But more important are the Xhosa, the Pondo, the Tembu and the Fingo. They've always been there, and they always will. They're also increasing, and we must act to keep everyone on balance.'

'Can this be done?' Sir Peter asked, and before there could be a reply to a question that permitted no reply, Emma came rushing across the lawn, and when she reached the oak trees she gasped, 'Hilary! It's Mrs. Saltwood. I think she's dead.'

In the aftermath of the funeral Mrs. Lambton said, in the presence of the two Saltwood boys and their wives, 'Hilary, get back to Africa. You should be forever ashamed of yourself. You killed your mother.'

'Now wait!' Sir Peter said.

'She sat with me day after day, weeping. Once she broke into wild laughter and said, "The fault's all mine. I bought that black girl for him. Yes, I sent him the money and he bought himself a wife." '

'Now, Mrs. Lambton,' Sir Peter interrupted, but she had scorn for him, too: 'If you'd had any love for your mother, you'd have thrown this pair out—'

'Mrs. Lambton, just last week my mother told me that it was God's providence that sent Hilary home, and not Richard. We didn't want Hilary to come. We were embarrassed when he did. But as we lived with him— and these were my mother's words . . .'

He broke down. All he could do was grasp his wife's hand and nod to her, indicating that she must continue.

Lady Janice said, 'There was a reconciliation. Among all of us.' She reached for Emma's hand, welcoming her at last to Sentinels. But at the door Mrs. Lambton cried, 'You killed your mother. Go back. Go back.'

It could never be determined who murdered the two missionaries. Before dawn one morning in 1828, when Hilary was only forty-three but looked sixty, distant herders saw fire at the hut, and when they reached it they found the two Saltwoods with their throats cut and all their possessions gone.

Fire consumed the place, so that gathering clues proved impossible. Speculation centered on six groups of suspects: Bushmen who liked to creep into such settlements and steal cattle, but none of the mission cattle were gone; Hottentots who rebelled against authority, but the local Hottentots loved the Saltwoods, who had no servants; Kaffirs who were quick with their assegais, but the Kaffirs in the area were mission hands who knew only peace; Boers who despised most missionaries, but the only Boers in the area lived sixty miles away and they rather liked Saltwood; Englishmen who hated the Saltwoods for besmirching the good reputation of the LMS through their miscegenation, but there were none in the area; and wandering Singhalese thieves off some ship, but the nearest harbor was seven hundred miles away. Perhaps society in the abstract had finished with them.

They had fallen victims to that terrible affliction which brings certain crucifixion: they took religion too seriously; they trusted Jesus Christ; they believed that the bright, soaring promises of the New Testament could be used as a basis for government; and they followed these precepts unfalteringly in the one part of the world where they would cause offense to three powerful groups of people: the old Boers, the new English, the timeless blacks.

In one of his most perceptive sermons Hilary had told his mission: 'The perpetual problem of government remains, "Am I safe at night when I go to sleep?" ' Like many others asleep in South Africa, he had not been safe.

It was an act of God, many alleged, that the three Saltwood children were absent when assassins struck. They were trekking in the Great Karroo with a Hottentot family, gathering ostrich plumes for sale in Paris. When they returned, their parents were already buried, and there was heated discussion as to what should happen to them. Some said they should be freighted down to Grahamstown on the next wagon heading south, but word was received that they were not wanted there. So there was some talk of sending them along to LMS headquarters in Cape Town, but they already had a flood of Coloured orphans and abandoned children. It would be quite improper to ship them off to England, where their ancestry would damn them.

Put simply, there was no place for them. No one felt any responsibility for the offspring of what from the start had been a disastrous marriage. So the children were left with the Hottentots with whom they had hunted ostrich plumes.

For a few years they would be special, for the older ones could read and write, but as time passed and the necessity for marriage arrived, they would slide imperceptibly into that amorphous, undigestible mass of people called Coloured.

VII. Mfecane

THE boy Nxumalo, like his distant ancestor, the Nxumalo who left the lake for Great Zimbabwe, had been reared to believe that what his chief said was law, no matter how contradictory or arbitrary. 'If the chief speaks, you leap!' his father told him, and the boy extended this sensible rule to all who gave orders. He was born to obey and trained to do so instantly.

One bright, sunny day in 1799, when he was eleven, he learned the real meaning of obedience. It would be an especially bitter lesson, since it came about because his father, an energetic man who loved the bursting flowers of spring, felt such a surge of joy that he could not keep from whistling whenever he walked through the fields near the kraal.

The sound of Ndela's happiness reached the ears of a suspicious woman who had concealed herself next to the footpath. A gnarled hunchback, she was the most powerful diviner in the region, a woman who held in her hands the balance of good and evil, of life and death. Now satisfaction spread across her face, for the spirits who lived in darkness had finally given her a sign. 'Ndela whistled!' she cackled to herself. 'Ndela whistled!' At last she knew why sickness lay like a cloak of winter mist over the herds of the Sixolobo. She was ready to act.

That afternoon the entire Sixolobo clan was summoned to the chief's place and the exciting word was passed: 'The diviner is going to smell out the wizard who has infected our cattle.'

Ndela arrived with no reason to suspect that he might be connected with the sick animals, but even so, when the divination began he behaved with his usual circumspection, because there was always the possiblity that it was in his body that the evil forces hid without his knowing it.

A divination was a fearful experience. The old woman's body was smeared with a loathsome mixture of animal fats; her arms and parts of her face were streaked with a whitish clay; her hair was rubbed with red powder; and about her neck hung strings of roots and bones. Animal bladders dangled from her waist and in her hand she carried a weapon of dreadful power: a switch of wildebeest tail. About her shoulders, obscuring her hump, was draped a cloak of black material, while strips of animal skin were fastened to various parts of her body.

'I bring words, my people,' she intoned in solemn accents. 'I have dreamed these many nights and I have seen the evil that attacks our cattle. I have walked in darkness and Lord-of-the-Sky has made all things known.'

She began to dance, her bare feet slapping the earth, and when her pace had increased to leaps and bounds, the onlookers sang to give her encouragement, for they knew that she was reaching out for the spirits of the clan's ancestors. There was not one in the audience who doubted a life after death; they were also convinced that spirits who had gained more than the normal wisdom of the earth guided the destinies of the clan through the being of the diviner. Words that fell from her mouth were not hers, but the wishes and judgments of their forebears; they must be obeyed.

Suddenly she stopped dancing to take from a gourd at her side a pinch of snuff. When this caused a paroxysm of sneezing, the onlookers applauded, for they knew that spirits of the dead dwelt deep within the body of the living, and any tempestuous sneeze released their powers. Now came a hysterical screech of laughter, following which the diviner slowly and dramatically sank to the earth. Squatting, she took the cloak from her shoulders and placed it over her knees so that it cast a shadow before her. Opening a skin bag, she exhaled into it a pungent odor of the herbs she had been chewing and then removed from it the charms which would encourage the spirits to identify the contaminating wizard. For each item she laid before her she chanted words of praise:

> 'Oh, Claw of Great Leopard
>   slayer of the weak . . .
> In my hand, Little Rock,
>   trembler of the stream of sorrow . . .
> Fly to me, Talon of Hawk,
>   watcher of all from above . . .
> Hear my voice, Flower of Night,
>   keeper of eternal darkness . . .'

With a flourish she threw the items on the ground in front of her, swaying above them. Keeping her head downcast for a long time, she muttered and moaned, then pointed with her left forefinger at one grisly treasure and another. All were silent, for the terrible moment was at hand. Finally she rose and walked boldly toward the chief, and many gasped, for it seemed that she was about to accuse him.

'They have given me the answer, my Chief!'

'What did they show?'

'A great black beast with a hundred legs and a hundred eyes and the mightiest of horns. And it was revered by my chief, for it was the fattest animal in the land, because in it dwelt all those that had gone before. But this great beast was grieved. At a time when your cattle are ailing, one of those men out there'—and here she pointed generally at the silent crowd

—'one of them, at this time of sorrow, did not lament. One of them was happy that the animals are sick.'

'Who was that one, Mother-with-Eyes-That-See-Everything?'

'The one who sings like a bird has brought this evil.'

When the diviner had said these fatal words, Nxumalo remembered immediately that his father sometimes 'sang like a bird' with his whistling, and he had a terrifying premonition that Ndela might be the man carrying the evil spirit that caused the cattle sickness. He watched with horror as the diviner began to stalk among the people, her wildebeest switch dangling loosely at her side. Whenever her eyes met those of another, the one under scrutiny would shake with fear, then breathe again as she passed on.

But when she reached Ndela, the whistler, she leaped high in the air, screaming and gesticulating, and when she came down, the switch was pointing directly at him. 'Him!' she shrieked. 'The happy one! The ravager of cattle!'

A cry rose from the crowd, and those nearest Ndela moved away. The great hump beneath the animal skins on the diviner's back was accented as she twisted about to address the chief: 'Here is the wizard, the one who has brought the evil.'

Briefly the chief consulted with his councillors, and when they nodded, four warriors seized Ndela and dragged him forward. 'Did you whistle?' the chief asked.

'I did.'

'While my cattle were dying?'

'Yes.'

'Did you have this dark evil in your heart?'

'I must have had it.' It was impossible for Ndela to doubt that he was guilty, for if the spirits of the clan had advised the diviner that he was the guilty one, it must be so.

'Why did you do it, knowing it was wrong?'

'So many flowers. The birds were singing.'

'So you sang too, while my cattle were dying?' Ndela had no explanation, so the chief growled, 'Isn't that true?'

'Yes, my Chief.'

'Then let there be judgment.' As he turned to consult his councillors, the men of the kraals moved closer while the women and children drew back.

'Ndela,' intoned the chief, 'the ones who came before have pointed to you as the wizard.'

'Praise them!' cried the crowd, paying deference to the spirits that guarded this clan.

'What shall be done with him?'

'Death to the wizard!' cried the men, the women ululating their assent. So the chief delivered the sentence: 'Let the lips that whistled, whistle no more. Let the tongue that pushed air, push no more. Let the ears that heard birds, hear no more. Let the eyes that were made drunk by the flowers, see no more. Let the wizard die.'

As soon as the words were out, the four warriors grabbed Ndela and rushed him toward the stout poles encircling the kraal, where the cattle languished. The screaming victim was hoisted up, his legs pulled apart, and with one downward thrust, impaled so that the sharp pole entered deep into his body.

Nxumalo, watching this without uttering a sound, wanted to run to the hideous scarecrow figure to mumble a farewell to his singing, loving father who had been so good to him, but any show of sympathy for a wizard was forbidden. Later, the corpse, the pole and even the ground at its base would be burned, and the ashes thrown into the swiftest river so that nothing might remain.

Nxumalo could bear no resentment against the chief or the diviner, for they had merely carried out the customs of the clan. No one in the audience that day could have questioned the fairness of the judgment: the spirits had advised the diviner; she had exposed the guilty man; and he had been executed in the traditional manner.

Hundreds of intricate rules governed a Sixolobo from birth till death, and beyond. Unquestionably the spirits of past members of the clan existed; unquestionably there was a Lord-of-the-Sky who had placed all men on earth. No phase of life could be without regulation: a man's hut must bear a certain relation to the chief's; women must move only in certain areas; a child must watch carefully his attitude toward elders; a man must observe formalities when approaching a stranger's kraal; and the treatment of cattle was minutely supervised. For any infringement of any of the rules, there was instant punishment, and death was obligatory for some fifty or sixty offenses, about the same number as applied in Europe at this time.

Deeply ingrained in a boy like Nxumalo were the beliefs that differentiated good and evil; these were notions which had come down from his earliest ancestors in Africa, observed by the Nxumalo of Great Zimbabwe, and brought by his descendants southward. These rules could be as petty as where cooking utensils were to be placed at night, or as grave as an accusation of wizardry, for which death by impaling was prescribed.

Nxumalo conceded that his father had been possessed by an evil spirit; he understood how Ndela could confess to a crime of which he had no knowledge; and he fully agreed that his father must die.

He had observed that the chief never killed for sport, or whimsically, nor did he exact cruel punishment or torture; he did only what tradition dictated must be done. He was a good man, burdened with duties and responsible for the lives of his thousand followers.

There existed, in this paradise tucked in between the mountains and the sea, some two hundred clans, many smaller than the Sixolobo, some larger, and the chief had to behave according to his status: imperious to the smaller clans, obsequious to those with more cattle, and most careful with any group that might raid the Sixolobo. Whatever decisions he made must be for the security of the clan, and chiefs before him had learned that even the slightest infringement of law had best be dealt with immediately.

The diviner was subsidiary to the chief, but as the earthly communicant with spirits, she wielded immense power and at moments of crisis might even overrule the chief. But the majority of her days were spent treating cuts and bruises, or relieving headaches, or brewing concoctions to ensure the birth of a son. But if a wizard crept into the tribe, spreading evil, she must seek him out, and then medicines were of no avail: that wizard must be impaled and burned.

Nxumalo understood all this and felt no bitterness, but since he was a bright lad he understood one thing more: that when a boy's father had been executed, the boy lived under a shadow. It was quite probable that one day the diviner would come for him. He had not the slightest idea as to what it would be that he would do wrong, but experience warned him that the son of a man who had been impaled ran a strong chance of repeating that prolonged death.

Caught in a conflict between obedience and self-preservation, he solved it in this manner: If I stay with the Sixolobo, I must do what the chief says, and I shall, but here the dark spirits are against me. So I shall run to a new tribe where I can start afresh, and give my allegiance to its king. He told no one of his decision, not even his mother, and before the moon showed midnight he was moving swiftly through the glorious valleys which led to the tribes of the south. To the west rose the forbidding peaks reaching eleven thousand feet into the sky, to the east swept the waters of the ocean.

He did not know where he was running to, but he was certain that there would be a welcome for a sturdy lad who showed promise of becoming a good warrior. But he wanted his new home to be at a safe distance from the Sixolobo, because he knew that if they ever found him fighting against them, he would receive a much harsher punishment than his father had suffered. Traitors were punished with four bamboo skewers.

He was headed for a river whose fame he had always known, the Umfolozi, which drained some of the most handsome land in Africa, tumbling out of the great mountains and running almost eastward to the sea. It marked a division between the tribes of the north and those to the south. It was not a massive river; few of the rivers of southern Africa compared to the great waterways of Europe or America, but it brought richness to all who lived along it, for its fields yielded good crops and its banks were crowded with animals of all description.

When moist and heavy winds blowing in from the south warned Nxumalo that he was approaching water, he concluded that he had come to the legendary Umfolozi, and he began to look for kraals to which he might report his presence, but there were none, and for two nights he patrolled the land well back from the river; on the third morning he came upon a group of nine boys his own age, naked like him and herding cattle.

With trepidation, but also a determination to protect himself regardless of what the boys attempted, he warily picked his way among the rocks guarding the pasture where the cattle grazed, and from a fair distance, prepared to announce himself. But at this moment the herders launched into a cruel game of throwing one of their younger companions into the center of a circle, while they kept a tough round tuber the size of a ball away from him, tripping him as he lunged for them and kicking him when he fell.

'Little penis!' they screamed at him. 'Little penis! Can't do anything!'

The boy in the center was himself not little; he was quite handsomely proportioned in all but his genitals, and probably able to handle any one of his eight tormentors taken alone; but when the entire group conspired against him, shouting words that wounded, he could only stand them off in a kind of blind rage.

His fury gave him added strength, and the incessant jibes about his penis drove him to extraordinary efforts; at one point he leaped high in the air, almost intercepted the ball, and did succeed in driving it off course and over the fingertips of his enemies. He, seeing its flight, was able to break through the circle of bullies and leap for it before any of them could change direction.

The ball rolled directly to Nxumalo's feet, and when the abused lad reached it he found a stranger handing it to him. In this way Nxumalo, a voluntary outcast from the Sixolobo, met Shaka, an involuntary exile among the Langeni.

With Nxumalo as his ally and ready to defend him, Shaka, a twelve-year-old, moody, difficult boy, received less tormenting. True, the entire Langeni clan continued to make fun of his undersized penis, and there was no way this particular abuse could be halted, but whenever rough play was involved, the newcomer and the moody one formed a resilient companionship. Yet, strangely, they were not friends, for Shaka would admit no one to that privileged position.

Yet he must have someone to talk with, and one night, his voice bursting with pride, he told Nxumalo, 'I'm a Zulu.'

'What's that?'

The tormented one could not mask his disgust at such ignorance: 'Zulu will be the most powerful tribe along the Umfolozi.'

'In the north we haven't heard of them.'

'Everyone will hear when I'm chief.'

'Chief! What are you doing herding cattle in this small tribe?'

'I was cast out of the Zulu. I'm son of their chief, and he banished me.' Then, with a bitterness Nxumalo had never witnessed before, Shaka unfolded his account of the intrigue which had driven him from the tiny, inconsequential tribe of the Zulu:

> 'My mother Nandi—you'll meet her one day. Look at her well. Remember her face, because before I die she's going to be proclaimed Female Elephant. People will bow down to her. [His voice trembled.] She was the legal wife of the chief, and he rejected her . . . cast us both out of his kraal, but I'll go back, and take my mother with me. [He clenched his fists.] I'm an outcast. You hear them make fun of me. Remember their names. Nzobo, he's the worst. Mpepha, he's afraid to hit me. He uses a club. Mqalane, remember him. I will always remember Mqalane. [He named the other five, repeating some.] They laugh at me. They refuse me permissions. But most of all, Nxumalo, they ridicule my mother. [Here he began trembling furiously.] I tell you, Nxumalo, one day she will be the Female Elephant. [Silence, and then the real burden.] No, the worst isn't that. It's the way they make fun of me. [It was impossible for this boy, tenser than the string of a bow, to weep, but he did tremble, grinding his heel in the dust.] They make fun of me.'

The simple sentence that Nxumalo uttered next would save his life on the day of retribution, but now it seemed only a gesture of decent friendship.

He reached out, touched Shaka on the arm, and said, 'Later it will grow bigger.'

'Will it?' the older boy cried impetuously.

'I've often seen it happen.' He had no authority for what he was saying, but he knew it must be said.

Shaka said nothing more, just sat there in the grass, pounding his fists against his knees.

Like any confused boy his age, Shaka had shaded the truth, so far as he was able to understand it. Senzangakhona, chief of the Zulu clan, had impregnated Nandi, a virgin of the Langeni. When the elders of the latter tribe heard of this shocking breach of tribal custom, they insisted that Senzangakhona do the proper thing and accept her as his third wife, which he did, but she proved more disagreeable than sand in the mouth. Her son was worse, and at the age of six allowed one of his father's favorite animals to be slain, a mistake which precipitated banishment. Shaka was no longer a Zulu; he and his mother must take refuge in the kraals of the despised Langeni.

On the day they left, Senzangakhona was most pleased; they had given him nothing but trouble, and he recalled what his councillors had said that first day when Nandi claimed she was pregnant: 'She had no baby in her. It's only the intestinal insect they call iShaka.' The king agreed, and now watched with undisguised pleasure as his unwanted wife disappeared, taking her 'insect' with her.

In 1802 famine swept the valley of the Umfolozi, the only time that men could remember when the richest of rivers betrayed her children, but now the lack of food was so critical that the chief of the Langeni began to drive unwanted persons out of his kraals, and among those who had to leave were Nandi, mother of Shaka, and her son, who was liked by no one in the clan. As they were departing southward, using a ford that crossed the river, the outcast boy Nxumalo overtook them, saying that it could not be long before he, too, would be forced out and asking permission to join them in their exile. Nandi, a powerful woman who wasted little effort in sentiment, said, 'Stay behind.' But her son, remembering various behaviors of the younger boy, said, 'Let him come.' And the exiles moved south.

In time they straggled into the lands of Dingiswayo, most important of the southern chiefs, and when he saw the two stalwart fellows he wanted them for his regiment: 'You look like warriors. But can you fight?'

Long-shafted assegais were produced, but when Shaka hefted his he disliked its balance and demanded a replacement. 'Why?' asked the chief, and brusquely Shaka said, 'A warrior must have confidence.' And not until he had a spear he liked did he say, 'I'm ready.'

Dingiswayo laughed at his impudence, saying to his attendants, 'He looks like a warrior. He boasts like one. Now we'll see if he can fight.'

Hearing this implied insult, Shaka pointed to a distant tree: 'There is your enemy, Great Chief.' And with a short run he launched his assegai far and true, so that Dingiswayo laughed no more. 'He fights like a warrior, too.' To the young man he said, 'Welcome to my regiment.'

For the next years Shaka and Nxumalo shared a wild experience. As members of the region's greatest regiment, the iziCwe, they helped fortify their tribe's position, participating in the vast raids that kept the territory pacified and augmented. Nxumalo was content with his good fortune in gaining a position, however menial, in the land's finest fighting unit, but Shaka was as disconsolate and irritable as ever: 'There's a better way to fight. There's a much better way to organize a regiment than this. If they made me commander for one month . . .'

For example, in the great battle against the Mabuwane he was outraged, even though it was judged that he had been the foremost warrior. What happened was a standard battle, which, in Nxumalo's opinion, the iziCwe regiment had dominated.

Four hundred of Dingiswayo's troops marched north in noisy stages, announcing at every stop that they were about to engage the Mabuwane. Two hundred women, children and old men trailed behind, throwing a cloud of dust that could be seen for seven miles. In the meantime, the Mabuwane, who had known for two weeks that a battle was to be fought, had been scouting not the enemy, whose dispositions they always knew, but for a suitable spot on which to fight. One of the major considerations was that on the Mabuwane side at least, and on both sides if at all possible, there be commodious hills from which the audience could watch, and a comfortable and level place on which to place the chief's chair as he followed the ebb and flow of the battle.

The Mabuwane did their job well, and an ideal battleground was selected, a kind of pleasant amphitheater with exactly the kind of sloping sides the spectators preferred. When the two armies lined up, there were dances, formations, shouted insults and a good deal of foot-stamping. Then from each side four men moved forward, brandishing their shields and shouting fresh insults. The mothers of the opposing warriors were excoriated, the condition of their cattle, the poor quality of their food, and their known history for cowardice.

Each warrior carried three assegais, and at maximum distance each threw one that came so far in such good light that the big shields had ample time to deflect them. Unfortunately, one of the Mabuwane warriors shunted a spear aimed at him right onto the foot of one of his own men. It didn't pierce the foot, but it did bring blood, whereupon the multitude on Shaka's side cheered wildly. Nxumalo was especially excited, dancing up and down until Shaka, standing beside him, grasped his arm in a terrible grip. 'Stop that! This isn't warfare.'

Then, from a distance almost as great as the first, a second flight of assegais was released, again with no consequences. At this point it was obligatory for the four warriors on each side to run forward and to throw their last spears from a distance of about twenty-five feet. Again they could be fended off easily.

Now the main bodies of the two armies were required to mingle; however, they did so under carefully understood rules: vast flights of assegais, thrown from far distances so they could be easily deflected, and when both armies were thus disarmed, a fragmentary melee without weapons in which one side pushed a little harder than the other and took a few captives. The observers could readily see which side had won, and when this was determined the other side fled, leaving its cattle to be captured and a few women to be taken home by the victors. Of course, in the scuffling some warriors were injured, and now and then some inept fighter would be killed, but in general the casualties were minimal.

A convenient feature of such a battle was that when it ended, each side could pick up about as many assegais as it had carried at the beginning, but of course they were not the same ones.

Disgraceful! Shaka brooded. This is no way to fight. Imagine! And he kicked his right foot in the air, sending his cowhide sandal in a wide arc: Men fighting in sandals. It slows them down. They can't maneuver. And it was after this fight that he began running up and down hills barefooted, until his feet were tougher than sandals and his breath inexhaustible. He also required Nxumalo to stand in the sun hour after hour, holding a big shield in his left hand, an assegai in his right.

Forty times, fifty Shaka told Nxumalo, 'I am your enemy. You must kill me.' And with a wild leap Shaka sprang forward, bringing the left edge of his shield far to his right. When Nxumalo tried to throw his assegai, as warriors were supposed to do, Shaka suddenly swept his own shield-edge brutally to the left, hooked Nxumalo's shield and half-spun him around so that the entire left side of his body stood exposed. With one swift lunge, Shaka thrust his spear at Nxumalo's heart, halting it inches from the skin.

'That's the way to kill,' he cried. 'In close.'

One afternoon, when he had slain Nxumalo many times, he took his own assegai and in a rage broke the shaft, kicking the halves in the dust. 'Spears are not the weapons for a fight. We need stabbers.' And in fury he grabbed Nxumalo's spear and shattered it, too.

'What's the matter?' Nxumalo asked.

'So stupid!' Shaka cried, kicking at the spears. 'Two armies approach, like this. You throw your first spear. I throw mine. Second spear. Third spear. Then when we have no weapons we rush at each other. It's madness.'

Retrieving only the metal points of the two spears, he went with Nxumalo to the best iron forger along the river and asked him whether he could combine these two points into one—a massive, heavy, blunt stabbing sword. The artisan said that might be possible, but where would Shaka find a haft heavy enough for such a spear.

'It's no longer a spear,' Shaka said. 'It's something quite different.' And he worked with all the blacksmiths, trying to find the man who could make the terrible weapon he visualized.

In these days, when the two were still living in mutual exile, Nxumalo noticed several unusual aspects of his friend's behavior, and once when they talked idly of their possible futures in this alien chiefdom, where warriors were respected but where real warfare was unknown, Nxumalo was goaded into telling Shaka of those obvious curiosities.

'For one thing, you cleanse yourself more than anyone I've ever known. Always under the bowl of thrown water.'

'I like to be clean.'

'I think you like to stand naked before the others. To show them that your penis is now big, like theirs.' Shaka frowned, but said nothing. 'And with girls, you're not like the rest of us. You often avoid the pleasures of the road.'

This was a lovely euphemism for one of the most gracious of the local

customs. Since among these clans premarital intercourse was severely forbidden, the habit had evolved of 'taking the pleasures of the road,' meaning
that youngsters were permitted to reach out for a likely love and take her
into the bushes for any imaginable kind of frolic so long as pregnancy did
not result. The men in the iziCwe were notorious for their gentle debauches,
and none enjoyed them more than Nxumalo, but he had noticed that Shaka
was indifferent to this love-play.

'No,' Shaka said reflectively on this particular day, 'I am destined to be
a king. And it's perilous for a king to have children. They fight for his
throne. When he grows old they kill him.' He was in his mid-twenties when
he said this, and so far as Nxumalo could remember—and he knew this
moody warrior better than anyone else—Shaka had never once boasted of
his sexual exploits as other young men did. Nxumalo suspected that his
friend had never lain with a woman, even though he was six foot three, with
no fat about his middle, and the target of many eyes.

'When it's time to marry,' Nxumalo predicted, 'watch out! You'll be the
first.'

'No,' Shaka said quietly. 'For me no children.'

'We'll see,' Nxumalo said, whereupon Shaka gripped him by the shoulder: 'You say I lie?'

'Oh, no,' Nxumalo replied, brushing his hand away. 'But you love
women more than any man I've ever known. Your mother.'

In a rage so violent that the grass trembled, Shaka leaped up, sought
madly for a stone, and would have crushed Nxumalo's head had not the
latter slithered away like a frightened snake.

'Shaka!' he cried from behind a tree. 'Put that down!'

For several moments the warrior stood there, gripping the stone till his
dark hands showed pale at the knuckles.

As the routine of army life absorbed them, disclosing no alternatives for the
years that loomed, Nxumalo saw with some anxiety that his friend was
becoming almost suicidal, dreaming hopelessly of goals he could never
attain, and he felt that he must help him assuage this corrosive bitterness:
'When you said, "One day I'll be chief"—of what? There's no chance here.
There's no chance of returning to the Langeni.'

'Oh! Wait!' Shaka said with fiery determination. 'One day I will return
to the Langeni. There are men there I want to see again.' And he began to
recite the names of the boys who had tormented him in the pastures:
'Nzobo, Mpepha, Mqalane.'

'You want to become chief of the Langeni?'

'Chief of them?' He laughed, and began to stride back and forth. 'I want
to be king of a real tribe. And with my men to march upon the Langeni.
And ask them about their laughter.' Suddenly he changed completely and
asked Nxumalo, 'Wouldn't you like to go back and be chief of the Sixolobo?'

'I don't even remember them.'

'Don't you want to meet the men who killed your father?'

'I wouldn't know them. My father broke a rule. He was executed.'

'But if we could take the iziCwe and march into Langeni land one year,
then Sixolobo the next . . .' His big hands had their fingers extended and

slowly he brought them together. 'There's only one clan I want to lead,' Shaka said. 'The Zulu.'

Nxumalo grew grave: 'You must forget the Zulu. They banished you. Your father hasn't seen you in years, and he has many other sons. What are the Zulu but a tiny flea compared to this clan?'

'But if I were King of the Zulu . . .' He hesitated, reluctant to share his aspirations. Lamely he concluded: 'The Zulu are real men. By the end of the first day they'd understand my dreams.'

In 1815 he revealed his vision of what warfare in his territory was to become. It was an engagement with the Butelezi, and everyone else supposed it was to be an ordinary confrontation, with the two chiefs seated in their chairs as thousands applauded the desultory skirmishing, but when the ground was selected and everyone was in place, a single Butelezi warrior stepped forward with mocking, insolent gestures. From Dingiswayo's ranks a tall man, lean as lion sinew, dashed barefooted at the enemy, hooked his shield deftly into his opponent's, twirled him about like a top, and plunged his short, terrible assegai into the heart.

Then, with a wild yell, he bounded toward the front ranks of the Butelezi, a signal for the rest of the iziCwe to swarm upon the amazed enemy and slay them.

Fifty enemy dead. Kraals burned. Nearly a thousand cattle led home in triumph. More than a dozen women captured. There had never before been a battle like this, and there would never again be a battle in the old style.

As a consequence of this stunning victory, Shaka gained Dingiswayo's favorable attention and was promoted rapidly to regimental commander, a post of honor which he should have held in quiet distinction for the remainder of his life. But such limited achievement was not what Shaka had in mind, not at all. At night he whispered to Nxumalo, 'This Dingiswayo goes to battle as if it were a game. He returns cattle to the vanquished. Leaves them their women.' In the darkness Nxumalo could hear him gritting his teeth. 'This isn't war. This is the quarreling of children.'

'What would you do?'

'I will bring war to the world. Real war.'

In 1816, when Reverend Hilary Saltwood, many miles to the southwest, was teaching the little Madagascan girl Emma the geography of Europe, Shaka's father, chief of the Zulu, died, and after an obliging assassin had removed the son intended for the succession, Shaka at last seized command of the clan, one of the smallest, with a total population of only thirteen hundred and an army, if all the able-bodied were mustered, of three hundred, plus two hundred novices.

It was a clan of little distinction, smaller than either the Sixolobo or the Langeni; it had no special history, had expanded its lands not at all during the preceding hundred years, and had provided no regional leadership except Shaka's promotion to command of the iziCwe. Normally the Zulu would have remained of these dimensions, crouched along one of the better reaches of the Umfolozi River.

But when Shaka assumed command, he moved in with an iziCwe regiment to support his takeover, and one of the first things he did was to require that every Zulu soldier throw away his three long-shafted assegais and replace them with one short stabbing weapon. He then increased the height and width of their shields, until a standing man, with knees only slightly bent, could hide his whole body behind two layers of rock-hard cowhide. But in some ways the most important thing he taught was how to dance.

First he appointed a knobkerrie team of six, choosing the tallest, strongest and most brutal men from his new recruits. Brandishing their clubs, they would stand behind him at all future public functions, awaiting his instructions. Then he assembled his Zulu regiment at the edge of a flat piece of ground well covered with three-pronged thorns. When they stood at attention in the moonlight he stepped before them, barefooted as always.

'My warriors,' he said quietly. 'Four times I have told you that if you want to be the greatest regiment along the Umfolozi, you have got to fight barefooted. And four times you have returned to your sandals. Now take them off. Throw them in a pile. And never let me see them again.'

When the recruits stood barefooted before him, he said, in the same low voice, 'Now, my warriors, we're going to dance.' And he led them onto the thorn-studded land and began a slow dance, accompanied by a chant they knew well. 'Sing, my warriors!' he cried, and as the rhythms began to throb, he danced upon the projections, which caused him no trouble, for he had made his feet tougher than leather. But for his soldiers those first tentative steps were agony, and some began to falter from a pain greater than they could bear.

Now came Shaka's first lesson to his Zulu. Watching hawklike, he spotted a man whose legs simply could not force his feet down onto the piercing thorns. 'That one!' Shaka cried, pointing at the soldier.

What happened next became invariable. Two of the knobkerrie team grabbed the offender from behind, pinioning him with great force. Another dropped down and grasped his ankles, spreading his legs apart. Reaching around from in back, the burliest of the gang seized the man's chin, and with a terrible swing of his arms, twisted it halfway around till the face was looking backward. Then an equally powerful man from in front grasped the chin and continued the awful wrenching until the man's face was again looking forward, having made a complete circle. The face looked the same, but the man was forever altered.

'Now dance!' he cried, and twice more he detected soldiers who were less than enthusiastic, and when he designated them, the slayers descended upon them, twisting their heads about in full circles.

Faster and faster Shaka set the beat until even he was tired. Then, with a gentleness that Nxumalo would never forget, he looked up at the moon and said, 'My dear warriors. It's three nights till the moon is full. Now go and harden your feet, for at the full moon after this, we shall all dance again. You have thirty-one days.'

When they resumed, at the next full moon, only one soldier's neck had to be twisted; the rest kept pace with Shaka until at the end all were jumping up and down on the thorns, driving them into the ground, and singing their regimental songs, and shouting with joy as they danced with their chief.

The next day Shaka explained to his troops why the foot-hardening had been necessary: 'We shall have an army unlike any that has ever swept along the Umfolozi. And its power will be speed. You and I will fly over the rocks, body-arms-head.'

That would be the secret of Shaka's irresistible army of Zulu: 'The body is the big concentration at the center. This is all that the enemy is allowed to see. The arms are swift outreaching movements on the flanks. These are concealed from the enemy.'

'And the head?' Nxumalo asked.

'You are the head, trusted friend. You're now in charge of my best regiment, and during the first stages of a battle your men hide behind a hill, at the center. With your backs to the fighting. You sit with your faces away from battle.'

'But why?'

'Because you must not know how the battle progresses. You must be neither excited nor dismayed. At the crucial moment I'll tell you what to do, and without thinking or trying to adjust, you roar forth and do it.'

It was the kind of commission at which Nxumalo excelled, for it required only allegiance and blind obedience, the two virtues that characterized him. Some men require a leader in whom they can place absolute trust; in his shadow they grow strong. And Nxumalo was such a man. Convinced that Shaka was a genius, he found it rewarding to obey him, and in doing so, became the young chief's only trusted advisor. One morning when the two stood before the regiments the difference between them was obvious. Both were dark of skin, both were battle-hardened. Shaka, only a year older, stood much taller than his aide, broader of shoulder and quicker of movement. In all ways he seemed superior, until the observer looked at Nxumalo's stocky middle, and then he saw a powerful heaviness: a massive chest that would never tire, a belly that could stand punishment, very stout legs prepared to climb hills, and a general endurance that was unmatched. They formed a good pair: Shaka the mercurial planner, Nxumalo the stolid executor.

Early in their strategy discussions they realized that if Shaka's battles were to depend upon fluidity, swift communication among the various segments was vital; equally important was accuracy. So one morning they assembled the four regiments that had been formed, and Shaka initiated this training exercise: 'Speed and accuracy. They're to be the heart of our success. Now the vice-commanders of our regiments are to go one mile from here, each in a different direction, then stand and wait. Each regiment, nominate four signal-runners, place one here with me, the other three at intervals along the way. When you're all in position, I'll give the signal-runners here a message. And off you go. Run to the first waiting man, give him the message, and he carries it to the second, and so on till it reaches the end of the line. Then you vice-commanders dash back here and tell me what the message was. Speed and accuracy.'

When the sixteen outlying men were in position, Shaka studied the field as if this were a real battle, and with Nxumalo and three other regimental commanders at his side, he said in a loud, clear voice, 'Run forty paces forward. Turn and go to the three trees. Leave half your men there. Move forward eighty paces.'

As soon as he had said this he clapped his hands, and the first signal-runners were off. With amazing speed these barefooted men, their feet inured to rocks and thorns, sped over the difficult terrain, ran up to the first waiting men, and delivered their messages. With some satisfaction, Nxumalo saw that his runners were doing rather better than the others, but this was to be expected, and when the final runners carried their messages to their waiting officers and those men began their dash back to Shaka, again Nxumalo saw that his vice-commander was in the lead.

Running at breakneck speed, this man approached the chief, knelt and delivered the message exactly as it had been stated earlier, and so did the next two officers, but the fourth not only lagged in speed but also in the accuracy of his message; indeed, it was badly garbled.

Shaka showed no displeasure. Instead he waited for the sixteen signal-runners to come gasping back to the center, whereupon he praised Nxumalo's men, nodding graciously to him as he did so. The second and third teams he also praised, but when he came to the five delinquent men, he merely pointed at them, whereupon the knobkerrie team grabbed them one by one and burst open their skulls.

'Speed and accuracy,' he said grimly, leaving the field.

Shaka placed major reliance upon Nxumalo because of his unflinching obedience. Some commanders questioned orders, but never his old companion: 'If I told the iziCwe to swim a river, climb a mountain and fight five thousand enemy along the way, Nxumalo would do it.' And he confessed to the other regiments that he depended upon the iziCwe as his one certain arm in battle, for its performance was terrifying.

Shaka's vision of the campaigns that would make him king required total war, total obedience to his personal rule, total destruction of anyone who raised even a whisper against him. He saw Dingiswayo's limited forays as a perpetuation of the petty rivalries which allowed every minor chief a separate development that made him weak and without direction. He was determined to sweep all clans into one great Zulu nation, and to do this his warriors must move like vast herds of antelope, leaving no blade of grass untouched.

While Shaka drilled his regiments, his mother, Nandi, asserted herself in the Zulu kraals. She became indeed the Female Elephant, trampling on those who had rejoiced at her departure years before. The long years of exile which mother and son had shared had forged an extraordinary bond of love and understanding, and now Nandi pushed her son ever forward toward the mighty destiny she saw for the outcast they had called 'that insect.'

Thus, when Shaka judged that his amaZulu were ready for the massive tasks ahead, he told his commanders one evening in 1816, 'We move against the Langeni,' and he was so determined to humble the clan which had treated his mother badly that he rehearsed his battle plan for three tiring days: 'Nxumalo, you were a dog of the Langeni. This time your regiment will form the body. I'm giving you that position because I want total discipline. No Langeni man is to be killed unless absolutely necessary. The two flanks. You must move with greater speed than ever before and capture the enemy alive.' Ominously, on the final evening he commissioned four additional bullies to serve in his knobkerrie team and gave one of them a club suitable for driving stakes. With all steps planned, he went to sleep.

Shortly after dawn Nxumalo assembled the four regiments in a hollow-square formation, each in its distinctive uniform, with headdress of identifying color and large shields of different-colored cowhide.

When all was ready, with a bright sun creeping over the hilltops, Shaka himself stepped into the center of the square, a giant of a man, completely naked, conspicuously muscled, and at a signal from Nxumalo the waiting soldiers cried 'Bayete' and gave foot-stomping applause.

His three personal attendants now dressed him for battle. First they put on a loincloth apron of tanned leather, then a girdle of bright leopard skin about two inches wide fastened tightly to support an ashy gray kilt made of twisted genet fur which ended well above his knees. About his shoulders they placed a loose garland of animal tails kept so short they would not flop when he ran, and on his head a kind of crown formed by tufts of small red feathers and topped by a backward-curving blue-crane feather at least two feet long.

He was barefooted, of course, and carried in his hands only two things: his massive shield almost as tall as himself and pure white, except for a small black dot in the middle; and his stabbing assegai with haft two feet long and iron point one foot. But what imparted a sense of awful majesty were the four adornments the attendants now attached. About each arm, just below the shoulder, an armband of white cowtails was tied, the tips reaching down to his elbows and very full, so that they fluttered when he moved. And below each knee, reaching to his ankles, a similar band was fastened, and it was these white ornamentations, combined with the stark whiteness of the shield, that caused his brown-black body to glow with imperial grandeur.

'We march!' he cried as he faced his regiments, and his five hundred warriors replied, 'Bayete!'

Like a serpent the Zulu army snaked through the hills, and at dawn next morning the Langeni were surprised to find, upon waking, that enemy regiments surrounded their kraals. Shaka's orders were obeyed, and the amazed Langeni, expecting their huts to be fired, their people slaughtered, found no assegai raised against them except in silent warning. Could this be Shaka, whose heralds referred to him as The-One-Who-Will-Swallow-the-Land? The answer would come with shocking clarity.

Nxumalo was sent quietly among the huddled Langeni, nodding at one, then another, until he had identified more than thirty. These men were taken to the main kraal, where they looked up at a face that seemed strangely familiar. 'I am Shaka, son of the Female Elephant Nandi, whom you reviled.' He sang out the names of the tribal leaders, and as each was shoved forward, the knobkerrie team began the slaughter.

The execution squad worked in different ways. If a victim had ever displayed one redeeming virtue, his head was swiftly and almost painlessly twisted in a complete circle. Death was instantaneous. But if there were remembered grudges, without extenuating circumstances, clubs were used, a heavy rain of blows to all parts of the body except the head, and this death was painful. The older Langeni died in this manner.

But when Shaka pointed out those who as herd boys had tormented him, he ordered the guards to stand them aside, and in the end he had eleven, and when he looked at them, his face grew dark as a thundercloud and reason seemed to leave him, for he was a boy again, back in the fields, and when he saw his chief aide and most trusted friend, Nxumalo, he shouted, 'You, too, were one of them!' and the knobkerrie team seized him and threw him with the others.

'Nzobo,' he now screamed at one of the former herd boys. 'Did you not scorn me?'

The Langeni, now a man of substance, stood silent. 'Take him!' Shaka bellowed, and in that instant Nzobo was taken hold of and stripped. Then two men held him by the knees while another two bent him forward in a final, terrible bow, as if he were a suitor seeking Shaka's approval. Another produced four bamboo skewers, each about fourteen inches long, fire-hardened and needle-sharp. One of these was inserted into Nzobo's rectum, and with a wooden pounder the last member of the knobkerrie team hammered it home deeply, slowly.

Another, and then another, and then a fourth was hammered in, where-upon a rope was slung under the armpits of the screaming victim and he was pulled aloft to hang from the limb of a tree. After sixteen hours of mortal agony he would be dead.

Nxumalo, seeing this horrible punishment and aware that he was destined for it, tried to make some appeal to Shaka, but the awful judgment was proceeding: 'Mpepha, did you not throw rocks at me?' A list of grievances, kept alive for twenty years, was hurled at the terror-stricken man, who was then stripped and skewered.

Mqalane was next, and when he, too, dangled from the tree, Shaka was finished with the three whose long-ago behavior rankled deepest. The next eight were impaled on the poles of the cattle kraal, where he could not see them. 'It's repugnant to watch traitors die,' he told his men, but now two were dragged forward whose death he would cherish. 'Did you abuse me?' The men nodded. For that he would forgive them, and they sighed, but then he asked, 'Did you abuse my mother?' and when they stood, heads down, he screamed, 'Let them die as women!' whereupon the death squad fell upon them and tore away their privates.

Now only Nxumalo remained, and at him Shaka looked with loathing, but also confusion. He had been one of the herd boys; clearly Shaka remembered that, but he could not recall what exactly the Sixolobo refugee had done that merited skewering. The guards were already stripping him when the king's mind cleared slightly and he realized that his regimental commander ought not to be included, and with humility he brushed the guards aside and stood facing Nxumalo.

'What did you do against me when we were herd boys?'

And Nxumalo replied, 'Nothing, my Chief.'

'What did you ever do for me?'

And this time Nxumalo said, 'I cannot speak it, Mighty One. But I will whisper it.'

So Shaka moved everyone back, ordering the guards to let Nxumalo have his uniform, and as the naked commander stood with his leather skirt in his hand, he whispered to the chief, reminding him of that afternoon when they sat upon the grass and Nxumalo had assured him that one day he would have a penis of normal size.

Shaka put the fingertips of his left hand over his eyes and bowed his head. 'Are you Nxumalo of the iziCwe?'

'I am.'

'Dark spirits are on this field,' Shaka mumbled, and with a great stran-
gling cry he demanded that the diviners conduct a smelling-out to identify
the men in this gathering who housed these spirits, and the wild ones with
snake skeletons dangling about their necks, dried gall bladders in their hair
and black wildebeest tails in their hands ran helter-skelter among the Zulu,
sniffing and listening and finally touching with their switching tails those
who had brought evil upon the chief. As soon as a victim was designated,
the knobkerrie men killed him.

Toward midnight, as Shaka sat drinking beer with Nxumalo, he began
to feel pity for the impaled men. 'It would be too cruel to leave them
hanging through the night,' he said, and he directed his people to gather
huge mounds of grass and sticks to pile under the dangling men. 'See,' he
cried to his victims, 'I no longer hold bitterness against you.' And he lit the
grass so that the men might die quickly and escape the terrible agonies that
would otherwise have come with the morning, when the hot sun began to
shine upon them.

As a gesture of conciliation Shaka absorbed the Langeni regiments into his
growing army, launching a policy that would result in a powerful force.
When Dingiswayo, to whom he still owed nominal allegiance, died in battle
with a northern tribe, the entire iziCwe contingent marched over to the
Zulu, and Shaka said, 'Nxumalo, my truest friend, from this day you eat
with the iziCwe.' This thrilling announcement had nothing to do with the
manner in which the new general of the regiments would take his meals;
it referred to the terrifying battle cry that would soon echo through the land
whenever a Zulu warrior killed an enemy: 'I have eaten!'

In every direction Shaka lashed out with devastating speed, devouring
small clans, and one morning he cried brusquely, 'Today we destroy the
Ngwane,' and within a few hours the regiments had crossed the Umfolozi
River and were dashing north to the kraals of a tribe which had given
repeated trouble. Without signals or warning, other than the cries of astonished herd boys who saw the amazing army approaching, the Zulu took
battle position, body-arms-head, and fell upon the community.

The Ngwane, like all subsidiary tribes in this region, were stalwart men
and they did not propose to lose their cattle easily, for they supposed this
to be another cattle raid in which two or three men might get hurt. So they
quickly formed into their rude battle formations, with their throwing assegais at the ready. They saw the body of Shaka's army, and it looked much
like any traditional raiding party, but as they moved forward to engage it,
they suddenly discovered that the wings were widespread, like the horns of
some enraged buffalo, so that wherever they turned they confronted swift-
running Zulu.

'They'll take all our cattle!' the Ngwane commander shouted, but it was
not cows that the Zulu sought this time. With terrifying force they fell upon
the Ngwane, stabbing and killing, and when the latter bravely tried to
regroup and fight in earnest, from out of nowhere sprang the iziCwe, their
brutal assegais slashing like the knives that slaughtered oxen for the sacrifice.

Under this tremendous onslaught the Ngwane defenses crumbled, and those warriors who were spared the Zulu cry 'I have eaten!' scattered and kept on running. In their flight from terror they would become outlaws, seeking in the blood of others vengeance for their own crushing defeat. The kraals from which they fled were now in ashes, their herds driven off, their boys dragooned into Zulu regiments and their women distributed among the Zulu kraals.

The old people were 'helped along to the other place,' their slayers killing them with joy, for the Zulu saw nothing cruel in shortening the days of any who were aged or infirm. But when this savage battle was over, the Ngwane had ceased to exist as a clan.

Their extinction had been made possible by the disciplined performance of the iziCwe, and when the regiments returned to the Zulu kraals, Shaka praised the men and told them, to the envy of the other warriors, 'You may now enjoy the pleasures of the road.'

Shaka had introduced his own variation of that sexual custom: no warrior could marry until his chief gave him permission, and this was usually delayed until the soldiers were in their mid-thirties and growing too old for the crack regiments. Then, in a grand ceremony, they were permitted to search the woods for a combination of vine, gut and gum, from which they made a wide headband, woven into the hair when moist and worn for the rest of life as proof of marriage.

But since it was illogical to expect grown men, and the bravest warriors at that, to remain continent till they donned their headbands, the soldiers were granted the 'pleasures' after any battle.

So Nxumalo's warriors fanned out through the community, looking for young women, and the girls, long wondering about husbands and lovers, eagerly allowed themselves to be found. For three long days the men reveled in the glades, loving the women with passion born on the battlefield, yet practicing an almost savage restraint because they knew the fearful penalty they must pay if they got the women pregnant.

Nxumalo, no less excited about the fraternizing reward than his men, had gone seeking his pleasure of the road at a kraal whose daughter he had been noticing for some time. He was now a powerfully organized man who had been in the forefront of seven battles; he had a right to assume, therefore, that one of these years he would win permission to take a wife, but he knew that in Shaka's regime, sex was utilized as the ultimate weapon of control.

So he was determined to excel in battle so that he could go to Thetiwe to ask her to be his wife. Thetiwe, sixteen years old and the daughter of a neighboring chieftain, a girl of lovely demeanor and flashing eyes, had expected the iziCwe to perform well, which meant of course that its commander would come calling. So she waited alone, and when night fell she heard his steps.

'How was the battle?' she asked as he led her into a scattered wood beside the river.

'They are no more, the Ngwane.'

'They were a troublesome people.'

'No more.'

They spent three exciting days together, and often they talked of how soon Shaka might allow them to marry. Nxumalo, better aware than most of Shaka's intentions, was not overly hopeful: 'Consider the situation. More than anything else, Shaka wants to build the Zulu into the commanding nation, of which he will be king. To achieve this, constant warfare is necessary. And in battle he must have one regiment he can rely on. It'll always be the iziCwe. And I shall be fighting at its head until I'm fifty.'

'Oh, no!' Pressing her small hands against her face, she pondered the empty years till Nxumalo could claim her, and with great sadness, asked, 'Doesn't he know that his men should marry?'

'Thetiwe,' he replied gravely, 'you must never let anyone hear you ask such a question.'

'But why not?'

'Because Shaka is different. He doesn't think of families. He thinks only of armies and the glory to come.' He paused, wondering if he dare discuss this matter honestly with an untested girl of sixteen, but his passion for her was so intense that he felt he must. 'How many wives does the chief have now?'

'In the various kraals, sixty . . . I think.'

'Are any of them pregnant?'

'Oh, no!'

'But the last chief. Shaka's father. Were his wives usually pregnant?'

'He had scores of children.'

'The difference is that Shaka never sleeps with his wives. You know what he calls them? "My beloved sisters." Always he calls them his sisters. You see, he fears women for two reasons. He wants no children, especially no sons.'

'Why not? You want sons, don't you?'

'I do. I would quit the army now . . .' He dropped that dangerous topic and continued speaking of his chief: 'And the other reason he fears women . . . it goes back to when he was a boy. The others teased him. Told him he could never have babies. They laughed at him constantly and said no wife would ever want him.'

'Now he has sixty wives,' Thetiwe said, 'and they'll probably put twenty of the captured Ngwane girls aside for him.'

'But you mustn't speak of this to anyone,' Nxumalo warned, aware of what might happen to her and to him if Shaka suspected them of irreverence.

She laughed. 'I've known everything you've said. What do you think the women in the kraals joke about when no one can spy on them? That Shaka keeps his beloved sisters aside till a real man comes along to claim them.'

'Thetiwe! Never speak of that.' And having observed the wrath of Shaka, the lovers were afraid even to think such thoughts, let alone voice them.

Shaka had now absorbed four troublesome tribes, 'embracing them in my arms,' as he said. In his utilization of the body-arms-head tactic he had become incredibly deft. Sometimes he sent one of his flanks far out and thinly spaced, their broad shields with the edges forward and thus nearly invisible. Hidden in the grasses behind lurked a second group. As his army advanced, the opposing general spotted the undermanned flank and wheeled his principal force against it, but when the enemy was committed, Shaka flashed a signal, whereupon the front line of Zulu whipped their shields front forward, while the hidden men leaped into position, showing the full width of their shields also. In an instant, what had been a line of stragglers became a solid phalanx looming two or three times larger than it actually was. Often this struck such terror that the enemy soldiers who had been marching confidently to engage an outnumbered foe fled in panic, disrupting the lines behind and inviting the massive body of the Zulu army to overwhelm them.

Zulu messengers, in reporting victories, gave details in rigorous order: so many cattle taken for the chief's pastures, so many boys for his regiments, so many girls for his kraals. The watchmen of the women selected twenty or thirty of the choicest maidens and turned the others over to the clan, and although Shaka appeared to pay little attention to his wives, any male caught lurking about the women's compound was instantly strangled, and if the girl to whom he had been making advances could be identified, she, too, was slain.

Nxumalo, obedient to each rule Shaka promulgated, spent whatever time was legally allowed with Thetiwe, and told her many things: 'Shaka is the greatest man who ever lived. A genius like no other. I've known four chiefs, and beside him, they were boys. It's in his plans for our nation that he excels. All tribes combined into one. From the rivers on the north to the rivers on the south. One family, one king.' He paused as he said this, then added, 'Shaka, King of the Zulu.'

'But you said he almost impaled you.'

'It was the evil spirits, not Shaka himself. They came and blinded him, but as soon as I told him who I was and his eyes opened, he spared me.'

'But didn't you often tell me that when the tribes were united, there'd be no more war?'

It was the kind of probing question that Thetiwe often asked him. But he knew there must be an answer: 'It's like this. We're still faced by many tribes that we must defeat. This will go on for some years, but one day there will be peace. Shaka has said so.'

The king's next actions belied this, for he authorized the formation of two new regiments. The first was composed only of girls Thetiwe's age, and because of her impeccable lineage and her bright intelligence, she was made vice-commander of this new regiment. The girls were not intended for battle; they were kept to the rear, performing services such as cooking, the mending of weapons and the nursing of the wounded, and quickly they learned the basic rule of Shaka's battle plan: 'If a Zulu is wounded, speak to him. If he can understand what you're saying, mend him. If he can't, call the guards.' When the girls did summon the knobkerrie men, the latter studied the case briefly, then usually took the wounded man's assegai and plunged it into his heart, for as Shaka said, 'If he can't walk, he can't fight.' And this the nurses understood.

The second new regiment was of quite a different character. It was almost laughable to look at, a collection of older men halt of leg and bad of eye. It was inconceivable that they could move with the alacrity demanded of Shaka's regiments, but gradually the king's strategy became evident: 'These men are to receive half-rations. They're to be worked constantly, and the sooner they die off, the better the Zulu nation will be.'

Now everyone, except the child-bearing women, was in a regiment and the nation was at last efficiently organized. Nxumalo liked the certainty this provided, the orderly progression through life with no chance for accidental deviation: a boy was born; he tended cattle; at eleven he was assigned a place in the cadets, a kind of pre-regiment that performed tasks for the king; at fourteen he joined the youth's regiment, carrying water and food to men in battle; at nineteen he could, if he were fortunate, become a member of some renowned regiment like the iziCwe. For the next quarter of a century he would live in barracks in an orderly way, traveling to far parts of the nation where enemies existed; and if he proved obedient, the time would eventually come when he could marry; he would have a brief, happy life with his wife and children, and then pass on to the old men's battalion, where he would die decently without prolonged imbecility. It was the way life should be managed, Nxumalo thought, for it helped men avoid erratic behavior and produced a disciplined, happy nation.

Nxumalo also appreciated the advantage that came from having the young girls collected into their own regiment: at the conclusion of some harsh battle, when the warriors were exhausted, these girls would be sent to the proper area, and for three or four days the victors could sport with them and thus avoid the burden of returning long distances to the kraals, where girls would have to be searched for. In later days Nxumalo was astounded by an additional simplicity the king's strategy permitted: once when the amaWombe regiment had performed especially well, Shaka rewarded it brilliantly. He marched the entire force to the parade ground, then summoned one of the girls' regiments and announced: 'The men may marry the women.' And by nightfall the pairings had been made and six hundred new families were launched without interrupting army procedures.

By 1823 Shaka had consolidated the major portion of his nation, bringing into carefully defined order what had previously been a mass of contending chiefdoms. He was an excellent administrator, offering positions of considerable importance to any gifted members of defeated tribes, and recalling his own unhappy days as an alien among the Langeni, he made the newcomers totally welcome, so that within a few months they began to forget that they had ever been anything but Zulu.

Nxumalo saw that iron rule was necessary if such a patchwork of clans was ever to become a unified kingdom; brutal punishments were accepted, for in the black tribes the chief served as father of the people, and what displeased him displeased his children, who became almost eager for retribution. Shaka started his reign in accordance with tradition; his rule was no more bloody than that of his predecessors, but as his authority widened he was tempted, like all burgeoning tyrants, to make his whim the law of the land.

In this he was encouraged by a curious personal motivation: he looked with scorn at all diviners and witch doctors, for although he knew they were necessary, he also knew they were a sorry lot. But the more he denigrated them, the more he was tempted to usurp their power; he became his own diviner, and those about him lived in terror. A nod when he was speaking, a belch, an injudicious fart, and Shaka would point to the offender, signaling his knobkerrie team to strangle that one.

But never in the early days was he a senseless tyrant; he gave the Zulu an able, generous government. He was especially careful to ensure that his people had reliable water supplies, stable sources of food, and his care of cattle would never be excelled. His personal herds numbered above twenty thousand, and he expressed his love for them in various ways. As a Zulu, he cherished cattle above any other possession, for he knew that a man's stature depended on the number of cattle he had been able to accumulate and that a nation's welfare was determined by the care with which it protected its animals.

His herds were so large that he was able to segregate them by color, which had not only an esthetic result but also a very practical one, because the cowhide shields of various regiments could be differentiated. The iziCwe, for example, carried only white shields with black fittings. Others had black, a choice color, or brown or red, the red finding little favor, for it was thought to be unlucky.

He was most careful with the animals intended for sacrifice, for upon them depended the spiritual safety of his kingdom, as well as his own. He never felt more secure than when he attended a ritual slaughter, stripped naked and washed himself in the still-warm chyme of a freshly slain bull. This thick liquid, the contents of the animal's stomach at the completion of the digestive process, was life-giving, and to feel one's self cleansed by it was an assurance of immortality.

Even more important, however, was the precious little sac, about as big as a child's fist, which fastened to the dead animal's liver. This was the gall bladder, in which rested the bitter fluid that symbolized life: it was acrid, like the taste of death, yet the bladder in which it lived was shaped exactly like the womb from which life sprang. Also, mysteriously, it resembled the beehive hut in which man lived, and the grave in which he ultimately rested, so that the whole of life was encompassed in this magical appendage. Once its bitter contents had been sprinkled to consecrate, it was dried into a thin leather, inflated and worn in the matted hair of witch-seekers.

He was extremely loving with his mother, turning over to her the supervision of the kraals in which he kept his wives, and it was because of her attentiveness that he became aware of Thetiwe, vice-commander of one of his women's regiments.

The Female Elephant was beginning to show her age, and Shaka was terrified by the possibility that one day she might die, so he tended her lovingly, and once when she caught something in her eye and could not dislodge it, she began to wail so loudly that messengers were sent for the king, and when he found her in despair, he summoned all his herbalists, but before they arrived, Thetiwe, whose regiment barracked nearby, was called to the queen's hut, and with the deftness she exhibited on so many occasions, extracted the thorn-tip which had tormented the queen. Nandi was ecstatic, and told her son, 'There's a splendid woman. I've waited all these years for you to give me a grandson. There's the one.'

When Shaka studied his young military leader he saw quickly that his mother was right, and this frightened him, for he did not want a Paramount

Wife nor did he want any children by one. On both accounts his thinking was clear and accurate. A king, when he was making his way, could have as many wives as he wished; Shaka had twelve hundred now. And with them he could have as many children as he was capable of siring; some chiefs had sixty or more. But none of this counted; the early mothers had no special standing, for among the Zulu there was no primogeniture.

What a prudent king did was wait till his reign had been securely established; then he carefully chose from some family that could assist him in time of trouble a young woman of proved stability. She became his Paramount Wife, acknowledged by all others, and her sons stood in line to inherit the kingdom. And that's where the trouble came, for in Zululand princes killed kings.

So as soon as the Female Elephant announced that she had selected Thetiwe to be this Paramount Wife, Shaka bowed, backed out the door of his mother's kraal, and had Nxumalo summoned: 'Didn't you tell me that you fancied the girl Thetiwe, of the women's regiment?'

'I did.'

'You're to marry her this afternoon.'

'Mighty Lion, I haven't cattle enough to pay lobola for such a woman.'

'I give you three hundred cattle.'

'But her family . . .'

'I will command her family to approve. Now!'

Hasty and flimsy arrangements were made on the spot, and before the Female Elephant could protest, a wedding was arranged. The king himself officiated, and when the witch doctors had shaken their matted locks and rattled their dried gall bladders, blessings were said and the surprised couple were married. Then, to spirit them away from Nandi's wrath, they were sent north to conduct a negotiation which would determine the future course of their lives.

Their quarry was Mzilikazi of the Kumalo clan, an extraordinary young commander who even now, at the youthful age of twenty-seven, was betraying signs of challenging Shaka. This Mzilikazi had refused to send Shaka three thousand cattle captured in his raids, and twice he had rebuffed emissaries sent to collect them. Now Nxumalo and Thetiwe, armed with plenipotentiary powers and one hundred warriors, went to recover the cattle.

They found Mzilikazi at his unpretentious kraal in the northern forests, and when they saw him they simply could not believe that this reticent, whisper-speaking young warrior would dare antagonize the King of the Zulu. But that was the case. Bowing in servility, the young leader extended every hospitality to his guests, but no cattle. Whenever Nxumalo raised the question of the cattle—'The lion grows impatient, Mzilikazi, and he wants to eat'—the young leader smiled, blinked his hooded eyes, and did nothing.

They stayed with him for two weeks, and the more they saw, the more impressed they became. One night, upon retiring, Nxumalo made a final threat—'If we don't take the cattle home with us, Mzilikazi, the regiments will come north'—and when he wakened next morning he found that all his men had been surrounded by the commander's warriors and were immobilized.

Mzilikazi ruled wisely and with a minimum of passion. He was so considerate of his subjects that he kept about him no gang of assassins to inflict his will. No rhinoceros whips were allowed to sting his cattle; supple reeds from the river had to be used. In all things he was gentle: speech, movement, the giving of orders, his manner of dress, his love of singing. He was so utterly different from Shaka that whenever Nxumalo looked at him he thought: How pleasant it would be for a warrior to serve in the retinue of this noble man.

But in the end Nxumalo and Thetiwe returned home without a single cow. At the final meeting Mzilikazi said in his silken way, 'Tell Shaka not to waste his energies sending for the cattle. They will never be released.'

Nxumalo knew that he was obligated to resist such arrogance, but he said, without raising his voice, 'Then you must build high fences of thorn to protect them.'

And Mzilikazi replied, 'The love my people bear me is my fence of thorn.'

When Shaka heard of this insolence he ordered his regiments to assemble, and within the week Nxumalo was at the head of his iziCwe marching right back to Mzilikazi's kraals. The siege was short . . . and bloody, but the boy-general with the quiet manners escaped in some safe direction that could not be detected.

Now the beneficial results of Shaka's approach to government manifested themselves. An area larger than many European nations, which had festered for centuries in petty anarchy, became a unit, orderly and prosperous. The two hundred tribal loyalties which had previously rendered sensible action impossible were now melded into one, and families that two decades ago had not even heard the word Zulu now proudly proclaimed themselves as such. Whatever new triumph Shaka attained brought a shared glory to them, so that what had begun as a small clan of thirteen hundred Zulu was magically transformed by his genius into a powerful nation of half a million.

Order reigned in the land, and advancement was open to even the latest convert to the Zulu cause. A boy from the Sixolobo tribe entering his Zulu regiment at fourteen had just as fair a chance of becoming its commander as did any son of a distinguished Zulu family. In fact, by the time he was fifteen, with a year's training behind him, he was a Zulu, and no one ever again referred to him as a Sixolobo. And such citizenship was not reserved for the young; this boy's parents could come into Shaka's court and demand justice the same as anyone else, and his sisters could enter the kraals as wives to men who were born Zulu.

Peace also prevailed, and the central kraals along the Umfolozi River would pass years without experiencing attack, so that Shaka's name became revered throughout his kingdom. Citizens cheered when he appeared, waited on his commands, and were gratified with the benefits he brought them.

Nxumalo, for example, had scores of reasons for loving his powerful friend. He had already served as general of the finest regiment and as plenipotentiary in arranging peace with outlying clans. In 1826 Shaka gave further proof of his affection for the man who served him so well.

'Nxumalo, you must come to my kraal,' the king said, and when they reached the sacred area two beautiful Zulu girls were waiting. 'These are your brides,' Shaka said, ordering the seventeen-year-old girls forward.

'This time, Mighty Lion, I have the cattle to pay for them.'

'Their parents have already received their lobola . . . from me.'

'I am most grateful.' It was a considerate thing Shaka had done, for in Zulu custom a husband was not permitted to go near his first wife, or any other for that matter, so long as she was pregnant or nursing a baby, and since she continued to nurse till the child was four and a half, this meant that the man was without sexual affection for about five years at a stretch. The problem was solved by allowing the man to take multiple wives, always supposing that he could pay for them in cattle, because this meant that as one wife after another became pregnant, there would be replacements, and one of the standard jokes in Zulu regiments dealt with the fiery commander who had seven wives, all pregnant at the same time: 'He might as well have been unmarried.' Now that Thetiwe had a baby, it was helpful to her for Nxumalo to take additional wives; Nxumalo, on his part, was made additionally beholden to his king.

But in a wonderfully subtle and corrective way Nxumalo's good fortune was beginning to produce its own penalties, for an ancient black tradition had been amended to provide a clever strategy for leveling society and cutting off any upstart whose popularity and power might begin to threaten the king's. This was the smelling-out ritual; now when witch-seekers coursed through the crowd, they were identifying those subversive persons whose removal would purify the tribe.

A smelling-out was conducted on sound psychological principles: as the witch-seekers with their gall bladders, snake skeletons and wildebeest tails dashed through the assembly, the crowd uttered the low, throbbing sound of a thousand voices moaning. If the seekers approached someone who by common consent ought to be removed from society, the humming increased to an audible roar, assuring the seekers that this man's death would be popular. In this way Zulu society cleansed itself. With subtle tactic it announced a consensus that was immediately enforced, for as soon as the witch-seekers nominated a man by waving their wildebeest tails in his face, he was grabbed, bent double, and destroyed with four bamboo skewers.

Nxumalo, as he accumulated fresh proofs of the king's favor, realized that he was moving into the realm of danger when the witch-seekers could mysteriously decide that the Zulu had had just about enough of him. Rumors were already circulating: 'Nxumalo? He came from nowhere. Connived against better men to win leadership of the iziCwe. Failed in his mission to Mzilikazi. Now has more cattle than a man should dream of owning. Nxumalo, like the white stork, flies too high.' So now whenever the Zulu were summoned for the next batch of removals, he began to sweat, appreciating like an ancient philosopher the transient nature of human glory.

In spite of this encroaching danger, he was needed by the Zulu, for although Shaka's system was well-nigh perfect, it had one self-destroying weakness: if a nation is totally geared to the waging of war, it had better ensure that war keeps occurring somewhere; and if incessant warfare is the rule, then trusted leaders like Nxumalo are essential. Every improvement that Shaka made obligated him to seek opponents against whom to test it, for he dared not allow his war machine to rest. It had to be housed and fed and armed with iron-tipped assegais: whole communities did nothing but forge iron; others spent their days fabricating stinkwood shafts.

So, like the emperors of Rome dispatching their legions to the far frontiers in search of new enemies, Shaka sent his regiments to distant valleys, where tribes that had committed no offense found themselves surrounded. And because Zulu warriors needed constant practice with their stabbing assegais, they collected few prisoners, but many cattle and women. This increased the wealth of the victors but not their stability, and many men discovered that as they acquired more cattle and wives, they also acquired the enmity of their friends. Many a prospering Zulu who was nominated by the witch-seekers wondered as he died in skewered agony how it all happened. War threw men upward, but the moaning of the populace dragged them back down.

It was in 1826, when Hilary and Emma Saltwood were entering Salisbury to visit his mother, that Shaka became acutely aware that he, too, formed part of this vast, impersonal process of advance and decline. He did not have to fear the diviners, for they were his agents; by subtle means he indicated whom he wanted them to remove, so that the leadership of the kingdom would always remain at a dead level, with no new heads rising suddenly above the multitude. What did threaten him, and all men, was the inexorable passing of time, the loss of a tooth now and then, the death of an uncle, the sad, sad wasting away of a man's life. Diviners were the enemy of Nxumalo; time, the enemy of Shaka.

By now a set of daring British traders had settled on the coast well to the south of Zululand, and among them was a tough, ingratiating Irish-Englishman named Henry Francis Fynn, a man whose personal courage equaled his brazen ingenuity. He introduced Shaka to Western ways, instructed him regarding the powers of the English king, and doctored his sick followers in the kraals. The extraordinary details of Shaka's final years might never have been known to the world at large had it not been for the recollections of Fynn, and the colorful journal of an imaginative eighteen-year-old, Nathaniel Isaacs, who had also made his way into the area.

No one will ever know what really went on in the minds of these traders as they observed customs and ancient traditions so utterly alien; their remembered response was clear, though, and in their writings they created the portrait of Shaka, the monster, driven by an unconquerable lust for slaughter:

> His eyes evinced his pleasure, his iron heart exulted, his whole frame seemed as if it felt a joyous impulse at seeing the blood of innocent creatures flowing at his feet; his hands grasped, his herculean and muscular limbs exhibiting by their motion a desire to aid in the execution of the victims of his vengeance; in short, he seemed a being in human form with more than the physical capabilities of a man; a giant without reason, a monster created with more than ordinary

power and disposition for doing mischief, and from whom we recoil as we would at the serpent's hiss or the lion's growl.

Confronted by such a horror, Fynn, Isaacs and the other Europeans who joined them were nevertheless to stay in Shaka's domain up to four years, unharmed, desperately trying to make money, and conniving constantly to have the British Colonial Office bail them out.

If Fynn and Isaacs were horrified by Shaka's killings, he was appalled to learn that the British imprisoned their offenders: 'Nothing could be more cruel than to keep a man lingering, when one swift blow would free him forever.'

But Fynn was a clever man, seeking any chance to gain the approval of the Zulu ruler, and after studying the man, he came up with a brilliant approach: a promise of liquid which prevented hair from turning gray.

'Yes,' said Fynn, 'you rub this magic liquid in your hair, and it never becomes white.'

'Immortality!' Shaka cried, demanding to know what this elixir was called.

'Rowland's Macassar Oil,' Fynn said.

'Have you any?'

'No, but a year from now, when the trading ship comes in . . .'

It was a year of anxiety. To all parts of his realm Shaka sent messengers seeking to learn if anyone had Rowland's Macassar Oil, and his tragic countenance when none was produced alerted Nxumalo to the king's confused state of mind: 'If I could live another twenty years . . . forty . . . I could have all the land ever seen under my control. Nxumalo, we must find the oil that prevents a man from growing old.'

'Do you really think there is such a thing?'

'Yes. The white men know of it. That's why they have guns and horses. The oil!'

When the oil did not arrive and gray hairs multiplied, Shaka had to face the problem of a successor. He was only forty, with death far off, but as he said to Nxumalo, 'Look at my mother, how she fades. I don't want the magic oil for myself. I want it to save her life.'

'She's old—' Nxumalo started to say, hoping to prepare the king for his mother's eventual death, but Shaka would hear no such words.

In terrible rage he shouted at his aide, 'Go—leave me! You spoke against the Female Elephant! I'll kill you with my own hands.'

But two days later Nxumalo was summoned back: 'Trusted friend, no man can rule forever.' As Shaka uttered these bitter words tears filled his eyes and he sat with his shoulders heaving, finally regaining enough control to add, 'If you and I could have another twenty years, we'd bring order to all the lands. We'd even bring the Xhosa into our fold.' With bitter regret he shook his head, then seemed to discharge his apprehensions: 'Nxumalo, you must go north again. Find Mzilikazi.'

'My King, I've seen your hatred for this traitor who stole your cattle.'

'It is so, Nxumalo, but you will take ten men and find him. Bring him to me. For if he rules the north and I the south, together we can protect this land from strangers.'

'What strangers?'

'Strangers will always come,' Shaka said.

Nxumalo's secret mission involved a long trip into land that no Zulu had ever entered, but they were guided toward Mzilikazi by the battered clans who trembled in the wake of the fleeing Kumalo commander, and at the end of a most tiring journey the kraal was located, and in it waited not a regimental commander but a self-proclaimed king.

'King of what?' Nxumalo asked.

'King-of-All-He-Will-See. Is that not enough?'

Nxumalo looked at the eyes still hooded, the face still handsome and delicately brown, but it was the voice that haunted—soft, whispery, extremely gentle, like the man himself: 'Why would Shaka invite me, an enemy, to his kraal?'

'Because he needs you. He knows you are the greatest king in the north, as he is in the south.'

'If I stay here, I'm safe. If I go there . . .' He indicated an assegai in his side.

'No, Shaka needs you.'

'But I hate battle. I want no more of killing.' He spoke with such intensity, in that silken voice, that Nxumalo had to believe him, and at the end of six days' talking it was apparent that Mzilikazi, in many ways as able a king as Shaka, was not going to combine forces with the Zulu.

'This time, Mzilikazi, no threats from me,' Nxumalo said.

'Friends don't threaten each other. But because I know that you will listen to my reasoning I have a gift for you. Look!' And when the lion skins decorating his kraal—an indulgence Shaka would never have permitted—were parted, there stood a lissome girl of twenty prepared to go with Nxumalo as a gift.

'Shaka will think that you gave me the present because I did not argue diligently.'

'Shaka knew I would not join the Zulu. He'll understand the gift,' said Mzilikazi, and while Nxumalo stood next to the attractive girl he studied this strange king, so different from his own. Shaka was tall, iron-hard and lean; Mzilikazi seemed to be getting fat and soft. When Shaka spoke the earth seemed to cringe in obedience, but Mzilikazi smiled much more than he frowned and his voice never rose in anger. Furthermore, Shaka was a brilliant but violent man, somewhat distant even to his friends, while Mzilikazi was frank and open to all, a man who seemed always to do the right thing. He was much too clever to be trapped by the great King of the Zulu, and told Nxumalo, as the latter started south with his fourth bride, Nonsizi, 'We shall not meet again, Nxumalo. But I shall always remember you as a man of good heart. Tell Shaka that the conversations are ended. I shall move far from his reach.'

The pudgy king was right; Nxumalo never saw him again, but remembered him often and with the warmest feelings, for he commanded respect. As Nxumalo told his new bride, 'I can't understand it. Mzilikazi started out with his people like a band of brigands on the run. Now he's forming a kingdom.' Among the clans Mzilikazi's followers touched in their wild movement they became known as the fugitives—the Matabele—and under that name they would flame through the generations, the tribe that out-smarted Shaka of the Zulu.

When Nxumalo crossed the Umfolozi River in the spring of 1827 he found the Zulu tense and frightened, for the Female Elephant had fallen ill, and her son was dispatching messengers to all parts of the kingdom to see if anyone had found a bottle of Rowland's Macassar Oil which would darken her hair and prolong her life. A member of Nxumalo's kraal, seeing the master returning with a new wife, hurried to him with a warning: 'Three messengers who returned without the oil have been strangled. If you say you have none, you may be killed. So tell him immediately that you heard of a source at the north.'

'But I didn't.'

'Nxumalo, if the Female Elephant dies, we'll be in great trouble.'

'But why should I lie to him? He will soon learn the truth.'

The matter was solved by the grieving king; he did not ask for Fynn's magic liquid. What he wanted was news of Mzilikazi. 'He has fled,' Nxumalo said bluntly. 'He feared you as the king and knew that he could not stand against you in battle.'

'I didn't want to fight him, Nxumalo. I wanted to enlist him as our ally.'

He had much more to say; with his mother's illness reminding him of his own mortality, the succession to his throne was uppermost in his plans, but at midafternoon all this was swept aside when a trembling messenger came with the awful news: 'The Female Elephant has died.'

'My mother? Dead?'

Shaka withdrew into his hut, and when he walked out an hour later he was in full battle dress. His circle of generals and the nation's elders watched anxiously, but he betrayed no sign of the titanic grief welling up inside him. For half an hour the great leader rested his head on his tall oxhide shield, keeping his eyes on the ground, where his tears fell in the dust. Finally he looked up, wild-eyed, to utter one piercing scream, as if he had been mortally wounded. That scream would later echo to the farthest reaches of his kingdom.

With Nxumalo and three generals close behind, he went to his mother's kraal, and when he saw her dead body, with one sweep of his arm he ordered every serving woman to be readied for her final journey: 'You could have saved her, but you didn't.'

When Nxumalo saw that his beloved wife Thetiwe was among those pinioned by the knobkerrie team he shouted, 'Mighty King! Do not take my wife.' But Shaka merely looked at him as if he were a stranger.

'They could have saved her,' he mumbled.

'Mercy, Companion-in-the-Battles.'

With a powerful hand Shaka gripped his advisor by the throat: 'Your wife cured my mother's eye. Why could she not cure her now?' And Nxumalo had to stand silent as lovely Thetiwe was dragged away. With nine others she would share Nandi's grave, but only after all the bones in her body were broken in such a way as to keep her skin intact, since the Female Elephant demanded perfection in her dark place.

Now word flashed along the riverbanks that Shaka's mother was dead, and almost as if they were being driven by unseen herdsmen, the Zulu came out to mourn. Wailings pierced the air, and lamentations filled the valleys. People threw away their bead adornments and tore their clothes, and looked askance at anyone whose eyes did not flow with tears. The world was in torment.

All the rest of that day and through the night the wailing continued until the earth itself seemed to be in anguish. Some men stood transfixed, their faces upturned, repeating over and over the shrieking dirges, and others spread dust over themselves, screaming all the while.

At noon next day, 11 October 1827, the awful thing began. It was never known exactly how it started, but one man, crazed by thirst and lack of sleep, seems to have stared at his neighbor and cried, 'Look at him. He isn't weeping,' and in a flash of hands the indifferent one was torn apart.

A man who sneezed was charged with disrespect for the great mother and was slain.

A woman coughed twice and was strangled by her own friends.

The madness spread, and whoever behaved in any conspicuous manner was set upon and killed by the mob. A woman who looked like old Nandi was accused of having stolen her countenance, and she perished. A man moaned his grief, but not loudly enough, and was clubbed.

On and on, throughout all that long afternoon, the grief-stricken citizens wailed their laments and watched their neighbors. Five hundred died near the hut of the Female Elephant. The footpaths were strewn with bodies, and as the late-afternoon sun struck the maddened faces, spies looked to see whether the eyes held tears, and if they did not, the owner was strangled: 'He wasn't weeping for the mother.' Soon a thousand lay dead, then four thousand.

In sheer exhaustion some finally had to sit down, and when they did so, they were slain for lack of veneration. Heat of day caused some to faint from lack of water, and they were stabbed with assegais as they lay. Others wandered to the Umfolozi for a drink, and as they bent to reach it they were stabbed. Two unfortunate old men with weak kidneys had to urinate and were pierced with spears for their irreverence.

Gangs raged through the area, peering into every kraal to see if any had failed to honor the dead woman, and when recalcitrants were found, the huts were set afire and the occupants roasted. A mother suckled her child, whereupon the crowd roared, 'She feeds when the great mother lies dead,' and the pair were slain.

Through the day Shaka remained in the royal kraal, unaware of the killings as he received a file of mourners who tried to console him with chants honoring the Female Elephant. Their bodies trembled with fever; they fell to the ground and tore at the earth; and each expressed an honest grief, for Nandi had indeed been the mother of the nation. Beyond the kraal the hills rang with cries, and toward sunset Shaka rose: 'It is finished. The great mother has heard her children.'

When he left the kraal he saw for the first time the extent of the madness, and as he passed over bloodstained earth he muttered, barely coherently, 'It is finished.' He ordered two regiments to put an end to the mass killings, but undisciplined bands now rampaged far into the country-

side, acting on their own and killing anyone who showed inadequate remorse, even in distant villages where news of Nandi's death could not have
penetrated. 'You should have known,' the fanatics cried as they wielded
their assegais.

Shaka's Dark Time the Zulu named these last three months of 1827, and
the outside world would never have known the extent of the tragedy had
not Henry Francis Fynn been visiting with Shaka on the day Nandi died.
He would report seeing seven thousand dead himself, and from the distant
countryside he received additional reports.

When the first spasm ended Shaka turned to the normal procedures for
national mourning, and Nandi was accorded the full rites given a great
chief: 'For one year no man may touch a woman, and if any woman appears
pregnant, having made love when my mother lay dead, she and the child
and her man shall be strangled. From all the herds in this kingdom no milk
shall be drunk; it shall be spilled upon the ground. No crops shall be
planted. For one year a regiment shall guard her grave, twelve thousand in
constant attendance.' Initial hysteria was forcefully channeled into absolute
obedience, and now additional people were killed if they drank milk or lay
together.

At the end of three awful months those closest to Shaka convinced him
that the nation he had worked so diligently to construct was imperiled by
these excesses, and he terminated all prohibitions except the one against
pregnancy, for he could never comprehend the need for sex. At a vast
ceremony ending the Dark Time, herdsmen were ordered to bring their
beasts, one hundred thousand in all; their bellowing would be the final
salute to the Female Elephant. When they were assembled, Shaka demanded that forty of the finest calves be brought for sacrifice, and as the
little creatures stood before him, their gall bladders were ripped out and
they were left to die. 'Weep! Weep!' he shouted. 'Let even animals know
what sorrow is.' Then he bowed his head as the contents of the forty gall
bladders were poured over him, purifying him at last of the evil forces that
had hastened the death of his mother.

The diviners and witch doctors, seeing a chance to reestablish their
authority, seized upon Nandi's death as a way to chasten the king: 'We
know what caused her death, Mighty Lion. A cat walked past her hut.'

Shaka listened avidly as the diviners revealed what dark spells had been
cast by women who owned cats, and when the indictment was complete he
roared, 'Let all with cats be found!' And when these women were assembled,
including one of Nxumalo's wives, he screamed at them, demanding to
know the poisons they had disseminated through their cats. When the
terrified and bewildered women, three hundred and twenty-six of them,
could make no sensible reply, he ordered them slain, and they were.

One morning Shaka took Nxumalo aside, seeking to recapture the
friendship he knew he needed: 'I'm sorry, trusted guide, that Thetiwe and
the other died. It was necessary.' When Nxumalo nodded, acknowledging
the king's power, Shaka pointed out: 'I gave you the women. I had a right
to take them away.' Again Nxumalo assented, and Shaka said, 'I wanted
the world to see how much a son could love his mother.'

And that speech was the beginning of the final tragedy, for when the
king endeavored to assure Nxumalo that all was again well between them,

the latter thought not of his words but of a gentler king far to the north with whom sanctuary might be found. Shaka noticed his lack of response, and his dissatisfaction with the one man who might have saved him was launched.

Ironically, Shaka decided to cast Nxumalo aside at the precise moment when he was needed most, for the Zulu were beginning to see that the welfare of their recently established nation depended upon a man subject to irrational behavior; they also saw that since he had no sons, he had no direct heirs, and that if he died in one of his paroxysms, the kingdom would be adrift.

Unlucky chance also worked against him, for if the Female Elephant had pushed him to glory, another woman of equal determination was now ready to destroy him. Mkabayi, his father's sister—whose name meant Wild Cat, an ominous portent—had nursed a smoldering resentment against Shaka from the moment he usurped the Zulu leadership, and now, seeing the disarray of the kingdom, she infected two of Shaka's half brothers with her poison. Dingane and Mhlangana began to meet secretly with her, and after a few tentative discussions, realized that they must enlist the support of some military leader. The fact that Nxumalo had lost two wives—killed by Shaka's orders—made him a likely candidate.

The brothers had to approach him with caution, for if he betrayed a single intimation, Shaka would kill them all. So Dingane, a clever, conniving man, asked, 'Nxumalo, has it ever occurred to you that the king might be mad?'

He had been expecting just such an opening from someone, but he, too, had to be cautious, not knowing the true temper of the brothers. 'You saw him at the punishment of the Langeni,' he said. 'He forgot who I was.'

'Advise us straight. If anything happened to the king—his biliousness, I mean—would the iziCwe run violent?'

'My men love their king.'

'Were . . . two of your wives . . . slain?'

He did not like the devious way Dingane asked his questions, so once more he was evasive: 'Shaka gave me three women. He said he had a right to take two of them back.'

The brothers were satisfied that Nxumalo wanted to join them but was fending them off, so Dingane said bluntly, 'You must know you're to be smelled-out at the next gathering.' Nxumalo only looked at him, unbelieving, so Dingane whispered, 'One witch-seeker said to me, "That Nxumalo, two wives dead. It must be an omen." Your bamboo skewers are being hardened. Before this year is out, you'll hang screaming in the tree.'

Nxumalo properly interpreted this as a suggestion that he take up arms against the king, but even though his allegiance to Shaka the man had begun to erode, his tradition of obedience to the concept of kingship remained, and he could not at this first meeting abandon it, so with great daring, well aware that the brothers might feel they must kill him to preserve their secret, he said, 'Dingane, I know what you're plotting. And I understand. My heart is broken by what Shaka has done to me, and I hate his madness. But I'm his general and I can't . . .'

It was a fearful moment, with lives in balance, but the brothers had to risk it, for to succeed in their conspiracy, they must have this general: 'Would you be able to forget that we have spoken to you?'

'As a soldier I cannot act against my king, but I know he is destroying the nation. I will remain silent.'

When he left, the brothers smiled, for they were certain that Shaka would do some additional outrageous thing that would alienate even Nxumalo. The king was marked for murder.

Shaka sensed that the dynamics of the situation required him to keep his army on the move, so he advanced into new territories, well to the south toward the Xhosa, and for the first time his regiments gained only a modified success; he executed more warriors than ever before for cowardice. He allowed his regiments no rest, but sent them feverishly to new lands in the north, and again they encountered disaster.

'Where's Nxumalo?' the king cried in anguish one afternoon.

'He's with his regiment,' a knobkerrie said, not wanting to irritate Shaka further by reminding him that he had ordered Nxumalo to be confined.

'Never here when I need him. And Fynn fails to bring me the magic oil.' He almost whimpered. 'So much work remains, I must not die.'

And the executioners wailed, 'Deathless-Stomper-of-the-Rhinoceros, Fearless-Slayer-of-the-Leopard, you will never die.'

'What is death?' the tormented king asked. 'And before you answer that, what is life?'

Four attendants who were accustomed to nod gravely at everything he said were suddenly seized by the knobkerrie gang, and two were stood to the left of the king, two to the right. 'Kill those,' Shaka said, and the two on the left were slain. 'They are death,' the king said, 'and these are life. Tell me—what is the difference?' And he kept this grim tableau in place for three hours, staring and pondering.

Then with a leap high into the air he roared, 'Fetch me the women who were pregnant before my edict,' and more than a hundred women in all stages of pregnancy were dragged before him. With sharp knives he began to slice open their bellies to see for himself how life progressed, and as he continued his studies with the later women, the first ones lay dying in a corner.

When word of this hideous experiment flashed through the kraals, disseminated by men whose wives had been taken, Dingane exulted: 'Now we'll have Nxumalo with us!' And he took his brother to the kraal where Nxumalo was being held and told him, 'Shaka has taken Nonsizi. He's going to cut her apart.'

'What!' Like a bull elephant crashing through trees, Nxumalo burst out of the kraal to save the lovely girl Mzilikazi had given him, and when he ran in maddened circles, Dingane said, 'Over there!' pointing to Shaka's kraal.

Nxumalo arrived in time to see the knobkerrie men pulling the hundred and sixth woman to Shaka's table, and it was as Dingane had warned— Nonsizi of the Matabele. 'Shaka—she is my wife!' he cried, but with an impatient shake of his head the king indicated that his helpers were to remove this interruption.

'Shaka!' Nxumalo repeated. 'That's Nonsizi, my wife.'

In a kind of stupor, the king looked up, failed to recognize his general, and said, 'She cannot be your wife. All women belong to me.' And while Nxumalo was pinioned, the king dissected Nonsizi, then hurried to the last three women, crying, 'Now I will know. I won't need the hair oil!'

In that awful scream-filled moment any vestige of allegiance or obedience vanished, and as soon as Nxumalo could break away, he sought the brothers and said, 'Shaka must be killed.'

'We knew you'd join us,' the king's brothers said, and they took him to their aunt, Mkabayi the Wild Cat, who said grimly, 'We must strike the tyrant now.' And it was her force of character, allied with Nxumalo's, that sealed the king's fate.

Had the plotting been left to Dingane, Shaka might have escaped, for when that shifty fellow realized that he might actually have to stab the king, he began to vacillate, until one night Nxumalo grabbed him by the strands about his neck and whispered, 'We shall kill him together—the three of us. He must be removed.' Forever obedient, he was now obedient to the needs of the Zulu.

But he had still to face two extreme tests, in one of which lay a bitter irony. In a kraal near his, in which the king kept some four hundred of his wives, there was a girl named Thandi, who had served briefly in a women's regiment before the king selected her to be his wife. Once during a lull in maneuvers Nxumalo had encountered her while she was resting beside the Umfolozi, and they had invited each other to enjoy the pleasures of the road, and several times after that Thandi had contrived to be in the vicinity of the iziCwe, and on two different nights they had run a terrible risk by making real love, with the possibility that she might become pregnant.

He found her so delightful, so fresh in her attitudes, that he had started accumulating cattle to pay her lobola, when the king abruptly chose her for his own. True to his custom, Shaka rarely came near her; once during their years of marriage he had spent part of an evening talking with her, boasting of his prowess in battle, but even though she had listened attentively and said several times, 'How brave you must have been,' she never saw him again. That brief encounter was supposed to suffice for the fifty remaining years she would spend in the royal kraal.

Now, through the agency of servants, she let Nxumalo know that she would brave any death if he were willing to run with her to find some home less pitiful, and one night while Nxumalo was brooding upon this matter, it occurred to him that one of the worst things his king had done was this imprisonment of so many beautiful girls, thus keeping them in fruitless bondage till their years were wasted, and he decided that if with the others he must kill the king, he would at the same time put his life in triple jeopardy by stealing one of the king's wives. In great secrecy he drafted plans, and felt as if life were starting anew when Thandi came boldly to the kraal fence to smile at him, indicating her assent.

Next day came the severest test, for the king abruptly summoned him, and as Nxumalo entered the royal kraal, came toward him with tears in his eyes, and confessed: 'Oh, Nxumalo! In my madness I thought of sending the witch-seekers after you, but now I see that you're my only friend. I need you.'

Before Nxumalo could reply, the king led him to a cool spot and shared a gourd of beer. Then, taking Nxumalo's two hands in his, he said, 'My brothers are plotting against me.'

'Not likely.'

'Oh, but they are. I dreamed I was dead. It's Dingane. I see him whispering. Mark my words, he's not a trustful man.'

'He's of royal blood. He's your brother.'

'But can I trust him?' And without awaiting a reply, Shaka sighed. 'I am cursed. I have no son. No one to trust. I'm growing old, and still the magic oil fails to arrive.'

Nxumalo could feel no sympathy for this slayer of women, and a response too dangerous to utter leaped to his mind: Shaka, you could have had a score of sons. Nine years ago, if you had accepted Thetiwe instead of throwing her at me, you could have had six sons.

Again Shaka gripped Nxumalo's hands. 'You're the one honest man in this nation. Promise me you'll watch over me.'

With a lingering pity Nxumalo looked at the stricken man, this violent giant whose leadership had been corrupted by madness, and as he tried to formulate words that would allow him to depart, the king cried with deep remorse, 'Oh, Nxumalo, it was wrong of me to kill your wives. Forgive me, old friend. I killed them all, and learned nothing.'

'You are forgiven,' Nxumalo said grimly, and with a deep bow he left the royal kraal, marched, ostensibly, back to his own, then slipped away to join the Wild Cat, who was instructing her nephews for the kill. 'Shaka knows your intentions!' he cried. 'He will kill you soon.'

Dingane, although of royal blood, was no Shaka. He lacked courage, and, as the king had said, he could not be trusted. 'What shall we do?'

'Slay him now.'

'Now?' Dingane asked, looking at his brother.

'Now,' Nxumalo repeated.

They would strike at dusk—all three of them—when the king was more or less detached from his knobkerrie guards. 'I'll fetch my assegai,' Nxumalo said, and as he went toward his kraal he realized that Dingane had modified the plan so that only he, Nxumalo, would be seen by anyone watching. This meant that when the tumult erupted, he as a commoner could be thrown to the maddened crowd. 'We'll have none of that, Dingane,' he muttered, and he diverted his course to the wives' kraal, where Thandi was waiting for his signal, and he told her that within the hour she must try to escape, prepared to flee north.

He then went back and told his remaining wife, 'Be ready to leave at dusk.' She did not ask why or where, for, like the others, she had deduced that he was soon to be impaled. His survival was hers, and to be saved she must trust him.

As the sun started its descent on 22 September 1828, the three untrusting conspirators met casually, checked one another to be sure the stabbing assegais were ready, then walked like supplicants with a petition for their king and brother.

'Mhlangana, what do you seek?'

The answer, a lunging assegai under the heart.

'Dingane! From you I expected treachery . . .'

Another leaping assegai.

And then Nxumalo, trusted advisor, driving his assegai deep into Shaka's side.

'Mother! Mother!' the great king cried. Clutching at air, he tried to steady himself, went dizzy, and stumbled to his knees. 'Nandi!' he wept. 'My father's children have come to kill me.' But when he saw the blood come spouting from his wounds he lost all strength and toppled forward, crying, 'Mother!' for love of whom he had erected a mighty kingdom.

In the mad confusion following the assassination, Nxumalo, accompanied by one wife, the gift of Shaka, and the lovely Thandi, scrambled across the Umfolozi River and headed northwest. They hoped to overtake their friend Mzilikazi, rumored to be building a new sanctuary there for his fugitive Matabele.

With them they had four children, two by Thetiwe, the first wife, and two by number two, who had died because she owned a cat. They had with them a small herd of cattle, some cooking utensils, and not much else. Four other fugitives joined them, and this complement of eleven were prepared to live or die as accidents and hard work determined.

By the end of the first week they had become a resolute band, skilled in improvising the weapons and tools needed for the endless journeys ahead. They traveled slowly, stopping at likely refuges, and they foraged brilliantly. Thandi, the youngest, was especially good at thievery from kraals they passed, and kept the family in a reasonable supply of food.

They ate everything, killing such animals as they could and gathering berries and roots like grubbing creatures in a forest. At the end of the first month they were a tight, dangerous group of travelers, and when one of the men caught himself a wife from a small village, they became twelve.

Like thousands of homeless blacks in this period, they had but two ideas, to escape what they knew and to grasp at anything that would enable them to exist. Nxumalo hoped to overtake Mzilikazi and take service in some capacity with a king who promised in almost every respect to be superior to Shaka. 'Not as handsome,' he told his wives, 'and not as brave in battle, but in everything else a notable king.'

From time to time the little family stopped at some kraal, risking the dangers involved, and by so doing they discovered that Mzilikazi had moved far to the west, so they set out in serious pursuit.

And then they learned the meaning of the word Mfecane—the crushing, the sad migrations, for they came upon an area, fifteen miles wide and stretching endlessly, in which every living thing had been destroyed. There were no kraals, no walls, no cattle, no animals, and certainly no human beings. Few armies in history had created such total desolation, and if Nxumalo and his family had not brought food with them, they would have perished.

As it was, they began to see signs indicating that hundreds of people had been slain, their bodies left to rot; for mile after mile there would be strands of human bones. Nxumalo thought: Even the worst destruction wreaked by

Shaka could not compare with such desolation. And he began to wonder what kind of all-consuming monster had wrought this ravishment.

It was half a year before he found out. With an instinct for preservation, he led his family back to the east, and after a hurried march, went beyond the swath of total destruction; here in the wooded area where streams ran, only the kraals had been destroyed, not the land itself, and one afternoon they came upon the first surviving humans. They were a family of three living in trees, for they had no weapons to defend themselves against the numerous wild animals that prowled their vicinity at night. They were so wasted they could hardly speak, but they did utter one word that perplexed the travelers: 'Mzilikazi.'

'Who was pursuing him?' Nxumalo asked.

'No one. He was pursuing us.'

'Mzilikazi?'

'A monster. A life-eating monster.'

'Feed them,' Thandi said. 'Don't question them when they're starving.'

So Nxumalo's men caught antelope for the wretched ones; they ate like beasts, the boy gulping the raw meat while he protected his portion by covering it with arms and legs. When the family slowly returned to human condition Thandi allowed Nxumalo to query them again, and he said, 'Surely Mzilikazi did not do this.'

'He slaughtered everything—trees, dogs, lions, even water lilies.'

'But why?' Nxumalo asked, unable to comprehend what he was hearing.

'He summoned our group of kraals . . . told us he wanted our cattle. We refused . . . and he started the killing.'

'But why slay everyone?'

'We didn't want to join his army. When we ran away he didn't even send his soldiers after us. They didn't care. They had enough to do killing those at hand.'

'But what was his purpose?'

'No purpose. We weren't useful to his moving army. In his rear we might cause trouble.'

'Where was he marching?'

'He didn't know, his soldiers said—they were just marching.'

After long consultation with the men in his group, and also with his wives, it was agreed that the family should be allowed to join them; the man could help with the hunting and the boy could prove useful later on, but when the enlarged group had been on the road three days, the new man died. Nxumalo assumed that one of his own men had killed him, for immediately the wife was taken into that man's care, without much protest from her.

When they had traveled as a unit for several weeks, they came upon the ultimate horror. They had been traversing mile after mile of total desolation —fifteen kraals without a sign of life, not even a guinea hen—when they came upon a small group of people living in a half-destroyed hut, and after a cursory inspection Thandi came to Nxumalo, trembling: 'They have been eating one another.'

The miserable clan was so desperate that they had resorted to cannibalism, and each wondered when the next would die, and at whose hand.

For these people there was no hope. Nxumalo would have nothing to do with them—they were untouchable. And he was about to leave them to their misery when Thandi said, 'We must stay and make them some weapons so they can kill animals. And our men must bring back some antelope to give them fair food.'

So at her insistence the group halted, and the men did go hunting, and after a while the cannibals, fourteen of them, began to fill out from their eating of antelope, and with their spears they now had a chance of fending for themselves. But despite Thandi's pleading, Nxumalo would not permit this group to join his, and when the family moved north the former cannibals stood at the edge of their desolate village, looking after them with strange expressions.

After a long time the signs of destruction diminished, and then stopped. Mzilikazi's armies had moved sharply westward, and for this Nxumalo was grateful, for it meant that he could now proceed northward without running the risk of overtaking the dreadful devastators or being caught in one of their chance sweeps to the rear. Of course, even this new land contained no people, for Mzilikazi had slain them all—hundreds upon hundreds—but there had been no general devastation, and the wild animals had returned.

Finally, after more than a year of this wandering, with two additional children being born to Nxumalo's wives and two to the other women, they came to a chain of low hills that looked much like the lovelier parts of Zululand, except that rivers did not flow through them. There were small streams, and Nxumalo began to think that beside one of them he might stop and build his kraal, and then one day as he came out of a valley he saw a pair of hills shaped like a woman's breasts, and they seemed a symbol of all the joys of the past and his dreams for the future: the deep love he had borne Thetiwe, his first wife; the tenderness he felt for his second, killed because of her cat; the passion he had known with Nonsizi of the Matabele; and the delight found in his two surviving wives, who had accepted the hardships of this journey without complaint. His six children were prospering and the men who had joined him in the flight had made themselves indispensable. The family deserved a halting place; it was with hope that he ascended the pass between the two hills, and when he reached the high point he looked down upon a lake and saw beside it the marked grave of the Hottentot Dikkop, buried there sixty years before by that wanderer Adriaan van Doorn.

'This has been the living place of men,' Nxumalo said, and with joy he led his people down the hill to take possession.

The Mfecane that raged through southeast Africa in the early decades of the nineteenth century produced excesses which went far in determining the development of an immense area.

The rampaging of the two kings, Shaka of the Zulu and Mzilikazi of the Matabele, set in motion sweeping forces which caused the death within a short period of time of huge numbers of people; chronicles unfavorable to blacks estimate two million dead within a decade, but considering the probable population of the area in those years, this seems grotesquely high. Whatever the loss, and it must have been more than a million, it was irremediable and accounted in part for the relatively weak defenses the surviving blacks would put up within a few short years when white men, armed with guns, began invading their territory. Starvation, cannibalism and death followed the devastation of the armies, while roving bands of renegades made orderly life impossible. Entire clans, which had known peaceful and productive histories, were eliminated.

The principal contributor to this desolation was not Shaka, whose victories tended to be military in the old sense, with understandable loss of life, but Mzilikazi, who invented the scorched-earth policy and applied it remorselessly. Why he slaughtered so incessantly cannot be explained. Nothing in his visible personality indicated that he would follow such a hideous course, and there seems to have been no military necessity for it. He killed, perhaps, because he sought to protect his small band, and the surest way to do so was to eliminate any potential opposition. Young men and male children became targets lest when they matured they seek revenge against the Matabele.

The widespread slaughter did not seem to alter Mzilikazi personally. His manners did not become rough, nor did he raise his voice or display anger. The young English clergyman who came out to Golan Mission in 1829 to replace Hilary Saltwood stayed there briefly, then, like his predecessor, felt obligated to move into the more dangerous northern territories, where he became a permanent friend to Mzilikazi; of him he wrote admiringly after the Mfecane had run itself out:

> The king is a likable man of only medium height, fat and jolly, with a countenance so serene that it seems never to have known vigorous events or dangers. He speaks always in a low voice, is considerate of everyone, and has proved himself most eager to cooperate with white men. He told me himself that he wanted missionaries to come into his domains because he felt that at heart he had always been a Christian, even though as a boy he could have known nothing of our religion. Indeed, he gave me for our mission one of the finest pieces of land in his capital city and sent his own soldiers to help me build it. Detractors have tried to warn me that I must be on guard, because Mzilikazi's soft ways hide a cruel heart, but I cannot believe this. He has known battle, certainly, but in it, so far as I can learn, has always conducted himself with propriety, and I consider him the finest man I have met in Africa, whether Englishman, Boer or Kaffir.

It must not be supposed that Mzilikazi and Shaka were personally responsible for all the Mfecane deaths. In many instances they merely set in motion vast dislocations of people whose ultimate exterminations of minor tribes occurred at distances far from Zululand. If ever the domino theory of inter-tribe and inter-nation response to stimulus functioned, it was during the Mfecane. A few hundred Zulu started to expand in all directions, and when they moved south they disturbed the Qwabe, who themselves moved farther south to disrupt the Tembu, who moved on to dislocate the Tuli, who encroached upon the Pondo, who pressured the Fingo, who impinged upon the secure and long-established Xhosa. At that moment in history the land-hungry trekboers were beginning to encroach upon territory which the Xhosa had long used as pasture; and caught between two grinding stones, the Xhosa sought relief by attacking kraals like Tjaart van Doorn's, whose owners brought pressure on Cape Town, which caused questions to be asked in London. Similar chains of dominoes collapsed in other directions as tribes moving outward dispossessed their neighbors of ancestral lands.

That Shaka slew hundreds with merciless ferocity is historical fact. That the Mfecane set in motion by Shaka and Mzilikazi caused the death of multitudes is also fact. But the behavior of these kings must be judged against the excesses which others, sometimes better educated and Christian, had perpetrated along the shores of the Indian Ocean. In 1502, when Vasco da Gama, the enshrined hero of Portugal, was angered by the officials of Calicut, he slaughtered a shipload of thirty-eight inoffensive Indian fishermen, dismembered their bodies, packed heads, arms and legs into a boat and sent it drifting ashore with the suggestion that the ruler 'boil the lot into a curry hash.'

The results of the Mfecane were by no means all negative. When it ended, vast areas which had formerly known only petty anarchy were organized. The superior culture of the Zulu replaced less-dynamic old traditions. Those who survived developed an enthusiasm they had not known before and a trust in their own capacities. In widely separated regions, deep loyalties were generated upon which important nation-states could be erected.

For example, the Sotho, who were never attacked by Shaka, consolidated a mountain kingdom first known as Basutoland and then Lesotho. The Swazi anchored themselves in a defendable redoubt, where they built their nation of Swaziland. One tribe, under terrible pressure from both Shaka and Mzilikazi, fled north into Moçambique, and helped form the basis of a state that would attain its freedom in 1975.

Even in that year the lasting effect of the Mfecane could not be determined, since the vast movement was still having its repercussions, but perhaps the principal result was the forging of the Zulu nation under Shaka, who took a small tribe with only three hundred real soldiers and about two hundred apprentices and within a decade expanded it with such demonic force that it conquered a significant part of a continent. In area the Zulu kingdom magnified itself a thousand times; in population, two thousand; but in significance and moral power, more like a million.

Had Shaka died before his mother, he would be remembered in history only as another inspired leader who, in accordance with the harsh customs of his time, had brought discipline to an unruly region; his accomplishments would have been respected. But he died after his mother, and the savage excesses of his Dark Time, plus the heroic manner of his death, elevated him beyond mere remembrance and into the realm of legend.

In the most remote corners of southern Africa huddling blacks would dream of the day when mighty Shaka would return to lead them into their heritage. His military prowess was magnified; his prudence as a ruler exalted. Out of his personal tragedy Shaka offered his people a vision.

At Vrijmeer, well north of Zulu power and safely south of Mzilikazi's burgeoning kingdom, Nxumalo, one of the few men who had known both kings intimately, came to realize as he grew older that the really glorious time of his life had been when he led Shaka's iziCwe into battle in its new formation of body-arms-head. Then he and his men, held in vital reserve with their backs to the fray, waited for the imperial command to storm forth. 'What a moment!' he told his children as they sat beside the lake, watching the animals come down to drink. 'Spears flying, men hissing as they killed the enemy, consternation, turmoil, then the calm voice of Shaka: "Nxumalo, support the left flank." That's all he said. And with a cry we leaped to our feet, turned to face the battle, and sped like springboks to destroy the enemy.'

The children were ordered to forget the rest: Shaka's murder of their mothers; the savagery of the Dark Time; the terrible denouement when assassins stalked the king in order to save the nation.

'The thing to remember,' Nxumalo said one evening in 1841, when he had white hair and his children were older, 'is that Shaka was the noblest man who ever lived. The wisest. The kindest. And never forget, Mbengu. Carry yourself tall, because Shaka himself was once married to your mother Thandi.'

When the children asked why, if he loved Shaka, he had not returned to Zululand, he explained: 'You've heard the old rumors. Dingane murdering his own brother Mhlangana, who had helped him gain the throne. If we had gone back, Dingane would have murdered us, all of us. He was always treacherous.'

He preferred nobler thoughts: 'When our nation falls into trouble, Shaka will return to save us, and we'll shout "Bayete!" and if you are men and women of character, you'll respond and Zululand will throb with marching feet, for he will always be our great leader.'

'But didn't you kill him?' a grandson asked.

There are some questions that cannot be answered intelligently, and Nxumalo did not try.

VIII. The Voortrekkers

I N 1828 Tjaart van Doorn was about as happy as a man could be. His farm at De Kraal was flourishing. His second wife, Jakoba, had begun to soften her harsh ways. And his daughter Minna was as pleasing a child as a father could have in his middle years. He was thirty-nine, stout, stocky, with a full black beard that started near his ears, covered his cheeks and chin, but left his upper lip clear. He wore heavy clothes: short jacket, calfskin vest, tieless shirt and stiff pants made of moleskin, with a huge flap that came across his middle and buttoned at his right hip. The pants were held up by a wide belt and stout suspenders, but the characteristic that identified him immediately, wherever he stood, was a low-crowned hat, with a very wide, sloping brim, whose underside was bright blue.

Since he was a man of few words most of the time, having been over-awed by his volcanic father Lodevicus, he gave the impression of a gruff, grumpy man with a firm-set countenance. He did not, however, seem a large man; there were many in his district who were taller, but few were more sturdy.

He had a right to take pride in his farm; from the fine start his father had given, he had augmented De Kraal in all respects. The basic holding was still that splendid valley set within protecting hills, with the copious stream running from the southwest right through the middle of the land to an opening at the northeast, from which it wandered on to make junction with the Great Fish River some miles farther on.

What Tjaart had done was to acquire from the government the right to use pasturage beyond the hills, and with the proceeds from his large herds, add to the clay-and-stone buildings that formed the heart of the farm. The house now had a spacious kitchen in which Jakoba could supervise the cooking; the servants and slaves occupied a chain of eight small huts linked together; calves had kraals with stone walls; and hay was stored in a spacious barn. Smaller buildings had proliferated for the safe holding of farm tools, feed and chicken roosts.

The farm contained the original nine thousand acres within the hills, but it now controlled an additional sixteen thousand acres to which he did not have legal title, but which his Coloured stockmen could use in herding cattle and flocks of sheep. Although he rarely saw much formal money, he had made himself into a man of considerable wealth and could look forward to a prosperous and placid old age.

Of course, most Boers grumbled about the English administration, its creeping modifications of law and custom, but such complaints were offset by the fact that the stalwart English settlers were now sharing the dangers of frontier life. The struggle had been harsh, as one Englishman noted in his diary:

> My wheat, two months ago the most promising I ever saw, is now cut down and in heaps for burning. The rust has utterly destroyed it. My barley, because of a grub which attacks the blade and the drought, produced little more than I sowed. All my other crops have practically been destroyed by the caterpillar and lice. My cows are dry from want of grass. Twenty of my flock of twenty-seven sheep were killed in a single night by a pack of wild dogs. My little girl has been bitten by a snake. I stood for a moment thinking of my misery, of my dying child, of my blasted crops, of my ruined flocks. God's will be done! I have need of fortitude to bear up against such accumulated misery.

And always there were the blacks invading the lands of Boer and Englishman alike. Tjaart, veldkornet of his district, had frequently taken his men to Grahamstown to help those settlers repel cattle raiders, and in many actions, had fought beside Richard Saltwood, ivory merchant, and Thomas Carleton, master wagon builder. He had found them an honorable pair and had invited them to hunting parties at De Kraal. Saltwood had proved himself not only a fine shot but a congenial guest who lacked all the mannerisms that irritated the Boers. He had even told Tjaart on departing at the end of the last hunt, 'This must be the best farm I've ever seen,' and with that he handed Mevrouw Jakoba two bottles of Trianon wine he had been hoarding.

And then the camaraderie was endangered. Lukas de Groot, Tjaart's neighbor nineteen miles to the north, stopped by one day on his way home from the port on that wild stretch of coast at which the English settlers had come ashore, and shocked Tjaart by showing him a copy of the Grahamstown newspaper: Dr. Simon Keer, the philanthropic leader in London, had published his second book, called *The Infamy of the Dutch Slaveholder*, and its appearance was guaranteed to cause trouble, for it was a savage assault against South African life and a shameless emotional appeal to the English Parliament to pass laws which Keer had long been advocating.

Keer's pressure came at a time when agitation for abolishing slavery throughout the British Empire was gaining momentum; it signaled the beginning of the final battle to demolish what many Boers considered their God-granted right: that all men of color should labor for them six days a week and sometimes seven, whether slave or free.

Keer's grand strategy of waging this war with propaganda in England had thus triumphed over Hilary Saltwood's tactic of cherishing and saving souls on the spot. The inspired lecturer with his flaming oratory had vanquished the modest missionary who had actually married one of his charges to prove that he loved them all. What Keer said in his new book was this:

> The oppression of free persons of color under the yoke of their Boer masters makes the idea of English fairness and justice a mockery. From birth till death the suffering native is held in bondage through a system of apprenticeship of his children born on Boer farms and through a contract that binds him and his family to Boer servitude. He is unable to move freely about the land, he is unequal in the eyes of the law, he is without protection from the scourge of Boer tyranny.

Was there any truth in these charges? Some. Was there gross exaggeration? A great deal. But from the indictment came a law which radically altered life on the frontier. 'Look what Keer and his fellow saints have done to us!' De Groot raged as he showed Tjaart the new provisions. 'It makes the Coloureds, the Hottentots, the Bushmen the exact equal to us Boers. They have all the rights we have. No further apprenticeship of the young. No work contracts. They don't have to have fixed abodes. Magistrates can no longer whip them as won't-works. From now on, damnit, Van Doorn, a man of color has all the rights I have.'

'That's terribly wrong!' Jakoba interrupted as the men talked. 'That's not what God intended at all.'

What Reverend Keer intended was a softening of the harsh laws that restricted servants; what he got was a disastrous dislocation; and the immediate burden fell on Lukas and Rachel de Groot, for when their herders and farm hands got word of their new status, twenty of thirty-six laborers took off, and it was a group of these homeless, roaming vagrants who ravaged their daughter.

To the big Boer she was Blommetjie, 'Little Flower,' a fragile girl of fourteen who spent most of her time among the trees and blooms of the veld. The three men found her beside a small stream, humming softly. She did not get home for the midday meal, and when she still wasn't back by late afternoon, De Groot went looking for her—and found a wild, deranged creature dragging herself across a mealie field.

He left the child with Rachel, said not a word and asked no one to accompany him as he rode out at dusk. Two of the guilty men had fled and would never again be seen in that district, but the third lay drunk in one of the deserted huts on De Groot's farm—and when the Boer discovered him, he pulled the man into the open, and for a moment stood over him.

'Get up, you devil!' he said grimly, and the man stood, swaying unsteadily, looking dazedly at his baas. With a wild cry of anguish, De Groot brought his gun up, and then the man realized what was happening, but as he backed away, a bullet slammed into his chest. He fell to the ground, not quite dead, and as he lay there De Groot pumped bullets into him, again and again.

As veldkornet, it was Tjaart's duty to report on the incident, and he duly swore that the vagrant had been shot while attempting to flee after having stolen mealies. The case was closed, but the wound in De Groot's heart remained open.

The seasons passed and no one said much about Blommetjie; they trusted that one day soon she would be able to move about the veld again. There was no improvement, either, in the labor situation, and increasingly Tjaart and his sons had to go out with the herds, much like the Van Doorns of four generations ago. And then, on a certain day in October when spring flowers made the veld a garden, Tjaart said at table, 'We shall go to the next Nachtmaal.'

The news created wild happiness among the women: Jakoba would be able to see friends she had not talked with for two long years; the slave women who would go along to do the cooking would enjoy the chance to meet with other slaves and to cook dishes they preferred; and little Minna, now thirteen and already worrying about how she would find a husband in this great emptiness, conjured up visions of a bright lad named Ryk Naudé, whom she had last seen at the Nachtmaal: 'May I have a new dress, Mama? I mustn't go in my old one.'

So the slave women, who cherished the girl, set about the pleasant task of fitting her out for a dress which would compare favorably with the fashions in Grahamstown: turned-down collar, wide sleeves fastened at the wrists, flounces around the lower part of the skirt, and a general sauciness to catch the eyes of young men. As they worked, Tjaart saw how much joy his daughter was deriving from the process. She was not a beautiful child, no one had ever claimed that, but she was a fine stout lass, strong in body and character. The fact that she was illiterate did not mean that she was stupid, for she could recite long passages from the Bible. There was little in the repertory of a good Boer *vrouw* that she could not do, and whereas in the western part of the colony girls her age often had two or three slaves of their own and never raised a finger except in rebuke, Minna was an industrious young woman, adept at anything from making soap and candles to spinning her father's wool into strong thread.

By rumor she had learned that several of the girls she had met at the last Nachtmaal were already married at ages fourteen and fifteen, and two were mothers, so it was understandable that she should become apprehensive about her prospects. She had only one, really, the Naudé boy from a farm far to the northeast, and she began to worry each night when the family went to bed that the Naudés might not be attending this Nachtmaal, and one night when Tjaart could not sleep he heard her whimpering and strode over to her room: 'What's the worry, Minnatjie?'

'I dreamed it was already Nachtmaal and Ryk Naudé didn't come.'

'Don't you worry, little lady. Lukas de Groot assured me he'd tell Ryk.'

'Oh, Father!' That her father had anticipated her concern without her voicing it was most unexpected and it pleased her greatly. Grasping his hand in the darkness, she brought it to her lips and kissed it. 'Such a Nachtmaal we'll have! And I with a new dress.'

Touched by her childish gratitude, he bent down and kissed her twice. 'Did you think Mama and I would forget the necessary things?'

The next days were marked with butchering and the first steps in making an abundance of biltong for the trip to Graaff-Reinet, ninety-two miles to the northwest. Tjaart owned three transport wagons, long flat-bedded affairs, and he kept them in fine condition for journeys to market, but the family wagon was a rickety bone-shaker. As it was being washed down and greased, Tjaart instructed the servants as to how they must mind the farm during his absence and care for his mother, Ouma Wilhelmina, who would remain behind.

When all was ready, an English settler came posting in with disturbing news: a band of Xhosa had broken across the Fish and were committing depredations. The messenger said that Lukas de Groot was collecting Boers to the north and would meet Tjaart halfway to form a substantial commando for assistance to Grahamstown.

Without hesitating, Tjaart saddled up, called for four of his Coloureds to join him, and galloped east. Counting the massive battle of 1819, when he had helped save Grahamstown, this was the sixth time he had joined with fellow Boers to quell a border disturbance.

There were two reasons for their being so willing to help defend the English. As sensible men, they knew that in protecting the forward English farms they were protecting their own. But also, there was the acknowledgment that deplorable English mistakes, such as Slagter's Nek and the recent turning of Coloured servants loose to become vagrants and banditti, were the acts of English officialdom and the philanthropicals and not those of Englishmen on the frontier. Indeed, the settlers in Grahamstown suffered as much from these laws as did the Boers, which is why they cheered whenever the Boer commandos reported. There was harmony of interests.

The Stevens Affair of 1832 was a brief, fierce clash, and as unfortunate an incident as could have been devised. On a small farm six miles west of the Great Fish, there was an outcropping of red-paint earth with such a powerful impregnation of pyritic elements that it glowed handsomely when dried on a black man's skin. For generations untold the Xhosa had come to this spot to collect the clay treasured by circumcision boys and warriors, and the fact that a family from rural England had crossed the ocean to establish Stevens Farm did not diminish their desire—one might say spiritual need—to scrape up the earth and carry it back across the Great Fish.

Usually the expeditions were silent affairs, a few warriors braving considerable dangers to penetrate what had become English property and sneaking away without having done the white men harm. But in the spring of 1832 careless Xhosa, some drunk on Kaffir beer, had gone to the Stevens farm to collect not only red earth but also quite a few white sheep. A scuffle had ensued, with dead bodies, and now the Xhosa must be punished.

'What we'll do,' Major Saltwood of the Grahamstown Irregulars proposed as the men assembled, 'is ride east, cross the river at Trompetter's Drift, and take them in the rear.'

But the local Xhosa who rallied to the defense of the raiders were a battle-hardened group, a hundred veterans of many skirmishes with the English and Boers, and were not likely to be surprised by any flanking action. So when Saltwood led the men forward at a gallop, Xhosa warriors in ambush peppered them with spears and bullets from the few guns they had been able to beg, trade or capture.

That was the first skirmish, with the white men losing. The second was inconclusive, but the third was quite a different affair. Major Saltwood, Tjaart van Doorn and Lukas de Groot concocted a plan that would smash the Xhosa from three sides, and everything worked to perfection except that a hiding spearman stabbed Thomas Carleton deeply in the left thigh, dragged him from his horse, and was about to kill him when Van Doorn saw the danger, wheeled in midflight and roared back to brain the black with his rifle butt. It was a near thing, and when Carleton realized that he was saved, and that the wound in his leg was much bigger than he could tend, he quietly fainted in Van Doorn's arms, and the two men stayed on the ground till Saltwood and some others doubled back to find them.

When they returned to Grahamstown—victors, but with serious losses —Carleton was so effusive in his praise of Van Doorn's heroism, and repeated it so often, that Richard Saltwood told his wife, Julie, with some asperity, 'You'd think he'd let it rest.' Then he added, with no malice, 'But of course, poor Carleton's not a gentleman. He hasn't had the training.'

'Nor am I a lady,' Julie snapped. 'So I can't be expected to know, either. And I think it's a thrilling story. So does poor Vera, because without it she'd be a widow.'

'But you must admit, he does overplay it, rather.'

'If I'm in trouble, first I'd want you to come riding up to rescue me. But next in line, Van Doorn.'

The victory celebrations were so congenial, with many of the English volunteers offering toasts in reasonably good Dutch, that Van Doorn and De Groot lingered, and this delayed their arrival at the Graaff-Reinet Nachtmaal.

When De Groot and Van Doorn, accompanied by their Coloureds, who had fought bravely, prepared for the ride home they were joined by a veldkornet who had conducted himself, as always, with notable dignity. It was Piet Retief, a farmer from the Winterberg far north; thin, tallish, with a small beard, he was a friendly, outspoken man in his fifties, but when Saltwood and Carleton came out to bid the Boers thanks and farewell, he stood apart.

Carleton hobbled over to Van Doorn's horse, grasped Tjaart fervently, and said, 'Old chap, you carry my life in your saddle. May God bless you for what you did.'

'I'd expect the same from you,' Tjaart said, and the Boers left town.

For a day and a half they were accompanied by Retief, and came to understand the perplexities that gnawed at him. He was a strange mixture, an esteemed commando leader from a Huguenot family, but also a reckless business adventurer who seemed destined to overreach himself. 'The English sued me when the barracks collapsed,' he grumbled, referring to a disastrous construction venture in Grahamstown.

'But you had it complete,' Van Doorn said, 'I saw it, and you did a fine job on the magistrate's office.'

'I ran out of money. And do you know why I hadn't any? I was always absent fighting the Xhosa to protect the very people that sued me.'

'You lost everything?'

'Everything. It always seems to happen that way.'

Van Doorn thought it best not to ask about the other disasters; what he wanted to hear was Retief's attitude toward the English government, for he was a man whose voice was being heard more and more. He spoke often about what he considered 'the persecution of the Boers.'

'The English will never give up until farmers like the three of us are ruined. Finished.'

'Why would any government adopt such a policy?'

'Because Keer will make them. His pressure will never cease until the Kaffirs control all the land. Look at your servants running wild over the veld . . .' His voice tapered off at the sight of De Groot's expression. 'They're not satisfied with robbing us of belongings and blood. They want to steal our good name, too. I see that as the English program.'

'Wait, wait!' Tjaart protested. 'You've seen that men like Saltwood and Carleton are decent.'

'They are good men, but they're here in Grahamstown. Keer is in London, and every law he proposes favors the Kaffirs at our expense. The philanthropist ladies in their London parlors will continue to bleat when they hear we Boers are trying to defend our wives and children against their Kaffir darlings.'

Van Doorn was unable to decide how much of Retief's grievance was justified, how much an understandable animosity springing from his ruined business contracts, but before they parted, Retief raised a new bold topic about which there could be no ambiguity: 'Tjaart, would you contribute rix-dollars to a project that Pieter Uys is contemplating? You know Uys, a very good man.'

Van Doorn did not know him, but De Groot did, and most favorably: 'Maybe the best Boer along the sea. What's his plan?'

'He thinks to go on an exploring trip. Up the coast into the fertile valleys along the Indian Ocean.'

'Why?'

'He thinks that one day the Boers might have to move there. I don't want to quit my farm. And I know you wouldn't want to, Tjaart. But it might be prudent if we looked.'

'To what purpose?' Van Doorn asked, and in years that were to come he would never forget Retief's reply. They had reached a landmark where Retief must turn north for his farm among the mountain ranges. Up there lay the kind of place no man would willingly leave, but Retief said, 'I fear the English are determined to drive us into the ground. Did you read Keer's reports?'

'You know I can't read English,' De Groot said.

'Well, I read them all,' Retief said with great force, 'and you know what I think? After next year there will be no more slavery. They'll take our Coloureds away from us, too, and then how will we farm?'

'What has Pieter Uys to do with this?' De Groot asked.

'A wise man considers many plans,' Retief replied. 'Not for me or you. We can manage. But for the poor Boers who are going to be pressed down by English laws. Uys will look at the lands in Natal and tell us if we can farm them.'

'Aren't the lands already taken?' De Groot asked.

'To the north, the Zulu. To the south, a few Englishmen. But in between, magnificent valleys with ample water, trees, good land.'

He asked again for contributions to the Uys expedition, and Tjaart had to say, 'I have no money now. Advance it for me and I'll pay back.' The English had recently introduced their own monetary system, thinking to replace the Dutch that everyone used, and De Groot did have some of the crisp notes. When he handed his offering to Retief the latter took it, held it in his two hands, and allowed the sun to play upon it.

'I do not like this money,' he said.

Nachtmaal (night meal) was Holy Communion. It was held four times each year, and those living near the church were expected to attend each one. But Boers in remote areas were forgiven if they missed entirely for three or four years, because at the first opportunity they would come swarming in on pilgrimages that might last a month. With them they brought children to be baptized, young lovers to be married, and elders who whispered, 'This might be my last Nachtmaal.'

For such travelers, there could be nothing more exciting and spiritually satisfying than this joyous celebration of the Dutch Reformed Church, for in its companionship there was social renewal and in its religious services a deepened pledge to Calvinist doctrine. A week of Nachtmaal lent grace and harmony to the lives of the Boers and explained why they formed such a cohesive group.

The rite was carefully structured: church service each day for four days, the one on Sunday lasting four hours; public weddings and baptisms; acceptance of new members into the fellowship; much time set aside for buying and selling of properties; and wonderful singing parties at which youths were almost challenged to fall in love.

But what everyone cherished about Nachtmaal was the strengthened friendship of families who had shared common struggles: almost every man had been on commando; almost every woman had lost a baby, or a husband; and all had pondered during the difficult years their relationship to God. In the English community there was nothing similar to Nachtmaal, which was one reason why the English could never be mistaken for Dutchmen.

In 1833 the Van Doorn wagon was not of the best for this long journey: ninety-two miles over a demanding terrain, with the sixteen oxen able to do at best eight miles a day. The cart had worn wheels and such a tattered canvas that Tjaart had been saying for some years, 'We must find ourselves a new wagon.' Upon his arrival at Graaff-Reinet, capital of the northeast, he was determined to acquire the best wagon possible, even if he had to trade all the sheep he was driving to the town to get it.

But his excitement in heading north was nothing compared to his daughter's, for she had convinced herself that when the Van Doorn wagon overtook the De Groots' in the far middle of nothingness, they would form a kind of royal procession, and at the entrance to Graaff-Reinet, near the miraculous mountain, they would meet Ryk Naudé, who would be waiting for her like a young prince. She had practiced her speech of welcome: 'Good afternoon, Ryk. How pleasant it is to see you again.' She would speak to him as if their parting had been two days ago, not two years. She experimented with charcoal to make her eyebrows darker and red clay from the Stevens farm to touch her cheeks. She pestered her mother and the slave women to convince herself that she would be acceptable in Ryk's eyes, and they assured her that she was a proper little lady whom any man would be pleased to have.

She was experiencing the wonderful days of awakening, and no one watched her with more approval than Tjaart. And he told his wife, 'Jakoba, when a girl is almost fourteen she better think about catching herself a husband. You almost waited too long.' She had been all of sixteen when the Widower van Doorn rode seventy miles to find her, and she could remember how worried she had been. 'Minna's just right for her age, Tjaart. She has a good head.'

The senior members of the family had also been attending to their appearance: Jakoba had made herself a new dress, a new bonnet, and had ordered new shoes for herself and Tjaart from Koos, an old cobbler who moved from farm to farm. Tjaart, in turn, had unpacked his one fine suit of dark clothes: coat, vest, trousers with a big front flap, felt hat with enormous brim. On the final evening, when all the attractive things were spread on the floor prior to being wrapped for the dusty journey, he took down the brassbound Bible and opened it to Isaiah, where he read: ' "Who is this that cometh from Edom, with dyed garments from Bozrah, this that is glorious in his apparel, traveling in the greatness of his strength?" ' And he answered the rhetorical question by saying in his own words, 'It is the family of Tjaart van Doorn. Traveling to Graaff-Reinet for Nachtmaal, to do You honor.'

In the morning they started—father, mother, two sons and their families, and the girl Minna—all in their oldest, roughest clothes, the three men in broad-brimmed hats, the women in sunbonnets to protect their complexions from the sun. Four Coloureds accompanied them to tend the sixteen oxen, pitch the tents at night, and guard the large flock of sheep Tjaart intended to trade for his new wagon, and three women slaves to do the cooking and watch after the needs of the travelers. They stopped by midafternoon, for the oxen had to be outspanned in daylight hours so they could forage on the rich but sparse grass.

They were traveling over a route with which the Van Doorn people had been acquainted for many years. Their course was a strict north-northwest, but it deviated sharply at times to allow the crossing of ravines or the circumvention of large hills; so at night, when the Southern Cross appeared, Tjaart had to correct his heading, which he did with confidence that on the morrow they would see familiar hills.

The slow movement of the oxen—each of which responded only to its individual name—the swaying of the wagon, the soft singing of the slaves and the rhythmic walk of the men produced a kind of timeless lethargy in which there was constant movement but little change, just the grand emptiness of the veld across which not even animals moved at this time of year.

But there was excitement! Minna, alert to the increasing nearness of Graaff-Reinet, began to display nervousness; for one thing, she kept strictly in the shade so that her complexion would be as light as possible, for she knew that Boer men treasured this in their women. When the afternoon sun threatened her face, she produced a light goatskin mask which she wore as a shield. At intervals she also smoothed her rough traveling dress as if she were already preparing to meet young Naudé. And often she joined the slave women in their singing, for her heart was fluttering and sought release. She might not be beautiful, but she was inspiring to see as she blossomed in the veld like a gray flower expanding after a long drought, and Tjaart reveled in her happiness.

Her nervousness was caused in part by the delayed departure for Nachtmaal, which meant that the Van Doorns and De Groots would arrive not on the Wednesday as planned, but only on Friday itself, when the ceremonies would be beginning; and it was in those preliminary days, before the preaching began, that the young people conducted much of their courting.

'Minna!' her father assured her. 'He'll appreciate you more when you do arrive. He'll be hungry to see you.'

And then came the small miracle which enlivened the prospect of Nachtmaal as nothing else could have done, for out of the east, at a far distance, rose a faint sign of dust: it must have been fifteen miles away, two days of travel, but there it was, a mark in the sky. And all that first day the Van Doorns watched the pillar of dust, and at night they strained their eyes for any indication of light—a campfire perhaps—but none showed, and on the second day they looked with joy as the pillar expanded and assumed the thickness that would be caused by a large team of oxen.

It was the De Groots, coming out of the northeast, leading a herd of cows to Nachtmaal, converging their course with that of the Van Doorns, and before evening the juncture had been made. There were kisses among the women, backslapping for the men, and the jollity of renewed friendships for the servants and slaves.

The two wagons rode together for the next four days, at the end of which De Groot said with some confidence, 'Tomorrow we'll see Spandau Kop,' and Minna was walking at the head of the procession when she cried, 'There it is!'

Tjaart had first seen this incredibly beautiful hill as a child, traveling to Nachtmaal with Lodevicus the Hammer, and to him it signified the beacons which God had placed in all deserts of the world for the guidance of His people. Abraham, coming out of Babylonia, had seen such reassuring signals, and Joseph, traveling home from Egypt, had seen the same. But what Tjaart had not appreciated as a child was the many-turreted chain of taller mountains that rimmed Graaff-Reinet, forming a kind of amphitheater of protection. When one came in from the flat veld, the physical appearance of this little town was overwhelming, and Tjaart saw with pleasure that his daughter was relishing the sight as he had done at her age.

The entire town was given over to the canopied wagons of men and women who had traveled vast distances for this religious ceremony: sixty groups had already arrived, their canvas tents pitched beside their wagons, their oxen grazing in the nearby meadows, attended by the herdsmen, who were enjoying the noise and the beer as much as their white masters.

The large square in front of the church was crammed with wagons by the time the Van Doorns arrived, but there was a tree-lined street leading to the parsonage which in some ways was preferable, for one's wagon was not surrounded by neighbors, and here the Van Doorns and the De Groots settled down.

It was Friday morning, and before Minna had time to seek out young Ryk Naudé, everyone had to convene in the famous white-walled church. The Van Doorns arrived just as the first long service was to begin, and they met with two situations that shocked them. The resident dominee, a Scotsman who had married a Boer girl, spoke more Dutch than English, and would have six sons, five of whom would be ordained at Graaff-Reinet, and five daughters, four of whom would marry dominees—this beloved man, a better Boer than many Boers, was absent in Cape Town, and in his place served a large, red-faced preacher from Glasgow who could barely speak intelligible Dutch; it was something to hear the burgeoning local patois delivered in a heavy Scots accent.

And then Minna saw to her horror that Ryk was sitting with a family that had a girl fifteen or sixteen years old and of remarkable beauty.

'Oh!' she sighed, and when her father asked what was the matter, all she could do was point with trembling finger across the church. It was unfortunate that she did so, for now Tjaart saw the girl, and for the duration of the service he could not take his eyes away. She was a glorious child, and at the same time a woman; her skin was fair, but touched with red at the cheeks; her face was broad and perfectly proportioned; her neck and shoulders were frighteningly suggestive, and despite the fact that he knew he was committing sin, he began to undress her in his mind, and the fall of her clothes was more provocative than anything he had previously known.

'Look at her!' Minna whispered, and he blinked his eyes and began to look at her in a different way, and what he saw boded unhappiness for his daughter, for this girl, whoever she was, had obviously decided that she was destined to marry Ryk Naudé, and by every feminine device, was ingratiating herself to him. Tilt of head, movement of arm, deep convincing smile, flash of white teeth—she used them all until the young man seemed quite bewildered by what was happening. Tjaart, himself so profoundly affected by the girl, knew that Minna had lost her young man, and to quieten both himself and his daughter he took her hand, and felt its trembling.

None of the Van Doorns paid much attention to the Scots minister, who was delivering one of the dullest sermons they had ever heard; he lacked the fire of a true Calvinist predikant, keeping his voice to a monotone, with none of the tumultuous raging the Boers liked, and often his words could not be easily understood. The true fire that day rested on the benches occupied by Ryk Naudé and his new girl.

When the sermon ended and the Boers had come out into the square, Minna, without any sense of shame, moved swiftly toward Naudé, posted herself where he could not escape her, and said boldly, 'Hello, Ryk. I've been waiting to see you.'

He nodded bleakly, well aware that he had promised two years ago to attend Minna at the next Nachtmaal they shared, but also aware that any such promises had been obviated by the dramatic arrival in town of the girl he now presented: 'This is Aletta.' He did not give her last name, for he had already determined that before this Nachtmaal ended, she would take his.

Aletta was as charming to Minna as she had been to Ryk during the service, and when Minna's father lumbered up, she was equally gracious, extending her hand and greeting him with a ravishing smile: 'I'm Aletta Probenius. My father keeps a store.'

'He's the man I seek,' Tjaart said, pleased that his business would keep him in touch with this exciting girl. 'Is it true that he has a wagon for sale?'

'He has almost everything,' Aletta said with a fetching toss of her head, and in the various events that accompanied Nachtmaal she demonstrated that, like her father in his store, she, too, had almost everything: smiles, witticisms, grace, and enormous sexual magnetism.

For Minna that first Friday was agony. One close look at the radiant Aletta warned her that chances for catching Ryk Naudé had vanished, and this so confused her that she did a series of things that made her look quite foolish. First she sought Ryk at his wagon to remind him of what he had promised her two years ago . . . 'We were children then,' he said.

'But you told me.'

'Things have happened.'

'But you told me,' she repeated, clutching at his hand, and when he tried to pull away, she grabbed at him. She wanted him, desperately she wanted him, terrified by the prospect of returning to isolated De Kraal for another span of years, after which she might be too old to catch herself a husband.

Ryk, at eighteen, had never experienced anything like this, for Aletta had permitted him only to hold her hand; he became so confused he did not know what to do, but his mother came up, deduced what was happening, and said calmly, 'Hello, Minna. Hadn't you better be joining your parents?'

'Ryk said that he—'

'Minna,' Mevrouw Naudé said, 'you'd better go—now.'

'But he promised—'

'Minna! Go home!' And she thrust the bewildered child away.

The following days were torment. In church Minna, like her father, stared at Aletta, and one evening as service ended she followed the girl to her father's store and confronted her: 'Ryk Naudé is promised to me.'

'Minna, don't be foolish. Ryk and I are going to be married.'

'No! He told me . . .'

'Whatever he told you,' Aletta said with a sweetness that would have mollified anyone else, 'was two years ago. You were children, and now he's a man and he's going to marry me.'

'I won't let you!' Minna cried, her voice rising so sharply that Mijnheer Probenius came out from his shop to see his daughter being assaulted by a strange girl much her junior in years.

'What goes on here?' he cried, and when it became apparent that the girls were fighting over a man, he laughed heartily and said, 'You ask me, that Ryk's not worth the trouble. You'd both be better off without him.'

Placing his arms about the two girls, he sat with them, telling Minna, 'You can't be more than thirteen. In Holland, where I came from, girls don't marry till they're twenty. Minna, you have seven years.'

'Not in the wilderness. And Ryk promised me . . .'

'Men promise a lot of things,' Probenius said. 'In Holland right now are three girls I promised to marry when I returned home to Haarlem. And here I am in Graaff-Reinet with a daughter sixteen years old who's to be married on Tuesday.'

'Married!' Minna cried, and she dissolved into tears, the shattering, soul-wrenching tears of a little girl striving to act like a woman.

To her surprise, Probenius took her round, tear-spattered face in his two hands, brought it up, and kissed it. 'Minna, this world is full of young men who need a wife like you.'

'Not in the wilderness,' she repeated stubbornly as Probenius got her to her feet, saying, 'Let's no one speak of this.' And he gently moved her along toward her parents' wagon.

Of course, everyone spoke of it, and when Tjaart reported at the store to dicker about the exchange of his sheep for a new wagon, he found Probenius, a man somewhat older than himself, disturbed that gossip should have struck so hard at little Minna: 'She's a fine child, Van Doorn, and I'm sorry this has happened. But she'll find a host of young men.'

'Her heart was set on Ryk. What kind of fellow is he?'

'The usual. Talks big. Acts little.'

'Are you happy with him?'

'Are parents ever happy with anyone?'

'Aletta's an impressive girl.'

'I sometimes fear for her. Back in Haarlem she'd be all right. Many young men to court her, for she is pretty. But also many young women just as attractive to break her heart now and then.'

'How are things in Holland?'

'Like everywhere, confused.'

'Will you go back?'

'Me? Leave paradise for those cold winters?' He came from behind his counter and stood with Tjaart. 'They warned us that after Jan Compagnie gave your land to the English, no Dutchman from Holland would be welcomed here. We came anyway. You should give thanks every day that you live in this wonderland.'

In trading, Probenius was a hard man, which accounted for his conspic-uous success, but Tjaart was equally difficult, which explained his successful farm. At the end of the Friday negotiation no agreement had even been approached: Tjaart had some of the finest sheep Graaff-Reinet had seen, and Probenius had a new wagon superior in every way to what Van Doorn had been using.

'You don't build wagons,' Tjaart said. 'Where'd you get it?'

'From an Englishman in Grahamstown named Thomas Carleton.'

'I know Carleton. I could get it cheaper by going to Grahamstown.'

'True, but your sheep are here. So you must trade here. And the price is what I said.'

On Saturday, Tjaart brought his family to inspect the wagon, and they found it to be even better than Tjaart had reported. It was a handsome piece of workmanship, so constructed that it could be disassembled for transport-ing down ravines, and then reassembled easily. It was nicely balanced, too, and the disselboom was so attached to the front axle that the whole would respond quickly to any turning of the oxen. Even the curved hoops that covered the body and to which canvas would be applied were nicely sanded to remove rough edges. It was in every respect superior, and the Van Doorns needed it.

There could be no bargaining on Sunday, of course, nor would there have been much time for it, for in addition to the four-hour service and the acceptance of new members, the predikant offered to conduct a special service for the baptism of those babies who had missed the Saturday rite, and the entire Van Doorn family had to attend because the De Groots were offering their new son for baptism. He was Paulus, a lusty, squared-off little boy with powerful lungs and a rowdy nature. The Scots minister was so taken with him that at the conclusion of the service he kissed the little fellow on the forehead, saying, 'This one will be a staunch fighter for the Lord.' The De Groots were not entirely happy that their son had been welcomed into the Boer church by this Scotsman, but nevertheless they gave the dominee two sheep in thanks for the special service.

On Monday, Tjaart returned to the store for some serious bargaining, and as it happened, Probenius himself was not there, but his daughter Aletta was, and for the better part of an hour Tjaart talked with this lively, attractive girl, noting every particular. She had a musical voice and laughed easily when assuring him that her father never reduced a price, once set: 'You'll face difficulties, Mijnheer, if you pursue that line.'

'I face difficulties in all I do,' he assured her, watching the enchanting way her gingham dress defined her figure when she reached for articles on the higher shelves. 'You people in Graaff-Reinet—you're getting to be a real town. Must be three, four hundred houses here.'

'But it's not like Cape Town, is it? That's where I'd like to go.'

'I wouldn't know. I've never been there.'

At the conclusion of their conversation Tjaart thought that he had never before met a girl so totally charming, and he was somewhat irritated when her father appeared to talk about the wagon: 'Let's get one thing straight, Van Doorn. Once I set a price, I never lower it.'

'Let's get a second thing straight,' Tjaart responded. 'I am perfectly prepared to herd my sheep right back home and go to Grahamstown myself. You may not know it, but last month I served on commando with young Carleton, and when I left, his wife said that I would always be welcomed back. Can you guess why she said that?'

There were in South African life two events that struck terror in the hearts of ordinary men: when two bull elephants raged in low scrub, knocking down trees in their feud; and when two Boers engaged in a business deal. Awed Englishmen, watching the trickery, the deceit, the conniving, the bluster and the outright falsification of evidence that occurred when one artful Boer was trying to outsmart another, sometimes wondered how the new nation survived the passions and near-strangulations. 'I do believe,' Richard Saltwood wrote home to his brother in Parliament, 'that they are the most contrary people I've met. Rather than yield the slightest advantage, they dig their heels in like a dozen stubborn mules and won't budge, neither back nor forward, not till kingdom come.'

'The reason why the Carletons would welcome me back,' Tjaart was saying offhandedly, 'and offer me their best wagon at a low price, is that during the commando I saved his life.'

'Then you should certainly drove your sheep back one hundred miles and drove them another fifty for the slight advantage you'd get.'

'I'm prepared to do just that,' Tjaart said, and at this point he should have left the store to allow Probenius time to consider his folly—for he knew that the storekeeper needed the sheep—but now Aletta returned, and she was so like a gazelle resting along a stream that he was imprisoned. He stayed, and her father quickly understood why, and while she was there he did not mention the wagon, but when she left he said, 'Now, when will you be delivering the sheep?' and Tjaart said, 'Never, at your prices.' And he stomped from the store, exactly as Boer custom required.

On Tuesday there was no negotiation, because that was the day of the marriages, when gaunt couples in from the distant hills stepped before the predikant with their three and four children to have their unions recognized of God and confirmed by the community. It was a solemn time; the frontier church was filled with witnesses who used this ceremony to renew their own vows, and girls nine and ten watched wide-eyed as the words were said and the marriages were blessed.

But the highlight of the day was more traditional, for at the conclusion of the marriages already in existence came the young couples, and on this Tuesday, Ryk Naudé, a handsome fellow, was taking as his bride the bewitching Aletta Probenius. They stood before the predikant like two golden creatures, blessed in all ways, and their youthful beauty lent grace to all the ceremonies that had gone before; they represented what marriage should be, and Minna van Doorn wept as they were wed.

On Wednesday, Probenius the storekeeper came to Tjaart's wagon, kicked at the wheels and said, 'Do you seriously think you could get this thing back to De Kraal?'

'Yes,' Tjaart said, 'because once you tell me our business is ended, I drive my wagon to Viljoen the blacksmith and have him tighten it up.'

'Did you see Viljoen at Nachtmaal? Didn't anyone tell you that he is carting ivory back to Cape Town?'

'Didn't anyone tell you that I knew this, and made arrangements for my boys to use Viljoen's forge to make the repairs?'

Who was lying? In a Boer negotiation that could never be determined, for truth was elastic, and what men hoped would happen became a prediction which had to be weighed in scales quite different from those used by a jeweler in weighing gold. Boer commercial truth was negotiable, and after judging the situation carefully, Probenius said with a show of honest summation, 'Tjaart, you need my wagon.' Here he kicked a wheel with such force that it nearly fell apart. 'And I could use your sheep, scrawny though they may be. Let's talk seriously of a proper price.'

'But we must not think only of Graaff-Reinet,' Tjaart countered with the same display of absolute honesty, 'because I am not forced to trade my fat, prime sheep. I can still take them back to Grahamstown for a better bargain.'

'I don't want to see you waste your time,' Probenius said as if he were engaged in a transaction with his own mother. And he offered a new price.

Fortunately, at this moment an extraordinary man came along looking for Van Doorn, and this gave Tjaart an excuse to defer the negotiations: 'Think it over, Probenius.' And he threw out a price markedly lower than the one the storekeeper had just proposed, but not enough to be insulting. 'I promised to talk with this gentleman.'

It was a curious use of words, for if there was anyone at the Nachtmaal who was not a gentleman, it was this odd fellow Theunis Nel, forty-eight years old, short, rumpled, unshaven, poorly dressed, and with a pitiful little mustache that made his upper lip tremble when he talked. Three times during Nachtmaal he had come seeking guidance from Tjaart, and thrice he had been put off. Now he arrived at a time when Tjaart found it convenient to interrupt his bargaining with Probenius, and to the little man's surprise, he was welcomed warmly.

'Theunis, my trusted friend, what can I do for you?'

In addition to his other infirmities, Nel had two which irritated many persons: he lisped slightly, and his left eye was both cocked and watery, so that anyone speaking with him had a confusing time looking first at one eye and then the other without ever knowing which one was functioning, and whenever a decision was reached, Theunis would interrupt the conversation by taking out a grubby handkerchief and wiping his eye: 'I have a cold, you know.' Now he said in pleading voice, 'Tjaart, please speak one more time with the predikant.'

'It's quite useless, dear fellow.'

'Maybe things have changed. Maybe he'll be more compassionate.'

'Haven't you got a job? Aren't you eating?'

'Oh, yes! I'm teaching school . . . for several families . . . beyond the mountains.'

'I'm very happy that you have work, Theunis.'

And then the terrible fire that burned in the heart of this little man manifested itself. In words that tumbled upon each other, and with his lisp worse than usual, he said, 'Tjaart, I am indeed called of God. I have a mission. I feel driven to pass through this community, helping and praying. Tjaart, God has spoken to me. His voice echoes in my ears. For His sake if not for mine, beg the predikant to ordain me.'

He was a pitiful man; refused entrance to any real theological school back in Holland, he had been half trained at a kind of missionary school in Germany. He was certainly not a predikant, which was why he sought ordination so compulsively, but he was not a layman either, because he had been on his way to Java to work in a mission when the last Dutch governor at the Cape had plucked him off his ship to serve in that capacity in South Africa. Itinerant teacher, wandering scholar, frontier sick-comforter, busybody, aspirant, his only virtue was that of all the Dutch sick-comforters in Africa and Java, he was the one who truly brought comfort to the dying. Insignificant, without pomp or pretense, but convinced that he was touched directly by the finger of God, he came into the meanest frontier hut and said, 'Life runs its course, Stephanus, and now the commando saddles up for the last charge. I have watched you for a dozen years, down and up, and I am convinced that God has His eye upon you. Death has not yet come. You have days and days to reflect upon the providential life you've enjoyed. Those children. The fields. Stephanus, you are quitting one glory to enter another, and I wish I could go with you, hand in hand, to see what you're about to see. Spend these last days in reflection. Would you like me to read you a sermon preached in Amsterdam about the nature of heaven?'

And that was the constant anguish! As a sick-comforter, Theunis Nel could read the sermons of others but never preach one of his own; the church laws which governed his deportment were severe. If he had ever presumed to preach in those early days when Holland governed, he would have been thrown in jail; now, under English law, he would escape jail but not the ostracism of his own people. So he carried with him always a small book of sermons, which he had memorized but which prudently he continued to read, because only this was permitted.

'Please, Tjaart, the years slip by and I am not yet ordained. Will you speak with the predikant?'

'Have you a Bible?' Tjaart asked. Theunis nodded eagerly, so they went to his wagon, and there in Leviticus, Tjaart found the citation he needed; it was terrifyingly explicit:

> And the Lord spake unto Moses saying . . . Whosoever . . . that hath any blemish, let him not approach to offer the bread of his God . . . Or crookbackt, or a dwarf, or that hath a blemish in his eye, or hath his stones broken . . . he shall not come nigh unto the altar, because he hath a blemish; that he profane not my sanctuaries.

Leaving the book open so that Theunis could see for himself, if he so wished, Tjaart said, 'There it is. You have a blemished eye. You give the impression of being crookbackt. It's impossible for you to be a predikant.'

'It's just a cold,' the little man said, daubing at his offending eye. And then the pretense ended and he scratched at his eye, crying, 'I would to God I could pluck it out.'

'Then you'd be blind,' Tjaart said, 'and the blemish would be even greater.'

'What can I do?' Nel pleaded, and all Tjaart could say was 'You're a teacher. You are God's sick-comforter. That's the way you must serve.'

'But I could do so much more. Tjaart, did you hear those dreadful sermons the fat Scotsman gave? No fire. No touch of God. It's a disgrace.'

'For reasons of His own, God has forbidden you to preach. Be content.'

And he shoved the difficult little man away, watching him as he returned to the wagon that would carry him to the four farms where he conducted his school, and when those children were grown, to four other farms, and then four others, until some younger sick-comforter should in due course come to him to ease his dying. He was the man of God whom God rejected.

On the way back to De Kraal in the new wagon, Tjaart thought several times that he would burst into tears before his entire family, something he had never done. But his anguish over the despair of little Minna was almost more than he could bear, and even as he tried to console her he felt himself coming apart, and he would leave before he made a fool of himself. Walking beside the lead oxen, he would try not to think of her sorrow, and his mind would fix on Aletta as she worked in the store, stretching to find a box, or as she appeared on the day of her wedding like a spirit risen from the veld, all gold and smiles and enchantment. He was entertaining such visions one afternoon when he heard a sudden cry from the wagon, and when he rushed back he found that Minna had undone the cloth in which her new dress was being carried and was tearing the garment apart, throwing the bits upon the veld.

'Daughter!' he cried in rage. 'What are you doing?'

'It's no use! I am lost!'

Climbing into the wagon beside her, he took her in his arms and told the slave women to recover the bits of cloth and take the dress away; it could be mended. He was not so sure about his daughter's heart, for in the days that followed she fell into a fever and lay in the wagon shivering and not caring whether she lived or died. The women had several remedies for such afflictions, but none sufficed, and on the third night Tjaart crept into bed with her, and kept her warm and comforted her, and when the dawn broke he said a strange thing: 'We must both forget Nachtmaal.'

Ironically, it was Van Doorn's oldest slave who announced the long-awaited decision on slavery. 'Baas, Baas!' he cried. 'Die big baas Cuyler, he here.' And that remarkable man from Albany, New York, Colonel Jacob Glen Cuyler, strode heavily into the De Kraal farmhouse. The two men with him did not presume to enter, but remained respectfully outside: Saul, the Xhosa deacon at Golan, and Pieter, son of Dikkop. The first was old and gray, the second hastening in that direction.

They were at the first stage of an incredible venture: Cuyler had fetched them from the mission village and was taking them to Port Elizabeth, whence they would go by ship to London as guests of Dr. Simon Keer, who wanted them to participate in one of his grand lecture tours. Hesitant about entering the home of a Boer, they would be entertained at Buckingham Palace.

Colonel Cuyler, now a respected magistrate and soon to be a lieutenant-general, had a message which was brief and shocking: 'Parliament have passed a law that says all slaves will be emancipated next year. On December 31, 1834, every slave in the empire will be freed.'

'Good God!' Tjaart cried. 'That's revolution!'

'Oh, you'll be compensated, fully. Every penny you spent. And the slaves must work for you during the first four years, so they can move in an orderly way into their freedom.'

Cuyler saluted and departed. For three days the Van Doorns and their neighbors discussed the new laws, and at the end of that time they still could not grasp the full meaning of this radical change—that it defined a whole new way of life—and to their surprise it was not any of the men who saw clearly the new landscape, but Jakoba van Doorn, the quiet, unlettered woman who had been ignored both at Nachtmaal and in these discussions. Now she spoke with fierce determination: 'The Bible says that the sons of Ham shall work for us and be our slaves. The Bible says there shall be a proper difference between master and slave. The Bible says we shall keep apart, His people to themselves, the Canaanites to themselves. I have never struck a slave. I have always tended my slaves and my Coloureds when they were sick. And I think I have shown that I love them. But I do not want them at my table and I do not like the sight of them in my church. For God has ordered me to live otherwise.'

Driven by her forcefulness, the illiterate men urged Tjaart to consult the Bible, desiring to hear for themselves what the strictures of good Christian life ought to be, and he found and recited those satisfying passages upon which their social order was so securely founded:

> 'And he said, Cursed be Canaan; a servant of servants shall he be unto his brethren . . . Now therefore ye are cursed, and there shall none of you be freed from being bondmen, and hewers of wood and drawers of water for the house of my God . . .'

After he had read a dozen such passages, which proved conclusively that God had ordained and blessed the institution of slavery, Jakoba, a woman fierce in righteousness, demanded that he seek further for two verses which predikants had explained to her, for upon them she based her belief that the Boers were special people, set free by God to behave in their own special way. After some searching in Leviticus, a book whose laws governed Boer life, Tjaart uttered the statement:

> 'And ye shall be holy unto me: for I the Lord am holy, and have severed you from other people, that ye should be mine.'

'See,' Jakoba cried with grim satisfaction, 'God Himself wanted us to be apart. We have special obligations, special privileges.' And she urged her husband to uncover that particular verse on which she hung the main body of her belief. He could not find it, and with some impatience she riffled the large pages of the book she could not read, then pushed the Bible back to Tjaart, with the command: 'Find it. It deals with tribute.'

It was this word that reminded Tjaart of a passage in Judges dealing with the establishment of Israel in a new land—an exact parallel to the situation of the Boers—and with a good deal of useless help from the men, he finally located what Jakoba wanted to hear:

> 'And it came to pass, when Israel was strong, that they put the Canaanites to tribute, and did not utterly drive them out . . . but the Canaanites dwelt among them and became tributaries.'

'And that,' said Jakoba, 'is how it should be. We have conquered the land. We live here. We are to be just to the Kaffirs, but they are tribute to us.'

'The English say that's all done for.'

'The English know nothing about Kaffirs,' Jakoba said. She was a small woman, daughter of a trekboer who had defended his land eleven times against black marauders, and in the harshness of her family's hut she had learned the principles by which a Christian lives, and to such a life she was committed. She was honest, hard-working, a good mother both to her own daughter and to Tjaart's children by his first marriage, and although she could not attend church each Sunday, for the nearest was many miles away, she did hold personal services in which she thanked God for His merciful guidance. What He wanted in the matter of relationships between white masters and black slaves was so clear that an idiot could understand, and she proposed that she, her family and her nation obey those precepts.

'We will not abide by English laws,' she said as she left the men, 'if they run counter to the word of God,' and when she was gone, Tjaart called after her, 'What have you in mind?' and from the kitchen she replied, 'Leave here. Go over the mountains and form a nation of our own.'

Late one morning as Tjaart returned from inspecting his flocks he was alarmed to find five horses tethered at his house, and he assumed that new troubles had erupted on the frontier: 'Damn! Another commando!'

But when he entered the kitchen he found no sense of urgency. Five neighbors were drinking gin and joking with Jakoba and Minna as the two brought large platters of food. 'Veldkornet!' the men cried noisily as Tjaart entered, and there was ribald joking as to why he had been absent when they arrived.

Leader of the group was Balthazar Bronk, a man Tjaart instinctively distrusted. Bronk endeavored to be two quite different persons at the same time: with superiors he was obsequious; with others he tried to dominate in various pompous ways; and sometimes he was downright objectionable. He could never be simply Balthazar Bronk, farmer.

'Veldkornet,' he said humbly as Tjaart reached for a glass of gin. 'We've come to enlist your services.'

'No commando. I'm tired of fighting those damned Xhosa.'

The men laughed, for they knew that the first man to saddle up if trouble came would be Van Doorn, but Bronk continued: 'We're worried, Veldkornet. With English rule—'

'Stop right there!' Van Doorn snapped, slamming his two hands down on the table. 'The English are in command, and slowly they're learning to do things right. Accept them.'

'Exactly what I said,' Bronk cried eagerly, and when he looked to the others for confirmation, they nodded. Then he coughed, adjusted things on the table, and went on: 'Under English rule our children will have to know more—to compete, to make us proud.'

Tjaart could not guess what would come next, but a quiet member of the group said, 'You're the only one of us who can read. None of our children can read—'

'We need a teacher,' Bronk interrupted. 'Find us a teacher.'

'Who would pay him?' Tjaart asked cautiously.

'All of us. We have so many children.'

A census was taken, and when the numbers were announced they gave a good picture of Boer life: 'Eleven, nine, nine, seven.' And proudly Bronk declared: 'Seventeen.'

'You mean they all want to go to school?'

'Only the young ones,' Bronk said. 'Six of mine are married.' Then he smiled unctuously at Tjaart and said, 'You have how many?'

Tjaart swigged on his gin, then said, 'First wife, two boys. They're past schooling, but they have children. Jakoba, tell them how many you have.'

Wiping her hands on her apron, she said, 'Minna here.'

Five heads turned toward the girl, who blushed deeply, for she could see that they were thinking: Why isn't she married?

'Mejuffrouw Minna is not for school,' Bronk said with a wide smile, and the others returned to the task of finding a master, and as expected, Tjaart was of help: 'At Nachtmaal, I was speaking with Theunis Nel . . .'

Bronk groaned. 'We want a real teacher. Not a squint-eye.'

Another said, 'We must have a school. Go see him, Van Doorn.'

When Tjaart reined his horse at the northern farm of Gerrit Viljoen, he was astonished by what the owner said: 'Welcome! Have you come to talk with us about emigrating north?'

'Why do you ask that?'

'Six wagons passed here the other day. Men like you and me.'

'Why would you go north?'

'Freedom.'

'I'm staying where I am.'

'I'd expect you to. All those good stone buildings.'

'They are good,' Tjaart agreed, not catching the challenge to his worldliness.

'You might have to reach a decision sooner than you think, Tjaart.'

'Why?'

'Freedom. Boers love freedom. And ours is being stolen from us.'

'Gerrit,' Tjaart said abruptly. 'I came here to steal your schoolmaster.'

'No complaint from me. He's about done his job at these farms.'

'Do you recommend him?'

'I do. I do. Knows his numbers. Knows his Bible.'

'Have I your permission to speak with him?'

'I'd be relieved if he found a good job.' He paused. 'A man so ill-favored needs help.'

Viljoen dispatched a slave to fetch the itinerant teacher, and when Tjaart saw the man again—crookbackt, and almost fifty years old—he shuddered: This man could never teach! But when he consulted the families, he found that all spoke of Nel with affection. One mother said, 'He's small and he has a high voice, but he's a man of God,' and the oldest Viljoen boy said, 'Any of us in class could have whipped him, but he kept order.'

'How?'

'He told us that Jesus was a teacher, too, and we listened.'

That night Tjaart offered Nel the job, and the little man wiped his watery eye and blessed him. 'But if I handle the children well, will you ask the predikant to ordain me?'

'Theunis,' Van Doorn said as if talking with a child, although the schoolmaster was older than he, 'you'll never be a dominee. I've told you that. We need you as a schoolmaster.'

'How many children?'

'Thirty, maybe.' Tjaart was afraid this might sound like too many, but Nel smiled broadly.

'It's better when there's lots. Then the school doesn't end too soon.'

'How many schools have you conducted?'

'Eleven.' Quickly he added, 'I was never discharged. The children grew up and I moved on.' He looked at the two farmers. 'I move on,' he said.

During Tjaart's absence it had been agreed that the new master, if found, would live with Balthazar Bronk and his many children, but when Jakoba heard of the arrangement she snorted: 'No charity there. Bronk wants him to help discipline the children. They're rhinoceroses.' And when Nel saw where he was to domicile, he, too, understood.

Bronk's farm lay nine miles east of De Kraal and proved quite suitable; it was central to the participating families, and had a small whitewashed storage shed that could be converted into a schoolroom. Here Theunis collected his thirty-three youngsters to teach the alphabet, the Bible and the counting tables. Nel had only the slightest knowledge of history, literature, geography and such related subjects, so he did not presume to teach them, but whatever he did attempt carried a heavy overlay of moral instruction.

'Bronk, Dieter. Stand and recite the First Psalm.' After the oafish lad had stumbled through, Nel would ask, 'Bronk, Dieter, suppose you walked in the counsel of the ungodly. What would you be doing?'

'I don't know, Master.'

'You would be breaking commandments.' And here Nel would launch into a small sermon about not lying, not stealing, not coveting another man's wife; though forbidden to deliver large sermons in church, he was free to deliver small ones in school.

All his pupils, age five to fourteen, met in one squarish room furnished only with benches, and often the school seemed more riot than rote, but patiently Nel established order, and with various groups sequestered in odd corners, he taught first the five-to-seven, then the eight-to-eleven, then the twelve-to-fourteen, but the best part came each morning at eleven and each afternoon at three, for then he assembled the students in one big group. In the morning he discussed the Bible, especially the Book of Joshua, which proved that God had chosen the Boers for some special task; in the afternoon he taught Dutch, or rather, the semi-Dutch of the frontier. He was a lively actor and would tell his children, 'I can speak English as well as anyone at Graaff-Reinet.' And here he would become a magistrate or a Scots minister, offering a fairly garbled English. 'But when I am a true man, I speak Dutch. Learn this manly language. Hold on to it.'

In a year of Nel's teaching a child might learn what he or she could have mastered in two weeks at a real school, but would certainly learn a wealth of moral instruction which children in better schools never acquired.

He had one weakness as a schoolmaster, and the farmers who employed him could not correct it. 'I am,' he told them, 'first and last a sick-comforter,' and if anyone in the region fell ill or approached death, he felt obligated to appear at the bedside. This meant that his school went unattended, and for this he was rebuked, but he told Balthazar Bronk, 'God has two concerns in the Graaff-Reinet district. That his young people get started right on their journey through life. That his old people get started right on their journey to heaven. In both instances I am the teacher.'

He was indeed a sick-comforter. With dying men he recalled their vigorous contributions to Boer society; with women he reminded them of the essential role they played in producing and rearing good people. He made the termination of life respectable, proper, inevitable, a thing to be as much appreciated as a beginning: 'You have seen the meadows fill with grain. You have seen six cattle multiply to sixty-six. These have been the signs of a good life, and through them God has marked you for salvation.'

In strict obedience to John Calvin's teaching, he was convinced that every human being he met was destined either for heaven or for hell, and he usually knew which; but this did not mean that he treated the condemned with any less benevolence than he treated the saved, and in the final moments whenever a dying person asked, 'Dominee, am I to be saved?' he replied, 'I am not a dominee, and I often wonder whether I am saved. This crooked back. This blemished eye. All I know about you is what I know about myself. In this life God has been just to me, and I'm sure He will be so in the next.'

The Van Doorns became personally affected by Nel's dual functions when the old grandmother fell ill. Wilhelmina was past sixty and her life was ending in a painful sickness. Nel, hearing of this, closed school and rode the horse his farmers had given him over to De Kraal, where he said simply, 'I am told Ouma is dying.'

'She is,' Tjaart said, tears marring his broad face and beard. 'She built this farm.' He led Nel to the dark room in which the old woman lay, and the first thing Theunis did was open the blinds and the windows. He then stepped to the bedside and spoke to Wilhelmina as if she were one of his scholars: 'Now tell me how you got this farm,' and when she had spoken only a few words, he interrupted, ran to the kitchen and told Tjaart, 'You must assemble all the children, immediately. Ouma wants to talk with them.'

She had in no way indicated that she wished to speak with her grandchildren, but Nel recognized that she possessed words of importance which ought to be passed from one generation to the next. So when they were all assembled, Nel arranged them in the sickroom and said, 'The generations of man are but as the winnowing of grain, and when the chaff is blown aside, the wheat must be treasured.'

'What in hell is he talking about?' Tjaart whispered.

'This Ouma who lies here with us has had a powerful life, and you must know about it, and tell it to your children's children.' And with this he started Wilhelmina on the story of how she had come to De Kraal.

In a wispy voice, sensing that she had only hours to live, she began: 'I lived by the sea in a family that knew not God, and a passing smous told me that up north a good man had lost his wife, so I got on my horse, and without saying goodbye to anyone I left that wrong house, rode north and told your father . . .' She was speaking to Tjaart, who listened dumfounded.

'They called your father the Hammer, which was an ugly name, really, and not at all the proud one he thought. But we needed a Hammer. Forty times or more he rode off, and always I prayed that I would see him come back.'

One thing worried her: 'Lodevicus died because he did a wrong thing. He offered to betray his government. I am ashamed . . .' Here she broke down momentarily, then said an unfortunate thing: 'I want to tell you about Nachtmaal at Graaff-Reinet. We went four times, I think, and the farmers were always glad . . .'

At the mention of Nachtmaal, Tjaart thought hungrily of that exquisite girl, but he stopped when he became aware that someone near him was sobbing. It was Minna. Death she could tolerate, but Nachtmaal carried memories too bitter to accept. Dashing from the death-room, she ran from the house and toward the hills that protected De Kraal.

'You must find her a husband,' the dying Ouma said. 'I rode alone more than a hundred miles to find your father, Tjaart.'

One of the children asked, 'Were there lions when you rode, Ouma?'

'There were lions,' she said.

When Theunis Nel began riding over to the Van Doorn farm after the death of Wilhelmina, it was ostensibly to report on the progress of the children, but after a third visit Jakoba took Tjaart aside: 'When he first came I thought it was to have a good meal. You know how the Bronks scrimp on food.'

'He eats practically nothing.'

'Do you know why? He's courting Minna. It's ridiculous. Tell him to stay away.'

'Minna!' Tjaart sat down heavily. 'Do you think . . .'

That afternoon he rode over to the school and invited Theunis Nel to dine, and the eagerness with which the little schoolmaster accepted convinced Tjaart that Jakoba had made a shrewd guess. That night both the Van Doorns scanned the teacher as he toyed with his food, and after he departed they whispered together.

'It's wrong, Tjaart. He's older than you.'

'I'm not so old.'

'But Minna's—'

'I know what Minna is. She's nearly sixteen, a woman without a man. And she's not so well-favored that she'll easily catch a good one now.'

These blunt truths brought tears, and Jakoba asked, 'What can we do?'

'We can encourage Theunis Nel.'

'You can't mean to marry her?'

'That's exactly what I mean.'

'But she's a girl. He's an old man.'

'Any woman past fifteen is thirty years old, or forty, or fifty, or whatever is required. When Nel comes to sit with Minna, you make him welcome.'

But how to inform the schoolmaster that he was free to sit with Mejuffrouw van Doorn in the opening stages of a formal courtship? Tjaart solved the problem in what he deemed a subtle way: 'Theunis, I've ridden over here to tell you that you've done wonders with our grandchildren. I have a daughter, you may have met her, I think. She ought to learn her letters, too, and we will pay you extra . . .'

'I'm sure I could arrange some free time,' Nel said, and he entered upon the most hectic period of his life: school all day, sick-comforting many nights, nine miles to De Kraal; instructing Minna at night; and helping everywhere on unforeseen tasks.

Sometimes Tjaart and Jakoba would peer into the kitchen, and there would be the schoolmaster, gazing raptly at Minna as she laboriously copied her alphabet. 'I wonder if she knows?' Tjaart asked, and Jakoba said, 'Women always know.'

And one night after Nel had departed, so weary that he fell asleep on his horse and allowed the beast to take him back to the school, Minna told her parents, 'I think he wants to speak with you, Father.' But having reported this, as she had promised Theunis she would, she burst into tears. 'But I'm in love with Ryk Naudé. I always will be.'

'Minna,' her mother said sternly, 'he's gone.'

'But I can't marry that schoolmaster.'

Jakoba shook her and said, 'When a woman's past fifteen she must make the best bargain.'

'You want me to marry him?'

'You heard what Nel said. "The generations of man are but as the winnowing of wheat." '

'I still don't know what that means,' Tjaart protested.

'It means a woman must do what she has to,' Jakoba said.

Two nights later Theunis Nel, wearing the best clothes he could command, appeared in the kitchen, and when Minna spread her papers, he brushed them aside: 'Tonight I speak with you, Mijnheer van Doorn.'

'Yes?' Tjaart said.

'Mijnheer van Doorn'—the schoolmaster spoke as if he were sixteen and Tjaart seventy—'I have the great honor of asking whether I might have the hand of your daughter Minna . . .'

When Minna heard these fateful words and saw the pitiful man that spoke them she might have broken into a sob had not her mother anticipated such a scene and grabbed her daughter's wrist furiously, as if to say, You cannot.

'I am older,' Nel continued, 'and have no farm . . .'

'But you're a good man,' Jakoba said, and she pushed her daughter forward.

'Theunis,' Tjaart said, 'we welcome you into our family.'

'Oh!' the schoolmaster gasped. Recovering his composure, he said, 'Can we all ride to Graaff-Reinet for the wedding?'

'Not in these troubled times,' Tjaart said. 'But you can start the marriage, and whenever a dominee comes this way . . .'

'I could not,' the devout little man protested, unable to imagine living with a woman before vows had been solemnized. 'I must pray on this.'

'Go ahead,' Tjaart said, eager to have his daughter married. 'But I've noticed that whenever men pray on this subject, the answer's always yes. Do you want Minna to ride with you to Bronk's?'

'I must pray.'

It was Minna who answered that particular prayer. 'You heard what Wilhelmina did when she married Lodevicus. She rode one hundred miles.

The school's nine miles. I'm riding with you.' Tjaart van Doorn had found a son-in-law.

In December 1834 it seemed as if all of Tjaart's uncertainties were laid to rest. Theunis and Minna returned to help run the farm, and the English government began to show common sense in running the country. But almost immediately trouble resumed, for the Xhosa launched a series of forays deep into Boer country, and all commandos were summoned to Grahamstown to strengthen the English regular troops and their civilian helpers like Saltwood. 'We're dealing not with hundreds of Xhosa warriors,' the commanding officer said, 'but thousands. An invasion of our colony is under way.'

After fourteen rugged days in the saddle, Tjaart's men were given a week's furlough; they were farmers, not soldiers, and their first responsibility lay in ensuring the safety of their homestead and flocks. As the tired men rode back to Grahamstown, a place Tjaart had grown to love for its hospitality, Saltwood spoke seriously: 'Piet Retief is talking about pulling out of here and emigrating north. If that good man leaves, it's obvious to me you'll all go. I think that's a mistake. You and I have proved that Boers and Englishmen can live together.'

'Your laws go against the Bible.'

'Against the Old Bible, not the New.'

'It's the Old that counts.'

'Be that as it may, if you ever decide to go north, I'd be very interested in your farm. It's the best in this area.'

'I'd not care to sell.'

'Then why did you buy that new wagon?'

Tjaart reflected on this. He refused to concede that he had acquired the wagon in order to emigrate, even though his wife had been counseling this for some time. 'I bought it because a farmer needs good tools,' he had told his sons. But gradually he admitted that he might also have done so because there was in the air a desire for life unimpeded by English law and custom. Perhaps Jakoba had been right. Perhaps they should go north and form a new nation.

But such thoughts fled from him when he and De Groot came over the last hill to De Kraal, for from its summit they looked down on a scene of devastation: all parts of the barn that were not of stone were burned away; the wooden shed attached to the house was burned; and in the space between barn and house stood what had been the new wagon, all parts charred and shattered.

'Great God!' Tjaart shouted, spurring his horse to find what might have happened to his family. 'De Groot!' he cried from the ashes. 'They've all been killed.'

But a search of the ruins uncovered no bodies, and now Tjaart feared that his family had been take captive. A wide-ranging search for spoor finally disclosed a trail leading to a faraway glen, and there they found Theunis Nel, the women, the children and the slaves—safe and hungry. His sons had been slain.

'Theunis saved us,' Jakoba said quietly when Tjaart embraced her. 'How?'

A Coloured servant, grateful that he was still alive, replied, 'Two guns. We fight one hour. We move back, step by step. We kill many. They go.'

Theunis had supervised the brilliant retreat which had saved the remnants of the Van Doorn family. Curiously, he had fired neither of the guns; Jakoba had used one, a Coloured shepherd the other. But it had been Theunis who had kept the group together and picked the route of their escape.

When Tjaart asked the would-be dominee, 'How did you find the courage, Theunis?' Nel replied, 'I had to. Minna's pregnant, you know.'

Six hundred miles away in Cape Town it was New Year's Eve, and guests at the Governor's Ball were saying it was the finest entertainment ever staged at the Cape. The ladies and gentlemen of the capital were resplendent in modish suits and gowns, but what really gave dazzling romance to the occasion were the immaculately uniformed English officers who moved through the festive crowd like valiant princes. The guests had come from every corner of the western Cape, and among them were the Trianon Van Doorns, one of the most prosperous of the older Cape Dutch families.

There were now more than twenty thousand people in the bustling town, a chaotic mix of wild irreverent seaport and nascent commercial center. Shops offering the fashions of Europe, fine blended teas and spices of Ceylon and Java, exquisite silks from China; little nooks where silversmiths crafted their precious wares; and a gentleman like Baron von Ludwig, who could advise on snuffs and tobaccos—all flourished. Comfortable hotels and clubs where the latest news from 'home' could be pondered at leisure stood alongside bawdy taverns with their Gentoo hostesses, stable yards, chandlers, the workshops of Malay carpenters, alleys jammed with the shacks of Coloureds and poor whites.

The gentry lived well in their fine town houses or in the gabled grandeur of their farms, devoting their energies to establishing the great Cape families of the future while debating such disparate subjects as the vexatious loss of their slaves and the newfangled bathing machine that would enable them to immerse their bodies in the Atlantic, 'a process which guarantees medicinal benefit.'

Much of the talk on this night at the ball centered upon the hunt, that New Year's Day event featuring scarlet-jacketed men led by the governor himself in thunderous pursuit of the fox of the veld, the jackal. 'Damn good job, too,' one crusty major cried. 'Gives one a touch of the old country, eh, what? Helps rid the farmer of his pests. Sporting show, what? Takes an English countryman to show these Boers how to make the best of this country.' He sealed his opinion with a mighty draught of port.

Outside the Castle, this New Year's was special too; the black and brown slaves were enjoying their first day of freedom. A huge crowd of these persons, with a horde of children, had gathered at the Lutheran church, their eye on the steeple clock that would announce the New Year. The children were whooping and yelling, impatient for the giant fireworks promised for midnight. At dawn next day they would receive their presents, as always.

At Government House the regimental band, augmented by the best town musicians, struck up another waltz, and there was an enthusiastic cheer as the garrison's lieutenant-colonel led his pretty wife onto the floor. Henry George Wakelyn Smith was a reedy, hawk-faced young officer whose reputation pleased both his soldiers and the Cape civilians. He had conducted himself with rare bravery while serving under the Duke of Wellington in the Spanish campaign against Napoleon, and had been honored, but he insisted upon being known as plain Harry Smith, one of fourteen children from an impoverished family. And he positively loved playing at war.

If the locals were proud of Harry, they adored his wife. Everyone knew of the gallant manner in which he had won her. At the siege of Badajoz, when he led his troops in their final assault on that city, two Spanish children, one a young girl, came running from the French-held lines in tears: 'Soldiers have killed our parents. And look! They've ripped the rings from our ears.'

Young Smith took one look at Juanita and declared to a friend, 'There has never been a lovelier lady.' And forthwith he married her, even though she was only fourteen and a Catholic. They formed one of the notable married couples in history, a marvelous, well-matched pair. He entertained the public with his bravery, she with her guitar. Years after this first sojourn at the Cape, Sir Harry would return as governor, and Juanita would be worshipped by everyone.

On this night, as he waltzed with her, Harry saw one of the governor's aides enter the hall and with grave gestures beckon him. Graciously he deposited his lady with friends, and without betraying any excitement, walked slowly to the governor's study.

'The Kaffirs have broken through all our frontier lines. Grahamstown and the Boer commandos can't hold them back. They're destroying everything in their path. Burning and pillaging.'

Without hesitation Harry said, 'I shall go.'

'It will be weeks before a warship can get you there.'

'Forget the damned navy. I'll ride.' Then he bowed slightly. 'Sir, midnight is almost here. Would it not be proper for us to rejoin the ladies?'

In the ballroom, as the eleventh hour ended, a great cheer went up and the band played that exquisite song of nostalgia 'Auld Lang Syne.' Harry Smith, aware that he must soon be off across the continent, clasped Juanita tightly as he voiced with her the words of Robert Burns:

> 'We twa hae run about the braes,
> And pu'd the gowans fine;
> But we've wandered mony a weary foot
> Sin' auld lang syne.
>
> We twa hae paidl'd in the burn,
> Frae morning sun till dine;
> But seas between us braid hae roar'd
> Sin' auld lang syne.'

From outside came the explosion of fireworks and cries of delight from those who welcomed 1835.

Harry and Juanita left the dance immediately. After a brief three hours' rest he kissed her farewell, buckled on his saber, picked up dispatches for the frontier, and rode out into the night as the citizens slept soundly in preparation for the next day's revelry.

At dawn Smith was well east of Cape Town, and in six days he covered the six hundred miles to Grahamstown, where, without resting, he took command.

The governor, Sir Benjamin D'Urban, sorely frightened by the Xhosa invasion, arrived himself on January 14, and soon Englishmen and Boers, two thousand strong, were ready, accompanied by their three hundred Coloured militiamen. 'We shall thrash the Kaffirs,' Smith said, but it took seven months to make good his threat. However, with men like Tjaart van Doorn and Richard Saltwood at his side he proved tireless . . . and merciless. After one three-week push, he announced with satisfaction, 'I have burned two thousand, seven hundred and sixteen huts. That'll teach 'em.' But in a more sober mood he estimated correctly: 'It would take me one hundred thousand of England's finest to crush these Xhosa.'

When finally he had forced them back to their own territory he returned to Grahamstown, where triumphal arches lauded him as the victor of the frontier, the subduer of the rebellion. 'We shall now have peace,' he declared.

But peace depended primarily upon the actions of Sir Benjamin, who had arrived at the Cape filled with the preachments of Dr. Simon Keer. However, service with a realist like Harry Smith, plus personal experience on the battlefront, had induced a radical change of mind. In his perceptive report on the Sixth Kaffir War he informed London that 'this fertile and beautiful province is almost a desert, and the murders which have gone hand in hand with this work of pillage and rapine have deeply aggravated its atrocity.' He added that in his opinion the Kaffirs were irreclaimable savages: 'Merciless barbarians who have driven our seven thousand farmers to utter destitution.'

Desirous of preventing a repetition, and eager, as an honest man, to formulate a just settlement, he annexed a vast territory, erected a chain of forts, and moved every man he could to garrison the land. Friendly blacks who had not participated in the war were invited to remain where they were, and new lands would be opened up for Boer and English settlers.

It was a sensible solution and went a long way toward compensating the farmers for their grievous losses, but when the costs of the war had been totted up, Sir Benjamin stuck assegais in a large map to indicate the extent of the huge losses suffered by the white men: 100 slain, 800 farms burned, 119,000 cattle stolen, 161,000 sheep missing. Coloured suffered comparably.

When news of this prudent settlement reached London, Dr. Keer stormed Parliament: 'The blacks were fully justified in their attempts to reclaim lands that were rightfully theirs. Three thousand of these gentle, helpless people are dead, martyrs in their struggle against the systematic injustice of the Boer and his new ally, the scum of England who live along the frontier.'

Keer won the propaganda war. The sensible peace arranged by D'Urban and Smith was annulled, with the annexed territory being returned to the blacks. D'Urban was recalled in semi-disgrace, and Harry Smith was left powerless: 'How am I to eat up Kaffirs with a lawbook?'

Keer and his philanthropicals had a simple answer: 'Send considerate English officials to live among our black friends and make good English citizens of them.' They also suggested the establishment of a dozen new Golans in which missionaries could offer refuge.

It didn't work. The frontier slipped back into tension and anxiety, and in region after region the Boers, now smitten by a vicious drought that withered their crops, met quietly, some amid the ruins of the farms, and said, 'To hell with these Englishmen!'

Tjaart's attention to these grievances was diverted when his daughter Minna, about to deliver her first child, became persuaded that because of her husband's imperfect appearance, her baby would be a misshapen monster: 'I can feel him in my belly. He's fighting to get out. Because he's grotesque and evil.'

She became so convinced that she was about to bear some hideous thing, and that the fault was her husband's, that she could not tolerate his presence. 'I look at him,' she whimpered, 'and all I see is that crookbackt. Then he stares at me like a wounded bird and I see that pitiful eye, always weeping. God cursed him, and now Theunis has passed the curse along to our son.'

She often became hysterical, and when Tjaart heard of her rantings he grew angry: 'Damnit, Minna, thousands of women have babies every year. Mevrouw Bronk has how many?'

'This wife has twelve'— Minna sniffed—'but her husband is a whole man.'

'So is your husband. He saved your life, didn't he?'

'He couldn't even fire a gun. Mama had to. I know my son is going to be all bent and twisted.'

Her obsession grew so strong that as time for delivery approached, Theunis had to leave the poor hut that served as their temporary home, taking residence with a Du Toit family that had three boys in school. These boys heard about their teacher's troubles at home, and even the cause, and rowdier lads began to torment Nel, but when Tjaart heard of this he stormed into the school, brusquely told Theunis to wait outside, and threatened to thrash the entire student body if there was any more of this nonsense.

'Your teacher is my friend,' he growled. 'A good, decent man, and as you've been whispering, he's going to be a father in a few days.'

'Du Toit says the thing's going to be a monster.'

'Who's Du Toit?' And when that boy stood, Tjaart rushed at him, stopping with his face close to the boy's: 'If I hit you, you'd bounce through that wall.'

No one laughed, for the menace was real. But immediately Tjaart relaxed and said quietly, 'Du Toit, go fetch the master.' And when the bewildered teacher returned, dabbing at his eye, Tjaart said, 'Boys, his son will be my grandson. And my father was Lodevicus the Hammer. We raise only the best.'

He quieted the schoolboys but not his daughter, and now her apprehensions contaminated him, so that when Minna was about to have her baby, and women filled the hut, he fell into a sweat greater than any he had known when his own children were being born. As he paced near the doorway during the agonizing wait, he could see ill-formed cripples drifting across his vision, and he prayed that this child would be whole: God, this is an empty land. We need all the young ones we can get, and we need them strong.

Cries came from inside, then women running out: 'A beautiful baby girl!'

Brushing people out of his way, he rushed into the hut, then slowly went to the cot and picked up the naked infant. Holding it aloft by its heels, he inspected it from all angles, satisfied himself that it was perfect, then returned it gently to Minna's arms: 'Thank you, daughter. Not a blemish. I must tell Theunis.'

He galloped the miles to the school, where he crashed into the room, shouting, 'Theunis! It's a girl. Perfect in every detail.' Then he pointed at the Du Toit boy who had led the disturbances: 'You, fetch some water.' For although Theunis was grinning happily, it was apparent that he might faint.

The Boer frontiersmen could have withstood the drought and resisted the renewed Xhosa incursions, but now the English government insulted them with the disgraceful business of the slave payments. The Van Doorns and their Boer neighbors had been long prepared for the ultimate freeing of their slaves, and they did not object in principle, but they did sometimes wonder why England was so insistent when countries equally moral—Holland, the United States, for example—were content to hold on to their slaves.

What happened was difficult to explain and impossible to justify. The English Parliament, even though Sir Peter Saltwood, M.P., as manager of the bill had promised otherwise, refused to provide the £3,000,000 which would have compensated the Cape slaveholders for their financial losses. Such a miserly amount was voted that Tjaart would receive for his six legally owned slaves not the £600 promised, but a grudging £180. And then, because the rules were mindful of London-based magnates with vast holdings in the West Indies, it was stipulated that no Cape farmer could receive even his diminished allowance unless he traveled personally to London to collect it.

'I don't understand,' Tjaart said, endeavoring to unravel these incredible instructions.

'It's simple,' Lukas de Groot said as he listened to the law with a group of Boers. 'Instead of six hundred pounds, you get one-third. And to get this, you have to trek to Cape Town, six weeks, then take a ship to London, four months, then back by ship, then trek back home. Better part of a year.' And the reader added, 'Look at this line at the bottom.' There it was: *Any*

claimant who comes to London must pay a filing fee of £1-10-6 per slave to
cover the cost of drafting the papers.

Tjaart was outraged. Under these insane regulations, there could not be
in the entire region east of Stellenbosch one Boer slaveowner who could
collect the compensation due him, and it became obvious that this had been
London's intention. Who could absent himself from his farm for most of
a year? And who, if he did get to London, could argue before the claims
court in English, the required language?

It was such a gross injustice that it encouraged a brood of unsavory
types to circulate through the hinterlands, offering to buy up the farmers'
rights at nine shillings to the pound; some of these scavengers were Englishmen who had failed at proper work and who saw this as a device for paying
their passage back to London. The chances that any Boer would receive his
funds from this gang of thieves was remote. 'But look, Tjaart,' one of them
weasled, 'I make the trek to Cape Town for you. I sail to London for you.
I spend days in the claims courts and urge your case in English. I earn my
fee.'

'But the government owes me the whole amount,' Tjaart argued in
Dutch. 'Why should I have to pay you more than fifty per centum?'

'Because you will be here, on a farm, and I'll be in London, in court.'

'It's so unfair.'

'It's the law,' the would-be agent said with a bland smile, and Tjaart,
realizing how impotent he was to press his legal rights, would probably have
accepted the offer and received less than one-sixth of what he had originally
been promised had not a deputation ridden in from Grahamstown to prevent this injustice.

It was composed of three Englishmen at whose side Tjaart had fought
in the Xhosa war, and two of them were his special friends: Saltwood and
Carleton. 'Have you signed any papers?' Saltwood cried as he rode in.

'No.'

'Thank God. Now you, sir, leave this district or be horsewhipped.'

'I have my rights,' the man whined.

With a snap of his short hippopotamus whip, Saltwood flicked the
intruder's saddle and called to Carleton, 'Show him what you can do.' And
with a somewhat longer whip the wagon builder also struck the saddle.

'You'd better ride on,' Saltwood said, and when the man started to
protest that he had legal rights, Saltwood snapped his whip and caught him
on the leg. 'Thief, ride out of here,' he said, and the man, now thoroughly
frightened, hurried away. Throwing threats, but only after he was at a safe
distance from the whips, he started across country to other farms whose
rights he would try to buy at nine shillings to the pound.

'Disgraceful,' Saltwood said as he explained what he and Carleton were
proposing to their Boer friends: 'You've been our good allies. Without you
we'd have no town back there, and we can't stand by and see you robbed.
So you give us your claims and I'll send them to my brother in Parliament.
I promise you nothing, Tjaart, except an honest deal. We may win, we may
not, but at least you have a chance.'

As they were discussing the matter, Carleton happened to see Van
Doorn's scorched wagon and identified it as one of his: 'How did you get
it?'

'Traded for it at Graaff-Reinet.'

'You should have come to me. I'd have given you a proper price.'

'My sheep were in Graaff-Reinet.'

Carleton picked up one of the charred timbers and pointed to a small rubric carved into the wood: TC–36 (Thomas Carleton–Wagon 36). Had he been satisfied to work rapidly and without careful attention, this wagon might have been numbered in the 80s.

'You'll need a new wagon,' he said. 'When you trek north.'

Tjaart looked at him strangely. First it had been Jakoba, years ago; then Saltwood, when they were returning from the Xhosa war; and now Carleton —all saying that the Van Doorns must emigrate north, as though there were no alternative.

'Who's trekking north?' he asked.

'Haven't you heard? Hendrick Potgieter departed last week.'

'For where?'

'The north. That's all he said.'

'Alone?'

'No, he had forty or fifty people with him. Sarel Cilliers left with him, you know. And Louis Trichardt left with Van Rensburg. Months ago. Maybe ninety people and seventy or eighty servants.'

Tjaart felt weak. Things were happening at a speed and magnitude he could not comprehend, and reluctantly he conceded that perhaps his neighbors were right.

Saltwood said, 'We thought that if men like you and Piet Retief do finally decide to leave us, you must not depart with ill feelings toward us. Hell, Tjaart, you fought with us—side by side.'

So an agreement was made, whereby Saltwood took the warrants of several Boers—among them, Van Doorn and De Groot—promising to send them to Sir Peter in London to collect whatever the government might allow, but in order for the transaction to be legal, it was necessary for the Boers to sign away their rights for one shilling each, relying upon the good faith of their English friends. This the men did with absolute assurance that an honest reporting would be made, for the participants in this arrangement had fought as brothers in defense of their homes. That the Boers were now thinking of quitting those homes was as distressing to the Englishmen as it was to the Boers themselves.

Tjaart was deeply moved by the sympathy shown by Saltwood and Carleton during their visit to his still-ruined farm. In the war he had volunteered to protect the English establishments, yet the government had shown itself powerless to save Boer farms; hundreds had been ravaged, and now the government sided with the Kaffirs. However, he was convinced that the Grahamstown fighters like Saltwood genuinely sought his friendship and deplored the losses they had suffered. As he moved among the charred timbers of his barn he pondered seriously what he should do. Seeking Jakoba's counsel, he asked, 'Shall we build a new house?'

'We must go north,' she said bluntly. 'To seek free land.'

When Lukas and Rachel de Groot came south to report on the sad condition of their farm they fortified Jakoba's advice: 'We haven't the heart to build again. We're leaving.'

'To where?'

'Cross the Orange River. Then down into Natal.'

'I think I shall stay here,' Tjaart said deliberately. 'This is a good farm in a good region. I think the English will govern it well, one day.'

When the De Groots volunteered to stay and help him rebuild, he had an opportunity to see what a fine lad their boy Paulus had become. He was four, a stocky little man who wore heavy trousers like his father's. His copious blond hair was cut straight across his forehead, bobbing this way and that when he ran, and his sturdy limbs indicated the strength he already had.

In the repairs to the farm the boy took to himself many tasks that might have gone to men, such as struggling with broken timbers and keeping the cattle to their proper areas. Tjaart, looking at the lad, thought: How splendid it would be if that boy married Minna's daughter. But when his thoughts ran in this pattern they were sooner or later diverted to that dazzling girl up north, Aletta Naudé, and he wondered if he would ever see her again. He pictured the inadequacy of Ryk, and imagined various ways in which he might come to a bad end: he proved a coward and Xhosa slew him; he stole money and an English officer shot him; he led a hunting party and an elephant crushed him. Always he disappeared, leaving Aletta to be saved by Tjaart van Doorn. The years would pass, but she would never age; never do household tasks. She was forever the nubile girl he had seen in her father's shop at Graaff-Reinet.

That name came up in the conversation quite often these days. From the first Theunis Nel had felt uncomfortable about living with a girl to whom he was not married, and when she became pregnant he felt downright immoral. But now that he was the father of the beautiful girl Sybilla, he began to nag Tjaart about taking the family to Nachtmaal, 'so that we can become acceptable in the sight of the Lord.' But Tjaart had no wagon and he was loath to borrow a neighbor's; still, Theunis was so insistent in his desire to sanctify his marriage, that Tjaart had to respect him, for in his own marriages he had experienced the same emotion. He was not an overly religious man, and certainly his two wives were rugged, rough women accustomed to frontier exigencies, but they had felt vaguely uneasy until their marriages were solemnized; there was something about living with a person of the other sex which had mysterious overtones: the passing of the month, the spacing of fertility, the birth of a child, the establishment of a home, the blessing of a barn to prevent lightning. These mysteries deserved attention, and prudent men gauged their lives accordingly. If Theunis Nel, a man of God, found himself enmeshed in these human complications and sought verification, Tjaart van Doorn was not going to ridicule him, even though sanctification lay ninety-two miles away, with no wagon to cover the distance.

Slowly, slowly in the rugged mind of this stubborn Boer his enthusiasm for rebuilding De Kraal waned and another stratagem began to coalesce: If we did go to Nachtmaal, Theunis and Minna could be married and Sybilla baptized, and we'd already be well on our way to the north. Three days' turning to the east, we'd be on the track the others took. The De Groots could ride in their good wagon. And I'm sure he'd help me build something usable on the burned frame.

Once he came close to weeping when he thought of that fine wagon, charred to dust in the ruin of his farm. But something could be built. The rims of the wheels were there, some of the fittings.

Very cautiously he said to Theunis, 'You are right. We must have a marriage and a baptism. In Graaff-Reinet.' That's all that was said, but everyone within the enfolding hills at De Kraal understood that the Van Doorns were preparing to abandon the farm they had spent sixty years in perfecting. The women began to sort away things for which they would have no space. The men sold off the weaker cattle. And little Paulus, approaching five, carried a hammer and banged away at everything.

No one mentioned a date for their leaving, but someone said casually that Nachtmaal would start in seven weeks. No one picked up the comment, yet day by day departure became more inevitable, and one day when Tjaart came upon his wife gathering eggs he saw that she was close to weeping. 'What a woman! You shout at me, "Go north!" and when I start, you weep.' She denied this.

He had a bad moment himself one morning when two Coloured herdsmen shouted, 'Baas! Baas! Look what come!' There, entering the farmlands from the hills at the southwest, came seventeen sable antelope, the most beautiful creatures in Africa, stately dark animals with white blazes across their faces and incredible scimitar horns that curved backward from the head, reaching forty, fifty inches. No purpose for these horns had ever been demonstrated; they swung so far back that they could not possibly be used in fighting. Perhaps, just perhaps, they were intended merely to be beautiful.

All the Van Doorns came from the house to witness this elegant parade. 'They must be the last ones south of the Orange River,' Tjaart said. 'See how gently they lift their feet.' How beautiful they were, how stately, this remnant of a great herd now diminished. Never before had they been seen at De Kraal, and their quiet passage across the farm seemed to presage a similar movement of the Van Doorns.

That night, while the majesty of the sables lingered in the valley, Tjaart said simply, 'We'll be following them north. Our life, too, has been used up here,' and once these words were thrown into the air, Jakoba and Minna felt free to weep.

If ever a group of people entered their exile with heavy hearts and moral reluctance it was the Van Doorns, and they spent one night drafting a letter of justification to their English neighbors in Grahamstown and their Boer friends in Graaff-Reinet. Tjaart began by saying, 'I think we've all heard the statement the Americans made when they broke away from England. I'm sure we must do the same.' And with ample guidance from Theunis, plus an occasional strong remark from Lukas de Groot, he compiled these thoughts which appeared in the papers of each community:

When in the course of human events a group of people decide to leave their homes, they must, out of decent respect for their neighbors, explain why they are doing so. We leave our farms with sadness, our neighbors with deep regret, but we can do no other. Our reasons for leaving will be adjudged by all good men to be just and reasonable.

The ravages of the past war show to the world that this Government is incapable of protecting our farmers against invasions of the Kaffir, and it has removed the last hope for an effective barrier to keep these hordes out of the colony.

Government has taken our slaves from us without compensating us adequately or honestly. It has ridiculed our traditional way of handling slaves and has listened only to contumelious adversaries who parade up and down England preaching lies and defamations. The honest citizens of this land, who live with the problem, have not been listened to.

Government has placed in the pulpits of our church predikants unfamiliar with our language. It has sent us officials to try our law cases who cannot understand the words we speak in our defense. It fills our schools with teachers who erase our children's knowledge of their mother tongue.

We leave soil claimed by the English Government without rancor, or threats, or ill will. We pay testimony to the good people of English heritage who have befriended us and we wish them and their nation well. We are satisfied in our hearts that we owe England no further obligations, and we are sure that the Government will allow us to depart in peace, for all we seek is to establish in the north a nation more obedient to God's rule.

Well after midnight, when five of the six participants judged that they had made a complete and honest statement, Jakoba startled them by pointing out that they had omitted their most important grievance, and when Tjaart asked, 'What might that be?' she explained. And after prayerful discussion her husband obediently added this paragraph, which came closer to the truth than any of the others; for that reason it would be widely quoted throughout the world:

Through a series of unfortunate laws Government has tried to alter the natural relationship between the races, exalting the savage and debasing the Christian. It has asked us to form a society in which the proper distance between master and servant is not respected. This is against the teaching of God Himself and we cannot surrender to it. God has said that there shall be master and servant, and that each shall keep his proper place, and we propose to form a new nation in obedience to that law, one in which people of all color shall have their proper place, under the guidance of those whom God has elected to lead them.

At four that morning the Van Doorns and De Groots, a trivial group in the large movements of mankind, confirmed with prayer the fact that they were heading not only to the Nachtmaal at Graaff-Reinet, but on to a world they could not even imagine. The Great Trek was under way. The Voortrekkers were in motion.

On the afternoon that Tjaart's letter appeared in the *Graham's Town Journal,* Major Richard Saltwood and Thomas Carleton saddled their horses, rasped out a series of orders to their servants, and galloped westward to intercept the Voortrekkers before they left De Kraal.

They arrived in time to see the wagons loaded, and they stood in shock to witness the pitiful thing in which Van Doorn proposed to carry his worldly goods into exile: 'Those wheels won't get them to Graaff-Reinet.' But of this they said nothing.

'We can't let you go away like this,' Saltwood said. 'You've been our brothers-in-arms.'

With a sweep of his hand Van Doorn indicated the ramshackle buildings: 'This is what is left of generations of Van Doorns.'

'I know,' Saltwood said.

'And the slave money. Will we ever get our share?'

'There's no word from London, Tjaart. These things take time.'

'We have no more time.'

'Tjaart, how old are you?'

'Forty-seven.'

'I thought so. You and I are twins. Same year. You are my brother, and I want to buy your farm, because I respect it.'

'This?' The two men looked about them.

'Yes. I can finish rebuilding it. I want my home here.'

'You would pay for this?'

'Yes. We made a kind of deal, last year. It wasn't your fault the facts changed.'

So they spent that day discussing what a fair price would be, and where the road north would take them, and whether they would ever return. Evening prayers were held, with Theunis Nel translating the Bible in his own inspired way, one-third Bible, two-thirds Theunis.

In the morning it became apparent that for some reason the Englishmen were reluctant to depart, and their stay was so protracted that finally Jakoba asked bluntly, 'When are you leaving?' and Carleton said, 'We have a present for you,' and after a painful hour, over the eastern rim of hills appeared twelve oxen dragging a new Carleton wagon with a tidy disselboom, a fine set of patented brakes, and a double canvas cover to keep out the rain and heat. On a board under the body was burned the rubric TC-43.

'I need my sheep for the journey north,' Tjaart said.

'You owe us no sheep,' Carleton replied. 'You helped us start our colony. We help you start yours.'

'I think we should have a prayer,' Theunis said, and from Exodus he wrenched four timely texts about Israelites moving across the Red Sea and toward their promised land. 'We are the new Israelites,' he said, whereupon the men who had fought together so many times started their farewells.

When the new wagon was packed and the five men were preparing to go their separate ways—two Englishmen back to Grahamstown, three Boer families north to lands unknown—an incident occurred which seemed at the time to be of no significance, whereas in fact it altered the history of South Africa.

A bold and cunning Xhosa prophet named Mhlakaza, with a ridged scar across his forehead, had taken advantage of the confusion following the war to slip into the area to spy out the amount of damage done in the recent raids. Not realizing that five armed men were ahorse, he suddenly appeared on the horizon in a silhouette so exposed that any one of the men could have shot and killed him.

Automatically Tjaart van Doorn raised his rifle to do so, but his son-in-law Theunis grabbed at his arm and cried, 'No! He's done nothing.' So Tjaart lowered his gun, and the Xhosa, laughing derisively, disappeared from view.

If Tjaart had killed him, and in the presence of two Englishmen, word would certainly have filtered back to London; Dr. Keer would have asked persistent questions; a scandal would have ensued, proving once more the heartlessness of the Boer; and quite possibly Tjaart would have been hanged. So it was fortunate that Theunis restrained him.

On the other hand, if Tjaart *had* killed this crafty man, the lives of many thousands of Xhosa would have been saved, a noble people would have been preserved at full strength, and the history of this area would have been dramatically modified.

On 15 March 1836 the Van Doorn party, as it came to be called, crossed the Orange River—that moody giant between banks of sand—leaving the jurisdiction of England and heading into those vast lands which Mal Adriaan had explored seventy years earlier.

Through gradual accretions the group now consisted of nineteen families with seventeen wagons. The latter number was most significant in that it was the smallest number that would allow the formation of a proper cordon, or laager, inside which women, children and cattle could be protected.

The emigrant party contained nineteen grown men, but this included Theunis Nel, deemed largely useless despite his heroic performance when the Xhosa overran De Kraal, and an equal number of mature women, making thirty-eight adults, all battle-tested. They had among them ninety-eight children: some, like the daughter of Theunis and Minna, mere infants; others, like the older sons of some of the families, almost men, well capable of handling a gun.

So there were a hundred and thirty-six white people, but they were attended by two hundred Coloureds and blacks. In most cases these servants had received reasonably good treatment on the farms and had come to accept that they belonged with the Boers, not in the way a slave belongs to an owner, but in a paternalistic pattern, as much a part of the white family as the children.

These servants had remained loyal when others had run off, and they saw no reason to leave the baas now. His life was theirs; they would find no other work they liked better; they were as excited as he by this adventure of heading into unexplored lands. They'd accept an old pair of shoes or a tattered jacket with a smiling 'Dankie, Baas,' a scolding with a great show of misery. And between the good and the bad, if they met with other Coloureds or blacks, they would argue that their baas was the best in the land. To show that they meant it, most were prepared to die for 'their' white people.

Each of the seventeen wagons had a span of from twelve to sixteen oxen, plus half a dozen spares; all men, most boys and many of the Coloureds had horses. And the party as a whole had two thousand cattle and eleven hundred sheep, which explained why the Voortrekkers were lucky if they covered six miles a day.

Of the hundred and thirty-six Boers, only two men could read, Tjaart van Doorn and Theunis Nel, but all could recite long passages from the Bible, and as they prepared to enter a new land, they compared themselves constantly with the ancient Hebrews who appeared in the Book of Joshua. Night after night, when the wagons were assembled, not in laager, for there was as yet no enemy, Theunis Nel, in the manner of a predikant, would read from that chapter and apply the lessons of that noble journey to conditions faced by the Voortrekkers. Inevitably the Boers came to believe that they were a reincarnation of Joshua's army and that God watched over them, too:

> Now therefore arise, go over this Jordan, thou, and all this people, unto the land which I do give to them, even to the children of Israel. Every place that the sole of your foot shall tread upon, that I have given unto you . . . There shall not any man be able to stand before thee all the days of thy life . . . I will not fail thee, nor forsake thee . . . Only be thou strong and very courageous, that thou mayest observe to do according to all the law . . . turn not from it to the right hand or to the left, that thou mayest prosper withersoever thou goest.

One other characteristic of the Voortrekkers applied particularly to the Van Doorn party: all the adult men, except the unfortunate Theunis Nel, had had more than one wife, and he was lucky to have any. If one took seven leaders of seven representative groups, the number of their wives would be 2-2-3-3-3-4-5, and seven typical ages for the brides would be 13-13-14-15-29-31-34, the first series proving that men liked their wives young, the last indicating that no woman was allowed to remain a widow long. When men were Old Testament patriarchs, as these men were, they used up their women.

They were in general an intransigent, opinionated group of Dutchmen whose isolation had caused them to turn their backs on the liberalizing influences of the eighteenth century, except that Tjaart himself had quoted

from the American Declaration of Independence in laying forth his reasons
for emigrating. They felt no need for Rousseau, Locke, Kant or the German
theologians who had begun to expose the mythological elements in the Old
Testament. They were satisfied with the fundamentals their Dutch and
Huguenot ancestors had brought with them in the middle 1600s and rejected
any new ideas imported by the English. Above all, they were self-confident,
so that when one Voortrekker came upon a little stream running due north,
he had no hesitation in announcing, 'This is the beginning of the Nile River,'
even though that body lay a good two thousand miles away—and forthwith
he christened it Nylstroom (Nile Stream).

The wagons in which they would live for the next two or three years
were special affairs, not at all like the great lumbering things that crossed
the American prairies. They were small, only twelve to fifteen feet long, and
rather low to the ground, except that when a canvas shelter was thrown over
the top, they appeared higher. They were surprisingly narrow, and were so
packed with family possessions that there was no room to sleep inside,
except for the mother, who made a rough bed for herself atop the baggage.
The iron-banded wheels were invariable: small front ones with ten spokes,
larger back ones with fourteen.

A superior feature of the Voortrekker wagon was its disselboom, the
pivoted main shaft that was so fixed to the front axle that it provided
maximum flexibility in both guiding and in riding easily over the bumpy
trail. But only the last pair of oxen were harnessed to the disselboom; all
others pulled against chains and harness that were attached to the wagon
in various ways.

Since nearly two thousand wagons would participate in the early move
to the north, trails became marked across the veld, but many parties like
the Van Doorn struck off on their own, making their way over the veld from
one conspicuous flat-topped hill to the next.

It was a habit of the Voortrekkers to linger at any congenial spot,
sometimes for a week, at other times for a month. Then the wagons would
be brought into proximity, but not in laager, and the men would ride far
afield to hunt while the women tended to sewing, and the making of needed
articles, and the baking of special dishes. Jakoba was particularly pleased
when the wagons halted at some spot which contained a good supply of ant
hills, for as a girl she had learned how to utilize these remarkable constructions that rose two and three feet above the veld, shining like little red-sand
mountains.

Selecting a sturdy one off by itself, she would take a heavy stick and
break open a small hole at the spot where the side of the dome touched the
earth; she was careful not to disturb the upper part of the ant hill, for it was
this dome which ensured fruitful use. When the hole was broken, a flood
of small black ants scurried about the landscape and soon disappeared.
Then the opening was crammed with sticks, leaves and other flammable
debris and set afire; for an hour or so it blazed and smoldered, becoming
in due course an effective, excellent oven in which all kinds of food could
be prepared.

Jakoba liked to bake her bread in such ovens, but she also knew how
to prepare a delicious toasted curry dish made of antelope strips bathed in
a sauce flavored with dried onions. The men were so fond of this that as

they traveled they kept an eye alert for ant hills, and the women learned that when such were plentiful, there would probably be a restful halt. And if there were no hills, they prepared a bobotie.

The determined movement of these Voortrekkers must not be thought of as a gallop across the landscape toward a known, specific destination; it was more like the slow displacement of a small village—with all the utensils, the babies' cribs, and the cattle moving patiently along.

But in one startling aspect the trek did not resemble the slow displacement of a town: among the fourteen thousand Boers who would ultimately travel north, there was not one clergyman. The Dutch Reformed Church, which had played, and would play, so significant a role in the history of the Boers, refused to sanction the mass exodus, and for substantial reasons: it suspected that the exiles represented a revolutionary spirit, and Calvinism could not tolerate that; it feared that the farmers were moving away from church influence, and this had to be opposed; and it felt uneasy about unauthorized movement into unexplored territory, since in such unfamiliar land the dominance of the church might be diminished. Resolutely the church turned its back on the emigrants, castigated them as revolutionaries and ignored their pleas for assistance.

More remarkable was the fact that in the most significant event in South African history, individual predikants also cut themselves off from the people, with many dominees flatly refusing to accompany the wanderers. The Voortrekkers, one of the most religious people on earth, with a profound reliance upon the Bible, were thus rejected by their own church. There could be no baptisms, marriages, solemnized burials, or even weekly services, yet at the end of the travail the Voortrekkers would be even more solidly supportive of their church than they had been at the beginning, and after having refused the travelers the services of religion, the Dutch Reformed Church would gather the emigrants back into its hands, converting the whole nation into a theocracy.

The man who suffered most in this strange development was Theunis Nel. Acutely aware of the Voortrekkers' spiritual needs, and grieved by the refusal of his church to help, he volunteered at various intervals to serve as substitute predikant, but invariably the majority rejected him on the grounds of his blemished eye and crookbackt.

He did not complain. Patiently he bore his wife's scorn, the ridicule of his fellow travelers, the lack of support from leaders like Van Doorn and De Groot. He tended the sick, tried to teach the children, and recited prayers at the graves of those who died. At one funeral, when an old man was being buried short of the new home he had hoped to reach, Theunis was overcome by emotion and launched into a graveside homily, a sort of informal sermon about the transitory nature of human life, and after the burial party had left the site, Balthazar Bronk, who took religion most seriously, asked Theunis and Tjaart to stand aside, and when the others had left, he berated the sick-comforter.

'You're not to preach. You're not a predikant.'

'We were burying a poor old man.'

'Bury him. And keep your mouth shut.'

'But, Mijnheer Bronk—'

'Tjaart, tell this simpleton to obey the rules.'

And when two young people from another party wanted to marry and came to Nel soliciting his assistance, he was willing to comply, but again Bronk intruded: 'Bedamned, I've warned you five times against posing as a predikant.'

'But these young people want to start their new life—'

'Let them wait till a real minister comes along.' And he was so adamant that the couple had to depart, their union unsanctified. But when Bronk was not spying, Theunis rode after the pair and told them, 'God wants his children to marry and multiply. I name you man and wife, and when a true predikant does arrive, ask him to bless your marriage properly.' When one did come after three years, he was able to baptize two children also.

Where was this exodus heading? No one worried. The families were more concerned with leaving English rule than with their destination: some proposed to cut east across the Drakensberg Mountains, which had hemmed Shaka's empire. Others, like Tjaart van Doorn, were determined to head north, cross the Vaal River and settle in remote valleys.

But where in the north? One of Tjaart's earliest memories was of the tales told about his grandfather Adriaan, who had gone into that northland with a Hottentot named Dikkop and a tame hyena named Swarts: 'He said he grew frightened at the Limpopo River and turned back, and found a lake which he called Vrijmeer, and on its bank he buried Dikkop.' Tjaart believed he was destined to reach that lake.

But regardless of whether a Voortrekker elected Natal as his destination or the unexplored north, all trails converged at the foot of a mountain with a fanciful name, Thaba Nchu. The Voortrekkers called it *Ta-ban'-choo,* and so many wanderers found rest here that for some years it formed a major settlement.

It was here that they met the first major black tribe north of the Orange River. In the first days of their trek they had encountered small groups of blacks and a few Coloureds, but at Thaba Nchu, there was a tribe of five thousand who welcomed them as allies against a mortal enemy to the north: Mzilikazi, Great Bull Elephant of the Matabele, one of the architects of Mfecane.

On 13 June 1836 wagons of the Van Doorn party rolled into Thaba Nchu, where five or six hundred earlier arrivals were waiting for their leaders to reach some decision, and they rested there, and there was time for new friendships to develop. Especially active was young Paulus de Groot, who ran with boys twice his age and wrestled with them, too. He talked little, was savagely protective of his rights, and seemed to prefer the companionship of Tjaart van Doorn above that of his own father, and this was understandable, for the lad showed signs of growing into the kind of man Tjaart was: solid, cautious, devout. When young Paulus said his prayers his large squarish face glowed with religious fervor, for it seemed to him that God was listening.

Despite this natural inclination toward devotion, Paulus disliked Theunis Nel, the self-appointed representative of religion, for the boy sensed the ridicule in which the sick-comforter was held. One morning, when Tjaart suggested that Paulus start learning his letters from Theunis, the effect of

Tjaart's sponsorship was destroyed when Minna came out of her tent screaming at her husband, calling him disrespectful names and conveying to the boy the community's reaction to the cockeyed fellow. No man could discipline a strong-minded boy like Paulus de Groot if he could not first discipline his own wife.

Tjaart, hoping to see this promising lad grow into a leader of men, took it upon himself to teach the alphabet and instruct in numbers, and one morning he was seated on a log drilling the boy when Lukas de Groot came past, taking offense at the idea of another man's instructing his son: 'He don't need to read. I don't read and I do all right.'

'All boys should learn to read.'

'Your boys didn't.'

'That's right. They were to live at De Kraal all their lives, and it didn't signify.'

'Why does it signify now?'

'Because we're moving into a new world. Your son may be needed as the leader of a great community. If he can't read, the leadership goes to someone else.'

The discussion might have become ardent had not Minna wandered by to inform her father that he must go out to shoot antelope, for the supply of biltong was depleted; and as she stood speaking to the two men, they saw that of a sudden her face changed from its normal sullen expression, and a frown gave way to a smile of broadening radiance. They turned to see what effected this change, and De Groot spoke for both men: 'Look who comes to join us!'

Among the newcomers to Thaba Nchu were sixteen families who had joined the main stream of Voortrekkers just south of the Orange River, and in the lead was Ryk Naudé, the handsome young farmer, and his pretty wife, Aletta. For Minna Nel, the return of the one man she could love was prophetic: God had used this exodus to bring them back together; for Tjaart, the arrival of Aletta meant that his tormented imaginings were given life. She was even more enticing than he had remembered, older now and more the woman, and his eyes would never leave her.

Wherever Aletta Naudé moved in these days when the leaders were trying to reach decisions, Tjaart endeavored to place himself so that she would have to see him, and after a while she became aware that he was doing this. It irritated her. She was nineteen years old and happily married, while he was forty-seven, with a second wife and a grandchild. He looked silly when he mooned at her, and one afternoon when he had succeeded in interposing himself between her and her tent, she said sharply, 'Mijnheer van Doorn, you're making yourself ridiculous,' and this so embarrassed him that he kept away from her for some days, but then the terrible fascination manifested itself again, and once more she had to avoid him.

The arrival at Thaba Nchu of so many new emigrants caused other troubles. Ryk Naudé and his wife announced that they had decided to cross the Drakensberg and go down to Natal, and this encouraged Lukas de Groot to choose the same option, which meant that Tjaart would be separated both from the girl he loved and from his long-time associate. With profound seriousness he contemplated relinquishing his idea of settlement in the north so as to remain with people he preferred, and he might have surrendered to this temptation had not the affair of the lion skin shown him what fearful temptations threatened his family.

Minna had been less discreet than her father. She was overjoyed to meet with Ryk again and was not ashamed to display her affection. She did everything but embrace him in public, and when he told the clustered emigrants that he and some friends were moving east to see if they could shoot some lions for their skins, she openly ran to him, imploring him to be careful, and when he was gone she moped. This so irritated Jakoba that she told Tjaart, 'You must speak with her. She's becoming a Jezebel.'

So Tjaart took his daughter aside and gave her blunt warning: 'You're married to a good man. He cherishes you and little Sybilla, and you owe him a decent respect. Minna, behave yourself.'

'But Ryk promised me. In the new land, somehow he will be set free.'

'You're married forever. In the eyes of God. Before the predikant at Graaff-Reinet. Obey your vows.'

Tearfully, but with stubborn determination, she said, 'Father, if Ryk and Aletta were separated. Somehow. In God's wisdom. How happy you and I would be.'

Tjaart was stung by her probing of his secret, by her shrewd connivance in bringing it out. What he replied was 'They're heading east over the mountain, we're going north over the Vaal—and we'll never meet again.'

But when Ryk came back to camp with four lion skins and gave Minna one of them, she was certain that this proved his devotion to her, and she convinced herself that he was as hungry for her as she was for him, and at night, when others were asleep, she crept to his tent and quietly, lest Aletta hear, called him out, and coaxed him beyond the wagons. There she poured out her love, and helped him to undress, and encouraged him to join with her three times. It was an explosion of love unlike any he had ever known with Aletta, beautiful as she was, and an invitation to endless future repetitions.

In the days that followed, even Tjaart, who was not quick to perceive nuances, became aware that something gravely wrong was occurring in his family, and one evening he followed Minna, and from a hiding spot, saw with astonishment his daughter's brazen conduct. Shame prevented him from breaking in upon the lovers, but next morning, after the cattle were tended, he went to his daughter's tent, told Theunis to go teach his class, and then confronted Minna.

'I know what you're doing. I saw you behind the wagons.'

'I can't live without him, Father. I'm going down into Natal.'

The possibility that a child of his should be guilty of disobedience was more than he could tolerate; a red haze flooded his eyes, and he recalled instructions from the Bible: 'If a child be disobedient, he shall be killed. If a woman commit adultery, she shall be stoned to death.' In his befuddlement he knew not what to say, so with a wild sweep of his arm he knocked her to the ground, then stormed at her, calling her names from the Old Testament, threatening to drag her before the public to be humiliated.

When his rage subsided, and some kind of sanity returned, he lifted her from the earth and held her as she trembled from the fury of his blow: 'Minna, God has tempted you and me. We have both been guilty of great sin. Tomorrow we go north to prevent the destruction of our souls. And tonight you sleep in my tent, because you are precious to me and I cannot bear to lose you.'

Next morning, 6 July 1836, Tjaart van Doorn, Theunis Nel, Balthazar Bronk and four other families not in the original group formed a new unit to cross the Vaal River and start a fresh community dedicated to the rule of God, the proper relationship between master and servant, and the strict separation of races. It took them eighteen days to reach the river, and with each tramp of the oxen's hooves, Minna Nel and her father felt more and more desolate, for they would never again see the persons they loved.

Only once did either of them mention the mournful separation; Minna said as she walked beside her father, 'My heart seems to break at every step. I realize now that he is gone. I heard a trekker describe the Drakensberg. Once a man crosses those mountains, he will not come back.'

Tjaart, desperately hungry for someone to talk with at this crisis in his life, confessed: 'Because of what you saw, you will find this hard to believe. But my heart yearns for three people. Most of all, little Paulus de Groot. I should love to watch him grow into a man. His possibilities are endless. And I will miss Lukas, too. And after them, Aletta, in a different way.'

'We'll never know.' And that was all she said, plodding her way toward the Vaal.

When they reached the river they found it swollen by an unexpected flood, and were forced to camp on the south bank, where they found several other parties also waiting for the water to subside. At first Tjaart was vexed by the forced delay, but one day the assembled Voortrekkers saw a heavy cloud of dust to the south, and as it approached they discerned four wagons accompanied by the complement of Coloureds, blacks and cattle.

It was Lukas de Groot, hurrying north to overtake his friend, and when the two men met, there was unspoken apology, silent acceptance. 'When I thought about it,' De Groot said, 'I knew my fate was to the north.' He did not add, 'With you,' but the joy his son Paulus displayed at being reunited with Tjaart spoke for the entire family. It was a happy, sensible reunion, and not even when De Groot spoke thoughtlessly of the Ryk Naudés— 'They're heading into Natal, fine pair'—was there any recurrence of the earlier irritation.

Indeed, when the river lowered and the seventy-odd Voortrekkers completed the crossing, Lukas easily consented when little Paulus asked, 'Can I stay with Tjaart tonight?' The Van Doorns camped much farther to the west than the De Groots, so that late at night when frenzied messengers galloped in from the northeast, they reached the latter family first.

'Where'd you come from?' two dusty, tired men shouted, scarcely halting to rest their horses.

'Thaba Nchu,' De Groot replied.

'Go into laager immediately. Kaffirs on the rampage.'

Before Lukas could interrogate the men they disappeared, spurring their horses westward and leaving the De Groot family with a difficult decision. They had nine wagons, not enough for a proper laager, and even these were well scattered. To assemble them would necessitate much maneuvering, and there was no certainty that blacks would come their way. Besides, the hurried trek up from Thaba Nchu had tired the men, so it was decided to wait till morning.

When the messengers took a last look back and realized that the Voortrekkers were not protecting themselves, they were appalled; reining in their horses, they returned to shout, 'Damnit, go into laager—now!' But again the De Groots ignored the warning, for as Lukas pointed out, 'Those men are not our friends. They're Englishmen, and they're trying to scare us into turning back.'

In disgust the messengers galloped westward along the Vaal River until they came to the Van Doorn encampment: 'Go into laager at once. Kaffirs.'

'What Kaffirs?' Tjaart shouted back.

'Mzilikazi!'

It was a name to strike terror among those acquainted with the north, and although the Van Doorns had known no one who had contact with the Bull Elephant, as he was now called, they had heard around the campfires at Thaba Nchu reports of his annihilations. One hunter who knew the area north of the Vaal had said, 'Mzilikazi was the shrewdest of the Zulus. Three times they came after him and three times he beat them off. To protect himself he has cleared an area, maybe two thousand square miles. Killed everything. Men, women, cattle, wild animals. Only thing I saw in fourteen days' travel—hyenas, jackals, a few small birds. I've spotted his scouts south of the Vaal, not far from here. He's watching us every day, the Great Bull Elephant.'

'Is that the Mzilikazi we were warned against?' Tjaart asked.

'The same. He has twenty thousand warriors.'

'Good God! If they all come at us . . .'

'They're spread across the area. It will be only a small detachment.' The two Englishmen, who had been hunting in the north, accepted a drink of water, and asked, 'Any other companies of you Dutchmen?'

'Three others. Farther west.' So off the two messengers went, spurring their horses.

Even before they were gone, Tjaart had started bringing his eleven wagons into an abbreviated laager, and this consisted of jamming the front of one against the rear of the one ahead, guiding the disselboom almost completely under the front wagon and fastening it with the trek chains, then lashing the wheels together and sending children out to gather thorn bushes, which the boys cut and the girls carried back to their mothers, who wove the prickly wood into spokes and wheels and each crevice along the outside perimeter. When they were finished, no enemy could sneak up to the laager and force his way either through or between or under the wagons, for he would face a wall of wood and canvas and thorn. One small opening was provided, and for it a gate of thorn was hastily built. Nine of the sixteen Coloured servants were sent back toward the river with the cattle and sheep; the other seven would fight alongside their masters.

Two people watched the construction of the laager with keen interest: Tjaart van Doorn and little Paulus de Groot, too young to help cut the thorn branches, not old enough to herd the cattle. What he did was stay at Tjaart's heels, running errands for him. Later he would carry lead to the women so that they could swiftly reload the rifles. Each adult man needed three guns, because as soon as he fired one it was useless, and he would have to pass it with his left hand to his daughter, while reaching out with his empty right hand to his wife. 'Give!' was all he would say, and the loaded second rifle would be slapped into his hand for the next shot. Tjaart's two women could load the guns just fast enough to keep one of them ready, and little Paulus could ran bags of powder to them.

Dawn came without any sign of Mzilikazi's men, but toward nine Tjaart heard a dreadful hissing sound to the east and then the ominous stamping of heavy feet on the earth, and a deafening cry of 'Mzilikazi!' followed by a titanic rush of near-naked soldiers and a flight of deadly spears.

'Do not fire!' he ordered the thirteen trekkers and the seven Coloureds. 'Let them come closer . . . closer.' And he heard the hissing sound again, the stomp of many feet and the same cry 'Mzilikazi!' Also, he heard one lonely voice inside the laager praying: 'Almighty God, we are few, but we wear Your armor. We are not afraid, for we have tried to be righteous men. Almighty God, they are many but You are with us. Guide us in this battle.' It was Theunis Nel, gun in hand, waiting for the charge.

'Mzilikazi!' shouted the warriors, rushing at the small concentration of wagons, expecting to overrun it.

'Fire!' Tjaart cried, and twenty guns blazed directly into the face of Mzilikazi's men.

The carnage was horrendous, but after the first ranks fell, wave after wave replaced them.

'Fire!' Tjaart cried again, and then the Voortrekker men passed along their empty guns, reaching back for the next loaded one.

'Fire!' Tjaart cried again and again, but still the intrepid enemy kept rushing at the laager.

'Tjaart!' a boyish voice called. 'Under the wagon!' But before Paulus could attract his captain's attention, Jakoba had chopped at the head of a black crawling into the laager, cleaving his skull.

For ninety terrible minutes the assault continued, with every man holding his position between the wheels of the wagons, continuing to fire while women loaded the rifles.

When the Matabele warriors slowly retreated, a few infuriated veterans of other battles refused to believe that this handful of trekkers had been able to stand them off. Enraged by their defeat, they re-formed at a safe distance, shouted for the last time 'Mzilikazi!' and dashed right into the muzzles of the guns. They died with their hands touching the wagons, but none broke through.

At dusk Tjaart went out with little Paulus to find the dead and count them: 'One hundred and sixty-seven. On our side, none.'

Theunis Nel, hearing these figures, called upon the entire party to kneel, and as they did he intoned an impassioned prayer, rocking back and forth, daubing his left eye now and then with his fingers. He reviewed the godliness of the Voortrekkers, the loyal faith of their grandfathers, their heroism in entering a strange new land, and he concluded:

'Almighty God, when we looked across the veld and saw those dark and fearful forms, more than the mind could count, against thirteen of us, we knew that victory would be possible only if You were with us. The victory was not ours, but Yours.'

And every man and woman and child listening, even the seven servants not included in the prayer, knew that what Theunis was saying had to be true.

But when the final tally was taken, the Voortrekkers had gained no victory. Not at all. Of the two companies camping to the west, one had been overrun, the other had not been annihilated but had lost four men. And at the De Groot camp, which had refused to go into laager, all fifty-two people were slain—children, Coloureds, former slaves—and all were horribly mutilated.

'You mustn't go there, Paulus,' Tjaart said, tears in his eyes at the horror of the massacre. 'Your father and mother and sisters are dead.'

'I want to go,' the little survivor said, and he rode back with Tjaart and the gravediggers to see what was left of his family. He recognized them, and did not vomit at the sight the way some of the adults did. He walked solemnly along the line of their eight bare feet, for they were stripped naked, and saw the manner of their deaths. Not a tear came to his eyes, and as the shallow graves were dug—just enough to keep the hyenas away—he placed a stone upon the chest of each person he had loved.

The rampaging of Mzilikazi's regiments forced all Voortrekkers to change their plans. The few like Tjaart who had ventured north of the Vaal River had to retreat hastily well beyond the south bank, and all along the line of advance the emigrants took stock of their perilous state as they awaited the Great Bull Elephant's next move.

Two members of a black tribe suppressed by Mzilikazi crept down with reports that the Matabele were assembling a mighty army that would overwhelm the Boers, with a superiority of one hundred and fifty blacks to one Voortrekker.

The English government chose this moment of dread to deliver, by means of late arrivals at the camp, its latest proclamation against the Voortrekkers; it stated that even though the fugitives had fled English soil, they must not think that they had escaped English law, because any wrongdoing committed south of the twenty-fifth parallel would be construed as having taken place within English jurisdiction and would be punished accordingly. Since the Vaal River lay well south of that parallel, the battle in which the Van Doorns had defended themselves could be interpreted as an unwarranted aggression, and Tjaart could be hanged.

The document was of course printed in English, but after it had been translated to the astonished Voortrekkers, Tjaart asked to see it. Even though his English was sparse, he could pick out some of the insulting words, and as his lips framed them they created in him a violent bitterness, for he could still envision the mutilated bodies of Lukas de Groot and his people.

It was typical of Tjaart's slow, stubborn awakening to any problem that for two days he said nothing, just carried the proclamation with him, pausing occasionally to reread the offensive lines, but on the third day he assembled all members of his party, and such others as he could reach, to deliver his judgment:

> 'We know from the Book of Joshua that we are doing God's work, in obedience to His commands. But at every turn we are opposed by the English. My father, whom you knew, Lodevicus the Hammer, he was dragged before the Black Circuit and accused by English missionaries of murder. Bezuidenhout here, his people were hanged at Slagter's Nek after God Himself broke their ropes and granted them reprieve. The English have stolen our language, the pulpits in our churches, our slaves. And now they send these laws after us to warn us that we can never escape them.
>
> 'I say "To hell with all the English." I say to my son Paulus, "Remember this day when the Voortrekkers, facing death at the hands of Mzilikazi, swore an oath to be free men." '

Somberly the members of the party whispered, 'I swear!' And all knew that any further compromise with any Englishman had become impossible. From that day, the break must be total.

But on the very next day a smous arrived from Thaba Nchu, and Tjaart was thrown into sad confusion. The peddler brought not only supplies, but also small packets addressed to Tjaart van Doorn and Lukas de Groot.

'Major Saltwood in Grahamstown asked me to deliver these,' the nervous little trader said.

'De Groot's dead.'

'Oh, dear!' The smous was terrified. 'Mzilikazi?'

'Yes. What shall we do with this?'

'Did any of his family survive?'

'His boy, Paulus.'

'Then we'd better give it to him. Because I made a solemn promise to deliver . . .'

They called Paulus and handed him the last message ever sent to his father, and when the boy opened the wrapping, there lay a pile of crisp English pounds. Every penny owed for the De Groot slaves had been paid in full, with no commission subtracted.

When Tjaart opened his packet he found the same. He was perplexed. His English friends had proved their trustworthiness, yet he had sworn open enmity toward them, and he did not know what to say, but after he gave Jakoba the two bundles of money for safekeeping he walked for long hours alone, then sought out the smous and asked, 'Did Major Saltwood pay you for bringing me the money?' And the peddler said, 'Yes, two pounds.' Awkwardly Tjaart translated this into rix-dollars, and he was amazed that Saltwood had spent so much of his own money to forward the funds.

He was confused on other matters, too, for in these days of anxiety when no one knew how soon Mzilikazi would strike again, he learned to his disgust that Ryk Naudé had not crossed the Drakensberg but had encamped some miles away. On several nights Tjaart had ridden over to seek Minna, and again spied on their love-making and he was bewildered: Why would a man with a wonderful wife like Aletta bother to plow the furrow with someone like Minna? He loved his daughter and had worked diligently to find her a husband, but he could never delude himself into thinking that she was in any way the equal of Aletta. Yet here was this young no-good imperiling his marriage by sneaking out at night to make love to a plain and married woman.

Tjaart became so disturbed by his daughter's misbehavior, relating it always to his own renewed infatuation for Aletta, that one day he resolutely confronted Ryk to upbraid him for his adultery: 'Ryk, we're about to engage Mzilikazi in a battle where we might all die. If God turns against us for our sins, we might perish. Don't you feel any responsibility?'

'I feel love for your daughter.'

'Love?'

'Yes, I should have married her, as she said.'

'But you have a beautiful wife . . .'

'Old man, tend to your battle. Guns will win it, not commandments.'

This was so blasphemous that Tjaart could not decide how to respond, but Ryk saved him: 'In two days we march north—to face Mzilikazi. We may all be killed, but I'll be happy knowing that Minna . . .' He did not finish this extraordinary statement, just walked off to prepare his horses.

Tjaart was angered by the young man's insolence, and surprised, too, for he had not thought of Ryk as brave enough to oppose an elder. More tantalizing were some of the deductions that could be made from what the young husband had said: if Ryk did not think much of his wife, if he did not want her, what wrong could there be if someone else approached her? None, he concluded, and as to the adultery he would be committing, he avoided any consideration of this by simply erasing Jakoba from his mind.

So he resumed his old habit of placing himself in Aletta's path, a foolish, dumpy man in belt and suspenders offering himself to the most beautiful young woman among the trekkers. He was ridiculous, and he knew it, but he was powerless to stop. One afternoon he waited till she was apart from the others, then grabbed her, pulled her behind some wagons, and started kissing her furiously.

To his surprise, she did not resist, nor did she participate. She simply leaned against him, even lovelier than in his dreams, smiling between the kisses and whispering at the end, 'You're not such a silly old man, after all.' And with that she walked slowly away, completely untouched by his embraces.

The encounter was an agony for Tjaart. During one spell he railed silently against his son-in-law: Why doesn't that damned fool Theunis manage his wife? Where in God's hell did I find such a man to bring into my family? And for more than an hour he mentally reviled the little sick-comforter as the cause of his own malaise.

Then he envisioned the forthcoming battle against Mzilikazi, and when he recalled the fearlessness with which those first Matabele had kept storming the laager, he grew frightened: If twice that many, three times that many, come at us, what shall we do? Then he recalled the mutilated bodies of De Groot's people, and a sickening rage overcame him: We must slay them, slay them! No Voortrekker ever raised a finger against Mzilikazi, and he did that to us. We must destroy him.

And then he paused, and like all Boers, reflected on the fact that even self-protection, let alone victory, would be impossible without God's help, and he became totally contrite, taking upon himself the burden of sin that he had tried to throw upon the adulterous Ryk Naudé. Lighting an oil lamp, he took down his Bible and looked through Proverbs till he came upon the passage which spoke definitively of his transgression:

> For the commandment is a lamp; and the law is light; and reproofs of instruction are the way of life: to keep thee from . . . the flattery of the tongue of a strange woman. Lust not after her beauty in thine heart; neither let her take thee with her eyelids . . . Can a man take fire in his bosom, and his clothes not be burned? Can one go upon hot coals, and his feet not be burned? So he that goeth in to his neighbour's wife; whosoever toucheth her shall not be innocent.

He was about to close the book when he realized that he required much more help than he could find by himself, and he sought out Theunis Nel, sleeping alone, for his wife was away committing sin, and he said to the sick-comforter, 'Come read the Bible with me and instruct me.'

Always prepared for such calls, Theunis rose, wrapped himself in a blanket, and accompanied Tjaart to where the Bible stood open under the lamp, and he grasped at once the significance of Tjaart's having been reading Proverbs Six. But he said nothing of adultery or lusting in one's heart.

'Theunis, this time we face terrible odds.'

'We did last time.'

'But then we didn't know. Now, with the De Groots dead, we do.'

'God rides with us.'

'Are you sure?'

The little man quickly turned the pages from Proverbs and closed the book, then placed his hands upon it and said, 'I know that God intends our people to establish a new nation in His image. If He sends us on this mission, surely He will protect us.'

'Then why didn't he send his predikants to accompany us? To give us guidance in His word?'

'I've wondered about that, Tjaart. I think He sent common folk like you and me because He wanted His word to work up slowly from the ground. Not thundering down in sermons written by learned Scottish predikants.'

'Is that a possibility?'

In the flickering shadows the sick-comforter said, 'If we had with us a learned dominee, we'd put all the burdens on him, let him tell us what God intended. This way, it's simple people like you and me. And when we work out our solutions, they will come from the heart of the Voortrekker, not from outside.' Rising and striding about the tent, if a man so slight could be said to stride, he told Tjaart, 'You will gain victory. You will slay the Canaanites. You will lead us across Jordan into our inheritance.'

And these two unhappy men—the stronger torn apart by sin and confusion, the weaker desolated by the misconduct of his wife—knelt and prayed.

In these years Mzilikazi commanded fifty-six regiments of highly trained infantry, so that had he wished, he might have sent twenty thousand men against the Voortrekkers, but despite his losses at the Van Doorn laager, he still could not believe that white men with guns and horses and interlocked wagons could prevail against his power. So he sent south only some six thousand men, not all of whom would be in position to attack the main laager when the battle joined.

A resolute body of Voortrekkers, consisting of some forty men, an equal number of women, about sixty-five children and the normal proportion of Coloureds, had moved to institute a massive laager of fifty-one wagons securely tied together and protected by solid interweavings of heavy thorn. Peculiar to this laager, where all participants knew that they must triumph or they would perish in hideous mutilation, was a block of four wagons kept at the center and covered with boards and heavy canvas: in these the women and children would take refuge during the battle, but it was foreseen that steadfast women like Jakoba van Doorn and Minna Nel would stay outside to help in the fighting, while many boys like Paulus de Groot would be at the barricades, firing guns at times and running powder to their mothers.

The leaders had chosen a flattish area at the base of a small hill, which meant that Mzilikazi's regiments would have to attack up a slight slope or down a steep one; at either point they would be at a disadvantage. To the surprise of the Voortrekkers, the enemy chose the steep southwest slope, and there they established an enormous camp, preparing methodically for the assault that must destroy the laager and all within it.

For two days the regiments sharpened their assegais and perfected their signals for the big thrust. During this time the Voortrekkers could see the enemy and hear him attending his duties; at night the Matabele campfires flared, and men wondered: Will the attack come at dawn?

On 16 October 1836 the Matabele were ready, and started slowly toward a position opposite the laager, whereupon Tjaart asked Theunis to lead the defenders in prayer, but once again Balthazar Bronk objected on the grounds that the defense might be imperiled if an improper clergyman was allowed to utter his own prayers. To this Tjaart responded, 'The enemy is ten minutes from us and we need God's help,' but Bronk was insistent: 'God is perfect. His church is perfect. Neither can tolerate a blemished man.' So Theunis was silenced, but Tjaart himself was encouraged to lead a prayer, which was short, impassioned, and a mighty solace to those who kept one eye open to watch the remorseless approach of some six thousand battle-hardened Matabele.

The leaders resolved to approach the Matabele in a startling way. A fearless patriarch named Hendrik Potgieter, famed for having had five wives in rapid succession, proposed that a sortie of twenty to thirty men—more than half the entire force—ride out into the middle of the black commanders and try to reason with them. It was this kind of action only an idiot would devise, or a man who felt the touch of God upon his shoulder.

'I'll go!' Tjaart said.

'I'll go!' Theunis Nel echoed.

Soon Potgieter had twenty-four volunteers besides himself, and then a twenty-fifth. It was Balthazar Bronk, whom Jakoba had shamed into joining: 'Are you afraid to die?' Reluctantly accepting the gun she thrust at him, he joined the suicide patrol.

On signal from Potgieter, these daring men left the safety of their laager, spurred their horses, and rode at breakneck speed directly at the heart of the enemy. One of the Coloureds in the laager had served with a hunter in Matabele lands, and through him, Potgieter addressed the warriors: 'Why do you wish to attack us? We come in friendship.'

'You come to steal our lands,' a commander shouted.

'No! We come to live in peace.'

'Mzilikazi, the Great Bull Elephant, is angry. His word is that you must die.' One commander raised his assegai and shouted the war cry 'Mzilikazi!'

At this signal the regiments started running toward the Voortrekkers, who sped back to the safety of their laager. That they made it could only be attributed to God's providence, for the odds against them were crushing. But they succeeded, firing from the saddle at the advancing Matabele.

Not all entered the laager. Five men, totally demoralized by the hordes of black warriors and withered by fear as assegais flew about them, reached the entrance with the others, but then ahead of them they saw an escape route which would carry them all the way to Thaba Nchu and safety. Without consciously intending to be cowards, they accepted this invitation so enticingly put before them. They took flight.

Young Paulus de Groot, standing by the entrance to welcome the returning Voortrekkers, saw with amazement that they were quitting the fight, and cried, 'They're running away.' And these five became known in Voortrekker history as the Fear Commando. In their lead as they fled was Balthazar Bronk, his face ashen with awful dread.

'May God have mercy upon our children,' Jakoba muttered, and then no further prayers were said, for with a single, terrifying scream the black soldiers fell upon the laager.

At every moment for more than a hour it seemed that the chain of wagons must crumble, and so many assegais fell upon the four wagons in the middle that Paulus ran out and collected more than twenty. Selecting the one that seemed strongest, he took position at a point where the wagons seemed most likely to collapse and stabbed at any Matabele who tried to penetrate.

The laager held. The barrels of the guns were burning hot from overfiring, but those courageous women who were helping in the fight kept on— exhausted, sweating, fearful. And the wagons held. One group of six was pushed back two feet, so powerful were the attacking Matabele, but in the end even those wagons held, their disselbooms shattered, their sides peppered with assegais, their canvas torn.

Veg Kop, they called this fight, Battle Hill, where less than fifty determined Voortrekkers, aided by their remarkable women and their loyal Coloured servants, defeated more than six thousand attackers. When Tjaart rode over the battlefield he counted four hundred and thirty-one dead Matabele, and he knew that only two Voortrekkers had been killed. But he also knew that there was hardly a member of the laager that did not have some wound to show; Paulus de Groot had been cut twice by flashing assegais, and he was proud of this, but he had to agree when a girl pointed out that he had given himself one of the wounds by his awkward handling of an enemy spear which he was trying to wrench free from the wagon it had pierced.

Jakoba had a painful cut in the left hand, but this had not impeded her handling of ammunition, and Minna had a gash in her leg which required bandaging. Tjaart was untouched, but he found to his dismay that during the attack Theunis Nel had taken two serious stabs. The man who comforted the sick was himself put to bed, and during the waiting period, when the Matabele had quit the fight but not the battlefield, he was visited by many who told him that as a man of courage and devotion he ought to be proclaimed the Voortrekkers' dominee; but there were just as many, and more obstinate, who refused to countenance such a move, for as they repeated: 'God Himself forbade such an ordination.'

The Voortrekkers had won the Battle of Veg Kop, but when the cost was counted, they found that the Matabele had slain every Coloured herdsman and had driven off every animal they possessed. For eighteen hungry days they were unable to move from their laager, and their plight might have grown even more perilous had not help arrived from an unexpected quarter: the black chief at Thaba Nchu, hearing of their predicament, decided that he must help the brave people who had smitten his enemy. He sent trek oxen north with food for the Boers, oxen for their wagons, and an invitation to return to the safety of Thaba Nchu, which they accepted.

Despite the loss of their livestock, they felt such joyousness of spirit that there was celebration for many days, with the somberness that marked the aftermath of battle giving way to drinking and raucous singing. When Tjaart growled, 'What I want is to find Balthazar Bronk and those others who fled,' he was told to forget them: 'They galloped in here telling us what heroes they had been. Then scuttled across the mountains, where they can still be heroes.' The smous, relieved that he had escaped the Matabele, produced a French accordion, which he hoped to sell to some wandering family, and on it played a series of old Cape ballads, and while the others danced, Tjaart took from the peddler's wagon a random supply of sugar, raisins, dried fruits and spices, to which he added such odds and ends as Jakoba could supply. In his brown-gold pot he baked a bread pudding which, with some pride, he contributed to the festivities.

Among those who took a cupful was Aletta Naudé. Carefully adding a little milk, she dusted her portion with sugar, then, keeping the mug close to her lips but not eating, and with a spoon clutched in her right hand, she looked over the rim at Tjaart and smiled. Slowly, provocatively she lowered the mug, dug out a spoonful of the pudding and took it to her lips; she delicately tasted the stuff and smiled again.

Tjaart was so entranced by Aletta, so held by the spell of her smile, that when he finally reached for his share of the pudding, there was none, but he could taste it whenever Aletta took a spoonful, and as she neared the end of her portion he moved toward her, and without speaking, indicated that she must accompany him.

Once clear of the celebration, he guided her behind a set of wagons, and while the accordion filled the night with revelry, pulled her to the ground and hungrily tore aside her clothes. Never before had he known what an overwhelming thing sex could be, and he was so preoccupied with his own violent experience that he failed to notice that Aletta was merely smiling at his ridiculous performance.

When it ended, and he lay back watching her impassive dressing, he made no attempt to reconcile his adulterous action in taking another man's wife with his profound gratitude to God for having protected the Voortrekkers in their laager. These were two unrelated things, and he was not obligated to harmonize them, for as he said to himself: King David had the same problem.

In April 1837 Tjaart encountered once again the man who was to become the memorable figure of the trek, Piet Retief, the frontier farmer with whom he had ridden so often on commando, and they talked of those heroic days: 'Remember how we did it, Tjaart? Fifty of us, two hundred Xhosa, a skirmish, a retreat. I understand that with the Matabele, it was different.'

Tjaart shivered. 'Five thousand coming at once. Six thousand. And every man prepared to die. For hours we fired point-blank into their faces.'

'That's finished,' Retief said. 'You're to come down into Natal with me. The Zulu will leave us alone. They have a sensible king, Dingane by name. We can deal with him.'

'I would hate to leave the plateau. Mzilikazi remains a threat, but I still want to go north.'

'The ones who did, they didn't fare too well. I think they're all dead.'

Retief was right. The toll had been heavy, and he advanced so many other sound reasons in support of Natal that Tjaart wavered, but Jakoba stiffened his determination to cross the Vaal: 'You've always wanted to search out that lake your grandfather spoke of. Do it. Natal is for weaklings like Bronk and Naudé.' It was the first time she referred to the family with which her own was so sorely enmeshed, and she said no more.

He accepted her counsel and informed Retief that the Van Doorn party would not go down into Natal, but that evening as he was heading back to his own tent, Aletta Naudé appeared mysteriously from behind a row of transport wagons, and almost before he knew what was happening, he was clutching at her, rolling with her in the stubble. When he lay exhausted, she ran her fingers through his beard and whispered, 'We're crossing over the mountains. Come down into Natal with us.'

That night he informed Jakoba that Retief had convinced him; they were moving east. She said, 'It's a mistake,' and in the morning she learned that Ryk Naudé and his wife were going, too.

It was a journey into springtime and into some of the most difficult land the Van Doorns would traverse. In their slow migration from De Kraal they had climbed unnoticed from near sea level to well over five thousand feet, so that for some time now they had been operating on what the men called 'the plateau.' It was high land, dipping to lower levels where rivers passed through. But now they were required to climb toward eight thousand feet, then drop precipitously down to sea level. The upward climb would be easy, the downward plunge frightful.

Eleven wagons gathered to make the attempt, and as they climbed the gentle western face of the Drakensberg they could not foresee the problems that awaited them, because Ryk Naudé assured them: 'Retief has gone ahead to scout a safe pass down. It can be done.'

But when they reached the summit and saw for the first time what lay ahead, even Tjaart blanched. To take a Voortrekker wagon down those steep slopes would be impossible, regardless of how many oxen a man had to help hold the wagons back. And when the beasts saw the cliffs they refused to go down them even without the wagons. On this route, Tjaart had to agree, descent was hopeless.

So he and Theunis searched for other trails. They found them, plenty of them. They descended easily, ran along relatively flat ground, then *boom!* A sheer cliff two hundred feet high.

Try the next trail. Fine descent, a reassuring spread of land sloping easily down, then a fairly sharp but negotiable stretch ending in another cliff.

For three weeks, as spring continued to blossom—a wild assortment of mountain flowers and baby animals and birds all around them—the Voortrekkers tried fruitlessly to locate that one pass through the mountains that would allow them to reach the lush pastures they knew existed below. Always the enticing avenue, always the sheer cliff.

In the fourth week Tjaart saw a lesser trail leading well to the north, and its conspicuous difference reassured him, for at no point was it inviting or easy; it was cruelly difficult, but as he descended, scraping shins, he gave a shout of triumph when he saw that the pass continued right down to level land. But could wagons traverse it? He thought so.

Accordingly, he hurried back to his beleaguered group and told them, 'We can go much of the distance in our present condition. But for about two miles we'll have to take the wagons apart and carry them, piece by piece.' Ryk Naudé thought this impossible, whereupon, with disgust, Jakoba pointed back over the route they had come: 'Then go back.' After much hemming and hawing, he decided to trust his luck with the others.

For two difficult days eleven wagons slipped and slid down grassy inclines, then rattled over stony ones. Theunis Nel conceived the good idea of reversing wheels, so that the big ones were in front of the wagon, where they could be better controlled on the really steep slopes, and another man devised a trick for replacing the big aft wheels altogether, and substituting heavy timbers which would drag along the ground under the axletree, providing an effective brake: the oxen did not like this, and when they saw the heavy branches being moved into place, grew restless; the Coloureds talked to them by name, treating them as pampered individuals, each with its own catalogue of complaints. It was remarkable how a few soothing words gave the hard-worked beasts the encouragement they needed.

But every yard that was successfully traversed brought the Voortrekkers closer to the low cliffs that could never be negotiated by any wagon. There the procession halted while Tjaart pointed out the grand and easy path that awaited them, once they cleared these cliffs, and when he had consoled them with his assurances, he led them off to the north to a prominence below which lay the rolling pasture lands that reached to the Indian Ocean. It was an introduction to a homeland that would never be excelled, a promise of grandeur and fruition: 'There lies Natal. There rests your home.' He did not, Jakoba noted, refer to it as their home, and for this she was grateful, for she remembered the cleaner, harder land of the Transvaal.

It was a hellish nineteen days. Theunis discovered a footpath by which he could lead the oxen down to the pastures, where they flourished. Every man, woman and child, Boer and servant alike, strained and sweated on the horrendous descent of the berg.

It was murderous work. Unpacking a heavy wagon and then disassembling it was difficult enough, but back-packing all items down the steep inclines where feet slipped on pebbles was exhausting, and reassembling the wagons and then repacking them was exhausting. The Voortrekkers accepted the challenge; even Paulus de Groot, hardly as tall as a wheel, sought responsibility for guiding one of Tjaart's wheels down the grade, but did not listen when Van Doorn warned him not to let it get going too fast. Before long Tjaart saw with dismay his precious wheel thundering down the grade and about to break to pieces. Fortunately, it stopped itself in bushes, and Tjaart had to laugh as he watched the lad wrestling with it to get it back on the path.

Ryk Naudé was less energetic. He complained of the route Tjaart had chosen, arguing that one farther south would have been better, and when he grudgingly carried an item down the cliff, he was most tardy in returning for another, and on one of his own trips Tjaart spotted Ryk and Minna kissing behind some rocks. He was turning out to be what Jakoba had predicted, a selfish, inconsiderate young man, and the older Voortrekkers were disgusted with him.

Jakoba was indefatigable, slipping and sliding as she descended with baskets, puffing with determination as she climbed back. For all those days she worked harder than any of the oxen, supervising the passage not only of her own wagon but also those of her neighbors. When she saw Aletta shirking, she spoke harshly: 'You needn't linger so long down there. Work's to be done.' But Aletta only smiled at her with the knowing grin of a younger woman who has captivated an older woman's man.

When this part of the descent was accomplished, the Voortrekkers were so exhausted they rested for five days, during which Tjaart made a fortunate discovery. While checking the last portion of the trail, to satisfy himself that it would be as easy as he had judged at first, he came upon a place so majestic that he had to conclude that God Himself had set this aside for his weary travelers. Because of its cathedral shape, he named it Kerkenberg (Church-in-the-Mountain), and to it he led his people.

It was a series of shallow caves and beautiful flat areas rimmed by towering granite boulders. From the outside it appeared to be a collection of mighty rocks assembled in accordance with some plan; from the inside it was a cathedral with the boulders inclining slightly toward the center and open to the sky; from every aperture the worshipper could look down to see the beautiful plains of Natal.

When the Voortrekkers entered this sanctified place, they were over-awed by its rough majesty and almost simultaneously they knelt in prayer, thanking God for His many deliverances, and while they were on their knees, Tjaart summoned Theunis Nel and uttered the words the little man had waited so long to hear: 'Theunis, by your valor and devotion you have earned the title *predikant.* You are now our dominee, and you are to lead us in prayer.' And this time no one tried to deny him.

Nel, fifty-two years old, rose and stood with his blemished face looking upward; this was a church beyond his greatest hope, an ordination nobler than any he had dreamed of, for it came from the people in the heat of their travail. His prayer was short, an acknowledgment that these Boers could not have survived the regiments of Mzilikazi, the dangers of the veld, the descent of these hills without God's assistance. The joy they felt at their deliverance was attributable to Him, and they thanked Him in advance for leading them into this land of peace and prosperity.

'Amen!' Tjaart cried, and when the people rose, he said, 'We have missed many Sundays. Theunis, you shall preach to us.' The crookbackt man looked apprehensively at the congregation and became unnerved for a moment when two older men led their families from the church in the rocks, for it was against their belief that a man so marked should serve as dominee. But when the noise of their departure subsided, Tjaart nodded quietly toward his little friend, and Theunis, set free at last, entered upon a sermon of transcendant power, and when he finished he left the worshippers and walked to where the dissident families stood beside tall rocks.

'Please join us now,' he said. 'The preaching part has ended.'

In November, Van Doorn terminated theological discussion; he was re-quired to leave Kerkenberg and go alone to the lower levels, where he hoped to find a permanent home for his people. He was not happy about leaving, for Balthazar Bronk, the craven hero of the Fear Commando, had returned, and in Tjaart's absence, would assume charge, and he was a man not to be trusted. But Tjaart had work to do, so he descended to the Tugela River, along whose banks Shaka had conducted so many of his battles, and there he met again with Piet Retief: 'What a fearful descent we made over the mountains.'

'Once down, never up,' Retief said.

'Has the king agreed to give us the land?'

'No. And that's why I am so pleased to see you here with me, because soon we shall go to see Dingane.'

Retief was now fifty-seven years old, whip-thin, bearded, and eager to put a capstone to his life's work: he would establish the Voortrekkers in a solid, fruitful home, then send to the Cape for predikants and watch the founding of a new nation obedient to God's instructions. To accomplish this, he needed only the final approval of the King of the Zulu, who had already agreed in principle to the proposal which Retief had offered.

The two men, accompanied by assistants, rode north from the Tugela River toward the Umfolozi, the historic river of the Zulu, and near its southern banks they came upon Dingane's Kraal, the established capital town of the Zulu.

Dingane was no black Napoleon like his half brother Shaka; he was a Nero, a tyrannical despot caring more for entertainment and intrigue than solid governance. His town was big, a dwelling place for forty thousand people. It contained row upon row of beehive huts, large parade grounds, a royal hut with ceilings twenty feet high and a reception hall with a vast dome roof supported by more than twenty pillars, each completely covered with intricate beadwork.

Retief and Van Doorn were led to the cattle kraal, the center of Zulu life, but before they could enter it and stand in the presence of the king, they had to divest themselves of all arms and come as humble supplicants. They were astounded by the extent of the place and the obvious desire of the king to impress any visitors. 'When the king appears, you must fall on your bellies and crawl like snakes to his feet,' an attendant explained in good English, acquired from a mission station.

'That we will not do,' Retief said.

'Then you will be killed.'

'No. Because you will explain to the king that Boers do not crawl.'

'But I could never address the king, unless he spoke first. He would kill me.'

'And if you don't, we will kill you.'

The man began to sweat so copiously that Tjaart realized he could never bring himself to tell the king anything, so he was dismissed, and the two Boers remained standing.

In a flurry of excitement, a score of lesser attendants rushed about the far end of the kraal, whereupon all the Zulu present fell to their knees while King Dingane entered, smiled at the Boers, whom he had expected to remain standing, and took his seat in a remarkable throne. It was an armchair ornately carved in Grahamstown and presented to the Zulu king by an English trader.

It was now nine years since Dingane had murdered his half brother Shaka, and then his fellow conspirator and full brother, Mhlangana, and then his uncle, and his other full brother Ngwadi, and nineteen other relatives and counselors. The years had been good to him; he weighed some two hundred and sixty pounds, had over three hundred wives, and an insight and a sense of what might happen next, which compensated somewhat for his treacherous ways, and it fell to him to confront the white men who kept coming over the Drakensberg.

He had already mastered the art of dealing with the Englishmen who clustered at the seaside; since they had ships which kept them in contact with London and Cape Town, they had to be treated with respect on the one hand and harsh indifference on the other. As he explained to one of the head councillors, Dambuza, with whom he often shared responsibilities: 'With the English it's all right to kick them, so long as you salute their flag and speak well of their new queen.'

The Boers were a much different problem. They owed no allegiance to any ruler in Europe, and apparently none to the government in Cape Town. They were self-ruled and obstinate. They did not wear badges like the English, and they did not summon ships from across the ocean to assist them in time of trouble. As he told Dambuza, 'They are like their oxen, patient and pressing. I can live with the English, for I know what they will do next. But I am afraid of these Boers, who come at me from across the mountains that you told me could not be passed.'

When Dingane was seated in his great chair he signaled, and sixteen of his brides were brought in to arrange themselves at his feet. A dozen of the women were beautiful, dressed in silky garments which the king had personally designed, but the other four were tremendous women, weighing almost as much as their king; on them the garments seemed ridiculous.

The king indicated that he was now ready to open his bargaining session, whereupon six older men were summoned to flank him, and while he smiled at the Voortrekkers these official flatterers, as they were called, poured forth their praises: 'Oh, Great and Mighty Slayer of the Matabele, Wise Master Elephant of the Deepest Jungles, He whose Footfall Causes the Earth to Tremble, Wisest of the Planners, He Who Orders the Wizards to be Impaled . . .' The interpreter, in bored monotone rattled off an additional dozen descriptions, after which Dingane silenced the flatterers, who were prepared to go on all day if necessary; they knew how to keep a ruler happy.

When Dingane finally spoke, Retief learned with disappointment that no real negotiation would occur that day; what the king had in mind was a series of displays calculated to impress the visitors with his power and their own insignificance, and to launch this exhibition, he used a device that had awed earlier visitors. In a compelling voice he cried, 'Tell the warriors to appear.' And then he raised his left hand to his mouth and spit upon his wrist. 'And all is to be done before the spit dries on my wrist.'

'What happens if the spit dries?' Tjaart asked the interpreter.

'The messenger who received the order is strangled.'

The warriors were ready. From numerous openings more than two thousand Zulu fighting men rushed into the cattle kraal bearing tall white shields, which they flashed this way and that in a dazzling display. Then, with three mighty stompings of their right feet, they shouted 'Bayete!' and the earth reverberated. They then began a warriors' dance, swaying gently at times, leaping into the air at others; it was an awesome performance, kept in such perfect synchronization that Retief whispered, 'I doubt if any European army could do the same.'

The first day was spent in this manner, and when it ended Retief said, through the interpreter, 'Tomorrow we shall talk.'

That was not Dingane's plan, for on the morrow he sat with his guests in the royal cattle kraal, where, like an Oriental ruler showing his jewels to impress a visitor, or a European his collection of paintings, he prepared to display his conspicuous wealth. Again he spit on his wrist, whereupon servants led enormous herds of cattle past in silent defile. One herd of more than two thousand consisted of alternate rows of black and red; another of somewhat smaller size was all brown.

When the handsome beasts departed and a scurry of men cleaned up the droppings, Dingane signaled once more, and now came an incredible performance. Filing through the entrance to the kraal came two hundred snow-white oxen garbed majestically in garlands and caparisons and all without horns. Each was attended by an ebony warrior who stayed at the beast's head but never touched it.

Tjaart assumed that this was another march-past, and he was sufficiently impressed by the beauty of these matched animals to nod approvingly to the king, who held up one hand to indicate that the real performance would now begin.

Slowly, to the Boers' amazement, the two hundred oxen began to dance with the warriors, following a set of rather intricate steps, forming large patterns and then regrouping, without ever a command that Tjaart could hear. Gradually, as Dingane had intended, the effect became hypnotic and wonderfully African: these huge beasts delicately stepping off their patterns, turning majestically and coming back, hesitating, twisting, and then moving forward at their slow purposeful pace. Each animal looked as if he alone were performing the dance, as if the eyes of all spectators were following him, and each displayed obvious satisfaction in dancing so well.

That night Retief told Tjaart, 'Tomorrow we talk.'

This time he was right. They talked, but not about the grant of land. Dingane, listening attentively to every word the interpreter said, asked, 'What happened when your people met with Mzilikazi?'

Delighted at this opportunity to instruct a pagan king, Retief expounded enthusiastically on the Boer triumphs: 'A handful of us . . . Van Doorn here was one of them. He'll tell you—'

'Tell me what?' the king interrupted.

Tjaart knew instinctively that he must not boast of his victories over the Great Bull Elephant, even though Mzilikazi was Dingane's enemy, for to do so would raise questions in the king's mind, so he replied modestly, 'We fought him twice, and he was powerful.'

'That's not the story!' Retief protested, and while Dingane kept his pudgy fingers pressed against his lips, the Boer leader cried, 'Forty of our men held off five thousand of his. Wave after wave of his soldiers came at our men, and we shot them down till they lay like ripe pumpkins in the veld.'

'So few of you, so many of them?'

'Yes, Mighty King, because when a ruler disobeys the commands of our God, he is struck down. Remember that.'

Dingane did not change his expression, but Tjaart noticed that he kept his fingertips pressed hard against his lips, as if he were controlling himself lest he say too much, and when the two Voortrekkers took their seats for this day's entertainment, Tjaart said, 'I wish you had not been so bold,' but Retief, in some exhilaration, replied, 'From time to time you must teach these pagan kings a lesson.' When Tjaart tried to remonstrate, Retief said, 'Look!'

More than two thousand Zulu warriors in full battle dress, with distinctive ox tails tied about their upper arms and knees, had run onto the parade ground, taken position and stamped their feet, shouting 'Bayete!' Then came a stylized battle show replete with cries, stabbing exercises and mock attacks. Tjaart, who had experienced the real thing, was repelled by the display, but Retief was riveted by the performance, and told the king, 'Your men are mighty warriors.' Dingane nodded, then replied, 'They live at my command. They kill at my command.'

On the fourth day the king finally consented to talk seriously with the Boers, and assured them that he was viewing favorably their application for a large grant of land south of his own domains. He asked Retief to prove his responsibility as a possible settler by recovering some cattle stolen from him by a distant chief, and more or less assured him that once this mission was accomplished, the land grant would be quickly arranged during Retief's next visit. After a long speech of farewell, with foot-stomping and a graceful exit of his sixteen favorite wives, the king nodded and departed, leaving Retief and Van Doorn free to return to their company of waiting Voortrekkers. But before the men left the area, an English missionary, who had been living near Dingane's kraal for some months, hurried up to them and said, 'Friends, your lives are my concern.'

'Ours too,' Retief said lightly, for he was pleased by the promising results of his first official visit with the king.

'Did he invite you back for another visit?'

'Yes, in January, if we could complete a small matter for him. If not, in February.'

'Friends, in the name of God, do not come back.'

'Foolishness. He's going to give us the grant we seek.'

'Friends, believe me. I live with these people. Every sign I saw proved to me that he intends killing you.'

'We Boers do not hold much with missionaries,' Retief said, and Tjaart nodded. Neither of the men could tolerate the philanthropists, and they saw in this meddling man one more troublemaker.

'Friends, regardless of what you think of me as a missionary, I warn you as a guide. Dingane means to kill you. If you return to his kraal, you will never leave.'

Retief had grown impatient with the intrusion. Brushing the missionary aside, he said as he strode past, 'Say no prayers on our account. We're not Englishmen. We're Dutchmen. We know how to deal with Kaffirs.'

When Tjaart returned to the Kerkenberg he found the place deserted except for one boy shepherding a flock left there for utilization by chance travelers. He said that Mijnheer Bronk had prevailed upon the group to complete the descent into the valley of the Blaauwkrantz River.

Tjaart was at first angry that Bronk should have made such a bold decision alone, but when he saw the new site he had to admit that it was an improvement on the aerie in the hills. Kerkenberg had been for resting; the Blaauwkrantz was for living. It had ample water, good drainage, and a promise of the fine pastures which the Voortrekkers would occupy for the remainder of their lives. Tjaart went to Bronk and said, 'You have chosen well.'

In December 1837 new arrivals struggling down the Drakensberg brought the Voortrekkers an unexpected Christmas present: 'We have defeated Mzilikazi. He's fled north of the Limpopo, gone forever.' And three men who had participated in the final running battle elaborated: 'We caught him in retreat and kept at his heels. Overpowered him. Four thousand of his men dead. Two of ours.'

Brave beyond the demands of normal warfare, these black troops without guns or horses had tried to combat a white army that had both, and the day had come when the Great Bull Elephant had to face the fact that his regiments could no longer dominate the vast area they had delineated for themselves, and his kraals could not hold out against the Boer and Coloured horsemen who came thundering through the huts at dawn. As one of the arriving Boers said, 'Like an enraged elephant, he thrashed about the veld, then slowly withdrew.' He crossed the Limpopo, passing that grand and gloomy collection of ruins at Zimbabwe and establishing his permanent kingdom of the Matabele in the western reaches of that olden empire. For Mzilikazi, the great odyssey of his people, which had left such a trail of blood, was ended.

But even as Jakoba heard of this victory, she shared with Tjaart her apprehensions over the way things had been going ever since Balthazar Bronk had led the Voortrekkers to lower ground: 'I don't feel safe here. We've worked so hard to come this far, and I think it's all wrong.'

'What do you propose?'

'We should go back to higher ground.'

'We can't move all these people back to the Kerkenberg.'

'I mean all the way back. To the plateau where we belong.'

Tjaart was astounded. 'You'd go back up that mountain?'

'I would. Right now.'

'We'd never get our wagon up.'

'Leave it. Let's go back to Thaba Nchu and join some other group moving north.'

The idea was appealing. Tjaart had not liked what he saw at Dingane's Kraal, for if the Zulu king controlled that number of well-trained men, what would keep him from acting like Mzilikazi if he became angry? And why had he been so nervously concerned about the defeat of his arch-rival in the early skirmishes if he were not applying that experience to himself? Surely, if the Voortrekkers had heard of the Bull Elephant's final expulsion, Dingane must have heard too, and must be wondering whether a handful of Boers could do the same to him.

'I fear the English missionary may have been correct,' he confided to Jakoba. 'I think Retief might do well to avoid that kraal.'

'Warn him.'

'He listens to no man. Never has.'

'Tjaart, I think we should leave here. Let Bronk command. Did you know that during your absence he expelled Theunis from the Kerkenberg?'

'He what?' Such graceless behavior in the name of religion nauseated Tjaart, and he sought the sick-comforter to assure him that many of the men in the company, those who had faced death repeatedly and had not run away, appreciated his spiritual assistance: 'Theunis, when a man faces odds of a thousand to one, and when the cattle have been stolen and the horses stampeded, he needs God's assurance. On this trek you have been more important than four guns. Stay close to us, for I fear that harsh days lie ahead.'

'As bad as on the Vaal River?'

'Worse. Mzilikazi was wily and brilliant. Dingane is terrible and undisciplined. If I'm ever absent, keep the wagons in laager.'

'We haven't been in laager for months.'

'I've seen Dingane,' Tjaart said. 'I've seen his kraal. This man is a king, and kings invade.'

Three times in the next days he contemplated following his wife's advice and leaving this encampment, and he even went so far as to consult with his son-in-law: 'Theunis, how would you respond to Jakoba's belief that we should leave here, climb the mountain and go north, as we proposed?'

'I would go tomorrow.'

'Why?'

'Balthazar Bronk, he's a tyrant. He's not a man to lead other men.'

Tjaart laughed. 'You're angry with him for demoting you.'

'That's one reason,' Theunis confessed. 'But we're in a new land, new problems. Desperately this people needs a predikant. Our church has refused to countenance us, so we should establish our own rules.'

'I tried. You saw me try, and we were defeated.'

'I would like to go north with you, Tjaart, and find our own land. Believe me, this Natal is contaminated.'

It was contaminated in ways that the sick-comforter either did not know or refused to recognize, for Minna, always fearful that the trek might split and take Ryk Naudé from her permanently, was stealing out to see him at every opportunity, and he seemed as eager as she for these assignations. This left Aletta free, and for reasons that no one could have explained, and certainly not the participants, she threw herself in Tjaart's way, knowing that he was hungry for her. It was a strange and ugly situation, the more so in that the aggrieved parties, Jakoba and Theunis, were among the strongest of the Voortrekkers, and the best. They never spoke to each other of their private griefs, but in their family prayers little Theunis, twisted to one side, sometimes became eloquent when he invoked God on behalf of the Voortrekkers, seeking for them a strength unusual, a devotion unworldly. Often at the end of his protracted prayers tears would spring from both his eyes, not only from the blemished one.

The Van Doorns were not able to leave Blaauwkrantz, because Piet Retief came riding into camp with an urgent request: 'I need a hundred men to accompany me to Dingane's Kraal. And they must be good horsemen.'

'Why?' a murmur of voices asked.

'Tjaart knows why,' and he asked Van Doorn to describe the exhibitions Dingane had provided for his visitors during the last meeting: the military drills, the dancing of the oxen. 'I want our horsemen to show that king something he's never even imagined. Boer strength. Our horsemen in their speediest drill.'

He was not able to enlist the full hundred, but he did get seventy-one skilled horsemen, including himself and his son. Of course, some thirty-one Coloureds rode along, for the Voortrekkers engaged in not a single operation, warlike or peaceful, without their usual complement of assistants. Besides, some of the Coloured were exciting horsemen, and Retief was counting on them to adorn the display he had in mind.

Added to the roster were Tjaart and Paulus de Groot, two weeks short of six years old and already a practiced horseman; as Tjaart said farewell to Jakoba and the Nels, he promised them that he would protect the boy and be home soon with an agreement giving the Voortrekkers rights in Natal. Plans for seeking a safer home in the north were abandoned.

It was a beautiful summer's journey down to the Tugela and across it into the heart of Zululand, but it was dangerously seductive, for the Voortrekkers had convinced themselves that no harm could befall them. Even

Tjaart, who had been warned by the missionary and cautioned by his wife, forgot his apprehensions.

'What could happen to us?' he asked his friends. 'Dingane wanted us to recover his stolen cattle, and there they are, trailing along behind us. He'll welcome us and sign the papers we want.'

They arrived at the great kraal on Saturday morning, 3 February 1838, and the festivities began at once. Paulus encountered a pleasure of which no one had told him, for in the royal town there had been for some time an English lad named William Wood, twelve years old, whom King Dingane treated as a kind of pet, a precious curiosity who lived with the nearby missionaries but who had the run of the capital. This lad took Paulus under his protection, showing him the intricacies of the royal huts and even the forbidden quarters, vast in extent, in which the king's wives were sequestered.

At the end of the first day Paulus was exhausted but delighted: 'Father Tjaart, this is the best.' And memories of his parents' mutilation by the regiments of another king like Dingane were dulled.

On the second day Retief offered the king a surprise, calling upon his horsemen to go through their maneuvers. Into the vast arena, populated by at least four thousand Zulu warriors, came the Boer horsemen, two by two, rifles across their saddles, blank loadings in position. Slowly the horses circled the arena, came down the middle, performing convolutions and raising a stirring clatter. The warriors were entranced, for although they had danced with the oxen, their beautiful beasts had been slow and ponderous; these horses flowed with magic, leaping and twisting at command.

And then, again from a signal by Retief, which Dingane carefully noted, the horsemen broke into a gallop, formed one phalanx, dashed straight at the ebony armchair-throne and discharged their rifles. The effect was overwhelming, and so startled Dingane that he whispered to an attendant, 'These men are indeed wizards.'

William Wood overheard this remark, and as soon as the affair ended he sought out Tjaart and told him of the awful thing the king had said: 'He whispered that you were indeed wizards.'

'In a way we are,' Tjaart agreed.

'Ssssh! It means he's going to kill you.'

Tjaart frowned. 'What's your name again?'

'William Wood. I know Dingane. Mr. van Doorn, he's going to kill all of you.'

The boy's face was so woebegone that Tjaart felt he must inform Retief of the incident, but the commander laughed it off: 'One of the English missionaries said the same thing. But you must remember they're English. They're afraid of Kaffirs.'

But Tjaart was so impressed by William's warning that he suggested leaving the area that night, and he argued so persuasively that Retief might have ordered his people home had not King Dingane himself suddenly appeared: 'I want to ask two questions. First, is it true that your people have finally defeated Mzilikazi?'

'Yes,' Retief replied expansively. 'We killed five thousand of his men. Drove him right across the Limpopo.' He looked threateningly at Dingane, and added, 'A similar defeat awaits any king who opposes the will of God.'

'Who decides that the will of your God has been opposed?' the interpreter asked.

'We will know,' Retief said.

'My second question. Is it true that your Coloured people can ride horses the way you do?' Retief answered, 'Tomorrow you'll see. And as you watch them, remember that you might be given horses, too, once we move into our land.' Dingane nodded.

On Monday, February 5, the show was held, and although the Coloured riders lacked the military precision of the Boers, they rode with such joyous abandon that they more than compensated for the deficiency. William Wood, sitting near the king, heard him grumble to his advisors, 'If the Coloured can ride horses, so can the Zulu. We must keep careful watch on these wizards.'

When the performance ended, William hurried to the Voortrekkers, warning them for the second time: 'Dingane means to kill you either tonight or tomorrow.' But again Retief refused to heed the caution, pointing out: 'A treaty is to be signed in the morning. We'll leave immediately thereafter.'

'Too late,' the boy said, but Retief dismissed him, turning to Tjaart: 'What we might do, Tjaart, is for you to speed back to the Blaauwkrantz. Tell our people that we've been granted the land. Get them packed and ready to take possession before Dingane changes his mind.'

From a small leather pouch he brought forth the precious paper, showing it to Tjaart in a kind of triumph. 'Tell them you saw this. Tell them the Kaffir will sign it tomorrow and then the land is peacefully ours.'

So Tjaart and Paulus saddled their horses, and prepared to serve as bearers of sweet tidings. At last the Voortrekkers would have a home of their own, but before Paulus mounted his horse, William Wood slipped up to him, grasped his hand and whispered, 'I'm glad you're going. Because tomorrow the others will all be dead.'

On Tuesday morning, 6 February 1838, Piet Retief, accompanied by seventy Boer horsemen, rode up to the gates of Dingane's Kraal, where Zulu commanders ordered them to dismount, tether their horses and deposit their weapons in a pile, which would be guarded by one of the regiments: 'Out of respect for the king. He was frightened by that sudden blast the other day.' To these arrangements Retief, as a gentleman, agreed.

The seventy-one white men, including Retief, entered the great arena, followed by their thirty-one Coloureds—one hundred and two in all. Since the day was extremely hot, the visitors were given those areas where the breeze was most likely to move the air, and they seated themselves and accepted the gourds of sorghum beer provided by Dambuza, the king's chief councillor. The land deed was presented to Dingane, who with a flourishing gesture put his mark on it and returned it to Retief. Then the dancing began, two regiments unarmed and wonderfully muscular performing intricate steps and maneuvers.

It was as peaceful a dance as the Zulu could have offered, and it pleased Retief and his men, but the boy William Wood, seeing that beyond the dancers three other regiments were silently moving into position, ran from the arena and told the people at the mission station, 'They are all going to be killed.'

'Hush,' a woman said. 'You've been reprimanded before for spreading rumors.'

The king, watching carefully the progress of the dance, decided that it had reached the designated moment, so while the steps continued he rose and proposed a toast, putting it into Zulu verse, which he composed on the spot:

> 'Let the white lips that thirst,
> Thirst no more!
> Let the eyes that want everything,
> See no more!
> Let the white hearts that beat . . .
> Be still!'

Retief, understanding none of the words, nodded graciously to the king and raised his gourd. At that instant Dingane shouted, 'Seize them, my warriors! Slay the wizards!'

A thousand voices repeated the king's command, and the dancing regiments stepped aside, allowing the real soldiers to leap forward, assegais in hand. With these daggers pointing at their throats, the bewildered Boers stumbled to their feet, whipped out what knives they had, and tried to defend themselves. It was useless. Four, six, ten Zulu grabbed at each Boer, wrestled him to the floor, then, holding him by the legs, dragged him out of the kraal and along a climbing footpath to the place of execution. There on a hill, as William Wood and the missionary women watched from their homes, the Boers were clubbed to death, one by one, knobkerries rising and falling.

The Coloureds also were slain to a man. Piet Retief, pinioned, had to watch his own son being tortured to death before he, too, was clubbed mercilessly until his skull was shattered and he fell upon the heaped bodies of his comrades.

The Zulu commander who had supervised the killings cried, 'Cut out the liver and the heart of this man. Bury them in the middle of the road he traveled.'

So ended Piet Retief, a man who had led his people into the wilderness to build a country of their own, a man who trusted those he met and placed his faith in God. His laager was destroyed; his son was slain; his far designs left unattained. A failure in much that he attempted, he came to a terrible end, but it was also a noble beginning, for his legend would inspire a nation.

On the day ten months later when other Boers came upon his body, they would find in the leather pouch near his bones a document carefully marked by Dingane, King of the Zulu, granting him:

> the Place called Port Natal together with all the Land annexed, that is to say from Dogeela to the River westward and from the Sea to

the North as far as the Land may be Useful and in my possession for their Everlasting property.

De merk + + van de Koning Dingane

Tjaart and Paulus, riding quietly along the banks of the Tugela River, could not know that their fellow Voortrekkers were being massacred, but the boy suffered powerful premonitions and said, 'Father, I do think the king is going to kill all our men. Should we turn back to warn them?'

'No one would dare do a thing like that.'

'But William knows the king. Twice he heard him say that we were wizards.'

'He meant wise men. Because we defeated Mzilikazi.'

'But William has seen wizards put to death. Men hammer stakes into them.'

The boy was so insistent that Tjaart had to pay attention; he became more alert, and it was fortunate that he did, because toward noon he detected to the rear a rise of dust along the trail they had just traveled, and from a hiding place, saw with horror the better part of two regiments, assegais glistening, flash past, headed in the general direction of the Blaauwkrantz River.

Instantly Tjaart realized that they must somehow move ahead of the running column to alert the encampments and the hundreds of Voortrekkers who would not be in laager, but no matter how cleverly they tried to speed along unused trails, invariably they were forestalled by detachments of Zulu who were fanning out across the countryside, murdering any Boers they found.

At four different isolated camps, Tjaart and Paulus found only smoldering ruins and gutted Boers. In an agony of fear, they fought to circumvent the Zulu lines and sound an alarm, but always they failed; once when it seemed that they could slip down a canyon, they watched in dismay as a third regiment of Dingane's men crept in, attacking a lonely wagon and killing everyone.

Belatedly, Tjaart had to acknowledge aloud that Retief and all his men were probably dead. He looked blankly at Paulus, and the boy nodded. He had known all along how great would be the disaster, for William Wood had told him, and now, distraught, he said, 'And before we left, William told me that every Boer in Zululand would be killed. We must hurry to the river.'

'I've been trying!' Tjaart cried, and once again he sought to outflank the Zulu lines, and failed.

At sunset on Friday, 16 February 1838, they were still far short of the Blaauwkrantz, their warning signal undelivered. That night, along an unprotected stretch eleven miles in length, the scattered wagons of the Voortrekkers stood in formless array, and near them the women and children of the men already slaughtered went carelessly to sleep. Additional families, only recently arrived from Thaba Nchu, were spending their first nights in their promised land and staring at the stars which had brought them safely home. It was a quiet night, with only a few dogs barking sporadically.

At one o'clock in the morning three full regiments of Zulu warriors stormed forth in a surprise attack and reached the sleeping wagons and tents before anyone could sound an alarm. In the first wave they slaughtered everyone at the eastern end of the line, except two members of the Bezuidenhout family. The younger Bezuidenhout, barely able to grasp the fact that all but one of his kin were slain, enabled others farther westward to survive the assault by heroically riding through the night, breaking miraculously through one concentration of Zulu warriors after another.

Among the groups he wakened was the Van Doorn encampment: Jakoba, Minna and Theunis, their three-year-old daughter Sybilla and their five servants. These nine had just enough time to take frenzied precautions before the screaming Zulu fell upon them, and in these moments of terror Theunis Nel did a remarkable thing: he took Sybilla and hid her behind a tree, well away from the wagons, and as he left her, trembling with a fear he could not control, he whispered, 'Sybilla, remember when we played the game? You must not make a sound.'

Running back to the wagons, he supervised the distribution of guns and knives and boards, and with these futile weapons and a heroism unmatched, his people defended themselves, the women firing their rifles until there was no more gunpowder, then standing side by side with their Coloureds, chopping at the deadly enemy. Minna went down first, cut to pieces. One by one the fearless, faithful Coloureds died. Then Jakoba and Theunis stood with their hands touching in love and farewell, fighting with whatever they could grab, and finally there was Theunis alone, a pathetic little man swinging a club.

When he saw fresh hordes descending upon him and realized that they might stumble upon his hidden daughter, he ran before them, leading away from her tree, and as the warriors overtook him, each stabbed at him with an assegai. But still he ran, to lead them as far away as possible, and shouting to warn the other wagons. When he felt his knees failing and blood choking his lungs, he turned to face his assailants, grabbed at their assegais, and died of many wounds.

Balthazar Bronk, who had so relentlessly denied him his ordination, had managed, as such men often do, to be at the far end of the encampment, where the Zulu did not reach.

Tjaart arrived at Blaauwkrantz before dawn, and searching in the ghostly light, he and Paulus saw the awful desolation: men hacked to pieces, women and children chopped down, brown and black servants who had surrendered their lives defending the people for whom they worked.

'Father!' Paulus cried. 'Our wagons!'

Recognizing the burned-out frames, Tjaart rushed over—and found his family massacred: Jakoba lay with six dead Zulu at her feet, Minna with three, all the servants, their bodies slashed by assegais. But no Sybilla. And no Theunis.

'Child!' Tjaart roared, hoping that she might somehow have escaped. There was no response, so he started shouting for Theunis, cursing him for having run away and deserted his women.

'Goddamn you, Nel!' he bellowed, and then suddenly he was surrounded by women, jabbering that Theunis had saved their lives: 'He was dying, but he ran nearly half a mile, shouting to us, warning us . . .' 'He was stabbed so many times . . .'

'Was Sybilla with him?'

'He was alone with the spears.' They led him to where the crookbackt sick-comforter lay, uncovered, and Tjaart fell beside him and cried, 'Theunis, where is your daughter?'

Paulus de Groot, now six, looked at the dead body of his second mother, then at Aunt Minna, and he was about to move on to see where Uncle Theunis lay when he sensed a movement among the trees, and although he was terrified by the dreadful things of this night, he walked toward the sound, and there beneath a tree sat Sybilla. She had witnessed everything that happened, but she knew from what her father had told her in those last moments that she must not make a sound.

She made none now, and even when Paulus reached down to take her hands, she followed him mutely, and with Paulus walking backward and guiding her, they left the tree and started to where Tjaart was grieving over the body of her father. But when Paulus had her well on the way, she suddenly halted, pulling her hands free, and when she was thus released she walked purposefully to where her mother and Ouma Jakoba lay. When she stood over them she did not weep, nor did she kneel to kiss them. She simply stood there, and after a while she turned to her friend Paulus and placed her hands again in his. Vaguely she had always known that his father and mother had been killed, and now she knew that hers had died, too. He was the person she could trust. He was the one who understood.

They were standing thus when someone informed Tjaart that his granddaughter was alive. 'Sybilla!' he shouted, but when he dashed back to lift her in his arms, crying, 'Thank God, thank God!' she merely looked at him. Her father had warned her not to speak, and it would be some days before she did.

As soon as Jakoba and the Nels were buried, Tjaart headed for the far end of the wagon line to ascertain what had happened to the Ryk Naudés, and as he walked, dozens of Voortrekkers halted him to ask, 'What news of Retief?' and he was afraid to tell them of Paulus' conviction that the entire party had been slain.

When he found the Naudé wagon, the people of that group were engaged in burying thirteen of their dead. Among them was Ryk; that feckless youth had refused to put his wagons into laager, had been out sporting with some new girl, and had rushed back in time to face a circle of Zulu, who hacked him to pieces.

At the end of the common grave Tjaart found Aletta, her arm in a sling, her face scarred by a long gash; as always, she stood there betraying no emotion, and even when Tjaart signaled to her across the fallen bodies, she merely nodded. Since the Voortrekkers were still without a clergyman, a layman was needed to read from the Bible, and Balthazar Bronk volunteered; he offered a fine prayer and the mass grave was closed.

Then, as if a mighty hand were pushing him from the back, Tjaart stepped around the grave, walked solemnly to where Aletta stood, and addressed her before some other womanless man might lay claim: 'You can't live alone, Aletta.'

'It would be impossible,' she said.

Her husband was dead. Her wagon was burned. She had no place to sleep, no clothes other than those she wore. She had no money, no food, no relatives. She was alone on unprotected land which the Zulu might overrun at any moment, so with a last tearless look at the grave, she held out her good hand, encouraging Tjaart to take it and guide her down the long line of wagons till they reached his.

With dismay she saw that he, too, had nothing: no bed, no box of Jakoba's clothes, no wagon ready for the road—nothing but a brown-gold pot and a Bible. There was no Dutch minister to marry them, but this widow and this widower were wed of their own determination; and as they started retrieving the possessions scattered about, messengers came crying: 'Retief and all his men are slain.'

It was obvious that God had struck His chosen people with a series of punishing blows. For their arrogance and their sins he had chastised them, and as they huddled in their depleted laagers, awaiting the next assault of the Zulu, they tried to unravel the mystery of their wrongdoing.

Every man who died at Dingane's Kraal had loved God and had endeavored to live according to His laws, yet all had perished. Every woman and child murdered at Blaauwkrantz had been faithful to the Bible, but they had been slaughtered. If ever an assembly of people had just cause to rebel against their deity, it was the Voortrekkers that summer of 1838, but they reacted quite differently.

Spiritually they sought within themselves the reasons for their reverses, and decided that they had been lax in their attention to worship and in the keeping of the commandments. For example, Tjaart van Doorn knew in his heart that the adulteries in his family had been the cause of the savage retribution he had suffered, and yet—why had he been saved and faultless Jakoba punished?

Aletta continued to perplex him. In the days following the massacre, her principal concern had been with the cut across her cheek: 'Will it leave a scar?' Wives showed her how to sterilize the wound with cow's urine and salve it with butter, and when she was assured that it would heal without a major blemish, she was satisfied. In her relations with Tjaart she continued as she had always been—completely passive, interested in nothing, absorbed only in herself. Once when he returned to their tent exhausted from digging trenches, he wanted to discuss the problem of finding someone who might lead them against the Zulu, but she had no opinions on any of the men. In some exasperation he asked, 'How about Balthazar Bronk?' and she put her hand to her chin, studied the matter, and said, 'He might be the one,' even though she knew he had run away at Veg Kop.

In the hard task of erecting some sort of defense he noticed this peculiarity: that the boy Paulus toiled like a man while the woman Aletta behaved like a child. He could not help comparing her with Jakoba, who would have been at his side as the new barricades were being built, and he began to understand why Ryk Naudé, married to this extremely beautiful girl, had nevertheless preferred Minna.

When, thanks to Tjaart's stubborn work, these Voortrekkers felt moder-

ately safe from Zulu attack, they returned to the Book of Joshua to review
the steps by which he had triumphed at Jericho over his Canaanite enemies,
and now the loss of Theunis Nel was felt, for he would have been eager to
explicate such matters. In his absence, Tjaart had to serve as principal
guide, bending over the charred cover of his Bible to read the relevant
verses:

> 'And it came to pass . . . that the people went up into the city, every
> man straight before him, and they took the city. And they utterly
> destroyed all that was in the city, both man and woman, young and
> old, and ox, and sheep, and ass, with the edge of the sword.'

Then he swore grimly: 'That's what we'll do to Dingane's Kraal. Total
destruction.' By what specific steps this would be accomplished he did not
know, for he considered himself inadequate to lead. What he could do was
reflect the stubborn Boer determination to see this job finished, and if any
man wavered, he laid forth the damning statistics: 'At the kraal, one hundred and two of our men killed. Here at Blaauwkrantz, two hundred and
eighty-two. Out in the countryside, at least seventy more slain in their sleep.
We demand retribution.'

'How can we attain it,' Balthazar Bronk asked, 'when we are so few and
they so many?'

'I don't know,' Tjaart said, 'but I'm sure God will show us a way.'

And then into camp rode the man who would achieve miracles. He was
Andries Pretorius, clean-shaven, younger than the other leaders, a person
of substance in Graaff-Reinet. He was extremely tall and bulky, slow to
reach decisions but resolute when he had done so. Like most of the leaders,
he had been married more than once, with eight children by his first wife,
three by his second. A grave, thoughtful man, he had hurried north in
response to a summons from the beleaguered Voortrekkers. With his gun,
his pistols and a thick-bladed cutlass, he strode into camp on 22 November
1838 and said simply, 'I have come to help you. Within the week we shall
ride forth to destroy Dingane.'

The first thing he did was follow the cautious precept of Joshua: 'I want
two men to spy out the enemy,' and he designated a curious pair—Tjaart
van Doorn, whom he trusted because of his determined commandos against
the Xhosa, and Balthazar Bronk, who had behaved so badly in previous
battles. He wanted Tjaart because he knew how to fight, Bronk because he
was a clever, wily man.

Together the two men left Blaauwkrantz, eased themselves cautiously
northward, and returned to camp with the somber news that Dingane had
begun to assemble his regiments for a massive strike: 'He will have twelve
thousand men to throw against us. How many will we have?'

Pretorius, like Joshua, had gathered all available soldiers, and he told
them, 'The odds against us will be thirty-to-one. But we will carry the fight
to them. We will select the place of battle.'

Only five days after the arrival of this dynamic man, the commando was
in motion. It consisted of four hundred and sixty-four men, with the usual
complement of Coloureds and blacks. About half had fought against the
Zulu in one capacity or another; half had never opposed any black regiment.

With them they had sixty-four wagons, absolutely essential in the plan Pretorius had devised. In the forefront was the rebuilt TC–43, now a sturdy, clean war vehicle with reinforced sides and fourteen highly trained oxen who seemed to take pride in setting the pace; if another wagon threatened to assume the lead, these oxen quickened their steps to stay in front.

By this swift movement General Pretorius appropriated tactical advantage; the battle would be fought where he decided, and on terrain favorable to his design. With brilliance he selected a steeply banked corner where a deep gully joined a small river; and in this fortunate area he placed his laager beside a deep pool which recently had been used by hippopotamuses for their bathing (Seekoei Gat, the Boers called it, Sea-cow Hole). He was thus protected on the south by the deep gully, on the east by the hippo pool, and to the north and west by the chain of sixty-four wagons, which he lashed together with enormous thongs, trek chains and great accumulations of thorn bush. At points along the perimeter, and positioned so they would face the maximum number of Zulu rushing to attack the laager, he placed four small cannon capable of firing an immense load of pellets, iron bits, chain links and rocks.

'We are ready,' he said at dusk on Saturday, 15 December 1838, and that night was the longest that these embattled Boers would ever know. They were few, and on the hills surrounding them on all sides gathered the Zulu regiments, men who had fought across the face of Africa, sweeping all before them. Inside the laager the nine hundred trek oxen lowed, hundreds of horses fretted, disturbed by the fires the Zulu maintained, worried by the sounds that encroached on all sides. Pretorius, moving among his troops, told them, 'We must station our men along the entire perimeter, for if we fire only from one direction, the animals, especially our horses, will swarm away from the noise, and they might escape through upset wagons. Without horses, tomorrow we would be lost.'

When all the details were perfected, the time was ripe for the crucial moment in Boer history. With the death of Theunis Nel, the Voortrekkers had no one who even presumed to be a predikant, but they had numerous men who knew the Old Testament almost by heart, and one of these was Sarel Cilliers, an educated farmer of deep religious conviction, and upon him fell the responsibility of reminding his fellow Voortrekkers of the sacred mission upon which they were engaged, and he recited those passages from the thundering Book of Joshua which presaged the forthcoming battle:

> 'And the Lord said unto Joshua, Be not afraid because of them: for tomorrow about this time will I deliver them up all slain before Israel: thou shalt hough their horses and burn their chariots with fire . . . One man of you shall chase a thousand: for the Lord your God, he it is that fighteth for you, as he hath promised you.'

Then Cilliers climbed upon the carriage on which a beloved cannon named Ou Grietjie (Old Gertie) rested, and repeated for the last time the covenant upon which the Voortrekkers had agreed:

'Almighty God, at this dark moment we stand before You, promising that if You will protect us and deliver the enemy into our hands, we shall forever after live in obedience to Your divine law. If You enable us to triumph, we shall observe this day as an anniversary in each year, a day of thanksgiving and remembrance, even for all our posterity. And if anyone sees difficulty in this, let him retire from the battlefield.'

In the darkness the Voortrekkers whispered their Amens; they were now a nation established by God, in pursuit of His objectives, and those who were able to sleep the few hours before dawn did so with easy consciences, for they knew that God Himself had brought them to this river to face odds that would have terrified ordinary men.

The Battle of Blood River, as it came understandably to be called, had no parallel in recent world history. Twelve thousand, five hundred highly trained and capable Zulu threw themselves over a period of two hours at a cleverly entrenched foe, and without modern weapons of any kind, attempted to overwhelm a group of tough, resolute men armed with rifles, pistols and cannon. It was a hideous affair. The Zulu warriors stamped their feet, shouted their war cries, and drove straight at the laager. The men inside stood firm, waited for the enemy to come within six feet of the wagons, then fired into their chests. Those warriors fell, but others replaced them, expecting their cowhide shields to protect them, and they, too, marched right into the muzzles of the guns, and they, too, fell.

A thousand Zulu died in this way, then two thousand, but still they came on. Within the first hour the Zulu generals, supposing that the white men inside the laager must be depleted, decided to throw at them their two finest regiments, those entitled to wear all-white shields, white armlets and knee decorations, and it was awesome to see these excellent men, all of an age and a height, march unswervingly over the bodies of their fallen comrades, straight at the laager.

Inside, General Pretorius told his men, 'This may be the flood tide. Hold your fire.' So the riflemen waited while the gunners loaded Ou Grietjie with a murderous load of scrap and leaden slugs; and when these crack regiments had marched directly to the muzzles of these creaking guns, Pretorius gave the signal. Ou Grietjie and her three ugly sisters spewed out their lethal dose right into the faces of the Zulu, while riflemen from the flanks poured hot fire at them.

Not even the White Shields could absorb punishment like this, but they did not falter or run. They simply came on, and died.

Now Pretorius made an astounding decision: 'Mount your horses. We shall drive them from the field.' So about a hundred Voortrekkers leaped upon their steeds, waited till riflemen opened a gateway through the laager, and galloped out in a firing, slashing foray that startled the Zulu. Down one front the Voortrekkers rode, killing at a fantastic rate; then along another, cutting and firing; then deep into the heart of the enemy concentration, galloping like wild avengers; then back and forth three times, as if they were immortal.

After slaying hundreds of the enemy, they galloped back inside the laager; the only rider in this amazing sortie to suffer a wound was General Pretorius. He had his hand cut by an assegai.

Now Ou Grietjie was moved from her position along the wagon arc and dragged by hand to one of the corners, from which she could fire straight down the gully into which four hundred Zulu had crept, hoping in this way to cut in behind the wagons. Then the cannon was loaded with an assortment of nails and scrap, and pointed directly into the gully and discharged. It was loaded again, and fired. And before the hidden Zulu could clamber out, a third salvo hit, killing the remnants.

Still the amazing Zulu pressed on; the ground was littered with broken bodies, but on they marched, throwing themselves against the wagons, trying in vain to move close enough to use their stabbing assegais, and falling back only when they were dead.

At the end of two hours the black generals sought to rally their regiments by gathering in one spot all White Shield survivors and giving them the simple command: 'Break through and slay the wizards.' Without hesitation these splendid warriors adjusted the shields, borrowed extra assegais, and began a stately march right at the spot from which Ou Grietjie had been removed. They came in panoply, they fought in glory. Wave after wave marched almost to the wagons and fell to the blazing guns. Yet on they came, men trained all their lives to obey, but when the final ranks hit the wagons, they accomplished nothing. Silently the generals signaled retreat and the punished regiments withdrew, defeated but still obedient to command. A new power had replaced them in Zululand, and it had come to stay.

Before dusk the Voortrekkers came out of their laager to inspect the battlefield, on which they counted over three thousand dead. Another seven hundred died of wounds at a distance and could not be verified. Still others would die later.

What can be said of a battle in which the casualties were over four thousand dead on one side, a cut hand on the other? Not one man in the Voortrekker laager was killed; not one was seriously injured; counting even the scratches, only three were touched in this incredible battle. Four thousand-to-nothing, what kind of warfare is that? The answer would come years later from a troubled Dutch Reformed minister: 'It was not a battle. It was an execution.'

But Blood River, terrible though it was, must not be considered by itself; it was merely the culminating battle in the campaign that included the massacres at Dingane's Kraal and Blaauwkrantz. If those unwarranted deaths are counted, plus the many casualties at unprotected farms, the real nature of this continuing battle can be apprehended: at first, overwhelming Zulu victories; at the end, a Voortrekker triumph so one-sided as to be grotesque; but on balance, a ferocious battle with many casualties on each side.

The real victor at Blood River was not the Voortrekker commando, but the spirit of the covenant that assured their triumph. As Tjaart said when he led prayers after the battle: 'Almighty God, only You enabled us to win. We were faithful to You, and You fought at our side. In obedience to the covenant You offered us and which You honored, we shall henceforth abide as Your people in the land You have given us.'

What the Voortrekkers failed to realize in their moment of victory was that they had offered the covenant to God, not He to them. Any group of people anywhere in the world was free to propose a covenant on whatever terms they pleased, but this did not obligate God to accept that covenant, and especially not if their unilateral terms contravened His basic teachings to the detriment of another race whom He loved equally. Nevertheless, in obedience to the covenant as they understood it, they had won a signal victory, which confirmed their belief that He had accepted their offer and had personally intervened on their behalf. No matter what happened henceforth, men like Tjaart van Doorn were convinced that whatever they did was done in consonance with His wishes. The Boer nation had become a theocracy, and would so remain.

General Pretorius knew he must not allow King Dingane a chance to regroup his regiments; he realized that Zulu learned quickly and that in the next great battle they would present him with difficult tactics, so he scoured the landscape, seeking the devious ruler who had committed the murders. He did not catch him. Before fleeing, Dingane set fire to his famous kraal, destroying the treasures accumulated since the reign of Shaka. Among the items found by the Boers in the kraal were two cannon, a gift from a treaty-seeker. They had been allowed to rust, unused; had they been operating at Blood River, they might have offset Ou Grietjie and her three sisters.

Dingane fled far to the north, where he established a new kraal and waited in fright for the Boers to come seeking retribution. A younger brother, Mpande, seized the chance to ally himself with the Boers and suggested a joint expedition against his brother's battered regiments. But before this campaign could be launched, Dingane sent his chief councillor, Dambuza, and a subordinate to the Voortrekkers, offering them two hundred of his finest cattle.

'Dingane seeks peace,' Dambuza entreated. 'The lands Retief sought are yours.'

Mpande, who attended this meeting, always seeking an opportunity to increase his standing with the whites, screamed at Dambuza, 'You lie! There will be no peace if Dingane lives. Who are you to speak, Dambuza? Were you not at his side when he killed Retief and his men? Were you not shouting, "They are wizards"? '

So ferocious was Mpande's indictment that Pretorius ordered the envoys stripped naked and cast into chains. Shortly, both were on trial before a military court, where the chief witness was Mpande. On his testimony, both envoys were sentenced to death, even though they were diplomats visiting a host country, as it were.

Dambuza did not beg, but he did plead for his subordinate: 'Spare him. He's a young man with no guilt.'

There was no mercy. Tjaart van Doorn, present throughout the hearing, saw Balthazar Bronk, eager to serve on the firing squad, prepare his rifle. The two condemned blacks were dragged into the open, and Bronk's marksmen lined up.

'Wait!' Pretorius cried. Striding swiftly toward the envoys, he said, 'Dambuza, you must ask forgiveness from God. Tell Him you're sorry, and He'll listen.'

The tall, powerful black said slowly, 'I know not your God, Boer. King Dingane is my chief. I did what he ordered. But I do plead for my aide. Release him.'

'Shoot them,' Pretorius barked, turning away from the scene of execution.

Bronk and his men assumed position. Their gunfire splattered, and the two blacks fell. Then the miracle happened. Councillor Dambuza, only slightly wounded, rose to his feet.

'He is spared,' someone shouted. 'God has saved him for his courage.'

'Reload,' Bronk shouted.

Tjaart van Doorn said not a word as Dambuza faced the firing squad for a second time, but he did think of a grim day long ago at a place called Slagter's Nek, and in his mind he saw a scrawny English missionary, brother to his friend in Grahamstown, pleading for mercy for men whom God had reprieved when the ropes at their necks broke.

'Fire!' Bronk shouted, and this time the aim of the executioners was sure.

Within months Dingane himself was dead, assassinated perhaps at the instigation of his brother Mpande, who ascended the throne with the help of his Boer allies. It had been Dingane's fate to wrest the kingdom from his half brother Shaka at the time in history when confrontation with a new and powerful force was inescapable, and he had never had a glimmer as to how adjustments should be made. He was an evil, pitiful man; he was also a powerful, wise and cunning manipulator; and the best that can be said of him is that his errors did not destroy the Zulu people. On the ashes of Dingane's Kraal a mighty nation would arise, powerful enough within a few decades to challenge the British Empire, and within a century to contest with the Boer nation for the leadership of southern Africa.

When victory was complete, Tjaart studied the situation carefully; desperately he wished that Lukas de Groot were still alive so that he might compare assessments with that sage farmer, for he needed help. He also missed Jakoba, whose stubborn advice had always been so sensible; she would have been a good one to talk with, but her successor, Aletta, was quite hopeless. Whatever Tjaart elected to do suited her; her principal concern was finding enough cloth and stiffeners to make a sunbonnet large enough to keep the sun's rays from her face, which she hoped to keep as fair as possible.

Once, in dismay, Tjaart said, 'Aletta, I think we ought to go back over the mountains to land we know. I don't like it here. Sooner or later the English are going to come at us . . .'

'That's a good idea,' Aletta agreed, but when he took the first steps to effectuate the plan, she whimpered, 'I wouldn't want to carry our wagon back up those cliffs.' He did not remind her that she had carried precious little down, but he was confused by her vacillations, and one day he asked, 'Aletta, where would you like to spend the rest of your life?'

The bluntness of this question startled her, for she had not reached the age when the phrase 'the rest of your life' had any meaning; it was then that she awakened fully to the fact that she was married to a man over fifty years old and that he had only a limited number of years remaining. But where would she like to live? 'Cape Town,' she said honestly, whereupon he ended the discussion.

He had about decided to stay in Natal with General Pretorius, whom he admired immensely, when two trivial things intervened: an English merchant came up from Port Natal with news that an English force would soon be arriving to take the port under their command; and young Paulus, now a tall and vigorous lad, said casually, 'I would like to go hunting lions.' And the vision of an untrammeled veld came back to haunt Tjaart. He appreciated Natal, especially these good fields along the Tugela River, but like many Voortrekkers, once he had seen the vast open sweep of the Transvaal, all other land seemed puny. He, too, longed to see lions and rhinoceroses and perhaps the sable antelope. He was homesick for loneliness, and the presence of so many Boers erecting villages and towns oppressed him.

Even so, Aletta's obvious preference for the maturing life of Natal might have kept him there had not a ridiculous situation developed: one morning he was awakened by a clatter outside his tent, and there was Balthazar Bronk, a man he despised. 'Van Doorn,' he said as soon as Tjaart wiped the sleeping-sand out of his eyes, 'what they say is true. "Wherever a ship can sail, an Englishman will come." I think we ought to get out of here.'

'To where?'

'Back up on the plateau.' From the tent, young Paulus cried, 'Hooray! We'll go back and hunt lions.'

The more Balthazar talked, the more sense he made, and by the time Aletta got out of bed, the two men had convinced themselves that they must start quickly toward the mountains; Natal was not for them. But when Aletta heard the decision she began to pout and said that she did not intend to help carry this wagon back up those hills. 'No necessity,' Bronk assured her. 'There's a good trail now. General Pretorius crossed the peaks in three days.'

'Why didn't we use it?' she said.

'It wasn't known then.'

For a three-day period it looked as if Aletta might leave Tjaart; she was not legally married to him yet, and there were other men in the new settlements who needed wives. It was her strong desire to remain here with the other women and not climb back to the highveld where her life would be lonely and short. But then an American missionary—a gawky young Baptist from Indiana—wandered into the settlements, and the hunger of the Voortrekkers for a predikant manifested itself. Tjaart joined a committee of five which interrogated the young man to see if he might be willing to perfect his Dutch and transfer his allegiance to the Dutch Reformed Church.

'I am not too good at languages,' he said in English.

'Did you attend seminary?' Tjaart asked in Dutch.

'Yes.'

'And were you approved?'

'Yes.'

'Then you can learn.'

'But you ought to have a Dutch minister.'

'That's right,' Tjaart said, 'but the Dutch ministers have outlawed us,' and he showed the young man the latest copy of the Cape Town newspaper, *The South African Commercial Advertiser,* in which spokesmen for the church reiterated the charge that the Voortrekkers were fugitives acting in disobedience to organized society, that they were no doubt spiritual degenerates and should be shunned by all good people.

'Of course it would be better if we had Dutch predikants,' Tjaart summarized, 'but what we want to know is can you accept our doctrines?'

'Well,' the young fellow said brightly, 'seems to me that the Dutch Reformed Church is pretty much what we in America call Lutherans.'

'Nothing of the kind!' Tjaart roared. 'That's Martin Luther. We're John Calvin.'

'Aren't they the same?'

'Good God!' Tjaart grumbled, and he took no further part in the interrogation, but when the other four had completed their questioning, it became apparent that here was a true man of God, called to the frontier from a vast distance, one who would grace any community. Without consulting Tjaart, they made him a definite offer, and he finally accepted.

But it was Tjaart who gave him his first two commissions: 'Will you perform a marriage?'

'I would be proud to do so, Mr. van Doorn.'

'I'm never a mister,' Tjaart growled, whereupon the young minister said, 'But you are a man of strong calling, and that I like.'

The two men walked to Tjaart's wagon, where Aletta was summoned, and when she heard that this strange fellow was a minister she turned pale, for during the past several nights she had been secretly meeting a young man whose love-making she fancied, and she had been about to inform Tjaart of her new preference. He, seeing her paleness, surmised what the situation might be, for he had met with her when she was married to another and he knew her irresponsibility; but he also knew that moving to the north without a wife would be impossible, and he was still captivated by her beauty. So he reached out, grasped her harshly by the wrist, and pulled her before the new predikant.

'Marry us,' he said, and there in the Natal sunlight the new clergyman performed his first ritual, knowing well that it was somehow faulty and that this was not a good union.

His second rite was a strange one. Tjaart, with the approval of some of his neighbors, asked the missionary, 'Sir, can you honor us by ordaining a dead man?'

'Quite unheard of.' But when Van Doorn led the party to a narrow grave marked by a few stones and explained to the new predikant who Theunis Nel had been, and how he had died, and why he had always wanted to be an ordained clergyman, the young fellow said, 'He won his ordination of God. It would ill behoove me to deprive him of it.'

So at the graveside he prayed for the soul of . . . 'What's the name again?'
'Theunis Nel,' Tjaart whispered. ' . . . The soul of Thy servant Theunis Nel.
I became a minister by studying at seminary in Pennsylvania. Theunis
became one by sacrificing his life for others.'

'Can you pray in Dutch?' Tjaart asked.

'I'm learning.'

'Well, say a few words. Theunis spoke Dutch.'

In halting phrases the young predikant asked for the blessing of all upon
this man who had served so faithfully, the true minister of the faith, after
which Tjaart said defiantly, 'Now he's a predikant,' but Balthazar Bronk,
following this nonsense from a distance, whispered to his cronies, 'He was
Tjaart's son-in-law. That explains it.'

Nevertheless, when Tjaart and his legal wife inspanned their oxen and
set their rebuilt wagon on the journey west, Bronk was with them, and six
other families. With the English once more breathing down their necks, this
time in Natal, they knew they had yet to find the promised land they sought.

On 26 March 1841 they reached the foothills of the Drakensberg, where they
rested for three weeks prior to the assault. Bronk had been correct in stating
that a new pass had been found over the peaks, but even so, it required
almost a month for the wagons slowly to retrace their way to Thaba Nchu,
where hundreds of Voortrekkers had assembled. Here, too, they rested
through the cold months of June and July, acquiring goods, listening to tales
about the land across the Vaal River.

Two of their families defected, but four new ones joined, and it was in
a party of ten wagons that they started their serious penetration of the veld.
Vast areas depopulated by Mzilikazi's early depredations had slowly started
their recovery, but the journey in late winter of that year was still appalling:
they came upon the roots of villages which had been totally destroyed. Not
a hut remained, not an animal, only bleached bones. Tjaart said, 'It's as if
a Biblical plague had wasted the land and its people.'

One morning as the wagons moved across the empty veld with Tjaart
and Paulus in the lead, Aletta broke into laughter, and when others asked
the reason, she pointed at the two figures and said, 'They look like two
flat-topped hills moving across the landscape,' and when the others studied
them, they did indeed resemble walking mounds: heavy shoes, thick ragged
trousers, bulking shoulders and flat hats with enormous brims—Tjaart
ponderous and heavy, Paulus a true child of the veld. They were the walking
mountains on whom a new society would be built.

In October they reached as far north as the Pienaars River, where
Paulus shot a large hippopotamus, providing meat for two weeks of their
stay in that congenial place. They had now been in uncharted territory for
three months, with no idea at all of where they would settle, but no one
complained. This was so much better than the early days of the Mzilikazi
terror, or those later days in Natal when massacres were frequent; here
there was only loneliness and swift death if illness attacked; there was also
food, and safety at night, and the incredible beauty of the veld.

On 17 November 1841 Tjaart reached a major decision: 'We're going up
to the Limpopo. I've always been told it's the best part of Africa.' Such a

journey might require six months, eight months. But there was nothing else to do, so the ten wagons slowly pressed northward, into the land of the baobabs, the land of enormous antelope herds. On the southern shore of the river Paulus de Groot shot his lion. Of course, Tjaart and Balthazar stood behind him and shot at the same instant so as to avoid leaving a cripple to ravage the area, but they did not tell Paulus of this and all agreed that he had brought down the beast.

These Voortrekkers spent from January 1842 to September exploring north of the Limpopo, moving out cautiously to ascertain whether or not the land which looked so peaceful contained enemy tribes, and at the conclusion of the fourth such probe, Tjaart said, 'The Kaffirs we've met all speak of a great city to the north. Zimbabwe. I think we should go see.'

The other families, including Aletta, counseled against this, saying, 'Mzilikazi lies in wait up there.' But to Tjaart's surprise he was supported by Balthazar Bronk, who had heard rumors that Zimbabwe was paved with gold: 'I've asked the Kaffirs. They say Mzilikazi moved far west.' So Tjaart, Balthazar, Paulus and two blacks set forth with six horses to reach Zimbabwe, and as they traveled through low scrub, decorated with euphorbias that looked like Christmas trees with a thousand upright candles, they caught something of the grandeur of this region; it was quite unlike land to the south of the Limpopo, but they noticed also that their horses were weakening, as if some new disease were striking them, and they began to hurry, eager to see Zimbabwe with its golden streets.

At last they could view on the far horizon the vast hills of granite with their exfoliated layers of smooth stone, and they guessed that they were in the general region of the city, but when their horses faltered, they felt that they must turn back, and a serious conclave was held, with Balthazar wanting to return and Tjaart wishing to forge ahead just a little farther. Paulus, too, wanted to try, and his vote decided; Bronk would stay with the sick horses while the two others walked for three days: 'If you see nothing by then, you must come back.'

'Agreed.'

So Tjaart, Paulus and the two servants walked the last miles, and from a hill they saw Zimbabwe, not the flourishing city paved with gold, but the ruins of a notable site, overgrown with trees, captured by vines, and populated by a tribe that knew nothing of past glories. On the ruins where great kings had knelt and along the overgrown streets which Arab traders had trod with bags of gold, baboons played and warthogs shuffled along, grunting and rooting among the fallen stones.

It was a gloomy, sad place and Tjaart said, 'Poor Balthazar. No gold here.'

When they rejoined Bronk, he informed them that two of the horses had died: 'I think a fly is biting them.'

'It's not biting us,' Tjaart said.

'The trip's proved nothing,' Balthazar complained.

'It's proved we don't want to live up here. No gold for you, either.'

So they returned south, three Voortrekkers leading four sick horses, and by the time they reached the Limpopo, two more were dead. Something in the vicinity of this river was inimical to horses, and when they rejoined their families, they found that the oxen were wasting away, too.

'We must leave here,' Tjaart said, and on 20 September 1842 they started slowly south, oppressed by a sense of defeat, which was exacerbated for Tjaart when Aletta began to show a distinct dislike for her granddaughter Sybilla. Because the little girl, now seven years old, was so extraordinarily beautiful, so fragile and so enticing, Aletta saw her as a reminder of her own aging. She was twenty-five now and the hated life of the frontier had attacked both her beauty and her figure, so that she sometimes considered herself actually ugly. 'Won't we ever settle in some town, Tjaart? I want to live with other people.' When he rebuffed her, she took her discomfort out on little Sybilla, who proved a most infuriating child; for when Aletta berated her for some imagined fault, she merely looked at her grandmother, listened obediently, then walked away to find Paulus, who comforted her after such assaults.

It angered Aletta to see the two children together, for obviously they inhabited a private world from which she would always be excluded; Sybilla's habit of clinging to the boy's hand, as she had done that awful night, irritated her, and whenever she saw this she shouted, 'Sybilla, come in here. Girls don't play with boys that way.' And the little girl would just stare at her.

On the southward journey Tjaart kept his group well to the east, and by the middle of November 1842 they had reached a protected valley some hundred miles south of the Limpopo. Here they camped for three months, collecting ivory from the vast herds of elephants that roamed off to the east in the dense forests that presumably led down to the distant ocean. They were quite content to stay clear of those rich lands: 'We want no more lowlands. Boers are meant to live on the highveld with the gazelles.'

On 10 February 1843, in the middle of a promising summer, the ten wagons, loaded with ivory, resumed their drift south, and after four weeks of easy travel, Paulus shouted one dawn, 'Look at them come!'

Startled, still half-asleep, they did not know what to expect. They had been so long removed from enemy tribes that they were quite unprepared for laagers, and none were now necessary, for from the veld to the west came a line of the finest sable antelope any of these wanderers had ever seen. They were larger, sleeker than those that had crossed De Kraal before the trek, and their coats were of a warmer hue. The white of their bellies shone in the morning sunlight, as did the distinctive blaze across their faces. But it was their horns which dominated—forty, fifty inches long, gracefully back-curved and awesome.

'Look at them!' Tjaart said, echoing the boy's delight. Even Aletta showed interest in the splendid beasts as they moved gracefully, uncon-cernedly away from the wagons.

'Where are they going?' Bronk asked, and Tjaart said, 'I think they're leading us home.' And he turned the wagons eastward, not trying to follow the sables, for they might gallop off at any moment. For some reason, the animals were not frightened by the wagons, so for part of that morning the two groups moved together, sables majestically in front, their horns shining in sunlight, the men and women behind, praying that they might soon reach the end of their wandering.

And then from the low and level fields that lay to the west of the lake, the Voortrekkers saw for the first time the quiet beauty of Vrijmeer, with its protecting mountains and the two signal hills. After seven full years of wandering, they had come home to what in the developing new language would henceforth be called Vrymeer.

They were not alone, for as they approached the lake they saw at the eastern end the collection of huts and lean-tos occupied by Nxumalo and his complicated family.

'Enemy!' Bronk cried, reaching for his gun.

'Wait!' Tjaart advised, after which he walked forward cautiously, gun at the ready, primed to defend himself if need be but also ready to accept friendship if that were proffered.

From his rondavel Nxumalo saw the white people approaching, and prudently he took down his stabbing assegai, and almost naked, strode forth to meet the newcomers.

Slowly, cautiously the two men approached each other, and in the heart of each there was a weariness with killing. Tjaart wanted no more rivers of blood and sorrow; Nxumalo had fled the excesses of King Shaka and the evil force of Mzilikazi. They were older men now, Tjaart fifty-four, Nxumalo one year more, and they sought repose beside some lake. Fate, at the end of wars and tribulations, had brought them to the same spot, and it would be madness for them to contest it.

Passing his gun back to Paulus, Tjaart extended his hands to show that he carried no weapons, and at this gesture of friendliness, Nxumalo, now white-haired, handed his assegai to his son. Paulus and the black boy waited as the two men moved cautiously forward, stopped an arm's length apart, and stared at each other. Finally, Nxumalo, on whose land this meeting was taking place, pointed to the lake and said that it was a safe, strong place. Tjaart, knowing little of the Zulu language, said haltingly that he had had this lake in his heart for all the years of his life, that his grandfather had discovered it and passed along remembrances of it. Pointing to the rondavels, he indicated that his people would build theirs at this spot, too, and this Nxumalo understood.

'There is room,' he said. In the days before King Shaka had run wild he had seen many tribes living side by side, and it could be done again.

But Tjaart, whose ten wagons represented just about the same population power as Nxumalo's accumulation, felt it necessary to demonstrate that the white men had certain advantages which the blacks would be wise to respect. Turning to Paulus, he told the boy, 'Shoot us a bird. Or an antelope.'

At that moment the sables elected to move on, and in doing so, came into range of the little fellow, who took careful aim, fired, and dropped the last in line. Nxumalo was dutifully impressed by two things: that the white man could kill at such a distance and that he would want to kill an animal as splendid as the sable antelope.

When the hartebeest huts were finished, identical with the rude sheds occupied by Hendrik van Doorn one hundred and forty-nine years earlier, a most fortunate thing occurred, one which Balthazar Bronk was able to utilize to the general advantage of the white community.

Relations with Nxumalo's tribe had prospered, and it was apparent that whites and blacks could share Vrymeer in harmony. There was no trouble about land, nor hunting rights, nor anything else; Nxumalo tried to make it clear, as he learned bits of Dutch, that his Zulu would in no way become vassals of the white men, nor would they work for them on any regular basis like their Coloured servants; they, too, were free and proud of that. But when during the building of the huts the blacks volunteered much labor and showed the newcomers how best to utilize the terrain for drainage, Tjaart said confidently, 'They'll soon be working for us.' It was a happy, prosperous relationship, with the Voortrekkers providing an occasional antelope for Nxumalo's pots and with certain women of the tribe volunteering to care for the white babies while their mothers worked at other tasks.

The situation did not exactly please Bronk and his group; they wanted the blacks to become slaves, as the Bible directed, and there was even some talk of eliminating Nxumalo's tribe altogether, in obedience to the precepts of Joshua, which Balthazar was skilled in quoting:

> 'And they smote all the souls that were therein with the edge of the sword, utterly destroying them: and there was not any left to breathe: and he burnt Hazor with fire . . . And all the spoil of these cities, and the cattle, the children of Israel took.'

To the surprise of all, Tjaart opposed this draconian solution, whereupon Bronk countered with the suggestion that the blacks be converted into servants, as the Bible ordered in so many places, but this, too, Tjaart rejected, saying, 'We have searched so long for a place in which we can live in peace, let us do so here.' And since he was the acknowledged leader of the group, this counsel was accepted.

But then the fortunate stroke came, and the whole problem was neatly settled. One night cattle thieves broke into the Van Doorn kraal and made away with some twenty oxen, half of them belonging to Balthazar, who threatened to annihilate the black settlement, but when Tjaart and Paulus went to investigate, they found that none of Nxumalo's people had touched the cattle: 'It's the village far over the hill. They steal our cattle, too.'

So a retaliatory commando was enlisted, and under the leadership of Balthazar Bronk it ranged far, following the spoor of the stolen cattle and coming at last upon a meager village of some forty people. There, in the kraals, stood the Van Doorn cattle, so with a mighty shout the horsemen burst into the heart of the village, massacring everyone.

'Not the children!' Bronk shouted. 'Save the children!'

In obedience to his command, eleven black children were saved, and these were driven back to the white camp, where they were distributed among the families to work for the rest of their lives. They were not slaves; the law forbade any further slavery and every Voortrekker constitution for a new republic outlawed it. But the Bible had expressly authorized Israelites to take children from the Canaanites and raise them as servants:

Moreover of the children of the strangers that do sojourn among
you, of them shall ye buy, and of their families that are with you,
which they begat in your land: and they shall be your possession.
And ye shall take them as an inheritance for your children after
you, to inherit them for a possession; they shall be your bondmen
for ever . . .

Cleverly the Voortrekkers reconciled this Biblical injunction with the new
English law: No slavery, but if a black child is left orphaned in battle, it
must as an act of charity be taken into a white home, where it shall serve
as helper till the age of twenty-one, without wages but with Christian
instruction and wholesome Kaffir food. After that, of course, the black
would have nowhere to go, really, so it would be logical for him to stay on,
at whatever compensation the master saw fit to offer.

So the sensible thing to do on commando was to see that there were
orphans, and Balthazar Bronk had done so. Tjaart argued mildly against
what seemed to him an evasion, but his wife was so pleased to receive the
two children assigned to her that he said nothing, for even though he was
disposed to ask Aletta not to keep them, there in his Bible were the instructions commanding him to keep the children, and to accept others when they
came his way.

Now that the great fixed battles had ended, Tjaart could think of the blacks
against whom he had fought so incessantly—Xhosa, Matabele, Zulu—as
men of enviable courage. He had been awed by their willingness to keep
coming forward into the face of certain death, and he prayed that the time
had come when blacks and Voortrekkers could share peace. In both religion
and tradition he had been taught that no black could ever attain the cultural
or moral level achieved by the most ordinary white man, and he was now
satisfied that they were intended to be servants. The Boer leaders referred
to them as 'the inferior race,' and he saw no reason to alter that assessment,
but he also knew they could be wonderful friends and trusted associates. In
his lifetime he had been forced to kill well over one hundred and sixty
individual blacks himself, and he could think of not a single instance in
which he had been in any way at fault. It was strange that not once did
he fire a gun at a black without having at his elbow one of his Hottentot
or Xhosa servants, who had helped him track the enemy and prepare the
guns. And no matter where he traveled, in peace or war, he never went
anywhere without blacks who had elected of their own volition to stay with
him. On numerous occasions he risked his life to preserve his personal
freedom, but if anyone had told him that blacks would do the same, he
would have been dumfounded, for he believed that they welcomed the
coming of the white man and preferred an orderly progress in servitude and
self-development, much as the oxen yoked to his wagon liked to be told
where to go.

Aletta was now completely disenchanted with Tjaart, finding him a monot-
onous, single-minded man whose rigorous attitudes toward life grew tedi-

ous. He had been exciting as an alternative to her pusillanimous Ryk
Naudé, but as a legal husband, he was tiresome. Much more to her taste
was a man like Balthazar Bronk, younger, livelier, more fun by the lakeside,
and before long she was seeing this flamboyant gentleman with some regu-
larity.

Paulus alerted his father as to what was happening: 'Aletta goes to the
fields.'

'Who with?'

'Balthazar.'

As always, Tjaart studied the matter cautiously, and when he proved
to his satisfaction that his wife had returned to her customary deceptions,
he went into seclusion for several days, during which he calculated the
remaining probabilities of his life: I'm an old man now, and all my children
are dead. My two sons slain at De Kraal. Minna dead at Blaauwkrantz. If
I lose Aletta, I'll never leave any sons. This Paulus is a man among boys,
finest lad I've ever known. I'll care for him and get him started, but damnit,
he's not mine.

Here he paused, for from his window he could see Paulus and his
grandchild Sybilla, twelve and nine, walking beside the lake, and as always,
she held on to his hand. Impulsively, Tjaart set aside his own miseries and
prayed: God, protect those two. They are the seed of our nation.

Then he returned to himself: The years roll past so swiftly, and we are
so many miles from the families we knew at De Kraal and Graaff-Reinet.
I'm alone, and I need this woman, whatever her behavior, and I shall keep
her.

Strong in his resolve, he stormed back into community life with fire and
terror. Grabbing his gun and marching to the hut of Balthazar Bronk, he
called him out, aimed the rifle directly at his heart, and cried in loud voice,
'Balthazar, pack your wagon and leave within the hour. Elsewise, I shoot
you dead.'

'But what . . .' It was Bronk's wife, peering out from the hut.

'He knows' was all Tjaart would say. And he stood there while the
Bronk family packed and sorted out their cattle from the common herd.

'Where shall I go?' Bronk said in a whining voice.

'I care not,' Tjaart snapped, and he called for Paulus to fetch another
gun and stand guard with him till the wagon was rolling.

'Give them our biltong,' Tjaart growled, and Paulus ran to fetch the Van
Doorn supplies. When the wagon started to move, Tjaart waited till it was
well under way, then fired shots over it to warn the Bronks that they must
not turn back, but on the second volley Aletta appeared, crying that she
must run to join them.

Once again Tjaart, who could manage men so ably, flew into a red fury
when called upon to reason with a woman. Throwing his gun to Paulus, he
grabbed his wife by the arm, swung her about, and used the only logic he
knew: he struck her three times across the face, and when she fell into the
dust, he reached down, pulled her back to her feet, and struck her again.

'Into the hut!' he commanded, and all that day the neighbors watched
as he sat by the door, gun in hand, saying nothing.

At sunset he went inside, and when he undressed for bed and stood before his wife, she burst into uncontrollable tears: 'You're old and fat and you have a big belly. Ryk was so young and strong. I despise you.'

With a great swing of his arm he knocked her down once more, so that she ran screaming from the hut, with him chasing her in only his pantalets.

'I shall go after him,' she wailed.

'Do,' he shouted. 'Go into the darkness, with the lions waiting.'

And when she had taken only a few steps, she saw the eyes of those animals who came to the lake at night, and she heard strange sounds and the muffled roaring of a distant lion, so terrifying that she hurried back to the protection of the village, and after a while, into her own hut.

Tjaart was waiting. With compassion and a profound unexplainable love, he took her in his arms and said, 'Ryk was young and beautiful, but he's dead. I'm old and fat, but I'm alive. That's how it is.' And that night Aletta conceived the boy Jakob, named after Tjaart's revered second wife.

IX. The Englishmen

I N the middle years of the nineteenth century a chain of unlikely events
inspired Queen Victoria to confer a knighthood on Major Richard Saltwood, of De Kraal, Cape Colony, and when this occurred, cartoonists
of South Africa and England lampooned him in a congenial way as Sir
Cupid. He was a hero, and his investiture became an act of warm celebration, uniting the colony more firmly to the mother country.

Saltwood's personal good luck began in 1856 when he was catapulted
into national prominence because of a disaster which riveted the attention
of the world. It began one autumn morning in May 1856 when a short, frail
girl of fourteen went to a pool in a stream east of the Great Fish River
and saw therein a ghostly assembly of figures accompanied by swirling
mists.

This might have had no aftermath had not the girl, Nongqause, happened to be the niece of that cunning seer Mhlakaza, whom Tjaart van
Doorn had come close to shooting back in 1836. Now, after twenty additional years of chicanery and nefarious behavior, this shifty man saw in his
niece an opportunity to set himself up as the great prophet of the Xhosa
people.

Mhlakaza interrogated the child at length, but found her answers confused and vague. She recited a rambling account of her walk to the pool and
kept referring to a hornbill that had flown near her—'certain omen of
disaster, for it brings droughts'—but he did not interrupt her until she said
something startling: 'They were strangers, my Uncle. Some with black skins
like Xhosa. But others in the mists . . . I am frightened!'

'What others?' he asked reassuringly.

'White men rising from the mists, my Uncle.'

Mhlakaza did not press her. Placing his hand gently on her shoulder,
he said, 'Go to your hut, Nongqause, and tell no one of this.' He watched

until she disappeared through the low entrance of her parents' place; then he stole from the village to inspect this pool.

It was four hours before he returned, and his slightest movement was watched, especially by older men and women who concerned themselves in such matters. For months he had been promising that the Xhosa would hear words of importance from his lips, and now his secretive behavior indicated that the prophet was ready.

When he stalked silently to his hut, word spread that no one was to approach him for two days and nights: the spirits had ordered him to do certain things. No questions were to be asked of the diviners, and young people were not to speculate on what his forthcoming revelation might be. If they did, their chatter might interrupt his communication with those who dwelt in the sky.

Alone, within his hut, Mhlakaza burned herbs and medicines to thwart witchcraft, then sat naked as the acrid smoke fumed about his body, causing his eyes to stream. He swallowed powerful emetics to purge himself, daubed his skin with red ocher and white clay, and entered into long incantations, begging the spirits to unleash forces that would prepare him for the great role he was about to play.

On the third day he came out from his seclusion, and with the entire village at his heels, strode to the cattle kraal, where he chose the plumpest beast from his own herd. Prodding it with an assegai, he pierced the skin until the animal bellowed with rage. He loved that sound; it meant the spirits were speaking to him. Then, with a vicious thrust, he drove the iron tip deep into the neck of the ox. Next he cut out the stomach and bladder, anointing his body with their contents, and to the delight of the witnesses, ordered the ox to be roasted and eaten. He was purified.

On the fourth day Mhlakaza returned alone to the stream long before first light, and his vigil ended when he uttered a mighty cry, as if things deep within him were released. There in the gray dawn stood an older brother who had died in the 1835 war against the English. 'Draw near, Mhlakaza, my good brother who is chosen for great deeds' came the voice. 'Our child Nongqause is chosen with you to lead our people to victory. To you, members of my family, will be shown the Xhosa strength.'

And then, just as Nongqause had seen the strangers in the pool, so did he! Regiment upon regiment of Xhosa heroes, risen from the dead, marched triumphantly through a great valley where no English or Boer face was to be seen. But with the black legions rode the white strangers who had come from overseas to help the Xhosa.

A dazed, wild-eyed Mhlakaza staggered back to the village, where his followers were not disappointed, for he told them that he, too, had seen the strangers who had first shown themselves to Nongqause. They had, he said, ordered him to purify himself before talking with them, and had not everyone seen him do this?

'We saw! We saw! The nights of smoke. The days of prayer.'

'Those that wait by the pool say this: "There is a valley of desolation, with the bones of many animals, with baskets empty of grain." '

A frightful cry rose from the listeners, wails and groans at so grim a vision.

'But look further, my friends. Open your eyes. And this land of death begins to blossom like a paradise. The cattle rise and are fat. The fields burst with the finest corn.'

'Aieee, Mhlakaza! How wonderful!'

'Say the ones at the pool, "All this is yours if you obey us." I saw a million Xhosa ready for battle. And with them came a regiment of strangers who fight alongside us as brothers.' Flecks of spittle hung at the corners of his mouth as he revealed his startling visions: 'They will slay the English! They will trample the Boers!'

When the roar of approval died, he added, 'The Xhosa will inherit everything. All the farms in this land will be yours. You will never again know a cattle shortage. Your grain baskets will overflow forever.'

Now, it so happened that Mhlakaza had recently traveled through the frontier districts, moving along the fringe of settlement as on that morning at De Kraal when Van Doorn wanted to shoot him. And as he moved about he listened: 'In lands beyond the sea there is a body of warriors called Russians. They are like the Xhosa, except they have white skins, but like us, they fight the English.'

'They're afraid of these Russians,' a servant whispered. 'In one battle they struck down the best commando of the English. Killed six hundred when the English ran at them on horses, with stabbing sticks.'

He picked up what additional information he could about the disastrous charge of the English brigade at Balaklava, and one fact began to burn in his mind: his enemy England had another enemy, the Russians.

Mhlakaza took Nongqause aside and explained the mystery of her visions: 'The Xhosa will be reinforced by the white strangers you saw, the Russians. We must hurry to the pool to get further instructions.' And when these words were locked in her childish mind, he took her to the kraal of the great chief, Kreli, where she stood before the councillors of the area: 'To prove your faith in the ancestors who spoke with me, you must do two things. Kill all your cattle. Burn all your mealies. Only when you are purified in this way will the ghosts march to help us.'

Chief Kreli, bewildered by such instructions, said, 'Step forward, child, and let us see who it is our ancestors speak with.'

Nudged by her uncle, Nongqause moved timidly toward Kreli, her large hazel eyes meeting those of the great chief.

'Tell them the white soldiers are ready to march with us,' Mhlakaza said.

'It is so, my Chief.'

'They have come across the sea to fight for us?' Kreli asked.

'They have,' she said quietly, going on to describe in detail the heroics of the Russians in their battle against the English. As she spoke, a chatter ran through the crowd, for if Mhlakaza vouched for her as a true Mother of Greatness, she must be listened to.

'The cattle are to be killed,' she said again. 'The baskets empty. The land bare. When that is done, the Russians and the Xhosa will drive the English and the Boers into the sea.'

The idea of slaughtering all cattle was so infamous, threatening as it did the very existence of the Xhosa, that older councillors scorned both Nongqause and her prophecy. One white-haired advisor protested: 'Where was this nonsense seen?'

'At the pool,' Mhlakaza said. 'She saw it first. Then I did.'

'This talk of a day when all people, dead and alive, shall come together. Isn't that what they say at the Christian mission at Golan?' the old man asked. 'Isn't that where you heard it?'

'It is the word of our ancestors,' Mhlakaza insisted.

'You bring us missionary ideas,' the old councillor persisted. 'The tribes of the dead coming back to earth, bringing paradise with them.'

'Our ancestors told me. At the pool.'

Chief Kreli, an artful, determined leader, had long sought some tactic that would unite his Xhosa, and he surmised that this young girl's visions might be the answer. Organizing a pilgrimage to the pool, he allowed his councillors to see Nongqause talking with the departed leaders and hear her speaking with the waiting Russians. When she reiterated the ghostly commands, that all foodstuffs be destroyed, he began to believe that if this were done, the Russians would arrive by ship and unite with the long-dead chieftains to expel the white men from the land.

'We shall do it!' Kreli announced, and for nine months Nongqause and her uncle paraded west and east, to the Xhosa and all adjoining tribes, assuring everyone that the day of revelation was at hand and the miracle about to occur, if only they would slay their cattle and let their fields lie barren. 'The ghosts wait there behind the clouds, all the victorious warriors of the past, eager to help us regain our pastures. But you must do as they command.'

It was a powerful doctrine, made more compulsory when Mhlakaza boldly predicted the precise day on which the miracle would happen: 'On the eighteenth day of February 1857 the ghosts will return, driving millions of plump cattle before them and bringing us untold baskets filled with grain.'

When reports of the cattle killing reached government agencies at Grahamstown, there was initial disbelief that such hysteria could ensnare an entire people, especially on the word of a child who could not possibly know where Russia was or what the name represented, but a tremor did run through the colony, for twice before, fanatic prophets had incited the Xhosa masses, whipping the kraals into a frenzy and leading them to disaster. In the first attack on Grahamstown a prophet had assured his people of victory, and not long ago another prophet had convinced his warriors that white men's bullets would be no stronger than raindrops if only the Xhosa killed all cream-colored cattle.

Now the government received proof indisputable that entire villages were engaging in an orgy of cattle slaughter, and serious attention had to be paid, for the people in Grahamstown had now lived side-by-side with the Xhosa for two generations and knew how much they revered their cattle. 'If they're actually killing them, something desperate's afoot,' a new district officer said, and Major Saltwood of De Kraal was sent for.

'What's it all about?' he asked when he reported for consultations.

'A crazy prophet named Mhlakaza has been preaching that the Xhosa must slay their cattle.'

'Mhlakaza?' Saltwood asked. 'Isn't he that fellow who gave us so much trouble over access to one of the rivers? Ten, fifteen years ago?'

'The same. This time he claims his niece, a stupid little girl of fourteen or fifteen . . . I've seen her. Squinched-up face. Doesn't weigh ninety pounds. She claims she was visited by all the dead Xhosa chiefs—Hintsa, Ndlambe, the lot. She says they told her to slay all the cattle, burn all the crops, and they'd come storming back to throw us English into the sea.'

'What's this about the Russians?' Saltwood asked. He was sixty-eight years old, tall, lean, white-haired, very much an English military man in retirement, and because of his service on the Afghan frontier, perpetually interested in Russian trickery.

'Oh, Mhlakaza seems to have picked up some nonsense about the Crimean War. All he knows is that Russia fought against us. Because of our loss at Balaklava, he's convinced himself that Russia won and that she wants to invade Grahamstown to complete her victory. Frightful mess he peddles.'

'Don't underestimate their prophets,' Saltwood warned. 'They can whip a countryside into frenzy.'

'To what purpose?'

'They're in cahoots with the schemers and plotters in the nation. Men like Kreli. I've survived two wars launched by fanatics, and it's serious business. If they do kill all their cattle, they'll have to find others. I hardly need tell you where they'll start looking.'

'What about the little girl?'

'She's a mystic of some sort. Hears voices. He's using her.'

'As simple as that?'

'Carson's the only one who's actually seen her. What's your story?'

A young Oxford graduate, whose first job had been at Grahamstown, had made a minor name for himself by learning the Xhosa language and something of the tribe's internal politics. The Xhosa trusted him, and on one of his recent trips into the heartland of the region they had allowed him to talk with Nongqause. 'She's illiterate, has no idea of our government at Cape Town, and couldn't possibly have any concept of Russia. But she has been remarkably consistent in her visions and has told only one clear story: "Kill everything, burn everything, and the spirits will come to free us." '

'Does she speak specifically against us?' Saltwood asked.

'Never heard her say as much. She has only a generic enemy, but it's got to be us.'

'She's not preaching armed rebellion?'

'The spirits are going to handle that end of it. But of course, the living Xhosa must be prepared to follow them, so I suppose that in the end we must expect armed invasion.'

'Good God,' the new district officer said.

'Do you take it that seriously?' one of the officials asked Saltwood.

'I do. You must remember, gentlemen, that these men you're talking about have been fighting us for nearly half a century. They've learned all the tricks. They're brave, and when their prophets preach a holy war they can become quite fanatical. I think we're in for trouble.'

Saltwood's perceptive observation about blended heroism and fanaticism gained such wide circulation that the government asked him to see what he could do to minimize or even halt the cattle killing, and he left Grahamstown with two Xhosa men who worked for him at De Kraal to enter the regions where Nongqause's preachments were having their strongest effect.

He was not prepared for what he saw. Entire fields lay covered with dead animals, and anyone who knew the Xhosa had to be appalled at this wanton sacrifice. On two different occasions his Xhosa companions broke into tears at the sheer waste, but when Saltwood talked with the men who had done the killing, he found them in a state of euphoria—smiling, happy, marking time till the eighteenth of February when every dead animal would be returned a hundredfold.

'Tell them it cannot happen,' Saltwood urged his men, but when they endeavored to persuade the other Xhosa not to kill any more cattle, the tribesmen smiled benignly and said, 'You wouldn't understand,' and the slaughter continued.

At the end of five days Saltwood had seen more than twenty thousand dead animals, and he sent one of his companions running back to Grahamstown with this brief message: 'The rumors we heard were one-tenth of the story. I truly fear that all cattle may be slain and that thousands of people will face starvation. Begin to assemble foodstuffs immediately.'

Distraught, uncertain, he decided to seek out a village where one of his former workers lived, a man named Mpedi, fine and trustworthy, hoping to use him as a wedge into the heart of the problem. But when he reached Mpedi's hut he found the man, a sensible fellow in his sixties, mesmerized by the glorious thing that was about to happen: 'Baas, you cannot know what we shall be doing. All the great chiefs coming back to help us. A hundred . . . a thousand warriors waiting in the rivers to rise up and lead us into our inheritance.'

'Mpedi, wake up!' Saltwood begged. 'Do you think your dead cattle will be replaced? Do you think food will come from the sky?'

'It will come, Baas.'

'Can't you see that you're about to starve?'

'There will be food for all, Baas.'

'Goddamnit!' Saltwood raged. 'Open your eyes!'

'They are open, Baas. And on the eighteenth of February yours will be opened, too.'

Saltwood shook his old herdsman, a man who loved cattle. 'Mpedi, if you kill the rest of your cattle, you're going to starve.'

'Baas,' the herdsman said with deep affection, 'I want you to leave this village and go back across the Great Fish, where you belong. Go to De Kraal and get your family. Hurry to Port Elizabeth and get aboard a ship and go away. Because the risen chiefs are going to march right to headquarters and kill all the white people who have stolen our land from us. I don't want you to die, Baas, because you've been a good man to us.'

Saltwood was so shaken by his inability to bring sense into the discussion that he tried a new tack: 'Mpedi, I'm not here as your friend. Remember how many times I went out on commando against you men.'

'Ah!' the herdsman said with a broad smile. 'That was war, Baas. I shoot you. You shoot me. Who cares? It was in peace that you were so good to us. Now please leave.'

And while Saltwood stood there, this man whose life had centered upon the building up of a small herd of cattle went back into his fields and resumed slaying the docile creatures whose existence represented the only chance of keeping that village alive in the awful days that loomed.

During the first two weeks of February, Saltwood penetrated to most areas of the western Xhosa, and what he saw sickened him so that he returned to Mpedi's village, now stripped of all food except what was in the pots for the few days remaining till the miracle. 'Can you take me to Nongqause?' he asked his former workman.

'No good, Baas. She sits by the pool waiting for the generals to rise from the waters.'

'I must talk with her.'

'No good, Baas. She just sits there, waiting!'

'Damnit, Mpedi. I'm trying to save enough animals to keep you idiots alive.'

'No good, but if you want to hear from her own lips . . .'

He led Saltwood a day's journey eastward to the Gxara River, where a delirious crowd of Xhosa had gathered to be near the prophetess when the chiefs arose to greet her, and enough people knew Saltwood's good reputation to allow him to pass through the multitude to talk with the little girl. She had a pinched face, no beauty whatever, and large watery eyes. She was quite oblivious of the furor she was causing, and when Saltwood had been in her presence only a few minutes he was satisfied that she did indeed see visions. When he spoke to her, she did not respond coherently but rather with a dreamy indifference, for she knew that the day of revelation was at hand.

'Nongqause, there's still time to save enough cattle to feed the people during the coming winter. Stop the killing, I beg you.'

'When all are dead, then the new will arrive.'

'Can't you see that you're bringing desolation to the Xhosa?'

'When the grain is all burned, the new will arrive.'

'Nongqause! You're destroying your people.'

'When the chiefs arise, it is the enemy who will be destroyed.' She pointed to the calm, dark surface of the pool as if she expected Saltwood to see what she saw: the cattle waiting to fill the pastures, the boundless supplies of grain, the great chiefs dressed in battle array, with the Russians somehow behind them.

'Do you know where Russia is?' Saltwood asked.

As soon as he said this word, an older man moved in to insert himself between the little prophetess and this English intruder. It was Mhlakaza, but neither he nor Saltwood was aware that they had met one fateful morning back in 1836 on the hill at De Kraal when Tjaart van Doorn was prevented from shooting him.

'Why do you come here?' he asked in good English.

'I come to beg the little girl to stop the cattle killing.'

'The spirits demand it.'

'Who are you?' Saltwood asked.

'Mhlakaza, he who speaks for the spirits.'

'Don't you realize that you're all going to starve?'

'There will be two hundred cattle for every Xhosa.'

'Don't be a damned fool. Your meadows couldn't hold them.'

'There will be food for all.'

Saltwood was so disgusted with this crazy man that he tried to return to the little girl, but this Mhlakaza would not permit. Keeping himself face-to-face with the Englishman, he nudged him farther and farther away from the pool. In desperation Saltwood asked, 'Mhlakaza, do you know who I am?'

'Are you Saltwood of De Kraal?'

'Yes. And Mpedi here will assure you that I'm a friend of the Xhosa. I've fought against you in clean battle. I've worked with you. Tell him, Mpedi.'

Mpedi nodded, whereupon Saltwood asked, 'Mhlakaza, do you know where Russia is?'

'The ships are already on the sea, coming to join us.'

'But do you know what it is? A city? A town? A group of kraals?'

'It is Russia,' the prophet said. 'They will be here next week.'

'And what will you do?'

'Greet them at the shore. Then march to Grahamstown.'

Having said this, Mhlakaza spoke in Xhosa to Mpedi: 'Take this man away. See that he reaches home safely.' In English he said, 'Saltwood, hurry home and leave the country. We do not wish to kill you when the Russians come.'

In frustration and despair Saltwood left the Gxara River and its magical pool. Wherever he moved through Xhosa land he saw the slaughtered cattle, the burning piles of grain. He calculated that about twenty-five thousand blacks would starve in the months ahead, and that figure represented only the western lands which he had seen. In the eastern areas, where white men rarely penetrated, there would be, he supposed, perhaps another fifty thousand. Mpedi would surely die, and Nongqause the innocent cause, and Mhlakaza the effective cause. The Xhosa nation would be so prostrated that it could never recover, and this was happening in the year 1857 when sensible nations ought to be able to halt such insanity.

When he returned to Grahamstown he dispatched reports to Cape Town and London, warning the governments that by the first week in March starvation would be rampant and that at least fifty thousand deaths must be anticipated. He urged immediate shipment to Grahamstown of all surplus food supplies and suggested that they be doled out slowly, for the starving period was bound to last at least a year and a half.

Tired, weak from inadequate food and sleep, he felt both his advanced age and the dreadful tragedy about to descend upon this region. He wanted very much to hurry back to De Kraal and prepare his farm for the wandering skeletons who would soon be spreading over the countryside, but he felt obligated to go back among the Xhosa, and he was at Mpedi's desolated village on the evening of 17 February 1857. It was one of those calm, sweet summer nights when birds sang and the earth seemed impatient for the coming of dawn.

The eighteenth was a bright, clear day, with visibility so unsullied that every mountaintop stood clear. If ever there was a day for beneficent miracles, this was it. The sun rose without a cloud across its face; the air was quiet, with no hint of storm; and had any cattle been alive in the valleys, they would have been lowing.

Ten o'clock came, and the sun reached toward its apex, increasing in strength. Since it was generally believed that the dead would rise at high noon, crowds began to gather, looking in various directions to catch the first sight of marching armies and the arriving cattle.

Noon came, and silence. Slowly the sun passed its zenith and began its long descent to the horizon, and with every hour the suspicion grew that neither the chiefs nor the cattle were going to arrive. By five o'clock, when shadows were conspicuously lengthening, Mpedi came to Saltwood and asked, 'Will they come in darkness? They wouldn't do that, would they?'

'They are not coming,' Saltwood said, his eyes touched with tears.

'You mean . . .'

'I mean that when the hunger strikes, old friend, come back to De Kraal.'

At six, while there was still plenty of daylight if the chiefs and the Russians wanted to fulfill their pledges, everyone became anxious, and by seven there was panic. When the sun vanished and the fateful day was gone, many began to wail, and by midnight there was consternation throughout the little villages. All food was gone; the Russians had not come; and slowly the Xhosa realized that on the morning of the nineteenth they were going to face problems more terrible than any they had so far imagined.

The next two months were horror. To the headquarters in Grahamstown came reports that chilled even the most hardened veterans: 'I visited six villages and found only seven people alive.' Entire river systems, including even their tiny branches, had not a single person surviving along their banks. Corpses of people rotted in the veld beside the older corpses of their cattle. The land lay devastated, as if Plague had swept in with his Scythe.

Many who survived owed their existence to Richard Saltwood, who marshaled his inadequate food supplies with brilliance, squeezing the maximum good from the mealies allowed him. He organized relief teams, went himself into the bleakest areas, and prevailed upon his neighbors to accept on their farms as many wandering Xhosa as they could.

He became inured to death, and hardened himself to make decisions which meant that this village would survive and that perish. For vast numbers in the Xhosa heartland, there was simply nothing to be done; there death was universal.

When he surveyed the western areas in late April he found that his estimates of the tragedy had been accurate: at least twenty-five thousand corpses could be seen lying about unburied; and he had been correct in guessing that a greater number lay dead in the eastern areas to which he could not go. Seventy, eighty thousand of the finest blacks in Africa had probably died, some two hundred thousand cattle were slain, because a little girl had visions which her unscrupulous uncle had used to reach for goals not even he could fully understand.

In the midst of this desolation Saltwood kept thinking of his old friend Mpedi; the herdsman had not reported to De Kraal, where some fifty Xhosa were being sheltered at Saltwood's expense, so he set out to rescue Mpedi —if he still lived.

The journey to that village was one he would later try to strike from his mind: corpses scattered in the sun like dead autumn flowers; pastures forlorn and empty of cattle that should have been producing calves; stench and dust and loneliness. But at the village itself the ultimate horror, for there he found six adults who had survived, and Mpedi off in a hut by himself, trembling and near death from starvation.

'Old friend,' Saltwood cried, tears coming to his eyes despite the fact that he had seen thousands of others dying. Mpedi was an individual man, a good herdsman who had tended De Kraal cattle faithfully, and his death would be a personal grief.

'Old friend,' Saltwood repeated. 'Why are you not sharing the food with the others?'

Shivering in terror, the herdsman drew back. He could not trust even his old baas. He wanted only to die.

'Mpedi!' Saltwood said, somewhat irritated at this rebuff. 'Why do you lie here alone?'

'They are eating their children,' the old man said, and when Saltwood stormed from the hut and kicked the ashes under the pot and upset everything, he saw human bones.

Mpedi starved to death, as did the fool Mhlakaza, responsible for it all. Nongqause did not starve; as a frail child she required little food, and her admirers supplied that. She lived another forty-one years, a curiosity gossiped about but rarely seen, for the Xhosa eventually realized that she was the instrument of their disaster. In the midst of a later famine she fled for her life when her identity became known. Among her intimates, however, she was pleased to talk about the great days when all the world listened to her preachments, and she seemed to have no realization of what she had done. In later years she assumed a new name, which she felt was more appropriate to her position. She rechristened herself Victoria Regina.

The Crimean War had been in part responsible for agitating the mind of Mhlakaza and creating the fatuous idea that Russia would shortly invade the Cape Colony; one year later it was directly responsible for Richard Saltwood's new name, Cupid.

When the Russians in Sebastopol stubbornly held out against the British, causing thereby the infamous Charge of the Light Brigade at nearby Balaklava, a serious crisis developed in the British army. Enlistments at home failed to provide enough new troops to replace those dying from Russian bullets and English malfeasance. Various devices were suggested for replenishing the ranks, but in the end the only thing that made sense was a return to the system used so effectively in 1776 against American rebels and in 1809 against Napoleon: the English army sent recruiting agents to Germany, where for substantial bonuses a first-class mercenary legion was employed.

The Germans had to be under twenty-five years old, over sixty-two inches tall, and unmarried. They proved a superb lot, and would surely have conducted themselves bravely in the Crimea except that peace came before they could be shipped out of England. This created a serious problem; the English had an army, trained and paid for, with no war in which to engage it.

Queen Victoria, herself of German extraction, and her husband Prince Albert of Saxe-Coburg-Gotha were naturally concerned about what might happen to their young compatriots and were delighted when plans were announced whereby the entire contingent was offered passage to the Cape as military settlers, to establish homes and secure posts along the recently disrupted Xhosa frontier. A strategy somewhat like this had been advocated in 1820 with English colonists, and there was no reason why it could not be duplicated in 1857 with Germans.

A vast scheme was initiated whereby nine thousand of the mercenaries, plus such new wives as they could acquire, would be shipped to the same port used by the English when they landed. But now a snag developed. The Germans had such an excellent reputation for soldiering that numerous other nations were eager to employ them; they received offers from the King of Naples, the Dutch in Java, the Argentinian government and seven revolutionary juntas across Europe, who felt that if only they could enroll these crack troops, they could overthrow reactionary governments. About a quarter of the recruits, 2,350 officers and men, were left over to emigrate to the Cape.

Since Queen Victoria and her husband were most eager that this settlement prove successful, they wrote to South Africa, asking that Major Richard Saltwood, who had distinguished himself during the cattle killing, come to London to supervise the emigration. He was delighted with this opportunity to visit with his brother Sir Peter, and within two days of receiving the invitation, was on his way.

To his astonishment, when he disembarked at Tilbury, he was whisked immediately to Buckingham Palace, where the queen herself discussed the emigration. She was a shortish, round woman with no chin, and when meeting strangers, liked to defer to her husband's judgment; they both displayed a keen interest in her South African colonies—Cape and Natal—and were enchanted by the various stories told of Saltwood's life on the frontier. They said that he must hurry to Southampton to make certain that the German embarkation moved smoothly, and Victoria added that she would hold Richard personally responsible.

She was in the process of adding that she preferred only married emigrants, for this ensured family stability, when a charming boy of thirteen burst into the room, stopped in embarrassment, and started to withdraw. 'Alfred, come here,' the queen said, 'this gentleman is from the land of lions and elephants.' The lad stopped, turned, and bowed low like a Prussian officer.

'I am most pleased to meet you, sir,' he said, whereupon Major Saltwood extended his hand, took the boy's, and drew him back into the room.

'You must come to my farm one day, and see the animals.'

'That I should like to do,' Alfred said, and the brief meeting ended.

In Southampton the authorities were mustering the mercenaries for the voyage to the Cape, and they found themselves with a sterling group of husky young men, but they were not having much success with getting wives. This omission worried Saltwood, since the queen had specifically stated that she preferred complete families in her colonies, so he made a special effort to visit all the nearby towns, seeking women for the young Germans. He was not successful, and when the last of the ships was ready to sail, the rickety old *Alice Grace,* he informed the captain that it must not depart until a final effort had been made to find more brides.

'Who am I?' the captain demanded. 'Cupid?'

'No,' Saltwood replied evenly, 'but you do have a commission to perform.'

'My commission is sailing this ship,' the captain replied. 'Not finding wives,' and the adventure would have ended poorly had not Saltwood been a man of ingenuity and humanity.

'You have over two hundred fine young men aboard this ship,' he told the captain. 'I want them all on deck. Now!'

When they assembled on the afterdeck he told them bluntly, 'Men, it would be most improvident to travel to the Cape without women, so the captain has agreed to hold his ship here for two days. You must circulate through the town and find wives. You'll be married before we sail.'

Saltwood added his own imaginative touch to the quest. Finding himself only a short distance from Salisbury, he hurried there by train, burst into Sentinels and cried, 'I can use all the spare women in town.' His brother was absent, attending Parliament, but his wife was there, and she organized a hunt which produced five young women who had only bleak prospects at home. One ill-favored lass named Maggie began to whimper, 'I don't want no South Aferkee.'

'That's where you're going,' Saltwood said sternly, herding his charges onto the train, which frightened them just as much as the prospective sea voyage.

At the ship two chaotic days were spent in a grand sorting-out, but since many of the Germans and some of the women were drunk, when dawn came on the third day and the passengers awoke to see the horrible choices they had made in the dark, there was rebellion.

This man did not intend to spend his life with that woman, and this woman who could speak no German knew that a substitute husband had been fobbed off on her in the confusion. A wild scene ensued, which the two German ministers aboard could not resolve, and it seemed as if the whole plan might go smash when Saltwood grabbed a whistle, blew it shrilly, and ordered the men to line up on one side of the ship, the women on the other. Then he addressed them: 'Gentlemen, do you wish to spend your lives alone?' When the interpreter repeated this question, many men said 'No.' And Saltwood continued: 'Well, if you don't find your wives this day, you won't find any out there for three or four or a dozen years. Is that what you want?' The interpreter handled this message with brutal frankness, and the German men looked at the deck, saying nothing.

Saltwood then directed his words at the English women: 'You haven't had good lives here. I can see that. Now you have a chance to go to a bright new land, with hope and a good husband. Are you daft, that you would surrender this?'

Before his chastened listeners could dredge up excuses, he ordered the men and women to remain in lines, facing each other, upon which he blew his whistle three times, then said, his finger pointing, 'You, at the head of the line. This is your woman!' And that couple moved forward.

'You!' the interpreter repeated in German. 'This is your woman.'

He went down the entire roster, arbitrarily deciding who was to be married to whom, and at his signal, Reverend Johannes Oppermann stepped forward and in one grand ceremony married the lot. The two hundred and forty couples spent three months together aboard the old *Alice Grace,* and when they reached their destination they established some of the strongest families in South Africa.

The London press delighted in the spectacle of a brother to the sober-sides member of Parliament, Sir Peter Saltwood, engaged in so amorous a royal commission, and a *Punch* caricaturist fleshed Richard considerably, plumped up his cheeks, stripped off his clothing but added a discreet diaper, gave him a little bow and arrow, and christened him Cupid.

When officials at Cape Town implored Queen Victoria to send some member of the royal family out to the colony to show the flag and instill patriotism in the hearts of the English segment of the population, she found herself in something of a quandary. She herself would not think of leaving England, and Prince Albert was in failing health. Five of their nine children were girls, and deemed unsuitable for foreign travel among lions and elephants. That left four sons, but the youngest two were ten and seven, hardly appropriate for diplomatic service, while the oldest boy, the Prince of Wales, was visiting the United States and Canada that year. That left only the second son, Alfred, but he was only sixteen. Still, South Africa was a country of farmers and shopkeepers, not a real country like Canada, so little Alfred might do.

He was a popular lad, and within the royal family it had been agreed that he would be the Sailor Prince, with newspapers making a great fuss over the fact that while serving as a midshipman he went barefoot on deck. He was not very bright, which was never a handicap in the English system, but he did love guns; all in all he seemed a sensible solution to the South African problem, and the queen wrote to her friend Major Richard Saltwood of De Kraal, asking him to look after her boy and to 'arrange for him a grand battue, if that be possible.'

It would indeed be possible. Richard knew an English farmer near Bloemfontein who could enlist enough blacks to put on a real battue for the young prince, and all was arranged. Saltwood was at the dock at the Cape when the young fellow landed, and after a round of receptions he sailed with him along the coast to Port Elizabeth, where the royal party disembarked and mounted horses for an adventure inland which would cover twelve hundred miles of saddle-riding over the roughest terrain.

When Saltwood first saw the entourage that proposed to make this

journey, he was appalled by its magnitude: the prince, his toothy equerry
Friddley, a company of fourteen from the ship, a company of twenty-six
from the local government, several score of grooms to tend the spare horses,
twenty-seven wagons with drivers to haul the gear, and a professional
photographer, Mr. Yorke, to record events on a ponderous camera that
required a wagon of its own. All this to enable a boy of sixteen to enjoy a
battue.

But it was a no-nonsense expedition, as the riders learned that first day
when they rode twenty-two miles without a major stop. The next day they
covered forty-six and were dusty-tired when they pulled into De Kraal,
where they would rest for two days with the Saltwoods.

It was a splendid respite, with the prince delighted by his first acquaintance with an African farm. De Kraal had been much improved in recent
years when the Saltwood fortunes prospered. All the stone buildings dating
back to the 1780s had been enlarged and beautified; the grounds had been
spruced up with flower gardens; and the fences had been regularized; but
the charm of the place, as young Alfred remarked, was still the handsome
setting within the hills and the wandering stream that cut diagonally across
the holding.

In acreage the farm was somewhat diminished since the days when
Tjaart van Doorn operated it: still the nine thousand acres within the hills,
but only four thousand outside. 'What I enjoy so much,' the boy prince told
Saltwood, 'is the mix of closed-in and open.' He also enjoyed the hunting
and proved his reputation by bringing down several smaller antelope.

At dinner on the first night the young man was embarrassed when one
of the black maids brought in a bawling white infant to be presented to
royalty. 'It's my grandson,' Saltwood explained. 'Seven months old and lord
of the manor.'

'What's his name?' the prince asked, holding the baby awkwardly.

'Frank.'

'Frank, I christen thee Sir Bawler,' and that became the child's nick-
name.

From De Kraal the party headed east to Grahamstown, where Friddley
cried, 'What a delightful place! So English. Even the Dutchmen who live
here look like our Surrey squires!'

Friddley was a new experience for Saltwood; as the nephew of a duke,
he felt entitled to say whatever came into his mind, and he did so in a flush
of patriotic emotion which often raced ahead of his grammar. At the
opening reception in Grahamstown he gave a far-ranging toast: 'To the
loyal citizens of this brave frontier city whose English pluck and heroic
perseverance, which shall ever animate our noble race, and who love the
queen with a devotion unparalleled and thank her for sharing with you her
son, the gallant Sailor Prince . . .' He dropped that sentence and launched
fervently into another: 'I say, it was your loyalty to our beloved queen and
her beloved consort, the father of our beloved Sailor Prince who does us
such honor by this timely visit to the most loyal of his mother's colonies,
and I have seen him barefooted on the deck of his ship, discharging his tasks
like any other decent, red-blooded sailor on whom the safety of our nation
depends . . .' He seemed to run out of breath, but then shouted, 'I drink
to the brave English hearts that protected this town against fierce savages.'

'Hear, hear!' the audience cried, but Saltwood asked his neighbor, Carleton the wagon builder, who served as mayor of the little town, 'What about the Boers?' and Carleton whispered, 'Tonight Boers don't count,' and Saltwood chuckled. 'Without them, he wouldn't be standing here tonight.'

At each step Friddley was eager to orate, dwelling upon the nobility of the queen in allowing her young son to come so far to receive the plaudits of the colony; he served the same purpose as the official flatterers at the court of King Dingane and his words were equally empty. But the prince was not diverted by this constant aggrandizement. 'When do we get to the battue?' he asked repeatedly, and once Grahamstown was passed, he stayed in the saddle for fifty miles a day.

Behind him the entourage rode in clouds of dust; the wagons creaked; the grooms helped along the horses gone lame; and Mr. Yorke performed heroics in keeping his cumbersome photographic wagon within striking distance of the others. When they slept in cots in their tents, he lay curled up in his wagon.

After a final ride of fifty-six miles in one day, they came at last to a large farm east of Bloemfontein, where an enormous plain a hundred miles in circumference lay hemmed in by low hills. Days before, at every pass through which game might escape, blacks had been stationed, one thousand in all, and on the late afternoon of 23 August 1860 these beaters began slowly moving toward the central area which the prince would occupy next morning. As they moved, they drove ahead of them from all compass directions a monstrous herd of zebras, blesbok, eland, hartebeest, wildebeest, kudu, ostriches and the soon-to-be-extinct quagga. How many animals did the herd contain? Perhaps two hundred thousand, perhaps less, for no one could count the beasts as they moved in toward the center, then out to the perimeter. Some escaped through unguarded valleys; most were kept penned in by the multitude of beaters.

At dawn the prince, accompanied by twenty-four other guns, moved to the hunting ground, where Friddley laid down the rules: 'I shall ride at the prince's left, Major Saltwood to his right. We will not shoot. Our job will be to hand the prince freshly loaded guns as he fires at the beasts. Your Royal Highness, reach first to me on the left, then to Saltwood on the right. Now I want six good shots to ride behind us in a semicircle. You gentlemen may fire at the game occasionally, but your main task is to protect the prince, should any beast come at him. Is that understood?'

Just as the sun came up, the twenty-five guns took their positions, plus Friddley and Saltwood as handlers, plus ninety black servants, many with guns, plus eighteen white factotums, plus one thousand beaters out on the plains to get everything in readiness for 'the greatest hunt in history.' Only then did Friddley flash a signal, and the grand battue was under way.

The beaters close in raised a hullabaloo, whereupon the frightened animals in that quarter started to rush in the general direction of the waiting hunters. First a score of zebras rushed past, then a scattered flight of leaping springbok, then the main body of the herd. They came in turmoil, hundreds of them, thousands. At first they veered away from the hunters, and many escaped, but when the crush became sheer chaos, they galloped by within ten paces of the gunners, great concentrations of large animals running in terror.

The firing never ceased. 'Here, your Highness!' Friddley cried as he took the prince's empty gun, thrusting a freshly loaded one into his hands. After firing from ten inches into the side of a zebra, the prince would thrust his gun in Saltwood's general direction, and without even looking, reach for a fresh one, which he would again discharge at animals not ten paces away.

Meantime, the twenty-four other sportsmen were also surrounded by fleeing beasts, often throwing up dust in their faces, and they, too, were firing as rapidly as they could, right into the chests of the rushing animals.

After an hour of incessant slaughter the herd reeled in confusion, where-upon the factotums rode their horses out into various parts of the plain, encouraging the beaters to accelerate their movement, and this threw a really tremendous flight of animals right past the waiting prince. Indeed, the great beasts now came so close that firing guns at them was senseless, if not impossible, for the barrels could scarcely be raised against the pressure of the animals.

This delighted Friddley, who shouted, 'Your Highness, let's use the blades!' And he took away the prince's gun, thrusting into his hand a short-handled hog-hunting spear, so sharp that Friddley had named it 'the Paget blade,' after the surgeon who attended Queen Victoria and her family. The young prince used it with some skill; he and Friddley spurred their horses and charged the stampeding beasts, stabbing at them as they roared past. Within minutes both Friddley and the prince were splattered with blood from the frequent stabbings and the fall of the animals.

The two men used their lances for the better part of an hour, with the six precautionary gunmen ranged behind them to fire in the event that some confused beast turned to threaten the royal hunter. Saltwood, without either gun or hog-spear, watched with a kind of detached horror as one great animal after another stumbled to its knees, gushing blood; at numerous times he could hold out his hand and touch the stampeding antelope sweep-ing past. The only danger a child would have had in that mad affair would be if it stumbled beneath the flying hooves or got in the way of some sportsman's rifle.

'Enough!' someone finally shouted, and when Saltwood got to the prince to take away the bladed-spear, he saw that he was completely covered with blood, like some inept country butcher. In the celebration that followed, one local gentleman shot off his own arm while firing a salute in honor of the heroic young visitor, and Friddley gave a stirring address of thanks to the hundreds of Bloemfontein people who had arranged the shoot: 'On this day we have slain six hundred and forty animals, each larger than a horse, plus thousands of smaller beasts we will not bother to register. Our glorious Sailor Prince proved that he is as brave on land as he is at sea, and we can assure the queen that we watched with manly pride the extreme courage he displayed when faced by the thunder of those enraged beasts. We are sorry that His Royal Highness was deprived of his lion, which we have no doubt he will confront and shoot before he leaves these shores.'

As an afterthought he added, 'This great onslaught was no willful waste of God's creatures. Our faithful Kaffirs need not go hungry this night.'

And since there was no stopping Friddley once he got going, he went on to observe: 'It was a very exciting day, and were His Royal Highness to live for a hundred years, I do not believe he could ever see such a scene again, for the game in these parts is fast disappearing.'

Prince Alfred sent his mother such a glowing account of Richard Salt-wood's hospitality that when her prime minister raised a matter of importance which concerned both India and Natal, she put forward the name of the master of De Kraal, pointing out: 'Saltwood's familiar with both places. Give him the job.' And thus she granted Cupid one more chance to launch his arrows.

At the age of seventy-one Richard was approached by the Natal government on a negotiation which would require some delicacy: 'Natal's a great land for sugar, but there's damned little we can accomplish unless we find labor.'

'You've got the Zulu,' Richard said. 'Put them to work.'

'Zulu don't tame easy, old chap. Not like your Xhosa after this cattle madness. No Zulu will work in the fields; won't use his hands. Says it's undignified. Women do such work. We've brought in a couple of Chinese, but the damned Chinamen won't work for the ten shillings a month we offer. They want to save money and buy their own shops.'

'So you're suggesting Indians?'

'Couple of thousand of them, ten shillings a head, we won't know what to do with all the sugar. They've been a success in Mauritius and the West Indies. Why not Natal?'

'What am I to do?'

'The necessary laws have been passed. Now we must go to India and collect them in an orderly way. You did a fine job with those German chappies, and we're sure you can do the same with Indians.'

At his age, Richard would have preferred keeping close to De Kraal with his young grandson, but he had the energy to accept this arduous task, and when he learned that the queen herself had recommended him, he had to accept.

More than forty years had passed since he fought in India, and when his ship reached Madras he was struck by the changes, for he entered that port barely eighteen months after the terrible Indian Mutiny. That bloody uprising had been suppressed after grievous loss on both sides, and it was a jittery peace that prevailed.

'Soldiers that we trained,' an officer at Government House recited, 'turned against us. Burning, looting, murdering. And do you know why? Because of those damned bullets at Dumdum.' Noticing Saltwood's quizzical look, he added, 'The new cartridges for the Enfields were greased at one end and had to be bitten—before use in muzzle loaders, that is. Rumor spread that the grease was pig fat, and the Muslims wouldn't touch it. Said we did it to humiliate their religion.'

'Our problem was red earth,' Saltwood muttered to himself.

'Whassat?'

'Our Kaffirs fought us because they needed red earth from one of our farms for their ceremonies. Hundreds died for red earth.'

More significant for Saltwood was the disappearance of John Company from the Indian scene. Even before the mutiny was quelled, Queen Victoria had signed the act which transferred the subcontinent to the crown, and after two centuries of deadly rivalry with the Dutch, the English company was dead.

'Maybe the businessmen should have retained power,' the officer said. 'Why?'

'They'd have dealt differently with the rebels.' The bitterness of the traditional colonial officer came through: 'A few of the leaders—the really bad ones who killed our people—they were hanged. But we have hundreds walking around with the blood of Englishmen on their hands. "Clemency Canning" they call our viceroy. By gad, his father, the real Canning, he'd have given them clemency at the end of a rope. Our Canning said it wouldn't do to make martyrs of them. More trouble than greased cartridges. Saltwood, I saw our women and children at Allahabad—hacked to death or tossed into a well still breathing. "Clemency Canning," damn him.' Saltwood was to hear endless repetition of these complaints.

He was furiously busy during his stay at Madras, ironing out the hitches in the labor contracts, consulting with recruiting agents; nevertheless, he was able to accomplish his commission, and one afternoon he stood in a large compound at the edge of town where nine hundred Indians squatted on the ground, each praying that he would be chosen to fill one of the two hundred vacancies that would enable him to escape the poverty of India. In less than two hours Saltwood had made his selection, but as he strode out of the compound, the three Desai brothers grabbed at him: 'Please, Sahib, Great Master, we go to your country, too.'

'All places taken. You'll have to wait for the next ship.'

'Please, Great Sahib!' And in the time remaining before his departure, these Desais dogged his steps, walking for miles behind his carriage, waiting at the gates to Government House, desperately striving to keep themselves before him. They would nod, break a pathway for him through crowds, repeat their names, tug at his arm: 'Please, Great Sahib, it is a matter of life and death.'

And always they grinned, showing very white teeth. Eventually they wore Saltwood down, so that he asked the captain of the *Limerick,* 'Got space for three more?'

'Well, my friend, that's a question,' the captain said. 'This is not a slave ship I run.'

'Captain, Captain!' the three Desais cried, bleating like injured sheep. 'You are a very great captain. Surely you can arrange . . .'

'Well, maybe I can fit them in.' The Desais kissed his hands, came weeping to do the same with Saltwood. 'You will never regret this,' they assured him.

So two hundred and three Indian men were certified for passage to Natal on ten-year contracts, after which they were to return home, but when Saltwood reported to the *Limerick* to see her off, he found some five or six hundred Indians ready to sail, many of them women. The three Desai brothers, grinning happily, had five extremely attractive women in tow.

'Our wives,' they explained.

'You're not Muslim,' Saltwood growled. 'You don't have more than one wife.'

'These two,' the Desais said. 'Our wives' sisters.'

'They can't sail with you. Men only. You work ten years, then come back to your wives.'

There was no great wailing. Life in India, especially after the mutiny, was difficult, and if this was the way these men were to earn their living, so be it. But that night at Government House, Saltwood raised the question with an official, who coughed and said, 'Well, there is some rubbish in the law about taking wives to Natal. But you certainly don't want that, do you? Take wives along, every man will have ten children in ten years.'

'Do you want them to live without women for ten years?'

'Do some of them good.'

'We have found in South Africa that it's inhuman to keep men separated from their women, and I'll have none of it.' His arguments prevailed; the government conceded that in future, women should accompany their men and work with them in the sugar fields, and it was then that some wag posted a letter to *Punch* detailing the further adventures of Cupid Saltwood, and soon the caricaturist had a new series showing the diapered Saltwood hovering with his bow and arrow over Indian couples working the sugar in the fields of Natal.

His successful mission to India, and the subsequent landing of young, healthy coolies with their wives, added the final complexity to the South African racial crucible: Bushman, Hottentot, Xhosa, Zulu, Afrikaner, Englishman, Coloured, and now the Indian.

When the cane workers, arriving under contract, were in place, 'passenger Indians' who paid their own way to Natal set themselves up as shopkeepers, and together, these initial groups grew to three-quarters of a million within the century. And though all were repeatedly offered free passage and bonus money if they would return to India, few were foolish enough to accept. They had found life so sweet in the land of Shaka that they intended staying.

Richard had succeeded beyond expectations. The Indians were happy to be in Natal and the white farmers were glad to have them. For his enterprise in handling this migration, and especially his foresight in also bringing wives, he received from the queen herself a letter which formed the capstone to his life: 'Because of your generous services to the Royal Family and the Throne, and in so many capacities, we wish you to come to London to receive a knighthood from our hands.'

When the ceremonies at court ended, Sir Richard Saltwood of De Kraal boarded his first train and rode down to Salisbury, where in the ancient hang-tile house beneath the sentinel oaks and chestnuts he sat with his older brother, Sir Peter, looking across the river at the still-glorious cathedral. They spoke of many things; Sir Peter was no longer in Parliament, having surrendered that seat to his son, but like all the Saltwoods, he was interested in everything.

'Tell me, Richard, what's to be done with the Dutchmen out there?'

'The Boers, or Afrikaners as some call them. They're a special breed. A real Dutchman came out not long ago, a clergyman from Amsterdam, intending to make his life there. I knew him well, and after six months he sat in my house and said, "I'm going back to civilization. These people don't even speak proper Dutch. They worship in a fashion we discarded two centuries ago. Few have read any book but the Bible, and even there, only the Old Testament." And he returned to Holland.'

'What did the locals say?'

'That's where it gets complicated. You've got to understand that the visiting Dutchman was talking about emigrant farmers who trekked— maybe fourteen thousand of them. But you must remember there were other thousands who did not trek. They still form the majority in the colony, and they don't know whether to love or hate their brothers up north. Our Amsterdam clergyman was trying to change the trekker Boers, but they are set in their ways. It'll take more than a Holland predikant to push that lot into the nineteenth century.'

'Are their ways so old?'

Sir Richard sat with his fingers propping his chin, and hesitated about answering, because what he said next would determine the nature of his reply to Sir Peter's major question about the probable future, and he knew that Peter still carried much weight in London. Very carefully he said, 'The ways of the Boer are very old indeed. And the ways of the Englishman are very modern. Sooner or later the two must come into real conflict.'

'War?'

'I don't know. If somehow we could maintain relations with them, the chasm could be bridged. But look at what happened to Tjaart van Doorn, the man who sold me his farm. Peter, you should come to South Africa and see it. No cathedrals visible from it, but a glorious place.'

'What about Van Doorn?'

'Same age as me. Same degree of energy. Splendid fellow—he stood at my side in forty skirmishes against the Kaffirs.'

'But what about him?'

'When he emigrated from our area . . . wrote a first-class letter giving his reasons. He battled Mzilikazi, then stormed down into Natal and helped destroy Dingane. Then fled to some valley far and gone. Lives there with Kaffirs, a few families like his own. No books, no newspapers, no ideas. None of the children can read. Lost. Lost.'

'But if he's fallen back into the bush, why fear him?'

'Because the Tjaart van Doorn I knew was a powerful man. You don't have men like that in England. Carved out of solid rock. Peter, if your government insults this man, or enrages him, there could be hell to pay.'

'What do you want us to do?'

'Conciliate.'

'Bosh.'

Without discussing the matter openly, the brothers agreed that since this would probably be the last time they would ever meet, they ought to take a traditional family excursion to Stonehenge and perhaps on to Oriel College in Oxford, where Sir Richard's grandson would one day be a student, like the three grandsons of Sir Peter. They arranged their schedules, told the grooms to prepare the horses, and one morning Peter said, 'Shall we saddle up and see the Stones?'

'Capital!' And within the hour they were on their way with a small retinue of servants.

They halted at Election Elm at Old Sarum, and under its branches Sir Peter said, 'I was the last member of Parliament to come from this wonderful borough. Back in 1832 I think it was. When Sir John Russell proposed his bill outlawing the rotten boroughs, I amazed everyone by supporting it. The day for that kind of privilege had passed.' He sighed. 'But this old tree sent some sterling men to Parliament, none better than Father.' He chuckled. 'Did you hear how I got the seat?' He told how the Proprietor had brought him here, grumbling all the while, then handed him the ballot with his name inscribed. 'He said he feared I was one of those young radicals. I must have been forty, but he liked members to be in their seventies. Said that by then they had some sense.'

By the time they reached Stonehenge the two old men were tired, and they decided not to try the longer ride to Oxford. 'It was a dear place,' Sir Peter said. 'I collected all my ideas at Oriel. They weren't very good, really, but they sufficed. My son feels the same way. And your grandson will, too. How old is the boy?'

'Two.'

'Is he bright?'

'Average, like all of us.'

After Richard said this the brothers fell silent, and finally Peter, with tears in his eyes, asked, 'Did you ever hear anything about David in America?'

'He disappeared somewhere in Indiana.'

There was prolonged silence as the brothers looked at the fallen stones on which their mother and their grandmother had sat during family picnics. Then Peter said, 'Tell me about Hilary,' but before Richard could speak, he added, 'You know, I suppose, that his visit home with that nigger wife was a disaster.'

'It was a disaster everywhere,' Richard said. 'Poor fellow, they both had their throats cut one night. No one ever knew who did it.'

'Those two dead. We two, knights of the realm. I think Mother would have been satisfied. She was dreadfully practical, you know.' He stared at the ancient stones so loved by his family and repeated what he had told Richard almost sixty years ago: 'This is always to be your home. I mean, here and Sentinels. Do come back.' But each brother knew there would be no revisiting, not for them. But for their children's children this would always be a lodestar.

When Frank Saltwood, grandson of Sir Richard, attended Oriel College during the years 1879–1881, he found it to be a luminous center for theological discussion, but like his forebears, he avoided any deep intellectual discussion. In the Michaelmas Term of his final year he began to take notice of a curious scholar who flitted in and out of Oxford, now attending lectures, now arguing in pubs, and then disappearing for months. Frank was not even certain what college this person belonged to, or whether he was a tutor or a fellow student.

Since he appeared so much older, Frank assumed he must be some itinerant lecturer attached temporarily to a prestigious college like Balliol or Christ Church, a retiring man of poor family whose clothes seemed out of place, whose coat was always buttoned to the chin, and whose trousers were invariably of an odd fabric. He had dark reddish hair, a heavyset body and watery blue eyes, which he shifted away from any direct stare.

As the time approached when he must take his final examinations and leave Oriel, Frank felt keenly the unique beauty of Oxford, and on days when he should have been studying he wandered along the Thames, listening to birds he had not known in South Africa, and wasted his time looking back at the profile of the city, with its domes and towers standing as proudly as they had four hundred years ago. He was oppressed by the ancient dignity of this place as compared to the raw youth of his homeland, and he began to generate that ambivalence which all South Africans experienced who came here for their studies.

In fact, he fell into quite a funk, the sharp direction which he had known up to now blunted by his oscillations between Oxford and De Kraal. For whole days he wandered the streets of Oxford, leaving his rooms at Oriel and aimlessly visiting the nearby colleges, not for intellectual enrichment in preparation for his exams, but rather to look at the great quadrangles as if he were leaving a place he cherished, never to see it again.

He would enter the gateway to some college in which he had never attended a lecture and stand there like a tripper down from London, staring at the beautiful façades of the buildings that outlined the square, imagining the great men who had lived in those rooms or studied in those halls. He was not good at political or literary history, and he certainly could not associate the notable graduates of Oxford with their colleges, but from the conversation of his father and from hints picked up during his residence at Oriel, he vaguely knew that great men of England had come to their studies in this city: Samuel Johnson, Cardinal Wolsey, Charles James Fox and the two Williams, Penn and Pitt, who had left Oxford to represent Old Sarum in Parliament.

When he returned to his own college and entered its gate and saw the low, squat outline of its rugged buildings, he could not believe that any famous men had come from its confines. Legend said that Sir Walter Raleigh had studied here, but he doubted it. Some of the professors made a fuss over an Oriel man named Gilbert White, but Frank had no idea who he was or what he had done. No, what came from this college was an endless procession of Saltwoods, men of solid worth who never stood at the head of any list but who had a penchant for doing the right thing. They had managed their business in Salisbury, and extended it into various profitable fields; they had served in Parliament when Old Sarum was a rotten borough and then stood for honest election when it was abolished; and like his grandfather's brother Hilary, they had followed God into strange and tragic callings.

Three weeks before his examinations were to begin he fell into a deep melancholy, obsessed by his thoughts of Hilary Saltwood, and he wondered what had motivated him. He had died with his throat cut, Frank knew, and images of the old man . . . He assumed that Hilary had been old, for he had lived long ago, and the old man's ghost haunted him so persistently that he began to wonder if this might not be a call to holy orders. Was God speaking to him, soliciting his assistance in some distant missionary field?

He might have gone quite sour and missed his examinations altogether had not the curious scholar come bursting back to Oriel, feverishly preparing for his own final examinations, as strange as ever, those watery blue eyes still deceptive. They seemed somnolent, like a snake's; actually, they burned with an incandescent fire on the few occasions when he looked directly at a newcomer.

This happened one afternoon at tea when a friend said in banter, 'Saltwood, you're beginning to look like a missionary.'

Frank blushed, but was spared the embarrassment of reply by the peripatetic scholar, who hunched his shoulders forward, stared right at him, and asked in a soft, high-pitched voice, 'Why would you elect to be a missionary in strange quarters when there's so much real work to be done in your homeland?'

'What do you mean?' Frank stammered.

'I mean South Africa. Don't you live there?'

'I . . . I do. But what's that got to do with it?'

Suddenly the stranger put down his cup, rose awkwardly and stomped from the room, volunteering not another word.

'Who is that fellow?' one of the Oriel men asked.

'Odd duck. Been studying here for his degree since 1873.'

'Eight years to do three years' work. Is he stupid?'

'I don't know. Those are the first words I've ever heard him speak.'

A younger student interrupted: 'He's not stupid at all, although he sometimes seems so.'

Another disagreed: 'He tried to enter a real college, you know. Balliol, I think, but he couldn't pass the exams. So Balliol sent him over here, and our provost said, "It's always the same. All the colleges send me their failures." And Oriel accepted him.' The speaker laughed nervously. 'Same thing happened with me.'

The first young man continued: 'He lives in South Africa, I'm told, and that's why he's been able to attend only on a hit-or-miss basis.'

'I don't understand,' Frank said.

'His health fails. His lungs. Our Oxford climate threatens him and he must hurry home to recuperate. He's had a very broken career, you know.'

'I'd hardly call that a career,' one student said derisively. 'I say, Saltwood, you're from South Africa. You know the blighter?'

'First time he spoke to me,' Frank said.

'Well, he owns diamond mines in South Africa, and caring for them's the real reason he flits back and forth.'

Three days later Frank again met the stranger, and was impelled to speak with him: 'You said I should not become a missionary?'

'What I meant to say—why don't you knuckle down and quit this foolishness? Why don't you act like a man, pass your examinations?'

The stranger's tone of voice was so peremptory that it sounded like a father's, and Frank said rebelliously, 'They tell me it's taken you eight years to pass yours.'

The man showed no resentment. A bright smile animated his face and he grasped Frank by the arm. 'You spend three years and come away with a degree. I spent eight years and return home with an empire.'

'What kind?'

'Every kind you can imagine. Political, business, mining, but mostly power.' The man started to leave, then turned back, taking Frank's arm again and holding it firmly. 'For God's sake, man, buckle down, finish the job, pass your examinations. Then brood about what to do.'

He spoke with such force and moral imperative that Frank became curious and tried to find out by what strange route this man had come to his final week at Oriel, but none of Frank's friends knew, or even whether he was English-born or a native South African. Later, when everyone dressed in formal attire—black suit, bow tie, black shoes, cap and gown—and filed into the stately Examination Schools adjoining the Bodleian Library, there was the stranger, older than any of the other examinees and older also than many of the proctors. For an entire week he scribbled furiously, never looking up, and when the ordeal ended he disappeared.

Because of this man's rude intervention, Frank had pulled himself together, accomplishing exactly what all his Saltwood predecessors had achieved at Oriel: a pass without distinction or honors of any kind. He had not been exactly educated at Oxford; he had been ordained into the fellowship of English country gentlemen, not bright enough to lead but steady enough to be good followers.

With his degree in hand, Frank hired a horse and wagon and started the long journey to Stonehenge, then south to Old Sarum, and finally into the stately cathedral town where his ancestral home stood quietly beside the river. For generations the South African Saltwoods would bring their diplomas home in this way, for until they were registered before admiring family at Sentinels, with John Constable's fine watercolor of the cathedral filling the hall with radiance, they were not truly graduated or ready to start their life's work in the colony.

Frank was so enchanted with the Saltwood home, and he enjoyed so much the civilized life of taking tea under the great oaks, that all thought of becoming a missionary vanished, but he did tell his cousin, Sir Victor Saltwood, M.P., of the curious experience he had had of going into a blue funk, from which he was rescued only by this forceful stranger. 'I'm indebted to him. He quite saved me, you know.'

He was therefore surprised and not a little pleased when he boarded his ship at Southampton to find that one of the first-class cabins was occupied by this belated graduate of Oxford, and with uncharacteristic boldness he presented himself before the man, saying, 'I must thank you for having saved my life.'

The stranger knew immediately who he was and remembered the brief conversation. 'I saw you buckling down to your examinations. I was pleased.'

'I say, if we're to travel so long together, shouldn't I know your name? Mine's Saltwood.'

'I know. De Kraal. Sir Richard, the old fool Hilary. I'm C. J. Rhodes.'

'Thank you for what you did, Mr. Rhodes.'

The brusque man extended no invitation either to call him by something other than Mr. Rhodes or to walk with him, and the conversation ended. Since Frank's quarters were at the farther end of the ship, during the first week he saw his fellow graduate no more, but during the second week some older men were gathered in a salon, engaged in heated conversation, and when they saw Frank passing, one of them called, 'I say, Saltwood. You live at De Kraal, don't you?'

'I do.'

'Stop with us a moment.' Place was made for him, and when he was seated, the man who had hailed him said, 'Do you think of South Africa as rich or poor?'

For several moments Frank compared images of rural England as he had come to know it with those of the veld, and he had to confess: 'I would say on the poor side.'

'He's right!' an excited, high-pitched voice cried. 'I tell you, South Africa's an impoverished land. Only hard work and imagination will save it.'

Mr. Rhodes spoke with a book of maps on his knees, and as the men listened he outlined his basic thesis, slapping at the maps with a stubby hand as he made his points. 'Look at the map, man. Look at what nature did.' And with a pudgy forefinger he showed how South Africa ended at a degree of latitude where the more fortunate continents were just beginning. 'Nature robbed us, savagely.' And he demonstrated how Africa was the continent that hugged closest to the equator, as if afraid to venture down into colder waters. 'We're the only continent that lacks a substantial percentage of its land in the temperate zone where farming can flourish and industry thrive. Look how we compare with South America, which shares the same oceans with us. It reaches south to the fifty-sixth parallel. We're cut short at the thirty-fifth. Measure it out on the scale. They extend fourteen hundred miles farther into the good climates than we do.'

As he became more excited, his voice rose until it was a complaining wail. Flicking the maps, he invited his companions to see for themselves how their continent had been defrauded. 'It's only when you compare us with Asia, Europe and North America that our impoverishment becomes clear. If those continents had been cut off the way we've been, look at the civilization they'd have lost!'

With the men following his finger closely, he demonstrated how Asia would have had to surrender Kyoto, Tokyo, Peking, Tehran and most of Turkey. 'Every good thing done in those civilizations lost forever. But look at Europe!' Here he showed how the entire continent would have been lost had it been as truncated as South Africa. 'And when we reach America, the same story.' Carefully he drew the line which would have run south of Chattanooga, Memphis, Oklahoma City, Amarillo and Albuquerque. 'Those cities and all the places to the north that you've heard of— St. Louis, Seattle, Detroit, New York, Boston. None of them would have existed.'

He passed his atlas to his listeners, and as they studied the facts he said solemnly, 'If the rest of the world were as deprived as we are, civilization would consist of Los Angeles, Mexico City, Jerusalem and Delhi. Our cathedrals would not have been built, our plays would not have been written, and neither Beethoven nor Shakespeare would have existed.'

He spoke with great passion, then recovered his atlas and opened it to South Africa itself to make his final points. 'We've been sorely cheated by nature . . .'

'Why are you afraid to say that it was God who cheated us?' a man asked.

'God?' Rhodes said, twisting the palm of his right hand up and down like a bargainer. 'I give Him fifty-fifty. He may exist. He may not. I never fight with Him, and if you want to say God where I say nature, so be it.' He returned to the map and said, 'We can't move northwest because the Kalahari Desert impedes us. And we can't move south because our land ends. What we can do, is make the most of what nature has given us.'

He became quite poetical as he outlined the South African promise: 'We have people with wonderful vitality. Forests with some of the most fertile lands on earth. Flowers that have no equal. And herds of great animals that are inexhaustible. In a week's journey you can see hippos and rhinos, lions and elephants. I've seen the land rolling with zebra and eland and gemsbok. It's a treasury with boundaries unlimited.'

Then he plumped his fingers upon the area about Kimberley, where his mining interests lay. 'Nature is rarely unfair. If she cheats us in extension, she compensates by allowing us to dig deep. She's given us the finest concentration of diamonds in the world. And they've already found gold, too. But the real gold lies up here.'

As he said this, he pointed to the empty lands north of the Limpopo; at least the map showed them as empty, a vague Matabeleland governed by a son of the famous Mzilikazi. 'And here, too,' he said gravely, indicating land north of the Zambezi. With a sudden movement of his right hand he covered the entire segment of Africa with his palm. 'This map should all be red.' He meant that it should become part of the British Empire.

'How could that happen?' one of the listeners asked.

'It's your job to make it happen,' he said.

The next weeks determined the pattern of Frank Saltwood's life. He had intended going to South Africa for only a brief visit with his parents, then returning to London for legal training, but as he moved about the ship he became aware that Mr. Rhodes was keeping an eye on him, and at various intervals they met in discussion, and once Rhodes asked bluntly, 'Why would you pursue the law when you could be exercising your power directly?'

'What do you mean?'

'When you were at Oxford, did you ever read John Ruskin's charge to the young men of the university? You didn't? You should have been required to memorize it. Wait here.' He ran to his cabin, a rather heavy man moving with agility, and within a few moments was back with a dog-eared pamphlet of Ruskin's famous Oxford address of 1870, a few years before Rhodes matriculated. 'Read this,' he said peremptorily, 'and we'll talk about it after dinner.' In Mr. Rhodes' chair on deck, Frank read the intoxicating challenge:

> Will you youths of England make your country again a royal throne of kings, a sceptered isle, for all the world a source of light, a center of Peace; a mistress of learning and of the Arts, faithful guardian of time-tried principles? This is what England must do or perish. She must found colonies as fast and as far as she is able, formed of her most energetic and worthiest men; seizing any piece of fruitful waste ground she can set her foot on, and there teaching these her colonists that their chief virtue is to be fidelity to their country, and their first aim is to advance the power of England by land and sea. All that I ask of you is to have a fixed purpose of some kind for your country and for yourselves, no matter how restricted, so that it be fixed and unselfish.

When Mr. Rhodes returned after dinner, the sun had set behind the western horizon, but its invisible disk still sent golden rays to illuminate the clouds that stood guard over Africa, making the eastern Atlantic a scene of glory. He asked only one question: 'Saltwood, have you discovered your fixed purpose?'

'Not really, sir.'

'Isn't it about time you did?'

'As you know, I've been thinking of law.'

'You've *been thinking of*!' He spat out the words with distaste. 'At Oriel you were thinking of missionary work. And next week you'll be thinking of something else. Why not come to solid grips with real problems?'

'What do you mean, sir?'

'Come to work for me. There's so much to be done, so little time to do it.'

Darkness fell upon the ship, and as it sailed southward to the realm of stars that Frank knew well, Rhodes talked insistently. 'I need help, Saltwood. I need the energy of young men.'

'How old are you, sir?'

'Twenty-nine. But I feel thirty-nine. Have you any idea, Saltwood, of the empire I control?'

'No, sir.'

'I told few at Oxford. I was embarrassed. But I mean to control all the diamonds in the world.'

'To what purpose?'

'The map, Saltwood. The map. I mean to turn it all red. To make places you and I have never seen part of the British Empire.'

'Can that be done?'

'Never ask such a question!' Rhodes exploded. 'Anything can be done if men of good principle determine that it shall be done. Have you the courage to strike for immortal goals?'

In the darkness of midnight Frank had no estimate whatever of his courage, and he said so. 'Then you must come to work for me,' Rhodes said, 'and I'll show you how much courage a young man can develop.'

Through the night they talked of the Limpopo and the Zambezi, of the

Matabele, and when the moon hung low upon the waves Rhodes introduced a new word: 'Zimbabwe. Ever heard of it?'

'Yes.'

'A fabulous city. Some idiots are beginning to argue that it was built by blacks, but those who know are convinced it's Ophir of the Bible. The Queen of Sheba may have built it, or the Phoenicians. One day we must go to Zimbabwe to show the world that this is the Queen of Sheba's city.' Immediately he enlarged on the subject: 'Matabeleland, ancient cities, gold mines . . . They're nothing, Saltwood. The obligation of mankind is to improve society, and no people have stepped upon this earth more quali-fied to perform this task than well-bred Englishmen. Will you work with me?'

The night was gone, the sun was coming up over Africa—and young Saltwood was bewildered. 'I must discuss these matters with my parents.'

'Saltwood! A man forges his destiny of himself, not of his parents' wishes. If I'd listened to my father—' He stopped abruptly. 'Fine old man. Village preacher. Nine children. Much loved by his parishioners, and do you know why? No sermon he ever preached was more than ten minutes long.'

'You have eight brothers and sisters?'

'Yes, and a half sister.'

'All of them married?'

'One,' and he said this with such fierce finality, as if a sore point had been touched, that Frank was not surprised when he stalked off. Then he recollected that not once during the entire voyage had he seen Rhodes talking with any of the lady passengers or acknowledging in any way that they existed.

In the days that followed that conversation Rhodes spent his time with a group of male passengers, discussing only one topic: England and her glory. 'Join us,' he called one morning to Saltwood, and when Frank sat with the men he was peppered with questions about South Africa, the future of ranching at De Kraal, and the likelihood that Zulu warriors might once more challenge English armies.

Rhodes liked his answers, and when the others left he kept Saltwood beside him: 'You're the only one who made sense.' Then he became excited. He did not speak, he orated—in a high voice that grew higher as his enthusiasm flamed. He sat on his hands, rocking back and forth, and always he returned to the subject of Africa and the extension of empire: 'Germany is coming at us from the west, and Portugal's dug in on the east. It will be our responsibility to fend them both off. Push the channels north. Always north till we reach Cairo. The world can be saved only by Englishmen standing together. Saltwood, I need your help.'

'What about the Boers?' Frank evaded. 'Can they, too, be used?'

'The Boers are some of the finest people on earth. United with them, we could form a nation of unsurpassed strength.'

'Why don't we invite them to join us?'

Mr. Rhodes frowned and rubbed his chin. 'You know, I'm a member of Parliament. And what kind of district elected me, if you please? Heavily Boer. I work with them, I collect their votes—and damnit, I know them no better than when I started. And those who emigrated north I understand even less.'

'Is there a mystery?'

'Yes. They huddle in their little republics and refuse to join the main-stream of the human race. They keep away on their farms and leave the running of the world to us.'

'You speak as if you intend to rule the world.'

'Nothing less.' Quickly he added, 'If that sounds arrogant, I mean that the empire I shall put together for England must rule the world.' He dropped his voice: 'So your task will be to bring the Boers in with us.'

Then he became so impassioned on this point that he asked Salt-wood to wait by the railing, and while other passengers were heading for the dining room, he ran to his cabin and returned with a rumpled piece of paper. It was a holograph of his will, and when Saltwood read it he was shocked: C. J. Rhodes was donating all his possessions to two minor officials of the English government, commissioning them to bring into the British Empire countries as diverse as the United States, the east coast of China and the whole continent of Africa, the Voortrekker republics not excluded.

'Can this really be done?' Frank asked.

'It must be,' Rhodes said, 'and you're to be part of it.'

When the volatile man disappeared into his cabin, Saltwood reflected on his curious behavior: he was offering a young Oriel graduate, whom he scarcely knew, a part in governing the world, but he never invited him to his cabin, or to his table, or to any other event of which he was a part. And one afternoon when he saw Frank talking with an attractive girl on her way home to Cape Town, he actually scowled and turned away in disgust. For some days thereafter he did not speak to Frank, and when he finally did he muttered, 'I hope you're not making silly promises to some silly girl,' and only when Saltwood replied, 'Hardly,' did he resume his friendship.

When the ship docked at Port Elizabeth, Frank headed immediately north for his family's farm, and he supposed that he would never again see C. J. Rhodes, but one afternoon as he and his parents sat at tea on a veranda overlooking the pastures and the stream, a dusty cart clattered up to the gate, and Mr. Rhodes strode up to the porch. After the most perfunctory acknowledgment of Frank's parents, he asked bluntly, 'Well, Saltwood, are you prepared to come with me?'

'I haven't really . . .'

'You're not mooning about the law, are you? With so much work to be done?'

Frank tried to avoid a harsh answer that would send Mr. Rhodes away permanently, and once he vacillated, Rhodes sprang at him like a tiger: 'Good! We're off to Kimberley in the morning.' Only then did he bother with the older Saltwoods: 'I'll watch over him. He'll be at the heart of things, and when you next see him he'll be a man.'

The next day they drove to Graaff-Reinet, where they caught the stage-coach to Kimberley, whose violent activity was bewildering. Frank would never forget his first sight of the diamond mines, for as he wrote to his mother, they were like nothing else on earth:

> Each prospector is entitled to a square of precious land, thirty-one feet to a side, but of this land he must leave a narrow path for others to use. Since Miner A had dug his plot forty feet down, and Miner B twenty feet, poor Miner C who has not dug at all finds himself atop a square with such precipitous sides that any fall is fatal. Also, at night irresponsible men cut underneath the footpaths, causing them to collapse. All is chaos.
>
> But what catches the eye is a massive nest of cobwebs which looks as if ten thousand Arachnes had been spinning. They are the wires and ropes leading from the edge of the mine down to each of the individual holdings. On them buckets are drawn up, bearing the diamantiferous soil, and this immense tangle of lines, the buckets rising and falling are the signs of a diamond mine at Kimberley.
>
> It is Mr. Rhodes' fervent hope that he can bring some order into this madness, and to this end he has quietly been buying up plots here and there, endeavoring to consolidate them into some kind of reasonable concentration. If he can do so, he will command the industry and will become even more rich and powerful than he now is. It is my job to cut down to the same level all the contiguous plots he acquires, and I am finding many diamonds in the soil left for the footpaths. But for the moment the chaos continues, with one block fifty feet up in the air, the one beside it fifty feet down, and no order anywhere except in those areas he controls. It is a race between reason and anarchy, and he assures me that where men of good sense are concerned, reason always wins. He intends to.

Frank did not tell his mother what might have been the two most interesting bits of information. In the cottage occupied by Mr. Rhodes just as much chaos reigned as in the mines; a tin-roofed affair, it was Spartan-like, with not a single adornment to grace it, clothes pitched everywhere, dishes unwashed and furniture about to collapse. No woman was ever allowed in the house, which Rhodes shared with a gifted, sickly young man a few years younger than he. Frank found that he wasn't the only one in his early twenties selected to advance Mr. Rhodes' many interests; a squad of bright, eager recruits submerged their personal interests in those of this dreamer who visualized a Union Jack over every territory from the Cape to Cairo.

He invariably called his young men by their first names: Neville, Sandys, Percival, Bob, Johnny, and often he encouraged them to engage in hearty pranks, as if they were in grammar school. They were free to entertain such women as they could find in the diamond town, but there was an unwritten law that ladies were to be flirted with, and perhaps frolicked with, but quickly forgotten. Far greater things were in store for 'my young gentlemen,' as he referred to them, and like Shaka, he wanted his regiments to keep their hearts on the great tasks ahead and not on the bosoms of their wives.

Frank noticed that up to the time of his formal employment, Rhodes addressed him with a curt 'Saltwood,' but once he accepted his assignment he became 'Frank,' and so he would remain, perpetually young, perpetually smiling. Like all the young gentlemen, he was paid well.

The second interesting bit involved Mr. Rhodes' chief rival in diamonds, an extraordinary chap who never stopped amazing the young gentlemen and the public at large. He was as different from Mr. Rhodes as a man could be, but was equally ruthless in hounding a business opportunity, and he alone stood between Rhodes and true riches.

Barnett Isaacs was a year older than Rhodes, a Jew born in one of the worst slums of London; in the midst of an undistinguished career as a frowzy vaudeville comedian and tap-dancer, he decided in a stroke of pure genius to make his fortune in the mines of South Africa. With only his nerve and some boxes of cheap cigars purchased near the docks at Cape Town, he talked his way north to Kimberley, peddled his 'six-penny-satisfiers,' and earned a pitiful living entertaining the miners with deplorable jokes, ridiculous acrobatics, and whatever else came to his mind when he stood before them in one cheap hall or another.

But Barnett Isaacs was an inspired listener, and while he clowned he picked up choice bits of negotiable information: who was going broke, who wanted to return to London, who had stolen whose claim. And bit by bit he pulled this information together, acquiring a horse and cart and prowling the diggings as a kopje-walloper, a kind of money-minded vulture looking to snap up the discarded pickings off other men's sorting tables. He soon got his hands on valuable rights, and one day Kimberley woke to find that Isaacs was one of the richest men on the diamond fields.

He thereupon changed his name to Barney Barnato, bought himself several suits of slick clothes, and indulged in a fancy which had tantalized many an earlier vaudevillian.

At a considerable personal cost, he assembled a moderately good theatrical company, purchased himself a set of Shakespearean costumes, and offered South Africa its first performance of *Othello,* with himself in the title role. Frank arrived at the mines too late to see the opening performance, but when all the young gentlemen purchased tickets to a subsequent exhibition, he went along to a steaming tin-roofed shed crowded with a noisy audience that cheered madly when 'Our Barney' strode onstage. His Desdemona, unfortunately, was six inches taller than he and appeared to be wrestling with him whenever they embraced; also, his makeup was so black and so thick that when she touched him her skin came away smeared while his showed white empty spaces.

'But he's rather good!' Frank whispered to the men beside him.

'Wait till the afterpiece!'

'What happens?'

'You won't believe it.'

When the final curtain fell, with Desdemona dead and pretty well besmudged, the young actor who played Cassio came forward to announce that in response to unusual demand, Mr. Barnato, who had already excelled in *Othello,* would now give his classic rendition of Hamlet's soliloquy, at which the crowd began to roar and whistle. After a few minutes Mr.

Barnato, his face wiped clean, appeared in a whole new costume. 'Watch this!' the young gentlemen whispered.

While Frank gaped, Mr. Barnato nimbly gave a flip-flop and ended standing on his head. Maintaining perfect balance for a surprisingly long time, he began to recite the soliloquy, but as he came to the better lines, he gave wild gestures with his hands, stabbing at 'bare bodkin' and waving madly at 'fly to others that we know not of.' At the concluding words 'and lose the name of action' he gave an amazing flip and landed back on his feet. The applause was shattering, for as Mr. Rhodes admitted acidly when his young men returned, 'The remarkable thing is not that he can do it, but that whilst on his head he can speak so powerfully and deliver such convincing gestures. I've never seen a better Hamlet.'

These two titans, Rhodes the taciturn plotter, Barnato the vaudevillian, fought each other for years, and then one night they stood face-to-face in the cottage of a man destined to be famous in South African history: Dr. Leander Starr Jameson. At four in the morning, after eighteen hours of tense bargaining, a deal was struck whereby Othello would eventually surrender all his control to Mars for a check whose photograph would be widely displayed throughout the world: £5,338,650. As Barnato capitulated, bleary-eyed and worn down, he said, 'Some people have a fancy for one thing, some for another. You, Rhodes, have a fancy for building an empire. Well, I suppose I must give in to you.' But he refrained from doing so until Rhodes promised that he would personally sponsor Barnato for membership in the ultra-exclusive Kimberley Club, where no Jewish Othello from Whitechapel would normally be welcomed.

If Barney's recitation of *Hamlet* had been surprising to Frank, his campaign for election to Parliament was stupefying: he purchased a whole new set of Paris suits, an imperial landau pulled by four dappled horses, European gilded uniforms for six footmen, a handsome costume for a postillion who rode ahead blowing a long trumpet, and a brass band of eighteen to follow behind. 'I voted for him,' Frank told the young gentlemen, and to his delight he found that they had, too. And he suspected that Mr. Rhodes had done the same, for as he once said, 'There are few men in this world who achieve everything they seek. Barney Barnato is one. He's played *Othello* to applause. He's recited *Hamlet* on his head. He's won the boxing championship of the diamond mines for his weight. He's had his own imperial guard. He's been elected to office. And he's the richest Jew in the country, with a full-fledged membership in the Kimberley Club. What more could he want?'

The young gentlemen were saddened when they heard that this man who had conquered the world by courage and sheer brazenness had committed suicide by throwing himself off the England-bound *Scot* in the middle of the Atlantic.

When Cecil Rhodes acquired control of the diamond fields, his attention was free to focus on the greater goals of his life; mere money, of which he now had prodigious supplies, interested him little except as a path to power. In the years when he was one of the richest men in the world, he continued to live with his young gentlemen in austere surroundings. 'Every man has his price,' he assured Saltwood, 'and often it's a hankering for luxury. With enough money you can buy any man. For example, the king up in Matabeleland wants guns. Above everything else, he wants guns. So let's see that he gets them.'

Selecting a team from among his Kimberley staff, he began to suborn the king, and this left him free to study the perpetual problem: 'Frank, we have at our end of the continent a priceless land governed by three races. English—who ought to rule. Boers—who don't know how to rule. And Kaffirs—who should never be allowed to rule. What's to be done?'

He allowed Frank to study this problem for some days, then gave his own answer: 'It's clear that England was intended to govern all of Africa. We're people of vision, decency, honor. We know how to govern, and to everyone we govern we bring added virtues. So we must gain control.

'The Boers? I love them. In some ways they're sturdier than the English. But they lack vision. They will never be able to provide good government. The republics they occupy must become part of our enterprise, and I think I see ways of accomplishing this. When they join us, they must be given every consideration, for we need them. But join they must.

'The Kaffirs? I stand ready to offer full citizenship to any man regardless of his color, so long as he is civilized. Would it be proper for them to have the vote while they remain in barbarism? I say they must be treated as children, and we must do something for the minds and brains the Almighty has given them.' He added, 'We must lord it over them until they gain civilization. Above all, Frank, never let them have alcohol.'

Upon analysis, Frank found that all of Mr. Rhodes' basic beliefs were debatable: at Majuba the Boer armies had knocked the devil out of regular British troops; Germany was moving defiantly into Africa and had already annexed the southwest lands along the Atlantic Ocean, her moves outsmarting the English; in the mines, Kaffir workmen were proving at least as capable as whites. But Mr. Rhodes had several million pounds to support his objectives, and Saltwood had none, so it was the former's views that prevailed.

To Rhodes, diamonds were the fire of his life, the glittering foundation of his fortune, so it was not surprising that he had been lukewarm to the discovery of gold two years earlier on the Witwatersrand (White Water Ridge), some five hundred miles to the north in the heart of the Boer republics. He did, however, stake his claim to a share of the golden fortunes, launching a great company that made him a Croesus, with unlimited power to undermine the Boers, keep the blacks obedient, and drive his highway of empire straight to the heart of Africa.

What happened next was inexplicable. In the Cape Parliament, Cecil Rhodes invariably sponsored full partnership for any Afrikaners who resided in the province, and they reciprocated by electing him to office, and would do so till he died. They liked his courage and admired his abilities. But now he decided to destroy the Boer republics in the north because, as he explained to Saltwood, 'They must come in with us.'

'But if they don't want to?'

'Then we shall force them.'

His reasoning was simple. The diamond mines at Kimberley were located on farmland which the English by infamous chicanery had forced to become part of their colony; English law governed the diamond fields. But the gold mines were located within the boundaries of one of the Boer republics; here Boer law prevailed, and this raised problems.

In the gold fields, which proliferated at a rate far greater than that seen in either Australia or California, there were Englishmen galore, and hundreds of Australians, and many Frenchmen, and Italians and Canadians and not a few American citizens who flocked in on ships from all the ports of the world. They were noisy, undisciplined, and a menace to the stolid Boers who wanted to be left alone on their farms; they swooped down on Witwatersrand like vultures finding a carcass on the highveld, and with them they brought contention, violence and every possible threat to the phlegmatic Boer way of life.

The self-governing Boers retaliated with the most imprudent laws: an Uitlander (Outlander) could vote for the Volksraad only after fourteen years' residence; before that apprenticeship he remained a second-class citizen, entitled to cast his ballot only for a separate assembly subject to Boer veto; dynamite required in mining was made by a Boer-favored monopoly, and prices for it became prohibitive; any infraction of a score of meticulous laws must be judged in a Dutch-speaking court according to laws not promulgated in English. Investment of money, movement of men and the mining of gold all fell under Boer law, and no concessions to reason were granted.

Rhodes, with his relentless determination to bring disparate elements in Africa under English rule, was convinced that the arrogant conduct of the Boers was ill-advised and must lead to rebellion unless modified. He decided to intervene personally with the forbidding Boer leader, Stephanus Johannes Paulus Kruger, that rumbling volcano of a man who ruled his little world from the stoep of his unpretentious dwelling on a tree-lined street in Pretoria.

'I will go to him privately this time,' he told his young men, 'and invite him like a gentleman to join with us.'

'What can you offer him in return?' someone asked.

'Membership in the British Empire,' Rhodes said without hesitating. 'What more could a ruler of a petty state want?'

Before any of the young men could point out that many nations about the world wanted a good deal more, Rhodes continued: 'I will see President Kruger next week, and we will talk like two grown-up men. Frank, you will come with me, so make sure you learn all there is to know about him.' During the next days Saltwood sought out anyone in Kimberley with knowledge of the titanic man with whom Cecil Rhodes was about to grapple. The diamond magnate had met the Boer leader before, in his capacity as a Cape politician; this time he would go unofficially as a private citizen, with his eye not on local affairs but on world empire.

'First of all,' one of the young gentlemen told Saltwood, 'he's known as Oom Paul, Uncle Paul. He's twenty-eight years older than Mr. Rhodes and will demand due respect. He's very vain, you know.'

'And ugly as sin,' another said. 'His face is all crags without the grandeur of mountains. His nose is marked with bumps, and his eyes are hooded. He stands leaning backward, with his great belly projecting forward. But because of his height . . . He's much taller than Mr. Rhodes and will treat him like a little boy.'

The first instructor resumed: 'He was in the Great Trek, you know. Killed some of Mzilikazi's warriors. Extraordinary strength. Extraordinary bravery. He's fought in all the wars.'

'But what you must remember, in all his life he's had only three months of schooling. He boasts, "Only book I ever read was the Bible, but since that contains all knowledge worth knowing, it's enough." '

'Do not,' the first man warned, 'react in any way if he mentions the earth.'

'I don't understand,' Frank said, seeking to build up his portrait of the Boer leader.

'Oom Paul believes the earth is flat. The Bible says so. And if he finds that either you or Mr. Rhodes holds it to be round, he'll stomp out of the room. He's also convinced that the Boers have been given their republics by God Himself, so Mr. Rhodes will be forced to prove that joining our empire is what God proposed, not Mr. Rhodes.'

'The one thing in your advantage, Frank, is that even though Kruger hates colonial Englishmen, he despises Uitlanders. Calls them the atheistic rabble stealing his land. He sees the English miners, Australians and Americans as impious and immoral, and he's not going to concede them anything. But if Mr. Rhodes can insinuate that he feels the same way about the Uitlanders . . .'

'It must be done with tact,' the oldest of the gentlemen warned. 'Oom Paul is beloved by his Boers. He's a dictator, because he knows he has total support, no matter what he does. He'll be imperious, objectionable, insulting and infuriating. But consistently he outsmarts the Uitlanders sent to deal with him. He's a brilliant manipulator. You are not meeting an ordinary man.'

One of the younger men added, 'And remember, the world is flat.'

Frank went to sleep that Thursday night with three adjectives reverberating: *'Stubborn, opinionated, God-driven,'* and he concluded that in contesting with Oom Paul, Mr. Rhodes might be in for a difficult tussle, but then the adjectives that depicted Mr. Rhodes began echoing: *'Relentless, self-assured, empire-driven,'* and he began to wonder if perhaps it might be President Kruger who would need help. Before he fell asleep he recalled the description of Kruger's appearance: 'Ugly as sin,' and he reflected that spiritually Mr. Rhodes might be described with those same words.

Late on a Friday afternoon they arrived in Pretoria in Mr. Rhodes' private coach, and they retired early so as to be up fresh and ready for their important meeting; Frank observed that Mr. Rhodes took special care with his shaving, as if he were seeing a princess, and adjusted his tie and high-collared coat so as to make the best appearance. In a carriage they rode through this extremely Boer town until, on a handsome street, they came upon an unpretentious cottage, somewhat Oriental in style, marked by a wide stoep on which stood a comfortable armchair. In it, so that all Pretoria could see him consulting with his people, sat Oom Paul himself, a hulking giant of a man, shoulders hunched forward, belly out, legs spread wide, his hooded eyes inscrutable, his beard framing his massive face. He was holding court for whoever chanced to pass by.

Rhodes stopped the carriage a respectful distance from the cottage. 'He's a difficult man, Frank. You go and prepare the way. Be courteous.'

When Frank approached the stoep he was astounded at how massive Kruger was and how ugly; he seemed a cartoonist's caricature of an illiterate Boer farmer, but when Frank fell in line and had a chance to witness how Kruger handled his complaining burghers, it was obvious that here was a man of tremendous animal magnetism and resolute force.

'What brings you?' the president asked abruptly.

'Mr. Cecil Rhodes is waiting in the carriage. He asks permission to have words with you, sir.'

Without even looking in the direction of the carriage, Kruger grumbled, 'This is Nachtmaal.'

'I was not aware of that, sir.'

'My burghers are. For years they've known they can talk with me at Nachtmaal. Schalk Wessels here has come a hundred and ten miles, haven't you, Schalk?'

When the man nodded, Kruger said, 'This day is sacred to the burghers. I might have a few free minutes on Monday.'

'On Monday, Mr. Rhodes has other appointments. Can't he possibly see you today? Or tomorrow, perhaps?'

President Kruger rose from his chair, demonstrating the great dignity he could command when necessary, and in a gracious voice explained: 'Today is Nachtmaal Saturday. It's reserved for the burghers. Tomorrow is Sabbath. It's reserved for the Lord. No matter how important Mr. Rhodes' problems, they can wait till Monday, and so can he.'

Without thinking, Frank replied in words which imitated Kruger's urbanity: 'Mr. Rhodes waits for no man.' Turning smartly on his heel, he left the stoep.

But by the time he reached the waiting carriage, he was alarmed by what he had done and asked Mr. Rhodes, 'Shall I return and apologize?'

'Never! You behaved with spirit. I meant to give that old devil a chance, but I refuse to crawl on my knees. We shall proceed without him.'

Back in his offices, Mr. Rhodes referred so frequently to 'that obstinate, Bible-quoting Boer' that Frank speculated on what his response to his humiliation might be. Then he discovered that Mr. Rhodes was making many cautious inquiries on various aspects of Boer strength, for as he told his young gentlemen, 'A man must never move until he can assess the full power of his opponent.'

'Are you spying out the enemy?' one of the young fellows asked.

'I have no enemies,' Rhodes snapped. 'Only opponents. The day after we settle our differences we become mutual friends.' And Frank recollected a dozen instances in which this rule had prevailed. For three years Rhodes had fought Barney Barnato, and when the fight was settled, had welcomed him to his board of directors. Now Rhodes promised: 'The morning after President Kruger agrees to our plans, I will offer myself as his assistant in governing our joint territories.'

Suddenly, one morning, he wheeled about and fixed Saltwood with his watery eyes, which could become so fiery when he wished. 'Zimbabwe! Frank, I've always wanted to know who built it. I'm convinced in my own mind it must have been the Queen of Sheba, as the Bible indicates. What

I want you to do is organize an expedition to search out the place and report
to me what you find. Because we must nail down the truth before some
German adventurer proves that the stone castles were built by Kaffirs.
Hideous thought.'

Since Frank could not decipher what Mr. Rhodes was up to, he asked,
'What has this to do with your plans?'

'There's a man living far east of here, next to the farm they call Vrymeer. They say he went to Zimbabwe as a boy. Saw the turrets close up.
I want you to interrogate that man, check his truthfulness . . .' Rhodes
hesitated, then added, 'Take a measure of him.'

'Who is he?'

'Paulus de Groot.'

Frank did not allow his countenance to change, but like a bomb lighting
up the night, Mr. Rhodes' intentions became clear. 'I'll go see General de
Groot. Sound him out.'

Paulus de Groot was that giant of a man, six feet five, with stooped
shoulders and massive red head, who had led one of the charges at Majuba
in 1881 when the Boers defeated the best troops in the British Empire. He
was a man who could enlist the support of other men; he was also without
vanity, for when the great battles ended he returned to his farm, where he
was reported to be living in stark simplicity. The Boer rulers in Pretoria
begged him to join the government, but he told them, 'Riding a horse
up a hill doesn't make a man sagacious.' And he remained a farmer.

What Mr. Rhodes wanted to know was whether General de Groot had
the capacity and the fire to resist an English attempt at taking over the Boer
republics. 'He's said to be past sixty, much too old to be leading troops. But
he's also said to be a very active man, good with horses and guns. Find out
about him.'

'Then you're not interested in Zimbabwe? Not really?'

Mr. Rhodes changed his attitude completely. Grasping Saltwood by the
shoulder, he said quietly, 'Frank, I'm interested in everything. I want to
pursue everything. You're off to Zimbabwe in the morning. By way of
Vrymeer.'

It was this variety of interests which almost destroyed the pleasant
relationship between Mr. Rhodes and Frank, because that night a cable
from London reached South Africa, informing Rhodes that a business
friend of some importance was sending his niece on vacation to Cape Town
and using her to deliver a packet of documents that he wanted Rhodes to
study. Someone must meet the young woman, Maud Turner, not only to
receive the documents, but also to see that she was properly ensconced.

No one knew anything about Miss Turner except that her uncle was
powerful, but there was a strong suspicion that she must be rather unattractive, else why would her uncle be sending her to Cape Town? Through the
years English families had developed the pleasant and prudent habit of
managing by one device or another to ship their unmarriageable females
either to India or to Australia, on the principle that 'if she can't get married
out where the competition is so thin, she'll never make it.' This trickle of
gaunt, unlovely creatures was regularly dispatched to the far colonies in
hopes that most would never return, or at least, not till they had sons of
a proper age for Eton or Harrow.

'You must attend her, Frank,' Rhodes said peremptorily.

'But I'm heading for Zimbabwe.'

'It can wait. It's been waiting three thousand years.'

So Frank Saltwood, now in his thirties, clean and trim, with the affectations of an Oxford education, boarded the smoky train at Kimberley and headed south over the empty spaces of the Great Karroo.

He realized from the start that this could be a much more dangerous mission than going north to Zimbabwe, because of the inviolate rule that governed Mr. Rhodes' young gentlemen: once a man displayed serious interest in a young woman, he was quarantined from decisions of importance, and if he actually married her, he could be fired that day. Indeed, Frank wondered if Mr. Rhodes' choice of him to attend Miss Turner had not been some kind of signal that his days in diamonds and gold were nearing an end. Because he enjoyed his work and wanted to continue it, he was determined to handle the young lady with aloofness, accept her documents, sign her into the Mount Nelson, and hurry back to Kimberley and his more important work. He certainly would not risk employment he'd liked for so many years by becoming entangled with a woman.

He had not counted on the duplicity of his Salisbury cousin, Sir Victor Saltwood, who had ascertained that young Frank was still without a wife or prospects of any. It was he who had gone to Maud Turner's uncle, proposing that his charming, gifted niece, twenty-three years old, be dispatched to Cape Town with papers for Cecil Rhodes, and it was he who drafted the cable which Rhodes received. Families of importance saw to it that their young men and women met marriageable people of their own kind, and if girls had to ship all the way to Australia or Cape Town, so be it. Sir Victor could not have devised that Frank himself should meet the ship, but he certainly expected him to meet Miss Turner sooner rather than later.

He had a right to expect favorable results, for he had sent one of the finest young women of the Salisbury district, member of a strong family, heiress to a modest fortune, and recipient of one of the most practical educations possible: she had been allowed to listen to the lively conversation of her elders, who were interested in politics, morals, business and empire. She was reasonably pretty, unreasonably clever with her tongue, and a person to whom an adventure like Cape Town was irresistibly attractive as something to do before settling down in Salisbury.

She half suspected that Sir Victor and her uncle were conspiring in some way to get her to meet this or that young man; they were always conspiring about bills in Parliament or reforms in the church, but this did not mean that she had to accede to their rough-and-ready stratagems. She would deliver the papers, go on an elephant hunt, and return to England to marry whom she pleased. In performing these duties she would see as much of South Africa as possible, and have a rattling good time doing so.

At the end of the voyage out she could have married any one of three quite ordinary men who had courted her, and she felt confident that on the voyage home she could do better, so she was in no hurry to accept whomever it was that her uncle had selected for her, but when she saw on the dock awaiting her a young man of obvious charm and vitality, she was interested.

'Halloo!' she cried in a very unladylike shout. 'Are you Mr. Rhodes' emissary?'

'I am. Saltwood's the name.'

'Meet me over there, Saltwood,' and without assistance from the pursers she found the gangway and was one of the first off the ship.

Frank, watching her come skipping down the sloping stairs, saw at once what a remarkable young woman she was. 'She seemed all of a piece,' he wrote to his mother. 'From her buttoned shoes to the sway of her skirt, from the broad cloth belt about her waist to the perfection of her blouse, she was a harmony, but what I liked most was the way she coiled her hair. No man could have deciphered just how she did it, all auburn and glowing in the sunlight.'

Still, he might have resisted her allure had it not been for the added seductiveness of the Mount Nelson Hotel. This fine edifice stood at the edge of the gardens laid out by Jan van Riebeeck two hundred and forty years before. It was the glory of Cape Town, a spacious inn with lovely grounds, ornate hallways, excellent kitchens and muted servants who seemed to be either Malay or Coloured. A chilled Trianon wine from the Van Doorn vineyards, a small helping of a spicy bobotie, followed by roast duiker and an orange soufflé at the Mount Nelson might addle any young man's good judgment, but when a lively young woman like Maud Turner sat sharing it and throwing her witty barbs, it became a Lucullan feast. He telegraphed Mr. Rhodes: BUSINESS COMPLICATIONS NECESSITATE THREE MORE DAYS.

During these three days he was captivated by the levels of interest and understanding she displayed, and he found that she was honestly 'all of a piece,' as he had written, a beautifully organized person whose individuality matched her intelligence. In curious ways she resembled Mr. Rhodes, for absolutely everything interested her: 'How will the blacks ever learn if there aren't enough schools for them?' She developed a special affinity for the Cape Afrikaners and sought them out. 'How could you, Frank, have lived here so long and known so few of them? They're far more interesting than your English friends . . . What, for heaven's sake, have you been doing all this time?'

'Working with Mr. Rhodes.'

'What I mean, Saltwood. The English in South Africa. Another decade, you'll have been here a century, and what have you achieved? You've driven the Boers to set up their own republics. And the ones left behind here in the Cape are talking about an Afrikaner Bond, or something. What have you English got to show?'

Frank laughed. 'My dear Maud, almost everything you've seen has been the result of English effort. The port you entered. The railroad you took to Stellenbosch. The passes over the mountains. The schools, the hospitals, the free press. All English-inspired.'

'It may be as you say,' she conceded, inwardly proud of the accomplishments he kept rattling off. 'But the Afrikaners I met at the coffeehouse don't seem to recognize any of it.'

'Nor did they ever recognize what Hilary was trying to do.'

'Your granduncle, was it? The missionary with the . . .'

'Black woman?'

'I didn't mean to say it that way, Frank.'

'I understand. But don't be surprised if you live to believe that what Hilary tried to do was right. That he saw the salvation of this land.'

'Do you think of this as your land? The way the Boers say they do?'

'I was born here. I've made it my home, even if your Afrikaner friends won't acknowledge my joint ownership. Just because they were here first doesn't mean that God gave them the land in some kind of deal. That's what the Boers up north preach, but mark my words, the English progress they despise will catch up with them. Perhaps very soon.'

'You're getting too serious, Frank Saltwood. Tell me about elephant hunting. Is it dangerous?'

She really did want to go on an elephant hunt, and if that proved impractical, a lion would do. When he informed her that both animals had quit these parts generations ago, she said simply, 'Then let's go after them. I have a small allowance, but I think it might suffice.'

When he disappointed her by saying that he could not remove himself from Kimberley, she said, 'Good, I've always wanted to see how they dig for diamonds. Silly stones—wouldn't want one myself.'

He pointed out that it would be quite improper for her to journey to Kimberley either with him or by herself, but she snapped, 'Nonsense! I carry with me letters to the most respectable families on the diamond fields.' And she organized the delivery of her two trunks to the railway and the purchase of her sleeping compartment to Kimberley. Frank was free to tag along, if he so wished.

The journey north was as pleasing as any he would ever know, a revelation of what a young woman could be. She was neither flirtatious nor coy; whenever an interesting topic arose, her expressive face revealed pretty much what she was thinking; and she sought out people for animated discussion. In the dining car, on the first evening, she invited an older couple to join them. With charming frankness she explained that she was not married to Frank, then went on to say that he was an important part of the diamond industry. From them she elicited the fact that they had a nephew working the gold fields and that he believed there was need, in the new town of Johannesburg, for a tailor. Normally they could not have afforded first-class accommodations on the train, but he had sent so much money that they had decided to splurge.

'Are you Jewish?' Maud asked abruptly.

'Yes. From Germany, our fathers, years ago.'

'Would you ever consider returning to Germany?'

'No. That happens to other people, not us.'

'Do you think Germany will try to take South Africa from us?'

'Germany will try to take everything,' they said.

On the second day she invited an Australian couple to dine with them, and again she explained that she was not married to Frank, whereupon the wife asked, 'Isn't it a mite risky? I mean, traveling with a young man?'

'Not if he's a nice young man, like Frank.' But as she patted his hand she added, 'Of course, he's not so young, really. How old are you, Frank?'

'Past thirty,' he said.

'Time to be taking the plunge,' the man said, at which Frank blushed uncontrollably.

'He'll do the right thing at the right time,' Maud said.

'With you?' the Australian woman asked.

'Goodness, we hardly know each other.' And by the time the train reached Kimberley, all the passengers knew that this fine-looking young woman was traveling with a young man she scarcely knew.

Mr. Rhodes took one look at the couple and realized that young Salt-wood had better be dispatched at once, or he was going to fall into irreversi-ble error, so once the introductions were made, he said, 'Saltwood, your conveyances are waiting. You'd better be off . . . this afternoon.'

'I shall leave day after tomorrow,' Frank said with some force, and that was the beginning of the estrangement, for Mr. Rhodes realized with dis-may that one of his young gentlemen had got himself seriously mixed up with a woman.

In the time he had stolen for himself, Frank demonstrated attractively his deep feelings for Miss Turner. He deposited her trunks at the local hotel, then escorted her about the town, showing her the mighty hole in the earth where he had worked, and the donkey engines which kept the water out. He took her into the countryside and to the local church, and as the second day ended he asked, 'Are you promised to anyone?' When she said, 'I am not,' he asked, 'Would you keep yourself free till I return from Zimbabwe?'

'And where's that?' she parried. When he told her, she wanted to accompany him on the safari, but this suggestion he rejected forcibly. 'I understand,' she teased. 'Mr. Rhodes wouldn't like it.'

'Conditions are far too rough, Maud.'

'I understand. Mr. Rhodes lays down very strict conditions for his employees. No women.' She expected him to say something, and when he didn't, she said boldly, 'But if I did wait, wouldn't Mr. Rhodes discharge you?'

'Yes. So when I married you, I'd have to find other employment.'

'Could you do so?'

'I'm a young man. I can work. I know diamonds and gold.'

Very quietly she said, 'I shall cancel my steamship.'

'What will you do?'

'I am going on an elephant shoot.'

'With whom?' he asked in amazement.

'With three gentlemen at the hotel.'

'My God, Maud!'

'I said I would wait, Frank. I didn't say I was going to sit on my hands.'

'But . . . but, three men from the hotel!'

'My uncle sent letters to two of them.' And then she kissed him, not a peck on the cheek, but the full passionate kiss of a liberated young woman who had found the kind of man she was willing to wait for.

From Pretoria, Frank took the new train leading down to Lourenço Marques on Delagoa Bay, but after a full day's journey he disembarked at the small station of Waterval-Boven, where a wagon awaited him. It was a fifteen-mile drive south, with a black man who gave his name as Micah Nxumalo. The first part came from the Bible, he explained in broken

English, the second part from his grandfather, who had come here from Zululand in the time of troubles.

'Did Mr. van Doorn own the land then?'

'No. It was our land.'

'But how did Mr. van Doorn acquire it?' The word was too big for Micah and he asked what it meant. 'Get. How did he get the land?'

A puzzled look came over the black man's face and he said, 'At first it was ours, then after a while it was his.'

When they reached the town of Venloo, Frank expected to be dropped at a lodging place before visiting Vrymeer, but Micah informed him that he was to room at the lake. 'With whom?' Saltwood asked. 'The De Groots or the Van Doorns?'

'Nobody stays with the De Groots,' Micah explained. 'They have only a very small place.' And when the horses climbed to the top of the rise that separated Venloo from the lake, Frank understood, for to the north stood a mean collection of wattle-and-daub structures in the center of unkempt fields, while to the east unfolded a substantial farm with an interesting mixture of barns for animals, kraals for holding areas, a rambling white-washed farmhouse with a corrugated iron roof, and at some distance a handsome collection of rondavels for the Nxumalos and the other blacks who worked the land.

The farm was obviously prosperous and looked inviting, but what captured Saltwood's eye was the inconsequential little stream that debouched from the hills, ran among the farm buildings and broadened out to a beautiful lake on which ducks abounded and flamingos. What Saltwood could not see, approaching by this road, were the two rounded mountains that gave the site distinction; as they came slowly into view, Micah pointed them out and said, 'Sannie's Tits.'

'Who's Sannie?'

'Girl that used to live here. My father's time. She loved a young man. He died. She died.'

The little northern dwellings were occupied by General de Groot, the big farm by the Van Doorns, and it was to the latter that Micah led the horses. 'Hello, there!' a rough voice called from the barn. 'You that Mr. Rhodes' man?' The English words came uneasily and with heavy accent.

'Yes. Frank Saltwood.'

'We don't hold much with that Mr. Rhodes. He's a bad one. But you're welcome.'

The farmer held out a big hand and said, 'Jakob van Doorn. Mama!'

From the house emerged not an older woman but three of the prettiest little girls Frank had ever seen. With a bang they burst onto the edge of the stoep—and then behaved quite differently. The oldest girl, about fifteen, stopped shyly when she saw the strange man and stood by a pillar, her blond pigtails reflecting the light. The two younger ones, who seemed to be about the same age, seven or eight, were not abashed by the stranger; they came rushing right down into the yard to embrace him, their pigtails flying.

'The twins!' Jakob said proudly. 'Anna and Sannah, but which is which you'll never know.'

The girls did not try to be cute or tease about their names. They simply took Frank by the hand and led him toward the stoep, where through the front door appeared Mevrou van Doorn, in her late thirties, holding an infant on her hip. 'This is my wife, Sara, and the ruler of our roost, little Detlev.'

With delighted tugging, the twins carried their baby brother about the stoep. 'Come in,' Mevrou van Doorn said. 'We wondered about your telegram.'

'Yes, I came to see the general. I understand he went to Zimbabwe once.'

'He was there. But only as a little boy.'

'Will he remember?'

'The general remembers everything,' Mevrou van Doorn replied.

'My father was there, too,' Van Doorn said. 'He led a party north of the Limpopo. Tsetse fly drove them back.'

'Will I run into the tsetse up there?'

'You will.' The Van Doorns took him into their house and showed him where he would sleep. As the twins helped him unpack, their mother made coffee and rusks, and then Jakob opened a bottle of witblits (white lightning), a fiery homemade brandy. 'We drink to your coming. Do you speak Dutch?'

'Alas, not much. I was brought up in the Grahamstown area, you know, where there were few Boers.' And before they could respond, he added, 'Our family bought De Kraal, you know.'

'You did!' Mevrou van Doorn cried. Vaguely the family had known that trustworthy English settlers had purchased the farm, but their name had been lost.

'Are you the family that collected the money from London for my father's slaves?' Van Doorn asked.

'Yes. I've heard that story.' Frank shook his head in disgust. 'What a bad thing the London government did to you people on the slave deal.'

'What do you mean, *deal*?' Van Doorn asked.

'The cheap way the slaves were paid for. Or not paid for.'

'That was a bad time,' Van Doorn said, but then he added brightly, 'You'll want to see the general right away, I suppose?' When Frank nodded, he cried, 'Come along, children,' and led a procession around the end of the lake.

Saltwood was totally unprepared for the primitive conditions in which this great general, a hero of the Boer republics, lived. But when De Groot came forward to extend a rough welcome, any thought of meanness or privation vanished. The man was a giant, but hunched over like some mountain denizen in a German fairy story. When he gripped Saltwood by the shoulder, his fingers were like steel.

Then he laughed heartily and said, 'I want you to meet my wife,' and from the rude hut came a handsome woman in her sixties, erect, white-haired, blue-eyed. As a girl she must have been beautiful, and even now her dignity was striking. 'This is Mevrou de Groot,' the general said, and as he spoke he took her hand, and they stood facing their visitor.

But then they saw the three Van Doorn girls, and Sybilla de Groot bent down to embrace the twins while the general bowed gallantly to Johanna. At this point Jakob said, 'This is Frank Saltwood. It was his grandfather who got us the payment for our slaves. He took our warrants, sent them to London, and got us every penny to which we were entitled. Not all that we should have had, but all that was allowed us.'

With a great slap of his hand on Frank's leg, De Groot said, 'I remember the day at Thaba Nchu. A smous came up from Graaff-Reinet with two packets. One for Van Doorn, one for my father. But my father had been killed by Mzilikazi. So the packet was given to me, and I can remember tearing it open and seeing the new bills, English bills, and I didn't like them. And do you know what I did with that money, young man?'

Frank said, 'I can't guess,' and the old general said, 'I saved it. Year after year I saved it, and in 1881, when we fought the English at Majuba, I spent it all to outfit my own commando. English money fighting English soldiers. I liked that.'

'Was the fighting hard—at Majuba?'

'Fighting is always hard, especially against you English. Your officers are stupid but your men are heroic.'

'Were you in command of the Boer forces?' Before the old man could respond, Frank added, 'I mean, they speak of you as one of the heroes of Majuba.'

With a big forefinger De Groot poked at his guest. 'No one is ever in command of Boers. Each man is his own general.'

'But everyone speaks of you as the general.'

'Yes. I raised the commando. And at night I asked if this or that approach might not be best. But if I ever gave an order, someone would have asked, "And who in hell are you?" And that,' he said, punctuating his remarks with his finger, 'would be a very . . .' He fumbled for a word and asked Van Doorn for help, using Dutch.

'Relevant,' Van Doorn suggested.

'Yes, that would be a relevant question. "Who in hell are you to give orders?" '

'How did you fight the battle?'

'Our Bible tells us that one Boer can defeat one thousand Canaanites. So we did it, that's how.'

'I don't remember any mention of Boers in my Bible,' Frank said, to which De Groot replied, 'That's your Bible.'

For nine days Frank studied these two families, and as he watched them in action he concluded that people like these would never conform to Mr. Rhodes' plans for them. When his departure neared, the Van Doorns announced that the De Groots would come over for a farewell supper with a surprise at the end, and Frank was perched on the stoep, trying to guess which little girl was Anna and which Sannah, when they suddenly cried, 'Here comes Ouma!' and Frank looked across the lake to see the De Groots approaching.

They came in an old cart pulled by one tired horse. General Paulus sat in front, the great bearded patriarch usurping the entire seat, while Sybilla sat deferentially behind, a big woman crammed into a little space. She sat not on a seat, but in the well of the cart on a pile of animal skins, and Saltwood had to suppress a grin, for she resembled a Queen Victoria of the veld, regal and rugged and triumphant.

When he went to the cart, this impression was reinforced, for she said quietly, 'How pleased we are to be with you again,' and he would have helped her down except that General de Groot calmly intruded, extending his hands as if it was his privilege, and his alone, to help this woman.

It was a substantial supper, one of Mevrou van Doorn's massive offerings of lamb stew, and as it ended, each of the four children, and the old people, too, began to show excitement, which reached a peak when Jakob went into the kitchen, reappearing with a brown-gold pot over whose rim showed a crusty pudding marked with citron, cherries and raisins. 'Bread pudding, style of Van Doorn,' Johanna cried, and when Frank tasted it he complimented Mevrou van Doorn.

'Not me! My man!' And she nodded at her husband, reverently touching the old ceramic pot as she did.

'Yes, in our family the men make the pudding,' Jakob said. 'This pot, 1680 maybe. Made in China, no doubt. Came over the mountains. Two farms were burned with it on the shelf. You ever hear of Blaauwkrantz? Well, it went through fire there, too.'

'We're an old people,' General de Groot said. 'We've been here a long time.'

After the meal the family grew quiet, and Van Doorn produced a Bible even older than the crock. 'Amsterdam, I think. Maybe 1630. The first pages were burned away.' And he prayed with his hand on the book.

Frank, who was paying close attention, began to suspect that these two families were trying to warn him about something, and his feeling was confirmed when the old general spoke: 'We were here more than a hundred and fifty years before you came, Saltwood. More than two hundred before Rhodes. We would not like interruptions.' Combing his heavy beard with his fingers, he stared right at the young Englishman, never for a moment conceding that Frank might be just as much a part of Africa as he.

On the last day Frank asked Jakob for a free space at the table, and there, with the twins looking over his shoulder, he wrote a long report to his employer, the crucial paragraph being this:

> One cannot talk with these men without becoming convinced that they would again take up arms in a minute if they thought their freedom was endangered. Van Doorn is probably in his fifties, but he would ride forth tomorrow if called upon. The general is well into his sixties, and I suppose he would not actually go into battle, but I am sure he would lend every support. One night we rode into the little town of Venloo, where we met with another forty Boers who said specifically they were at all times ready to mount a commando on one hour's notice. I must therefore caution you doubly and trebly not to allow any of your associates to launch unwarranted or headstrong adventures. I would hate to see the rabble of the gold reef go up against these rocklike men, who would be fighting for their independence. I can hear you telling the others: 'Young Frank is frightened.' That would not be correct, because I am terrified. I am terrified that an imprudent or hasty action might bring disaster upon us all. I assure you that Paulus de Groot alone could take on eleven Australian and American floaters who have no concern with the

land except to bleed it, and I suspect he could handle five or six Englishmen, too.

I am off to Zimbabwe. General de Groot was there more than fifty years ago, but he says he can still see every wall, every edifice. I wish he were on our side.

By the accidents of history, Frank Saltwood was about to traverse in 1895 the route that young Nxumalo had taken in 1457. He left Vrymeer and headed for the Limpopo, near whose banks the copper mine still flourished. Once more high water impeded the crossing, and when the north bank was reached, the baobab trees exerted their magic. 'I was quite unprepared for them,' he wrote his mother. 'Trees which seemed to be planted upside down by some mysterious force, their uplifted roots filled with birds. On two occasions we have slept inside the trees.'

Like Nxumalo, he came upon the great slabs of granite, their layers exfoliated into perfect building blocks, but unlike him, he did not have to carry samples to the king. In proper time he reached the hills from which the ancient city became visible, and there he paused to see for himself, without distraction of any kind, physical or historical, just what it was this strange, lost city represented. Lacking all prejudice, he studied the ruins from afar and saw that they were long overgrown with trees and climbing vines, that they must once have been imposing but were now in poor condition, and that nothing in their sad, majestic profile betrayed their origin.

He descended into a valley leading to the ruins, and came after a while to an impoverished group of blacks led by a Chief Mugabe, who could speak neither the Zulu nor the Sotho language of the bearers, but after a while one was found who had once drifted down to the diamond mines, and he could speak a kind of lingua franca.

'Zimbabwe?' He knew nothing of it.

'Who rules now?' No one, but Chief Mugabe had his kraal on the side of the hill on which the citadel rested.

'Who built the towers?' That had often been discussed.

'Can we inspect it?' Why not?

For two weeks Frank climbed over the ruins, uncovering not a single clue which would indicate origins. The pictures in the Bible his parents had given him on his twenty-first birthday came to mind, but they looked nothing like this. However, suppose that all those pictures had been of Jewish structures? Could not these ruins have been those of the Queen of Sheba, who would have built in a different manner? Or of the Phoenicians, who would have had their own style? And what authority did the pictures in the Bible have? Were they not merely some artist's imagination?

Whenever he pursued such thoughts, he stopped before reaching a logical conclusion, because he had to keep in mind the fact that his employer, Mr. Rhodes, desperately wanted these buildings to be the ancient Ophir, not because that would prove the Bible to have been accurate, but for a much subtler reason: to justify his own wrongdoing.

When he got nowhere with President Kruger in his plan to have a joint

English-Boer occupation of the lands north of the Limpopo, he had leap-frogged the Boer republics and thrown his own pioneer column deep into Matabeleland, where Mzilikazi's son was overrun. When resistance developed, he dispatched a private army to crush it, then annexed the entire area. Even at this moment, grateful imperialists in London were proposing that this new British colony be called Rhodesia.

So now, if Rhodes could prove that no black society had ever been advanced enough to have built Zimbabwe, his theft of Matabeleland would seem more palatable. It would, after all, be rather ugly to have stolen a kingdom in order to bring it civilization if that kingdom had once been civilized.

Frank Saltwood was thus obligated to prove that Zimbabwe had been built far back, in the time of the Old Testament, and during his last three days on the site he remained in his tent, drafting another report to Mr. Rhodes:

> Every indication at Zimbabwe proves that it was of Phoenician origin. The grand design, the shape of the tower, the construction of the high citadel, the way the now-vanished huts of the city must have been arranged, and especially the work of the stonemasons, combine to demonstrate a Mediterranean provenance. I could not find a shred of evidence that would support the claims of some that these walls had been erected by primitive black men, and to so argue seems preposterous.

> I put these structures at the late Phoenician period, which means that they could well have been erected by artisans of that nation imported here by the Queen of Sheba in the days when King Solomon ruled in Jerusalem. Since there is strong and viable record of much gold coming from Zimbabwe, I think we can state with certainty that this is Ophir of the Bible and that from it Sheba obtained the gold she took with her on her journey to meet Solomon. The matter is closed.

But when the wagons were packed, and the last photograph taken, and the antelope shot for the food supply, Frank returned to the ruins alone, sickened by the shameful thing he had done, this profanation of everything he had learned at Oriel: 'A man must be true to the facts, and if the facts disprove his preconceptions, he must change his preconceptions, not the facts.'

What have I done? he asked himself as he studied the silent stones whose messages were crying out to be understood. Have I debased myself to curry favor with an irascible man who perverts everything to his own purpose?

Cautiously he climbed a platform next to the tower to inspect once more the stonework, which now seemed so primitive, so unlike anything the Phoenicians or the Jews of Solomon's time might have done. After all, the basic stonework of Rome was being laid down in that age, and Greek masons already knew the major principles. Men trained in those schools could never have built these edifices.

But he found no proof of anything until the final moments, when he had left the tower and was standing at a point where two walls abutted, and he saw with amazement that the stones were not interlocked, as they would have been in any Mediterranean building: that is, the stones of the wall running east and west did not bind themselves into the stones of the wall running north and south, making each wall stronger. In crude fashion, one wall merely leaned against the other, acquiring only such added strength as proximity provided, and it occurred to him that masons had not used that childish device in Rome or Greece or Phoenicia or the Holy Land or Persia or Arabia for the past four thousand years.

'My God!' he whispered. 'They're right. These buildings were erected by black men who never heard of Ophir or the Queen of Sheba,' and he ran to all the corners where walls abutted, and in every instance one wall merely leaned against the other. With this knowledge, he hastened to the foot of the steep hill on which the citadel rested, and, though exhausted, ran up, breathing furiously until he reached the lonely top where the goldsmiths had worked and the great Mhondoro conversed with spirits. And there, too, the walls leaned one upon the other, and the stonework was primitive, with no sign of Mediterranean sophistication. These buildings, too, had been built by the ancestors of the Xhosa and the Zulu. The nonsense about the Queen of Sheba was a fatuous dream generated by men who had never seen the stones, and kept alive by fanciers who loved the idea of ancient royalty and despised the actuality of black builders.

As he was about to leave the citadel he saw, partly hidden by the rubble, something he had missed on his earlier explorations: a beautifully carved narrow stone about six feet high, its bottom squared off for fitting into a socket, its top an intriguing bird, something like a falcon, something like an eagle. In not a single line did it betray Mediterranean influence; this was an artwork of black men, and when he called for servants to carry it down the hill for delivery to Mr. Rhodes, he thought: I have been forced to write that Zimbabwe is Phoenician, but this bird will proclaim the truth.

Back in his tent as it was about to be folded, he looked at his report and was tempted to destroy it, but he was restrained by the fact that Mr. Rhodes would like it in its present form and would be most distressed if he, Frank, modified it in accordance with his final discovery: I know what the truth is. Does what Mr. Rhodes thinks do any harm? And he carefully filed the papers that would set the intellectual patterns for the next eighty years. Zimbabwe had been stolen from the blacks.

When he neared civilization he began to hear rumors of turmoil, but exactly what caused them he could not ascertain. Black members of his safari spoke of a battle, but the white members could make nothing of this until a terrified English miner, obviously running for his life, intercepted them with the shocking news that Mr. Rhodes had shortly before declared war on the Boer republics. His ragtag army, led by the mercurial Dr. Leander Starr Jameson, had tried to take over the government but had been roundly defeated.

Anxiously, Frank interrogated the fugitive, who gave confirming details: Mr. Rhodes had done all the things which Frank had warned him against, and the consequences had been the disaster he had predicted.

When the safari reached Pretoria it was approached by an armed Boer commando whose leader shouted in English, 'You have a man named Saltwood?' and when Frank stepped forward, three Boers pinioned him, took his papers, and carted him off to jail.

'What's the charge?' Frank protested.

'You'll hear. Just before they hang you.'

He was thrown into a cell that contained an Australian member of Mr. Rhodes' revolutionary force, two Englishmen and a breezy, even-tempered American mining engineer named John Hays Hammond, who had helped organize the ridiculous affair. 'What happened?' Frank asked.

'Very simple,' Hammond explained. 'We had five hundred hand-picked men under Dr. Jameson, many more waiting in Johannesburg, but with no communication between them. We marched forth to capture the country, but suddenly Boer horsemen appeared from everywhere, led by this great whiskered brute of a man, General de Groot, riding a little Basuto pony. He said, "All right, boys, put down your guns." So our men put them down, and here we are—in jail.'

'You mean De Groot defeated your whole army?'

'Have you ever seen De Groot?'

'I have. They call him the Hero of Majuba.'

'He's a formidable man,' Hammond said.

'But what am I doing here?' Frank asked. 'I was north of the Limpopo when this happened.'

None of the prisoners, cell after cell of Uitlanders, who had called themselves Reformers, could explain why Saltwood had been arrested, but after days in the crowded jail he heard enough from the conspirators to assure himself that they were indeed guilty of insurrection and that the venture had been sorely botched.

'How could Mr. Rhodes have stumbled into this?' he asked repeatedly, and finally the Australian said, 'Because he had contempt for the Boers, like all of us did.'

'After what I wrote him?' Frank blurted out, and when these words echoed in the cell, all the prisoners looked at him.

'Oh,' one of the Englishmen said, 'you're the spy they kept asking about.'

'Spy?' Frank repeated. He suddenly realized that his prying visit to General de Groot, his chain of persistent questions and his note-taking could be interpreted as spying.

And at the trial, General de Groot and Jakob van Doorn both testified, with regret, that he had come to them some months before the raid as a friend, asking a series of probing questions relating to the rebellion. Van Doorn in particular could verify that he had written a long report which he admitted he was sending to Cecil Rhodes, and from hints that Van Doorn picked up, it concerned the military capabilities of the Boers.

'Did Mr. Saltwood appear at your farm in military uniform?'

'No, sir, he came as a spy.'

'Did he inform you that he was serving as the agent of a rebellion?'

'No, sir, he functioned as a spy.'

When the trial ended, the grim-faced judge placed on his head a small black cloth. One by one the prisoners were brought before him: 'John Hays Hammond, the court finds you guilty, and for your treasons you will be taken from jail and hanged.'

Frank felt his knees buckling as an ashen-faced Hammond was returned to the jail, and if the Australian had not held him, he might have collapsed. The Australian was sentenced, then the two Englishmen, and now it was Saltwood's turn, but as he was led into the dock a rude commotion erupted at the rear of the courtroom. Two policemen were trying to restrain an elderly Boer who was struggling with some heavy object.

When they led him before the bench, the judge looked down severely: 'Lang-Piet Bezuidenhout, what is this nonsense?'

'Forgive me, your Honor. But I bring something that might help your Honor punish these men.'

'Lang-Piet, this is a court for justice, not a place for cheap revenge. Go before I get angry.'

'But, your Honor, the men of my commando have been in the saddle many days to bring you this thing.'

'What thing?'

'Die balk van Slagter's Nek, Oom Gideon.'

And that was precisely what had happened. Lang-Piet Bezuidenhout and his cronies had ridden down to Graaff-Reinet to buy the wooden beam of the Slagter's Nek gallows from a family who had preserved the grim relic for some eighty years.

'The rebels must hang from this very beam,' the old man shouted as his cronies cheered. 'We want justice.'

The judge, Oom Gideon de Beer, said quietly, 'Lang-Piet, in these days we dispense a fairer kind of justice. Sit down and be silent.' Then he turned his attention to the man waiting in the dock: 'For your crimes you will be taken from jail and hanged.'

In this extremity, Maud Turner came to Frank's rescue. With bars separating her from the man she considered her fiancé, she listened intently as he told her every detail of what he had done since she had said farewell to him at Kimberley. When he explained what he had written in his Vrymeer report to Rhodes, she cried, 'But that would exonerate you!' And when he told her of the Zimbabwe report, which the Boer commando had taken from him, she was exultant: 'It proves you honestly were doing scientific work. That makes your Vrymeer questionings legitimate.'

But how to get possession of the two documents? The first was held by Rhodes, who would be further incriminated if its contents were revealed. The second was held by the Boers, who would not likely deliver it. There seemed no way to obtain the papers.

With no other recourse, and with the death of her fiancé imminent, she took the bold step of going directly to the president of the Boers, and she found him sitting on his stoep, wearing a top hat and making himself available to any complaining citizen. At first he terrified her: that face of monumental ugliness, the deep voice that rumbled like a volcano, the flecked beard that rimmed his features, the tight-fitting black frock coat. But after he heard her out, he spoke to her, in English, with a warmth that surprised her.

'You want me to save the young man's life?'

'I do!' she cried.

'You sit down here. You say two documents are in existence?'

'They are! They are!'

'And if I could see them, they would exonerate him?'

'They would, sir.'

'Then why don't you produce them?'

She took a deep breath. 'Because Mr. Rhodes has one. And you have the other. And you are both very stubborn men.'

He halted his interrogation and called for his wife to fetch them coffee, and when Mevrou Kruger appeared on the stoep, a heavy, wheezing housewife, she seemed more like a kindly grandmother than the first lady of a republic. Her Coloured servant handed Maud a gaudy cup and saucer, with a second saucer to hold a helping of rusks. To her husband, Mevrou Kruger handed a double portion of rusks, then sat beside him with hands folded.

'You say you are Miss Maud Turner?' the president asked.

'Yes.'

'And you planned to marry this young man? Before he was caught as a spy?'

'He was never a spy, sir.'

'But you yourself told me that in his first report he informed Mr. Rhodes of our strength.'

'That he did, but if you remember, he also warned Mr. Rhodes against any military adventure.'

Mevrou Kruger broke in: 'Do you still want to marry him?'

Before Maud could respond, President Kruger astounded her by breaking into a hearty laugh. 'My dear young lady! Do you think we Boers want to give the English a motive for revenge, such as they gave us at Slagter's Nek?' He paused. 'Have you ever heard of Slagter's Nek?'

'I've been there, twice. Do you know the role played by Frank's ancestor? Reverend Saltwood the missionary? Who tried to halt the hangings?'

'We Boers do not cite missionaries as evidence,' Kruger said, and again he broke into laughter. 'Miss Turner, early this afternoon I commuted all the sentences.' He reached over and patted her knee as Mevrou Kruger offered fresh coffee to both her husband and his guest.

'Yes,' Kruger said as Maud daubed at her eyes. 'He's free, if he can pay his fine.'

'How much?'

'Twenty-five thousand pounds.'

She gasped. This was more money than she had ever visualized, a vast fortune really, but she firmed her chin and said, 'Somehow I'll get it.'

'No need. Mr. Rhodes has already informed us that he'll pay it.'

'Then Frank is free?'

'Yes.'

Her fortitude deserted her. With trembling hands she put the saucers aside and buried her face in her hands. After a few moments Mevrou

Kruger came to her side and helped her to her feet. 'He was free when you arrived,' she said. 'My husband likes to talk with pretty women.'

When Mr. Rhodes learned that Frank was determined to marry Miss Turner, he was deeply distressed. The loss of any of his young gentlemen to matrimony was a calamity, but to have Frank leave when he was going to be so sorely needed was intolerable. Summoning Miss Turner to his offices in Kimberley, he put it boldly to her that she was ruining the young fellow's life by insisting upon marriage.

'Seems to me,' she snapped, 'it's you who've done the ruining.'

'Don't be pert, young woman,' he replied.

'I didn't land him in jail,' she retorted, and the debate was on.

Rhodes pointed out that if Frank stayed with him he would always have a fine job, at the center of things, helping to decide affairs of great moment, to which she replied, 'He decided how to get himself hanged.'

'I saved him,' Rhodes said, and he proceeded to depict the bright future that awaited this brilliant chap—

'He's not brilliant,' she cut in. 'He's not even bright, if you ask me, getting involved in your daydreams.'

Ignoring the interruption, Rhodes explained the dismal prospect that would await Frank if he married and lost his job, to which Maud asked, 'Why must he lose his job? If he does a sensible thing like marrying the woman of his choice?'

'Because no man can work as my personal assistant, and share the dreams I have, and cater to a woman, too.'

'Your dreams, Mr. Rhodes, are addled, and I'm taking Frank away from you before you turn him crazy, too.'

The threat was easier made than discharged, for when Frank was brought into the discussion, Rhodes pleaded for the young man's continued help, especially at this time of crisis: 'You must come with me to London. To help me face down the inquisitors.' And he made such a plaintive appeal, explaining the morass of legal problems he faced as a consequence of the rebellion, that Saltwood once more allowed himself to be entrapped by this man.

'Maud, I'll be gone only a short time. He needs me.'

'I need you,' she replied. 'And if you go, don't count on my waiting for you forever.'

'Maud!' It was a cry she did not hear, for she had left the offices, and in her stead Frank had in his hands a sheaf of legal papers which he must study before sailing from Cape Town.

Maud's patience was to be severely tested, for not only did Rhodes keep his hold on Frank during this time, with its involved lawsuits and frenzied meetings, but he dragged him into another set of extensive negotiations in an attempt to strengthen his empire. He had exited from his troubles with more power and money than before; he had engaged in criminal acts against both the Boer republics and his own government, but had emerged almost unscathed. He did have to resign as prime minister of Cape Colony, but he retained his seat in Parliament permanently.

He turned once more to his grand design. The map of Africa must be painted red; Rhodesia must be extended in all directions. German infiltrations must be halted and Belgium watched. He had a thousand schemes, plus a special one which lay entwined with his heart: this he discussed with Saltwood, whom he considered, all things in balance, to have been the very finest of his eighteen or so young gentlemen.

'What do you think of it?' he asked one morning during their second trip to London as he shoved at Frank a rumpled paper covered with ink scratches. It was the rough outline of a new last will and testament— seventh in line—explaining his involved plan for a perpetual trust. It would receive millions of pounds, to be doled out to bright young men in the British colonies and America to enable them to attend Oxford and there imbibe the instruction which would encourage them to go forth and make the world British.

Mr. Rhodes proposed four large criteria for identifying the perfect man: scholastic achievement; success in manly sports; exhibition of moral force and leadership; and what he called 'qualities of manhood,' which included truth, courage, devotion to duty, sympathy for the weak, kindliness, unselfishness and fellowship. Young men who exhibited these qualities were to be handsomely endowed with scholarship funds and given every advantage in gaining a start in life.

'Well?' Rhodes asked impatiently.

'You establish very high standards, sir.'

'You met them. All my young gentlemen at Kimberley met them.'

When this reference was added, Frank understood what Mr. Rhodes hoped to accomplish with his largesse: he wanted an endless supply of the young men who had served him so well—Neville, Richard, Edgar, Elmhirst, Gordon, Mountjoy, Johnny, and so on, through eternity, men with first names only, who did not bother with girls but who stood tall and tended the duties of empire. The list of attributes Mr. Rhodes had drawn up were those best calculated to produce just such men, and there would always be both a need and a place for them.

But even as Frank studied this description of himself he had to be amused by one incongruous aspect. 'What's funny?' Rhodes asked testily.

'Your criteria,' Frank said with a chuckle he could not repress. Tapping the paper, he said, 'Mr. Rhodes, you wouldn't qualify on a single item. You hate sports and ridicule us when we engage in them. You took nearly a decade to win your degree. You had little sympathy for the Matabele, until they were thrashed. And as for truth, I've heard you give quite wrong explanations of your acts. Courage you may have, but you weren't in the front line when your revolution took place. And damnit all, you showed no kindliness to Maud. Not only would you fail to win one of your scholarships, you wouldn't even be considered.'

Laughing heartily, Rhodes reached for his will, waved it under Frank's nose and said, 'These criteria are not meant to identify men like me. We who move the world are not pleasant people, but we need pleasant, inoffensive people to help us. These scholarships will uncover such people.' When Frank started to speak, Rhodes interrupted: 'Stay with me, most precious of my young gentlemen, and we shall attain the dreams. You're to administer the scholarships, you know.' As he started to leave the room he turned back to say, 'You're to find me an endless supply of decent chaps just like yourself.' Handing the will back to Frank, he said, 'Think about it.'

For some time Frank sat staring at the floor, anticipating the great times he could have in Oxford, administering the scholarships, but this opportunity vanished when two visitors to his hotel room changed everything.

The first was his cousin, Sir Victor Saltwood, M.P. for Salisbury. He was brief and harsh: 'You've behaved like a damned fool, Frank. I sent you one of the finest young women this world could produce, and what in hell do you do but leave her and go off to some pile of rubble in what they call Rhodesia. And when you come back you get yourself nearly hanged. Your life was saved by that girl, and yet you abandoned her.'

'Mr. Rhodes needed me. You've seen what happened in London.'

'Needed you, yes, but dictate to you how your life should be lived? If you had any gumption, you'd tell him to go to hell, get aboard the next ship, and marry Maud Turner.'

'I'm afraid I've lost her, Victor. I've hardly seen her these past years.'

'You haven't at all. She understands the pressure you were under. After you left her the first time she got herself involved with schools in the farm districts. She's done a splendid job. Her father tells me she's visited your folks at De Kraal, loves them, and is prepared to wait till you come to your senses. But she's only human, Frank, and others want to marry her. She writes me that she's giving you two months.'

'She is!' The world seemed to spin back from the abyss of loneliness which Frank had envisioned for himself. He had supposed that Maud was lost and his life was to be an endless extension of the present, but now his cousin was saying that he had been in communication . . .

'I want to send a cable,' he cried impulsively, and on the back of Mr. Rhodes' proposed will he scribbled: *Maud. Sailing home immediately. Marry me the day I arrive, please, please, and save my life.*

He was signing it when Mr. Rhodes returned to the room to fetch his will, but before he could reach for it, Frank thrust it at him, his words face up, and said, 'Sir, I think you should be the first to know.'

Displaying no emotion, the great financier read the proposed cable, smiled, and said to Sir Victor, 'Stated in plain language.' He summoned a bellhop and asked him to bring the manager of the hotel. When that gentleman arrived, Rhodes said, 'See that this telegram is filed instanter. And book us two staterooms on the *Scot* sailing on Friday.'

'No, sir,' Frank said with a firmness that pleased his cousin. 'I don't want you arguing with me all the way to Cape Town. My mind's quite made up, you know.'

'Of course it is, and properly so. I wish to be present at the wedding.' Turning to Sir Victor, he said, 'The best, I think. This boy was the best of the lot.'

'Was?' Sir Victor repeated.

'Yes. He won't be working with me any more. I had plans for him, but times change, plans change.' And he accompanied Sir Victor from the room, a bulky, tired man, only forty-six years old, whose weakened heart could not keep pace with his dreams.

Frank's second visitor was the managing director of the Union Line, which operated the mail ships to South Africa. It seemed strange that a man of such high position would be delivering the tickets, even to such a frequent customer as Mr. Rhodes, and Frank said so: 'I know he travels back and forth at least once a year, but this is most considerate of you. I shall tell him.'

'No! No!' the director said in real panic. 'My meeting with you is highly confidential.'

'What is it?' Frank asked.

'The princess. The Polish princess.'

'Who?'

'A lady of high rank. Berlin, Warsaw, St. Petersburg.'

'What's she got to do with Mr. Rhodes?'

'Ah, that's what we don't know.' Nervously he began to unfold an incredible yarn: 'I don't know whether it's a hoax or what. I don't know whether Mr. Rhodes is in some kind of danger or not. In fact, I don't know what I know.'

'Why not tell me what you think you know.'

'The Princess Radziwill—a real princess bearing a distinguished Polish name—for some time she's been visiting us to talk about a shadowy trip to Cape Town. Says she has interests there. It develops that her interest is Mr. Rhodes. She never buys a ticket. She's interested only in when Mr. Rhodes is sailing.'

'That seems harmless.'

'Yes, but yesterday, within fifteen minutes of your ordering the two tickets to Cape Town . . .'

'He did the ordering. Did it himself.'

'Even more suspicious. Someone in this hotel, or someone in our offices —someone notified Princess Radziwill. And as I said, within fifteen minutes she was in my office, wanting to know which stateroom he had and demanding the one next to it.'

'Now, that does pose problems,' Frank conceded. 'Who is this woman? Young? Adventurous?'

'Not at all. She is the true Princess Radziwill. Well vetted in the Almanaca de Gotha. Not young at all. In her forties maybe, fifties, and looks it. May have been a great beauty once, but too much Polish and Russian cooking. Dark hair, no streaks of gray. Speaks acceptable English, but also French, German and, of course, Polish and Russian.'

'Has she any funds?'

'There's my problem, Mr. Saltwood. I have absolutely nothing to go on, but from years of selling tickets for boat passages, I'd say the Princess Radziwill conforms in every detail to the typical woman passenger who is going to give us trouble. Why do I say this? I don't really know. But that woman has financial problems.'

'Is there any chance that I might see her before we sail? Not talk to her, you understand. Just see her. Because we don't want a scandal, do we?'

The managing director thought that he might summon her to the office at three, to confirm her passage, or something like that, and if Frank happened to chance by to pick up *his* tickets . . . 'You wouldn't approach my door, you understand. Just the outer office, like any ordinary passenger. You could see her as she exits.'

It was arranged, and from a shop across the street from the Union Line offices Frank watched a shortish, attractive, dark-haired woman step out of a cab and walk in to confirm her stateroom. Casually he crossed the street, moved to a counter, and engaged the young male clerk in conversation about a possible passage to Australia. From where he stood, he commanded a fine view of the manager's office and had a good chance to study the Princess Radziwill of Poland.

She seemed gracious, well groomed, interested in the details of her forthcoming voyage. She talked with animation, and whenever he caught sight of her face, it seemed quite pleasant. If she was an agent in some conspiracy against his employer, she masked it well.

She rose rather sooner than he expected, walked briskly from the inner office, spotted Frank immediately, and walked straight up to him. 'Frank Saltwood,' she said without hesitation. 'I am Princess Radziwill. And you are the cousin of my good friend Sir Victor. Liberal party. Salisbury. I believe we're to share the *Scot* together, this Friday. How very congenial.' With a slight bow she passed on.

Both the steamship management and young Saltwood deemed it best to inform Mr. Rhodes of this strange development, and he guffawed at their apprehensions. 'I like *grandes dames* like that. I talk to them roughly, introducing more profanity with each turn of the conversation. After a while they leave me alone.'

Frank had a premonition that this cavalier treatment might not succeed with royalty as determined as the Princess Radziwill, and he boarded the Union Line ship with trepidation, which was justified a few hours later at the evening meal. He cautioned Mr. Rhodes: 'We'll go in late, after she's chosen her table,' and they did so, but as they entered the salon Frank caught a glimpse of a lady in black waiting in the shadows, and no sooner had Mr. Rhodes taken his table, one with spare chairs so that he might entertain business acquaintances during the long voyage, than Princess Radziwill swept into the room, crying in a soft, ladylike voice, 'Oh, dear! Where shall I sit?'

Ignoring the chief steward, who hurried up to assist her, she let her hand fall upon one of the chairs at Rhodes' table and asked gently, 'Does this happen to be vacant?'

Frank started to say brusquely, 'It's taken, ma'am,' but before he could complete the sentence Mr. Rhodes said gallantly, but with obvious reluctance, 'It seems to be free, madam,' at which she seated herself with great firmness, indicating that this would be her place for the duration of the voyage.

She was an enchanting woman, much younger in spirit than her years, informed on everything and willing to deliver final judgments on politicians,

writers, musicians and the state of the world. When Mr. Rhodes attempted
to stifle her with his routine profanity, she responded with animated discussions of her digestive system, her bowel movements and episodes in her sex
life. Very quickly Mr. Rhodes retreated to more casual conversation.

From the first she demonstrated an intense dislike of Frank Saltwood, assessing him accurately as a bar to whatever designs she might
have on Mr. Rhodes. She scorned any statement he made, ridiculed his
Oxford insularity and lampooned his general deportment. Specifically
she wanted to know why he wasn't married, and when he tried to
counter with questions about her own status, she deflated him with a
forthright statement: 'I am the daughter of a great Polish nobleman, but
my father and I have always considered ourselves Russians first, Poles
second. I am married to a Radziwill, one of the proudest Polish names,
but he has treated me abominably, and I am soon to be divorced from
him. I am forty-one years old.'

She intimated that she was also a famous authoress: 'Five well-regarded
books.'

When he made inquiries among the other passengers, he found that she
was indeed a distinguished writer on political subjects and that she knew
everyone in European society. Sensing that he doubted her statement about
her writing, she appeared one noontime in the promenade café with two of
her books, solid affairs dealing with European court life and its political
intrigues. When she saw that Frank and, indirectly, Mr. Rhodes were
sufficiently impressed, she said casually, 'You know, of course, that my
aunt, Evelina Rzewuska, was the wife and financial salvation of Honoré de
Balzac.'

'Who was he?' asked a young man from Kimberley who had recently
been invited to join the Rhodes circle.

'Oh, my God!' she screamed so loudly that people at other tables turned
to look. This pleased her, and she appealed to them: 'This young fool asks
me who Honoré de Balzac was. It's like asking an Englishman who William
Shakespeare was.' And with this she launched upon a recitation, with wild
gestures, of the entire sonnet:

> 'When to the sessions of sweet silent thought
> I summon up remembrance of things past . . .'

When she was halfway through, Frank thought: What can this creature be
up to? At the closing couplet he found out, for with a sudden drop in her
voice, she gazed longingly at Mr. Rhodes and whispered:

> 'But if the while I think on thee, dear friend,
> All losses are restored and sorrows end.'

After a few demonstrations like this, Frank was so deflated that she could
speak right past him when she wished to address Mr. Rhodes. But if she
humbled the younger man, she exalted the older, praising him extravagantly
and placing herself in his way whenever she moved on deck. When he sat
down on a deck chair, he found that she had acquired the one next to it,

and if he sought to rest because of his increasing heart unease, there she was, prepared to argue politics with him.

'What does that woman want with me?' Rhodes asked Frank in some dismay at the end of the fifth day.

'I think she wants to marry you, sir.'

'She's already married. Said so herself.'

'But she's getting a divorce. Said so herself.' Rhodes caught the mockery in his young friend's voice and burst into laughter. 'You have only one commission, Frank. Protect me from that woman.'

Saltwood's first stratagem backfired: 'We'll take our meals in your cabin. Let her have the table.' But before the first meal ended, the princess burst into the cabin, eyes aflutter, to assure herself that 'dear Mr. Rhodes is not suffering.' Deftly she maneuvered Frank out of the stateroom, fluffed up the pillows, and sat close beside Mr. Rhodes to help him eat his meal.

'Frank!' came the anguished cry. 'You said you'd bring the papers.' Grabbing anything at hand, Saltwood hurried back into the room, where the beleaguered man said, 'Sit here beside me,' and the princess was edged away.

The next afternoon, in their deck chairs, she chided Mr. Rhodes for having been so ungallant, and as she rose to spread a blanket for him she was seized with a mild fainting spell, which threw her gently into his arms.

'Frank!' he bellowed, and when Saltwood hurried up, he found his master embracing the inert body of the Polish princess.

During the entire voyage this charade continued, for no matter what maneuver the two men devised, the princess knew how to outsmart them, and one evening when persons at the bar said in her hearing, 'I do believe Mr. Rhodes, the woman hater, is having an affair with the princess,' she smiled.

It was when the *Scot* was one day out of Cape Town that Cecil Rhodes made the second great mistake of his life. In the presence of Frank Saltwood and two guests at his table he said casually to these business friends, 'When we reach the Cape you must visit me at Groote Schuur.'

'I shall be delighted!' the princess said.

He had scarcely unpacked his bags when a telegram arrived from the Mount Nelson Hotel announcing that the princess would be coming to dinner that night. At the meal, a party for the colony's political leaders, she assigned herself the seat as mistress of the establishment, and before long, cryptic notices began appearing in the Cape Town newspapers, sent to them anonymously in a woman's handwriting:

> The mighty Colossus whose armor has blunted all the arrows of Cupid seems to have been wounded by that sly huntsman, and we understand that wedding bells may soon be sounding, but who the fair partner is to be we cannot at this time divulge except to say that she is a titled dignitary much accustomed to the royal circles of Berlin, Warsaw and St. Petersburg.

Who was this cyclonic woman who had risked everything on a boat trip to South Africa in pursuit of the world's richest bachelor? Princess Radziwill was everything she claimed to be, and one thing more. She was the daughter of one of Poland's noblest families; her aunt had indeed been the salvation of Honoré de Balzac; she had written widely popular books; and she was divorcing her husband, a process that would require many years. But the salient fact was that she was almost penniless.

At forty-one, her hectic behavior had caused her expulsion from the courts of Europe, and several nations had denied her reentry. A waspish gossip, she had frittered away a dazzling life until members of her two families, who did have great wealth, wished to see her no more. With her pen she might have made herself a good life with respectable income, but this talent, too, she abused, and her publishers were weary of her broken promises and unfulfilled contracts. Like her talents, her beauty had begun to fade, and she sensed that she had only a few more good years, which she must use to advantage.

It was remarkable that at the nadir of her career she should have devised a plan so bold, with risks so tremendous, but one day as she was sitting in her mean Paris lodgings this splendid thought had come to her: Why not marry Cecil Rhodes? Unfree to marry because of her dragging divorce, without funds, with fewer good dresses than ever before in her life, she had nevertheless launched her assault. Now, at Groote Schurr, Rhodes' fine Cape Dutch mansion that would become the equivalent of South Africa's White House, she behaved like a first lady and made it clear that she intended assisting Mr. Rhodes in governing the nation.

'I need help,' the great man moaned one afternoon. 'Beg Frank Saltwood to come back.'

In the hectic days when Princess Radziwill was intent on capturing Groote Schurr, Frank was having the tenderest experience of his life. Upon disembarking from *Scot* and bidding Cecil Rhodes farewell for what he assumed was the last time, since he had been dismissed, he caught a cab and hurried to the Mount Nelson Hotel, where Maud Turner had come to greet him. Ascertaining from the desk clerk where her room was located, he hurried through the stately lobby, bounded up a flight of oaken stairs, and thumped loudly at her door. Quickly it was opened and quickly he was down on his knees for anyone in the hallway to see: 'Maud, can you forgive me?'

'Get up, you stupid boy.'

'Then you'll have me?'

'Not if you act like this.' And with a swift reach of her hand she grabbed his wrist and pulled him into the room, then kicked the door shut with her heel. 'I am so glad we found each other again,' she said, and she maneuvered Frank to the bed, telling him, when the impassioned interlude was over, 'Now, damnit, you've got to marry me.'

They took the train up through the Karroo, then south to a small siding convenient to De Kraal. It consisted of an iron shed and stock ramp marked by a deeply carved sign erected by Frank's father: HILARY. On the long journey Maud had discussed seriously the manner in which they should lead their lives: 'Forget Mr. Rhodes completely. We'll have no more to do with him. What kind of work can you do, Frank?'

'I know the business world. Bankers, diamonds, Parliament.'

'Could you be a manager of sorts?'

'I think so. But where shall we establish our headquarters?'

She had been thinking about this for over two years, and every selfish desire urged her to say Cape Town, for she considered this the fairest city she had ever seen, a place incomparably lovely, with its ocean, its mountain, its deep indented bays, its gorgeous wealth of flowers. This was a city she could love, but her business sense warned her that South African industry was bound to center in the north, near the diamonds and the gold, and it was there that a young man could make his way: 'I think we should work in Johannesburg.'

'What a grubby place. Have you ever seen it?'

'Grubby now, but we must think of the future. It's got to be Johannesburg.'

'But couldn't we . . .' He hesitated, rubbed his nose, and asked tentatively, 'Couldn't we . . . maybe . . . maintain an office also in Cape Town?'

As if the idea had never occurred to her, she pondered it, tickled him under the chin with her fingernail, and said, 'Frank, I think that's a capital idea.'

In the Cape cart sent from De Kraal to meet them at the Hilary siding they devised a rough pattern for their future: a secure farm investment in the countryside; a business office in Johannesburg to watch over banking, insurance, trading and stocks, which Boers ignored because they had little interest in intricate financial matters; a political footing in Cape Town to protect one's holdings; and a permanent link with 'home,' a spot back in England crammed with memories.

'We must never forget our families in Salisbury,' Maud said.

'Naturally. What do you have in mind?'

'I'd like to slip back home as often as I can. I do cherish my English heritage.'

'Sounds reasonable.'

The decisions reached by Maud and Frank Saltwood represented those of many Englishmen in South Africa at that time. For them, some cathedral town like Salisbury was 'home,' Stonehenge their playground, Oxford or Cambridge their natural inheritance. No matter how diligently Frank handled his finances in Johannesburg or his political connivings at Cape Town, he and Maud would always be drawn back to Salisbury, spiritually if not physically; and whenever an opportunity for a trip to England arose, they would be eager to renew the umbilical tie.

The Van Doorns, on the other hand, never returned to Holland. Not one of them would have known his or her way around the canals of Amsterdam; they rarely knew who was governing the land or what political disposition it had. And if they had gone, they would not have understood either the religion or the language. Huguenot descendants were the same: none of the Du Preez family remembered the Oudezijdsvoorburgwal or its significance to their ancestors; and even less, the French village of Caix where their history began; nor could they speak French. Both the Dutch Van Doorns and the Huguenot Du Preez were now Afrikaners, and proud to be so.

The Saltwoods were Europeans; the Boers were people of Africa.

The Saltwoods would always have a refuge to scurry back to if trouble erupted; the Boers would not. If a Saltwood behaved moderately well, the English queen might call him back to London for a knighthood, but if a De Groot performed heroically, no royalty in Amsterdam would know of it, much less seek to ennoble him. Prudently the Saltwoods kept one foot in Salisbury; the Van Doorns kept both feet in Africa and did not even know of any alternative home to escape to. They rose or fell, lived or died according to what happened in Africa, and between these two types of people, the Europeans and the Afrikaners, the gulf would grow wider and wider.

Maud paid close attention to the wild rumors coming out of Cape Town regarding Mr. Rhodes and the Polish princess, and found naughty delight in the great man's discomfiture: 'Gossip says he told her she was not welcome at Groote Schuur and warned her to return to Europe.'

As the scandal worsened, Frank was forced to take notice, and he was grieved when the papers reported that the princess had forged Rhodes' name to bank paper to the extent of £23,000. 'Listen to this, Maud. "She seems to have copied his signature from a printed postcard sold in stationery stores." How bloody preposterous!'

'Who is this woman?' Maud asked.

'The most extraordinary liar I've ever met, except that everything she ever told me was true.' He delighted her with a brief sketch of the affair, explaining how the princess had maneuvered herself onto the *Scot* and into Mr. Rhodes' astonished arms. Then he became serious: 'If she claims she has letters which incriminate him, I'd say she has them. If she claims the financial papers are not forgeries, but were given to her by Rhodes, I'd hesitate to call her a liar in court. This woman is . . .' He fumbled for words, then came up with 'Stupendous.' He added that if the charge of forgery had to be ventilated in court, the entire Cape had better prepare itself for a hurricane.

'Should you offer your assistance, Frank?'

'To whom?'

'To Mr. Rhodes, of course,' she snapped.

'But he fired me.' He broke into laughter and fell into a chair, dragging his wife along with him. As she perched on his lap he said, 'You know, of course, that he has never in his life allowed a married man to work as his private secretary. You got me discharged, and it was damned well worth it.'

'But if he needs you . . .'

Maud Turner was the first of the famous Saltwood women; they formed a long line of strong-willed girls who had left secure homes in rural England, bringing with them to South Africa learning, musical ability, skill in drawing and high moral conscience. They accounted for the charity wards, the little schools tucked away in valleys, the libraries, the inadequate colleges, the books of reminiscences which would mean so much to later generations. Even during her stay in Cape Town, Maud Turner had already launched the Lady Anne Barnard Bowls Club, and near De Kraal she was using her own money to restore the ruins of Golan Mission. Women like her looked at their world, rolled up their sleeves, and tried to make it better.

Now Maud behaved with characteristic charity. Not forgetting that Mr. Rhodes had denigrated her and delayed her marriage for several years, she nevertheless told Frank, 'If that sad, confused man needs your help, we must offer it,' and they had already reached Grahamstown on their way to the Cape when a telegram intercepted them: NEED YOUR HELP. RHODES.

When they entered Groote Schuur they found it occupied only by a cadre of male servants and assistants, one of whom said, 'That woman's chasing him all the time. He's run away to Muizenberg.' At that little seafront village, well to the south of Cape Town, the great man had sequestered himself in a small corrugated-roof cottage wedged against tall trees. Viewed from the outside, it seemed to contain a few meager rooms and no amenities; it was scarcely a proper setting for what was becoming a major tragedy.

Maud expected to work in the cottage, providing what comfort she could, but as she walked up the narrow footpath two young men appeared at the door of the cottage, obviously determined to prevent her entrance: 'No women allowed.'

'But he sent a telegram for us,' and she produced the paper.

'That meant Frank, not you. Mr. Rhodes would be most distraught if you were to force your way in.'

'I never force my way,' she said quietly, but the men were adamant: 'No women.' So she drove back to Cape Town and her husband moved inside.

He was shocked. Mr. Rhodes, not yet fifty, sagged in all directions. His jowls were heavy and unshaven; his mustache, never attractive, was less so when untrimmed; his reddish hair was uncombed and matted with sweat; his arms and legs lay inert; but it was his eyes that sent the most alarming signals, for they were sodden, lids drooping and pupils unfocused. He behaved like a man in his painful eighties, forlorn and distressed. The bright young men still surrounded him; they seemed to come in endless supply: 'Yes, Mr. Rhodes. Yes, Mr. Rhodes.' But they gave him little sustenance.

'Is that you, Frank?'

'It is, Mr. Rhodes. What can I do to help?'

'You've already helped a great deal. See the Phoenician bird in the corner? He watches over me.' It would be intolerable to tell him now that the stone masterpiece was not Phoenician.

Rasping sounds came from the bed. It was Rhodes trying to make an important statement: 'Frank, to protect my honor I've got to defend myself against that damned woman.'

There was now no time for courtesies or blandishments: 'Sir, I must advise you most firmly that in proper English society a gentleman never brings suit against a lady.'

'I've never given a damn about English society. I'm not a gentleman. And that princess is certainly no lady. See the attorney-general, Frank, and urge him to file charges.'

'Oh, my God!' cried one of the young gentlemen. 'There she is again.'

And everyone in the cottage looked down the path to the roadway, where a woman dressed in stylish black, under an umbrella, walked slowly back and forth, staring at the cottage where the man she had wanted to marry lay dying.

'Drive her away!' Rhodes cried, but the young man said that they had tried this and the police had warned them that she had a right to walk on a public thoroughfare.

'But not to stare at me!' Rhodes wailed.

'She can walk and she can walk and she can look,' one of the young fellows said. 'All we can do is pray for rain.'

For weeks this tragicomedy continued. Rhodes lay in the cottage planning, while his lawyer and Frank Saltwood helped the attorney-general's office with their case against this brazen embezzler; she issued threatening releases to the newspapers and at dusk came down from Cape Town to walk back and forth, menacingly, silently before the cottage.

One evening Maud rode out to talk with the princess as she patrolled the roadway. 'Why do you torment him?'

'Because he has tormented me. He wants to send me to jail.'

'Did you forge the seven papers?'

'I have been Mr. Rhodes' staunchest supporter. He owes me enormous sums.'

'Didn't he pay your hotel bill when the Mount Nelson threatened to evict you?' Before the princess could respond, she added, 'And when you accepted the money, didn't you promise that you'd leave South Africa?'

'I did leave,' she protested like an insulted innocent, 'but I came back.'

'Princess, what can you hope to achieve by this ridiculous behavior?'

'Prison, I suppose. But men who ignore women, or treat them badly— they must be taught a lesson. When I'm through with Cecil Rhodes the entire world will be laughing at him.'

'They're already laughing at you. Have you seen the cartoons?'

'Cartoons are for today,' she huffed. 'I am for history.'

Maud achieved nothing, and when she drove off, the princess was still stalking back and forth in the shadows, casting a witchlike spell on the cottage and its inhabitants.

Despite all that the two Saltwoods tried to do to bring sanity into this mad affair, the criminal trial moved forward, complicated by civil trials on lesser matters, and the day came when the two protagonists faced each other before a judge sitting with his clerks at Groote Schuur, since Rhodes was too ill to appear in a regular Cape Town court. They met in bitterness, they testified in bitterness, with Rhodes stating categorically that he had never signed any papers on behalf of the princess, and that if she had peddled such promissory notes to the bankers and money lenders of Cape Town, she had done so as a forger.

His testimony, ungracious and unforgiving, condemned the woman to imprisonment; her testimony, malicious and biting, condemned him as a fool. Worse, it condemned him to death.

After appearing before the judge, he retreated to the miserable cottage, where Frank ordered a hole knocked in the bedroom wall so that Rhodes could catch the air for which he gasped continuously. If he lay down, he could not breathe; if he sat up, he could not rest. Still the princess marched back and forth, keeping her death watch; knowing that she could not escape incarceration, she showed no mercy. She would haunt this ungracious, unforgiving man to his death.

'Please go away,' Frank pleaded with her one night.

'This is my only freedom.'

'Have you any money left? Any at all?'

'I'm a pauper. I haven't enough to eat. I shall welcome the security of prison, for all my friends have abandoned me, a princess of the Russian court.' She pronounced the word *Rrrosshian.*

He gave her two pounds and told her to go to the Muizenberg Pavilion and eat, but she continued her vigil.

The breath of air Rhodes sought in that dreadfully hot March never reached him, and when he felt that death would overtake him before the criminal trial reached a conclusion, he dismissed her from his mind completely. Asking for his beloved atlas, he talked with Frank about those portions of his plans still to be realized: 'You must make the map red. Look how much we've done so far.'

When his hand fell upon Rhodesia, he looked up almost pitifully and asked, 'They never change the name of a country, do they?'

'No,' Frank said. 'That will always be Rhodesia. Your monument.'

But then Rhodes' eyes could not avoid the areas which represented his gnawing defeats: South-West Africa had fallen to the Germans; Moçambique still rested in Portuguese hands; the damned Belgians had proved their hearts were made of concrete. But worst of all, while Rhodes was suffering torment from the princess, a far greater agony had raged around him, for Boer and Englishman had finally come to fratricidal blows on the South African veld. His unwavering goal, the union of those two groups, seemed more impossible than ever, but his final words to Frank addressed that problem: 'Dear boy, when this war is over, spend your life trying to unite Boer and Englishman.'

When Rhodes died, Frank was in Cape Town giving a deposition in the trial, and when he heard of the death he felt an overwhelming sense of failure: he had tried to protect this great man from his blunders and from this fiasco with the princess, but he had accomplished little. He was told that Rhodes had died just at sunset on 26 March 1902, forty-nine years old, consumed by the volcanic fires that had driven him. As he died he uttered his own sardonic epitaph: 'So little done, so much to do.'

When the Princess Catherine Rzewuska Radziwill heard of Rhodes' death she was only forty-four, disgraced, penniless, and facing a two-year sentence in one of Cape Town's worst prisons. She said of Rhodes: 'I wanted only to help this lonely, miserable man. Had he attended to me, he might have been saved.'

In prison, her first demand was for a book of rules, which she mastered with such diligence that she became a notorious 'jailhouse lawyer,' arguing for the rights of all prisoners. Long before her sentence was completed, the warden petitioned the court that she be set free: 'Whenever I see her coming at me with that book of rules, I am threatened with twitches.'

The conniving princess would not accept freedom unless the government provided her with first-class steamship passage to London, and enough cash to allow her to live in a respectable London hotel for half a year. Since the senior authorities were also developing twitches, they bowed to her demands, then requisitioned a tug to ensure that she got aboard. To the Afrikaner lawyer who had enthusiastically defended her against the Colossus, they said, 'Do not give her a penny of the money. Hand it in a sealed envelope to the captain of the ship, to be delivered only when the vessel is far out to sea.'

She wrote more books, thirty in all; she lectured; when Prince Radziwill, her husband, finally died, she quickly married a Swedish gentleman whom no one ever saw; she was condemned by Russia to perpetual exile; and by some bizarre set of accidents she landed in New York, which she loved. As Princess Radziwill, she became the darling of royalty-hungry Americans and lived off them in various ingenious ways. Never once during her long stay in that country did anyone uncover the fact that she had spent nearly two years in a South African prison as an embezzler.

Finally she wrote her autobiography, not one chapter of which was true; she enchanted new generations of New York society; and in 1941, at the age of eighty-three, she sat propped up in bed writing long letters to the rulers of Europe advising them how best to prosecute World War II. She signed her pronouncements: Princess Catherine Radziwill—and when she died she was surrounded by three American ladies-in-waiting.

X. The Venloo Commando

FROM the throats of a hundred Boers, young and old, fair-faced and weather-beaten, came a merry song that carried far beyond the great barn at Vrymeer in which they were celebrating. The melody was that of an American Civil War song, 'Just Before the Battle, Mother,' but the Afrikaner version, popular in the eighties, had to do with love, not war:

> 'When will our marriage be, Gertjie?
> Why are you so very quiet?
> We've been betrothed so long, Gertjie!
> Now's the time for us to wed.
>
> Come then, Gertjie, for I shall not
> Be kept any longer on a string.
> Perhaps you think I cannot die,
> But my years are passing on!'

The grizzled warrior Paulus de Groot could not remember when last he had seen so many happy couples. 'Tonight, Jakob,' he shouted to the owner of the barn, 'there's many a heart will be lost under the stars of Vrymeer.' Van Doorn grinned back through a haze of smoke and dust.

General de Groot, as all thought of him, was guest of honor at the party, and with good reason, for in this very week back in February 1881 he had stormed Majuba Hill to thrash the English. And now, from fifty miles away and farther, as if it were Nachtmaal, Boers had packed their wagons and gathered up their families for a ride to Vrymeer.

The Van Doorn women, with Ouma Sybilla de Groot enthroned at their kitchen table, had prepared enough food for a commando. An ox was roasted on a spit opposite the barn; nearby were tables of bredies, vegetables, sweet dishes: tarts, koekies, pumpkin fritters, konfyts, and Jakob's contribution, the crock of bread pudding sensibly flanked by two bucketfuls of the same. Of course, there was a determined group who praised the pudding but passed it by in favor of the barrel of peach brandy.

It was a day the people of Vrymeer would not forget, and children bounded through the paradise like a troop of frisky baboons. Nothing was more exciting for a dozen robust little Boers than their encounter with the offspring of the Nxumalo family. Together they explored the secrets of Vrymeer, running screaming from the barn to the cave where the Bushmen's rhinoceros galloped. After a shouting circuit, they ran to the lake, tossed aside their clothes, and jumped in.

At nightfall the tallow candles along the walls of the barn were lit, the ant-hill floor gleamed, and a noisy trio of guitar, violin and concertina went to work. Even Ouma Sybilla managed, just once, to step out and do a few turns, not with her husband, who was tending the peach brandy, but with a young man who had his eye on Johanna van Doorn and thought courtesy to the old queen-buffalo would improve his chances.

The dancing was really for the young couples, and the floor was continuously crowded, for if the violin grew tired, the guitar and concertina kept going; and sometimes the squash-box performed alone. Johanna had agonized for some days over what to wear, and her efforts had proved most successful: she had donned a long skirt whose bottom hem was filled with kernels of corn to give it weight and make it flare out when she pirouetted.

'Watch your millstone, young fellow!' De Groot roared suddenly. 'You're grinding too rough.' He meant that the partner swinging Johanna had her dress so nearly parallel to the floor that bits of grain were flying loose.

It was past midnight and the concertina played a little more slowly as groups talked quietly or hummed old songs and Jakob mentioned the one sober question of this festive day: 'How long have our families lived here, Paulus?'

The general reflected: 'Fifty-eight years.'

'We should be grateful.'

'What for?' the old warrior asked.

'Many things, Paulus. Mostly we've been able to hold on to our ways ... keep the Englishmen from changing us. But with so many Uitlanders moving in . . .'

'Oom Paul—it's his job to watch the English. If he wants to see you, like the telegram said, it must be important.'

'Ja, my Generaal!'

Earlier that week Jakob had been summoned to meet with President Kruger in Pretoria; he would take the train Monday morning, for he knew that something serious was brewing.

Jakob found the great man on the stoep, deep wrinkles in his face, a black top hat perched on his head and a tightly buttoned coat covering his enormous belly. He did not rise to greet one of his most trusted burghers but showed his pleasure at the visit.

'Jakob, there are troubles, there are dangers we must face,' he said, indicating a chair.

'The English, Oom Paul?'

'Always the English. They mean to steal our republics, them and the Uitlanders.'

'Not while this Van Doorn has a breath. We'll never allow that.'

'Nice words, Jakob. Nice words.' He spat over the edge of the stoep. 'I have a task for you, broeder. You have family at the Cape, not so? Van Doorns of Trianon. I want you to visit them. Hear what they have to say. What's on their minds if the English take up arms.'

'There's been talk of rebellion down there. Against the English government.'

'Ja, ja. But what do the people really think?' He rocked back and forth. 'Talk isn't enough. Where will the Van Doorns, the Du Preez, the Hofmeyrs stand the day we have to fight for our lives?'

'We'll need them all,' Jakob said.

'You are visiting family down there. Understand? You're not Oom Paul's official. Talk with anyone you like, but keep away from government people. We have enough troubles with them already.'

'I understand, Oom Paul.'

'Ja, now that's good, Jakob. Let's have some coffee while you tell me about Paulus de Groot. How's the old devil these days?'

Jakob was fifty-five years old that February, a man of medium height, heavy build and deliberate movement. He was delighted at the prospect of traveling to the Cape in a first-class carriage and at government expense, for he had never seen the Trianon of his ancestors and looked forward to meeting its occupants.

He conducted his interviews in Cape Town first, and was pleased to find that the wealthy Du Preez had not forgotten their links with his family. They were most congenial when recalling those days when the first De Prés shared the Trianon vineyards with the Van Doorns. 'We've both moved a long way.' But when he discovered their attitude toward participation in a possible war, he was unhappy to learn that they had no interest whatever in taking up arms to defend the Boers.

'Don't misunderstand us, Van Doorn. We have much sympathy for the republics, but not for war. Look at what we have here. It's all come since the English arrived. I realize you might not like the Uitlanders as neighbors, but damnit, man, you Boers wouldn't know how to handle gold. Not even with all the Hollanders and Germans you bring in to run your government.'

Jakob tried to argue that the freedom not only of the northern Boer but of the southern Afrikaner, too, would hang in the balance: 'That is, if war comes. You Cape Afrikaners would certainly—' They cut him off: 'We have all the freedom we need here in the Cape. More than you seem to have up north. You may not believe this, but we like it here. We won't march in your armies.'

A schoolteacher named Carolus Marais invited Jakob to walk with him to see various Afrikaner establishments in the area: schools, big churches, solid homes built on the slopes of Table Mountain. 'Our forefathers never did so well under Dutch rule. We elect our people to Parliament, protect ourselves from the Englishmen. We don't want war.'

'Neither do we!' Jakob exploded. 'But suppose the English force it on us. Surely, if you have any decency or courage, you'll support the republics.'

'Would you ride out in some silly war, at your age?'

'Of course. And the other burghers at Venloo, we'd ride with our commando if they call us. We'd lose everything if we didn't.'

'Then you'd be very foolish. You and I can gain everything we want from the English without firing a shot. They have laws, Van Doorn. They're a great people for putting everything down in laws. And when they do, they obey them.'

'But always on their own terms.'

'Jakob, be sensible! We Cape Afrikaners are fighting our own war, not with German guns and Boer commandos. With the laws the Englishmen give us. Go listen to our clever politicians in the House and you'll learn how to keep the English rulers on the run.'

After eight days of this, it dawned on Jakob that Pretoria's hopes of a Cape Afrikaner uprising were pointless. These sturdy people with their schools and coffeehouses and politics were not interested in supporting a rebellion.

'Wait a moment!' Du Preez protested when Jakob voiced his disappointment. 'At first you asked, "Will you support the republics?" Of course we'll support them. We'll argue your case in Parliament. We'll speak out for you in every meeting. We'll back you up with letters in our newspapers.'

'But will you support us with arms?'

'Good heavens, no!'

He did locate three young Afrikaners who offered to volunteer, but when he asked around about them he learned they were a bunch of ruffians unable to hold a job with any respectable English firm. The schoolteacher, Mr. Marais, said, 'I was unlucky enough to have two of them in my school. They're wild, like old Rooi van Valck.'

'Maybe that's what we need.'

'Good heavens, no! There are plenty of decent Afrikaners here who'd want to help you keep your independence. Some may even want to join your fight. Perhaps the Boers near your borders. But don't count on it. And the three rascals you have found won't help your army much.'

'We have no army. Only commandos.'

'Then you'll lose the war. Because the English surely will have an army, and that makes a difference.'

Jakob was glad to be rid of Cape Town. The Afrikaners there seemed more interested in playing political games than in fighting for their freedoms. Little things had irritated him, too, like Du Preez and Carolus Marais saying 'Good heavens!' as if they were proper Englishmen. He saw other manifestations of this pervasive English influence, all making him think that the local Afrikaners were corrupted by their long severance from the Boers of the north. It was impossible to imagine Paulus de Groot in the Cape setting, or his own vibrant father, Tjaart. There were apparently two groups of Afrikaners now, and the southern had fallen into the hands of the enemy.

The train puffed across the Cape flats to Stellenbosch, out beyond the broken hedge of bitter almond: it passed suburban backyards, small settlements and numerous farms. He had left Cape Town with no promises, but he felt confident that when he got among his own people at Trianon his reception would be different, for these Afrikaners lived outside the debilitating influences of the city, and he would be able to talk with them in specifics.

When he saw the lovely tree-lined streets of Stellenbosch and the low white buildings, he felt that he had come to a town that had always been his. He stopped at a small, very clean whitewashed inn, where he had a room overlooking the central square and better food than he had enjoyed in some time. Three other travelers shared his table, men in from farms near Swellendam, and they wanted to know his business. When he told them that he was a farmer, too, but from Venloo in the Zuid-Afrikaansche Republiek, they all leaned forward: 'What's Oom Paul doing up there?'

'He's facing down the English, and he better, or you'll all be losing your freedoms.'

'I wouldn't know what to do with more freedom if I had it,' one of the farmers said.

'I mean freedom to worship as you wish. Have Dutch taught to your children.'

'We have that now.'

Another broke in: 'You say your name's Van Doorn? One of our Van Doorns?'

'The same.'

'You're not going to talk to them about joining Kruger's ridiculous war?'

'It's the duty of every good Afrikaner to support Oom Paul.'

'Agreed,' the three men said at once. And one added, 'I liked it when he took the strap and belted those lords of Johannesburg and their cheeky Uitlanders. But war . . . against England . . . With her navy? And her empire? Your people can't be serious about that?'

'Aren't you?' Jakob asked.

'Good heavens, no.'

There was the phrase again, spoken in accented English, betraying the corruption that had overtaken these good people; they lived so far from the heartland of the Volk, where great decisions were being made, that they could not comprehend the problems facing them. He rose to leave this depressing assembly, but as he walked away one of the farmers warned him: 'Don't go talking rebellion to the ones at Trianon. They sell their wine to London.'

The warning was perceptive, for next morning when he hired a cart to carry him west to the winery, he could see that its vineyards were so substantial and so ancient that whoever owned them must perforce be a cautious man; but when the driver swung about in a large circle to approach the house from the west, and Jakob saw for the first time that magnificent entrance, with the white arms reaching out in welcome and the great house standing in pristine loveliness, he gasped.

'These are the Van Doorns of Trianon,' he whispered respectfully. The place was like some palace he might have seen in a children's book, all green grass and blue hills, white walls of an older society. When the cart approached the big house the driver blew a small whistle, which brought the occupants to the stoep.

'It's Jakob come from up north!' the master of the house shouted to his children, whereupon he leaped off the stoep, rushed to the cart, and embraced this almost-forgotten cousin.

'I am Coenraad van Doorn,' he said, pushing Jakob back so he could see him better. 'And this is my wife, Florrie. The two boys are Dirk and Gerrit and the baby is Clara. Now come in.'

With real enthusiasm the young master of the vineyards, only thirty years old, led Jakob through the front door and into the spacious line of rooms which comprised the forward leg of the H. In the center of this line stood the reception hall; to the left, a lofty-ceilinged room for meetings; to the right, the guest bedroom in which Jakob would stay. But once his bags were deposited, he was led back through the crossbar of the H and into the warm, lively room where meals were served, off which the family bedrooms ranged. What was so very pleasing about the arrangement of this house was that gardens proliferated in both squares, so that all rooms were surrounded by flowers. The place had an air of elegance that almost overwhelmed Jakob.

Young Coenraad showed himself to be an able fellow: 'My father died too soon, and someone had to take command. I feel quite submerged. I've never been to Europe, you know, and most of our accounts are there. I must trust the opinions of others.'

'Does the business prosper?'

'Famously. But I'm worried. If this war talk continues . . .'

'I don't think it will stop. Up north many people believe that war with England is inevitable.'

'Wrong decisions, Jakob, are never inevitable. A wise man can always turn back from a precipice.'

'Are you telling me—you, a Van Doorn—that we Boers must not fight when an enemy wants to steal our lands and oppress us?'

'What oppression?' He almost laughed as he spoke.

Jakob had no opportunity to pursue the matter, because young Coenraad saw his cousin's visit as an opportunity to unravel the mysteries of the Van Doorns in South Africa, and before Jakob knew what was happening, a large sheet of white paper was laid down before him, with names and lines indicating the various members of the family: 'Willem and Marthinus in the 1600s I have. It's the next generation that confuses us, isn't that right, Florrie?' His wife came to sit with the two men, explaining from the chart how the two sons of Marthinus had separated, one to father the Trianon wine-makers, the other to go out into the veld to form the Vrymeer line. 'But what was your ancestor's name?' Coenraad asked.

Without having the family Bible at hand, Jakob could not trace his line so far back: 'My great-grandfather was a trekboer called Mal Adriaan. There's something they say . . . he discovered Vrymeer. His father may have been the one who left Trianon, but I don't recall his name.'

'That must have been Hendrik. Who was your grandfather?'

'A famous fighter. They called him Lodevicus the Hammer. He had two or three wives. One was a Wilhelmina, I believe. My mother died only last year. Aletta, eighty-one years old; I think her maiden name was Probenius.'

Carefully Coenraad drew in the lines, making estimates to account for the lost generations. It was a spotty genealogy they constructed, detailed in the case of the Trianon Van Doorns, inaccurate regarding the trekkers.

'But we are cousins,' Coenraad said expansively. 'That much we know.' When Jakob tried again to bring up the question of volunteering during the forthcoming war, the wine-maker laughed easily and cut him off: 'No one at Trianon wants war. We have no quarrel with the English.' And when Jakob started to argue that no Afrikaner would ever be spiritually free till the English were subdued, Coenraad drew his children to his side of the table so that they could inspect the diagram of their family, and said firmly, 'That'll be your war, Jakob, not ours.' And he would permit no further discussion.

In September 1899 England began moving troops up to the Orange River and ordering home regiments and units from other colonies to reinforce the Cape and Natal garrisons. The two Boer republics loaded their arsenals also, importing Mausers from Krupp's and long-range guns for the State Artillery, their only regular military organization. Late in the month the word went out to the commandos: 'Opsaal, burghers!' And when the Boers were told to saddle up, they knew that danger was at hand.

One of the first to respond at Vrymeer was Micah Nxumalo: 'Baas, the Kaffirs at Groenkop, they got ponies. You want me to see if they're any good?'

Jakob nodded. 'What will those Kaffirs do in the war?'

'Nothing, Baas. Sit in their kraals and talk.'

The Groenkop blacks were a small group who occupied a valley far to the north; some of their people worked for Boers, but they had never entirely surrendered their tribal roots the way Nxumalo had done. They were, of course, part of the Boer republics, but no one took much notice of these pockets of blacks so long as they 'behaved' themselves. This would not be their war.

'Will your older boy be riding with us?' Van Doorn asked.

'No. He stay with his mother. I go with you, Baas.'

It never occurred to Micah that he had an option in this matter; if war came, he would naturally ride with the Venloo Commando. His affection for Van Doorn and his respect for the old general would dictate that.

Next morning Paulus de Groot came over to Vrymeer; he and Sybilla had left their miserable house and would stay with the Van Doorns until decisions were reached. His only concern was whether the Venloo men would keep him as leader of their commando, and when Jakob said, 'Of course they will. You were a general at Majuba,' he replied with some anxiety, 'With a commando, you never know. The burghers of Venloo will make up their own minds.'

In each district a new commandant was elected every five years, and because of his heroics at Majuba, De Groot had won the post every time, but save for a few Kaffir raids and the rout of Dr. Jameson's invaders, there had been eighteen years of peace, and there were a dozen young men claiming that they would be better at fighting the English.

De Groot and Van Doorn rode in to Venloo to meet with two hundred and sixty-seven other men who comprised the commando. They were a tough lot, burghers mostly in their thirties, but anywhere between sixteen and sixty, with De Groot the oldest, ignoring his seven years past normal retirement. They met at the church, but not in it, for they were many and each wanted his say. Under the big trees, in the shade, these men of the Boer nation discussed the looming war.

'We beat them at Majuba,' De Groot said, eager to establish his credentials early, 'and we'll donder them again. With these!' And he held up a Mauser. A wagonload of guns had arrived from Pretoria, and they were handed out.

The new weapons caused much excitement, and there was so much free firing that the war almost ended for three burghers who got in the way of the fusillades. But the problem of who would lead remained unsettled, and this was of grave importance for a commando. Tonight it had two hundred and sixty-nine members; tomorrow it might have four hundred or, if things went poorly, it could relapse into a veldkornetcy with less than a hundred fighters. It all depended upon how the war was progressing, conditions in Venloo, and what the burghers thought of their leader.

The law said that every male citizen had to serve when summoned, unless officially excused. The commandant-general, his assistant-generals and the combat commanders laid down the regulations, but the Boers had lost none of their independent Voortrekker spirit, nor their disregard for meddlesome authority. They might be ordered to serve in a commando, and Oom Paul might have a law which said they would be thrown in jail if they refused, but once they were in the saddle, they would recognize their leader only as chief among equals.

If he made one serious mistake, half his troops might ride off in disgust, and even if he were continuously brilliant, his burghers still might go home if they grew sick of the war or apprehensive about its outcome. Also, every fighting man considered himself free to quit the commando he was in and transfer to another, if he liked its fighting style better or considered its leader more apt to win his battles.

It was crucial, therefore, to select the right man at the beginning, and one burgher said, 'Naturally, we would want you to carry on as commandant, De Groot, a former general and all. But you're an old man now, and I doubt you could stand the chases.'

'He can ride better than me,' Jakob said.

'We need someone who can think quickly,' another said. 'You know, the English are going to throw their best generals into this fight.' It was uncertain whether this speaker was for old Paulus or against him, but before he could clarify his statement, another said warmly, 'If De Groot did so well at Majuba, and when the Uitlander raiders came . . .'

'I think he's too old.'

Without a vote having been taken, it seemed that sentiment ran something like 180–89 in favor of the old man, but one of the complainants said with some force, 'This won't be Majuba or untrained Uitlanders. We need someone young, with strength in the saddle.'

The commando decided not to vote that night, but to think some more about the touchy problem; each burgher was convinced that war with

England was only days away, that it would be demanding, and that they must have the best leader possible.

Some of the men wished to consult with Jakob, since he had been to both Cape Town and Pretoria: 'How does it look with the Boers at the Cape?'

'I found three boys who'll be cleaning their rifles tonight. But we can forget about real help from the south. They will not fight. Say they'll win their war on the floor of their Parliament, and that we're wasting our time with commandos.'

'Verdomp! We'll show them. God alone knows, we'll show the whole damn world, too.'

'Tell me, Van Doorn,' a thoughtful burgher asked. 'Who do you want as commandant?'

'We already have one—Paulus. He's a true leader.'

They left it at that, and De Groot slept that night at the Van Doorns'; before going to bed he said fervently, 'I would like to serve, Jakob. I have ideas about how to handle the English.'

'We'll have to wait and see. A lot of them think you're too old.'

'I am,' De Groot conceded quickly. 'But I'm the one with ideas.'

Next morning the burghers resumed discussion, and sentiment swung strongly to a vigorous young man who farmed east of Vrymeer, but someone pointed out that he was always talking about how clever the Hollanders in Pretoria were and how the Boers could learn some culture from them. That finished him, for while most Boers supported Oom Paul in anything he did, they distrusted the Amsterdam clique around him, the hundreds who had been imported to serve in the Boer government. Some Venloo men said, 'The damned Hollanders are almost as bad as the Uitlanders.'

The vote was taken that afternoon, and old Paulus de Groot was retained as commandant, 201–68, grudgingly by some, who mumbled, 'We wanted someone younger. But we'll give you a chance.' All he said was 'Get your saddles ready.'

At Vrymeer the old man gathered everyone in the farmhouse kitchen, and with his hands resting on the ancient Van Doorn Bible, he said, 'When God chooses a people to do His work, He places on that people many demands, but in our response He watches over us and always brings us victory. Sybilla, are you ready?' The old woman, her hair drawn tight across her head, nodded. 'Sara, will you guard the farm and the children?' The younger woman nodded, bringing her young son closer to her side. 'Girls, will you defend this home against the Englishmen, if they come?'

'We will,' the twins said gravely, but Johanna, the older girl, merely nodded.

'Then your father and I can go to war with easy hearts. Let us pray,' and in the farmhouse, so far removed from conflict, the eight farm people bowed their heads and clasped their hands:

> 'Almighty God, we know that You have called us to this battle. We know that as Your chosen people we must obey the covenant You handed down to us. We are Your instrument in bringing Your kingdom into being on this earth, and we submit ourselves to Your care. Bring us the victory You gave us in the past.'

On the morning of October 7 word reached Venloo that their commando was to depart immediately for the Natal border, but not to cross it until formal commencement of hostilities: 'You can stand with the forefeet of your ponies touching enemy territory.' So the Venloo Commando formed up, and rode south.

This commando consisted of two hundred and sixty-nine Boers, each mounted on a sturdy pony which he supplied. Since each man dressed in whatever clothes he deemed appropriate for an extended stay in the field, the file looked more like a rabble than an army company. Some men wore heavy brown corduroys, some black, a few white. Most wore vests, unbuttoned, and about half had heavy coats of a wild variety. They wore veldskoen, heavy homemade field shoes of softened leather. The only item of clothing or equipment in which there was the slightest standardization was the hat: most of the men preferred the slouching Boer hat, which made them look like disgruntled sheepdogs. But even hats weren't uniform, for some men chose bowlers, tweed caps or almost any other available headgear. Behind them came some forty blacks, all mounted, leading twenty or thirty spare ponies.

What made the Venloo Commando unforgettable were the units front and rear. Ahead of his troops rode General Paulus de Groot, sixty-seven years old, big, hefty in chest and belly, bearded, wearing the uniform that had distinguished him at Majuba: a formal frock coat with silver buttons and a tall black top hat. The side of this hat was decorated with a small republican flag embroidered by Sybilla with the words: VIR GOD! VIR LAND! VIR JUSTISIE! His official rank was Commandant, but no one addressed him as anything but General.

At the rear, behind the blacks and the remounts, came the wagons containing the sixteen wives who would accompany their men to the front. Undisputed leader among them was Sybilla de Groot, sixty-four years old, who said, 'I must go with my man in his war against that woman across the sea.'

This was typical of the Boer army, little disciplined, less organized, paid not at all, but well able to live off the land it fought for, with a Mauser and six legs for each man, because everyone was mounted. Its task: to defeat the combined armies of the British Empire.

Ostensible blame for launching the Anglo-Boer War of 1899 was visible for all the world to see. At five o'clock on the afternoon of October 9 the Boer republics drafted an ultimatum which threw into the face of the British government demands of such an uncompromising nature that no self-respecting major power could possibly have accepted them.

Early in the morning of 10 October 1899 these demands were presented officially to the British cabinet, who reacted with surprise and delight: 'They've done it! They've given us a cast-iron case. They stand before the world as the aggressors.' That night the British government rejected the ultimatum, and when news of this reaction reached Pretoria on the afternoon of October 11, war officially began, and troops from both sides swung into action. A handful of rural Boers had brazenly challenged the might of an empire.

But the real cause of the war was much more complex than an exchange of cablegrams over demands for arbitration and troop withdrawals. It involved the same forces that had caused General de Groot's storming of Majuba in 1881, and those which had urged Cecil Rhodes to support the invasion of the Transvaal in 1895. The English wanted to control all of southern Africa in one grand union of states and peoples; the Boers wanted the freedom to conduct their own governments off to one side without interference from London. The English took up the case of the Uitlanders on the Golden Reef. The Boers saw these fortune-seekers as a threat to their way of life. These interests conflicted, aroused animosities, and inevitably goaded the two nations into combat.

If the Boers had not declared war on October 11, the English would probably have done so within a few days. The sanest judgment that can be passed on the genesis of this terrible war between two groups of friends is that it was the result of imperiousness on the English side and intransigence on the Boer.

Like rivulets wandering across a plain, coalescing at last to form a river, the various commandos heading toward Natal came together to create a Boer army. In time it contained some seventeen thousand men, and when they were assembled for the drive into English territory, old Commandant-General Joubert, in charge, decided to hold a review in honor of Oom Paul's birthday to inspirit the troops and put them in a military frame of mind, so while he sat astride his horse to take the salute, the commandos galloped past, each man executing what he called a salute in the distinctive style he favored. Some doffed their big hats; some merely touched the brim with a finger; some yelled Boer fighting words; some nodded; a few shook their own hands and grinned; and some made no other gesture than a wink. But each man signified that he was ready.

They galloped into Natal, prepared to sweep gloriously down to the Indian Ocean, capture Durban at the end of their ride, and deprive the English of a port through which to bring the reinforcements already on their way from London. General de Groot, with his Venloo Commando, tried to keep near the front of the advance, for he wished to lead the gallop down to the sea.

Two heavily garrisoned towns obstructed the path of the Boers as they entered Natal—Dundee and Ladysmith—and it was De Groot's urgent advice that they be by-passed: 'Give me a handful of commandos, we'll dash direct to Durban.' Had he been allowed to do this, he would have prevented English ships from landing reinforcements, and then, as he growled, 'Without supplies, the garrisons will wither up here and we can pluck them when we will.'

But the commandant-general felt that orderliness required that he capture these two strong points: 'We can't have thousands of English troops in our rear, can we?' De Groot insisted that his charging raid to the seaport might win the war, but he was silenced with a stern command: 'Take your burghers toward Ladysmith. You'll do your fighting there.'

So while thousands of Boers peeled off for the attack on Dundee, where the English commanding general was to be mortally wounded while his troops fled south, the Venloo Commando had to swing west, abandon the brilliant concept of a dash to the sea, and make for the hills overlooking Ladysmith.

The town acquired this remarkable name because of the exploits of a dashing young officer, Sir Harry Smith, who made his historic ride from Cape Town to the defense of Grahamstown back in 1835. He captivated the imagination of the local population. Later he returned to Cape Town as governor, and was enthusiastically welcomed by 'my children,' as he called the Boers and blacks. But just in case the Xhosa had any dream of re-creating the troubles they had caused him, he summoned two thousand to meet him, with their chiefs. Mounted on his horse Aliwal, he held in his right hand a brass-headed wand signifying peace, and in his left, a sergeant's stick representing war.

The chiefs were ordered to step forward and touch the wand or the stick, indicating the course they wished to follow. Peace was the victor, but at a price: 'Now, to show that you submit to me and my Great White Queen, you will kiss my foot.' They did, whereupon Sir Harry shook their hands and reported: 'We have secured permanent peace.' Alas, only three years later his Xhosa children invaded the frontier yet again, and once more he had to repulse them.

Sir Harry also had his troubles with the Voortrekkers who crossed the Orange River, but the dashing governor and his lovely Spanish wife continued to enjoy such adulation that the people named a series of towns after them: Harrismith; Aliwal, honoring his victory over the Sikhs at that place in India; and two different towns named Ladysmith, one of which Paulus de Groot and his Boers were about to invest.

Late on the second afternoon of the ride toward Ladysmith, a violent thunderstorm broke, making De Groot's drenched burghers curse as they pushed through the torrent. He rode up front with Van Doorn, head pulled in toward chest, a bitter anger darkening his face. 'Every step this horse takes,' he grumbled, 'we're farther away from the route to the sea. Damnit, Jakob! Even if we do reach Ladysmith in good order, we'll have to wait for the rest to catch up before we can attack.' Then he voiced his real complaint: 'We're missing the battles.'

He was mistaken. Two Boer scouts raced back and cried through the pelting rain, 'Die Engelese! They're fighting our men just beyond those gullies.'

'We join them!' De Groot shouted as he spurred his horse. The commando plunged into the eroded rift in the veld, ponies slipping and sliding in the quagmire, then struggling up the opposite side. They came out on the edge of a vast plain, but the rain cut visibility; through a small telescope De Groot could barely discern a company of Boers, far distant. To his dismay, they seemed to be retreating: 'Where in hell are they going? To the Transvaal?' Without waiting for an answer, he headed directly toward the fighting.

The Venloo burghers were thus projected into an experience which would go far in determining General de Groot's future actions. To begin with, their scouting had been inadequate: the two young fellows sent forward miscalculated the capacity of the enemy force, encouraging the Boer contingent to advance too rapidly, ill-prepared for the shock the English were about to deliver. Boer losses had already been heavy and the retreat was general.

De Groot judged that swift movement on his part might halt the rout, but as his men approached, the English commander unleashed a unit which up to now had been held in reserve: four hundred lancers roared onto the plain, sweeping toward the confused Boers. When they spotted the arrival of the Venloo Commando, half the force broke away and came directly at the new target.

The Boers rarely charged an enemy on horseback; they usually dismounted, tied their ponies, and fought on foot. Nor did they like the idea of one white man stabbing at another with bayonets and lances; to them, decent warfare permitted only bullets, with stabbing a savage tactic resorted to by Zulu and Xhosa. But now here came the English cavalry, galloping like fiends across the open space, their lances flashing in the sunlight that broke through the clouds.

It was a dreadful affray, those huge horses coming at the Boers, those long, sharp lances jabbing at the disorganized burghers caught unprepared in the open. Van Doorn narrowly escaped when a lance smacked into his saddle, jarring his pony to a deathly stop and tossing him to the ground. Luckily, he made it on foot to some rocks, but watched as a score of his fellow Boers were cut down. Because of the nature of a cavalry charge—fifteen, twenty, forty mounted men thundering one behind another along a single path—any Boer who was struck by one lance was apt to be hit by a dozen others, so that a dead body could be riddled.

The Venloo Commando was broken and scattered, which encouraged the Englishmen to launch a second and third charge. On and on they came, yelling and shouting and spewing obscenities; Van Doorn heard one young officer cry, 'What a glorious pig-sticking!' His khaki uniform was splattered with blood; this was a grand battue all over again, a wild and savage slaughter.

Aside from the group of rocks in which Jakob hid, along with five others, there was no cover for any Boers who lost their ponies, so the razor-sharp lances were free to pick them off at will as they ran screaming across the veld. Some of the commando did manage to escape on their ponies, and these closed ranks with De Groot; their rapid fire from the saddle diverted the English cavalry from destroying trapped men like Van Doorn, but nothing could stop the butchery of the Venloo men.

At last the victorious lancers withdrew, having lost only a handful of their men; but when ashen-faced Van Doorn inspected the bloodstained veld he found more than seventy Boers slain, most with more than six deep gashes in their bodies; one young fellow caught in the full path of the first and third charges had been punctured eighteen times. When De Groot saw this lad—the one who had dared to dance with Sybilla, who had kissed Johanna van Doorn in the barn—and witnessed the obscene manner in which he had been stabbed, he stood over his young fighter and swore an oath: 'I will destroy the English cavalry.'

He got his first chance during the ensuing battle for Ladysmith. Having learned his lesson, he used the best scouts available: Micah Nxumalo and two other blacks, who reported accurately the movements of the English cavalry. He moved his commando as close to the lancers' position as he could, praying that they would accept the bait he was about to throw before them: 'They'll never catch us in the open again. But let the swine think they can eat us up like they did before.'

Like an old and practiced spider, he spun his web. On five successive days he changed his guard an hour before dusk, instructing his men to walk from their posts slowly, as if weary from the November heat. Replacements were to arrive tardily and to appear listless. Six men or seven were to be visible between the tents, and there was to be desultory movement. Everything was to look like a poorly managed Boer camp, and for five days absolutely nothing happened. So he prolonged the drill, inventing new pieces of activity which would help create the illusion, and on the eleventh day the English cavalry came out again, with nearly two hundred men.

The roles given the forward actors were perilous indeed, for the thundering cavalry was allowed right into the heart of the encampment, with enough Boers running distraught to maintain the illusion, and these must be adroit enough to escape death from the stabbing lances. Two failed, and with great cries of triumph, the cavalrymen hacked them to death.

But when the sortie had passed through the camp, it found itself enfiladed not only by the survivors of the Venloo Commando but also by one hundred burghers from the Carolina contingent borrowed for this occasion, and from those grim Boers came a withering crossfire, aimed not at the lancers but at their horses. And as the beasts went down or ran wild in fury, Boer marksmen calmly shot any surviving cavalrymen. Only those who surrendered instantly were spared, and not all of them.

The Englishmen who made it through the fusillade regrouped at the far end of the camp and wanted to speed back to save their grounded comrades, and some daring horsemen tried, but when they were mowed down by concentrated rifle fire, their companions realized that this day's battle was over. In a wide sweep they galloped away from the laager, returning to Ladysmith a sadly depleted force.

There was other bad news for the English. After the fall of Dundee, many thousands of Boer horsemen had been released to join the assault on Ladysmith, and when the English infantry marched out to give battle, they were sorely thrashed, the Boers capturing more than nine hundred prisoners. This meant that henceforth the troops in the town must stay on the defensive. The English could hold on, but they could not swing over to the attack.

It was a notable victory for the Boers, but at the moment of triumph a fatal weakness manifested itself: the Boer generals began squabbling among themselves. Paulus de Groot, epitome of the daring commando leader, repeated his request to ignore stalemated Ladysmith and gallop south in wide, swinging raids, dashing right into Durban before reinforcements could be landed, but other commandants, who were frightened at the idea of leaving a redoubt in English hands, insisted that brash De Groot stay with them, help them mount a siege, and gradually wear away the English defenders.

'We must strike while we're free!' De Groot pleaded.

'Paulus,' the old commandant-general said, 'if God extends a finger to us in this great victory, we mustn't grab for His entire hand. He would not like it if you galloped off to Durban.' De Groot was ordered to remain, to dig in, and passively watch the English in Ladysmith.

That night he met with his veldkornets. 'I am sorely worried. Commandos were born to move, we should be galloping south.' When no one spoke, tears came to his eyes. 'I can see us roaring into Durban. Taking the port. Throwing the English back into the sea.' Still no one spoke. 'Once we let them land, they'll be like bulldogs. They'll never let go.' The Venloo men knew he was right, but they had their orders and there was nothing they could say, and again tears trickled down his beard. 'We sit here tonight, losing the war.'

Then came exhilarating news which assured the Boers that victory was still within their grasp: Boers on all the other fronts had won stunning victories, which encouraged De Groot to urge once more a dash to the sea that would end the war. This time permission was granted, but he was forestalled by precisely what he had feared: thousands of English troops had sailed into Durban harbor and were already entraining for the north. This mighty force would quickly lift the siege of Ladysmith and go on to destroy the Boers.

The preponderance of power would rapidly become so overwhelming —five, sometimes ten well-armed professional soldiers against one fighting Boer, ten heavy guns to one—that the Anglo-Boer War should have ended well before Christmas. In this opinion all the foreign military experts concurred.

It was the custom in these years for any army in the field to invite uniformed observers from friendly nations to march with it, observe its performance, and report to their own headquarters the quality of this army's fighting men. German officers rode with the Boers, and French and Russian and some South Americans, while the same nations sent other officers to report on the English.

At the end of 1899 these cautious experts concluded that despite initial Boer victories, the English on the Natal front would rather quickly lift the siege of Ladysmith and then, in an orderly fashion, bring in so many troops through Durban that victory was assured. But in early 1900, after an opportunity to assess the remarkable general London had dispatched to do the job, they became confused.

Said the German observer in his cable to Berlin: 'With this man the English will be lucky to win in four years.'

But the French major wired in code to Paris: 'He's the type who gives the enemy much trouble, the traditional English bulldog who holds on with every muscle in his body.'

Wrote the Russian: 'If this man is what the English War Office considers a general, I suggest you terminate our proposals for a military treaty with England.'

But the American reported: 'Do not underestimate him. He's the type of general who holds the British Empire together. The Boers will defeat him six times in a row, then realize with dismay that he has won the seventh, and final, battle.'

Sir Redvers Buller, scion of the noble family that had given King Henry VIII two of his queens, Anne Boleyn and Catherine Howard, was sixty years old, something over two hundred and forty pounds in weight, and chairbound at headquarters for the past eleven years. His appointment as commander-in-chief of the English effort in South Africa had been bitterly opposed by one faction in the War Office and the cabinet, somewhat tepidly supported by another faction that wanted a no-nonsense man in the field. He himself, when he heard of his impending selection, wanted to avoid it, judging himself to be inadequate, for he had never commanded a full army, but in the end he had accepted on the sensible grounds cited by many another man called to assume major responsibilities: 'I'm as good as any of the others.'

Prior to embarking on his great adventure, he had the bad luck to make an observation which would haunt him: 'I doubt I shall have to do much fighting against the Boers in the field. My only fear is that everything may be ended before I get there.'

But as his ship neared Cape Town, a passing vessel moved close, and without stopping, hung out a huge blackboard with alarming news about the confusion on the Natal front, so that when Buller reached Africa he was a much-sobered man, determined to do his bulldog best.

The troopship put into Cape Town about an hour after dusk on 30 October 1899, in a driving rain. Since this was too late for a gala entrance, the passengers slept fitfully while those ashore prepared to greet the man they relied on to protect them from the rampaging Boers.

Early next morning Cape Town was aflutter with excitement, thousands of citizens having gathered at the docks to greet their hero. Gangways threaded with ribbons led to the ship's deck, where a monstrous cinematograph was being worked by four men in cloth caps: the arrival of the great man would be recorded in motion pictures. Bands played, little girls carried flowers, every government official was present, and a bishop offered prayer.

Precisely at nine in the morning trumpets sounded, drums rolled, and Sir Redvers Buller stepped forth to command the war effort in Africa. He was of medium height, with an enormous belly, and had a strange head which once seen could never be forgotten. It was shaped like an eggplant, heavy and triple-chinned at the bottom, rising almost to a point at the top. His small eyes almost touched at the bridge of a very large nose, which guarded a huge, bushy mustache that smothered his weak upper lip. As if he sought to accentuate the odd shape of his head, he favored a small, tight military hat with a long visor that obscured his vision.

When he spoke, his one conspicuous asset manifested itself: his voice rumbled with deep, masculine authority, but what it said was rarely understood, for a rambunctious horse had kicked out his front teeth. An irreverent Capetowner, startled by Buller's appearance, whispered, 'He looks like a distressed walrus,' but a reserve officer who knew Buller's record for extreme bravery replied, 'Sir, you are wrong. He looks like John Bull.'

General Buller proceeded directly to Government House, where he was briefed on the shocking prospects facing the English forces, for as the local officer explained: 'We are threatened on two fronts. On the west our troops are besieged at Mafeking and the diamond town of Kimberley. On the east they can't break out of Ladysmith. And we hear rumors that the Cape Afrikaners are about to rise in rebellion.'

So instead of occupying a relaxed position in Cape Town and directing

his subordinate generals to dash this way and that, subduing the obstreperous Boers, Buller was faced with the awesome necessity of splitting his army
into two parts and taking field command of one of them. 'I'll need time to
study this,' he said, and forthwith he established his headquarters in a small
house on a side street; for his living quarters he chose rooms in the Mount
Nelson Hotel, and early one morning a tall, handsome man in a newly
purchased uniform of major in the local corps knocked on his door.

To provide Buller with maximum support, Her Majesty's government
in Cape Town had scurried about to find some young man with strong
business experience to serve as economic liaison, and upon the advice of
several older men, Frank Saltwood was chosen.

The men who selected him for this important post advised: 'You must
find out as much about Buller as you can. Always helpful to know how a
man's mind works.' For the past two weeks Frank had been doing just that,
and like the military observers at the front, he was getting conflicting
reports.

'Most important,' an English official said, 'he's of noble lineage. Duke
of Norfolk, and all that. True gentleman, but of the rough sort.'

An English military man said, 'Enjoys the absolute confidence of the
General Staff. Good Old Buller, they call him. He's welcomed at court, and
Queen Victoria rather dotes on him.'

But it was a South African of Dutch-Huguenot descent who contributed
the first important bit of information: 'Never forget that against the Zulu
in 1879 he won the Victoria Cross. Bravery beyond description. Just set his
jaw and walked right through enemy fire to rescue a group of wounded men.
A man of extreme bravery. Proved it again in Egypt.'

The encomiums continued, explaining why he had been selected and
constructing the portrait of the classic English general, and it was not until
the third or fourth day that nagging details began to surface. One enlisted
English soldier told Saltwood, 'You must remember, for the past eleven
years it's been mostly chair duty for that one.'

Another soldier who had seen Buller at the War Office in London
contributed: 'He's past sixty, I think, and gotten frightfully fat. Must have
weighed eighteen stone when I saw him.'

A major newly arrived said, 'Only hearsay, but I believe the Staff was
sharply divided about accepting him. Some wanted younger, harder drivers
like Kitchener or Allenby. Others wanted trusted older men like Lord
Roberts. There was grave suspicion that Buller might not be up to the
challenge.'

'Then why was he chosen?' Saltwood asked, scribbling rapidly to keep
up with the flow of words.

'It was the general impression,' the newcomer said, 'that he was a good
fellow who deserved a shot at high command.' He coughed, then added,
'He's never led an army, you know.'

'Why would they give such a man so important a job?'

'Well, he had been around a long time and it was his turn.'

A young Englishman who knew considerable about his country's military system, and who was obviously perplexed by the appointment of
Buller, said reflectively, 'It just occurred to me. Take all the leading generals

assigned to this campaign. Not one has ever led his troops against an enemy that wore shoes.'

This extraordinary statement produced a thoughtful silence, broken by Saltwood, who asked, pen still in hand, 'What do you mean?'

'They've fought barefooted Afghans, and barefooted Egyptians, and barefooted Sindi. "Shoulder-to-shoulder, men, and drive the pagan blighters back to the hills." I know nothing about the Boers, but I believe they wear shoes.'

'They do,' a South African conceded. 'But essentially they're a rabble. Buller should have no trouble with them.'

'But a rabble with shoes,' the young Englishman warned.

It was an older English officer who gave Saltwood the most helpful information: 'I knew him in England, after his days of glory in the field. He had only two objectives. Build the best army possible. Do everything to protect the welfare of the troops. I'm told in recent letters that he wasn't the unanimous choice of either the War Office or the cabinet, but he was a good choice. He had many Boers in his unit when he fought out here against the Zulu. He'll respect them.'

It was with this body of conflicting opinions that Frank Saltwood approached Buller's room that October morning, and before he had been with the general two minutes, he realized that all his research had been useless. Frank's major problem was understanding what the general was saying, for he had trouble pronouncing words because of his missing teeth, and those he did say were often lost in his mustache. Frank wondered if he had heard the opening words correctly.

'Glad to have you, young fellow. What I mean . . . hhmmph . . . you're to fetch me an iron tub.'

'Did you say iron tub, sir?'

'What I mean, if I have to go to the front meself. Man must have his bath, what?'

'You mean a tub to carry with you, sir?'

'Yes, damnit, what I mean, a man can't go dirty on bivouac, can he?'

He also wanted a mobile kitchen so large that it would require an entire wagon and eight mules. He wanted a feather bed with extra blankets: 'Don't want the cold to impede us, do we, hhmmph?' After a whole morning of this, in which Saltwood jotted down enough items to fill a small store, the general asked abruptly, 'How far to Stellenbosch?'

'The train might get you there and back in a day. But there are no troops, enemy or . . .'

'Damn. Well, you know, in London and all that.'

Saltwood was quite lost until Buller mumbled, 'Trianon, you know. One of the really good wines of the world. I shall want fifty dozen of their best sparkling wine.'

'That would be six hundred bottles, sir.'

'Six hundred is what I want.'

That would require an extra wagon and eight more horses, but when Frank demurred a second time, Buller raged at him, showing the force which had made him a general to be feared: 'Damnit, man, this is a campaign, don't you know? Out in the field. Months on end, perhaps. Man wants his comforts.'

Saltwood was to find that this phrase had specific meanings for Buller, because by the close of the second day he had encouraged his staff to fill the empty rooms at the Mount Nelson with the choicest free ladies of Cape Town, and with them on the scene, there was considerable revelry. On the third day Saltwood said, 'Sir, the officers want to consult with you. You're aware, I presume, that the fighting is not going well?'

Saltwood was astonished by what happened next; it was if a magician had waved a military wand, transforming this big, bumbling man into a tough-minded soldier. Buller stiffened, and with the riding crop he kept in his quarters, indicated a top-secret binder: 'I have me orders. Before I left London the wizards planned me entire campaign. Spelled out everything I was to do.' He rapped the folder twice, not arrogantly, but in a gesture of dismissal: 'And every plan they made was wrong. It doesn't apply, not with those damned Boers . . . My word, they can move fast, those Boers.'

'What are you going to do, sir?'

Buller rose, moved about his suite, then stopped and stared out the window at the confusing land he was supposed to conquer. Turning abruptly to face his new assistant, he said, 'Prepare to spend a long time in the field. I've got to do exactly the opposite of what they order.' He shoved the War Office directives aside. 'I'm splitting me troops. Half to Kimberley to rescue them up there. You and I will be going to Ladysmith.'

He made this bold move to inspire the troops, but as a member of the clique opposed to him said, 'He did inspire the troops, but the wrong ones.' And in London a wag circulated the rumor that the Boer high command had issued an order: 'Anyone who shoots General Buller will be court-martialed. He's our strongest weapon.'

Frank Saltwood, watching closely every move he made, believed at first that the critics and the comics were correct. Redvers Buller was an ass.

The Tugela River is that lovely stream which marked the southern limit of King Shaka's Zululand, and along which Piet Retief's people had waited while he and his men marched to their death at Dingane's Kraal. When these waiting women and children were slaughtered a few days later, their blood ran into the Tugela. Now, at a small hill far upstream, Spion Kop (Lookout Hill), General Redvers Buller was about to conduct a campaign which suggested that the German observer had been correct when he added to his first report: 'When you first meet Buller you instinctively like him. A real soldier. But when you study what he actually does in battle, you shudder.'

The town of Ladysmith was still under siege. Resolute Englishmen, lacking food, medicine, fire power, horses and sleep, protected the town against encircling forces. All England, which received telegrams direct from the town, wanted these brave defenders rescued, so when General Buller joined his massive army below the Tugela, he found himself less than fifteen miles from Ladysmith, with overwhelming superiority, twenty-one thousand against forty-five hundred, and he dispatched an unfortunate helio-graphed message to the besieged troops: 'Will rescue you within five days.'

There were two difficulties: he had to cross the river, and once that was done, his men would have to run a gauntlet through a chain of small hills.

As the German observer reported later: 'He might have accomplished either of these tasks if faced alone, but to require him to meet both of them at once posed a problem so complex that he seemed quite unable to grapple with it.'

Buller sat on the south side of the Tugela for five days, pondering the difficulties, finally telling Saltwood, 'A frontal attack would be quite impossible. Never break through there, eh, Frank? We face a long, hard fight.'

'You said in England that it would be over before you got here.'

'Would have been, if the other chaps had done their job. Now we've got to mop up.'

He worked night after night, going over and over his plans, but after he had swilled most of a bottle of Trianon, his eyes, already almost touching at the corners, seemed to come together, at which times he would drift away from battlefield problems and discourse on his theories of parade-ground military combat: 'Keep the shoulders touching, move forward in line, don't fire too soon, and the ruddy bastards will never stand up against an English march.'

'With the Boers, it's mostly cavalry, sir,' Saltwood reminded him.

'Don't like the cavalry. Never know where the devils will be going next. Give me foot soldiers every time.'

Sometimes late at night, when he was well under, he would grow sentimental: 'Worst thing ever happened to the English soldier, they put him in this damned olive-drab. Said it made him less a target. I say it killed his spirit. In Egypt you had six hundred gallant lads in bright red, marching in the sun. By gad, it struck terror, that's what it did. It struck terror.'

He never referred to his own bravery, which had been considerable, in all theaters of war, but if someone pressed him about his V.C., he would say, 'There's a job to be done, you press forward. No need to give a man medals. That's his job.'

After all his sound deliberations on the folly of a frontal assault on a river and a chain of hills, General Buller changed his mind on the eve of battle and elected to do precisely that. 'We'll roll back the Boers and lift the siege of Ladysmith,' he told Saltwood triumphantly, and as if the deed were done, he sent another heliogram assuring the defenders that he would be there within five days—with plenty of food.

With a shockingly inadequate map of the area and incomplete scouting sorties, he threw his men against the Boers, who stayed north of the river and picked them off in isolated batches. His fifteen-pounders, inspirited by the idea of the daring dash into the face of an enemy, rashly moved far ahead of their supporting infantry and were isolated. Rescue attempts failed and the guns were captured by the enemy, a loss of more than half the army's field artillery. By nightfall one hundred and forty English soldiers were killed, to the Boer's forty, and more than a thousand were wounded or missing. In dismay and confusion, General Buller ordered his first retreat from the Tugela and afterward dispatched one of the more shameful telegrams of military history.

Ordering the heliographer to his tent, he scribbled a message, which Saltwood begged him not to send: 'It will dash the hopes of the Ladysmith defenders, sir.'

'They're soldiers. They've got to know the worst.'

'But let it come upon them slowly, I beg you. Not from their own commander-in-chief.'

'Send the message!' Buller stormed, as if he were driven to prove himself an ass before the entire world, and it was sent, from an addled commander to a very brave man striving to defend a difficult position:

> It appears that I cannot relieve Ladysmith for another month, and even then, only by means of a protracted siege operation. I need time to fortify myself below the Tugela. When I'm in position I suggest you burn your ciphers, destroy your guns, fire away your ammunition, and make the best terms possible with the Boers.

A commanding general had advised one of his bravest subordinates to surrender while there was still a fighting chance to hold on. Buller himself, after a lengthy effort to pull his troops together, tried to ford the Tugela again and wound up in a second confused retreat. In desperation he told Saltwood, 'There must be a way to cross that river. I'll think of something.'

It was imperative that he do so, for the general commanding the defenses at Ladysmith had refused to surrender, and it was obligatory that Buller try once more to rescue him. Instead, in his report to London he complained that he had been repulsed at the Tugela because the Boers outnumbered him: 'They had eighty thousand in the field against me.' To this, London replied acidly: 'Suggest you check population of total Boer republics, men, women and children.'

The rebuff infuriated Buller: 'Damnit, Saltwood, back there they don't know these Boers. What I tried to tell them is that we're not fighting an army. We're fighting a nation. Men, women and children.'

With Buller ensnared, General de Groot sought permission to lead his commando on a wide sweep east of Ladysmith and deep into Natal: 'We can chop up the English supply lines.'

Permission was refused, and some of the finest horsemen in the world were held stationary to fight as unneeded foot soldiers. At the two battles of the Tugela they had conducted themselves with dignity, fighting from trenches and behind boulders, but slowly their numbers were eroding. From the original two hundred and sixty-nine, they had lost one hundred, and the waiting so irritated those remaining that more had simply gone home, leaving the commando a mere one hundred and fifty-one. De Groot was aware that unless they soon enjoyed some kind of success, even that number must diminish, and then he would be in serious trouble.

Therefore, when Christmas came, with all Boer troops still inactive, ten more Venloo men growled, 'To hell with this,' and returned home to tend their farms. De Groot was now reduced to one hundred and forty-one disconsolate men, but he was enormously encouraged when three young fellows of a different commando reported one day with the simple statement: 'Our fathers fought with you at Majuba. We'd like to join you.' It would be additions like these that would keep De Groot's commando up to strength for the major battles that lay ahead.

General Buller had been as humiliated as any general in history. His heliogram advising Ladysmith to surrender because he could think of no quick way to rescue it had been circulated to the cabinet, causing such a scandal that the War Office had to take action, and they had deprived him of the supreme command, handing it to an extraordinary man, Lord Roberts of Kandahar, approaching seventy, the hero of Afghanistan, five feet four inches tall, one hundred and twenty-three pounds in weight and blind in one eye. His chief-of-staff would be Lord Kitchener of Khartoum, and it was agreed that these two would really fight the Boers, while Good Old Buller could be left off to one side, wrestling with the Tugela River, which he had now failed twice to cross.

To compound his problems, the War Office had given him as second in command a general whom he positively detested and to whom he preferred not to speak. For Sir Charles Warren, nearing sixty, this would have to be his last command, and unless he performed with some brilliance, he could hope for no further honors, which probably did not worry him, for he had other loves, especially archaeology and the secrets of Jerusalem. He had also made an abortive run for Parliament and a more successful one for head of the London constabulary, a post he held for three years, losing it when he failed to uncover the mystery of the century: the identity of Jack the Ripper. Quietly he moved back to the army, and when war broke out he reminded everyone that he had seen much service in South Africa, had helped solve the ticklish question of who owned the diamond mines, and 'knew a thing or two about the Boers.'

Warren despised Buller, holding him to be an ass, but it was nevertheless essential that he keep close to the old general because Warren carried in his pocket a most dangerous piece of paper: it was called 'a Dormant Commission,' and it stated that if anything should happen to Buller, or if he should fall apart, as seemed likely, Warren was to assume command. Consequently, it was in Warren's interest to see that Buller did fail.

Relieved of responsibility for the other fronts in South Africa, General Buller was free to direct all his attention to the Tugela River, and as he rode back and forth along its southern shore, pondering how best to reach the northern, he began to see that his previous attempts had been doomed because he had been heading straight for Ladysmith along roads which had to be heavily defended. What he would do would be to dash far to the west, outflank the Boers, and swing into Ladysmith in a leftward charge. With Warren's troops he again had more than twenty thousand first-class men to face a Boer force of less than eight thousand. But he had Sir Charles Warren breathing down his neck, and he still had to cross the Tugela.

A flanking movement like this required speed and deception; unfortunately, Buller surrendered both those advantages by entrusting the most important part of the campaign to the 'ex-policeman,' as he contemptuously called Warren. Sending the difficult and unreliable Warren off to the left, he moved his own sybaritic tent some twenty miles upstream, and when his feather bed and iron bathtub were in position, he astonished Saltwood and his other aides by scouting the opposite shore with his French telescope.

He did this by lying flat on his back and propping his scope on his enormous belly and toes, moving it slowly through whatever arc his position permitted, and shouting his observations to Saltwood. By now, newspapers throughout the world knew that 'General Buller is once more thinking about crossing the Tugela.'

What he saw when he lay prostrate looking through his toes were three hills perched menacingly behind the north shore of the Tugela: Hill One, nearest at hand; Hill Two in the middle; Hill Three well to the west. The plan was for Warren to move far west of Hill Three and cut the Boer line, if he ever got his land-armada across the river, with his innumerable wagons and fifteen thousand trek-oxen; this incredible train was fifteen miles long and required two days to pass a spot, even when moving sharply. Buller would then make a drive for Hill One and join up with Warren, opening the pathway to Ladysmith. A tremendous amount of staff work was done to prepare the English forces for these carefully planned moves.

At Warren's crossing point, four huge wood-fueled steam tractors had been maneuvered into position, and as they huffed and puffed, belching fire, wagons were pulled across small crevices while engineers sought low spots in the river at which pontoon bridges might be built. They isolated three such spots, and their officers chose each one in turn, abandoning it as soon as any difficulty arose. The delay was intolerable.

Saltwood had found it a memorable experience to watch these two elderly generals, Buller and Warren, go about their planning of this crucial battle, for it became apparent that in their extreme jealousy, neither was backing up the other, and each was holding his choice cards tight to his chest without permitting his colleague to see them. One of Buller's most ambitious young assistants told Frank, 'We're going to witness three great battles. Us against the Boers. Buller against Warren. And Warren against Buller.'

'Dreadful way to run a war.'

'Ah, but the last two battles will be well matched, because our two generals are of equal intelligence, somewhat higher than a mule but markedly lower than a good bird dog.'

'Buller told me yesterday we'd be ready to strike tomorrow.'

'It won't happen. General Warren has this curious fixation that armies should be allowed to get into position and face each other for three or four days. Get the feel of contest.'

'We've been trying to get the feel of it for two months now,' Frank said. 'Those poor devils in Ladysmith.'

'They've nothing to worry about. Buller heliographed them again yesterday that he'd be there within five days.'

'Any chance?' Frank asked.

'If Warren punches west through the Boer line, I'm sure we can make it. But if he swings over to Hill Two in the middle, we'll be in deep trouble.'

'Would he do such a thing?'

'With these two generals, anything can happen.'

'Tonight we should pray,' Saltwood said, and he did.

It did not help. For days Warren plodded along until Buller, who had watched helplessly since giving the man an independent command, could no longer contain his anger. Riding over to Warren's headquarters, he said gruffly, 'For God's sake, move!'

'There are thousands of Boers out there waiting.'

'There were only ten hundred when you started.'

'I've decided to go for Hill Two,' Warren said.

The young officer had been correct in his fears that these two generals would dissipate their great opportunity: the 'ex-policeman' was swinging to his right to club the Boers on Spion Kop. With incomplete orders to the troops involved, the vast plans were scrapped and whole battalions were ordered to march right when they had planned to go left. What seemed incredible then, and even more so now, they were to attack a sizable hill that no one had scouted and for which only the roughest maps existed. This error could easily have been corrected had General Buller authorized his balloonist to go aloft, for the man was a skilled observer and from twelve hundred feet, his optimum operating level, could have informed the generals of exactly what lay ahead. Buller did not hold with balloons and other such nonsense, so this invaluable tool was not used; the troops would march up Spion Kop with no concept of where they were going or what they might face when they got there.

What was worse—much worse, as it turned out—General Warren kept his headquarters far to the west, which would have been reasonable had the drive continued in that direction, while General Buller kept his far to the east, removed from everything. When Major Saltwood protested this wide separation of the two headquarters—seven miles with crude communications—Buller growled through his enormous mustache, 'It's his show. He's in charge of the troops.'

'But you're the commander-in-chief, sir.'

'Never meddle with another man's fight.'

'But it's your battle, sir.'

'It's Warren's day. He's got the finest English troops to win the battle.'

Frank wanted to cry, 'Then God save the empire.' But he did not. He rode the seven miles to General Warren's headquarters, where he arrived in time to witness an incomprehensible performance.

Warren had in his command a brilliant, headstrong cavalry leader named Lord Dundonald, a charismatic type whom the older generals distrusted, and when this fiery chap, leading fifteen hundred of the finest mounted troops, was set loose on the left flank, he launched a glorious charge which quite neutralized Hill Three and gained access to an unpatrolled road along which Warren's infantry could advance directly into Ladysmith. By this daring and gallant maneuver he opened the way to an English victory, and the younger officers were cheering when Frank reached their headquarters: 'Dundonald's done it! He said he would.'

But then Warren sprang into action. Gray with fury, he stormed into the room where the younger men were cheering and cried, 'Bring that damned fool back here. We need cavalry to protect our oxen. Let him keep a few men on his damned road, but I want the rest back here in camp!' and on the spot he deputized Major Saltwood and two others to ride posthaste after the cavalry and bring them back. 'Damned young fellows! Put them on a horse, they think they know everything.'

Saltwood, not being a member of General Warren's force, was not afraid to confront him: 'Sir, I believe Lord Dundonald should be allowed to hold the road, and we should rush men to ensure he keeps it.'

'He'll come back here, and he'll obey my orders. My God, I'll take his horsemen away from him. Insubordination.'

So Frank Saltwood had the miserable task of riding west to inform the gallant young Lord Dundonald that he was to pull back the bulk of his men. On this day Dundonald had beaten off a series of Boer patrols in savage encounters; he had won a notable victory; but now he must retreat. The burghers would win this segment of the battle without having fired a shot!

On the night of 23 January 1900 General Warren sent his men up the south face of Spion Kop; they were led by a major-general, but he was fifty-five years old, had weak legs and did not take easily to steep places, so that he had to be shoved up them by his troops. Poor man, he was soon dying from a shell fragment.

What ensued must have been orchestrated by some mad genius, because both Warren and Buller, from their separate headquarters, appointed different replacements to the vacant major-general's slot. Unfortunately, communications collapsed and no one knew who was in charge. There were, as a consequence, two British officers conducting the fight, each unaware of the other and assuming that he was in supreme command.

Two additional officers were sent in to take charge, one by Buller, one by Warren, and once again each assumed that he was in sole command. One way or another, the hill now contained four commanders leading nineteen hundred of the empire's finest, while another eighteen thousand were kept in reserve; they would be sorely needed as the terrible struggle developed, but no one would command them to march.

In grandeur General Buller sat in his tent like a sulking Achilles, out of contact with the progress of the battle and doing nothing to sort out the mess his 'ex-policeman' was getting his men into. 'It's Warren's fight,' he insisted when Saltwood galloped back from the other general's camp, begging for clarifications.

On the other hand, Buller was not loath to intervene whenever a particularly brilliant idea occurred to him, and he issued commands that would have bewildered generals as quick-minded as Hannibal and Napoleon. As for Warren, he was a fool who moved at a snail's pace, fighting a night battle on a hill he did not comprehend. Not once did he move to Spion Kop; not once did he try to see for himself the dreadful slaughter occurring there.

He issued some twenty crucial orders, half to one of his commanders on the hill, half to others battling toward it. A German observer watching this amazing battle said, 'The English army is composed of ordinary soldiers who are lions of bravery led by officers who are asses of stupidity.' And he said this before the two generals had an opportunity to display their true talents.

General de Groot chafed. Much against his counsel, his truncated commando was being held in reserve behind Spion Kop. 'We'll throw you in at the crucial moment,' he was told, but two more of his men, seeking action, had slipped away.

The scene behind the hill was extraordinary. Row after row of sleek Boer ponies stood with their halters tied to trees or rocks while their masters fought on foot up the steep hill. Some five hundred wagons huddled at a distance, field ambulances and Red Cross units outspanned among them, their oxen peacefully grazing. Near them waited the wives who had accompanied their husbands, and in one tent Sybilla de Groot tended such men as were dragged to her impromptu hospital ward. Other women helped their servants do the cooking, and from time to time everyone would stop to listen to the raging battle which was taking place less than a quarter of a mile from where they worked.

When, toward noon, General de Groot walked back through the dust to talk with his wife, the women learned that whereas the English troops had captured the top of the hill, they had placed their trench so poorly that the Boers had a good chance of taking it away from them. 'Will there be many dead?' Sybilla asked.

'A great many,' the old man said.

'Will you be going up?'

'Soon as they set us free.'

'Be careful, Paulus,' she said as he shuffled back to the hill.

It was men of the Carolina Commando, from the small town east of Venloo, who won the honors for bravery this day. They were led by Commandant Henrik Prinsloo and a short, stocky veldkornet named Christoffel Steyn, almost as thick through the belly as he was tall; when Steyn ran forward, rolling from side to side, men muttered, 'If he can do it, I can do it.' What he did was run straight through a heavy barrage to the top of Hill Three, a kopje opposite the summit of Spion Kop, where he positioned his men behind rocks so that they could fire directly into the side openings of the English trenches. This fat fellow, who had never fought before, could not believe that the highly trained English officers opposing him could have allowed him to occupy this fatal hill, but he accepted his luck and ordered his men to increase their fire into the exposed English ranks.

Whole trenches were wiped out, not a single man surviving, and of ten dead soldiers, nine had been shot not through the front of their bodies, but through the side of the head. Christoffel Steyn's men had made the difference, but they did so from a hill they should never have been able to occupy for as long as they did.

Why the ragged line of burghers was permitted to hold the strategic kopje was one of the disgraceful incidents of this battle. While eighteen thousand crack troops still remained in reserve, powerless to aid their brothers dying in such numbers on Spion Kop, a commander of the King's Royal Rifles, on his own initiative, dispatched his two finest battalions, ordering them to rush another hill opposite to the one held by Steyn. If they were successful, they could drive Steyn out with gunfire, and thus save the men on Spion Kop.

It was an impossible ascent, almost straight up, in heat of day, with Boers firing down at them from above, but these brave men, goaded by their energetic officers, somehow made it to the top, drew much of the fire away from their exposed comrades, and began to batter the Carolina burghers. It was a triumph of courage and grit, giving the English their first victory of the day.

Saltwood, witnessing the triumph, hastened to inform General Buller, but when this confused leader heard that a commander of troops had acted on his own, and had, furthermore, split his men into two groups, he fell into a fury and began to heckle his commander. At this moment a message reached Buller, warning that the Boers were in such firm control that if the King's Royal Rifles tried to cross over to Spion Kop, they would be annihilated.

'Bring them back down!' Buller fumed.

'Sir!' Saltwood objected. 'They've performed a miracle. Let them stay.'

'They should never have been split into groups.'

The commander, seeing his general in such confusion, lost all confidence in the daring action and signaled his men to climb down: 'Get off the hill! Come back immediately!' At first the men refused to believe that such a stupid order could have been issued, and one colonel refused to obey it. 'Damn them all,' he shouted, whereupon a Boer bullet struck him below the heart, killing him instantly. The retreat began.

Night fell as the beleaguered soldiers on Spion Kop watched with dismay as the King's Royal Rifles abandoned the neighboring hill. For a few more hours the officers on Spion Kop held their positions, but finally one of the finest commanders signaled a retreat. This heroic man, Colonel Thorneycroft, had been breveted general in the midst of the battle; he weighed about twenty stone—two hundred and eighty pounds—most of it hard muscle, and he was afraid of nothing. Only his courage had kept the trenches in English hands, despite the awful slaughter, but now he lost his nerve.

He led his brave men down the hill, conceding defeat, just as one of the other commanders was climbing up with fresh troops, hoping for victory. They passed in silence.

When the new commander reached the crest of Spion Kop, in darkness, he found an amazing situation: the Boers, who had faced tremendous fire that day, had decided, half an hour before General Thorneycroft began to evacuate troops down the hill, that Spion Kop could not be taken. The constant pressure of the English gunners had been more than even these Boers could absorb, and they had deserted the hill. They knew they were defeated.

In other words, two heroic armies who had fought as bravely as men could fight, had decided within fifteen minutes of each other that the day was lost. Their two retreats occupied the same moments. After deaths innumerable, Spion Kop was deserted.

The Englishman climbing up as Thorneycroft went down was the first to discover this; he was another of the four in command that tangled day, and now he had a chance to save the day for the English. All he had to do was rush back down the hill, signal his superior, General Warren, and convince him to send more troops scurrying back to the summit. Full victory rested in the hands of the English if only this officer could contact General Warren.

This could not be done. The officer framed an excellent message, calling for quick reinforcements to occupy the abandoned hill and explaining how victory was assured, but when he summoned the signalman and told him to use his night lantern to flash the good word to General Warren's head-quarters, the man said, 'I have no paraffin.'

'Try the wick. It may burn. Even for one minute.'

The signalman lit his wick. It did not even sputter. For want of a thimbleful of kerosene, the fateful message was not sent. The Battle of Spion Kop was lost.

While those futile efforts were being made to get English soldiers back onto Spion Kop, on the northern side of the hill a few of the defeated Boers consulted at two in the morning concerning their fate, and as an occasional rifle shot echoed from some distant place where soldiers were nervous, they whispered in the darkness, 'General de Groot, what did you think of the battle? Could we have won?'

'I wasn't allowed in the battle. They never called for our reserve.'

'Our losses were heavy, General. But not like the English. Did you hear about the Carolina Commando? They had a clear shot, right down the English trenches. They killed everybody.'

It was another young fellow, only a boy, really, who asked the question that saved the day for the Boers: 'I was on the eastern hill when the English crawled up and took it. Why did they go back down?'

In the darkness General de Groot asked, 'You saw them go down?'

'Yes. They were very brave. One officer . . .'

'But they went back down?'

'Yes, they drove us off the hill. We lost sixteen, seventeen men. Jack Kloppers standing beside me. Right through the forehead.'

De Groot took the lad by his shoulders, pulling him into the flickering light of a small fire. 'You say they held the hill, then abandoned it?'

'Yes. Yes. I covered Jack Kloppers with a blanket and I went back to the summit. They went down and we didn't even fire at them.'

For some minutes General de Groot stood in silence, looking up at Spion Kop. Finally he said in a very low voice, 'Son, I think you and I should go back up that hill. I think that maybe God has been holding me in reserve for this moment.' He asked for volunteers, and Jakob van Doorn, of course, stepped forward.

So the three tired Boers, at two-thirty on that dark, forlorn morning, set out to climb the hill where so many had died. In front, walking faster than the others, was Paulus de Groot in top hat and frock coat. Behind him came the lad who had occasioned this expedition, and behind, puffing heavily, came Jakob van Doorn, who had been quite content to have his commando held in reserve: death terrified him.

They climbed slowly, for there was no moon, and from time to time they trod on the face of some fallen comrade. When they approached the crest, where the fighting had been most hazardous, they stepped on many bodies, and then the old general, his hat still in place, rose upon the horizon in a position which would have been fatal had English troops been on the hill. Slowly the other two joined him, and like scouts reconnoitering some dismal field of death, they moved forward, coming to the trench where the English lads lay stacked, bullets through the sides of their heads, and all the way to the other edge of the plateau, where they could look down upon the silent camp of the enemy.

Running back to the center of the silent battlefield, where he assured himself that this miracle had taken place, Paulus de Groot removed his hat, placed it over his heart, and kneeled in the bloody dust: 'Almighty God of the Boers, You have brought us victory, and we didn't know it. Almighty God of the Boers . . . dear faithful God of the Boers . . .'

The sky was brightening when he straightened up and walked to the edge of the hill to alert his comrades below: 'Boers! Boers!'

In their bivouac the commandos had watched as sun began to break, uncertain as to what they might have to face this day from that bloody embattled mount.

An incredible sight greeted them. On the summit, outlined against the sky, stood an old man, the victor of Majuba nineteen years before, waving his top hat triumphantly. General Paulus de Groot had captured Spion Kop.

There had been at the hill that twenty-fourth day of January 1900 three young men of radically different character; no one of the three saw the other two, but each would live to play an outstanding role in the future history of his particular country.

The oldest was a Boer officer, only thirty-seven, on whom fell the burden of rallying his troops when all seemed lost and sustaining them when the leadership of the older generals proved defective. Had some young English colonel of comparable ability managed to insert himself in place of his own wavering and slow-witted generals, that side would probably have won this crucial battle; fortune dictated that it would be the Boers who would act intelligently. This splendid military genius was Louis Botha, who would become the first Boer prime minister of the new nation that would emerge from this battle. At Spion Kop young Botha, who ended the day in overall command, became convinced that Boer and Englishman would do better if they worked together. In the rage of battle he knew that this internecine warfare was senseless, and that unless the two white races coalesced in their common interests and humanity, South Africa must be torn apart. He became the great conciliator, the prudent counselor, the head of state, and few names in the history of his country would stand higher.

The youngest of the men was a rowdy newspaperman whom nobody could discipline. Reporter for a London paper, he wrote penetrating, irreverent accounts of men like Warren, so that proper military men shuddered when he approached. He was then tallish and slim, and spoke with a lisp that caused merriment among the sturdier types. He had not done well in school, had avoided university altogether, and was thought of as pretty much a freak. Because of carelessness, he had already been captured once by the Boers but had escaped through sheer brazenness. There was a kind of price on his head, not to be taken seriously, perhaps, but had he been captured at Spion Kop, things might have been rather sticky. In spite of this, he climbed three times to the crest of the hill, where he was revolted by the confusion and inefficiency. He was Winston Churchill, twenty-five years old, already the author of several fine books and desperately hungry to get into Parliament. A brief fourteen years after this day on Spion Kop, young Churchill would find himself in the middle of a much greater war, and in the war cabinet, and in charge of naval operations. At Gallipoli he would interfere in military matters so disgracefully that he would ensure the tragic defeat of a major English operation, so that his name became synonymous with civilian incompetence. On Spion Kop that day he had learned a lesson from defeat, for when the battle was dismally lost, General Buller at last took complete charge, and in rallying his men he was superb, a stubborn man with iron courage who stared into the face of catastrophe and assured his troops: 'We shall win this war.' And his men were willing to support him. Of Buller, Churchill wrote: 'It's the love and admiration of Tommy Atkins that fortifies him.' In 1941 this lesson in bulldog tenacity would lead Winston Churchill to immortality.

The third young man was a curious type; scrawny, short, spindly-legged, very dark of countenance, with even darker hair, he served that day as an ambulance runner. If Louis Botha had seen him, he would have ignored him as an unwelcomed immigrant; had Winston Churchill seen him foraging among the dead to ascertain if even one man still survived, he would have dismissed him as inconsequential. Born in India, he had surveyed that impoverished land and decided that it held no promise for young lawyers, so he had eagerly emigrated to South Africa, where he fully intended to spend the remainder of his life. His name was Mohandas Karamchand Gandhi, volunteer stretcher bearer to the English forces. Aware that the ruling castes, Boer and Briton, held all Indians in disdain, he had persuaded his fellow Hindus in Durban to volunteer for the war's most dangerous service to prove their worth; on this day he had escaped death a score of times, and two of his associates had been killed. On Spion Kop, Mohandas Gandhi learned that warfare was unutterably stupid, that it solved no problems, and that when the dead were collected and the medals distributed, the warring parties still faced their insoluble problems. How much better had they avoided violent discourse and taken resort to peaceful non-resistance.

There was a fourth man on Spion Kop that day, or rather that night, but no one paid him any attention, and he did not rise in later years to lead his nation, but on this encrusted battlefield he did learn the first and only of his great lessons. When General de Groot, at two-thirty in the morning of the day following the battle, climbed back up Spion Kop, there were two men with him, the young fellow who alerted the move and Jakob van Doorn, his constant companion. There was a fourth man, but since he was black he didn't count. He was Micah Nxumalo, who would never be far from the old general in the days of this war. He did not have to participate, and he had no gun to defend himself; he merely tagged along because he loved the old general and had served him in various capacities. He could tend horses, scavenge for food, help the women, serve as scout when conditions grew tense, and tend the sick commandos. On Spion Kop, Micah Nxumalo began to develop a great truth which he would later quietly pass along to his people. As he moved through that fiery day, seeing the troops who seemed so numerous, he noticed that taken altogether, they numbered far fewer than his Zulu tribe, or the Xhosa, or the Swazi, or the Basuto, or the Bechuana, or the Matabele. He saw that the English and the Boers were playing tremendous games, but that when the battles were finished they would be brothers, a few white men set down amidst a vast congregation of blacks: When the games are ended and the mighty guns are silenced, the real struggle will begin, and it will not be Englishman against Boer. It will be white man against black, and in the end we shall triumph.

For the duration of the present episode Nxumalo would continue with the Boers; they were his proven friends; and he hoped they would win this time. But he was struck by the fact that an equal number of blacks served with the English, hoping, no doubt, that they would win.

When the disaster of Spion Kop was ended, with the land-armada once again south of the Tugela, and the fifteen thousand trek-oxen pulling the massive wagons back to where they started, Frank Saltwood had to evaluate the performance, which he had witnessed mainly at Buller's elbow: He had rotten luck. Having that Warren thrust upon him. What a dunderhead! The battle could have been won four different ways, and he rejected them all. But then the question arose: I wonder why Buller didn't discharge him? Buller was in command.

The more he thought about this the more he realized that as a South African not reared in the English military tradition, he could not appreciate the reticence one general would have in ever bringing criticism upon another: They're a fraternity of aging warriors, each supporting the other, each attentive to the traditions of the service. Losing a battle is far less important than losing relative position in the hierarchy.

But even Saltwood had to admit that not all the blame could be thrown on Warren; Buller, too, had participated in the gross errors: He gave Warren command, then intervened a score of times. After all, it was my man Buller who heckled the commander of the King's Royal Rifles until those brave men were ordered to retreat.

When he had lined up in his mind all the pros and cons, one fact persisted: Buller's foot soldiers consider him the best general they ever served under. I've asked a score of them. Always the same answer: 'I'd go anywhere with Old Buller. He looks after his men.' And now Saltwood realized that many of the horrendous decisions he saw Buller make were done to preserve lives. He might drink too much Trianon sparkling, and as one correspondent wrote, he did eat gargantuan meals; but where human life was concerned, he was Spartan. 'Train them hard,' he had told Saltwood. 'Drive them hard. But bring them back in good order.' When Frank asked about this, the old man said, 'Most important fact of war? Keep your army in existence. Lose the battle, but keep your eye on winning the war.'

But everyone in Buller's command had to be aware of the attacks being made upon their general by the experts in Europe. London newspapers began calling him 'The Ferryman of the Tugela.' In Parliament he was known as 'Sir Reverse Buller.' After the last debacle he humphed and mumbled, 'By gad, they're splendid troops. Retreated without losing one gun carriage.' To which Saltwood said, 'They should do it well, sir. They've had plenty of rehearsal.' General Buller looked at him with his tiny pinched eyes and laughed. 'Yes, yes. What I mean, yes. They are great troops.'

He sent another smashing heliogram to the besieged heroes at Ladysmith, assuring them that he would rescue them within five days, and with fortitude he crossed the Tugela yet again, only to get a shocking bloody nose which sent him reeling back across that pitiful stream once more. In Ladysmith the rations were diminishing, and at the end of twelve weeks Buller was no closer to the town than when he started. Still he had the gall to heliograph yet again that he would succor the town at any moment now.

In view of the growing criticism, Saltwood sometimes wondered why the British authorities allowed him to retain command. There was one reason, tragic and accidental. In Buller's first attempt to cross the Tugela, that masterpiece of ineptitude, a gallant young officer volunteered to rescue some heavy guns that were about to be lost to the Boers. He was killed, and he happened to be the son of Lord Roberts, who would shortly become Buller's superior. Now, lest Roberts appear vengeful over a death for which Buller was in no way responsible, he remained silent, when otherwise he would have recommended his removal.

A more subtle explanation was given to some French and German observers one night by a young English officer: 'The War Office wants generals like Buller. They're never comfortable with uncertain types like Kitchener and Allenby. Buller is steady, which they like, and not too clever, which they prefer. As a young man he obeyed orders and plunged ahead. You should have seen him, they tell me, wading into Egyptians. Very forceful. They like it that he can't speak clearly, that he harrumphs all over the place. That's how a proper general should behave. Look at Raglan and Cardigan at Balaklava.'

'But why in God's name don't they dismiss him when his deficiencies become known?' the German asked.

'Ah! That's why we're English. That's why you'll never understand us. Who appointed Buller? The establishment. The older generals. The older politicians. Probably some of the archbishops had a hand, if the truth were known. They like him. They trust him. He's one of them. Good family, you know.'

'But he's destroying the army,' the Frenchman protested.

'The army! What's the army? The important thing is that men like Buller be protected. He is England, not some damn-fool lieutenant who got his legs blown off.'

'In Germany he wouldn't last a week.'

'In England he'll last forever.'

'You speak as if you love the old fool.'

'I do,' the young man confessed. 'He's a doddering ass, and I love him. Because most of the people at home I love are just like him, and somehow they always do the right thing. You watch, when the decisive battle of this war is fought, Buller will be there, pushing his way ahead, just as he did with the Egyptians.'

'I wish to God he were forty years younger,' the German said.

'Why?'

'Because when our war against England comes, and it will, I would like him to be in command.'

'He will be,' the young man said. 'Under a different name. And beware of him.'

As he spoke, he tacked onto the bulletin board a notice from Lord Roberts on the other front; it referred to some of his associate officers in the South African war: Douglas Haig, John French, Julian Byng, Edmund Allenby, Ian Hamilton. They would be the General Bullers whom the Germans would have to face.

With these confused judgments rattling in his head, Major Saltwood watched with pride as General Buller finally figured a way to cross the Tugela, and that night he wrote to Maud, who was busy organizing charities for the wives of Cape men serving with the English forces:

> It was damned brilliant, really. Old Buller moved his heavy guns, we get them from the navy, you know, put them on his flank and laid down a hellish barrage, right ahead of our advancing troops. Like a fiery broom he swept away the Boers. So at least we're across this damned river, but I cannot bring my pen to say, 'We'll lift the siege of Ladysmith in five days.' We've said that too many times before. But soon we shall be there.

On 28 February 1900, ninety-five days after he assigned himself the task of relieving Ladysmith, the siege was lifted. Three memorable incidents marked the stirring occasion.

Lord Dundonald, always eager for acclaim, dispatched a unit of his cavalry to be first into town. He followed, and in his company was Winston Churchill, almost a full day ahead of General Buller.

Later, when the general's more pompous entrance was made, he got his maps mixed up and marched to the wrong gate; the heroic defenders, military and civil, were waiting on the opposite side of town, and when it was pointed out to him that since he and his men were fresh, and on well-rested horses, it might be gracious if he rode to the other side, he said, 'I enter here,' and the multitude had to hurry across town to greet him.

And finally, when the defeated Boers were in retreat, some of the cavalrymen saw a chance to chase and destroy. When they started from the town, some of the men who had withstood the siege wanted to join, but could not: 'We have no horses. We ate them.'

'Where are those cavalrymen going?' Buller asked Saltwood.

'Pursuing the enemy.'

'Pursue an enemy who's been honorably defeated? Good God, call our men back. Give the poor devils decent time to lick their wounds.'

'Sir, we've been chasing those damned Boers for months. This is our chance to eliminate them.'

From beneath his tight little hat General Buller stared at his South African aide. 'Sir, you have none of the instincts of a gentleman.' When Frank tried to protest, Buller put his heavy arm about his shoulder. 'Son, if we lose honor in warfare, we lose everything.' And he canceled the pursuit.

General de Groot was bewildered. For more than four months his commando had been abused and misused, and he could do nothing about it. Instead of riding hard and fast in a strike-and-hide tactic, at which his horsemen would have excelled, he had been held in rein and used in assault efforts. It occurred to him, as he sat with Sybilla after the defeat at Lady-smith, that almost never in these four months had his pony been at a gallop, and rarely a trot.

'You know, Sybilla, we're losing men all the time. Our burghers won't tolerate this sort of thing.'

'They'll come back, when your kind of fighting begins.'

'You can't have a commando with nine men.'

Then shocking news from the western front reminded them of the harsh possibilities of this war: General Cronje, an obstinate man who believed that the best defense against English arms was a laager, had surrendered.

'What could he have been thinking of?' De Groot asked Jakob. 'With four thousand men, you and I could take Durban.'

'It's a different war over there. General Roberts is in a hurry. He's no Buller.'

This doleful news, coinciding with Ladysmith, generated a vast depres-sion among the retreating Boers, so that the Venloo Commando was re-duced to one hundred and twenty, and when the time came to hand out assignments, those in charge looked at De Groot with pained tolerance: 'What can you do, Paulus, with so few?'

'We can attack the cavalry installation,' he replied with that bitter animosity he held for the English lancers.

'They'd slaughter you!'

'We wouldn't take them head-on.' He was so persuasive that permission was granted for what could only be a suicide attempt, except that he had no intention of allowing it to become so.

He would take his men, including, of course, Van Doorn, and they would move quietly across the Orange Free State to where Generals Rob-erts and Kitchener held their troops after their big victory over Cronje, and they would ride daringly close to the cavalry cantonment, trusting the natural confusion of a large assembly of horses to mask their approach. They would then dismount, wait till three in the morning, when attention was always at a minimum, sweep in, disrupt the horses, and fight any personnel that might be afoot. In the confusion they would run to their ponies and be off due north, in a direction which the English would not anticipate, because such a move would carry them directly into English lines. De Groot had a plan for what would follow.

'Sounds possible,' Van Doorn said.

'You wouldn't want a force much bigger than ours,' De Groot said enthusiastically.

'We'll need expert scouting.'

'I've thought of that. We've got to know exactly where the English troops are. That's where Micah comes in.'

Micah proved himself a good scout, always moving with caution. One morning he haltered his pony far beyond English lines while he slipped around sentries, entering boldly the small town upon which the British were centered. Moving freely, he estimated the size and character of the forces, making shrewd guesses as to the length of time they expected to remain in this favorable location.

He stayed in town two days, losing himself within the black population, several of whom guessed his identity; they did not betray him because they were indifferent as to which side won, and if he was to be well rewarded for his mission, they were pleased.

When he regained his pony, satisfied that he knew fairly well the disposition of the army men, he rode south and toward the west to where the cavalry were billeted, and now he faced a much more difficult problem. Again tying his pony at a distant spot, he set out on foot to approach the camp, but this time there was no small town into which he could infiltrate, masking himself among the blacks. He had to move from hillock to hillock, running always the risk that a sortie from the barracks would sweep out across the veld on some practice mission and find him spying upon them.

So he moved with extreme caution until he came within some two hundred yards of the lines where the mounts, big Argentinian horses, were tied. There were more than he had ever seen before, a massive command. The Boers are in trouble, he thought as he studied the fall of the ground, but General de Groot knows what he's doing.

He had doubts about his own wisdom when a contingent of young men left their tents, sauntered over to their horses, and casually mounted. After tightening straps, they waited for the arrival of their officer, who came at last on a striking red horse much larger than the others. What a fine animal, Micah thought as he watched what had to be a development of considerable danger.

'Heh!' he heard the young officer cry, and the forty-six troops lined up behind him. Using his bare right hand instead of the saber which he kept at his side, he indicated the direction his sortie was to make, and Micah saw with dismay that it would be headed in his general direction. He flattened himself between two rocks that provided some cover.

A bugle sounded and the men came forth. They rode to within thirty yards of where he hid, not one of them looking right or left; since this was a practice session, they felt no need to stay alert, but suddenly they stopped, looked in his direction, and burst into laughter. For one awful moment he thought they were preparing to lance him as a fixed target, but then he heard at some distance a slight scratching sound. Three little meerkats had come out of their burrows to look at the horsemen, and when one of the men made a lunge at them, they scampered. One of the men shouted, 'Bravo, Simmons. Stick three little Boers like that and there'll be a medal in it for you.'

When they continued their canter they headed right into the area where Micah had left his pony, and he expected at any moment to hear a 'Halloo!' There was no cry, and after a long while they galloped back to their camp. He breathed deeply when he saw that they had no pony with them.

Because of his careful scouting he was able to inform General de Groot precisely as to the nature of the two bodies of men: 'The soldiers will be there for many days. The cavalry horses stand at the edge of the veld, the men's tents behind them. They expect an attack from the other side, where the Boers are supposed to be.'

The Venloo Commando did not form a line as they set out on their mission; they straggled over the veld in positions from which each man could dash forward or retreat according to his own judgment. They were engaged in a perilous effort and knew that maximum mobility would be essential. Slowly they covered the neutral ground, then tensed as they approached the land that held the two English contingents. Finally they reached a spot some six hundred yards from the cavalry camp, and here they dismounted.

'Guard the horses,' General de Groot told his blacks, and they were left behind; that is, all stayed with the horses except Micah Nxumalo, who crept forward with the commando to guide his general to where the enemy horses rested.

It was now dusk. Keeping low, they stooped and scurried from rock to rock across the veld, zigzagging their way till they were close upon the English encampment. They would hold these positions for at least six hours during this fine summer night, during which they must not talk or smoke. Insects attacked and there was a good deal of scratching, but in general the men remained silent.

Stars appeared, and the moon, and in the distance a hyena grumbled, then laughed. Familiar constellations climbed to their apex and began their leisurely descent, and over the camp silence reigned. At midnight some cavalrymen came out of a mess tent, stood talking for a while, and bade each other a good rest as they separated.

'Sssst,' De Groot signaled, and his six followers crept forward. They were on a mission which disturbed some of them, for the butchery they contemplated went against the grain of farmers, but a chain of recent defeats had impressed upon them that they were engaged in a struggle which would not end in truce; one side or the other was going to be totally defeated, and it had better not be the Boers, for the penalties they would pay in lost freedom and even the loss of their republics would be terrifying. They must do what had to be done.

So as they approached the encampment, De Groot touched those nearest him, saying nothing but indicating that he expected them to perform their tasks. Some of the men brushed his hand with theirs; others simply nodded in the darkness. When they were within ten yards of the horse corral, he leaped forward boldly and his men followed.

Three of them knocked down barriers and turned hundreds of horses loose. Others grabbed the bridles of seven big horses saddled for emergencies and led them outside. General de Groot and Jakob moved methodically to the line where the officers' choice mounts were kept and shot them methodically, one after another, killing them in most cases, immobilizing them permanently in others.

There was no panic, no hurry when bugles began to sound, only the piling of inflammables and the striking of matches. Before any English cavalryman could get to the stores, they were ablaze and dark figures were riding away. What infuriated the Englishmen as they rushed onto the scene, powerless to retaliate, for their horses were gone, was that in the light from leaping flames they could see Boers on horseback, galloping among the free horses and shooting them down.

'M' God!' one young officer cried. 'They're shooting the horses!' In rage he began firing at the retreating Boers, and although everyone knew that the invaders could not be reached, the entire cavalry contingent blazed away at them, firing and cursing as they watched their great steeds go down. When dawn came, both the Englishmen and the Boers realized that the remainder of this war was going to be excessively ugly.

'An inhuman act,' General Kitchener cried when he saw the dead horses. 'No civilized man would do such a thing.'

He had no right to be sensitive about what civilized men would do or not do; in the fiery battle that had led to the surrender of General Cronje and his four thousand Boers, a critical moment had come when the English line seemed to be wavering. It could be stabilized only by some drastic action which would command the attention and respect of all. Kitchener had seen the solution.

'Cavalry, charge up the center, and even if you do not reach the Boer laager, blaze away at them.'

'Sir,' the Scottish commander of the horsemen protested, 'that would be suicidal.'

Kitchener stiffened. He knew that by ordinary standards the order was insane, but this vast battle was not ordinary. 'I command you to charge the laager.'

The Scotsman saluted briskly. 'Very well, sir.' He realized that if he disobeyed, he would be court-martialed and perhaps shot, but he also knew that if he obeyed, two hundred of his best men would be slain. He solved the problem in a heroic way. Turning to the brigade, he said, 'Retire twenty paces and regroup.' To his four officers he said, 'Return to camp and fetch us more ammunition.' When all were safely behind him, he turned to face the distant enemy and started riding slowly toward the laager, as ordered.

On and on he came, far ahead of his men, riding on a tall white horse that stepped forward with stately caution. Suddenly he spurred his horse and ranged forward, closing upon the enemy guns, well hidden behind bulwarks, and it became apparent to both the English and the Boers what he was doing. He was obeying orders. He had been told to charge, and he was about to charge, but his obedience did not mean that he had to carry his men to their death. There was a hush, and then he whipped out his sword, tilting it at the proper angle, and as his handsome animal leaped forward he bellowed, 'Charge!'

Boers, watching him gallop into the muzzle of their guns, could not bring themselves to fire, but one burgher who had read Sir Walter Scott understood the traditions of chivalry and knew that from such a charge there would be no retreat, nor any place in English life after such insubordination. 'Fire!' this man shouted, but no one responded. 'Fire,' he cried again, 'we must help him,' but once more there was awed silence. But when the rider was almost to the guns, the burghers opened fire at him, and he fell dead.

For General Kitchener to order a Scottish officer and his men to certain death was warfare, and as a consequence of such discipline, he had been enabled to destroy General Cronje; but for Paulus de Groot to kill two hundred Argentine horses was, in Kitchener's words: 'A show of barbarism, an inhuman act of madness outside the rules of civilized warfare.'

From now on, the war would be marked by many inhuman acts, but it would depend upon which side was speaking as to where the inhumanity lay. The English attitude was well summarized by General Kitchener: 'Damnit all, stands to reason, what I mean. Why don't they dress in khaki,

like a proper army, so you can see them, and get down off those damned
ponies and fight like men? What's all this hitting a man and then running
away—are they cowards, or what? The damned Wogs fought better than
these fellows. The lot of them need a proper hiding.'

General Roberts, a more temperate man, objected to three things about
the Boers: 'They don't obey their commanders, so it's impossible to make
a truce with them. They lack discipline, so you never know what they're
apt to do next. And I don't like to bring this up, but they are careless, very
careless indeed about the use of the white flag.' When asked by a correspondent from a Paris newspaper what he meant by this, he sought to avoid
controversy and remained silent, but when others pressed him, with their
pencils ready, he said bluntly, 'They approach you with the flag. Lull you.
Then drop it and are back in the battle.'

'Certainly not, sir.'

'I saw it with my own eyes. I've had various reports. Couldn't believe
them. After all, these are decent human beings. But at the Battle of Driefon-
tein, I watched as they did it.'

What Kitchener objected to, and most strenuously, was the Boer habit
of ransacking the bodies of dead English soldiers and appropriating articles
of needed clothing: 'The ghouls appear in our khaki. At fifty paces can't tell
they're enemy. That's breaking the rules of civilized warfare.'

The English leaders made a great fuss over these rules of civilized
warfare; they felt that an enemy should behave much like the barefoot
Indians and Egyptians: stand in line with their rusty guns; wait as the
phalanx of red-coated battalions marched at them; fire; run when the cavalry charged; surrender and go back to their land when the war was declared over. It was disturbing to think that men of European heritage would
fight the way the Boers did, with trickery, speed, and the nasty habit of
dissolving back into the landscape instead of surrendering. And the fact that
these Boers were well supplied with the best German Mausers and French
Martini-Henri rifles was distressing.

But the Boers, too, had their grievances. Like General de Groot, they
felt it to be inhuman and far beyond the principles of civilized warfare for
men to sit astride big horses—like those from the farms of America and the
Argentine—and to ride them in among the commandos, cutting and slashing as they came. Hundreds of Boers, who started with no more than sullen
resentment against the English, grew to detest them because of the cavalry
charges, and when De Groot and his men destroyed the Argentine horses
they applauded.

Even worse they deplored the English habit of firing their guns at two
hundred yards, and then a hundred, and then fifty, and finally charging in
with bayonets, a weapon the Boers never used. 'To come at a man with cold
steel,' De Groot said, 'that's inhuman.' Many an Englishman who should
have been captured and led away to safe imprisonment lost his life because
he fought with a bayonet, for Christian men did not do that.

Between the combatants a kind of chivalry did exist, based on real
respect: the English were redoubtable foes, willing to absorb tremendous
losses; the Boers were often willing to go up against unbelievable odds, and
many of the most unusual gestures of courtesy were extended by these rude
farmers. But on two points of difference they were adamant, and when

the English refused to concede on these, a deep bitterness was engendered, with each side actually flogging and shooting prisoners captured from the other.

The deepest difference, perhaps, concerned black troops; each side used African scouts, but increasingly those with the English turned up with arms, whereupon word would flash through the countryside: 'The English are arming the Kaffirs.' This was intolerable, for no matter how desperately the two white armies fought each other, in the backs of their minds the real enemy was the black man watching from the side.

English commanders were aware of Boer feelings on this point, but that did not prevent them from enlisting and arming Coloured units from the Cape, and for this the Boers would never forgive them.

Besides, for the English to use these Coloureds only deepened the Boers' resentment of the fact that so few Afrikaners from the Cape volunteered to help. Many still hoped for a massive rebellion against the English in the two colonies, Cape and Natal, but no more than thirteen thousand crossed over. What was especially galling, thousands of Cape citizens of Dutch ancestry joined men of English descent in colonial regiments which fought in British armies against the Boers. Many in the north would die hating their brothers in the south for this treachery.

The other Boer grievance was less complex. Because of their stern religiosity, they tried to avoid any activity on Sundays, and once during a protracted engagement, when General de Groot had his men at Sunday prayer, their guns silent, one of the Venloo men rushed into the service, shouting, 'They're playing cricket!'

De Groot stalked to a vantage point and looked through his glass at the green field upon which the English officers were having a merry game. He was appalled at this sacrilege and ordered a heliographer to send a message commanding the game to halt, this being the Sabbath. When the English signaled back the score, 'Eighty-seven for three wickets,' he fell into a dark fury and ran breathlessly to a large gun.

'Fire on them!' When the Creusot monster was loaded and aimed he cautioned: 'But not too close.' The shell landed well off the cricket field and killed no one. Phlegmatically the officers continued their game, so a second shell had to be launched, and this came so close that the young men flew helter-skelter. When white-flagged emissaries came to protest the breaking of a tacit truce, De Groot replied, 'On Sundays you are to pray like us, not play at cricket like heathens.'

This matter of religion always perplexed De Groot and Van Doorn. They knew they were men dedicated to God and were convinced that He looked after them with special regard; they also knew that since the English were indifferent to the Bible, God must despise them, yet there were contradictions, as De Groot pointed out in a report to the council:

> I cannot understand it. The English have what they call a chaplain attached to every unit, and braver men I have never seen. To aid a fallen comrade or give last prayers to a dying man, they will cross open areas of gunfire with such fortitude that our men sometimes cheer them in admiration. But we Boers, who live and die under a special covenant with God, have some predikants who jump if even

a pistol shot goes off. Our spiritual welfare was being looked after by Predikants Nel and Maartins, but not for long. As soon as the first gun fired, both these dominees quickly found that commando life was not for them. No member of my commando felt their loss, as we provide our own prayers.

One bitter point was never discussed in public; it appeared in no news dispatches from the front, but it caused the harshest animosities, as General de Groot learned one morning when his commando captured six Englishmen. The young officer, a blond lad from Oriel College with his first commission, protested grievously: 'Sir, why do you Boers stoop so low as to use dumdum bullets?'

De Groot did not change his expression. 'Did we use them?'

'Yes! Yes!' the young man cried in near-hysteria. 'Chalmers was struck in the jaw. Should have been merely a nasty wound. Dumdum expands, makes a mess of his head. Atkins hit in the abdomen. Normally might pull through. Dumdum opens up his whole belly.' When De Groot made no response, the young fellow shouted, 'It's monstrous, Meneer.'

Quietly De Groot nodded to Van Doorn: 'Hand him three.' And from a special pouch Jakob produced three dumdum bullets, tossing them into the young man's lap. The Englishman studied them and blanched. In consternation he looked at De Groot and asked, 'Is this correct, Meneer? Our own Woolwich Arsenal?'

'Tell him where we got them,' De Groot said, and Van Doorn said, 'You heard about our raid against the cavalry? The seven big horses we kept? Those bullets you hold came from this pouch, found attached to one of the saddles.'

The young man apologized: 'They were intended for the Afghan frontier. Not for civilized warfare.'

In the autumn of 1900 such incidents receded in importance, for the massive strength of the English began to tell. They now had about two hundred fifty thousand men in the field against a maximum of sixty-three thousand Boers, and there was no way that the few, however gallant, could continue to hold off the many. With bold yet carefully prepared strikes, Generals Roberts and Kitchener rolled their choicest troops across the veld to Johannesburg and Pretoria. Town after town fell to the Tommies, and on the seventeenth of May even the tiny settlement at Mafeking was relieved at the end of a siege which had lasted interminably. General Robert Baden-Powell, who had used his scouting tactics to keep the town alive, was hailed throughout the world as a proper hero, and his manly deportment gave the English troops added courage as they headed for Johannesburg, which they captured on 31 May 1900.

Now came that most popular of all war songs, and in many ways the best, 'We're Marching to Pretoria.' Thousands of men chanted this as they closed in upon the Boer capital, and their triumphant voices could be heard as a last railway train left Pretoria on its solemn way down the line that led to Lourenço Marques in Moçambique. This was the only line the Boers still controlled, and in Car 17 that gloomy day rode Oom Paul Kruger in desperate flight.

It took the English only five days to capture Pretoria; it fell on 5 June

1900, and the great Anglo-Boer War was almost over. There was such joy in England that the police feared rioting, and families which still had sons in Africa—and there were many of them—wept openly to know that their boys would now be coming home.

There was a little mopping up to be done. General Roberts did not want to leave for London until the last railway line was in his hands, for that would mean that any further resistance, even from guerilla units like Paulus de Groot's dwindling commando, would be impossible. Like the good soldier he was, the little one-eyed genius refrained from announcing victory until President Kruger was driven completely out of South Africa, and to achieve this, he proposed that he and Kitchener march east along the railway while General Buller came up from the south to close the final pincers.

There are in existence some fifty telegrams in which Roberts from the north begged Buller in the south to speed up his approach, and to each the Ferryman of the Tugela replied with faultless logic, explaining why he could not move a whit faster. When Roberts sent an English colonel to find out what in the world was restraining this warrior, it fell to Major Saltwood to escort him, and as the two officers inspected General Buller's operations, Frank became even more aware of the considerable change that had taken place in his estimate of Buller.

For example, the visitor exploded at the number of wagons in the train, saying, 'My God! We're in the closing stages of a war. He ought to abandon four-fifths of these and gallop north to help us.'

'Now wait!' Saltwood replied defensively. 'Buller moves slowly, but I've observed that he accomplishes his missions with minimal losses of men. No general protects his troops the way this old man does.'

'But at what cost? He refuses to take chances.'

'I used to think so, too. But watching him in action—'

'What action? Know what they're calling him at headquarters? Sitting Bull.' The colonel laughed heartily at the mess-room joke.

Saltwood stiffened. 'Sir, we have a dozen funny names for the old fellow. But do you know what his men call him? John Bull.'

The colonel was not impressed, but when he challenged Buller about his excessive wagons, all he got was a harrumph: 'Damn me, man, troops can't march forward with empty bellies.'

'General Roberts says you think too much about your men.'

'No general ever lost a battle because he defended his men.'

'When you began this campaign,' the colonel pointed out ungraciously, 'you promised it would be over by Christmas. That was last Christmas, sir.'

Buller showed no resentment. Squinting his tight little eyes beneath the brooding visor, he said simply, 'Damn-fool statement. Made it before I'd met the Boers in battle. They're formidable, sir, and if Roberts thinks . . .' The rest of his rebuttal was lost in his monstrous mustache.

The formal meeting accomplished nothing, but when Buller withdrew, mumbling to himself, Saltwood remained with the colonel. 'In our march north I've seen a remarkable man at work. Victory after victory, with almost no casualties. He seems to have an uncanny sense of what his men can do, where they should strike.'

'At Spion Kop he was a disaster.'

'At Spion Kop he relied upon General Warren. Now he relies on himself.'

'Are you defending Sir Reverse?'

'I am. He's no Roberts, flying off all over the place. He's no Kitchener, blustering into cannon fire. He's an elderly general with a smart sense of warfare and a devotion to his men.'

Buller proved this in an embarrassing way, for in the hearing of the visiting colonel he said, 'Saltwood, we're facing the final push. Go down to Trianon and fetch me five hundred of their best sparkling. It may not be champagne, but it does taste good at the end of a long march. And fetch some beer for the men.'

When the two junior officers were alone, the visitor said, 'He never took a long march in his life.'

'I can assure you of one thing,' Saltwood said. 'On the day of victory, Old Buller will be the one marching in. Not fast, mind you. But very steady.' And when the sneering colonel had departed, Frank realized to his amazement that he had grown to love the Ferryman of the Tugela, for Redvers Buller, with his squinting eyes and eggplant head and telescope between his toes, knew what war was, how it should be fought, and how it could be won.

When he reached the Trianon vineyards to commandeer the best part of their bottling, Saltwood found that his wife had come east from Cape Town to share a few days with him, and from her he learned that the war had taken a dramatic turn, about which he had heard nothing.

Maud was worried: 'Frank, do you think General Roberts is justified in this move?'

'It's brilliant. Two armies concentrating on the last railroad the Boers have. It'll end the war.'

'I don't mean the railroad. I mean the scorched earth.' He would always remember that she was incredibly beautiful as she first uttered these words: the sunlight of Trianon fell on her auburn hair, outlining the wondrous curls and twists she used for controlling it, and her eyes glowed with that intensity she had shown when first he met her. War and decisions were forgotten as he leaned over to kiss her, but after a kind of routine compliance she returned to her concern.

'Yes, he's given orders to the burghers: "Lay down your arms or we will burn your farms and devastate your fields. If you fight, you will starve." ' She took a deep breath. 'Really, Frank, is that decent warfare?'

'Well, they're a difficult enemy. You scotch them here, they break out there. I hadn't heard of the new order . . .'

She produced a copy, signed by General Roberts, and he saw that she had reported it correctly. 'Looks sensible to me. We've defeated them, you know—totally defeated them—and these regulations apply only to the scattered remnants.'

'But they sound so barbaric. They don't sound like my England at all. They sound like Genghis Khan.'

'These are the mopping-up days of the war, Maud. We're gleaning the last sheaves.'

'Then why are you here buying wine for your stupid general?'

'Maud, he's not stupid. He's a man who knows exactly what he's doing, although I didn't use to think so.'

'But why the wine?'

Her chin tilted forward, and the hardness which she could command when confronted by stupidity showed itself. Frank became irritated by her questioning and blurted out: 'Because he likes to have an orderly mess, even in wartime. And he does so because he's the nephew of a great duke, who gives him the money to spend as he sees fit. He sees fit to buy champagne, that's why.'

It was a silly answer and he realized this as soon as the words were spoken. 'It's been a long, trying year,' he said. 'But I've grown fond of Old Buller, and you'd be ashamed of me if I deserted him now.'

'I'm sorry if I spoke harshly,' she said with such sweet innocence that he had to embrace her, but even as he kissed her, she returned to her concern: 'Is General Buller burning farms?'

'He could never do that. He fights armies, not women and children.'

'But it's an order. From Roberts.'

Frank laughed. 'I've learned one splendid lesson from Buller. If a stupid order comes down, ignore it.'

'But is he burning farms?'

'Darling, he's a wonderful, bumbling old fool, who has more sense of warfare than all the others. He'll fight this war his way, with good food, and sparkling Trianon, and plenty of rest for his men. And do you know what? In the end he'll win.'

On his side of the battle lines, General de Groot was encountering difficulty. Despite an occasional dashing sortie like his attack on the English cavalry, he was so stuck in routine that more of his commando had left him to affiliate with larger units engaged in the serious efforts of the war. The Venloo Commando now consisted of the general himself and ninety horsemen, plus their blacks. To keep it any longer in existence was ridiculous, and one afternoon the council told him so.

Standing before his men in his double-breasted frock coat—tattered and ruined, its silver buttons gone—and his tall top hat, he was a forlorn figure, a fat old man of sixty-eight whom the world had passed by. 'Commandant-general says we must join Tobias Brand's commando.'

'We're ninety men!' Van Doorn protested. 'We can still fight as a unit.'

'No. We must obey orders. Our commando is no more.'

'But it would be humiliating—to take orders from someone else, after you've been a general.'

'Not to me. I don't care where I fight.' He summoned Sybilla, and in the presence of his men, said, 'Old lady, they tell me I must surrender my command and fight under Tobias Brand.'

'He's a good man,' she said. 'I'll fetch the wagon.'

But when they rode over to Brand's camp, with Van Doorn sharing the

wagon, the younger general said, 'You understand who's in command?'
And De Groot said, 'You are, Tobias.'

Now Brand objected to having Sybilla along, for she was much older
than the women in his commando, but Paulus pleaded: 'This beaten wagon
is her only home. We have fought side by side for sixty years.' So she
resumed her position at the rear of a column, this one commanded by a
stranger. On hot days when she could shoot an antelope she would make
biltong for the long treks that she knew lay ahead.

Anyone who looked even casually at the map of South Africa could see
what the strategy of the English forces had to be, and De Groot listened
as the combat generals explained what they must do to keep the Boer
republics alive: 'The railroad to Lourenço Marques is our only link with the
world outside. It must be kept open. We've already lost it east of Pretoria,
but we dare not lose this part.' A brief flick of the finger indicated all that
remained: only the area between Middleburg and the Portuguese border,
including the two remarkable villages of Waterval-Boven (Above-the-
Waterfall) and Waterval-Onder (Under-the-Waterfall), for here in the space
of a few miles the whole face of Africa changed.

The Elands River, coming down off the high plateau, cut a deep gorge
through soft rock, creating a beautiful tumbling waterfall from which the
villages took their names, but this was not the spectacular character of the
place. Waterval-Boven, at the edge of the high plateau, was a typical veld
settlement, with harsh landscape, wide stretches of almost barren land and
a forbidding aspect. Then came the plunging drop, and at Waterval-Onder
one was in the lush lowlands, with high humidity, twisting vines and a
richness of grass and tree that was startling.

In the winter of 1900, when the Transvaal republic was falling apart, the
two Watervals became the focus of world attention, for to the high one came
Oom Paul Kruger, seventy-five years old, stooped and weary, a president
losing his country. From his railway carriages, he tried to hold his nation
together, wincing when he learned that districts upon which he had depended were gone. He had not wanted to leave Pretoria and was especially
grieved at being forced to abandon his old wife, but here he was near the
end of the railway line.

Men leading the commandos came to see him and spoke reverently of
his accomplishments in the past: 'Oom Paul, we're near the park you set
aside for the animals. The lions and giraffes send you thanks.'

'Little help you voracious men gave me in arguing for the park. All you
wanted to do was shoot elephants for their tusks.'

When General de Groot came by to pay his respects, Kruger said, 'I
hear you're keeping Sybilla with you. Splendid idea, Paulus. Boer women
thrive on battle.'

'You and I are the only ones left who were in the Great Trek,' Paulus
said, and tears came into his eyes as he recalled those days.

'Wasn't Mzilikazi a fearful enemy?' Kruger asked. 'He fought us all day,
killing and slaying, then prayed with the English missionaries all night,
telling them how his heart bled for his people.' The weary president shook
his head, then added, 'I must say, I've never cared much for missionaries.
How can the Bible produce such a bad lot?'

'They use a different Bible,' De Groot said.

Kruger slapped his leg. 'I agree, Paulus. The Bible in English, it doesn't sound the same. They do something to it.'

'What will you do, Oom Paul, if the English come down the railway line?'

'They want me to go to Europe. To stir up the nations. Find allies for us in our struggle.'

As the two old Pauls spoke, a cadre of officers came to the railway coach to inform them of disturbing news: 'We're taking you down to Waterval-Onder. Safer down there.'

At the new headquarters, De Groot was assigned the pleasant job of serving as a kind of liaison between the Boers up on the veld and President Kruger sitting in a small white house down among the tropical growth, where the air was soft and warm. But within days news of the war grew ominous: 'Oom Paul, General Roberts is coming at us along the railway line. General Buller moves up from the south.' And then Paul Kruger demonstrated just how deeply he believed in the covenant his people had made with the Lord.

'De Groot, I want you to help me draft a last message to your Venloo burghers,' he said, and laboriously, but with a kind of grandeur in their hearts, the two old men, veterans of the Great Trek to freedom, lined out the message, parts of which would be memorized by the Venloo men to whom it was read:

> Burghers, in all ages the Craven Beast has had the power to persecute Christ. Today, when God's nation put here by Him to defend the Word is assailed by His enemies, every man who loves God must rise to defend Him. The time is at hand when God's people are to be tried in fire, and those who are true to the faith and fight on in the name of the Lord shall be received in Heaven and enter into everlasting Glory. To those who talk of surrender I say that is a falling away from God. To those who are forced to lay down their arms and take an oath I say, 'Go in again at the first opportunity and continue fighting.' And to all I say that we fight on the side of God, and He will surely protect us. Read this message to officers and burghers at every opportunity.

When General de Groot took the message up to be copied and circulated, he learned that Waterval-Boven was in peril from approaching English forces. When he returned to Oom Paul's little house, he stood for some moments among the trees, looking through the window at the bearded man who was about to lose the republic he had worked so diligently to bring into being, and tears started to his eyes, but he fought them back: Nou is nie de die tyd, De Groot! (Now is not the time.)

Entering the room Kruger used as his office, he said brusquely, 'Oom Paul, you've got to go. A ship will meet you at Lourenço Marques.'

'I cannot go,' the old man said, but he went.

In doing so, he created a profound moral problem for Boer historians. They would find it impossible to say flatly that in time of deepest crisis their president had fled his country, abandoning it to the enemy. They would devise all sorts of explanations, all kinds of justifications: 'He went to enlist allies. He went to represent us in foreign capitals. He took our gold to safekeeping. We sent him away, he didn't go.' But the fact would always remain that history was replete with examples of other beleaguered leaders who had refused to quit their native lands in time of crisis—so many, that it had become the honorable tradition. When William the Norman invaded England, Harold the Saxon felt it incumbent upon him to resist, and he did, to the death. When the Muslims invaded Spain, the Spanish king held fast, and from a cave battled back. When Pizarro sacked the Inca empire, the Inca did not flee; and when Cortez attacked Mexico, Montezuma stayed to defend his land. Even in South African history, when Colonel Gordon surrendered Cape Town to the invading English, he felt it necessary in the tradition of military honor to commit suicide, which he did; and when Marthinus Steyn, president of the Orange Free State faced utter defeat, he sent the English a telegram: 'We shall never surrender!' and he fought on with his commandos. It would be difficult to find another major example in which the elected ruler of a country abandoned it, and his old wife, and his trek companions, but Oom Paul Kruger did, and the explanations he gave while wandering futilely from court to court in Europe sounded hollow.

For his strange behavior there might be political justification; an effort did have to be made to keep his nation alive, and help from Europe might have been the only practical solution. But it is impossible to conjure up any explanation as to why an old man like this would abandon his wife of many years. When word reached him in Europe that she had died back in Pretoria, he wept.

Boer intelligence, which was usually good because of a more intimate knowledge of the battle terrain, saw clearly what the English generals were up to: 'Roberts marches east along the railway line. Kitchener reinforces his rear. That's the approach we must protect.'

'What about Buller moving up from the south?'

'He never gets anywhere on time. You can forget that approach.'

So near Bergendal Farm the Boers fortified a big red hill upon which the security of their entire line depended. If that hill was captured, English cannon could destroy the Boer lines, and the war would be over.

It was a formidable target, sloping sides leading up to a plateau about three acres in size and covered with huge scattered boulders, like an untidy playground of giants. It was held by one of the stoutest of the Boer units —a group of Johannesburg policemen, the toughest in the nation, who were prepared to die.

With his bumbling instinct for seeing simple solutions to complex problems, General Buller, arriving belatedly as the battle loomed, saw that the big red hill formed the hinge of the Boer forces, and that if it fell, the entire enemy position must collapse. 'It looks like Spion Kop,' he said as his heavy guns swung into position. 'But this time I'll be in charge.' So while Lords Roberts and Kitchener approached from the west with copybook tactics, Buller thundered ahead on his own and invested the hill.

This time his tactics were impeccable, and while Roberts and Kitchener stared with mouths agape, his horde of naval guns blasted the hill with lyddite for three awful hours, blowing entire boulders apart. Then his men stormed the redoubt, slew most of the Johannesburg policemen, and fractured the Boer lines.

It was the last pitched battle of the war, and when it was over, Buller wrote to his wife: 'Here I am, as happy as a pig . . . Today I have a very nice telegram from the Queen . . . I defeated the army . . . while Lord Roberts' army, which had got there before me, had missed the chance and had to sit looking on. What a beast I am!'

Redvers Buller had won the war.

In London there were fantastic celebrations. The old queen, fresh from her Sixtieth Jubilee, decided on her own that her personal friend, Lord Roberts, had been responsible for the victory. She insisted that he be elevated to the rank of earl, admitted into the Order of the Garter and promoted to commander-in-chief. As Field Marshal Lord Roberts, he received from a grateful nation a vast estate and a cash gift of £100,000, a huge fortune in those days. He had brought the war to an end, and England rejoiced.

But General Buller was not forgotten. As soon as the war ended he was whisked aboard ship and hustled to England, where he was given a prestigious job in the military and a score of resounding state dinners, in which one city after another handed him ornate silver testimonials in the form of old-style Roman marshal's batons inscribed with the roster of his victories: 'Conqueror of the Tugela, Relief of Ladysmith, Hero of the High Veld.' His picture in tight little battle cap appeared everywhere, and it was agreed that he was perhaps the finest fighting general that England had ever produced.

Of course, some years later, when the facts of Spion Kop surfaced, all hell broke loose, and generals in the military establishment hounded him, charging him with lack of leadership. He was dragged before boards of inquiry, where his testimony was not inspiring. These attacks by envious rivals seemed not to worry him, for he surrendered none of the public acclaim which he adored, and to his home in the country came a constant queue of men who had fought under him in South Africa to assure him that he was the finest general they had ever known. As one conscripted soldier told the press: 'When you fought under Buller, things went slower, but you did eat well.'

On the morning that Lord Roberts knelt before his sovereign to become an earl and a Knight of the Garter, a group of tired flop-hatted Boers met secretly at a farm west of Pretoria. Louis Botha was present, Koos de la Rey the brilliant improvisator and Paulus de Groot the bulldog, and a brilliant young fellow all ice and steel, Jan Christian Smuts.

They had no settled government, no railway line to the outside world, no guaranteed arms supply, no replacement of horses, no system of conscription to fill their ranks, and no money. They were as defeated a group of men as military history provided; they had been mauled and chased almost off the continent, but there was not one among them prepared to put his hands up.

'The situation is this,' Louis Botha said. 'Lord Kitchener has two hundred thousand men in arms right now. And he can get two hundred thousand more. We have maybe twenty thousand burghers in the field. That's twenty-to-one against us, plus their ships, their heavy guns, the support of their empire. But what we have is knowledge of this land and determination.'

For some hours the discussion continued, and there was still not a leader there who was not ready to continue the conflict perpetually against the English. They drafted plans which only a fool would have accepted, and they applauded the daring. When someone said, 'The sensible thing to do is attack Cape Town; that will encourage the Cape Dutch to join at last,' four different commandants volunteered to undertake this incredible mission.

'The bulk of Kitchener's force will have to play policeman,' Botha predicted. 'He'll need a hundred thousand, maybe two hundred thousand, just to hold on to what they think they've got.'

On and on went the wild discussion, until a listener might have thought that these were victors planning their next campaign, and as they talked and encouraged one another, the tremendous determination of these Boers manifested itself: 'Our women will be with us. Our children will find a way to help.'

Paulus de Groot took no part in formulating these soaring plans, but they were confirmed when he jammed on his worn top hat, fastened his coat with the two safety pins that had replaced the lost silver buttons, and said, 'The battles are over. Now the war begins.'

It began with an action that reverberated around the world. It would have been a remarkable adventure had General de Groot done it alone, but it so happened that two newspapermen, a Frenchman and an American, hearing of the dissolution of the commandos now that the war was over, sought out old De Groot, thinking that he would provide a colorful story: the old veteran of the Great Trek who had fought first as a general, finally as a mere private. Also, since he had long ago been one of the heroes at Majuba, his return to civil life would be interesting to older readers.

But when they found De Groot and asked their first battery of questions about the impending surrender, he looked at them in amazement. 'Can you men ride horses?'

'We can.'

'Are you afraid of bullets?'

'Like everyone.'

'Good, because I don't like heroes. Ride with me and see how we surrender.'

He had regrouped with ninety men, mostly from the old Venloo Commando, but including sixteen older burghers from other districts who had little to go back to and wanted a chance to twist old Kitchener's tail. They had fine ponies and, of course, the usual complement of black retainers. They also had two wagons carrying three of the wives, and when the reporters saw Sybilla de Groot, in her sixties, they gasped.

'What's she doing here?'

'I don't go to war without my wife.'

'But the war's over.'

'Only the preliminaries.'

When the newspapermen finally grasped De Groot's plan of action, they were shocked both at the boldness and at the fact that a man nearly seventy should have concocted it.

'We want to give old Kitchener a signal that his war is still under way. He thinks he took over to receive salutes and break down the camps. He has a dreadful task ahead of him, and we want you to tell him so.'

'If you do what you threaten,' the Frenchman said admiringly, 'he won't need us to tell him.'

What De Groot proposed was to swing far west of Pretoria and Johannesburg, drop down some twenty-two miles below the latter city, and cut the railway line to Cape Town. Then, when English troops were everywhere, to gallop north as he had done before, right into the heart of their strength in Johannesburg district, there to cut the line again. Then, after a forty-six-mile gallop south, to strike the line again far from the first blow. Three nights, three directions, three strikes. It was confusing even to listen to; for an English general basking in victory it would be appalling.

Far out in the veld they left the two wagons and the spare ponies. As they prepared to ride in for their insane adventure, old De Groot took off his hat, kissed his wife, and told her, 'One day, old woman . . . one day it will end.'

Casually, the Boers and the two correspondents rode east, calculating so exactly that at two in the morning, when guards were sleepy, they would have time in which to blow up the Johannesburg–Cape Town railway. They accomplished this with dispatch—a wild, violent eruption filling the night —then galloped at breakneck speed right toward the heart of Johannesburg, taking cover just before dawn.

All that day they watched English troops hustling back and forth, 'In rather a panic,' De Groot said.

At dusk they stayed where they were, but well before midnight De Groot, Van Doorn and Micah again led a dozen burghers up to the railway, lugging a huge supply of dynamite, which they fastened to the rails, detonating it from a distance. The explosion ripped the entire rail system apart, but before the debris settled, the Venloo Commando was galloping south over back roads to their third appointment. Again they spent daylight hours watching the frustrated troops, and once more at nightfall they resumed their riding. This time they galloped till almost dawn, when De Groot said, 'They won't expect us this far south.' Calling upon his same team, he had one hundred yards of rail mined, and when the early dawn was shaken with the vast outburst, throwing lengths of rail high in the air, the Boers retreated out over the veld, then far north to where Sybilla waited with the wagons.

The American reporter wrote a story which covered front pages in all states: WAR IS JUST STARTING SAYS DE GROOT. He was so factual and outlined the daring Boer strategy with such detail that the reader had to be impressed. When the report reached England a shudder passed through the nation, with editors asking soberly: WAS CELEBRATION PREMATURE?

But it was the French report that captured the world's imagination, for it told of Sybilla waiting in the veld, of Paulus taking off his top hat before kissing her, of the unbelievable daring in riding right into English strength, and of the coolness with which De Groot and his men handled their dynamite. What caused the story to be remembered, however, was the happy phrase the Frenchman coined to describe De Groot and his mission: AVENGER OF THE VELD. It sounded better in French *(Vengeur du Veld)*, but even in English it was telling, and its effect was reinforced by something that General de Groot had whispered on one of the night rides. 'He told me,' read the report, 'that now that the gaudy battles are over, the real war begins. Having seen him in action for three Scheherazade Nights, I can believe it.'

Now the old man faced a different problem. All the adventurers wanted to join him, and the name Venloo Commando flashed across the world. It struck in the north. It appeared out of the mist in the far reaches of the Orange Free State. Newspapers fought desperately to catch photographs of Sybilla de Groot driving her old wagon, or of her husband standing beside her with his tall hat in his hand.

He had ninety men, then a hundred and fifteen, and finally the maximum he felt he could handle, with Van Doorn's help: two hundred and twenty. They were the best riders, men who could load and fire at a gallop, and they had no reason to halt anywhere, for they could not return to their homes.

When Kitchener found to his grim dismay that the Boers did not intend to surrender, as a defeated rabble should, he became distraught and issued orders that the farms of dissident commando members be burned to the ground, their fields ravaged and their livestock driven away: 'They may fight, but they won't feed.'

Before he left South Africa, Lord Roberts had applied this scorched-earth policy selectively, putting to the torch only those farms known to be collaborating with the commandos, but by the time Major Frank Saltwood was transferred from Buller's defunct command to Kitchener's, the practice had spread. 'I really don't think it will have much bearing upon the burghers,' Saltwood warned when he studied the figures, but Kitchener was adamant, and for the first time Saltwood saw the steel in this man's fiber. Clean-shaven except for a distinctive mustache, trim, rigid, accepting no nonsense from anyone, he seemed the right man for the unpleasant task of cleaning up the few recalcitrant rebels like old Paulus de Groot.

'Shall we burn his farm?' an English aide asked, and before Kitchener could reply, Saltwood volunteered: 'That would be a mistake, sir. Already the man's a hero. Simply create more sympathy.' When these prudent words were spoken, Lord Kitchener stared at his South African liaison, trying to assess him: Is this man to be trusted to put England's interest first, or is he infected with local patriotism? This time, however, what he says makes sense.

'Do not burn the De Groot farm,' Kitchener ordered, and for the moment it was spared, but when the wily old man continued to strike at unforeseen places, making fools of the English, Kitchener became coldly furious, and although he did not yet burn De Groot's farm, he ordered a wide swath of desolation on either side of the railway leading to Lourenço Marques. As soon as this was done, the Venloo Commando swept in and cut the railway in four places, to the intense delight of the French correspondent who accompanied the raid.

This was important, because the press of the world, especially the cartoonists, turned savagely against Great Britain, lampooning both her and Kitchener as murderers and bullies. Hardly a day passed that the influential papers in Amsterdam, Berlin and New York did not crucify Kitchener, showing him as a tyrant burning the food needed for starving Boer women and children. When one of the noble lord's English aides saw a selection of the worst cartoons, he grumbled, 'Damned few of those great fat Dutch women are starving.' But the corrosive propaganda continued, until it appeared that the entire world was opposed to England's performance in South Africa, as indeed it was, save for countries like Canada, Australia and New Zealand, which retained legal ties to the mother country.

The hero in this ceaseless barrage of pro-Boer propaganda had to be General de Groot—*Vengeur du Veld* and a cartoonist's delight. He was an old man in a frock coat and top hat, and he was accompanied by a woman whose stately demeanor under all circumstances had won the admiration of all newsmen. Together they formed an irresistible pair, especially when an American photographer caught them holding hands beside their battered wagon. In London a brazen Cockney paperboy bought himself a stack of white envelopes, labeled them PORTRAIT OF GENERAL DE GROOT and sold them for sixpence. When the purchaser opened the envelope to find nothing, the cheeky lad cried, to the delight of those in on the joke, 'Damn me, Guv'nor, 'e got away again!'

Who was chasing De Groot in these eight frustrating months of 1901? Instead of the troops going home at Christmas, 1900, as Lord Roberts had said they would, some two hundred thousand had to stay on. To them, at one time or another, were added another two hundred forty-eight thousand, not all of whom were in the field at one time. De Groot had two hundred twenty men, but of course there were other equally insolent commandos operating; however, the disparity between forces was both enormous and enraging. The vast numbers of English troops ought to have been able to catch the commandos, but they didn't; old De Groot and his wife ambled their way right through the traps set to catch them.

At one point when the summer heat was most unkind to the imported troops unaccustomed to the highveld, the following units, among many others, were striving to catch the Venloo Commando: from England, the Coldstream Guards; from Scotland, the Argyll and Sutherland Highlanders; from Ireland, the heroic Royal Inniskilling Fusiliers; from Wales, the Royal Welsh Fusiliers; from Canada, Lord Strathcona's Horse; from Australia, the Imperial Bushmen; from New Zealand, the Rough Riders; from Tasmania, the Mobile Artillery; from India, Lumsden's Horse; from Ceylon, the Mounted Infantry; from Burma, the Mounted Rifles; from Gibraltar, the 1st Manchesters; from Mauritius, the King's Own Yorkshire Light Infantry; from Egypt, the 1st Royal Fusiliers; and from Crete, the 2nd Rifle Brigade.

Earlier in the war the Boers, too, had help from outside. Adventurers from all nations, believing themselves to be fighting for liberty against aggression, had flocked to South Africa, and one important French colonel died in their ranks. There was an Irish regiment always eager to take a thrust at the English; a German and a Hollander contingent. Most tragic was a volunteer unit composed of one hundred and twenty-one idealistic Scandinavians, mostly Norwegian; in one of the earliest battles of the war almost the entire force was exterminated.

Such events were brilliantly reported, especially in the English press, for in addition to Winston Churchill, Rudyard Kipling came out to write about the conflict, championing the English cause in prose and verse; Edgar Wallace was a frenetic legman; Conan Doyle was afire with patriotism; H. W. Nevinson showed patrician restraint, and Richard Harding Davis the opposite; Banjo Patterson, who would become Australia's Poet Laureate with 'Waltzing Matilda,' did excellent reporting; and in the closing days quiet John Buchan looked things over. A strange assortment of visitors filtered in as observers; Prince Kuhio, heir to the throne of Hawaii, appeared one day, and as the scion of a family always strongly pro-English, was invited to the front, where he pulled the lanyard of a big gun, firing his blast at the hidden Boers.

In August 1901 English pressure became so powerful that the Boer command decreed that wives must no longer ride with their husbands, and on a bleak hillside Paulus de Groot had to inform his companion since childhood that she must leave. She did not want to go; that mean farm at Vrymeer was much less attractive to her than riding with her husband into battle. She had no fear of war's rigors; she wanted to share all things with Paulus, even though she suspected that sudden death or slow disillusion must be their fate. When Paulus remained firm, she became disconsolate.

'You are my life,' she said.

'It's the others. They made the decision. You must go home.'

'Where you are is home.'

'The rides will grow more difficult. The lines tighter.'

Thinking that this might be the last time she would ever see him, she knew that she must not cry. Instead she broke into an infectious chuckle. 'Remember when we were married? After the last battle with the Zulu? And the dominee said in a loud voice, "Does any man know why this man and woman should not be wed?"'

'Good God, what a moment!' the general cried, and then he, too, laughed.

'And Balthazar Bronk, always a troublemaker for other people, shouted that the marriage was forbidden. That we had been raised as brother and sister.'

They stood silent on the dark veld, and then she took his hand and whispered, 'You were never my brother, Paulus. After that night at Blauuw-krantz, I loved you always. And I always will.'

De Groot tried to speak, but no words came.

'Get sleep when you can,' she said, and they walked to the old wagon. He kissed her and helped her up, and she started up the hill.

Paulus remained holding his hat as she climbed to the crest. He did not expect her to look back, nor did she, but when she was gone, he prayed: Almighty God, forget the battles for a while and look after that woman.

When De Groot saw the first one, he shuddered. It was Lord Kitchener's invention for ending the guerrilla war. It was perched beside a vulnerable stretch of railway track, a device of admirable simplicity. It was made of corrugated iron and looked like one of those circular Spanish barns called silos, except that it was squatter. It consisted of two iron cylinders, one fitted inside the other, with enough room inside to house armed patrolmen. In the narrow space between the two cylinders rocks and debris had been jammed to give both protection and insulation. The top was enclosed by a conical roof, so that from a distance the contraption resembled a heavy, blunt cigar jammed into the earth.

Since the new device was obviously lethal and intended to halt the depredations of commandos, De Groot wanted to know as much about them as possible, and a man from the Carolina Commando, who had seen one after it had been blown up by a large force of dynamite, told all the burghers, 'Very difficult to destroy. Manned by seven soldiers. Three little beds. Place to cook. And some have telephones to the next blockhouse.'

As the commando looked down the tracks they had expected to dynamite, they saw six more of the blockhouses, cheap to build, easy to erect, and effective in breaking the open veld into manageable units out of which a mounted commando would have difficulty in moving.

'Look!' Jakob cried, and at the far end of the line of blockhouses, soldiers were stringing barbed wire from one house to the next. 'Kitchener's building a fence across Africa.'

This was correct. Goaded by ridicule, the commander had given orders that the railway system be protected by these new-style blockhouses, and when the first hundred proved successful, he called for eight thousand more, some of them built of stone. Once a commando found itself driven against one of the fortified barriers, its retreat could be so cut off that capture seemed inevitable.

Not for Paulus de Groot. When he was trapped the first time, in southern Transvaal, there was no escape; barbed wire flourished everywhere, but the English troops still had to find him. At the darkest moment he told Van Doorn, 'No army in the world ever found a way to keep all its enlisted men awake. Somewhere there's a blockhouse sound asleep.' He sent Micah to test the line for a weak spot, but when the Zulu scout crawled back he reported: 'All manned. All awake.'

'Try again,' De Groot growled, and this time the scout isolated one iron fort in which all seven men seemed to be asleep. With a swiftness that amazed some of the commandos, De Groot, Van Doorn and Nxumalo crept up to the house, worked their way under the barbed wire, and rushed the loopholes four feet above the ground, pouring in a deadly fire, killing all the occupants. Within minutes the Venloo Commando were cutting the wires that had restrained them, and after they had regained the open veld, one newspaperman quoted De Groot: 'Lord Blockhead's little toy houses cause us no worry.'

When cartoons across the world showed the noble lord playing with blocks while old General de Groot slipped away behind him, an enraged headquarters in Pretoria commanded: 'That man must be brought in.'

Regiments from eleven nations applied pressure, and once again the old man was trapped within a barbed-wire hedge, with Canadians, Irishmen, Australians and Welshmen closing in. This time he adopted a simple device: rounding up all available cattle from unburned farms, he stampeded them toward a spot between two blockhouses, and as the frightened animals piled up against the barbed wire, they simply carried it away, while the Venloo Commando swept off to freedom yet again.

This time the cartoonists were merciless: 'LIKE ULYSSES . . .' And they showed De Groot and his men tied to the bellies of the steers as they galloped past a sleeping Polyphemus who looked exactly like Lord Kitchener.

'All of them!' he thundered. 'I want all of them thrown into camps.' So his men moved out to corral every woman and child belonging to the fighting Boers. They would be herded into camps of concentration, to keep them from feeding and supporting their menfolk. It was pointed out to Kitchener that there were already more than fifty thousand refugees in camps, many there at the behest of Boers themselves, for they had been unable to survive on farms without their men. 'I don't care if there are fifty thousand more!' stormed Kitchener.

When the drive against the commando-homesteads was well under way, and the Boer territories further denuded of women and farms and cattle, leaving only smoking ruins, Kitchener began to see good results. Three commandants, unable to survive against starvation and barbed wire, voluntarily surrendered, but before doing so their top men crept away to join up with General de Groot, whose forces now reached their maximum: four hundred and thirty hardened men, a hundred extra ponies and fifty blacks. This would be the final army, led by an old man approaching seventy.

Pleased with the apparent effectiveness of the concentration camp, Lord Kitchener summoned Major Saltwood one morning and gave him an order: 'Burn Vrymeer and herd the women into the camp at Chrissie Meer.'

'Are you sure you want to do this, sir?'

'I am,' the steely-eyed general said, 'and I deem it best if you lead the men, rather than an Englishman.'

'I think of myself as an Englishman, sir, and I don't relish assignments like this.'

'I consider you a local, Saltwood. It'll look better.'

So with a mixed detachment of seventy, including troops from various colonies, Saltwood rode east on the Lourenço Marques train, disembarked his horses at Waterval-Boven, and rode slowly south toward the lake—a journey he had taken in happier times. When he reached Venloo and saw the heavy price it had paid in this war, all windows shattered, a feeling of despair came over him, and he remembered what Maud had said that day at Trianon: 'Seems more like Genghis Khan.'

Then he turned west on the pleasant rural road leading to the lake, and when he crested the hill he could see the two farms at which he had once been so happy and so well received. It pained him to think that these good people had later considered him to be a spy, but he supposed, upon reflection, that he had been, in a general way of speaking. He did not want to go on, but when the men behind began to rein up near him he sighed and headed for the rickety buildings of the De Groot farm. 'Not much lost if they burn,' a Welshman said.

Sybilla was in the kitchen, and when she saw the troops she knew what to expect. Without saying a word, she packed a few belongings, reached for her sunbonnet, and appeared on the stoep. 'General Kitchener's orders,' a soldier said. 'Men, set the fires.'

In a way the flames were merciful; they were erasing farm buildings that had long since served their day, and removing them was an act of good husbandry, but as the fire spread, Saltwood became aware of voices behind him, and turning, saw the four Van Doorn children: the girls Anna, Sannah and Johanna, and the handsome little boy Detlev.

'Sir, sir! What are you doing?' one of the girls screamed.

At this moment Major Saltwood chanced to look down from his horse and catch the eye of the oldest girl, Johanna, twenty-one years old, and he saw in her such hatred that he almost shuddered, yet with this fierce animosity she was also studying him, as if she had seen him before. She did not seem to remember, for which he was grateful.

'I suppose you'll burn ours, too,' she said through teeth that were almost clenched. 'My father rides with the general.'

'Be gentle with the old woman,' Saltwood shouted at his men as Sybilla was placed in a wagon. 'Gather the children.' The three youngest were lifted up by soldiers and deposited beside her as the troop wheeled its horses and made its way to the Van Doorn farm—with Johanna walking grimly through the dust.

This was no outmoded collection of shacks. It was one of the stoutest farms in eastern Transvaal, a place of stone buildings and excellent rondavels for its blacks. To burn this would be to destroy the heart of a rich agricultural district. 'Burn it!' Saltwood said, but before the torch could be applied to the wooden parts that would ignite, a woman appeared at the kitchen door.

'What are you doing?' she demanded.

'Lord Kitchener's orders, ma'am. You're to get in the wagon.'

'That I will not do,' Sara van Doorn said, and when the Australians guarding the wagon relaxed their attention Johanna ran to join her mother. Together the two women blocked the entrance to the house.

'Remove them!' Saltwood commanded, and a detachment of Irish cavalrymen grabbed at the women, but they broke away and dashed into the house. When soldiers forced them out, the women carried in their arms the chief treasures of the Van Doorn family: Mevrou van Doorn held the brassbound Bible; Johanna, the ceramic pot in which her father made his bread pudding.

A good fire was now burning in the shed, and one of the soldiers tried to snatch the book, intending to throw it in, but Mevrou van Doorn struggled to retain possession, and there was a scuffle until Saltwood saw what was happening. 'Good God, man. That's a Bible. Stand off.' He was too late, however, to protect the pot that Johanna held, for a brutish soldier brought the butt of his gun around in a circle, caught the pot, and smashed it. When the dozen pieces tumbled to the boards of the stoep, it was apparent that a clever person with the right glue could reassemble the precious old thing, and Johanna stooped to gather some of the pieces, but this enraged the soldier, who brushed her aside and ground the remaining fragments under his boot.

'Stand back, you fool!' Saltwood cried, but as he did so he looked into the eyes of this embittered girl, and she remembered who he was: 'Mother! He's the spy.'

From her wagon, Sybilla looked out to inspect the man in charge of this destruction, and she, too, recognized him: 'The spy!' The twin girls, peering from beneath the canvas, saw who he was and they joined the lamentation: 'The spy! He's Saltwood the spy.'

When Frank dismounted to reassure the two Van Doorn women on the stoep, Johanna spat in his face: 'They should have hanged you.'

'They should have hanged you!' the twins shouted, and Detlev, finding sticks in the wagon, started throwing them at their betrayer. Meanwhile, the fires raged.

It was only thirty-eight miles from Vrymeer to the cluster of large lakes which the English called Chrissie Meer. Here the concentration camp had been established, but in that distance Major Saltwood's column had collected five additional wagons filled with women and children from farms en route. Since all buildings had been burned, the women were sooty and weeping as they turned the last corner; then they looked with awe at their destination. Their camp lay at the edge of one of the loveliest lakes in Africa: a surface shimmering in sunlight, hills rising softly from the shore, flowers in beds, and a hint of animals hiding in the glens. Saltwood said to a member of the Welsh Fusiliers, 'If you must have a prison camp . . . the clean air . . . the sunlight . . .' In months ahead when the name of this camp echoed with shame, he would concede that it was at least a place of physical beauty. To it he delivered Sybilla de Groot, Sara van Doorn and the four Van Doorn children, but as he did so he noticed by sheerest accident a tent in which three young children lay sleeping, he thought; on closer inspection he saw that they were awake, too emaciated to respond when he spoke to them.

Rushing to the commandant's office, a doctor from the English Midlands, he cried, 'Sir, those children in the tent at the bottom of Row Eighteen. Sir, those children are starving.'

'There is no starvation here,' the doctor said sternly, as if reporting on his hospital to a village committee of inspection.

'But those children! Legs like matchsticks!'

'We are all like matchsticks,' the doctor cried, his voice suddenly rising almost to a scream, as if his earlier composure had been tenuous. 'And do you know why?' He uttered a string of obscenities Saltwood had not heard for years; they were not used at officers' headquarters. 'It's your goddamned Lord Kitchener, that's who it is. Go back and tell him what you saw.'

'I can't leave my women here . . .'

'You're right, Colonel . . . What's your name?'

'Saltwood, and I'm a major.'

'English?'

'I'm from the Cape. And I'd appreciate your telling me where to take these women.'

'Where? Yes, where?'

'Doctor, lower your voice. You sound demented.'

'I am demented!' the little man screamed in a Lancashire dialect. 'I am demented with shame.'

With a sudden swipe of his right arm, Saltwood knocked the agitated man against a wall, then pulled him up and sat him at his desk. 'Now tell me without bellowing—what's the matter?'

'Typhoid's the matter. Measles are the matter. And dysentery, dysentery's the matter.' He broke down and sobbed so pitifully that Saltwood had to cover his own face in compassion.

'Tell me in an orderly way,' he said, touching the doctor's shoulder. 'I can see it's horrible, but what can we do?'

The doctor jabbed at his eyes, rumpled through some papers, found a report, and covered it with his hands for a moment. 'We're at the end of the supply line here, Colonel. Headquarters can't send us enough food. But the diet would sustain life, except for the incessant illness.' And here he repeated his litany of death: 'Typhoid, measles, dysentery. We could fight any one, but a body already weakened by stringent diet, it hasn't the strength. These figures tell our story.' And he shoved the paper forward. 'Deaths per thousand, months of February, March, seven hundred and eighty-three.'

'My God!' Saltwood cried.

'Those were the bad months. Chrissie Meer's average is usually less than three hundred.'

'But even so, that's one in three.'

'Yes,' the doctor said. 'Of the thirty-seven women and children you delivered today, maybe fifteen, maybe twenty will be dead at the end of six months, if dysentery runs wild again, if the food supply weakens.'

'Doctor, you are in very sore condition yourself. I think I should take you back to Pretoria.'

A nurse heard this proposal and stepped forward, an extremely gaunt woman. 'Dr. Higgins controls his feelings most of the time. We all try to. And when we get fresh vegetables or meat from the countryside, we keep many people alive. But without medicines . . .' She shrugged her shoulders. 'Dr. Higgins is a very strong man, spiritually. He does what he can.'

'What do you need?' Saltwood asked.

She hesitated, looked at Dr. Higgins, and saw that she would get no help there. He had withdrawn from the discussion. 'We need everything. Hospital beds. Medicines. We have no toilet paper. Dysentery runs wild, and children seem to starve, as you saw. If we don't get help soon, and I mean nourishing food in better supply, all the children you brought us will be dead.'

Two nights later, when he was back in Pretoria, he found that there were no additional supplies for Chrissie Meer, at the far end of the line: no extra food, no medicines, no sanitary aids, and he could see his children, the ones he had taken to the camp, dying. Retiring to his room, with dull anguish assailing him, he wrote a love letter:

> My dearest darling Maud,
>
> I have never before addressed a letter to you like this, because I did not appreciate how desperately I love you and how much I need you. I have been to Chrissie Meer, to the big concentration camp there, and I am shattered. You must do all you can to alleviate the condition of these pitiful people. Food, blankets, medicines, trained people. Maud, spend all our savings, volunteer yourself, but for God's sake and the reputation of our people, you must do something. At this end I shall do whatever I can. An evil fog has fallen over this land, and if we do not dissipate it promptly, it will contaminate all future relationships between Englishman and Boer.
>
> When I rode back from Chrissie Meer, I reflected on the fact that the three men who were spoilers of this land, Shaka, Rhodes, Kitchener, not one of them had a wife. I fear that men without women are capable of terrible misdeeds, and I want to apologize to you for having allowed Mr. Rhodes to delay our marriage as he did. I was as evil as he in conforming to that hateful posture, and I bless you tonight for the humanity you have brought into my life.
>
> Your most loving husband,
> Frank

When word circulated at headquarters that Maud Saltwood was creating disturbances—'Not riots, you understand, but real annoyances, questions, and all that, you know'—Lord Kitchener was enraged. It infuriated him that one of his own men should be unable to control his wife, permitting her to make a fuss over the camps, where, as he pointed out again and again, 'the women and children are much better off than they would be in their own homes.'

'Bring Saltwood in here!' he thundered. When the major stood before him he used his baton to indicate a pile of papers. 'What's all this—these reports—about your wife, Saltwood?'

'She's doing what she can to alleviate conditions—'

'Alleviate? There's nothing to alleviate.'

'Sir, with all respect, have you seen the death rate—'

'Damnit, sir, don't you be insolent with me.' The noble lord looked as if he could bite Saltwood in half, and would relish doing so. 'You sit down there, and listen to someone who knows.'

He summoned a Dr. Riddle, from London, who had just returned from a tour of the forty-odd camps. He was a cheery man, obviously well-fed, and seemed full of enthusiasm. With alacrity he took the report Lord Kitchener held out to him. 'I wrote this, you understand, Saltwood. Done on the spot.' From it he read his major conclusions:

'The Boer women and children are noticeably better off than they would be if left on their abandoned farms. They receive adequate supplies of the most healthful foods, on which they seem to prosper and if—'

'Did you get out to Chrissie Meer?' Saltwood interrupted. 'Listen to the report,' Kitchener snapped. 'I wasn't able to get that far east,' Dr. Riddle said.

'Whatever illness appears in the camps is due primarily to the Boer women themselves. Having been raised on farms without privies, they cannot learn to adopt the sanitary measures which alone prevent the spread of epidemics. And when illness does strike, they insist upon resorting to country measures that have not been used in civilized nations for the past sixty years. They wrap a measled child in the skin of a freshly slaughtered goat. They grub in the countryside for old herbs which they claim can reduce fever. They recite rhymes as if they were witch doctors. And they will not wash their hands.'

'I am seriously thinking of bringing criminal charges against some of these mothers,' Kitchener said with great irritation. 'They should be tried for murder. It's all their fault, you know.'

'So I must conclude that the English authorities are doing everything humanly possible to protect the women and children in our charge. I found them in good condition, reasonably happy, and with every probability of leaving the camps in better condition than when they entered.'

'What would your precious wife make of that?' Lord Kitchener asked, fastening his hard eyes on Saltwood.

Saltwood, having once denied his wife in the presence of a strong man, had no intention of doing so again: 'I think, sir, she would say that such a report does both you and the king an injustice.'

An explosion without specific words erupted, after which Kitchener roared, 'Are you impugning the integrity of Dr. Riddle?'

Taking a deep breath, Saltwood replied, 'I am saying that his report does not begin to cover conditions at Chrissie Meer, and, I suspect, at a lot of other installations I haven't seen.'

'But your wife has seen them?'

'Sir, the day may come when you will be eternally grateful that my wife spoke out in these bad days.'

'Bad days, damn you! We're winning along the entire front.'

'Not in the camps, sir. You run great risk of damaging your reputation because of what's happening—'

'Show him, Riddle,' Kitchener said. 'Show him the other page.'

'I'll read it,' the ebullient doctor said, not wishing this secret part of his report to fall into other hands, even temporarily:

'The complaint of the Boers that their women and children are dying at an excessive rate is belied by the statistics of our own forces. To date 19,381 such Boers have died in the camps, but it must be remembered that in the same period 15,849 of our soldiers have died under similar circumstances. It is not our barbarity that kills, nor starvation on the diet we provide; it is the physical nature of the camps and the hospitals, the incessant spread of dysentery and typhoid, and these strike Boer and Englishman even-handedly.'

'And what do you think of that?' Kitchener snapped, but Frank was too ashamed of the mendacity of this report to say what he thought: The English soldiers went into their hospitals wounded or already near death from disease. Most Boer women and children went in healthy. Both died, and at equal rates, but from much different causes.

'Well?' Kitchener asked. 'They're equal, aren't they?'

'In war, unarmed women and children do not equal men in uniform.'

'Get out of here! You're dismissed from my headquarters. I will not have a man around me who cannot control his own wife.' When Saltwood remained at attention, Kitchener repeated, 'Get out. You're dismissed with prejudice. You can never again serve with an English unit. You are unreliable, sir, and a disgrace to your uniform.'

In a calm such as he had not known since he began serving under General Buller, Frank Saltwood looked down at Lord Kitchener at his desk, arranging reports which proved that England was winning the war. 'Permission to speak, sir?'

'Granted—then begone.'

'If you pursue the war along these lines, you'll be remembered as the general who lost the peace.' With that he saluted, marched from the room, and headed for the Johannesburg railway. At Cape Town, hungry for the civilizing spirit of his wife, he burst into their quarters to find her gone. The maid said, 'She's out to inspect the camps, Mr. Saltwood.' When the girl left, he bowed his head and mumbled, 'Thank you, God, for showing at least one of us his duty. I mean her duty.' In the morning he would find where she was working, and join her.

When Sybilla de Groot and the Van Doorns were deposited at their concentration camp, they were assigned to a small bell tent that already contained a family of four, the two youngest of whom were near death. Sybilla, white-haired and somewhat stooped, came into the tent, saw what needed to be done, and said quietly to the Van Doorns, 'We can make do.'

She moved the cots of the dying children to where they would catch a breeze, then did what she could to encourage the women to get up and see if they could scrounge even a little extra food for the children, but she saw to her amazement that the women lacked not only the stamina to do this, but also the will. In a daze of terror she left the three youngest Van Doorns in the tent and drew Sara and Johanna out into the open, where she took each by the hand, squeezing until her own fingers hurt. 'We must not surrender. The children will live only if we live. We must never give in.'

Looking alternately at her two friends, she asked them, 'Do you swear?' They swore that they would not surrender.

When the first of the two children died, in terrible emaciation caused by a combination of typhoid, dysentery and inadequate food, Sybilla tried to mask the fact from Detlev, only six years old, but he knew what death was, and said, 'The little girl is dead.'

The entire tent—that is, those who could walk—attended the funeral. Camp attendants, who seemed to be quite healthy, came down the lane between the tents, collecting bodies, and at Sybilla's they lifted up the little corpse, then reached for the other child, who lay inanimate. 'That one's not dead yet,' Detlev said, and the attendants passed on.

The attendants carted the bodies to a busy burial ground, where a carpenter from Carolina had volunteered to build rude caskets from whatever odds and ends he could scavenge. He was Hansie Bronk, descendant of that Balthazar Bronk who had protested the marriage of Sybilla and Paulus de Groot; big, round-shouldered, blessed with a rural sense of humor, he was a civilizing force, his most appreciated contribution being not his caskets, but his ability now and then to find extra meat and vegetables in the countryside.

When Detlev appeared at the burial ground, Hansie chucked him under the chin and said, 'Nou moenie siek word nie, my klein mannetjie.' (Now don't you fall sick, little man.)

This day there were four caskets, and beside their shallow graves stood Dr. Higgins holding a Bible. He despised every moment of his service in this horrible place but felt obligated to oversee all that happened, as if he were both the cause and the participant, and he strove to make the burials decent. Detlev listened as the doctor prayed.

The boy was in the tent three days later when the other little girl died, her arms like threads, and he walked with the attendants as they collected the bodies of those who had died of fever in the preceding hours. He was always present at the burials, and always Hansie Bronk told him, 'Nou moenie siek word nie, my klein mannetjie.'

His watchful eye noticed when the older of his twin sisters—Anna, who boasted of her precedence—began to waste away, but he was not prepared for what happened when he said to his mother, 'Anna needs medicine,' for Mevrou van Doorn uttered a piercing scream and started running down to the doctor's quarters—but there were no medical supplies.

'My God!' Sybilla cried, running after her, slapping her and bringing her back to the tent. 'We swore an oath, Sara. We have got to protect the children.' When food was doled out, a meager amount, the hungry women apportioned much of it to the twin, who nevertheless grew weaker each day.

'Is Anna going to die?' Detlev asked.

'Don't say that!' his mother cried, whereupon old Sybilla shook her again and made her sit down, and she became quiet.

In time Anna did die, just as Detlev had expected, and at the funeral he watched attentively as Hansie Bronk placed her thin body in one of his caskets. On this day there were four other children to be buried, and when Dr. Higgins tried to read from his Bible he could not control his voice, so Sybilla took the book and finished reading the Psalm. Detlev listened to the sound of earth pitched upon the caskets.

The death of her child had such a debilitating effect on Sara that she seemed to wilt in the intense heat like one of the flowers. At night it was extremely cold, and this sharp fluctuation aggravated whatever illnesses the internees contracted, but in Sara's case it was merely lack of will power.

One week the supply of Boer meal increased noticeably, and everyone in the tent received an extra portion, but this did little good for one of the women whose children had perished. She ate a little, smiled at Detlev, and died. At her burial he wept for the first time.

But if Lord Kitchener believed that by imprisoning the Boer women he would break the spirit of their men, he misconceived the nature of these people, for when the women were thrown together, their resolve doubled and they, even more than the men, grew determined to see this war through to victory. When four had already died in her tent, Sybilla de Groot wrote a letter, which was reprinted in hundreds of newspapers:

Chrissiesmeer, Transvaal

Christmas Day 1901

General Paulus de Groot,

Never surrender. If you have to fight on foot, one against five hundred, never surrender. Carry fire to all parts of the land, but never surrender. They think that because they have thrown us here and because they deny our children food to eat that we will urge you to stop. They miscalculate. From the bottom of our hearts we cry to you, never surrender. We send you our kisses and our love, and we pray for your victory. Run, hide, retreat, burn, dynamite, Paulus, but never surrender.

Sybilla de Groot

Sara van Doorn

and 43 others

Lord Kitchener's relentless pressure began to produce limited results. Certain weary men, contrary to their wives' pleas, did surrender. They were called contemptuously 'hands-uppers,' and in the early years of the war would have been shipped off to imprisonment in Ceylon or Napoleon's St. Helena. But now, with the war approaching an end, it was deemed economical to incarcerate them within the country; with their farms burned and their families scattered, the only reasonable solution was to add them to the concentration camps. This was a dreadful mistake, for when two of these men were billeted at Chrissie Meer, Sybilla, Sara and the other incarcerated wives marched to the doctor's office and warned him: 'Get those "hands-uppers" out of here or they'll be murdered.'

'Now wait, that's a fearful thing to say. These men—'

'Get them out of here,' the women cried in unison.

'Ladies,' the doctor said in an attempt to restore sanity. Death from disease was one thing, but planned murder was another. 'Will you listen to reason?'

'If they sleep here tonight,' Sybilla said slowly, 'I myself will murder them.'

The doctor gasped. This was not a wild phrase thrown out in the heat of protest; this was the calm threat of a resolute old woman who could be depended upon to fulfill it. 'We'll move them away,' he said, and the women departed.

That was the last gesture Sara van Doorn was able to make. She was so weakened from continued fever that one morning, on a fearfully hot day, she had not the strength to rise, and Detlev went running for Sybilla, who was always up early to see if she could add a little food to the ration. 'Tant Sybilla,' the boy cried. 'I think Mother is going to die.'

'You're not to use that word.'

'She can't lift her head.'

'Then we must see what's the matter,' the old woman said, and she led the boy back to the tent. He was right, his mother was about to die. The long ordeal of keeping her family together without a husband, and now without proper food and medicine, had been too demanding. Her strength was gone, and even when Sybilla and Johanna pleaded with her, reminding her of her promise, she was powerless to respond, and toward noon, in the blazing heat, she expired.

Five in this tent had now died, so after the attendants took away her body they moved a new family of four in to take their places, and Detlev watched with equal interest the departure of his mother and the arrival of these four doomed women. But then he realized that he would never again see his mother, and with a half-wail he ran after her, clinging to Johanna's hand as the body was placed in one of Hansie's caskets. When Detlev sought consolation from this kindly carpenter, Hansie had to turn away, for he was weeping.

'Almighty God,' intoned the weary doctor, 'take these Thy children to Thy bosom.' He looked as if he might topple into the grave with them.

Of the four newcomers, two died quickly, and Johanna, watching her brother carefully, worried that he had now witnessed seven burials of people with whom he had shared the tent, two from his own family, and she asked Sybilla what the effect might be. 'Children can stand anything, if even one person loves them,' she said, remembering the days after Blaauwkrantz. 'You and I must love that boy, Johanna.'

'What about Sannah?' the girl asked, and the old woman said harshly, 'Death is upon her.'

And with dreadful speed it came. Her frail body, fourteen years old and at the height of its beauty, wasted so swiftly that even Sybilla, who had anticipated this, was aghast. The child was laughing wanly one day, unable to move the next.

'Oh, Sannah!' the little boy wept. 'I need you.'

'I need you, Detlev, my dear, dear brother.' Limply she extended a hand, and he sat holding it through the night, but before dawn he crept to where Sybilla slept and whispered, 'I think she's dead.'

'Oh, God,' Sybilla sighed.

'Shall I tell Johanna?'

'No, she needs her sleep.' She rose wearily, near fainting from lack of food, and went to the cot on which the dead girl lay and sat beside her, taking her lovely head in her lap. Detlev joined her, not crying, just sitting there in the dark. When he took one of her hands he could feel no flesh, only bones, and as he clasped it the hand grew cold.

'You are very dear to me, Detlev,' Sybilla whispered. 'You are my own son, the son of General de Groot, too. He and your real father, they fight for us, and in the years to come you must fight for us, too. You must remember these nights, Detlev. Never, never forget how Sannah felt in your arms this night. It is nights like this, Detlev, that make a man.'

They were sitting there when the attendants came, but when Johanna, waking tardily, saw them reach down for her beautiful sister, she started screaming 'No! No!' and it was Detlev who had to tell her that the girl was indeed dead. But this time at the grave he could no longer constrain himself, and when the attendants placed her in a box he started shivering as if this were some entirely new experience, and Sybilla took him in her arms.

With three of the Van Doorns dead, and both Johanna and Detlev obviously weaker each day, Sybilla de Groot realized that the salvation of this camp depended upon what women like her accomplished in the perilous days ahead. If they flagged in their dedication, the death of despair could sweep the camp, but if they sustained hope, and encouraged discipline and fortitude, lives of enormous value could be saved. She took as her litmus paper young Detlev: If I can save him, I can save the Boer republics.

Weak though she was, and close to her own death, she rallied the children of the camp about her. 'I am General de Groot's wife,' she told the parents, 'and while he is on commando in the field, you and I are on commando in this prison camp. I want your children.'

With indomitable force she organized a system whereby the children could receive just a little bit larger share of the daily ration. She persuaded Hansie Bronk to steal just a bit more food, then teased him about his notorious grandfather. But most of all she concentrated on the children, instructing them in the legends of their people.

'I was at Blaauwkrantz,' she told them. 'I was no older than you, Grietjie, when Dingane's men came after me. And do you know what I did?' The hollow, ghostly eyes of the children would stare at her as she acted out that night. 'My father placed me under a tree, in the darkest hours, and what do you think he told me?' And she would watch quietly as the children pondered, and always someone, enchanted by the story, would guess that her father had told her to be quiet, and she would smile at that child.

She told them of the long years she and Paulus de Groot had waged their battles, and of Majuba, where she saw the charge up the hill, and of recent Spion Kop, where a handful of Boers had beaten back the entire English army. She sang songs with the little ones, and played easy games that required no motion, for they were too weak, but always she returned to the theme of heroism and the simple things one man and one woman could accomplish: 'The battle was lost, no doubt about it, but General de Groot saw a weakness in the line and drove his men right at it, and we triumphed.'

'Were you afraid?' a girl asked.

'I am always afraid,' Sybilla said. 'I am afraid that I will not be brave, but when the test comes, we can all be brave.'

And at some point in each session she spoke directly to Detlev, whose salvation was paramount in her plans. She told him of how Boer boys were supposed to act, of how they had sometimes run at night to alert the villages, and of the joys they had known during long treks. Day after day she hammered into his soul the binding nails of patriotism, and reverence, and persistence. And each day she saw him grow physically weaker.

When Jakob heard that his wife and the twins were dead, and that his son Detlev was near death, and his farm totally destroyed, he became a somber madman, eager to support the wildest schemes of his general, and when De Groot suggested that the commando make a swift foray through English lines and down into the Cape, he was first to volunteer.

'I want no more than ninety men,' De Groot said. 'Forty extra horses and some of the best scouts. There's little chance we can return. Five hundred miles down, five hundred back.'

'What are we going to do?' one young fellow asked.

'Burn Port Elizabeth.'

The crowd cheered, and within a minute the old man had his ninety, but enthusiasm was tempered when plans showed that they would be forced to cross both the Vaal and the Orange . . . twice. Some wanted to know if that could be done, and he said sharply, 'It has to be.'

The Vaal, smaller of the two, would present most dangers, because the drifts were heavily guarded with extra blockhouses and mobile troops who patrolled it constantly; Lord Kitchener, having driven the various commandos into pockets, did not want them coalescing. During a dangerous reconnoiter Micah Nxumalo located a spot where the guard seemed to be relaxed, but as he explained to De Groot: 'That's because the riverbank there is steep. Difficult to ford.'

'We can't have everything,' De Groot said, but since he treasured his men, he wanted to see the terrain himself, so he went out with Micah and saw that what he had said was true: weak defense but perilous crossing. For a whole night the two men searched the area, concluding in the end that Micah's spot was best.

'We go!' De Groot said.

It was to be a brutal affair. Cut the barbed wires, overwhelm two blockhouses, killing all the guards, and gallop the ponies over the steep banks and into the Vaal River, trusting to luck that no mounted English patrols would be astir. They would do it at twelve thirty-five, an odd and arbitrary hour, and as it approached, the ninety whispered among themselves, 'On to Port Elizabeth,' and they laughed to think how surprised those people would be when their town was ablaze. That the odds against such a success were in the order of five thousand-to-one did not distress them.

At midnight they approached the blockhouses, each with seven soldiers, two ordinary posts among the eight thousand. At twelve-thirty no armed patrols had appeared, and at twelve thirty-five the Boers rushed forward.

The wire cutters went to work, and the men reached the corrugated-iron silos before those inside could fire. All fourteen were slain before they could signal the next blockhouse in line.

But soldiers in the distant houses had detected that something was wrong, and they telephoned for help. An armed patrol in the district asked for directions and began galloping across the veld, but as they reached the threatened area, they saw only the flanks of many ponies thrashing through the dark waters. There was firing, but not to much account—and in Pretoria, Lord Kitchener was awakened with the news that General de Groot had broken loose once more.

'Do the correspondents know?'

'Everyone knows.' As Lord Kitchener had said several times, 'I'd like to shoot every damned newsman. They make these damned Boer banditti the darlings of Fleet Street.'

It was a gallop for two days, then a canter for seven through the loveliest parts of the Orange Free State. They bivouacked for some time near Thaba Nchu and listened to De Groot tell about his first great battle, when Mzilikazi's men killed his entire family: 'I was a coward hiding in the wagons of this man's father.' And he slapped Van Doorn.

They rode in a kind of dream world, with the veld stretching in all directions, never a tree in sight, only the sweeping valleys, the lovely flat-topped hills, with now and then a herd of antelope moving against the slow motion of the horsemen. Thousands of skilled soldiers were hunting for this little group, but still they rode in comparative safety, the distances were so vast. When the meerkats spied on them, De Groot called down from his pony, 'Hurry and tell Lord Kitchener you saw us. And demand more pay.' Only the sky, and the distant hills, and the gentle sweep of the barren land. 'This is earth we must keep,' De Groot told his men as they rode easily, one foot in the stirrup. 'We could ride like this forever,' Jakob said quietly to a friend. There was no war, no chase, no sudden death.

The crossing of the Orange was not especially difficult because no one dreamed that a Boer commando would try anything so preposterous as an invasion of the Cape, but when the news flashed that Paulus de Groot had forded the river between Philippolis and Colesburg, the world came to attention, and diverse reactions were voiced. Those who wished England well were disgusted that the Avenger of the Veld had been allowed to run loose yet again, while those who hoped to see England humiliated, the greater part, reveled in his escapade. It was predicted that he would head west to pick off some town like Swellendam, but instead he turned sharply east to avoid Graaff-Reinet, which would be well defended; he came at last upon his original De Groot homestead, now owned by an English family.

'Each of you, select two horses,' he told the Englishman.

'What are you going to do?'

'Take two horses and anything you especially prize. Ride to Grahamstown.'

'What are you going to do?'

'This was my farm. My family's farm. And I'm going to burn it to the ground.'

'That's insanity.'

'I'll give you thirty minutes to pick the things you want. You women, gather your personal possessions.' When the Englishman protested, he said quietly, 'That's more than your Lord Kitchener gave my wife.'

When the people were herded away, he set fire to everything, adding to the combustibles when the flames threatened to go out. When the farm was reduced to ashes, he rode to the next one and then the next. At last he told Van Doorn, 'Over that hill, if I remember. I was only a child then, and maybe I don't remember. But over that hill . . .' When they reached the top there was nothing, and De Groot said, 'I was afraid. But aren't those tracks? It'll be the next hill, maybe.'

At the top of the fourth hill Jakob van Doorn saw, for the first time in his life, the splendid farm put together by his ancestors: 'I think Mal Adriaan must have started the place. The house was built by Lodevicus the Hammer. Those additions were Tjaart's, God bless that fighting man. He'd understand.'

'When this one goes up,' De Groot said with soaring enthusiasm, 'all the Cape Boers will rally to us. It'll be a whole new war.'

'All who intend to are already riding with our commandos,' Jakob warned. 'There'll be no more.'

'Of course there will. They're patriotic . . .'

'They have money, Paulus, not patriotism. I was here, remember?'

'At this farm?'

'No, but at the Cape. They talk politics, not war.'

As the commando came down the hill, the men began to shout, and from the farm buildings numerous people appeared. 'Get ready to leave!' the Venloo men cried as they began to light their torches, but before General de Groot could give the signal, a woman in a gray linsey-woolsey dress appeared at the door of the principal house.

'What do you want?' she asked as the men approached.

'I am General de Groot, of the Venloo Commando, and we are going to burn your farm.'

'I saw your wife at Chrissie Meer,' the woman said quietly. 'And aren't you Van Doorn? I saw your son and daughter.'

There was a long silence as the two men looked at this fearless woman, and finally De Groot asked, 'Are you the woman of the camps?'

'I am Maud Turner Saltwood.'

Both of the Boers spoke at once: 'The traitor?'

'The man who quit Lord Kitchener because he could not tolerate the camps.'

'You are that lady?' De Groot asked again. When she nodded, he hesitated, then wheeled his horse about and led his men, still with their flaming brands, away from the farm. He rode farther south for two days, but during that time he began to realize the futility of attempting to reach the Indian Ocean; from three directions young Boer scouts reported the presence of enemy troops, and Micah Nxumalo, who had gone in the direction of Grahamstown, said that a force of English and Cape colonials were massing there. At dawn on the third day De Groot told his commando, 'We could never get to Port Elizabeth. Let's go home.'

They left behind them a flame of glory and wonder, the commando that almost reached the sea, the men from the tiny town of Venloo who rode through the heartland of the conqueror and then turned back, untouched by the four hundred thousand who searched for them.

When Maud Saltwood returned to Chrissie Meer to complete her documentation on the concentration camps, she wanted to examine, as dispassionately as possible, the actual conditions, and she sought out Sybilla de Groot, knowing her to be a sensible woman. But she found her so emaciated from dysentery that she wondered how she could stand, let alone converse intelligently.

'Was Frank Saltwood a spy?' the old woman asked.

'We've never discussed it.'

'We know that Lord Kitchener's a monster.'

'He's not a monster. He's a foolish, bullheaded man who has no heart. Now we must get you some medicine.'

'There is none,' the old woman said, and she was right. The English could bring into this tight area four hundred and forty-eight thousand soldiers, but they could not find space in their ships for the extra medicines and food needed to save emaciated women and children. They could import a hundred thousand horses for their cavalry, but not three cows for their concentration camps. Guns bigger than houses they could haul in, but no hospital equipment. It was insane; it was horrifying; and in her news reports Maud Saltwood said so.

'That woman should be shot' was Lord Kitchener's sober evaluation of the affair. Many members of Parliament felt the same way, and her husband's cousin, Sir Victor, kept a low profile, for she had besmirched his name. But on she went, one woman exposing to the world the monstrous wrong of these camps. In Cape Town many English families stopped speaking to her husband, while others commiserated with him over his wife's misconduct, not realizing that he supported her enthusiastically. His income, which she spent lavishly, kept alive some three hundred women who would otherwise have perished, and for this he would be forever grateful to his vigorous wife.

While Kitchener raged, Maud quietly continued interrogating women at Chrissie Meer, spending much time in the associated camp where blacks were being held. There she talked with women of Micah Nxumalo's family, and they were suffering as sorely as the whites.

'Why we here?' one woman asked plaintively, showing her thin arms.

'Isn't your father fighting with the Boers?' Maud asked.

'Your husband fight with English. They throw you in jail?'

Her most fruitful discussions were with Sybilla de Groot, for the old woman sensed that she would soon die and was eager to have her views spread before the world: 'Like many wrong things, it was all wrong. There should have been no camps.'

'Some say,' Maud argued, 'that the camps were good for you women. They gave you security.'

If Sybilla had been strong, she would have raged and stomped about the little bell tent; she was so weak she had to remain seated, but she did point to the entrance: 'Through there we have carried eight dead. Detlev counts them for me. What kind of security is that?'

But when Maud asked about sanitary conditions, the old woman did make certain concessions: 'We were farm families, far from towns. We didn't have privies like they say we must. We didn't have these new medicines. In the free veld we were never sick. In these tents, these dirty barracks, we die. Eight of us, and soon me.' She rocked back and forth, tears streaming from her eyes. 'That's why I say it was wrong from the beginning. It was all wrong.'

'Did you get enough to eat?' Maud asked.

Sybilla held out her arms for inspection. 'You don't get enough. You grow weak. So you get sick. Then, no matter how much you eat, it does no good.' She pointed to the field not far from her tent where women and children, driven mad by dysentery, were squatting and wrenching their insides. 'It's all wrong,' she said.

Desperately Maud wanted to keep this great woman alive, as a symbol of the fact that English women, at least, would do everything in their power to save a Boer woman, even though she was the wife of their country's principal aggravator. She failed.

In April 1902, when the imperial armies were at last closing in upon Paulus de Groot, pinning him against the barbed-wire fences but never catching him, Detlev woke early one morning to find his Tant Sybilla gasping. Since it was a clear autumn day, with the air somewhat fresher than usual, he knew the old woman was in distress, and he wanted to awaken Johanna, but his sister was deep in sleep, exhausted in the cool morning air, so he went to Sybilla's cot alone.

'Are you awake?'

'I hoped you'd come.' She turned her head weakly, and when he looked at her arms, thin as the reeds beside their lake, he realized that she was powerless to move. 'Fetch Johanna.'

'She's still asleep.'

'Let her rest.'

'Are you all right, Tannie?'

'I'm resting, too.'

'Shall I sit with you?'

'Oh, I would like that.' She lay quietly, his hand in hers. Then she showed renewed vitality and clutched him tighter. 'They say the war's almost over, Detlev. For you it's just beginning. Never forget these days. Never forget that it was the English who did these things. You must fight, fight.'

He wanted to say that he had no horse, but she continued: 'Detlev, you may never see the general again. Remember, he did not surrender. Even when they came at him from all sides . . .'

She seemed to fall asleep, then awakened with a start. 'Whether she's sleeping or not, I must speak to Johanna.' When he roused his sister, the old woman said brusquely, 'Now you go out and play.' He walked slowly from the tent, but there was no play. There were more than seventy young children in the camp that morning, but there was no play. They sat in the sun and breathed deeply, as if they had strength only for that.

On her deathbed Sybilla admonished Johanna: 'If I die before noon, tell no one. That way you can get my ration for today. And, Johanna, it's now up to you to see that Detlev survives. Women are stronger than men. You must keep him alive so he can carry on the fight. Even if you must starve yourself, keep him alive. Never surrender.'

This effort exhausted her, and she was near death, but suddenly her entire face became animated, not only her eyes. Clutching at Johanna, she gasped, 'And if they bring "hands-uppers" into this camp, kill them. Find long needles and kill them. In this camp heroes lived, not "hands-uppers." '

She was dead. Johanna called Detlev because she knew her brother loved this old woman, and he understood when she pledged him to secrecy. They sat all morning on her bed, talking to her, and got her ration, and when the attendants finally came to take her away, Detlev did not cry; many children in this camp never cried. But toward evening, when Johanna was apportioning the stolen ration, something happened that he would never forget: years later, generations later, he would remember that instant. Johanna broke the food into two equal pieces, weighed them in her two frail hands, then took from one and added to the other, making it much bigger. 'This is yours,' she said, and she handed him the larger share.

When the remaining Boer generals met to consider what they must do in the face of the overwhelming pressure brought against them by Lord Kitchener, they realized that in order to have an orderly discussion they must somehow muzzle Paulus de Groot. They knew that he would bellow 'No surrender,' and they were willing to have him say this once, to clear his conscience, but they did not want him repeating it every ten minutes to the detriment of sensible evaluations.

'We are not defeated,' one of the younger men said. 'The English have lost six thousand men killed. Sixteen thousand more dead in their hospitals. Twenty-three thousand more or less seriously wounded.'

'What have our losses been?' an older man asked.

'Maybe five thousand killed, but they were our finest.'

'How many children have died in the camps?' the old man asked.

'Twenty thousand.' From the rear of the room a man sighed. It was Jakob van Doorn, there to support his general.

'More than all the men on both sides, we have lost our children.'

'There was nothing we could do about it,' a young general said.

'There's something we can do about it now,' another man said. 'We can surrender.'

This was the word that De Groot was waiting for. Quietly he said, 'We shall never surrender. We can carry this fight for another six years.'

'We can indeed,' one of the younger generals said. 'But can our children?' And the debate continued.

On a day in late April an event occurred at the Chrissie Meer camp which worsened, even more, English-Boer relations. As Detlev van Doorn was about to eat a spoonful of meal, his sister Johanna rushed into the tent and knocked the bowl away.

'Don't touch it!' she screamed.

He was so ravenous that he automatically fell to the floor, grabbing for the mealies, but again she cried, 'Don't touch it!' and although her own body was wasting away with hunger, she ground the food into the dust.

'Johanna!' he pleaded, bewildered by her action.

'They've mixed ground glass in our food. Mrs. Pretorius ate some and died.'

There were sixteen good medical reasons why Mrs. Pretorius should have died that day, and the seventeenth was most forceful of all: typhoid. But the prisoners began to believe that she had died from eating powdered glass, and no amount of logical persuasion could convince them otherwise. Thus the hideous legend festered and spread.

The little doctor, whose voice so often rose to a scream in this charnel house, came out to the women to swear upon his sacred honor that the English would never do anything like that. He himself ate the pap. Would eat another dishful right now, taken from anywhere. 'The English,' he insisted, 'do not put ground glass in people's food.'

'Kitchener would!' a woman cried, and all his efforts were fruitless. As Johanna told her hungry brother that night, 'Always remember, Detlev. When we were starving the English tried to kill us with ground glass in the mealies.'

At the final meeting of the generals it was agreed that Paulus de Groot be kept away. They had heard his speech on bitter-ending; they respected his heroism; but the time had come when further resistance was futile. The Boers were ready to surrender.

After the painful decision was reached, they sent the young lawyer Jan Christian Smuts to inform the old man. Smuts, having been a courageous commando leader himself and one of the youngest, carried good credentials, and when he appeared, De Groot could guess his mission: 'It's all over, Paulus. You can go home.'

'I would like to fight once more, Jan Christian.'

'So would we all. But the children . . .'

'The children most of all would understand.'

'You must go home.'

'Let me have my Venloo men and we'll go.'

'No.' Smuts laughed. 'None of that, old man. We've sent the Venloo men on ahead. We couldn't trust you.'

'Can I be at the surrender? I'd like to smash that Kitchener.'

'No, it's best if you go home.'

'Perhaps so,' the old man said, and without farewells he called for Van Doorn, and together they sought out Micah Nxumalo, and the three veterans headed north. When they reached the crest from which they could first see the lake, they looked down at the awful desolation of what had been their homes. Of De Groot's farm, there were no signs except the charred stumps of the buildings, not six inches above the ground. Of Vrymeer, only the shells of the structures built by Tjaart van Doorn were visible. Of the place where Micah Nxumalo's huts had stood, only the base of the ronda-vels remained.

The two white men did not speak. Sybilla was dead, and Sara, and the twins. Johanna was lost somewhere, and Jakob prayed that the boy Detlev was with her. When he turned to look toward the direction of the concentration camp, as if to find the children, he saw the matched peaks of Sannie's Tits and they reminded him of the twins, those precious girls. He dropped his head. He had not the courage to go down the hill to that ruined farm, those vanished hopes.

General de Groot tugged at his arm: 'Come, Jakob, much work to be done.' And as the ponies moved forward, the old warrior said with clenched determination, 'We lost the battles. We lost the war. Now we must win in other ways.'

XI.
Education
of a Puritan

THE education of Detlev van Doorn began on the day he came over the hill with his sister from the concentration camp at Chrissie Meer and saw the devastation of his home. His father and old General de Groot were waiting in the ruins, and after the briefest greetings they led him to a grassy slope where Nxumalo's five huts had stood. There he saw, sticking up from the earth at regular intervals, four wooden tombstones bearing in ill-formed letters the names: SYBILLA DE GROOT, SARA VAN DOORN, SANNAH, ANNA.

'Never forget,' the general said. 'These women were murdered by the English, who fed them powdered glass.'

Detlev was seven, a little boy with the pinched features of an old man and the cautious wisdom of someone in his forties. 'They were buried in the camp. They can't be here.'

'Their tombstones,' De Groot said. 'For remembrance.'

'Those aren't stones,' Detlev said.

'Later, when we have a farm again,' his father said. 'We'll have proper stones.'

'Wood or stone,' De Groot said, 'you must never forget.'

'Where shall we stay?' Johanna asked.

'We've fixed up the old wagon,' her father said, and he led his children to that frail relic in which his father, Tjaart van Doorn, had taken his family across the Drakensberg, then north of the Limpopo, and finally back to Vrymeer. Van Doorn and the general had locked the big wheels and used boards to form a kind of shelter on the wagon bed, but it clearly could not hold a young woman like Johanna, a boy and two grown men. When De Groot saw her look of perplexity, he laughed. 'You two sleep up here. We two down below.' And she saw that under the wagon body, her father had arranged boards on the ground, where he and the old man would make their beds.

On the first wintry night that the four spent together—no pillows, no blankets—Jakob awakened at dawn, and in the dim light saw over his head, carved into the heavy wood of the frame, the rubric TC–43 and he wondered what it signified. When De Groot awakened, Jakob asked, 'What do you suppose this means?' The old general squinted his eyes, studied the marks, and remained silent, as though brooding over something. Finally he grumbled, 'One of the only two decent Englishmen I ever knew. Thomas Carleton built this wagon and he and Richard Saltwood gave it to your father. Yes, gave it.' He reflected on the enormity of having taken refuge under an English wagon, then added, 'I rode two thousand miles in this wagon . . . walking beside it most of the way.'

Detlev, who was already awake, called down from above, 'How could you ride and walk at the same time?'

Reaching into the wagon, General de Groot pulled the boy out and tossed him in the air. When he set him on the ground he said, 'You do what you have to do. Once I helped carry this wagon down the Drakensberg.'

'What will you do, sleeping down there, if it rains?' Detlev asked.

'I won't let it rain,' De Groot promised, and during the four weeks it took to assemble a kind of roof over one room of the ruined farmhouse, it did not.

In the second week they stopped work when Detlev cried, 'People coming!' Across the veld they saw a distant file walking toward them, and ominously Jakob reached for his gun. 'Kaffirs,' he said, indicating that his son must stand behind him.

In the chaos after the war, bands of homeless hungry blacks had started raiding Boer farms in the district, stealing what they could find and roughing up any farmer who tried to protest, but there was nothing to fear from this company, for Detlev shouted, 'It's Micah!'

At the sight of only three Van Doorns and one De Groot, tears began to roll from Micah's eyes, for he knew that the absence of the others could mean only one thing, for he, too, was returning from a camp, one for blacks, in which his family and friends had been interned, and of his four wives, only two had survived; of nine children, only three were left.

The suffering of these black Boers would go unrecorded. Even Maud Turner Saltwood, who had done so much for Boer women and children, had to admit, in a final report, that the situation of the black internees had been without hope: 'Beyond affording a little relief to the sick in the few camps I visited, we were able to do nothing.' More than one hundred thousand blacks and Coloureds had been herded behind barbed wire; how many came out alive would never be known.

When De Groot learned of Nxumalo's heavy loss he was overwhelmed. In a gesture from the heart he held out his arms to his saddle companion and embraced him: 'Kaffirtjie, as true as there's a God in heaven we'll not forget what they did to both of us. Stay close and one day we'll ride again.'

Nxumalo nodded.

'This what's left of your family?' the general asked, and when Nxumalo nodded again, the old man took a step back to survey the land where the handsome rondavels had once stood. 'We must all start over. But this time, by God, they'll not be able to burn down what we build.'

So Nxumalo and his people returned to their security at Vrymeer, and he sketched in the ruins how his women must build the new huts. Early next morning he led the men who'd accompanied him from the camp to the Van Doorns' farmhouse, where they all started work. They did not ask what the arrangement would be for their employment. They just carried on as before.

The Van Doorns were surprised at the end of the first month when the old general informed them that since they now had protection from the weather, he would like to start rebuilding his farm. 'But you're to live with us,' Johanna protested with great warmth.

'No, I want a place of my own.'

'Who will cook? How will you live?'

The answer came from one of Nxumalo's wives. 'He is old,' she said. 'He needs help. We go to his place.' And Micah agreed that the woman and a young girl must accompany the old warrior to his shattered home.

Utilizing the foundation of what at best had been a miserable house, they put together what could only be called a hartebeest hut, a pitiful affair with a flap-door and no windows. One morning as Jakob surveyed the astonishing place he thought: In our barbarism we retreat many centuries. A hundred years ago our people lived better than this. Two hundred years ago they surely built better huts.

Could he have gone back to the year when Mal Adriaan, Dikkop and Swarts lived here beside the lake, he would have found them in simpler but better quarters than these, and certainly in the days of the first Nxumalo the village and fine rondavels that stood here were superior to what the old man occupied. The centuries pass, Jakob thought, and men stay about where they were.

The rains were coming late this year, producing a drought so severe that many farmers in the area, faced by the necessity to rebuild and also to fight dust, were giving up and moving to Johannesburg, where they could at least find some kind of employment in the mines. 'I don't like this,' the general complained when he heard that four families had pulled up stakes and headed for the city. 'Boers are farmers. Our name says that. We don't do well in cities. The damned mines, they're for the Englishmen and Hoggenheimer.'

'Who's Hoggenheimer?' Detlev asked.

'The Jew who owns the mines,' and he produced a newspaper which had been circulated avidly from farm to farm. It contained two biting cartoons by a persuasive artist named Boonzaaier, showing a bloated Jew, fingers bejeweled, vest enclosing a gigantic belly, cigar at an angle, wearing a derby while gorging on the food for which starving Boers pleaded in vain. That was Hoggenheimer, and on him was thrown the blame for everything ill that was happening in the conquered republics.

'If you ever run away to Johannesburg,' the old man said, 'you'll meet Hoggenheimer.'

The old general came over to the Van Doorn farm quite often, riding his pony, wearing his frock coat and sometimes his top hat. He came not for food or companionship, but to supervise the education of young Detlev: 'You must remember that your great-grandfather, one of the finest men who ever lived, was dragged to an English court, where a Kaffir was allowed to bring testimony against him . . .' Night after night he reviewed with Detlev the vast wrongs done by the English at Slagter's Nek and at Chrissiesmeer, where they put ground glass in the meal. 'Never trust an Englishman,' De Groot reiterated. 'They've stolen your country.'

'But Mrs. Saltwood was English,' Detlev said. 'She brought the food that kept us alive.'

De Groot, remembering how he had confronted Mrs. Saltwood on the stoep at De Kraal, would concede only that 'some few English ladies, yes, they had hearts.' But having granted this, he would proceed with the litany: Slagter's Nek . . . Kitchener . . . glass in the meal.

The education was fiercely effective and achieved precisely what De Groot intended. 'Detlev, your father and I fought our battles, and we lost. You will fight other battles, and you will win.'

'I can shoot straight.'

'Every Boer boy can shoot straight,' and he would digress to tell the boy of how his men, always outnumbered, would hide behind rocks and pick off Englishmen one by one: 'Ten bullets, you ought to get at least eight Englishmen.'

'I could shoot an Englishman,' Detlev insisted, whereupon the old man clasped him tight and whispered, 'Pray God you never have to. You'll win your battles in more clever ways.'

'How?'

De Groot tapped the little boy on the forehead: 'By learning. By becoming clever.'

And that was to be the foundation of Detlev's formal education, which began one day when there rode up to the farm a remarkable man: tall, thin, with very big hands that he used awkwardly and knees that protruded from his heavy trousers. He had yellowish hair, not at all becoming a man of his size, and one of the kindest faces Detlev had ever seen. He told the Van Doorns, 'My name is Amberson, Jonathan Amberson, and I've been sent by the new government to open a school at Venloo. I should be most happy to see your son in my classes.'

'He can't ride into Venloo every day,' Jakob protested.

'Nor shall he. Mrs. Scheltema will be running a hostel—'

'Are you English?' Johanna broke in.

'Of course. It's the new school, the new government.'

'We wouldn't want any English here,' she said bitterly.

'But—'

'Out. Get out of this house and off this farm.' Detlev, watching everything, feared that she might strike the tall stranger, who bowed, backed down off the stoep, and departed.

When General de Groot heard of this some days later, he became quite agitated: 'No, no! Not that way at all.'

'He was English,' Johanna snapped. 'Do you think we want our boy to learn English ways—'

'That's exactly what we want.' And for the first time young Detlev heard the strategy of his life spelled out—and he comprehended every word.

'The problem is this,' the old man said, while Detlev sat on his knee. 'The English know how to run the world. They understand banks and newspapers and schools. They are very capable people . . . in everything but war. And do you know why, Detlev?'

'At the camp, Dr. Higgins cried a lot.'

'Who was Dr. Higgins?'

'The man who was supposed to keep us alive. When we died, he often cried. Men don't do that.'

'Answer my question. "Why are the English so clever and we Boers so dumb?" '

'My father isn't dumb,' Detlev said quickly. 'And you're not dumb, Oupa.'

'I mean in books and banks and things like that.'

'I don't know.'

'The English are clever because they know things we don't.'

'What things?' Detlev asked, all attention.

'Books. Figures. Big ideas.' These words landed like Krupp shells in the little kitchen. No one spoke, and Detlev looked at his three elders, each of whom nodded. He would never forget this heavy moment.

'So what you are to do, my young clever one, is go to the English school and find out everything they know.' When Detlev nodded, the old man continued: 'You are to be the brightest boy that teacher has ever met. You are to learn everything.'

'Why?' the somber little boy asked.

'Because when you know as much as they do, you can declare a new kind of war against the English.' The old man's hands began to tremble. 'You are the generation that will win this country back. You will win the war that your father and I lost.'

General de Groot felt so strongly about this that he personally led Detlev in to Venloo, and he was impressed by the efforts taken to improve the old house that now served as schoolroom and hostel, and by the care with which Mr. Amberson had arranged things. There were books, and slates, and pictures on the wall . . . When he saw the florid portrait in color of King Edward VII he turned away.

'We are honored to have with us this morning,' Amberson said in hesitant Dutch, 'a great hero of this country, General Paulus de Groot, the hero of Majuba, the Avenger of the Veld. We never did catch you, did we, General?'

De Groot was astounded by such words coming from an Englishman, and when the nineteen children applauded he dropped Detlev's hand and retreated.

At the end of the second week, when De Groot returned to fetch Detlev, he asked no questions on the short ride to the farm, but that evening when supper was ended, the three adults sat the boy in a chair, faced him, and asked, 'What happened?'

He liked school and especially he liked Mr. Amberson, who was patient with his young scholars. 'He explains everything,' Detlev said enthusiastically, 'but sometimes I can't understand his words.'

'Does he teach in Dutch?' Johanna asked.

'Of course. We don't know any English.'

'What does he teach you?'

'That King Edward is now our king . . .'

Johanna stomped out of the room.

'Does he teach you how to figure?' De Groot asked.

'Oh, yes!' And with some enthusiasm the little boy began to recite the two-times table, but in English.

'What are you saying?' De Groot cried.

'Two-times,' the boy replied.

'But in what language?' the old man roared.

'In English. Mr. Amberson says that after he learns our language and we learn his, all classes will be in English.'

De Groot was so agitated that he began pacing about, but after a while he calmed down and lifted the boy up, sitting him on his knee. 'Of course. You must learn English as fast as you can. Every week you must learn more English, because that's how they conduct their affairs.'

But at the half-year mark, when General de Groot went to fetch Detlev, he found the boy quite distraught but unwilling to talk, so on the way back to the farm he did no probing, but when they were assembled that night Detlev suddenly burst into tears. 'What is it?' Johanna asked with great solicitude. She allowed the old general to mastermind the lad's education, but she felt responsible for his safekeeping, and when he wept in this manner she knew that something most serious had occurred, for he was a boy who did not cry.

'What is it, Detlev?'

'I had to wear the dunce's cap.'

He knew the word only in English, and when the three demanded further explanation, he fashioned with his hands the long, thin paper hat he had been required to wear four times that week.

'What for?' the general exploded.

'Because I used Dutch words.'

'You what . . .'

'Yes. New rules. Any boy or girl who speaks Dutch instead of English must stand in the corner, with the tall hat and a sign which says "I spoke Dutch today." '

'But Mr. Amberson himself speaks Dutch. You said so.'

'Not any more. He said we'd been in class half a year now and must never again speak Dutch.'

'That monster!' Johanna snapped. She was twenty-three, a fierce, hard-working young woman, and if this schoolmaster was mistreating her brother, she would teach him a lesson.

'No,' Detlev said quietly through his tears. 'He is not a bad man. He is very kind, and he helps me with my numbers. But he says that our country is now English—the war decided that—and we must forget we were ever Dutch.'

'Good God!' Johanna cried, but to her surprise it was General de Groot who pacified her.

'We must remember that this is still war,' the old man said, and he took from his pocket a newspaper containing a new set of Hoggenheimer cartoons, proving that the Jews were stealing the country. It carried also a statement by the English high commissioner, which unknowingly outlined the nature of the insidious battle the Boers now faced:

If ten years hence there are three men of British race to two of Dutch, this country will be safe and prosperous. If there are three of Dutch and two of British, we shall have perpetual difficulty.

Coldly, De Groot explained the next level of strategies: 'The English are doing everything they can to bring in more of their people. Bring them in and drown us in a wave of English books, English plays, English education.'

'But you said you wanted me to learn English,' Detlev said.

'I do. Detlev, I want you to learn all of everything. Whenever he offers you a new English word, take it and say to yourself, "This is a knife I shall use against you." '

'When?'

'Every day of your life from now on. When you are twelve, use your knowledge against the English boys that age. At eighteen, use it against the young men in college. At thirty, against the Hoggenheimers in Johannesburg. At fifty, against the government people in Pretoria. And when you're an old man like me, keep using it. The enemy is the English, and they can be destroyed only by cleverness.'

Johanna, deeply angered by the psychological abuse heaped on Detlev by the dunce's cap and the degrading sign, wanted to ride right in to Venloo and confront Mr. Amberson, but the old general had more to say: 'Accept English in your mind, but keep Dutch in your heart. For if a conqueror once makes you accept his language, he makes you his slave. We were defeated . . .'

He had never voiced that admission before. He had said, 'We've lost the battles. We've lost the war.' But he had never conceded that he had been defeated. Now, as he uttered the terrible words, he rose from his chair and stamped about the little kitchen. 'We have been defeated—your father, I, Oom Paul, General de la Rey, General Smuts . . .' He stopped speaking, for the words were grinding in his throat. Then with a great roar he cried, 'But the next war we shall win. The war for ideas. You and I will see the day when Dutch is the only language in this land—the only one that counts. There will be no English spoken where men of power assemble.' Towering over Detlev, he pointed a long finger at him: 'And you will be responsible.'

Johanna felt her own responsibility, and early Monday morning when the time came for General de Groot to take the boy back to school, she surprised him by saying sternly, 'I take him today.'

She arrived at the school half an hour early and found that Mr. Amberson was there, arranging his materials. The first thing she saw, waiting in the corner, was the dunce's cap and the elegantly lettered sign: I SPOKE DUTCH TODAY. Walking directly to them, she said, 'Why would you dare use these?'

'I use the cap every day. For numbers missed, for words misspelled.'

'But this?' she demanded, shaking the sign at him.

'It's half a year now, Miss van Doorn. The children must begin seriously to learn the language under which they will live for the rest of their lives.'

'It won't be English, Mr. Amberson.'

He was astonished by this statement, for it had never occurred to him that Dutch could persist in competition with the victors' language, but he surprised both Johanna and Detlev by the gentlemanly manner in which he reacted. 'Sit down,' he said graciously, and when she elaborated her complaint, he listened attentively, endeavoring to catch the full meaning of her words, for she would speak only in the language of her people, the vital adaptation of Dutch by generations of her ancestors.

'There is something else we must take into account,' he said courteously, as if reasoning with a child. 'I'm told that the Dutch you do speak —in these parts, and throughout the country—I'm told it really isn't very good Dutch and should not be perpetuated.'

'Who told you that?'

'Mr. Op t'Hooft, who comes from Amsterdam and works in the education department.'

'Another Hollander! Damn them all, they come out here, take a job and then lord it over us.'

'But Mr. Op t'Hooft intends taking out citizenship. He prefers it here.'

'We don't want him.' The mention of another Hollander who was riding roughshod over the local Boers enraged Johanna and sidetracked her from her main complaint.

'Miss van Doorn, I'm sure President Kruger's government didn't want to hire so many Hollanders, but it had to, because your people out on these farms . . .' He felt that he was getting into deep water, and tried again: 'The Boers were simply wonderful at warfare, maybe the best free fighters on earth. My brother fought against General de Groot, you know. King's Own Royal Rifles, you know.' Johanna stared at him as if he were an imbecile, and he ended lamely, 'You Boers refuse to learn business procedures, so President Kruger had to invite the Hollanders in to run the government. Absolutely essential.'

'They can go home now,' she said tartly. And then she changed the subject: 'Mr. Amberson, I wish you would not again hang that sign about my brother's neck.'

'He must stop speaking Dutch in class, really he must.'

'Why? If this is to be a Dutch country?'

'Ah, but it's to be English.' He hesitated. 'The language, that is.'

They had reached an impasse, and when she returned to the farm she sought out the general, asking him if he thought the Dutch spoken by the people of Venloo was as corrupted as Mr. Op t'Hooft, whoever he was, seemed to think.

'Yes. We have a different language now. Our own. Your father and mine fashioned it. Simpler and better.'

'Should we allow the Hollanders who run everything to stay on?'

'Kick them all out. They despise us, and God knows, we despise them. Just because they can speak like Amsterdamers, they think they're lords and ladies. I say, "Kick their asses out." ' He apologized for his rough speech, then repeated it.

But any worry over the insolent Hollanders, most of whom were going home anyway, since they deplored the barbaric level of society they had to suffer in towns like Pretoria and Bloemfontein, vanished when the real menace showed itself. Word of this disastrous decision had reached Venloo, and when Detlev came home from school he astonished his elders by announcing, 'They're bringing in sixty thousand Chinese workmen.'

'What?' the general shouted.

'Yes. The mine owners say that since the war they can't get any more Kaffirs, so ships are sailing into Durban with Chinese.'

'Who is doing this?' the old man bellowed, but despite his fevered questioning he could find no rational answers, so he decided to take the little money he had and ride the train in to Johannesburg and see for himself what the crisis amounted to.

'You're to come with me,' he said to Detlev, and when the boy protested that he must report to school, the general said, 'More important that you see the enemy,' and he rode with the boy to Waterval-Boven, where they caught the train.

It was a stunning adventure for Detlev—travelers eating their meals while they sped westward, the sweep of the veld, the farms struggling back into production, and on the far horizon the first sight of a major city. De Groot was welcomed wherever he went, both by his former Boer cronies and by the English, who held him in high regard for his heroic conduct in two wars. From his acquaintances he learned that yes, the government was in the process of importing sixty thousand Chinese to work the mines, and he also heard disturbing rumors about the behavior of these coolies.

The government and the Englishmen who ran the mines seriously believed that it was possible to import sixty thousand vigorous young men, all of them under thirty, and have them work deep in the gold mines— without their wanting any recreation, or association with women, or any kind of reasonable relaxation for a period of ten or twenty years. When the young men began to gamble, the Dutch Reformed Church was horrified. When they began to form liaisons with black or Coloured or lowly white women, the predikants screamed from their pulpits that God would scourge this land if that were permitted. And when some enraged coolie actually killed another, Englishmen and Boers alike claimed that this proved the Chinese were a gang of animals.

Nothing that the government would do in the first decade after the English victory would so excite the Boers as this importation of Chinese, and when Paulus de Groot actually saw the yellow men going down into the mines he experienced an anger that would not be assuaged. In fact, he was so outraged that when he returned to his quarters in the city, a Boer friend, who shared his emotion, suggested that they go see General Koos de la Rey, who had tormented the English for three years during the late war. When Detlev met this famous man, not so tall as General de Groot but gentler of face, he realized that he was seeing a significant part of his nation's history, and when later General Christiaan Beyers joined them, Detlev saw a grand triumvirate.

They discussed how they might force the government to rescind the law which allowed the importation of the Chinese. 'More important,' De la Rey said, 'is how we kick those already here out of the country.' It was agreed that everyone must work for the repatriation of the Chinese, but then talk turned to an even more serious point.

'I am disgusted with the mistakes this government is making,' De Groot said bluntly. 'Do you know what they're doing with our children? Tell them, Detlev . . . about the dunce's cap.' When the little boy did, the generals listened soberly, but then De Groot said, 'The sign. Tell them about the sign.' When this humiliating incident was related, they shook their

heads, and after a long while De Groot said quietly, 'One of these days we
will all be riding again. Against the English, for they do not know how to
govern.'

Neither of the other generals responded to this, but De Groot repeated
his prophecy: 'You will be back in the saddle, both of you. And do you know
why? Because Germany is stirring. Germany is on the march, and sooner
or later we'll see an expeditionary force landing in South-West Africa.
What'll they do? They'll march this way and consolidate with their colony
in East Africa. And what do we do? We join them. And in that moment
we kick the English out of here forever.'

Detlev would remember that somber moment: De Groot, De la Rey,
Beyers looking ahead to the wild twists and turns of war, and he suspected
that each man hoped that when Germany began to play a vital role in
Africa, all decent men would side with her against the hated English.

'If it were to happen,' General Beyers asked carefully, 'would the others
join us?'

De Groot was sure that the great hero De Wet would support Germany,
and so would others. 'The man we'd have to fear is that young upstart Jan
Christian.'

'Who is he?' Detlev broke in.

'Smuts,' De Groot said. 'A brave general, but I despise his politics.'

After this informal meeting, De Groot walked the boy around Johannesburg, pointing to the large buildings dominated by the English business
leaders. When they came to one group of important offices he made Detlev
stand there and read off all the names of the lawyers, the insurance men,
the business negotiators, and when the boy reached FRANK SALTWOOD,
AGENT, he said, 'That was the spy who burned our farms. Never forget.'
And once more the boy symbolized the contradictions in which nations and
people find themselves, for he said, 'Mrs. Saltwood saved my life.'

The most important lesson General de Groot taught Detlev came not from
what he said but from what he did. When the English government released
the captured Boers who had been interned in distant places like Ceylon,
Bermuda and St. Helena, from the latter island came a great hulking man,
taller than De Groot, on whose sloping shoulders rested a heavy burden.
He was General Pieter Cronje, who in 1900 had surrendered at Paardeberg
his entire army of nearly four thousand troops, the most disastrous loss in
the war.

A photographer had happened to catch a stunning shot of the surrender, from which an artist working for the *Illustrated London News* made
a most effective sepia wash, which eventually was seen throughout the
world, becoming the traditional depiction of Boer-English relationships.
There came Cronje, looking six feet seven, in rumpled field trousers, vest,
coat and overcoat, bearded, dirty, and wearing a huge broad-brimmed hat.
Waiting for him stood little Lord Roberts, one-eyed, one hundred and thirty
pounds, bristling mustache, all spit-and-polish boots and leatherwork,
jaunty expeditionary cap at a sharp angle. 'The Giant Surrendering to the
Midget' the picture was sometimes called.

The copy which General de Groot kept on the wall of his house showed signs of having been spat upon; it was also punctured where the old man had thrown a fork at it. This version was titled 'Cronje Meets His Master,' and when De Groot explained its significance to Detlev he said, 'A man should rather die with six bullets in his belly than face such a moment. Don't ever surrender.'

Detlev was surprised, therefore, when he looked up one morning at the farm and saw the gigantic figure of General Cronje waiting on the stoep. It could be no one else, and when the deep voice rumbled, 'Waar is die generaal?' Detlev replied, 'He lives at the house.' He led Cronje to De Groot's place and was present when the two generals met. They did not embrace in the French manner, but stood respectfully apart, inclining their heads slightly out of mutual respect.

'Come in, Cronje,' De Groot said, ushering him into the sparsely furnished room. 'How was St. Helena?'

'Napoleon died there. I didn't.'

'What happened at Paardeberg?'

The general seated himself uneasily on an upended box and shrugged his shoulders. 'From babyhood we were taught "When you face trouble, go into laager." I faced trouble, Kitchener hammering at me like a madman, Roberts waiting. So I went into laager, but the old rules no longer applied. Not when they had cannon to rim the laager and blow its insides to bits.'

'Now, that's curious,' De Groot said. 'My family lost its life against Mzilikazi because it didn't go into laager. You lost everything because you did.'

'Times change.' He shook his head, then got down to business. 'Paulus, you're living like a pig. Things aren't good for me, either. But we both have a chance to earn a lot of money.'

'How?'

'Have you ever heard of St. Louis? The American city?'

'No.'

'I'm told it's important, bigger than Cape Town.'

'What's it got to do with us?' De Groot asked suspiciously.

'They're having a large World's Fair. Biggest of its kind.'

'Yes?'

'They've seen the drawing of me and Lord Roberts. They've sent a man here, untold funds. He wants me to collect a small commando of Boers who can ride well and shoot from the saddle. Blanks, of course. They'll have American soldiers dressed like Englishmen, and in a big arena you and I will come in riding and shooting. There'll be a mock fight, and then there'll be a tableau.'

'A what?'

'Everybody stops . . . dead still. And the audience sees that it's a representation of my surrender to Lord Roberts.'

De Groot simply sat there, arms folded, legs spread apart, staring at his old companion. Cronje had helped storm Majuba back in 1881. He was a verified hero, but he was also the man who had behaved poorly at Paardeberg. If such a tragic twist in fortune had been forced upon De Groot, he would have shot his brains out. Cronje was proposing to go to St. Louis, wherever that was, and ride his pony into an arena firing blank cartridges, and then surrender again, twice a day, six days a week, to Lord Roberts.

Slowly the old man rose, indicating that Cronje must do the same. Sternly he edged the huge warrior to the hut doorway, where he said, 'Piet, dear comrade, as you can see, I need the money. But there's never been a time in my life when I fired blank cartridges, and I'm too old to learn.'

Cronje had no trouble in conscripting other fine horsemen, who went to St. Louis and put on an exhibition that dazzled the locals, improving considerably their estimation of Boers. But whenever the band stopped dramatically, and two small cannon roared, and the lights came on, General Cronje stepped forward in the costume he had worn in the photograph and surrendered to a taut little major on detached duty from Fort Sill who wore a fake mustache and a replica of an English uniform.

When photographs of this tableau filtered back to South Africa, they caused anguish, but in St. Louis the approval was so marked that Cronje's contracted salary was raised. General de Groot found one of these photographs and tacked it to the wall, beside the original version.

'Remarkable,' he told Detlev when the boy first compared the two. 'How could they get the surrender so accurate?' Detlev was afraid the old man was going to tear the wall apart, so strained became the muscles on his neck, but all he did was tap the two pictures gently, as if they were of value. 'Never surrender, Detlev,' he said. 'Not even in play.'

The people at Vrymeer were so obviously concerned about Detlev's education that Mr. Amberson fell into the habit of riding out from Venloo now and then to report on their boy's progress, and as he sat in the kitchen at the farm, Detlev noticed two things about him. Unlike the hefty Boer farmers of the area, this thin young man could sit in a chair, twist his left leg over his right knee, and then hook his left toe under his right ankle, as if he were made of rubber. Detlev could imitate this, but none of the chubby larger boys could, and certainly none of the elders. Also, Mr. Amberson was interested in everything, and that was why Vrymeer acquired an additional beauty which made it somewhat different from the other farms.

'They have a new system now,' he said with some excitement. 'They come from Australia, mostly.'

'What does?' the general asked suspiciously. He did not like Mr. Amberson, but Detlev noticed that he appeared whenever the tall Englishman visited, because he enjoyed arguing with him.

'The trees. The government are importing millions of trees to spruce up the veld.'

'Who pays for them?'

'I think they're free. Eucalypts, I believe, and something they call wattle.'

'Free?'

'Yes, but you must plant them. That's only fair.'

Mr. Amberson used that phrase a good deal, for he saw many things in life that could be adjudicated easily on that principle: 'It's only fair.'

'Is it fair for you to make our boys learn English?' De Groot asked, as usual.

'I've learned Dutch.' He coughed modestly. 'Such as it is. I do this out of respect. But Detlev must learn English for a better reason. Because the world runs on English, that's why.'

On this basic point he would make no concessions. English was the language of the great world, and provincial Boers stuck off in their corner must learn it, if they presumed to participate in world affairs. On all else he was conciliatory, granting that the Boers probably won the war through their obstinate heroism and conceding that Dutch cooking was much better than English. He was really rather a likable chap, and when he sat with his legs twisted in knots, rocking back and forth on his haunches, arguing abstruse points, he lent a touch of congeniality and culture to what was otherwise a dull existence.

The farm was in good condition now. With help from Nxumalo's people, all buildings were roofed; the Herefords were maturing; the wool clip was coming in at a satisfactory level; and the black farmworkers had gouged out two small lakes, or catchments, below the big lake, so that on sunny days the three bodies of water shone like a necklace of jewels. Detlev was especially pleased with them, for he saw that by this device the water that came down from the hills behind the farm was used three times—four, really: 'It runs past the house as a stream, then builds our big lake, then goes on to make the two smaller ones for the cattle.'

It was to the north shores of these attractive lakes that Mr. Amberson brought the thousand saplings when they arrived at Durban from Australia. They were, as he predicted, mostly eucalypts, those shaggy-barked wonderful trees whose leaves when crushed had a minty odor. But he also delivered some two hundred wattles, the bushlike trees whose golden flowers would adorn the landscape.

'That many trees is a monstrous task,' he warned the men, and to help them with the planting he excused his entire school one Thursday and Friday, bringing all the boys out to work by the lakes. 'Practical learning' he termed it, and he worked hardest of all, dashing here and there to satisfy himself that the trees were in line. The only charge to the Van Doorns for this unusual service was a barbecue for the lads, and it was after the boys and their teacher had returned to Venloo that Detlev first voiced his suspicion. The two older men were sitting in the kitchen while Johanna cleaned up, and when she left the room, Detlev said quietly, 'I think Mr. Amberson is in love with Johanna.'

'What did you say?'

'He comes here to argue with you, General de Groot, but he really comes to be with Johanna.' He mimicked the way in which the Englishman pronounced her name, not Yo-hon-na, like a Boer, but Jo-hann-a, in the English manner.

This news was so frightening that General de Groot whispered 'Shhhhhh' lest Johanna hear that they were discussing her indiscretion, and when she returned to the kitchen six eyes studied her cautiously. When she left again, De Groot snorted: 'Unthinkable! A Boer girl in love with an English . . .'

'I didn't say that,' Detlev protested. 'I said he was in love with her.'

'A fine girl like Johanna,' the general said. 'She'd never do a thing like

that.' He uttered the words with such contempt that he might have been
speaking of prostitution.

'She is twenty-six,' Jakob said thoughtfully. 'She's a precious girl and
ought to be finding herself a man.'

'You need her here,' De Groot said, meaning that he needed her.

'She mustn't wait much longer, though,' Jakob said. 'But I agree I don't
want an Englishman in my family.'

Everything these three male spies saw in the next weeks confirmed their
suspicion that Johanna van Doorn was falling in love with an Englishman,
and one weekend when he appeared at the farm to inspect the young
eucalypts, General de Groot bearded him: 'Young man, did you come here
to see the trees, or did you come to see Johanna?'

Mr. Amberson blanched, then turned bright red. 'Well, I . . .'

'It would be better if you didn't come here any more.' When the young
man started to defend himself, Jakob entered the discussion: 'Yes, it would
be better if you stayed away.'

'But . . .'

'Starting now,' the general said firmly, and the two men remained
at Amberson's side, edging him toward his horse. The general said, 'We
don't want an Englishman making up to one of our girls. Now get!'
And he slapped the horse, sending the long-legged teacher back toward
Venloo.

At lunch, when it appeared that Mr. Amberson would not be joining
the family, Johanna asked why, and the general said bluntly, 'We don't
want him fooling around with a decent Boer girl.'

Johanna blushed, but did not retreat. 'Did you send him away?'

'We did,' the general snapped.

'Who are you to send people away, General de Groot? You're a guest
here.'

'I am the protector of this house,' he said firmly.

'I don't want your protection.' She wanted to cry. Badly she wanted to
weep, for there were no young men in Venloo, and Mr. Amberson had
proved himself to be a generous, understanding human being. The war was
over; the camps were over; and she felt a great urge to get on with life, to
start a farm of her own with children of her own, and if no one else came
along, she was prepared to marry an Englishman, repulsive though it
seemed.

But the three men in her family would not allow it. Detlev spoke for
them all when he said, 'Johanna, you can wait.'

This observation surprised her. 'But you like him best of all. You
brought him here.'

'As a teacher,' the boy said. 'Yes, he is a fine teacher.'

'Unthinkable,' General de Groot pronounced as the final verdict, and
Mr. Amberson was seen at Vrymeer no more.

At school he betrayed not a single indication of his disappointment; if
anything, he treated Detlev with added consideration, which was natural,
since this boy was one of the best. In numbers and history and clear
handwriting he received good marks, and Mr. Amberson gave him much
encouragement, stopping by Mrs. Scheltema's sometimes at night to assign
him further tasks so that he could excel.

What he did to sublimate his rather strong feelings toward Johanna revolutionized Venloo; it would not be the same after that summer. The metamorphosis started slowly, with his bringing an ovoid football to the school and telling the bigger boys, 'You must play rugby. And one day, even though you come from this small town, you may be famous like Paul Roos.'

Up to then the Boers of this little community knew little of the vigorous game that was sweeping the country. Before the war they had heard of the visits of teams from England, first in 1891, when the visitors won every match, and again in 1896. But it had remained an exotic game played principally in the Cape.

Through rugby Mr. Amberson endeared himself to the locals. Day after day he went onto the playing field, in boots, knee-length socks, short pants and jersey, to go up against the strongest boys in his school. They would race up and down the area, bend down in scrums, and play till they were exhausted. 'My word,' he often said as the games ended, 'that was a good effort. Boys, you're becoming first rate, absolutely world class.'

Older men in the community ridiculed the schoolmaster: 'He's a man among boys and a boy among men.' But when he suggested that the older youths, those now out of school, also form a team, he assured them that he was prepared to play with them, and now the entire male population of the town came out to watch the gladiatorial games.

He was remarkable, a tall, somewhat frail fellow who showed no fear of slamming into the biggest and toughest of the local Boers. Some boy would break loose with the ball and be on his way to a score when Amberson would detach himself from the pack, fly across the field, and tackle the brute with bone-crunching force, knocking the ball loose, then scrambling to his feet and running with it himself until some mighty Boer brought him down.

At the end of a game he would sit on the sidelines, panting, his body bruised, his mouth showing flecks of blood, and the hefty men would come by and slap him on the shoulder and say, 'You know how.' And he would reply, 'It was a mighty game.'

His principal interest, however, remained the boys in his school, and he was delighted when Detlev showed signs of becoming a first-class stand-off halfback, the capable lad who received the ball from the scrum half and passed it along to the speedier backs.

He had a natural aptitude for the game, and while he did not love it with the passion Mr. Amberson exhibited, he did appreciate the fellowship, considering it an attribute to a good life. This was helpful, because South Africa was in the process of becoming one of the world's fanatic sports centers, and if a boy like Detlev ever made a national team, his future would be assured.

It was this mania for sports which made it necessary for Frank Saltwood to issue an edict which went far in determining the social structure of his country. Like all Englishmen, he was dotty about games and served as chairman of the board governing cricket. He was a good player himself, having been a sometime member of the Oxford eleven, and in South Africa, had dedicated his spare time and surplus funds to encourage the game. Whenever a team was chosen to play visitors from Scotland and Wales, he was apt to serve as manager of the tour, ensuring that his men comported themselves within the grand traditions. He was insistent on this: 'Cricket is the game of gentlemen, and its rules apply even more to life than to the playing field. I like to see men extremely energetic, but within the set rules.'

This posed a dilemma in the postwar years when the great clubs of England extended an invitation to their former enemies to come home and play a set of gala matches; more than anything else, this would make the peace treaty a conclusive fact to families who had lost sons in the war. But a serious problem arose, in the person of Abu Bakr Fazool, a Coloured Muslim gentleman from Cape Town who was probably the best bowler in the world. When C. Aubrey Smith, himself a stalwart bowler and future motion picture star, captained his cricket team on a tour of South Africa, he said of Fazool, 'Has the fastest riser I've ever seen. Much better at the tricky stuff than I am.' He promised Fazool that if the latter ever came to England, he'd find a place for him on one of the county teams.

So now the question was: Should Abu Bakr be a member of the team visiting England? And at first it was assumed throughout South Africa that he should. Local enthusiasts predicted that he would mow down the English batters; but gradually people in rural areas began deploring the possibility that a Coloured might represent South Africa abroad, and articles appeared in the better papers, asking: 'Have the board really sorted this thing out?'

The burden fell squarely on Frank Saltwood, and had he stood before his board and said, 'We would appear stupid before the world if we omitted Abu Bakr,' they would have agreed, but after he had studied the matter from all angles, he became cautious and gave the board members craven advice:

'It is acknowledged here and abroad that Abu Bakr Fazool is perhaps the best bowler alive today. As C. Aubrey Smith said at the end of his successful tour, "That young man is ready for county cricket right now." So we would be doing our side, and the mother country, a favor by including him. I am enthusiastic about doing so. But we must consider carefully certain objections to such an act. The scars of our recent war are slowly healing, thanks to the good conscience of both sides, and it would be almost criminal to do anything at this early date which would reopen those scars. Our Boer brethren have certain clear-cut traditions about handling their Coloured and Kaffir neighbors, and it would ill-behoove us to offend those traditions. Such consideration would dictate that we not take Fazool to England with us.

'A more serious aspect, in the long run, is "What kind of impression do we wish to make upon the mother country when our team takes the field?" I know that dark-skinned Indians have played at Lords with distinction, but all England knows that India contains Indians, and it would be ridiculous if none appeared. In the same way very dark West Indians have represented the Caribbean colonies, but again that is the color of those colonies. With South Africa it is different. It is important that we present ourselves to the mother country in garb as like hers as possible. This is a white man's country

and always will be. Our welfare depends upon the good opinion the
mother country holds of us, and when our team appears on its sacred
pitches, it would be better if it represented what we want to be:
England's white colony, safe, secure, well-educated, loyal to European tradition, and to be trusted. I am afraid the appearance of Abu
Bakr Fazool among our players would not enhance that image.'

Had Frank Saltwood in that moment of great, though unrecognized, crisis
come out in favor of sending Fazool to England, and had the gifted athlete
performed as might be expected, a whole pattern of acceptance might have
been launched. There were other Coloured cricket players who could have
made those touring teams, and when their white colleagues observed how
well they played and with what ease they fitted into mother country festivities, an attitude of approval would have been generated throughout South
Africa; and if gifted blacks had been trained for the rugby teams, smashing
their opponents about in the scrums and running like antelope for scores,
the nation would have seen that they were little different from the Boers and
the Englishmen who played beside them.

But time was not ripe for such acceptance. Frank Saltwood convinced
his board and kept Fazool off the team. He did not appear in England to
take his place beside the fabulous bowlers from India, the immortal batsmen
from Australia. He continued to play in the darker neighborhoods of Cape
Town, and as the rules against interracial competition stiffened, he quit the
game altogether. He could often be seen at the docks, in the fish market,
tallying not runs but the daily catch of snoek.

Often in the biographies of important women and men one comes across
the phrase: 'Like a burst of light, the idea which would animate her life came
upon her.' In the case of Detlev van Doorn this simile was literally true.
A flash of light struck him, and the course of his life was set.

It happened because of a packet of powdered jellies imported from
France. When General de Groot and her father forbade Johanna to see Mr.
Amberson, she was left with little to do and began to occupy her spare time
with knitting and embroidery. The arrival at the Venloo store of the imported powders excited her, and swiftly she presented her men with acidy
orange and lemon desserts. They liked them, and asked for more, so she
returned to the store and purchased the large-size packets, and when she
reached home she found that she now had some six or seven different
flavors. She experimented with each, and the men found them so tasty that
they encouraged her to continue.

She was a resourceful young woman, nearing thirty now, and one day
as she was pouring the jelly into her glasses it occurred to her that if she
poured only a small portion into each glass, allowing it to harden, she could
then pour on top of it another jelly of a different color, and repeat the
process until she had a multilayered glass which would be not only quite
tasty but also attractive to look at.

On her first tries she failed, because she poured the succeeding colors
while they were too hot and thus melted any that had already firmed and
cooled. Being a provident woman, she mixed the mangled jellies into one

mélange and decided to try again later, but when the mixture hardened and
she served it to her men, Detlev protested: 'This doesn't look right and it
doesn't taste right.' She offered no explanation, but did agree with him. That
experiment had failed.

Next time, however, when the first jelly was well firmed, and she made
the next flavor, she allowed it to cool almost to point of hardening, then
poured it in, and her plan succeeded. Indeed, it produced a result much finer
than even she had anticipated; it was really quite handsome, for with artistic
taste she had placed the black currant layer at the bottom, the light brown
apple atop it, then the reds, and finally the orange and the light lemon. The
glasses were almost works of art.

When Detlev came into the kitchen they were perched on a window
ledge, with one well off by itself, and when rays of sunlight struck that glass,
the layers scintillated, each color showing to maximum advantage, throwing delightful patterns of black, brown, crimson, orange and lemon on the
opposite wall, and in that moment Detlev understood the grand design of
life.

'Look!' he cried, bringing the general and his father into the room. 'How
each color keeps to itself. It doesn't muddy the other. It shines like a
diamond.' And with one finger he outlined the nature of humanity as God
had ordained it: 'Here at the bottom the black. Then the lighter brown.
Then here the Indian . . .' Already he had translated the colors into racial
groupings. 'Up here the Englishman, he's orange. And on top of them all,
the Afrikaner, clear and . . .'

'You are a Boer!' De Groot said.

'They keep telling us at school we're not Boers any longer. We're not
fighting anybody . . .'

'We're always fighting the English,' De Groot said. 'In your lifetime we
will never stop.'

Detlev returned to the jellies: 'Each color in its own level. Order.
Neatness.' He had found the guiding secret of life. 'We're Afrikaners, that
nice clean color on top.'

'That's the way it should be,' De Groot said, and that week he launched
his campaign to get rid of Mr. Amberson as the Venloo teacher. He had
learned to like the Englishman and told him so openly, but he also felt that
the time had come for the education of Boer boys . . . 'Afrikaner boys
deserve Afrikaner men to teach them.' He liked this Afrikaner business. It
bespoke the true heritage of his people. They were not Englishmen, and God
knows they were not Dutch. They were men and women of Africa, and the
word carried crisp meaning.

Mr. Amberson reacted as one would expect: 'I think you have a legitimate concern, General de Groot. Besides, you should be bringing up a
generation of your own teachers. I've been offered two appointments to the
English schools in Grahamstown. My rugby training, you know.'

Even when public meetings were convened to discuss the necessity of
dismissing him, he continued with rugby games, striving in his final weeks
to instill his boys with the abiding principles of sportsmanship: 'Don't
crybaby . . . A tooth can be replaced . . . Be gallant when you win and extend
your hand to the man who played opposite you . . . Fight to the very
last second, then give a cheer for the goodness of the game . . . Be

manly . . . If the other man is bigger, you be more clever . . . The goal is to win . . . Always you must win . . . You must drive for that score . . . But there are rules you dare not break in trying to score . . . Be manly . . .'

In the grand exhibition prior to his departure he was about as capable as a stand-off halfback could be, diving straight into the biggest bully on the town team and being knocked so silly that when he got the ball he ran in the wrong direction. In his farewell speech he paid resounding tribute to General de Groot: 'Just as this noble captain led his men through every difficulty, so our team has fought against all the odds presented by bigger schools and heavier opponents. To General de Groot I give my fullest admiration. He is the spirit of Venloo. To my boys I give the eternal challenge. Be manly.'

It was the consensus that this small town had been lucky in having this scrawny Englishman in the period of transition. He had helped make boys into men, Boers into Afrikaners, and former enemies into relaxed allies.

The week after he departed, the new schoolmaster appeared, a young man of much different stamp. He was Piet Krause, graduate of the new college at Potchefstroom, which would become the most Afrikaner of the universities, and he let it be known on his first day that the nonsense about instruction in English was ended. To the delight of the local farmers, this tense, crop-headed young fellow announced: 'The spirit of a nation is expressed in its language. This nation is destined to be Afrikaner. Therefore, its language must be Afrikaans.' This was the first time that word had been used in Venloo, and when he saw the confusion on the faces before him, he explained: 'Just as we have created a new people in this cauldron, steeped in Slagter's Nek, Blood River and Majuba, so we are building a new language, simpler than the old, cleaner, easier to use. It's our language now, and with it we shall conquer. One day we shall give thanks for this victory, using our own Bible in our language, the Afrikaans Bible.'

General de Groot applauded all but the last sentence; he was not sure that the Bible should be in any language other than Dutch: 'That's the way God handed it down to us. Those are the words He used when He spoke to us. He gave us our covenant in Dutch, and we should keep it that way.'

He and others like him raised such a howl about printing the Bible in anything but pristine Dutch that the project was dropped, nationally, but not in Venloo. Krause rode out from Venloo to meet with the Vrymeer people, and told them, 'We must eliminate all areas in which we are subservient. No more English, except what the law demands. No more Dutch. All the damned Hollanders thrown on a ship and sent back to Amsterdam. We are Afrikaners, and whether General de Groot likes it or not, one of these days we'll have our own Bible.'

He spoke with such force, and in defense of a program so needed in this community, that Johanna van Doorn listened with growing joy. This was what she believed. Her liking for Mr. Amberson had been physical only; spiritually she had been repelled by his Englishness. But here was a fiery young man whose eye was on the future, the only future that made any sense for South Africa.

She resumed taking Detlev to school on Monday mornings, arriving even earlier than she had in those first tender days with Mr. Amberson, and she came with a firmness Detlev had not seen before. Her eyes glowed as she supported the new teacher in all he attempted, and three times she invited him to Vrymeer for long discussions and good boboties. 'I think Mr. Krause has lost the battle,' Detlev joked one night after the schoolteacher had left for Venloo. Johanna, disregarding his teasing, said nothing, and during Krause's next visit at the lake, Detlev himself fell under the spell of this dynamic man.

'What we must have in this country,' he cried with expanding excitement, 'is a system of order. Indians, Coloureds, blacks, all in their proper place, all obedient to the wise laws we pass. And I don't want Englishmen passing them, either. I want Afrikaners in all positions of decision.' When Detlev heard these words he realized that Mr. Krause, starting from his own experiences, had discovered the principle which he, Detlev, had seen in the glass of jellies. They both believed in discipline and the ascendancy of the Afrikaner Volk.

'What was that?' General de Groot asked when Detlev first used the phrase in the kitchen.

'Mr. Krause uses it all the time. It means the People, the secret force of the Race that makes us different from the English or the Kaffir.'

'I like that word,' De Groot said, and soon he was speaking about the mission of the Afrikaner Volk.

Detlev was not surprised when at the end of only five weeks Mr. Krause came nervously to the kitchen to inform the men: 'Johanna and I seek to marry. I know she's four years older, but we love each other. We have work to do, and I ask your permission.' It was granted—by the general, by her father, and most enthusiastically by her brother.

The wedding ceremony was performed by a newcomer to the community, a man who added much to the quality of Venloo. He was the Reverend Barend Brongersma, a graduate of Stellenbosch, the prestigious university of the Cape, and a most excellent young man. He was thirty-one when he took over the Venloo church, tallish, well proportioned, with very black hair and deep-set eyes to match. His outstanding characteristic was a resonant voice which he had carefully cultivated so that it could range downward from a high, impassioned plea to a thundering middle accusation to a solid reassuring affirmation. It was obvious, when one heard him preach, that he gave much thought to his sermons and that he was a young man who would surely go far in the management of the South African church. He spoke with great conviction, outlining his arguments so that anyone could follow, and buttressing them so firmly that everyone had to agree. He was as fine a predikant as the Dutch Reformed Church offered in this period, and his stay in Venloo would be limited, for he would be needed in some larger community.

He was married to a woman much like himself: solid good looks, eager, a winning smile, and unafraid to say what she thought. They made an impressive couple, and the three men at Vrymeer were pleased to have them in Venloo.

It was customary now to speak of three men at the farm, because Detlev was growing into such a hefty young fellow that he was assigned a position in the forward line at rugby, where his weight and more than ordinary strength would prove an advantage. Several times his father had said, 'Detlev, you're built just like your grandfather Tjaart. He was a strong man.' There had been a photograph of the old man, with belt and suspenders, tight-trimmed beard from ear to chin, flat black hat, staring straight ahead; it had gone in the flames, but Detlev could remember it and hoped that one day he would look the same.

Venloo had now fallen solidly into place as the prototype of a small Afrikaner community: it had in General de Groot its hero of past wars; in Piet Krause, a fiery teacher who wanted to remold the world; in Dominee Brongersma, a charismatic predikant who could both instruct and censure; and in Detlev van Doorn, the typical young lad of promise. At times it seemed that all the forces of this community conspired to make this boy more intelligent, more dedicated.

At the moment his brother-in-law, Piet Krause, had the greatest influence, for Detlev tended to see society through this vibrant young man's eyes. Once, coming over the hill, Piet stopped their carriage, looked ahead at the broken farm occupied by General de Groot, and began to rant: 'Never forget that scene, Detlev! A man who led us in battle living like the swine, forgotten, unloved, a castaway.'

'He wants to live that way,' Detlev explained. 'Every year Father asks him to move in with us. He says he likes the old place, the old ways.'

'But look at him, a great hero forgotten.' When the teacher spoke like this to De Groot, the old man laughed. 'Detlev's right. I like it this way. You should have seen how we lived on the trek.' He told of his family on that last evening when he elected to stay with the Van Doorns, and thus escaped being killed by Mzilikazi's men. 'Halt the wagon. Spread some blankets. Draw a canvas out from the wagon. Three poles to form a kind of tent. Go to sleep, and have your throats cut before morning. That's how we lived.'

'General,' Krause said with brimming emotion, 'Johanna and I want you to come in town and live with us.'

'Oh, no! You two would be arguing with me all the time. I'm happy where I am. If I get hungry, I come over to Jakob, here.'

The Vrymeer farm, with no white woman in attendance now that Johanna was married, faced problems which were solved when Micah Nxumalo and two of his wives moved back from the old general's place. This did not leave De Groot bereft, for two younger black women looked after him. Five rondavels existed again at Vrymeer, looking much as they had for the past fifty years, and they were occupied by some twenty blacks, half of whom had drifted up from Zululand. They worked at the farm, but it was Nxumalo who remained in charge.

With Van Doorn's encouragement he had patiently coaxed a herd of blesbok, more than sixty of them, to lodge permanently beside the three lakes. A stranger coming to the farm would see these handsome animals, white blazes gleaming in sunlight, and think that they had wandered in from the veld, but as day waned and they stayed fairly close to the house, he would realize that they lived here. How beautiful Vrymeer was, with the blesbok and the fattening Herefords and the eucalypts attaining enough height to form tall hedges, and sunlight falling across the lakes.

Four or five times a year Van Doorn harvested one or two of the older blesbok, turning the meat over to Nxumalo's wives for making biltong, and this seemed to help the herd rather than hurt it. Van Doorn usually shot unwanted bucks, but with such care that the other members of the herd scarcely knew that a shot had been fired. Certainly he never stampeded them, for he loved these beasts and felt that they helped tie him and De Groot more tightly to the soil of their ancestors. Nxumalo felt the same.

Piet Krause saw it as his duty to keep the farm and the town of Venloo at the center of Transvaal activity; he forced everyone to follow with careful attention everything that happened, and was always ready to explain its significance. On the memorable day in 1910 when the four disparate colonies —the English Cape and Natal, the Afrikaner Orange Free State and Transvaal—were united by the Act of Union into one nation, with its own governor-general, prime minister and parliament, Krause exulted: 'Now we're set on our own course. What we accomplish is up to us. Think of it, boys! Someone in this school may be a future prime minister of a country that is totally free.' He looked at each of the boys, endeavoring to inspire them, but he was thinking of himself.

'We're not totally free,' one bright lad said cautiously. 'We're still a union which owes allegiance to the king.' Seeing his teacher frown, he added, 'We're part of the British Empire.'

'Don't use that word!' Krause stormed. 'We have no quarrel with Britain. Do we fight against Scotland or Wales or Ireland? Not at all. Our fight is with England.' And from then on, his students used only that word.

'Will we always owe allegiance to the king?' the same boy asked.

'That will change,' Krause said firmly, but for the moment he was not prepared to explore details. However, on his next visit to the farm, Detlev recalled that brief exchange and asked, 'Do you think we will break away from England,' and to his surprise, Krause did not respond, but Johanna did. With a fierceness Detlev had not seen before, she orated: 'We shall never be free until we do break away. We must have our own flag, our own anthem, our own president, and not some bedamned Englishman like Governor-General Gladstone making believe he's our king.' On and on she went, outlining a program whereby the Afrikaners would take over control of the nation, as free men and women: 'In Pretoria only Afrikaans will be spoken, only Afrikaners will hold positions of power.'

'Will the English allow this?' Detlev asked.

'We will find ways to make them allow it,' Johanna said, at which General de Groot applauded.

'There will be ways,' he agreed, slapping Detlev on the knee. 'And this young fellow will discover what they are.'

In private conversations Johanna Krause was always the one who gave fiery direction, but in public, as in any good Afrikaner family, she allowed her husband to take the lead, and one morning in school he excited his pupils by announcing, 'I want everyone who can do so to bring his parents and his wagon, and we'll ride up to Waterval-Boven to see a magnificent sight.' He would not tell them what, but when he insisted that General de Groot come along, the old man predicted: 'He wants you to see where President Kruger ruled this country in the last days,' and when they reached that revered spot, De Groot lectured the children: 'The great man lived on these railroad tracks, in Car Number 17, first up here above the waterfall, then down below in the little house next to the hotel. And you must remember one thing,' he warned them in a voice quivering with anger, 'no matter what lies the English newspapers print, Oom Paul Kruger did not run away with half a million pounds in gold. It left Pretoria somehow, but he never took it.'

It was neither the waterfall nor the lost gold that had attracted Piet Krause. His attention was reserved for the clock, and at three he assembled everyone at the railway station.

'We're about to witness a glorious moment in our national history,' he said, and when the train from Pretoria appeared around a bend he and his wife led the children in wild applause, though what they were clapping for, the students did not know.

Piet had arranged with the stationmaster that the train would halt for six minutes, but when the first three customary carriages drifted slowly past, showing no special passengers, General de Groot told Detlev, 'I don't understand.' But now fifteen roofless cattle trucks creaked to a halt, allowing the amazed schoolchildren to stare into the yellow faces of seven hundred Chinese coolies. They were the last contingent of workers imported from Shanghai in 1904. All were being expelled from the country, and when this train slid down the grade to Moçambique, South Africa would be cleared of this menace.

'Out they go!' Piet Krause exulted as the wagons stood in the sun. 'A fearful wrong is being corrected.'

The Chinese, bewildered when they left Canton years ago, bewildered by their treatment in the mines, and now bewildered by this enforced exodus, looked out impassively at the boys they had never understood and the grownups they had never known. One schoolboy picked up a stone and threw it at the hateful exportees, but Piet Krause halted that: 'No abuse. Just cheer when the train starts.' And when it did, and the trucks moved again, everyone applauded, for a heavy burden was being removed from the homeland. 'Die Volk,' said Krause, 'is nou skoon!' (The Volk has been purified.)

When the boys returned to their school, Krause said, 'Our next task is to repatriate all the Indians. Gerrit, what does *repatriate* mean?'

'To send back a person to where he belongs.'

'That's right. Every person on earth has a place where he belongs. He should stay there. We've sent the Chinese back to China. We must send the Indians back to India. And the English should go back to England. This is the land of the Afrikaner.'

'What about the Kaffirs?'

'They belong here. They're as much a part of Africa as we are. But they're inferior. They know nothing. It's our responsibility to protect them, and explain to them how they must obey our laws. The Kaffirs will always be with us, and we must treat them with respect, but also with firmness.'

Whenever Detlev heard such preachments he thought of that glass of layered jellies, each color in its proper place, each clearly demarked from the other, and as he recalled that moment of revelation, he remembered the earlier day, when Johanna's experiment had not worked and she had mixed all the jellies together. That result had been pleasing neither to the eye nor to the taste: It was a jumble without character and I didn't like it. But when it was done right, look what happened! It was beautiful to see, and when you dipped your spoon in, each layer had its proper taste. The orange was the way orange should be, the lemon on top tasted right, and even the currant on the bottom preserved its real flavor. That's the way races should be.

Not long after the disappearance of the Chinese, Piet Krause invited three of his best students to accompany him to an important meeting near Johannesburg: 'You are to hear the one man in this country who knows what he's doing.'

It was General J. B. M. Hertzog, a hero during the Boer War, a brilliant lawyer afterward. He was not overpowering, like old General de Groot, for he was only of medium height and weight. He was a handsome man, with a close-clipped mustache and neatly parted hair. He wore steel-rimmed glasses and a business suit, and spoke softly as he offered a justification of his recent behavior:

'I said that South Africa must be for South Africans, and I make no apology. By South Africans, I mean those persons whether of Dutch or English heritage who have committed their lives to this country, and who do not think fondly of some place else as "home." [He spoke this word derisively.]

'I said that I wanted my country to be ruled by men who are totally South African at heart, and I make no apology. By this I mean that we should be governed only by men who understand this land and its language, who are working for its welfare and not for the welfare of some empire. [Here there was both applause and boos.]

'I have been accused of wanting to make the Afrikaner baas in this country, and I confess to the charge. I certainly don't want some newcomer who knows nothing of the land or the language or the religion to be my baas. I want South Africa to be ruled by South Africans.

'I have been accused of not being willing to conciliate, and I confess to that charge also. On what principle should I conciliate, and whom? I have done no man any wrong, others have done me wrong by invading my country, and I await conciliation from them. If conciliation means that Dutch-speaking South Africans must always make concessions to English-speaking South Africans, I say that we are not ripe for conciliation, and I refuse to sacrifice the future of one child of the true South Africa on that altar.

'I have been accused of putting the interests of South Africa ahead of those of the empire, and to this accusation I most gladly plead guilty. I will always place the interests of my country first, for unless we are strong, and good and able to govern ourselves, we shall be no use to the empire or anyone else. [At this Krause and many others applauded.]

'Finally, I have been asked by many in authority to dissociate myself from the striking statement made some months ago by a great hero of our country, General Paulus de Groot of the Venloo Commando.

He said, while standing on a pile of manure at his farm, "I would rather be here on this dunghill with my people than in the palaces of empire." I say the same. This is my country, such as it is. This is the country of those who love South Africa. [Here Krause led wild cheering.] First, foremost and always.'

Detlev had never before heard such a speech, so rational, so carefully organized, and with such a constant appeal to the crowd's emotions. 'He must be the finest mind in South Africa,' he whispered to Piet Krause when the cheering stopped.

'He is. He will lead us to freedom.'

'What does he think about the Act of Union?'

'What I think. That it should be used intelligently as a weapon to attain our freedom.'

'Does he agree with you about the Kaffirs?'

'Absolutely. South Africa must always be a place of white supremacy.' Detlev had not heard this phrase before. 'We shall assume fatherly responsibility for the Kaffirs, who will never be able to govern themselves. But we must rule them, for they are children and we must tell them what to do.'

In these days, when Piet Krause was promoting such ideas, no one noticed that Micah Nxumalo was sometimes away from Vrymeer for the better part of a week. His wives were so capable that they kept things moving forward in his absence, assuring Jakob that their husband was over at General de Groot's, and telling the latter that he was working the far fields.

He would actually be on his way to Waterval-Boven to catch a train to Johannesburg, where he ducked down alleys to a ramshackle building. For these trips he wore an old dark suit which Van Doorn had given him, shoes, a white shirt with high collar, a four-in-hand tie and a stiff felt hat made in England. He was in his forties, and except for his good clothes, in no way conspicuous. Of medium height and weight, he looked like any of the blacks who worked in Johannesburg offices.

The dozen blacks who met with him in secret one night in 1912 looked the same. 'This is Reverend John Dube,' a man explained, introducing him to the persuasive chairman of the African National Congress.

'This is Solomon Plaatje. He served with the English forces during the siege of Mafeking.' Nxumalo nodded toward the famous newspaperman and said, 'I served with the Boers at Ladysmith.' Whereupon Plaatje, a small, nervous man, laughed. 'Two rather ugly affairs.'

Of the other ten, all men as prominent in black circles as Dube and Plaatje, Micah noticed that each spoke English with beautiful ease and pronunciation. Plaatje, of course, had worked for the *London Times*, so that his mastery was not remarkable, but it was curious that some of the others had acquired such fluency. Nxumalo had only the most meager vocabulary and felt himself at a disadvantage, but not when the discussions started, for by listening to General de Groot and especially young Piet Krause, he had acquired a solid comprehension of what the new laws signified.

Plaatje was speaking: 'We are in the position Thomas Jefferson was in in 1774, prior to the revolution. By that I mean, we must utilize all the legal processes open to us to protect our position and to gain such advantage as we can.' Those were the exact words he spoke, and when others took the floor, they referred in comparable phrases to conditions in England, France and Germany.

They were bitterly opposed to the sections in the Act of Union which denied Coloureds and blacks the right to vote in three of the four provinces; only in the Cape was such voting allowed. There was strong feeling that this provision must be attacked, but as one of the men pointed out: 'Keeping us off the rolls was one of the principal clauses in the peace treaty that ended the war. It is defended not only here in South Africa but also in London. We are stuck with it, I am afraid.'

Talk then turned to a new bill which these men saw as a serious step backward in relations between the races; the Natives Land Act established the principle that some lands were reserved for the blacks, some for the whites, and that the law itself protected and ensured this division. 'The land should be for us all,' Plaatje argued, and others joined in so forcefully that it was unanimously agreed that a delegation of five be appointed to travel to London to present to the king their plea for protection. 'We cannot look to the Afrikaner for fair treatment,' one of these men argued, 'because his custom and his church deny that we have rights—'

'Now wait!' another interrupted. 'They recognize our rights. Even Hertzog does that. What they want to do is restrict them.'

The first speaker ignored this interruption; in the crowded little room with inadequate light he reasoned: 'So we must depend upon England and the liberal opinion there. We must keep constant pressure on them to accord us the same privileges they grant native-born New Zealanders and Australians.'

'In the long run,' one man predicted, 'the English of this country will prove no different from the Afrikaners.'

When the rules were spelled out for the conduct of the commission to the king, the members wanted to hear from Nxumalo about conditions on the frontier, those little Afrikaner towns where the ideas which would later sweep the cities germinated, and now he spoke, slowly, while the others listened. He had not their command of English, and more than half of them would not have difficulty in understanding his Zulu had he used it; none wanted him to speak Afrikaans, even though he was proficient in it, and they too.

'We have a new teacher, very forceful. Took his boys to see the expulsion of the Chinese. Some came home wanting to expel the blacks, too. But he calmed them down. Took another group to hear General Hertzog. They came home wild-eyed with patriotism. They want to fight the English again. General de Groot encourages them. He says war must come. He speaks of Germany a good deal. He is in contact with other generals, and they may cause trouble one day.'

He spoke of many things, displaying an uncanny understanding of what was motivating the sturdy Afrikaners in the Venloo district, but it was when he came to matters of real importance that he showed his sensitive awareness of probable trends: 'The young schoolteacher is like the general; he wants to go to war now. But his ideas come from his wife. She is four years older. Was in the camp at Chrissiesmeer. She is strong, wanted to marry an Englishman but her family wouldn't allow it. She makes no senseless challenges. She thinks.

'But the true power in Venloo is the new predikant. Very good man. Has a strong mind like yours, Plaatje. Preaches careful sermons, very logical. He has an orderly view of what is going to happen and takes no risks. When I drive the people to church, I stand outside and listen. Powerful voice. Good man. But he is totally against us. He uses the Bible to club us. And in the long run he will be more dangerous to us than anyone you have mentioned.'

'What can he do to hurt us in Venloo?'

'Soon his voice will be heard throughout the land. He is like Jan Christian Smuts. To see him is to know that he will one day command.'

The other men took notice of the name, Barend Brongersma, of Stellenbosch.

In 1913 Detlev received the first letter that had ever been addressed to him specifically, and it came in such form that it overwhelmed him, as well it might, for his response would go far in determining a major part of his life. It came from a committee of women in Bloemfontein, and said:

> We have erected a noble monument in remembrance of the Boer women and children who perished in the infamous concentration camps of our Second Freedom War. Since you were in a camp and lost a mother and two sisters, and since your teacher Mr. Krause has given us your name as an able scholar, we deem it proper for you to join us at the dedication of a monument that will stand forever as a reminder of your mother's heroism and the cruel deaths of your sisters.

The letter went on to say that he would be one of a group of twelve survivors of the camps, six girls, six boys, who would stand at attention as the monument was dedicated. He was eighteen that year; the others would be younger.

Bursting with pride, he showed the letter to Mr. Krause, who said, 'It is proper for the Volk to honor its past. This is a profound honor, and I trust you will conduct yourself appropriately.' He added that he would not have recommended Detlev had he not been sure of the boy's loyalty and patriotism. Detlev walked several inches taller when he carried the letter out to Vrymeer, where General de Groot explained that Detlev would be standing as surrogate for all the young heroes who died in the camps: 'You escaped the ground glass in the meal. They didn't.'

For the first time Detlev traveled on a train alone. He carried with him four books of South African history, which he read so assiduously that when he paused for a bite to eat, a young man traveling to Cape Town asked, 'What preoccupies you?'

'I am reading about the English settlement of Grahamstown. That's where my family lived in the old days.'

'That was a bad period,' the young man said in fluent Afrikaans. 'If we hadn't allowed those extra Englishmen ashore, they wouldn't have been able to steal our country from us.'

'One of the Englishmen, man named Saltwood . . .'

'One of the worst. Do you know anything about that infamous family? They rob this country blind. Offices in the cities, stealing Afrikaner money.'

'Mrs. Saltwood saved my life, I think.'

'She was all right. That I grant. But every family has to have one decent member. Her husband, you know. The big sportsman. Cricket and tennis. He was one of Cecil Rhodes' worst young men. Horrible spy, and all that.'

After a long and confused tirade, he asked Detlev where he was going, and when he learned about the dedication of the Vrouemonument his manner changed completely: 'Wonderlik, wonderlik! And you're to stand there representing us all! How ennobling! Oh, I do wish I could go with you!'

'Why?'

The young man, who had been so authoritative only a moment ago, could not reply. His eyes filled with tears, and when he tried to speak he choked. He blew his nose, looked out the window at the highveld, glowing in the sun, and tried again to speak. Finally he surrendered and wept for some moments. Then he muttered, 'My mother. My brother. All my sisters. They died at Standerton.'

When he recovered he told Detlev about the last days, when food was scarce: 'There was an English hospital nearby. Their troops wounded or knocked down by the enteric. I was sure they must have food, so I sneaked out of our camp and crept along to theirs, but they were dying too. It was a horrible war, Detlev.'

He spoke with such an unusual mix of deep feeling and wide knowledge that Detlev deemed him the appropriate person to answer a nagging question: 'You don't believe those stories about ground glass in the meal, do you?'

'Absolute rot. I just told you, the English died the same way we did.' Abruptly he asked, 'Detlev, what a curious name. What's it mean?'

'German. Along the Rhine. My mother was a very beautiful woman who had a German uncle or something.'

'Detlev! It's not a Dutch name, you know.'

'I said it was German.'

'Why do you keep it?'

'You keep the name God gave you. Look at General Hertzog. Nobody more Afrikaner than he . . .'

'Now, there's a man, not so?'

'Do you know his name? No? Well, it's James Barry Hertzog, that's what it is.'

'He ought to change it. With his ideas, he ought to change it.'

'It's the name God gave him.'

'It isn't at all. Some damn-fool English name, that's what it is.'

The young man seemed to have so many positive ideas that Detlev wanted to know what he was doing on the train to Cape Town. 'I'm going down to work in Parliament. I'm to be a clerk of some sort, and one day I'll be head of a ministry, telling you farmers what to do.'

'How did you get the job? How old are you?'

'I'm twenty-one, and the country is hungry for bright young men who can speak Afrikaans and English. You might say that I am needed in Cape Town.' He said his name was Michael van Tonder and that one day he would be as famous as Jan Christian Smuts, but Detlev never heard of him again.

At Bloemfontein he was met by a committee of women wearing sashes; they were in charge of the ceremonies and had brought with them bold sashes for the twelve young survivors of the camps to wear. Across each was lettered in red: CONCENTRATION CAMP SURVIVOR, and when Detlev was handed his the woman said, 'Wait here. We have to find a girl coming down from Carolina. Her father was a hero of that commando and her mother and two brothers died in the camp at Standerton.'

So he stood alone on the platform, his sash across his chest, while the committee searched for the girl; and when they found her, they placed a ribbon on her, too, bearing the same words but in blue. She was introduced as Maria Steyn of Carolina. 'We're neighbors,' Detlev said and she nodded.

For three days they were together, young people caught up in the tormented memories of the camps and proud of the performances of their mothers and their siblings struck down by disease and hunger, and especially their fathers, who had served in the great commandos. 'My father,' Maria said, 'is Christoffel Steyn. Of the Carolina Commando. Many said they were the finest unit in the war.'

'We all know Christoffel Steyn and Spion Kop. My father rode with General de Groot in the Venloo Commando. They didn't accomplish much at first.'

'Oh, but they were heroic! That dash down to Port Elizabeth.'

'That didn't accomplish much, either, from what they tell me.'

'But such willingness!'

At the dedication they stood facing each other, Maria with the young women, Detlev with the young men, and he noticed that when the solemn words of remembrance were spoken, she had tears in her eyes as he did in his.

'I wouldn't want to do that again,' she said, but then they were taken to a church where a very old predikant delivered a marvelous oration, preaching forgiveness and the love which Jesus Christ extended to all his children:

> 'And I would say to you young people who bear across your bosoms the sash that tells us that you were in the camps, that Jesus Christ personally saw to it that you were saved so that you might bear witness to the forgiveness that marks our new nation.'

This was followed by a sermon of a much different stripe, for at the conclusion of his prayer he announced that one of the most brilliant of Stellenbosch's recent ministerial candidates had been asked to speak of the new South Africa that would be erected upon the spirit of the Vrouemonument. It was Barend Brongersma, who spoke in a deep, controlled voice of the dedication 'which we the living must accept from the hands of those dead':

'Not a day dare go by without our remembering the heroic dead, the loving wives who would see their husbands no more, the beautiful children who were destined to cruel death before they could welcome their fathers home from defeat.

'Yes, it was defeat, but from such defeat great nations have risen in the past, and a great one will rise today if you have the courage to ensure it. You must build on the crucifixion of your loved ones. You must take to your hearts the covenant your forefathers received from the Lord. You must ensure and send forward the convictions of the devout people who formed this nation . . .'

His voice rose to a powerful thunder as he challenged every individual in that audience to do some good thing for her or his nation so that the martyrs represented by the Vrouemonument should not have died in vain. Detlev, looking across the aisle to where the young women sat, saw that Maria was sobbing, and he felt his own throat choke with patriotic emotion, so forceful had been the peroration of the predikant from Venloo.

During the final session on a vibrant spring day Detlev found himself with Maria constantly, under various circumstances, and while eating a hearty breakfast provided for the young people or walking to a church service with her in central Bloemfontein, he had an opportunity to study her closely, as he did with all people who interested him. She was three years younger than he, but mature for her fifteen years. She was a heavy girl, not beautiful, and even though she had lovely blond hair, which she might have dressed in some attractive way, she ignored it, pulling it back tightly in the old fashion. None of her features was distinctive, each being marked by a certain rural grossness, and she moved with no special grace. She was not a lumpy peasant type, not at all, for she had a quickness of mind which showed itself constantly; she was, indeed, much like Johanna Krause, and since Johanna had served as Detlev's mother, he had a predilection toward that type of woman. But the essential characteristic of this girl, which even Detlev was old enough to perceive, was the gravity of her deportment. She was a serious young woman in all the best meanings of that word, and any young man who came into contact with her at an emotional level would have to be impressed by her moral solidity. She was not a person forced by the tragedy of the camps into a premature adulthood, worn and withered; she was naturally adult.

Therefore, when the young couple walked to the Vrouemonument for the farewell picnic they walked together, their conversation falling into the pattern of grave thoughts. 'How were you chosen for the honor?' Detlev asked as they strolled across the grassy mound. 'I mean, I know about your father. We learned about him in school. I mean, who chose you?'

'I think it must have been the dominee.'

'In my case it was the schoolteacher. He's married to my sister, you know.'

'I was not aware of that.' She spoke cautiously and in a somewhat old-fashioned way.

'What do you propose doing after we return?' Anyone talking with Maria Steyn found himself quickly falling into her stately patterns.

'I shall continue to read. And work on rebuilding the farm. My father remarried, did I tell you?'

'No.' He reflected on this, then said, 'I wish mine had. I think Father has been very lonely.'

'War alters people,' she said. 'Perhaps he had no further need of a wife.'

'All men need wives.' He said this with such speed that he felt embarrassed. He had not yet touched Maria, not even by any accident, other than shaking hands one time at the railway station, and he was deeply impelled to take her hand now, but as they turned a corner in the path they came upon another young pair who were kissing rather ardently and bumping into each other, and, as Detlev later expressed it to himself, 'perhaps doing other things even more awful,' so that he and Maria backed away in deep confusion. The lively eroticism of the other couple did not, as it might have done with another pair, inspire them to kiss, too; it shocked them; and they returned to the monument, in whose grim shadow they finished their conversation. They were, in other words, both puritans of an especially tenacious character: Huguenots imbued with the living spirit of John Calvin and the intellectual and moral torments that come with that persuasion. But they were also lusty Dutch peasants, close to the soil, and had they once kissed there on the mound, they would have expanded with happy love. The moment gone, they talked, reverently.

'Detlev,' Maria said. 'That's a curious name.' When he explained its German origin, she said with some force, 'But if you're to be an Afrikaner, working on the things your brother-in-law . . . What was his name?'

'Piet Krause.'

'Now, that's a proper Afrikaner name. You should have one too. Detleef, that's what it ought to be, here in a new land.'

'Do you like it as Detleef?'

'I do. It sounds proper and responsible.'

Whenever their conversation might have taken a lighter tone, the shadow of the monument fell across them, and they would study its well-carved figures and envision once more the episodes of the camps, or they would look up at the monitory obelisk rising one hundred and thirteen feet above them, summoning them back to serious matters.

'If the Germans should arrive from the west and the east, would you join with them?'

'Is there reason to believe . . .'

'Oh, yes! My father is sure there will be war in Europe, and that the Germans will mass their forces in South-West Africa and Tanganyika and come toward us like pincers.' She hesitated. 'You'd join them, of course?'

Detlev didn't know what to say. He'd heard such rumors frequently in recent years, when things seemed to be going badly in Europe, but he had never believed that Germany would actually strike at South Africa. If she did, he would leap to her support, of course, because any enemy of England's had to be a friend of his, but he was not prepared to commit himself openly.

'My father will be the first to join them,' Maria said. 'We pray that they will come soon to liberate us.' Detlev understood this enthusiasm but still remained silent. 'It would be rather wonderful, you know, to be a free country again,' she said, 'under our own rulers, with a strong Germany on either side to protect us.'

When Detlev made no response, she changed the subject: 'Will you make your name Afrikaans?'

'I've been thinking about that. I don't much like it the way it is.'

'Detleef,' she repeated. 'I like that.'

'Done!' he said. 'I prefer all things Afrikaans. I am now Detleef van Doorn.' He was sorely tempted to take her hand, or even to kiss her to mark the solemnity of his rechristening, but the mournfulness of the monument prevented this, and they spent the rest of that meaningful day talking of sober subjects.

When he returned home he found himself something of a hero, for he was invited to speak at various communities, telling of the splendid monument which memorialized their hardships in the camps. He was asked to come even to Carolina, an invitation he accepted eagerly, since it enabled him to renew acquaintance with Maria Steyn and to meet her father. When in his talk he alluded gracefully to the heroic performance of Christoffel Steyn and the Carolina men, everyone applauded.

After his speech he shared supper with the Steyns, and in later years he remembered this affair as one of the most important in his life. It had nothing to do with Maria, and was a silly thing, really, but as he watched Mrs. Steyn, almost as plump as her husband, moving easily about the kitchen and displaying her love for her family, it occurred to him that she was a second wife, not a first, and he wondered if his childhood would not have been happier had his father married again. He saw Mrs. Steyn as the epitome of what a loving Afrikaner woman could be, and it was important that he see this.

When he returned to his own home he was struck by its bleakness, and he felt depressed, but his thoughts were diverted by a series of mysterious incidents. Unidentified horsemen arrived at Vrymeer asking where General de Groot lived, and when they were told, they galloped off into the darkness. Excitement was caused by the appearance of an automobile containing three serious-looking men who wanted to consult with the general, and one afternoon Maria Steyn's fat little father appeared on the stoep, asking to talk not only with General de Groot but also with Jakob. Van Doorn was now sixty-nine years old, white-haired and somewhat stooped, but still mentally alert, and after the meeting ended he was obviously disturbed.

One evening in midwinter, 1914, when supper was over, he pushed back his plate and looked at his son. He said nothing, reflected for some moments, then stalked from the room, and Detleef could hear him walking back and forth across the stoep. Much later he returned to the kitchen and said brusquely, as if his thoughts had suddenly clarified, 'Son, England has declared war unrightfully against Germany. We must all make decisions. Let's go see De Groot.'

In the moonlight they walked to the other farm, where they found the old general in bed, a weary man past eighty, very thin, his long white beard rimming his sunken face. He had not been eating well, and it looked as if his sheets had not been changed for weeks, or even months, but the fire in his eyes had not abated. 'Have you heard the glorious news?' he cried in weakened accents. 'We have a chance to fight England again!'

'We come asking your advice, Paulus.'

'Only one thing to do. Take this country into the war on the side of Germany. Only that way can we win our freedom.'

'But won't Smuts try to make us fight in the English armies?'

General de Groot got out of bed and began to stride about his little room. 'There's the man we have to fear. That damned Jan Christian Smuts. He will try to make us fight on the wrong side, because he loves everything English. Uniforms. Medals. The king. People bowing to him. I wish I could shoot him tonight. Save us all a lot of trouble.'

They talked long about the strategies they must follow to assure that South Africa joined this war beside Germany, and what great steps they would take when German victory set them free of the bondage in which they were convinced they languished. Toward dawn De Groot said, 'By tonight I'll have the commando assembled again, and if they'll take me as their leader, we'll ride out to battle once more.' And from a pile of clothes in a corner he found his frock coat and top hat, donned them, and rode off toward Venloo to start training his men.

In the last weeks of August, when the big guns were firing salvos across wide fronts in Europe, the schoolteacher Piet Krause was marshaling public opinion in Venloo, and he was most persuasive: 'There is no reason on God's green earth why we Afrikaners should fight on the side of England against Germany, the land of our brothers, to whom we have always looked for deliverance. We must tell Jan Christian Smuts that he cannot bludgeon us into this war on the wrong side.' Constantly he harped on this theme, convincing most of the Afrikaners in his region that they must join with the Germans. In a show of hands in his classroom he found that some fifty-two boys out of sixty would volunteer for war against England. 'Wonderful! It proves that the spirit of the great commandos is not dead.'

'What will you do, Mr. Krause?' one of the boys asked.

'What could any self-respecting man do? I shall ride with the commando.'

Detleef, hearing this response, thought: They all speak of riding their horses with the commando. This time it'll be automobiles, and trucks, and the government will have them. He alone among his friends was apprehensive about the outcome. He considered Jan Christian Smuts a clever man who would defend the imperial cause effectively; but despite his caution, he knew that if the Afrikaners did not rebel now, they might never win their freedom. When Mr. Krause asked, 'You, Detleef, what will you do?' he responded promptly, 'I shall fight in defense of South Africa.'

'Which South Africa?'

'The Afrikaner homeland my father fought for.'

'Good, good.'

Now the night visitors to General de Groot increased in number, and Detleef came to know the great heroes of his people: General de Wet, General de la Rey, General Beyers, tough Manie Maritz, big as an ox, ferocious as a leopard. But the hero who impressed him most was Christoffel Steyn, who showed himself to be a man of iron courage and sober judgment.

Said he during one meeting with De Groot: 'The tides of history run tempestuously. This has always been a storm-tossed land, and where the currents will sweep us now, we cannot foresee. But to stand on shore and watch others breast them would be disgraceful. De Groot, you have the Venloo Commando in excellent condition. Visit the others. Get them ready. And when the time comes, you must lead your horsemen into battle. This time we shall regain our freedom.'

From that strong position Steyn never retreated. When others wavered, pointing out the considerable advantages the government forces would have, he persisted on one steady course, freedom, and he expected all about him to do the same. But Detleef noticed that even in his most stubborn moments, he sought guidance from General de Groot and insisted upon the old man's approval and allegiance, as if he knew that he himself lacked the leadership qualities to head a revolution, whereas De Groot had them in marked degree.

'Keep your eye on Smuts,' the old man warned. 'Christoffel, you will succeed or fail insofar as you can outsmart Slim Jannie.' When De Groot used *slim* he did not intend the English word, although Jan Christian was that—slim and tall and handsome—but rather the Afrikaans word pronounced the same way: clever, shrewd, sly, not to be trusted, devious, tricky, deceitful, treacherous. It was a wonderful word, used often in connection with Smuts, whom no republican-minded Afrikaner could trust. 'Be careful, Christoffel, of that Slim Jannie.'

It was sound advice, for Smuts, perhaps the keenest brain that South Africa had ever produced, was convinced that the destiny of this country had to lie with England, and stood ready to repel any German invader from the outside or discipline any German sympathizer who sought to operate secretly on the inside. Supporting him were English-speaking South Africans and many like-minded Afrikaners who were eager to forget the past and wanted to unite the two white tribes of the land. Paulus de Groot was shrewd when he perceived that the battle of his commandos would be not against England, but against Slim Jannie. It would be a precarious revolution and he said so.

But he was impatient to lead it. He fed his Basuto pony extra rations, oiled his rifle, and consulted constantly with leaders of the other commandos. He was in Venloo church that Sunday morning, tall and straight for all to see, when Predikant Brongersma delivered his famous sermon on patriotism:

> 'The Bible is replete with instances in which men were called to defend their nations, in which they rode forth to protect the principles upon which their homeland existed. The Israelites in particular had to protect themselves against Assyrians, Medes, Persians, Egyptians and Philistines, and whenever they fought in accordance with God's principles, they were victorious. When they raised their own false banners, they were defeated.

> 'What words appear on the banner of God? Justice, fortitude, obedience, charity to the defeated enemy, reverence, prayer, and above all, sacred respect for the covenant under which our nation exists. If we,

in moments of crisis, can comport ourselves in harmony with those commands, then we can be assured that we fight on God's side. But if we are arrogant, or seek what belongs to others, or are cruel, or behave without respect for the covenant, then we must surely earn defeat.

'How can a man discern, in time of crisis, whether he is in harmony with God's commands? Only by searching his own heart and comparing his proposed behavior with instructions he has learned in the Bible. And only by subjecting himself to that comparison constantly. It is in the Bible that we find our instructions.'

After the sermon, when De Groot asked him point-blank if he would be riding with the commandos, the predikant said that his duty lay with the community, to help guide it regardless of the outcome. 'Then you are afraid we'll lose?' De Groot asked.

'I am,' Brongersma said.

'You mean our cause is unjust?'

'I mean, General, that I have heard you say a dozen times, "We have lost the battles. We have lost the war. Now we shall win in other ways." You were right when you said that. But now, at the first chance, you go back to the battles. Why?'

'If a bugle sounds against the English, who can stay home?' As he asked this, the old warrior stared straight into the eyes of the predikant, recalling the dismal fact that in the great moments of his life—the trek, the frontier, the battles—his church had never supported him. He did not expect it to now.

The first two weeks of September 1914 were a hectic and dazzling experience: Paulus de Groot dispatched emissaries to the other commandos, advising them that he expected them to rise as soon as the great generals declared themselves in favor of Germany; Christoffel Steyn assembled seventy-two men out of a possible ninety, each ready to mount his pony and ride forth; Piet Krause had already put away his books and was eager to fight; Jakob van Doorn, at seventy, had purchased an automobile; and his son Detleef, at nineteen, was up in the hills behind Vrymeer, practicing with a Mauser.

Beginning on Friday, September 12, De Groot convened a series of leader-meetings attended by a secret agent of the German armed forces in South-West Africa, who assured the locals that all was in readiness. The uprising was to start on Tuesday, September 16; wild Manie Maritz would lead his commando across the border into German territory; General Beyers would resign his position with the government after releasing a fiery condemnation of Smuts; and General de Groot would summon the men in the northeastern Transvaal. Pretoria would be taken, the government would be captured; and German power would reach from the Atlantic on the west to the Indian Ocean at Tanganyika. Combined with victory in Europe, this would herald the dawn of Germanic hegemony, in which Afrikaner nationalism would dominate southern Africa, under German guidance.

On the night of Sunday, September 14, Detleef van Doorn rode slowly eastward to Venloo, where his brother-in-law, Piet Krause, had assembled twenty-two men of the local commando. They rode through the starry night to a meeting point where others were gathering for the uprising; when morning came and he saw the masses of men willing to fight once more for a republican South Africa, his excitement soared and he cried to Krause, 'Nothing can stop us now!' He gained additional reassurance when he found that these men were to be led by Christoffel Steyn.

And then the blows of misfortune began to fall. As Barend Brongersma had foreseen, God was not with these Afrikaners this time. The general on whom they depended most to lead them, Koos de la Rey, a fine and brilliant man, had the horrible misfortune to be riding out of Johannesburg to convene his segment of the rebellion when a policeman, suspecting that the speeding car might contain a team of gangsters who had committed many depredations, including murder of policemen, fired a shot at the Daimler's tire. It should never have hit the car, but it ricocheted off a rock, smashed into the head of De la Rey and killed him. Sometime later, capable General Beyers, who might have taken the dead man's place, tried to flee across the Vaal River and was drowned. Tough Manie Maritz was neutralized across the border, and even brave General de Wet, noblest of the lot, was surrounded and forced to surrender.

Slim Jannie Smuts made not a single mistake. When the rebellion appeared to be powerful, he did not panic; instead, he called up loyal Afrikaner troops to confront their defiant brothers, keeping the English section of the nation out of the fight. And when the rebellion began to fizzle, he did not exult. He simply maintained one pressure after another, and in the end, found himself victorious on every front: the German invading force from South-West Africa was beaten back; the Germans in Tanganyika were immobilized; and within the country only Paulus de Groot and Christoffel Steyn held out against him, pinned down, as in 1902, in a wee corner of the Transvaal.

'We must fight to the death,' De Groot told his men, and if any showed an inclination to despair, young firebrands like Piet Krause disciplined them, saying, 'In Europe, Germany is winning everywhere. Victory will still be ours.'

But then they were crushed by the most devastating blow of all. One night in November 1914, after a tiring ride across the highveld, General de Groot said to Jakob and Detleef, who had ridden with him, 'I feel tired.' A bed was made for the old man, the first he had slept in for the past ten days, and he began to breathe heavily. He said a most curious thing: 'I would like to see my Basuto.' So the little horse was brought to where he lay. Sixteen, eighteen, fifty . . . how many of these wonderful beasts had he ridden and out of how many traps? He tried to pat the munching animal, but fell back, too exhausted to complete the effort.

'Take him away,' Jakob told his son, but the old man protested: 'Leave him with me.' Toward midnight he rallied somewhat and told Christoffel, 'Lead the men toward Waterval-Boven. We always fought well there.' In some bewilderment he looked at Jakob and could not remember who he was, but then he saw Detleef, who had been so kind: 'Are you Detleef with the new name?'

'I am.' The old man tried to speak, fell back, and died. Born in 1832, he had witnessed eight decades of fire and hope, defeat and victory.

With his death, the last commando more or less dissolved. Christoffel Steyn made a valiant effort to hold the men together, and Piet Krause threatened to shoot any who deserted, but finally, even men like Jakob and Detleef drifted away, for as Van Doorn told his son-in-law, 'Piet, it's time to get back to the farm.'

'No!' the young schoolteacher pleaded. 'One more battle, just one big victory, and the Germans will come storming up from Moçambique to save us.'

'There are no Germans in Moçambique,' Jakob said, but Krause was so determined to pursue this logic that he maneuvered the men into a position from which they could not escape without giving battle, and in this fight Jakob van Doorn caught a burst of .303 bullets right between the eyes. Little of his head was left to be buried with the shattered trunk, and after prayers were said at his improvised graveside, Detleef said, 'Piet, I think we'd better go home.'

It was fortunate they did, for the very next day government troops surrounded the remnants of the commando and arrested Christoffel Steyn.

Then began the worst agony of this abortive affair, for Jan Christian Smuts discovered that Christoffel, in the years of peace following the end of the Boer War, had accepted a position in the South African army which he had never resigned. Technically he was a traitor, and while hundreds of other rebels had been dealt with leniently, Smuts was determined to prosecute charges against this officer. On an awful day in December 1914 a court-martial condemned Steyn to be executed. From the Afrikaner community, including many who had not supported the rebellion, came a cry of protest, voicing respect and admiration for this brave man who had conducted himself with such integrity during the forays of the Carolina Commando. But Smuts would not listen.

Piet Krause led a delegation of schoolteachers to Pretoria to plead for Christoffel's life, and Reverend Brongersma preached four tremendous sermons, two in Johannesburg, begging the government to show clemency, but to no avail. Only a few days before Christmas, Steyn was taken before a firing squad in Pretoria Central Prison, where he sang an old Dutch hymn: 'When we enter the Valley of Death we leave our friends behind us.' As the soldiers took up firing positions he refused a blindfold and continued singing until the bullets silenced him.

Detleef was torn apart by this tragic culmination of the rebellion: De Groot dead on the battlefield; Jakob buried in strange soil; Christoffel, of them all the most chivalrous, executed on a summer's morning; his own life shattered. That night he wrote to Maria, the rebel's daughter:

> I fought alongside your father. I saw him at his noblest and his memory will always abide with me. He was executed most unfairly, and if I ever see that Slim Jan Christian Smuts, I will put a bullet through his brain, if he has one, which I doubt.

She, being a prudent young woman, showed the letter to no one, for she realized that if it were seen by the police, the young man she loved might be in serious trouble. She folded it carefully and placed it with mementos of her father: a handkerchief worn at Spion Kop, his cartridge belt, a book of Psalms in Old Dutch that he had carried with him in all his Boer War battles.

Christoffel Steyn was dead, but his memory would be kept alive not only by his daughter but also by a whole people longing for heroes. Slim Jannie Smuts had created a martyr out of this little commando and left a burning wound in the soul of Afrikanerdom. It would flame alongside the charred memories of Slagter's Nek, Blaauwkrantz and Chrissiesmeer—a bitter legacy upon which the sacred history of a nation would be built.

Detleef would surely have married Maria Steyn not long afterward, except that Reverend Brongersma came to the farm with news that carried him off to wholly new adventures in education: 'I have the most exciting development to discuss with you, Detleef. Some time ago I wrote to a group of professors at Stellenbosch, telling them two things: that you were good at studies and unusually good at rugby. They want you to come there to pursue your studies.'

'What studies?'

'I would say philosophy and the sciences. And it would please me greatly if you found it in your heart to enter the ministry. You have a strong character, Detleef, and I think you could be of notable service to the Lord.'

'But who will tend the farm?'

'Piet Krause and Johanna. I've spoken to them.'

'He can't live here and teach in Venloo.'

'Recent events have spoiled him, Detleef. He no longer wants to be a teacher.'

'He won't be very good at farming.'

'No, but he'll look after the place till you get back. And then we'll see what happens.' He paused and rubbed his chin. 'You know, Piet is a remarkable man. He could move in any direction if God ever shows him the right one.' He laughed. 'You have found your path.'

'And what is it?'

'To get an education. To serve God and your society.'

It was a long journey in miles from Vrymeer to Stellenbosch, a much greater one in mental and moral significance, for this quiet town with tall trees and white buildings had become a beautiful and seductive educational center like Cambridge in England, or Siena in Italy, or Princeton in America, a town set apart to remind citizens of how splendid colleges and libraries and museums could be. It was an Afrikaans-speaking place, heavily tinged with religious fervor, but also imbued with an intense speculation about the nature of politics in South Africa, and its professors were some of the most astute men in the nation.

At first Detleef was merely a big, bumbling oaf from the country, forced to compete with the sharper minds of lads who had matured in places like Pretoria, Bloemfontein and Cape Town, but when he settled down in the home of a clergyman's widow and navigated his first term of advanced trigonometry, beginning philosophy and the history of Holland in the golden century, all of which he fumbled rather badly, he found his sea legs, as it were, and proceeded firmly into his second set of courses, in which he began to display the solid learning he had mastered in the good school at Venloo.

He was especially attracted by his older professors, those men of learning, some from the university at Leiden, some from Oxford, who saw their nation as it actually was, a mix of cultures striving to achieve a central tendency, and he found to his astonishment that two of the classes he enjoyed most were taught by Englishmen, in English. But he appreciated them as he might an especially provocative class in Latin; these men were dealing in historic materials that were long since dead, and if they did so brilliantly, they did so nevertheless with a sense of the mortuary, and he knew it.

The men who exerted the deepest influence were the younger professors who discussed contemporary values, the future of South Africa, its current crises. There were no courses in such subjects, but the better professors knew how to slip relevant teaching into their lectures. In 1916, for example, there was much discussion of how the war in Europe would terminate, with some professors still convinced that Germany would win, but conceding that her victory would not mean much constructively to South Africa, which would face a new set of problems. One man warned: 'I cannot see Germany surrendering Lourenço Marques to us when she conquers it from Portugal. It will be her port, not ours, and indeed, she may drive a harder bargain for its use than the Portuguese did.' Hardly a day passed but what some challenging idea was extruded, sometimes painfully, always cautiously, and his mind expanded with this new aspect of learning.

Living in the house of a predikant's widow, and buttressed by constant pressure from Reverend Brongersma back in Venloo, it was natural that Detleef should fall into the orbit of the professors of religion, and they quickly saw in this able young man a likely prospect for the pulpit. He was inherently devout and well informed on Biblical matters; both his father and the old general had taught him from the time-scarred Bible, and the predikants of Venloo had been a virile lot, preaching a durable version of the Old Testament, while Barend Brongersma had introduced him to the subtleties of the New, so that by the end of his first year it was generally assumed that he would be heading for the ministry.

As had been the case for the past hundred years, one of the most influential voices in the Dutch Reformed clergy at Stellenbosch was a Scotsman, a devotee of John Knox named Alexander McKinnon, whose ancestors had been Dutch-speaking Afrikaners since 1813. It was he who introduced Detleef to the persuasive teachings of the conservative prime minister of Holland, Abraham Kuyper, who had promulgated new theories on the relationship between church and state. It was from McKinnon that Detleef first gleaned an appreciation of the fact that South Africa might soon have to evolve new patterns for contacts between the races. On this subject McKinnon was most conservative, going back to a strong Calvinism to support his contention that races, like people, were foreordained to either salvation or damnation: 'Obviously, the Bantu are the children of Ham, as the Bible explains.' Detleef noticed that like most cultured people these

days, he avoided the pejorative word *Kaffir,* using instead the curious word
Bantu, which more accurately was the name of a language, not that of a
tribe or nation. 'Obviously, the Bantu as a group cannot be among the elect,
although individual Bantu can become highly educated and just as favored
of God as the finest Afrikaner. Individuals can be saved, but the race as a
whole is certainly condemned.'

But in the latter part of his first year at Stellenbosch all such matters
faded into insignificance, for the university discovered that in Detleef they
had a natural-born rugby player, and in a nation increasingly mad about
sports, this attribute superseded all others. He was a thick-necked block of
granite, tested in real battle, and extremely quick in adjusting to the movements of the enemy. He played forward, and in the scrum his shoulders
disrupted the opposition, breaking holes in their line, while his feet were
unusually nimble at hooking the ball or sending it forward. He was a
stubborn chunk of aggression who could absorb punishment without flinch-
ing, and as such, he was invaluable.

The Stellenbosch fifteen were known as the Maties because of their
strong sense of fraternity; they were a formidable combination, capable of
playing the best regional teams, but their special delight came in defeating
the Ikeys of Cape Town, so-called because that university admitted a goodly
number of Jews, who were not exactly welcomed at Stellenbosch. Any
Maties-Ikeys game was apt to be exciting, and in the first one Detleef
played, he excelled. From then on he was accepted as a member of the
Afrikaner group that specialized in sports, and by virtue of this he traveled
to many parts of the country, playing against the men who would later
occupy positions of leadership, for in South Africa there was no passport
to preferment more effective than membership on the Stellenbosch rugby
team.

These were the years when the game was dominated by one sensational
family, the Morkels, and sometimes Detleef would go up against a team that
fielded six players with that name, or seven. Twenty-two Morkels were
playing in this decade: brothers, cousins, unrelated solitaries, all of them
stout lads. Detleef knew it was going to be a strong game whenever he bent
over in the scrum and found himself facing two or three of these rugged
types. Once, the four biggest men facing him in the tight confrontations
were Morkels, and he left that game, as he told his coach, 'as if I had slipped
by accident into a threshing machine.' He was not surprised when an
entrepreneur announced plans to invade Europe with a team composed only
of Morkels; it would be formidable.

It was as a rugby player that Detleef finished his first year at Stellenbosch, and it was principally because of this reputation that he attracted the
attention of the Van Doorns who operated the famous vineyards at Trianon.
One afternoon, to the house in which he boarded, a Bantu came bearing an
invitation to Detleef van Doorn to take dinner that evening with his Trianon
cousins. It was the day after a game in which five horrible Morkels had run
up and down his spine, so he was not exactly lively, but he had heard so
much about Trianon that he accepted, and rode out to the winery.

Like many before him, he gaped when he approached the western
entrance and saw for the first time those enchanting arms reaching out and
the pristine façade of the main house waiting to welcome him. The war

years had been good to Trianon; General Buller had paid top prices for its premier wine and other officers did the same for the lesser blends, so that the Van Doorns had sold their entire pressings for European prices without having had to pay freightage to get the bottles to that market. In all respects the place had been improved, and now looked pretty much as it would through the twentieth century.

On the stoep, resting on one of the tiled benches built two centuries earlier by Paul de Pré, waited Coenraad van Doorn, head of the establishment, who had extended a similar welcome to Jakob in 1899, on the eve of the Boer War. He was heavier now, a man in his late forties, and his manner was even more affable, for life had been exceedingly good. He loved sports and was proud to have a member of his family, even one so remotely associated as Detleef, playing well at Stellenbosch.

'So this is the hero I've been reading about, the Matie who sweeps them aside!' Extending both hands, he drew Detleef up to the stoep and in through the front door. In the wide hallway between the rooms Detleef saw for the first time the Van Doorn daughter, Clara, nineteen years old and so pretty she caused him to gasp. Her face was beautifully oval, with cheekbones just a bit too wide, and framed by carefully brushed amber hair worn in a kind of Dutch-boy bob. She smiled warmly as she stepped forward to greet her distant cousin, and said, 'We are so happy to see such a rugby player in our home.'

At dinner her two older brothers, Dirk and Gerrit, who had by now graduated from Stellenbosch, asked a barrage of questions about the university and their chances of beating the Ikeys again, and the evening proved to be one of the most pleasant Detleef had ever spent. It was fortunate that it was occurring at the end of his first year, because by now his success at rugby had transformed him from an awkward country lad into a self-confident university man, quiet-spoken and interesting. When talk turned to the war in Europe, he repeated some of the things he had heard in class, predicting a German victory in Europe but no significant change in the countries bordering South Africa.

'What I feel precisely,' the older Van Doorn said, and as Clara walked with Detleef to the automobile that would take him back to his lodgings she said, 'You've been learning something at the university. Come back and share your knowledge with us.' He started to protest that he really knew very little, but she halted him: 'No! My brothers went to Stellenbosch and they learned precious little.' It was as if she rode in the car with him back to town, so vivid was his recollection of her lovely bearing.

He spent two weeks trying to invent some excuse for returning to Trianon, and then one night the driver was there again with a note: 'Dr. Pretorius of Paarl is coming to dinner and would like to meet you. Clara.' It was the beginning of a thrilling experience, for Pretorius was active on a committee agitating to have Afrikaans accepted as the legal equivalent of Dutch and he was excitable about the matter: 'Acts of Parliament must be printed in Afrikaans. Our major newspapers should convert to it immediately. I've been speaking with our leading clergymen. I want our Bible to be in our language.'

'Are they ready for that?'

'No. In that quarter I receive much opposition. But consider. For three centuries in the late Middle Ages people spoke one language and read their Bible in Latin. That had to change.'

'The Catholic church still conducts its Masses in Latin.'

'That will change, too. The day will come when your daughter here is married by a predikant reading the service from an Afrikaans Bible.'

'You think so soon?' Mrs. van Doorn asked. 'I'm afraid you'll be an old maid, Clara, if you wait for that.' Clara did not blush, but Detleef did.

After one agitated flight of speech, Dr. Pretorius looked about the room as though to command close attention, then said in a softer voice, 'I want to speed the acceptance of our true language because it can become the chief agency in uniting the Afrikaners of this land and inspiring them to wrest the government from the English.'

'We have the numbers already,' Coenraad pointed out.

'But without a central soul, numbers are nothing. And what is the soul of a people? Its language. With Afrikaans we can capture this nation.'

At a subsequent meeting, at which he especially wanted Detleef to be present, Pretorius faced up to the accusation, launched by Coenraad, that Afrikaans was a second-class peasant language: 'Exactly, and that's why its vitality is assured. It will be precisely like English. And why is that language so effective?'

Each listener offered some reason: 'No declension of nouns.' 'Few subjunctive verbs.' 'Strict word order, which assures meaning.' 'A lot of quick short words to indicate case.' 'A simplified spelling.'

Clara said, 'And if English spots a good word in another language, it takes it . . . with no apologies.'

At each idea, Dr. Pretorius nodded approvingly, then asked permission to read from the work of a distinguished Danish scholar who was exploring this subject: 'He is Dr. Otto Jespersen, world-famous authority, and he says, "The English language is signalized by order and consistency . . . Simplification is the rule." And here he makes a point which relates specifically to our new Afrikaans: "Whenever I think of English and compare it with other languages, it seems to me positively and expressly *masculine*. It is the language of a grown-up man and has very little childish or feminine about it." '

He asked Clara to pass out slips of paper, and when they all had pencils he directed them to write this sentence in English: *We ourselves often took our dogs with us.* 'Four pronouns to express the first person plural. Now see what happens when we write the same sentence in Afrikaans: *Ons onsself het dikwelf ons honde saam met ons geneem.* One word—*ons*—to convey all those meanings.'

'But isn't the English more precise?'

'It is indeed. Just as the Latin forms *agricola,* by the farmer, *agricolae,* to the farmer, are more precise than *the farmer.* But we refuse to bother with such niceties. Prepositions are so much simpler. One word for *farmer.* Sixty prepositions to define relationships.'

From another pocket he produced a handful of sheets on which verses from Matthew, Chapter 6, had been printed in English:

9.   Our Father which art in heaven, Hallowed be thy name.
10.   Thy kingdom come. Thy will be done in earth, as it is in heaven.

11. Give us this day our daily bread.
12. And forgive us our debts, as we forgive our debtors.

He pointed out how relatively simple this was, and how direct. He then asked the Van Doorns to study other sheets of paper, where the same verses appeared in the Old Dutch of their 1630 Amsterdam Bible.

9. Onse Vader die daer zijt inde Hemelen: uwen name worde geheylicht.
10. Drijckje kome. Uwen wille ghejchiede op der Aerden gelijck inden Hemel.
11. Gheeft ons heden ons daghelijcks broodt.
12. Ende vergheeft ons onse schulden. Gelijch wy oock vergheven onsen schuldenaren.

He read this aloud twice, stressing the beauty of the flowing Dutch they had learned as children and still used when reciting their prayers. He obviously cherished the rhythms of this version, but indicated that it would be better when translated into Afrikaans, of which he gave a sample:

9. Onse Vader wat in die hemele is, laat u Naam geheilig word;
10. laat u konindryk kom; lat u wil geskied, soos in de hemel net so op die aarde;
11. gee ons vandag ons daaglikse brood;
12. en vergeef ons ons skulde, soos ons ook ons skuldenaars vergewe . . .

'Ah!' he cried triumphantly. 'How excellent!' And he went over the new translation, line by line, indicating its superiority: 'See how much simpler the Afrikaans is, how purified of old encrustations. This is to be the language of the future, believe me.'

When the two older Van Doorns protested that they did not want their Bible tampered with, he said bluntly, 'The generation that is forty years old when the change comes will know an agony of the soul. After that we will be a new people.' When Coenraad tried to voice another doubt, he said abruptly, 'Remember, if John Calvin were alive today, he would be using a Bible in Afrikaans.'

Detleef, back in his room, balanced the two versions of a word he loved: The old *Nachtmaal* becomes the new *Nagmaal.* I don't like it. The mystery of *night* is lost. And for the first time he sensed that many great good things of ancient virtue might be lost during a normal lifetime: the women he had loved so much in the concentration camp, the sturdy virtues of General de Groot. He stared at the night and could not sleep, but as dawn broke he thought: It's my duty to save the good old things.

While Detleef was enjoying these varied experiences, the young men of the Saltwood families were pursuing their studies in a much grimmer classroom. Near the city of Amiens and east of the great battle site of St. Quentin was a hunting preserve known as d'Ellville Wood, and both the Allies and the Germans realized that this grove of trees would prove crucial in the tremendous Battle of the Somme.

The German high command issued the order, 'D'Ellville shall be taken, regardless of cost,' at exactly the time when the Allied command said, 'The wood must be held at any cost.' A titanic battle to the death had become inescapable.

On 14 July 1916 Colonel Frank Saltwood, fifty-six years old and one of the first volunteers in his country's expeditionary force, received orders to take and hold d'Ellville Wood. In his command were four of his nephews —Hilary and Roger of the Cape Town Saltwoods, Max and Timothy of De Kraal—and they, too, had volunteered early.

Throughout four unbroken days the two armies battled, calling upon every great gun in the area until the trenches shuddered from explosives. Without any rest or hot food, the five Saltwoods defended their terrain heroically, with Colonel Frank moving from spot to spot to encourage his nephews.

On the second day Hilary was shot through the head. On the third day young Max led a valiant charge, which was annihilated. And on the last day Colonel Frank, rushing to an endangered point, was struck full in the face by seven German bullets, and with his death the South African position was doomed.

But into his place leaped Roger, who at twenty years old assumed command of the battle. He would have led his men to defeat had not Timothy gone totally berserk, as heroic young men sometimes will, and held off a platoon of Germans, killing most of them. And now the two cousins, surrounded by innumerable dead, including three Saltwoods, rallied the South Africans. Ignoring the hailstorm of German shells, grimly preparing for the next attack, they staffed the command post and defended the woods which they had occupied at such fearful cost and held so tenaciously.

When the South Africans were finally relieved on the fifth day of battle Roger Saltwood, as senior in command, reported: 'We took 3,150 men into the wood five days ago. We are marching 143 out.'

Delville Wood, as the battle became known in English, represented perhaps the high spot in human courage during this war. The South African volunteers had given new meaning to the word *heroism,* but the cost could not even be calculated by critics who were not there. In the pompous tradition of the time, British headquarters issued a statement that was supposed to compensate for the terrible losses, as if this had been a kind of rugby game: 'In the capture of Delville Wood the gallantry, the perseverance and determination of the South African Brigade deserve the highest commendation.'

This suicidal action had been devised and ordered by Sir Douglas Haig, one of the young generals who had learned their trade with Redvers Buller during the Boer War. Unfortunately, few of them had acquired his concern for the fighting man.

The two surviving Saltwoods, Roger of Cape Town and Timothy the V.C. from De Kraal, managed leaves together. They spent them at Sentinels with their Salisbury cousins, and as they sat beside the River Avon and looked across at the timeless cathedral, it was Timothy who told the local

Saltwoods, 'We did lose three of us, yes. But it was only what we should have done for England.'

At Stellenbosch, as the war in Europe stumbled to an end, there was considerable commotion. One of the university's most promising recent graduates was announced as offering a series of four lectures on the moral bases upon which any government of the country must rest. Detleef was especially interested in the event because the speaker was Reverend Barend Brongersma, his own predikant. He invited Clara to hear the lectures with him, and her parents asked to come along, as did one of her brothers.

At Brongersma's request, the assemblies were held not at the university but in the largest of the local churches, and all seats were taken. Brongersma was now thirty-seven, at the threshold of his powers and the apex of his appearance. He was tall, slim, with a head of dark hair, and he appeared modern in every way as opposed to the older Dutch and Scottish theologians who normally occupied podiums at the university. He was different from them, too, in that he did not address himself to abstruse philosophical problems, but to the down-to-earth difficulties a politician met in running a proper government. His voice was equal to the task; Dutch Reformed congregations appreciated a predikant who could storm and thunder, and he could.

He was certainly not a coward. At the opening of his first lecture he said that the future of this nation depended upon the way it managed its relationships with the various racial groups, and so that his listeners would know what he was talking about, he invited them to write down the figures he was about to recite: 'They deal with the actual and projected populations of this country.' And he gave these data:

THE UNION OF SOUTH AFRICA

Group	Actual Population	1950 Estimate	2000 Estimate
Afrikaner	800,000	2,700,000	4,500,000
English-speaking	400,000	900,000	1,500,000
Coloured	525,000	1,200,000	4,200,000
Indian	150,000	366,000	1,250,000
Bantu	4,100,000	8,600,000	33,000,000

Without comment on the relative strengths of the five groups, he launched into a review of the positions the Dutch Reformed Church had taken on the matter of race during the past two and a half centuries, reminding his listeners of things they might have forgotten:

'Under Jan van Riebeeck, whites and blacks worshipped together, which was sensible because there was no alternative. In the frontier churches at Stellenbosch and Swellendam, similar conditions prevailed.

'Problems arose with the rite of communion, many whites not wishing to drink from the same cup that blacks used, but various ways were devised to get around this, and in general, worship continued to include both white and black. At mission stations especially this was the custom, with whites being invited to attend churches that were primarily black.

'But at the Synod of 1857 pressure was exerted to change this, and a curious solution was proposed. The leaders of our church confirmed that Jesus Christ intended his people to worship as one, and this was to be preferred, "but as a concession to the prejudice and weakness of a few, it is recommended that the church serve one or more tables to the European members after the non-white members have been served." It was further recommended that whereas it would be healthy and in accordance with Gospel for all to worship together, "if the weakness of some requires that the groups be separated, the congregation from the heathen should enjoy its privilege in a separate building and a separate institution."

'So in certain districts separate church organizations were established whose members worshipped in separate church buildings, and in time this custom became universal. It was found that most white church members preferred to worship only with other whites, on the sensible ground that health could thus be protected and the dangers of miscegenation avoided.

'As a result of such pressures, a policy developed of having separate church buildings and church organizations for each of the various racial groups, and this lent strength to the Christian movement, for the Coloured and Bantu now had churches of their own which they could operate according to their own tastes, yet all were united in the brotherhood of Christ.'

He said much more, of course, in this historical lecture, but he left the impression that the Christian church was one and undivided, that the Coloured and Bantu preferred to have their own church off to one side, and that the present division of the church into its various components was something ordained by God, approved by Jesus, and eminently workable in a plural society. He certainly did not apologize, and would have been astounded had anyone asked him to do so.

'That man is an asset to any community,' Coenraad van Doorn said when he assembled his family and Detleef at Trianon. 'He speaks with a clarity one seldom hears.'

'He told me things I didn't know,' Clara said. She looked as if she had been crying, and Detleef asked what had happened.

Her mother answered, 'The awful deaths in Europe. Clara has many friends there, you know.'

Detleef said, 'I didn't know there were very many Afrikaners fighting in that silly war.'

'There are,' Clara snapped, 'and it's not silly.'

'Any men we have there are certainly fighting on the wrong side. Germany's bound to win, and a good thing, too.'

Mr. van Doorn intervened to quash a difficult subject: 'I wonder what Brongersma will tell us next time?'

'He said in passing that it would deal with the New Testament,' Clara's brother said.

'Good. None of us know that section of the Bible well enough.'

'The Old Testament is sufficient, really,' Detleef said, and again the atmosphere chilled, but when it came time for him to say goodnight, Clara volunteered to walk with him to the car, took his hand and squeezed it. 'You mustn't be so contentious, Detleef. A living room isn't a rugby field.'

'But if a man has beliefs . . .'

'All men have beliefs. And sometimes they adhere to theirs as firmly as you do to yours.'

'But if theirs are wrong . . .'

'You feel obligated to correct them?'

'Of course.'

To his astonishment she leaned over and kissed him. 'I'm glad you're strong, Detleef. You're going to need it.'

He was trembling, and clutched her hand. 'I don't want to be obstinate, but . . . well . . . even Reverend Brongersma can be wrong sometimes.'

'For example?'

'Well, I felt he was apologetic about the way our church separates into white, Coloured, black. But that's what God intended. Even the whites separate. Afrikaans for the true believers. English for the others.'

'Detleef, how can you say that?' When he looked blank in the pale light, indicating that he had no concept of what she was talking about, she said, 'The Afrikaners and the English as being different religiously.'

'Well, they are!' he said forcefully. 'They believe quite differently from us. They don't pin their faith on John Calvin. They're almost Catholic, if you ask me.' He trembled again, this time from the terrible force of his convictions. 'And surely God entered into no covenant with them.'

To this extraordinary body of belief, Clara had no comment; her family had developed under quite a different body of faith and had often gone to the Church of England for services when that was more convenient. But now it was time for Detleef to return to the university, and as he held her hand he asked shyly, 'May I kiss you goodnight?' but she deftly pulled away.

'No, no! When I kiss you that's one thing, but when you kiss me that's another.' And before he knew what was happening, she touched him lightly with another kiss and skipped away.

Reverend Brongersma's second lecture was a revelation to Detleef and a surprise to others who thought they knew the Bible. It dealt almost exclusively with the teachings of the New Testament and the nature of Christ's church on earth. It was highly theological, but also intensely practical to those Afrikaners who sensed that with a German victory in Europe, and perhaps in Africa, relationships were bound to be different from what they had been in the past. The audience sat in deep, religious silence as he spoke with that fluid breadth of concepts which would characterize this series:

'I told you last time that the orderly development of our church from the days of Van Riebeeck to the present was a good thing, approved by God and consonant with the teachings of Jesus Christ, and that we must always be proud of the high mission of our church. But since it exists in the bosom of Christ, it behooves us to know what exactly He said about our responsibilities and conduct.'

With this he launched into a patient hour-and-a-half analysis of New Testament teachings, drawing upon the soaring texts in which Christ set forth the essence of his thought. He said, when introducing the focal passage from Matthew, 'If we live in a land with divided populations, almost every question we face will pose special problems which other more homogeneous nations can evade. We cannot, and how we solve these problems of race will determine the character of our existence.' He then read the passage:

'Master, which is the great commandment in the law? Jesus said unto him, Thou shalt love the Lord thy God with all thy heart, and with all thy soul, and with all thy mind. This is the first and great commandment. And the second is like unto it, Thou shalt love thy neighbour as thyself. On these two commandments hang all the law and the prophets.'

He cited so many passages in Christ's teaching bearing on this issue that Coenraad whispered to Clara and Detleef, who sat together, 'He sounds like an LMS missionary,' and none could discern what he might be driving at:

'For as we have many members in one body, and all members have not the same office: so we, being many, are one body in Christ, and every one members one of another.'

And if anyone felt reluctant to accept this teaching, he threw at them a text which emphasized the message. It came from Colossians:

'Where there is neither Greek nor Jew, circumcision nor uncircumcision, Barbarian, Scythian, bond nor free: but Christ is all, and in all.'

This led him to what he warned was the key text of his entire series, the noble passage on which a God-fearing nation should build its patterns. It came from Ephesians and summarized, he said, the whole teaching of Jesus:

'There is one body, and one Spirit . . . one Lord, one faith, one baptism, one God and Father of all, who is above all, and through all, and in you all.

'The spirit of Jesus Christ resides in the bosom of every man and woman and child living in this nation,' he said in rising voice to indicate the conclusion of this lecture. 'It takes no cognizance of white or black, of Indian or Coloured, of woman or man, and certainly it does not distinguish between Englishman and Afrikaner. We are all one in Jesus. He loves us equally, He cares for us evenly.'

There was some restiveness in the audience at this revolutionary doctrine, for members felt that whereas these precepts did undoubtedly occur in the New Testament, their application was a more delicate matter than Reverend Brongersma appreciated. When he concluded with the stern warning that Christianity required its adherents to apply these fundamental strictures in their private and public lives, and especially in the organization of their societies and nations, there was actually a rumble of disapproval, but he stalked from the podium without taking cognizance of it.

That night there were no hearty invitations for him to join suppers at Stellenbosch homes, and the Coenraad van Doorns were so agitated that they did not even invite Detleef to Trianon; before they parted Mr. van Doorn said, 'Your predikant hasn't learned much up north,' and Detleef, without endeavoring to defend him, admitted, 'It all sounded so woolly. I like more order in society than that,' and even Clara, who had liked parts of the lecture, grumbled, 'He doesn't seem to understand his audience. We face real problems in this country, and he talks mealie pap.'

But Barend Brongersma did not graduate from Stellenbosch with honors because he was stupid. He had intended his long second lecture to create the effect it did because he wanted it to serve as preparation for what he knew would be one of the most important performances of his life, and when he stepped boldly to the podium for the third lecture he quickly told his audience why:

> 'Tonight I am addressing the young men who in the years to come will govern this nation. Look about you, I pray. The lad sitting next to you may be your prime minister one day. That fellow over there will preach in the mother church at Cape Town. You will be chancellor of this university, and you will be ambassador of our independent country to Paris. It is important that you think about the future, that you ponder the nature of a free society.

> 'Jesus addressed himself to this grave problem, and so did St. Paul, and in the New Testament they provide us with guidance. To govern well, we must govern justly, and to govern justly, we must govern wisely. What does Jesus tell us to do?'

Before he cited the relevant texts, he asked his audience a series of blistering hypothetical questions, until everyone present was aroused, leaning forward to catch what solutions he was about to propose. Then, with low voice and gentle patience, he began to unfold the teaching of Jesus, and the text he chose was so recondite and arbitrary that someone not from South Africa would have been at a loss to understand its application, but he claimed it to be the very foundation of the law, the most vital text in the entire Testament, insofar as the governance of nations was concerned. It came from the second chapter of Acts:

> 'And when the day of Pentecost was fully come, they were all with one accord in one place. And suddenly there came a sound from

heaven as of a rushing mighty wind, and it filled all the house where they were sitting . . . And they were all filled with the Holy Ghost, and began to speak with other tongues, as the spirit gave them utterance . . . every man heard them speak in his own language.'

What could be profound about that? How could the policy of a nation be built upon such an esoteric base? As he elucidated the text, it became clear: God created all men as brothers, but he quickly divided them into distinctive groups, each man to his own kind, each nation separate and off to itself, and here he thundered forth that wondrous sequence of names appearing in this all-important chapter:

'Parthians, and Medes, and Elamites, and the dwellers in Mesopotamia, and in Judea, and Cappadocia, in Pontus, and Asia, Phrygia, and Pamphylia, in Egypt, and in parts of Libya about Cyrene, and strangers of Rome, Jews and proselytes, Cretes and Arabians, we do hear them speak . . .'

He explained that God willed this diversity and applauded the strangeness that existed among nations. He wanted tribes to be different, to retain their distinctive qualities, and Brongersma suggested that if South Africa had been in existence when Acts, Chapter 2, was delivered, the litany might have ended thus:

'Afrikaners and Englishmen, Coloureds and Asians, Xhosa and Zulu, all spake in their own tongues.'

Detleef snapped bolt upright, for these local names were recited in the exact order he had seen them that morning when sunlight struck the glass of jellies. His world was in order; the races were distinct and they were separated, each in its proper place. He heard the remainder of this remarkable oration in a kind of majestic stupor; this was a confirmation that would last a lifetime, and others in the audience that evening would say the same when they governed this nation, as Brongersma had predicted they would: 'One lecture unfolded the future for me.' Brongersma now cited some fifteen pertinent texts, one of the most powerful coming from another chapter in Acts:

'God that made the world and all things therein . . . hath made of one blood all nations of men for to dwell on all the face of the earth, and hath determined the times before appointed, and the bounds of their habitation; that they should seek the Lord . . . and find him, though he be not far from every one of us.'

From this passage he derived the principle that God wanted each race to have its own boundaries and not to trespass on the territory of others; this applied both to physical boundaries, such as where people lived, and to mental, so that each race retained its own customs and laws. He then pointed out that religion asked all groups to accept the limitations placed upon them, especially people in the lower ones:

'As the Lord hath called every one, so let him walk . . . Let every man abide in the same calling wherein he was called. Art thou called being a servant? care not for it: but if thou mayest be made free, use it rather. For he that is called in the Lord, being a servant, is the Lord's freeman: likewise also he that is called, being free, is Christ's servant.'

And then he came to the crucial issue: 'Are all groups equal in the eyes of God?' He reminded his listeners of what he had said in Lecture Two, that unquestionably all men were brothers, but he went on to say that not all brothers stand equal in the sight of God. On this the New Testament was most specific; there were good nations and bad nations:

'When the Son of man shall come . . . then shall he sit upon the throne of his glory: and before him shall be gathered all nations: and he shall separate them one from another, as a shepherd divideth his sheep from the goats: and he shall set the sheep on his right hand, but the goats on the left. Then shall the King say unto them on his right hand, Come, ye blessed of my Father, inherit the kingdom . . . then shall he say also unto them on the left hand, Depart from me, ye cursed, into everlasting fire . . .'

He ended superbly, looking with flashing eye at his listeners, as if to challenge each one personally: 'In the time of judgment, which is now, will Jesus Christ set our nation on His right hand among the sheep, or throw us on His left side, among the goats? For the nature of our society we must look to the Old Testament, which I shall do in my concluding lecture.'

That night the audience was ecstatic as it left the church, for listeners could be sure that the Afrikaner nation was saved, while the English and the Bantu were probably lost. More than a dozen families wanted Brongersma to come with them to share supper, but he elected to go with the Van Doorns, and it was then that he saw the dangerous waters into which his young friend Detleef from Vrymeer was heading. He said nothing that night, but he wondered what good could come from this country boy's falling so blindly in love with a young woman who obviously lived in a much different world, and thought in much different ways. Detleef had said nothing about his deep affection for Clara, nor did he need to.

In his last lecture, like a healing balm, the predikant soothed all spiritual strains by reverting to the marvelous texts of the Old Testament, reminding his Afrikaners of who they were and the special obligations they owed God. He started by assuring them that in the Calvinistic sense they were among the elect, for God had specifically said so:

'Now therefore, if ye will obey my voice indeed, and keep my covenant, then ye shall be a peculiar treasure unto me above all people: for all the earth is mine.

'If you are a peculiar treasure, what follows?' he asked, and in the thundering passage from Leviticus he provided the answer:

'But I have said unto you, Ye shall inherit their land, and I will give it unto you to possess it, a land that floweth with milk and honey: I am the Lord your God, which have separated you from other people.

'It is right that you should be separated, for you have special tasks to perform'—and he elucidated them: 'To rule justly. To be fair to all men. To love your neighbor as yourself.' On and on he went, instructing the future rulers of the country as to how they must behave when they assumed power. 'I tell you these rules, young men,' he cried in his most powerful voice, grasping his lapels with two hands and leaning far forward, 'because God is most specific as to how he will punish you if you ignore his teaching,' and he set forth the unmistaken call for obedience:

'If ye forsake the Lord, and serve strange gods, then he will turn and do you hurt, and consume you, after that he hath done you good.'

He concluded this lecture and his series with a crisp twenty minutes of what this all meant to the governance of a church, and specifically the Dutch Reformed Church of South Africa. He dealt briskly with the most trying problems, brushing them away as if adherence to basic principles eliminated difficulties. When he came to the question as to whether it was proper for the white church to prevent blacks from worshipping side by side with them, he cried, 'Certainly it is proper. What does Deuteronomy say? "When the Most High divided to the nations their inheritance, when he separated the sons of Adam, he set the bounds of the people." Almost the last words of the Old Testament, the final verse of Zechariah, address this problem: "And in that day there shall be no more the Canaanite in the house of the Lord of hosts." We are separate. We are wonderful each in our way. God has assigned us our proper places and our proper tasks. Let us live accordingly. But I would close with these words of Jesus Christ which launched these talks: "Thou shalt love the Lord thy God. Thou shalt love thy neighbour as thyself. On these two commandments hang all the law and the prophets." '

In these four lectures, among the most important ever delivered at Stellenbosch, Brongersma spelled out the dilemma facing any theocracy: How does one organize a society so as to attain the order of the Old Testament and the freedom of the New? Detleef van Doorn, whose advanced education started with these lectures, heard only the first half of that question.

When the speculative and philosophical aspects of Detleef's education fell into place, thanks to that penetrating series of lectures by Barend Brongersma, and when his position at the university was securely established because of his excellence as a rugby player—at Stellenbosch that would always be determinative—he felt that it was time to start thinking seriously about a wife. He was twenty-three now, much older than the Voortrekkers when they married, and his thoughts turned to two young women.

He had not seen much of Maria Steyn, for she had remained on her family farm at Carolina. With her mother dead in the camp, and her father shot as a traitor, she had to assume heavy responsibilities and was able to travel little. She had never visited the university, and from the nature of Detleef's few letters she deduced that they were growing further and further apart; she pondered most carefully how best to reveal through the post her continued affection for him, but she found no womanly way to do this. She simply could not write: 'I love you deeply. Please come and rescue me from this prison of the spirit.' But that is what she felt, and as the years passed and she realized that she would never want to marry anyone but him, she experienced all the anxieties an uncertain young woman of twenty could feel. Desperately she awaited his letters, weighing each phrase to detect hidden meanings, but she found little to console her. Morning after morning she awakened at the farm, dreading the possibility that on this day she would learn that he had married someone else.

Far in the back of his mind, Detleef sensed that this must be the situation, and he sometimes admitted that in a proper world he would long since have been married to this stalwart girl he had liked so much that spring in Bloemfontein; whenever he mailed her a letter he visualized her as a married woman in church, or attending her duties, or caring for children. He never thought of her as beautiful, which she was not, but as some fine, solid human being for whom he had a steady affection.

But with Clara! That was different. For one thing, she was here in Stellenbosch, not in some distant Transvaal country town. She was alive with information, awake to changes occurring in the countryside. Her family had a new car, imported from America, and in it she loved to tour over the mountains to Fransch Hoek, where the Huguenots had clustered, or down to Somerset West, where the fine houses were. She was one of the first to learn that the war had ended in Europe, not with a German victory, as many had supposed, but with a smashing Allied triumph. For her own reasons, this gave her considerable satisfaction, but she did not annoy her father or her brothers by expressing this preference.

During the victory celebrations, in which the English settlers around the Cape were downright obnoxious, Detleef confided to her his disappointment: 'It would have been much better had the Germans won. They would have brought order to Europe.'

'And here, too, I suppose?' When he realized that she was goading him, he said no more, but when church services were held at the university to give thanks for the cessation of battle, he stayed away.

He began his serious courtship of Clara at Christmas time, 1918, spending most of his pocket money on a present for her. After considerable reflection he decided upon a small, fine leatherbound Bible published in Amsterdam, in which he wrote, facing the page on which their marriage and their children would be recorded: *To Clara, the best of the Van Doorns.*

She was embarrassed by the gift and wanted to return it, deeming it most inappropriate, but her father would not permit this: 'He gave it to you as a sincere expression. Accept it on that basis.'

'If I do,' she said, 'it can only mislead him.'

'That's the risk we all take when we give or accept things,' he said, and that night at supper he said to Detleef, 'I cannot imagine a finer gift.'

As the year drew to an end, Detleef became quite tense, rehearsing how he could best make his declaration to this exciting girl: I surely have the money to support a wife. Even Piet Krause, who doesn't farm very well, is showing a profit at Vrymeer. I have an education, so I can talk with her. I'm accorded a certain respect because of rugby. And I'm a good Christian.

But then he would in honesty list his deficiencies, and they seemed to weigh down the balances, but nevertheless, he decided to plunge ahead. However, there was to be no New Year's celebration, at least not with the Trianon Van Doorns, for they all drove in to Cape Town to greet a troop-ship that arrived on the last day of the year. It brought back to South Africa those gallant men who had volunteered to fight for king and country, and among them were some forty soldiers who had fought at Delville Wood.

As they came down the ramps, led by Timothy Saltwood, V.C., there was a curious silence. Most men and women in the crowd, English and Afrikaner alike, were overcome with emotion; but a few Afrikaners were, like Detleef, silent because of perplexity. These men were heroes, unquestionably, but they had fought on the wrong side. Then a wave of sentiment swept over the crowd as the men actually landed on home soil, and cheers deafened the Van Doorns as they applauded the men.

When the party returned to Trianon, with the tidy buildings appearing more secure than ever, there were celebrations, to which Detleef was not invited, but on the third of January, 1919, he bicycled out to the vineyards, prepared to make his formal proposal: I'll speak to Coenraad first, and then Clara's mother, and when I have their permission, I'll go to Clara herself. But as he pedaled his way down the long lane, he saw at the end of the little houses on the left a young woman who looked much like Clara kissing rather ardently a young man in military uniform. In great confusion he rode on, staring ahead, but from the corner of his eye he saw the woman break away when she noticed him, then move quickly back for another kiss.

'It's you!' Coenraad cried happily from the stoep. 'Come in, Detleef. It's a real celebration. Timothy Saltwood's home, covered with medals.'

'Is he in uniform?'

'Of course.'

When Clara and young Saltwood came into the hallway, Detleef felt weak, for the officer was a handsome fellow, lean, bemedaled, eager. 'This is Timothy Saltwood, of De Kraal,' Clara said. 'He tells me your family used to own his farm.'

'Long ago,' Detleef mumbled, and as soon as he could manage it, he whispered to Clara, 'Can I speak with you?'

'Of course! What?' She must have guessed what he was about to ask, but she gave him no help, standing firm in the middle of the room.

'I mean, can we talk . . . alone?'

'Of course,' she said brightly, leading him into her father's office.

'Clara,' he said. 'I gave you the Bible . . . I mean . . .'

'What is it?' she asked.

'I want to marry you.'

She placed her fingers on his lips: 'Don't, Detleef.'

'To ask you to marry me,' he muttered.

'Detleef, I'm so sorry. I'm going to marry Timothy.'

He gasped. 'But he's an Englishman!'

'He's a very brave young man.' When Detleef tried to speak, she placed her hand over his mouth and said firmly, 'If you do care for me, come out now and behave like a gentleman.'

'I am not a gentleman,' he said harshly, pushing her hand down. 'I'm not some fancy Englishman.' He looked at her in anger, and said accusingly, 'You knew this all the time. You let me make a fool of myself.' He fumbled for words and said a most stupid thing: 'You let me give you that Bible.'

'I think,' she said with asperity, 'that you had better take your damned Bible back,' and she hurried from the room.

He was aghast that a young woman he loved should use such a word in such a connection, and when she flounced back into the office, thrusting the Bible into his hands, he dumbly accepted it, then watched as she recovered it, opened it, and ripped out the page on which he had written his dedication. 'Give it to someone else,' she said sternly, and with that she left him.

For some minutes he stood there, holding the maimed book. He did not know what to do. He heard voices in the house, people talking gaily as if nothing embarrassing had happened, and then he made up his mind. Stalking from the room, looking at no one, he went out the front door for the last time in his life, and marched to his bicycle. Holding the Bible first in his right hand, then in his left, he pedaled down the long driveway, then jammed the book under his belt and went back to Stellenbosch.

Two days later Coenraad van Doorn came to see him, and said quietly, 'Detleef, things like this happen to everyone. My wife and I want you to attend the wedding. Clara wants it, for she considers you her good friend.'

With a hatred that burned his throat, Detleef said, 'All you English-lovers will be driven from power.'

Coenraad was a man who had worked hard to keep his vineyards solvent through war and peace, and to him such talk was shameful, for Afrikaners could prosper best if they cooperated with the English who had made South Africa their home, and he for one was pleased that his daughter was forming an alliance with one of the strongest English-speaking South African families. He wanted such conciliation to be repeated across the country, and since it was imperative that young Afrikaner men appreciate this, he swallowed the rebuke and begged Detleef to reconsider: 'Lad, don't you see that sometimes a gap can be too wide for ordinary measures to bridge? You saw Christoffel Steyn shot because he sided with Germany. The Saltwoods saw their men slain at Delville Wood because they sided with England. Such wounds can only be healed by men of good will—like you and me.'

'I hope England perishes.'

Coenraad would accept no more. With contempt he snapped, 'Detleef, you're a tight-minded fool. Get out and see the world. I'll have no more of you.'

As Detleef might have guessed, the Van Doorn–Saltwood wedding did not take place in Stellenbosch. It was performed with high ceremony and lavish celebration in the English cathedral in Cape Town.

Like many a young man before him, Detleef found vengeance in sports. He played rugby with a fury that astounded older men, throwing himself about with special abandon when pitted against teams like Somerset West, which had a more than average proportion of English players. Against the Ikeys he played like a wild man, for he suspected that somehow the Jews were involved in his loss of Clara. In fact, he played so magnificently that several newspapers predicted that when South African rugby teams resumed touring England and France, he would have to be included: 'Pound for pound, he may be the best forward playing today.'

At the same time he did well in his studies, and there was renewed interest in having him transfer to divinity school. Indeed, Reverend Brongersma himself came down to Stellenbosch to talk with him, but not on that subject. In fact, for the first half-hour of their conversation Detleef could not fathom what the visit was about.

'Your brother-in-law Piet is no farmer, Detleef. You must come back and take over, because he wants to find other employment.'

'He's not paying much attention to the farm?'

'You're not to worry.' He coughed, then said in an entirely different voice, 'What you should worry about, Detleef, is finding yourself a wife.' Before the bewildered young man could respond, Brongersma said hurriedly, 'Detleef, I have great affection for you. No boy from Vrymeer has ever shown more promise. I've heard about you and Clara van Doorn. I could see it happening when I gave my lectures. You've behaved miserably, Detleef. Like a damned fool, if you'll forgive me that word. But you have been a damned fool, and I'm ashamed of you.'

It was a blast Detleef had not expected. On the rugby field he had been knocked about by the biggest—mouth cut, eyes blackened—but the dominee's words were blows to his pride, and he gasped.

'There's a fine young woman in Carolina who is wasting her life for love of you. Maria Steyn, daughter of heroes, a heroine herself. For God's sake, Detleef, open your eyes. It was never intended that you marry Clara van Doorn. It would have been wrong. It would have ruined your life to have beat your head against that wall. And all the time you had a sweet, good woman waiting for you, and you were too blind to see.'

After a long silence Detleef asked weakly, 'Did she send you?'

'I heard about her, and I came on my own, as your friend.' When Detleef made no comment, the predikant asked in a low voice, 'Detleef, shall we pray?' And on his knees beside the young man for whom he had such high hopes, he talked with God about the extreme difficulty men face when they want to lead a Christian life.

The wedding was to be held in the Dutch Reformed church at Carolina, where numerous Steyns from the region gathered to honor Christoffel's memory. At the strong suggestion of Reverend Brongersma, Maria's predikant was asked to perform the ceremony, but on the evening before the wedding Detleef went to the church in Venloo and said, 'Reverend Brongersma, I wouldn't feel properly married unless you helped,' and when the pastor said that he would drive Detleef down to the wedding, the young man fumbled with a package and asked hesitantly, 'Dominee, tell me. I paid a lot of money for this Bible. Could I give it to Maria?'

Brongersma took the book, opened the cover, and saw that a page was missing; it required no cleverness to deduce what had happened. He thought for a moment, then asked gently, 'Don't you think that a bright girl like Maria might guess about Clara?'

'Yes, I suppose she would,' he said dejectedly.

'I'll tell you what we'll do, Detleef. I've always wanted a leatherbound Bible. I'll trade this for a new one of mine.' And next day Brongersma printed in firm clear letters on the page reserved for family records:

DETLEEF VAN DOORN–MARIA STEYN
Kinders van ons helde. Getroud 14 Maart 1919
(Children of our heroes. Married 14 March 1919)

And then Detleef was thrown out into the world, just as the Trianon Van Doorns had advised; the committee that selected rugby players for a team which would tour New Zealand chose him to be one of the principal forwards, and Venloo expanded with more pride than it would have done had he been elected general of the armies. For a small town to provide a Springbok was a glory that rarely came.

A Springbok was any athlete of world class who wore the green blazer with its golden springbok emblem while representing South Africa against another nation. A cricketer could be a Springbok, so could an Olympic runner, and as such they were entitled to full honors; but it was generally understood that only a rugby Springbok was a true immortal. This was especially true in 1921, because the New Zealand All-Blacks, so called because of their ominous uniforms, were regarded as the finest team that had ever played the game, and it was agreed that the winner of the forth-coming matches would be world champions.

Detleef was twenty-six that year, the father of a boy, the master of a growing farm. When his picture appeared in the city papers, it showed a stocky farmer, feet wide apart, rope around his ample stomach as a belt, and with absolutely no neck. The line from the bottom of his ear to the break of his shoulder was straight and unbroken, and when he posed next to his heaviest pair of oxen, he resembled them.

The problem of who would tend the farm while he was absent was conveniently solved: when Piet Krause left Venloo he had expected to find work quickly in Johannesburg, but these were hard times, and at one industry after another he was rebuffed. Chastened, he was glad to accept Detleef's offer of a free home and meals for himself and Johanna: 'But only during the rugby tour. I know I can find work in Johannesburg. This nation needs men like me.'

When Detleef, accompanied by five of the horrible Morkels, stepped ashore at Auckland, he was like some gape-eyed child, for the people of New Zealand were immersed in frenzy over this championship series. The South Africans were allowed to warm up, of course, against regional teams, and in the first match Detleef discovered what he was going to be up against. When he hooked arms in the scrum, he looked into the face of a gigantic New Zealander with the sloping shoulders and quick moves of a true athlete; he was Tom Heeney, soon to fight Gene Tunney for the boxing championship of the world, and when he slammed into Detleef, the latter felt his knees jump backward. In the afternoons to come, he would face Heeney often.

When the regional warm-ups were finished, the two nations played a series of three games, the first on the southern island at Dunedin, the last two on the northern island, at Auckland and Wellington. Detleef would never forget that opening game: 'When we lined up for the photographers to take pictures, I was like a little boy. I had to go to the bathroom. So I went and was almost late for the whistle. I remember nothing about the first half, except that I kept bumping into some very strong men. We ended the half ahead by five-to-nothing.' Whenever he spoke to audiences about that game he stopped at this point, laughed and said, 'But I certainly remember the second half. New Zealanders kept running up and down my spine. The crowd kept roaring. The ball kept slipping away, and at the end of the game New Zealand won thirteen-to-five.'

But he was blooded. Like an animal that has gone up against a lion and escaped with its life, he knew what fear was; he understood the meaning of pressure and became indifferent to the roar of the crowd. Before the opening of the second game he gathered the five Morkels on his team and said, 'We show them no mercy.' It was an epic struggle, tied at five-all until the gang of Morkels made superhuman plays to eke out a 9–5 victory. 'That night,' Detleef often said in later years, 'was the high point of my life. Nothing could ever excel that victory over New Zealand.'

The third and deciding game should never have taken place, for the field was so water-soaked and the rain so incessant that play resembled swimming more than rugby. The score was a frustrating 0–0, but the last seconds were a kind of majestic triumph for Detleef; a huge New Zealander broke away for what seemed the game-winning score, except that Van Doorn made a diving tackle that slowed him down. Boy Morkel rushed up to help hold him, whereupon six New Zealanders piled on. In the tangle and mud, Detleef's leg twisted, then broke. His rugby days were ended, but as he was carried off the field, refusing to surrender to the pain, he was able to tell Tom Heeney, 'Well, you didn't beat us,' and the Hard Rock from Down Under laughed and said, 'We nearly did.'

In the ensuing years Detleef was remembered wherever he went as 'the man who saved the day in New Zealand.' He treasured his green jacket with the emblazoned antelope and kept it on a special hanger in his wardrobe, taking it out occasionally for some sporting event. It became a sacred object, replacing the ceramic crock in which the men of his family had long made their bread puddings.

XII.
Achievement of a Puritan

WHEN Detleef limped home on crutches in 1921 and saw how ineptly Piet Krause had managed Vrymeer during the rugby matches in New Zealand, he was tempted to show his disgust, but Maria calmed him by pointing out: 'Piet kept worrying about Johannesburg. Don't blame him for what he overlooked here.'

Krause had found—or more accurately, Johanna had found for him—a minor job as labor advisor to the government. He specialized in gold-mine problems, and when he returned to Venloo for a visit, Detleef, seeing the excitement with which he attacked his new duties, forgave him: 'You were never meant to be a farmer, Piet. Tell me, why do we hear so many rumbles from your city?'

That was all Piet needed. In wild bursts of words, interrupted by Johanna with her own interpretations, he explained why the burgeoning city had become the focus of the country: 'It's there the real battles are being fought. Our excursions up north, where General de Groot died and you and I took part, they were nothing. Echoes of the nineteenth century. But in Johannesburg . . .'

'Who's fighting?'

'The Afrikaner. He's fighting for his soul.'

He insisted that Detleef come back with him to witness the struggle of the white Afrikaner workman against the English mine owner, the Hoggenheimer financier, and especially the Bantu worker, but Detleef said that until he could move without crutches that would be impossible. However, he did want to understand the gold mines and promised that he would read whatever Piet mailed him in preparation for his later visit.

Johanna made the selection, and what she sent was startling. One gang of workers wanted to establish a soviet in which laboring men would take control of the mines, overthrow the government, and establish a Communist dictatorship in harmony with Russia. One group of mine owners wanted to fire all white workers and use only Bantu to work the gold, but when Maria read the literature more carefully, she pointed out: 'That's not what the owners said, Detleef. That's what their enemies said they said.' But then he received other mailings which proved that many owners wanted to cut back the number of white workers and increase the number of black.

From a distance, the city seemed such a jungle of competing forces that Detleef was actually eager to get there, and as soon as his leg mended he informed Johanna that he was ready. She advised him that if he caught a train at Waterval-Boven they would meet him at the railway station in central Johannesburg, and when they did they led him into a miasma of urban horror.

His education up to that moment, except for Chrissiesmeer, had been romantic: old generals fighting lost battles, gallant young men on the playing fields of New Zealand, sentimental remembrances of the Vrouemonument, unrequited love. Now his realistic instruction was to begin; he experienced it first in the section of Johannesburg called Vrededorp, where thousands of rural Afrikaners, driven off their farms by rinderpest and drought, had collected. They stopped at a small house occupied by a family named Troxel: tall, gaunt husband who should have been back on the open veld; scrawny wife with flat, sagging breasts; unkempt children, their faces drawn with hunger. In that dwelling there was little hope.

'Will you take us to other homes?' Piet asked, and Troxel led them to much worse hovels, whose occupants were desolate. After talking with these forlorn people, Detleef felt sick at the stomach, not figuratively but actually, almost to the point of vomiting. 'We've got to do something, Piet. These people are starving.'

'Tomorrow we'll see what lies behind the starving,' Piet said, and on this day he took Detleef to a workers' hall, where there was much agitation about new rules which the Chamber of Mines had promulgated.

'They're cutting back the proportion of white workers,' an agitator explained. When Detleef asked what this signified, the man screamed, 'Extermination, that's what it means. Extermination of the white Afrikaner,' and he explained that tradition in the gold fields had been that for every eight Bantu diggers, there had to be one white man. 'Now they want to make it ten blacks to one white. We can't accept that. It would cost too many Afrikaners their jobs.'

A stronghold of the strikers was Fordsburg, a working-class district near Vrededorp, and here Detleef was taken to an inconspicuous shed in which the future soviet was being planned. Here rabid Afrikaners met with Cornish miners imported to do the basic work down deep and three fiery Englishmen who were determined to take South Africa into the Communist orbit: 'There'll be blood this time! Are you with us?' When Detleef said he didn't work the mines, but was a farmer, four excited Afrikaners surrounded him, demanding to know why he did not bring food into the city to feed his starving compatriots.

That night he could not sleep, seeing the pinched faces bearing in upon him, for he knew what starvation was, and when on the third day Piet took him back to Vrededorp to talk quietly with Troxel and the other Afrikaner families, and he heard their pitiful tales of perished hopes on the farms, the doleful trek to the city, the cruel exploitation in the mines, and the endless struggle to maintain their rights against the pressure of the blacks, his earlier sickness returned, and abruptly he informed Piet and Johanna that he was going home. When they accused him of rejecting his own people, he assured them: 'I'll be back.'

And he was, with a convoy of three large wagons bringing all the spare food he had been able to collect in Venloo. He drove the lead wagon, Micah Nxumalo the second, and Micah's son, Moses, the third. They brought the food into the center of Vrededorp and started to distribute it, but they occasioned such a disturbance that a riot would surely have ensued had not the Communist workers swept in, taken charge, and told the hungry miners that this food came from their committee.

This second visit had one by-product neither Detleef nor Piet had intended; Micah, left in charge of the three empty wagons, drove them out to a different section of Johannesburg where his people clustered. It was called Sophiatown, and when Micah came back to tell Detleef where he had been, Van Doorn decided to go with him to see how urban blacks lived.

Sophiatown had come into existence some two decades earlier, planned as a suburb for whites but spurned by them when a sewage works was located nearby. It was only four and a half miles from the center of Johannesburg, and the owner of the land had to do something with it, so he started renting and selling land to the blacks who were pouring in from the countryside to fill jobs in the postwar industrial boom.

For Detleef it was a journey into hell, for Sophiatown had no proper streets, few proper houses and no proper water supply. It was a mélange of prostitutes, tsotsis, and decent mothers trying to maintain a home against phenomenal odds while their husbands worked ten and twelve hours for a daily wage of twenty pennies.

When Detleef looked at Sophiatown he saw a festering sore, dark and malignant, threatening to spread over a clean white city. It reached dangerously toward Afrikaner communities, as if it intended to engulf them. He was shocked to learn that blacks could actually own land here, which meant that they could stay permanently. 'A hideous sore,' he muttered to himself. 'It must be removed.'

This conclusion was intensified when he saw the home Nxumalo's relatives occupied. The Magubanes had a house with walls of real wood and a secure watertight roof made of paraffin tins. One of the Magubanes told him, 'Yes, when our people get the money they will make a lovely place of Sophiatown. Just like the homes of the rich people in Parktown.'

'Where do your people work?' Detleef asked.

'Offices, factories. And if the new rules come for the mines, thousands of our people back in the kraals will be eager for jobs. Fifty thousand, a hundred thousand if you need them.'

So Detleef left Sophiatown with the certain knowledge that the blacks would insist upon improving their lot, but he saw that this would be possible only at the expense of the white Afrikaners already trapped in poverty. He found that Troxel and the other white miners were willing to express themselves quite forcefully: 'We want this to be a white nation run by whites and not a black nation run by blacks.' Detleef could not imagine the huddled blacks of Sophiatown running anything; they would be lucky if they survived. His sympathies lay with the white miners, and when the callous owners announced even more stringent rules which might cost four thousand additional white men their jobs, he knew there would have to be a strike, although he himself did not want to support any moves which might turn this country into a soviet.

When the strike began, he knew he ought to hurry back to the safety of Vrymeer, but he was hypnotized by the intricacy of the struggle and curious to see how it turned out. So Piet Krause, whose job made it logical for him to stay on the scene in Vrededorp, asked the Troxels whether he and Detleef could board with them during the trouble, and the destitute Afrikaners were eager to have paying guests.

This was a battle much more fundamental than the pro-German rebellion of 1914. Miners were fighting for survival; owners were fighting for financial control; and the government, led by Jan Christian Smuts, was fighting for continuation of an orderly society. The hatred Krause and Van Doorn felt for Smuts clouded their vision of what was right, and they tended to cheer for whatever group opposed him.

It was real combat. Detleef turned a corner and saw sixteen civilians mowed down by machine-gun fire. A government building was dynamited and fourteen soldiers were killed. Police were gunned down, and on one awful day airplanes flew over the city, dropping bombs on concentrations of miners.

The death toll was fifty, then a hundred, then a hundred and fifty, with food running low and arson becoming common. There was talk of shutting off water, and children in the streets were slain by stray bullets.

'Why are Afrikaners fighting Afrikaners?' Detleef asked in anguish, and Troxel growled, 'Because we Afrikaners want to keep this nation white.' He was a brave man, and when General Smuts in total frustration warned that heavy artillery would shell the heart of Vrededorp at eleven the next morning, he refused to move his family. 'Shells matter nothing,' he muttered, but when they began to fall, monstrous things intended for shattering forts, he quivered. Detleef, comforting the Troxel children, could not believe that his government was doing this, and as the dreadful concussions continued he thought: This is insanity. There must be a more sensible way.

In the midst of the barrage, Troxel left his shelter and ran directly across the open square where the shells were falling. He was heading for strike headquarters, and when he returned through the smoldering debris he was weeping: 'They committed suicide!'

'Who?' Detleef asked.

'Our leaders. The Englishman, the other. Pistol shots through the head.'

The armed rebellion was over, with the competition between the very poor Afrikaners in Vrededorp and the totally poor blacks in Sophiatown no closer to settlement than when the strike began. Only one poverty-stricken Afrikaner came out of the affair better than when he went in: after the fighting, when Nxumalo reassembled the three wagons for the trip back to Vrymeer, and Detleef saw them standing empty, he impulsively ran to the Troxel house and said, 'Come with me. This town is no place for an Afrikaner.' And on the spur of the moment he and Piet Krause threw into one wagon the pitiful collection of goods this family had accumulated after ten hard years in the city; it did not begin to fill it.

'They can use the De Groot place,' Detleef said as the bewildered cavalcade started eastward. He had seen Johannesburg and was appalled.

One Sunday, Detleef received the distinct impression in church that Reverend Brongersma was preaching directly to him, not in the long ordinary passages of the sermon, but whenever something of special import had to be said. Then Brongersma would stare in his direction, sometimes looking at others in his vicinity but again and again coming back to Detleef to make his points.

He said nothing about this to Maria and even doubted if she had been aware of it, but when on two following Sundays the same thing happened, he asked casually on Monday night, 'Did you notice anything strange in church yesterday?'

'No, except that Reverend Brongersma seemed to be preaching to you more than anyone else.'

'You noticed it?' When she nodded, he said, 'Did you not see it on the past Sundays?' and she said that she had. 'Why didn't you speak?' he asked, and she said, 'I thought that perhaps you had done something wrong and would tell me at such time as you deemed best.' In some anger he asked her what she thought he had done wrong, and she laughed.

'Detleef, I only said *perhaps*. You're not the kind of man who does wrong things. And if you have done something, it couldn't be very big.'

'There you go. What have I done?'

'Detleef, I only said *if.*'

But he was troubled, and every time his brother-in-law visited the farm and asked probing questions, Detleef became even more irritated, especially since the dominee continued preaching at him.

He was about to confront his two tormentors when Piet said abruptly one day, 'Detleef. Can you come to a special meeting tonight?' Hoping that the mystery would be revealed, he said quickly, 'Yes,' and that evening he was taken to a house he had never taken much notice of before, where the owner, a man named Frykenius, sat waiting, with Reverend Brongersma standing by a table.

'Sit down, Detleef,' Frykenius said. 'We want to ask you some questions.'

'What have I done?'

'Nothing, except being a good citizen. We want to find out how good.'

'I've done nothing wrong!' Detleef protested, and this was ignored.

'Tell me,' Frykenius said. 'In the rebellion against the war in Europe, would you have fought on, even though your father was killed?'

'I would have fought the English forever.'

'Do you speak Afrikaans in your home?'

'Nothing else.'

'Do you insist that your children speak it?'

'I allow them to speak no English.'

On and on came the questions, covering all aspects of what might be called his political, emotional and patriotic life. At the end his three interrogators asked him to step out in the yard, and while he looked at the glorious stars of the Southern Cross, they whispered among themselves.

After about fifteen minutes Piet Krause came out and said with obvious pleasure, 'Detleef, please come in!'

When he entered the room, both Frykenius and Brongersma rose to greet him: 'Detleef. You are one of us.' When he asked what this signified, Frykenius said, 'Sit down, Brother.' And when he was in his chair the three men, speaking alternately, informed him that a powerful and secret band of brothers, a Broederbond, had been quietly operating for the past five years, accomplishing much good. After the most careful investigation of his credentials by men in Pretoria, he was being offered a chance to join.

'Are you members?' he asked.

Frykenius said, 'I helped start it.' This seemed strange to Detleef, for he could recall no instance in which this quiet man had ever played a major role in anything; he knew that he attended church, but was not even an elder. He had heard that he had ridden with the Venloo Commando but had accomplished nothing of note. He ran the butcher shop in town, but obviously never made much money. And he never spoke in public. But it was clear that he was now in command.

'Reverend Brongersma has belonged almost from the first,' Frykenius said, 'and Piet here, one of our best, has been with us for three years.'

'What would I be supposed to do?'

'Advance the Afrikaner,' Frykenius said.

'I already try to do that. But how?'

Piet was eager to explain, but was interrupted by Frykenius: 'I already know the answers to these two questions, but we must have sworn statements. "Have you ever been divorced?" No. That's good. "Is your wife English?" No again. You're eligible.'

'Morally, we're very strict,' Piet said.

Satisfied that Detleef had committed no serious breaches, the three men placed before him a program of simple integrity: 'Whatever you do, from this moment till you die, must work toward making the Afrikaner supreme in this country. In politics you must elect men who will carry us away from English domination.'

'That I would like,' Detleef said.

'In education you must insist that every teacher become an agent for the supremacy of Afrikaans. They must teach our national history in the patterns we provide.'

'In the armed forces,' Krause said excitedly, 'we must remove every English officer. In government we've got to clean out the English officeholders.'

'But it's in the spiritual realm,' Brongersma said, 'that we must do our hardest work. Cultural societies. Work groups. Festivals. Patriotic gatherings. If there is to be a speaker, it must be one of us.'

'You saw the fighting in Johannesburg,' Frykenius said. 'Jan Christian Smuts using Afrikaner soldiers to fight Afrikaner workmen. That must never again be allowed.'

'Can we drive Slim Jannie from office?' Detleef asked.

'We must,' Frykenius said. 'Are you with us?' When Detleef nodded, as enthusiastically as if he were going to war with General de Groot or to a rugby game against New Zealand, Frykenius in his dry, unemotional voice administered the oath of the Broederbond, and Detleef swore to uphold its secrecy, advance its purposes, and live each moment of his life so as to achieve the dominance of the Afrikaner. That night he rode home with a greater sense of mission than he had ever before experienced. The other war that General de Groot had so often referred to was under way and he had enlisted for life.

In the weeks that followed, Detleef developed an enormous respect for his brother-in-law. He was no longer the somewhat flighty schoolteacher or the man who had quit the Vrymeer farm after discarding responsibility; instead, Piet Krause showed himself as a fine strategist. Frykenius was a staunch administrator and Brongersma a source of the spiritual strength which such a movement needed, but Krause was downright brilliant: 'Let us look honestly at the condition of the two groups. The English are educated; we aren't. The English control the money; we don't. The English are in command of the armed forces; we hold no high appointments. The English know how to manage; we don't. And above all, the English are supported by an entire empire; we stand alone.'

When Frykenius protested that the Afrikaners had strengths, too, Krause brushed him aside, and Detleef noticed that whereas Frykenius issued operational commands, which Piet obeyed, in the field of ideas Piet accepted guidance from no one. 'Yes, we have strengths,' he agreed impatiently, 'but not the ones you think.'

And he outlined a program of daring character: 'We can't take control of business away from the English. They're too clever to allow that. And we can't dictate in politics yet. But I can see two areas which employ a lot of people where we can dominate. Trains and schools. From now on, every trainman who is hired must be an Afrikaner. Every schoolteacher, too.' He explained that if the Broederbond could control the railway union, it would have a solid base from which to operate; and if it controlled the teachers, it could monitor what the young were being taught: 'Out of a hundred boys leaving school, ninety would be potential Broederbond members.'

'No, our membership must always be restricted,' Frykenius said, and when Detleef was taken to meet with cells in other areas, he found that this was true. Of a hundred members, thirty were schoolteachers, thirty were predikants, and the other forty were mostly farmers of solid position in their communities. There were, of course, no members who were bankers, lawyers or elected officials, for few Afrikaners had yet attained such positions.

After three years of the most exciting participation, Detleef saw with satisfaction that every teacher appointed in a vast area had been an Afrikaner, and eleven of the best had been permitted to join the Broederbond. Of a hundred new employees of the railway system, all had been Afrikaners. There had been musical exhibitions arranged by the Bond, art displays, barbecues, lecture series and sports events. Whenever an Afrikaner in rural South Africa stepped out of his house, he fell unwittingly under the influence of the Broederbond, but it was the new proposal offered by Piet Krause to a plenary session in Pretoria that moved the Bond onto an even more effective level:

'We have won the railways and have triumphed in the battle of the schoolroom, but in business and politics we have accomplished nothing. I cannot yet see how we can gain any victories in politics, but

I do see clearly how we can gain effective control of business. We Afrikaners are not yet smart enough to run the insurance companies and the big banks. That will require time and education. Let the English continue to control the businesses which appear on the stock market. What we'll do is control the stock market. And how do we do that? We become the officials who make the rules, who supervise the operations, who stay in the background as watchdogs.'

He launched an ingenious program aimed at filling every available administrative position with Afrikaners: 'Of course, the Englishmen will continue to occupy the flashy front offices. We'll take the unseen jobs, none of them attractive or well paid. And once we have Afrikaners inserted in the system, we'll promote them quietly, until they attain positions of real power.

'Then do you see what will happen? The insurance company will still be owned by Englishmen. But our people will pass the little rules by which they operate. And in time we will control everything—not own it, control it.'

He preached that an essential factor in such a strategy was the proliferation of minor administrative jobs: 'Where one man is needed, let us appoint three. If an old office falters, let us establish two new ones, staffed always with our people. Jobs, jobs, jobs. Whether they're needed or not, create more jobs because they must pay for them. And always in the legislation creating them insert the phrase "The occupant must be bilingual." With Afrikaans we will strangle them to death.'

As a consequence of this policy, South Africa would become one of the most overly administered governments on earth, and gradually, because of the bilingual requirement, this plethora of officeholders became predominantly Afrikaner. Piet Krause had shown far-seeing wisdom: the English insurance company did continue to make money, but it operated under rules promulgated by Afrikaner functionaries, who drafted these rules in accordance with the wishes of the unseen Broederbond.

While cells of the Broederbond in all parts of South Africa were convening secretly to determine the future character of their nation, awakening young black men were meeting, also in secret, to decide what patterns should be followed when they attained the leadership to which they felt entitled.

Micah Nxumalo was not a great man, but he had always associated with great men, and that was almost as good. Paulus de Groot, Christoffel Steyn, the various Boer generals during the war—he had worked with them all. Usually they had not been aware of him, but in his quiet way he had been intensely aware of them, and had learned from them lessons which would have amazed them had they known the depth of his perception.

He was bewildered by white men. They lived surrounded by blacks, but made no effort to understand them or to profit from the association. The whites were outnumbered in many areas forty-to-one, but they continued living as if they alone possessed the landscape and always would. He watched them making decisions which had to be against their own best interests, and doing so only to maintain control over the larger number of blacks who surrounded them.

For example, Micah was astounded that the two white tribes, Boer and English, should have fought each other so viciously for so long, when at any time each could have achieved everything that came out of the peace treaty and at one-fiftieth of the cost. For him the insanity of their behavior was epitomized by the Battle of Spion Kop, in which he had played a major role. 'I tell you, Moses,' he said to his son, 'one side marched up to the top of the hill, then the other side marched up, then one side marched down, then the other side marched down. Then, long after midnight, General de Groot and I walked up, and we captured it. And three days later it didn't make a bit of difference who held it, but hundreds of white men lay dead and wounded.'

He saw also that it made very little difference, really, which side won: 'We fought for the Boers, Moses. They were good people and we could trust them, men like Jakob from this farm, and the old general. But when it was over, we got no thanks. They made laws against us just the same. And don't you ever believe that the Kaffirs who fought on the English side came off any better. Because the English abandoned them as soon as peace came. "We will never desert you," they promised in 1899 when they needed black help, but at the peace treaty they forgot about our rights. And now they're just as eager as the Afrikaners to hold us down.'

Micah, who could not read or write, could formulate such sophisticated analyses because he had for many years been quietly associating with that remarkable group of black leaders who moved through the countryside talking about actual living conditions, legislation and civic rights. These few men were well educated, some in England, one or two in the black colleges of America, and some of them had even visited the Parliament in London with petitions drawing attention to the worsening conditions in South Africa. 'It would be improper for England to interfere with the internal relations of a dominion,' they were always told, and helplessly they watched the deterioration.

These men, who would be the leaders of their race in coming years, first brought Nxumalo's attention to the problem of the poor white Afrikaner, the numerous people like the Troxels, who had been driven off their inherited farms by drought and rinderpest and who had taken refuge in Johannesburg. 'I assure you,' Sol Plaatje said at one meeting, 'in their hovels they live worse than the blacks do in Sophiatown. Every law that holds us down, holds them down too. In a sensible world the Troxels would combine with us to improve everyone's condition, but they stay off to themselves, the poorest of the poor, and we stay off to ourselves, the dispossessed.'

What perplexed these leaders was the contradictory policy of the white government: 'They spend enormous sums to bring in white settlers from Russia and Germany and Poland, when they have right on their doorsteps better labor and cheaper, which they refuse to use.' John Dube, in one of these meetings, offered the statement which Nxumalo would always remember: 'The worst thing a nation can do to itself is to cultivate and maintain a supply of cheap labor. When salaries are kept down, money stops circulating, taxes bring in diminished funds, and everybody loses. The white man thinks he's hurting us when he keeps our wages low. Actually, he's hurting himself.'

At one meeting a young Swazi who had studied in London said, 'In our worst industries, the white man earns sixteen times as much as the black man doing the same kind of work. Now, I don't mean the same work. As you know, certain jobs have been defined by law as too complicated or pivotal for a black man to master. Such jobs must be held by whites only. What I mean is that whites and blacks work together, the whites doing the so-called critical work, which a schoolboy could learn in fifteen minutes, the blacks doing the manual labor, which the white could do more efficiently because he's usually better fed and stronger. Taking all industries, the white worker gets nine times the wage of a black, and they propose to build a sensible society on that basis!'

Nxumalo understood such reasoning; he would never have elucidated such thoughts himself, but when others did he approved. However, on one point he was as obtuse as the white man: when he contemplated the long future of South Africa he could not visualize any logical place for the Coloureds. The white man had stated in a hundred different laws and regulations that the Coloureds were not white; the blacks knew intuitively they could never be black. Almost never was the problem discussed; once Plaatje said after returning from London, 'The white men, if they had any sense, would embrace the Coloureds instead of importing white immigrants at great expense.'

'Should we embrace them?' Nxumalo asked.

Plaatje thought a long time, then said, 'I think not. They want to do what they call "moving up to whitehood" and would never be satisfied with doing what they would call "falling back to Kaffir status." Why distract our attention by bothering with them, when we can argue directly with the whites?'

It was from such discussions that Micah Nxumalo acquired his obsession: 'One day our boy Moses will attend the college at Fort Hare.' To that end he terminated his own practical education; no longer would he waste his few rand by attending the secret meetings in Johannesburg. That money would be saved for the boy. He went to the Van Doorns, asking them to help toward the fees Moses would have to pay, but Detleef growled, 'He needs no further schooling, he has a job here,' and the meager funds that Micah could accumulate were inadequate for so bold a venture, and the dream of sending a black lad from Vrymeer to college vanished.

But not the dream of learning: 'What you must do, Moses, is read the books that educated men read. You must associate with men who have traveled to America and Europe, and you must listen to what they say. Most of all, son, you must get off this farm. You were not meant to be a peasant.'

Using some of the money he had saved, he returned to his friends in Johannesburg and asked them for books that would start his gifted son on the right track. They gave him one book by Marcus Garvey, the American black; two books by Plaatje on the South African condition; one by George Bernard Shaw; and a splendid volume on the golden age of the Dutch Republic. As he was about to depart, the young Swazi who had recited the figures on comparative wages at the earlier meeting, had an afterthought: 'What might do him the most good—this novel about Java.'

'What is Java?'

'It used to control South Africa.'

'Why should he read about that?'

'Because you never know, Mr. Nxumalo, what will ignite a boy's mind.' And he handed over a Dutch novel, *Max Havelaar,* by a man who had been a civil servant in Java in the 1800s; he wrote under the name of Multatuli, Latin for Many Sorrows, and although he spoke only of conditions in Java, everything he said applied to South Africa.

The five scholarly books Micah brought back to Vrymeer were helpful, but *Max Havelaar* sharpened the mind of Moses Nxumalo. He was in his twenties when he read it, bewildered by the flood of ideas that had been coming at him from his own observations, the canny wisdom of his father and the lessons from the serious books; the novel tied these scattered concepts together in a way that was almost magical. It was poorly written, really, forcing upon the reader more instruction about plantation life in Java than he needed, but in the end it left a residue of emotion and moral commitment that would otherwise have been unobtainable. After an absence of two hundred years, the power of Java had returned to South Africa.

When he finished the six books, Moses told his father, 'I want to try it in Johannesburg.'

'You should,' his father said. 'And I suppose you know that the chances are good that you'll be dead before the end of the year.'

'I've heard.' In *Max Havelaar* a young Javanese much like Moses had gone to his Johannesburg and died with a belly full of bullets. As in the past, Java was instructing South Africa.

So in the mid 1930s Moses Nxumalo of Vrymeer went quietly away from the farm and into the city, a journey of ninety-nine miles in physical distance, an incalculable distance spiritually.

He sought out his cousin, Jefferson Magubane, somewhat older than he was, and found him living in Sophiatown, and on the first night he was there, police came hammering on the rickety door, demanding to see all documents. By a miracle of timing, Jefferson managed to slip Moses into an alley leading to the communal privy, and there he hid while the others presented their papers for inspection. Although his sheltered life at Vrymeer had not prepared him for this indignity, his experiences with Max Havelaar had, and he thought how strange it was that he, whose ancestors had lived on this land for a thousand years, should be restricted by incomers as to where and how he could travel.

Next morning Jefferson, who had not been distressed by the police visit, for that was a common occurrence, said brightly, 'Moses, I think we can get you the proper passes.' And he took his cousin some miles out toward the country to a large suburban house called New Sarum. There, deferentially, he went to the back door and informed the black maid who tended it that he had brought her a first-class houseboy. With nudges and winks he instructed Moses in making proper responses, with the result that a black man was summoned, who led the applicant through the kitchen to a kind of office where a white husband and wife waited. They introduced themselves as Mr. and Mrs. Noel Saltwood, whereupon Mrs. Saltwood, a tall, fine-looking English woman, asked him a series of questions, using English, Afrikaans and Zulu interchangeably.

'Can you read and write?' she asked. When he nodded, she asked him where he lived; he panicked, not knowing what to say, but she perceived this and said quickly, 'I know you have no papers. Jefferson told us. We'll arrange for your passbook.' She spoke as if she were a conspirator.

'I'm from Vrymeer.'

'I don't know that. Is it a small place?'

'It's near Venloo.'

'Ah, yes. The Venloo Commando. Who doesn't know about that!' She looked at her husband approvingly, and Moses wondered if he should volunteer further information, but his quandary was solved by Laura Saltwood. 'Did you know, perchance . . . No, you'd have been too young. But a very brave man came from Venloo. General de Groot.'

'My father rode with him. I used to live with him.'

Both the Saltwoods gasped, and they spent the next fifteen minutes asking about his father's experiences on commando, after which Mrs. Saltwood said, 'Noel, we really must put someone to the job of compiling the record of the black commandos. On both sides. Their stories must be incredible, and they'll be lost if we don't do something.'

Then she became strictly business: 'We'll get you your papers, Moses, but you must work here faithfully, because if you don't, back you'll go to the farm. Is that understood?'

'Yes, Baas.'

'We don't use baas here. I'm ma'am, he's mister.'

His pleasure at the prospect of both a job and the papers to prove it was diminished that night when he sat with Jefferson in the cramped room the Magubanes called home and heard the sound of running feet, then screams, then ugly grunts and more screams.

When he rose to intercede in whatever was happening, his aunt Mpela raised her hand and stopped him. 'It's the tsotsis,' she said, and before she could lower her hand, there came the long terrible scream of a woman, then the echo of runners retreating.

In the morning the police came, tardily, indifferently: 'Another Three Star killing.' They ordered a cart to haul the corpse away, and after they had departed and Moses had inspected the blood, he asked what a Three Star killing was.

'The tsotsis carry knives made in England. Three stars on the handle.'

'How do I avoid them?' Moses asked.

'Play the coward. They run in gangs, and if you see them coming, get out. Do anything—hide, run, stand behind a woman—but get out of their way.'

'Don't the police . . .'

'The police say, "The tsotsis do our work for us." You see, Moses, they kill only Bantu.'

'Does this happen often?'

'All the time,' Jefferson said.

So whenever Moses detected these youthful murderers, pimps, scavengers, thieves, dagga-peddlers and bullies in the area, he quietly disappeared. He was eager to keep himself safe because of the consuming interest he had in the things that Jefferson was doing: the political meetings, the long discussions with knowledgeable men and women. He was enchanted to find that one black woman, a handsome person older than he, had actually been to America and won a college degree; she was Gloria Mbeke, a bold and forceful speaker, and although he was too shy to approach her directly, he did frequent her discussions, listening attentively as she outlined her principles:

> 'The one thing we can be certain of is that if we endeavor to confront our oppressors with any kind of force, they will not hesitate to mow us down with their machine guns. That realization must be the foundation of our policy.

> 'When Enoch Mgijima encouraged his Israelites, following their own interpretation of the Bible, to claim land at Bulhoek, the police warned him once to move them off. They warned him twice, then they opened fire on people who carried not even sticks. One hundred and sixty-three dead, one hundred and twenty-nine wounded for life.

> 'When a remnant of Hottentots in the deserts of South-West Africa a few years ago wanted to continue hunting while the government wanted them to work on farms at almost no pay, what did the government do? They placed a huge tax on dogs, and when the Hottentots refused to pay, they sent in airplanes that bombed them as they ran across the veld. One hundred and fifteen killed, three hundred wounded for life.

> 'Our policy must be the policy of Mahatma Gandhi, who originated it when he lived among us. Passive resistance, legal pressure, and the constant education of our young people.'

At another meeting he heard Miss Mbeke say something which influenced him deeply. She returned to the slaughter of the Israelites at Bulhoek:

> 'There are two lessons to be learned from this. The white police will never hesitate to shoot us down if they don't like what we're doing. But also, we blacks get ourselves into trouble when we listen to messianic leaders. Remember how Nongqause led thousands of Xhosa to commit suicide in 1857? You agree now that that was insane. But how did Enoch Mgijima get his hypnotic hold on his Israelites? When Halley's Comet passed overhead in 1910, leaving a long trail of star dust, he said it was a message from God to him.

> 'Do not believe outside messages. Many of the gold miners who were shot down during the strike in Johannesburg had been listening to leaders just like Nongqause and Mgijima, except that their revelations came from Moscow. Communism will not save us in South Africa. The silly teachings of Marcus Garvey in America will not save us. We will save ourselves.'

Thirty minutes after hearing this constructive speech, as he and Jefferson were drifting home through the alleys of Sophiatown, discussing Miss Mbeke's theses, they were suddenly attacked by a gang of sixteen tsotsis wielding Three Star knives. 'Give us your money!' the tsotsis screamed as if demented, and quickly Jefferson did so, but Moses hesitated, and in that flash of a second, the knives came at him. It was a miracle that he was not killed, for even after he had fallen, horribly cut, the inflamed young men kicked at him viciously, and would surely have finished him off had not Jefferson yelled at the top of his voice, 'Police! Over here!' There were no police, but the tsotsis dared not take the risk.

Many had heard the fracas, but none would help. Behind closed doors they thought: In the morning they'll come and clean it up. It's not our affair.

So Jefferson took his cousin home, where his aunt Mpela was always prepared for such an event. She washed the wounds, borrowing from a neighbor a vial of concentrated iodine, which caused Moses to faint, and when she satisfied herself that no arteries had been cut, she went to bed and advised her son to do the same.

In the days of his recuperation, Moses had an opportunity to evaluate the experiences which had been cascading down upon him. He saw the farm at Vrymeer as a system whereby white employers were able to control black peasants with wages preposterously low. Essentially good-hearted men like General de Groot had never in their lives considered that what they were enforcing was Old Testament slavery, and had they been advised of this, they would not have understood what was wrong. He saw Detleef van Doorn as doing practically the same thing but from sanctimonious motivations, and he found that he had little regard for his father's employer. He realized that Van Doorn's associates might force him at any time to return to the gentle slavery at Vrymeer.

He was impressed by the generosity of the Saltwoods and hoped that he might be able to continue working for them, but he had little faith that they would stand by him when the confrontations that Miss Mbeke foresaw came to pass. The English were excellent people, but too concerned with pleasing others.

Sophiatown was no worse in his eyes than Vrededorp: in both places he found strong, honest men fighting to uplift their people and give them hope. Again and again he was struck by this parallel between poor Afrikaners and poor blacks: both groups grappling for roots in an alien city, both sharing poverty and dispossession. He constantly hoped, like old Micah, that blacks and Afrikaners alike would escape their wretchedness. But even as he perceived these relationships he had a terrible fear that what Miss Mbeke said was right: 'The victory of the poor Afrikaner will be at the expense of the blacks.'

Of the young black intellectuals he had listened to, he found to his surprise that he valued most not Miss Mbeke, who was so fluent in both speech and idea, but the young Swazi who had been to London and who had studied economics. He talked sense. Again and again he laid out the limits of a problem and indicated how it could be solved. It was he who uttered the sentences that influenced Moses most deeply: 'In South Africa last year thousands of black men and women were arrested because they moved about with improper documentation in a country which they own as much as the white man.' And 'Sometimes it seems that we have more black children in jail than in school.'

It was not long after he recovered from his stab wounds that the permanent wounding of Moses Nxumalo began. One morning he was stopped by police on Eloff Street, Johannesburg's glittering shopping avenue, and his documents were demanded: 'I see you haven't paid your annual tax of one pound. You must come with me.'

With sixteen more black tax-dodgers he was hustled into a police van, but he never got to jail. He was taken instead to a vacant lot, where a different policeman snarled, 'Now, you damned Kaffirs, you listen. Tomorrow you go before the magistrate, he'll give you jail, three months. You know what it's like in there.'

'Yes, Baas.'

'But I'm willing to give you a chance.'

'Yes, Baas.'

'That truck you see over there belongs to a farmer from Hemelsdorp. He needs strong men who can work well. You sign a two-month contract with him, I'll forget about the magistrate, you can forget about jail.'

Moses and most of the others chose Hemelsdorp, Village of Heaven, but the farm to which they were headed lay not in heaven. For twelve hours a day they toiled in the fields; at night they were thrown into a stinking cattle shed, where they lay awake listening to two of their crew who had pneumonia. One morning the older of the pair was dead.

At the end of one fearful month Moses tried to run away, but was captured in the hills beyond Hemelsdorp and dragged back to the farm.

'Miserable Kaffir bastard!' the farmer screamed. 'Time you learned a lesson.'

The punishment was administered by two of the black overseers, who stripped Moses and bound him about a forty-four-gallon drum. With the rest of the workers forced to watch, he was thrashed with sjamboks till he fainted.

Two days later he was sent back to the fields, but on the first night, when others were asleep, he made another dash for freedom. A black overseer spotted him, but before the man could raise an alarm, Moses knocked him to the ground. When the overseer tried to rise, Moses smashed him in the temple with a large rock, then fled.

For six months he hid in lands along the Limpopo River, then crossed over into Rhodesia, following an ancient route which took him to the Zimbabwe ruins, but he did not tarry there. For two years he worked as kitchen 'boy' in a Bulawayo hotel, and he was at his job one day when a man from Vrymeer found him: 'Your father died last Christmas.'

Moses waited till the end of the month, took his pay and journeyed south, for he was now head of the Nxumalos, and his place was with his people. He slipped in quietly, said nothing to the Van Doorns, who hadn't even noticed his absence, but his family saw the scars on his back. Within a few weeks he was the acknowledged boss boy, and any dream of a more meaningful life vanished.

He said little as he went about his work, but sometimes when he was alone he would look across the veld and swear: 'If I have a son, he will go to college at Fort Hare, and get started right.' This hope compensated for the pain he felt at his own failure.

The Saltwoods made efforts to trace Moses, but when he stayed away for months they supposed that he had merely gone back to his kraal. 'You

can never trust a native,' a neighbor said. 'You do everything in the world
for a boy like your Moses, and when your back's turned, he steals you blind.
How much did he take?'

'I rather think something terrible happened to him,' Laura said. 'He was
so willing, so keen to please.'

'No doubt the tsotsis got him.'

'Could be,' Mrs. Saltwood said, but for a long time she continued to
wonder about Moses Nxumalo.

In the heady atmosphere of Johannesburg, when the grand strategies of the
Broederbond showed their initial signs of succeeding, Piet Krause was
thinking one day about the opportunities that would present themselves for
a patriotic outburst in 1938, the hundredth anniversary of the Battle of
Blood River, the culminating event of the Great Trek.

'We must think of something,' he told Johanna as they came home from
a meeting of schoolteachers, 'that will stir up the nation and remind the
Afrikaners of their heritage.' They discussed a master rally at the site of
Blood River, but that location was so far removed from major centers of
population that only a devoted few would be able to attend. They thought
of a celebration at Blauuwkrantz, but since that lay in Natal, which was
notoriously pro-English, they quickly dropped it.

In fact, they could think of nothing original, and then one morning
Johanna read that a committee of Afrikaners was considering the erection
of a massive monument on a hilltop outside Pretoria, a memorial to Blood
River and the covenant that was entered into on that sacred day. This
excited Piet, and the couple talked of inviting huge numbers of people, even
from Cape Town, to the dedication of this proposed monument, and when
they saw a sketch of how the building might look—a splendid, blunt affair
reminiscent of the structures at Great Zimbabwe—they became positively
dedicated to the task of making this a historic affair.

Johanna said, 'We must see that all parts of the nation cooperate, all
the Afrikaner parts, that is,' and she began to construct patterns for the
celebration. As a woman, she was of course not allowed to participate in
the Broederbond, but since her husband talked everything over with her and
respected her opinions, it was easy for her to feed her ideas through him.
She suggested a convocation of religious leaders from all over the world, but
discarded this when Piet pointed out that she would have to invite the Pope
and certain rabbis. 'What we could do,' she countered, 'is ask the leaders
of the Dutch and German churches to join with us.'

On and on went the planning, and then one day Piet suggested the best
thing of all: 'What might be a splendid idea—we could see if any of the old
ox wagons still existed. There'll be plenty of oxen. Why not build repli-
cas of the old wagons, we have their dimensions, and have two or three of
them travel from Graaff-Reinet to the monument. People could dress in
the old style—men could let their beards grow like Piet Retief and Gert
Maritz . . .'

For two days the Krauses imagined this cavalcade winding north over
the old route, and then Johanna proposed a brilliant concept: 'Piet! Not a
cavalcade. Five or six separate wagons. Each starting from a major point.

Detouring slowly to every small town en route. And all converging on Pretoria on December 16. Every Afrikaner in the nation would have to be there.'

It was this plan which Piet Krause presented to the Broederbond leadership, and he was astonished to find that several prominent members of the railway cultural society had proposed an identical program, except that they visualized only two ox wagons starting from Cape Town. The advantages of Piet's scheme of five or six were recognized and he was assigned the task of organizing the 1938 trek.

'It can be,' Reverend Brongersma predicted to an English newspaper, 'a great outpouring of the Afrikaner spirit. It can at once both unite and ignite.' To a reporter he said, 'It will rejuvenate Afrikaner politics as nothing else could do. I expect wonders from this trek.' In private he added that if sufficient spirit were generated, the Afrikaners might at last succeed in taking South Africa out of its present Union status, making it republican. To any Afrikaner who asked, he said, 'That is the goal we seek,' and if they asked further whether this would mean an exodus or expulsion from the British Empire, he replied, 'Not necessarily. England might like us better as completely equal partners.'

There was, however, one question which he never answered frankly. One night Piet Krause, flushed with his success in launching the wagons, asked, 'Dominee, this time will we join Germany when war comes?' Brongersma did not like to discuss this ticklish situation, for he saw much in contemporary Germany which bothered him. In 1914, like many intelligent Afrikaners, he had felt strongly that his country's future lay with Kaiser Wilhelm's Germany; the latter had good leadership, power, intellectual force and a strong Lutheran tradition. In retrospect he still believed that it would have been better for the world had Imperial Germany won and imposed her version of peace on troubled areas, but he certainly did not believe that about Adolf Hitler's Germany. He saw too much that disturbed, for if in his great series of lectures at Stellenbosch he had educated the young leaders of his nation, he had also educated himself. He believed every word he spoke in those four carefully reasoned discourses, and believed it even more now. South Africa was a Christian country. It endeavored to combine the best of the Old Testament and the New. It believed in justice for all peoples, and if it insisted upon the separation of races, that was only because God had done the same, and he believed that his country managed its separation with firmness and justice. He did not like what Hitler was doing and felt that he would have to oppose an intrusion of his concepts into South Africa.

'Will we join Germany this time, Dominee?' Piet repeated.

'I pray the whole world can avoid war,' he replied.

In early 1938 Detleef astounded the committee supervising the trek by announcing that he had found on his farm the only surviving ox wagon that had been used by one of the important leaders of the 1838 period, and when it was dragged forth, the wagon he had slept in during the weeks following the end of the Boer War, carpenters said that whereas it was obviously in ruins, it could easily be restored, and they set about doing so. For weeks various newspapers printed photographs showing the progress of rehabilitation, and when the rubric TC–43 was uncovered, correspondents in Grahamstown were able to state what it signified, and recalled the generosity of the English settlers of that period toward a man they trusted. Because of where the wagon had originated, it was proposed that it start its journey to Pretoria from Grahamstown, but Detleef would not permit this; he wanted his wagon to have no contact with Englishmen, so it started from Graaff-Reinet.

The journey north, in those winter days of August 1938, began on a high emotional pitch, with the central square of Graaff-Reinet looking much as it had during the historic Nachtmaals: tents pitched, women in sunbonnets, children playing, men in beards and suspenders. As the wagon moved slowly forward, a tremendous visual remembrance of heroic days, people came from fifty miles to see it pass, its sixteen sturdy oxen walking slowly, as their ancestors had done a century ago.

The *Tjaart van Doorn* did not go to Bloemfontein, for another wagon was starting from there, but it did move east through the historic sites: Thaba Nchu, Vegkop, the site on the Vaal where the De Groot family was assassinated, then east through the concentration-camp towns of Standerton and Chrissie Meer. In early December it headed west to Carolina, where the members of Christoffel Steyn's family paid it honor, and then on to Venloo, where descendants of the commando of Paulus de Groot formed an honor guard. When it reached Waterval-Boven, from which Oom Paul Kruger had left for his exile, the emotional strain was intense, and thousands prayed along the roadside as it passed. This was a wagon in which women and men of stature had risked their lives and fortunes in the building of a nation, and to see it move so slowly, with such strain and with so cramped a space for survival, brought tears.

On December 13 the *Tjaart van Doorn* slowly approached the vast field at the foot of the mound on which the future monument was to stand, and when Detleef and Maria, in their 1838 costumes, saw the throng that awaited them, they stopped the wagon and bowed their heads. What had started as a topic of conversation had expanded to a mighty outpouring of the Voortrekker spirit. Two days before the event, more than eighty thousand Afrikaners camped at the site, and that night Detleef led his wagon into a simulated laager with six others. The oxen were turned loose to graze, as in the old days, and children brought thorn bushes to weave among the wheels to keep away the Zulu. When the moon rose late, and the silhouettes of the wagons stood against the dark horizon, men wakened their families to witness the sight, and improvised choirs chanted the Psalms in Afrikaans.

On December 17 Piet Krause rode among the wagons already in position, assuring the men that all was in order; the two major wagons from Pretoria and Cape Town would arrive next morning. By now the crowd approached a hundred thousand—families camping on the slopes, as in the old days—and friendships that had languished for years were renewed with pledges to maintain them.

On this day rumors began to circulate: 'The mayor of Benoni will not be allowed to participate. He's Jewish. They've told the general not to appear. He's English. Best news of all, Jan Christian Smuts will not be coming. They want nothing of him in this celebration. He's more English

than he is Afrikaner. No speeches in English will be allowed tomorrow.'
Piet Krause, the originator of most of these rumors, had personally decreed
that what would be the major monument in South Africa must be a purely
Afrikaner affair.

On December 18 some two hundred thousand people gathered on the
hill south of Pretoria to consecrate the spot on which their monument
would rise. If, despite everything they had heard, General Smuts and other
Afrikaner supporters of the government did appear, the occasion would
become an affair of state, and 'God Save the King' would have to be played,
but Piet Krause openly avowed that if the band played one note of that
anthem, he and a gang of toughs would smash every instrument. Aware of
the bitterness of the issue, Smuts prudently stayed away, and to the joy of
the Afrikaners only 'Die Stem van Suid-Afrika' (The Call of South Africa)
was played, and many swore that it would soon be the official anthem of
the Afrikaner republic when the new nation came into being.

The orations in Afrikaans, one delivered by Reverend Brongersma,
were dignified but charged with heavy implications. Hardly any words of
historic evocation could be spoken without producing cheers from the
massed throng, and when symbol-words like Slagter's Nek, Black Circuit
and Christoffel Steyn were uttered, the crowd cheered automatically. When
heroes were recalled—Pretorius, Retief, De Groot—the crowd yelled till it
was hoarse, and as the day waned and the leaders realized how far beyond
their expectations their success had been, it began to penetrate to all involved that something more than a celebration had occurred here this day.
'This is the opening gun of our campaign to break away from England
altogether,' Piet Krause cried in an ecstasy of patriotism.

He became so mesmerized by that assembly of two hundred thousand
Afrikaners that it was not long before he began to have visions of a vast
national uprising, and to discover how this could be orchestrated, he slipped
down to Cape Town, boarded a ship for England and quietly crossed to
Germany, where he quickly made contact with Nazi leaders.

He was overwhelmed by what he saw. At a tremendous rally in the
stadium used by the 1936 Olympics he realized how amateurish the Voortrekker thing had really been. 'We had all those people in one place,' he told
his Nazi guide, 'and did nothing with them. They went away with the same
thoughts they had when they came. Next time it must be different.'

He was so intelligent, and appeared to be so highly placed in South
African politics, that the men about to launch a total war in Europe were
captivated by the possibilities he offered: 'Could you arrange an uprising
against the English government—if war happened to come to Europe?'

'Look at what we did in 1914, without help or guidance from you,' he
reminded them. When they admitted that they were ignorant of that affair,
he told them of the courageous effort made by men like Paulus de Groot
and Jakob van Doorn, who devoted their lives to the struggle for freedom.
'Van Doorn was my father-in-law. De Groot you've heard of, naturally.'
They hadn't, so he dropped that subject.

'But what can you do this time?' they asked.

'I give you my solemn promise that Jan Christian Smuts will not dare
call for mobilization. No one would report.'

'The police?'

'They'll fight for Germany.' Recklessly he promised everything, implying that he spoke for all segments of the population. If he did not convince them of his interpretations of South African politics, he did persuade them to invest a modest amount in a potential subversion of that government. They granted the funds on the sensible basis of disrupting the English power at all points, provided the cost proved not too high; they never expected the southern tip of Africa to become a German enclave, but they could reasonably hope for enough disruption to impede the war effort.

With these assurances, Piet Krause, who spoke miserable German, went to Nuremberg for one of the frenzied rallies of mid-1939, when the leadership knew that war was inevitable, though the people did not. The stadium was filled with ecstatic young men who would shortly die in Greece and Italy and Russia and the North Atlantic and in the skies above England. He heard eleven preliminary speeches, pounding into him the need to exterminate Jews and cleanse the bloodstream. He appreciated the enormous appeal of the word Volk and decided to increase its use in South Africa. But when the lesser orators were finished, Herr Goebbels appeared, and after him, Adolf Hitler, the man who would save the world.

Piet Krause stood enthralled as Hitler unfolded his plan for regeneration, and each word he said applied to conditions in South Africa, so far as Piet was concerned. He was hypnotized by Hitler's force, his clear logic; and when the wild cheering died, he still stood there, trying to determine how best he could assist this man in bringing the same kind of order and enthusiasm to South Africa.

That night, in his Nuremberg room, he drafted the blood oath which he would administer to all who later joined him in his enterprise:

> In the presence of Almighty God and on the sacred blood of the Volk, I swear that my higher authority will find me obediently faithful and eager to obey in secret any command given me. I shall fight constantly for the victory of National Socialism, because I know that democracy has become like an old shoe which must be thrown away.
>
> If I advance, follow me!
> If I retreat, shoot me!
> If I die, avenge me!
> So help me God!

When he reached home in midsummer, 1939, his wife could see that he had undergone some thunderclap experience, for he was not the man she had known before. When he confided the responsibilities that had been placed upon him, she knew that she must assume responsibility for the family, since he would be preoccupied with a score of duties. He started with the police, talking quietly against the local custom of conscripting the whole force into the armed services: 'Don't let them make you go to war. If Jan Christian Smuts wants you to fight his battles in England, don't permit it. This time England must lose, and when that happens, you and men like you will be in command.'

He was also active with young Afrikaners: 'Do not allow the government to force you into uniform. And for the love of God, don't volunteer. When the Germans recapture South-West Africa, there'll be a place for you in a real army.'

He asked certain trusted clergymen to preach against participation in this impending war, and he did effective work among the unions. He talked with schoolteachers, advising them what to say to their pupils, and when war did come, in September of that year, Smuts found himself unable to order conscription, or to move policemen bodily into the armed forces, or to argue young men into volunteering. In fact, when Smuts sought to take his country into the conflict on the side of England, he was strongly opposed by those who insisted that it remain neutral. At the final moment South Africa joined the Allies by a vote of only 80–67.

'He is taking us onto the wrong side,' the principal members of the Broederbond cried in dismay, and some of the future leaders of the nation went into detention camps rather than fight against Germany. Piet Krause, escaping police attention, swung into violent action, organizing disruptive squads, which secretly attacked military installations, power lines and even military training camps. Men loyal to the Allies, especially young Afrikaners seen as traitors to the Volk, were assaulted and some were killed.

The government was in pitiful shape to fight a war. It dared not call for nationwide conscription, and those soldiers and policemen who volunteered to serve outside the country were required to wear orange swatches, which distinguished them from others who announced that they would not fight abroad; this presumably divided the men into heroes and cowards. But there was a disadvantage in such a system; Piet Krause's young hoodlums who were against the war could easily spot the men with swatches who were willing to fight for the Allies, and it became fashionable to beat such soldiers up, killing them on occasion.

Piet and his wife did whatever they could to exacerbate such situations, and in the heady days of Nazi victories on all fronts, they received a cryptic message from Berlin: 'Meet Wyk Slotemaker Mafeking.' He was a minor South African actor who had appeared in several German films, absorbing propaganda as he worked, and when Piet encountered him at a ramshackle hotel he whispered, 'I have weapons, fifteen thousand American dollars, and plans to assassinate Smuts.'

'The hour is at hand!' Piet exulted.

It was a sorely divided South Africa that tried to prosecute this war. Johanna van Doorn and her sister-in-law Maria prayed daily for a German victory and hoped that it would be of such magnitude that England would be crushed forever. Detleef agreed with them in principle, but had reservations about Adolf Hitler and real doubts as to whether South Africa would gain much from a German victory in Africa.

The Saltwoods of New Sarum, led by Maud Turner Saltwood, now a feisty sixty-nine, were totally supportive of the Allied cause and were overjoyed when the United States joined in. Her daughter-in-law, Laura

Saltwood, Noel's wife, organized canteens to help England and was distraught when some of them were vandalized by Piet Krause's storm troopers.

The Saltwoods of De Kraal and the Van Doorns of Trianon faced difficulties in determining their allegiances, for Timothy Saltwood, V.C., was married to Clara van Doorn, a stalwart Afrikaner. Like many similar families, they prayed quietly that the war would end and did not parade their emotions.

The Nxumalos were perplexed. As a family that had always been loyal to General de Groot, they at first favored a German victory, but when the African National Congress pointed out that Herr Hitler thought even less of blacks than he did of Jews, they realized that in his moment of victory they were going to be in trouble, so gradually they transferred their moral support to the English. They were astounded as they watched contending elements within the white population fight each other, and slowly they realized that the Afrikaners would win, here in South Africa if not in Europe, and that when they did, they were going to be very harsh with the blacks. Old Micah, at the end of a long, wild life of fighting great battles without weapons—Majuba, Spion Kop, the raid into the Cape—had sadly assured his family: 'Whoever wins, we lose.'

The heaviest burden of moral decision fell upon Reverend Brongersma; as the son of a family that had provided five commandos in the Boer War, he was staunchly pro-Afrikaner and his whole sympathy had to be with their nationalist and republican aspirations. His lectures at Stellenbosch had not dealt with this aspect of South African life; he had avoided the issue lest he give offense to the English half of his community. But on balance, and looking at the entire world as he was permitted to understand it, he could not see that England had ever exhibited any great moral superiority. Their record in India and South Africa did not impress him, and he suspected that most of what was commendable in the United States stemmed from its non-English immigrants. So he would be quite content to see a German victory—except for the fact that no Christian could remain blind to the awful excesses of Hitlerism. The Nazis had perpetrated crimes against the family, the church, the youth of the nation, and certainly against the Jews. Sitting alone in his study, his tall body hunched over at times, at other times thrown far back as he propped his legs on his desk, he wrestled with this problem: Nazism, using the most exalted impulses of the human race, seems to release the lowest urges of the human animal. Leave Germany out of it. There must be millions of people in America who would gladly staff a Nazi prison. God knows we could find them here in South Africa. And one of the ugliest, I am afraid, is my good friend Piet Krause. Like a dog, he grabs hold of one idea, gnaws at it, worries it, and allows it to obsess him.

He felt that in common decency, but also for the good name of the Broederbond, which did not sponsor such behavior, he must talk with Piet, but when he tried to reason with him, he found the former schoolteacher glassy-eyed with dreams, and in the end he dismissed him as hopeless. But after the disappointing session he did consult with Frykenius, who was still

Piet's superior in the brotherhood, and implored him to summon Krause back to Venloo, where together they might knock some sense into him. This Frykenius agreed to do, because he, too, was worried by the excesses Piet was engineering.

Krause, as an obedient member of the Broederbond, came down from Johannesburg, but as soon as he saw that Reverend Brongersma was with Frykenius he bristled: 'Dominee, we do not seek your counsel.'

'Piet,' Frykenius said, 'sit down.'

But even after the two older men had spread before him their analysis of the harm he was doing, he refused to accept their rebuke: 'Have you two any idea of the great forces set in motion by the ox wagons? This country is seething with patriotism.'

'Don't use anything as precious as patriotism for a wrong purpose,' Brongersma cautioned.

'Dominee, there's to be a great uprising!'

When he heard these words the predikant sat back, his hands folded in his lap. He knew that what Piet had just said was true: there was going to be a tremendous uprising of the Afrikaner spirit, so vast that it would sweep Jan Christian Smuts and his English ways right out of office and keep them out forever, so vast that every aspect of life in the country would be modified. Because of the spirit generated by the ox wagons, the Afrikaner was on the verge of victories which only the idealist had dreamed of. South Africa would quit the empire. No more would bands play 'God Save the King,' no more would Englishmen sit in the cabinet. The Afrikaner nation would be free to solve its racial difficulties in its own just way. And strife would end.

'Piet,' the predikant said softly, 'you've won your victory. Don't contaminate it with violence.'

'Dominee, the real victory is just beginning! Herr Hitler is about to sweep the English from the seas. America can do nothing, he'll sink their ships. His principles will rule this land.'

When Frykenius tried to soften this tirade, Piet cried, 'You men have a choice you must make in a hurry. Are you for the revolution that's breaking, or against it?'

'Piet,' Frykenius reasoned, 'you know what the aims of the Broederbond have always been. Of course we're for an Afrikaner triumph. But not on your violent terms. The rioting in the streets, that's got to stop.'

Piet drew back as if dissociating himself from the timid approach of the Bond. 'You men in the Broederbond. I see your kind in Pretoria and Johannesburg all the time. You're like a pretty girl who gives a boy a kiss, three kisses, a dozen, then runs away when he wants to get down to business. Well, I'm getting down to business. I have work to do, and I doubt that we'll be meeting any more.'

In a frenzy he dashed out and went to Vrymeer, burst into the kitchen and presented Detleef with an ultimatum: 'Either you join us this night or you miss your chance to lead the nation when we triumph.' When Detleef asked for details, Piet thrust a typed card into his hand, crying excitedly, 'Take this oath. Now. And tonight you ride with us . . . if we get instructions from Berlin.' Before Detleef could respond to such a commitment, Piet said with urgency, 'I must use your radio,' and through the shortwave screeching he listened to Radio Zeesen:

> 'Good evening, dear and loyal friends in South Africa. This is your favorite program, By Kampfuur en Ketel [By Campfire and Kettle]. Today our glorious Führer has enjoyed victories on all fronts. The decadent democracies cringe and crumble. [Here came a series of coded instructions, at which Piet Krause leaped with excitement.] Trusted friends in South Africa . . .'

Neither he nor Detleef heard the final words, for Piet snapped off the radio and asked bluntly, 'Well, Brother, do you join our revolution?' and faced with that moment of decision, Detleef finally concluded that he distrusted Adolf Hitler and doubted his ultimate victory.

'I can't accept such an oath,' he said.

'Heroes can,' Piet said, and he was off.

He drove recklessly from Venloo to Waterval-Boven, where he picked up two conspirators who had taken the oath, then west to Pretoria, where Wyk Slotemaker, the one-time actor eager to assassinate Smuts, joined them, then down to an army base south of Johannesburg, where they were scheduled to blow up a major ammunition dump. When the actor saw the intricacy of the barbed wire, he drew back, and this also deterred the other two, but Piet, inflamed with memories of Nuremberg and Berlin, and visualizing the same kind of glory breaking over South Africa, crept forward alone, dynamite strapped to his back.

His careless use of wire clippers activated a warning bell in the guard-rooms, and seven sharpshooters streamed out as huge searchlights flashed on. An Afrikaner from Carolina who had volunteered for Smuts' army drew a bead on the dark figure creeping toward the ammunition, and fired. His bullet struck the package on Piet's back, detonating it and blowing him to shreds, but even so, Krause gained a limited victory, for he had reached a spot so close to the dump that his explosion ignited combustibles—and through the long night shattering concussions threw flames far into the sky.

In 1946, when Detleef and Maria van Doorn were once more peaceful farmers at Vrymeer, they were visited by his sister Johanna, a widow with a minor job in Johannesburg. She came with a proposal from a group of persons much interested in the welfare of the nation, and although Detleef was suspicious of almost anything she did these days, he had to listen, for whenever he met with her his first impression was of that evening in the camp at Chrissiesmeer when she apportioned the food delivered to the dead Tant Sybilla, and weighed it in her pale hands, giving him the larger share. He was alive today because of her courage and generosity.

'Detleef, and this concerns you too, Maria. In business the English are proving much more clever than we suspected. We've made almost no headway in penetrating their offices of power. We just don't have enough trained young men. Damnit all, our best people go down to Stellenbosch, and what do they study? Religion, of which we have far too much. Philosophy, which is of use to no one. Some history. Some literature. A little science. What we need is accountants and bankers and managers.'

'I certainly have no capacity in those fields,' Detleef protested.

'Of course you don't. Because you wasted your time at Stellenbosch. Playing rugby.'

'Wait a minute! Don't you say anything against rugby.' When she had railed against religion a few moments before, he had remained silent, but he could not do so if she spoke against rugby.

'Forget that. We've decided that what we must do is place men like you who can speak good English . . . Well, what I mean is . . . you must take one of the permanent secretaryships with the committees in Parliament.'

'That pays nothing!'

'Of course it doesn't. That's the point. We slip you in there. Nobody notices because no Englishman would want the job. And you serve there twenty-five or thirty years . . .'

'I'm already fifty-one.'

'So you serve twenty years. In time you make enormous inroads. It's you who will be drafting the laws. And we will gain by indirection what we can't win head-on.'

She had with her a list of some forty inconspicuous vacancies, not one of which would be mentioned in the newspapers when it was filled: a series of jobs which might have tempted a boy out of high school, but not Detleef. They were mostly in agencies of the government dealing with financial or business affairs, in which he felt no competence, but as he was returning the paper to her, his eye fell upon one line, off to itself, relating to an office so small it provided only one vacancy: Commission on Racial Affairs. Idly he said, 'Now, if a man had to accept an assignment . . .'

'Which?' she pounced.

'That one.'

'A man could do much good there, Detleef.'

'No! No!' He dismissed the invitation absolutely and would say no more about it, so dutifully she gathered her papers, smiled at Maria, and left.

Three days later Mr. Frykenius summoned him to Venloo. The two Broederbonders had grown so close since the deplorable death of their mutual friend, Piet Krause, that they attacked any subject without formalities: 'Detleef, they want you take the position with the Commission on Racial Affairs.'

'I can't leave the farm.'

'But you can. The Troxels can manage, and you and Maria can divide your time between Pretoria and Cape Town.'

'Really, I can hardly . . .'

'So many times have you and I discussed what to do with the Bantu and the Coloureds. Here's a chance to put our principles into operation.'

'I don't want to leave Vrymeer . . .'

'Detleef, you and I have only a limited number of years remaining. Let's spend them on things important.' When Van Doorn hesitated, the butcher said, 'Remember when you told me about your vision for this country? The sun striking the glass of jellies. Each on its own level, clean and separated? Now you have an opportunity to achieve that dream.'

'I shall have to speak with Maria.'

'Detleef, on crucial matters, leave the women to themselves.'

'But how did you hear about this job? Surely it was my sister Johanna who told you.'

'I never speak with women. This came as an order from Pretoria.'

Detleef smiled and thought: But who told Pretoria to send the order? It had to have been Johanna, and he remembered the debt he owed her: She broke the rations in half, then added to one portion and gave it to me. She kept me alive. She helped form my beliefs.

'So the problem we have is of our own making,' Frykenius was explaining. 'In order to get the little jobs in government, we insisted that every employee must be bilingual. It worked. We got all of them because the English wouldn't bother to learn Afrikaans. But now the big jobs are opening up and we damned Afrikaners have too few bright people who can speak English well. We'll get them when our universities get going. But right now we must depend on people like you.'

When Detleef remained silent, the butcher said, 'I have written this letter for you, accepting the assignment. Sign it.' And he pushed forward the document that would ultimately make Detleef van Doorn one of the most influential men in the nation.

Because there had been fierce antagonisms among cities when the Union government was established in 1910, each insisting that it be the capital, Detleef's new position required him to maintain three homes: the permanent farm at Vrymeer, a six-month home in Cape Town, and a year-round pair of rooms in a Pretoria hotel. Fortunately, he had the funds for such extravagance.

The reasons for this proliferation were complex. The contest for the capital had been solved rather neatly: Pretoria housed all executive operations; Cape Town hosted the Parliament; and Bloemfontein had the Appellate Court. Financial and business interests, although not forming a recognized branch of government, more or less ran the country from Johannesburg, which left poor Natal with nothing except a semi-tropical climate and breathtaking views of the Indian Ocean.

As a consequence, the South African government resembled the Indian, which during hot months moved entirely from steaming Delhi to cool Simla in the Himalayas. During the half year that Parliament was in session most of the executive branch boarded trains and went down to Cape Town, and during the other half, parliamentary offices moved up to Pretoria.

The Commission on Racial Affairs was in those years a trivial Cape Town operation dealing mostly with housing; it was chaired by an elected member of Parliament and staffed by officeholders of little distinction. There was a secretary, an Englishman who had held the position for twenty routine years, and a pettifogging assistant of equal service whose resignation because of failing eyesight had created the opening which Detleef was filling. His salary was £900 a year, scarcely enough to live on if one had to move back and forth between the cities.

In 1946 the commission had so little work to do that Detleef slipped into place with no notice of his appointment appearing in any newspaper, but in early 1947 an event occurred which projected him into permanent attention; after that, whatever his commission did attracted notice.

In that year Jan Christian Smuts, as filled with honors as a man could be—Prime Minister of South Africa, Field Marshal of the British Empire, Chancellor-elect of Cambridge University, sponsor of the United Nations and co-drafter of the noble preamble to its charter—decided that to cap his career and at the same time increase his chances for reelection, he would invite the King and Queen of England to visit their dominion; and he had the happy idea of asking them to bring along their two charming daughters. All four accepted, and when they landed at Cape Town there was an outpouring of loyalty to the royal family by all but a determined group of Afrikaners who were working assiduously to take South Africa out of the empire.

Detleef became involved in the royal tour when his prize bull, a gigantic beast called Oom Paul, won the blue ribbon at the Rand Agricultural Show. This meant that Vrymeer could charge sharply increased fees for Oom Paul's services, and Detleef was delighted.

But then he found that to receive his blue ribbon, he must accept it from the hands of King George VI, who would be attending the Rand show, and this infuriated him. As Maria said bitterly, 'My father was executed by soldiers of the king. Your father was shot by his soldiers. How could you accept a prize from his bloodstained hands?'

'It was soldiers of King George V,' Detleef corrected, but this was unfortunate, because Maria said, 'The English killed most of your family at Chrissiesmeer.'

The word inflamed him: 'Chrissiesmeer! Do you know how they spell it on their maps? Chrissie Meer. They're even stealing our names from us.'

'Detleef, you cannot accept a prize from that man.'

Painfully aware of the money he was sacrificing, Detleef stormed down to the cattle pens and told his manager, Troxel, 'Take Oom Paul home.'

'But the blue ribbon!'

'I will accept no prize from the hands of a bloodstained king.'

A newsman heard the fracas and recognized Detleef as a former rugby great. Sensing a great story, he shouted for his cameraman, who was photographing sheep. When the man ran over, he quickly grasped the situation and dragooned Detleef into posing beside his champion. At that moment Oom Paul, irritated by the commotion, assumed a sneer almost as contemptuous as Detleef's. The scene was frozen on film: an honest Afrikaner and his bull defying the empire.

As the 1948 election neared, the stately English homes in Johannesburg suburbs glowed with color portraits of the royal family standing with Jan Smuts, while the Afrikaner homes displayed the shot of Detleef standing with Oom Paul. When the agricultural attaché from the American embassy visited eastern Transvaal to check crops, he listened for two days to the scathing accusations lodged against Smuts, then broke into laughter. 'You people feel about him the way my father in Iowa feels about Roosevelt. Smuts won the war for you, and now you want to kick him out. Roosevelt won the war for us, and men like my father wanted to hang him.'

The voting took place on 26 May 1948, and that evening the Van Doorns invited to their Vrymeer home their sister Johanna, Mr. Frykenius and their

dominee, Reverend Brongersma. As a cool autumn night descended over
the lakes, the five people sensed that this could be a day of majestic change.
The king and queen were going to be banished. Slim Jannie Smuts' party
would be tossed out. The days of smug Englishmen like the Saltwoods were
numbered. And those wavering Afrikaner families, like the Van Doorns of
Trianon, half Dutch, half English, would be forced to make up their minds
and nail their colors aloft for others to see.

Frykenius spoke: 'I see a tremendous nationalism assuming power in
this country tonight. Smuts? Forget him. The king? He'll be gone in ten
years. The English language? Now it falls to second place. Tonight we take
revenge for Slagter's Nek and the concentration camps. I pray we have the
energy to capitalize on the victory we're about to win.'

When the first returns came in they were from strongly English areas,
and Smuts' tenure as prime minister seemed to be secure, but as the night
wore on, startling upsets were reported, with men who had been in intern-
ment camps during the war because of their pro-Hitler stance winning
astounding victories. When it became clear that Daniel Malan's National
party was winning, Detleef began to cheer, and said to his sister, 'I wish Piet
Krause were here to see this night. All he dreamed of we're getting, and
without one rifle shot.'

Toward two in the morning, when neighbors dropped by to share
sandwiches and coffee, the really glorious news reached them: 'Jan Christian Smuts has lost even his own seat at Standerton. The field marshal leaves
the field of battle.'

'Thank God!' Maria Steyn van Doorn cried, and she knelt. Johanna
joined her, and the two women prayed in thankfulness that they had seen
the fall of this man who, they believed, had hurt them so grievously.

When they rose, Frykenius turned to Brongersma and asked, 'Dominee,
would you lead us in prayer? This is a night to be remembered.' And the
tall man, who would shortly leave Venloo to occupy the pulpit in the leading
Pretoria church, asked his four listeners to pray with him:

> 'Almagtige God, ons dank U. From 1795 when the Dutch first lost
> their colony at the Cape, through vicissitudes untold, we have fought
> to establish a just society in this land. In those troubled years You
> extended a covenant to us, and we have been faithful. Tonight You
> bring us great victory, and our only prayer is that we may prove
> worthy of it. Help us to build here a nation in Your image.'

Fervently the others cried 'Amen,' and that very afternoon Detleef and
Maria headed for Cape Town, where with a new majority in Parliament
they would begin their arduous work of reorganizing the nation.

The first thing Detleef did was to make life so miserable for his superior,
the senior secretary to the Commission on Racial Affairs, that the only
sensible thing that Englishman could do was to resign. For several weeks
he tried to avoid this drastic step, trusting that the new member of Parliament who was taking over the chairmanship would protect him, but this
man was a tough-minded farmer from the Orange Free State, and instead
of defending the aggrieved secretary, he treated him even more contemptuously than Detleef had, and in disgust the man quit. He left government

altogether, beginning the hemorrhage that would drain every department until the civil service at all levels became almost totally Afrikaner-minded and -managed.

With Detleef in position, the commission was ready to tackle the vast problems of whipping the various elements of society into shape, and it fell to Van Doorn to draft the preliminary directives, then construct the proposed laws that would convert them into a permanent discipline. He worked endlessly for this goal, at first a faceless bureaucrat, but as his accomplishments became known, a nationally acclaimed hero in the movement to protect the race.

Like puritans in all countries, he started with sex. He saw that in a decent society white men should marry only white women, Coloureds marry Coloureds, and so on down to the Bantu, who would marry among themselves. Whenever he thought of these matters, or discussed them with his wife, who heartily approved of what he was trying to do, he started at what he visualized as the top with Afrikaners, working his way down to the Bantu, who represented the vast majority at the bottom. Afrikaners were entitled to top position because they respected God and were faithful to the directives of John Calvin; Coloureds stood higher than Indians for two reasons: they had some white blood and they usually believed in Jesus Christ, and even those who didn't, accepted Muhammad, who was higher than the Hindu gods; and Bantu were at the bottom because they were black and heathen. Of course, a large proportion of them were Christian, hundreds of thousands being enrolled in their own Dutch Reformed churches, but this was a complication which he ignored.

His first proposal was simple: no white person, regardless of his or her situation, could marry a non-white. If he attempted to do so, he would be thrown in jail, and if he actually entered into such a marriage, it would be invalid.

This presented little difficulty in the Afrikaner provinces of Transvaal and the Orange Free State, but in Cape Town, where more than half the population was Coloured, it created havoc, and there was great outcry. But that very year in Durban, blacks and Indians engaged in wild communal rioting in which nearly one hundred and fifty people were slain, and Detleef could tell his people, 'See, races should be kept apart.' To those in his confidence he often spoke of his vision: the glass with the perfect separation of jellies.

In 1950 he carried this marriage ordinance to its next logical improvement: he pulled out an old immorality act of 1927, which had struggled ineffectively to deal with the matter, and gave it new teeth, so that sexual relations between persons of unequal color were criminalized; any man embracing a woman of different color would be jailed. His wife and sister approved of this law and said it would perform miracles in purifying life in the Union.

The use of this word *Union* irritated Detleef, and he wondered how soon the Afrikaner majority would officially break ties with England. When he asked his superiors about the timetable for freedom, they told him gruffly, 'One thing at a time. Get along with your own tasks.' He was diverted temporarily when at the United Nations, Madame Pandit of India launched a bitter attack on South Africa's racial policies, particularly the treatment of Indians. He was enraged that a woman should presume to speak so, and that a Hindu should so make a fool of herself by criticizing a Christian country. At his suggestion, he was given time off to draft a reply to Madame Pandit, but it was so discourteous to an ambassador of another Commonwealth nation that it was not dispatched, but for many weeks he continued to mutter to his Afrikaner friends, 'Imagine. A woman and a Hindu daring to say those things. She should be muzzled.'

When his superiors ordered him to forget India and get back to work, he produced for them four smashing proposed bills, all of which became law. As one newspaper said of this herculean output: 'Rarely in the history of the world has one nation opened its floodgates to such a torrent of legislation.' When he and Maria surveyed what they had accomplished, they could take pride in the fact that they had achieved through quiet application of their talents what their fathers had failed to attain through battle. 'Think of what we've made happen in such a short time!' Detleef said after a six-month stint in Cape Town, and like a professor he ticked off the changes.

One, he had begun to codify customs and rules forbidding contact between whites and non-whites in any public amenity. Toilets, restaurants, trolley cars, taxis, elevators, post-office windows where stamps were sold, station platforms and even park benches had to be clearly designated with large signs as to who could patronize them, and across the nation WHITES ONLY proliferated. Maria was particularly gratified by the post-office restriction: 'I would hate to stand in line behind some big Bantu, waiting for my stamps.'

Two, he had helped his cohorts in Parliament pass a Group Areas Act that would enable the government to divide the entire nation, and especially every city, into segments allocated to specific groups. Thus, the central urban areas would be cleared of any Indians or Bantu so that whites alone could live there. Huge areas now occupied by Coloureds in Cape Town would be reserved for whites only; the Coloureds would be removed to new housing tracts on the windy Cape Flats. The Bantu would be confined to vast locations outside the limits of white cities and towns, and would be allowed to stay even there only so long as they provided meaningful labor for white interests. 'With these reasonable actions,' said Van Doorn, 'the racial cleanliness which is the mark of any good society will be both defined and enforced.'

Three, he aided in drafting harsh, good laws for the supression of Communism, making them so sweeping that almost any activity the Afrikaner majority did not approve could be punished by extremely long prison terms, often without due process of law. 'This is needed,' he assured any who questioned him, and when certain liberals, often Englishmen, pointed out that for every Communist thrown into jail without trial, sixteen non-Communists who wanted better schools or labor unions would be so penalized, he answered with a remark he had only recently heard: 'You can't make an omelet without breaking eggs.'

Four—his major achievement—he conceived the law which came closest to his heart, and in the formative stages, long before it had passed, Maria and Johanna had applauded the far-sightedness of his planning. 'What we propose,' he explained to the parliamentary members who would push the bill through, 'is that every human being residing in this country shall be listed in our records—available always to police and government—as to his or her specific racial identity.'

'What I mean,' an English member fumbled, 'if this classification is to follow a man all his life, oughtn't we to be fairly careful—'

Detleef did not let him finish: 'Sir, the utmost care will be taken. White people of the finest reputation will do the classifying, and of course we can expect a few mistakes. You know that and I know it. But when they're pointed out, and any man can challenge his classification, a committee of three responsible white persons will meet with that complainant, look at his skin color, study his background, even take testimony from his close friends and neighbors, and reclassify him upward, if the facts warrant.'

'And if the facts are unclear?'

'Then it will be better if the classification stands.'

'And what if a man you classify as white wants to be classified as Coloured?'

'Downward?' Detleef asked. The question was so preposterous that he could think of no answer, but what he did reply was interesting: 'I can see the day when a man classified tenuously as Coloured will have lived such an exemplary life and so clearly have acquired civilized habits that his community will assent to allowing him to change his classification upward to white. Everyone can aspire to upward movement, especially if his skin is on the light side.'

Because Detleef exulted over these new laws, it must not be assumed that he had much to do with their actual passage through Parliament. He never forgot that he was only a bureaucrat working out of a small Cape Town office, and many members of Parliament, especially those of the opposition parties, almost forgot that he existed, for he never appeared on the floor. But through persistent pressure and the fact that he kept his job while the members often lost theirs, he gradually acquired a leverage quite out of proportion to his position.

Even so, when the bells of Venloo marked the beginning of a new year, he knew that despite his victories, he had failed to deal with the worrisome nettle that would torment his nation into the next century, and on New Year's Day 1951 he posed the dilemma to Maria and Johanna: 'What are we going to do about the Coloureds?'

The question was most perplexing. The Bantu were clearly black, with historic areas to which presumably they belonged: the Transkei of the Xhosa, Zululand, the lands of the Tswana and the Sotho. It wasn't really as neat and tidy as that, for there were millions of Bantu living loosely throughout the nation, but it was a definable problem that could be solved.

Since the Indians kept to their crowded ghettos, mainly in Natal, they, too, could be handled logically. 'Give them a shop, restrict them, and don't allow them too many liberties' was Detleef's prescription.

But the Coloureds—what to do about them? They were not of any one clear race—white-black-Malay-Indian-Hottentot—nor of any one religion, for many were Muslim. They had no specific terrain, for they lived everywhere. And they were certainly not primitives, for most of them had the intellectual and technical capacities of whites. But they were in a sense unidentified, unspecified, and as such they could be ignored.

They were needed. In every industry, jobs went unfilled because Coloureds were not allowed to take them. In every aspect of growth there was inhibition because Coloureds were forbidden to associate equally with whites. Constantly they were restricted to lower levels of achievement when obviously they had the capacity to do much better. In these years a marvelous opportunity was lost.

All nations make mistakes, terrible miscalculations which once adopted can rarely be amended. In England it was social categories that inhibited normal development in many areas, creating animosities that festered. In India it was rigid stratification of caste, descending even to untouchability. In Japan it was the persecution of the Eta and the denigrating of the Okinawan. And in America it was the blundering incapacity to deal with blacks. In South Africa the fearful miscalculation occurred in the 1920–1960 quadridecade when the white ruling classes could have reached out and embraced the Coloureds, welcoming them into a respected partnership.

Only by following the logic of Detleef and his two women on New Year's Day 1951 can one approximate an answer to this enigma of a nation's casting aside a major treasure. Detleef opened the conversation: 'It occurs to me that we are far from solving the big problem.'

'The Bantu?' Johanna asked. She was seventy-one now, no longer employed in Johannesburg, but nevertheless a major factor in Afrikaner women's circles. 'We know very well what to do with the Bantu. Treat them justly but keep them in their place.'

'I mean the Coloureds.'

'That is a problem,' Maria agreed, and she set the tone for the discussion: 'They are the children of sin, and God must despise them.'

'They are mongrels,' Johanna said, 'and I wish we could cleanse the nation of them as we did the Chinese. Remember that day, Detleef, when you saw the last Chinese go down the cog railway to Waterval-Onder. That was a wonderful day in our history.' Longingly she thought of this, then said briskly, 'In Cape Town the other day I walked about District Six. That could be made into one of the finest sections of Cape Town, but it's crowded with Coloureds. They must all be moved out.'

'To where, Johanna? Where?'

That line of discussion ended, but the three puritans were not finished with Maria's opening statement. 'They really are children of sin,' Detleef agreed. 'They're a rebuke to God-fearing Christians, a reminder of our fathers' transgressions.'

'Not our fathers,' Maria protested. 'It was sailors from the ships that stopped here.'

Detleef and his sister nodded. The existence of the Coloureds was an affront to them, and it was a blessing, the gathering felt, that the original Dutch and Huguenot settlers had not been involved. 'It was the sailors,' Detleef repeated, and as he thought of this blot on the nation he resolved to do something about it. Accordingly, when he returned to Cape Town and the session of Parliament, he labored far into the night, week after week, trying to devise some cauterization of this ugly moral wound.

When the year was well spent he discovered one area in which he could introduce reform, but it was so controversial that it would occupy major attention for five years. In 1910, when England had engineered Union between its colonies, two clauses in the enabling legislation were entrenched —that is, they were judged so vital that they could be altered only by a vote of two-thirds of the two Houses of Parliament sitting together. Section 137 protected English and Dutch (later Afrikaans) as languages of equal legal merit; Section 35 assured the Coloureds that they would always have the right to vote in Cape Province.

Although no Coloured men could stand for Parliament—that would be repugnant—they did vote on a common roll with the whites, casting their ballots for the white candidate who would best represent their interests. In 1948 more than fifty thousand had voted, almost all for Jan Smuts' party, and in seven crucial constituencies their vote defeated the Nationalists. They were a growing power, and the vote must be taken from them.

'They pollute the political process,' Detleef warned again and again. 'This is a white man's country, and to allow those damned Coloureds to vote dilutes our purity.' He located parliamentarians to bring onto the floor the bills he masterminded, but trouble ensued. 'It's that miserable Section 35,' he growled to his women. 'I'm afraid we can't muster a two-thirds vote.' He was right. When his men carried to the floor their bill stripping Coloureds of their voting rights, it failed to win the majority required, and it seemed as if the attempt was dead, at least for the 1951 session.

But Detleef was resourceful, and spurred by a suggestion thrown out by his sister, he convinced his supporters in Parliament to try a daring gambit: 'Because of changes in the laws governing the British Empire, Section 35 is no longer operative. We can pass our bill with only a simple majority.'

With excitement and joy his men did just that, and the Coloureds were disenfranchised. But the Appellate Division of the Supreme Court, sitting in Bloemfontein away from the pressures of the Cape, declared the new law unconstitutional, and 1951 ended with Coloureds still allowed to vote, a most offensive situation.

Detleef would not surrender, and his next move was downright ingenious. He did not dislike Coloureds personally; he knew some of excellent reputation and wished them well. But he was galled that these offspring of sin should have equal rights with white people, and now he came up with a master plan: 'Maria, I think I have it! We will supersede the Appellate Court!'

'I shouldn't think that would be possible. It's in the constitution.'

'We'll leave it there. What we'll do is establish Parliament itself as the "High Court of the Nation." If the two Houses, sitting together, approve a law which they themselves have passed—and it seems to me they always would, having just passed it—then it becomes law and the Appellate Court can say nothing in the matter.'

It was clean and simple. It passed Parliament quickly and the High Court, composed entirely of Nationalist members, reversed the decision of the nation's highest court of justice. With blazing speed the Coloureds were thrown off the common rolls, and with almost equal speed the Appellate Court annulled the whole process, pronouncing it a mockery. So 1952 ended in another defeat.

Elections in 1953 gave the government more Afrikaner seats in Parliament, so once more Detleef shepherded his bill toward a two-thirds majority, and once more he failed. At this point the average man would have quit, but Detleef was so offended by those who resisted his attempts to simplify matters that he barged ahead with still new devices. As he told Johanna and Maria after this third disappointment: 'The damned Coloureds don't seem to realize that we're doing this for their own good. It's our job as white men to study the nation and determine what's best for all, and then to pass the necessary laws.'

'They don't really need the vote,' Maria agreed. 'They can't possibly be interested in the things that concern us. They should fall back into place and be quiet.'

Johanna, feeling her life slipping away, was more bitter: 'Detleef, you must eliminate them from national life. Clear them out of the cities. Keep them off the work force. They're an affront to the nation, and if you don't keep trying to get rid of them, I'll be ashamed of you.'

'You speak as if you wanted us to ship them out, the way we did the Chinese.'

'I'd like that.'

'But don't you see, Johanna, there's no place to ship them. They have no homeland. They're the bastards of the world, and we're stuck with them.'

'Well, think of something!'

'I will. I promise you I will, but I must have time to plan.'

National attention was diverted from the Coloured question by 'Virtue Triumphant,' a rather florid statue that was placed in front of the government buildings in Pretoria. It had been carved by a promising young Afrikaner much influenced by Michelangelo and sculptors of the Quattrocento; it showed a woman of rather heroic proportions fending off lions, pythons and a politician who looked remarkably like Hoggenheimer. As with the work of many great sculptors, the woman was nude.

Many Afrikaner housewives, especially those from the Transvaal country districts, questioned the propriety of such a statue, and Johanna van Doorn, now seventy-four, came rushing down to the Cape, where Parliament was in session, to share her outrage with Detleef: 'It's immoral! There's no place in the Bible that condones naked women. St. Paul is emphatic that they must remain covered.'

'I think that refers to wearing hats in church,' Detleef said.

'If he could see this statue, he'd include it, believe me.'

She got nowhere with Detleef, but her feeling was so intense that Maria said, 'When we return to Pretoria, I must see this thing.'

'You won't like it,' Johanna predicted, and later, when the two women went to inspect the offending sculpture, Maria was even more incensed than her sister-in-law, and when she reached her rooms she penned a sharp letter to an Afrikaans newspaper:

All Afrikaner womankind is insulted by having such a statue in such a place. It is offensive to the spirit of the Bible and treats with contempt the noble traditions of our people. Women in Afrikaner statues should wear long dresses, like the ones shown in the Vrouemonument in Bloemfontein. For them to appear naked embarrasses not only all Afrikaner women, but also most of the men. The damage it does to children is incalculable. On behalf of all Afrikaner women, I demand that either the statue be taken down or that Virtue wear a dress.

Of course, the English-language press, always eager to embarrass its Afrikaner opposition, had a frolic with Mrs. van Doorn's proposals, and cartoons appeared showing Virtue wearing a Mother Hubbard, or a chain of fig leaves, or bending over to protect herself. One especially scurrilous cartoon depicted Oom Paul Kruger as this excellent statue, completely nude except for his top hat and one rather large oak leaf.

Foreign newspapers, ever on the alert for a story that would symbolize the curious happenings in South Africa, quoted Mrs. van Doorn's strictures about art, and when, under pressure, she gave an interview about the statue, editors had a joyous time:

'Ninety percent of Afrikaner women feel the way I do about that horrid statue. A few spineless art critics who defend it say that Michelangelo carved such statues for the prominent plazas in Italy. All I can say is that Michelangelo may be all right for Italians, who have a very low standard of morality, but he has no place in South Africa. Besides, what was this woman doing fighting a snake with no clothes on?'

She won her battle. The matter was resolved rather neatly—by converting 'Virtue Triumphant' into a man, who fought the same enemies naked but behind a shield that protected the sensibilities.

While his wife was defending the moral purity of the nation, Detleef was laboring yet again to save its political purity, and this time, with the help of some very able parliamentarians, he came up with a totally new stratagem, which he explained to the leadership in this way: 'No more struggling with minor problems. We take this thing head-on. We need a two-thirds majority in the Senate and can't get it. Simple. Create forty-one new senators guaranteed to vote our way. And if you're still afraid that the Supreme Court might overturn the vote these new men give us . . . Simple—add six more judges pledged to vote for us.'

It was, as he assured them, a simple solution, a steamroller so monstrous that any possible opposition would be crushed, and the government proceeded. It might have gone into effect without undue publicity except that a group of Afrikaner women with a social conscience united with a similar body of English women to activate a political-action committee called the Black Sash, as heroic a group as the world at that time knew. Against the full flood of national opinion, these women opposed every unlawful and restrictive measure of their government, never hysterically, never aimlessly.

They protected people who could find no other protection and kept a relentless spotlight on the irresponsible acts of their government.

Their president was a forceful woman, Laura Saltwood of New Sarum, the Johannesburg residence of this important industrial family. Born in Salisbury, near the cathedral, she had met Colonel Frank Saltwood's son Noel under memorable circumstances. As a resident of Salisbury she knew the local Saltwoods, of course, and did not like them; Sir Evelyn, a staunch conservative, made such an ass of himself in Parliament that she and her brother Wexton vowed they would run a liberal candidate against him when they were old enough. Her brother went to Cambridge University, a site she loved; whenever an opportunity presented, she went up to visit with him and his brilliant associates, and while on such a visit in 1931 she met a quiet young man from Oxford to whom she was much attracted. 'It's so nice to be with you, when the others talk so much and say so little,' she told him, and he blushed. He was Noel Saltwood, of the South African branch, and after a leisurely courtship in two of England's most enchanting towns, Cambridge and Oxford, they were married.

She had the good luck to reach Johannesburg while Maud Turner Saltwood was still alive, and from that stalwart woman, who had done so much to make South Africa habitable, she acquired the custom of direct speech and timely intervention. Like her mother-in-law, whom she revered, she was afraid of nothing: literally, she hunted lions with the same verve that she tracked down the latest restrictive laws of Detleef van Doorn. He despised her for the opposition she continually mounted against his best projects, and as for her Black Sash, he believed it should be outlawed and its members thrown into jail. He would look into this possibility after he settled with the Coloureds.

For the present he fenced with Mrs. Saltwood, who had accurately identified him as a major force behind the previous legislation and the current effort to strip the Coloureds of their vote. She spoke at meetings, gave interviews, appeared on radio whenever possible, and maintained a constant scrutiny. She was such an effective opponent, that at one strategy session held in Detleef's Pretoria home, Johanna wanted to know why a woman like that should be allowed free speech. That was a relevant question, for which Detleef had a quick answer: 'Because this country is not a dictatorship. Your husband, Johanna, had dangerous ideas, about Hitler and all that, but men like Brongersma and me drew back. We did not want Hitler then, and we don't want him now.'

Johanna began to cry, thinking that her dead husband's martyrdom was being denigrated, but Detleef consoled her: 'We're aiming at the same goals, really, but by legal means. We will perform no un-Christian act, but in the end we'll have a regulated society. Almost exactly what Piet and I talked about years ago.'

In 1956 Detleef van Doorn engineered one more assault on the Coloureds, and this time, with a vastly enlarged Senate and a Supreme Court more than doubled, the law was passed by Parliament and certified by the Court, but Detleef's sense of triumph, to which he was entitled, was diminished by the severe illness of his sister. He was with her when she heard the joyous news that Coloureds were to be thrown off the common roll, first step in their total disfranchisement: 'It is our duty, Detleef, to make decisions. We must see that they are just, but we must also see that they are enforced strictly so that we retain control. I wish our father and mother could have seen this day.' She passed into a mumbling period, then called for Maria: 'Detleef lacks will power. When the time comes, he won't want to fight to take South Africa out of the Commonwealth. Pressure him, Maria. We must be free.' And she died, never for a moment perceiving that Coloureds and blacks might also want to be free.

In the sad wake of his sister's death Detleef worked diligently on the next chain of laws which would bind the nation together. Only whites could attend the great universities. Bantu education was severely revised, taking it away from religious organizations and missionaries and placing it under the control of politicians: 'Blacks must not be troubled with subjects which they have not the brain power to comprehend, or trained for jobs which will never exist for them. They should be taught only those skills needed to enable them to support the dominant society. Instruction should be in Afrikaans, since that is to be the language of the nation of which they will form a helpful part.'

He then directed his attention to living areas, for it angered him to see attractive spots in the big cities still occupied by Bantu. In sweeping regulations, which he drafted but which appeared over the signature of others, he authorized the evacuation of such areas and gave special attention to one particular eyesore in Johannesburg—Sophiatown—where he called in the bulldozers to start leveling the place; the black occupants were sent out into locations he had set up in the countryside. These blacks, all of whom worked for white families and establishments in Johannesburg, joined the masses of workers herded together southwest of the City of Gold. High-speed railway lines soon carried nearly half a million black servants into the city at dawn, out to the countryside at dusk.

In 1957 Detleef played no part in two major decisions, but he supported the men who made them: 'God Save the Queen' was dropped as the national anthem, to be replaced by 'Die Stem van Suid-Afrika,' a fine, stirring song; and the Union Jack no longer flew as a national flag. Maria was especially gratified by these changes, for they proved to her and others that the country was at last becoming the Afrikaner republic it should always have been: 'The bad years since 1795, when the English first intruded, are almost over. I was just a little ashamed of myself for cheering when Jan Christian Smuts died, but I was glad to see him go. He betrayed the Afrikaner, and it was only just that he should have died rejected by his own people.'

And then the euphoria of the Van Doorns was shattered by an act they could not comprehend. Their son Marius, an excellent rugby player at Stellenbosch, with every promise of graduating to Springbok status, was selected to be a Rhodes scholar and offered a sumptuous grant of money to study at Oxford.

'It's reassuring to know he was eligible,' Detleef told his friends in Parliament. 'He's one of the best.'

'Will he accept?'

'Certainly not. There's talk of his being selected for the next tour of New Zealand.'

'A Springbok?' the men asked excitedly.

One man who followed sports avidly broke in: 'Detleef's too modest. I've heard rumors that they might choose Marius to captain the side.'

'Well,' the father said deprecatingly, 'he'd be a little young for that. Those New Zealanders . . .' And the rest of that day was spent reminiscing about the 1921 tour and the way Detleef had handled, or not handled, Tom Heeney, the Hard Rock from Down Under.

Maria was pleased that her son should have received such recognition from the Rhodes committee, but like her husband, she said she would be offended if he showed any signs of accepting: 'We don't need a son of ours going to Oxford . . . like some Saltwood with divided loyalty . . . living here and calling Salisbury home.'

Both the Van Doorns wrote to Marius that night, congratulating him on the honor, but telling him also that they had heard whispers of his becoming a Springbok, perhaps even the captain, but before their letters could be delivered, he appeared in Cape Town to inform them that he had accepted the scholarship and would be leaving soon for England.

Detleef was so shocked he could hardly speak: 'You're not . . . passing up a Springbok blazer . . . for a Rhodes scholarship?' When Marius nodded, Detleef cried, 'But, son! A scholarship comes every day. To be a rugger Springbok, that comes once in a lifetime.'

Marius was firm. He was twenty-one, taller than his father, and without the bull neck. He played not as a rugged forward in the scrum but as a fleet, elusive back. His intellectual brilliance, inherited mostly from his maternal grandfather, Christoffel Steyn, shone in his face, and he could not mask his delight at going to Oxford and competing with the best.

'But, Marius,' his father pleaded. 'You can learn things out of books anywhere, but if you have a real chance to captain a Springbok side—that would be immortality.'

'There's more to life than rugby,' the young man said.

'What?' Detleef demanded. 'I've done many things in my life. Seen the camps. Had the prize bull at the Rand Agricultural. Fought with De Groot and Christoffel. And watched the triumph of my people. But nothing comes close to stepping on a rugby field in New Zealand wearing the Springbok jersey. For God's sake, Marius, don't throw away that opportunity for something Cecil Rhodes devised as a trick to seduce our Afrikaner lads.'

'I can still play rugby. I'll play for Oxford.'

'You'll what?' Detleef looked at his wife in blank stupor.

'Did you say you'd play for Oxford?' Maria asked.

'Yes, if I can make the team.'

'A man who could be a Springbok . . . playing for Oxford?' Detleef choked a bit, then said, 'You realize that the way things fall, you could one day be playing against South Africa?'

'It's only a game.'

Detleef rose to his full choleric height: 'It is not a game. It's how we instilled patriotism in this nation. I would rather be captain of a Springbok team in New Zealand than prime minister.'

No argument could dissuade Marius, and when, three years later, he informed his parents by cable that he was going to marry an English girl, they wept for two days.

The marriage of Marius van Doorn, Oriel athlete and scholar, to Clare Howard was solemnized on 20 March 1960 at the home of her parents in a village northwest of Oxford. His parents were not present, for although they had been invited, they refused to set foot on English soil, and this accounted for the fact that they were at home in Pretoria the next day when South Africa was torn nearly apart by a fusillade of police bullets at Sharpeville, a black township near the Vaal River.

For the past year black indignation had swelled against the laws that placed increasingly severe restrictions on black freedoms: Albert Luthuli, soon to win the Nobel Peace Prize, had been confined to his home district for five years; African women marching in demonstrations had been baton-charged; in the Transkei and Zululand, uprisings had left dozens dead and injured.

At Sharpeville the blacks decided to try peaceful protest: they would turn in their passbooks and offer themselves for arrest, holding it to be an insult to carry such identification in their own country; some ten thousand converged on the police station. Without a warning shot to turn them back, the front line of police opened fire on the crowd. Sixty-seven were left dead and more than one hundred and eighty men, women and children were wounded.

'It was inevitable,' Detleef said when he heard the news. 'We do what is right for the country and they refuse to cooperate.' When he heard that blacks were massing in various other cities, he told Maria that any uprising must be stamped on without mercy. He was not a vicious man, but he did believe in order, and when Parliament, after due deliberation, decided that the country should be organized a certain way, it was everyone's duty to conform: 'You cannot have Bantu deciding whether they will obey the laws or not obey them. The laws have been passed. They must be obeyed.' It was his opinion that white agitators, especially women like Laura Saltwood, were responsible for these disturbances, and he began pondering ways whereby people like her could be restrained.

Detleef was sixty-five and considering retirement, but the chain of dramatic events in 1960 convinced him that his lasting achievements still lay ahead. Not long after Sharpeville a maniac, overwrought by the anxieties thrust upon him by recent changes in national life, fired a revolver point-blank into Prime Minister Verwoerd's head. Miraculously, that brilliant political leader survived, and this, said the Van Doorns, proved that God wanted him preserved for noble tasks. In October, Verwoerd accomplished one of them: he engineered a plebiscite which authorized the government to break all relations with the English crown and declare itself a republic.

With enormous vigor Detleef and his wife had worked at erasing all vestiges of what they termed 'a century of English domination.' Earlier, a series of modest changes had been made—no more knighthoods like Sir Richard Saltwood's; Jan van Riebeeck's face on coinage instead of king or queen; *lieutenant* changed to *veldkornet*—but now Detleef moved among his colleagues pressuring them for the most important change of all.

'We must eliminate the last remnant of past degradations,' he preached. 'We must leave the British Commonwealth of Nations, for it's only an English stratagem to keep us subservient.'

Many who heard him say this were aghast that he should carry his obsession so far: 'When we voted to break ties with the monarchy, we certainly did not intend to leave the Commonwealth.' To such objections he had a rigid answer: 'When you start on an honorable course, pursue it to the end. Our end is complete freedom.' And when he came home at night to discuss these matters with his wife, she supported him: 'They shot my father. They killed my people in the camp. We must end every association.'

In March 1961, when the Van Doorns were at Vrymeer, the glorious news arrived. An assistant at Pretoria telephoned: 'Sir! Sir! We're free at last. Verwoerd has taken us out of the Commonwealth!'

Detleef was cautious, so before he shared the triumph with Maria he made two calls to confirm the news, and when he was satisfied that his country was at last free, he did not run exultantly to his wife or start a celebration. Instead, he left the house and walked gravely to the largest lake, where blesbok were grazing, and he looked across to where the hartebeest hut of General de Groot had stood in the bad years following the end of war, and he could hear the old warrior predicting: 'You are the generation that will win this country back. You will win the war that your father and I lost.'

Raising his fist, as he had done years ago when celebrating a rugby victory, he shouted, 'Old man! We've won! We've won!'

Detleef was retired now, with no office in either Cape Town or Pretoria to report to, and he might have rested, for the laws he had sponsored had specified proper behavior for all residents of the republic, but sloth was alien to his puritanical nature, and he began to fret over another mammoth task which he felt needed to be done: 'I could die happy, Maria, knowing that we have our great file in Pretoria showing everyone's proper racial classification. The green identity cards are good, too. But what we really need is an identification document covering a person's entire life—everything he does. He'd carry it with him at all times, so that the authorities could see exactly who he was and what he's done.'

The small booklet he devised, 4 ¾ x 3 ½ inches, was a masterpiece of sound planning. It contained forty-eight pages—which summarized a life and provided in one convenient place all kinds of helpful data. Long coded numbers indicated racial derivation, status and domicile. Space was provided for a series of photographs covering different ages and styles. Four pages were given to marriage records, with the printed assurance that if the holder was embarrassed by a proliferation of divorces, she or he could apply for a new booklet and start fresh. Included was a complete record of immunizations, allergies, blood group and any other medical information that might prove helpful to an ambulance attendant or a hospital nurse. It was also a driver's license, reserving pages 18 through 21 for police endorsements as to arrests; it was also a license to carry firearms, with four full pages to record weapons. Pages 26 through 46 were marked 'For official use,' without any clue as to purpose, but available for insertion of whatever information the authorities might in the future wish to include. The last two pages contained a voting record, and a pocket at the rear was to hold a list of all real estate owned.

Every white citizen, under Detleef's plan, was obliged to carry this document at all times. 'Now we will know who everyone is,' he said, 'and we can have an orderly state.'

He was congratulating himself one afternoon when Reverend Brongersma, white-haired and failing, stopped by to pass the time of day. He no longer preached, but he did try to follow the activities of the Broederbond; along with the church, that fellowship had been the high point of his life: 'I often think back to the vigorous days, Detleef. You and Frykenius, me and Piet Krause. That was a lively foursome. We accomplished so much.'

Then he said, almost abruptly, 'Call Maria. I want to see the girl whose life I saved.' And when stout, squat Maria came into the room, he rose and kissed her. 'I rode all the way to Stellenbosch to tell this young fellow he had to marry you, and this fine Christian home resulted. I wish I could have visited Marius before he married that English girl. Now he can never join the Broederbond . . . never play a major role in our society.'

That was regrettable. He talked of Piet, too, then said something which disturbed Detleef profoundly: 'Piet was a radical on the left, and he destroyed himself. You were a radical on the right, and you've destroyed many of our freedoms.'

'What do you mean?'

'Detleef has worked only for good,' Maria said defensively.

'I'm sure he has,' the old man said, 'but I fear he got things out of balance. The fellowship of Christ is meant to bring freedom, not restraint.'

'But society has to be disciplined,' Detleef protested. 'You know that.'

'I do. But if we read the Old Testament too grimly, we miss the love-making, the adventure, the wild triumphs, the dancing and the sound of flutes.' He shook his head. 'I was to blame, too. I sought a new world so forcefully I forgot the goodness in all worlds. Do you know my favorite verse in all the Bible, now that I approach death? "Word wakker, word wakker, Debora: Word wakker, word wakker, hef 'n lied aan." *Deborah, sing us a song!* You have killed the singing, Detleef.'

When he left, Maria said, 'Poor old man, his mind's wandering.'

A few moments later men rushed into the house, shouting, 'The prime minister's been assassinated!'

The Van Doorns, trembling, rushed to the radio. Detleef tuned it so nervously that he could not locate a station, so Maria took over and found the awful verification: 'Today as he was attending his duties in the House of Parliament, our prime minister, Hendrik Verwoerd, was stabbed to death by an assassin who approached him in the guise of a uniformed pageboy. Three knife wounds entered the throat and chest and he died before he could reach the hospital.'

In darkness the Van Doorns sat silent, contemplating the nemesis that seemed at times to hang over their nation: a splendid patriot assassinated in the halls of government; foreigners making accusatory speeches at the United Nations; blacks obstinately refusing to accept their assigned positions; and Marius married to an English girl.

In the days that followed, Detleef's tightly organized world seemed to fall apart, because the very laws which he had structured to defend the state had been used to destroy its elected leader. 'It seems as if God Himself willed this tragedy,' Detleef wailed, and in mounting fury he shared the evidence with his wife.

'Who killed him? A man who should never have been allowed entrance into the country. A nobody from Moçambique.'

'How did he sneak in?' Maria demanded, voicing the anger of two and a half million Afrikaners.

'You won't believe it, but four people I trained myself—immigration officials who were supposed to check all entering aliens. The man had a criminal record. It was in his papers and no one saw it.'

'But how could such a man get a job as messenger, right in the heart of Parliament?'

Detleef shuddered. 'His papers specifically stated that he was half-white, half-black. Everyone in Moçambique knew it. Our embassy knew it. But what happens? He walks in here bold as brass, and my office gives him an identity card stating that he was white. After that, everything was easy.'

'But why did he want to kill our prime minister?'

Van Doorn lowered his head and covered his eyes. He did not want to answer this ugly question, but in a weak voice he confided: 'He said he became bitter over the fact that as a man with a white card, he was forbidden to have sexual relations with a Coloured girl he liked.'

In a sullen rage Detleef stormed about the kitchen in which his early lessons had been learned. He could hear the voice of old General de Groot, who had never stopped fighting. He listened to Piet Krause, who had such a clear vision of the future. And from the corner came the powerful voice of his sister Johanna, who had been the backbone of the family and of the nation. He was embittered by the sardonic trick whereby his own laws had been used against him, but he could find nothing wrong with those laws.

'What we must do,' he told his wife, 'is pass stricter laws. And then enforce them better.'

XIII.
Apartheid

THE complex fabric of old custom and new law woven by Detleef van Doorn and his peers came to be known as *apartheid,* a classic example of the misfortune Afrikaners had in naming things. The word meant *apartness,* and did not appear in older dictionaries of the language; it was invented, and reflected their belief that God willed the races be kept separate, each progressing properly at its own speed within its own confines.

The word should have been pronounced *apart-hate,* appropriately ominous, but by foreigners it was usually *apart-hite,* which is merely ugly. Either pronunciation was unfortunate, for it connoted offensive intentions which its authors did not contemplate.

As the years progressed, so did the names used to describe apartheid: *guardianship, separate development, separate freedoms, separate amenities, indigenous development, multinational development, self-determination, plural democracy.* No matter how diligently they tried, the architects of these laws were unable to erase the first, correct name they had given their grand design.

No one could study the instrumental role played by Van Doorn in drafting these laws without being impressed by the planner's oft-repeated assertion: 'I acted from the best and most honest motives, and without personal rancor, in accordance with His will.'

He certainly wished no harm to the Coloureds, Asians and blacks whose lives he circumscribed; he often said, 'Some of my best friends are the Bantu who work on my farm,' and although it was true that he had always refused to alter the conditions under which they worked, he did constantly examine his Christian conscience when deciding what was right and wrong for them. Often he paid them higher wages than they might have got elsewhere. He insisted that he did not regard them as inherently inferior human beings, only different; he did not want to dominate them, only act as their well-intentioned guardian.

But even honest intentions sometimes create problems which the promulgator of a law could not have foreseen; apartheid became so pervasive that it dominated the lives of ordinary people from birth to death to resurrection.

AT BIRTH

The Afrikaner was never afraid to fly against the winds of history, and usually with success. Other nations had learned to utilize, and sometimes condone, the mixture of their races, with enviable results. No more beautiful people exist in the world than the languorous, able Chinese-Polynesians of the South Seas. The black-white mixture in Brazil produces offspring of extraordinary quality, while the Japanese-white children of Hawaii are exceptional in both talent and appearance. The Indian-Spanish mix in Mexico is a good one, and so is the Indian-black in Trinidad.

The Afrikaner saw the hand of God in the creation of his small nation, and was determined to isolate it from admixtures that would dilute its purity. Indeed, it was difficult to find a more homogeneous, handsome and dedicated body of people than those Afrikaners nurtured on the veld and in the valleys of the continent's southern tip. Of course, the pure Dutch strain had been infused with contributions from the gifted Huguenots who filtered in, never many in number, and with heavier contributions from the Germans, who at times actually outnumbered the Dutch. But these were peoples of roughly the same physical and mental inheritance. Additions from the English were inescapable; they came to form a large part of the white community. And it would have been impossible for the Afrikaner not to draw, too, from the Hottentot, the black and the Coloured. In pioneer days he acknowledged this, but his descendants were determined to prevent any further penetration of their white laager.

His jealous guarding of blood purity did exact a social cost, for the Coloured peoples that had arisen, here as elsewhere in the world, had to be savagely excluded from national life. Not only were they forbidden to intermingle with whites socially; they were also cut off economically, professionally, creatively, until the loss to the nation was incalculable. How much poorer the United States would have been without the contributions of persons whose light skins would cause them to be classified as Coloured in South Africa: Frederick Douglass, Ralph Bunche, Martin Luther King, O. J. Simpson, Harry Belafonte, Lena Horne, Diahann Carroll, Senator Brooke and Congressman Powell. Or how the world's creative pool would have been diminished without the work of Coloureds such as the poet Pushkin, the painter Pissaro, and the flamboyant storyteller Dumas.

South Africa silenced in the cradle all such potential contributions from its Malay-Hottentot-black-Afrikaner-English-Coloureds, and its loss was never greater than when it rejected young Heather Botha, twenty-three years old and of such a mixture. She was exotic, like a palm tree bending beside a lagoon, or a tawny pearl held in a Balinese hand. She combined the most attractive features of all the wanderers who had figured in her background: the fiery-tempered Malay slave woman who had fought her Compagnie master for nine years, then slept with his son for eleven; the Dutch sea captain who had fought storms in too many seas to give a damn about what Compagnie officials said regarding fraternization with girls of mixed breed; the Hottentot herdsman who had protected with a gun the forty-seven cattle he owned, plus the fifty-seven stolen from Compagnie herds; the black warrior who had defended himself against both Zulu and white man; the fair-faced English officer, India-bound, whispering love to a young Coloured maiden beside a brook on the slopes of Table Mountain. Heather was the child of lusty forebears, and all of them would have been proud of her, for as she said on various occasions, echoing her Dutch sea-captain ancestor, 'I don't give a damn.'

At the university in 1953 she had openly dated white men, despite warnings from the faculty that she might fall into danger and from the police that such action was criminal. It would have been difficult for her to refuse the numerous invitations she received from white students, for she was a spectacular young woman and one of the liveliest on campus. She had a rowdy laugh, a provocative manner of walking, and a smile which showed white teeth against a golden complexion.

But she was condemned. At birth she had been classified Coloured, which meant that for the remainder of her life this would be her outstanding characteristic, outweighing her intelligence, her beauty and her capacity to contribute to society. Where she lived, the quality of her early education, what job she could hold, whom she could fall in love with, and the role she could play in South African life were all sharply proscribed. Everyone in the nation would know Heather's limits, everyone, that is, except Heather.

At twenty the police arrested the young student for 'inciting white men to have interracial carnal intercourse or to commit an act of indecency,' and rarely was a miscegenation charge more correct—she certainly was tempting, to white men or those of any other color—or more fallacious, for it was not she who did the tempting; it was the men. On that charge she was given three months in prison, suspended on condition that the tempting cease. She was warned that if she was again brought before a magistrate on a charge of immorality, she would suffer the consequences.

'I don't give a damn,' she told her fellow students after the trial, and continued to behave with an insolence that was charming to those who knew her, insulting to those who merely watched. She went where she wished in Cape Town, ate wherever her crowd stopped for food, and when late October came around she frequented the beaches reserved for whites, where her striking figure, her sun-tanned skin and her lively manner gained attention, if not always approval. Twice white sunbathers warned her that in using beaches legally reserved for their group, she was breaking the law. She tossed her head and smiled at them.

At Christmas vacation, which marked the height of the summer season, Heather was sunning herself at a white beach when Craig Saltwood, aged twenty, came home from Oriel College at Oxford for a visit with his family, and it was not remarkable that he met her. They talked about college classes, and of recent developments in South Africa. He poured warm sand upon her legs, then gallantly brushed it off, one grain at a time. She told him to be careful where his fingers went, and soon they were kissing in hidden corners where the police would not see them, and on the third afternoon young Saltwood drove her home in his Morris Minor.

He was delighted with her parents. Simon Botha was a skilled builder, head of his own construction company. His wife, Deborah, was a quiet homemaker who took pride in caring for Simon and their three children, of whom Heather was the oldest. Mrs. Botha was often to be found in the kitchen of their home in Athlone making the boboties and sweet confections her family had always prepared with elegance. Like her daughter, she had a glowing complexion, but unlike her, she was shy.

'I often worry about Heather,' she said softly. 'Going to the white beach. She's bound to get into trouble.'

'I'm not trouble,' Craig said.

'For my daughter you are,' Mrs. Botha replied.

Then Mr. Botha talked about the letting of recent contracts to build houses in a new township, and of how white officials discriminated against Coloured artisans, awarding large constructions to certain white builders who really lacked expertise and experience. 'They won't let me build those new boxes, yet when one of the great old houses like Trianon needs attention, they call me.' He laughed. 'Then it's "Botha, can you fix that gable in the old way?" Or "Botha, we want to restore that barn built when Jan Compagnie was here. We've got to protect our cultural heritage." And who protects it? I do.'

There was much laughter in the Botha home, and many books and quite a few records by Wilhelm Fürtwangler and Arturo Toscanini, plus a shelf of His Master's Voice operas. The Bothas spoke English, but were at ease in Afrikaans, and on Sundays they worshipped at the Dutch Reformed church (Coloured) where Simon and Deborah had been married and their children confirmed.

The Korean War had just ended, and Simon spoke proudly of the South African fighter planes in the Far East, but he could not mask his disappointment when reflecting on his own four-year service during World War II. 'Jan Smuts came personally to thank our Coloured unit when it was over, and I can still see the Oubaas standing not ten feet from me, telling us we were needed back home to build a new South Africa. "God bless you all," he said. "May you prosper in peace even more than you did in these years of conflict." Fifty thousand men like me fought against Hitler. For freedom, they said. But when we got home, Smuts forgot every promise he made, and now they're even trying to take away our right to vote.'

When Heather saw how sympathetically Craig participated with her family, her response was so warm that all suspected that she might be spending the next nights with him in the Sea Point boardinghouse he was using for his vacation, but on the second night a suspicious woman in a room opposite telephoned the police to warn them that a crime was being committed in Room 318. The case was handed to two policemen, a sergeant fifty-five years old who was revolted by such duty, and a gung-ho young fellow of twenty-two from a country district who was greatly excited by the prospect of bursting into rooms where nude couples were in bed. At four-fifteen one morning, having kept the premises under observation for several nights, they crashed their way into the room, took photographs, and arrested the naked couple, the older policeman blushing with shame.

'The sheets! Don't forget the sheets!' cried the younger man as he watched Heather while she dressed, and the sergeant was forced to strip the bed and wrap the sheets in a bundle. The investigators would send the linen to a medical research institute, where highly paid technicians using ultra-modern equipment would ascertain scientifically whether miscegenation had truly occurred.

'I'm sorry for this,' the older policeman apologized as he led the lovers down the corridor and past a doorway in which a triumphant woman demonstrated her pride in having served as guardian of her nation's morals.

'You pitiful creature,' Heather said to the watchdog, and this 'act of arrogance and spite against a decent citizen' was cited against her at the trial.

'Insolent and unrepentant, even though guilty of a major crime,' the magistrate thundered at her, after which he delivered a sentence standard in these cases: 'Craig Saltwood, you come of a good family and have a respectable university record. You have clearly been influenced by alien ideas in England, and your behavior is a disgrace. The example set by you and other white men of your ilk cannot but be seen as shocking in the eyes of decent Coloured people, whose daughters must be protected against such liaisons. Three months, sentence suspended for three years' good behavior.' The magistrate glowered. 'But if you ever again consort with any woman outside your own race, you will go to jail.'

He studied Heather for a moment, balefully, then said, 'You have chosen to ignore the warning I issued at your previous appearance. I have pity for what your parents must feel as a result of this disgraceful act. But the court has no alternative. Prison, three months.'

It was assumed that the white man, feeling the sting of censure from his society, would slink off and keep his mouth shut. But Craig Saltwood was so outraged by the gross unfairness of Heather's sentence that instead of hurrying back to Oxford and forgetting his vacation escapade, he phoned his mother and asked her, 'Will you help correct a grave injustice?'

'I would like nothing better,' Laura Saltwood said.

She had already battled, with little success, for the rights of black and Coloured ex-servicemen and was appalled by the injustices that were being perpetrated under the new laws promulgated by the Nationalists since their 1948 victory. When Craig explained how he had been excused and Heather thrown into jail, she was outraged.

'Clear up one thing, Craig. Is she a prostitute?'

'Hell no! She didn't entice me, like the court said. I chased her.'

'You visited her home?'

'Had dinner with her parents. As I would with any girl I liked.'

'Isn't her father Simon Botha, who restores the old Cape Dutch houses?'

'He is.'

That was all Laura Saltwood needed. Convening the small group of women who had joined her in her efforts to protect the rights of ex-service-men, she laid the facts before them, and they were disgusted, but when she suggested ventilating the story in the newspapers, a Mrs. van Rensburg asked her if she thought this prudent: 'Hasn't your son suffered enough publicity?'

'We Saltwoods have never worried much about that,' Laura said, and she hurried to Cape Town, where she poured out her anger to the *Argus* and the *Times*. She visited Heather's parents and told them to be of good courage, but she also advised them that if her fight to get this infamous sentence revoked was successful, Heather should leave the country.

'And go where?' Deborah Botha asked sadly.

'Canada. There they behave like human beings.'

She also visited Heather in jail, ignoring the snide remarks the authorities threw at her when she sought permission. She found Heather to be the kind of young woman a mother hopes her son will meet—attractive, strong and with a robust sense of humor. 'We'll get you out of here, Heather.'

'In three months,' the girl joked.

'I mean out of the country. You must get leave.'

'I like it here.'

'You have no future in South Africa. Elsewhere you could lead a normal life.'

'I lead a pretty normal one here.'

'In a prison cell? For loving a young man? Don't be a fool.'

Heather had only a week to ponder this advice. In that time Craig Saltwood returned to Oxford, and his mother sought out the one person she thought would listen to her, Detleef van Doorn, chairman of the Committee on Racial Affairs, architect of the new laws. He did listen to her, attentively, then patiently explained that white South Africa had to protect its racial purity against the hordes that were trying to destroy it: 'Heather Botha's sentence is appropriate to the grave damage she might have done if she gave birth to yet another Coloured child.'

'What about my son's crime?'

'She tempted him,' and he cited several instances from the Bible in which honest young Israelites were tempted by the daughters of Canaan, and when Mrs. Saltwood smiled indulgently, he reached in his desk and produced an English Bible, which contained many paper markers. Searching for the applicable one, he opened to Genesis 28:1, which he read in sonorous English: ' "Thou shalt not take a wife of the daughters of Canaan." ' Closing the Bible triumphantly, he stared at Mrs. Saltwood.

'He did not, so far as I know, intend taking Miss Botha as his wife.'

Van Doorn, like any proper puritan, was incensed by this flippancy, but after a moment's silence, he said quietly, 'Mrs. Saltwood, if you continue along the path you've chosen, you'll find yourself in great difficulty.'

'No,' she said evenly, 'I shall find myself raising merry hell wherever I can about Heather Botha's disgraceful sentencing.' Laura was a resolute woman who feared nothing, who intended her closing years to be meaningful. The contributions of her family to this nation had not been minimal, and she did not propose surrendering her moral positions to the judgment of Afrikaner Nationalists, whom she considered excessively bigoted.

Van Doorn, looking at her determined face thrust forward toward his, could imagine that he was confronting Hilary Saltwood, that first and worst of the difficult clan. Whenever the trekboers tangled with that demented missionary, they had come away scarred, and Detleef suspected that in any open contest with Laura Saltwood, he would be scarred too.

'I'll talk to the proper authorities about commuting her sentence,' he said.

'As of today?'

'I can't speak for others.' Then he dropped his voice and pleaded with his difficult visitor: 'Could we keep this a secret between the two of us?'

'We certainly shall. Detleef, I knew you were a man of common sense.'

'No, I'm a poor Boer, madam, incapable of combating you bedonderde Saltwoods.'

Heather was set free, and six months later, on a visit to Cape Town, Laura found the young woman packing. 'I'm off to Canada,' the girl said happily, and she kissed Laura for having shown her how a free woman should behave.

She took up residence in the best of Canadian cities, Toronto, where her style and beauty attracted people of diverse qualities, including several young men captivated by her exotic appearance and spirited wit. Friends helped her locate a job as secretary to a firm with overseas connections, where her facility with languages proved an asset.

In Toronto she was prized for those qualities which at home had made her a criminal: a saucy indifference to outworn custom and an infectious acceptance of people, whatever their station. She was free to contribute to Canadian life to the extent of her capabilities, but she never became pompous or pontifical. When well-meaning travelers tried to inform her about current happenings in South Africa, she smiled graciously and said, 'I no longer give a damn what those poor sick people do to themselves down there.'

But she did care, for she never threw away a small green plastic identity card which proved she had been a South African citizen. In red letters it also informed the world that she was COLOURED-KLEURLING.

Heather Botha married a young Canadian lawyer, had three fine children and became a patron of the musical arts in Toronto. She kept the plastic card at the bottom of a drawer in her bedroom as a sober reminder of the prison from which she had escaped.

AT SCHOOL

At Venloo there developed alongside the school founded after the Anglo-Boer War by Mr. Amberson, the rugby player, a girls' school with a notable reputation for producing excellent Afrikaans-speaking graduates who did well at university. It had a patriotic tradition of which its students and teachers were proud. Said the principal, Roelf Sterk, 'My grandfather started this school in a cattle shed back in 1913, when our people were in the years of their suffering. He had no money and his scholars had none, either, but he gathered girls from the neighborhood and told them, "We will not be able to build a free nation in which Afrikaners can live in dignity unless you future mothers master the skills practiced by the English. You must learn to figure and write and reason. You must study." I now tell you the same thing. We've won our rightful place in the government of this land, but to keep ahead of those English, we must study as never before.'

He was especially proud of the way in which two girls in Standard Two took his lectures to heart. Petra Albertyn, aged nine, and Minna van Valck, aged ten, were the kind of students teachers pray for. They were eager and attentive; they behaved themselves without being subdued; they did well in classes requiring memory, but just as well in singing and drawing; and in whatever good thing was afoot, they could be depended upon to take the lead. In addition, as if God sometimes gave certain chosen persons too much, each child was unusually attractive—Petra a handsome dark-haired girl, and Minna a striking blonde with classic Dutch features.

It was arithmetic that started the trouble. Minna, being older than Petra, excelled in most branches of study, which in no way distressed the latter, who told her parents, 'I love Minna. She's so sweet and kind.' But in arithmetic little Petra had uncanny skill; she was really quite brilliant, and her teacher, a woman from Pretoria University who recognized brains when she viewed them in action, reported: 'This girl is a precious little genius.' Obviously, she received highest marks, well ahead of her friend Minna.

This did not disturb Minna, for she told her mother, 'I don't like numbers anyway, and I'm not very good at them.'

'But you allowed Petra to excel,' Mrs. van Valck complained with some irritation. 'Have you no pride?'

'I beat her in everything else!' Minna exclaimed, but her mother suspected that something might have gone amiss at the school, and she was determined to ascertain whether or not her brilliant daughter had been improperly treated. Accordingly, she marched to the school and demanded to see the principal.

Roelf Sterk was accustomed to meeting distraught parents; in fact, he rather liked it when they thought enough of their daughters' progress to interrogate him, but he was not prepared for the harshness with which Mrs. van Valck assailed him: 'I'm convinced that Minna must have done better than this Petra, whoever she is, because I myself corrected her exercise book every night.'

'You mean, you helped her?'

'I did not say that. I said that when her work was done I checked it to be sure she understood the problems. And she never had an incorrect solution.'

'That's why she received such a high mark,' the principal explained.

'But this Petra received a higher. My daughter was penalized . . .'

'Mrs. van Valck,' the principal explained patiently, 'in Petra Albertyn we have a near-genius in arithmetic. She's extraordinary. There's no way your daughter could equal her in this one field. Remember, Mrs. van Valck, Minna got highest in all her other subjects . . .'

Mrs. van Valck was still not satisfied and demanded to see who this superior child was, so Dr. Sterk consented, hoping in this way to defuse the mother's suspicions. Since Petra, like many of the scholars in this school, lived in a town many miles away, she stayed in a dormitory, which differentiated her from other children like Minna, who stayed at home, and this aroused Mrs. van Valck's suspicions: 'Who is she? Why does she come so far to school?'

Patiently Dr. Sterk explained that more than two-thirds of his best students came from considerable distances: 'It was the same in my grandfather's day. Most of those first scholars who earned this school its reputation, well, they came here by wagon in January and never returned home till June.'

The simplest way for Mrs. van Valck to see what was happening in the school was for her to peek in the door of the classroom, but when she reached that spot from which this would have been possible, Dr. Sterk pushed open the door, interrupted the class, and announced: 'This is Minna's mother.' The students rose and bowed, whereupon Dr. Sterk pointed to a girl in the first row, saying, 'And this is Minna's good friend, Petra Albertyn.'

Later, when he testified before the Race Classification Board, he would recall: 'When Mrs. van Valck first saw Petra Albertyn her jaw dropped and she froze. I noticed it at the time but could think of no reason for this strange behavior.'

That morning in the classroom she said nothing, just stared at Petra, then hastened from the school, going straight to the magistrate's court, where she swept past clerks, burst into his room, and dropped into a chair. 'Leopold,' she said, 'there's a Coloured girl in Minna's school.'

'Not likely,' her husband, the magistrate of Venloo, said.

'Leopold, I saw her. Not ten minutes ago. If that girl isn't a Hot-not, I'm not a Potgieter.' She used her maiden name, one of the most revered in Afrikaner history, as verification of her own pure lineage.

'Mother,' her husband said quietly, 'Dr. Sterk does not allow Coloureds into his school. The law forbids it. Parents have to show their white I.D. cards before any child is accepted. Sterk and all his teachers are most circumspect in such matters. Now you go—'

'Leopold! This Coloured girl has become Minna's closest friend. Minna wanted to bring her to sleep in our home last week.'

'Are you still angry about the arithmetic grade? Forget this silly accusation, and let's go home.'

That night the Van Valcks interrogated Minna, who said, 'Well, she's darker than me. But she talks like me.'

'You mustn't say anything about this, Minna. This is an important secret, but tomorrow ask her about her parents. Where do they live? What do they do?'

So Minna became a spy, and after much interrogation, was able to report to her parents: 'Her family is all right. Her father is foreman in a garage. Her mother runs a store. She says that's where she learned to add so fast, in the store.'

This did not appease Mrs. van Valck, who arranged for her husband to visit the school so that he, too, could see the suspected child, and when he did, his jaw dropped and he would utter no further words inside the school, but when he joined his wife in their car he said, 'My God! That girl is Coloured.'

The Van Valcks stayed awake most of that night, trying to decide what decent course they must pursue. For a Coloured child to pass as white was immoral, illegal, and crucially dangerous to their daughter, since the two were not only thrown together, but had established bonds of friendship, if not downright love. A thing like this could ruin a white girl, could tarnish her for life if it became known in the community. And it was not only the

Van Valck family that was endangered; any school had to be constantly protective of its reputation, and the easiest way to lose it would be for it to harbor children of the wrong color.

Toward morning the Van Valcks decided that they must place this difficult problem in the lap of Dr. Sterk, a man of demonstrated competence and a stout defender of Afrikanerdom. Indeed, many supposed that he must be the head of the the local Broederbond. So after Minna was safely in her classes, they drove inconspicuously to the school and slipped in to the principal's office. 'Dr. Sterk,' Mrs. van Valck said sternly, 'we have reason to believe that Petra Albertyn is Coloured.'

He choked. 'Mevrou van Valck! That's a serious charge to make.'

'We're making it. That girl is not white.'

'Impossible.'

And then something happened that sent a chill down his spine. The two Van Valcks simply sat there, firm in their chairs, their fists clenched, staring at him. They said nothing, made no threats, just waited. Finally he coughed, then said, 'You really are serious about this.'

'We are,' Leopold van Valck said.

'You're charging Petra Albertyn with being Coloured?'

'We are.'

'You're aware of the grave consequences? To the girl? To her parents? To the school?'

'We are.'

'Let me consult with her teachers.'

'That's not necessary,' Mrs. van Valck snapped. 'You can tell by looking at her that she's trying to pass. And she's endangering our daughter.'

'I need time to consider this,' he said firmly. 'Now you return home and I'll visit you tonight, after I've spoken with my people.'

That night, at half past eight, he came to their door, accepted the coffee and biscuits they offered, and reported: 'Not one of our teachers ever suspected Petra of trying to pass. She's a splendid little girl—'

'She's Coloured,' Mrs. van Valck said firmly.

'We find absolutely no evidence—'

'Have you checked her family?'

'I do not know her family,' Dr. Sterk confessed. 'Their I.D. cards say they are white.'

'I shall visit them tomorrow,' Mrs. van Valck said. 'Can you give me their address?'

'They live at Blinkfontein.'

On Friday afternoon she drove forty-eight miles north of Venloo to a crossroads village with a single store, Albertyn Super Shop. Parking her car, she looked for the police, but there were none. She walked to the post office and asked to see the man in charge, whom she swore to silence: 'It's a most important matter, Meneer. Things are being said about those people across the road. Back in Venloo. Their child Petra is in school there.'

'What are you talking about, Mevrou?'

'What do you know of the Albertyns?' Shrugging one shoulder toward the store, she added, 'Over there . . . '

'They've lived here for—'

'Where'd they come from?'

'They've always lived here.'

Receiving no help from the postmaster, she went to the store itself, in search, she said, of Trotter's jellies. The assistant, a man suspiciously dark, said he had none, and she asked, 'Will you have some later, Mr. Albertyn?' and he replied, 'I'm not Mr. Albertyn. He works at the garage. I just help here.'

'Could I see Mr. Albertyn? Or Mrs.?'

'You can see them both. They're out back.'

When she met Petra's parents they seemed as white as any Afrikaner, but she noticed something she found most ominous: in spite of the sun, Mrs. Albertyn had no freckles.

Back home she told her husband, 'As clear as the lines in the palm of your hand, that woman's Coloured.'

'How can you be sure?'

'No freckles.'

The Van Valcks returned to the school to present their hard evidence to Dr. Sterk, who laughed nervously and said, 'Really, I can't act upon freckles.'

His use of this word angered the Van Valcks, who rose to leave. 'My husband knows what to do,' Mrs. Van Valck said. 'The life of our daughter is endangered.'

'Now wait,' the principal said, inserting himself between them and the door. 'A public charge could hurt this school. It might even rebound against your daughter.'

'It's our daughter we're thinking of,' Mrs. van Valck said.

'Will you grant me two days? Please?'

'We'll grant you two months,' Leopold van Valck said generously. 'But only if you take this seriously.'

'I do. I do. I'm thinking of the great damage that might be done to the Albertyn girl if your charges are made public . . .' He tried vainly to find some good way to end this sentence, but none surfaced. 'And are found insubstantial,' he added.

This angered both the Van Valcks, but it was the wife who replied, 'They are substantial. That girl's Coloured. Now get her out of here.'

'It had better be two days,' Mr. van Valck said sternly.

That afternoon Dr. Sterk held a meeting with three of his wisest teachers, two women and one man, good Afrikaners all, and their counsel was crisp and clear: 'The Van Valcks are troublemakers, especially the mother. She raised the merry devil last year when Minna received a caution on her deportment. If she's threatening to bring public charges, she'll do it. Better get the Albertyn girl out of here quietly and forget the matter.'

'But is the girl actually Coloured?'

'No sign we've ever seen,' the arithmetic teacher said, 'but she'd better go.'

'Mrs. du Plessis, you've always told me what a splendid child Petra is.'

'I did and I love her. But in a case like this, it may be best for the child's sake if she leaves.'

The three teachers were adamant. The welfare of this important school superseded all other considerations, and whereas to suspend Petra might be heartbreaking for the girl, even the rumor that she was Coloured might have disastrous consequences for the school if circulated by determined people like the Van Valcks.

But Dr. Sterk refused to accept such advice, and next afternoon drove out to the Albertyn store, where he asked the owners to get into his car so that he might take them to some isolated spot on the veld where they could talk privately. As they drove in silence the Albertyns could only speculate on what painful thing might have happened at school: Petra had done something warranting punishment, and they were distressed, but they were also prepared to support Dr. Sterk and school discipline. Mrs. Albertyn placed her hand in her husband's and took deep breaths as the car stopped and the principal turned toward them. He looked ill-at-ease, distant, and finally he came out with it.

'Charges have been made that Petra is Coloured,' he said.

'Oh, Jesus!' Mr. Albertyn gasped.

'Most serious charges, by persons prepared to press them publicly.'

'Oh, my God!'

The anguish expressed by Mr. Albertyn was an indication of the gravity of this accusation. To make such a charge in South Africa was not like someone saying in Hungary, 'I think Lazlo's a Rumanian.' Or saying in the west of England, 'If you look into it, you'll find that Masterson is really Irish.' In normal countries such charges were matters of social judgment; in South Africa they determined life and sometimes death.

'Is there any foundation to the charge?' Dr. Sterk asked.

'None whatever,' Mr. Albertyn said, and right there the great suspicion began, for the principal noted that whereas Mr. Albertyn leaped forward to defend his family and his daughter, Mrs. Albertyn did not, and he said to himself: Why is the woman so quiet? She must be hiding something. I do believe Petra is Coloured!

At the conclusion of the interview on the veld Dr. Sterk suggested, 'I think under the circumstances you'd better take your daughter out of our school.'

'I refuse,' Mr. Albertyn cried. 'Have you any idea what it would mean to the child? Thrown out of school for doing nothing wrong?'

'I understand your sensitivities,' Dr. Sterk said with a certain unctuousness. 'But have you considered the consequences if a public charge is made? There would have to be a Race Classification inquiry. The effect on Petra . . .' He paused, not ominously, but with just the hint of a threat: 'The terrible consequences to yourselves?'

Belatedly Mrs. Albertyn spoke, and she did so with quiet force: 'Have you been thinking of the consequences, Dr. Sterk? Of persecuting a poor little child?'

These words had just the opposite effect to what she had intended. Dr. Sterk interpreted them as a challenge to his integrity, and said crisply, 'I'm always mindful of my duty, Mrs. Albertyn, to my pupils and to my nation. If you are attempting to pass into a white society, that is against the laws of our country, and a board will determine the facts.'

He took them back to their cottage, then speedily returned to Venloo, where he joined a meeting of the school committee: 'A most serious charge, not yet formalized, has been made that our child Petra Albertyn is a Coloured. Have any of you evidence bearing on this?'

Two of Petra's teachers had asked to be present and volunteered their assurances that Petra Albertyn was one of the finest— Dr. Sterk cut them off: 'We're not testifying to her quality. We're interested only in her race.' And the way in which he spoke these words conveyed the clear impression that he now considered the accusations against this child justified. This encouraged the vice-principal to say that he had been watching Petra for some time, and she not only looked suspiciously dark, but she also behaved in distinctly Coloured ways.

'What do you mean?' Dr. Sterk asked.

'The way she says certain words.'

Venloo's dominee, Reverend Classens, was a committee member, and he asked ponderously, 'Do we appreciate what we're doing here tonight? This child's entire future is at stake.'

'No one could be more sympathetic than we are, Dominee,' Dr. Sterk said. 'But if she is Coloured, then one of her parents must be Coloured, too. They can have a future among their own people. Not here in Venloo.'

'Does this mean,' the dominee asked, 'that you plan to examine every child who seems a bit dark?'

'They are examined every day. By their fellow students. By everyone who sees them. This is a Christian nation, Dominee, and we obey the law.'

'That is what I preach. But I also preach "Suffer the little children to—" '

'We don't persecute little children. But we must keep serious priorities in mind.'

'Such as?'

'The moral welfare of every child in this school.'

After the meeting a grim-faced Dr. Sterk went to see the Van Valcks, and reported: 'I've seen the Albertyns and there is foundation for your accusations. The vice-principal has also had his suspicions.'

'That's what we told you,' Mrs. van Valck said smugly. 'What are you going to do about it?'

'I've asked the Albertyns to remove their daughter.'

'And they refused?'

'They have.' There was a long pause, in which each of the three considered the inevitable next step, the one that would throw the community into turmoil. Twice Dr. Sterk made as if to speak, then thought better of it. In a matter of such gravity the decision must be made by the people involved, and he would wait upon them.

Finally Leopold van Valck asked in a low voice, 'You want to know whether we're prepared to lodge formal charges?'

'We are,' his wife interrupted with great force. Having made the decision for all of them, she sat primly in her chair, hands folded, chin jutting out as if she were already bringing her testimony before the Race Classification Board.

Dr. Sterk felt that he was the only one in this mess who appreciated the terrible confrontation that threatened; only he foresaw the consequences, once this social avalanche was torn loose, and he wanted to give the Van Valcks time to consider. He said nothing, and in the silence Mr. van Valck might have wavered, except that his wife rose suddenly, smoothed down her dress, and said, 'Well, that's that. It is our job to inform Pretoria.'

'You're sure you want to?' Dr. Sterk asked one last time.

'We are,' she said firmly, and next morning she went early to the Venloo post office to buy a money order for £10, which she carried to her husband's office. He had been in since seven, preparing two affidavits detailing the grounds for their complaint. When she filled out the forms, she took them back to the post office and mailed them to the Director of Census in Pretoria. At home she told her husband, 'I'll be proved right. They're trying to penetrate white society. And when the verdict's in, I'll get my ten pounds back.' This deposit, the government believed, was required as an indication of good faith on the part of accusers: 'It stops malicious persons from bringing frivolous or vexatious complaints.'

A tornado broke over the school, for rumor quickly spread that Petra Albertyn was Coloured; her father was white enough, but her mother was Coloured, maybe even a Bantu, and the inquisition to which children are prone ensued. Two teachers, unusually mindful of the race laws, told the principal they did not wish to have any Coloured child in their classes, that to do so was not only illegal but also personally offensive. By midafternoon the school was polarized, a few older students and the two younger teachers defending Petra, the rest ostracizing her.

It was obvious to Dr. Sterk that such a situation could not be tolerated during the weeks it would require for a Race Classification Board to be appointed, so once more he drove out to the Albertyns', imploring them, for the welfare of their daughter, to remove her from school. Mr. Albertyn, keenly aware of what could happen to his family if his daughter was declared Coloured, was disposed to comply, but his wife said, 'No. If a cruel charge like this can be made against Petra this week, it can be made against others next week. Let's settle this once and for all.'

But next day a deputation of parents stormed Sterk's office, demanding that the girl be removed immediately. One was the wife of the sergeant at the Venloo police station, and her husband stepped forward: 'Wouldn't it be best for all if if I drove Petratjie to her home?' So Petra's things were collected from the dormitory and placed in the sergeant's car. On the way to Blinkfontein he said little, but he did offer her several of his extra-strong white peppermints: 'Don't worry, Petratjie. These things always work out for the best. You'll be much happier with your own people.'

The Race Classification Board was appointed by Pretoria, for this was one of the early cases under the new regulations and it was important that precedents be established. The membership was curious: the chairman, Detleef van Doorn, the lawmaker, who had at one time or another headed every important local organization and was still head of the committee of the Paulus de Groot High School; Mr. Leopold van Valck, the magistrate, who in another country might have been disqualified as being partner to the litigation; and the Venloo dentist with the good English name of John Adams, to avoid charges that the commission was overloaded with Afrikaners judging their own special laws.

They met in one of the town's two courtrooms and spent the first days taking testimony from any interested parties: teachers who had always suspected the child, playmates who might have observed suspicious behavior, village gossips interested in the Albertyns' personal life. The intention was to learn whether their friends and others regarded them as white persons. The testimony was conclusive that they did.

But the vital evidence was taken on the third day, and the community watched grimly when a motorcar brought the Albertyns, including two older children, to be inspected visually by the three commissioners. This was all-important, for what the investigators were endeavoring to decide was whether the Albertyns as a whole were Coloured or not, and looking at them face-to-face was one of the best ways to judge.

The four Albertyns, lacking Petra, were lined up before the commissioners, who studied them minutely prior to questioning. Mr. van Valck, whose name meant *falcon,* rose from his chair behind the prosecutor's table, where the commissioners sat, and suggested that they move onto the bench used by judges 'so we can look more impressive.'

'No,' Detleef objected, 'this is a simple family matter, so let's handle it that way. Our job is to start sorting out our nation, putting everyone in his place. This wouldn't have been necessary if the English had kept people properly separated, but once those first fatal steps of intermixing occurred, the damage was done. Now we must move back to an honest base.'

Detleef van Doorn began: 'Who were your grandparents?' He placed great store on lineage.

'Have you any Coloured friends?'

'What is your minister's name? His initials?'

'Is his church exclusively for whites?'

'Are you and your husband registered as voters?'

'Have your names ever been removed from a voters' list?' Here Magistrate van Valck interposed gravely: 'Remember, you are under oath, and one false answer will put you in jail.'

'Have you ever traveled in a train for Coloured persons?'

'When you go on holiday, where do you stay? What hotel? Is it for whites?'

On and on, for three hours, the questioning went, inconclusively. The Albertyns seemed much like any other South African family, mostly Dutch, with a strong strain of German and perhaps a Huguenot ancestor far back. No English. Probably no Malay or Hottentot or Bantu.

Now the fascinating part of the investigation approached, when the commissioners actually inspected the bodies of the suspects. Each commissioner had his or her special clues for detecting Coloured blood, the result of rural superstitions. Mr. van Valck, coached by his wife, placed emphasis on freckles and ear lobes: 'White people freckle. Coloureds don't. It's as simple as that.' But when he examined the Albertyns, he found Mrs. Albertyn and one son with no freckles, Mr. Albertyn and the other son with a copious supply. 'Now, with ear lobes,' he explained to everyone in the room, 'with whites, there's an indentation. With Coloureds, there isn't.' But again the Albertyns divided two and two.

The dentist had heard that something about the half-moons at the base of fingernails furnished some clue to racial origin, but he could never remember what it was. He considered an investigation like this offensive but felt he had better go through the motions, so he carefully studied forty Albertyn fingernails, and said, 'Hmmmmmm!' The other two commissioners were relieved that he was taking his assignment seriously.

Van Doorn trusted only hair, especially on the backs of hands, where it could not be tampered with, as it often was on the head: 'Hand hair that twists in a certain way.' Eight Albertyn hands were carefully inspected, after which Detleef asked for a pencil, which relieved Mr. van Valck, since he placed considerable store in the pencil test. 'We twist the hair over the ears tightly around this pencil,' Van Doorn explained to the watchers, 'and if the subject is white, it unravels quickly when the pencil is withdrawn. With blacks, as you know, it remains crinkled.' Studying the pencil to see that the hair was properly drawn, he jerked the pencil away and watched with satisfaction as the hair responded. 'You may sit down,' he told the Albertyns.

Now came the time to investigate the little girl herself, the one who had technically committed the offense. Petra was brought into the room and told to face the interrogators, who went through the tedious business of asking her profound questions when everyone knew that it would be the physical examination that counted.

Even so, little Petra responded with answers that were innocent and sometimes charming. Yes, she understood this was a serious business. Yes, she knew that if she were indeed Coloured, she would have to go to a school with her own people. Yes, she knew that every group had its own place in South Africa so that it could be happy. In fact, she knew a great deal and demonstrated the intelligence of which her teachers had spoken, even those who wanted her expelled.

'Now, Petra, walk to the end of the room and back.' It was clear to Mr. van Valck that she walked like a Coloured.

'Now we come to the most important part.' It was Mr. van Valck speaking in a rather conciliatory voice, for he was about to impose the one inspection that some people deemed foolproof. 'Slip down your dress,' he said as gently as he could.

So the little girl, shyly but with no fierce embarrassment, dropped her dress and then her petticoat until she stood practically naked before the commissioners. Since her breasts had not yet formed, she felt no need to cover them with her hands; nervously she twined her fingers over her flat stomach. 'Drop your hands to your side, Petra, so we can see how you stand,' Detleef said, and the commissioners examined her, paying special attention to the small triangle at the base of the spine, for as Mr. van Valck had assured them: 'If that's dark, you can be sure she has Bantu blood.' Dr. Adams, ashamed of himself for participating in so ghastly a ritual, looked at the triangle and saw only the properly developing spine-tip of a little girl.

When the Albertyns, all five of them, were dismissed from the room, the commissioners excused Dr. Sterk and the two policemen and started their deliberations, and it became quickly evident that Mr. van Valck was determined to find the family Coloured, while Dr. Adams, a naturally sardonic type, would have none of it; indeed, he appeared to be contemptuous of the whole affair. The deciding vote would therefore be cast by Van Doorn, and he intended to be as just as Solomon.

'I think we should begin our deliberations with prayer,' he said in Afrikaans.

'Why?' Adams asked in English.

'Because we're about to decide the fate of a family,' Van Doorn replied.

'Seems to me it's already decided,' Adams said. 'Not a shred of evidence that family's Coloured.'

'That's what we're here to decide,' Van Doorn reminded him, and he launched into a long, fervid supplication to God, asking Him to monitor their deliberations as they endeavored in good conscience to protect the nation.

Before the voting could begin, an investigator from Detleef's office broke into the room without having been invited and handed the chairman a report: 'It's what you asked for, Mr. van Doorn.' For three weeks this man and four of Detleef's assistants in Pretoria had been scrutinizing the Albertyn past, because the government was determined that this important race-classification hearing be conducted so as to evoke maximum impact.

'Mr. van Doorn, sir,' the investigator whispered. 'I don't think you'd better let anyone see our report.'

'The other members are entitled . . .'

'It was the other members I was thinking of.'

Moving apart from Van Valck and Adams, Detleef read the document and became ashen. He was astonished that detectives could uncover so much and appalled at the possible consequences of what they had learned. The detective, seeing his dismay, whispered, 'Shall I burn the report, sir? I made only one copy.'

It was the severest moral test Detleef would ever face. His whole being urged him to quash this report, but the dignity of his office and its obligation to purify the race took precedence. If at this first hearing he smothered evidence, all subsequent ones would be suspect, and the good that such procedures might otherwise accomplish would be aborted. Wiping the sweat from his forehead, he cleared his dry throat and said, 'Gentlemen, I think we should hear a rather remarkable report. It bears directly on our case. Mr. Op t'Hooft here is an investigator from my department, and he's been looking into the heritage of the Albertyns. You may proceed, Mr. Op t'Hooft.'

The detective squared his shoulders and read a concise account of the Albertyn record:

'The charge that Mrs. Albertyn is Coloured is completely false. There is no blemish of any kind on her family record. The possibility that she may have had sexual intercourse with a Bantu is remote, for not only does she have an impeccable reputation, but we can find no occasion when she could have been in contact with a Bantu. Also, since her other children all look like Petra, there would have to have been repeated acts of intercourse with the same black man, and that seems positively impossible.

'Mr. Albertyn, however, is another matter. He is contaminated doubly, and proof of the contamination is contained in a straight, unbroken, demonstrable line back to 1694 when the Coloured slave Bezel Muhammad married the Trianon spinster Petronella van Doorn.

'Bezel and Petronella had four children who carried no last name, and they might have been lost in the general Coloured population except that neighbors kept track of them, knowing them to be Van Doorns. We have found numerous families well regarded today containing the blood of Bezel and Petronella.

'In or about the year 1720 their daughter Fatima, named after Bezel's mother, became the third wife of the notorious frontier outlaw Rooi van Valck, who had four wives, one yellow, one brown, one black and one white. Fatima was the brown one, and she became the progenitress of a large unruly breed.

'One of her daughters married an early Albertyn and was thus the direct ancestor of our Henricus Albertyn. Without question, he is doubly Coloured. Without question, his daughter Petra must be so classified.

'Our investigators could not avoid remarking upon the extraordinary fact that our Petra thus becomes a lineal descendant of the original Petronella, who broke the rules of her community. Could this be an an example of Divine intervention?'

When Mr. Op t'Hooft finished reading the report, he waited in some confusion as to what he should do next. He looked in vain at Chairman van Doorn for instructions, but Detleef was too shaken to act intelligently, and as for Mr. van Valck, whose redoubtable ancestor Rooi had been dragged from his stormy grave, he was in a state of shock.

Dr. Adams reached for the report, but Mr. Op t'Hooft was not sure he should deliver it to a man known to be difficult where Afrikaner matters were concerned. Dr. Adams solved this by snatching the paper and holding it aloft. 'Did you say this was the only copy?'

'Yes. Not even one carbon was made.'

'Good. I want you to watch what happens to your one copy.' Crumpling it in his left hand, Dr. Adams produced a match, scratched it across the top of the polished table, and set fire to the report. Holding it by one end, he watched the flames creep closer to his fingers, then dropped the burning paper on the table, where it vanished, leaving a scar.

'I think we should all forget this report,' Adams said. 'It can do no one in this room any good, and it could do distinguished citizens outside a great deal of harm.' When Mr. Op t'Hooft, completely bewildered, left, Adams said, 'It looks to me as if I'm the only one here who is not related to this little Coloured girl.'

Van Valck and Van Doorn glared at him, but he ignored them, saying brightly, 'I propose we declare the child white and end this farce.' He supposed that the shaken men, in order to hide their own involvement, would agree, but he underestimated Detleef's moral tenacity.

In silence the Commissioner on Racial Affairs lowered his head and pondered what to do. In his anxiety he could hear the voices of his family orating savagely on the problem of the Coloureds:

> Maria van Doorn: 'They are the children of sin, and God must despise them.'
> Johanna Krause: 'They are mongrels.'

But then he heard his own voice: 'They're . . . a reminder of our fathers' transgressions.'

He was sorely tempted to follow Dr. Adams' advice and terminate the investigation, for he knew that if the facts became public, the sins of his ancestors must surface; but to evade his responsibilities would be craven, so he decided to plow ahead.

He was about to voice his decision when he saw, shimmering in air, that decorated page of the ancient Bible on which the data of his family were inscribed, and on it in blazing letters stood that second entry, the one that was never discussed in his family: *Son Adam van Doorn born 1 November 1655.* Generations of Van Doorns had tried to ignore that cryptic passage, avoiding the question of who the boy's mother could have been. And there was the later entry: 'Petronella'—but with no statement as to whom she had married. Always the Van Doorns had suspected that they were related to Coloureds; always they had submerged this truth. Now the gossip-whispers were about to rampage, and Detleef was sick with shame.

But he *was* the Commissioner on Racial Affairs, he *was* the chairman of this Race Classification Board, with a duty to perform. In a voice scarcely more than a whisper he said, 'Clearly the child Petra has contaminated blood from both the Van Valck and the Van Doorn lines. Clearly she must be classified as Coloured.'

Van Valck shuddered: 'All along I thought it was Mrs. Albertyn who carried the fatal strain.'

'What in hell do you men mean?' Dr. Adams exploded. 'Words like *contaminated* and *fatal strain*?'

'We mean the defilement of Afrikaner blood,' Detleef whispered. 'We have all been defiled this day.'

From the moment the date 1694 was mentioned, Dr. Adams had started doing calculations and now produced his results: 'At least eight, and possibly more, generations separate the slave Bezel Muhammad from our little girl . . .'

'She's not my little girl,' Mr. van Valck interrupted. 'She's a Coloured trying to penetrate our community.'

'Eight generations would mean that back in the 1694 period she would have had no fewer than two hundred and fifty-six potential ancestors in existence. And because two of them were Coloured—'

'More,' Detleef interrupted. 'You're forgetting Rooi van Valck.'

'I was just coming to Rooi. By the way, Van Valck, from which of his wives were you descended? Don't bother to answer. Whichever it was, Petra's your cousin.'

Leopold leaped from his chair, and would have assaulted the dentist had not Van Doorn intervened. 'Gentlemen, sit down. We have a vote to take. The evidence against this girl is overwhelming. Do I hear a motion to declare her Coloured?'

'I so move,' Van Valck said firmly.

'Do I hear a second?'

Dr. Adams stared at his fingernails, trying to guess how he would be evaluated a decade from now when this movement for racial purity became a mania and some ill-spirited neighbor denounced him.

'Dr. Adams, do I hear a second?'

'Not from me.'

'Please, we must conduct this meeting in orderly fashion.'

'Then I move that you two men vote to declare your cousin Petra Albertyn white, for I am certain that she's as white as any of the three of us.'

'I second the original motion,' Detleef said, his blood raging and his mind taking note of this man Adams. He would be dealt with later. The medical commission should look into that man's credentials.

'Moved and seconded that this commission finds the girl Petra Albertyn Coloured.'

'No!' Adams called in a loud voice.

'The vote was not called for,' Detleef said, trying to control his anger. 'Now I ask for the vote.'

'Ja,' Van Valck cried. Van Doorn did the same, then looked at Dr. Adams, who was again studying his fingernails. 'And you, Adams?'

'Record it that I was ashamed in the sight of God to vote upon such a motion. That I refused to condemn your cousin Petra.' He rose and started to leave the room, but Detleef intercepted him.

'Please! It's of major importance that we start this procedure correctly. You must be seen sitting with us when we deliver our decision.'

So, reluctantly, Dr. Adams resumed his chair and watched as the Albertyns and the spectators were brought back into the room. The family was ranged neatly along one wall, and little Petra, hands primly at her side, was again asked to stand facing her judges, who looked down upon her.

'Petra Albertyn, you are Coloured.'

She made no response, but did turn slightly to see what the noise was to her left. Her mother had fainted.

The fateful decision in Petra's case launched a time of terror for the Albertyns. She was immediately dismissed from school, and when her family appealed to the courts they were turned down: 'Clearly Coloured.' In a few months the board declared Henricus Albertyn Coloured, too, so he could no longer work at the garage, since his foreman position was classified 'whites only.' Nor could he find work elsewhere; he was unemployed and would remain so for more than a year.

It was absolutely forbidden for the Albertyns to continue living where they had for the past forty years; as Coloureds they must move into some township reserved for their race, but no such group area existed in Venloo, so they decided to uproot their entire family and move down to Cape Town, where the vast majority of Coloureds lived. Because they were forced to sell their house under crisis conditions, they received £2,000 for a £4,500 investment.

When they reached Cape Town the only accommodation they could find was in a collection of three-story hovels originally designed as a transit camp for the military. It was now one of the shames of South Africa, with multiple families crammed into each flimsy-walled apartment.

When the shattered Albertyns moved into Orchard Flats they contemplated suicide. The cleanliness of Blinkfontein was gone, the neatness of their home, the warmth of their relationships in the tiny community—all lost. In their place was filth, criminality and social hatred. That anyone should have to live in such surroundings was disgraceful, but that proven good citizens could be forced into them by a government acting in the name of God and racial purity was criminal.

Henricus Albertyn discovered how criminal one evening when he came home from his job as grease-monkey in a distant Cape Town garage. As he climbed the stairs to his third-floor room, assailed by the smell of cheap wine and urine, he racked his brain trying to devise some tactic whereby he could organize a decent life for Petra, for upon her he now fastened all his dreams.

But when he reached his door he heard sobbing, not Petra's but his wife's, and he burst into the room—to find her quivering in a corner, with a pair of long scissors, covered with blood, in her hand. For one terrible moment he suspected that something beyond words had happened to his daughter, but when he looked about in frenzy, he saw Petra seated by the lone window, reading a book. Whatever foul thing had happened, she had remained untouched.

Quickly embracing her, he asked, 'What's happened?'

'Just the skollies,' Petra said, apparently unconcerned. 'Mama stabbed them, and they ran away.'

From her corner Mrs. Albertyn said softly, 'No skollies will rape my child. We'll never surrender to this dreadful place.'

And Petra, putting aside her book, showed her father the long knitting needle she had for some days kept secreted in her dress: 'I stabbed them too. Shamilah downstairs told me how to jab at their eyes.' And without any sign of agitation she returned to her homework.

She was in school again, at a much bigger institution in nearby Athlone, staffed by a group of dedicated Coloured men and women. When her father attended a parent-teacher meeting, the chairman of the school committee, a prosperous builder named Simon Botha, sought him out: 'Albertyn, our teachers tell me that your little Petra is a near-genius. You must give thought to her future.'

'In this country what can a Coloured do?'

'You mustn't limit your horizon to this country. My daughter in Canada tells me the universities there have many bursaries. They're hungry for children like Petra. Australia, too, or even London.'

Such thoughts were beyond Albertyn's ken, but he realized that he must learn to grapple with them, for as Botha said, 'To leave a girl like Petra in this country is to commit her to death.'

Even though Venloo had been cleansed of the Albertyns, the Van Valcks could not feel victorious, for they were assailed by haunting questions. One night Leopold asked bluntly, 'Do you think that English atheist would dare to start rumors about us? I mean, about Rooi van Valck and his three dark wives?' Later he asked plaintively, 'Could I possibly be carrying contaminated blood?'

They spent much time inspecting the half-moons on his fingernails, and although these were inconclusive, Mrs. van Valck did find comfort in his many freckles. After convincing themselves that he was safely white, they relaxed and invited Principal Sterk to dinner and listened as he reported on the final outcome of their crusade to purify the community. When they heard of the area in which the Albertyns were forced to live, Mrs. van Valck said without rancor, and even with a sense of forgiving them for the trouble they had caused, 'It's only what they deserved, trying to be something better than they were.' Then she added brightly, 'Yesterday I had a letter from Pretoria. They sent me back my deposit.'

AT HOME

February 8, 1955

Greetings,

Further to my previous letter this is to advise you that my Board will provide transport free of charge for yourself, members of your household, and property belonging to you on February 9, 1955.

Will you kindly pack your belongings and be ready to load by 6 A.M. on that morning.

Attached hereto is a letter which, please, hand to your employer. It explains why you cannot be at work on February 9, 1955.

I. P. van Onselen
Secretary to the Native Resettlement Board

February 9 was the kind of crisp summer's day Johannesburg often provided, but this year it carried special significance, for the government had announced for the last time that the bulldozers were going to move; no further legal complaints would be tolerated. The first batch of blacks to be evicted from Sophiatown were to obey the secretary's letter to the last word.

Barney Patel, a clothing dealer aged forty-six, and his friend Woodrow Desai, aged fifty-nine, owner of a grocery store, had traveled from their shops in Pageview, an Indian trading and residential area in Johannesburg since the days of Paul Kruger. They were standing on a hill overlooking Sophiatown, where bulldozers were lined up, awaiting the signal. From their vantage point the two Indians were able to look down into the township which blacks had occupied for decades; fifty-seven thousand of them now lived here, some in ugly slums, many in fine houses which they owned. In a last-minute appeal that failed, an expert in housing had testified: 'Only one structure in eight is a slum that warrants complete demolition.'

It had to be admitted, however, that the slum area was an amazing collection of buildings divided into five easily recognized categories: at the bottom, cardboard walls acquired by flattening grocery boxes; next, tin walls made from hammering out paraffin cans; next, corrugated iron siding; next, actual wood to protect the walls; and finally, cinderblocks to replace everything that had served before. But whatever the building material, all the houses were jammed together along narrow streets or dark alleys, and from this assembly came not only the patient black workers of the area but also the incorrigible young tsotsis, the peddlers of dagga, as marijuana was called, the prostitutes and the horde of petty criminals.

Sophiatown was a tightly knit community, and for every tsotsi who prowled the streets, there were a dozen good youngsters; for every father who staggered home drunk to a tin shack, there were a dozen others who cared for their families and supported the churches and schools and traders. But this black township had had the poor foresight to situate itself in the heart of what would become a predominantly Afrikaner white suburb. It must now be bulldozed off the face of the earth not for the sake of honest, if somewhat overzealous, urban renewal, as might have happened in many other countries, but because it stood in the path of white aspirations.

'There must be no confusion of thinking,' a cabinet minister said. 'Sophiatown counts as a black spot on our land.' He then explained that a black spot was a place where Bantu had acquired land ownership under old laws. Under apartheid, such offensive spots had to be rubbed out. Thirteen percent of the land, traditional sites for kraals, had been set aside, and there blacks could own land. 'At Sophiatown, and spots like it that we need, their temporary sojourn in our midst is over.'

'I can't believe they're going to knock it down,' Barney Patel said as the bulldozers revved their engines.

'The paper said they start today.'

'But all the people living there?'

'Out in the country. To the new settlements.'

'You mean they'll have to travel all those miles?'

'That's not the government's problem [he pronounced it gommint]. Out they go. Gommint says they shouldn't have been here in the first place.'

A bell started ringing in a Protestant church right in the middle of the slum area, and continued for some minutes until a policeman hurried through the crowd to silence it. 'They don't want any trouble,' Patel said. 'They've banned meetings of more than twelve people.'

'They won't have any trouble,' Desai said. 'Look at the police.'

To deal with the first one hundred and fifty families ordered to abandon the homes they owned, the government had brought in two thousand policemen armed with Sten guns and assegais, backed by troop carriers, signal units and squads of military police.

When the bulldozers were ready, two men to each machine, a Resettlement Board official gave the signal, and the powerful scrapers moved forward, their blades lowered, their snouts hungry.

'I just don't believe this,' Patel said, his throat suddenly dry.

'Look!' the older man said, and they watched as the monstrous machines ripped a path through a group of shacks. A single bulldozer would wipe out an entire house, but this was no great accomplishment, for that one had been cardboard and planks.

'Look over there!' Desai cried, and as he pointed, a bulldozer chewed its way into a substantial home of wood and brick.

'That house must have been worth . . .' Patel did not finish his sentence, for the bulldozer, having attacked something it could not easily subdue, hung in the air for a moment, then slid sideways, endangering the driver but not upsetting. Angrily it backed up, sped its engine and tore back into the house, which collapsed in a cloud of dust.

'Look at the people!' Desai said softly, and the two Indians turned to the south where large groups of blacks gathered silently to watch the demolition, mindful of what was in store for them. They stood with anguish on their dark faces, their hands clenched, powerless to obstruct either the bulldozers or the officials who directed them. This black spot could not be tolerated by whites in neighboring Mayfair; it must be cleansed of its vermin and converted to higher purposes.

'There come the trucks,' Patel said as a line of vehicles moved in to carry away the residents, and while the 'dozers knocked down the unwanted houses, the trucks carted off the unwanted people, free of charge, as the letter had promised.

There were, of course, those few blacks who refused to quit their homes; these were routed out by the police but no harm was done them. From one house near where Patel and Desai stood, a team of soldiers carried away an old man who had stubbornly refused to budge. 'Come on, old grandpop, we're in a hurry!' the soldiers said in Afrikaans ('Kom, Oubaas, ons is haastig'). Almost gently they bore him to a waiting truck and sat him down among the others, and he was scarcely seated before a bulldozer eliminated the house in which his children and grandchildren had been born.

The two Indians remained on their prominence most of the morning, gripped by the drama of this vast removal and weighing the possibility that they might be next. 'Do you think they'll really knock down our houses?' Patel asked as the bulldozers ate into Sophiatown.

'Gommint policy,' Desai said. 'All Indians to get out of Johannesburg.'

'You think they'll move us miles out in the country, like they say?'

'Look, Barney. Mukerjee told me yesterday the surveyors were out there, laying out streets.'

'Who can believe Mukerjee?'

'Well, he kept warning us that one day Sophiatown would be knocked down. Then I laughed. Today I believe.'

'But blacks are different from Indians. There are so many of them. So few of us.'

'Numbers mean nothing to apartheid. It's only interested in color.

Today it hates this black spot. Tomorrow it'll be a brown spot, and off we go.'

'But Kruger's gommint gave us the land we have. I own my land.'

'Yes, they put us there for what they called "sanitary" reasons. Today their grandsons will kick us out for economic reasons. Believe me, Barney, the bulldozers will come down our streets, too.'

They stood in silence, watching the destruction, marking the exodus of black families, and as they knew themselves to be powerless to protest this brutal maneuver, they thought back upon their own curious history in this fertile land.

Woodrow Desai's grandfather had been one of the three Desai brothers shipped to the sugar fields by Sir Richard Saltwood. When their contracts had been worked out, they had stayed on and were soon joined by 'passenger Indians' like the Patels, who had paid their own way to serve the rapidly growing community as shopkeepers and traders.

The Indian immigrants settled mostly in Natal, near the port of Durban, and there they proliferated: Patels, Desais, Mukerjees, Bannarjees. Unlike the Dutch before them and the Chinese, the Indian men would have nothing to do with black women, or white either, for that matter. They remained strictly aloof, and in the first forty years of their work in mine and field, few Indians married persons of another race. Woodrow's father and others moved to the Transvaal, and in the smallest towns they opened shops to which all customers were invited, but in their homes they kept to themselves, with their dishes of ghee and lamb and rice and curry. They were clean, usually law-abiding, and the other people of South Africa hated them.

'Without the little one,' Patel reflected, 'Indians would have been in even worse shape.'

The little one was a skinny lawyer with a high whining voice who emigrated to Durban in 1893. His name was Mohandas Karamchand Gandhi, intelligent enough to have made a good life for himself in South Africa had he been free to operate there. Indeed, when he arrived at age twenty-four he intended to remain, but the disadvantages which Indians suffered so irritated him that he found himself constantly at war with the authorities.

'He was a fighter,' Desai mumbled, recalling this contentious man who had defied the entire white establishment.

'And clever too,' Patel said admiringly. 'When the Boer War was at its worst, what does he do? Organizes an Indian ambulance corps. Helps the English, even though they've been harrying him. Very brave, you know.' He chuckled to think of little Gandhi issuing orders to the white government.

'My father knew him well,' Desai said. 'But Father was much like me. Never wanted trouble. So when Gandhi started sending letters to General Smuts, like he was head of an Indian gommint, my father warned him: "You watch out, Mohandas. Gommint's going to throw you in jail." That was when he invented Satyagraha, right here in South Africa.'

'If he were watching this disgrace now, he'd do the same for the blacks as he did for us. Peaceful resistance. Just lie down in front of the bulldozers.'

'The bulldozers in India were British. They stopped. These are Afrikaner bulldozers and I don't think they'd stop. Not even for Gandhi.'

'I love him,' Patel said. 'Not for what he did in India. For what he did here.' He paused and shook his head. 'I often wonder what might have happened if he'd stayed in Durban. To help our people.'

'He'd have been shot. I don't think Afrikaners understand Satyagraha.'

The mention of shooting saddened the two Indians, for the Desai and Patel families back in Natal had suffered grievously when the Zulu, infuriated by government laws restricting them, had taken vengeance not on the whites who had passed the laws but on the Indians with whom they traded daily. For three days the tall Zulu had chased little Indians through the streets, slashing and killing, while some whites even looked on with approval, shouting at times, 'Kill 'em, Zulu!' More than fifty Indians were slain; more than seven hundred required medical attention. It was a different South Africa after that, with many whites muttering that it would have been better if the Zulu had been allowed a free hand to settle the Indian Question once and for all.

Desai, who had lost an uncle in the riots, smiled sardonically. 'Well, we had a chance to get out. Remember when gommint provided boat fare and leaving funds so that every Indian could go back to India? I think three old men accepted. Wanted to be buried in their native villages. The rest . . .'

'My father told me,' Patel said, 'that any Indian who left South Africa for India could be certified insane. This was so much better than what he had known . . .'

As the sun approached its zenith, and the blacks' houses crumbled to dust, the two Indians went soberly home to Pageview, where they stood at an intersection and stared at the rows of houses and shops occupied by their compatriots; Indians always preferred living in tight communities for mutual protection. 'Do you think they'd dare knock all this down?' Patel asked nervously. 'Five thousand people. Homes, businesses. Insurance told me ten million pounds, at least.'

Before he could answer, Cassem Mukerjee came running. He was a small nervous man, much like Gandhi in appearance, and he spoke with that agitated enthusiasm some men display when circulating bad news: 'My cousin Morarji saw the papers at his office. They're going to bulldoze this place, too. All our houses are to go. And they'll take our shops too.'

Barney Patel did not like Mukerjee, and now he shook him. 'You stop that rumoring! Your cousin knows nothing.'

'He knew they were going to bulldoze Sophiatown,' the little man said, almost gleefully. 'Are the houses gone?'

'It'll take years,' Patel snorted, but Desai wanted to know about the supposed papers: 'Did Morarji actually see anything?'

'The orders have been drafted. All Indians to be cleaned out of Johannesburg.'

'My God!' Desai said, and he leaned against the wall of a solidly built brick house, and as he stood there, sick in the sunlight, he could see the dust of the future, and thought:

They will move the bulldozers here, and these houses of warmth and love will go down. The stone ones like mine and Barney's, they won't

destroy them, but we'll be forced to sell at government price—
twenty cents in the rand. The school where my children went will
be razed, and all the little houses where the old people expected to
live until they died. Our stores on Fourteenth Street . . . My God,
I worked so hard.

And we'll be moved far out into the country. Miles, miles from all
our friends, all our customers. There'll be new houses at prices
people can't afford, and new stores with no customers, and hours on
the train each day, and all our money wasted on transportation we
don't really need. And we'll be off to one side where no one can see
us, and the streets we once knew will have vanished—and for what
great purpose?

Woodrow Desai decided that night to form a committee to visit Pretoria
for a serious talk with the government official whose office was responsible
for planning the future of the Indian community. He took Barney Patel with
him, but not Morarji Mukerjee, who was something of an alarmist. Patiently they explained the folly of such an evacuation, pointing out that it
would accomplish not one single economic advantage, but the official assigned the task of dealing with them cut them off: 'We aren't really talking
about economics, are we? We're talking about instilling some order in the
community. Each group secure in its own place.'

'But if you put all of us in this so-called Lenasia so far out into the
country . . .'

'That's for your protection. All the Indians in one spot.'

'But so far out. We'll waste hours and rand every day.'

'My dear friends,' the official, a Natal-born Englishman, said with
warmth but also with a certain stiffness, 'our country has no finer citizens
than you Indians. We wouldn't dream of doing anything to your disadvantage. But we must bring order into our lives. Pageview is intended for
whites. Look at the map!' And he showed them how where they lived and
traded intruded into areas that could better be used for whites.

'And you can have nice new shops out there,' he assured them, waving
his hand in some vague direction. 'You'll like it better when it happens.' He
paused. 'We're doing this for your own good,' he said. And before they
could reply they were out on the street.

'I wish Mohandas Gandhi were here again,' Patel growled. 'He'd know
how to stop this.'

AT WORK

The Golden Reef Mines southwest of Johannesburg needed a constant
supply of black workers to man the deepest shafts where blasting of the face
rock occurred. From all over southern Africa planes and trains and buses
brought almost illiterate black men to the compounds within which they
would live for the six to eighteen months of their contract. Critics of the
labor system likened these compounds to harsh prisons in which the blacks

were incarcerated; management spoke of them as well-run dormitories in which the laborers lived infinitely better than they did at home.

There was one clue to the truth of these contrasting claims: black men in the bush of Moçambique, Malawi, Rhodesia, Lesotho and Vwarda fought for a chance to work at the Golden Reef, and for good reason. Though the wage was trivial, it was much more than they could get in their home villages; the food was better; there was more of it; beds were covered with good blankets; and doctors provided health care. Black nationalists in surrounding countries would publicly inveigh against South Africa but privately see to it that planes which came flying into their airstrips were loaded with workers, for only in this way could some of the economies be kept afloat. Black families also encouraged their men to fly to the Golden Reef for the sensible reason that a good percentage of a man's wages was paid only when he returned home, and his wife and children could temporarily escape their poverty.

When blacks from thirty or forty different tribes, speaking radically different languages and dialects, had to work together, it was necessary to construct some simple language they could all understand. Fanakalo was the ingenious solution. The word came from pidgin Zulu and meant roughly 'do it like this,' and the lingua franca it represented was a marvelous mélange of Bantu, English, Afrikaans and Portuguese. It consisted mostly of nouns, with a few essential verbs, some profanity for adjectival emphasis and a great many gestures. One linguist who tried to analyze it said, 'You don't speak Fanakalo. You dance it while shouting.'

Few things in the world worked better, for a tribesman could master simple instructions in three days: 'This here wrench, fanakalo.' (You do it like this.) And once learned, it served as a magical passkey to all the levels of the mine, so that a man from Malawi speaking a unique dialect could work deep in the shaft beside one from Vwarda speaking his. One white supervisor asked an associate what the workers on his shift meant when they referred to 'Idonki ngo football jersey,' and the second man said, 'Simple. They mean *zebra.*'

A miner could renew his contract again and again, but it was found better to have him return home after a long stint in the mines, see his family back in his home village, and return rested up. These returnees usually spoke well of the Golden Reef, especially the food. Once when Vwarda's representative at the United Nations was addressing the Security Council and asking for sanctions against South Africa, the government was filling six planes with Vwarda men who wanted to get back to work.

Not all the black mine hands came from foreign countries; the Golden Reef, along with sister mines, maintained a vast network of some forty recruiters who were engaged only in the enlisting of South African blacks, who comprised a third of the mines' work force. One such recruiter came to Venloo, set up his table, and counseled with young blacks from that area. Since jobs were scarce, he was able to sign up a score of workers, among them Jonathan Nxumalo, oldest son of Moses, who had been so long associated with the Van Doorns.

Jonathan was a bright lad of twenty, eager to see something more of the world than the restricted view available to a farm hand at Vrymeer, but as soon as he passed through into the Golden Reef compound, where five thousand other black men lived, sixteen to a room, he heard the gates slam behind him—and realized that he had gained not freedom but a new kind of restriction. To learn Fanakalo became essential.

It took the white overseers only a few weeks to promote Jonathan as the best of this gang, and they designated him to work at the face, more than ten thousand feet down the rocky shaft. This paid more money, but it demanded more intense work in a constant temperature of 114° F. Water to cool the body and salt to protect it became almost as important as the gigantic jackhammer drill Jonathan handled, and when the long shift ended and the men from below shot up in the elevator they had the self-satisfaction of knowing that they had completed one of the world's hardest jobs.

White men shared the heat and the danger. No black was ever assigned a job more treacherous than what the white overseer was willing to do, so that a kind of camaraderie developed among the teams, with each white boss settling upon one or two superior blacks on whom he could rely. Jonathan became an aide to Roger Coetzee, an ambitious Afrikaner who loved the mines and would one day become the big boss.

Jonathan's job was an exciting one. At the start of each shift he entered the cage with the rest of his gang, bolted the doors, and dropped a sickening ten thousand feet straight down. Occasionally some visitor from Johannesburg or overseas would want to inspect how the men worked, and then the cage was lowered at a much slower rate, which irritated Nxumalo, for he had grown to like that awful drop; it was a badge of his profession. He could take it, whereas a stranger could not.

Below, he would meet up with Coetzee, who came down only with other white miners; the two men and their helpers walked about one mile hunched over, their heads protected by hard hats, which bumped against jagged rocks, their bodies exuding perspiration. After a long drink of water and some salt pills, they followed a narrower tunnel, in which the noise became shattering. Now they were approaching the face of the gold-bearing rock, and here huge pneumatic drills were sending steel probes far into the rock, prior to the placement of the next charges of dynamite.

It was hellish work. Jonathan would creep into the working hole feet first, lying on his back and never able to sit erect. When he reached the drilling machine, a heavy instrument with cross-bar handles and stirrups for the feet, he would adjust himself, check the electrical lines, then jam his feet into the stirrups and deftly point the six-foot diamond-tipped drill at the spot to be dynamited. Then, taking a deep breath, which always stimulated him, he would squirm about for a comfortable position, thrust his feet forward, and flick the switch. With incredible power and noise, the water-cooled jackhammer drill would eat into the rock, throwing spray and slush until Jonathan looked like a white man.

When the hole was drilled, Nxumalo would squirm back out and signal to Coetzee that all was ready. The Afrikaner would then replace Nxumalo in the cramped tunnel and fix the dynamite, the cap and the connecting wires. Whistles would blow. Sirens would whine. And all men would retreat from this area as Coetzee plunged the detonator, exploding the charge and breaking away the next burden of gold-bearing rock.

When the dust settled and it seemed probable that no last rocks would tumble down from the new ceiling, Jonathan Nxumalo and Roger Coetzee would creep back into the tunnel and start calculating how long it would take for the ore to be hauled away from the stope face to the breaker and then to the refinery. It was hard work, dust-filled and exciting, and the men deep below developed respect for each other's capacities. Of course, when they left the danger area to go aloft, their lives changed radically. Coetzee could jump into his car and drive where he wished; Nxumalo was restricted to the compound, where all needs were provided by the company.

He was not exactly a prisoner. During any eighteen-month contract, workers were allowed into Johannesburg six times, but only in a group, with some white like Coetzee holding the passes of thirty-six workmen. Should one want to break away from the ensemble, he could risk it, but he would then find himself with no pass, and since spot checks for pass inspection were quite common, sooner or later he would be detected and packed off to jail.

Several times, however, Jonathan did receive, through Coetzee's intervention, a special pass allowing him to visit a Vrymeer friend who, with sheer duplicity, had contrived to land a job in Johannesburg without proper papers. 'What I did,' he confided, 'was to grab on to this white family that had to have help. They protected me.' He added, 'Of course, since we're both breaking the law they pay me less than proper wages. But I don't complain.'

'You like Johannesburg?' Jonathan asked.

'Good food. Work not too hard. And look at these clothes.'

Jonathan was so enticed by city life that he tried on other visits to find an illegal job, to no avail. During the final moments of one leave he pleaded for more information as to how he should proceed, and his friend asked, 'You know anybody important might help you get a pass?'

'My father works for Detleef van Doorn.'

'You crazy? He's the one behind these laws. He's no friend. He's your worst enemy.'

Back at the mine, Jonathan asked Coetzee if he could help, but he said firmly, 'You're a mine worker now. You'll never be able to change because we need you.' And when Jonathan inquired at the pass office about getting an endorsement that would enable him to work in Johannesburg, the official snapped, 'You have mine papers. You'll never have anything else.'

Since he was sentenced to the underground, as it were, he decided to strive for the best job possible, but here again he was forestalled: 'You're qualified for drilling. Wasteful to try you anywhere else.'

Back in his quarters, Jonathan talked with men from Malawi and Vwarda: 'I'm going to apply for a job like Coetzee's. I know all he knows, or any of the other white bosses who work our deep shafts.' But in cautious Fanakalo the black workers warned him not even to whisper such a possibility: 'That job whites only. No matter how stupid, they smarter than you. No black ever be boss.'

Coetzee must have suspected Jonathan's concern, for one day as they crept out of the tunnel he volunteered: 'You could do my work, Nxumalo, but the law is rigid. No black must ever hold a job in which he might give orders to a white.' Before Jonathan could comment he reminded him of the Golden Reef work rules, which stipulated that dynamite placers had to be white. No black could ever aspire to that job, for the intelligence required to tamp dynamite into a hole drilled by a black was entirely beyond the capacity of non-whites. The fact that black workmen throughout the rest of the world easily performed that function was ignored; in South Africa they could never learn enough to do it properly.

Sometimes the white bosses didn't do it properly, either. One terribly hot and dust-choked day Roger Coetzee placed his dynamite carelessly, and Jonathan Nxumalo started to point this out, but before he could persuade Coetzee to correct it, the charge went off and an unplanned leaf of ceiling rock fell, trapping the Afrikaner behind a mass of rubble. The rock did not fall directly on him, or he would have been crushed. A sliding fragment did break his leg. He was trapped in a pitch-black, airless, waterless crevice with the temperature at 114° F. It was imperative that air and water pipes be got to him in a hurry, and with no white bosses in the vicinity, the task of doing it fell to Nxumalo. He probed through the fallen rock, lifted aside the chunks that he could handle, and called for other blacks to help with the bigger slabs. Within a few minutes white rescuers appeared on the scene, and proceeded exactly as Nxumalo had planned it. They succeeded in breaking Coetzee free, and from his hospital bed he asked to see Jonathan, who was ushered in by nurses who resented his being in the white hospital.

Coetzee was lucky to be alive, for there was no more deadly work in South Africa than that performed by men like him and Nxumalo. Each year more than six hundred men died in the gold mines—nineteen thousand in thirty years—and more than ninety percent were black.

'I know it was you that got me out,' Coetzee said, and before Nxumalo could say anything, he added graciously, 'And you were about to warn me not to do it that way.' He grinned and extended his hand. 'I wish I had a cousin in Johannesburg who needed a houseboy.'

No such luck. With Coetzee hospitalized, Nxumalo's shift got another boss, a tough Afrikaner who despised blacks. Once, when he saw Jonathan resting after a particularly stiff spell at the face, he growled at him, 'You work-shy idle black bastard.' Another day, when Nxumalo suggested approaching the face from a different angle, the boss yelled, 'No lip from you, you cheeky Kaffir bastard.'

Since Nxumalo's contract had only five more weeks to run, he tolerated the new man's insults, and when the compound manager said, at the termination of his eighteen months, 'I hope you'll sign on again,' he was noncommittal, but he was satisfied that he wanted no more of the Golden Reef. What he would do, he didn't know.

AT DEATH

Old Bloke, who delivered lawyers' letters at the Cheston Building in Johannesburg, was only fifty-four years old, but his life had been so demanding that he looked older than he was. His name was Bloke Ngqika, and in his early years he had worked at heavy labor in industry, where he had acquired numerous skills that could have been utilized in several advanced positions, but since he was a black he was prohibited from taking any of them.

After an accident in a tool-making foundry, which left him with a shuffle, he was extremely lucky to land a job delivering important papers by hand. It paid little, and the hours it took to commute to work and back home were intolerable, but he dared not quit because of a peculiar law which was severely enforced: it was possible for a black to qualify for a legal pass to remain in Johannesburg and permission to occupy a house in Soweto, but to do so he had to work for one employer only for a period of ten years. If he quit or was fired, he lost the endorsement in his pass book, lost his house and his right to remain in Johannesburg. He was like a medieval serf, bound perpetually not to the land, as the serf had been, but to a specific job. This meant, obviously, that his employer could pay him scant wages, and he was powerless to protest, for if he were fired, he would lose not only his job but his entire pattern of living. As his employer often reminded him, 'Bloke, it isn't only wages I'm paying you. It's your house, your pass, the permission for your wife to be here too. Mind your step.'

He did not mind his step one blustery August day when he stepped off a curb in Commissioner Street into the path of a truck, not immediately in the path, for the driver might have avoided him had he been attentive. As it was, the truck hit him hard, and the last words he heard before he fainted were the familiar ones: 'Bloody stupid Kaffir.'

He did not have to die. He could have been saved, except that the first ambulance on the scene was marked WHITES ONLY, and of course it could not help. It did radio for a NON-WHITE; however, Old Bloke lay on the sidewalk for nearly half an hour before the proper ambulance arrived, and on arrival at the non-white casualty ward of Jo'burg hospital he was certified dead.

The anguish that showed on his face just before he fainted was not caused, as some thought, by extreme pain; nor was it resentfulness at the muttered cursing of the truckdriver, for he got that all the time. It was his instant realization of what his death might mean to Miriam, his wife of more than thirty years. In a flash he saw her patient acceptance of the hardships thrown her way, the years of separation, the hard work of rearing children alone. Whole decades had passed with only brief visits from her husband; she could not join him, apartheid laws forbade that. So she had lived a meager life in one part of South Africa, he in another, and when Bloke at last gained the right that enabled her to live with him, she was so grateful that she advised him to accept any injustice regarding hours and wages: 'We got each other at last. You do the work, we say nothin'.'

On the third day after the funeral, Miriam was summoned to the office of Pieter Grobbelaar, director of the subdivision in Soweto where the Ngqika home was located. He informed her that since she was no longer married to a workingman with a legal right to remain in Soweto, she had become what the law called 'a superfluous appendage,' and as such, lost all right to remain in Johannesburg. He used the language well and outlined the steps of her expulsion.

'You can stay here to collect your things, but then you must leave for Soetgrond.'

'I've never been there. I don't even know where it is.'

'But you're a Xhosa. Your papers say that.'

'But I was born in Bloemfontein. I never been in Xhosa country.'

'The law says that you are now a temporary sojourner . . .'

At least ten times that first day Mr. Grobbelaar used the phrase 'the law says.' On every point raised by Mrs. Ngqika the law had anticipated her. Did she want to hold on to a house which she and her husband had occupied for ten years and had improved significantly? Mr. Grobbelaar could cite a law which said that the widow of a man lost all her rights when her husband died. Did she want to stay for six months in order to find some alternative place to stay? Mr. Grobbelaar could quote a law which said that he could order her to clear out within seventy-two hours. Did she want permission to take with her the new kitchen sink which Bloke had given her last Christmas? Mr. Grobbelaar had a law which said anything attached to the walls of government-owned property had to be left behind.

The first interview had miserable results. When she left Mr. Grobbelaar with his pile of papers, Mrs. Ngqika wept for two hours, then sent a young boy into Johannesburg to find her son, who had a 'location in the sky,' that is, quarters atop the apartment block in which he worked as cleaner. When this young fellow heard that his mother was being dispossessed and shipped off to a country location which she had never seen, he hurried out to Soweto.

'Mom, they can't send you to a place like Soetgrond. That's just a bunch of shacks in the veld.'

'Super says I got to go.'

'To hell with Super. I won't let you go.'

'He told me to come back to his office next week. You talk with him?'

And there was the difficulty. Her son's right to stay in Johannesburg, where he had not been born, depended upon his remaining invisible to the law. Were he to complain to Super, his papers would be inspected, the police would be summoned, and he, too, would be banished to Soetgrond. He was powerless to help his mother.

'Mom, there ain't nothing I can do,' and he was off to his location in the sky. If he could somehow hang on for ten years, he might earn a pass permitting him to remain in the area.

On the second visit Mr. Grobbelaar was as patient and as understanding as he had been on the first. He listened quietly to each of Mrs. Ngqika's frantic requests, then leafed through his gray canvas notebook till he found the relevant law and quoted it. He never raised his voice, and spoke not in Afrikaans, which she might not understand, but in English. He merely leafed through his papers and produced the law. When she got home she felt weak, and now she had only three weeks before she must quit this place into which she had poured so much of herself.

She was not being evicted because Bloke had been careless with his money; he had even gone to Super to ask if he could buy their little home, but the law book was explicit: 'No non-white may own land in Soweto.' And since Johannesburg non-whites were forbidden to live anywhere but Soweto, home ownership was impossible. As Mr. Grobbelaar explained: 'Bloke, you are allowed to remain here only so long as you do meaningful work to help the whites. And your wife is welcome only so long as your pass remains valid.'

That evening a group of black ladies met in Miriam Ngqika's kitchen to console her and to bid her farewell, and there was an awesomeness about the gathering, for each of these women knew that when their husbands died, they, too, would be exiled to some distant black spot which they had never seen and with which they had no affiliation whatever except by dictate of the new laws.

There was, however, in the group a schoolteacher who said, 'The Black Sash ladies have been asking us to find a case which they could fight. I think this is it.'

'I don't want to fight,' Miriam said quietly.

'But we got to fight,' the teacher said, and she warned the black women that it could become ugly and that reputations could be injured. 'Is there any scandal in your family?' the teacher asked, and the women stayed late at night, reviewing Miriam Ngqika's history, and it was blameless.

Early next morning the schoolteacher reported to the Black Sash society, and it happened that Mrs. Laura Saltwood was in attendance at a meeting of the national board, and when she heard the facts in the Ngqika case she exclaimed, 'Just what we've been waiting for!'

The committee agreed that Bloke Ngqika's fine record would be an asset in protesting this eviction, and the respectable manner in which he and his wife had lived would also help. Miriam Ngqika had an admirable reputation in the township, and it was assumed that Superintendent Grobbelaar would not be able to testify adversely against her.

He didn't. He listened carefully as Mrs. Saltwood made her plea, then in good English explained that the law . . . Here he turned the leaves to the applicable law: 'Mrs. Ngqika was always well behaved . . .' He sounded like an elementary-school teacher reporting on some infant; in fact, he was saying that he approved of the conduct of a woman fifteen years older than himself: 'She was neat, didn't drink, and I had no occasion to reprimand her.'

'Then why can't she stay?'

'Because all the Bantu are temporary sojourners, in a sense. She has become a superfluous appendage and must go.'

For an hour Superintendent Grobbelaar patiently glossed the laws, patiently explained that when a non-white family ceased to be useful to the white community, it must get out.

'But she's never been to Soetgrond,' Mrs. Saltwood protested.

'That may be so, but the law says that we must begin to get those non-useful people back to their own homelands.'

'Johannesburg is now her homeland.'

'Not any more.'

Mrs. Saltwood became almost offensive in her pressure for a humane concession, but Grobbelaar never lost his temper. When Mrs. Saltwood cried in moral outrage, 'Can't you see, Mr. Grobbelaar, that this is a great human tragedy?' he replied gently and with no bitterness, 'Mrs. Saltwood, every decision I have to make, week after week, involves what to the people concerned seems a great human tragedy. But we're trying to get our society sorted out.'

'At what human cost!'

'The cost may seem excessive to you, now. But when we have everyone in his place, you'll see that this is going to be a splendid country.'

With a wave of her arm she asked, 'Are you going to evict a million people here in Soweto?'

Superintendent Grobbelaar smiled. 'You English always exaggerate. It's five hundred and fifty thousand.'

'You don't count the illegals?'

'They will be dealt with.'

'You're going to evict them all?'

'Certainly not. Those who are essential to the operation of our businesses and industries will be allowed to remain. The rest? Yes, we'll evict them all. They'll have their own cities in their homelands.'

'How many black servants does Mrs. Grobbelaar have?'

'Two, if that's relevant.'

'You'll allow those two to stay?'

'Of course. They're essential.'

'Mr. Grobbelaar, can't you see that if you evict the blacks, Johannesburg will collapse?'

'We'll keep the ones we need.'

'But not the wives? Nor the children?'

'We want to avoid the clutter. They'll stay behind in the homelands.'

'Is there no appeal I can make in this matter?'

'Mrs. Ngqika is what the law calls a temporary sojourner, and she must go.'

He would make no concession. Never raising his voice or showing any irritation, he rebuffed every suggestion this difficult woman made, but when she was gone his face went livid and he roared at his assistant, 'I want three men to look into every aspect of that Ngqika woman's record. I'm going to teach that pair a lesson.' And forthwith he phoned a friend in the Security Branch: 'I suggest you take a close look at this Laura Saltwood. She consorts with Kaffirs.'

In the case of Mrs. Saltwood, secret police in various cities turned up only the facts that had appeared in newspapers. For some years she had been a thorn, defending non-whites against the just application of the new laws, but she had always acted in the open, so that no reasonable charge could be made against her.

'We'll keep close watch on her,' the Security Branch assured the Johannesburg police. 'One of these days she'll trip.'

In the Ngqika case something was found; a black living in Soweto informed the police that Miriam had a son occupying a location in the sky, but when they went to the address given they found that living there was an official of the government, whose wife protested that Miriam's son was the best and strongest cleaner she had ever employed and his continuance in the job was essential, so he was allowed to stay in Johannesburg, for the time being.

On a night in the third week, the last that Miriam Ngqika would spend in the house she had possessed for more than ten years but which she had not been allowed to own, the black women met in prayer and consolation. Afrikaners believed and tried to indoctrinate foreigners with the thesis that blacks of South Africa could never coalesce because they were tribal, with one group hating the other, but on this sad night Miriam's kitchen housed Xhosa, Zulu, Pondo, Sotho, Tswana and Shona. True, they were sometimes suspicious of one another, the way a respectable Episcopalian worries about a hard-shell Baptist, or the way a Catholic looks askance at a Jew, and sometimes that mistrust flared into faction fights, but that they were engaged in mortal combat was preposterous. These women shared a common destiny, and they knew it.

But as the night wore on, a remarkable event occurred. The schoolteacher who had enlisted the futile aid of the Black Sash crept through the streets leading a white woman, whose presence in Soweto was illegal and whose willingness to come at night was downright revolutionary. 'This is Mrs. Saltwood,' the teacher said. 'You've heard of her.'

The women had, especially the Shona woman who had been paid by Superintendent Grobbelaar to attend this meeting; she would report this criminal act, and the dossier on Mrs. Saltwood would note that at last this dangerous English woman had stepped across the boundary line from open defiance to criminal conspiracy.

What did the conspiracy consist of? Mrs. Saltwood told the black women, 'There are women all over the world who are fighting to stop such injustices. We've lost this battle, and Mrs. Ngqika will have to go this time, but . . .' Suddenly her stalwart manner vanished and she came close to tears, but she controlled herself, thinking: Tonight they need no white woman's tears. In a low voice she said, 'Miriam, we shall pray for you. In our hearts you will always have a home, even if they take this one . . .' Now she was almost crying, but she bit her lip and sat silent, the black women taking no notice of her emotional reactions.

In the morning Superintendent Grobbelaar appeared with a government truck, and Miriam's possessions were thrown into the back. Grobbelaar checked to be sure she did not take the kitchen sink, which was now government property, and at ten o'clock the truck pulled away, with Mrs. Ngqika and two other dispossessed women sitting atop their goods.

When the truck reached the Johannesburg railway station, the driver was surprised to see Mrs. Laura Saltwood waiting to accompany Mrs. Ngqika to her new home. She would, of course, have to travel in the WHITES ONLY coach, but there was nothing to prevent her watching over the dispossessed woman; if Mrs. Saltwood wanted to waste train fare to cry over one black woman no longer needed by the white community, that was permitted; but the driver did make note of the fact, and when he reported it to the superintendent, Grobbelaar had this latest evidence of rebellion forwarded to the secret police.

It was a tedious trip south; in the rude third-class compartments provided by the South African Railways for their black customers, women from various towns, whose husbands had died, were heading for homelands they had never seen. Young men who had tried to establish themselves in cities like Pretoria and Johannesburg were being sent back into their Bantustans. Most pitiful, in many respects, were the young married women who had wanted to live with their husbands in a real home, but who had been sent away; their husbands would work in Johannesburg for six or eight or ten years without their wives. In the end they might get legal papers; they might not.

'What is so wrong,' one young woman with a college education obtained in the black nation of Lesotho said, 'is that in Alexandra the government will build a six-story building for black men working in the city, and a mile away, surrounded by a high fence, another six-story building for black women, and they honestly believe that they can keep those men locked up at night in their building and the women locked up in their building, with no communion between them. And this is supposed to continue forever. Men and women aged twenty are to live like bees in these cells, without love between them, in a temporary sojourn that could be prolonged for forty years.'

Late on the second day the train reached a small station—Hilary Siding —in eastern Cape Province, and there the women destined for Soetgrond were ordered into trucks. Mrs. Saltwood was determined to stay with Miriam, but a white policeman said that that was impossible, and he refused to allow her to ride on the government truck. So she watched in angry silence as Miriam's few belongings were thrown on the ground. Then she phoned the Saltwoods at De Kraal to borrow one of their cars, and when it arrived, she drove with Miriam sitting beside her.

They followed the route of the truck to its miserable destination, and shuddered as they saw how bleak the area was. Soetgrond became even more forbidding as rain began to fall and darkness deepened, with the car sliding this way and that in the glassy mud.

They came at last to a village, some two hundred flimsy houses recently erected on eroded land, without a tree, without one square of grass or garden. There was a store, lit with kerosene lamps, and the beginning of two roads, mostly mud. Evacuees who had been moved down during the preceding year gathered to greet the newcomers and give them such encouragement as was possible. A government official took note of names, and when he came to Mrs. Ngqika he said, 'You have Lot Two-four-three.'

'Where's that?' Mrs. Saltwood asked.

It was now evening, and the official pointed down one of the dark and muddy roads. 'Down there. You'll find a placard.'

'Is there anyone to help us with these things?' she asked.

'Help?' The official laughed. 'You carry your own. Down there.'

So the two women, one black, one white, lifted the bundles and started down the almost impassable road. In some of the shacks lights shone, and this helped them to pick their way, but in others there was nothing, forcing Laura and Miriam to stumble about. They found shack Two-three-nine, then Two-four-zero, and Laura said, 'It can't be far.' But at Two-four-one the shacks stopped. Beyond, there lay only darkness and mud.

'We must be on the wrong road,' Laura said, and they went to the last house and inquired as to where Lot Two-four-three was, and an old man said in Xhosa, 'Just down there.' And he pointed to open space.

'What did he say?' Laura asked, and Miriam said, 'My lot is down there.'

'But there's no house!' Laura exclaimed.

In the gloom the two women stared at the vacant lot, and again Laura was tempted to turn back and ask for clarification, but a faded cardboard tacked to a leaning stick said clearly: Lot Two-four-three.

Good God! This was it. This woman who had worked so hard for so many years, this woman who had reared her children and educated them, who had mended her husband's clothes so that he could hold his precious job, received this as her reward.

'There really must be some mistake,' Laura said brightly. 'I'll ask.' And leaving Miriam, she trudged back to the official at the truck. He laughed again and said, 'That's how they all started. They got their lot and made something of it.'

'But where's she to sleep?'

'That's her problem.'

'No,' Laura said quietly. 'It's my problem, and it's yours.'

'Lady, get in your car and go home. These people find a way.'

She wanted to argue with him, but he turned his back and left. Standing in the drizzle, she thought: It is his problem. Government has plans to move three million eight hundred thousand people. One in six. In America that would be forty million people uprooted from good homes and moved to bad. And tonight I'm responsible for one of them.

Slowly, refusing to cry in her anguish, she trudged back through the mud, unable to believe that what she was experiencing could occur in a civilized society. A sovereign state, in the latter half of the twentieth century, believed that this was a solution to a problem involving human beings. In the muddy darkness, with soft rain slanting at her, she could visualize Superintendent Grobbelaar leafing through his canvas-backed book, finding the applicable law. It would be there, and it would be enforced.

'We'll sleep in my car,' Laura said softly when she joined Miriam.

In the rain the women wept.

In a valley not far to the north, on an eroded hillside, stood two stone cairns marking the graves of Mal Adriaan, who talked with hyenas, and Seena van Doorn, lusty daughter of old Rooi van Valck. Close by was the grave of Lodevicus the Hammer, to whom God had sent two faithful wives. Those Afrikaner pioneers had paid a terrible price for a foothold in this land, and they had done it in order to be free. In sentencing Miriam Ngqika to this awful place, their descendants had become prisoners of their own restrictive laws.

AT RESURRECTION

Despite the deprivations imposed by apartheid, the blacks of South Africa never lost their courage. They dreamed of a resurrection when they would again be free, and it is important to differentiate between the character of this dream prior to 1975 and after. The crucial change can be perceived in the contrasting lives of two men from the Vrymeer area: Daniel Nxumalo, grandson of Micah who had ridden with General de Groot and served the Van Doorns for so many years; and Matthew Magubane, whose parents worked on a farm near Venloo.

As a child Daniel Nxumalo showed such promise that as soon as possible he went not to the mines, like his brother Jonathan, but to the black college at Fort Hare. Since 1911 this institution had grown from little more than a high school to a full-fledged university with a faculty like no other in all Africa, composed of informed blacks who glimpsed the possibility of an awakening among their people. 'Teach as if the destiny of a free South Africa depended upon you alone' was the whispered motto of these teachers, and each devised tricks of speech and emphasis to signal to their wiser students: 'The police won't let me say what I ought to say next, but ask yourselves if Napoleon ever destroyed the national aspirations of any land he temporarily conquered?' A clever student at Fort Hare learned that what happened in the rest of the world might also happen in South Africa.

It was in a class in world history that Daniel first caught these signals. A woman professor who had never impressed him one way or other was teaching about the Norman Conquest of England; the curriculum was heavily loaded with developments in Holland and England rather than with pertinent events in South African life. She was explaining how Frenchmen had stormed across the Channel to impose their rule on the Saxon peasants of England, and Nxumalo was dozing.

She spoke in a singsong voice, reciting meaningless dates and genealogies, and then without a cue of any kind she stood quite still before the class and began to tell in her own words what it had been like in one small Saxon village when the conquerors arrived, and she used such vivid images and so many parallels to the trekboer invasion of frontier villages that all students became attentive. No papers rustled as she spoke on and on, treating of Saxon women with babies who could no longer own a cow for milk, and of the marching of Norman soldiers, and of the payment of taxes, until at the end she just stood there, tears streaming down her dark cheeks, not moving a muscle of her body as her voice continued with overwhelming passion the story of alien occupancy and lost freedoms.

For three months there was no other day like that, but its harrowing into the students' lives was deep and fertile, and word passed among the beds in the dormitory that this woman knew. She also knew that if she said anything specific relating to the condition of blacks in South Africa she would be spirited away by BOSS (Bureau of State Security) and perhaps never be seen again. Therefore, she had to convey her inner convictions without ever spelling them out, educating her pupils while keeping clear of BOSS. She played an intricate game, knowing that her history classes waited tensely for the next revealing lecture.

It came some fourteen weeks after she spoke of the subjugation of the Saxons. She was dealing with the difficult times America faced in 1861, when the nation was ripped apart by civil war, and meticulously she avoided the question of slavery or brutality, focusing instead on the movement of the battles, as was required in schools at that time. But when she came to the end of the war, she began to speak of what it meant to the blacks in one small town in South Carolina, and again she seemed to go into a trance and stood quite rigid as she imagined the impact of freedom on a community that had been so long in bondage, and she aroused in her students such wild visions of a different pattern of life that her small classroom became like a bomb, fused and eager to explode.

No young black, listening to her that day, could fail to comprehend her message, and among her students was one put there by BOSS, and this girl reported secretly to the police the subversion her teacher was practicing. There was no third lecture, because officials appeared, took the teacher away, and questioned her for three days before she was released. That was only the opening salvo of their harassing, and before the term's end she vanished. Her students were convinced she'd been sent to Robben Island; the fact was, she had fled the country on a forged exit permit and was teaching at the university in Nairobi, where she did not have to use Norman and Saxon as evasions for trekboer and Xhosa.

From this incident Daniel Nxumalo derived two generalizations which would determine his life pattern: It is imperative for me to learn what is happening to blacks elsewhere in the world, but I must do it so that I never attract the attention of BOSS. The first generalization was easier to carry out than the second, for as he learned more and more about Africa and Europe, he moved ever closer to the danger line.

BOSS was a semi-secret agency with power to arrest and detain without warrants of any kind. Any black or Coloured or Indian or even white who did anything that might conceivably endanger society could be investigated, and if shown to be a threat to apartheid, imprisoned on Robben Island, a speck of rocky land in Table Bay with a fine view of Table Mountain. Because of its mysteriousness, the legend grew that it was a hellhole. 'It makes Devil's Island look like a *fête champêtre,*' a French journalist wrote, but he was wrong. It was merely a strongly guarded prison for political dissidents, and was much more lenient than Alcatraz or even the best jails in Russia.

Blacks were sent there with shocking frequency, and there they stayed for having promoted the concept that their people should be freed from serfdom . . . or for having imported machine guns from Moçambique. Some were Communist revolutionaries, but too often that label had been pasted onto men who merely sought to be the Martin Luther King or Vernon Jordan of South Africa. Had Andrew Young been a citizen of the Transvaal, he would more likely have ended up on Robben Island than as an ambassador in the United Nations.

It was not easy for an involved black scholar to stay clear of BOSS, and by the time Daniel Nxumalo left Fort Hare he had entered their notebooks in four instances: (1) at a student gathering, as reported by the same spy who had turned in the history professor, he had given a rather pointed talk when someone mentioned Brazil; if he had said nothing, the topic in itself would have alerted suspicions, because Brazil had a mainly black population, but he reviewed a book by the Brazilian professor Gilberto Freyre, *The Masters and the Slaves,* which contained ominous parallels to South Africa; (2) at a mock United Nations convention he was assigned the role of Gromyko; he hadn't sought it, but someone had to be the Russian, so he accepted, and as a good student, studied Gromyko's life and opinion; his speech was quite Slavic; (3) at a cricket match in Port Elizabeth he was noted as having cheered not for the South African team but for England; (4) on several occasions he was observed singing the Freedom Hymn, popular with students, 'with more than necessary enthusiasm.'

At the end of his student days at Fort Hare it seemed pretty clear that eventually Daniel Nxumalo would be sent to Robben Island, but when he reported to Witwatersrand University to take his master's degree in sociology he fell in with quite a different kind of professor, a white man trained in England who summoned him to his office one day and roared at him, 'You damned fool! Keep your mouth shut. How can you exercise any leverage if you're in jail? Your task is to learn. Make yourself the brightest black in South Africa, then teach others.'

The professor was careful to avoid stating specifically the end purpose of such education and never explicated his ideas of revolutionary change through superior knowledge, for this would project him also into BOSS territory, but he did defuse Nxumalo's exhibitionism, converting him into a solid, knowing scholar.

The days at Wits were like the rich summer days of February in a good year; the enthusiasms of spring were gone, but the fruition of the ripening season was at hand. Daniel met students from all over the country, and professors of extraordinary brilliance from all over the world. Many of the students were Jewish, a group he had not known before, and their keen analysis of things he took for granted enlightened him; he was particularly impressed by the way many Wits students ridiculed apartheid, defying the segregation laws in private and infuriating the more conservative citizens of Jo'burg by lining the sides of Jan Smuts Avenue outside the university and waving at them, as they streamed home from work, amusing placards of an abusive nature.

But his real education came not from Wits, where he acquired an M.A., but from a university unique to South Africa and one of its most commendable inventions. The University of South Africa had no campus, no buildings, no classrooms in the sense of a regular university. Its campus was merely a post-office address in Pretoria and a faculty of learned men and women capable of supervising students throughout the republic. By mail Nxumalo registered for his doctoral studies and by mail he conducted them. He rarely met his professors, posting them each week the results of his study. He worked in silence, spending large sums on books published in London and New York, and if he lacked the advantage of arguing with students in dormitories, he achieved a comparable intellectual stimulus when his professor wrote: 'Interesting, but apparently you haven't read what Philip Tobias says on this subject. Can you dismiss Peter Garlake's theory on Great Zimbabwe?' In fact, he read rather more widely than young men his age at Stanford or the Sorbonne.

UNISA enabled any bright young man or woman in even the most remote village to acquire an advanced degree, and from government's point of view this produced two desirable results: South Africa was becoming one of the most capable nations on earth; and the lack of a central campus prevented potentially rebellious students from congregating at one spot, where ideas offensive to the proponents of apartheid might germinate. It also avoided the problems that would arise when the government ordered other universities like Wits and Cape Town to segregate.

At the conclusion of his doctorate-by-mail, Daniel Nxumalo, having utilized the system to maximum advantage, was an educated man with a burning determination to effect revolutionary change in his birthplace, and a firm resolve to escape entanglement with BOSS. Few men graduating that year from universities like Harvard or Oxford were undertaking a more difficult, tightrope assignment, but unexpected assistance from Matthew Magubane enabled him to fulfill it.

In his early years this Matthew had showed little promise—a bull-necked boy who resented discipline—and his education might well have ended at fourteen, except that his father knew the Nxumalos and asked young Daniel, already studying for his doctorate, to talk with his son.

Nxumalo found the boy quite difficult and was about to conclude that further education would be wasted, when the boy said suddenly and with great arrogance, 'Man don't have to go to college like you did to get what you want.'

'And what do I want?'

'Change things. I can tell by your face.'

'And you want to change things, too?' When the boy just sat there, refusing to answer, Nxumalo wanted to shake him as if he were a stubborn child, but he repressed the urge and said quietly, 'Matthew, to achieve what you want, you, too, must have an education.'

'Why?'

'Because I can see that you want to lead others. And you can't do this unless you know at least as much as they do.'

He arranged for Matthew's entrance to the black high school at Thaba Nchu, erected on the very site which Tjaart van Doorn and his Voortrekkers had occupied when they were seeking their freedom. There, like Nxumalo before him, he fell under the spell of an inspired woman teacher who kept on her desk a wood-carved motto: TEACH THIS DAY AS NEVER BEFORE. She was convinced that a revolution in values was under way across all of Africa; the Portuguese had been driven from Moçambique and Angola; South-West Africa would soon be black-governed; and great Rhodesia was crumbling. She never ranted about these vast changes, merely kept on the wall behind her as she lectured a large map of the area with three changes indicated by paste-on alterations: South-West Africa became Namibia; Rhodesia was Zimbabwe; and the fine port city of Lourenço Marques was now Maputo. Day after day her students saw those signals.

'You will be with me only for a brief time,' she told them. 'I must arouse enough enthusiasm to last your lifetime.' And she did, and underlying it all was a visible commitment to revolutionary change. On no student was her impact greater than on Matthew Magubane, whose marks never exceeded a low average but whose fiery convictions surged to an apex.

Magubane expressed himself not in sports, for he was awkward, nor was he much good in debating, which required an adroit mind. What captured him, sweeping his soul, was music. He had a resonant bass voice, unusual in a high school student, and an innate sense of how to use it to advantage. He sang alone; he sang in the quartet; and best of all, he sang in the school chorus. Four times a year the South African Railways offered black high schools concessions so that soccer teams and choruses could travel to various parts of the republic for competition with other black schools, and these safaris awakened Matthew to the possibilities of his country. He saw the rich ranching lands of the north, the Indian character of Durban, the majesty of the Cape. While other boys roughhoused in the S.A.R. coach, he stayed at the window staring at the endlessness of the barren Karroo, taking its brutal quality to heart, and with this awareness of the land he had inherited, even though it was not now his, he began to appreciate what Daniel Nxumalo had told him—that to accomplish anything in South Africa, he had to learn. In his final year he won the English and history prizes.

Magubane and Nxumalo arrived at the University of Zululand the same April, the first as a stocky fellow with the kind of hairdo that infuriated whites, the second as a gracile young man with a three-piece suit and neat haircut. They maintained a cool distance until the first term had almost ended; then Nxumalo went to the younger man's quarters, missed him, and left a note: *I would be pleased to see you in my room at five, Daniel Nxumalo.*

When Magubane in his rough clothes reached there, he found two upperclassmen seated on the floor, accompanied by three girl students, all drinking sweetish tea and discussing Gunnar Myrdal. It was a disconcerting experience, with Magubane conspicuously out of place but appreciative of the fact that Professor Nxumalo still retained an interest in him.

He did not want to become like the polished young men sitting on the floor; he was more at home with radical students who met around back tables at the café, and it was through association with them that he fell afoul of BOSS. It had started on a train excursion to Durban when Matthew led a gang of noisy students in a selection of revolutionary songs:

> 'There's a sun in the east
> Rising, rising.
> There's a moon in the west
> Falling, falling.
> I follow the sun, no matter how bright.
> There goes the moon, down into night.
> Oh, glorious sun!'

Police officials went to the university following this exhibition, for there were always spies, and the administrators asked Professor Nxumalo to warn young Magubane of the dangerous path he was pursuing, singing songs like that and encouraging others to join him.

When they were alone Daniel turned to Matthew: 'You're heading for trouble. You must pause and take a deep breath.'

'There can be no more pausing,' Matthew said.

'What do you intend?' Nxumalo asked evenly, not wanting to hear the response.

'I think many like me will have to go into exile. Into Moçambique.'

'No!' Daniel cried. 'That is not the way.'

'We'll go into Moçambique and get guns, the way the blacks in Moçambique went into Tanzania and got their guns.'

'South Africa will not be Moçambique. The Portuguese did not have the will to defend themselves. The Afrikaners do.'

'Then we will have to shoot the Afrikaners.'

'Believe me, they will shoot you down.'

'The first ten thousand, the second. But others will keep coming.'

'You expect to be in the first ten thousand?'

'I'd be ashamed not to be.'

They spoke in Zulu, and the phrases young Magubane used echoed the great periods of Zulu history; they were words from a past century applied to the one that was coming. He visualized himself as marching in an impi that dared not turn back, even though it faced certain annihilation. 'The others will keep coming,' Matthew said. He would not be among those others, and the victories they won would be unknown to him, for he would be dead, but they would be his victories, too.

Teacher and pupil ended this painful exchange centuries apart but with strong admiration each for the other, and when Professor Nxumalo discussed Magubane with the administration, he used empty and noncommittal phrases: 'I came away convinced that Matthew Magubane saw the error of his ways . . . There is no reason why he cannot return to what he was at Thaba Nchu . . . I see a bright future for this young man, for his commitment will match his grades . . .'

Before the end of the second term, Magubane was picked up by BOSS operatives and transferred to a police interrogation center in remote Hemelsdorp, where many infamous inquisitions had been conducted and where Jurgen Krause, grandson of Piet Krause, was determined to stamp out even the slightest signs of black insurgency.

He was a six-foot-three, broad-shouldered blond Afrikaner with a generous smile and powerful fists. As soon as the door closed behind Magubane, and the northern officers were gone, Krause said to his assistant, Sergeant Krog, 'Bring him here.'

With a mighty sweep of his right arm, Krog struck Magubane from behind, knocking him forward, and as the black stumbled toward Krause's desk, the latter swung his right fist with full power and smashed Matthew in the face. As the boy fell, both Krause and Krog leaped at him, punching and kicking until he fainted.

A security investigation anywhere in South Africa was a solemn affair; over the years some fifty men had fallen carelessly from eight-story buildings, strung themselves up with public-works blankets and died, but in Hemelsdorp, investigation was an art, and here such mistakes were avoided. When Magubane revived, his face wet with the water tossed over him, he found himself facing Sergeant Krog, who held an electric cattle prod.

'Undress,' Krog said.

When Magubane hesitated, the sergeant summoned two minor assistants, who ripped Matthew's clothes away, and as soon as he stood naked, Krog applied the prod to his testicles, watching with satisfaction as Matthew leaped and jumped to avoid the torture. When he ran into a corner, bending to protect his genitals, Krog jammed the end of the prod into his anus, applying such a heavy charge of electricity that the student fainted.

Year after year one black in four throughout the general population was arrested for some trivial offense or other, and it was fortunate for them that not all police were as determined and sadistic as the team of Krause and Krog. Their like could be found in most countries; Russia, East Germany, Iran, Argentina, Brazil, all had such interrogators. But the majority of South African policemen tried to be law-abiding officers of justice; Krause and Krog were officers of terror.

For three days Magubane was punched and kicked and tormented. He did get fed and he was allowed to go to the bathroom and drink as he required, but the torture was incessant. At the end of four days the only charge against him was 'You cheeky Kaffir bastard,' a phrase leveled against any black who had progressed as far as high school or who refused to behave deferentially. It was a terrifying charge, because almost invariably it was accompanied by some brutal punishment, so that the words actually meant 'Take that, you cheeky Kaffir bastard,' the *that* being a smash to the mouth or a prod with an electric probe.

Matthew had been told, on the playing grounds at Thaba Nchu, that 'white police officers are preoccupied with black genitals,' but in his innocence he could not conceive what this meant. Now he was learning, for Krause and Krog relished having him stand before them naked so they could jab his private parts with the electric tip, and once, as they prepared to do so, Matthew broke into laughter. He was recalling what he had heard a black man say after being released: 'They put so much electricity into me I was afraid I'd light up like a bulb.'

Matthew's laughter so infuriated Krause that he and Krog kicked him unconscious, and when he revived, still naked in the cold room, he heard the first serious charge against him. The officers were singing in cracked and unharmonious voice the freedom song:

'There's a sun in the east
Rising, rising.
There's a moon in the west
Falling, falling.'

The words were familiar, as Matthew came out of his daze, but not the tune, and he looked with pity at the two officers, for they were singing their own dirge and could not find the melody.

'What do you mean, "a sun in the east"?'

'Nothing, Boer.' A smash to the side of the head.

'Don't you mean Moçambique?'

'No, Boer.' Another smash behind the ear.

'Don't you mean the swine who have fled this country into Moçambique?'

'No, Boer.' Another smash.

'I suggest, Magubane, that you mean the terrorists with guns over there.'

'No, Boer.' This time he was jabbed so hard with the electric prod that he danced in the air, arms and legs in all directions.

'Running to Moçambique, are you?'

He was too numb to respond, so they jabbed him for almost two minutes, after which he fainted.

When he revived, too weak to stand erect, they propped him against a wall, and he felt blood oozing from his nose. He was positive that this had not occurred when he was conscious; they must have been kicking him while he lay on the floor, and he moved parts of his body to see if anything had been broken by their heavy boots.

'And what, pray tell, Mr. Magubane, is "falling, falling"?'

'Nothing, Boer.' More punishment.

'Stand up, you cheeky Kaffir bastard. Now you tell us what you mean by "falling, falling." I put it to you, Magubane. You mean that South Africa is falling, don't you?'

There was more punishment, the flailing out of worried men, and Matthew realized that he was being tortured so furiously because he had been overheard singing a song whose words the police could not interpret.

'All right, you cheeky bastard, you sing the song for us.' Krause began in his monotone to chant the words, joined quickly by Krog, whose efforts augmented the dissonance. 'Sing!' Krog screamed, and slowly, with deep powerful tones, Magubane picked up the song, lending it significance and beauty:

> 'I follow the sun, no matter how bright.
> There goes the moon, down out of sight.'

Krog, reading from a typed copy of the song, detected Magubane's change in words and halted the singing.

'You changed the words!'

'There are many verses,' Magubane said.

On the seventh day he heard the second serious charge: 'People say you're a black-consciousness activist.'

'I am for black power, yes.' Smash to the jaw.

'You're a Bantu, a stupid goddamned Kaffir Bantu, with no power at all!'

'Yes, Boer, I am an African.' Fist in the mouth.

Afrikaners like Marius van Doorn, the son of Detleef, looked forward to the day when there was one citizenship in South Africa; he felt himself to be a man of Africa—an African—and he did not want that honorable word applied only to blacks. But other Afrikaners were infuriated if any black claimed to be an African, as Magubane was doing, for they sensed a grave danger: the black was seeking outside help from his brothers in powerful black nations like Nigeria.

'Now, Mr. Magubane, I want you to explain what makes you think you're an African.' Prod with the electric tip. 'Dance if you wish, but go on with your explanation.' More prodding.

'I'm a native of Africa, as you are. We're both Africans.' Smash to the face. 'I'm willing to accept you, and you must accept me.'

'You cheeky bastard!' And the fury of the two officers at being linked in a brotherhood stemming from a common terrain was ungovernable.

Next morning Magubane awakened convinced that on this day Officers Krause and Krog intended killing him. He was mistaken. BOSS was never so callous as to plan a murder; all it sought was to intimidate potential troublemakers. 'Trimming the hedge,' Krause called it. 'When a cheeky Kaffir starts to stick his head up, like a wild branch in a hedge, what's the sensible thing to do? Knock it back.' This prevented trouble later on, so BOSS developed the system of bringing any black who was beginning to exhibit leadership into custody, kick him around a bit, and set him free. The danger was that after nine or ten days of interrogation the black man might be beyond freedom: 'Case No. 51. Verdict. Death while trying to escape.'

And this might have been Magubane's end except for the work of two men outside the jail who had never met Magubane. The first was André Malan, white, twenty-nine, and a reporter for the *Durban Gazette.* He was a courageous chap dedicated to the high quality of South African journalism and suspicious of why so many Hemelsdorp investigations ended in fatal attempts at escape.

On the day of Matthew Magubane's arrest two black men had slipped into Malan's office and expressed a premonition that the young man was exactly the kind of black who would prove so intractable that Jurgen Krause would be tempted to forget what the regulations said about avoiding undue pressure. 'Watch what happens,' the blacks warned.

So André Malan began writing articles about the detention of Magubane, and he asked the police to issue reports of the young man's well-being. In fact, he created so much pressure that officials became irritated and decided to apply one of their laws against him.

There was a law in South Africa which said that BOSS could invade the quarters of any writer at any time without a warrant, and if they found any notes or materials or photographs which *might* be used to write an article which *might* be offensive to the government, that writer could be detained indefinitely without any charges being brought against him.

On the morning of the eighth day one of Malan's two black informants ran to his apartment, shouting, 'Get rid of your papers!'

As a newsman who had watched three of his colleagues imprisoned by BOSS, he required no additional explanation; he destroyed the few papers he had allowed to accumulate, even those not relating to Matthew Magubane, then hastily scanned his bookshelves to see if any of the thousands of books banned by the government were there. Reasonably assured, he waited.

The BOSS crew did appear. They did ransack his quarters. And they did find one book published by the World Council of Churches in Geneva, and it was this which justified them in putting him in jail, on no charges, with no warrant, and with no right of self-defense.

News coverage of Matthew Magubane ended. The police were free to continue their probing of his life and beliefs as they wished, except that on a farm near Vrymeer the rebellious young black Jonathan Nxumalo, unemployed now but once a worker at the Golden Reef Mines, had been following in the newspapers the running record of Magubane's detention. Now he heard of Malan's arrest and deduced that Magubane was about to be murdered. Convening four friends, he took an informal vote: 'How many say we try to rescue Magubane?' All five voted yes. 'And then flee to Moçambique?' This time only four voted, the man who refrained explaining, 'My mother . . .'

'No explanations necessary. Tomorrow night we could all be dead.'

'Or on the way to Moçambique.'

Jonathan then cleared his throat and said, tentatively, 'My brother's home on vacation from university. I think we should have his advice.' Someone was dispatched to fetch the professor, and when he stood at the entrance to the small room in which they met, he realized that the men inside represented a conspiracy. To take even one step into that room would make him a part of the criminal movement, with the possibility of a lifetime in prison, or even death. His whole inclination was to turn and run, but the liveliness of their faces made that impossible. These were the young men he had been training, and now they were about to train him. He joined them.

'We're going to storm the jail at Hemelsdorp,' his brother said.

'I supposed that might be it.'

'We've a cache of guns smuggled in from Moçambique.'

'I wish you could do it without guns.'

'This is the year of the gun,' Jonathan said. 'If we get to Moçambique, what do you think we should do?'

If he had left the room even at this point he might have avoided incrimination, but like other blacks across the nation he felt a growing sense of the future. 'I would not storm the police station. You could all get killed.' As soon as he uttered these words he knew they were irrelevant; these men were prepared to die.

'About Moçambique,' his brother repeated.

'I can't go with you. My job is to teach young men at the university.'

'Daniel,' his brother cried. 'We don't want you to come. Men like you . . . stay here to build. Men like us . . . get out so we can tear down.'

Professor Nxumalo felt old and out of place; he was alarmed at where his teaching had led, but he was also profoundly excited by the challenge. 'When you reach Moçambique—and you will, I know you will—you've got to consolidate. Make no move till you can rely upon help from all the frontiers. Namibia, Zimbabwe, Botswana, Vwarda, and especially Moçambique. Then move subtly, a push here, a retreat there. In a dozen years, with help from Russia, East Germany and Cuba, the monolith will crumble.'

'We give it the first push tomorrow,' Jonathan said, embracing his brother. And when the professor was gone, he handed out the guns.

By separate routes the five young men journeyed to Hemelsdorp, having agreed to rush the detention center at one in the afternoon, when lesser policemen, like Krog, would be at lunch and their superiors, like Krause, so well-fed as to be lethargic. Jonathan's men would be armed, a fact which almost guaranteed their execution if apprehended.

Quietly they converged on the barracks, waited an interminable five minutes in position, then without any kind of juvenile exhibitionism, walked resolutely into the headquarters, took possession of the desk and the hallways, and hurriedly searched the rooms till they found Magubane.

'What's happening?' he asked through swollen lips.

'Off to Moçambique!'

As they ran from the barracks without having fired a round, the young man who had to care for his mother headed north, where he would function underground. The others concealed their guns and went into exile.

One of the most gratifying days in Van Doorn's life occurred on 16 December 1966, when he was invited to deliver the main speech at the Day of the Covenant celebrations at the new housing development that had arisen, under his direction, on the site from which the black township of Sophiatown had been bulldozed. The area had been renamed Triomf and was now occupied by white Afrikaner families who kept their little houses neat and their flower beds flourishing.

But as Detleef drove along the clean wide streets that had replaced the slum alleys he said somewhat sourly to his white chauffeur, 'I'll wager most people in those houses have no idea what the new name means.'

His chauffeur said quickly, 'But we know what a triumph it was, don't we?'

Van Doorn showed his appreciation for this support, then said, 'Sophia-town was a national disgrace. Crime, poverty, young tsotsis running wild.'

'A white man would be afraid to go there after dark,' the chauffeur agreed.

'Tell me frankly, isn't our new Triomf a hundred times better?'

Like any impartial judge, the chauffeur had to admit the new suburb was not only better, but was also inhabited by people of a much higher status: 'You did a wonderful thing here, Mr. van Doorn.'

Inspired by such approbation, Detleef showed real enthusiasm as he approached the podium in the church hall. Among the other dignitaries on the platform were four ancient men, oudstryders (old fighters), veterans of the Boer War, who nodded approvingly as he lambasted the enemies of the nation. In many ways his speech was a summation of his vision regarding the future of the Volk:

> 'Our beloved Voortrekkers, Retief, Pretorius and Uys, who an-swered the summons to freedom, saved this nation when it faced mortal danger. With pride I add my own grandfather, Tjaart van Doorn, who helped in handing to us the precious gem that is South Africa. They gave us more—their vision of God's will as it guides the destiny of the Afrikaner nation . . .

> 'Never forget, this is the land of the Afrikaner, paid for with our blood and held through our faith. When the father of this nation, Jan van Riebeeck, first set foot on this soil in 1652 he found it empty, absolutely empty, of any Xhosa or Zulu, who had not then reached south of the Limpopo. Oh, there were a few Bushmen and Hottentot who died tragically from smallpox and other diseases. But this land was empty and we took it . . .

> 'To protect what God gave us in His covenant we have fought and won great battles, and we shall forever be ready to move back into laager to resist any onslaught against us. This we must do, because we were placed here by God to do His work . . .

> 'But let us be always mindful that there are vicious forces arrayed against us, eager to break the spirit of our small proud people who sparkle like a diamond among the nations of the earth. These bitter enemies refuse to see the wisdom of what we are trying to accom-plish here. Who are these enemies? The anti-Afrikaner establish-ment. The priest establishment. The English establishment. The press establishment. The wealthy liberalists who still grudge us our glorious national victory in 1948 . . .

'When we occupied this empty land, we were a pitiful few, devout Christians unable to stem the entrance of Xhosa and Zulu into our country. Now that they are here, it is our duty to guide and discipline and govern them. When the English ruled, the blacks were like cattle moving over all the land, grazing here, grazing there, destroying the rich veld. We put a stop to that. We put them back in the kraal. And now we move them from places like the old Sophiatown to new quarters of their own . . .

'But we are told today that civilization means equality and that the Kaffir [his first use of this word] must be raised up and given a free share of everything the Afrikaner worked and died for. I have nothing against the black man. I have deep sympathy for his backwardness, but I do not want him as my brother. [Laughter from the audience] And I certainly do not want to hear him prate about "Africa for the Africans." This part of Africa is for the Afrikaners, and no one else . . . [This occasioned wild applause, and Detleef took a drink of water; he was sweating now and very red in the face; his voice shook with emotion.]

'I am the first to admit that the Kaffir has a place in this country, and our new laws will help him keep to it. We will never allow him to dictate: "White man do this," or "White man do that," for if we do he'll take our head. I say to the Kaffir and the brown man, "Out of the kindness of our hearts, out of our deep study of Divine Providence, we will chart a path for you along which you can find happiness and peace . . ." [More applause and cheering]

'My final message on this sacred day commemorating the death of our heroes in Dingane's Kraal is to our young people. Sons and daughters! Be physically and spiritually prepared for the assaults our enemies will make. Protect your identity as we protected your language. When I was a child they stuck a dunce cap on my head because I spoke Dutch. I fought back. You, too, will have to fight, as these veterans behind me fought. Allow no terrorist regiments on your soil, no Communist propaganda, no liberalist weakness, no Anglican bishops spreading lies. And when you fight, know that you are doing God's will, for he ordained that you should be here . . .

'If you are steadfast, you will triumph, as we triumphed over poverty and slums when we bulldozed Sophiatown to make way for this splendid development you see today with its white houses and neat gardens. In the darkest days of war Oom Paul Kruger said, "I tell you God says this nation will survive. Most certainly the Lord will triumph." Today, young people, look about you. This is the hour of Afrikaner triumph.'

As he moved away from the podium, he felt a pain in his chest; he swayed unsteadily, but reached his chair and sat down. Other speakers followed,

with one confining himself to 'Triomf over Sophiatown,' but it never occurred to anyone present to ask what it was that they had triumphed over
when they erased this black spot. Over the old women who had worked in
white homes for fifty years and hoped for a refuge in which to die? Over
young black children who had begun to learn in Father Huddleston's
missions? Over sturdy black workmen who had long manned essential jobs
in Johannesburg and who now had to travel many miles to work each
morning and back at night? Over the clergymen who had protested the
immorality of bulldozing serviceable homes so that favored whites could be
spared the sight of black neighbors? Over the good white women, English
and Dutch, of the Black Sash who had tried to protect the rights of black
mothers and their children? Over the attempts at reconciliation, which
should have prevailed in South Africa and didn't? Over what had Van
Doorn's system triumphed, except the forces of reason?

The pains assailed Detleef again, accompanied this time by a heaviness
in the chest which he had to recognize as serious. To the Boer War veteran
next him he whispered, 'Damnation! Just as we were getting things truly
sorted out.'

He was whisked to a private ward in the Johannesburg General Hospital, and his family was summoned from Vrymeer. When they assembled at
his bed and heard his labored breathing they waited for Marius to speak,
but Detleef did not want to hear from that one. He distrusted his son, and
as older people often will, leaped a generation and extended his shaking
hands toward his granddaughter, flaxen-haired Susanna. 'Come closer, Sannie,' he whispered, and when he kissed her hands, a gesture most inappropriate from him, the others realized that death must be near. Marius left
the room to call Vrymeer, asking that two things precious to the old man
be brought in at once.

'Sannie,' the dying man said, 'you must always do the thing that is right
for your country.' This had been the dictate of his life: the honest move, the
just act. He felt that the determination of what was just and honest had best
be left to the judgment of men like himself, who were above greed or vanity
and who acted solely in the interests of society.

'You're inheriting a noble country,' he told the girl. 'Now that people
have been told their place and can rely on just laws to help them keep it.'
He noticed that Marius had reentered the room and was wincing at this
summary, but he could not understand why. He could not conceive that a
son of his might ask, 'Who assigned the places? Can such allocations be
made without consultation with those who are being assigned?' Detleef was
convinced that since well-intentioned men, attentive to God's teachings,
had made these decisions, to question them endangered the republic. He
could not believe that his son would peck like a raven at a fabric so justly
woven.

As the afternoon wore on he again began to visualize the enemies who
had endangered his land; immortal adversaries, they ranged themselves
along the wall waiting for him to die. First were the blacks, who threatened
to engulf the nation, cursed offspring of Dingane and stained, like him, with
treachery. No! No! First there were the English. Always there were the
English enemies, with their clever ways, their superiority of language and
class. Two thousand years from now, when Great Pretoria lay crumbled in

dust, you could be sure that some Englishman had knocked down the stones. They were the permanent enemy, and he was about to cry out that he still hated them when his mind cleared and he said boldly to everyone in the room, 'I have never hated anyone. I have acted only from a sense of justice.'

He did not hate the English—he pitied them, with their lost empire and their doomed superiorities. Nor did he hate the Indians, either; they were a sad lot huddling in their stores. It was regrettable that they had not been expelled, as the Chinese were; then he smiled, for the vision of Mahatma Gandhi flashed across his mind. 'We got rid of that one,' he said. Nor did he hate the Jews, even though they had stolen the diamond mines and the gold. 'They contaminate our land. We should have expelled them, too.'

'Who?' his wife asked, but before he could respond, there was a commotion in the hall. An official of some kind, you could tell that from his voice, was warning someone: 'You can't go in there. Blacks are not allowed on these floors.'

Marius hurried into the hallway, offered explanations, and soon brought into the sickroom Moses Nxumalo, who carried in his arms the great brassbound Bible. It was impossible to determine which of these gifts from the country pleased the dying man most. He loved old Moses, who had shared so many of the important moments of his life, and he cherished the sacred Bible which contained the record of that life, reaching back through the generations to the young sailor who had planted this Holy Book, actually and figuratively, on South African soil.

He held out his hands to both the black and the Bible.

'I'm so glad you came,' he said weakly.

'I've been weeping for you,' Moses said. 'But now my eyes are cured, seeing you again.' They spoke of old days, of meaningful adventures, and it was impossible for the black to acknowledge that it was this white who had done so much to hedge in his sons, who had promulgated so many laws to restrict and emasculate them. Detleef was merely the good master, and to see him so near death was bitterness.

It was the Bible that brought Detleef back to reality, and he began thumbing its heavy pages, printed so long ago in Amsterdam, its heavy Gothic letters setting for all time the course of right and wrong. It was inconceivable that God had delivered these words in anything but Dutch . . .

He stopped. Not even at the doorway to death could he forgive one insidious enemy who fought both South Africa and God: the infamous World Council of Churches, which refused to see that what Van Doorn and his helpers had done was right and openly made cash contributions to murderous revolutionaries. 'How can they ignore the good things we've done?'

'Who ignores us?' Marius asked.

'Why do they all persecute us?' he whimpered.

And he began to recite the sufferings of the Boers: 'The Black Circuit. Slagter's Nek. Blaauwkrantz. Dingane's Kraal. The Jameson Raid. Chrissiesmeer Camp.' Bitterly he repeated that infamous name: 'Chrissiesmeer!' Then: 'Where's Sannie?'

Impatiently he gestured Moses and Marius aside and reached toward his granddaughter. When he saw her bright face outlined against the stark-white walls he whispered, 'Sannie, never forget what they did to us at Chrissiesmeer.'

Mention of that dreadful place so enraged him that blood drained from his brain and he passed into a strange kind of coma: He saw his bed ringed not with members of his family but with the timeless enemies of the Volk: Hilary Saltwood siding with the Xhosa. The man from America giving orders to the hangman at Slagter's Nek. Dingane giving his bloodstained signal. Cecil Rhodes, implacable foe. Teacher Amberson making him wear the sign: I SPOKE DUTCH TODAY. The Jew Hoggenheimer, who had monopolized the mines. The Catholics who had sought to destroy his Martin Luther church. Officials from the United Nations talking sanctions. Was ever a nation so beset by enemies? And among the shadowy figures he saw his own son, who had chosen a scholarship at contaminating Oxford rather than a captaincy of the Springboks. Enemies all.

Then blood returned to his fevered brain and a light seemed to enter the room, illuminating past and future. He rose on his arm and began shouting, 'Laager toe, broers— Draw the wagons into a circle!'

'Sannie, tell the drivers to draw . . .' He fell back, breathing heavily, and reached for old Moses: 'Warn your sons—everyone must hold to his assigned place . . .'

When it became apparent that he was dead, Marius leaned down to kiss the embattled face, then covered it with a blanket. Closing the old Bible, he said, 'Lucky man. He won't have to watch the consequences of his handiwork.'

XIV.
Diamonds

O N three hundred and fifty-five days a year you could smell Pik
Prinsloo at a distance of twenty feet. One old prospector who had
worked the diamond diggings with him said, 'Pik takes a wash once
a year. Twenty-fourth of December. Says it covers him three ways. Christmas, New Year's and the heat of summer. So for about ten days he's
tolerable, but come the middle of January, then it's the same old Pik.'

Had he been married, his wife would probably have made him bathe,
but he lived with a slatternly sister in a gypsy-type tin-walled house-wagon
drawn by eight donkeys. He was seventy-one years old, toothless, bearded,
stooped, with rheumy eyes and matted hair; he wore a flimsy undershirt,
sagging pants, untied shoes with no socks and an oil-stained khaki hat. He
had been haunting diamond fields since the age of ten.

He lived on canned foods, bits of meat and such mealie-pap as his
slovenly sister bothered to make; his house-wagon was such a disgrace that
other diamond hunters said, 'Even the bush lice won't go in.' Yet he lived
in a kind of odoriferous glory, because on six mornings a week, year after
fading year, he wakened with the conviction that on this day his luck was
bound to change: 'Today I find that diamond as big as a fist.' After a swig
of lukewarm coffee two or three days old, he would shuffle out the door of
his house-wagon, stand in the dust, scratch himself under both arms and
shout, 'Kom nou! Waar is die diamante?' And he would almost run to the
spot where his five sieves waited and his pick and shovel rested against a
tree. He was perpetually convinced that a day would come when he would
find his diamond.

He had little cause for optimism. As a boy of fourteen he had been the
main support of one of those marginal Afrikaner farms, and on this waterless land he had been expected to sustain himself and his sister. Four
dreadful drought-ridden years passed as they fought to grub existence from
the inhospitable acres, always urged on by their predikant, who cited vari-

ous parables relevant to their condition. One Sunday, after returning from prayers for rain to a noontime meal of pumpkin and mealies, Pik and his sister concluded that God did not intend them to struggle with land to which He sent no water, so they abandoned the farm and acquired the house-wagon and eight mules.

In 1926, as a youth of eighteen, he searched for alluvial diamonds on the Lichtenburg diggings, following a tributary of the Vaal, and there he found his first profitable gem: a flawed stone of just under four carats for which he received the intoxicating sum of £47. That night he announced himself as a diamond digger: 'Pik Prinsloo, diamonds.'

His luck had not held. For five desolate years he trudged the Lichtenburg diggings without turning up another diamond of any size. He found chips. He found trivial stones of less than half a carat. But the diamond as big as a fist eluded him, as did those as big as the tip of his little finger, and in 1932 he experienced the indignity of having to quit the diamond fields to test his fortune in the eastern Transvaal gold fields, but even when he did pan a few payable nuggets he derived little satisfaction from them. He was a diamond man; the lure of those beautiful gems tantalized him, so back he went with his spinster sister, his mules and his sieves to probe the smaller streams of the north.

He had no luck whatever, and 1937 found him on the emerald fields near Gravelotte, at the western border of the Kruger National Park. Sometimes at night, sitting in his house-wagon in some lonely spot, he would hear the lions and hyenas, but unlike the other diggers, he never ventured into the park to see the great beasts. 'I'm a diamond man,' he growled. 'I oughtn't to be here at all. A bucketful of emeralds isn't worth one good diamond, and some day . . .'

No matter where he went, or how his fortunes decayed, he had one treasure which differentiated him from most other men, and on the rare occasions when he left his sister to join the other diggers in some rural bar and strangers would intrude, he would be apt to place upon the counter a small flat object wrapped in dirty canvas and say ominously, 'Look in there and you'll see who I am.' And the stranger would rather gingerly unfold the canvas and find therein a Digger's Certificate, printed by the government in 1926, which stated that Pik Prinsloo, of Kroonstad in the Orange Free State, was a licensed digger. And on the back, in variously colored inks, stood the record of his having renewed this precious license each following year, at a fee of five shillings.

'I'm a diamond man,' Pik explained, and if anyone pointed out that he was working emeralds, he would apologize: 'Right now I'm gathering capital, because I got me eye on a stream up north . . .' He would hesitate, turn his rheumy eyes upon the stranger, and ask, 'Would you maybe want to back me? I know where there's diamonds for certain.'

In this way, in the summer of 1977, Pik found his fifth partner, a commercial traveler from Johannesburg who had always wanted to participate in the diamond madness. They had met in a bar, and when Pik displayed his Digger's Certificate with its endless renewals, the man said, 'I been looking for a fellow just like you. How much do you need?'

In the excited discussion which ensued, the Johannesburg man had the good sense to ask, 'By the way, has anyone else staked you? I mean, would there be outstanding claims ahead of mine?'

For Pik Prinsloo to lie about his diamond business was impossible: 'I owe four men ahead of you.' Then, grabbing the stranger's arm, he added quickly, 'But they was long ago. Maybe twenty years.'

The Johannesburg man drew back, looked at the old digger, and hesitated. But then he saw that wizened face, the lips without teeth, so that nose and chin almost met, the torn undershirt, the sockless feet and the deep fire burning inside the watery eyes, and he knew that if he intended gambling on some self-deceived diamond man, this was the kind he had been seeking.

'How much would you need to move north?' he asked quietly.

Without hesitation, for he had been calculating such problems for fifty years, Pik replied, 'Three hundred and fifty rand.'

'You have it,' the man said, and that was how in the New Year of 1978, Prinsloo and his nagging sister drove their donkeys north to the Swartstroom, parked their house-wagon in a field some miles north of Sannie's Tits, and started their prospecting.

Old Pik had been attracted to this particular stream by signs he had seen many years before, the harbingers of diamonds: agates and flecks of reddish garnet mixed in with ilmenite, the jet-black rock which had first been identified and named at the Ilmen Mountains in Russia. The more he studied the stream in those days, the more convinced he had become that it must be diamantiferous. 'The bantoms are heavy and black,' he told his sister in their filthy wagon. 'There's got to be diamonds here.'

'If there was,' she grumbled, 'somebody else would've noticed.'

'Maybe somebody else wasn't as smart as me,' he said, but when weeks passed without a find, she insisted that he head south to sites which had been proclaimed.

Now he still had more than three hundred rand, enough, counting his state pension, to live on for three years at the frugal rate at which he and his sister ate. One huge can of baked beans, the top knocked off by a dulled opener, a pot of mealie meal and some scraggy mutton would suffice for three days, bent forks scraping over the tin plates. 'Ek sê vir jou, Netje. [I'm telling you, Netje.] There's diamonds this time, and I'm the one to find the damned things.'

Jamming his beaten hat with its torn wide brim onto his uncombed head, he hunched up his shoulders as if marching to war, and went forth to probe the Swartstroom.

Fortunately, the level of the stream was low, so that he could concentrate on the meanders of this remnant of the mighty rivers which had cut away the earth. He worked only the inside of the bends, for there the water slowed and dropped whatever heavy objects it might be carrying. If there were diamonds, they would be hiding here, so day after day he dug the gravel and passed it through his sieves. When he eliminated the larger rocks, which he inspected fleetingly, he was left with a residue which might conceivably hide a diamond, and this he sieved carefully, with much water and a poetic, drifting motion that swirled the gravel about in such a way as to gravitate the heavier bantom to the bottom and into the center. Thus, when he flipped the sieve over onto a flat surface, any diamond would be on top, in the center.

On a hot morning in January 1978 he carried his sieve to the shaded area where he always did his inspecting, flipped it, and with a curious knifelike scraper, which he had been using for more than forty years, sorted the agates, certain that on this lucky day he was destined to find a diamond. None appeared. Had one been in the rubble it would have shone so brilliantly in the shadows that he would have spotted it within seconds, but none did. Instead he saw something which pleased him mightily, so that he ran from his pan to call his sister: 'Netje! Look at what we have!'

In her felt slippers and faded cotton dress she came grumbling from the house-wagon, picking her way along the rocky footpath to the stream, where she studied the mess left by the sorting and snorted, 'Gemors, man. Nothing!'

'The little ones!' Pik cried with bursting excitement.

She looked at the little ones and saw nothing, at which her exasperated brother shouted, 'The little red ones! They're garnets!'

Beside them she saw the ilmenite, too, glistening black, and then even she had to concede that this stream was worth searching.

January and February, the sweating months, were spent probing the inner banks where the water slowed, and although not a single diamond chip was found, garnet and ilmenite continued to show in faint traces, signs as positive as if someone had posted a notice: DIAMONDS HIDING HERE.

So he kept searching, and then one morning in October, after he had gobbled two spoonfuls of cold pap, he shuffled out, heart high and trousers dragging, to a new bend in the Swartstroom, and on the first panning, when he flipped the gravel, there in the middle of the small mound rested a shimmering gem larger than the end of his thumb.

There could be no mistake about it, for although the stone lay in shadow it glimmered like a light in darkness, vibrating even through the film of muddy deposit that clouded it. It was a diamond, the biggest old Pik had ever found in fifty-two years of searching, and he was so stunned by his discovery that when he tried to shout for Netje, no sound came from his throat.

And that was good, because as soon as he hefted the diamond, and cleaned it, and studied it in sunlight, seeing that it had pentagon-shaped faces and what appeared to be a good color, he realized that he must keep his find secret until such time as he had explored the vicinity. But this posed a problem. South African diamond law was bitterly severe where possession of uncut gems was concerned; and the most reviled profession a man could follow was I.D.B.—illegal diamond buyer.

The finding of even the smallest diamond became an act encased in legal paperwork. Within twenty-four hours Pik had, by law, to enter his diamond in his personal register, stating its site of finding, its approximate weight and likely value. Then within three days he must carry his diamond to some police station and register it, and he could not simply report that he had found such-and-such a stone of such-and-such weight; he must show it to them physically, and allow them to describe and weigh it. These details would be entered in both his register and the police record, and stamped. And as soon as that was done, the world would be informed that Pik

Prinsloo had found a diamond stream, and hungry men would flood the place.

Pik was familiar with this procedure; indeed, he had often dreamed of chaperoning a real diamond through the intricate process, but now that he had control of one, he sought to protect himself. He wanted four or five days to inspect this bend on the chance that it contained a parcel of equal gems, but to delay involved illegality, and he had seen too many men go to jail for ignoring the strict rules.

What to do? He sat for some time with the diamond in his cupped hands, convincing himself that it was as fine a stone as he had first believed: Hell, this one'll bring two thousand rand! The thought staggered him, so he studied the stone again. It was a good one and it really could bring as much as two thousand rand: God Almagtig! We're rich! Trembling, he spit on the diamond, polished it, and was sitting with it in the sun when he became aware that a drop of moisture had fallen upon it. He was sweating, and it was then that he buried the diamond beneath a well-marked rock and returned feverishly to the stream.

He dug and sieved and gravitated all that day, but found nothing. At dusk he returned to the house-wagon, tethered the mules, and came in to supper. 'Why you so nervous?' his sister asked, and he said his head ached. But when he got up twice during the night to stand barefooted outside the door, staring toward the rock where his diamond lay, his canny sister whispered as he came back in, 'You found one, didn't you?' And he could not repress his surging excitement.

In mumbles that came rushing forth through his toothless gums, he told her of his legendary find: 'Bigger than my thumb. Fine color, fine color. Netje, this one could bring two thousand rand.'

'Don't be a damned fool,' she growled.

'It could. Honestly it could. When you see it . . .'

'So you hid it under a rock?'

'I want to search the stream.'

'You want to go to jail. You enter it in the book, proper. You take it to the police.'

'I got to protect myself.'

But she was adamant, and as soon as enough light showed in the east for them to see, she marched to the rock, and when the diamond was placed in her hands, and its true weight and color were evident, tears came to her eyes. 'It's a real diamond,' she conceded, but the concept of two thousand rand was beyond her.

In the house-wagon it was she who took down Pik's register and in an almost illiterate scrawl wrote: 'Swartstroom, by the three acacias, 11 October 1978, about five carats, color good. Maybe two thousand rand.' That afternoon she and Pik walked six miles to the nearest police station to register their find.

Once the diamond was legally registered, it became Pik Prinsloo's property, to dispose of as he wished, but only through established channels. If he allowed this stone to fall into the hands of some I.D.B., both he and the buyer would go to jail; he must take it personally to the diamond market at Boskuil, two hundred and sixty miles to the west. The trip could be made by train—four hours to Johannesburg, five more to Boskuil—but old Pik felt that with such an impressive stone, he ought to travel by private auto, so with great difficulty, because he hated telephones, he called his backer in Johannesburg: 'We got the biggest diamond in my life. Let's go to Boskuil and sell it for two thousand rand.'

The man said he could break free late Friday afternoon— 'Stop right there!' Pik shouted. 'We got to be in Boskuil Friday morning. Only day the buyers come.'

So early Thursday his backer came for him and they got in the car and started for a location which had no equal in the world: a remote farm lost in the barren lands south of Johannesburg, where by tradition diamond buyers from all over the nation clustered in a collection of rough corrugated-iron shacks to see what the local adventurers might have found. The trip was not easy, for whenever Pik and his diamond left one magisterial jurisdiction to enter a new, he had to be prepared to produce his registration papers so that the authorities could trace this one diamond across the country and be assured that it made its way into the hands of a licensed buyer. And when Pik reached the jurisdiction in which it was to be sold, he must register it anew.

The halts were tedious enough, but this October day was turning out to be one of the hottest of the new spring season, so that the car steamed inside, and Pik's habit of not bathing now became a penetrating problem.

The Johannesburg man tried opening his window, then Pik's, then all the windows, but even this flow of fresh air failed to alleviate the awful smell, and the man began to wonder if even a five-carat diamond was worth the torment. But at last they came to Boskuil farm, at about the same time as the evening train which brought the buyers for the Friday market. Office Number One had for some years been occupied by H. Steyn, Licensed Diamond Dealer of excellent reputation, and early Friday morning Mr. Steyn, a small, knowing man dressed in a dark suit, posted his certificate on the outer door, donned cuff guards, and placed his German-made six-power loupe on the table upon which his elbows rested.

First man in line was Pik Prinsloo, grubby khaki shirt, sagging trousers, hat with broken brim. For fifty-two years the diamond merchants had known this fellow, a splinter diamond here, a fragment there, and always the promise that one of these days . . . No buyer had ever handed old Pik more than three hundred rand at a time, and on this meager flow of capital he had survived.

H. Steyn, seeing the old fellow approach, assumed that once again Pik had found himself a quarter-carat stone worth a few pounds, but when he noticed that the smelly old man was trembling, and there was a wild light in his eye, he realized that this day was special. And when Pik's backer started to enter the shack, Steyn noticed how the prospector waved him back: 'You stay outside. This is my job.' There was some muffled conversation, at the end of which the old man screamed, 'Of course I'll tell you how much, and if I don't, Mr. Steyn will. Now get out!'

'You have a stone?' Mr. Steyn asked.

Pik's hands shook, but after an awkward moment he produced a matchbox, which he slid open with difficulty, and placed upon the table a diamond large enough to make H. Steyn cough. 'You have your papers for this?' he asked.

'Papers?' old Pik shouted. 'You're damn right I got papers.' There was more fumbling, and when the familiar documents were spread before Mr. Steyn he pretended to read them, using this as an excuse for finding time to run through a series of hasty, silent calculations: Goodness, that looks to be at least five carats! It's makable. Possibly a brilliant. Can't see any big flaws. What's the color? Might even be an ice-white. Probably cut down to about one-point-four carats. I could sell this to Tel Aviv for maybe ten thousand dollars. They could sell it to New York for fifteen thousand. Ultimate buyer, as much as twenty-eight thousand dollars. So I could afford to pay him fifteen hundred dollars a carat or seventy-five hundred in all. But that would be shaving it a little close. Best I ought to go would be fourteen hundred dollars a carat, or seven thousand in all. I'll offer him thirteen fifty a carat, or sixty-seven fifty in all. Like all diamond buyers, he did his calculations in dollars, since America was the ultimate market, but since he had to pay in rand, he knew immediately what the exchange would be. It took $1.16 to purchase one rand, so that the final price of $6,750 worked out to about R5,800, and that was the figure he kept in mind as he prepared to speak.

While H. Steyn was completing his calculations, old Pik was pursuing his: It's a good stone. It's worth two thousand rand. And I saw his eyes light up when I placed it on the desk. Damn, I will ask two-five. Look at that diamond. He doesn't see a diamond that good in a month. It could even go for two-six. Damn, I'll go for two-six.

H. Steyn cherished his reputation as dean of diamond buyers, 'the man who never cheated anyone,' but did not feel that in order to sustain his good name he had to pay exorbitant prices. He had found it most effective to state an honest price, just a fraction less than some hungry buyer might offer, and then to adjust it slightly upward if he really wanted the stone.

The more he studied this one, the more he wanted it. This could be a fine stone, he said to himself. The color might turn out to be much better than I think. It won't cut to more than one-point-four carats, but when it's done, it could be an exciting diamond.

'Pik,' he said in the low voice he used in such negotiations, 'I won't fool around. You've got yourself a very good stone. I'm going to offer you top price. Five thousand, eight hundred rand.'

Pik stood silent. Mustering all his strength, he was able to keep from gasping or staggering backward. His head bent forward, so that Steyn could see only the broken rim of his big hat, and it was very still. Finally Pik gained control of himself, and in what he assumed was a normal voice he asked, 'Of course, that's an open offer?'

Now Steyn had to control himself, not from trembling but from laughing. Here was a man in his seventies, never had a real diamond in his possession before, would probably earn more from this one than he had from all his fragments in the past twenty years. And he was haggling. But Steyn enjoyed such men and wished them well, so if old Pik wanted to haggle, he'd go along.

'Wait a minute!' he said with a show of irritation. 'I make you a firm offer of fifty-eight hundred now. I am not making you an open offer, allowing you to go up and down the row, seeing if you can engineer a bid a little higher. I'm warning you right now you won't. So don't come back here at nightfall and tell me, "I'll take your fifty-eight hundred, Mr. Steyn," because at nightfall that offer don't stand. You accept it right now, or I withdraw it.'

Pik said nothing. Steyn's offer was almost triple what he had realistically expected, more than double his most sanguine hope, and desperately he wanted to accept it, pay off his five backers, and take Netje enough to live on for the rest of their lives. But as a diamond man he also wanted to play the whole game, to go from shack to shack, displaying his incredible find, to hear the other men whispering, 'Prinsloo's got himself a diamond,' and he would not be cheated of this exercise, not even by an offer of great wealth.

'Got to see what the others say,' he muttered, closing his matchbox and heading for the door.

H. Steyn rose to accompany him. Ignoring the horrendous smell that radiated like a halo, he threw his arm about the old man's shoulders, and said, 'I'm sorry to lose that stone, Pik. It's a good one. Don't let them cheat you.'

'Don't intend to,' Pik said.

By midafternoon the backer from Johannesburg was weary of the charade: 'Damn it, Pik, you got three good bids. Take one of them and let's get out of here.'

But Prinsloo was enjoying himself as never before. To walk into a real buyer's shack, to open the matchbox, to watch the buyer as he studied the find in disbelief, to hear the tentative offers, and then the real bid. Buyer Number Five had offered five thousand, nine hundred, and kept it an open bid: 'I'd like to get that stone, Pik. Come back, because I know you won't find any higher.'

At the seventh shack, Adams and Feinstein, the bid went to six thousand rand even, and this, too, was open. 'Six thousand rand!' Pik reported to his backer. 'God Almighty, that's more money than you earned in your whole life.'

'We're taking it, I hope.'

'Nope.'

The Johannesburg man exploded, did some cursing, then listened, amazed, as Pik said, 'All my life I dreamed of walking in to H. Steyn's and selling him a diamond. A real diamond.' So against the protests of his partner, the old man went back and told Steyn, 'I got me a bid of six thousand even. Would you consider going along with it?'

Without hesitation Steyn said, 'No.' But when the old man's face turned gray, he added, 'I made you an honest offer, Pik. But let me see the color again.'

With a rush old Pik produced the matchbox, fumbled awkwardly, and placed the stone once more upon the table. With a show of studious professionalism Steyn picked up his loupe, took the diamond in his left fingers, and studied it carefully. No detectable flaws. A color perhaps one grade higher than he had judged at first. The stone cut from this raw diamond might sell in America for . . . Who knows what the Harry Winston people could get for such a stone—$32,000?

Slowly Steyn put down the loupe, shoving the lovely diamond back toward the old man. 'Best I can do, Pik. Fifty-nine fifty.'

'Sold!' Pik cried with exultation. But when he reached the car his partner berated him: 'You damned fool! Adams and Feinstein offered you six thousand. Cash in hand. What in hell are you doing?'

'I want to act like a gentleman,' Pik said. 'I like to deal with them. You should know that. When you offered to back me, there in the bar—did I haggle over terms?' The Johannesburg man made no reply, so Pik finished: 'Tomorrow you and me find the others. Give them their share. Then we divide a fortune.'

'If you're going to be rich,' the partner said, 'would you consider taking a bath?' Pik said nothing. He was imagining the look on Netje's face when he told her that he had walked right into H. Steyn's office and demanded six thousand rand . . . and almost got it.

News of the Swartstroom find flashed across South Africa, and before nightfall was known in Tel Aviv, Amsterdam and New York. It alerted geologists at the Anglo-American offices on Main Street in Johannesburg, and especially the officials at Amalgamated Mines in Pretoria.

'This is our chance,' the president told the executive board that convened in special session on Saturday morning. 'What do we know about the Swartstroom?'

His men knew a great deal: 'Little stream flowing into Moçambique. Researched many times. Negative. It does lie in the general vicinity of the Premier Mine, but doesn't seem to be connected in any way. No logical pipe areas near it, and remember that it's cut off from Premier by those low mountains.'

'You think Prinsloo's find was an accidental?'

'No find is ever accidental, if it's been honestly reported.'

'What do we know about Prinsloo?'

'For over fifty years he's always prospected the possible streams. Never wasted his time where there were no signals.'

'What signals could he have seen?'

'Damned if I know. I've been up and down that stream six times. Never even saw garnets.'

'Well, he saw something. And we'd better go back.'

There was much discussion as to whom to send, and the geologist who made the earlier six explorations eagerly wanted another crack at it, but the president said, 'There's that American who's being expelled from our mines in Vwarda. Isn't he exceptionally good?'

When the young man's file was produced, the man from personnel summarized it rapidly: 'Born Ypsilanti 1948. University of Michigan. Graduate work at Colorado School of Mines in Golden. Worked at Broken Hill in Australia. Supervisor at Mount Isa. We offered him a job on the strong recommendation of all his professors and superiors. He worked at our place in Sierra Leone, then to Botswana, and finally as field manager in Vwarda.'

'His expulsion from Vwarda?' the president asked. 'Did it reflect on him. Morally, I mean?'

'Certainly not from our end. He did a splendid job for us.'

'I mean, was there a public scandal? Would we be hurt if . . .'

'Sir,' the personnel man said in a tired voice, 'it was the usual. I have the whole nonsense, too damned dismal to repeat. After independence he was kept on at our mines. When Richardson was fired on that trumped-up currency charge he became chief. Did a first-class job for us and for Vwarda. One of the few white men accepted by the new regime. But one day a committee went to the prime minister and accused him of racism. And he was expelled.'

'Is he racist? These southern Americans, you know.'

'I think Michigan is in the north. When Richardson was kicked out, the government insisted upon placing in all the second echelons Vwardians who could scarcely read or write. But they were cousins of the prime minister. So one day, when the entire operation threatened to collapse, our man fired them all. Said he had to have someone in command who could manage without coming to work at eleven in the morning in a Mercedes-Benz.'

'And those men,' the chairman suggested, 'formed the committee that charged him with racism.'

'The same,' the personnel man said.

'What's our chap's name again?'

'Philip Saltwood.'

'Related to that Saltwood woman who keeps provoking the government?'

'Not likely.'

'We can't afford to go looking for scandal, you know.'

'This Saltwood's an American.'

He was summoned from Zambia, to which he had fled after his expulsion from Vwarda, and he arrived one morning at the Swartstroom driving a white Toyota with the gold monogram AMAL. He was followed by two other white cars bearing the famous letters, and then by two white trucks carrying five workmen each. A team of eighteen would now work every bend of this little stream, for it was imperative that the industry know whether a new source of alluvial diamonds had been found, and if so, where the master pipe might be hiding that produced them. It would be Philip Saltwood's responsibility to answer these questions, and he had seventeen assistants and twelve months in which to do it.

When he first arrived at the Swartstroom that sunny November morning in 1978 he seemed ideally suited for the task. A theoretical geologist well trained in America and Australia, he had acquired broad experience in the oil fields of the former country and the gold mines of the latter. In recent years his specialty had become diamonds, as a result of his intensive work in places like Sierra Leone, Botswana and Vwarda, and he brought to his present task a considerable knowledge.

He was thirty years old, bright, hard-working, and because of his American-Australian diet, much more solid than the average South African Saltwood. He had always known vaguely that his family stemmed from Salisbury in England, with a major branch in South Africa, but none of his relatives had ever made contact with either branch.

He was divorced from an Australian girl, and since they had had no children, there were no lingering emotional ties. They had met while he was working at Broken Hill and had courted while chasing brumbies across the

Outback. They had spent their honeymoon on the ski slopes in New Zealand, and as long as Philip worked Down Under they were a happy pair.

But when he was sent back to America, she could not adjust. The oil fields of Oklahoma had broken her spirit, and prospecting in central Wyoming had proved intolerable, so one afternoon she fled those barren regions in a Quantas plane to Australia, informing Philip of her departure only when she reached the safety of civilized Sydney. There she obtained a divorce on the grounds that he had deserted her, and sometimes he could scarcely remember her name.

He established his camp quickly and with stern authority: 'At the beginning we work three weeks unbroken, then a week off. Spend that week as you will, but come back sober. Workday starts forty minutes after sunrise, so get up early and hit the chow line. Good on you.' His speech was an amalgam of Texan, Australian and African diamond field; his manner, international-mine-field. He was a bold man determined to whip this crew and this rivulet into shape, and when he surveyed the six white tents in which he and his men would live for the following months, he took satisfaction in the secure way they had been pegged to the ground and the orderly manner in which they lined up. He knew of no other way to work.

There was great excitement in surrounding towns like Venloo when it was learned that Amalgamated Mines was making a serious probe of the Swartstroom, and curious businessmen kept trying to discover whether any further diamonds had been uncovered: 'They work from sunrise to sundown, and they got all kinds of machinery. They've an American in charge, and he drives them.'

'But did they find any diamonds?'

'Not from what I hear. That stream's been worked before, you know. Back in the thirties, I been told. They found nothing then, either.'

But old Pik Prinsloo had found his diamond, now reported to have been eleven carats in size. 'Yes, but sometimes I wonder. He's a canny old coot. You suppose he salted it?'

Why and from where would a seventy-one-year-old man salt a trivial little Transvaal stream? From time to time Saltwood would hear rumors that he was hauling his house-wagon to some new site, but none of the workmen had ever actually seen the filthy old fellow. They attended their power-driven scoops, their mechanized gravitators as they moved methodically from one bend in the stream to the next, finding nothing.

'Hell,' a long-time Amalgamated field man growled, 'we aren't even finding garnet or ilmenite.'

And then, in late November, Pik Prinsloo, working on his own at an unpromising site, came up with a find that was in some ways more exciting than his first: at locations well separated he uncovered two diamond chips, the largest only one-tenth of a carat, both together worth only seventy rand. The significance of this find was that it confirmed the fact that the Swartstroom was indeed diamantiferous.

Saltwood's men, working at the Amalgamated camp, were even more pleased by this unexpected find than was old Pik, and although the week of their vacation was upon them, they agreed to work straight through and delay their off-time till December. For the first six days they found nothing, then, on Saturday, they produced a third chip, about one-eighth of a carat, so small the layman would barely have noticed it, and they telephoned the stirring news to Pretoria. They had confirmed a new diamond site.

Philip Saltwood spent his week of vacation in the small town of Venloo eating good food at the neat hotel run by a Jewish couple, and since on Sundays there was absolutely nothing to do there, he attended the morning service at the Dutch Reformed church, where he caught his first glimpse of the real South Africa.

He wandered in a few minutes after the service had started, and by good fortune the congregation was singing a hymn he had grown to love, popular in both Australia and America. It was Martin Luther's 'Ein Feste Burg Ist Unser Gott,' and although it was being sung in Afrikaans, its noble message was the same in any language, and he bellowed his version in English. As he did so, he became aware that a most lovely Afrikaner girl, her hair in Saxon braids, was laughing at him. Turning his head quickly, he caught her eye, and she blushed and buried her face in her hymnal. But since she knew this greatest of the Afrikaans hymns by heart, she soon looked up, and he saw the golden face that would haunt him during the remaining months of his dig. It was squarish, characteristically Dutch, with broad forehead, blue eyes, generous lips and pronounced chin. She was not a tall girl, but she gave the impression of being extremely solid, like some tidy Cape Dutch farmhouse nestled against the berg. She was dressed in white, so that her flaxen hair and golden complexion shone to good advantage, and in no way could she discipline her mischievous smile.

He ended Luther's rousing hymn, this battle cry of a new religion, with his voice in full power, then sat so that he could watch the girl with the Saxon braids, but before long his attention was drawn to the pulpit, raised high above the congregation, from which a young predikant with brilliant forcefulness had begun to deliver his sermon, leaning down in his black robes to castigate, implore, inspirit, deride, cajole, threaten and bless.

I haven't heard preaching like that since the Holy Rollers in the Oklahoma oil fields, Saltwood said to himself, and for the moment he forgot the girl as he tried to follow what the predikant was saying. He knew only such Afrikaans as an engineer would acquire in a mining camp, but this was sufficient for him to pick out the main ideas: Joshua was on a hilltop looking down at Jericho, facing a great obligation placed upon him by the Lord, and the people of this congregation, every man, woman and child, stood this morning upon a similar hilltop staring down at his or her obligation.

The theme of the sermon was powerful, but it was the delivery that overwhelmed Saltwood: This isn't your basic Episcopalian homily. This is by-God religion. That man's the best I ever heard.

And then he saw something which had escaped him at first. In a special section of pews at the right hand of the predikant sat a group of older men, solemn-faced and rigid, each dressed in somber black with white shirt and gleaming white tie, and each word that the young predikant uttered seemed to be recorded mentally by these thirty men, who nodded when they approved what he said, or sat grimly silent when they did not. Because they were seated well below the pulpit, which was hung suspended from the ceiling of the church, they had to raise their faces to see the predikant, so that they looked like a group from some Ghirlandaio fresco in Florence or the figures from a dark terracotta casting by one of the Della Robbias.

To the left of the preacher, in a similar collection of pews, sat a much younger group of men, also dressed in funereal black with the same type of white shirt and white tie. They, too, followed the predikant with intense interest, but their special function did not become clear until toward the end of the service, when they rose en masse, moved to the foot of the pulpit, and took heavy wooden plates in which to gather the collection. As the choir sang, the young men moved briskly along the aisles, and when Salt- wood saw how big they were he thought: I'd hate to tackle that gang on a rugger field. He smiled, then looked at the older men: Or try to pass a law that they didn't approve of.

The service ended with a brief, sweet prayer of consolation and recon- ciliation, and when Saltwood started for the exit he concluded: This could be the finest church service I've ever attended. He sensed that it had been a community affair, a gathering of like-minded persons who sincerely sought the message their predikant had to offer, and whose voices were raised in unison to give thanks to God for once more having demonstrated His benevolence and concern.

He was thinking in this manner when he felt his arm taken by a firm grasp, after which a strong voice asked, 'Aren't you Philip Saltwood, from the diggings?'

'I am,' he said, and turned to see a stalwart man in his forties, obviously Afrikaner, although why Philip thought so he could not have explained. The man smiled the warm greeting which Afrikaners always extended to strangers visiting their churches.

'I'm Marius van Doorn. We live just west of here, and we'd be honored if you'd take dinner with us.' With this the speaker reached back, clasped the arm of his wife and brought her forward, and she, in turn, reached for the hand of her daughter, and Saltwood saw to his delight that this was the girl with the Saxon braids who had been laughing at him.

'This is my daughter Sannie,' the man said.

'Susanna van Doorn,' her mother explained, and they headed for Vry- meer.

The original invitation had been for one dinner, after church, on one Sunday afternoon. It was extended to drop-in meals whenever Saltwood could detach himself from the diamond explorations, and whenever he drove the few miles from Venloo to Vrymeer and came over that last hill, his heart beat faster to see the white-faced blesbok grazing quietly. They seemed like unicorns of legend attending the lovely young woman waiting in the farm- house.

Because of the shape of the Van Doorn house and the way the road twisted, visitors were attracted automatically to the kitchen stoep, as if aware that here life centered. The front door was rarely used, and this was understandable, for at the Van Doorns', the family usually gathered in the big, inviting rear room. It contained a long plank table, two comfortable carver chairs, one for the master, the other for any honored guest, and nine sturdy chairs of lesser dignity. Against one wall stood shelves of Ball jars containing canned fruits and vegetables; opposite was a collection of old copperware. There was a big glass container, too, but only rarely did a guest learn of its contents: all that remained of the old brown-and-gold Dutch crock that had been in the Van Doorn family for generations. At the far end of the kitchen an electric range had long since replaced the old coal-eating monster, but the servants who had tended that area were still present: an older Nxumalo woman and two young girls. Most of all, the kitchen exuded a sense of warmth and home, as if here innumerable meals had been eaten, vivid topics discussed.

Sannie did not try to mask her pleasure in having the American geologist as an unannounced suitor; when he came to the farm she ran to the stoep to greet him, extending her two hands and bringing him into the kitchen, where hot coffee and cold beer were waiting. By the end of his second month at the dig he had begun to think of Vrymeer as his headquarters; he even took his telephone calls there. It was a constantly rewarding experience, for not only was Sannie a charming young woman, but her parents were helpful and instructive. Mrs. van Doorn was English and represented the thinking of that large segment of the population, but her husband was a true Afrikaner, and from him Philip derived his insights into the thinking of the men who directed the country. Debate in the Van Doorn kitchen was apt to be heated and prolonged, and as Saltwood listened to the conflicting points of view he realized that he was sharing a privileged introduction to South African life: the Afrikaner view; the English view; and in Sannie's bold opinions, the view of the new breed who represented the best of the two older stocks.

Like all visitors, Philip was astounded by the freedom with which the citizens of South Africa discussed their problems. The expression of ideas and the exploration of alternatives were totally free, and what was not said in the kitchen debates was spelled out in the very good English-language newspapers. This was no dictatorship, like Idi Amin's Uganda or Franco's Spain; within fifteen minutes of meeting the average Afrikaner family, a stranger was sure to be asked: 'Mr. Saltwood, do you think we can escape armed revolution?' or 'Have you ever heard anything more stupid than what our prime minister proposed yesterday?' What with his intense work at the diggings, where he was in contact with all types of South Africans, and his discussions at Vrymeer, Philip was learning much about this country.

But of course his real purpose in visiting the farm was not to gain an education; he was falling in love with Sannie van Doorn, and he had reason to believe that she was most seriously interested in him. In the third month, with her parents' obvious consent, she accepted his invitation to visit the diamond claims, and then to drive over to Kruger National Park, where they would spend two days watching the great animals.

At the diamond camp she asked, 'Philip, what is it you're doing?'

He showed her where they had found traces of diamond, and when she saw how minute the specks were she gasped: 'Why, they're not worth anything!' And he said, 'They're pointers, and diamond experts all over the world are thrilled that we've found them.'

'Pointing to what?' she asked, whereupon he honored her with a graduate seminar on diamonds. She understood only the highlights, but when he reinforced his lecture with a rough diagram, she grasped what he was up to.

'This is the Swartstroom, the little river we're exploring. It's yielded diamonds, so we know they exist. Our problem is "Where did they come from?" They didn't originate in this stream, that we know. It merely carried them here. But from where? This branch of the river is Krokodilspruit. After we finish here, we'll look there. Maybe they were carried down that stream. We'll look everywhere.'

'What for?'

'The pipe. My life is spent looking for the pipe.'

'And what's that?'

'About a billion years ago, give or take a million or two, one hundred and twenty miles straight down, somewhere near here, a kind of subterranean cave or area developed. We know its characteristics completely: twelve hundred degrees Celsius, pressure sixty-two thousand times greater than here at the surface. In that environment, and there alone, carbon transmutes into diamonds. In some circumstances down there this carbon becomes coal; in others, graphite. In ours it becomes diamonds.'

'But what's the pipe?'

'The diamonds form in a kind of blue clay, and when everything is just right, that clay, carrying its diamonds with it, roars upward through one hundred and twenty miles of intervening material and bursts loose, something like a volcano.'

'I still don't know what the pipe is.'

'The channel it leaves on its upward journey. Lined with that blue clay and sometimes diamonds. We call the blue clay kimberlite, after Kimberley. And my job is to find that pipe, lined with kimberlite, carrying diamonds.'

'Where do you think it might be?' Sannie asked, and he said, 'For this year I torment myself with only two questions: "Will Sannie van Doorn marry me?" and "Where in hell is the pipe that produced these diamond fragments?" '

'Where could it be?'

Returning to the diagram, he said, 'You can see that it can't be down at Chrissie Meer. Those mountains would prevent this river from coming this way. That region up there is too far north. It can't be over at Vrymeer, because those two little hills . . .' He paused in some embarrassment.

'You mean Sannie's Tits?' she asked demurely.

'You damned Afrikaners are very careless with words. We better get over to Kruger Park.'

At the close of their first long day with the animals they stopped at a camping site, whose manager asked routinely, 'One rondavel?' and Sannie said promptly, 'Two, if you please.'

So that night they slept apart, but on the second day of viewing animals they came upon a glade where giraffes were resting in shadows, some seventy of them, and two were in the courting mood. It was an extraordinary sight, these tall, ungainly animals, preserved by some freak of nature from ages past, standing under trees facing each other and twining their necks in the most lovely, slow, poetic way, as if they were weaving dreams. It was their love dance, unmatched in nature.

As they watched, Sannie moved closer, until at the conclusion of the giraffes' exquisite performance the human beings were duplicating the animals, touching and kissing and moving apart, then rushing together again. That night when they approached the same camping ground, it was Sannie who suggested: 'Let's drive to the other one. It'll be less embarrassing.' And when they reached the alternate and the caretaker asked, 'One rondavel?' she said, 'Yes.'

In succeeding weeks Sannie and Philip took excursions to various sites in eastern Transvaal—north to Waterval-Boven to see the cog railway, south to Chrissiesmeer to see the site of the concentration camp—and on one weekend they drove to Pretoria to see the capital, and the rugged beauty of this veld city was a surprise. Philip was excited by the imposing statue of Oom Paul Kruger in the center of town, with four handsome statues of burghers ready to ride forth on commando.

'It's heroic—the way a patriotic statue should be,' he exclaimed.

'Wait till you see the Voortrekker Monument!' she cried, pleased that he was respectful of her treasures. And again she was right. This great, brooding pile atop its mountain, this amazing echo of Great Zimbabwe, was such a perfect evocation of the Afrikaner spirit that he was almost afraid to enter. 'Do they allow Englishmen in here?'

'They're not welcome,' she joked, 'but I'll tell them you're my Afrikaner cousin from Ceylon.' When they went inside and Philip saw the fiercely patriotic bas-reliefs depicting Blood River and the other victories of the Afrikaner tribe, he was struck by the strangeness of a nation's having as its principal monument a memorial in which only a small segment of its population would feel welcomed. There were no blacks here, no Englishmen at ease, only Afrikaners reveling in their hard-won victories.

'How many people are there in South Africa?' he asked as they sat on stone benches in the lower crypt.

'About thirty-one million, all told.'

'And how many Afrikaners?'

'Let's say three million maximum.'

'Less than one-tenth of the total. Doesn't it seem odd to you, Sannie, to have your major national monument restricted to one-tenth of the population?'

'It's not restricted. On certain days, at certain times, blacks are allowed in.'

'Would they want to come? A monument dedicated to their defeat?'

She drew away from him for a moment, then said stiffly, 'We're a nation in laager and we cannot deny our past. It's from the scenes in this building that we derive our strength.'

From this vast, awesome structure they went back to the residential areas of the city, and it was here that Philip received his major shock, because whole avenues and scores of broad streets, reaching as far as he could see, were lined with jacaranda trees bursting with purple, not hundreds of them but thousands upon thousands, until the entire city seemed a bed of flowers. He had never seen anything to compare with this explosion of purple elegance, and when they slipped into bed that night he whispered,

'You're a blend of monument and jacaranda—fierce durability and soft elegance.' When she said nothing, snuggling closer to be kissed, he asked, 'Shall we be married?' but then she drew away, for she was not yet prepared to make such a commitment.

Wherever they went on their brief excursions she provided him with new revelations of her country. After they had visited some dozen little towns, each with its statue of some minor Boer War general, they returned to Pretoria, where she took him to the fine figure of General Louis Botha in front of the government buildings. Behind it stood a somber, handsome memorial to the 2,683 South African soldiers who had lost their lives in a single battle.

'Wasn't Delville Wood, back in 1916, the most important battle your troops ever engaged in?' Philip asked.

'Perhaps,' she said grudgingly.

'All those men lost . . .'

'It was the wrong war, fought on the wrong continent, by the wrong troops.' After reflecting upon this curt dismissal, she added, 'It was an English affair that played no part in our history, an incident well forgotten.'

He was struck by the exposed beauty of South Africa, the endless veld, the treeless reaches of landscape, the wonderful little flat-topped hills, the enclaves with elephants, and white rhinoceros, and eland, and the great blazing sky. 'Your roads, you know, are much better than those in the United States,' he told her once as they were driving across a far stretch of veld on a roadway that contained not a ripple.

Most of all he liked the little towns with their public squares, their low white-walled buildings and their jacaranda trees. He became familiar with a dozen other blossoming trees whose names he did not know: 'This is a land of flowers!' And of all those he saw, better even than the jacarandas, he liked the protea: 'You must have a hundred varieties!'

'More, I think.'

They were able to take these excursions because of his schedule at the dig: three weeks of dawn to dusk, then a week off, and once when he was entitled to a break she said, 'We have a remarkable village which you really must see,' and when he took out his map she said, 'You will find it as Tulbagh, but we like to call it by its old name, Church-Street-in-the-Land-of-Waveren.'

'What a delightful name!' and they drove two days to an enclave among tall hills where in a closed valley stood this remarkable thoroughfare, as beautiful as any in the world. It had been founded as early as 1700, one long street with a church at one end, a parsonage about half a mile away, and some fifteen houses connecting the two. As the centuries passed, the low houses seemed to settle close to the ground, and the place might have been remembered only as a fading echo of past times, except that on 29 September 1969 an earthquake shattered the area, knocking down some of the dwellings and damaging all of them.

'What happened,' Sannie explained, 'was that some energetic men and women, Father among them, got together and said, "This is a chance to rebuild the street as it was in 1750," and believe it or not, Philip, that's just what they did.'

When they approached the village, Philip saw a church of stubborn beauty and in the distance a stately parsonage, but what captivated him was the row of stark-white houses, all cheap adornment erased, standing pristine as they had two centuries earlier. It was as if a magician had waved a wand and restored patterns of living long since vanished. They stayed that night in one of the houses, whose proper owners were distressed at the idea of Sannie's traveling with a man to whom she was not married: 'What would your grandmother Maria Steyn have said?' The wife had clippings of Maria's famous altercation over the nude statue in Pretoria, and Philip guffawed at some of the statements the old lady had made: 'If the Israelites could destroy the statues of a golden ass, we women of South Africa can destroy this statue of a naked woman.' She had also told one newspaper: 'A naked man is not much better than a naked woman, but he's easier to fix.'

'Times change,' Sannie said, but the woman would not allow the couple to share the same bedroom. Late at night, in the darkness, Philip tried to reach Sannie's room, only to find that buckets had been placed across the hallway. He made a terrific clatter, at which the man of the house came out with a flashlight to be sure he returned to his own quarters.

As soon as breakfast was over and they were driving north, he said, 'Sannie, we've got to get married. I can find a good job almost anywhere in the world, and I need you.' But again she held him off.

He supposed that this was because she loved her own country too much to leave it, and he had to admit that it was magnificent in a great, brutal way, unlike any he had previously seen, but an observant traveler had to spot three grievous problems which warranted attention: 'Sannie, as a geologist I see one hell of a lot of your country is desert, and according to old maps, it seems to be spreading eastward.'

'You're right,' she conceded.

And whether in the countryside or in the small towns, he became increasingly aware that whites and blacks occupied two radically different worlds. The separation was constant, universal and severely enforced. Philip was by no means a liberal; as a practical engineer, he knew that separation was sometimes advisable: 'I was never much for interracial dating. I observed that the men in my class at college who dated girls of other races—Chicanos or blacks or Orientals—they were all alike. Aloof, bad complexions, and wrote letters to the editor advocating the abolishment of fraternities.'

'Here it would be intolerable,' she agreed.

'But I've also noticed that countries which support a cheap supply of labor always impoverish themselves.'

'We're certainly not impoverished,' she protested.

'In many ways you are. You ought to pay your blacks high wages, then tax them like hell to provide public services. That's the path to civilization.'

'Philip! They'd not be worth a penny more than they're paid.'

'Wrong.' He became quite excited on this point. 'I've worked in three different black nations. With all kinds of black workers. And whenever we had in our cadre a black from South Africa, especially a Zulu or a Xhosa, he was invariably the best in the work force. If blacks with much less experience can rule Moçambique and Vwarda and Zambia, yours could

certainly run this country.' It was a startling statement, which she did not
wish to discuss.

The third sad discovery came always at night. They would have had a
fine dinner with friends she knew from one past experience or other; the
conversation would have been lively, ranging over politics and economics;
the food would have been superb and the local wines even better; and then,
as they were about to depart, Philip would see on the mantel over the
fireplace three handsome photographs of young people Sannie's age.

'I didn't know you had children.'

'Yes!' And if the family was of English derivation, or Jewish, or enlightened Afrikaner, either the mother or father would say, 'That's Victor, he's
in Australia. Helen is married to a fine young man in Canada. And that's
Freddie, he's at the London School of Economics.'

They were gone. They were gone to the far continents. They would
never return to South Africa, for the pressures were too great, the possibilities too forbidding.

When the young lovers returned from one such trip Mrs. van Doorn asked
unobtrusively if she could speak with Philip, and when she had him alone
she said forthrightly, 'You must not lose your heart to Sannie. The Troxel
boys will soon be back from the frontier, and then things will be different.'

'Who are the Troxel boys?'

'Their families own the old De Groot farm. Their parents, that is.'

'Those people who live on the far side of the lake?'

'Yes. Marius' father brought them here from Johannesburg over fifty
years ago. Wonderfully sturdy people.'

'And they have two young men, Sannie's age?'

'Yes. They're cousins. On military service just now, but they'll be back,
and things will be different.'

'Sannie's said nothing.'

'I think she has, Philip. Didn't you ask to marry her?'

'Twice.'

'Why do you think she hesitated?'

'Had she some arrangement with one of the boys?'

'With both, I think. Point is, when they left she hadn't made up her
mind between them. But she will, Philip. She's Afrikaner to the core and
will marry an Afrikaner. Of that I'm convinced.'

'I'm not,' he said with laughter that softened the disagreement.

'Nor should you be. But remember my warning. Don't take this too
seriously, because, I assure you, Sannie doesn't.'

He was prevented from brooding about his courtship when his obligations at Swartstroom suddenly intensified. His men had come upon a reach
where the stream took a pronounced turn to the left, producing a bend
where diamonds ought to have been deposited had any ever existed in this
territory.

The crew found what it was looking for, two tiny bits of diamond,
glistening so pure in sunlight they seemed to create a radiance all the way
to Pretoria, Antwerp and New York, where word circulated that 'Amal-

gamated Mines may have something at Swartstroom.' The two tiny fragments were worth about four rand, enough to pay one black worker for one
day's effort, but they had the power to inflame men's imaginations, for when
taken in conjunction with Pik Prinsloo's earlier find, they confirmed that
at some time far distant this little stream had been diamantiferous. Saltwood's problem was to isolate the ancient source, but so far he could find
no signs of it.

A helicopter was flown in to take him aloft so that he might inspect
contiguous areas, but this disclosed nothing, and he had to revert to time-
tested procedures of following the little stream. He discovered no more
diamond chips, but in reality he needed no more. Those he had found
proved that somewhere in this vicinity there had been a source of diamonds,
and in time he, or someone like him, would uncover it.

So he was kept at the dig and for some weeks found no opportunity to
visit with Sannie, but his spare time was not wasted, for an unusual young
man came to visit him, and through this accidental meeting he was about
to behold rather more of South Africa than the average foreign geologist
would ordinarily have seen.

His visitor was Daniel Nxumalo, a black of about Saltwood's age; he
spoke the precise English of one who had been educated in a colonial college
by itinerant scholars from Dublin or London, and he was on a curious
mission: 'Mr. Philip Saltwood? I'm Daniel Nxumalo, associate professor—
as you would call me in America—at Fort Hare. I was advised to come see
you.'

'By whom?' Saltwood had the prejudices of a typical Texas engineer: he
would hire anyone, but he had an instinctive distrust of any black who spoke
in complete sentences.

'The people in Venloo. They told me you were interested in all things
South African.'

'How would they know?'

'They've seen you in church. They listen.'

'What was it you wanted?'

'Because you've seen so much of Africa, Mr. Saltwood, I thought it
would be courteous if I showed you the real part—our portion, that is.'

With this rather condescending introduction, Daniel Nxumalo, home
on vacation from his duties at the university, began to take his American
guest to little enclaves in eastern Transvaal occupied by blacks who, like his
own predecessors, had fled the Mfecane of King Shaka and Mzilikazi. They
had survived for the past century and a half in various settings, some
attached to white farms like Vrymeer, some living by themselves in hidden
valleys. Quite a few clustered about the environs of rural towns like Carolina and Ermelo, but all had made sensible adjustment, and Philip was
surprised at the substantial goods some of them had accumulated.

'But under the new laws,' Nxumalo said, 'we must move ourselves to
one of our Bantustans . . . By the way, ever met any Xhosa?'

'Had two of them working for me in Vwarda. Spoke with clicks.'

'In some ways they're more fortunate than the Zulu; in other ways, not.'

'I'm amazed to hear a Zulu confess that anyone is better.'

'I didn't say better.' Nxumalo laughed. 'I said "more fortunate." ' When
he grinned, his teeth were extremely white and his eyes glistened.

'Let me guess,' Saltwood said, for he was growing to like this somewhat cheeky fellow. 'It's something the white man did to the Xhosa and you, something very unfair to the Zulu.'

'You're perceptive, Mr. Saltwood. The Afrikaners have given the Xhosa a beautiful territory, compact and arable. The Transkei. And next to it another cohesive tract, the Ciskei. In that land the Xhosa have a fighting chance to build something good. But what did they give the Zulu? Fifty, a hundred unconnected fragments of land. They call it kwaZulu, and it's supposed to be a homeland for all the Zulu. But it's really a collection of junk. They want us to occupy that broken territory.'

'In time it'll coalesce, if the idea's a good one.'

'The idea's bad and the land's bad, because all the good parts have been preempted by white men.'

'I should think that could be changed.'

'You haven't lived here very long.' He altered his tone completely. Up to now he had been a college professor, outlining a general problem; now he became a human being, lamenting a wrong done him personally: 'In pursuit of their policy, Mr. Saltwood, they insist that we Zulu, who have made good lives in places like Vrymeer and Venloo, pick up all we have, leave all our friends and our ways of life, and move off to one of the fragmented sections of their kwaZulu.'

'I thought you said it was your Bantustan.'

'We don't want it. It was never our idea.'

'You're to be evacuated?'

'Yes, as if a plague had struck our land. As if locusts had eaten our little fields and we had to move on.'

When Saltwood argued that Nxumalo must be telling only part of the story, the professor agreed, heartily: 'I am indeed. And the reason I came to see you is that I wondered if you would like to see the other part.'

'I certainly would.' Philip Saltwood operated on the principle that governed many young scientists these days as they worked about the world: whether they were American or Russian, Chinese or Australian, they wanted to know what was happening in the lands which employed them at the moment, and often they moved far from their basic tasks, investigating possibilities that at the moment seemed remote but which, at some future date, might become all-important.

With Nxumalo as guide, Philip drove west to Johannesburg, where they toured inconspicuously up and down the handsome main streets of that thriving American-style city. Since it was four in the afternoon, the business areas were jammed with people, and half of them black. They were laborers, and messengers, clerks and minor officials, shoppers and dawdlers, and they could all have been in Detroit or Houston. 'Look at them,' Nxumalo said with some pride. 'They keep the wheels of this city spinning.'

At quarter to five he directed Philip to the area around the central railway station, and in the ensuing hour Saltwood saw something that was so shocking as to be unbelievable: from all parts of central Johannesburg streams of black men and women converged, more than half a million of them crowding to leave the city before sunset, after which it would be unlawful to be there. Like swarms of grasshoppers leaving a ruined field, the workers of Johannesburg hastened to that endless belt of steel that ran perpetually out of the city at sunset and back in at sunrise. It was a movement of people of such magnitude that he knew nothing with which to compare it.

At the end of the hour he thought: When I look at those streams of black people I see all the occupations of a major city. You have street sweepers and young men with briefcases. Sheep butchers and young women who work as doctor's assistants. There are draymen and junior executives. And they are all being expelled.

'Are you game to see where they're going?' Nxumalo asked, as if he could read Philip's mind.

'It's forbidden, isn't it?'

'Yes, it's against the law for whites, but it can be done.'

It was the kind of challenge a peripatetic geologist often faced: Strangers are not allowed in that temple, it's sacred to Shiva. Or, You're not permitted in that corner of Afghanistan, too close to the Russian border.

But always the daring ones went, and now Philip Saltwood was on his way to a clandestine visit to Soweto, a nonexistent city of at least one and a half million black people. South Western Townships was its official title, the first two letters of each word having been taken to form the acronym.

As they drove the twelve miles to it, with trains rushing past in orderly procession, each laden with workers, some clinging to the doors, Nxumalo said, 'It's the same problem as the little one we saw at Venloo. The Afrikaners honestly believe that no black people live in their all-white cities. They believe that we work there briefly during daylight hours, then vanish. Soweto up ahead does not exist officially. The million and a half people who live there, fifty percent of them illegally, are not really there. They're supposed to sleep there temporarily while they work in the city, but if they lose their jobs, they're obligated to move back to their Bantustans, which most of them have never seen.'

When Philip started to respond to this macabre fairy tale of the city twice as large as Boston that did not exist, Nxumalo grinned and jabbed him in the arm. 'I'll wager you didn't notice the most important fact about that exodus at the railway station.'

'As a matter of fact, I did. I saw that the crush contained all kinds of workers, from street sweepers to college professors.'

Nxumalo laughed. 'You failed your examination. The significant fact was that almost everyone carried a package of some kind. You see, because Soweto doesn't exist, and because it's seen as only temporary, ephemeral . . . Well, what's logical? It has no stores. No real ones, that is. They're not allowed, because they don't fit into the white man's plan. Everything except a few minor commodities must be purchased from white-owned stores in Johannesburg. Soweto is not a city. It's a dormitory.'

Saltwood's first impression was arbitrary and in a sense preposterous: 'Christ! Look at all those churches. I never heard of one of them before.' At frequent spots in areas that contained nothing but row upon row of uniformly dismal blockhouses, a flagstaff would display a torn ensign indicating that this building was the Church of Zion, or the Church of the Holy Will, or the Xangu Church, or simply the home of a holy man who had direct contact with God.

'After the beer hall,' Nxumalo explained, 'it's the best racket in Soweto. Maybe four thousand different churches preaching God-knows-what.' But now they were opposite a huge wire-enclosed shed, devoid of any charm whatever, where hundreds of workingmen sat at long bare tables guzzling weak Kaffir beer. That word was officially outlawed now, and if a white man called a black a Kaffir he could be charged with common assault, but the name for the beer persisted. It was a pernicious drink, strong enough to be expensive, weak enough to prevent a man from becoming dangerously drunk.

'The beer hall is the greatest anti-revolutionary instrument in Africa,' Nxumalo said, but even as he spoke, a force of much different character swept past, a gang of tsotsis running to some rendezvous that could involve theft, or rape, or one of the thousand murders each year, fifty percent unsolved because the victims were black.

Out of the vast miasma of this forsaken city, this purgatory that was not hell, for the houses were livable, nor heaven, for there was no ease or hope, Nxumalo led Saltwood to the small dark house that was the focus of this visit. Inside the curtained kitchen sat nine men in a kind of ring, into whose center Philip was thrust: 'This is my friend, Philip Saltwood, the American geologist who is highly respected by his workmen at Swartstroom. He is completing his education.' The men acknowledged him briefly, then turned to Nxumalo and started to press him with questions.

'What do you hear from Jonathan?' one asked, and Philip had no way of guessing who Jonathan might be.

'Nothing.'

'Any news at all from Moçambique?'

'From this side we know that the frontier patrols are penetrating into Mocambique every week. They must be doing damage.'

'Is your brother still alive?'

'I hear nothing from Jonathan.'

Philip judged that Nxumalo hedged on his reply, perhaps because he did not want to say anything incriminating in the presence of a white witness.

They discussed the situation on each of the other frontiers, where apparently they had men from Soweto in position among the rebels, and in no segment of the extensive border did their people seem to be accomplishing much. But when Philip analyzed what actually had been said, he realized that verbally at least these men were not plotters against the government; they were simply discussing events along the frontier, exactly as the white people at Vrymeer followed these affairs, but from a much different point of interest.

The talk was broad in scope and free in manner. These men were teachers, a clergyman, businessmen of sorts, and they were concerned about the directions their nation was taking. They were deeply worried about the forthcoming American presidential election and wondered whether Andrew Young would regain his position of power in a new administration. They were particularly interested in one aspect of American life. 'What accounts for your ambivalance?' a teacher asked. 'Your big newspapers are against apartheid, so is President Carter, so is Andy Young, but ninety-eight percent of the Americans who visit our country approve of it. Almost every American who comes here goes home convinced that Afrikaners are doing the right thing.'

'It's simple,' Philip said. 'What Americans come here? It's far away, you know, and very expensive. Businessmen come on company accounts. Rich travelers. Engineers. And they're all wealthy and conservative. They like what they see. They approve of apartheid, really, and would like to see it introduced in America.'

'You're an engineer. You're not a conservative.'

'On many things I am. I'm sure as hell no liberal.'

'But on apartheid?'

'I'm against it because I don't think it works.'

'Do you find the world turning conservative? Canada? England? Maybe America?'

'I do.'

Late in the evening they got down to cases, and now Nxumalo moved to the fore: 'I've been pondering what we might do to inspirit our people. To send a signal to the men in Moçambique that we're still with them. And it seems to me that the most effective single thing, under present conditions, is to organize a day of remembrance for our dead children who were gunned down in Soweto in 1976.'

'That has merit.'

'I would propose that on June 16 this year we have a national day of mourning. No disturbances, just some kind of visual remembrance.'

'Would that antagonize government?' a short man asked.

'Anything we do antagonizes government.'

'I mean, to the point of retaliation?'

Nxumalo sat silent. This was a penetrating question, for the tactic of committees like this had to be protest up to the edge of the precipice at which Afrikaner guns began to fire, as they had at Sharpeville, in Soweto and at a score of other sites. Judiciously he said, 'If the white man can make a national holiday of Blood River, where he slaughtered thousands of us Zulu, we can remember Soweto '76. I say let's go ahead.'

It was agreed, and when Saltwood left the meeting, and slipped out of Soweto, he was aware that his new friend Daniel Nxumalo had entered upon dangerous ground, but he had no idea that by this simple gesture of irritating the government the young educator would place himself in mortal jeopardy.

When Philip returned to Vrymeer he found his life much altered, for the Troxel boys were back from border duty and were out of uniform. One sight of them warned Saltwood that he was in trouble, for they were a handsome pair, with the fine looks and open smiles of the true Afrikaner. Frikkie was twenty-five, about six feet three, slim, easy in his movements and with a rather serious mien. When Mr. van Doorn introduced him he said, 'Frik's a rugby halfback and one of the best.'

Jopie was different. Well under six feet, he was built like a Roman wall, one massive building block set down upon another. He was broad, in all respects. He had a wide face and very wide mouth from which massive square teeth showed. His shoulders and hips were enormous, for although he was much shorter than Frikkie, he was also much heavier, but what startled Philip was the fact that Jopie had no neck. As with many of the historic rugby forwards, Fanie Louw and Frik du Preez among them, Jopie Troxel's head was set square upon his shoulders, giving his body a battering-ram quality which he used to powerful effect, but in no way was he a gross or insensitive person, and he had in the middle of his chin a deep dimple which quivered when he laughed. His humor was robust, and it was obvious that Sannie van Doorn appreciated it.

Her father had introduced Frikkie; she took charge of Jopie: 'This is my dear friend, who wears his hair forward, like Julius Caesar, and that isn't the only thing forward about him.' With a massive right hand Jopie grabbed Philip's and said, 'Did Jimmy Carter and Andy Young send you over here to tell us how to run our country?'

Philip stiffened. 'I came to find diamonds.'

'Finding any?'

'No. You damned people keep everything hidden.'

'We'd better,' Jopie said, 'or you and the English would steal it.'

'How was the border?' Marius asked, aware that these three young men were behaving like bulls caught up in the heat of spring. He suspected that daughter Sannie was about to experience a difficult spell.

Frikkie dropped into a chair and accepted the beer that Sannie brought. 'It's rotten work. You patrol fifteen days in the bush and see maybe one terrorist. Ta-ta-ta-ta. He's gone, but you know there's a dozen back there somewhere.'

'But we're holding our own?'

'Definitely. There's this Kaffir from here, this Jonathan Nxumalo. He issues a threat now and then on Radio Maputo, as you know. Going to storm Johannesburg. But he's damned sure to stay clear of our patrols.'

'You mean there was real fighting?' Sannie asked.

'Whenever the black bastards gave us a chance,' Jopie said.

'How long were you at the border?' Philip asked, and Jopie looked at his cousin to check whether this was privileged information.

'Six months. It's our obligation.'

'We certainly missed you on the team,' Marius said, hoping to change the conversation, but Philip asked, 'How long can this go on? I mean, with so many young men taken out of productive work?'

'You ask two questions which only an American would ask,' Frikkie said sharply. 'How long? As if everything had to be completed in a hurry. We can guard our borders for the next hundred years. And is it productive? No, it isn't, in the sense of making things at a factory. But what could possibly be more productive than protecting one's country?'

'That subject is closed,' Marius said. 'Now tell me, how soon can you men get back into shape for the big matches facing us?'

'On the border,' Jopie said, 'you're always in shape. I could play Saturday.'

'Do you mean that?'

'Me, too,' Frikkie said, and when Philip looked at the young commandos he knew that they were telling the truth.

The game was against a team from Bloemfontein, and when the Troxels ran onto the field the crowd cheered wildly, for newspapers had hinted at their exploits at the frontier. They displayed the poetic abandon for which they had been famous, but they lost, rather badly, as a matter of fact, 23–9. They did have a great time and in the drinking bouts after the game they smashed a few windows.

When they returned to Vrymeer, there was serious talk as to what they might be doing in the future, and as Philip listened he learned to his surprise that they were suited only for farming. Frikkie had been to the university at Potchefstroom but had learned nothing of practical value, nor much of anything else, while Jopie had shown no interest in going beyond high school. Their two families, offshoots of the Troxels whom Detleef van Doorn had rescued from the slums of Vrededorp, had not acquired much land, so that both boys could not look forward to farming their own fields, but they were capable, and Marius suggested, to Philip's dismay, that they think seriously of assuming responsibility for the extensive acres at Vrymeer. Logically, this would imply that one of them should marry the Van Doorn daughter, and this each was eager to do.

Sannie's intentions were not entirely clear. She was more than fond of her American geologist; her excursions with him had been instructive to her, too, and some of the nights in Kruger Park rondavels or country hotels had been rapturous. He was by no means an improbable suitor, for many South African girls of her generation had breathed sighs of salvation when their marriages carried them away from this turbulent cauldron; she had personal friends who proposed to spend the rest of their lives in places like Toronto and the University of Southern California, and those who wrote spoke often of homesickness for the veld, but more often of the freedom they enjoyed in their adopted homes. She could be happy in Texas and at times had a positive longing to see it.

Also, she might be tempted to emigrate with Saltwood because she was sometimes painfully reminded of her mixed heritage. Her father had sprung from impeccable Afrikaner roots but had gone whoring after a Rhodes scholarship, and in so doing, had acquired an English wife. This killed his eligibility for membership in the Broederbond, nor had he been selected an elder in the local church. Mrs. van Doorn was openly pro-English, but Sannie felt no attachment whatever to England and had refused two opportunities to spend vacations there.

As she matured, she found herself becoming more and more an Afrikaner. She understood why Frikkie and Jopie were willing to serve on the border, and she shared their love of this land. She had known these young men all her life, had played with them as a child, and felt she could be happy with either of them on this enchanting farm with its tumbling lakes and wild blesbok. Which of the cousins she preferred she could not say, for up to now she had never been required to choose between them.

There was one further complication. She was almost in love with Philip Saltwood. Intuitively she sensed that he was a finer-grained human being than the Troxel boys, a man who was going to take life seriously. Besides, she had enjoyed sharing a bed with him. For the time being she postponed divisions, trusting that things would sort themselves out.

They were in the kitchen drinking beer and telling Van der Merwe stories. Frikkie said, 'Van der Merwe and two rascals from Krugersdorp went to Paris to hold up a bank. But on the way to the job, Van der Merwe dropped the dynamite and the three were arrested. All of them sentenced to the guillotine. But when the knife came thundering down on the first man, it stuck and he was miraculously spared. French law declared him free. So the second man was strapped down, and again the knife came roaring down and again it jammed. He was set free. Now came Van der Merwe's turn, and he was so curious about what had happened that he looked up as they laid him on the plank, and just as the executioner was about to pull the lever that released the knife, Van der Merwe shouts, "Hold everything! I see what's wrong with this crazy machine!" '

Jopie said, 'Van der Merwe, as you know, always had a low opinion of Englishmen, and one day he watched in disgust as three of them spent more than two hours digging a hole for a fence post and setting it in the ground. "Lazy bastards! Two hours for a job like that. I could do that by myself in fifteen minutes, you give me nine Kaffirs." '

'Jopie!' Sannie warned. 'Government says we're not to call them Kaffirs any longer. The legal word now is Plural.'

Frikkie said, 'You know what Van der Merwe calls a Bushman rock painting? Under the new law, that is. "A rural plural mural." '

Jopie said, 'You know what Van der Merwe says to a Kaffir holding a machine gun? "Good morning, Baas." '

Frikkie said, 'Van der Merwe had a flagpole lying on the ground. He propped it in its hole, got a ladder and a tape measure and tried to climb up to measure it, but the flagpole fell down. Twice again he propped it up and tried to climb it. Finally a Kaffir said, "Baas, why don't you measure it when it's on the ground?" and Van der Merwe said, "Stupid Kaffir, I want to know its height, not its width." '

Jopie said, 'Speaking of width. Air France sent out its top pilot to see if Van der Merwe was ready to fly to Paris and London. Van der Merwe made one of the greatest landings in aviation history—his 747 touched down at the front edge of the tarmac . . . screamed to a braking stop, its front wheels three inches from the other end of the landing surface. "Absolutely *magnifique!*" the Air France inspector said. "This man is ready for any airport in the world. But tell me, why does South Africa make its runways so short?" "I can't explain it," Van der Merwe said. "And look at the crazy thing. It's almost five miles wide." '

Koos van der Merwe was the prototypical Afrikaner boob on whom all jokes about rural stupidity and childlike simplicity were hung. Everyone had his favorite, so that a session like this could run for hours, with an endless chain of hilarious insights into the stolid Afrikaner mind. It was interesting, Philip thought, that most of the jokes were told by Afrikaners themselves, and not by Englishmen, although he had discovered, from several such affairs, that any really ugly jokes were usually told by the latter.

After Frikkie, Jopie and Sannie had each reeled off half a dozen stories, some of them very rough on their fellow Afrikaners, they turned to Philip and asked him what his favorite was. 'I rather fancy one I heard at the diggings. "What do the numbers 1066, 1492 and 1812 have in common?" ' When Sannie pointed out that they were dates important in history, Philip replied, 'Wrong. They're adjoining rooms in Van der Merwe's motel.' Then he asked, 'Why do you tell such jokes?' and each of the three had a sensible explanation. Frikkie felt that any people who were essentially rural took refuge in two kinds of comedy: 'Barnyard-sexual, and the Afrikaners have some very funny stories in that style, and country-bumpkin. In the first we're laughing at the dominee and the domination of the church. In the second we're laughing at ourselves. You hear the same jokes in each category, I'm quite sure, in rural Germany . . . or Norway.'

Jopie had quite another theory: 'We know that the Englishmen laugh at us. So we beat them to the punch and do it better.'

Sannie thought otherwise: 'We do it out of affection. Every one of us has in his family somewhere a Koos van der Merwe. He never comes exactly into focus. But we love him just the same. How many pieces in Van der Merwe's jigsaw puzzle? Two.'

When Sannie said this, Jopie broke into wild laughter, quite out of proportion to the merits of the joke. Frikkie looked at him and asked, 'Have you gone bonkers?'

'No! I just happened to think of something terribly funny.' When the other three turned to stare at him, he said, 'I was in Pretoria when Andy Young and two of his assistants from the State Department were there making speeches and giving interviews about the rights of blacks in South Africa. And I burst into laughter.'

'Why?' Saltwood asked defensively. 'Sometimes Young makes sense.'

'Granted. But not that day. Because it suddenly occurred to me, when I had a chance to look at him, to see him . . . You know, he's not black at all. Neither of his two aides were black. I've never seen a black American. Everyone who comes here is Coloured.' Here he broke into convulsive laughter, and after a moment Frikkie joined him. The two athletes punched each other and almost gagged on their merriment.

'I don't get it,' Philip said.

'Don't you see?' Sannie explained as her two suitors tried to control their raucous behavior. 'If Andy Young and your other black leaders in America lived in South Africa, and if they got their way—one-man, one-vote—and the blacks took over, the very first people to be done in would be Andy Young and his gang.'

'Now wait!' Philip snapped. As a loyal American, he felt obligated to defend President Carter and former Ambassador Young when they were attacked, which in South Africa was almost daily. 'I don't approve of Andy when he shoots from the hip, but on basic African policy he makes sense.'

'How could he?' Frikkie asked. 'One-man, one-vote?'

'I mean his view of the continent as a whole. There are three million Afrikaners at most. Three hundred million blacks at least. Should we support you few against so many?'

'Of course you should, since our interests are the same as your interests,' Frikkie said.

'But what was your point about Young being in danger?'

'My dear stupid American,' Frikkie said, winking at Jopie. 'Don't you know that Zulu, Xhosa, Fingo, Pondo—all of them—dislike Coloureds even more than they dislike whites?'

'Why?'

'Because they feel that when decisions are made, Coloureds will side with whites. They're seen as traitors to the black cause.'

Jopie broke in: 'You may have heard. When the blacks rioted at Paarl. Quite a few dead. The Coloureds didn't raise a finger to help. Believe me, Philip, when the crunch comes, Andy Young would be in a lot more danger than me. The blacks know they'll need men like me to help organize their new world. But they'll have no place whatever for Andy Young and his light-skinned Coloureds.'

Frikkie became quite serious: 'We've watched this in many former English colonies. When the natives assume power, they ostracize the light-skins . . . if they don't slaughter them. The reason's simple. "If we must do business with people other than ourselves, let's do it with the best of the lot, the real white people." The Coloureds in this land—how many of them? Three million, perhaps. They have no future except with us. So if your Ambassador Young wishes to help his kind, he better come to Jopie and me and say, "Afrikaners, save me!" because the blacks will do him in.'

Jopie broke the tension by tickling Sannie under the chin as she finished her beer. 'You know, I don't believe I've ever seen an American black. I wonder if anyone in South Africa ever has. We made a big to-do over Arthur Ashe, and the rock musicians, and what not. But when the crunch comes, everyone like them will be dead. Because there'll be no place for those cats in the new South Africa.'

Sannie said, 'Would you like a Van der Merwe cocktail? Perrier and water?'

It was language, which tyrannizes us all, that converted Laura Saltwood into a major criminal. It began accidentally during a trip home to England; she had stopped at a store in Salisbury and the shopkeeper had said, 'I can't deliver it today, Mrs. Saltwood. My temp didn't report.'

'Your what?'

'My temp. The boy who comes in occasionally.'

On her way back to Sentinels she used a footpath through the cathedral grounds, and as she glanced about her she thought: How we English do corrupt our language. Mr. Dixon has a temp. I go to the hairdresser's for a perm. My cousin leaves the telly, goes to the fridge to get herself a snack of meat and veg. How awful.

In succeeding days she paid extra attention to what was being said around her, and heard such words as *perks* for perquisites, *grungey* for objectionable, *grotty* for distasteful, and what was probably the ugliest verbal invention of all time, *brolly* for umbrella.

When she spoke about this debasement with her cousin she noticed approvingly the precise English pattern of Lady Ellen's speech: 'Mustn't be put off by the odd bit of verbal invention, must we?'

'I was thinking of how the Dutch language deteriorated at the Cape. Became quite debased, you know.'

'I shouldn't wonder if they'd done a good thing, Laura. Mark you, languages change. You say the Afrikaners blotted their copybook. I say they've kept up with the times, and a good thing, too.'

'But there's a grandeur about language. I don't like to see it cheapened.'

'The odd bit of improvement never hurt any language. I relish some of the changes the Americans have made. *Mortician*'s a delightful word. *Custodian*'s much higher-toned than *janitor.* Not to worry about a few modifications.'

'It offends me to see signs in my dress shop which say, "Wear U get tru value," and in Afrikaans, "U is welkom." I may sound chauvinistic, but they seem silly.'

Since Lady Ellen knew nothing of Afrikaans, Laura dropped the subject, but three nights later when they drove north to see the Oxford Players do *King Lear* at Stonehenge, and the great monoliths glowed somberly in the night shadows, she surrendered to the glories of Shakespeare and actually trembled when the old king, huddling against the darkest pillars, shared his pity with those less fortunate:

> 'Poor naked wretches, wheresoe'er you are,
> That bide the pelting of this pitiless storm,
> How shall your houseless heads and unfed sides,
> Your loop'd and window'd raggedness, defend you
> From seasons such as these?'

It seemed to her that words could not be more glorious, and later, when the young man tried to frighten the crazy blind Earl of Gloster by describing the cliff and the workman climbing perilously down its face, she sighed with the terrible power of the words:

> 'How fearful
> And dizzy 'tis to cast one's eyes so low!
> The crows and choughs that wing the midway air
> Show scarce so gross as beetles: half way down
> Hangs one that gathers samphire—dreadful trade!
> Methinks he seems no bigger than his head . . .'

Unaware of the dangerous path she was treading, she sat there in the shadow of Stonehenge and gave herself over to the magic of great-fashioned words hurled into the night and became drunk on them, and when old Lear at the end confessed his weakness, she had tears in her eyes from suffering with him:

> 'I am a very foolish fond old man,
> Fourscore and upward, not an hour more nor less;
> And, to deal plainly,
> I fear I am not in my perfect mind.'

Three days later, still mesmerized by words, she borrowed Lady Ellen's Austin and drove by herself to Cambridge, where as a young woman of twenty she had enjoyed such flawless hours with her older brother, Wexton.

Parking the car in a municipal lot, she walked along King's Parade, ignoring the noble chapel of King's College, for she wanted to see again the austere entrance to Clare College, which her brother had attended. Walking as if in a dream, she entered the old surroundings which had housed scholars since 1326 and stood for a long time recalling ruefully those long spring days when she had visited Wexton here. How mercurial they were, how filled with surging ideas. Shaking her head in mournful recollection, she left Clare, nodding her head as she remembered the excellent education her brother had obtained here: You were one of the brilliant lads, Wexton. Oh, God, how I miss you.

She walked aimlessly south till she reached the gatehouse to King's College, where almost against her will she entered that stately court where Wexton had encountered the temptations he could not resist. She intended hastening through, wanting to see the Backs, where she and her brother's friends had enjoyed so many hours, but she was diverted to the right toward that grandest of England's self-contained chapels, King's, with its glorious arches reaching to heaven, its ornate choir reminding one of kings and princes. It had been spoiled somewhat since she first knew it by the installation of one of the best canvases Peter Paul Rubens ever painted, a gigantic adoration of the Magi worth millions of whatever currency might be in vogue: Damn, that's a fine painting, maybe the best he ever did. But it doesn't belong here.

She sat in one of the choir stalls, envisioning the days long ago when she and Wexton had come here with his friends to hear evensong: Those damned friends. Those accursed friends. Oh, Wexton, all life's a falling away, a dismal falling away, but why did you . . .

Tears came to her eyes and for some moments she wept, refusing to use a handkerchief, for these were not handkerchief tears. Pressing her fingers to her cheeks, she wiped the tears away, then left the chapel to walk slowly down one of the major sights of England and perhaps Europe, that expanse of green grass hemmed in by the walls of Clare, the chapel and King's. The buildings were admirably suited to each other, but it was the long sweep down to the River Cam and the Backs beyond that gave the place its nobility. Here she had been sitting on the grass one evening during the Mays—that week of frivolity which falls in June—when Noel Saltwood, from Oriel College at Oxford, drifted by in a boat with Cambridge friends he was visiting. They had met, fallen in love, and pledged a marriage which she had never once regretted. Life in Noel's South Africa had been rather primitive, and good conversation lagged, but often he encouraged her to get back to Salisbury, and from there to the theaters in London, with occasional excursions to Cambridge, and that had sustained her.

'Oh, Wexton, why in God's name did you do it?'

'Pardon, ma'am, but did you call?' It was a short little man wearing a rather long overcoat although the day was warmish, the kind of odd attendant one found everywhere.

'No. No. I was just thinking.' The man moved closer to assure himself that she was all right, then passed on. As he left she thought: I was indeed thinking. Of years gone, and of evenings on this grass when I first met Noel and his fine, unaffected approach to life. He listened like a country oaf to everything that Wexton and his clever friends and that brilliant young tutor said so glibly. And as he walked me back to my digs he said bluntly, 'I think your brother and his cronies are half-daft.'

'Don't you dare say a thing like that.'

'The way he ridicules everything. Don't you ever listen to him?'

So under Noel's tutelage she did listen, and Wexton and his friends, and especially the tutor, did ridicule everything. They despised Australia. They considered South Africa a blight. And they positively excoriated the United States. They also put George Bernard Shaw in his place, and John Galsworthy was beneath their contempt.

It was only then, spurred by Noel's sharp analysis, that she realized that her brother had fallen captive to a clique that idolized the young tutor, and in later years she watched with horror as they landed fine jobs in government, accelerated to positions of importance, then scurried off to Russia with high state secrets. Three of them, including Wexton, were living there now in lifelong exile. Two others had ended up in American jails, and one had committed suicide to avoid a treason trial. No one identified the tutor who had enlisted them, and so many others, in the revolution which was to eliminate excrescences like Australia, South Africa and America.

Oh, Wexton, I would travel to Leningrad on my knees if I could see you again! Once more she broke into tears, thinking of the dazzling manner in which this group of young brilliants had used the English language, and of the pitfalls into which it had led them. With them cleverness was four-fifths of the battle, she said to herself. Remember when one of them dismissed all of South Africa with a joke, even though he knew I was engaged to a South African: 'We had sense enough to let America win her war against us and got rid of that bad apple. We had to win our damned war against the Boers, and we're stuck with that atrocity.'

When she dropped her head in her hands, displaying an anguish that all could see, the little man in the long coat hurried back: 'Ma'am, I say, are you all right?' She was so preoccupied with her grief that she did not see another man, in a dark suit, who watched her from a far bend of the River Cam.

Very slowly she drove back to Salisbury, experiencing a vague presentiment that this might be the last journey she would ever make to Cambridge, or to England either: I'm old now. I should be visiting here as a dignified old lady coming to see my brother to talk about old times. But he's in Leningrad. God, he must be homesick.

When she tried to decipher how he had been seduced into committing his mortal sin—the betrayal of his nation and his peers—she began to think of the role words play in life: Our family was so keen on word games. Wexton and I played them incessantly. I think I first came to suspect him when he cheated one day. Altered the meaning of a word in order to win. At Cambridge he altered the meanings of the great words and ended a traitor. Back in Salisbury, walking within the shadow of the cathedral, she thought: Integrity in words protects integrity in life. If the word is corrupted, everything that stems from it will be evil. And this made her ponder word usage in South Africa, and it was then that she made her decision.

Immediately after she deplaned at Johannesburg she telephoned her son: 'Yes, tonight. I want you and Susan and the children over here at once.' When they arrived she took her son aside and said bluntly, 'Craig, I thought you were wasting your talents when you took science at Oxford. Now I thank God you did.'

'What are you prating about?'

'Your salvation. I want you to cable Washington tonight. Tell them that you've accepted the NASA position. Go to America. And take your family with you . . . forever. But first you must visit Salisbury—make arrangements for Timothy's college.'

'But why? You've always said you love it here.'

'I do, and that's why you must go.'

'To what purpose?'

'To get out of here. I'll put aside funds for Timothy's fees at Oriel, and Sir Martin can find him something in England when he graduates.'

Mrs. Saltwood asked her son to call in his wife and children, and when they were formally seated before her she said, cryptically, 'Very ugly things are going to happen in this country. They're beyond our control—beyond the control of any sensible people. If there was a chance that you could modify them, I'd want you to stay. I will.'

'We can't leave you here, Mother,' Craig's wife said earnestly.

'I'm expendable. You're not. I've had my life, you haven't—and it would be crazy to try to spend it in this insane atmosphere.'

'What makes you so agitated?'

'I went to a performance of *King Lear* at Stonehenge. I heard majestic words. And I dare no longer turn my back.'

'Mother, you're not making sense.'

'All you need to know, Craig, is that after the first of June it will not be wise for any Saltwood to be living in South Africa.'

'What happens on the first of June?'

'I go bowling. I go bowling in Cape Town with the Lady Anne Barnard Club, and I want you to be safely home in Salisbury.'

She would say no more. She bought four tickets on South African Airways: 'They have the best planes, you know, and the best pilots, too.' And she spent many hours at the Johannesburg offices of the Black Sash, discussing events with the ladies who were endeavoring to alleviate the tragedy and hardship engendered by enforcement of apartheid. She also sent four urgent letters to Sir Martin Saltwood at Sentinels, explaining the necessity for sending Timothy to England and asking him to watch over the boy. Finally she wrote to the principal of a black high school in the Transvaal, assuring him that she would speak at his school, as requested. After that she spent her spare time with the sonnets of Shakespeare, until a chain of those unequaled lines echoed in her head, building an eclectic sonnet of their own:

> When to the sessions of sweet silent thought
> I all alone beweep my outcast state
> Bare ruined choirs, where late the sweet birds sang
> Roses have thorns, and silver fountains mud

Like as the waves make towards the pebbled shore
When yellow leaves, or none, or few, do hang
Not mine own fears, nor the prophetic soul
Of the wide world dreaming on things to come.

At times the sheer beauty of the words overcame her, and she felt that men
and women give their lives for many good and noble causes, but none more
sacred than the keeping alive of words that thunder and sing and console,
and it was to such a mission that she now dedicated herself.

When word reached Vrymeer that Craig Saltwood and his family were
leaving, the Van Doorns were startled, for this was only the latest in that
flood of talent that was pouring out of South Africa. 'Craig must be out of
his mind,' Marius stormed. 'Good job here. Sound prospects.'

'And a clear view of the track ahead,' his wife agreed.

Philip Saltwood had dropped by to see Sannie, but she was out with the
Troxel boys, and Marius put the question to him: 'Would you be frightened
out of South Africa today?'

'I'd want to stay. But that's because I like crisis situations.'

'You imply that if you were Craig, you might leave.'

'I might. I doubt a non-Afrikaner has much future here. I'd probably
go back to where I was wanted.'

'You damned foreigners,' Marius growled.

'I'm staying,' his very English wife said. 'But of course, my life is here.
Sannie and the rest.'

'Are you also saying that if you were Craig, you'd take the chicken and
run?' her husband asked.

'I would, for the reasons Philip has just cited. It's not pleasant, Marius,
living where you're not welcome—'

'Rubbish. All my friends adore you.'

'And half our Jewish acquaintances have sent their children out of the
country. Never coming back. And we know many English who are doing
the same.'

Marius adopted a philosophical view: 'Every organism ought to cleanse
itself now and then. The brains we lose will be replaced locally.'

'But if you Afrikaners despise speculative thinking because it might turn
radical, how can the gaps be filled?' she asked. 'Have you heard what
Afrikaner professors and ministers are teaching these days? Not much
leadership there.'

'It'll come,' Philip interposed. 'I see some very bright young engineers.'

'One thing does worry me,' Marius said reflectively. 'Of all the places
in the world I've seen, the one that impressed me most was Princeton,
New Jersey. When I was there Einstein was in residence, and John von
Neumann, and Lise Meitner was visiting. All the brilliant scientists that
Europe had lost in the 1930s. They were the ones who paved the way for
the atomic bomb. Fermi, the others. And when the urgent need came in
World War II, the Germans looked around for their help and they were
gone. I wonder if we're alienating similar talent.'

But when Frikkie and Jopie arrived with Sannie, they put things back into perspective. 'To hell with all English fugitives,' Jopie said. 'They fight for nothing these days. Won't even play us in rugby.' But as soon as he said this he remembered that Mrs. van Doorn was English: 'I don't mean you.'

Frikkie said brightly, 'Let the Jews and the English hands-uppers clutter up Harvard and Yale. We have work to do here which they would never stomach. And we're going to do it.'

When the time came for the Craig Saltwoods to leave the country, Philip announced that he'd like to drive to Jan Smuts Airport to see them off, for this would give him a chance to meet Laura Saltwood, of whom several local people had spoken with regard. However, the journey was a hundred miles, and he might not have gone had he not received a surprising telegram from Craig Saltwood, whom he had never met: IMPERATIVE I SEE YOU JAN SMUTS AIRPORT PRIOR MY DEPARTURE.

Frikkie and Jopie volunteered to drive, because they knew that Sannie enjoyed seeing the 747s even if she wasn't flying in them, so as a foursome they drove across southern Transvaal, roaring into the airport well ahead of takeoff. They found Craig Saltwood anxiously looking for his American cousin. When Frikkie identified the Englishman, the three Afrikaners withdrew, leaving the cousins alone. Then Craig said, startling Philip even more, 'I know we're practically strangers, but . . . Philip, would you please watch over my mother. I'm sure she's up to something dramatic and I'm damned if I can learn what.'

Philip was at a loss for words. Stunned by the request, he finally said, weakly, 'I can't very well watch over her from Venloo.'

'I don't mean that. You can never stop my mother from doing what she wants.'

'What do you mean?'

'I think she's going to fall afoul of the law. Everything she says and does strengthens the impression.'

'Then why are you leaving?'

'Because she insists. Says things here are bound to go to hell— Here she comes.'

Laura Saltwood was sixty-seven that day, tall, white-haired, thin as in her youth, and clear-eyed. She was quite content to see her family leaving 'for a better climate,' as she phrased it, and she did not intend showing tears as they departed. She was somewhat disconcerted to meet Philip, for his unexpected presence made the departure one degree more grave than she had intended; however, she greeted him cordially and asked him to join them in the lounge to await the plane's takeoff.

'I have these friends with me,' he apologized, and when he called them over she widened her conversation to include them, using Afrikaans when introductions were made. The situation was strained, for the Craig Saltwoods were embarrassed at leaving the country, while Frikkie and Jopie were obviously disgusted with them for doing so.

Now the plane was wheeled into position, a modified version of the standard 747, shortened so it could fly non-stop to London, since South African planes were not allowed to refuel anywhere in black Africa. An all-white flight crew took their places in a land that was eighty percent non-white, and after formal goodbyes another family left the country, its children never to return to the land which had nurtured them and which sorely needed whatever contributions they might have made.

Jopie said as the plane soared off, 'The English—last to land, first to flee.' And Frikkie said, 'A wise farmer weeds out his weak mealies.' They made no attempt to hide their bitterness.

They might have been even more upset had they chanced to see at a far edge of the airport an unscheduled Boeing to which a sequence of small automobiles reported during the space of about an hour. No announcements were made over the loudspeakers regarding this plane; no uniformed stewardesses flourished through the airport, heralding it. Quietly it filled with passengers, quietly it taxied to the far end of the runway, and without notice of any kind it took off, circled, and flew directly westward on a very long flight to South America. It contained one hundred and eighty businessmen and farmers, most of them Afrikaners, who were going with their wives to visit Rio de Janeiro and São Paulo to investigate farmlands of the interior against the day when they might wish to quit South Africa for a new frontier. Of these passengers, forty-three families would like Brazil so much that they would make arrangements to purchase vast *fincas,* holding them in reserve for the day when they might be needed. The others would make their decisions later. As for the secret plane, after an appropriate rest it would load up with Afrikaner and English doctors and fly them to Australia to register with that country's medical association, so as to ensure a refuge . . . when the crunch came.

On May 30 Laura Saltwood appeared at the black school in the Transvaal to find that publicity regarding her visit had encouraged some thirty or forty black principals and school officials to drive substantial distances to hear her. They knew her to be a remarkable woman, a quiet worker in a score of worthy causes. She had the reputation for both good sense and fearlessness, and they knew she would not have come so far unless she had something pertinent to say.

Although she had written her speech in detail, suspecting that it might be the most important she would ever deliver, and perhaps the last, she did not refer to notes but spoke extemporaneously. She announced her subject as *Language,* one of the most mercurial topics in the world, and eased the apprehensions of the older conservatives by praising Afrikaans:

'As you know from the Old Testament, South Africa and Israel have much in common, especially their determination in creating and establishing a new language. Israel went back to ancient Hebrew. South Africa went to classical Dutch, adding a wonderful assembly of new words, new spellings, and new arrangements.

'Don't let anyone ridicule Afrikaans, just because it uses compact constructions. The greatness of English is that it simplified High German, made it more attainable, knocked out the silly declensions. A German purist would have every right to scorn English as a bastardization, just as Dutchmen scorn Afrikaans as a cheapening of their language. That's unfair. Two centuries from now Afrikaans may be a major language and Dutch may have disappeared, because Afrikaans speaks to simple needs, and therefore creates its own vitality.'

The more volatile younger teachers were disappointed by the conciliatory approach, and one history teacher whispered, 'She could be the spokesman for the Afrikaner universities.' But then she launched into the heart of her message:

'Before Soweto 1976 the black children of South Africa were advised that since their future lay in this country, they should adopt as their second language not English but Afrikaans. And they were ordered to use Afrikaans as the medium of instruction in half their subjects, when they clearly preferred to use English in all. They were right to demand English. To deny them that language would be a most grievous deprivation. [Here several teachers applauded.]

'English is a universal language, a lingua franca in all parts of the world. Airlines fly by English. Scholarly reports from all countries are circulated in English. To have this language is to have a key to the world's economies.

'English also has a literature probably richer than that of any other language, because in English you have not only the immortal contributions of Milton and Shakespeare, Dickens and Jane Austen, but you also have contributions made by people like Ernest Hemingway from America, Patrick White from Australia and William Butler Yeats from Ireland. To surrender English when you have a chance to acquire it is like throwing away the key to a treasury.

'Learn Afrikaans to help you in your daily life in this country, but learn English to help you live in the whole world. The conqueror who makes me learn his language makes me a slave. The edict that makes me learn a language spoken by only a few people puts me in a cage. The teacher who enables me to learn the lingua franca of the entire world sets me free. If you learn Afrikaans, you will be able to read a few fine books; if you learn English, you will be able to read the greatest body of learning and literature in the world.'

The principals applauded; the teachers cheered; the students went out and marched with banners. The police looked diligently for Mrs. Saltwood, but she had traveled by back routes to her home in Johannesburg; the next day she flew to Cape Town with a friend who served with her on the board of the Black Sash. What was more important, they made arrangements to bowl together on the Lady Anne Barnard team.

On June 1 Laura Saltwood rose at seven, read from the little book of Shakespeare's sonnets which she kept with her, and after a spare breakfast in her friend's kitchen, dressed in her bowls uniform: white stockings, white shoes with pale blue trim, white dress with heavy braided piping, white sweater with the Lady Anne Barnard colors on the pocket, and a stiff white straw hat with Barnard streamers. A selected group of women, most of them Church of England, had proudly worn this uniform for the past eighty years, and now twelve of them journeyed by different ways to the bowling green in the park, where they were to meet the distinguished Ladies of the Castle. During much of South African history this team had enrolled titled members.

Most of the players were in position when Laura arrived; some were much older than she; most were in their fifties. They were a handsome group of women, sun-tanned, each in proper uniform, each keen on the game which they had played for decades. The Ladies of the Castle could be easily differentiated from Laura's team: they wore brown shoes with very heavy rubber soles, and their hats had wide brims, down in front, up in back, with ribbons that hung neatly from the left side. It was obvious that they intended to win.

No one, either from the Barnards or the Castles, spoke to Mrs. Saltwood in any way other than their normal greeting on a June morning when the air was brisk and the sides of the playing field rimmed with beds of late-autumn flowers, but their tenseness indicated that this was not an ordinary day.

Laura was paired with the best bowler on the Barnards, Mrs. Grimsby, a stern-faced woman who intimidated her opponents by wearing on her dress a band of six medals she had won in international competitions. She was formidable, and shook Laura's hand firmly when they met: 'We'll have at them, yes?'

'It's our turn to win,' Laura said.

The teams bowled in sets of four, two opponents at one end of the rink facing two at the other. Today Laura would be bowling against Mrs. Phelps-Jones, who consistently beat her, but she felt that with Mrs. Grimsby at the other end, they just might pull off a surprise victory.

Laura won the right to send down the target bowl, the jack, which she did with some skill, landing it almost exactly the right distance from the backstop, but a little too much to the right. Since other foursomes would be playing at the same time on adjoining rinks, it was customary to move the jack into the center of the lane, at the distance set, and when this was done, the game began.

Laura and Mrs. Phelps-Jones were each to bowl four balls, Laura's marked with a small blue triangle inset into the wood, her opponent's with a green circle. A small mat was spread to protect the grass where the bowlers would be standing throughout the game, and on it Laura took two firm steps, swinging her right arm at the same time and delivering a ball with a decided spin. She launched it far to the left of her target, but since it was not perfectly round and since she had been careful to start it on its largest axis, it gradually twisted itself to the right, ending up not too far from the jack.

Mrs. Phelps-Jones was not daunted. Taking over the mat, she swung her first bowl well to the right, watching with satisfaction as it cut a large parabola toward the left, ending closer to the jack than Laura's. At the end of this first head, Mrs. Phelps-Jones scored one point, for her first ball rested closer than any that Laura could send down, but

Laura escaped disaster because one of her bowls was better than her opponent's second closest.

Now it was Mrs. Grimsby's turn, and she was a terror. Sending her wood right-to-left, she seemed to have implanted a magnet in the jack, for it drew her wood to it, and at the end of that head she had scored a cheering three. The game continued close through the twenty-one heads, with Mrs. Grimsby scoring the points that Laura failed to make. It was a splendid competition, with all four ladies delighted by the closeness.

It was Mrs. Grimsby who first saw them. She had delivered a smashing wood, sharp right-to-left, that knocked away two of her opponent's bowls, and when she looked up, they were standing off to one side, two men in dark suits watching the game, saying nothing.

Mrs. Grimsby's opponent saw them next, then all the women on the far ends of the rinks. No one spoke, but gradually their changed expressions alerted the women, whose backs were to the men. Finally Mrs. Phelps-Jones said matter-of-factly, 'Laura, I think they've come.'

Mrs. Saltwood did not look up. She was checking the position of the balls sent to their end by Mrs. Grimsby and her opponent, and she said, 'I think Esther has two, do you agree?'

Mrs. Phelps-Jones bent over to inspect and said, 'Two, right.'

The game continued, as the men intended it should, and although Laura did poorly, the remarkable bowling of Mrs. Grimsby enabled their side to win 25–21, but as Laura knelt to recover the bowls, she saw that Mrs. Phelps-Jones was weeping, and when she moved down the rink to congratulate Mrs. Grimsby, she found that she, too, was crying.

It was Mrs. Grimsby's opponent who spoke: 'Laura, you were the dearest woman in the teams. May I kiss you?'

Tears streaming down their faces, the women gave her their farewells, aware that they would probably never again compete with this fiery, wonderful woman. When they were finished, the two men moved forward, stood facing Mrs. Saltwood, and said quietly, 'Laura Saltwood, you are banned.'

She sat in her house, alone. For the next five years she must never be seen in the presence of more than one other person. She could attend no public meeting of any kind, nor address any gathering of even three, nor publish anything, nor consult with anyone except her doctor, her dentist and her lawyer, but not even them in unison.

No mention of her could be made in the public press; no quotation could ever appear in print of anything she had ever done or said or written or thought. She could not receive money from abroad, or appear on radio or television. If she went into town, she must never appear with more than one other person, and if friends stopped to talk with her, she was obliged to turn them aside.

It was because she had anticipated this imprisonment that she had sent her son and his family out of the country, for as a banned woman she would not have been free to meet with them or to travel with them on vacations of any kind, and she did not want them to share such painful limitations.

When anyone visited her, she had to leave her door open so that police or even strangers could satisfy themselves that she was not conducting a meeting, and if more than one person came to her house, with spying neighbors knowing that they were there, she had to provide chairs for the extras so that they could sit outside and be seen as not participating in the visit.

Since she would never be told what charges had been brought against her, there was no way to defend herself against the banning or clear herself once it had been imposed. Some eighty or ninety minor officials had the right to recommend to higher authorities the names of those they disliked, but the victims would never know who the accusers were or what had provoked them. In Laura's case heavy emphasis was placed on the report from the secret operations maintained by the South African government in London:

> Our agent 18-52 followed Mrs. Saltwood to Cambridge University, where her brother Wexton enrolled in the Communist Party prior to his escape to Moscow, and here she visited his old college Clare, from which she went to the banks of the River Cam at King's College, where a courier in a long coat approached her once, went to a telephone, and approached her a second time with messages not heard.

Only certain types of citizens were apt to be banned: newspapermen, writers, clergymen who strayed from the dictates of the Dutch Reformed Church, women who agitated, and of course any black who showed signs of potential leadership. The good thing about banning, from the government's point of view, was that it involved no prolonged court case, no publicity, and no obnoxious statements by the accused in their defense. It was clean, effective and final.

On the third night of her banning, Laura Saltwood was not surprised when at four in the morning a bomb exploded outside her door. When the government designated a person like Mrs. Saltwood as objectionable, she became a free target for every hoodlum in the neighborhood, and the police did little to discourage the rabble from bombing and firing the homes of banned persons. In recent years six hundred and seventeen such bombings and attacks had been made, and never once did the police track down the culprits. Always the authorities said, 'The bombing was despicable. Every effort is being made to identify those responsible.' In some of the cases, including Mrs. Saltwood's, fragments of the bomb contained serial numbers comparable to those issued to the police, but the best detectives in the country could not track down the perpetrators. They could trace a lone fountain pen sent into the country by a church in Geneva and know every person who handled it before it found its way to some black scholar, but they could not track down a bomb whose serial number indicated its place of manufacture, its designation, and who had signed for its receipt.

Of the previous attacks, many had resulted in disastrous fires, several had maimed and two had killed, but no suspect had ever even been listed, let alone arrested. In Mrs. Saltwood's case, the bomb destroyed a door and left a heavy fire-stain on the woodwork, but that was all. What the next one would do she could not know, but there would surely be a next one, which the police would investigate and the officials in Pretoria deplore.

The harshest aspect of Laura Saltwood's banning was that on the morning of the day when her five years expired, the same two men could appear at her door and say quietly, 'Laura Saltwood, you are banned for five more years,' and after that, there could be another five, and another.

That was why the members of the Lady Anne Barnard Club wept as they bade her goodbye that first day of June. They expected never to see her free again.

In his discussions with young Afrikaners, both at the fossicking and at Vrymeer, Saltwood was disturbed by the cavalier manner in which they dismissed world opinion. The United Nations would pass a resolution condemning South Africa for its racial policies, or its treatment of Indians, and the Troxel boys would laugh: 'What can they do about it? They need our minerals. To hell with them.' Newspapers in London and New York would print bitter editorials, and the young geologists working with Philip would sneer: 'What can England and the United States do? They've got to rely on us as bulwarks against Communism, so the bleeding hearts can bloody well drop dead.'

No outsider could talk with these vital young people without becoming convinced that they intended using military force to defend their way of life and were prepared to use their guns against either outside threats or internal ones. 'Let their armies step one foot across our borders,' Frikkie said, 'and we'll blow their heads off.'

Jopie made a much different point: 'If this Jonathan Nxumalo or any of his kind try to infiltrate us from Moçambique, we'll shoot them the moment they step on our soil. And we'll shoot any Kaffir inside our country who raises a finger to help them.'

'You sound like the Götterdämmerung Commando,' Saltwood said one Sunday afternoon at the farm.

'What's that?' Jopie asked.

'A German myth. The gods have loused everything up, hideously, so they go into laager, and to solve their problems, they burn down all of heaven.'

'I volunteer for that commando,' Jopie said.

'I, too,' said Sannie.

'You mean you would risk destroying the whole structure of South Africa to prolong your advantage?'

This was the kind of rhetorical question that would have been effective among university students in Paris or Berlin. At Vrymeer it evoked from Frikkie an answer which simply stunned Saltwood: 'No American could understand our situation. You have a problem with your blacks which you solve in ways harmonious to your history. But what you do bears no relationship to us. Because God placed us here to do His work. He put us here to serve as a bulwark of Christian civilization. We must stay.'

Philip gasped. In the United States, Frikkie and Jopie would be professional football players, and he could not conceive of a pair of athletes from the Dallas Cowboys or the Denver Broncos citing God as the sponsor of their political behavior. 'Do you believe what you just said?' he asked, and Sannie replied, 'We were placed here to do God's will, and we shall do it.' When Philip tried to question her, she interrupted: 'If Frikkie and Jopie were to be killed in the first battle, I'd take up their guns.'

'To do what?'

'To preserve our Christian way of life.'

'You would go out to your rondavels and shoot the Nxumalos?'

'I certainly would.' And almost imperceptibly she moved toward the cousins.

Silence fell in the kitchen. This was the first intimation that she had decided to cast her lot with the Troxels and against the American intruder, and Saltwood decided it was futile to speak further. Which of the cousins she would ultimately prefer was not discernible, but it was clear that she had enlisted in their Götterdämmerung Commando.

Later, when he was alone with her, he dared to reopen the difficult subject, but at the first tentative question she made her position clear: 'Philip, we're a small group of white people on the edge of a hostile black continent. God placed us here for a specific purpose and gave us a commission. I assure you that we will all perish before we prove false to that obligation.'

'Sannie, it seems to me you're overpowered by the attitude of Frikkie and Jopie. What do your parents think?'

'What Mother thinks isn't relevant, she's English. But if you want to ask Father . . .'

They went to Marius in his study, a room lined with books he had used at Oxford and others he had imported from London and New York through the years. 'In my father's day,' he said, 'this room contained one book, that old Bible. Now I can't even read the Dutch.'

'We've been having a sharp argument, Father. Philip accuses the cousins and me of being members of a Götterdämmerung Commando. Burning South Africa down to save it.'

'He's correct about your attitudes now. But as you grow older . . .'

'I'll grow more convinced. I have no patience . . .'

'Not now, but when you face the real alternatives.'

'What are they?'

Marius leaned back. For some time now he had been worried about Sannie's growing militarism; she behaved as if she thought a machine gun answered all questions. But he also wondered about his own attitudes; had his years at Oxford and his marriage to an Englishwoman contaminated him? Well he remembered his father's telling him what Dominee Brongersma had said about his marriage to a non-Afrikaner: 'Now he can never join the Broederbond . . . never play a major role in our society.' Brongersma had been right. No man who had chosen Oxford above the captaincy of the Springboks, and an English wife over a loyal Afrikaner, could be other than an outcast from the governing cadre; he had never been taken into the confidences of anyone seriously connected with government and had existed in a kind of limbo, neither Afrikaner nor English. He once said of himself, 'I'm like an Afrikaner Coloured,' and having admitted this, he realized that his daughter Sannie, who seemed bent on becoming pure Afrikaner, would hold anything he said in suspicion.

'I've been pondering this question constantly,' he said slowly. 'I've had to evaluate the things Father did in his long years on the Race Commission. And I've come to the conclusion that Afrikaners like Frikkie and Jopie will never change.'

'Hooray for them!' Sannie cried.

'And at her own request I must place my daughter in their camp.'

'Which is where I want to be.'

'So, Philip, I would be most happy, and so would my wife, if you married this girl and took her away with you.' He was speaking gravely, almost sorrowfully. 'I see no happy future for her here. Like the gifted children of so many families we know, she must make her home in Montreal or Melbourne.'

'Leave me out of it,' Sannie said abruptly. 'I can fend for myself. What future do you see for the country?'

'With the fall of Moçambique to black forces—Namibia, Zambia, Vwarda and Rhodesia—can we logically suppose that we can hold out indefinitely against . . .'

'I can,' Sannie said. 'So can Frikkie and Jopie and all loyal Afrikaners.'

'For your lifetimes, perhaps. Or for as long as your guns can find bullets. But in the long run, beyond our petty personal interests . . .'

He was hesitant about sharing his apocalyptic view with a foreigner who had no vested interest in the country, or even with his daughter, who might be alienated by it. But like all South Africans, he was eager to talk about the future, so he carried on: 'I think the blacks, like the Nxumalo brothers —Jonathan in Moçambique, Daniel at the university—will be willing in their moment of triumph . . .'

'You think they'll triumph?' Sannie asked contemptuously.

'Or their sons, who will be much like them,' her father said.

'My sons will shoot them down,' she said.

'Then their grandsons. History has time . . . It can wait.'

'For what?' Saltwood asked eagerly.

'As I was saying, I think the black victors will be generous. They'll want us to stay. God knows, their brothers haven't made much of the countries they now control. They'll realize they need us.'

'You really believe that?' Sannie asked.

'Without question. The black leadership in this country has been the most patient on earth, the most understanding. It's been a miracle of compassion and tolerance, and I think it will continue in that vein.'

'Then where's the trouble?' Philip asked.

'With us. With Sannie and Frikkie and Jopie. We won't be able to accept the change. We'll ride the Götterdämmerung Commando, as you predict, but we'll grow sickened of it, even if the rest of the world doesn't intervene. And then . . .'

Here he showed himself truly reluctant to spell out his vision, and neither his daughter nor his American guest could possibly have foreseen what he was about to say: 'At that moment of crisis the Afrikaner and his

English supporters, of whom my wife will be one, will go into perpetual laager. With the full connivance and even assistance of the new black rulers, we'll retreat to the western half of the Orange Free State and Cape Province west of Grahamstown. We'll keep the diamond mines at Kimberley, but surrender the gold fields at Johannesburg. That city and Pretoria will be turned over to the new black government, and in our compressed little area we will build our Afrikanerstan. The tables will be reversed. When we were in power we tried to concentrate all the blacks into little areas, while we held the vast open spaces and the good cities. In the future they'll hold the open spaces and the good cities, and we'll be compressed.'

'What will happen to the Coloureds?' Philip asked. 'They'll all be with you—in Afrikanerstan?' And Marius van Doorn gave the same answer his people had been giving for the past three hundred years: 'We'll deal with that knotty problem later.'

When Philip and Sannie, much sobered by her father's predictions, repeated them to the Troxels, the cousins guffawed, and Jopie said, 'When they try to capture Pretoria, they'll find us in the trenches at the monument, and they better be prepared to die.'

'Father said the real tests will come with your grandsons. They'll be smart enough to—'

'If one of my grandsons talks like your father, I'll beat him to a jelly.'

Frikkie sought to face the problem more philosophically: 'There was no one on this land when we arrived. God gave it to us. We found a primitive paradise and converted it into a great nation.'

'Just a minute!' Philip protested. 'I'm sure I read that natives greeted your ships when they arrived at the Cape.'

'There was no one here,' Jopie insisted. 'I heard Sannie's grandfather state this in a public meeting.'

This evidence so startled Philip that he asked Marius to join them to clarify the facts. 'Jopie says he heard your father . . .'

'On several occasions,' Frikkie added.

'. . . state that when the Dutch arrived at the Cape, they found the place completely empty.'

Marius laughed. 'My father was fond of claiming this in his orations. It was a basic tenet of his religion—still is for the average Afrikaner.'

'See, there were no people here!' Jopie cried triumphantly.

'Detleef was right, according to his definitions. There were no Englishmen, no Spaniards, no Portuguese. And certainly no blacks.'

'We took over a virgin land,' Frikkie said quietly.

'Not exactly. There were many little brown people. Bushmen, Hottentots.'

'They don't count,' Jopie protested. 'They weren't human.'

'They did die out,' Frikkie said. 'Diseases took them. And a few returned to the desert, and pretty soon they'll die, too.'

'Like we said,' Jopie concluded, looking fiercely at Philip, 'the place was empty. God called us here to perform a task on His behalf.'

The Troxel arrogance was somewhat shaken by two events which occurred not in South Africa but abroad, and when Philip saw how the cousins reacted, and the young men working for him, he thought: Maybe the outside world is beginning to penetrate, after all.

The first jolt came from a most unlikely source. Reverend Paulus van den Berghe, moderator of a group of French and Dutch Calvinists, came to South Africa to ascertain whether the rupture which had separated the mother church in Holland and the Afrikaners' church in South Africa could be repaired, and in the course of his investigations he asked permission to meet with the son of one of its principal architects. Marius, always eager for foreign contacts, agreed to have the distinguished theologian spend some days at Vrymeer, where in the gentlest manner Van den Berghe interrogated not only Marius, but also Frikkie and Jopie and then Daniel Nxumalo, home on vacation.

At the end of four days Van den Berghe knew something of conditions at Venloo from both the white and black points of view, and at the final session, to which Philip was invited and Nxumalo, too, he voiced a few of his tentative conclusions:

'What do you suppose the two biggest surprises were for me? Meeting two rugby players of international status and seeing for myself what sterling young men they are. I wish you good luck, Troxels, with your forthcoming games in Australia and New Zealand. The second big surprise was to find that I was on the farm once occupied, or shared, by Paulus de Groot, who was my hero when I was a lad. I was born the year he died, and how often I heard my parents talk about the heroic Dutchman—to us, Boers were always Dutchmen —who held at bay four hundred thousand Englishmen. It was a moment of deep affection when I was allowed to place flowers on his grave.

'As to the purposes of my visit, it must be obvious that clergymen like me in The Netherlands and France are disturbed by the course your Dutch Reformed Church has been taking since you Afrikaners assumed control of the nation in 1948. It has become a handmaiden not of a religion, nor of the republic, but of a particular political party, and that's always regrettable. A church should be the handmaiden of Jesus Christ first, the entire society second, and to align it on the side of faction is dangerous.

'Concerning its preachments regarding apartheid, it would be improper for me to voice my personal judgments before the whole commission has had a chance to evaluate and temper them. But I must confess that I leave your country with a heavy heart. I had not realized you had grown so far apart from us. It will now be the duty of all to conciliate our differences.'

When he was gone, Frikkie said with ill-masked fury, 'This land has always been cursed by missionaries. That man's an agent of the World Council of Churches and I should have shot him for a spy.'

'Oh, Frik!' Mrs. van Doorn protested.

'I mean it. What did the foreign churches do in Rhodesia? They gave money to terrorists. And how did they spend it? Killing women and children and missionaries. Is that Christianity?'

Jopie joined in: 'You watch what he writes when he gets back to Holland!' And the Troxels were right, for when the commission's report appeared, it was a devastating attack on the South African church:

> With mounting sorrow your committee must report that our Afrikaner brothers in the white Dutch Reformed Church of South Africa have strayed so far and so willfully from the path of Christian morality as evidenced in the preachings of Jesus Christ and St. Paul that reunion now between our church and theirs would be inadvisable and unproductive. Your committee therefore recommends unanimously that the present severance of affiliations be maintained until such time as the Dutch Reformed Church of South Africa manifests a Christian concern in ending its support of the system of repression known as *apartheid*.

Saltwood was surprised at the fury with which the Troxels reacted to this censure: 'We're the polecats of the world, and damnit, if they come at us, we'll squirt in their eyes.' Sannie agreed, and even though Saltwood cautioned the young people that they could not indefinitely ignore world opinion, Frikkie responded, 'We can if it's wrong.' Philip then asked if young men like him and Jopie ever admitted that anything was wrong with South Africa, and they replied together, 'No.' And Jopie added, 'We've worked out a decent, fair system of handling the races in our society. The laws have been passed, and they must be obeyed.'

'But in most countries,' Philip said, thinking of the drastic readjustments in America in recent years, 'provision is made for reassessment. A law tends to be applicable for only about ten or twenty years. The laws your grandfather passed, Sannie—'

'He didn't pass them. He proposed them.'

'Haven't they served their day? Shouldn't they be repealed?'

'Repealed?' the Troxel boys echoed. 'They should be strengthened!'

'You see, Saltwood,' Frikkie explained, 'we know the blacks. They're wild veld creatures like the antelope, and we won't allow them to be spoiled by modern ideas, no matter what the Dutch churchmen advise.'

Jopie was more blunt: 'To hell with the Dutch churchmen. They're today's missionaries.' And at this, Sannie grasped the hands of her young men and started a dance, chanting an improvised song:

> 'To hell with the missionaries!
> To hell with the men of Holland!
> To hell with all who interfere!'

Marius, hearing the clamor, came from his study, and Sannie danced up to him: 'We're consigning the missionaries to hell.'

'That was done long ago,' Marius said, and when he joined the young people in a beer, Saltwood asked, 'How do you see the church problem?'

and after some reflection he replied, 'When I accepted my Rhodes scholarship instead of playing rugby for the Springboks against New Zealand, I knew I was sacrificing a lot.' He smiled at the Troxels. 'These lads go against New Zealand next month. It'll be the great adventure of your lives.'

'Apparently you have regrets.'

'One you'd never expect. When I returned home with an English wife, I couldn't be a member of the Broederbond, but who cared? What did hurt was that I was denied the right to be a full member of the Dutch Reformed Church. I've never been an elder, you know.'

'Does that matter?' Saltwood asked.

'Grievously. I truly believe that our church is the most effective on earth today. It has spirit, meaning, force. It obeys the word of God and endeavors prayerfully to implement it. A real church.'

'But its support of apartheid? Surely . . .'

Marius rose and went to the refrigerator for another beer. 'Churches go through cycles. In America, if I understand correctly, your Catholic church is riding rampant on birth control and abortion. That's temporary, a fashion of the moment. It has very little to do with the ongoing operation of the church. Same with our church and apartheid. It's a problem for the 1980s. Fifty years from now it will all be settled.'

'So you support your church in all it does?' Philip asked.

'I do, because it's the moral force of South Africa. It's forever.'

'And in the meantime,' Jopie cried, 'to hell with the visitors from Holland.'

'And the World Council of Churches!' Sannie cried, resuming their dance.

A few days later Saltwood observed his arrogant young Afrikaners knocked flat by a much different kind of foreign intervention. He was alone in the Van Doorn kitchen, waiting for Sannie, when her father and Jopie burst into the room, looking ghastly. Without speaking, they fiddled with the radio, located a Pretoria station, and listened as the awful news was reported: 'There is an unconfirmed report out of Auckland that the governments of Australia and New Zealand will be forced to cancel the scheduled tour of those countries by a rugby team from South Africa.'

'Good God!' Marius said, looking at Jopie as if the latter's arms had been amputated. 'That would mean you wouldn't get your Springbok blazer.'

'Wait, wait! This can't be serious.'

But it was. A different newscaster announced in tremulous Afrikaans, his voice near breaking: 'We have nothing definite yet, but governments of Australia and New Zealand have explained that rioting in the streets protesting the tours have made cancellation advisable.'

'Have you heard?' Frikkie bellowed as he rushed into the kitchen. 'Tour's been canceled.'

'Not officially,' Jopie said, his hands sweating.

Then came the appalling bulletin: 'It is now confirmed that the Springbok tour of Australia and New Zealand has been canceled.'

Marius fell into a chair, staring pitifully at the brothers. 'It's like you said, Jopie. The world thinks we're skunks.'

The three rugby players huddled at the radio, shaken by the urgent bulletins that flooded the air, and when the ugly story was fully verified, Saltwood was amazed by the violence of the men's reactions.

'It's criminal!' Marius shouted. 'Using sport as a weapon of confrontation. A game's a game, and politics should have nothing to do with it.'

'I'll teach them politics,' Jopie thundered. 'I'll fly to New Zealand and break those protestors in half, one by one.'

'It's not the ordinary citizens,' Marius said. 'It's the damned press.'

'The press in all countries should be muzzled,' Frikkie stormed, but at this moment the minister of sports, came on the radio to console the nation, and he was bidding them be of good spirit despite the shattering blow, when Sannie burst into the kitchen, weeping. 'Oh, Jopie! Oh, dear Frikkie! They've stolen your glorious tour from you!' She ran to the cousins and kissed them; Jopie gulped so deeply that Philip feared he might burst into tears, but instead he went about the room, knocking his fist against doorjambs.

Then came more shocking news: 'In New Zealand the agitation against our Springboks was led by a South African citizen, one Fred Stabler, who himself used to play rugby for Rhodes University in Grahamstown. This agitator has moved through both North Island and South, spreading the poison about what he calls apartheid, and he raised such a virulent storm that the New Zealand government had to intervene and order the tour to be canceled. In Australia, at least, it was native-borns who led the agitation. In New Zealand it was one of our own.'

Gloom settled over the Van Doorn kitchen as the Afrikaners realized the full impact of this decision. A generation of fine young athletes would never know whether they could match courage with the ferocious All-Blacks. The great good feelings that welled up when a touring side ran onto the field against New Zealand would be lost. It was important when a South African tennis player was barred from competing in world tennis, a thing to be deplored, but when a whole rugby team was denied an opportunity to win the green blazer, it was a national scandal, and men of all stripe were finally driven to wonder if perchance their nation was on the wrong track.

This self-exploration was intensified next day when newspapers carried full reports from New Zealand, and one Auckland paper, long a defender of South African teams, editorialized:

Through the years this newspaper had prided itself on being a champion of restraint in dealing with the thorny problem of South African rugby. In 1960, when our Maoris were threatened with expulsion because their skins were not white, we apologized for the backward attitudes of a nation grappling with a serious problem. In 1965, when in the heat of one of our grandest victories Prime Minister Verwoerd announced that henceforth no New Zealand team containing Maoris would ever again be welcomed in South Africa, we discounted his threat as one given in despair over the unexpectedly poor showing of his Springboks. And in 1976, when all the world condemned us for sending the All-Blacks to perform in a country so ridden with racial hatred, we supported the tour. And even when the refereeing

proved disgracefully one-sided, we argued that any All-Black–
Springbok championship series was worth the effort, and we urged
our boys and our nation to enjoy it.

But we can no longer see anything to be gained by allowing sport,
however noble its intentions, to be used to shore up a racist regime.
Belatedly, and with the saddest possible regret, we support Government's decision that this tour must not be allowed to proceed. There
are some things in this world bigger than an All-Black–Springbok
match, and humanity among brothers is one of them.

Jopie Troxel folded the paper and shoved it over to Sannie. There was so
much he wanted to say, but he would not trust himself to speak. They don't
understand us, he thought. They accuse us of things we've never done. All
we want is to maintain an orderly society, and they protest.

While Sannie and Frikkie prepared sandwiches and beer, he sat staring
at his knuckles and brooding. The United Nations had condemned South
Africa, but that was a bunch of dark-skinned third nations flexing their
feeble muscles, and could be disregarded. The World Council of Churches
had condemned apartheid, but they were a gang of radicals. The French-
Dutch Commission had spoken harshly, but they were vexed because South
Africa did not follow supinely in their missionary-socialist trail. But when
Australia and New Zealand canceled a rugby tour, the heart and spirit of
the nation were endangered.

'Why can't they try to understand us?' Jopie cried. Sannie and Frikkie
kept cutting sandwiches.

A few days later Saltwood was introduced to a South African game even
more brutal than rugby, if that was possible. Daniel Nxumalo came casually
to Swartstroom and asked, 'You free tonight?'

'Let me phone Sannie.' But when the call went through, Mrs. van
Doorn said that her daughter had gone to Pretoria with the Troxel boys,
and Philip visualized them moving as a threesome beneath the jacaranda
trees. 'I'm free.'

By roundabout paths Nxumalo led Philip to a shack where three tall
blacks waited: 'This is my brother Jonathan. This is my cousin Matthew
Magubane. This is a new recruit, Abel Tubakwa.'

Philip gasped. A thousand police were searching for Jonathan and
Matthew; indeed, the Troxel boys had been on the border primarily to
pursue these two into Moçambique, yet here they were, boldly in the same
hills as those who were hunting them. 'They were in Soweto last night,'
Daniel said, 'and they go north tomorrow. Or at least that's what they told
me.' The conspirators laughed.

'We suggested the meeting,' Jonathan said in Afrikaans.

'Why?' Philip asked.

'So that you could tell the Americans, when you go home, that we are
far from defeated.'

'I may not go home.'

'You should. In a few years this could be an ugly country.'

Magubane interrupted: 'Marry the girl and get her out of here. All the bright young whites are leaving.' He spoke in such rapid Afrikaans that Saltwood failed to catch his full meaning, so Abel Tubakwa interpreted in fine English.

'How do you see the future?' Philip asked in English, and after that the men used this language.

Jonathan was obviously the tactician: 'If they caught us tonight, we'd all be shot. But they won't catch us. We move about pretty much as we wish.'

'Terrorism?'

'We don't call it that. Sporadic attacks. Harassment. Ridicule. War of nerves.'

'To what purpose?'

'To remind them always that we're serious. That we will never again go away and lie down like good dogs and not growl.'

'Will that accomplish anything?'

'It will gnaw at their minds. Saltwood, you've seen the enlightened Afrikaners. These people are not stupid. They know that accommodation must be made. I think they're ready to accept us now, on some radically new basis. Not total equality, not yet. And not one-man, one-vote. But a true partnership.'

'Look at what's happening in Pretoria right now,' Daniel said excitedly. 'They've built this new theater. With public funds. I understand it's as good as anything in Berlin or the one in Minneapolis.'

'I've been reading the stories,' Philip said. 'Public funds, and then they state that only whites will be admitted.'

Jonathan slammed the table. 'They doing that again?'

'Yes,' his brother said, 'but there's been this great outcry. From all parts of the public. People you'd never expect have stepped forward to demand that the theater be made available to everyone.'

'Goddamn!' Jonathan cried, and Magubane rose and walked agitatedly about the room. It was the situation they had fought against for the past three years. 'We no longer want crumbs from the master's table,' Jonathan said. 'We don't want a slice of bread. We don't want the loaf. We want the whole damned bakery. And we want it now.'

'We're not part of their society,' Magubane said sardonically. 'We would not appreciate Shakespeare or Goethe.' He kicked at the chair he had just vacated. 'I can recite whole pages of *Othello,* but I can never see it performed.'

Jonathan burst into laughter. 'Magubane, you ass. *Othello* is not really welcomed in South Africa. He's black, man. He's black, or didn't you know?'

Magubane brushed his chin as if embarrassed by his ignorance, then stood by the door, his right hand across his chest—'I am a Moor of Venice!' —and declaimed:

'Had it pleased heaven
To try me with affliction; had they rained
All kinds of sores, and shames, on my bare head;

    Steeped me in poverty to the very lips,
    Given to captivity me and my utmost hopes,
    I should have found in some part of my soul
    A drop of patience . . .'

He quit his oratory and said quietly, 'We have that "drop of patience," but only for so long.'

'What I was trying to say,' Daniel Nxumalo continued, 'was that right now in Pretoria booths have been set up in many spots. White people, women mostly, manage them . . .'

'For what purpose?' Jonathan asked.

'They're collecting signatures, petitioning the authorities to allow non-whites to attend performances in the new theater. And I understand the response has been overwhelmingly in favor.'

'Well,' Jonathan admitted grudgingly, 'change does come. Slow—but inevitable.' He rocked back and forth, then asked, 'Dan, do you think I'll ever be free to come back here and live like an ordinary workman?'

'Yes. Without the slightest hesitation I say yes. There's change in the air. Good things are happening, and I honestly believe we can attain our goals.'

'I don't,' Jonathan replied. 'Not without armed revolution, which will probably not come till I'm an old man.'

'You see yourself living a life of exile?' Philip asked.

'Yes. Magubane here will never see his birthplace free. Tubakwa, when you join us over the border you will never come home.'

'What will you do?' Philip asked.

'Maintain pressure. Goad the Afrikaners into taking an open Hitler stance until the world has to intervene.'

'If the government offered you amnesty—'

'We would reject it,' Magubane broke in. 'This is war to the finish. The evil tricks of these people must be ended.'

'But Frikkie and Jopie, the two rugby players. They say almost the same thing. War to the finish. To preserve the kind of government God willed them to have.'

Jonathan started to make a cynical denouncement, but Magubane cut him off, saying to Philip, 'That's why I advise you to marry the girl and get out of here. You Americans proved in Vietnam you had no stomach for the long fight. The Troxels do. And we do. This war will last forty years, and it can only increase in severity and barbarity. That's why the airplanes are filled with those young people leaving. That's why you should go.'

Philip turned to Daniel Nxumalo. 'But you think there's still hope?'

'I do! The people signing those petitions in Pretoria are proof.'

But when Philip reached his camp he found his workmen excited by a news flash from the capital. Rural Afrikaners calling themselves the Avengers of the Veld had stormed into Pretoria, dynamited the kiosks in which the theater petitions were being signed, and burned the rubble, threatening to donder the women if they persisted in this unpatriotic effort to mix the races. The spokesman for the Avengers explained: 'God has forbidden us to accept Canaanites in our midst, and if this effort continues, we shall have to burn down the theater.'

When Sannie and the Troxel boys returned home, they were elated.

Philip wasted much of his leisure time at the diggings trying to fathom why —above all else—the men at Vrymeer were so devastated by the cancellation of the New Zealand tour. He reached no conclusion, but one morning he was summoned to Pretoria for an evaluation meeting with Amalgamated Mines. The principal officers convened at the Burgers Park Hotel, and as they sat in the lounge with drinks, Philip saw coming through the door a man whose face was vaguely familiar. 'Who's that?' he whispered to one of his superiors.

'That's the minister of finance,' the Johannesburg man said without taking further notice, but apparently there was some kind of governmental meeting, for within a few minutes the new prime minister came bustling in. He had been in office such a short time that Philip only vaguely recognized him. 'Is that who I think it is?' he whispered.

'Yes, that's the prime minister.' And again no one moved.

A little while later an extraordinary man walked past them. It seemed to Philip that one of the Drakensberg Mountains had come to Pretoria, for the man was gigantic, not in height, although he was quite tall, but in the girth of his body, the enormous spread of hips, the lower jaw that jutted at least four inches farther than normal. He had black hair and great dark eyes.

'Who's . . .' Philip started.

'My God!' the chairman of Amalgamated cried. 'That's Frik du Preez!' At this, all the businessmen stood up and nodded at the great Springbok who had played in more international matches than any other South African. Like an Alp wading across the Mediterranean, he moved majestically through the lobby to enter the dining room, and everyone in Saltwood's party marked his progress.

'That was Frik du Preez,' the chairman repeated.

'I think my family had some doings with the Cape Town Du Preezes,' Saltwood said, and at this news all the men regarded him with additional respect.

The most revealing incident concerning rugby occurred one morning at the camp when Philip received a day-old Pretoria newspaper, across the front of which appeared four excellent photographs depicting one continuous play in Saturday's game against Monument. The left-hand picture showed Frikkie Troxel being savagely tackled by a Monument brute named Spyker Swanepoel, who was using what American football called 'the clothesline tackle,' in which a man with the ball running full speed east is grabbed about the neck by a bigger man running full speed west. In this photograph it looked as if Frikkie was about to lose his head.

Shot two showed him flat on the ground, unconscious, ball flopping away, while Spyker Swanepoel delivered a savage, heavily booted kick with full force right at his temple. It was a blow which would have killed a mere human being, but rugby players were something beyond that.

Shot three was the precious one. Frikkie lay almost dead, spread-eagled.

The triumphant Spyker was striding away. And up behind him could be seen Jopie Troxel, leaping off his left foot, his right fist swinging forward with terrifying force and striking Spyker so fiercely that it was clear that his jaw jumped sideways three inches.

Shot four was total bedlam. Frikkie lay dead, or almost so. Spyker Swanepoel lay unconscious, his jaw awry in such a way as to impart a beatific smile. And seven Monument men, engulfing Jopie, were knocking him to the ground and kicking him. In other parts of the photograph some half-dozen major fistfights were taking place, with one Venloo man neatly kneeing his opponent in the crotch. The series was entitled SPIRITED PLAY AT LOFTUS VERSFELD.

When Frikkie regained consciousness in the hospital, sports reporters wanted to know how he felt about the game, and he said, 'We should've won.'

'You did,' they told him.

'Hooray!' He tried to get out of bed, but could not control his movements and fell back.

'Did you know that Spyker kicked you?'

'What if he did?'

'Did you see the papers?'

'I haven't even seen daylight.' They showed him the four photographs, and he spent some time on the first one. 'That Spyker made a strong tackle, didn't he?'

'But the kick?'

'Jopie took care of that,' he said, pointing to the ferocious blow in the third shot. Then he studied the last picture: 'I'm down. Spyker's down. Jopie's going down. I'm glad we won.'

The kick to the head had temporarily deranged the mechanisms which enable a human being to maintain equilibrium; it was as if someone had set in motion a gyroscope which held to one course, no matter what the lateral pressures. Frikkie would start walking in a given direction, and when the time came to make a turn, he would continue straight ahead, sometimes going right into a wall.

The doctors were more alarmed than he. 'I'll get it back into control,' he said, and added that he fully intended to play in Saturday's fixture against a team from the Orange Free State, but by midweek it was quite clear that he would not even be out of the hospital. It was then that Sannie began attending him regularly, and as she observed the straightforward manner in which he accepted his punishment, and the determined way he went about recovering, she felt increasingly that he represented the best in South Africa. Was there a job to do on the Moçambique border? He would go do it. Was there a tackle to be made? He would make it. Did the government require some new approach to old problems? He was the man to effectuate it. He was direct, uncomplicated and trustworthy.

She was at his side when Spyker Swanepoel came to visit, his jaw wired back into place. 'That was a strong tackle, Spyker' was all Frik said.

'You still got ringing in your ears?'

'Something's out of balance. It'll fall into place.'

'What you need, Frikkie, I've seen it a dozen times. A little sharp exercise and a dop of brandy.'

'I think so, too,' and he allowed big Spyker to pull him to his feet, steady him, give him a drink, and then run him right at the farthest wall.

'Whoa!' Spyker cried, and back they came the other way.

'That feels great!' Frikkie said. 'Let's go out in the hall.'

'Frikkie!' Sannie protested, but she could not stop these two great hulks, and out into the hall they went. She watched as they started down the long passageway, running and dodging as if they were on a rugby field. 'Hey! Hey!' Spyker grunted, shouting encouragement, and soon he was in the lead, allowing Frikkie to run by himself, but as before, the internal gyroscope prevented Frik from making a turn and he ran right into the end wall.

'Jesus Christ!' Spyker bellowed through wired teeth. 'Don't run into the goddamned wall.'

'What in the world?' the matron in charge of the floor cried as she saw two huge men coming back down the hall, Spyker in front, Frikkie dodging along behind and going great until he again plowed into the wall.

'We've got to work on it,' Spyker said as he led Frikkie back to bed. 'How do you feel?'

'That damned wall . . .'

By now the hospital staff had crowded into the room, and the head doctor was upbraiding Sannie for allowing such a dangerous situation. 'You should have stopped them,' he blustered.

'Have you ever tried to stop them?' and when Spyker was led away, and she was alone with Frikkie, she went to the door and locked it. 'You're all right,' she said, returning to the bed, where she took his hands and pulled him to her. 'You're a little weak on turns to the left, but who cares?'

And as she slipped into bed with him she whispered, 'As soon as you can walk straight, we're getting married.'

'I'm playing next Saturday,' he announced, and it must have been the therapy she provided, because on Friday morning he left the hospital, on Saturday he sat with her watching his team play, and the next Saturday he was on the field against Natal. It was during the celebration following that game, which he played like a ghost looking for a lost glen, that Sannie announced that she was going to marry him.

Jopie poured champagne over his rival, then kissed the bride-to-be and said, 'I always suspected he'd be the one.' But when Philip Saltwood heard the news, he dashed in from the diggings to beg Sannie to reconsider.

'I did,' she said. 'In the hospital. I love you, Philip, and will never forget how good life with you could have been. But Frikkie is South Africa. And so am I.'

When Sannie van Doorn, firmly and finally, rejected Philip Saltwood's offer of marriage and indicated that either of the Troxel boys would have been accepted ahead of him, he slipped into a profound melancholy, unable to force his tangled values into sensible patterns. He felt discarded not only as a suitor but also as a human being; for some years now he had been working in suspension, not attached to any specific country, or enterprise, or woman. He was a man in limbo, and the growing affection he had felt for Sannie was caused partly by her unusual attractiveness, partly by her promise of being a solid anchor for his drifting boat. He liked her and he liked her country; its challenges did not frighten him, for he would enjoy participating in its violent development.

Even without Sannie he wanted to stay on, so he directed all his energies to an even more frantic search for the hidden source of the diamonds, and one day while looking at the map he saw that he should investigate the headwaters of Krokodilspruit, a minor tributary to the Swartstroom, and when he consulted the managers in Pretoria, they agreed. Since Daniel Nxumalo was acquainted with that lonely terrain, he was invited along. What made the trip memorable was that as they left the dirt road and walked quietly along the stream, they came upon a small valley encompassed by low hills, and there for the first time in his life Philip saw a herd of eland, some thirty majestic beasts, golden tan in color, with white blazes across the back and on the legs. They were so much bigger than the antelope he had seen in places like Wyoming and Colorado that he gasped and held out his right arm to halt Nxumalo's movement, but this was unnecessary, for no one who loved the veld of Africa ever took such a herd casually.

'Look at the dewlaps!' Philip whispered—certain of the bucks showed massive appendages to their chests that swayed gently as they walked.

For perhaps ten minutes the two men stood motionless, watching these noble beasts, dark glowing in sunlight, symbols of the Africa that had always mystified both strangers and those who knew it well. In every respect these were notable animals, for they were not of gigantic size like huge elephants, nor threatening like the rhinoceros, nor ethereal like the flamingos, nor utilitarian like the horse, nor repellent like the black mamba snake. They were among the regal beasts of the world.

'Jesus, they are beautiful,' Philip said, and then for reasons he could not have explained he started running toward them, shouting and waving his arms as if to dissolve this vision. At first only those at the rear were aware of him, but when they started leisurely to move on up the banks of the Krokodilspruit, the others realized that something untoward was occurring, and they, too, began moving off, until at last the entire herd was in motion, not frantically and not in leaping bounds, but with a dignity befitting their exalted place in the animal kingdom.

When Philip continued his running, they disdainfully acknowledged that something must be done to protect themselves from whatever danger he represented, so they ambled easily away from the spruit and into a sparse collection of low trees, where mysteriously their brown colors and white patches blended so perfectly with the shadows that they became invisible.

'They've disappeared!' Philip said, but when Nxumalo joined him the black could see colors which the white could not, and he pointed out the various large bucks who trailed behind protecting the herd, and when Nxumalo affirmed that they were still there, Philip could see them. It required the eyes of Africa to see Africa.

Daniel was so favorably impressed by Saltwood's enthusiastic response to the eland that when their exploration of the Krokodilspruit was completed, he studied the white man as if judging whether he could be trusted, then said abruptly, 'Saltwood, there's something I'd like to share with you.'

'What?'

'Something exceedingly precious. A surprise,' and he directed Philip to drive along narrow, unpaved roads. On the long ride the two talked seriously of matters to which they had merely alluded in previous sessions. Nxumalo was thirty that summer, Saltwood a year older, and he spoke first.

'When you court a girl in a strange land, seriously, I mean . . .'

'I know what you mean. I could see.'

'Well, it jolts you down to hard-rock common sense. Seeing those eland hiding off in a valley had the same effect. Christ, Nxumalo, what's going to happen to this land?'

'It has its own force, you know. The great revolving of the earth. The inescapable numbers of people. There are limits beyond which we can't go. And there are directions in which we must go.'

'Are you a fatalist?'

'No, a determinist.'

'A Marxist?'

'No, but in certain analyses Marx does make sense. Just as Frantz Fanon does. Or Thomas Jefferson.'

'What do you see happening?'

'Would I share my vision with a white man?' When Philip looked at him in astonishment, Nxumalo said prophetically, 'Must I not take into account the possibility that I will be arrested one of these days and that you will be required under oath to report what I said to you one summer morning as we rode to see the rhinoceros?'

Philip sat silent, acknowledging the heavy truth of what this man was saying: with a black, everything of day and night, of work and relaxation was subject to interrogation, with death and life hanging in the arbitrary balance. He was under no such constraints, not in his own country or in any other he visited, and that was the terrible, inescapable difference between being a white man in America and a black man in South Africa.

'Can you not imagine the prosecutor hammering at you: "Why in the world, Mr. Saltwood, were you going with this suspect black to see a rhinoceros?" except that he would call it *renoster*. And what could you say?'

Philip did not try to answer; instead he asked, 'What will be the future of the Coloureds?'

'Why do you ask such a question?'

'Because Frikkie and Jopie warned that once you blacks took control, the Coloureds were finished.'

'Frikkie and Jopie are right. There'll be no place for them. They had their chance to work with us, but stupidly they clung to the hope that one day the whites would accept them. They wanted to move up to catch the whites rather than down to work with us, and their decision was fatal.'

'Could it be corrected?'

'I think not, but maybe they will be given another chance to save themselves.'

'The Indians?'

'Who in Africa has ever solved the problem of the Indians? In Malawi, in Uganda, in Burundi—out! They've tossed them out. I could see something like Viet . . .' He stopped. He was confiding too much. Recently he had visualized crowded boats leaving the Natal coast burdened with Indians expelled from the country. England would no longer have them. No African nation would permit them entrance. Madagascar would fire upon the ships if they attempted to land there. And certainly homeland India would refuse them, for it already contained three bodies for each available space.

'How's your brother in Moçambique?'

That was another question that had better not be answered.

'Do you see any permanent place for the white man?'

'For the true Afrikaner, yes. He belongs to Africa and can learn to live with us. For the others, I'm afraid not. They'll never commit themselves to our soil.'

'What language will you be using?'

'Now, there we are.' He rapped his knuckles against the car door and blew out a heavy breath. 'It ought to be Afrikaans, really. That's a splendid, functional language. Most of my friends speak it, even though they don't like it. I'll tell you what Afrikaans is. Do you know Fanakalo, the made-up language of the mines? Afrikaans is the gentleman's Fanakalo.'

'Then you'll drop English?'

Nxumalo abruptly changed the subject: 'Did you follow the case of Mrs. Saltwood down in Johannesburg? She must be a distant relative of yours.'

'She is. Afrikaners who despise her behavior keep reminding me of it.'

'Accept her, Philip. Embrace her. She's one of God's rare women.'

Fleetingly, Philip thought of Craig Saltwood's request, and felt a twinge of guilt. 'But she's banned, isn't she?'

'She's sitting in silence at the foot of God.' He bowed his head for a moment, then said briskly, 'When our student group met the other day in Bloemfontein, black students, that is, we spoke nine different languages. Zulu, Xhosa, Swazi, Sotho, Tswana, Fingo, Pondo, Venda and Tonga. In self-defense we had to use English as the functional language.'

'Why didn't you use Afrikaans?'

'Could anyone use Afrikaans to discuss freedom?'

'Afrikaners do. They would die to preserve their freedom.'

'Isn't it curious?' Nxumalo cried. 'From the first day the Dutch landed at the Cape they struggled for freedom. Their whole history, as they teach it to us, was a ceaseless battle to be free. Yet when we say, "As major inhabitants of this land, we blacks would like to be free," they look at us with horror, call us Communists, and grab their guns to shoot us down.'

For some minutes they drove in silence over the veld, where tiny flowers in myriad colors looked like magical gems shining in the dust. 'Philip,' Nxumalo repeated, 'have you looked into the Laura Saltwood banning? Do you know why the government pounced on her?'

'No. All I saw was a formal announcement, then nothing.'

'That's what banning is—"then nothing." She advised blacks to cling to English and not permit the government to force Afrikaans upon us.' He paused, then laughed. 'You see, that's where the dilemma stands. Afrikaans could be a useful language for us. You know, I suppose, that it's the basic language for the Coloured, too? They helped invent it, and most of them speak it.'

'Sounds confused.'

'It is, philologically, historically, socially and politically.'

'Which will win, Afrikaans or English?'

'Contests between languages are always settled by poets. Most Coloured poets write in Afrikaans, and very movingly. But what black poet would care to do so?'

They now rode along a ridge from which vistas were immense, and to the south Philip saw a small conical mountain, and it was to this that Nxumalo directed him: 'There's only a small path. If many people knew of this, the place might have to be cordoned off. This is treasure, you know.'

After a brief climb the men came to a small flat area, bounded on one side by a large overhanging rock. At first Philip assumed he was being taken to a rude cave with some archaeological significance, but he found no signs of a dig, nor any potsherds to indicate that one had ever taken place. Then, gradually, he saw on the sloping wall the distinct outline of a rhinoceros, very large, with flecks of color still marking its hide fifteen thousand years after its completion. Aridity and remoteness had protected this masterpiece, so that it looked not significantly different from what it had been originally.

Philip leaned against a rock and studied the amazing work. As one familiar with engineering, he could appreciate the exquisite manner in which the long-dead artist, Gao of the Bushmen, had used so few lines to accomplish so much: 'Look at that! One unbroken line from mouth to tail! Look how he does the whole rear ham with one sweep! This was worth the trip.'

Pushing some rocks together, he formed a kind of chair on which he could sit and view this wonderful rhinoceros, and once or twice he broke into laughter. 'Hey! Hey! Rhino! Look at him gallop!' But then, after nearly an hour of looking, he covered his face with his hands, as if he wished to see the wall afresh, with no preconceptions.

'This is amazing, Daniel. I mean . . .'

In awe he studied this other vision of Africa: the timeless beauty galloping out of dark caves, the unknown wonders of the dark human soul, the sweep of line that captivated the senses, the overpowering sensation of being in the presence of vanished people who had come this way.

'Run, you sonofabitch—run, or they'll get you!' He bowed his head again and thought of Sannie, and the placid lakes at Vrymeer, and of Daniel Nxumalo's terrifying words: 'Must I not take into account the possibility . . . that you will be required under oath to report what I said one summer morning . . .' Africa was rather a bigger bite than one could chew.

When they left the rhinoceros still galloping across his timeless veld, Philip wandered around the side of the rise and saw to his astonishment that just a little distance to the west lay the buildings and lakes of the Van Doorn farm at Vrymeer. Nxumalo chuckled. 'That's why I brought you by the little roads. Yes, we're on one of Sannie's Tits.'

'Why didn't they tell me?'

'We Zulu keep it to ourselves. It's our rhinoceros. The Van Doorns are in Africa, but they aren't of it.'

Nxumalo's high praise for Laura Saltwood created in Philip a burning desire to visit the woman he had only glimpsed at the airport, and whose son had asked that he 'watch over' her. He had been remiss, but nothing he could have done would have altered what happened to her. He suspected that she might be something of a rhinoceros herself.

He sought permission from Pretoria to travel to Johannesburg on what he claimed was personal business, South Africa having infected him to the extent that he deemed it prudent not to confide that he intended speaking with a banned person.

When he reached her house he saw that it had been recently damaged by fire, for the façade was scarred; when he knocked, he heard a scurry of feet. Looking this way and that, he saw that he was being followed by a policeman, who was taking notes from across the street, and then the door opened.

Pointing to the scarred area, the white-haired woman said, simply, 'Bomb. This time they set the house afire. I'm sure they hoped it would burn me out, but as Louis Bromfield said in his good novel about India, "The rains came." '

'You mean this was a bomb?'

'Third in a row. Once you're banned, hoodlum patriots feel it's their obligation to bomb you or shoot you, or whatnot. Government encourages them.'

'Surely not!'

Mrs. Saltwood had made no move toward inviting him to come into the house, and he supposed this was because of the damage it had suffered, but she disabused him: 'Actually, they do little harm, the bombs. Scare hell out of one, but that's secondary to the greater indignity of banning.' She coughed and said, 'I'm going to meet with you out here, Philip, because the policeman over there must be assured that I'm meeting with only one person. That's my allocation, you know.'

She led him to a small lawn with a table and two chairs. 'We used to have four. Tea in the better afternoons. But we'll not have four again.' For the first time her voice trembled. 'Now, if you'll excuse me for just a moment.'

When she went back into the house, Philip felt an overpowering urge to confuse the watching policeman, so he rose as if in deep thought, walked to where the most recent bomb had struck, and took out a piece of paper. To his disgust he could find no pencil or pen, so he made believe he was taking copious notes on the damage, stepping back now and then to assess it. From the corner of his eye he could see that the policeman was becoming agitated, so he tucked away the paper and pretended to take out a camera, as though he were about to photograph the fire damage. This brought the policeman running.

'You can't do that, sir!' he cried in heavily accented English.

'I wasn't doing anything,' Philip said, showing his empty hands.

'You was taking a picture. That's forbidden, you know, at a banned site.'

'No, sir,' Philip said with great deference. 'I'm an architect. I was just taking proportions,' and he framed a box with his thumbs and fingers.

'That's permitted,' the policeman said.

'What's going on out here?' Laura asked as she appeared in the doorway with a silver tray containing tea things.

'I'm terribly sorry,' Philip apologized, more to the policeman than to

Laura. 'I was stupid. This good man feared I had a camera. I am sorry, sir.'
To Laura he whispered, 'I did it on purpose to throw him a scare.'

'I say, that's jolly! But we mustn't appear to be laughing. He has the power to be very unpleasant if he wishes.'

'Why the furor about the photograph?'

'When I'm banned, my house is banned. The evidence that it's being bombed is banned.' Abruptly she halted that chain of complaints and invited Philip to sit with her, and when he saw the exquisite silver service —tray, teapot, creamer, sugar, small tray for biscuits, little receptacle for marmalade, butter tray, spoons, little forks for the lemon—he almost burst into tears. It bespoke the long heritage of his people, and for the first time in his life he felt like an Englishman.

'Now tell me,' she said brightly, 'how did a decent Saltwood ever get to an outlaw place like America?' She laughed.

'As far as I can tell, there was a renegade brother far back. You English are wonderful in producing renegade brothers.'

'Woods are full of them.'

'So about the time your branch came out here, our branch, and a very lowly one it must have been, came to America. Massachusetts, Ohio, Indiana, Michigan. If you can visualize the map, they're stations west. My family was always on the move.'

'The sheriff?'

'I think so. I continued the tradition. Colorado, Texas.'

'You're a real American. Tell me, have you ever visited Salisbury? The old cathedral town west of London? No? Well, you must. The Saltwoods have a very ancient house there, with the tiles upside down or something. Quite wonderful, you know, with a river at the doorstep and a cathedral across the meadow.'

'This silverware . . .'

'A wedding gift in Salisbury, many years ago. My husband and I named this house New Sarum after the little hill where the members of Parliament used to be elected. Do you know about that? Well, we'll talk about that later. We liked to entertain and had plenty of servants. In the old days white people in this country always seemed to have plenty of servants. And my vanity was to have five complete tea services in silver.'

'Why?'

'Because in the morning we liked to serve our guests tea in bed. At seven o'clock sharp, bare feet came down the hall. Five servants, five tea services. Knock on the door, "Tea, Baas," and there was your tea.' Delicately she ticked off the silver pieces: 'Tea in this, hot water in this, toast in its silver rack, sugar, cream, lemon, one sweet biscuit.' Suddenly she rose and went inside the house, returning after a brief moment with four silver teapots, which she added to the tray.

'These were my only vanity. I wanted to remember Salisbury and tea in the shadow of the cathedral, and these enabled me to do so. But I also wanted to put away childish things and engage myself in Africa. So I helped found the Black Sash, and I spoke as I did, and now I'm banned. For life, I judge.'

Philip dared not speak. Staring at the five glistening teapots, he felt a chaos of thoughts rush through his brain, but there were none he cared to verbalize. Finally he asked, 'How do you keep these damned things so highly polished?'

She answered in a curious way: 'Do you know what I miss most? Not the meetings, where people say the same things over and over. And not the friendships, really, for people like you come by often. But I do miss the bowls. That's a wonderful game for relaxation—the proper uniform, you know, the lovely green grass. I miss that.'

'I don't follow you.'

'I can't bowl any more, of course, so whenever the urge strikes me, I polish my silver. Again and again I polish it. Everyone who comes here gets a cup of tea. It's compulsive, really, because I want to use a different pot each day. This one, then this one, then this one.'

Philip got up and walked away to hide his emotion, and of course Laura knew why he had done so. 'One must do something to keep occupied,' she said gaily. 'One can't read Solzhenitsyn week after week.'

'Good God! What are these?'

'Bullet holes,' she said matter-of-factly. 'At night sometimes they shoot at me.'

He wiped his forehead and sat down. 'What I'd really like,' he said, trying to sound casual, 'is another cup of tea . . . from that one,' and he pointed to one of the highly polished pots.

'That can be arranged,' she said, and with an elegant sweep of her hands she emptied the tea from the filled pot into the waiting one, then graciously poured Philip a cup. 'But I shall have my cup from this pot,' and once more she transferred the tea.

The policeman took notes.

'What's going to happen, Mrs. Saltwood?'

'Laura. We're cousins, you know.'

'How do you see things?'

'For me, a continuation of this until I die. For the country I see some hope. And do you know why? Because every decent and sensible man and woman in this nation knows that changes will have to be made. The Afrikaners who pass these horrible laws are not stupid people. They know this is a last gasp. Our blacks are among the most brilliant in Africa. They know time and pressure are on their side. There is enormous wisdom in this land, and one prays it will be granted the necessary time to manifest itself.'

'Will it? Moçambique, Zimbabwe, Vwarda, Zambia, Namibia pressing in from all directions?'

'The machine gun will guarantee reasonable time, I think. When you return to America assure your people that Afrikaners will use their machine guns if forced to do so. This is not Rhodesia, where retreat became epidemic. This is South Africa, where the gun rules.'

'That sounds rather hopeless.'

'Not at all!' She suggested that they utilize the final two teapots, pouring the cooling tea rapidly from one to the other, to the total bewilderment of the policeman. 'What I mean is, the machine guns will be used to buy time, probably through the remainder of this century. But with every moment gained, more wisdom is gained, too. And the day will come when the bright lads from Stellenbosch and Potchefstroom will lead the way in conciliation.'

'Can they do so soon enough?'

'The other great asset we have is the stability of our Zulu and Xhosa. They're the most patient, wonderful people on this earth. They make me humble, they have behaved so well for so long. Beside them I'm an uncivilized boor, and I think they can wait, intelligently, till the sick white man sorts things out.'

'Sick?'

Laura Saltwood pointed to herself, to the watching policeman, to the closed-in yard, to the bombed front of her house. 'Would any society invent banning if it wasn't sick?'

This seemed to be the period for Philip's intensive course in African realities, for when he returned to his hotel an urgent telegram was awaiting him from his superiors in Pretoria: FAVORABLE UPHEAVAL VWARDA. PROCEED IMMEDIATELY TEMPORARY DUTY KATOMBE TO PROTECT OUR INTERESTS. ANTICIPATE TWO MONTHS ABSENCE VRYMEER. INSTRUCTIONS AWAIT YOU THERE. PETERSEN. He caught a plane which took him to Zambia, where a smaller one belonging to the Vwardan government was waiting. Two other Anglo-Saxons who had once worked in that republic were aboard, and they informed him of the revolutionary decision President M'Bele had made last Friday: 'He informed London, Geneva and the United Nations that his country was plunging into chaos—industrial, financial—and he was inviting back at full pay plus bonuses some five hundred foreign technicians, mostly English, who had been in charge of technical details at one time or other during the past decade. I'm to head the distribution of flour.'

'Why?'

'You see, I was run out of the country three years ago. Pretty much like you, Saltwood, if I understand your case. My Vwardan understudy accused me of racism because I yelled at him one day. And why did I yell? Because he was supposed to watch the granary levels throughout the country, and he had allowed those in districts occupied by tribes other than his own to dwindle to zero. I really chewed him out and was expelled.'

'What happened when you left?'

'He became chief of grain procurement, and damned if he didn't continue to let his rival tribes starve.'

The other man had previously been in charge of Jeep and Land Rover procurement and had established a spare-parts replacement system based upon knowing calculations of what happened to vehicles in a primitive country. After drawing up a table of shrewd estimates, he proposed a law which would forbid the importation of any more Jeeps or Land Rovers until stockpiles of spare parts had been accumulated and stored in nine scattered warehouses, from which they would be efficiently distributed to broken-down vehicles that would otherwise stand useless.

'But a nephew of the president had the monopoly for importing Jeeps, and he demanded that he be allowed to bring in as many as he wanted, and to hell with spare parts. So what have they been doing? Cannibalizing perfectly good Jeeps to get a generator here or a differential there. The rest of the Jeep stands rusting, but the president's nephew doesn't give a damn.'

When their plane landed at Katombe they were hustled to a bright new hotel built with Swedish capital, where more than four hundred technical experts were herded together to hear an address by President M'Bele. He spoke with such eminent good sense that even men like Saltwood, who had legitimate grudges against him because of his earlier treatment, applauded, for it was quite obvious that he and they now had identical interests; they were men of Africa:

> 'Gentlemen, from the bottom of my heart I am most pleased to see you here. You are men of great experience in running aspects of our society. You are all men who performed well in the past and whom I can trust to perform equally well in the future. If I suspected for one moment that I could not rely upon you, I would not have called on you for help.

> 'We do need your help. The productive wheels of this nation are grinding to a halt. And why? Not because we haven't the brains to keep them going. And not because we are lazy or indifferent. The reason is simple. It takes time and long apprenticeship before anyone can master the skills necessary to keep a complex machine functioning. Our people, good-hearted though they may be, lack that long know-how, as the Americans term it. You men have it, and therefore we need you.

> 'Take bread. The citizens of many of our towns are close to rebellion because they have no bread. We have the money for it. Bread appears in our budget. And we have the grain. What do you suppose is holding us back? No one remembered to order yeast. No one purchased replacements for baking tins that wore out. And the damned flour is stored in the wrong places. How many bakers and grain experts are there in this room? Gentlemen, get working before nightfall.

> 'One vastly important thing which I know you will understand and remember as you go about your resumed duties. Vwarda has not changed its attitude toward racial equality one percent. We are not inviting you back because you are superior whites. We are asking you to help us because you are well trained in fields where we are not. We will not tolerate any racial-supremacy nonsense, and if you abuse our people, you will have to go. We are a black nation and proud to be so.

> 'But I promise you this. Our judges, our committees and my staff will not listen to wild charges of race discrimination. I know the injustices that occurred with some of you in the past, and they will not be repeated. It is more important that we get our bakeries functioning again than that my son-in-law drive a Mercedes from one plant to the other.'

Saltwood was shipped back to the mines he had once supervised, and when he reached them he was pleased to see that no chaos had resulted from his absence. Dynamite was being handled properly, with safeguards observed, and the lifts that shot workers down and up the deep shafts at incredible speeds were in order. Where the trouble lay was in planning, the subtle shifting of work forces and the movement of ores to logical locations. At the end of a week he reported to President M'Bele:

> The mines, when I reached them, were ninety-five-percent effective in their basic techniques. Your workmen were performing their jobs skillfully and responsibly, and Cornish miners could have done no better. There were, as you know, grave errors in scheduling. We require eight or nine men of broad grasp and firm decision. These are hard to come by in Vwarda, or America.

He found one young fellow who showed signs of catching on; he had acquired skills by working in the gold mines of Johannesburg. He asked the young man if he had any acquaintances who had shared that experience, and four were brought forward. Two had learned nothing in South Africa, but the other two were clever like the first, and around this cadre he began to build his staff. Fortunately, he found one older man who had had three years at the London School of Economics, and just as factories in South Bend, Indiana, profited by having young men from such provocative schools, so the mines in Vwarda began to function better when he assumed partial control.

Ultimate control remained in the hands of President M'Bele's son-in-law, who had been mainly responsible for Saltwood's firing in 1978. He was a much-changed man; having taken his mines almost to the point of bankruptcy, he now knew that he was not free to make decisions on narrow, tribal lines. He was scared, for he enjoyed his Mercedes and welcomed any guidance that would enable him to keep it. This time he listened when Philip outlined the need for a world view: 'You must know what Japan is doing with her metallurgy, and what Russia is up to. You've got to watch the markets, and you don't need a computer to do it. Your aim must be constant flow. Keep all parts in balance.'

At the end of his two months he was able to recommend a Belgian engineer with wide experience in Katanga Province over in Zaire: 'He's a knowing man. Works well with black nations. And he's better informed on your problems than I am.' When President M'Bele implored Philip to stay on till the Belgian was properly indoctrinated, he saw the sense of this and agreed to extend his stay, but only for three weeks.

When these passed, and he was confident that the Belgian was qualified, he sought permission to fly back to Johannesburg, but when the plane landed he was prevented from going directly to his job at Venloo by three BOSS officers. 'You must come with us,' they said, and he was whisked off to a small room at the airport.

'This in no way endangers you, Mr. Saltwood. We know why you were called to Vwarda and how competently you did your job there. We must

interrogate you about an important trial and would prefer that no one talk
with you.'

'Whose trial?'

'Daniel Nxumalo. High treason.'

The Terrorism Act of 1967, based on careful preliminary work supervised
by Detleef van Doorn the year he died, was both wonderfully vague and
terrifyingly specific. It was vague because it forbade any act or attempted
act which in any way embarrassed the state. Almost any behavior which
protested apartheid could be so construed, and the bases of proof were also
extremely vague. What was specific? The minimum penalty the court could
impose: five years, most likely on Robben Island. The maximum: death.

Twelve kinds of behavior fell under the ban, and of these the government conceded that nine did not apply in Nxumalo's case. He had not
interfered with the police; he intimidated no one; he did not cripple production; he did not lead any insurrection; he did not advocate cooperation with
any foreign government; he had caused no bodily injury; nor had he brought
financial loss to the state, or endangered its essential services, or obstructed
its land, sea or air traffic. On those counts he was patently innocent and the
indictment ignored them.

But on three other counts most threatening to the security of the state
he was presumably guilty: first, he had agitated blacks by asking disturbing
questions, so was accused of promoting disorder; second, by reminding
blacks of past grievances, he had encouraged hostility between races; third,
in various ways he had embarrassed the government. And for these offenses
he must be tried, and if found guilty, sent to prison or hanged.

Philip learned that the trial would be conducted in Pretoria by a crusty
old judge, Herman Broodryk, who had a record of handling such cases
covering more than two decades. Prior to his appointment to the bench in
1958, he had been a brilliant advocate who gained favorable attention in the
1940s by defending Afrikaner radicals charged with attempting to sabotage
Jan Christian Smuts' efforts to take the country into the war on the side of
England. He was a personal friend of all the recent prime ministers, and
Philip thought it disturbing that a man with such credentials should sit in
this case; but an Amalgamated Mines lawyer told him, 'The South African
higher judiciary is above reproach. We can be proud of two liberties—
judges like Broodryk and our free press.'

And then Philip made an even more startling discovery: 'Is it true that
Justice Broodryk will hear the case alone . . . without a jury?' And again
his lawyer friend defended the system: 'One of the best things we've done,
abolish the jury system. What chance would Nxumalo have against a jury
of twelve white men and women? I leave to your imagination what would
happen in the circuit court at Venloo, for instance, if a black appeared on
a charge of molesting a white farmer's daughter. With an all-white jury!'

Daniel Nxumalo was to be defended by Mr. Simon Kaplan, a Johannesburg advocate well experienced in fighting the battles of blacks who had
offended the mores of apartheid. The accusations of terroristic activity
would be presented by Mr. Martin Scheepers, a specialist in the Terrorism

Act; nineteen times he had prosecuted such cases, winning fourteen and sending a total of eighty-seven men and women to prison. In three recent cases involving armed insurgency, he had won the death sentence.

In England, in America and in most Western nations a judge could spend a lifetime on the bench without ever sentencing a man to death; year after year in South Africa some eighty people went to the gallows, more than in the rest of the Western world put together. When Saltwood asked about this, the Amalgamated lawyer said, 'Most of them are black. Murderers, rapists. We are forced to do this to maintain order. There's four million of us, twenty million of them.'

The courtroom was packed when Judge Broodryk took his seat. He was a large man, with heavy, bushy eyebrows, pendulous cheeks and a fearsome manner, but as the trial proceeded Philip would find him patient, attentive and considerate. When a judge had no jury to contend with, he had to be judicial, uncovering facts and judging character, for on him alone would rest the decision of innocence or guilt, death or life. In his years of mining experience Philip had attended trials in several African countries, and in none had he found a wiser judge.

Broodryk extended every courtesy to Nxumalo, listening with obvious attention whenever he spoke. In his opening address Advocate Scheepers spread before the court the essentials of his case against Daniel:

> 'The state will prove that it was this man who conceived the idea of having the blacks of this nation gather in large numbers to observe the anniversary of what he called Soweto '76. What was this but a device to engender bad relations between the races? The evidence will show that in a manner calculated to be provocative and conducive to disorder he organized such a gathering in Bloemfontein and harangued it. And why, pray, did Mr. Nxumalo choose to hold this meeting in Bloemfontein? Because he knew it to be the most loyal of our cities, where what he had to say would create the most inflammatory reaction.

> 'It is on another charge that he will be found most guilty. His every act is carefully premeditated to bring embarrassment upon our government. He appeals to the basest emotions of our cruelest critics in London and New York. He makes crude appeals to agencies like the World Council of Churches, and we will show that his acts and intentions are such as to bring discredit upon us, arguing as he does that our laws are unjust and our system of apartheid unfair. He is an evil man whose activities must be halted.'

Thus was set the tone for the clash between Nxumalo and Scheepers, a bitter division between two able men that flared on the first morning of the trial when Nxumalo began his careful campaign to place the grievances of his people on the record:

DEFENDANT NXUMALO: Only in recent years have our people begun to discover themselves, to seek an identity different from the one the white man says we must wear. We are in the position the Afrikaner was before he crawled out from under English domination, and we respect his struggle for his *volksidentiteit.* But from this reasoning I conclude that if the Afrikaner is free to celebrate his victory over Dingane at Blood River, we blacks ought to be free to recall the powerful events that shook Soweto in June 1976.

STATE ADVOCATE SCHEEPERS: What events did you have in mind?

NXUMALO: The deaths of our children who protested apartheid.

SCHEEPERS: Mr. Nxumalo, those schoolchildren rioted in the streets, burned down buildings, killed innocent civilians, and challenged just authority. You see that as equivalent to a battle fought between two armies?

NXUMALO: I agree that the circumstances are not the same—well, not entirely—but the end result, my people were left with anger and sorrow.

SCHEEPERS: And you wanted to use that anger to generate disorder?

DEFENSE COUNSEL KAPLAN: I must object to the way my learned friend phrases that.

SCHEEPERS: That anger and sorrow were at the basis of your wanting to celebrate Soweto '76 as a remembrance day?

NXUMALO: I believe we owe a great deal to those children. They showed us that change in this country must come from within. That we must make a stand against a system we abhor.

SCHEEPERS: You presume to speak for all blacks?

NXUMALO: Someone must. We have been silent for too long.

SCHEEPERS: In celebrating our great victory over Dingane, we Afrikaner people observe a solemn Day of the Covenant in which we pray for peace, not disorder; for unity, not chaos. Were those your aims in sponsoring Soweto '76?

NXUMALO: We also want peace and unity for all. And prayers for the children who fell at Soweto, victims of the unjust system which deprives them of a right to citizenship in the land of their birth.

JUDGE BROODRYK: Mr. Nxumalo, this court is not here to debate what happened at Soweto in 1976. We cannot decide whether the students were victims of injustice or not. Confine your answers to Mr. Scheeper's questions.

NXUMALO: My Lord, the Afrikaner in his schools, his churches, his celebrations of the Day of the Covenant is reminded by his teachers, his ministers and his political leaders of Slagter's Nek, of ground glass in the mealies, the execution of Christoffel Steyn. With deepest respect I submit that such constant remembrance of blood that flowed in the past engenders bad feeling between the races.

BROODRYK: Mr. Nxumalo, the Afrikaner and the Englishman are of the same race, so what you charge could not possibly take place. We are concerned only with the delicate balance between the white and black races in this country and the danger of fostering ill-will between them. By your irresponsible speeches, for example.

NXUMALO: I do not believe that the black people of this country can be denied the right to remember the Slagter's Nek of their history. I mean Sharpeville and Soweto '76. Until we find our own dignity and identity, we can never be free.

SCHEEPERS: What would have to happen, Mr. Nxumalo, for you to consider yourself a free man?

NXUMALO: Apartheid would have to end. Blacks would have to have a proper voice in running this country.

SCHEEPERS: Ah! You mean one-man, one-vote?

NXUMALO: Yes, I suppose I do.

SCHEEPERS: Do you think that by encouraging bitterness among your people, by waving Soweto '76 at them, you'll get your vote?

NXUMALO: A man has a right, surely, to remember ugly things that have happened to him. To us the dead children of Soweto were heroes.

SCHEEPERS: It's impossible to follow your reasoning. Those young people were undisciplined rioters. They were led by professional agitators.

NXUMALO: I must beg to contradict. The young black boys of Soweto were rather similar to the young Boer lads who fought the English in 1899. They took up arms against their oppressors, the English.

SCHEEPERS: Ah-ha! So you do advocate that young blacks take up arms against the Afrikaner? Against the legal government?

KAPLAN: My Lord, my client said nothing of the sort. I must object most strenuously to my learned friend's attempt to misconstrue the evidence.

BROODRYK: Sustained. Mr. Nxumalo, I can appreciate some of the points you are making, but it seems to me there is a danger that if your inflammatory remarks are constantly thrust before the public, a revolutionary climate will be fostered throughout this country.

NXUMALO: Yes, there is such a danger, my Lord.

BROODRYK: Then should you not pursue your objectives through a more peaceful method? By negotiation rather than violence?

NXUMALO: Most certainly that would be preferable.

BROODRYK: Then you agree that by working through established channels, and there are many, mass upheaval could be averted?

At this point the judge was so reasonable and conciliatory that Saltwood, listening carefully to every nuance, felt certain that if Nxumalo reciprocated, Judge Broodryk would be eager to find him guilty only to a limited degree, and his life would be spared, for everyone in the courtroom knew that Nxumalo had performed no overt act of real revolution. But to Saltwood's dismay, his friend refused the olive branch the judge had extended. Indeed, his rejection of Broodryk's invitation was cold and total.

NXUMALO: Your Honor, we cannot accept the status quo because we had no voice in establishing it. We will never accept it, for this is our land, too, and we of this generation cannot abdicate the rights of our children still to be born. We are opposed to apartheid now and forever.

BROODRYK: But people may not oppose it, Mr. Nxumalo, with actions that contravene the law of the land. They may not engage in acts of terrorism to upset what the government has patiently and justly ordained.

NXUMALO: Not justly, my Lord.

KAPLAN: What he means, my Lord—

BROODRYK: I know what he means. Let him continue.

NXUMALO: I stand before this court accused of terroristic activities. Every day in South Africa acts of terrorism are committed against my people through the harsh application of laws not justly ordained. To me it was an act of terror to banish an old woman to a resettlement camp. It is an act of terror to starve a young mind hungry for learning. It is an act of terror to force apart a man and woman who love each other. It is an act of terror to say to a black man born on this land, 'You cannot live here because white people want the land.' Or to tell that same man he cannot go to a town where he can earn a decent living for his family.

BROODRYK *(with great patience):* I am waiting for your point, Mr. Nxumalo.

NXUMALO: I will state it honestly, my Lord. We deny that the laws of apartheid are just or that this is a just society. We see it as a society with only one ambition—to maintain white supremacy.

BROODRYK: But that is the acknowledged goal of this society. If you have a solution that is better for all, this court would like to hear it.

NXUMALO: We might start with justice for the majority of people living here.

BROODRYK: And the minorities, who also deserve protection?

NXUMALO: A minority with machine guns can always protect itself.

Judge Broodryk was meticulous in according Daniel every opportunity to defend himself, and although some of the young professor's answers must have infuriated him, he betrayed nothing, and Saltwood saw that Nxumalo was going out of his way to antagonize the judge. What the young man's strategy was, Philip could not discern, and the trial proceeded.

Prosecutor Scheepers now turned his attention to two curious aspects of the case, returning to them again and again during the four days he interrogated the young teacher.

SCHEEPERS: Where did you first hear the phrases Black Power and Black Consciousness?

NXUMALO: I can't say. They were in the air.

SCHEEPERS: Could I put it to you that you heard them from Communist agitators? Men infiltrated here to agitate the unthinking blacks?

NXUMALO: Blacks do not need Communists to agitate them. Apartheid does that every day.

SCHEEPERS: But what does the phrase mean—Black Power? Doesn't this necessitate blacks opposing whites? Like your older rallying cry 'Africa for the Africans?'

NXUMALO: There's nothing subversive about that. You're a man of Africa. My counsel is a man of Africa. The learned judge—

BROODRYK: I will assign myself.

SCHEEPERS: If we are all Africans, why the emphasis on the power of black Africans?

NXUMALO: As I explained before, our people must develop pride in themselves—Black Consciousness. And if you force me—Black Power. We cannot negotiate with whites from a position of inferiority.

SCHEEPERS: I see your Black Power only as an agency with which to confront whites and embarrass this government.

NXUMALO: In the eyes of the civilized world, this government embarrasses itself.

BROODRYK *(sternly):* No flippancy, young man.

NXUMALO: The protests sounding around the world against this trial are not flippant. They are very real, and one day—

BROODRYK: No revolutionary threats will be tolerated. Mr. Kaplan, advise your client to mind his tongue.

KAPLAN: Believe me, my Lord, my client utters his words without any coaching from me.

BROODRYK: I believe you, Counsel, for this court has always found you to be a prudent, loyal and patriotic man. But you must warn your client that he damages his case by engaging in revolutionary threats. This court is not impressed by what happens 'around the world,' as he says. For some decades this nation has been endeavoring to act in accordance with God's dictates and not the yammerings of the discredited World Council of Churches.

After this resounding statement Judge Broodryk declared recess, during which Saltwood endeavored to talk with Nxumalo. No outsider was permitted to approach the prisoner lest the latter receive coaching, which was what Philip sought to offer, for he had seen signs that Broodryk wanted to avoid a severe sentence, if only Nxumalo would admit minor guilt and appeal for clemency. He suspected that for arcane reasons of his own Nxumalo would refuse to act humbly; this became evident when the prosecutor attacked him on language.

SCHEEPERS: May I put it to you, Mr. Nxumalo, that you borrowed your ideas about language from Laura Saltwood? It was her preaching, wasn't it, that encouraged you to advise your students not to accept any instruction in Afrikaans?

NXUMALO: With your permission, respected sir, there are two errors in your question.

SCHEEPERS: And what are they?

NXUMALO: I gave my advice long before Mrs. Saltwood was banned. And nothing in my advice was antagonistic to Afrikaans. What I said was, 'Learn English first, for it is the language of international communication.'

SCHEEPERS: But why should a Bantu . . . Excuse me, m'Lord. Why should a black child whose life is to be spent in South Africa bother with international communication?'

NXUMALO: Because it will be our international associations—I don't mean international committees, I mean the contacts we establish with people overseas—that will go far in determining the nature of our future government.

SCHEEPERS: You mean, of course, Communist Russia?

NXUMALO: I mean the civilized world. We cannot speak to them in Afrikaans, because nobody out in the world understands that language.

BROODRYK: You seem determined to insult this nation, Mr. Nxumalo. First you ridicule our most sacred holiday. Now you ridicule our language.

NXUMALO: I said merely the truth. That it is not used anywhere outside this small country.

BROODRYK: You consider South Africa a small nation? In comparison with Belgium, say?

NXUMALO: In comparison with Brazil and Indonesia. In comparison to the rest of Africa.

SCHEEPERS: When you advised your students not to study Afrikaans—

NXUMALO: I never advised that, sir.

SCHEEPERS: May I read from a transcript of your speech at Bloemfontein:

> 'Our program must be to insist that basic instruction be given in English, for then our young people will be able to communicate with the entire world and not only with a few bigoted Afrikaners stuck away in their little corner.'

Are those not inflammable words, Mr. Nxumalo? Are they not an incitement to the blacks to ignore the laws of this land?

KAPLAN: Your Worship, I wish you would direct learned Counsel to read the next sentences of his police report.

SCHEEPERS: I've read everything I have, and I assure you that it is—

KAPLAN: Your Worship, I happen to have the full text, and with your permission may I read a few additional sentences? I think you will find them instructive:

> 'I want every student to learn Afrikaans, for it is an excellent medium for conducting our affairs in this country. I speak Afrikaans, use it all the time, to my great profit, but when I do speak it I can communicate with less than three million. When I speak English, I communicate with the entire world.'

SCHEEPERS: Why would a black child in Venloo wish to communicate with the entire world?

NXUMALO: Because we are citizens of the entire world.

SCHEEPERS: But repeatedly we find evidence that you call yourself African. Is not your claim—

NXUMALO: I am a citizen of Venloo, which makes me a citizen of eastern Transvaal. That gives me citizenship in South Africa—

SCHEEPERS: Not South Africa. You're Zulu, I believe. You belong to kwaZulu, the Bantustan of the Zulu.

NXUMALO: I was born at the farm Vrymeer. I have taught in the University of Zululand, but Vrymeer is my home.

SCHEEPERS: Nevertheless, you are a citizen of kwaZulu and must eventually make your residence there. That is the law.

NXUMALO: So as a citizen of South Africa—

SCHEEPERS: M'Lord, I protest this insulting behavior.

BROODRYK: Let him make his point.

NXUMALO: As a citizen of South Africa, I automatically become a citizen of Africa the continent, and as a citizen of Africa, I am obligated to behave as a citizen of the world.

SCHEEPERS: With allegiance to Communist Russia.

NXUMALO: With allegiance to the total human race. It is because I want to share ideas with them that I advocate the learning of English.

SCHEEPERS: Then our language is not good enough for you?

NXUMALO: I speak your language, and it is certainly good enough for communication with Pretoria and Cape Town. But, your Honor, it is not understood in Paris or Madrid or Rio de Janeiro, and on certain occasions we require to speak with them, also.

As the trial droned on, with only such flimsy evidence as might have been appropriate in a public school if some obstreperous scholar had misbehaved, Saltwood began to realize that in this courtroom the real culprit was never mentioned. Daniel Nxumalo was being prosecuted not for what he had done but because his brother Jonathan in Moçambique was a thorn. Since Prosecutor Scheepers never charged 'You are guilty, Daniel Nxumalo, because your brother is a revolutionary,' Philip had to assume that the state had no proof of complicity; and because Judge Broodryk did not thunder 'We are going to imprison you, Daniel Nxumalo, because we can't get at your brother,' Philip supposed that the state wished this aspect of their case to be smothered. But that Daniel was being attacked because of Jonathan, there could be no doubt.

And that raised a fascinating point, which Philip contemplated many times as the trial progressed: Daniel did receive Jonathan in his house in Venloo. He did conspire with him, in a manner of speaking. Is he not guilty —if one accepts South African law? And when that rhetorical question had to be answered affirmatively, an even more perplexing one presented itself: I was there that night. I was at the clandestine meeting in Soweto. Am I not also guilty of conspiracy? When he first acknowledged this question, he was looking at Judge Broodryk, and it occurred to him with horror that on the facts, the judge would be justified in sentencing him, Philip, to imprisonment. Thus, at unexpected moments, the visitor to South Africa found the realities being driven home, and it was as a condemned man that Saltwood listened to the final two days of a trial in which he had subtly become a co-defendant.

This sense of unspecified doom intensified when Mr. and Mrs. Frikkie Troxel, accompanied by their cousin Jopie, entered the courtroom to hear the concluding testimony against their neighbor, the son of Moses Nxumalo. Arrival of these two distinguished athletes caused approving smiles, and Judge Broodryk welcomed them to this court. They sat not with Philip but across from him, indicating that they opposed his alien, socialist views, and this allowed him to see their undisguised satisfaction whenever the state made a telling point against the black man who threatened their comfortable way of life. They loved their freedom, those three Troxels, and were prepared to lay down their lives to preserve it, no doubt about it. What they refused to understand was that Daniel Nxumalo might feel the same way about his freedom.

It was deplorable, Philip thought, that these three fine white people should know so little about the Nxumalo family with whom they had shared their farms; had they reached out to form a partnership with Daniel and his brother Jonathan, they could have built a powerful force, able to lead their section of the country into better understandings and more logical arrangements, but they had remained enemies. Worse, they had remained strangers. Now they listened intently as Nxumalo was interrogated on his politics:

SCHEEPERS: Let us return to that provocative phrase 'Black Power.' Doesn't that mean black supremacy and the expulsion of whites?

NXUMALO: You seem to have a complete file on me, Mr. Scheepers. Nowhere in it will you find a word I have ever said advocating the expulsion at any time in the future of all white men. In the society I visualize, you white men will be needed, most urgently needed. Twenty years from now when—

KAPLAN: I must warn my client against completing that statement.

BROODRYK: I am most eager to hear what awaits us twenty years from now.

NXUMALO: Twenty years from now, when blacks have the vote, not one-man, one-vote, perhaps, but some reasonable concession for the moment, I would expect Prosecutor Scheepers to be serving exactly as he is serving now, and Defense Counsel Kaplan to be defending some business client—

BROODRYK: And the judge?

NXUMALO: I would expect the judge in this court to be black. *(Laughter)*

BROODRYK: I thought so.

NXUMALO: By that time, your Honor, you might well be in the Appeal Court, you and three black judges. *(More laughter)*

BROODRYK: You, as dictator, would appoint me?

NXUMALO: A consortium of the people, white and black, would want the best judges they could get.

BROODRYK: 'A consortium of the people?' That's Communism, isn't it?

NXUMALO: No, your Honor, that's democracy.

BROODRYK: Sounds more like dictatorship.

NXUMALO: No, we have a dictatorship now.

BROODRYK *(in towering rage):* I cannot allow you to denigrate this government.

NXUMALO: I meant no offense, your Honor. I was merely speaking the truth. In the great election of 1948 that threw Jan Christian Smuts out of office and brought your party in, that was against the wishes of white people. You might say you engineered a takeover, like the Communists in Czechoslovakia.

SCHEEPERS: That's a lie. We won that election fair and square.

NXUMALO: No, the record must be kept straight. You won seventy-nine seats in Parliament to seventy-one.

SCHEEPERS: A majority of eight, as I said.

NXUMALO: But in the popular vote you lost by a substantial majority. Something like six hundred thousand against you and four hundred thousand for. Many white people did not want your brand of government.

SCHEEPERS: How could that—

NXUMALO: You know very well. The white vote in this nation is heavily weighted in favor of the farmer, heavily skewed against urban dwellers. A farmer's vote may count as much as thirty-five percent more than a city dweller's.

SCHEEPERS: And rightly so. The virtue of a nation resides in its farmers. The rot that destroys a nation thrives in the cities.

NXUMALO: Then we blacks, who are mostly farmers, ought to have a larger vote than anyone.

SCHEEPERS: We're talking of civilized voters.

And there it ended, with Daniel Nxumalo having offended the judge, the prosecutor, his own advocate and most of the public. Even Philip Saltwood had to concede that he was guilty as hell—but of what? No overt act of treason had been proved; he had been in contact with no foreign power. He had said certain things which college professors and students around the world were saying, except in Russia and Uganda. He had organized a day of remembrance for the dead of Soweto. He had spoken in favor of English as the major language for students. He had used the phrases Black Power and Black Consciousness. And he had done certain things which might embarrass the government, which tried to hide the worst effects of apartheid.

For these trivial offenses he must be imprisoned?

Pursuing this line of thought, Saltwood then had to admit that his friend was guilty of two additional crimes which were not trivial: he had visited with revolutionaries in Soweto; he had provided refuge for his renegade brother. But these had not been discussed in court. The final, damning evidence was that Nxumalo had consulted with black leaders—and this was tantamount to conniving with an alien nation. Also, Nxumalo had advanced the disgraceful argument that when blacks honored Soweto they were doing only what whites did when they honored the Day of the Covenant. That was blasphemy; and in a theocracy, a mortal sin.

It was essential for the protection of the state that Nxumalo be severely punished, perhaps even hanged, but when the court convened in dreadful silence and the time came for Judge Broodryk, creature of the system, to defend the system, he surprised his listeners by intoning:

> 'Prisoner Daniel Nxumalo, this court finds you guilty on all counts as charged. You have, whenever an opportunity arose, sought to endanger the security of this state by furthering the aims of revolutionary groups plotting to overthrow the government of this republic. The court has listened with patience to your pleas about Black Consciousness and identity, but the good people of this nation have evolved an intricate system which ensures fairness for all. It is defined in sensible laws which you must obey, and for a man of your education to subvert them is criminal. The maximum sentence laid down by the Terrorism Act is death, but in your deportment during this trial I have seen repeated evidences of a superior mind and a solid character, and in this world that counts for something. I sentence you to ten years' imprisonment.'

So Daniel Nxumalo, thirty years old, whose only real crime was that he had spoken in terms used by people like Jean Jacques Rousseau, Abraham Lincoln and Winston Churchill, was sentenced to a decade on Robben Island.

He was not frightened by the prospect of imprisonment because he suspected that it would not be long before reason would prevail in his land; even if he were banned for five years after his release, he knew that a time would come before the end of this century when he and black men like him would know real freedom. At that time he would occupy a privileged position because of his martyrdom—as the prisoners Nehru, Mussolini, De Valera, Vorster, Kenyatta, Lenin, Hitler and Gandhi had done before him. He would use his time in prison as they had used theirs: to perfect his theories of government, coming out a much stronger man than when he went in. Nations tend to be governed by men who have been forced by adversity to clarify their thought; those who have enjoyed unbroken smooth sailing are often too lazy to speculate on how to manage their ship in storms.

In the military prison at Chrissie Meer, Detleef van Doorn had begun his education in restrictive puritanism; in the political prison on Robben Island, Daniel Nxumalo would undergo his apprenticeship in the strategies of freedom.

When Philip Saltwood landed his job with Amalgamated Mines he promised his favorite professor, Gideon Vandenberg of the University of Michigan, that he would not form any hard conclusions about South Africa until he had worked there a full year, but that when he had done so, he would report to Vandenberg. The professor was a member of that distinguished family which produced Senator Arthur Vandenberg and General Hoyt Vandenberg; he spent his summers in Holland, Michigan, tulip capital of America, and was a kind of professional Dutchman. Just as the senator had presented himself to the electorate as an incorruptible Dutchman, conservative but prudent, so Gideon yearly offered a course in 'The Golden Age of Holland, 1560–1690,' in which he extolled those creative pressures which had made this minute country one of the masters of the world, possessors of Java and Cape Town. He needed to know what was happening in the latter and had commissioned Saltwood to tell him:

> Dear Professor Vandenberg,
>
> One of the best bits of advice you ever gave me was to wait a year before reaching any conclusions about South Africa. Ten years would be a better study period. But I've worked diligently with Afrikaners, Englishmen and lots of blacks. I've also been in all parts of the nation. And I've reestablished contact with the local Saltwoods, whom our branch last knew in 1810. I offer you these tentative speculations.
>
> South Africa must be one of the most beautiful lands on earth, surpassed in my experience only by New Zealand. All thinking must start from this. It's a land worth keeping. For whites it also has one of the highest standards of living in the world, and if people in Europe and America knew how grand the daily existence was, they'd all emigrate. Compared to the upper South African white, rich people in Texas and Oregon live like serfs. If you taught here, at your salary, you'd have four servants, a life of ease, and all the amenities. The South African way of life is worth preserving (for whites) and even worth fighting for. I have never lived so well.
>
> For urban blacks the standard of living is also higher than I have seen in Nigeria, Zambia and Vwarda, and much higher, I'm told, than in any of the surrounding black countries, which is why hundreds of thousands of blacks in those countries would like to emigrate to South Africa. Personal freedoms, of course, are another matter, and much of what you hear in a liberal university like Michigan is true.

The people of South Africa perplex me. Even cursory investigation proves that what we call an Afrikaner is rarely of pure Dutch descent. The mix seems to be Dutch ancestry thirty-five percent, German a hefty thirty, Huguenot twenty, English five, other European five, and a submerged and denied five percent due to early miscegenation with slaves from Madagascar, Angola, Java, Ceylon and lots of Malays, with a liberal salting of brown Hottentots. But apparently one drop of Dutch blood supersedes all other European strains and can even mask black infusions, if they occurred long enough ago. A man who is demonstrably seven-eighths German, Huguenot and English will say proudly, 'My ancestors were Dutch.'

But in recent times the process seems to have been reversed, for now one drop of black blood contaminates ninety-nine percent of white blood, which accounts for the steady rise of the Coloured population. You could live here a thousand years, Dr. Vandenberg, and never understand this problem. The Coloureds, who should be the natural allies of the pure-white man—if ever there were a pure anything—are kept in limbo without any fixed place in society. The Afrikaner language evolved in large part because of contributions from the various languages spoken by the Coloureds, as did many of the social customs and habits, like the Afrikaner's love of spicy foods. Anyone with training in history, like you, would have to conclude that one of the saddest mistakes the Afrikaners made was to divorce themselves from people of great ability who are in effect their half brothers—these Coloureds.

Such argument would infuriate the Afrikaner, who is absolutely convinced by his historians, his teachers and his predikants that the white-slave mixture was the consequence exclusively of sailors and soldiers roistering into Cape Town on shore leave, and that no self-respecting Dutchman ever touched a slave girl. A naughty lad at Witwatersrand University has calculated that to achieve the amount of infusion that obviously occurred, every soldier and sailor would have had to come ashore with his trousers half down, go to work immediately, and not stop till the bo's'n blew his whistle to summon them back to the ship.

A phenomenon that you with your Dutch background might anticipate, but which I certainly didn't, is the Afrikaner's unshakable belief that God personally has ordained his state and its traditions. I cannot tell you how shocked I was in discussing a management problem the other day with two university graduates and hearing them tell me, 'But God wants us to do it that way. He entered into a covenant with us for that purpose.' Any prime minister taking office assures the people that he will keep the nation on the course outlined by God. Students in school are taught that God devised apartheid, and I even heard a rugby enthusiast say that God engineered South Africa's victories, because He wanted His chosen people to triumph. Any outsider who minimizes the influence of this belief in South African politics misses the core of the problem.

Of the four dozen Afrikaners I know well, forty-seven honestly
believe that God has directed them to stay on this land, run it exact-
ly as they are now running it, and defend it against blacks and
Communism. I have never known an American to be so sure that
God personally looked after American interests, which of course
He does.

Like most Americans, I know little about religion, but here one
cannot ignore it, it dominates government and gives sanction to
whatever the ruling political party decides. Aren't Presbyterians
Calvinists, too? I don't remember them behaving like this at home.
The Dutch Calvinists, you know, have rejected the South African
church, and recently a famous theologian from Holland came out
here to try to mend fences. I attended a thoughtful lecture he gave
in which he said that John Calvin was firm on this matter of government, and he quoted from Calvin himself, something to the effect
that all men are certainly subject to the magistrates that rule over
them, but only insofar as the magistrates obey the basic rules of God.
If they do otherwise, the citizens should not pay them any regard,
nor be overawed by the dignity they possess as governors. The visitor
didn't go so far as to call for revolution, but he sure did call for new
evaluations of government policy.

As a matter of fact, every sensible Afrikaner, Englishman and black
I have met knows that great changes must be made, and they know
what changes. But some eighty-five percent of the rural Afrikaner
population would rather die than accept even one of those changes,
and they are assured by their reactionary leaders, lay and cleric, that
they are right. The tragedy is that the philosophers of all sides are
prepared to make those changes now, but they will not be made, and
ten years from now, when they are grudgingly conceded at the point
of a gun, they won't be enough. In every conversation I have I hear
comparisons made with Rhodesia. Ten years ago the whites there
should have made certain concessions, but they refused. When they
became more than willing to make them, the time for accepting that
modest change was past.

Seems to me there are four alternatives. First, peaceful, gradual
change to a modern multi-racial state. The die-hard whites say
they will never accept this. Second, black revolution sweeping
the whites from power and perhaps from Africa altogether. The
blacks don't appear to be capable of this, yet. Third, continued
white domination, with more and more repressive measures as
surrounding black nations achieve the power to support infiltra-
tion guerrilla forces. The present nation becomes a white laager
defending itself from black Africa. Most of my workmen, white
and black, think this is what will happen, and that the whites
can get away with it for the remainder of this century. But if
they persist in rejecting the Coloureds, forcing them into alliance
with the blacks, the whites will endanger what chance they have.

In the short run, at least, events will be strongly affected by what the Coloureds do.

The fourth alternative shocked me, but since it was proposed by the finest mind I've met here, black or white, Afrikaner or English, I must take it seriously. He suspects that things are moving so swiftly that the Afrikaner will not be able to hold his country against a combination of outside pressure and inside urban warfare, and that if he tries, the land will go down in terrible revolution. He advocates that white men, all of them, retreat voluntarily into the old Cape Province, there to establish a real republic in which Afrikaner, Englishman and Coloured work together as full partners. I was really jolted when he drew the outlines for me on a map. Pretoria and Johannesburg would be surrendered, as would Durban. Port Elizabeth and Grahamstown would be retained, as would Kimberley and Bloemfontein. This beautiful, rational area would be as big as Texas. It would be ruled by those whites who refused to cooperate with the black government of the north, plus the many Coloureds. Safe on the southern tip of Africa, they would become a new Hong Kong. When I asked if the triumphant blacks would permit such a withdrawal and consolidation, he said something profound, which I want you to discuss with your students and all who are interested in Africa. I'll try to give it in his words:

'If the black men in Africa refuse, as they seem to have done elsewhere, to allow any reasonable partnership for indigenous whites, the result would be harmful to Africa but disastrous to the United States, because your country is in the throes of accepting and defining justice for its black minority. If it sees a black majority in Africa denying comparable justice to whites in countries that they dominate and slaughtering them on television, the backlash could be frightening.'

I said that he was asking blacks to define their behavior as a majority before they attained an equality, and he said, 'That's when the definitions should be made.'

Which of these four scenarios do I subscribe to? I've had pretty good luck as an engineer working on the principle that if I'm smart enough to see something, the people intimately involved must have seen it too. If every sensible man knows what concessions ought to be made right now, my constant hope is that they'll be made. Therefore, I incline toward the first solution: peaceful, accelerated change leading to a nation in which all men and women vote and in which the black majority safeguards a place for white participants—whom they might not like—because they are needed, just as today the Afrikaner accepts as a partner the English-speaker whose ancestors he opposed so bitterly.

I'm going to ignore the die-hard machine-gun type of Afrikaner who shouts, 'Over my dead body.' The Afrikaner leaders I've met are at least as prudent as the American politicians I know, and more so. I'm going to put my faith in them. And I want to make one point clear, which is never ventilated in the South African press. The blacks of South Africa are as capable as any people with whom I've worked. Wherever I've supervised a mine, I was relieved to find some South African black to take charge, because he was sure to be clever and hard-working and informed. If blacks inferior to him can run Zambia and Tanzania and Vwarda, however awkwardly they may do so at the moment, he can surely run South Africa. As a matter of fact, a grand coalition of black capacity, Coloured adaptability, English skill and Afrikaner force could forge a nation that would be one of the most powerful on earth, situated in one of the best settings, and with a way of life that most other people would envy. This is what I hope for.

If, as some fear, any rational solution becomes impossible because the stubborn Afrikaner refuses to yield any of his prerogatives, then I see great pressures along all the borders, encouraged and sometimes engineered by Communist-bloc countries, incipient and real civil war within those borders, with the Afrikaner able to defend himself for the rest of this century, after which other pressures which we cannot now foresee will alter the picture radically. On one thing I have been convinced. The young Afrikaners I know will use their guns. They will go forth fighting, to defend a way of life which God himself has ordained and which, for them, is one of the best on this earth. They will not hesitate to slaughter, because God Himself assured the Israelites, after whom they pattern themselves, 'One man of you shall chase a thousand: for the Lord your God, he it is that fighteth for you, as he hath promised you.' More frighteningly: 'And they utterly destroyed all that was in the city, both man and woman, young and old, and ox, and sheep, and ass, with the edge of the sword.'

The major impediment to rational solution is Afrikaner stubbornness, but a contributory one is the regrettable division within the white community. Smashing Afrikaner triumphs at the polls have meant that they can ignore the other sections of the community and throw them out of all official positions. There are no Englishmen in the cabinet, or at the head of major police units or the armed services. I asked a leading Afrikaner whether the nation he foresaw would have any place for Englishmen, and he said bluntly, 'Not really.' Then he remembered that I had English relatives here and he conceded, 'Well, if they quit running back to England every time there's trouble, we might find a place for them, and even trust them when the crunch comes.'

The key phrase in every serious discussion is *'when the crunch comes.'* Everyone expects it to come. Super-patriots argue that when it does, the English will somehow chicken out. Everyone is convinced that when it comes, only the Afrikaner will prove reliable.

And what is this mysterious *crunch?* The armed rebellion of the blacks.

You must not conclude from what I've just said that the English-speaking South African is much different from the Afrikaner. In fact, he profits equally from the present situation and might be even more reluctant than the Afrikaner to surrender his servants and his prerogatives. My English foreman confided the other day, 'Sure I talk liberal, and I vote liberal, but on election night, when the tally's announced, I'm damned relieved the Afrikaners have won again. They'll know how to handle affairs when the crunch comes.'

I hate to say this to a professor of history, and a very good one, but South Africa is a land cruelly wounded by its constant recollection of things past. At certain points the English did behave poorly; this is never allowed to be forgotten. At every memorial the same time-worn litany of incidents must be recited. Hatreds become enshrined as the most vital components of the national mythos, and no one is ever permitted to forget, or turn his attention to more creative tasks. I remember that day you told us what Santayana had said: 'Those who forget history are condemned to repeat it.' Well, those who remember it obsessively are poisoned by it.

After my third long trip through the country, friends at the mine asked what my most lasting impression had been, and I said, 'Just once I'd like to enter some South African town and see a statue to someone who wrote a book, painted a picture or composed a song.' I was weary of those dreadful monuments to minor generals who had fought battles involving thirty-eight men. It's as if our country were festooned with statues of Francis Marion, Pierre Beauregard and James Van Fleet. I'm sure they were meritorious fellows worthy of remembrance, but they would form a fragile base for constructing a national hagiography.

As for my final guess, if the Götterdämmerung Afrikaners do use their blazing guns to protect themselves for the rest of this century, I think they can get away with it. But any hope of later reconciliation would prove impossible. I would expect them, sometime around 2010, to retreat under pressure to the Cape Province enclave, there to become the Israel of Africa, surrounded not by Arabs but by blacks. I cannot see them leaving Africa, nor should they. They have no other homes. They have lived here much longer than most American families have lived in the United States.

You have probably detected that I write with more fervor than ever I dared exhibit in your class. The reason is simple. I fell in love with an adorable Afrikaner girl, much prettier than those professional models who appear in wooden shoes on your Holland, Michigan, postcards, and through her I saw the best of

Afrikanerdom, which I liked much better than I did my own
English strain. I saw them as excellent people trying to find their
way. Alas, she married the other guy, the one with the machine
gun at the ready, and I find myself speculating on what her future will be. I am desolate of spirit.

Philip Saltwood

He was indeed desolate. He had come to South Africa to find diamonds,
and had found none. He had tried to marry a beautiful girl, and had failed.
Most nagging of all, he had tried to comprehend a land with which his
family had many ties, but had finished his tour as ignorant of its real
construction as when he started.

He did not know why Frikkie and Jopie were so determined to settle
questions with their machine guns, nor could he guess how much longer
Nxumalo would be willing to make concessions. Indians, Coloureds, Zulu,
Xhosa, Afrikaners—he was puzzled by them all, and especially by Craig
Saltwood, who had accepted exile. Had he been Craig, he would not have
fled.

Yet he was leaving. His work was ending on a cascade of falling notes,
like a music box that has run down; his only reasonable next step was
toward the exit. He packed his gear at the camp, notified Pretoria that all
accounts with the workmen would be cleaned up as of Saturday, and made
inquiries about flights back to New York, where a group of oil men wished
to talk with him about problems in Texas.

By Wednesday he had things in order, with clean-up jobs assigned to
all men still on the payroll. He talked with each about plans, about his wife
and children. By now the blacks trusted him and were willing to explain
their uncertainties: 'Maybe a job here. Maybe we go to Zimbabwe to help
get their mines working again.' They were wonderfully resilient men, these
Zulu and Xhosa, and he felt that regardless of how badly the black and
white leaders messed things up, these technicians would keep their profi-
ciencies ready to serve whatever type of government emerged. They did not
seem sorry to see him go, but they did respect the high standard of his work
as they had witnessed it. He knew his job.

The white workers usually knew what they were going to do next; like
the blacks, they were not sorry to see the American go. He had never really
fitted in, never quite understood the reasons why they had to keep the blacks
in their place.

'Don't mess with any gangsters,' they warned him.

'Tell Jimmy Carter we're desperately awaiting his next words of advice.'

'If you see Andy Young, up his bucket.'

They were a competent, rowdy lot and he would be pleased to work with
them anywhere, anytime, but they did not represent the South Africa he had
grown to love. That was centered on Vrymeer, and when the camp was
fairly well secured he drove over the hills to Venloo and then out to the farm
nestling beside the lake. When he came down the approach and saw once
more that enticing cluster of buildings, the five rondavels, the step-lakes and
the herd of blesbok, he stopped his car, studied the relationship of each item

to the others, and thought: This is paradise, chopped out of rock, and rich even in time of drought.

He noticed that several months of dry weather had lowered the level of the lake considerably, so that the rather steep flanks were visible, one layer after another of seemingly different kinds of rock: More likely all the same rock, but stained different colors by different exposures to water and air. He was about to formulate additional thoughts when a large group of flamingos rose from the far end of the lake, wheeled about in breathtaking patterns for several minutes, then landed delicately on one of the smaller lakes, annoying a flock of guinea fowl that had been pecking at the sand nearby. Whatever thoughts he might have had about the lake vanished, so he drove down to the yard, parked the car, and shouted, 'Marius!'

Before he could reach the house Van Doorn was at the door, laughing uproariously and waving a newspaper. 'Philip! I'm so glad you arrived. This is so good it must be shared.'

'What have the Americans done now?'

'No fear. This is Afrikanerdom at its best,' and he dragged Saltwood into the main room, where the first thing Philip saw was a colored photograph of Sannie in her wedding dress. Quickly he turned away, but as he did so he caught Marius looking at him, so he asked casually, 'How's she doing?'

'Fine. Frikkie has a job with government. Everyone has a job with government.'

'What's the hilarity?'

'The drought.'

'I fail to see the humor. Things look rather barren out there.'

'Not here. Up north at Blinkfontein.'

'Let me see,' Philip said in total confusion as he reached for the newspaper.

'No, you must read the background story first. I have it here somewhere,' and Marius held on to the paper which had caused his mirth while rummaging through a pile by the window. 'Here it is.'

When Philip took the old paper he had no doubt as to which story had caused the merriment, for the first page was dominated by a carefully posed half-page photograph of a man completely nude, accompanied by the headline: NUDIST IDENTIFIED AS CAUSE OF DROUGHT. The straight-faced story explained that Mrs. Leopold van Valck, chairlady of the Blinkfontein Moral Action Committee, speaking on behalf of her forty-three members, had determined that the prolonged drought which had so harmfully affected her area was caused by God's anger at a man named Victor Victoria, who invited couples, not always married, to his farm near Blinkfontein to engage in nude sunbathing. Mrs. van Valck believed that if Mr. Victoria was allowed to continue his nude bathing, God would continue to afflict Blinkfontein, so her committee was handing down an ultimatum: 'Get some clothes on or face the consequences.' She did not indicate what these consequences were, but implied that they would not be pleasant. On the other hand, if Mr. Victoria would consent to get dressed, she assured him and the other citizens of Blinkfontein that rain would fall fairly soon, in accordance with II Chronicles, Chapter 7, verse 14:

> If my people . . . shall humble themselves, and pray . . . and turn from their wicked ways; then will I hear from heaven, and will forgive their sin, and will heal their land.

She concluded, 'So it's up to you, Mr. Victoria. Put on your clothes and bring us rain.'

Philip passed the paper back with a sigh. 'We have crazies in our country, too. And you ought to see what happens in Texas.'

'That's not the point!' Marius cried, slapping the later paper into Saltwood's hand, and there on the front page was another photograph of Mr. Victor Victoria, fully dressed, accompanied by the headline: NUDISTS DRESS, HEAVENS BLESS. On the afternoon of the morning on which Mr. Victor Victoria's guests put their clothes back on, a torrential rain arrived, not only ending the drought but also washing away two small bridges. Mrs. van Valck, chairlady of the Blinkfontein Moral Action Committee, was quoted as having said, in the midst of the storm, 'Mr. Victoria is a good neighbor. He pays his bills. And he listened to reason.' There was a second photograph of Mr. Victoria, fully clothed, at one of the washed-out bridges, with the caption: I MUST HAVE WORN TOO MUCH.

'Perfect ending for my visit.'

'Are you really leaving?'

'Reluctantly.'

'Amalgamated would certainly find you a job, the price of gold being what it is and diamonds doing so well.'

'Yes, but . . .' He indicated the photograph of Van Doorn's daughter.

'I know at least two dozen girls in Pretoria as pretty as Sannie.'

'But not Sannie. If things had worked out differently . . .'

He was standing at the big window, looking off toward the lake and the striations left around its sides by the drought. 'If it rained up in Blinkfontein, it'll be moving down this way within the next couple of days. Your lake should fill again.'

'Always has. Looks to me as if it's been there a thousand years, maybe a million.'

'Things here are very old,' Saltwood said perfunctorily. Then he stopped, turned, and faced his friend. 'What did you say?'

'I said it looked to me . . . Well, I know nothing about these things, but I've always thought the lake had been here for thousands or even millions of years.'

Grabbing Marius by the arm, Philip ran toward the lake, and when they stood at its edge, he said, 'Suppose this lake has existed for eons. Why did it settle—here in this declivity?'

'Why not?'

'The only explanation would be that it filled some natural dip in the earth. And what caused that dip? The mouth of an old pipe.' He knelt down, pecked at the striations with no purpose, for they could reveal nothing, then rose and cried, 'Marius! What I've been searching for could be right here.'

And he turned eastward toward the spot where old Pik Prinsloo had found his diamonds, far beyond the intervening hills, and with a sweep of hand obliterated the hills, for he supposed correctly that they had erupted millions of years later than the formation of this lake.

With the hills gone, he could visualize the river that had carried the diamonds downstream; it had come from the west, probably, along this chain of little lakes, and it had flowed eastward right over the roots of those hills, and it had not turned northward, along the path of the river that now existed, but always eastward in a logical direction, bearing the diamonds with it.

'Marius!' he cried. 'I think I've found it.'

'What?'

'The pipe that produced those diamonds. I've spent a year searching in the wrong direction.'

'You think it might be here?'

'I'm convinced of it. Not because of anything I've seen here today, but because I've exhausted all other possibilities.'

The words had a heavy impact on Van Doorn, for he saw his country in the process of exhausting *its* various possibilities before it came to grips with the towering one that threatened its existence. But as with Saltwood and the diamonds, preliminary exploration required time and the cauterizing of old animosities. If Philip had spent a futile year searching for his diamonds, South Africa could afford ten or twenty searching for its solution:

Let's say ten years' toying with the idea of a total, military-style repression, then maybe five with some kind of neo-fascism, then another five in a retreat to sanity, and then perhaps another ten in fumbling attempts at a shared democracy. Hell, time moves in vast cycles, but this whole thing could be solved in my lifetime. In my white-hair period I could see a splendid society here. We wouldn't have to scuttle down to the Cape enclave. Black and white, Coloured and Indian could participate equally.

'Marius, are you listening?'

'What?'

'I said I'd like to drill one more experimental hole. Over there at the margin of your lake.'

'For what?'

'I'm convinced I'll find kimberlite. Maybe five hundred feet down, through the detritus.'

Detritus, that's the word. The awful accumulation of wrong decisions, improper turns. You scrape away the excrescences of history—the hangings at Slagter's Nek, the awfulness of the prison camps, the sins we've committed with apartheid—and maybe you get down to the bedrock of human society, where diamonds hide. God of my fathers, how I wish we could bring in the psychological drills and probe down to bedrock.

'So, I have your permission?'

'To do what?'

'To drill the test hole . . . down to kimberlite?'

Kimberlite! This nation of mine will gamble a billion rand to find the next kimberlite in hopes that diamonds will be uncovered. But it won't spend ten rand to find the kimberlite of the human soul. We'll turn the clock back a billion years to find gems worth absolutely nothing in a reasonable world, but we ignore the flint-hard gems in the human conscience that are worth all the raw money in the world. It's an insane society, and if Saltwood does find the new cache of diamonds, everyone in Pretoria and London and Amsterdam and New York will say, 'South Africa has saved itself once more in its time of crisis.' We buy financial credits, but not intelligence.

'I'll keep the mess off to one side,' Philip said in great excitement. 'Not bring in too many vehicles. And the lake poses no problem. We'll go down two or three thousand feet, then fan out our shafts north and south.'

'And the detritus? There's bound to be a lot.'

'There always is when you find diamonds. Ten tons of rubbish for every carat. We'll pile it over there. Never see it from the house.'

The flamingos rose from their small lake, formed their ballet in the air, and danced about the sky in celebration of discoveries about to be made. At the end of one grand sweep, their red feathers blazing in sunlight, they passed the spot at which Philip would place his drills, then headed north. Next year when they returned, the lake would be quite different.

Glossary
and
Genealogical Charts

In writing of a people with a language as evocative as Afrikaans, the temptation is to lard the narrative with a spate of colorful short words like *kloof* (ravine) or astonishing compounds like *onderwyskollegesportsterreine* (education college sports fields). I try to avoid this device, judging it to be exhibitionism which does not aid the reader. However, to write of the Afrikaner without a seasoning of his language would be an injustice. I have, therefore, used those few words without which the narrative would lack verisimilitude, and in this glossary have marked with an asterisk those which can be found in our larger dictionaries as English adoptions.

*ASSEGAI   slender hardwood spear   *Arabic*
BAAS   master; boss
*BAOBAB   tree with swollen trunk   *Bantu*
BAYETE   royal salute   *Zulu*
*BILTONG   strips of sun-dried, salted meat (jerky)
*BOBOTIE   ground meat, curry, custard   *Malay*
*BOER   farmer (capitalized: South African of Dutch or Huguenot descent)
*COMMANDO   Boer military unit (member of such unit)
*DAGGA   marijuana   *Hottentot*
DANKIE   thanks
*DISSELBOOM   main shaft of ox wagon
*DOMINEE   minister of Afrikaner churches
FONTEIN   natural spring (fountain)
HARTEBEEST HUT   wattle-and-daub hut with low walls, no windows
*IMPI   regiment of Zulu warriors   *Bantu*
*INSPAN   harness draft animals
JA   yes
*KNOBKERRIE   club with knobbed head   *Hottentot*
*KOPJE   small hill, often flat-topped
*KRAAL   African village; enclosure for livestock   *Portuguese*

*LAAGER   defensive camp encircled by wagons

*LOBOLA   cattle paid for bride   *Bantu*

*MEALIES   British maize; American corn (hominy grits)

*MEERKAT   small mammal (resembles prairie dog)

MEJUFFROUW   Miss; young unmarried lady

MEVROUW   Mrs.; becomes Mevrou

*MFECANE the crushing (forced migration following Zulu consolidation) *Bantu*

MIJNHEER   Mr.; becomes Mynheer and Meneer

*MORGEN   land measure (about two acres)

NACHTMAAL   night meal (Holy Communion) (becomes Nagmaal in Afrikaans)

OUBAAS   old boss (old fellow; grandfather)

OUMA   grandmother

*OUTSPAN   unharness draft animals

*PREDIKANT   clergyman (especially of Dutch Reformed churches)

*RAND   unit of currency worth about one dollar (abbreviation of Witwatersrand)

*RONDAVEL   hut with circular floor plan

*SJAMBOK   short whip of rhinoceros or hippopotamus hide   *Malay* from *Persian*

SKOLLIE   hooligan (especially Cape Coloured)

*SLIM   clever; crafty; cunning; shrewd (the original English meaning of this word)

*SMOUS   itinerant merchant (peddler)   *German*

*SPOOR   track or trail of man or beast

*STOEP   stoop (porch)

*TREK   arduous migration (especially by ox wagon)

TREKBOER   nomadic grazier

TSOTSI   member of street gang   *Bantu*

*UITLANDER   outlander (capitalized: foreigner, especially on the gold fields)

*VELD   open grassland with scattered shrubs and trees (veldt is archaic)

*VELDKORNET   minor district official (in military: lieutenant)

*VELDSKOEN   rawhide homemade shoe (also veldtskoen)

VERDOMDE   damned; cursed

V.O.C.   Vereenigde Oostindische Compagnie (United East India Company)

*VOLK   nation; people

VOORTREKKER   forward trekker (member of the 1834–1837 Great Trek)

VRYMEER   Freedom Lake (in Dutch: Vrijmeer)

Pronunciation: In general, words are pronounced as they look, except that J = Y; V = F; W = V; OE = U. The name Van Wyk = Fan Vake; and for no reason that can be explained, Uys = Ace. Vrymeer, of course, is Fraymeer.

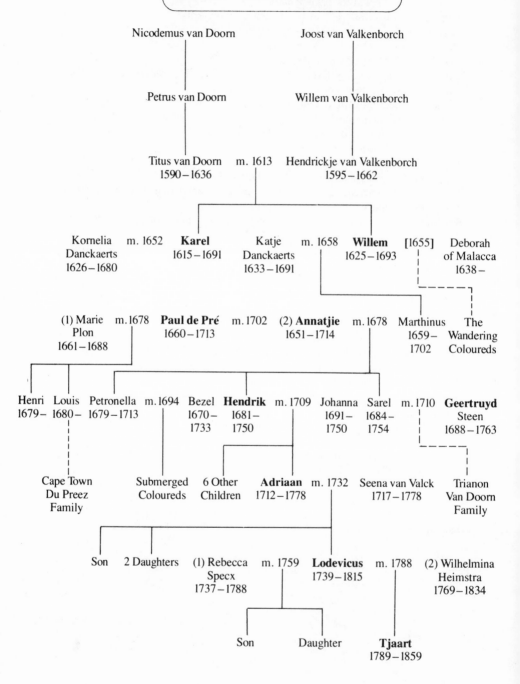

The Van Doorns

Nicodemus van Doorn — Joost van Valkenborch

Petrus van Doorn — Willem van Valkenborch

Titus van Doorn — m. 1613 — Hendrickje van Valkenborch
1590–1636 — 1595–1662

Kornelia — m. 1652 — **Karel** — Katje — m. 1658 — **Willem** — [1655] — Deborah
Danckaerts — 1615–1691 — Danckaerts — 1625–1693 — of Malacca
1626–1680 — 1633–1691 — 1638–

(1) Marie — m.1678 — **Paul de Pré** — m.1702 — (2) **Annatjie** — m.1678 — Marthinus — The
Plon — 1660–1713 — 1651–1714 — 1659– — Wandering
1661–1688 — 1702 — Coloureds

Henri — Louis — Petronella — m.1694 — Bezel — **Hendrik** — m.1709 — Johanna — Sarel — m.1710 — **Geertruyd**
1679– — 1680– — 1679–1713 — 1670– — 1681– — 1691– — 1684– — Steen
— 1733 — 1750 — 1750 — 1754 — 1688–1763

Cape Town — Submerged — 6 Other — **Adriaan** — m.1732 — Seena van Valck — Trianon
Du Preez — Coloureds — Children — 1712–1778 — 1717–1778 — Van Doorn
Family — Family

Son — 2 Daughters — (1) Rebecca — m.1759 — **Lodevicus** — m.1788 — (2) Wilhelmina
Specx — 1739–1815 — Heimstra
1737–1788 — 1769–1834

Son — Daughter — **Tjaart**
1789–1859

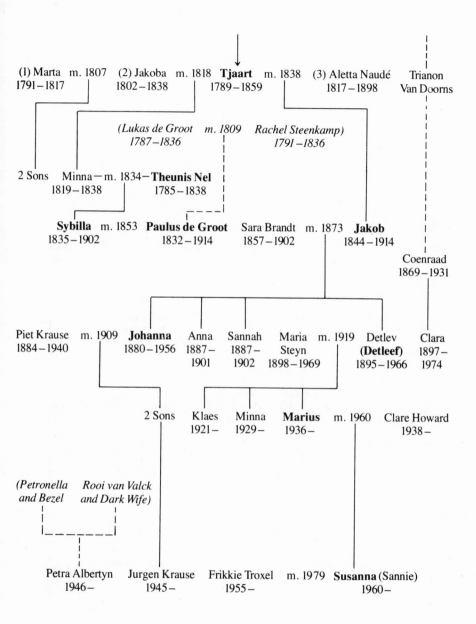

(1) Marta m. 1807   (2) Jakoba m. 1818   **Tjaart** m. 1838   (3) Aletta Naudé   Trianon
1791–1817   1802–1838   1789–1859   1817–1898   Van Doorns

(Lukas de Groot   m. 1809   Rachel Steenkamp)
1787–1836   1791–1836

2 Sons   Minna—m. 1834—**Theunis Nel**
          1819–1838   1785–1838

          Sybilla m. 1853 **Paulus de Groot**   Sara Brandt m. 1873 **Jakob**
          1835–1902   1832–1914   1857–1902   1844–1914

                                                                                    Coenraad
                                                                                    1869–1931

Piet Krause m. 1909 **Johanna**   Anna   Sannah   Maria   m. 1919 Detlev   Clara
1884–1940   1880–1956   1887–   1887–   Steyn   **(Detleef)** 1897–
                                   1901   1902   1898–1969   1895–1966   1974

                      2 Sons   Klaes   Minna   **Marius** m. 1960 Clare Howard
                                  1921–   1929–   1936–   1938–

(Petronella   Rooi van Valck
and Bezel   and Dark Wife)

Petra Albertyn   Jurgen Krause   Frikkie Troxel m. 1979 **Susanna** (Sannie)
1946–   1945–   1955–   1960–

The Nxumalos

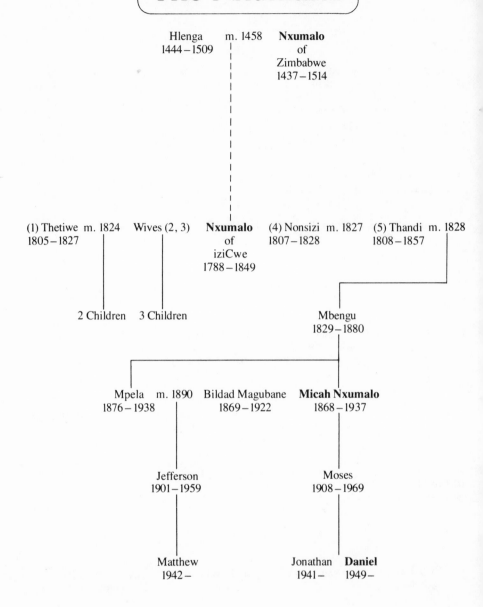

Hlenga   m. 1458   **Nxumalo**
1444–1509   of
Zimbabwe
1437–1514

(1) Thetiwe   m. 1824   Wives (2, 3)   **Nxumalo**   (4) Nonsizi   m. 1827   (5) Thandi   m. 1828
1805–1827   of   1807–1828   1808–1857
iziCwe
1788–1849

2 Children   3 Children   Mbengu
1829–1880

Mpela   m. 1890   Bildad Magubane   **Micah Nxumalo**
1876–1938   1869–1922   1868–1937

Jefferson   Moses
1901–1959   1908–1969

Matthew   Jonathan   **Daniel**
1942–   1941–   1949–

The Saltwoods

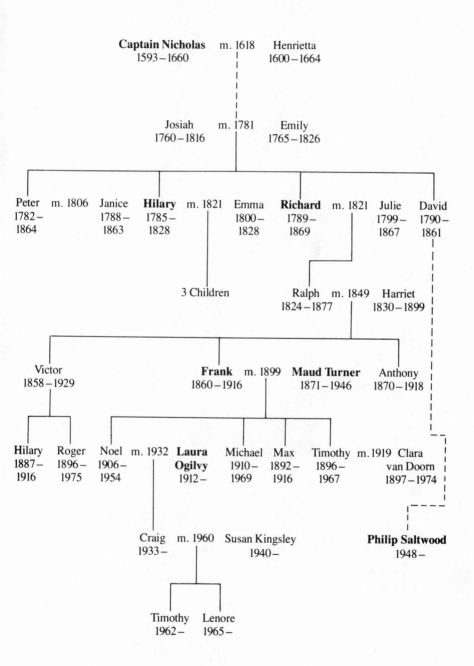

Travels and Treks

0 ————— 200 miles
0 ————— 200 kilometers

Orange River

DEATH OF
GUMSTO ×

Orange River

V

Rooi van Valck's ×

A T L A N T I C

O C E A N

1751
×

1742
×

Golan

Cape Town
1648 ● ×1662

×1692

1724
×

Jean Paul Tremblay